the GRAPHIC CANON

Volume 1

HA HA HA HA HA
YOU... YOU PROMISED...TO...
HA HA HA HA HA HA HA HA HA HA HA
FOLLOW ME.

Volume 1

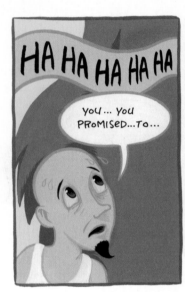

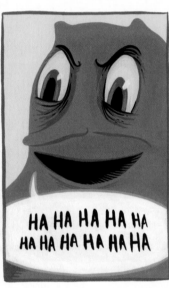

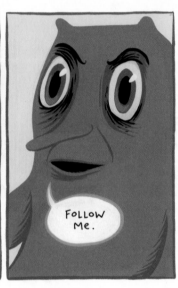

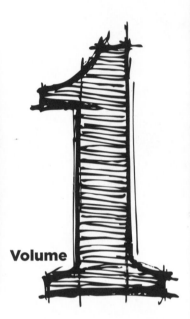

FROM *THE EPIC OF GILGAMESH*
TO SHAKESPEARE
TO *DANGEROUS LIAISONS*

the GRAPHIC CANON

Edited by
RUSS KICK

SEVEN STORIES PRESS
New York

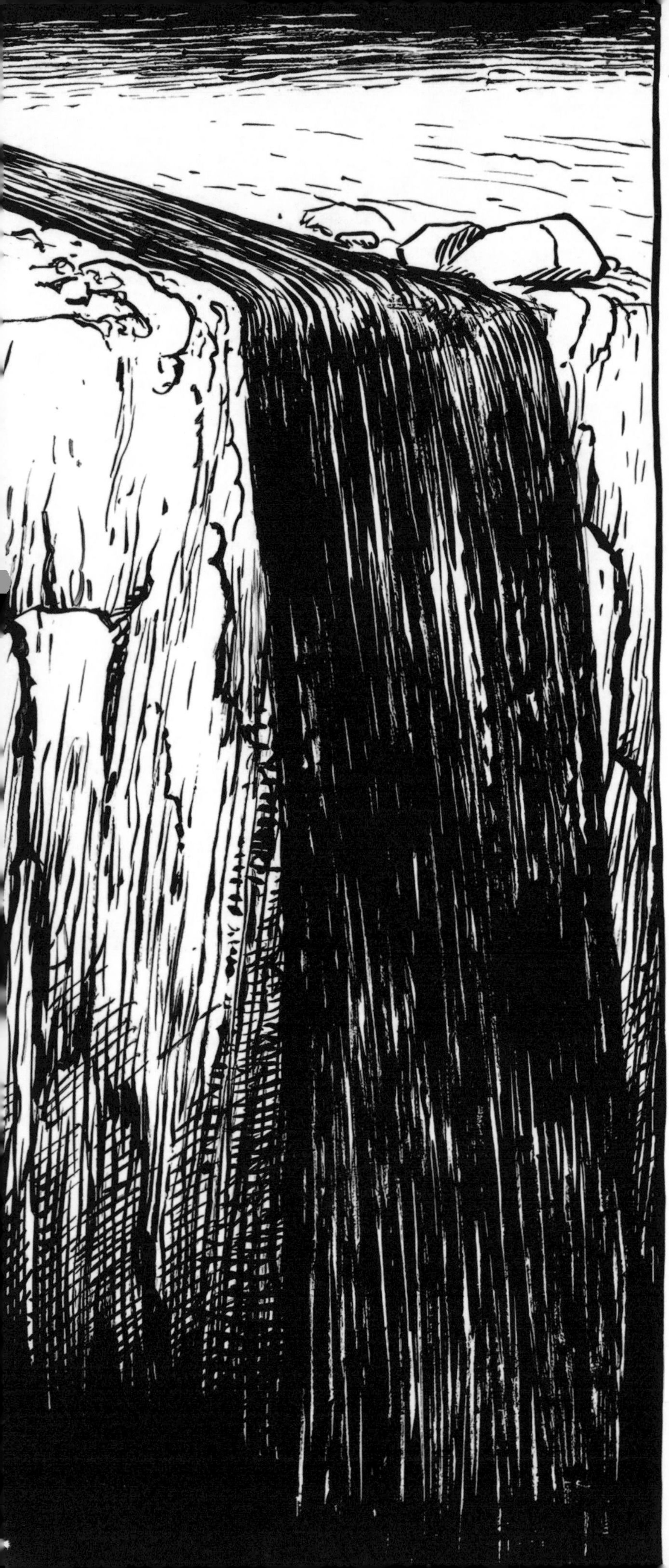

For permissions information see page 500.

A SEVEN STORIES PRESS FIRST EDITION

SEVEN STORIES PRESS
140 Watts Street
New York, NY 10013
www.sevenstories.com

College professors may order examination copies of Seven Stories Press titles for a free six-month trial period. To order, visit www.sevenstories.com/textbook or send a fax on school letterhead to (212) 226-1411.

Book design by Pollen/Stewart Cauley, New York

Library of Congress Cataloging-in-Publication Data
The graphic canon, volume 1 : from the epic of Gilgamesh to Shakespeare to Dangerous liaisons / edited by Russ Kick.—A Seven Stories Press 1st ed.
p. cm.
Includes index.
ISBN 978-1-60980-376-6 (pbk.)
1. Comic book, strips, etc.—History and criticism.
2. Literature—Adaptations. 3. Graphic novels in education. I. Kick, Russell.
PN6714.R57 2010
741.5'69—dc23
2012000276

Printed in China

9 8 7 6 5 4 3 2 1

CONTENTS

Three Panel Review
Lisa Brown

HAMLET
by William Shakespeare
KILL your UNCLE!
Should I kill my uncle?
© 2011 LISA M. BROWN | DIST. BY TRIBUNE MEDIA SERVICES, INC.
You know what? I think that I will.

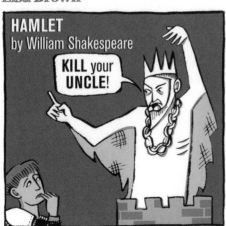

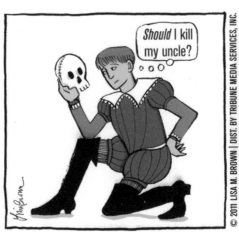

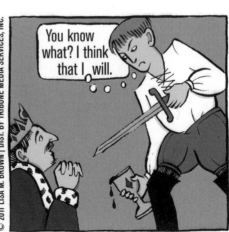

ACKNOWLEDGMENTS

IT TAKES A LOT OF PEOPLE TO MAKE A BOOK, ESPECIALLY a gigantic anthology. Endless gratitude goes to Dan Simon, founder and president of Seven Stories Press, who immediately shared my vision for *The Graphic Canon* and, by his second email to me, was already discussing the nitty-gritty details. I originally pitched an over-sized 400-page book, but much later in the process, when I later told Dan that it could easily be expanded to 500 or even 600 pages, he expanded it, all right—to two volumes. Then, weeks later, to three. From 400 pages each to close to 500. From some color to color throughout. From mostly reprints to mostly new material. We both like to think big.

Huge thanks to editor and fellow night owl Veronica Liu, who was so much fun to work with that it didn't feel like work at all, even when she found loads of errors I had embarrassingly overlooked or when she lovingly cracked the whip as I let this or that task fall by the wayside. Merci beaucoup to everyone on Seven Stories' all-star team: Liz DeLong, Phoebe Hwang, and Jon Gilbert on production; Ruth Weiner on promotion; and Linda Trepanier on bookkeeping. Gracias to Eva Fortes for fact-checking, and to Liz Byer for putting together a fantastic "Further Reading" section.

Hugs go to my parents, Ruthanne & Derek, Kiki, Sky, Terrence & Rebekah, Darrell, Billy Dale, Cat & David, Kelly & Kevin, Mary, Z, Hawk, Songtruth, Fred & Dorothy, Jeff & Christy, and Jenny. I raise a glass to Gary Baddeley and Ralph Bernardo at Disinformation. I bow to the artists who led me to other artists—Molly Kiely, Onsmith, Molly Crabapple, Ed Choy Moorman, and Zak Smith.

A tip of the hat to Lora Fountain, Denis Kitchen and Stacey Kitchen, Eric Reynolds at Fantagraphics, Melanie Blais at Candlewick Press, Charlotte Baron at Fulcrum Publishing, Claudia Cappelli at the Jewish Publication Society, Rosemary Kiladitis at Bloomsbury, Tobias Steed at Can of Worms Enterprises, and Charlotte Sheedy, Meredith Kaffel, and Mackenzie C. Brady at the Charlotte Sheedy Literary Agency.

Major thanks are due to everyone who gets this book made and into your hands: the paper-makers, the printers, Random House's distribution department, the truck drivers, the booksellers. . . . And of course the many trees who gave their all.

I'm grateful to all the authors, poets, and playwrights who gave us these works of literature. Many of them sacrificed their personal freedom, economic well-being, sanity, relationships, livers, and lives to illuminate the human condition. And I reserve a special place in my heart for all the artists here, who enthusiastically produced amazing work. Without you guys, *The Graphic Canon* couldn't exist.

EDITOR'S INTRODUCTION TO VOLUME 1

WE'RE LIVING IN A GOLDEN AGE OF THE GRAPHIC NOVEL, of comic art, and of illustration in general. Legions of talented artists—who employ every method, style, and approach imaginable—are creating such a flood of amazing, gorgeous, entertaining, and groundbreaking material that it's pretty much impossible to keep up with it all. What if a bunch of these artists used as their source material the greatest literature ever written?

That was the question that occurred to me several years ago, while in the graphic novel section of a bookstore. Specifically, I saw a graphic version of *The Trial* by Franz Kafka (adapted by Mairowitz and Montellier). That was the tipping point. It fully dawned on me just how many amazing graphic adaptations of literature had been published in recent years. My instincts as an anthologist kicked in. I needed to gather the best of what had already been done, commission lots of new adaptations, and put it all in one place. It seemed like an obvious idea, yet no one had done it: create a huge, brick-like book spanning centuries, countries, languages, and genres. Include novels, short stories, poems, plays, autobiographies, the occasional speech and letter, and scientific, philosophical, and religious works.

I quickly found a publisher who shared my vision—Seven Stories Press—and *The Graphic Canon* started gestating in earnest. Soon it became triplets. There was too much outstanding material to cram into a single volume, even a large one, so it split into three. *Gilgamesh* kicks off the first book, and David Foster Wallace's *Infinite Jest* closes the third. In between, almost every A-list work of Western literature is covered, but that's just the beginning. As I contacted more artists, the range of works expanded. Literature from the Eastern canon—Japan, China, India, Tibet. Religious/spiritual literature. Philosophy. Bawdy material. Ancient Greek drama. Medieval writings. Romanticism. Modernism and postmodernism. The Beats. Works from indigenous peoples. Fairy tales. Mystical visions. *Candide*. Poems from Emily Dickinson. *The Hasheesh Eater*. A rare, early story from Hemingway. *One Flew Over the Cuckoo's Nest*. And still there's more—190 works in all, with the first 55 (taking us through the end of the 1700s) in this initial volume.

Likewise, the range of artists became staggering. Legendary cartoonists—such as Robert Crumb, Will Eisner, Sharon Rudahl, S. Clay Wilson, Roberta Gregory, and Kim Deitch—were participating. More big names joined. Artists who have drawn for Marvel and DC climbed aboard. Bright lights from the alternative comics, mini-comics, and Web-comics scenes said yes. I recruited ridiculously talented newcomers. Artists from Brazil, Italy, Belgium, Sweden, South Korea, the UK, and Canada joined their US counterparts. Not only comics artists . . . I was getting stunning work from illustrators, painters, silk-screeners, a collage artist, a radical graphic designer, and two artists who create photo-dioramas.

I asked the artists to stay true to the source material—no setting it in the future, no creating new adventures for characters, etc. Longer works would of course be represented by excerpts or extreme abridgements. But within that framework, they were given carte blanche. Any approach, any medium, any style. I wasn't interested in a workman-like, note-by-note transcription of the original work. The adaptations are true collaborations between the original authors/poets and the artists.

Each piece stands on its own, but taken together they form a vast, rich kaleidoscope of art and literature. A rainbow of visual approaches has been applied to the world's treasure trove of great writings, and something wondrously new has taken shape.

And this is the main point of *The Graphic Canon*. You could look at it as an educational tool, and I hope it does get used that way. You could say that it will lead people to read the original works of literature; that would make me happy. But, at its heart, this titanic, multi-volume anthology is a self-contained artistic/literary work, an end in itself.

RUSS KICK

The Epic of Gilgamesh

Babylonian tablets

ART / ADAPTATION BY **Kevin Dixon**

RENDITION BY **Kent Dixon**

YOU'LL OFTEN HEAR *The Epic of Gilgamesh* referred to as the oldest work of literature, but that isn't strictly correct. There are many shorter works from the Mesopotamian region and Egypt—hymns, spells, collections of maxims, codes of conduct, creation stories, and even some short poems about Gilgamesh, among others—that predate *Gilgamesh*. But it is definitely the earliest epic poem, and the earliest sustained narrative work, in existence.

Like so many premodern works of literature, *Gilgamesh* has a convoluted and obscure history. The "standard version" of the epic is based on twelve clay tablets written in the Akkadian language around 1000 BCE, apparently inscribed by a scholar (who was also an exorcist and perhaps also a poet) in Babylonia, Sîn-leqi-unninni, who combined earlier written material, oral traditions, and his own imagination to create the epic as it now stands. Those tablets were buried for around 2,500 years, lost to the world from around 600 BCE until the 1840s–1850s, when an amateur British archaeologist and his assistant uncovered a buried Assyrian palace whose library contained more than 100,000 engraved tablets and fragments. It wasn't until 1872 that an assistant curator at the British Museum read one of the Gilgamesh tablets and realized he had discovered something amazing.

The tablets tell the story of the mighty demigod Gilgamesh, King of Uruk (which is now Iraq), around 2500 BCE. Gil is arrogant, and he tyrannizes his people, so the gods create a wild man, Enkidu, to distract the king and divert his boundless energy. After the feral Enkidu is tamed and civilized by a temple prostitute who brings him to Uruk after a seven-day sexathon, he gets into a raging fight with Gilgamesh, after which the two become inseparable friends. The buddy duo decide to undertake an adventure, traveling to the Cedar Forest and killing its monstrous guardian, Humbaba. Back in Uruk, Gilgamesh brushes off the sexual advances of the goddess Ishtar, who gets her father, the god Anu, to unleash the Bull of Heaven on Uruk as revenge. Gilgamesh and Enkidu make mincemeat of the monster, and Enkidu lobs part of the bull at Ishtar. As punishment, the gods kill Enkidu, which sends Gil into intolerable grief. Now fearing death, he goes on an epic journey across mountains, the river of death, and other hostile landscapes to find the secret of immortality from Utnapishtim, whom the gods have decreed will never die. Utnapishtim tells Gilgamesh that there is no way for him to become immortal but that he can regain his youth by eating a plant found at the bottom of the sea. Gil man-ages to retrieve it, but in one of the cruelest moments in literature, a snake eats it while Gilgamesh is bathing. More than a simple adventure tale, *Gilgamesh* also doubles as wisdom literature, with insights into friendship, death, and the meaning of life.

The adaptation in this volume relates the Bull of Heaven episode, beginning as Gil and Enkidu are cleansing themselves of the grime that slathers them after their battle with Humbaba. It comes from Kevin Dixon's self-published comic series adapting the entire epic. The text is supplied by his father, Dr. Kent H. Dixon, a professor of English at Wittenberg University, who explains:

My translation of the Gilgamesh epic is actually what is called a rendition, which is a translation made from other translations and not from the original. About half the translations out there of *Gilgamesh* are actually renditions, such as John Gardner's or the most recent and much-touted Stephen Mitchell's (a terrific translator of Rilke). However, I took a course called Cuneiform by mail taught by an Assyriologist at the University of Chicago's famous Oriental Institute, and learned to read about a third of the some 600 to 800 symbols that constitute the Assyrian syllabary. I also consulted more than two dozen translations and renditions in English, plus three in French, and one each in Italian and German.

I wanted a translation that would appeal to college students and general readers, so I biased mine toward the sensory dimension, in which the original is weak; hence, I call it "an enriched rendition," as if I'd doped it with diction and vocabulary that evoked the most vivid sensory world. See Alexander Heidel's 1948 translation for something in English closest to the original Babylonian and Akkadian, and if you do that, and compare it with other translations, you will see how much latitude scholars and poets working on this very first piece of great world literature take. My own effort, I maintain, while unabashedly biased toward the sensory world, is still one of the more accurate literally.

SOURCES

George, A.R. *The Babylonian Gilgamesh Epic: Introduction, Critical Edition and Cuneiform Texts* (Volume One). Oxford University Press, 2003.

Damrosch, David. *The Buried Book: The Loss and Rediscovery of the Great Epic of Gilgamesh*. New York: Henry Holt and Company, 2007.

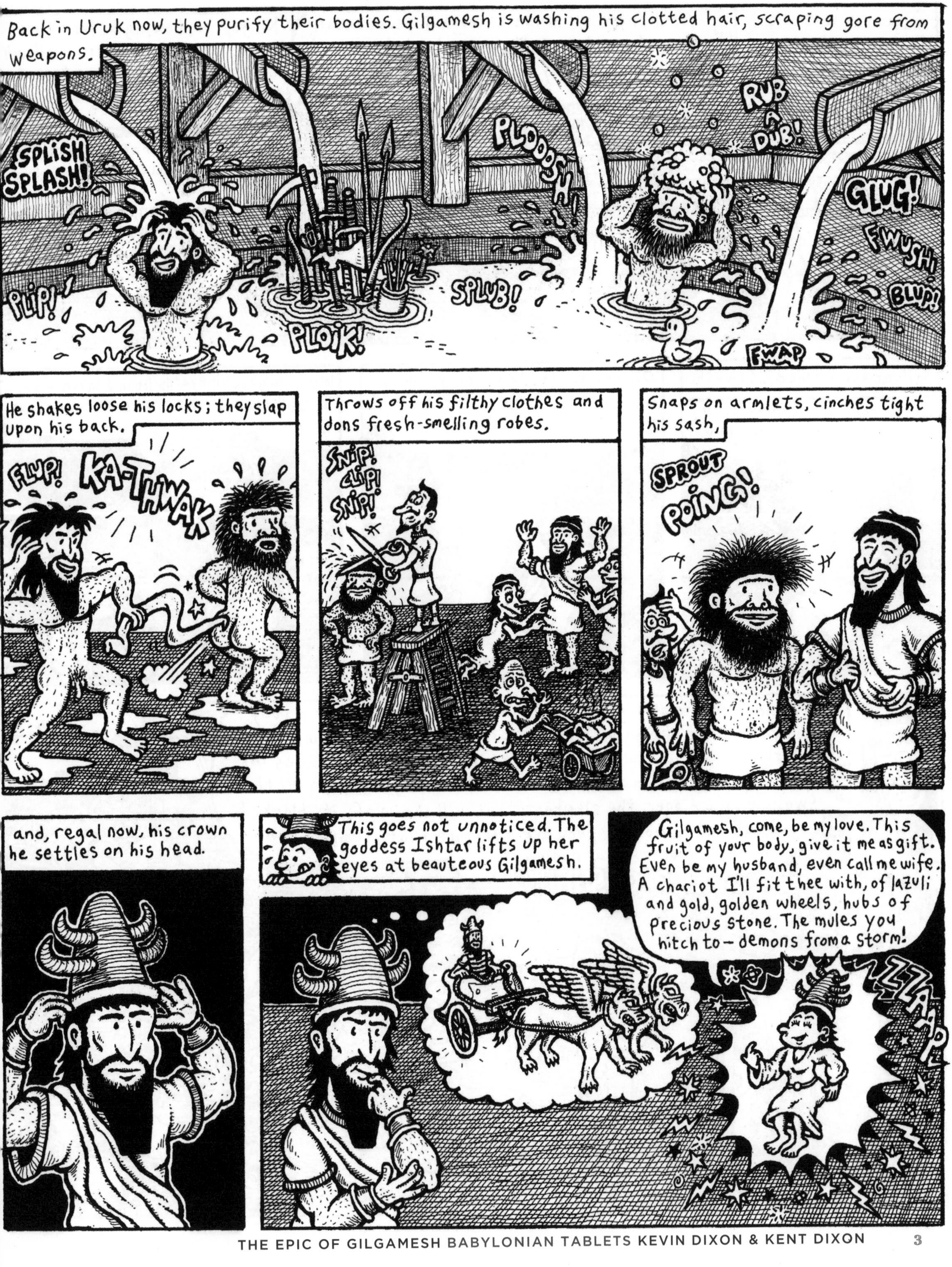
Back in Uruk now, they purify their bodies. Gilgamesh is washing his clotted hair, scraping gore from weapons.
SPLISH SPLASH!
PLOOOSH!
RUB A DUB!
GLUG!
FWUSH!
BLUP!
PLIP!
SPLUB!
PLOIK!
FWAP
He shakes loose his locks; they slap upon his back.
FLUP!
KA-THWAK
Throws off his filthy clothes and dons fresh-smelling robes.
SNIP! CLIP! SNIP!
Snaps on armlets, cinches tight his sash,
SPROUT
POING!
and, regal now, his crown he settles on his head.
This goes not unnoticed. The goddess Ishtar lifts up her eyes at beauteous Gilgamesh.
Gilgamesh, come, be my love. This fruit of your body, give it me as gift. Even be my husband, even call me wife. A chariot I'll fit thee with, of lazuli and gold, golden wheels, hubs of precious stone. The mules you hitch to—demons from a storm!
ZZAP!

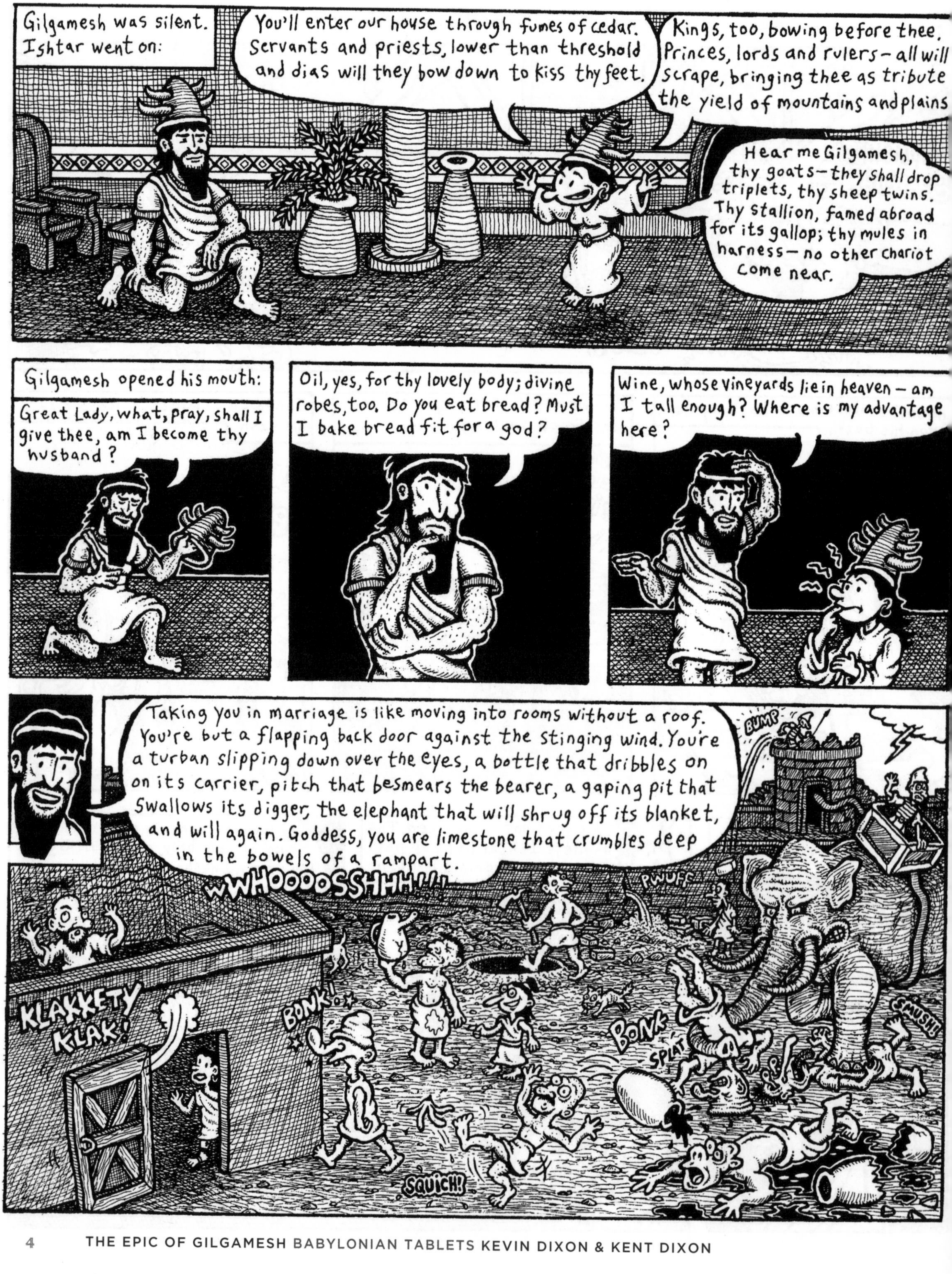
Gilgamesh was silent. Ishtar went on:
You'll enter our house through fumes of cedar. Servants and priests, lower than threshold and dias will they bow down to kiss thy feet.
Kings, too, bowing before thee. Princes, lords and rulers – all will scrape, bringing thee as tribute the yield of mountains and plains
Hear me Gilgamesh, thy goats – they shall drop triplets, thy sheep twins. Thy stallion, famed abroad for its gallop; thy mules in harness – no other chariot come near.
Gilgamesh opened his mouth:
Great Lady, what, pray, shall I give thee, am I become thy husband?
Oil, yes, for thy lovely body; divine robes, too. Do you eat bread? Must I bake bread fit for a god?
Wine, whose vineyards lie in heaven – am I tall enough? Where is my advantage here?
Taking you in marriage is like moving into rooms without a roof. You're but a flapping back door against the stinging wind. You're a turban slipping down over the eyes, a bottle that dribbles on on its carrier, pitch that besmears the bearer, a gaping pit that swallows its digger, the elephant that will shrug off its blanket, and will again. Goddess, you are limestone that crumbles deep in the bowels of a rampart.
BUMP
wWHOOOOSSHHH!!!
PWUFF
KLAKKETY KLAK!
BONK!
BONK
SPLAT
SMUSH!
SQUICH!

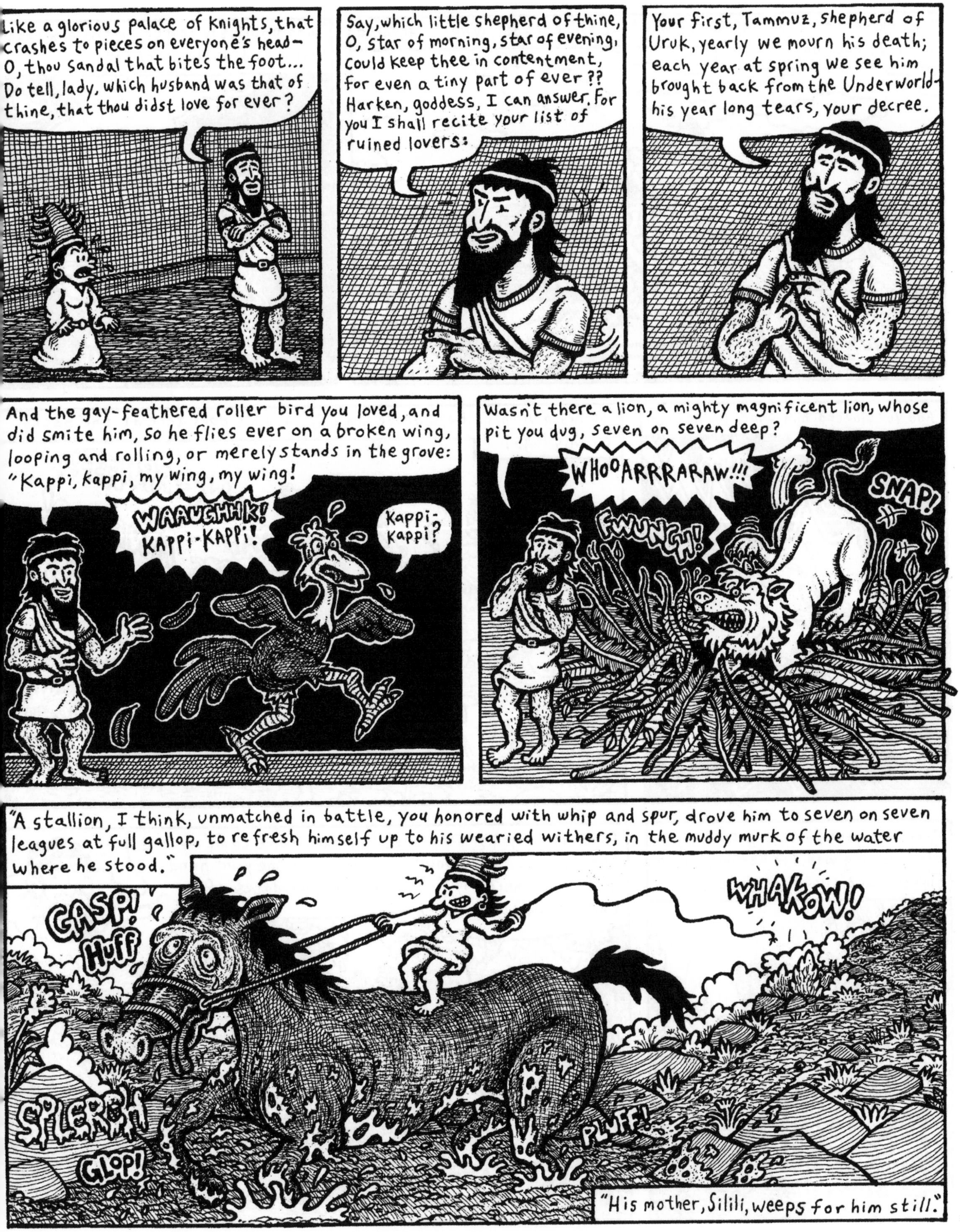
Like a glorious palace of knights, that crashes to pieces on everyone's head— O, thou sandal that bites the foot... Do tell, lady, which husband was that of thine, that thou didst love for ever?
Say, which little shepherd of thine, O, star of morning, star of evening, could keep thee in contentment, for even a tiny part of ever?? Harken, goddess, I can answer. For you I shall recite your list of ruined lovers:
Your first, Tammuz, shepherd of Uruk, yearly we mourn his death; each year at spring we see him brought back from the Underworld— his year long tears, your decree.
And the gay-feathered roller bird you loved, and did smite him, so he flies ever on a broken wing, looping and rolling, or merely stands in the grove: "Kappi, kappi, my wing, my wing!
WAAUGHHHK! KAPPI-KAPPI!
Kappi-kappi?
Wasn't there a lion, a mighty magnificent lion, whose pit you dug, seven on seven deep?
WHOOARRRARAW!!!
FWUNCH!
SNAP!
"A stallion, I think, unmatched in battle, you honored with whip and spur, drove him to seven on seven leagues at full gallop, to refresh himself up to his wearied withers, in the muddy murk of the water where he stood."
GASP! HUFF
WHAKOW!
SPLERCH!
GLOP!
PLUFF!
"His mother, Silili, weeps for him still."

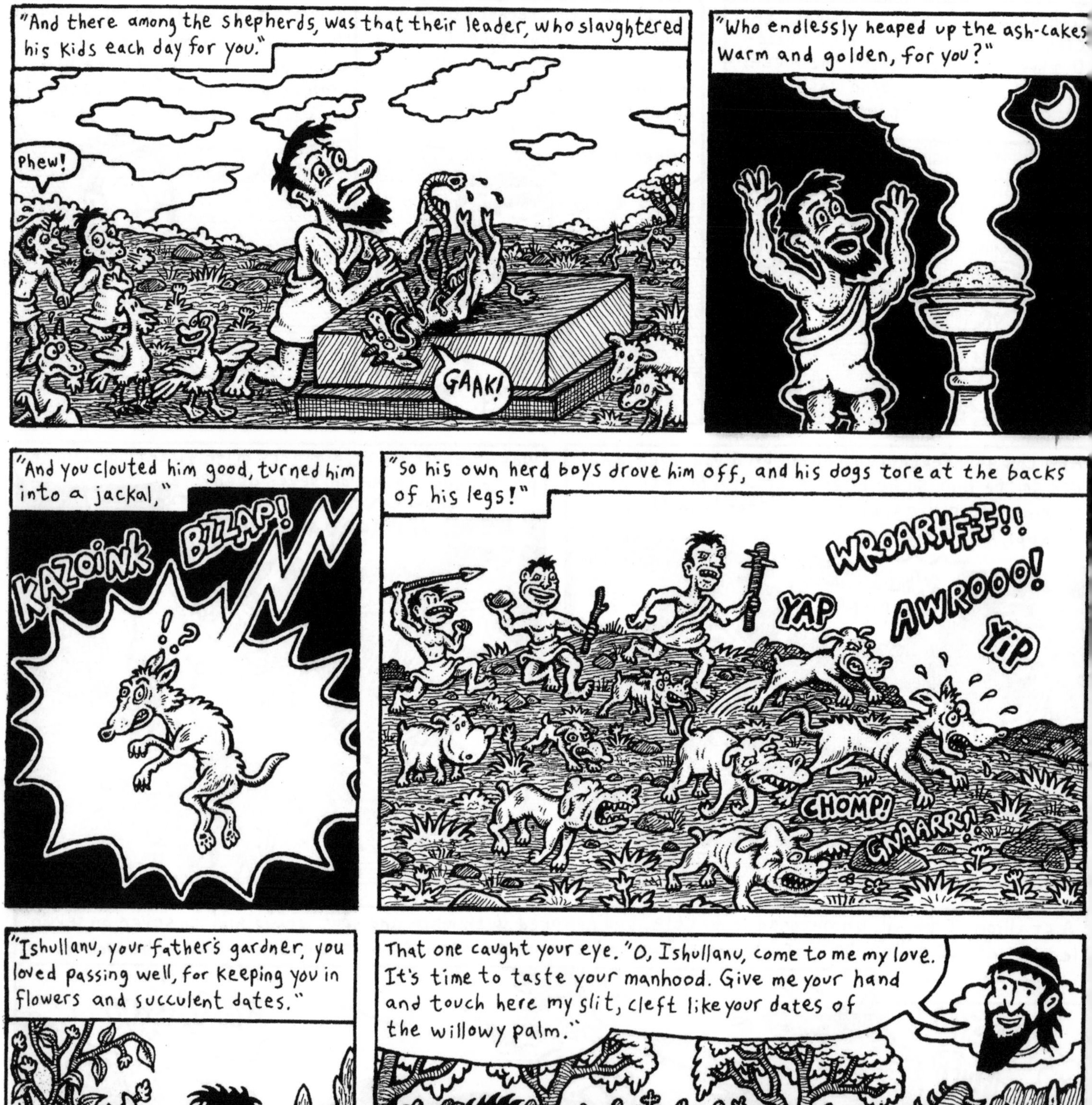
"And there among the shepherds, was that their leader, who slaughtered his kids each day for you."
Phew!
GAAK!
"Who endlessly heaped up the ash-cakes warm and golden, for you?"
"And you clouted him good, turned him into a jackal,"
KAZOINK
BZZAP!
!??
"So his own herd boys drove him off, and his dogs tore at the backs of his legs!"
WROARHFFF!!
YAP
AWROOO!
YIP
CHOMP!
GNAARR!!
"Ishullanu, your father's gardner, you loved passing well, for keeping you in flowers and succulent dates."
That one caught your eye. "O, Ishullanu, come to me my love. It's time to taste your manhood. Give me your hand and touch here my slit, cleft like your dates of the willowy palm."

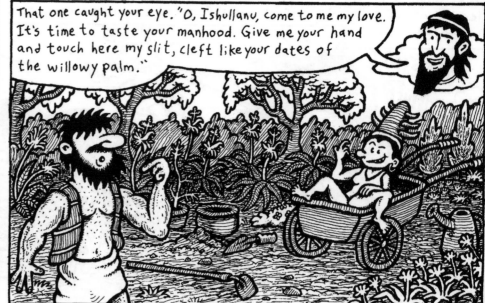

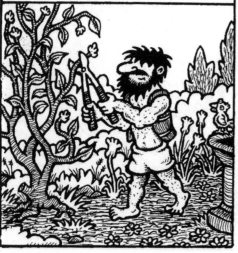

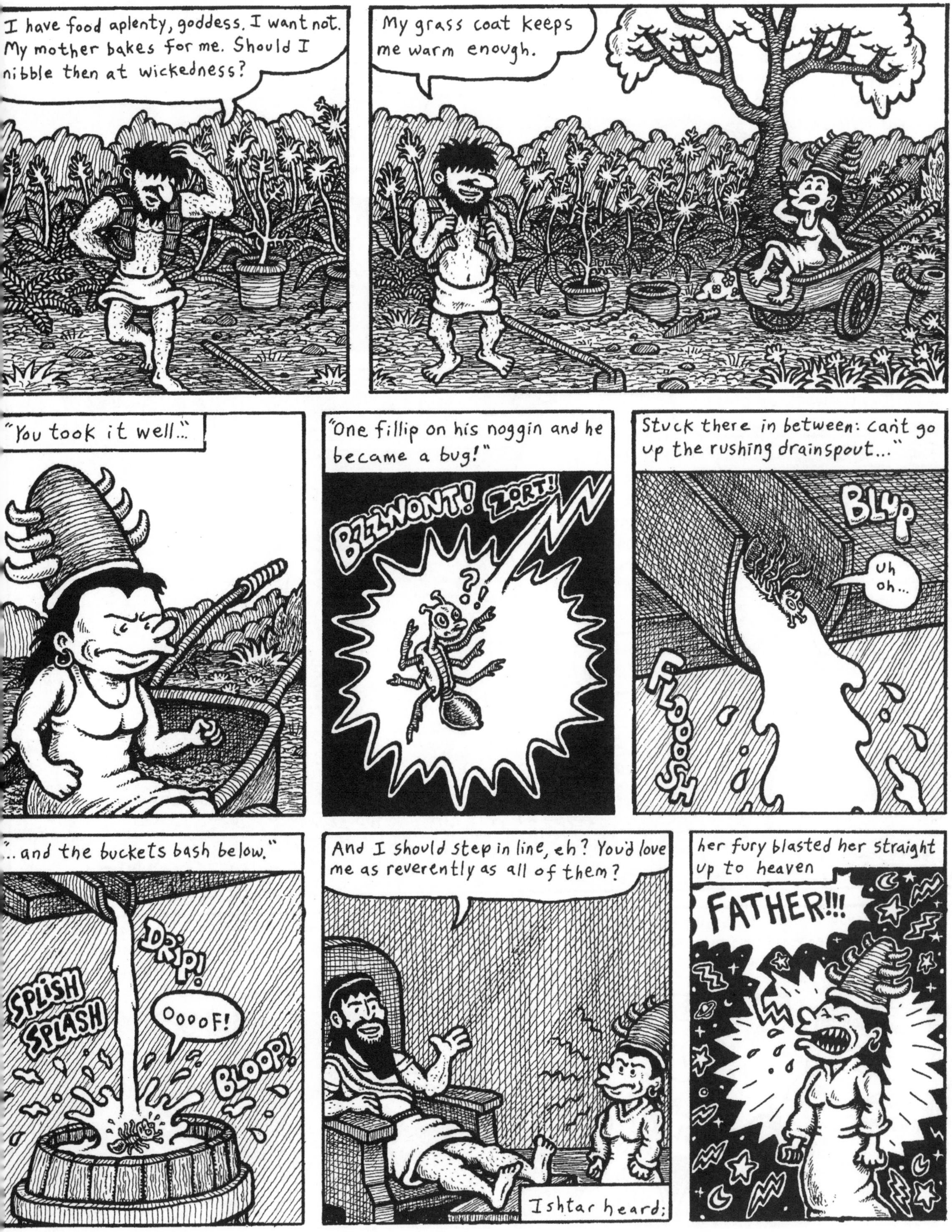
I have food aplenty, goddess. I want not. My mother bakes for me. Should I nibble then at wickedness?
My grass coat keeps me warm enough.
"You took it well..."
"One fillip on his noggin and he became a bug!"
BZZWONT!
ZORT!
?!
Stuck there in between: can't go up the rushing drainspout..."
BLUP
Uh oh...
FLOOSH
"...and the buckets bash below."
DRIP!
SPLISH SPLASH
OOOOF!
BLOOP!
And I should step in line, eh? You'd love me as reverently as all of them?
Ishtar heard:
her fury blasted her straight up to heaven
FATHER!!!

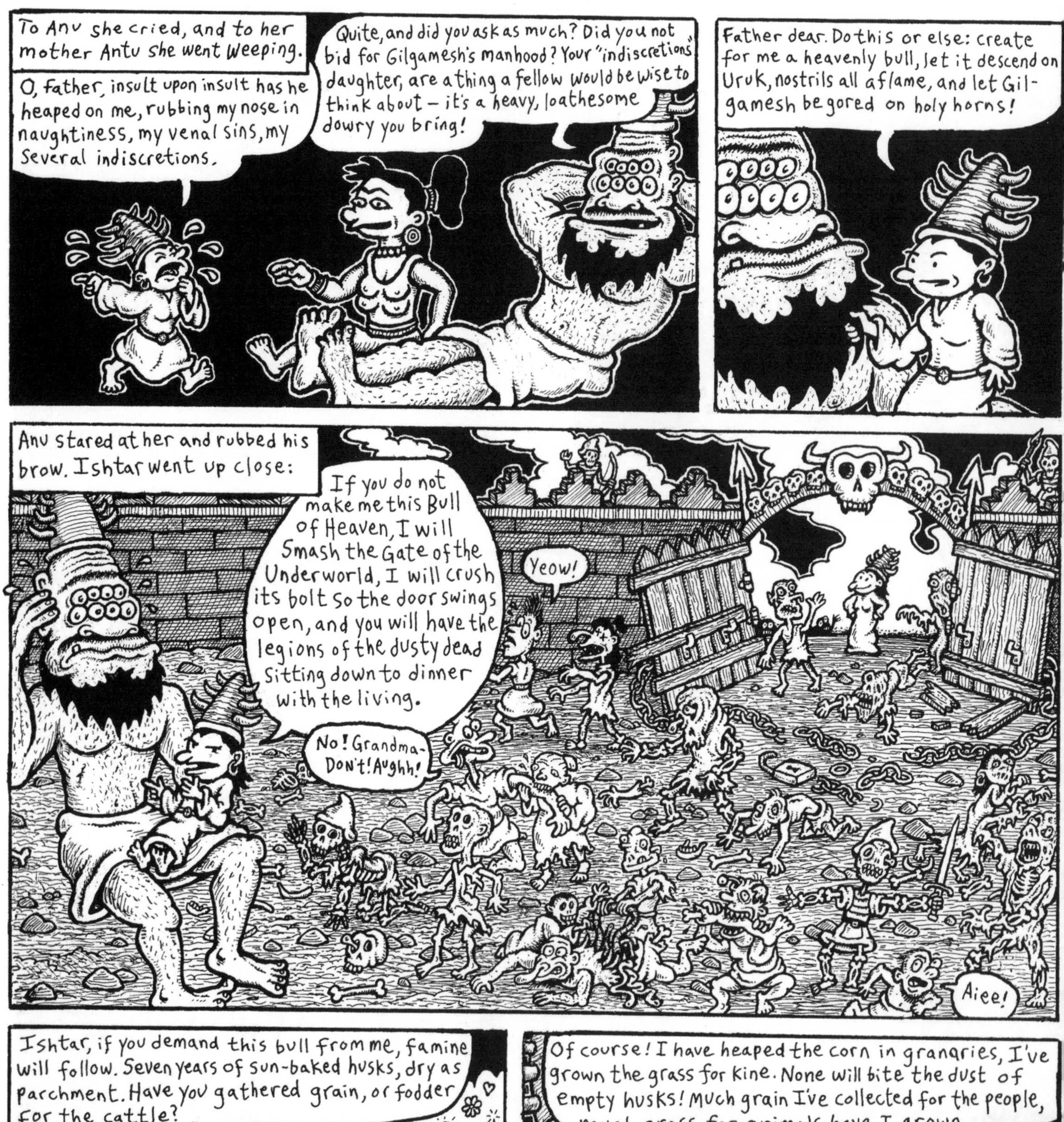

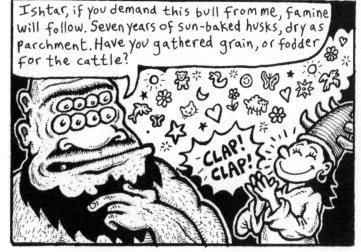

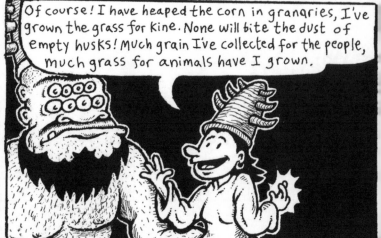

To Anu she cried, and to her mother Antu she went weeping.
O, Father, insult upon insult has he heaped on me, rubbing my nose in naughtiness, my venal sins, my several indiscretions.
Quite, and did you ask as much? Did you not bid for Gilgamesh's manhood? Your "indiscretions" daughter, are a thing a fellow would be wise to think about – it's a heavy, loathesome dowry you bring!
Father dear. Do this or else: create for me a heavenly bull, let it descend on Uruk, nostrils all aflame, and let Gilgamesh be gored on holy horns!
Anu stared at her and rubbed his brow. Ishtar went up close:
If you do not make me this Bull of Heaven, I will smash the Gate of the Underworld, I will crush its bolt so the door swings open, and you will have the legions of the dusty dead sitting down to dinner with the living.
Yeow!
No! Grandma-Don't! Aughh!
Aiee!
Ishtar, if you demand this bull from me, famine will follow. Seven years of sun-baked husks, dry as parchment. Have you gathered grain, or fodder for the cattle?
CLAP! CLAP!
Of course! I have heaped the corn in granaries, I've grown the grass for kine. None will bite the dust of empty husks! Much grain I've collected for the people, much grass for animals have I grown.

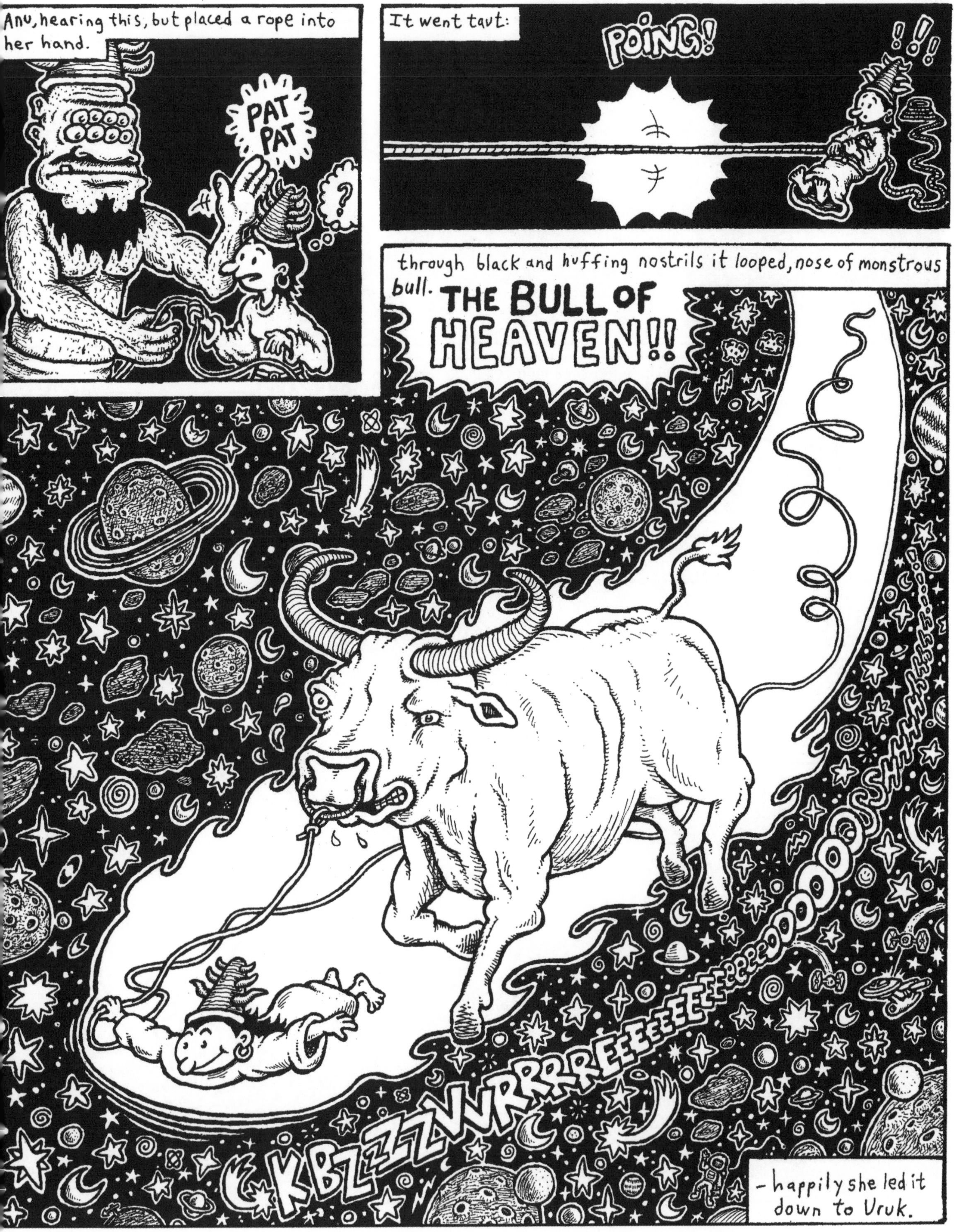
Anu, hearing this, but placed a rope into her hand.
PAT PAT
?
It went taut:
POING!
!!!
through black and huffing nostrils it looped, nose of monstrous bull.
THE BULL OF HEAVEN!!
KBZZZZVVRRRRREEEEEEEEEEEEOOOOOOOOSHHHHHH
-happily she led it down to Uruk.

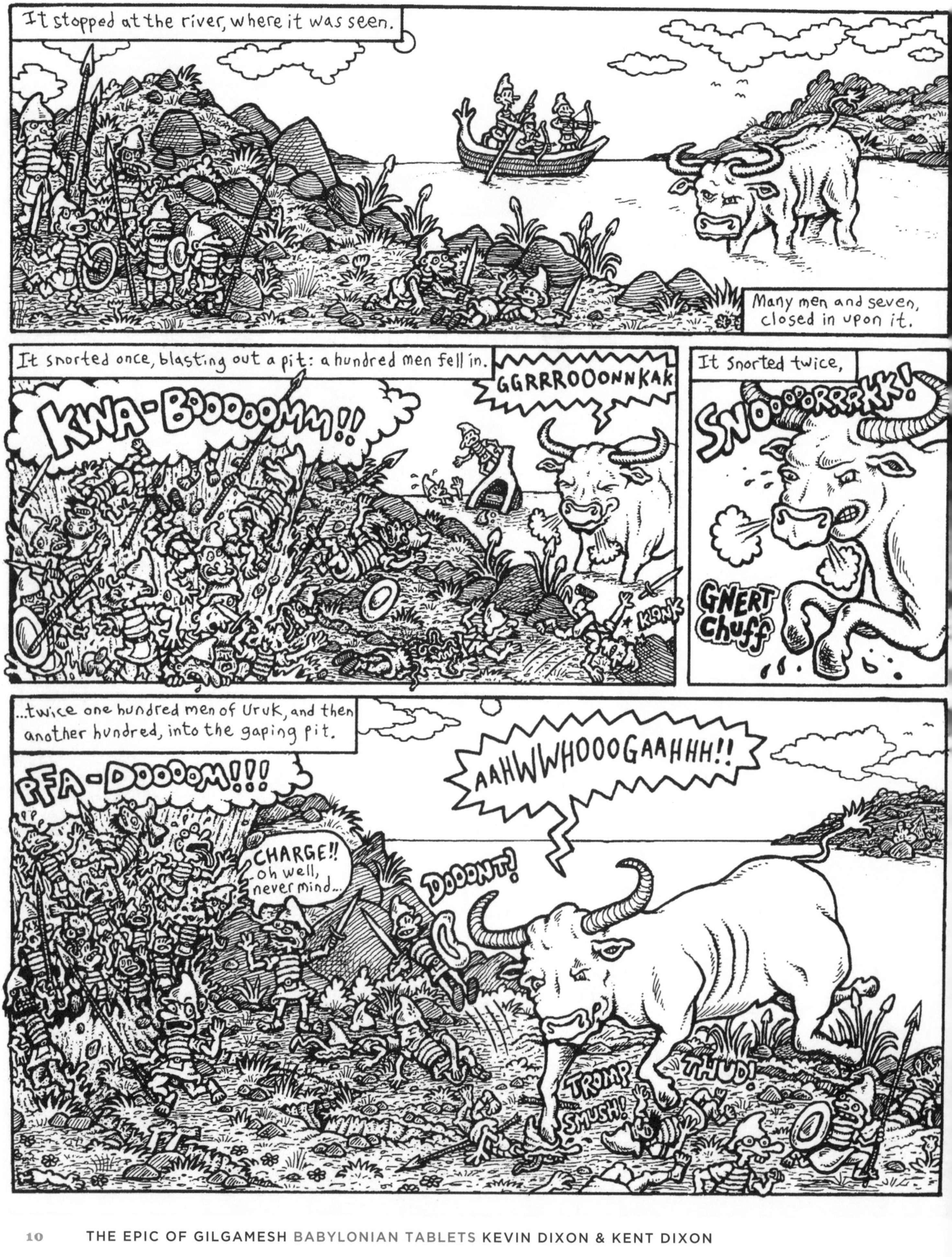
It stopped at the river, where it was seen.
Many men and seven, closed in upon it.
It snorted once, blasting out a pit: a hundred men fell in.
GGRRROOONNKAK
KWA-BOOOOOMM!!
KLONK
It snorted twice,
SNOOOORRRKK!
GNERT Chuff
...twice one hundred men of Uruk, and then another hundred, into the gaping pit.
PFA-DOOOOM!!!
AAHWWHOOOGAAHHH!!
CHARGE!! oh well, never mind...
DOOONT!
TROMP
SMUSH!
THUD!

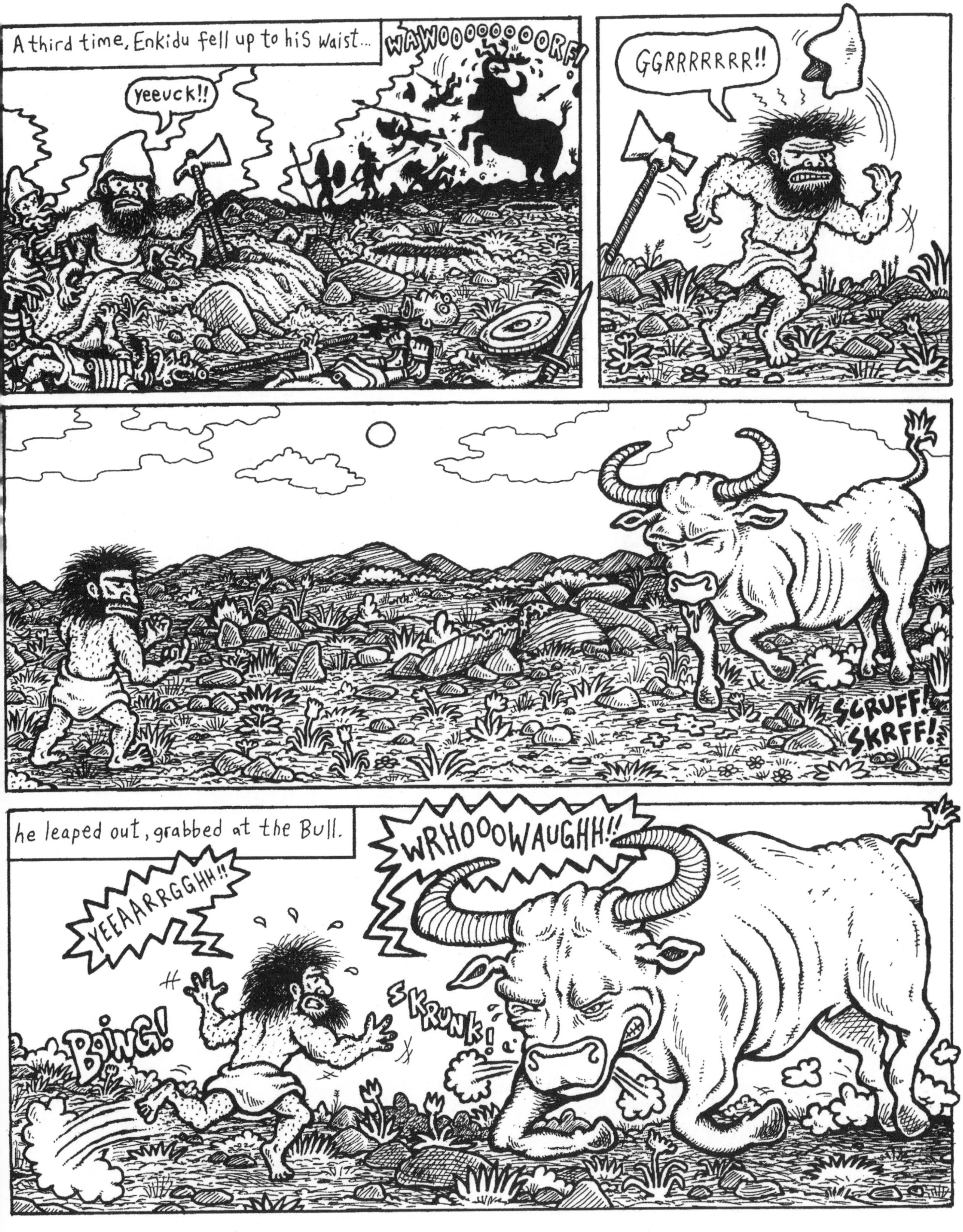
A third time, Enkidu fell up to his waist...
WAWOOOOOOOORF!
yeeuck!!
GGRRRRRRR!!
SCRUFF! SKRFF!
he leaped out, grabbed at the Bull.
WRHOOOWAUGHH!!
YEEAARRGGHH!!
BOING!
SKRUNK!

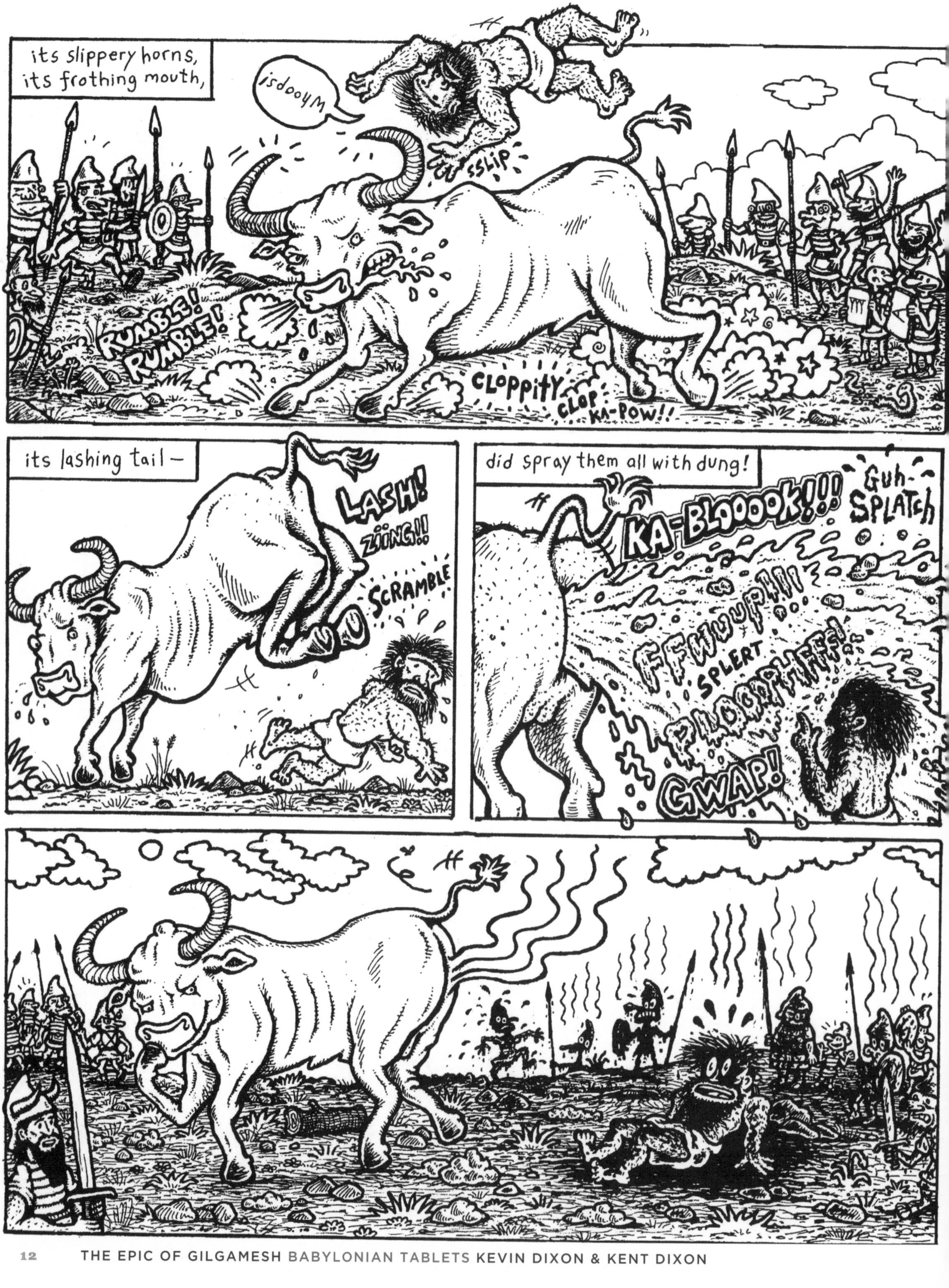
its slippery horns, its frothing mouth,
Whoops!
SSLIP
RUMBLE! RUMBLE!
CLOPPITY CLOP
KA-POW!!
its lashing tail—
LASH!
ZING!!
SCRAMBLE
did spray them all with dung!
KA-BLOOOOK!!!
GUH-SPLATCH
FFWUUUP!!!
SPLERT
GWAP!

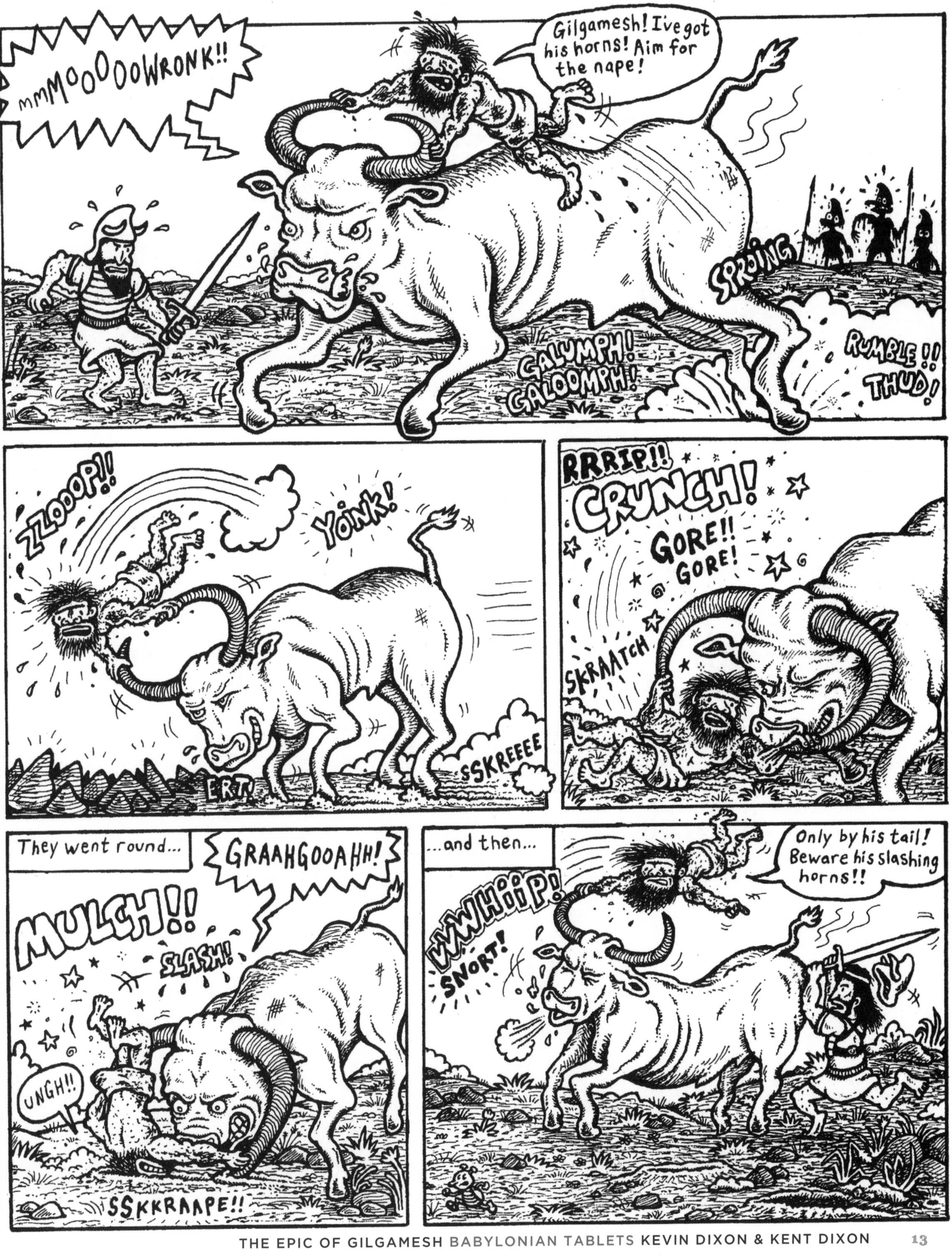
mmMOOOOOWRONK!!
Gilgamesh! I've got his horns! Aim for the nape!
SPROING
GALUMPH! GALOOMPH!
RUMBLE!! THUD!
ZZOOOP!!
YOINK!
ERT
SSKREEEE
RRRIP!!
CRUNCH!
GORE!! GORE!
SKRAATCH
They went round...
GRAAHGOOAHH!
MULCH!!
SLASH!
UNGH!!
SSKKRAAPE!!
...and then...
Only by his tail! Beware his slashing horns!!
WWHIIP!
SNORT!

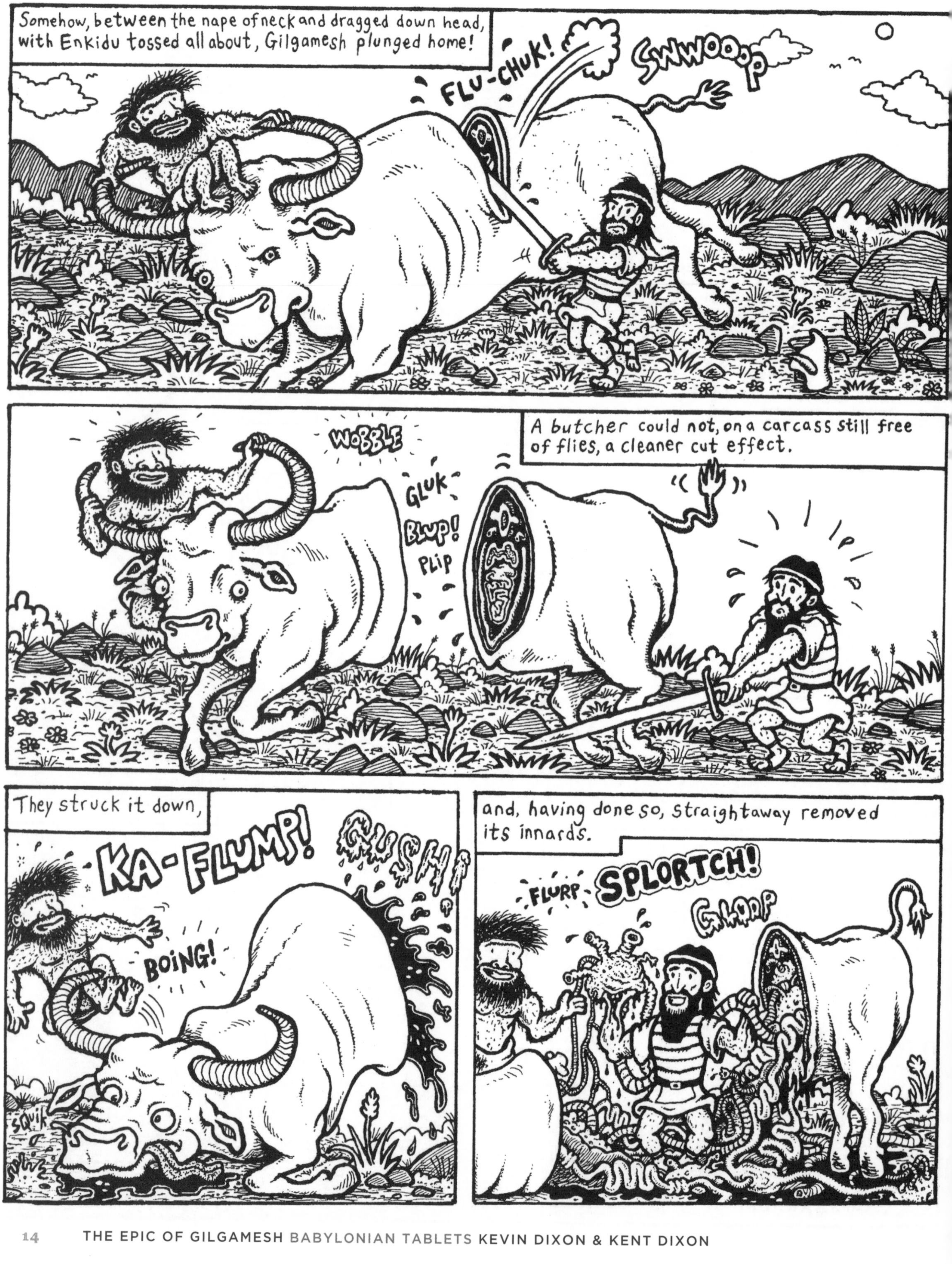
Somehow, between the nape of neck and dragged down head, with Enkidu tossed all about, Gilgamesh plunged home!
FLU-CHUK!
SWWOOOP
A butcher could not, on a carcass still free of flies, a cleaner cut effect.
WOBBLE
GLUK
BLUP!
PLIP
They struck it down,
KA-FLUMP!
GUSH!
BOING!
SQUIK
and, having done so, straightaway removed its innards.
FLURP
SPLORTCH!
GLOOP

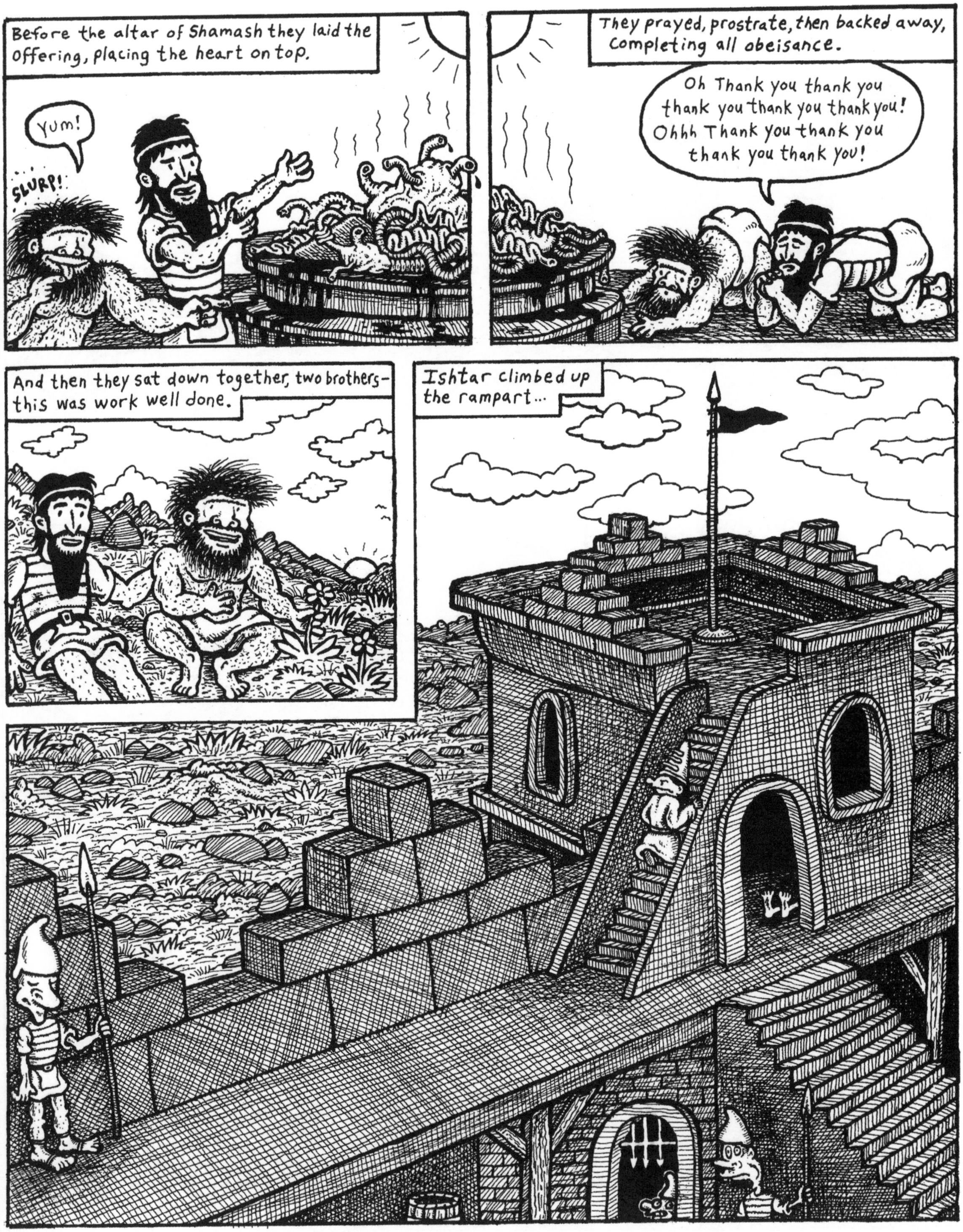
Before the altar of Shamash they laid the offering, placing the heart on top.
Yum!
SLURP!
They prayed, prostrate, then backed away, completing all obeisance.
Oh Thank you thank you thank you thank you thank you! Ohhh Thank you thank you thank you thank you!
And then they sat down together, two brothers- this was work well done.
Ishtar climbed up the rampart...

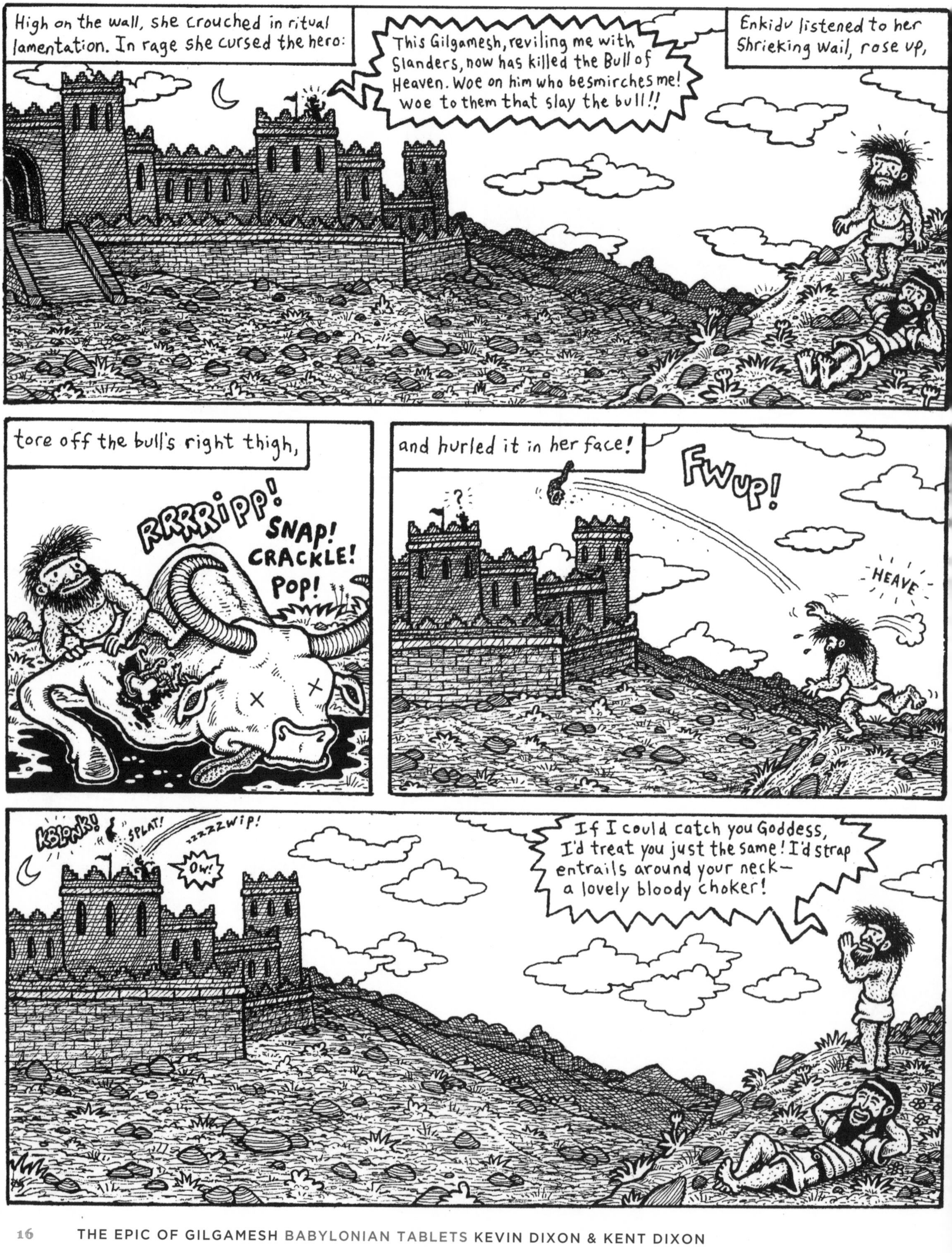
High on the wall, she crouched in ritual lamentation. In rage she cursed the hero:
This Gilgamesh, reviling me with slanders, now has killed the Bull of Heaven. Woe on him who besmirches me! Woe to them that slay the bull!!
Enkidu listened to her shrieking wail, rose up,
tore off the bull's right thigh,
RRRRIPP!
SNAP!
CRACKLE!
POP!
and hurled it in her face!
?
FWUP!
HEAVE
KBLONK!
SPLAT!
ZZZZZWIP!
OW!
If I could catch you Goddess, I'd treat you just the same! I'd strap entrails around your neck— a lovely bloody choker!

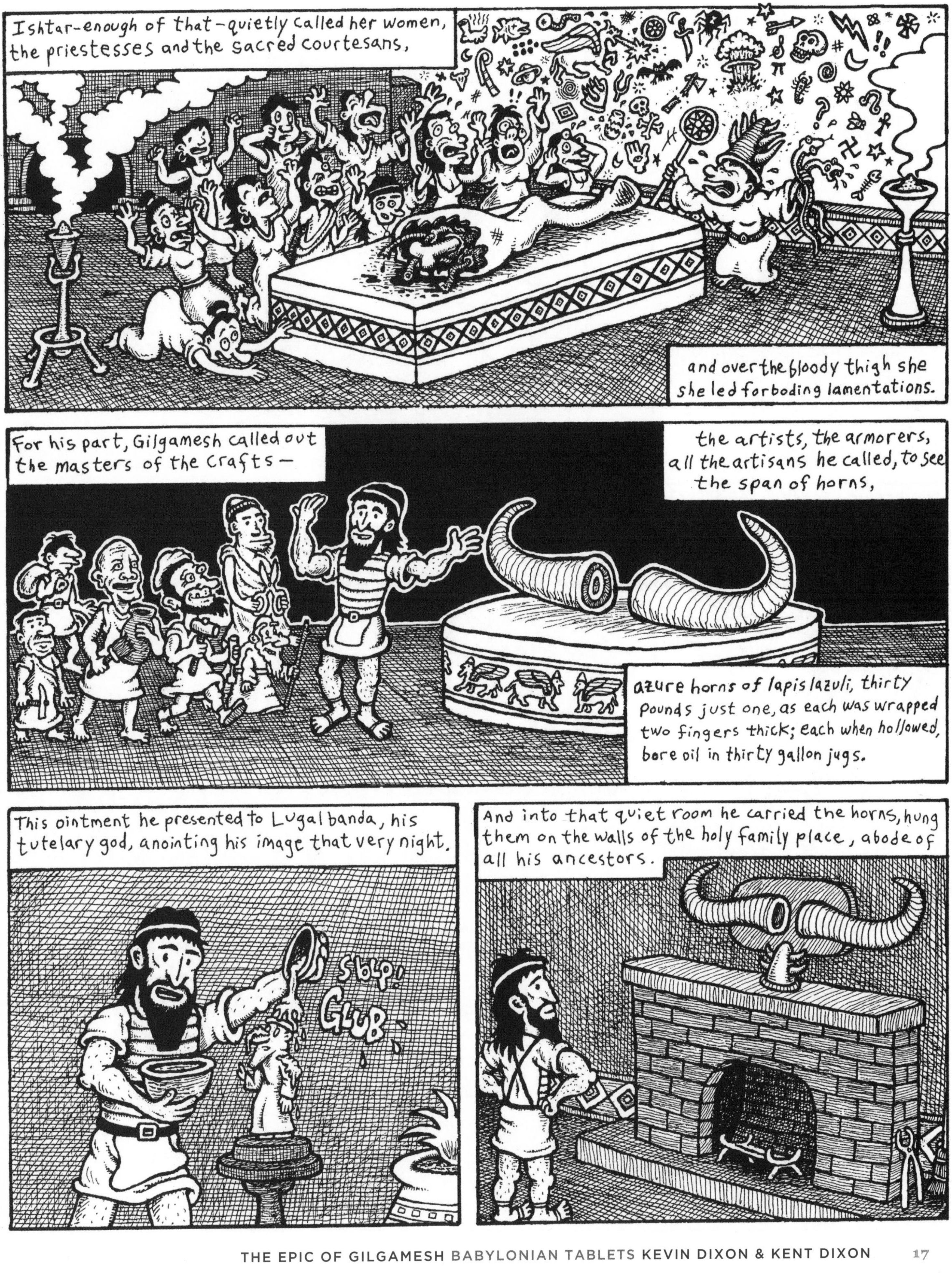
Ishtar–enough of that–quietly called her women, the priestesses and the sacred courtesans,
and over the bloody thigh she she led forboding lamentations.
For his part, Gilgamesh called out the masters of the crafts–
the artists, the armorers, all the artisans he called, to see the span of horns,
azure horns of lapis lazuli, thirty pounds just one, as each was wrapped two fingers thick; each when hollowed, bore oil in thirty gallon jugs.
This ointment he presented to Lugalbanda, his tutelary god, anointing his image that very night.
SBLP!
GLUB
And into that quiet room he carried the horns, hung them on the walls of the holy family place, abode of all his ancestors.

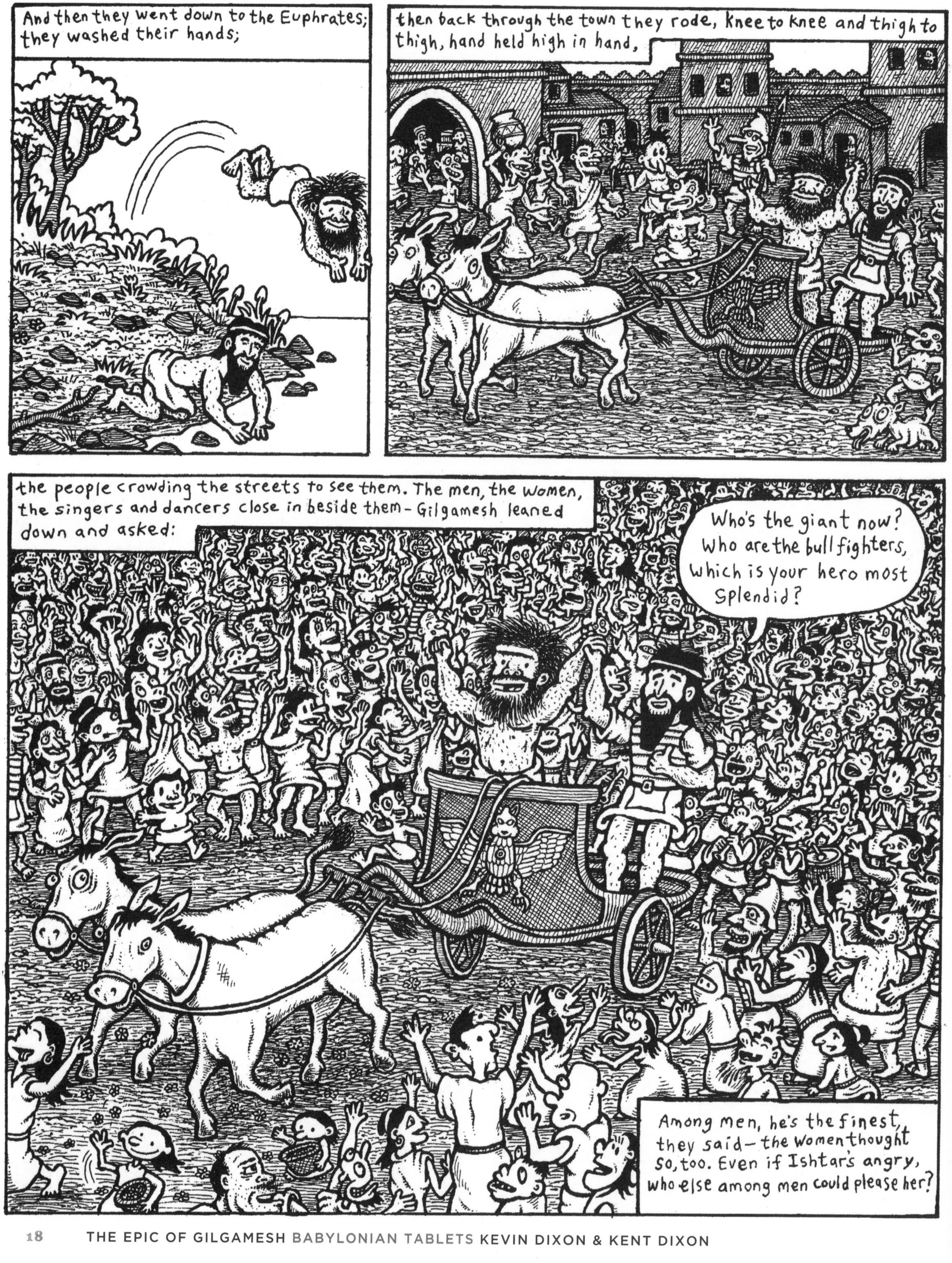
And then they went down to the Euphrates; they washed their hands;
then back through the town they rode, knee to knee and thigh to thigh, hand held high in hand,
the people crowding the streets to see them. The men, the women, the singers and dancers close in beside them– Gilgamesh leaned down and asked:
Who's the giant now? Who are the bullfighters, which is your hero most splendid?
Among men, he's the finest, they said– the women thought so, too. Even if Ishtar's angry, who else among men could please her?

"Coyote and the Pebbles"

Native American folktale

STORY BY **Dayton Edmonds**

ART BY **Micah Farritor**

BEFORE THE ARRIVAL OF EUROPEANS, NATIVE North American tribes had pictographs and petroglyphs but no alphabet-based written languages. Knowledge, entertainment, and wisdom were overwhelmingly passed along orally, resulting in a canon of stories that existed for millennia only in memories and voices.

Since the start of the European invasion, those stories, in countless variations, have been set down in text, and it was in 2010 that a group of Indian folktales was graphi-cally adapted, in the stunning book *Trickster*. Editor Matt Dembicki paired artists with twenty-one Native American storytellers, including Dayton Edmonds of the Caddo Nation, who told his tribe's tale of why the night sky looks the way it does (thanks to the arrogance and clumsiness of that trickster, Coyote). Micah Farritor—who has previously illustrated *The War of the Worlds* and *A Christmas Carol*—supplied the highly atmospheric artwork for this age-old work of oral literature.

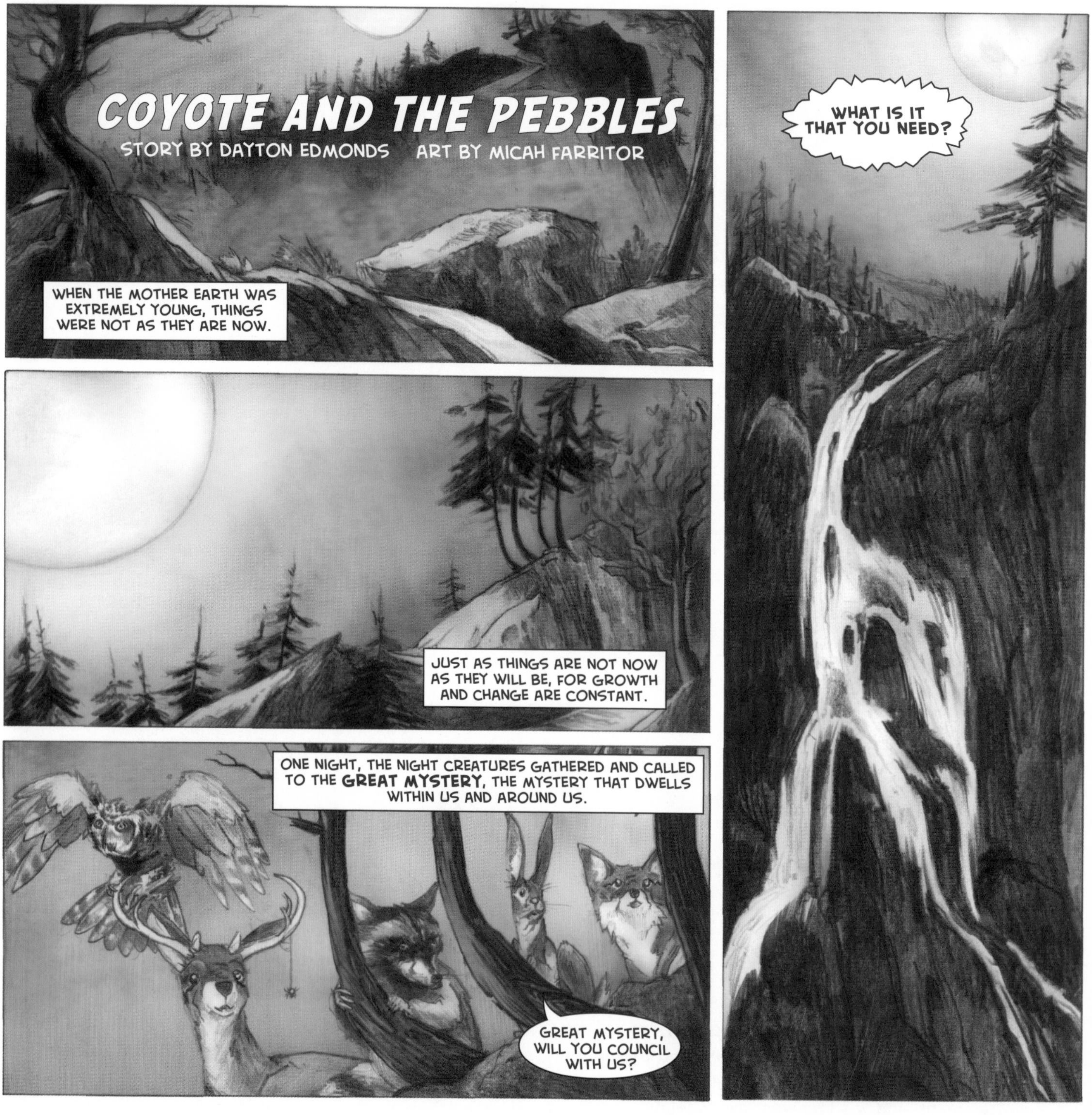
COYOTE AND THE PEBBLES
STORY BY DAYTON EDMONDS ART BY MICAH FARRITOR
WHEN THE MOTHER EARTH WAS EXTREMELY YOUNG, THINGS WERE NOT AS THEY ARE NOW.
JUST AS THINGS ARE NOT NOW AS THEY WILL BE, FOR GROWTH AND CHANGE ARE CONSTANT.
ONE NIGHT, THE NIGHT CREATURES GATHERED AND CALLED TO THE GREAT MYSTERY, THE MYSTERY THAT DWELLS WITHIN US AND AROUND US.
GREAT MYSTERY, WILL YOU COUNCIL WITH US?
WHAT IS IT THAT YOU NEED?

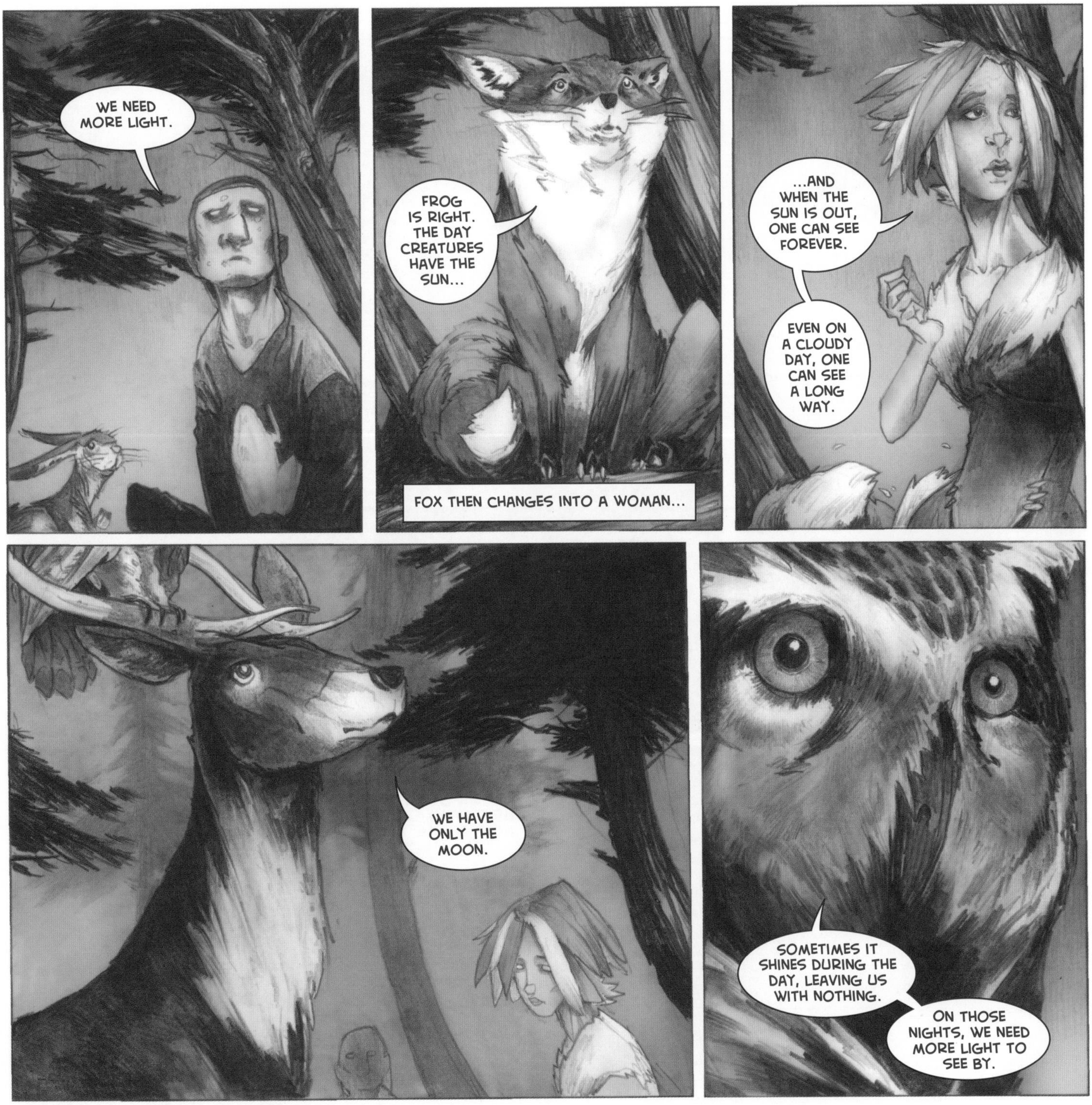
WE NEED MORE LIGHT.
FROG IS RIGHT. THE DAY CREATURES HAVE THE SUN...
FOX THEN CHANGES INTO A WOMAN...
...AND WHEN THE SUN IS OUT, ONE CAN SEE FOREVER.
EVEN ON A CLOUDY DAY, ONE CAN SEE A LONG WAY.
WE HAVE ONLY THE MOON.
SOMETIMES IT SHINES DURING THE DAY, LEAVING US WITH NOTHING.
ON THOSE NIGHTS, WE NEED MORE LIGHT TO SEE BY.

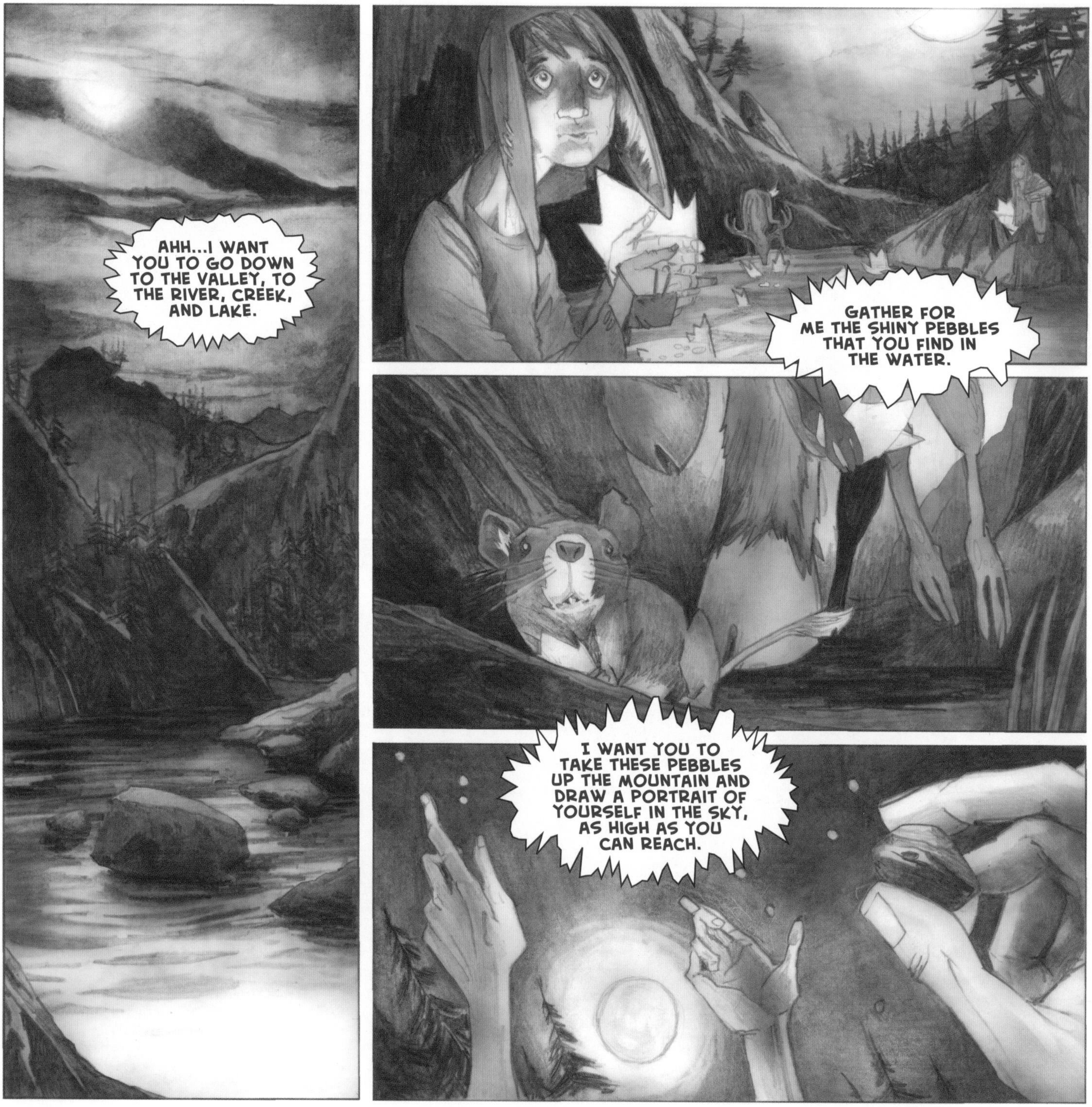
AHH...I WANT YOU TO GO DOWN TO THE VALLEY, TO THE RIVER, CREEK, AND LAKE.
GATHER FOR ME THE SHINY PEBBLES THAT YOU FIND IN THE WATER.
I WANT YOU TO TAKE THESE PEBBLES UP THE MOUNTAIN AND DRAW A PORTRAIT OF YOURSELF IN THE SKY, AS HIGH AS YOU CAN REACH.

COYOTE, A DAY-AND-NIGHT CREATURE, WAS A LITTLE LATE FOR THE MEETING.
SOME SAY HE WAS RUNNING ON INDIAN TIME.
WHAT ARE THEY DOING?
WAKE UP TO THIS, OLD MAN! THEY'VE STARTED WITHOUT YOU!
THE GREAT MYSTERY ANSWERED THE CALL FOR MORE LIGHT IN THE DARKNESS, AND BID ALL NIGHT CREATURES TO COLLECT PEBBLES FROM RIVER, CREEK, AND LAKE...
COYOTE TURNS TO HIS HUMAN FORM...
...AND TOLD THEM, "BRING THEM BACK TO THE MOUNTAIN, AND PAINT A PICTURE OF YOURSELF IN THE SKY."
LOOK AT THESE SELFISH ONES!

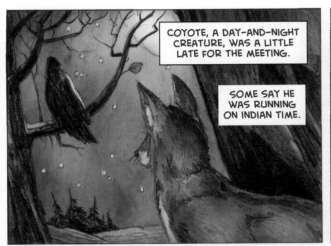

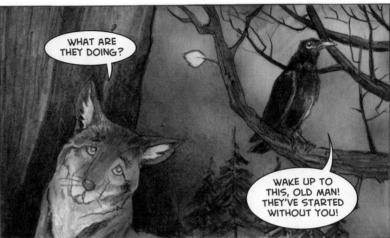

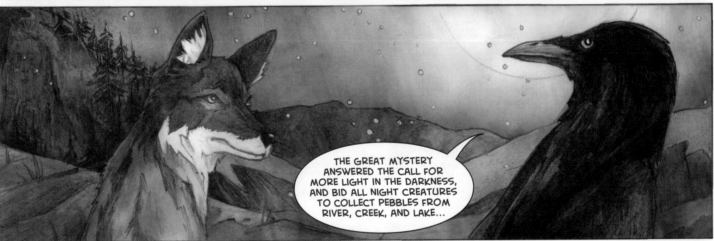

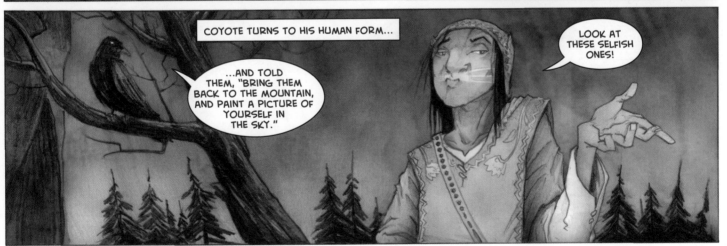

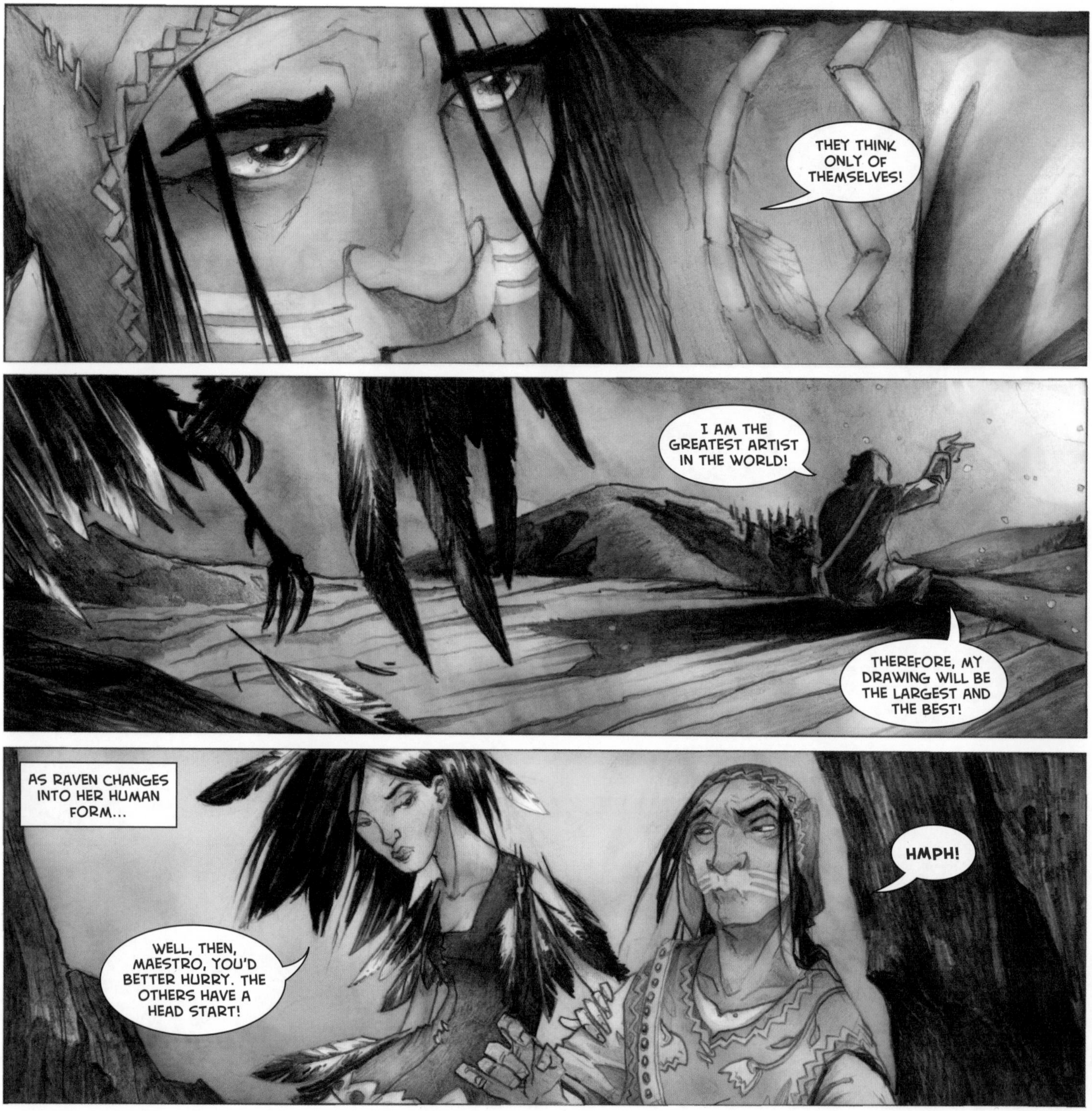
THEY THINK ONLY OF THEMSELVES!
I AM THE GREATEST ARTIST IN THE WORLD!
THEREFORE, MY DRAWING WILL BE THE LARGEST AND THE BEST!
AS RAVEN CHANGES INTO HER HUMAN FORM...
HMPH!
WELL, THEN, MAESTRO, YOU'D BETTER HURRY. THE OTHERS HAVE A HEAD START!

COYOTE DESCENDED INTO THE VALLEY.

FIRST, HE WENT TO THE RIVER.

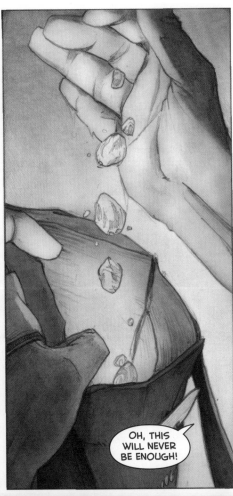

OH, THIS WILL NEVER BE ENOUGH!

HE TURNED BACK TO HIS ANIMAL FORM...

...AND THEN RAN TO THE CREEK.

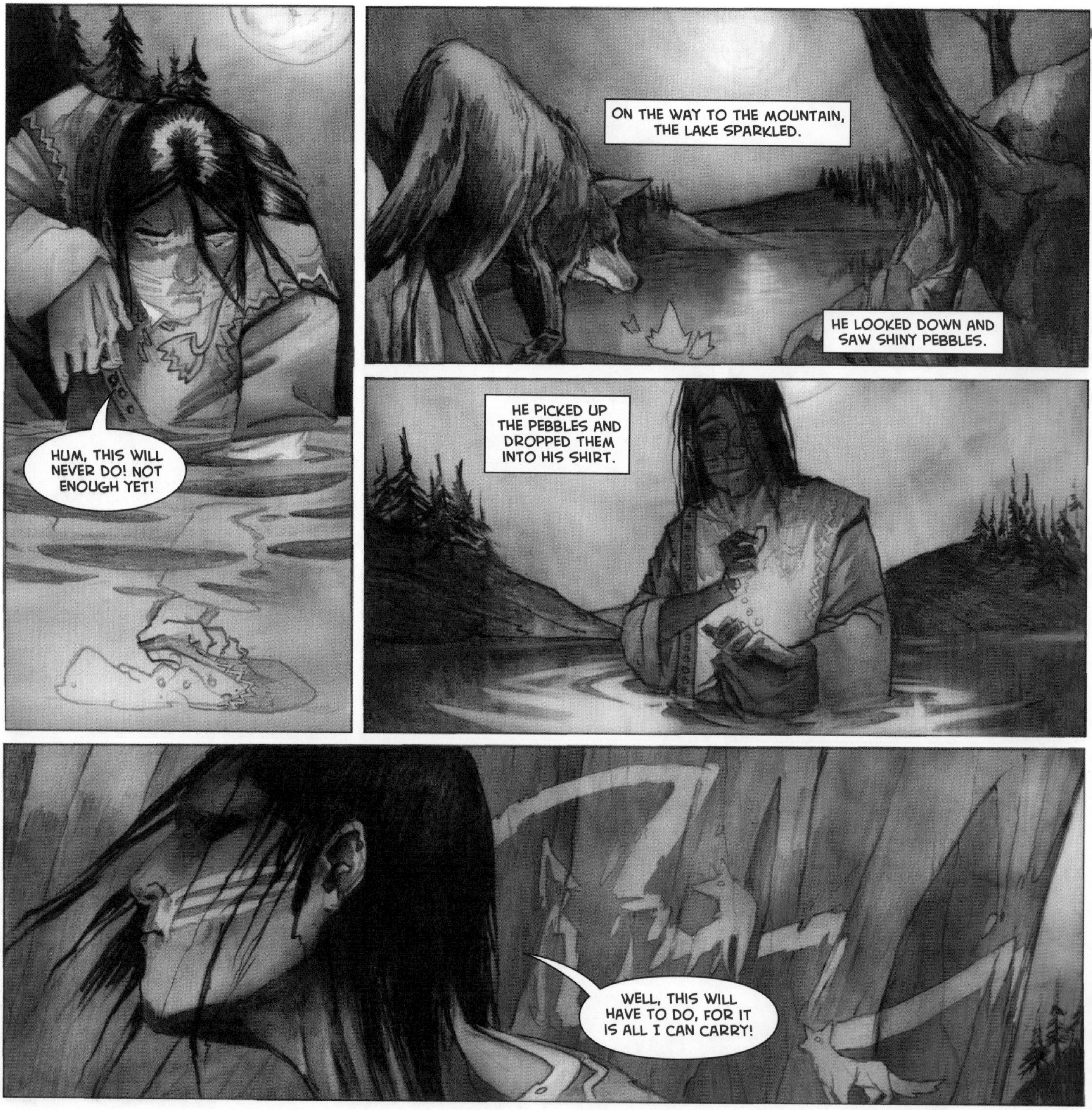
HUM, THIS WILL NEVER DO! NOT ENOUGH YET!
ON THE WAY TO THE MOUNTAIN, THE LAKE SPARKLED.
HE LOOKED DOWN AND SAW SHINY PEBBLES.
HE PICKED UP THE PEBBLES AND DROPPED THEM INTO HIS SHIRT.
WELL, THIS WILL HAVE TO DO, FOR IT IS ALL I CAN CARRY!

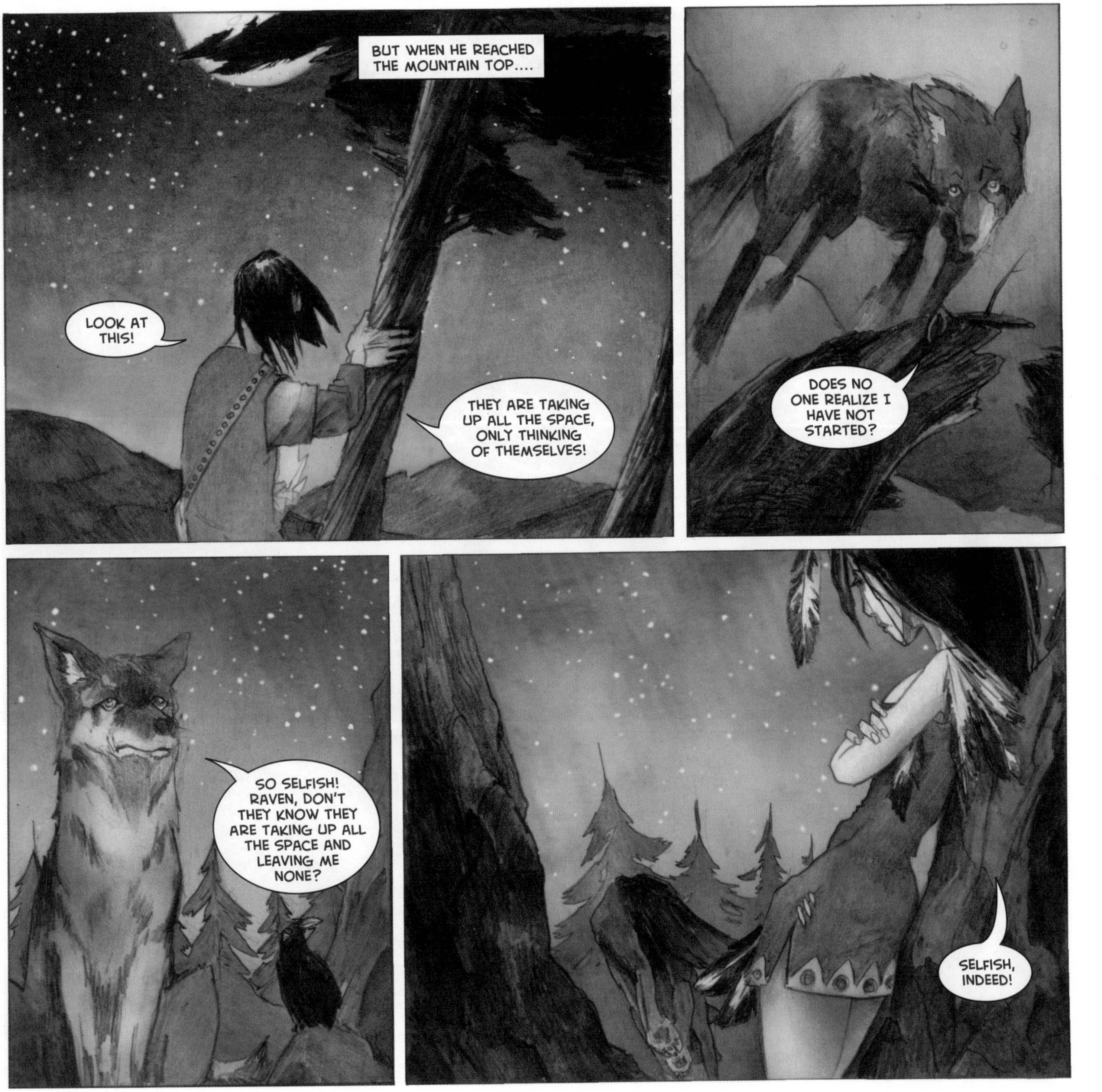
BUT WHEN HE REACHED THE MOUNTAIN TOP....
LOOK AT THIS!
THEY ARE TAKING UP ALL THE SPACE, ONLY THINKING OF THEMSELVES!
DOES NO ONE REALIZE I HAVE NOT STARTED?
SO SELFISH! RAVEN, DON'T THEY KNOW THEY ARE TAKING UP ALL THE SPACE AND LEAVING ME NONE?
SELFISH, INDEED!

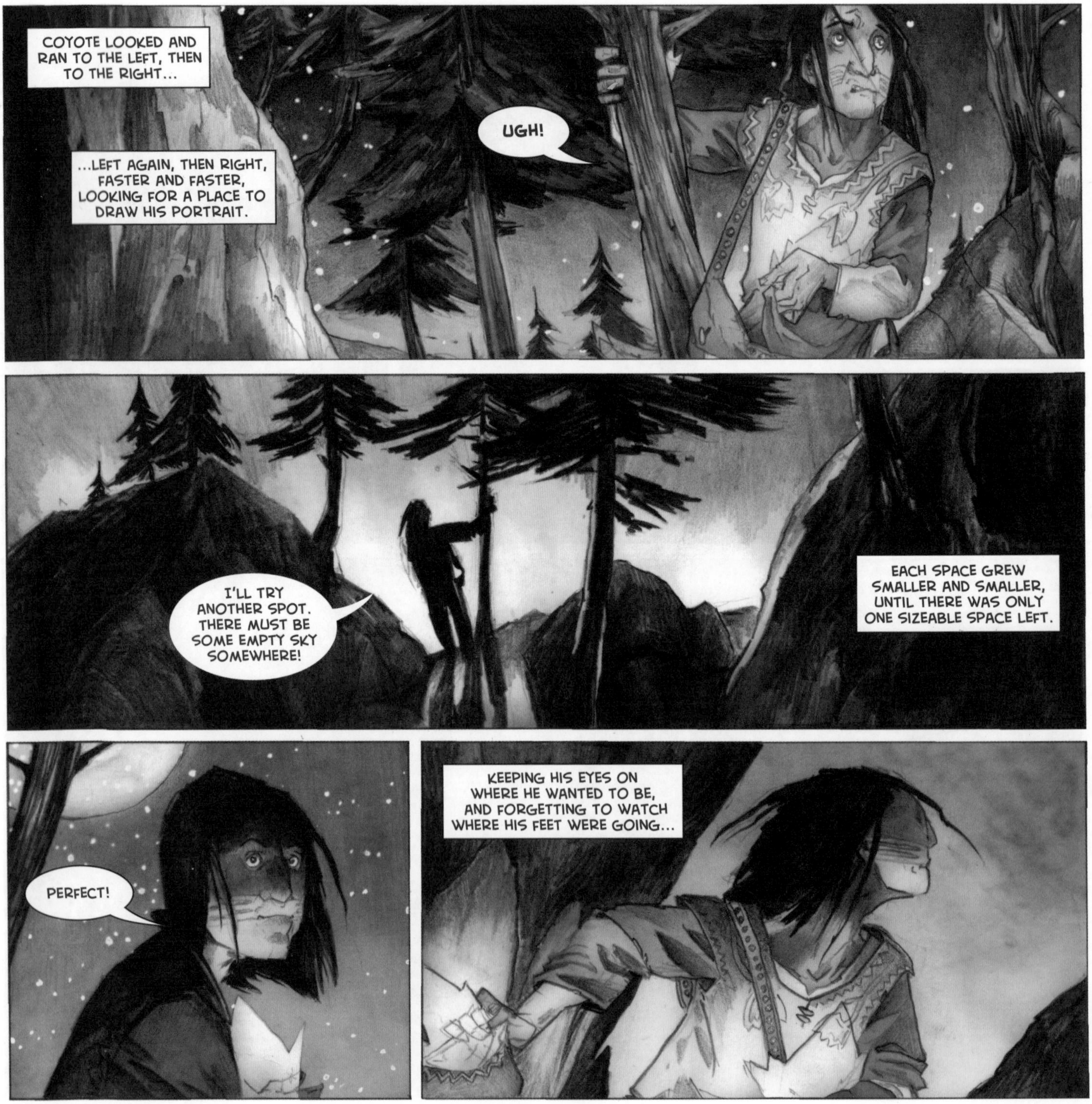
COYOTE LOOKED AND RAN TO THE LEFT, THEN TO THE RIGHT...
UGH!
...LEFT AGAIN, THEN RIGHT, FASTER AND FASTER, LOOKING FOR A PLACE TO DRAW HIS PORTRAIT.
I'LL TRY ANOTHER SPOT. THERE MUST BE SOME EMPTY SKY SOMEWHERE!
EACH SPACE GREW SMALLER AND SMALLER, UNTIL THERE WAS ONLY ONE SIZEABLE SPACE LEFT.
PERFECT!
KEEPING HIS EYES ON WHERE HE WANTED TO BE, AND FORGETTING TO WATCH WHERE HIS FEET WERE GOING...

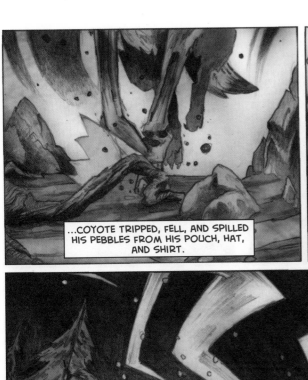

...COYOTE TRIPPED, FELL, AND SPILLED HIS PEBBLES FROM HIS POUCH, HAT, AND SHIRT.

OH, NO!

THE PEBBLES SPRANG AROUND, HIGHER AND HIGHER, HERE AND THERE, BUMPING INTO EACH OTHER, UNTIL THEY WERE BUMPING INTO EVERYONE ELSE'S DRAWINGS.

NO, NO, NO...

PEBBLE BUMPED PEBBLE, AND A CHAIN REACTION CAUSED EVERYONE'S ARTWORK TO EXPLODE.

THE NIGHT CREATURES COULD ONLY WATCH AS THEIR PORTRAITS WERE DESTROYED.

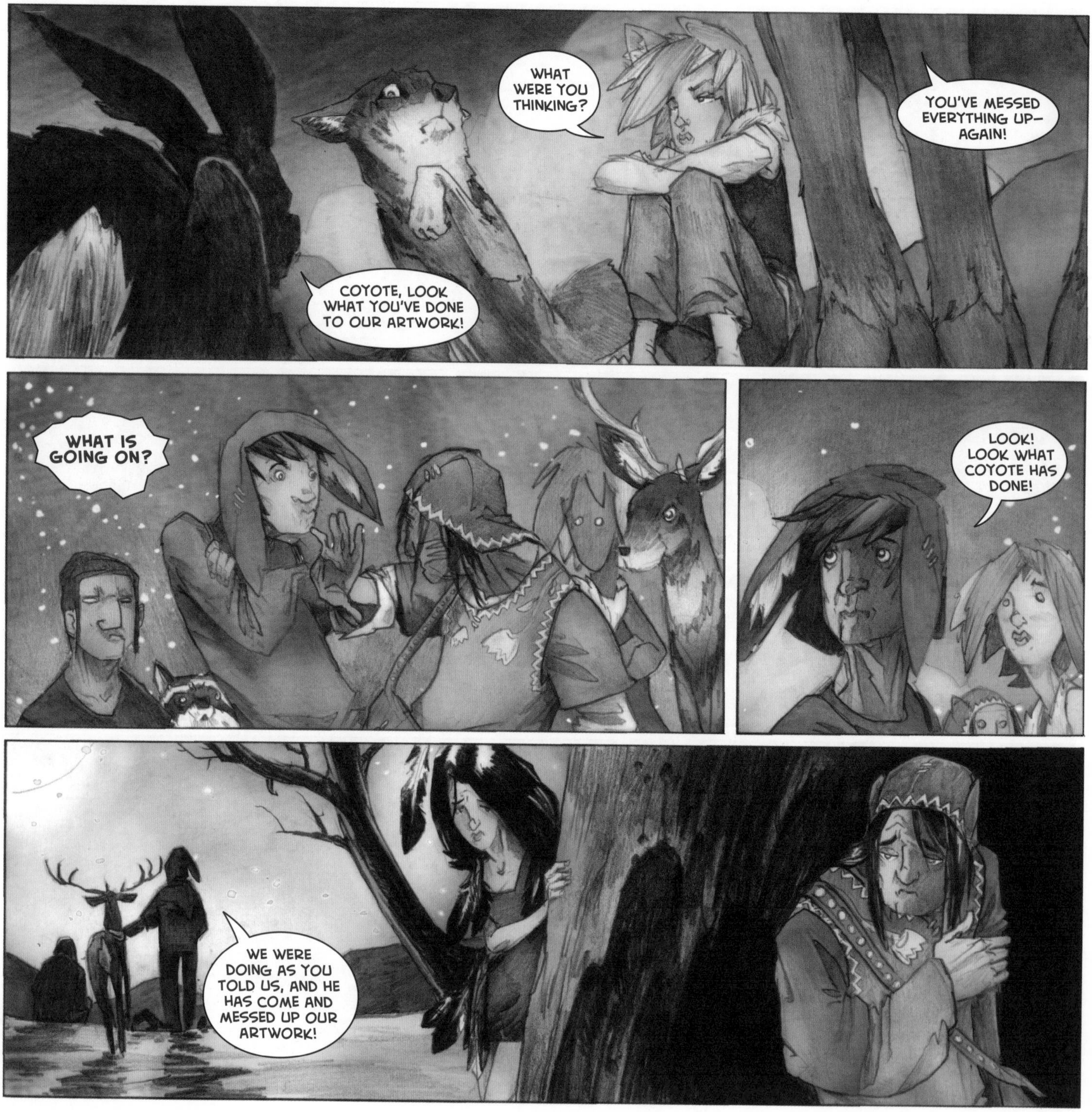
WHAT WERE YOU THINKING?
YOU'VE MESSED EVERYTHING UP—AGAIN!
COYOTE, LOOK WHAT YOU'VE DONE TO OUR ARTWORK!
WHAT IS GOING ON?
LOOK! LOOK WHAT COYOTE HAS DONE!
WE WERE DOING AS YOU TOLD US, AND HE HAS COME AND MESSED UP OUR ARTWORK!

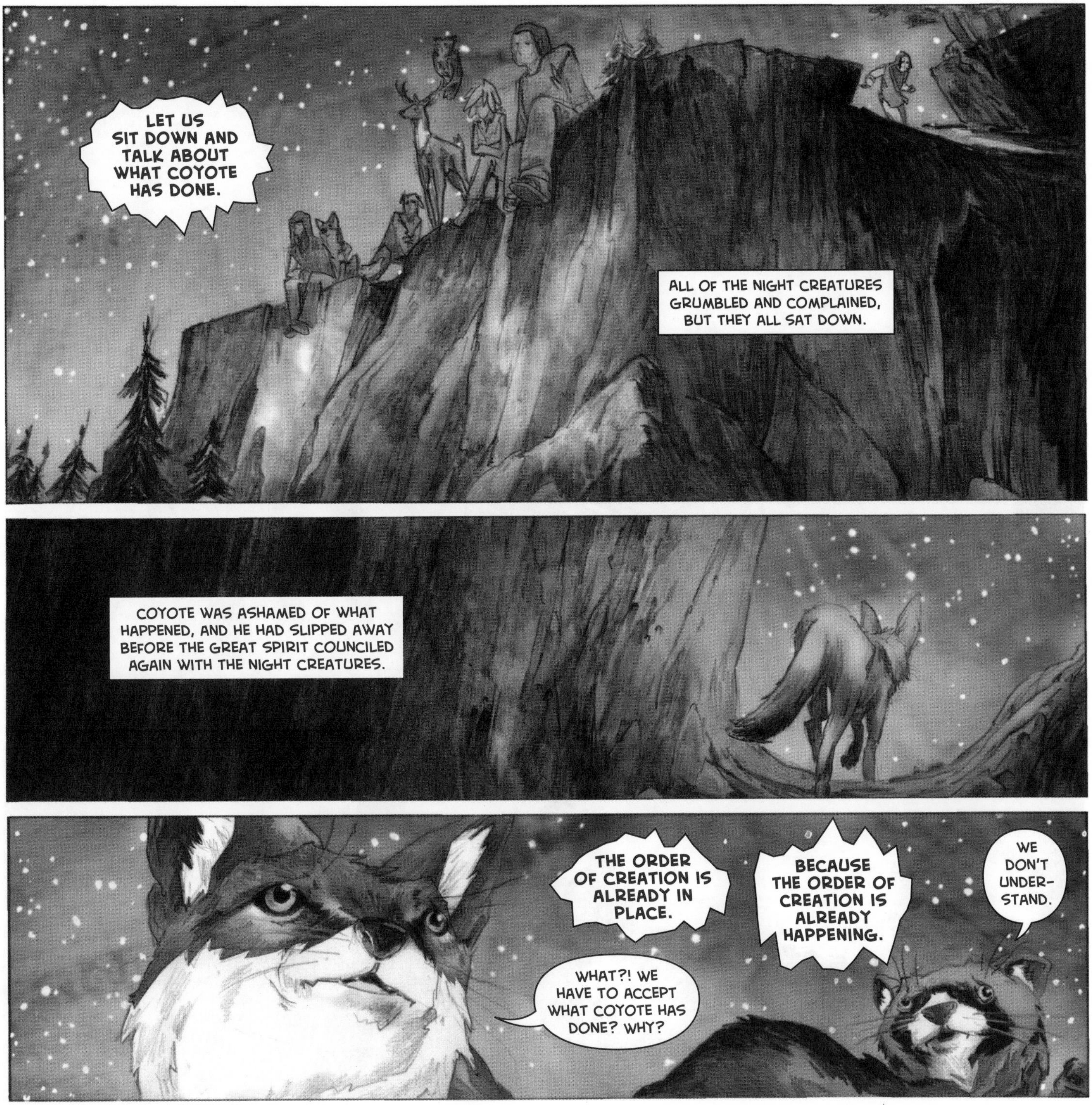

LET US SIT DOWN AND TALK ABOUT WHAT COYOTE HAS DONE.
ALL OF THE NIGHT CREATURES GRUMBLED AND COMPLAINED, BUT THEY ALL SAT DOWN.
COYOTE WAS ASHAMED OF WHAT HAPPENED, AND HE HAD SLIPPED AWAY BEFORE THE GREAT SPIRIT COUNCILED AGAIN WITH THE NIGHT CREATURES.
THE ORDER OF CREATION IS ALREADY IN PLACE.
WHAT?! WE HAVE TO ACCEPT WHAT COYOTE HAS DONE? WHY?
BECAUSE THE ORDER OF CREATION IS ALREADY HAPPENING.
WE DON'T UNDER-STAND.

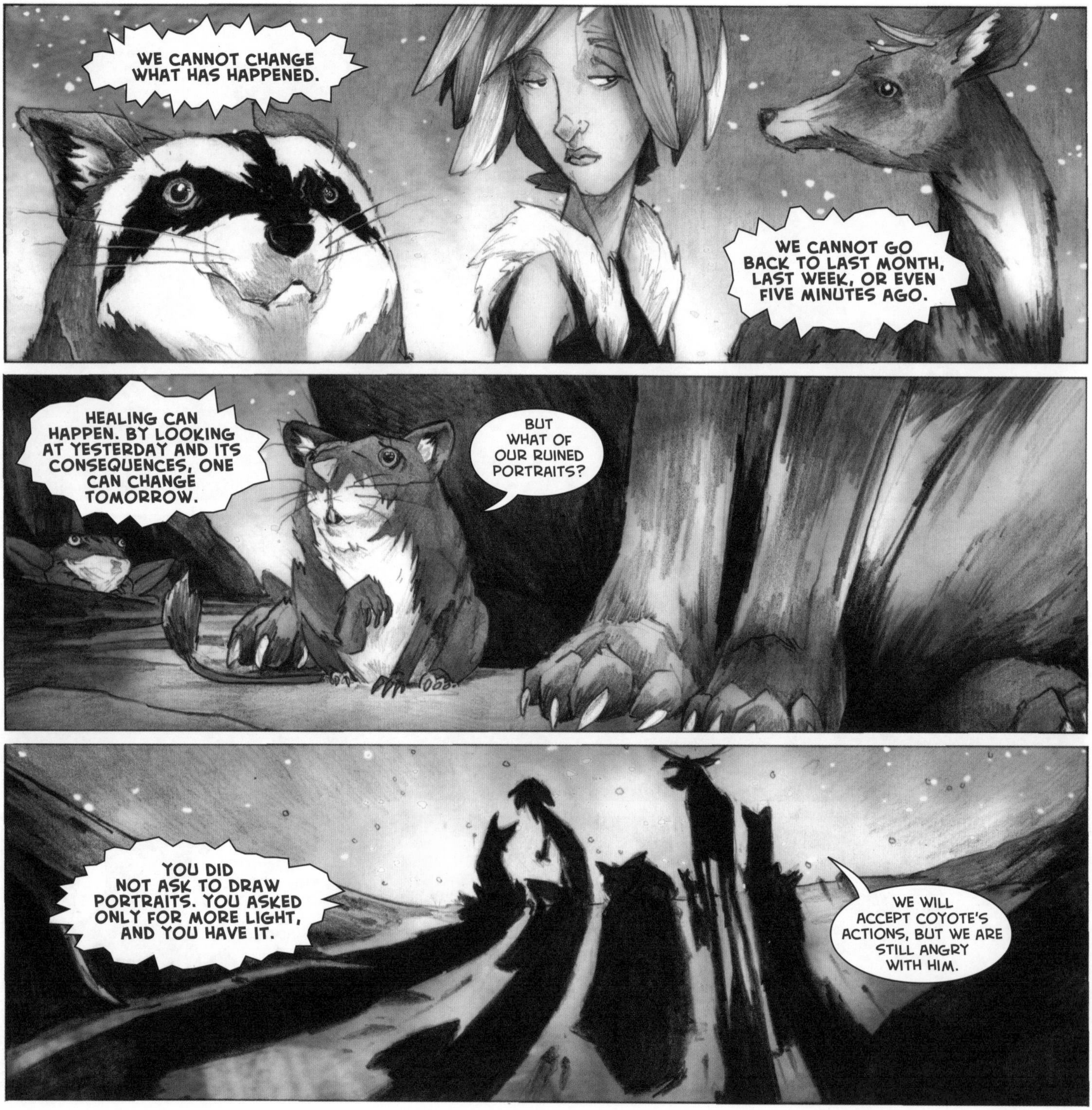
WE CANNOT CHANGE WHAT HAS HAPPENED.
WE CANNOT GO BACK TO LAST MONTH, LAST WEEK, OR EVEN FIVE MINUTES AGO.
HEALING CAN HAPPEN. BY LOOKING AT YESTERDAY AND ITS CONSEQUENCES, ONE CAN CHANGE TOMORROW.
BUT WHAT OF OUR RUINED PORTRAITS?
YOU DID NOT ASK TO DRAW PORTRAITS. YOU ASKED ONLY FOR MORE LIGHT, AND YOU HAVE IT.
WE WILL ACCEPT COYOTE'S ACTIONS, BUT WE ARE STILL ANGRY WITH HIM.

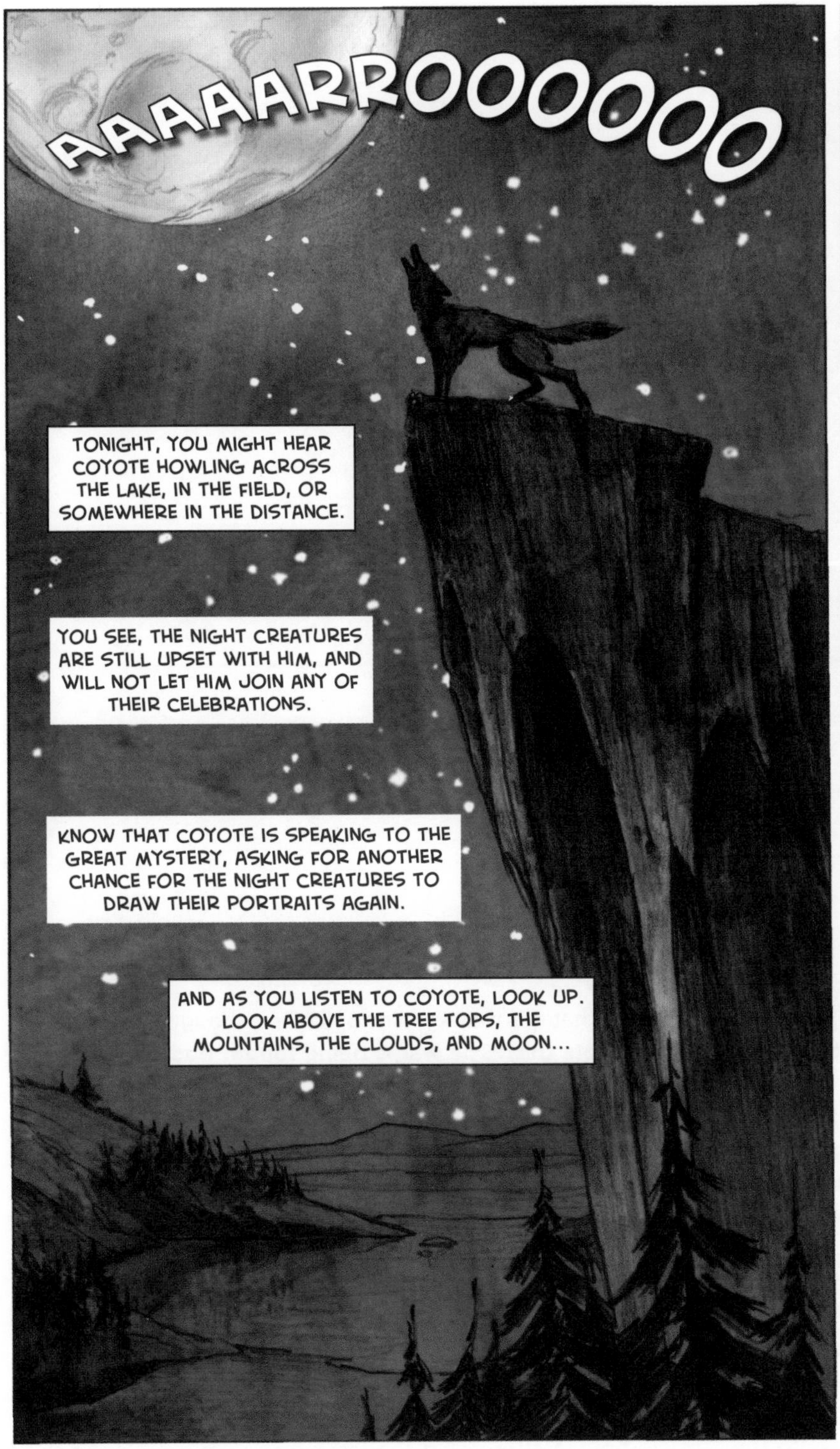
AAAAARROOOOOO
TONIGHT, YOU MIGHT HEAR COYOTE HOWLING ACROSS THE LAKE, IN THE FIELD, OR SOMEWHERE IN THE DISTANCE.
YOU SEE, THE NIGHT CREATURES ARE STILL UPSET WITH HIM, AND WILL NOT LET HIM JOIN ANY OF THEIR CELEBRATIONS.
KNOW THAT COYOTE IS SPEAKING TO THE GREAT MYSTERY, ASKING FOR ANOTHER CHANCE FOR THE NIGHT CREATURES TO DRAW THEIR PORTRAITS AGAIN.
AND AS YOU LISTEN TO COYOTE, LOOK UP. LOOK ABOVE THE TREE TOPS, THE MOUNTAINS, THE CLOUDS, AND MOON...

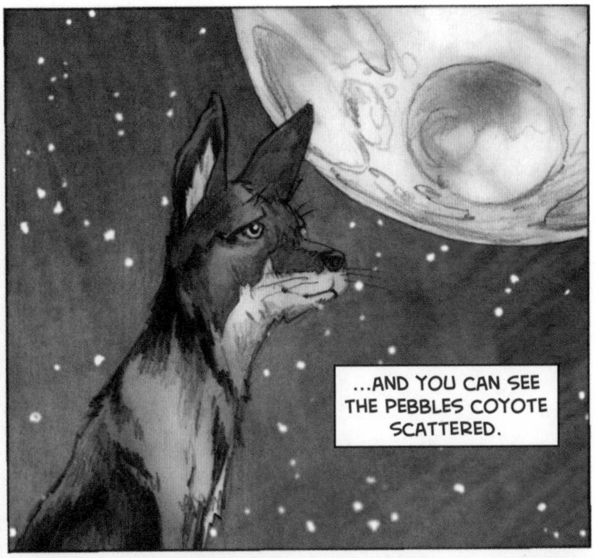
...AND YOU CAN SEE THE PEBBLES COYOTE SCATTERED.

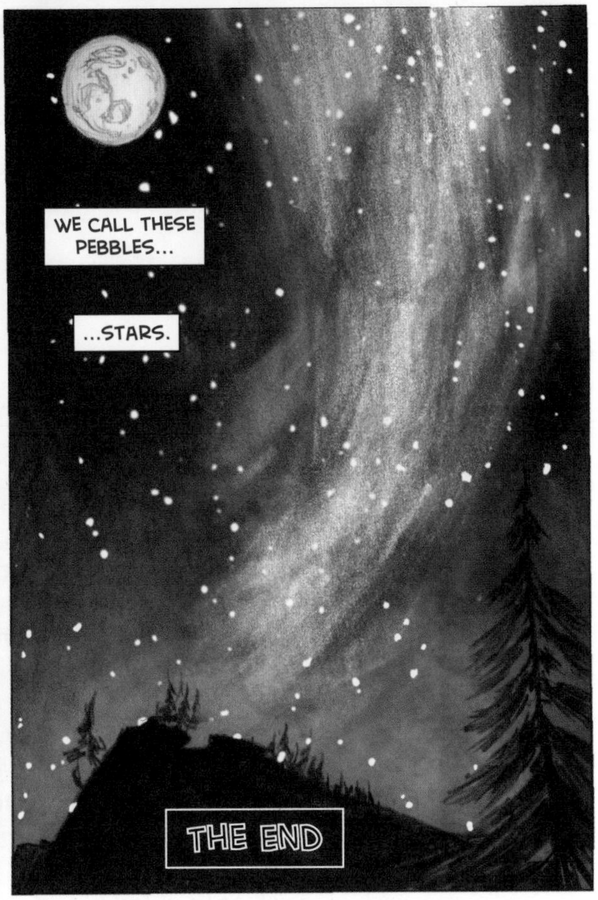
WE CALL THESE PEBBLES...
...STARS.
THE END

The Iliad

Homer

ART/ADAPTATION BY **Alice Duke**

THE ILIAD AND THE ODYSSEY ARE SUCH TITANIC, endlessly influential monoliths of literature that it's easy to overlook their humble and hazy beginnings. Professor Ralph Hexter reminds us that the twin summits of Western literature started "as sung entertainment in the banquet halls of petty chieftains in Greece and around the Aegean basin during a time often called the Dark Age of Greece (roughly the years 1150-800 BCE)."

He continues: "No matter what role a bard named Homer had in the final shaping and polishing of the epics, the enduring strength of the two works lies in the facts that they are the living productions of entire cultures, the culmination of the narrative talent of who knows how many bards and audiences, each of which contributed in some way to the drama, the images, the wisdom—in short, the humanity to be discovered in these poems."

The Iliad relates events during several weeks in the final year of the decade-long siege of Troy by Greek soldiers, sometime in the twelfth or thirteenth century BCE. (There's evidence that this war actually took place, though not everyone accepts this.) The war is being fought because Paris, the Prince of Troy, abducted the stunning Helen, wife of Menelaus, the King of Sparta. In Book Three, the portion being adapted here, Paris and Menelaus agree to settle the entire war with a personal duel (which is really how all wars should be fought—the two men with the beef slug it out; the winner's country is the victor). But, as is the case throughout *The Iliad,* gods and goddesses interfere with human events. . . .

Alice Duke, who specializes in illustrations of the fantastic, originally started a full-color treatment of this pivotal segment of *The Iliad* but eventually opted for monochromatic tints in alternating shades, which give the piece an older and starker feel.

SOURCE

Hexter, Ralph. *A Guide to The Odyssey: A Commentary on the English Translation of Robert Fitzgerald*. Vintage, 1993.

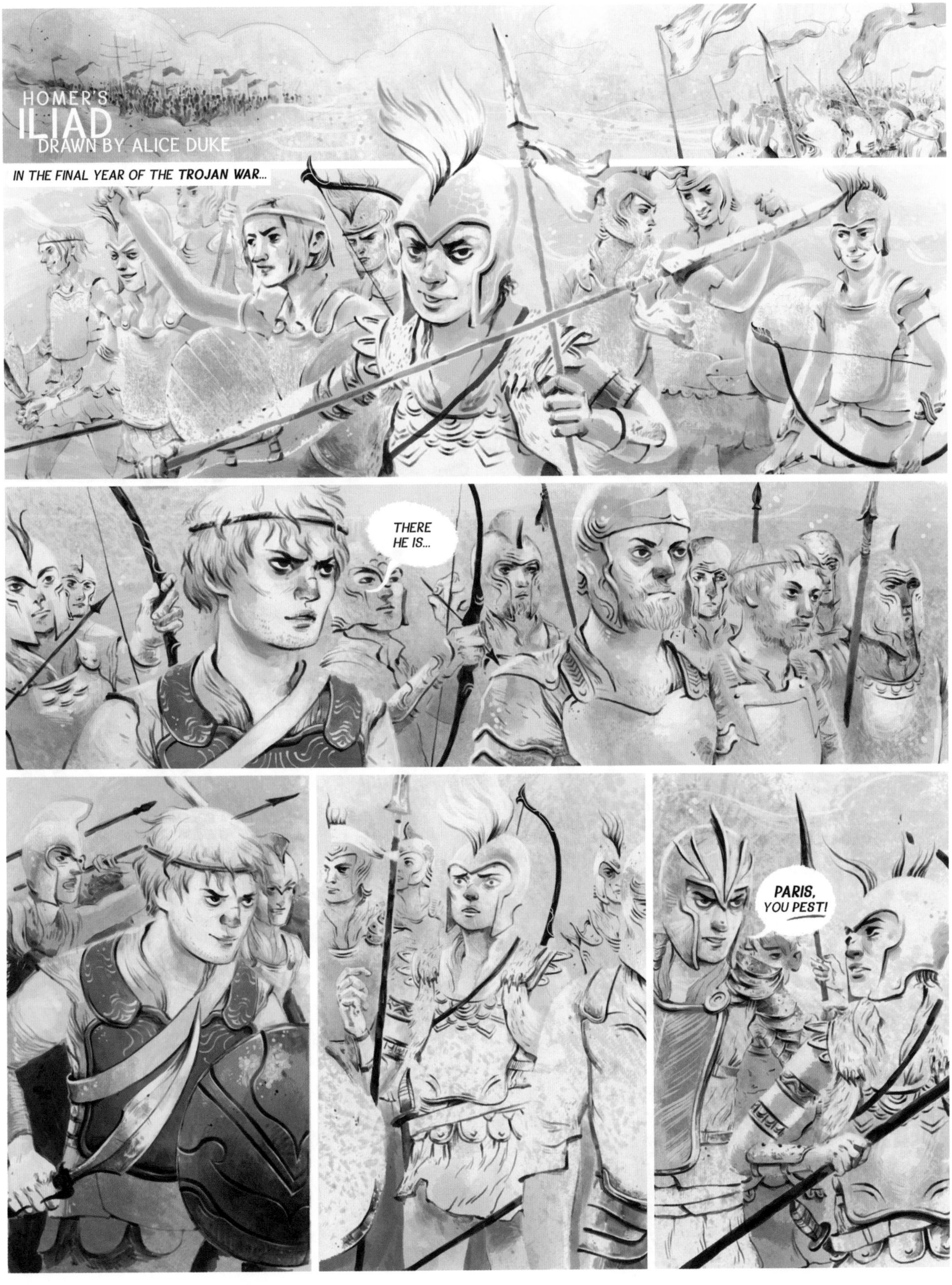
HOMER'S
ILIAD
DRAWN BY ALICE DUKE
IN THE FINAL YEAR OF THE TROJAN WAR...
THERE HE IS...
PARIS, YOU PEST!

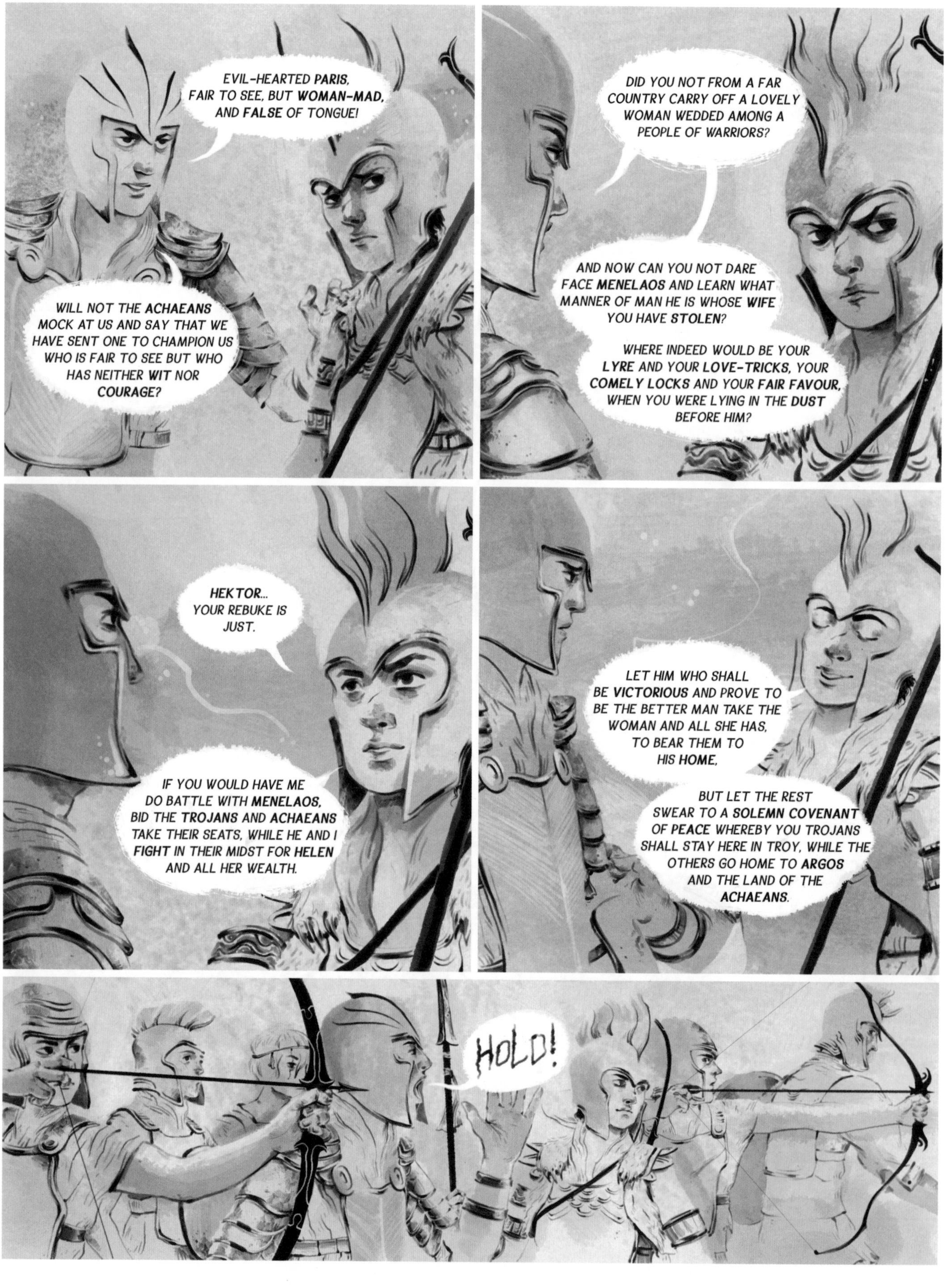
EVIL-HEARTED PARIS, FAIR TO SEE, BUT WOMAN-MAD, AND FALSE OF TONGUE!
WILL NOT THE ACHAEANS MOCK AT US AND SAY THAT WE HAVE SENT ONE TO CHAMPION US WHO IS FAIR TO SEE BUT WHO HAS NEITHER WIT NOR COURAGE?
DID YOU NOT FROM A FAR COUNTRY CARRY OFF A LOVELY WOMAN WEDDED AMONG A PEOPLE OF WARRIORS?
AND NOW CAN YOU NOT DARE FACE MENELAOS AND LEARN WHAT MANNER OF MAN HE IS WHOSE WIFE YOU HAVE STOLEN?
WHERE INDEED WOULD BE YOUR LYRE AND YOUR LOVE-TRICKS, YOUR COMELY LOCKS AND YOUR FAIR FAVOUR, WHEN YOU WERE LYING IN THE DUST BEFORE HIM?
HEKTOR... YOUR REBUKE IS JUST.
IF YOU WOULD HAVE ME DO BATTLE WITH MENELAOS, BID THE TROJANS AND ACHAEANS TAKE THEIR SEATS, WHILE HE AND I FIGHT IN THEIR MIDST FOR HELEN AND ALL HER WEALTH.
LET HIM WHO SHALL BE VICTORIOUS AND PROVE TO BE THE BETTER MAN TAKE THE WOMAN AND ALL SHE HAS, TO BEAR THEM TO HIS HOME.
BUT LET THE REST SWEAR TO A SOLEMN COVENANT OF PEACE WHEREBY YOU TROJANS SHALL STAY HERE IN TROY, WHILE THE OTHERS GO HOME TO ARGOS AND THE LAND OF THE ACHAEANS.
HOLD!

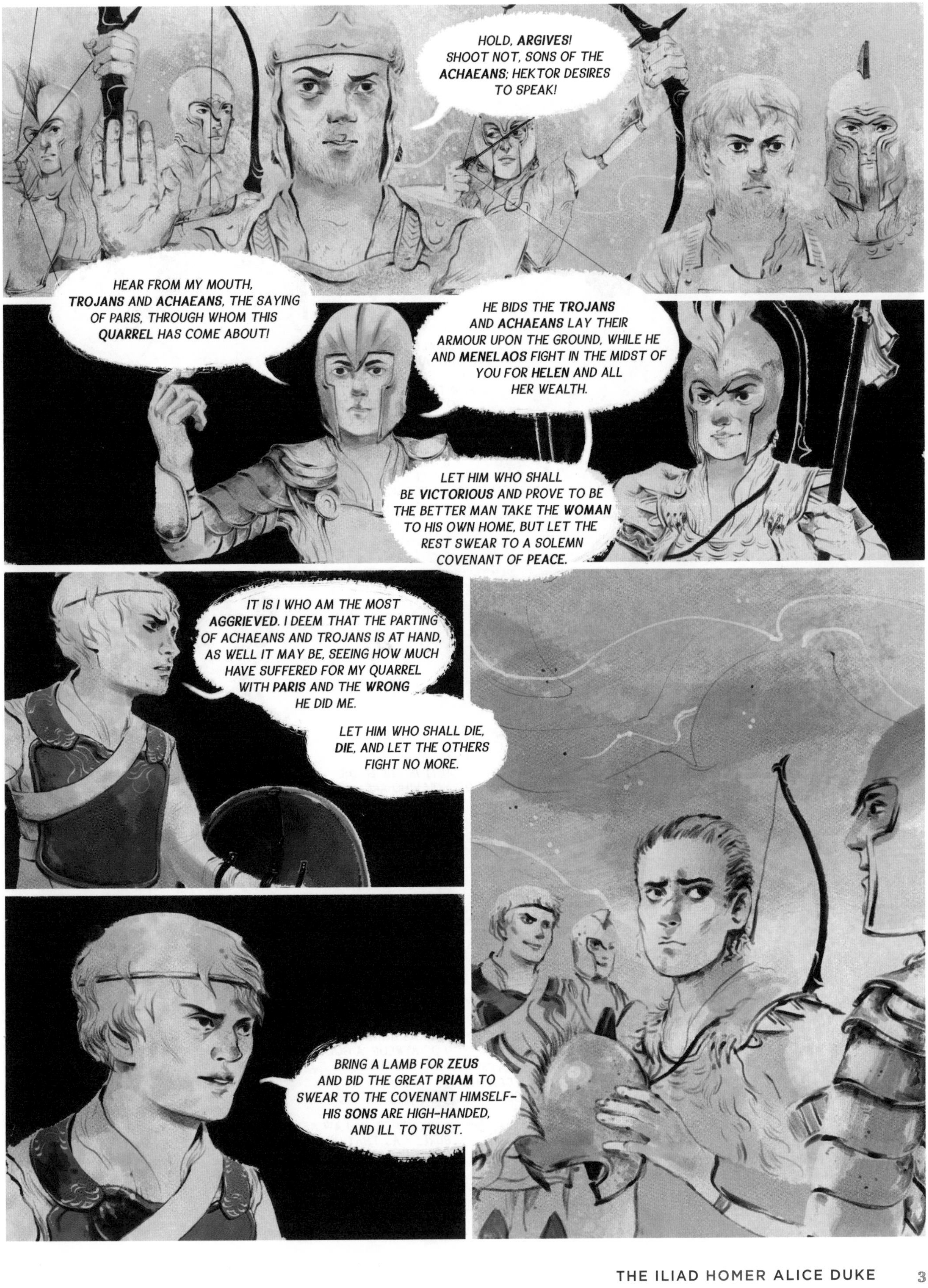
HOLD, ARGIVES! SHOOT NOT, SONS OF THE ACHAEANS; HEKTOR DESIRES TO SPEAK!
HEAR FROM MY MOUTH, TROJANS AND ACHAEANS, THE SAYING OF PARIS, THROUGH WHOM THIS QUARREL HAS COME ABOUT!
HE BIDS THE TROJANS AND ACHAEANS LAY THEIR ARMOUR UPON THE GROUND, WHILE HE AND MENELAOS FIGHT IN THE MIDST OF YOU FOR HELEN AND ALL HER WEALTH.
LET HIM WHO SHALL BE VICTORIOUS AND PROVE TO BE THE BETTER MAN TAKE THE WOMAN TO HIS OWN HOME, BUT LET THE REST SWEAR TO A SOLEMN COVENANT OF PEACE.
IT IS I WHO AM THE MOST AGGRIEVED. I DEEM THAT THE PARTING OF ACHAEANS AND TROJANS IS AT HAND, AS WELL IT MAY BE, SEEING HOW MUCH HAVE SUFFERED FOR MY QUARREL WITH PARIS AND THE WRONG HE DID ME.
LET HIM WHO SHALL DIE, DIE, AND LET THE OTHERS FIGHT NO MORE.
BRING A LAMB FOR ZEUS AND BID THE GREAT PRIAM TO SWEAR TO THE COVENANT HIMSELF- HIS SONS ARE HIGH-HANDED, AND ILL TO TRUST.

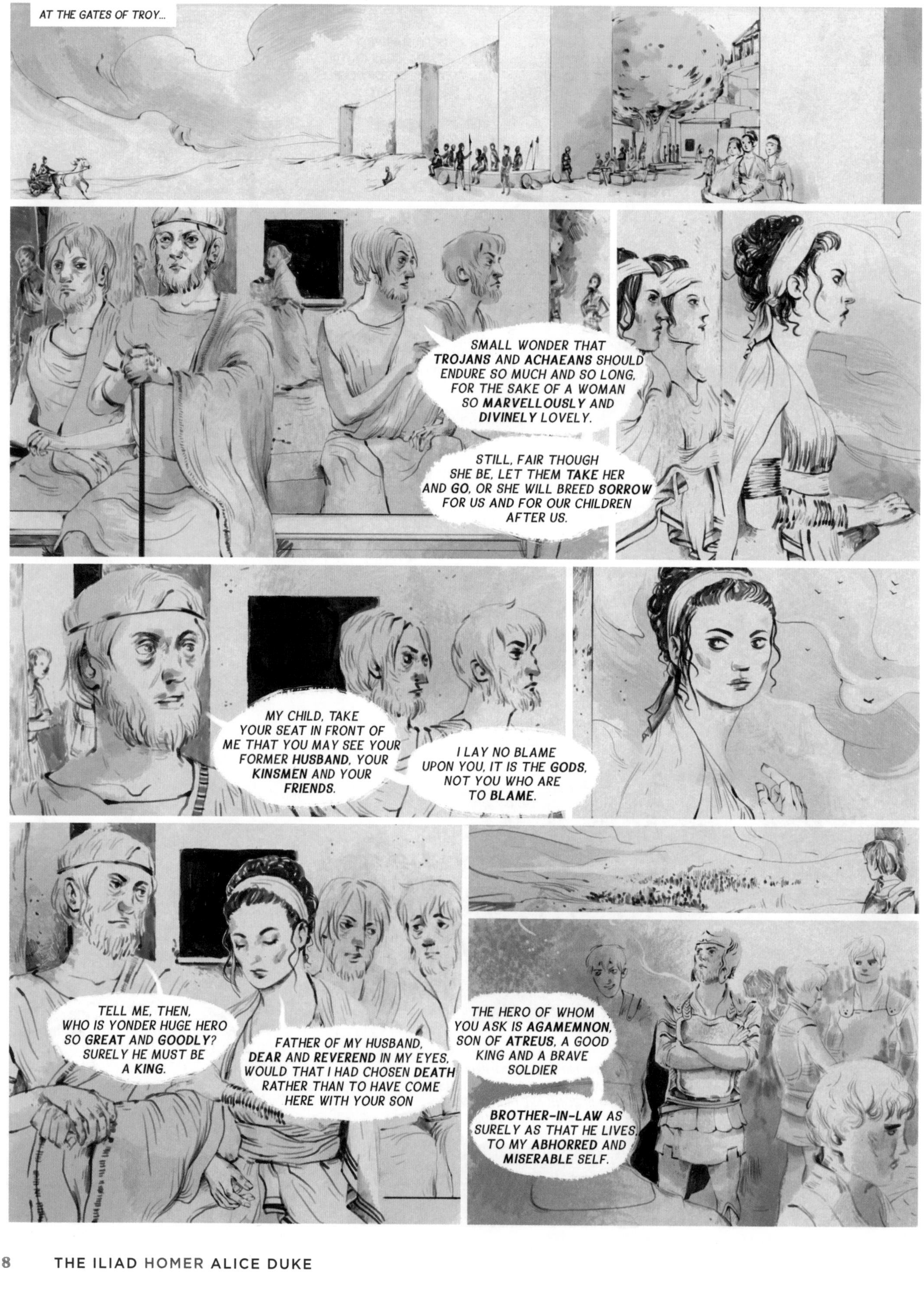
AT THE GATES OF TROY...
SMALL WONDER THAT TROJANS AND ACHAEANS SHOULD ENDURE SO MUCH AND SO LONG, FOR THE SAKE OF A WOMAN SO MARVELLOUSLY AND DIVINELY LOVELY.
STILL, FAIR THOUGH SHE BE, LET THEM TAKE HER AND GO, OR SHE WILL BREED SORROW FOR US AND FOR OUR CHILDREN AFTER US.
MY CHILD, TAKE YOUR SEAT IN FRONT OF ME THAT YOU MAY SEE YOUR FORMER HUSBAND, YOUR KINSMEN AND YOUR FRIENDS.
I LAY NO BLAME UPON YOU, IT IS THE GODS, NOT YOU WHO ARE TO BLAME.
TELL ME, THEN, WHO IS YONDER HUGE HERO SO GREAT AND GOODLY? SURELY HE MUST BE A KING.
FATHER OF MY HUSBAND, DEAR AND REVEREND IN MY EYES, WOULD THAT I HAD CHOSEN DEATH RATHER THAN TO HAVE COME HERE WITH YOUR SON
THE HERO OF WHOM YOU ASK IS AGAMEMNON, SON OF ATREUS, A GOOD KING AND A BRAVE SOLDIER
BROTHER-IN-LAW AS SURELY AS THAT HE LIVES, TO MY ABHORRED AND MISERABLE SELF.

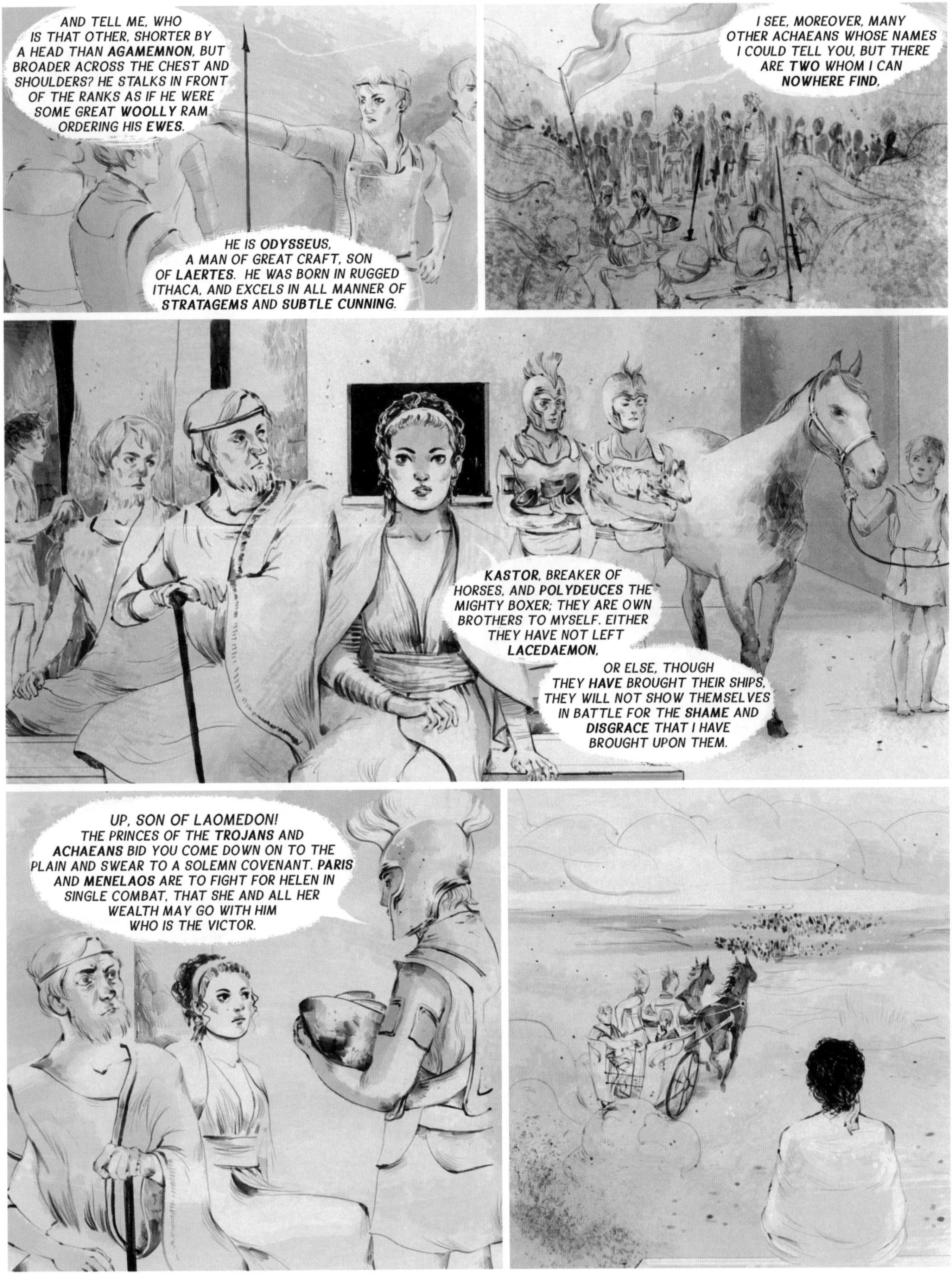
AND TELL ME, WHO IS THAT OTHER, SHORTER BY A HEAD THAN AGAMEMNON, BUT BROADER ACROSS THE CHEST AND SHOULDERS? HE STALKS IN FRONT OF THE RANKS AS IF HE WERE SOME GREAT WOOLLY RAM ORDERING HIS EWES.
HE IS ODYSSEUS, A MAN OF GREAT CRAFT, SON OF LAERTES. HE WAS BORN IN RUGGED ITHACA, AND EXCELS IN ALL MANNER OF STRATAGEMS AND SUBTLE CUNNING.
I SEE, MOREOVER, MANY OTHER ACHAEANS WHOSE NAMES I COULD TELL YOU, BUT THERE ARE TWO WHOM I CAN NOWHERE FIND,
KASTOR, BREAKER OF HORSES, AND POLYDEUCES THE MIGHTY BOXER; THEY ARE OWN BROTHERS TO MYSELF. EITHER THEY HAVE NOT LEFT LACEDAEMON,
OR ELSE, THOUGH THEY HAVE BROUGHT THEIR SHIPS, THEY WILL NOT SHOW THEMSELVES IN BATTLE FOR THE SHAME AND DISGRACE THAT I HAVE BROUGHT UPON THEM.
UP, SON OF LAOMEDON! THE PRINCES OF THE TROJANS AND ACHAEANS BID YOU COME DOWN ON TO THE PLAIN AND SWEAR TO A SOLEMN COVENANT. PARIS AND MENELAOS ARE TO FIGHT FOR HELEN IN SINGLE COMBAT, THAT SHE AND ALL HER WEALTH MAY GO WITH HIM WHO IS THE VICTOR.

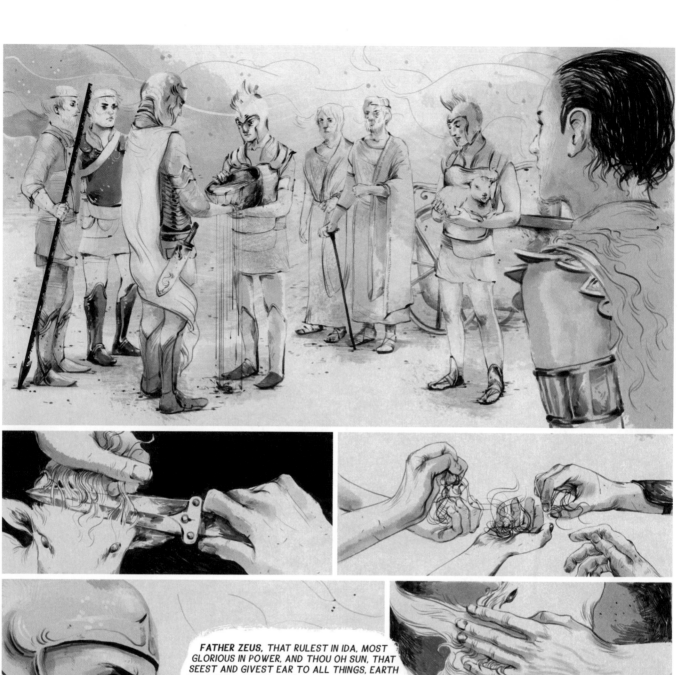

FATHER ZEUS, THAT RULEST IN IDA, MOST GLORIOUS IN POWER, AND THOU OH SUN, THAT SEEST AND GIVEST EAR TO ALL THINGS, EARTH AND RIVERS, AND YE WHO IN THE REALMS BELOW CHASTISE THE SOUL OF HIM THAT HAS BROKEN HIS OATH, WITNESS THESE RITES AND GUARD THEM, THAT THEY BE NOT VAIN.

IF PARIS KILLS MENELAOS, LET HIM KEEP HELEN AND ALL HER WEALTH, WHILE WE SAIL HOME WITH OUR SHIPS; BUT IF MENELAOS KILLS PARIS, LET THE TROJANS GIVE BACK HELEN AND ALL THAT SHE HAS; LET THEM MOREOVER PAY SUCH FINE TO THE ACHAEANS AS SHALL BE AGREED UPON, IN TESTIMONY AMONG THOSE THAT SHALL BE BORN HEREAFTER. AND IF PRIAM AND HIS SONS REFUSE SUCH FINE WHEN PARIS HAS FALLEN, THEN WILL I STAY HERE AND FIGHT ON TILL I HAVE GOT SATISFACTION.

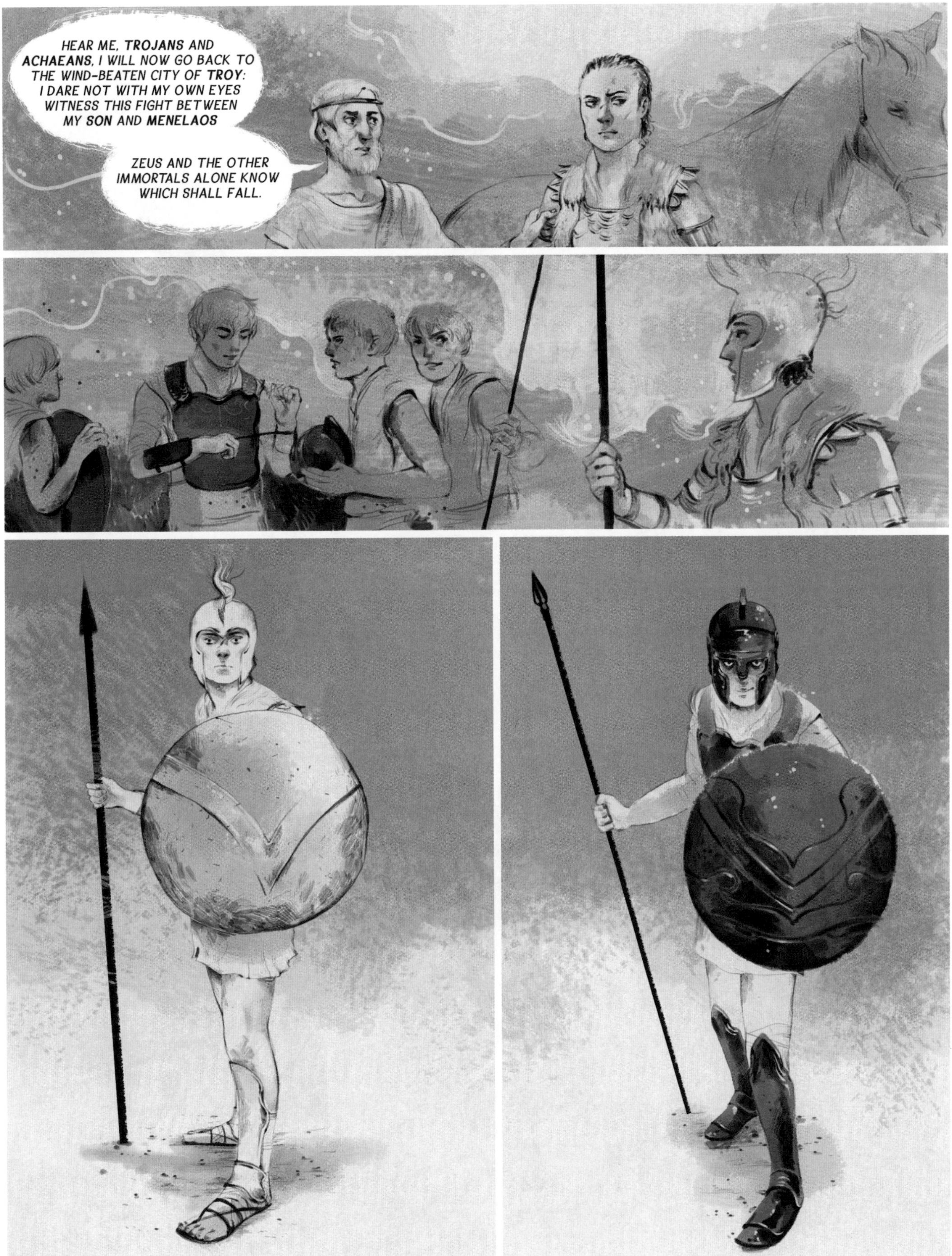
HEAR ME, TROJANS AND ACHAEANS, I WILL NOW GO BACK TO THE WIND-BEATEN CITY OF TROY: I DARE NOT WITH MY OWN EYES WITNESS THIS FIGHT BETWEEN MY SON AND MENELAOS
ZEUS AND THE OTHER IMMORTALS ALONE KNOW WHICH SHALL FALL.

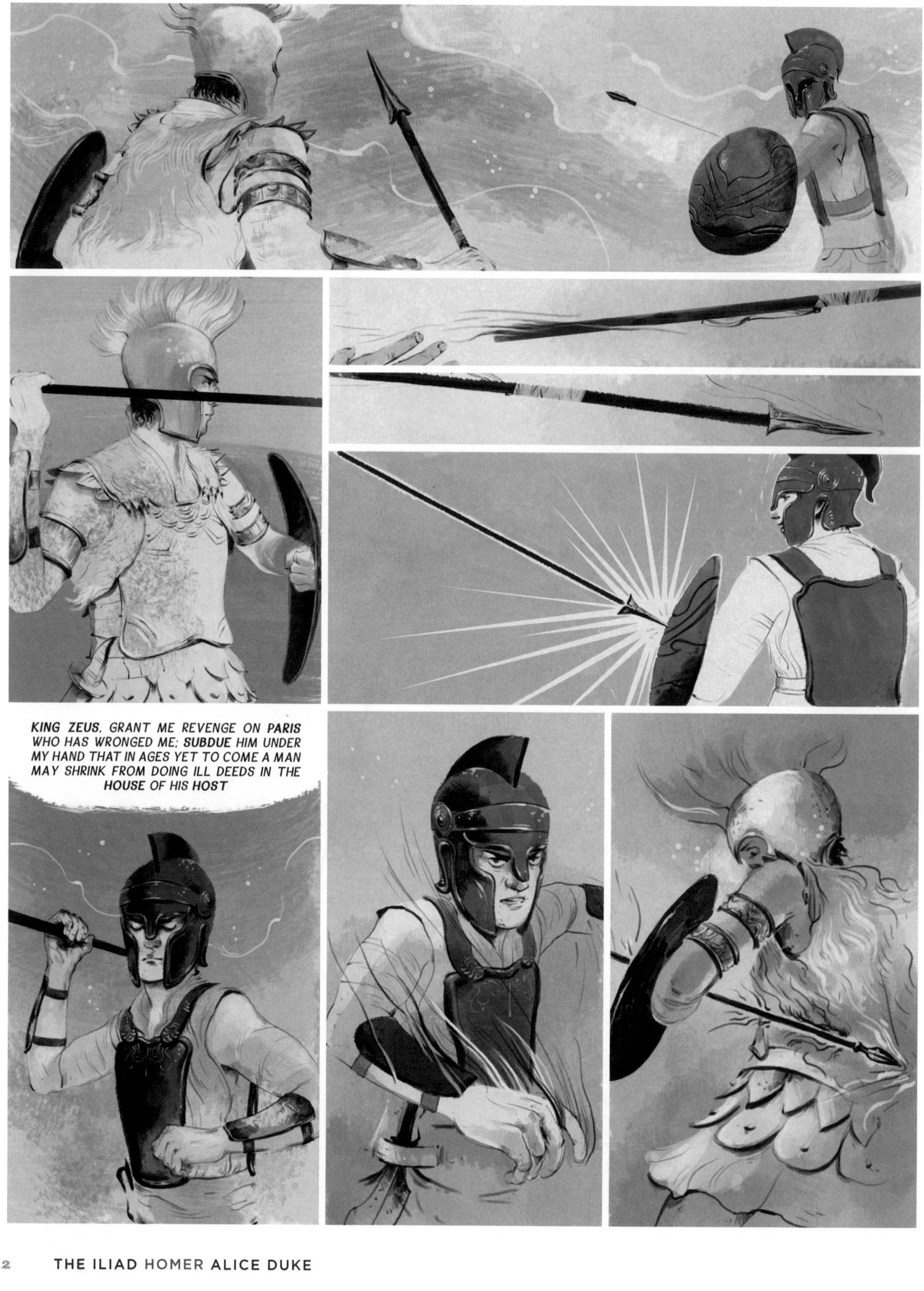
KING ZEUS, GRANT ME REVENGE ON PARIS WHO HAS WRONGED ME; SUBDUE HIM UNDER MY HAND THAT IN AGES YET TO COME A MAN MAY SHRINK FROM DOING ILL DEEDS IN THE HOUSE OF HIS HOST

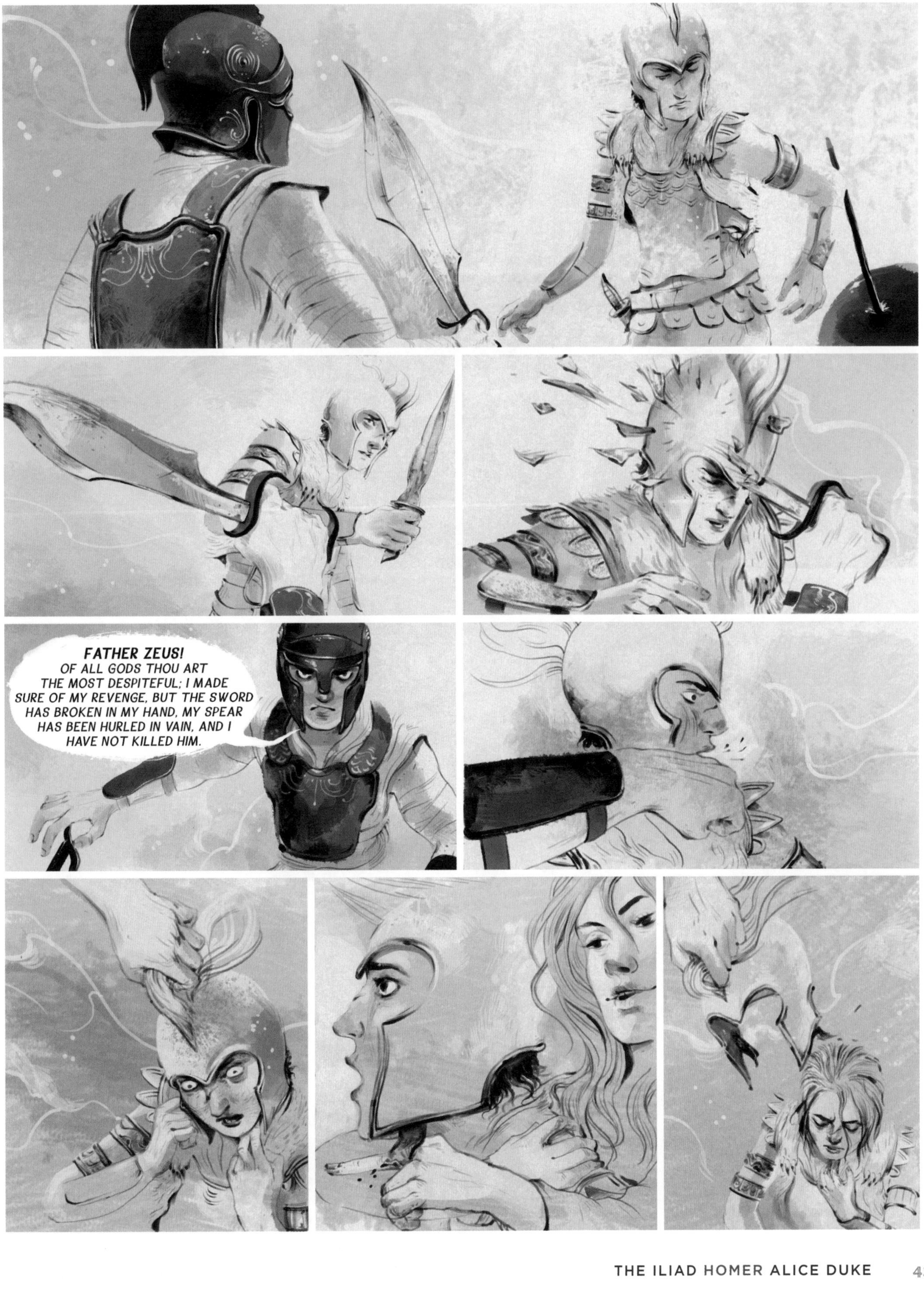
FATHER ZEUS! OF ALL GODS THOU ART THE MOST DESPITEFUL; I MADE SURE OF MY REVENGE, BUT THE SWORD HAS BROKEN IN MY HAND, MY SPEAR HAS BEEN HURLED IN VAIN, AND I HAVE NOT KILLED HIM.

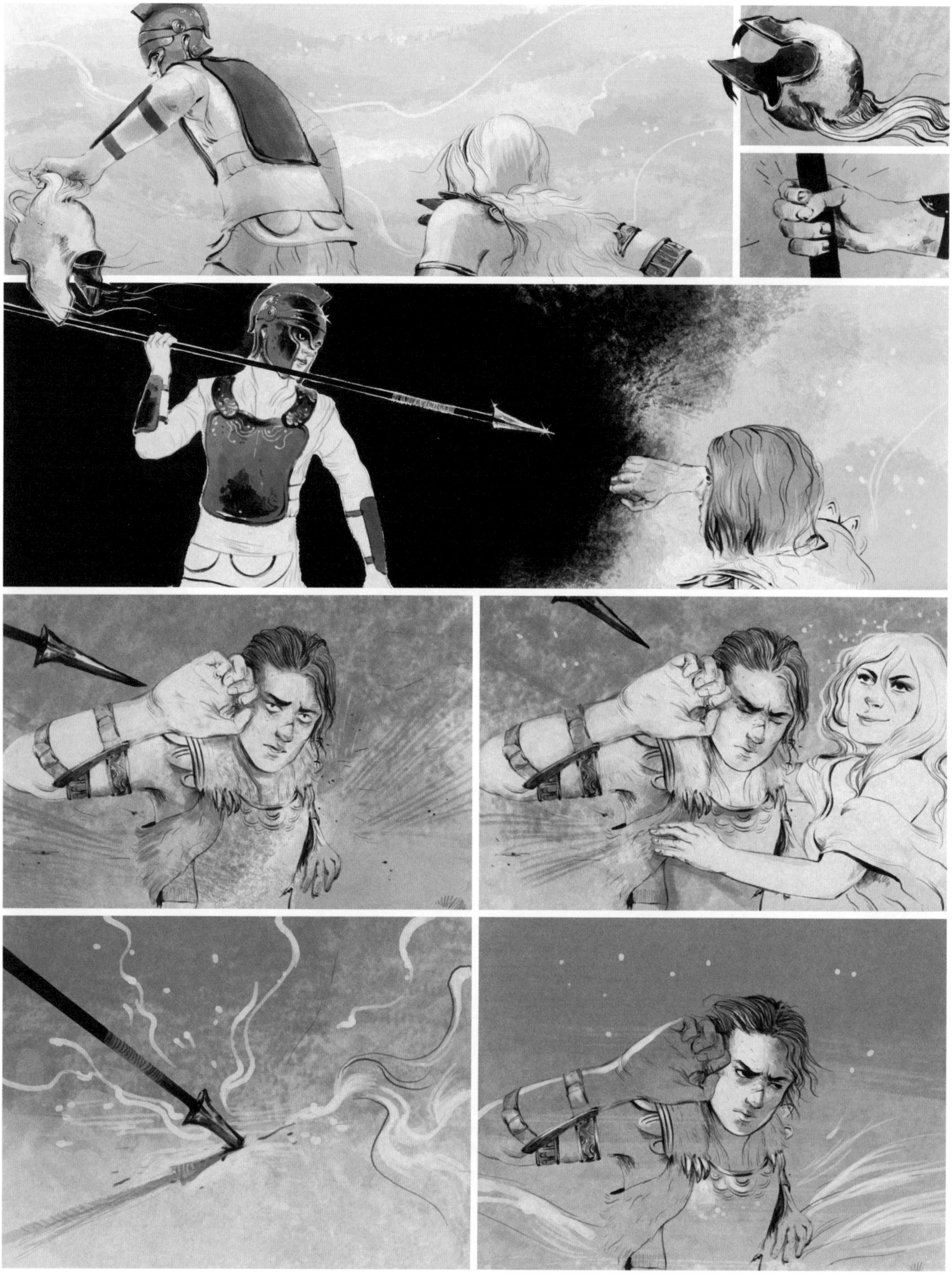

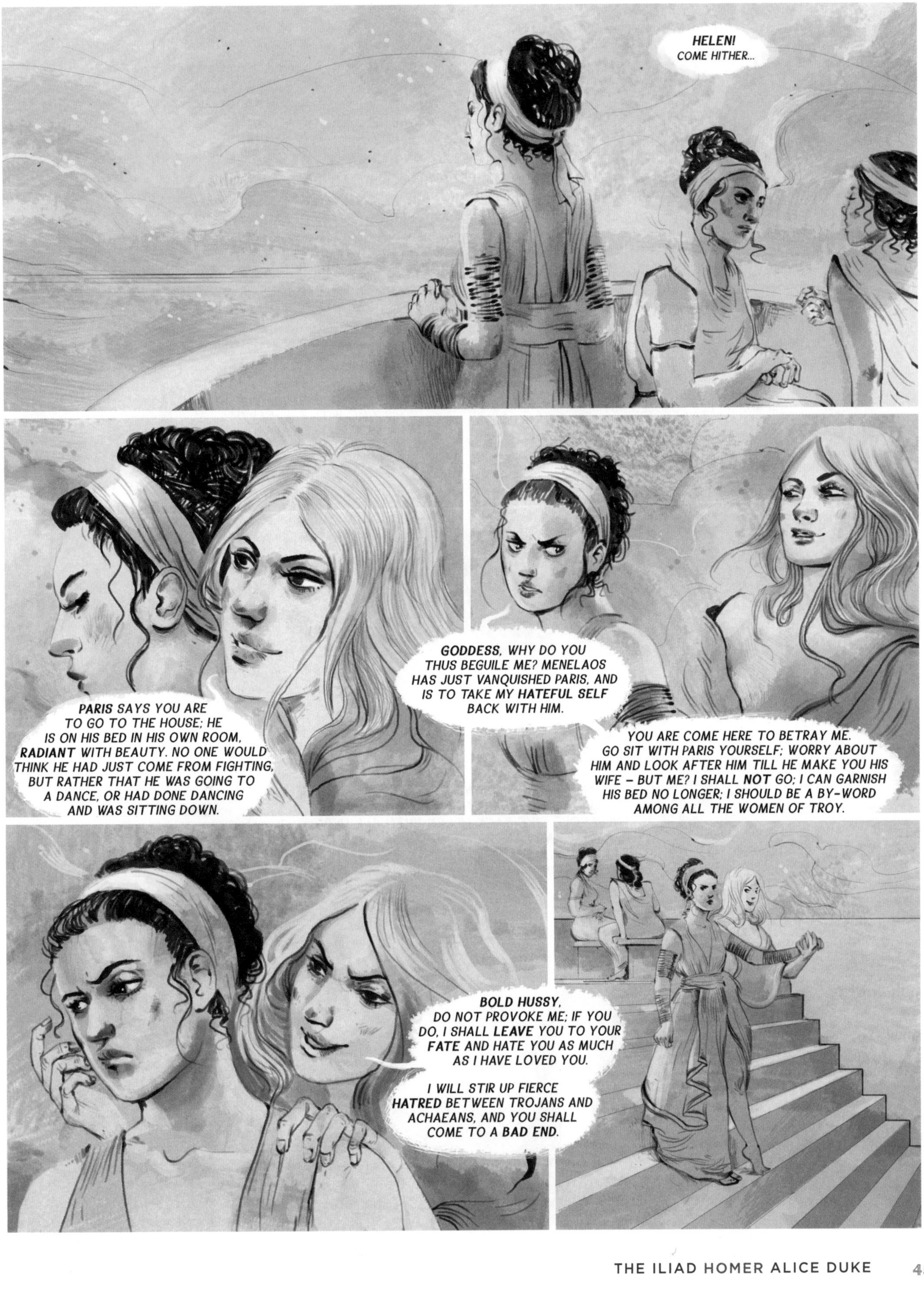
HELEN! COME HITHER...
PARIS SAYS YOU ARE TO GO TO THE HOUSE; HE IS ON HIS BED IN HIS OWN ROOM, RADIANT WITH BEAUTY. NO ONE WOULD THINK HE HAD JUST COME FROM FIGHTING, BUT RATHER THAT HE WAS GOING TO A DANCE, OR HAD DONE DANCING AND WAS SITTING DOWN.
GODDESS, WHY DO YOU THUS BEGUILE ME? MENELAOS HAS JUST VANQUISHED PARIS, AND IS TO TAKE MY HATEFUL SELF BACK WITH HIM.
YOU ARE COME HERE TO BETRAY ME. GO SIT WITH PARIS YOURSELF; WORRY ABOUT HIM AND LOOK AFTER HIM TILL HE MAKE YOU HIS WIFE – BUT ME? I SHALL NOT GO; I CAN GARNISH HIS BED NO LONGER; I SHOULD BE A BY-WORD AMONG ALL THE WOMEN OF TROY.
BOLD HUSSY, DO NOT PROVOKE ME; IF YOU DO, I SHALL LEAVE YOU TO YOUR FATE AND HATE YOU AS MUCH AS I HAVE LOVED YOU.
I WILL STIR UP FIERCE HATRED BETWEEN TROJANS AND ACHAEANS, AND YOU SHALL COME TO A BAD END.

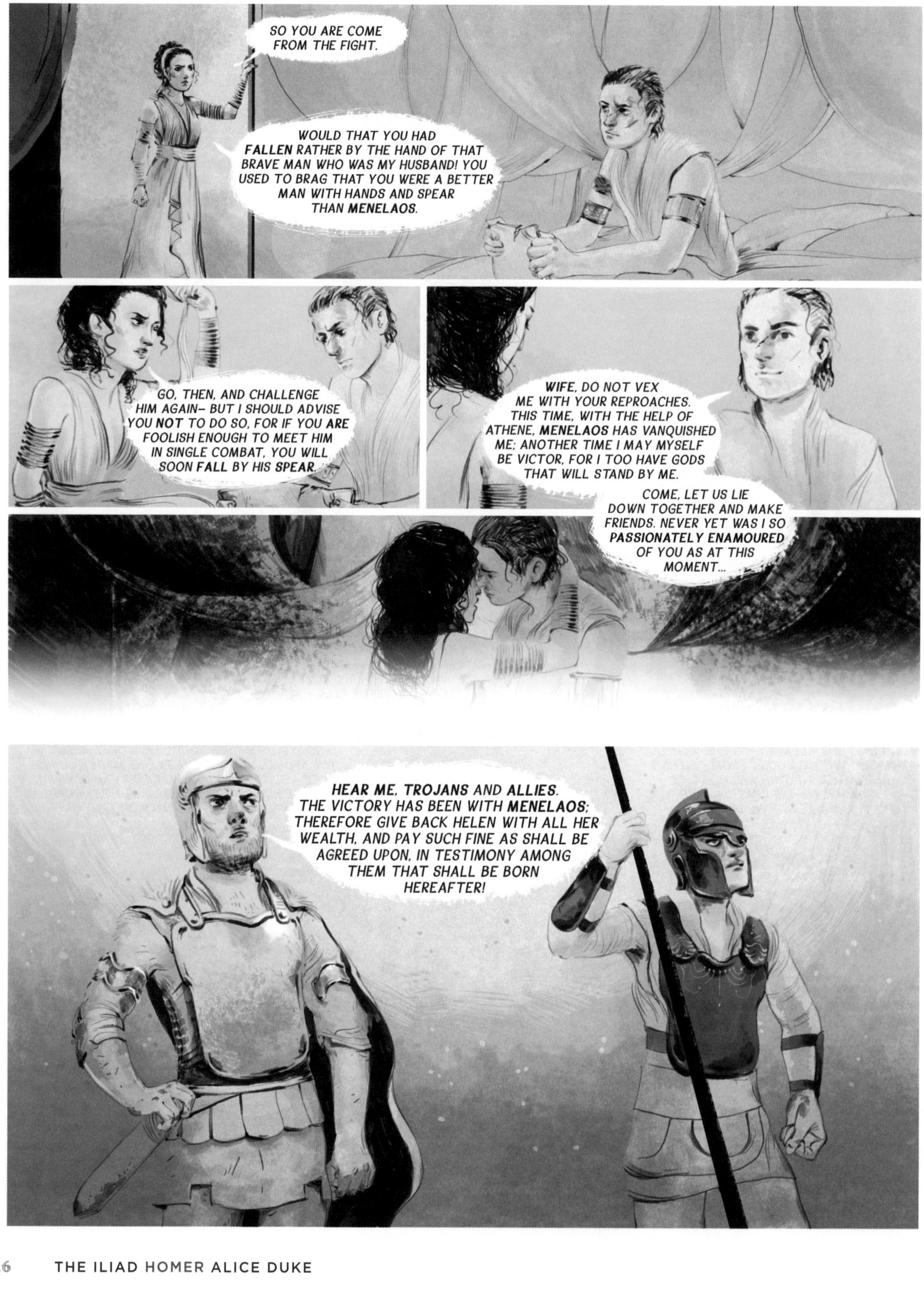
SO YOU ARE COME FROM THE FIGHT.
WOULD THAT YOU HAD FALLEN RATHER BY THE HAND OF THAT BRAVE MAN WHO WAS MY HUSBAND! YOU USED TO BRAG THAT YOU WERE A BETTER MAN WITH HANDS AND SPEAR THAN MENELAOS.
GO, THEN, AND CHALLENGE HIM AGAIN– BUT I SHOULD ADVISE YOU NOT TO DO SO, FOR IF YOU ARE FOOLISH ENOUGH TO MEET HIM IN SINGLE COMBAT, YOU WILL SOON FALL BY HIS SPEAR.
WIFE, DO NOT VEX ME WITH YOUR REPROACHES. THIS TIME, WITH THE HELP OF ATHENE, MENELAOS HAS VANQUISHED ME; ANOTHER TIME I MAY MYSELF BE VICTOR, FOR I TOO HAVE GODS THAT WILL STAND BY ME.
COME, LET US LIE DOWN TOGETHER AND MAKE FRIENDS. NEVER YET WAS I SO PASSIONATELY ENAMOURED OF YOU AS AT THIS MOMENT...
HEAR ME, TROJANS AND ALLIES. THE VICTORY HAS BEEN WITH MENELAOS; THEREFORE GIVE BACK HELEN WITH ALL HER WEALTH, AND PAY SUCH FINE AS SHALL BE AGREED UPON, IN TESTIMONY AMONG THEM THAT SHALL BE BORN HEREAFTER!

The Odyssey

Homer

ART / ADAPTATION BY **Gareth Hinds**

AFTER THE TROJAN WAR ENDED THANKS TO HIS brilliant hiding-soldiers-in-a-giant-hollow-wooden-horse trick, the cunning, egotistical Odysseus (a.k.a. Ulysses) set sail for his home in Ithaca and his abundantly patient wife, Penelope, in this sequel to *The Iliad.* Little did he know that it would take him a decade to make the trip, dodging monsters, angry gods, natural dangers, alluring females, soporific drugs, and other obstacles that threatened to kill or derail him and his crew.

Gareth Hinds has made a career out of highly lauded graphic adaptations of classic lit (you'll also find his *Beowulf* and *Gulliver's Travels* in this volume, and he's done Shakespeare and the Brothers Grimm). He considers his adaptation of *The Odyssey* to be his magnum opus, faithfully relating the ancient Greek epic poem with 250 pages of ink and watercolors. For *The Graphic Canon,* I chose the famous Polyphemus episode, in which the Greek warrior and his men are trapped in a cave with a giant cyclops. Not only is it a great self-contained mini-adventure, it once again shows Odysseus' sneaky brilliance and ends with a display of his arrogance. He tells Polyphemus his real name, a remarkably bad move considering that the blinded monster's father is Poseidon. When you're making a long journey by sea, you really don't want the god of the oceans mad at you, and sure enough, Poseidon becomes the reason Odysseus takes ten years to get home and loses his entire crew and ships along the way.

SOURCE

Hexter, Ralph. *A Guide to The Odyssey: A Commentary on the English Translation of Robert Fitzgerald.* Vintage, 1993.

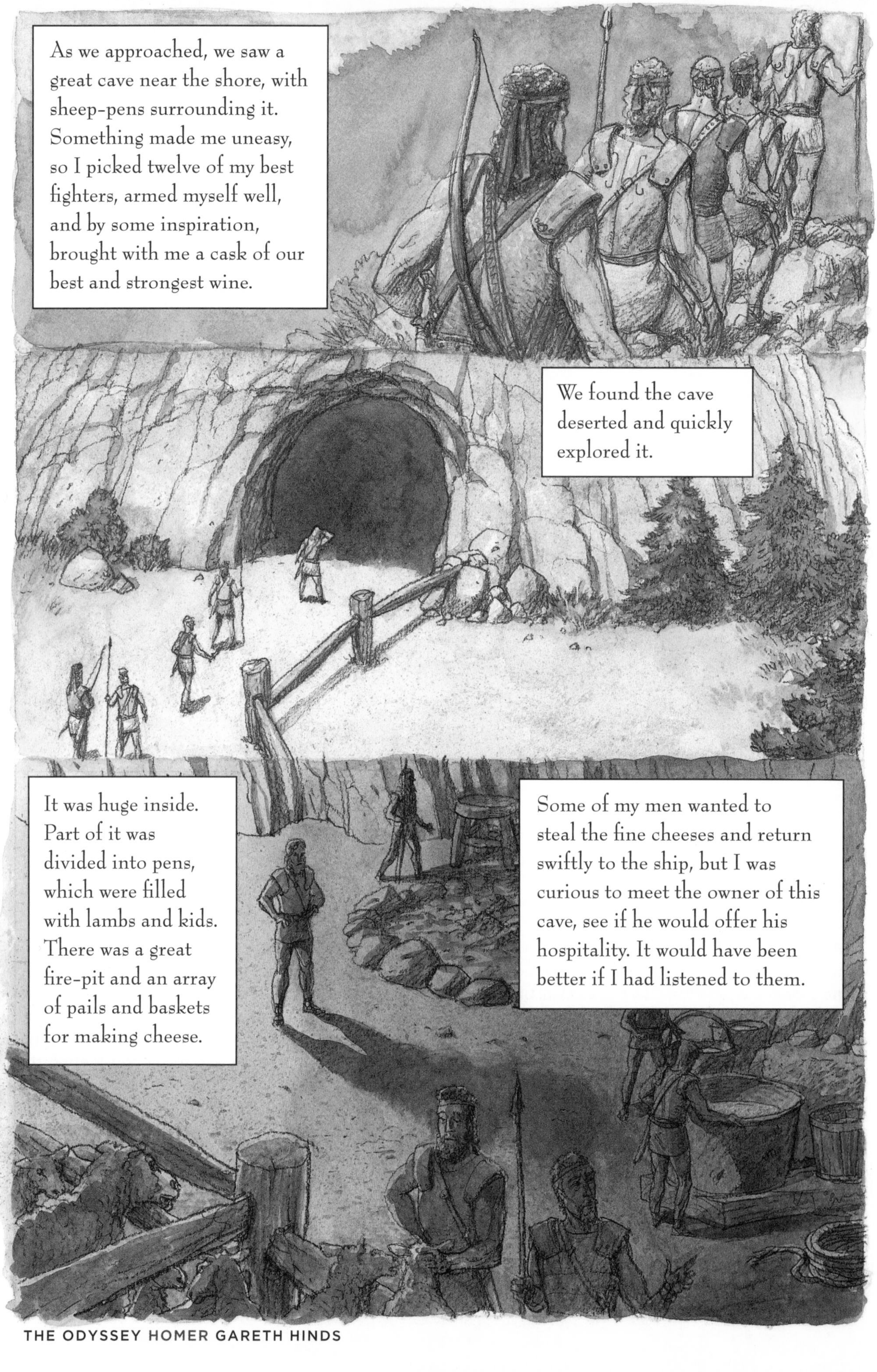
As we approached, we saw a great cave near the shore, with sheep-pens surrounding it. Something made me uneasy, so I picked twelve of my best fighters, armed myself well, and by some inspiration, brought with me a cask of our best and strongest wine.
We found the cave deserted and quickly explored it.
It was huge inside. Part of it was divided into pens, which were filled with lambs and kids. There was a great fire-pit and an array of pails and baskets for making cheese.
Some of my men wanted to steal the fine cheeses and return swiftly to the ship, but I was curious to meet the owner of this cave, see if he would offer his hospitality. It would have been better if I had listened to them.

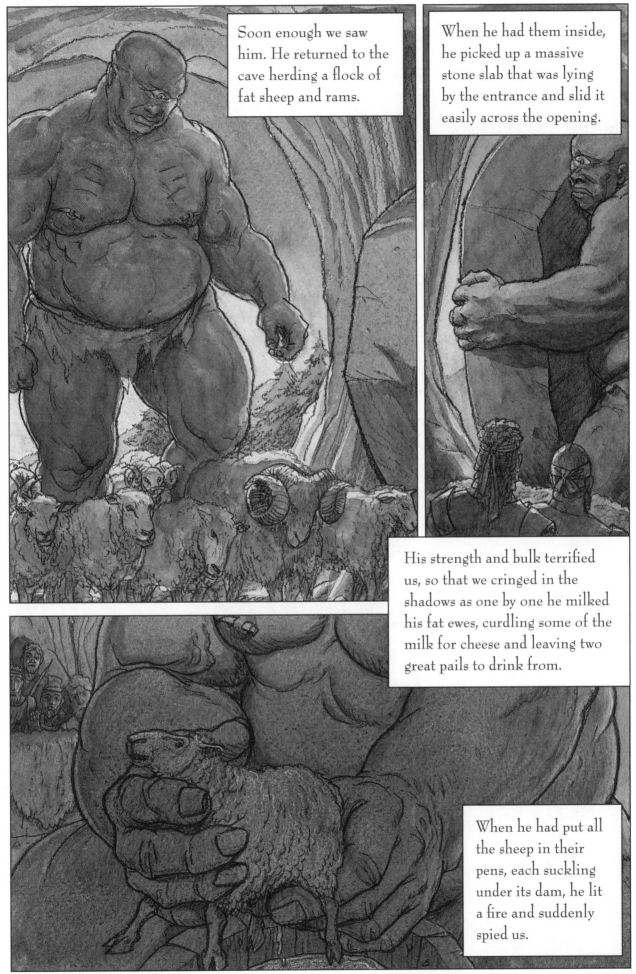

Soon enough we saw him. He returned to the cave herding a flock of fat sheep and rams.

When he had them inside, he picked up a massive stone slab that was lying by the entrance and slid it easily across the opening.

His strength and bulk terrified us, so that we cringed in the shadows as one by one he milked his fat ewes, curdling some of the milk for cheese and leaving two great pails to drink from.

When he had put all the sheep in their pens, each suckling under its dam, he lit a fire and suddenly spied us.

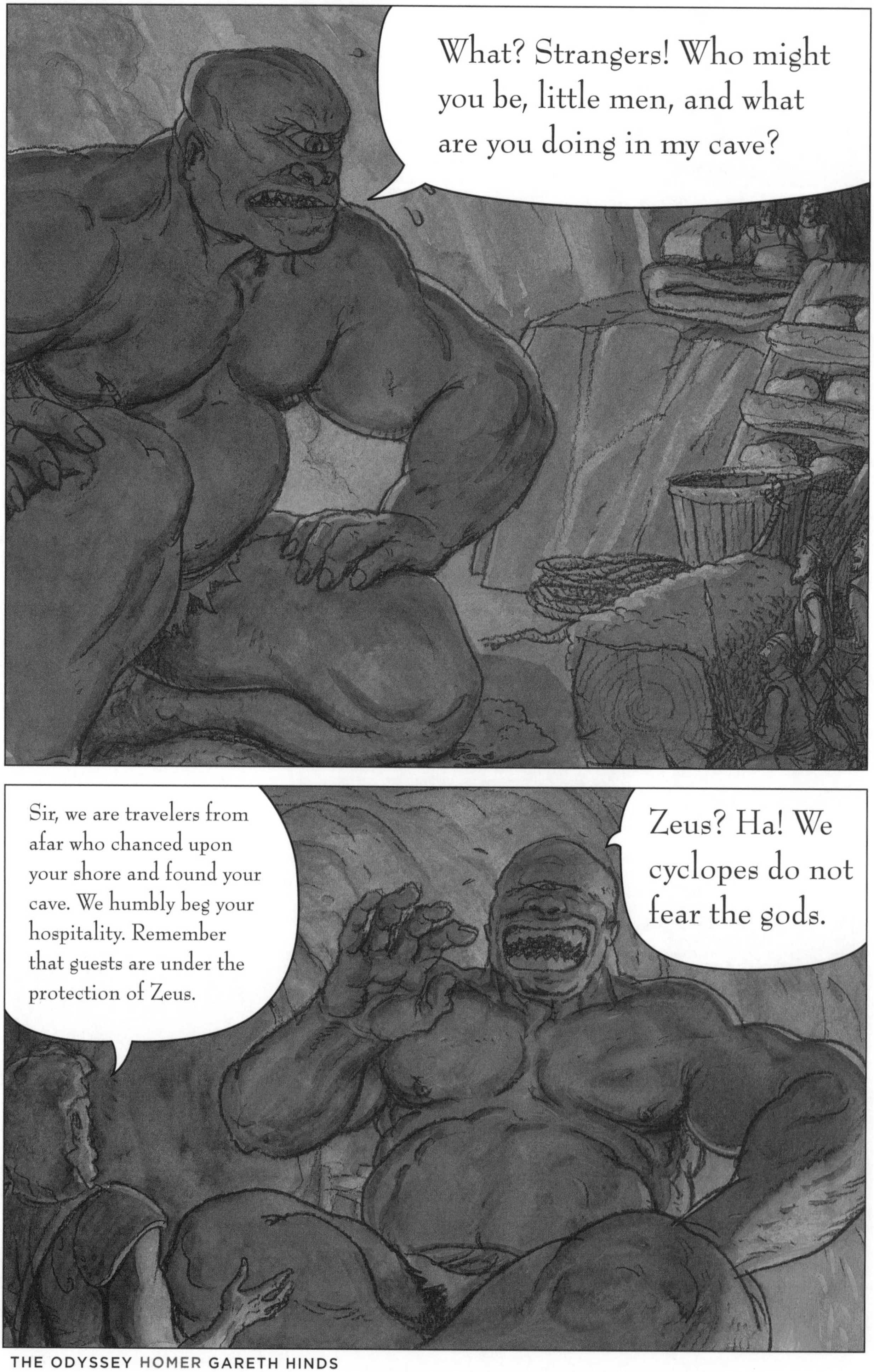
What? Strangers! Who might you be, little men, and what are you doing in my cave?
Sir, we are travelers from afar who chanced upon your shore and found your cave. We humbly beg your hospitality. Remember that guests are under the protection of Zeus.
Zeus? Ha! We cyclopes do not fear the gods.

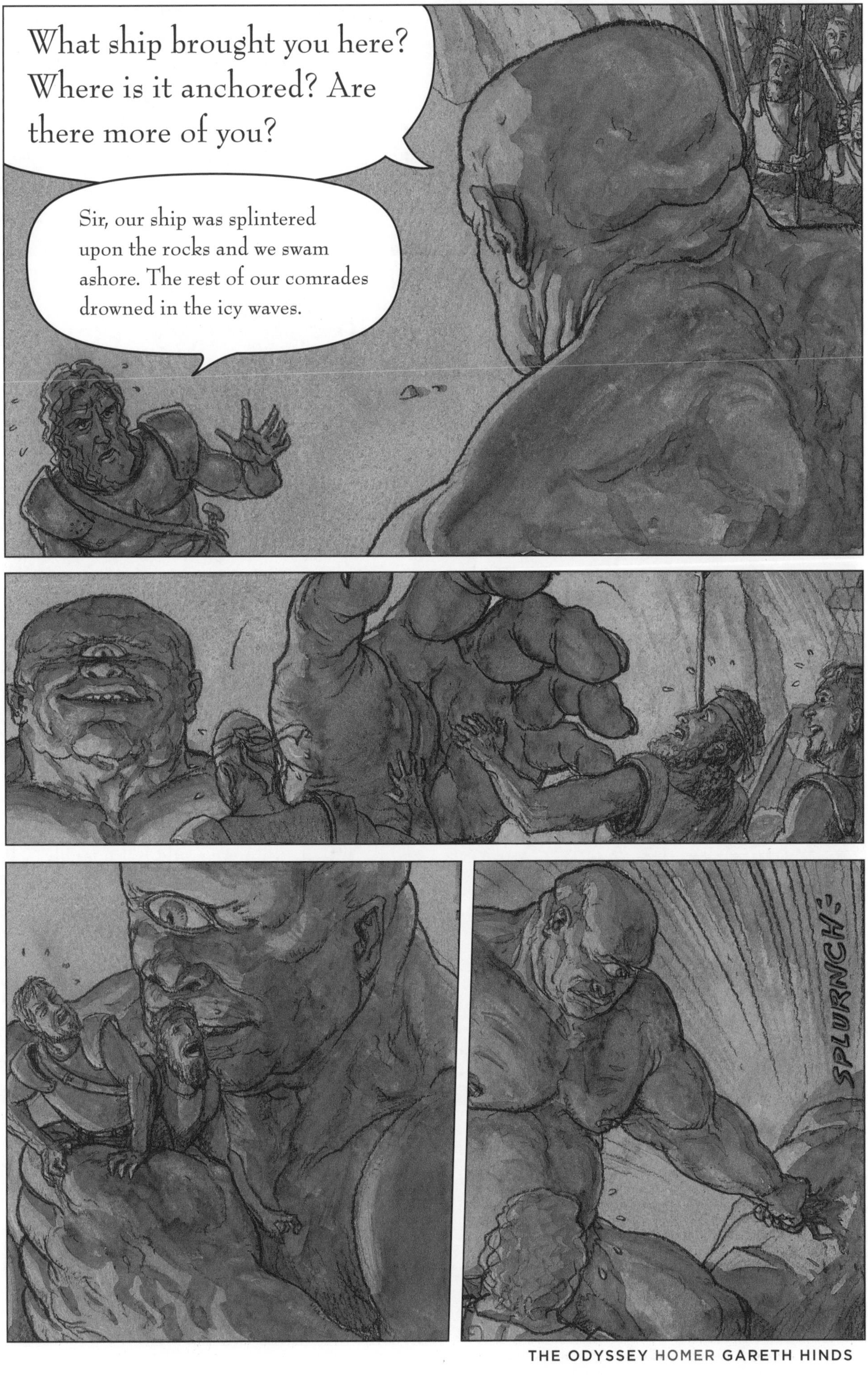
What ship brought you here? Where is it anchored? Are there more of you?
Sir, our ship was splintered upon the rocks and we swam ashore. The rest of our comrades drowned in the icy waves.
SPLURNCH!

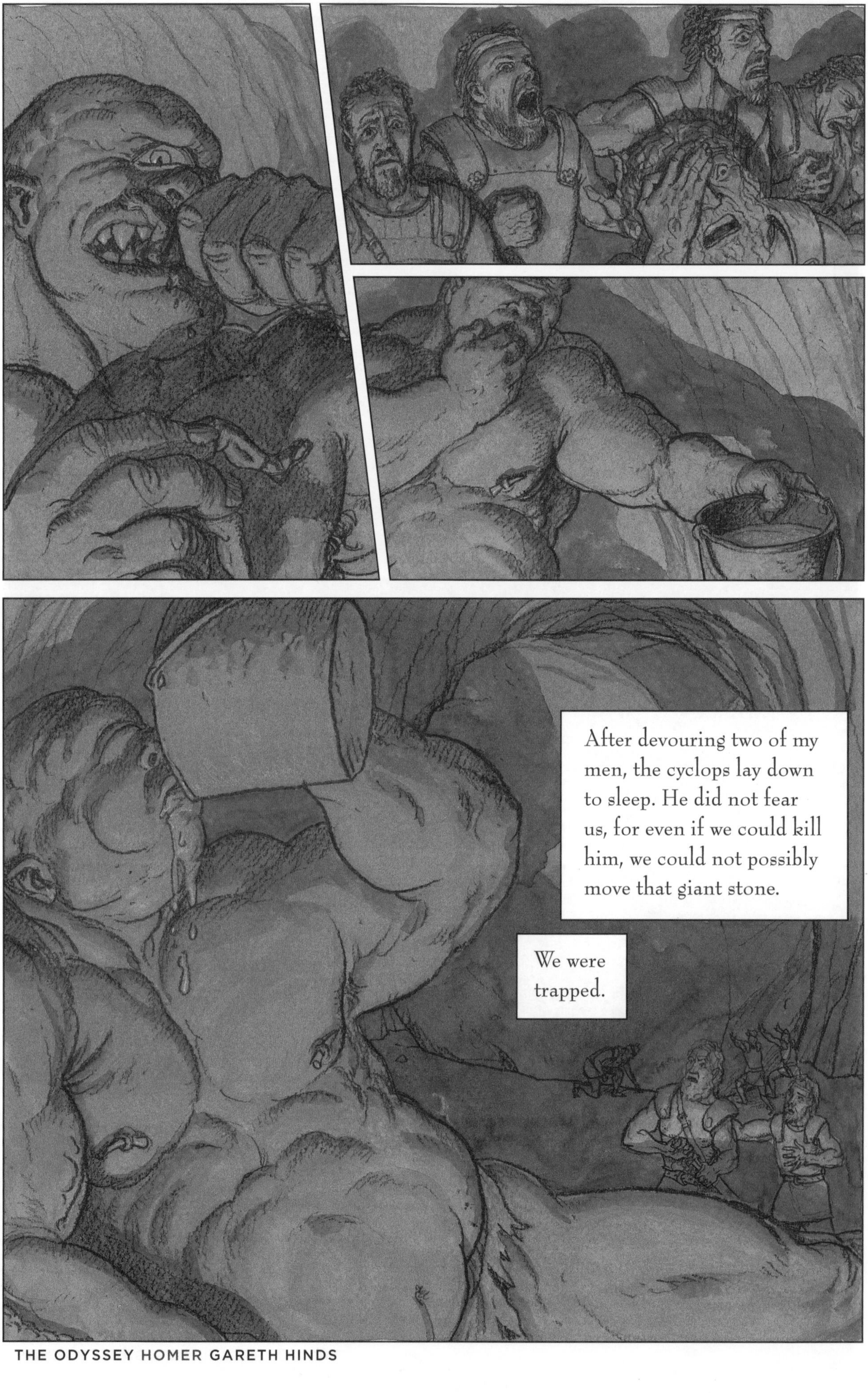
After devouring two of my men, the cyclops lay down to sleep. He did not fear us, for even if we could kill him, we could not possibly move that giant stone.
We were trapped.

In the morning, the cyclops killed two more men for his breakfast, then drove his sheep outside and replaced the stone across the entrance as easily as a man might cap a quiver of arrows.

I racked my brain for a plan that would let us escape alive from the clutches of that brute, and this was what seemed best to me:

There was a massive staff of green wood lying in the cave, and I whittled this down to a sharp point and hid it in the back of the cave. I picked four of my strongest men to help me wield it when the time came.

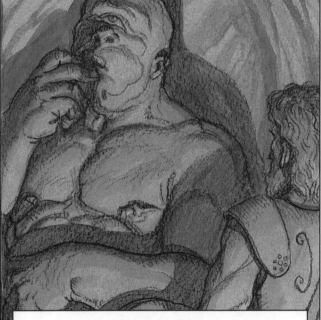

Once again I had to stand by and watch as he killed two more of my men to make his dinner. When he had devoured them, I approached him.

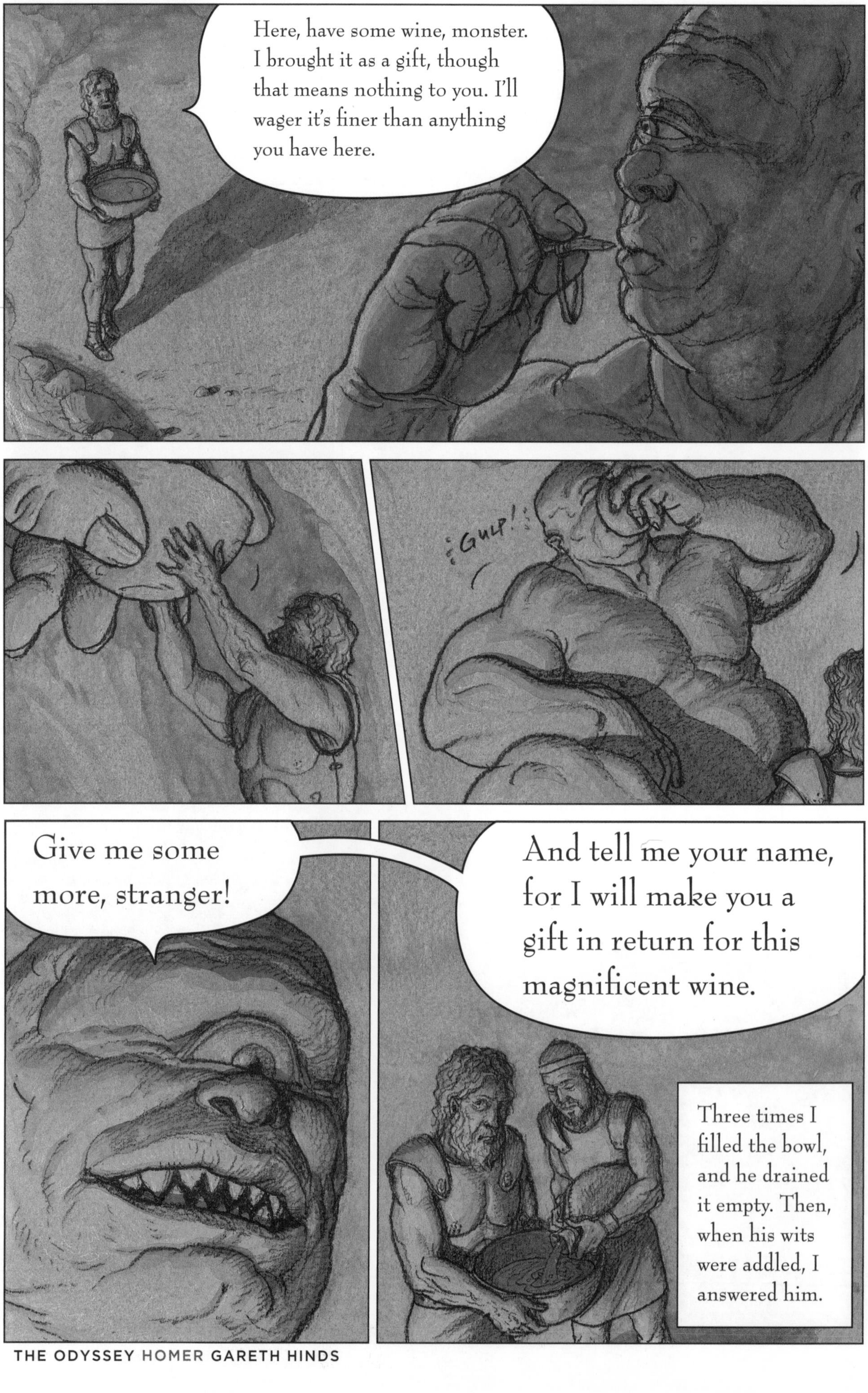
Here, have some wine, monster. I brought it as a gift, though that means nothing to you. I'll wager it's finer than anything you have here.
¡GULP!¡
Give me some more, stranger!
And tell me your name, for I will make you a gift in return for this magnificent wine.
Three times I filled the bowl, and he drained it empty. Then, when his wits were addled, I answered him.

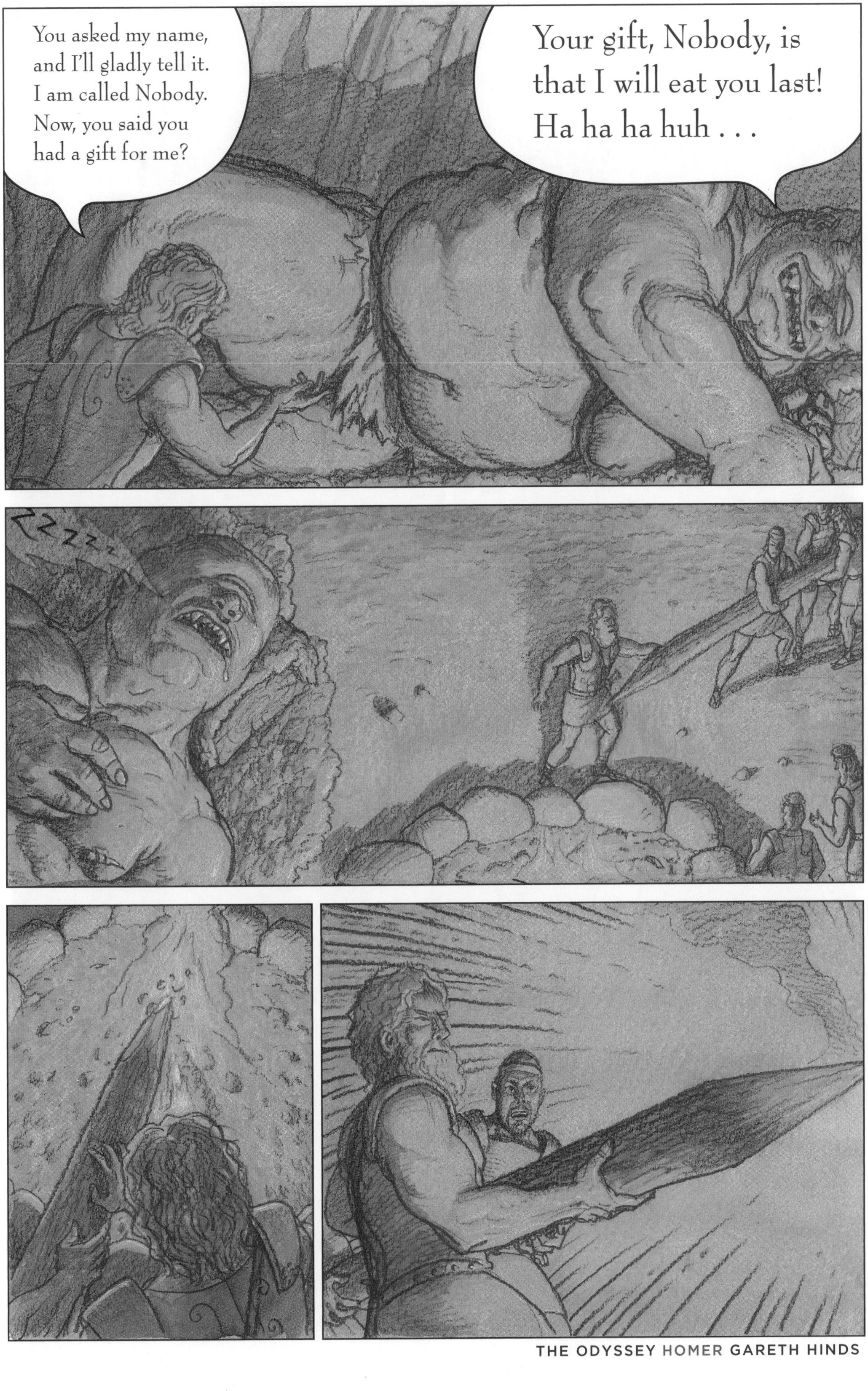
You asked my name, and I'll gladly tell it. I am called Nobody. Now, you said you had a gift for me?
Your gift, Nobody, is that I will eat you last! Ha ha ha huh . . .

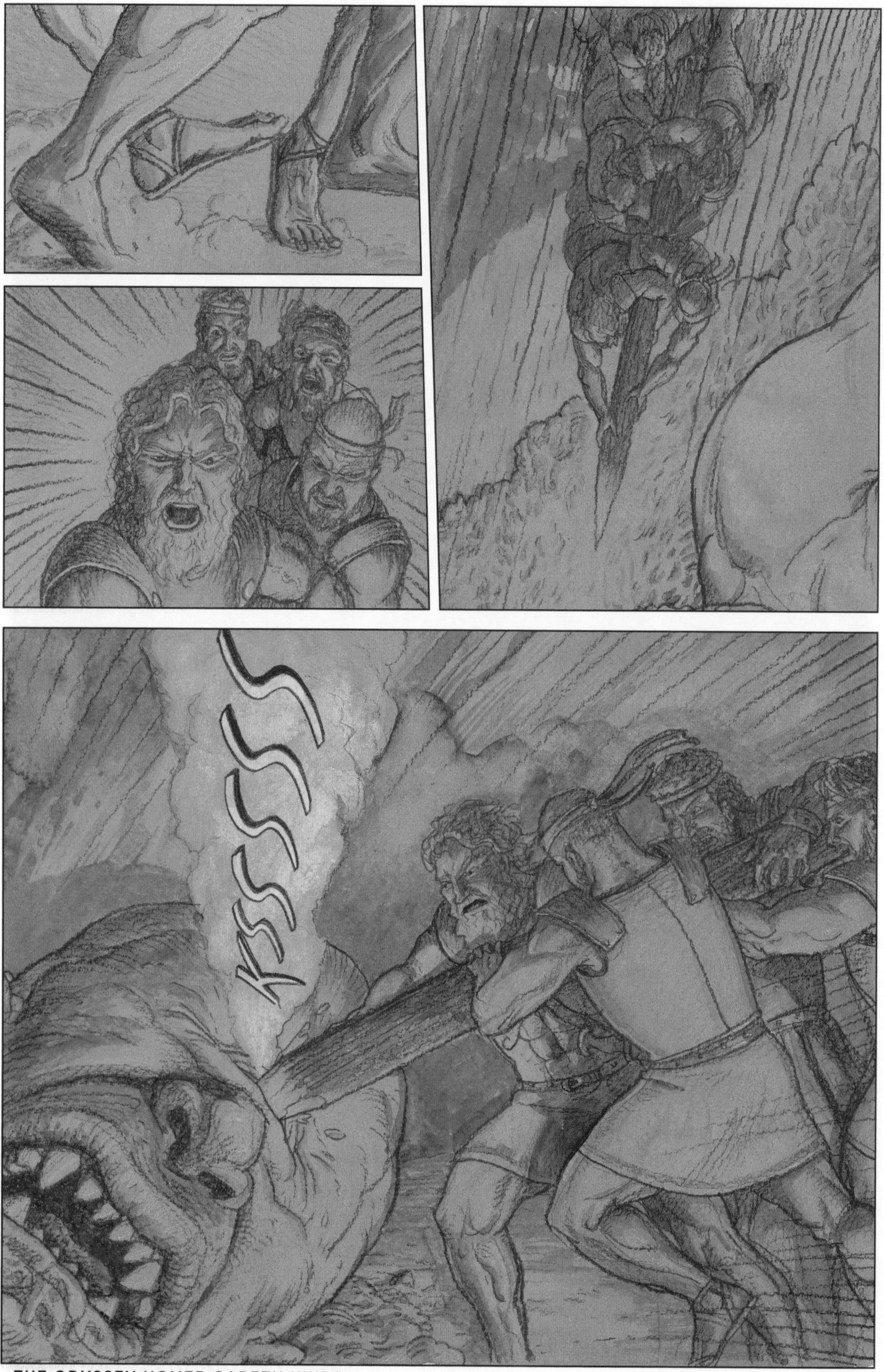
KSSSSS

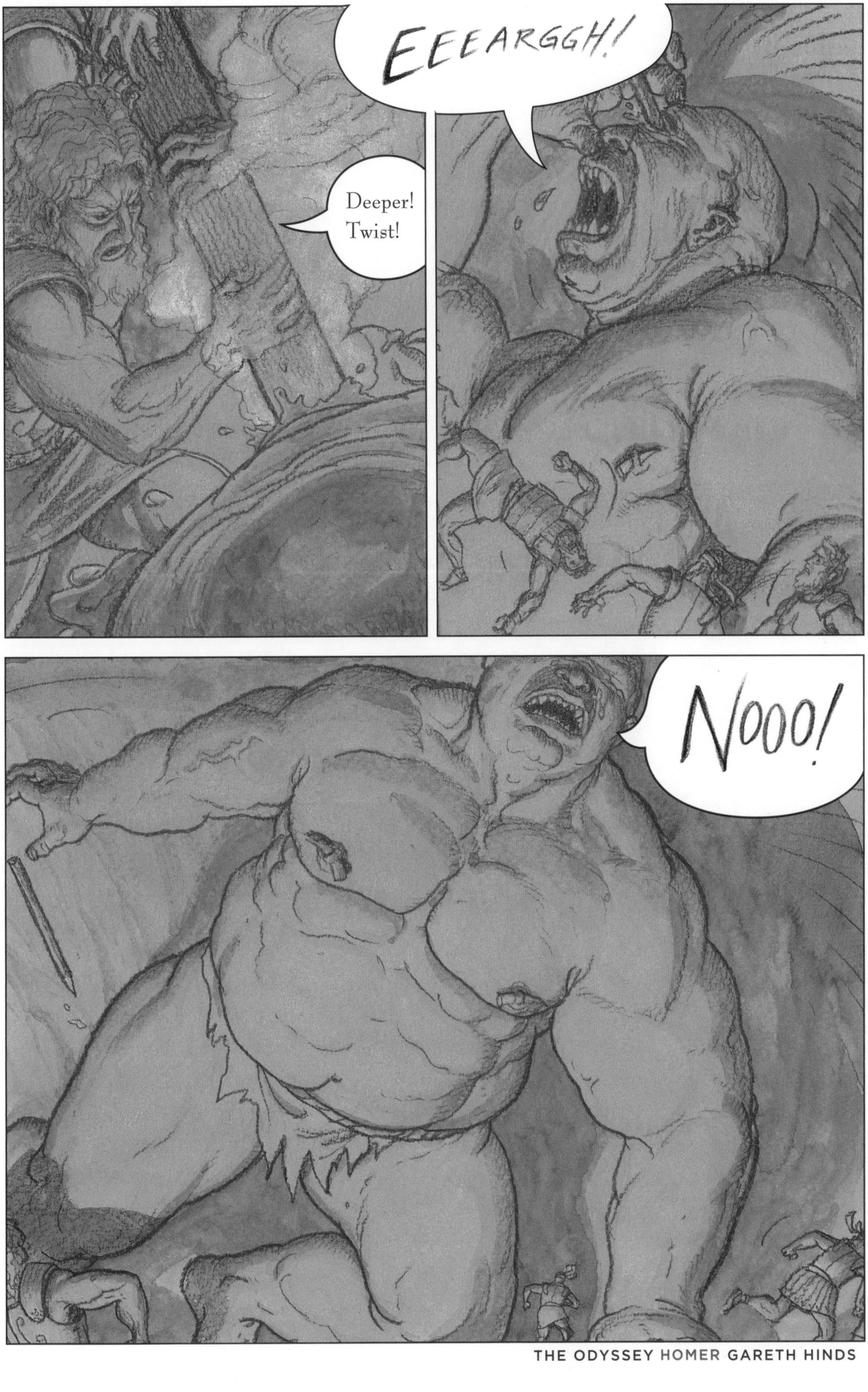
Deeper! Twist!
EEEARGGH!
Nooo!

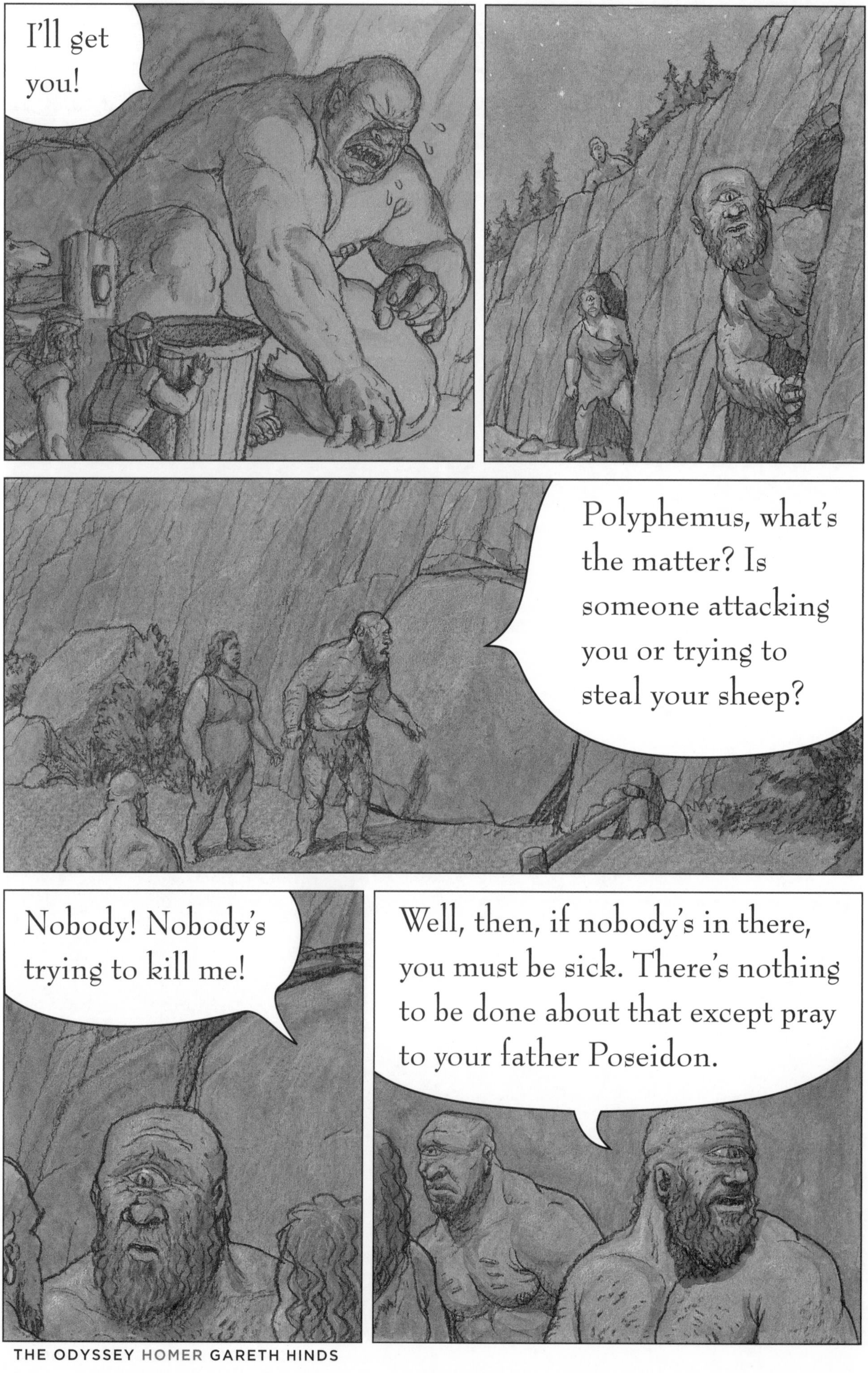
I'll get you!
Polyphemus, what's the matter? Is someone attacking you or trying to steal your sheep?
Nobody! Nobody's trying to kill me!
Well, then, if nobody's in there, you must be sick. There's nothing to be done about that except pray to your father Poseidon.

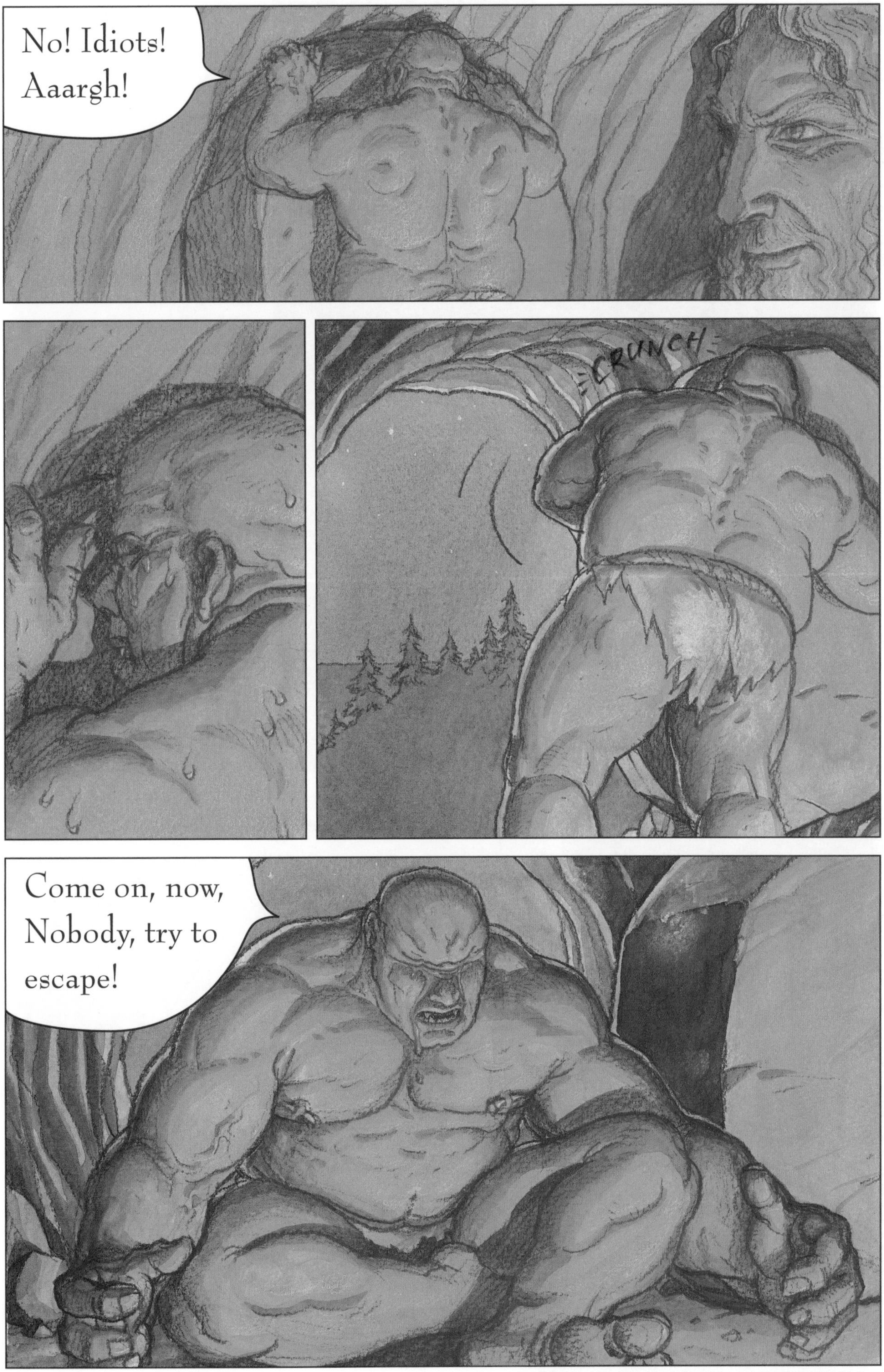
No! Idiots! Aaargh!
CRUNCH
Come on, now, Nobody, try to escape!

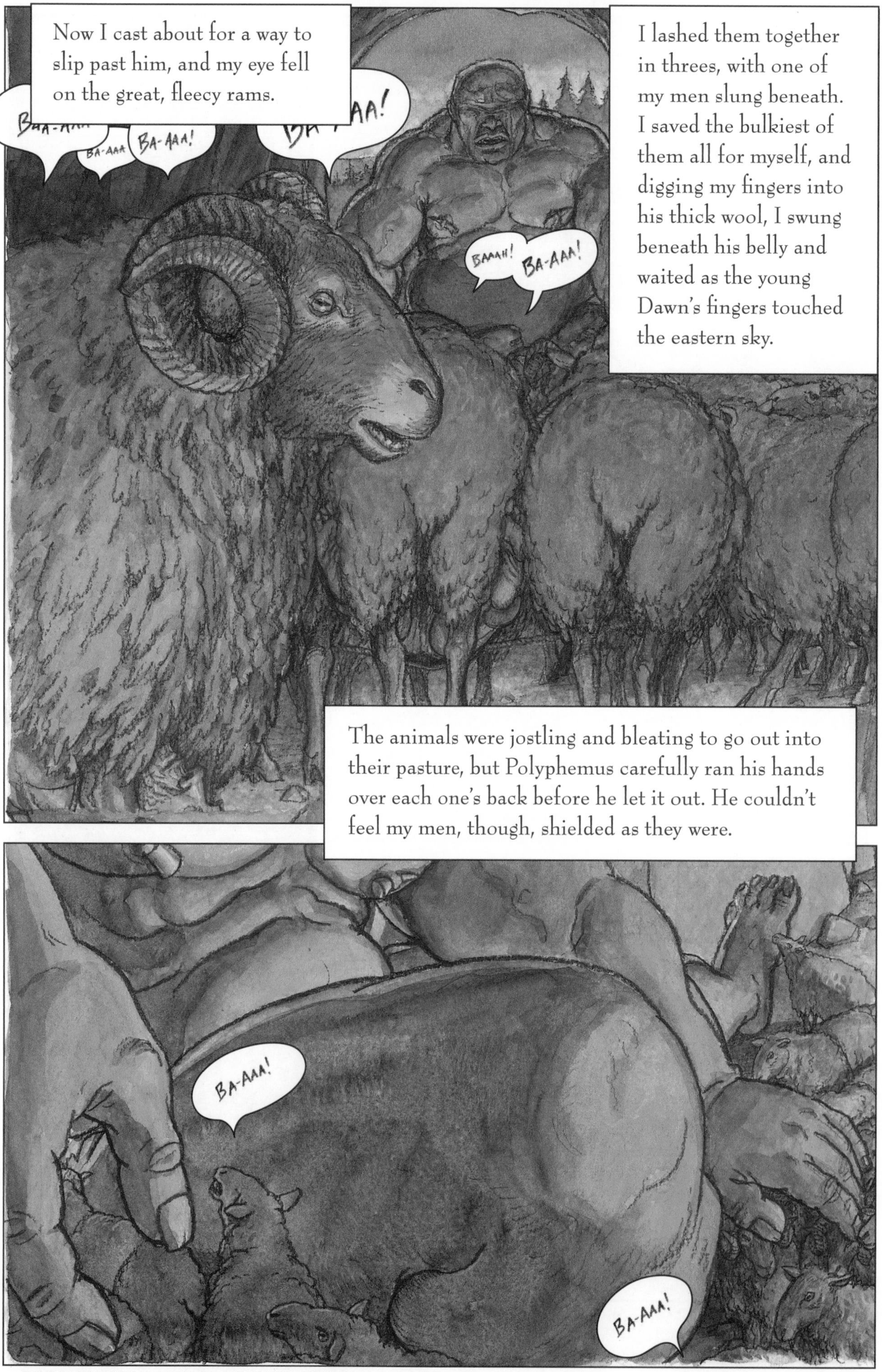
Now I cast about for a way to slip past him, and my eye fell on the great, fleecy rams.
BA-AAA
BA-AAA!
I lashed them together in threes, with one of my men slung beneath. I saved the bulkiest of them all for myself, and digging my fingers into his thick wool, I swung beneath his belly and waited as the young Dawn's fingers touched the eastern sky.
BAAAH!
BA-AAA!
The animals were jostling and bleating to go out into their pasture, but Polyphemus carefully ran his hands over each one's back before he let it out. He couldn't feel my men, though, shielded as they were.
BA-AAA!
BA-AAA!

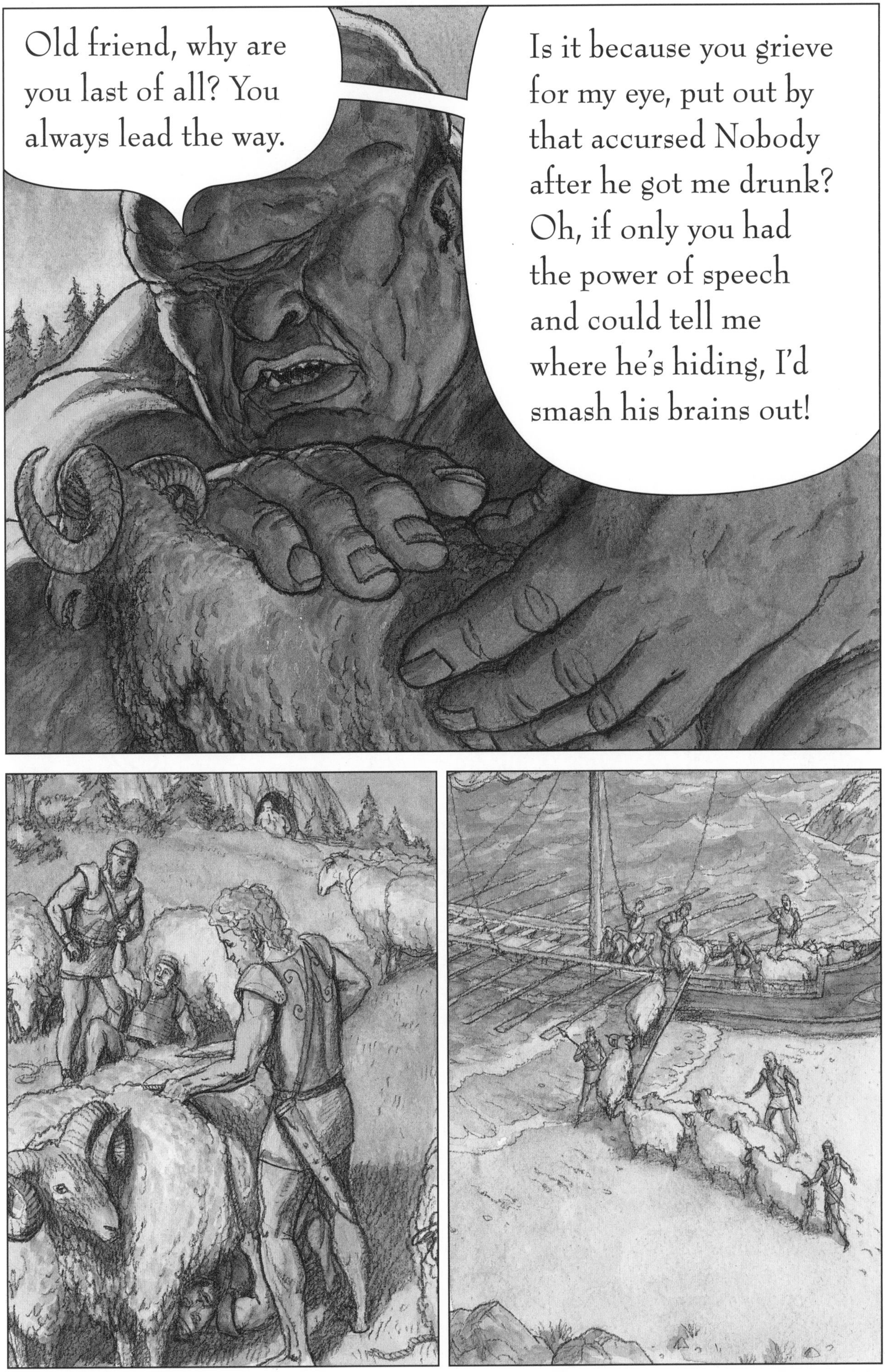
Old friend, why are you last of all? You always lead the way.
Is it because you grieve for my eye, put out by that accursed Nobody after he got me drunk? Oh, if only you had the power of speech and could tell me where he's hiding, I'd smash his brains out!

Cyclops! Your victims have escaped, and the gods have paid you back for your crimes!

CRACK!

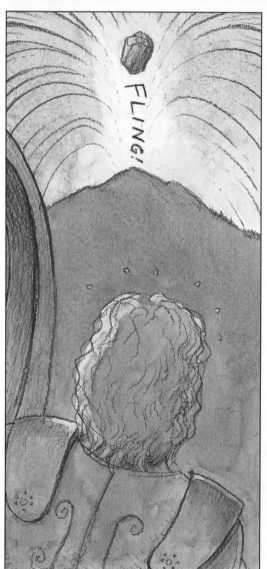

FLING!

!

BLOOSH

THE ODYSSEY HOMER GARETH HINDS

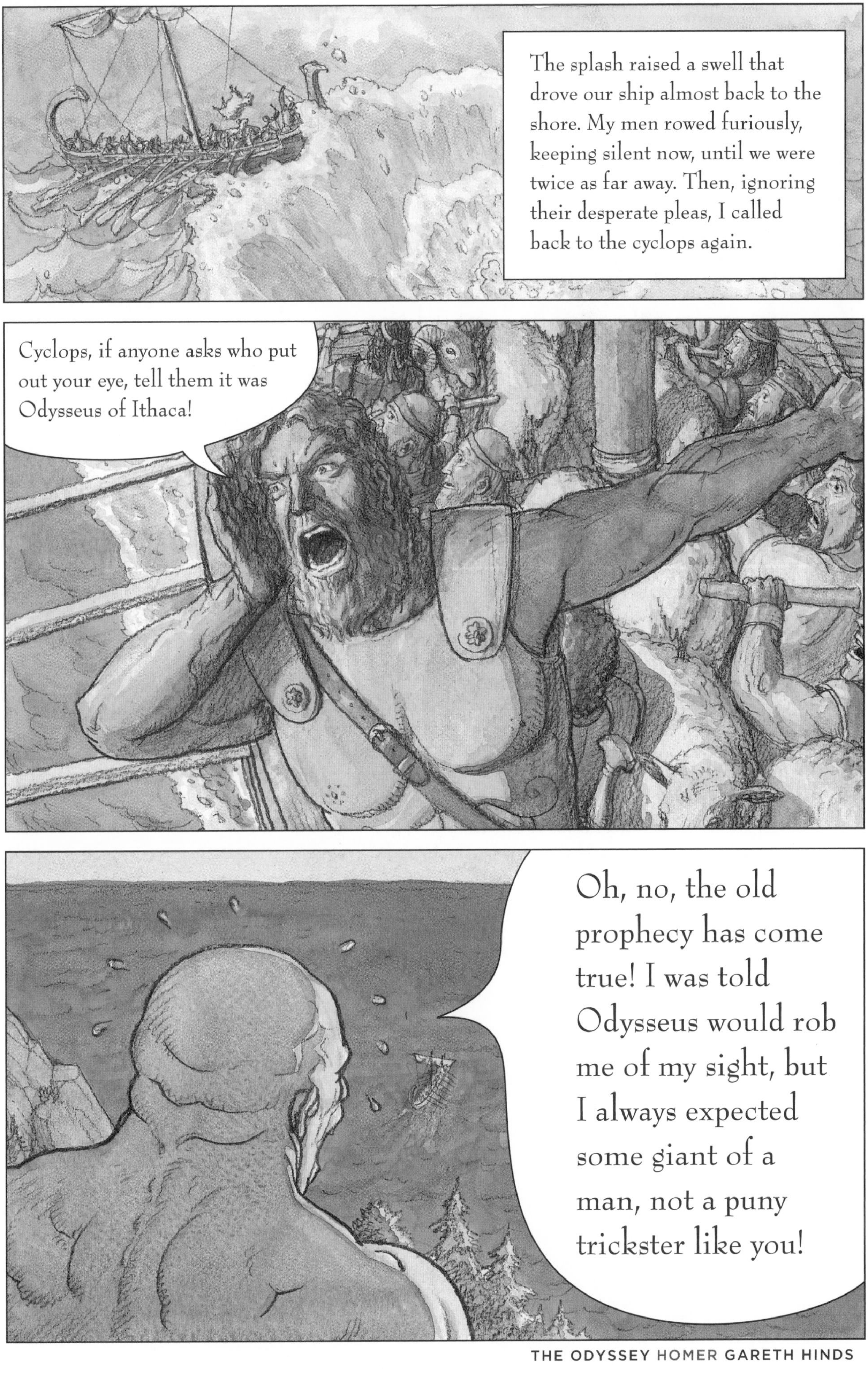
The splash raised a swell that drove our ship almost back to the shore. My men rowed furiously, keeping silent now, until we were twice as far away. Then, ignoring their desperate pleas, I called back to the cyclops again.
Cyclops, if anyone asks who put out your eye, tell them it was Odysseus of Ithaca!
Oh, no, the old prophecy has come true! I was told Odysseus would rob me of my sight, but I always expected some giant of a man, not a puny trickster like you!

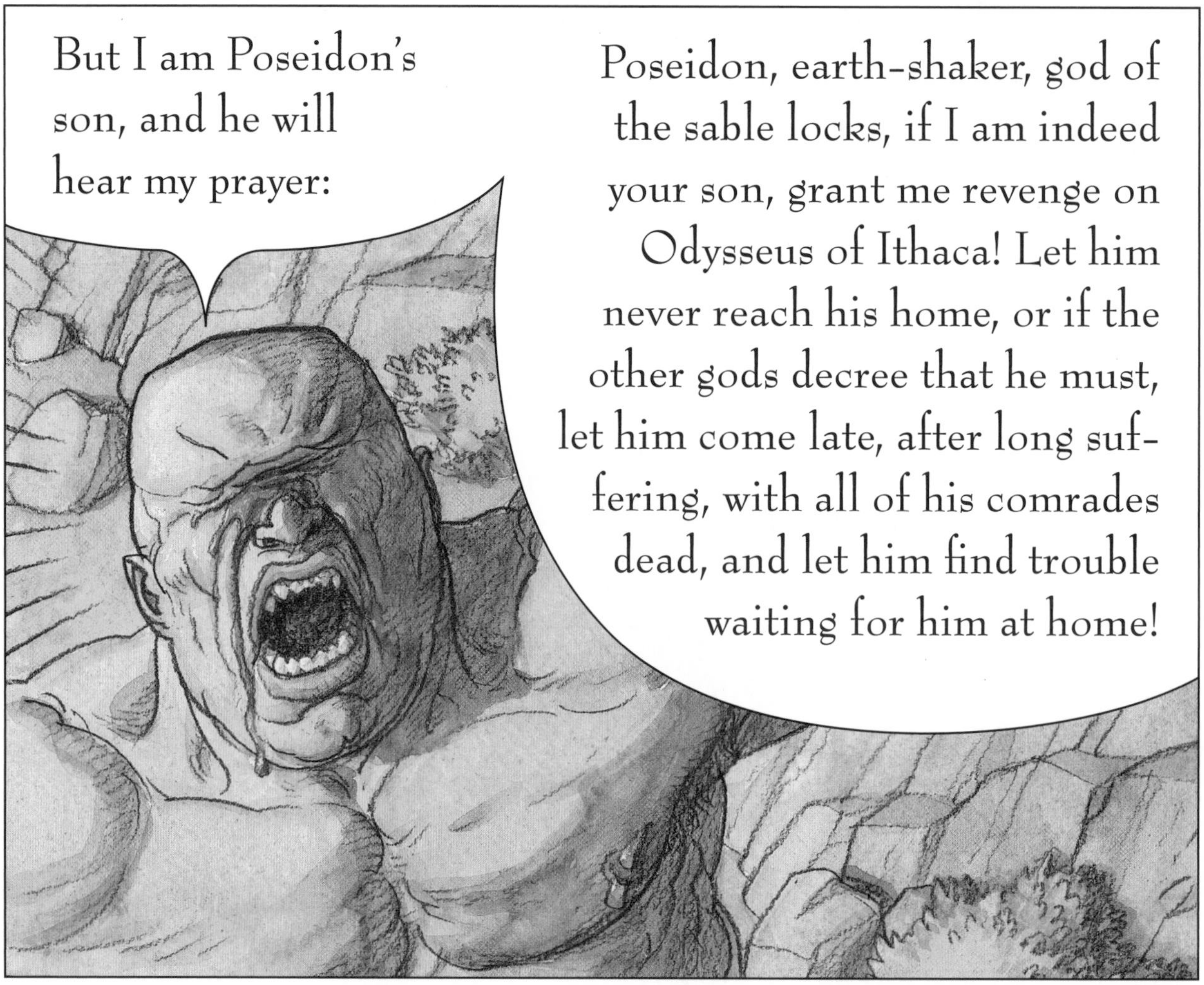
But I am Poseidon's son, and he will hear my prayer:
Poseidon, earth-shaker, god of the sable locks, if I am indeed your son, grant me revenge on Odysseus of Ithaca! Let him never reach his home, or if the other gods decree that he must, let him come late, after long suffering, with all of his comrades dead, and let him find trouble waiting for him at home!

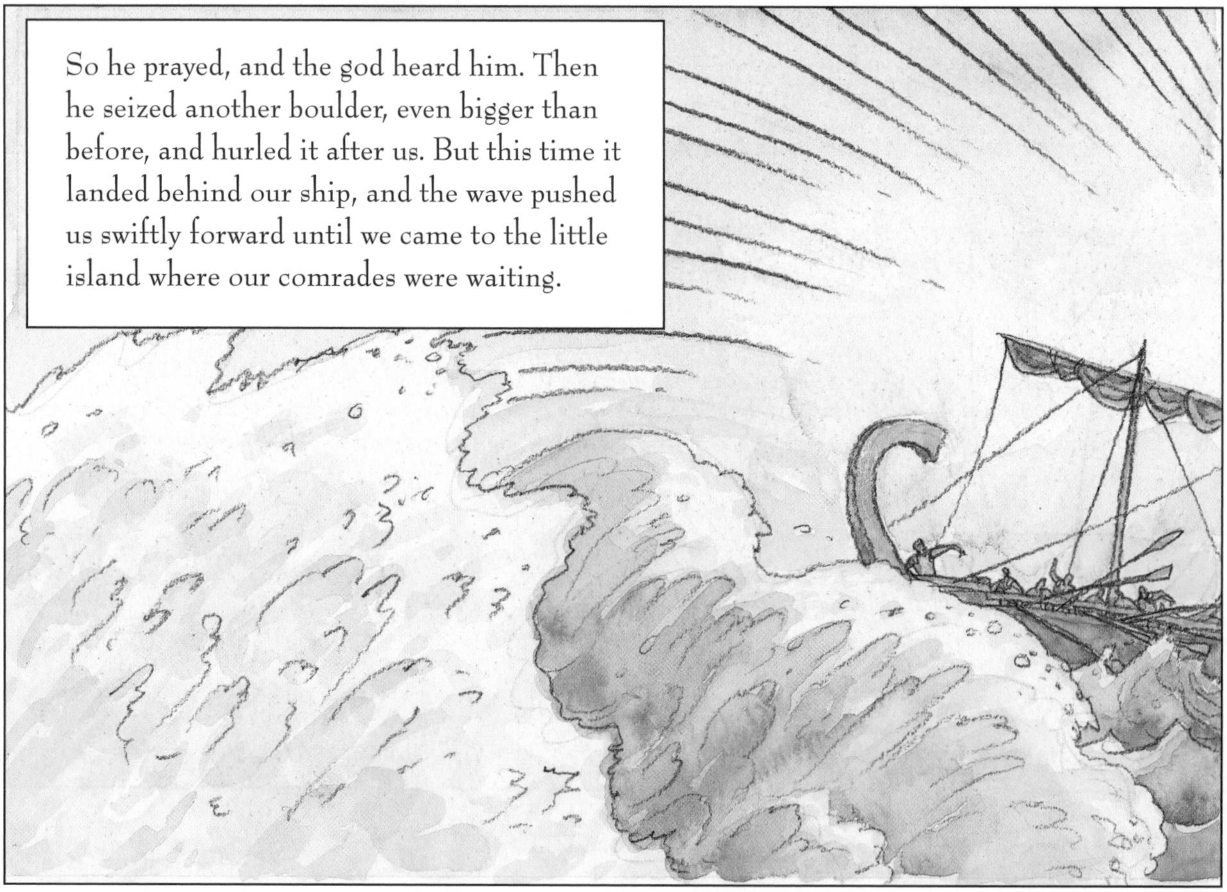
So he prayed, and the god heard him. Then he seized another boulder, even bigger than before, and hurled it after us. But this time it landed behind our ship, and the wave pushed us swiftly forward until we came to the little island where our comrades were waiting.

Poem fragments

Sappho

ART / ADAPTATION BY **Alessandro Bonaccorsi**

ONE OF THE GREAT POETS OF THE ANCIENT world—considered an equal of Homer and called "the tenth Muse" by Plato—Sappho was one of the first, maybe even the first, to stop using poetry for ritualistic and militaristic ends (war stories, funerals of VIPs, paeans to the gods) and start using it to express our inner lives, especially affairs of the heart. Sung to the accompaniments of a lyre at her highly esteemed school of poetry on the Isle of Lesbos, her poetry wasn't written down during her lifetime (circa 610–570 BCE), but when it finally was, over a century later, it filled nine rolls of papyrus. Of these literary riches, a paltry 200 fragments survive, along with one complete poem, the twenty-eight-line "Hymn to Aphrodite," which we have only because a Roman orator quoted it in its entirety in one of his manuscripts more than 500 years after Sappho's death. In fact, until the early 1900s, the only reason we had *any* of Sappho's verse was because ancient and medieval writers with access to the now-lost manuscripts would quote a line or two in their own works. At the beginning of the twentieth century some more fragments were recovered from strips of papyrus scrolls that were found in a town dump and had been preserved due to weather.

Sappho's poetry shows that love hasn't changed one iota in the intervening two and a half millennia. The joy, ecstasy, and excitement are there, as are the despair, jealousy, and confusion. The lines "I have two minds, / I know not what to do" could've been written by a poet earlier today.

Using fragments of the Edwin Marion Cox translation chosen by me, Italian illustrator and graphic designer Alessandro Bonaccorsi worked them into a silvery, moonlit design scheme.

SOURCE

Reynolds, Margaret (editor). *The Sappho Companion*. New York: Palgrave, 2002.

65

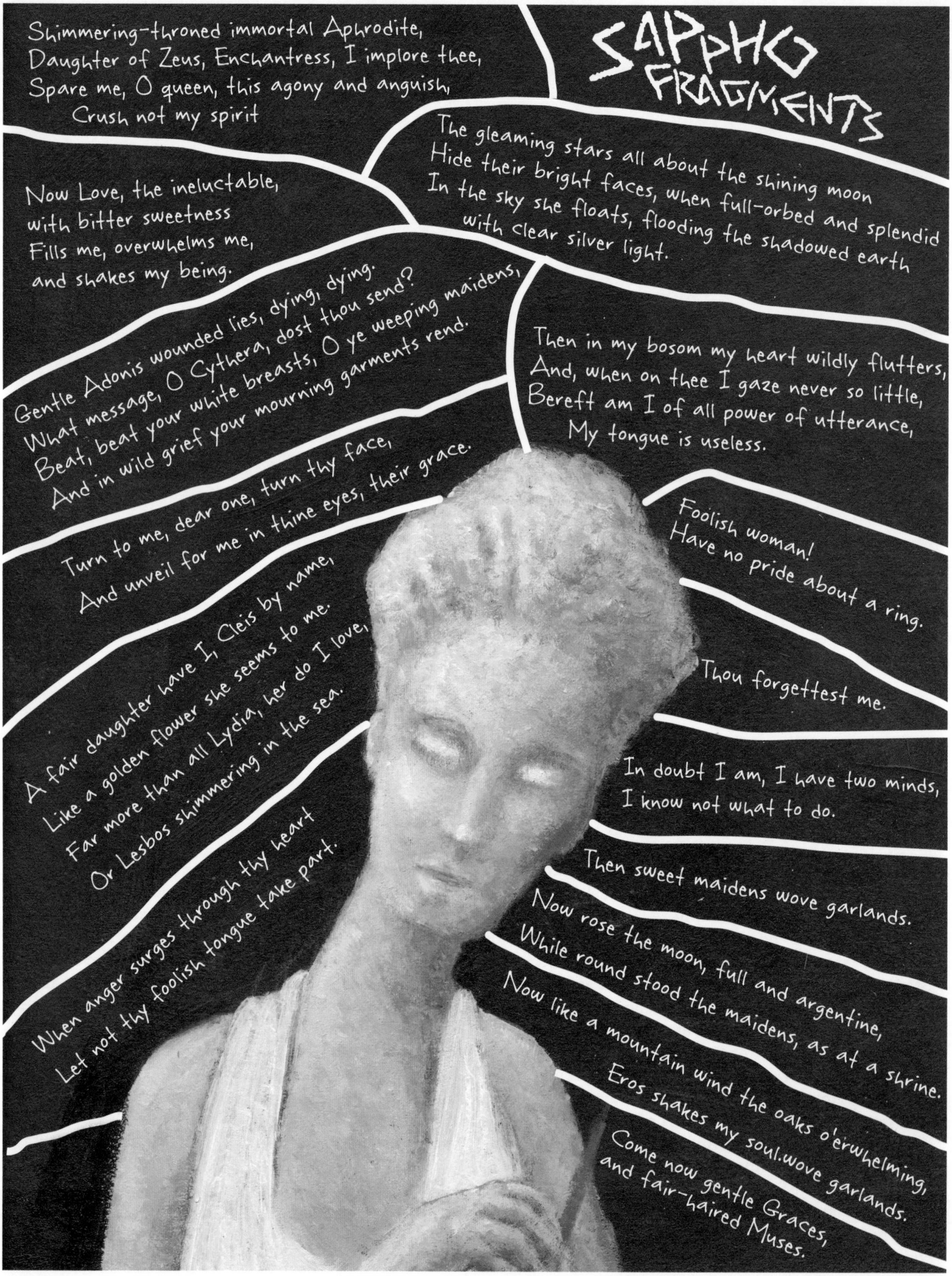
SAPPHO FRAGMENTS
Shimmering-throned immortal Aphrodite,
Daughter of Zeus, Enchantress, I implore thee,
Spare me, O queen, this agony and anguish,
Crush not my spirit
The gleaming stars all about the shining moon
Hide their bright faces, when full-orbed and splendid
In the sky she floats, flooding the shadowed earth
with clear silver light.
Now Love, the ineluctable,
with bitter sweetness
Fills me, overwhelms me,
and shakes my being.
Gentle Adonis wounded lies, dying, dying.
What message, O Cythera, dost thou send?
Beat, beat your white breasts, O ye weeping maidens,
And in wild grief your mourning garments rend.
Then in my bosom my heart wildly flutters,
And, when on thee I gaze never so little,
Bereft am I of all power of utterance,
My tongue is useless.
Turn to me, dear one, turn thy face,
And unveil for me in thine eyes, their grace.
Foolish woman!
Have no pride about a ring.
A fair daughter have I, Cleis by name,
Like a golden flower she seems to me.
Far more than all Lydia, her do I love,
Or Lesbos shimmering in the sea.
Thou forgettest me.
In doubt I am, I have two minds,
I know not what to do.
When anger surges through thy heart
Let not thy foolish tongue take part.
Then sweet maidens wove garlands.
Now rose the moon, full and argentine,
While round stood the maidens, as at a shrine.
Now like a mountain wind the oaks o'erwhelming,
Eros shakes my soul.wove garlands.
Come now gentle Graces,
and fair-haired Muses.

Medea

Euripides

ART / ADAPTATION BY **Tori McKenna**

THE MYTHOLOGICAL FIGURE MEDEA IS THE prototype of the betrayed woman who wreaks incalculably horrible, blood-soaked vengeance. The daughter of the barbarian King of Colchis (which is now Georgia), and granddaughter of the sun god Helios, Medea provides crucial assistance for the hero Jason in his famed quest to retrieve the Golden Fleece. He has agreed to marry her in return for her help, and he makes good on his promise. They even have a couple of children, but . . . well . . . now King Creon of Corinth wants Jason to marry his daughter, which would be a good political move for him, and he agrees. This is where *Medea* by Euripides—one of the great ancient Greek tragedies—begins.

In addition to this play, first performed in 431 BCE, Medea's story was told by numerous ancient Greek and Roman writers, and later formed the basis of operas, ballets, Broadway plays, and movies, including one by Pasolini. As professor Sarah Iles Johnston tells us in a collection of Medea essays that she coedited: "Ancient artists were mesmerized by her as well: we meet her image in Greek vase paintings, engraved Roman gemstones, Italian terracottas, and Pompeian wall murals." Now another artist has visualized Medea's story, this time in sequential comics form. Tori McKenna first adapted Euripides' play as a class project; several years later, when I approached her for this collection, she agreed to redo her adaptation from scratch, admirably presenting the entire work in fourteen pages.

SOURCE

Clauss, James J., and Sarah Iles Johnston (editors). Introduction. *Medea: Essays on Medea in Myth, Literature, Philosophy, and Art.* Princeton University Press, 1997.

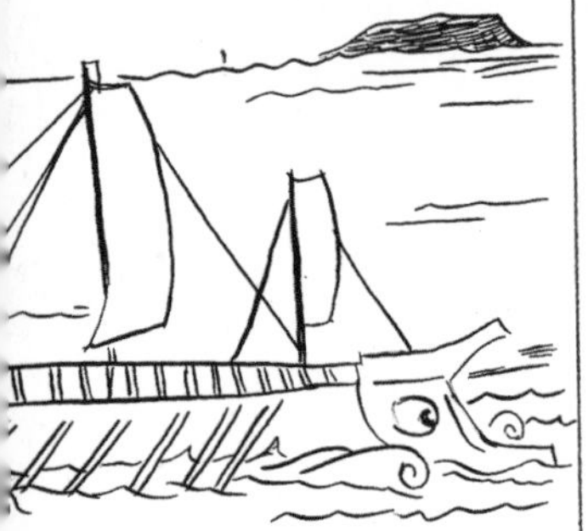

ripides'

EDEA

Adapted & Drawn by Tori McKenna

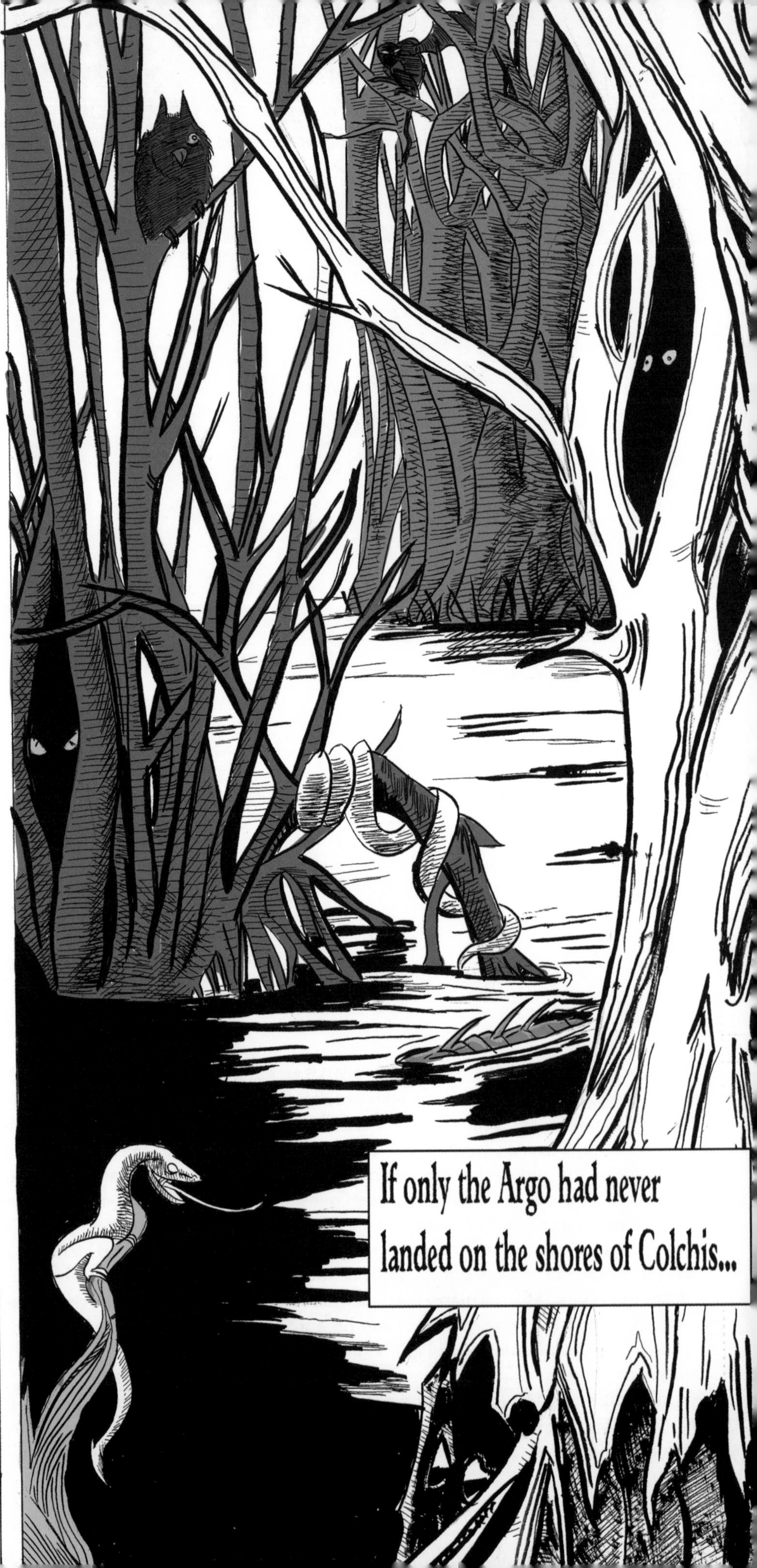
If only the Argo had never landed on the shores of Colchis...

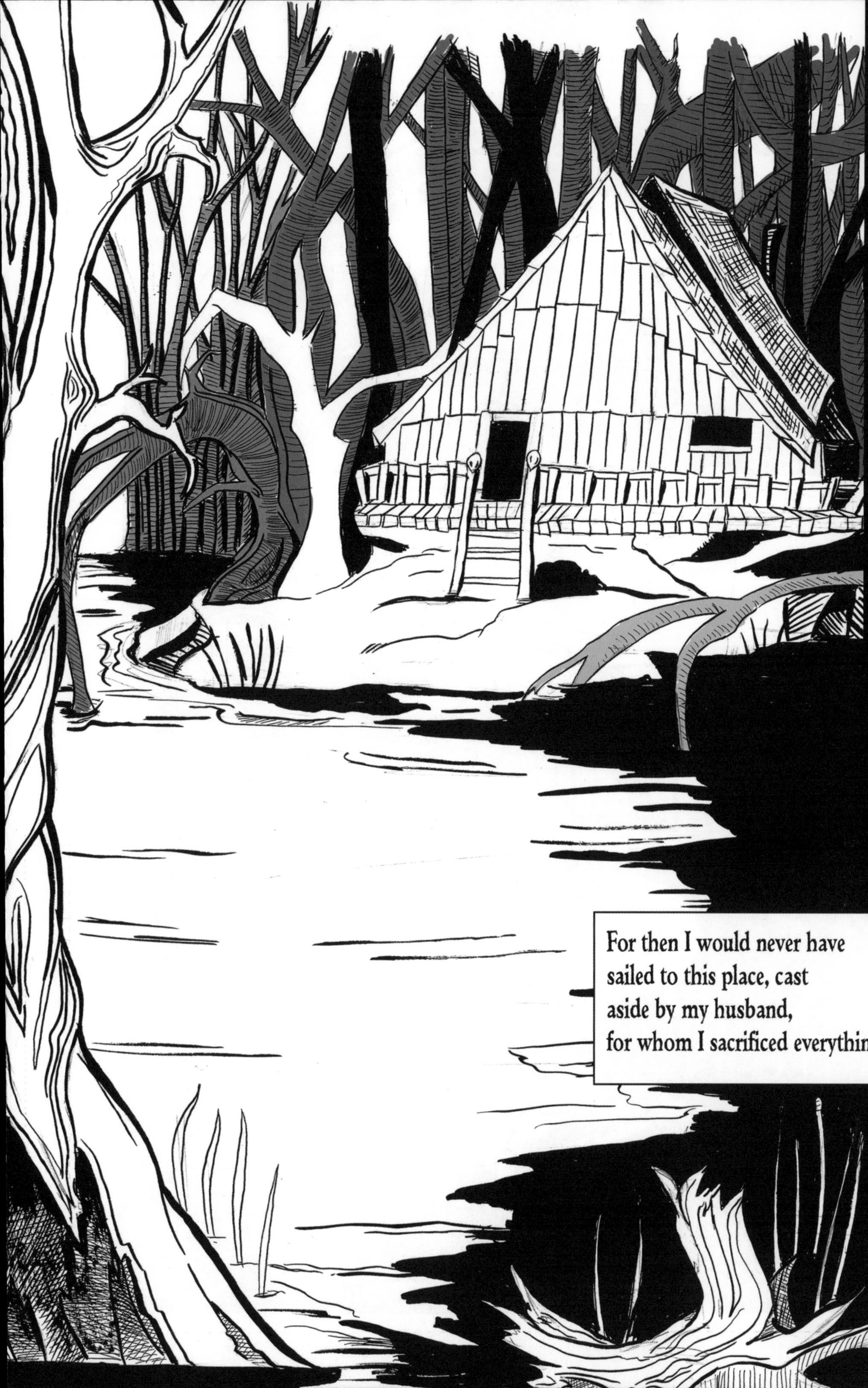
For then I would never have sailed to this place, cast aside by my husband, for whom I sacrificed everything

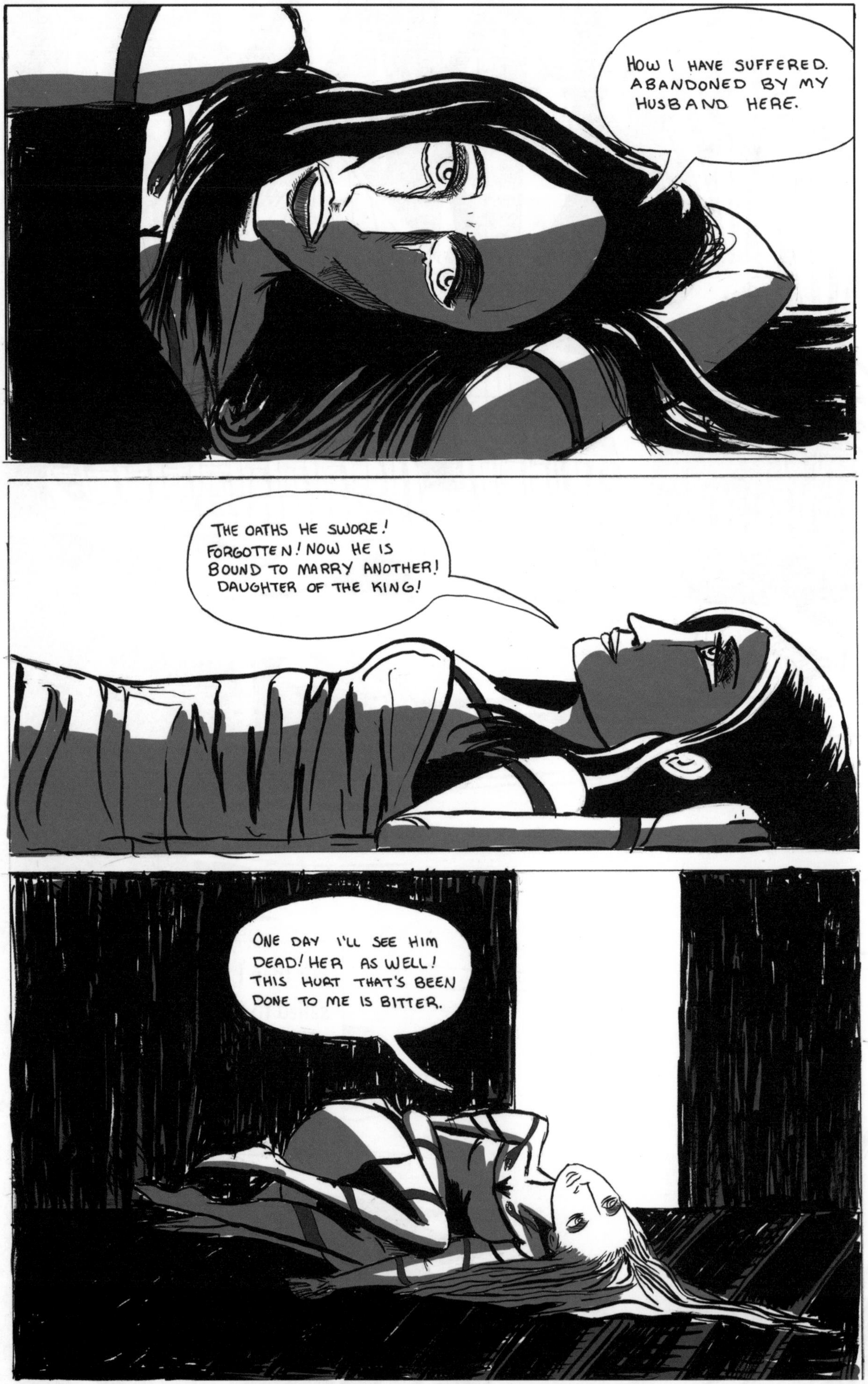
HOW I HAVE SUFFERED. ABANDONED BY MY HUSBAND HERE.
THE OATHS HE SWORE! FORGOTTEN! NOW HE IS BOUND TO MARRY ANOTHER! DAUGHTER OF THE KING!
ONE DAY I'LL SEE HIM DEAD! HER AS WELL! THIS HURT THAT'S BEEN DONE TO ME IS BITTER.

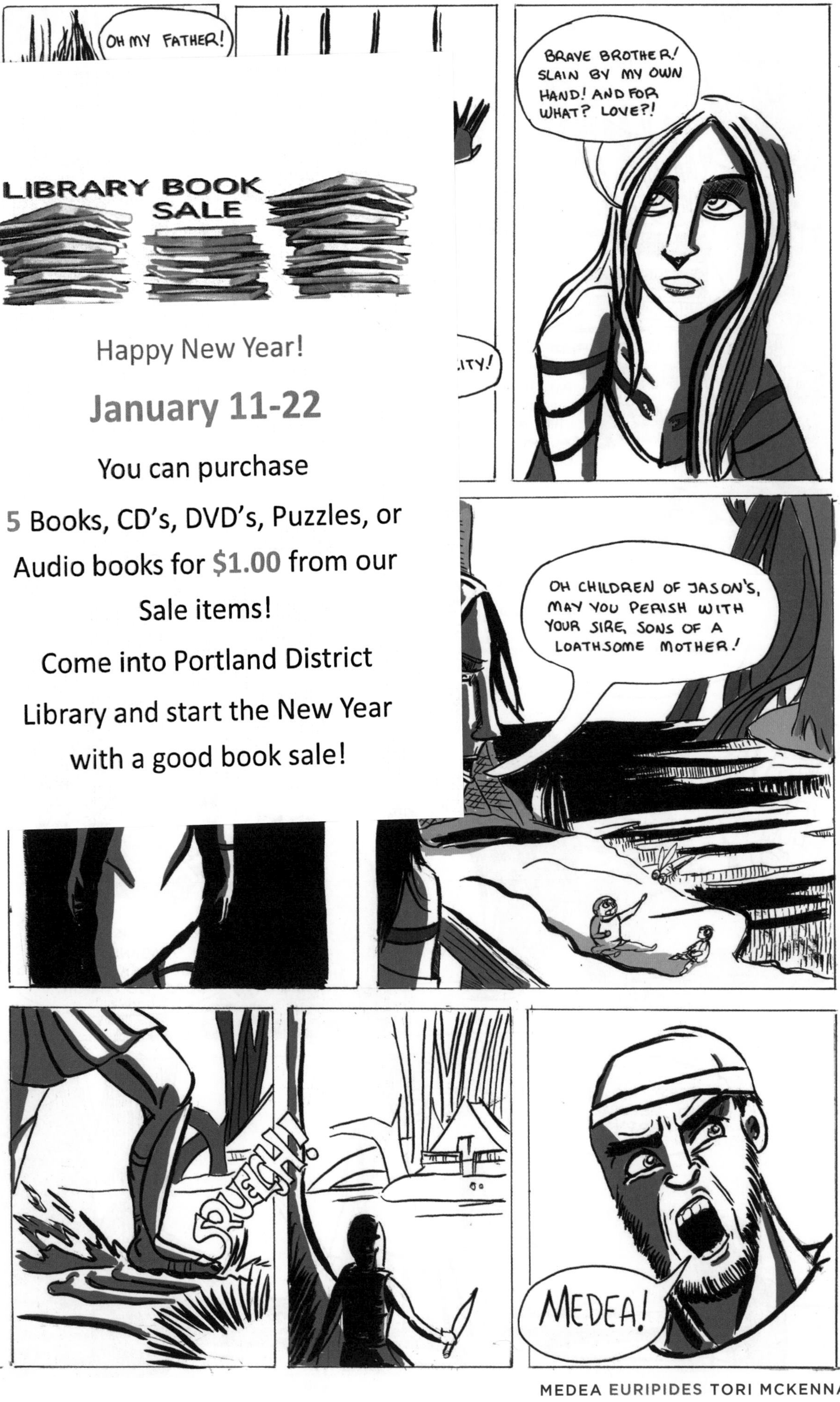
OH MY FATHER!
BRAVE BROTHER! SLAIN BY MY OWN HAND! AND FOR WHAT? LOVE?!
OH CHILDREN OF JASON'S, MAY YOU PERISH WITH YOUR SIRE, SONS OF A LOATHSOME MOTHER!
SQUELCH!
MEDEA!

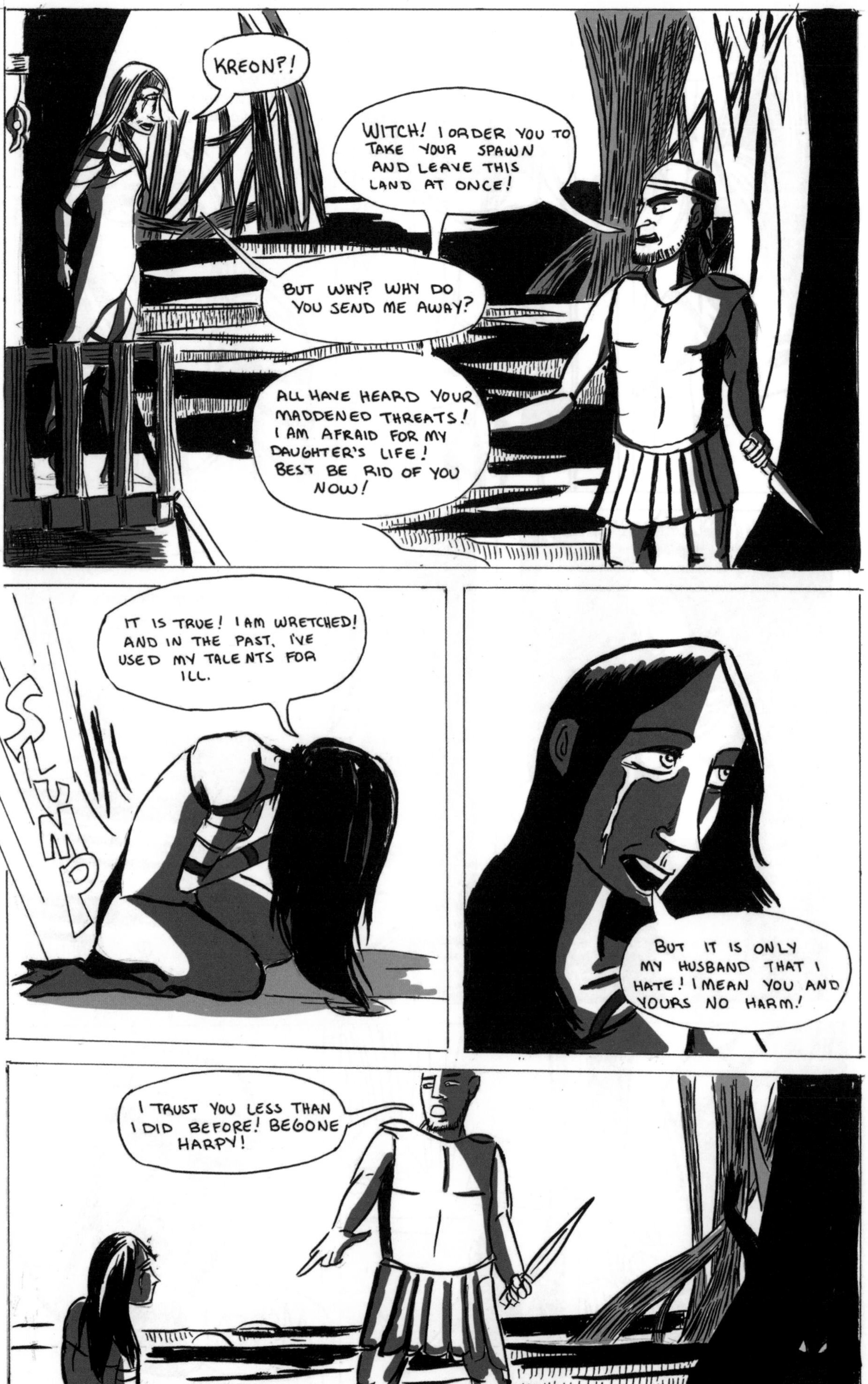
KREON?!
WITCH! I ORDER YOU TO TAKE YOUR SPAWN AND LEAVE THIS LAND AT ONCE!
BUT WHY? WHY DO YOU SEND ME AWAY?
ALL HAVE HEARD YOUR MADDENED THREATS! I AM AFRAID FOR MY DAUGHTER'S LIFE! BEST BE RID OF YOU NOW!
IT IS TRUE! I AM WRETCHED! AND IN THE PAST, I'VE USED MY TALENTS FOR ILL.
SLUMP
BUT IT IS ONLY MY HUSBAND THAT I HATE! I MEAN YOU AND YOURS NO HARM!
I TRUST YOU LESS THAN I DID BEFORE! BEGONE HARPY!

PLEASE! LET ME STAY! I BEG YOU BY YOUR KNEES!
YOUR WORDS ARE USELESS! YOU WILL NOT PERSUADE ME!
BUT MY CHILDREN!! GIVE ME ONE DAY TO ARRANGE THEIR FUTURES.
ONE DAY! AND THEN I WILL GO.
I BEG YOU... ...AS A PARENT.
VERY WELL.
BECAUSE OF THE LOVE FOR MY DAUGHTER, I WILL GIVE YOU ONE DAY. BUT IF YOU ARE STILL HERE, AFTER, I WILL SLAY YOU MYSELF!

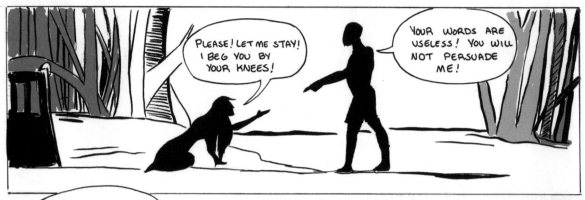

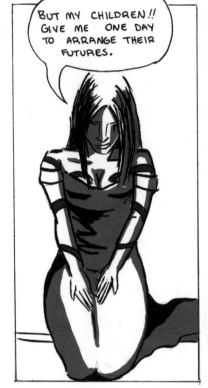

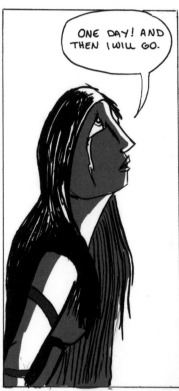

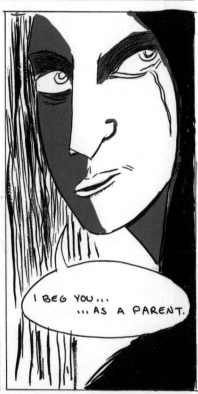

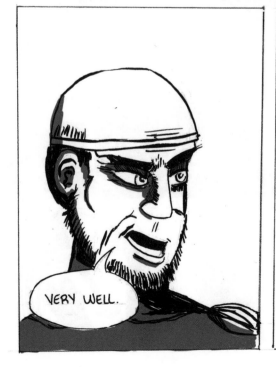

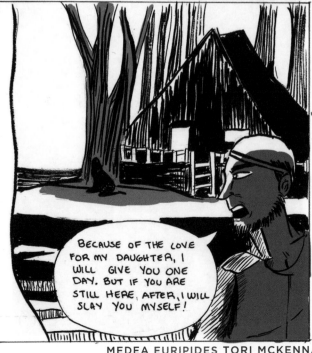

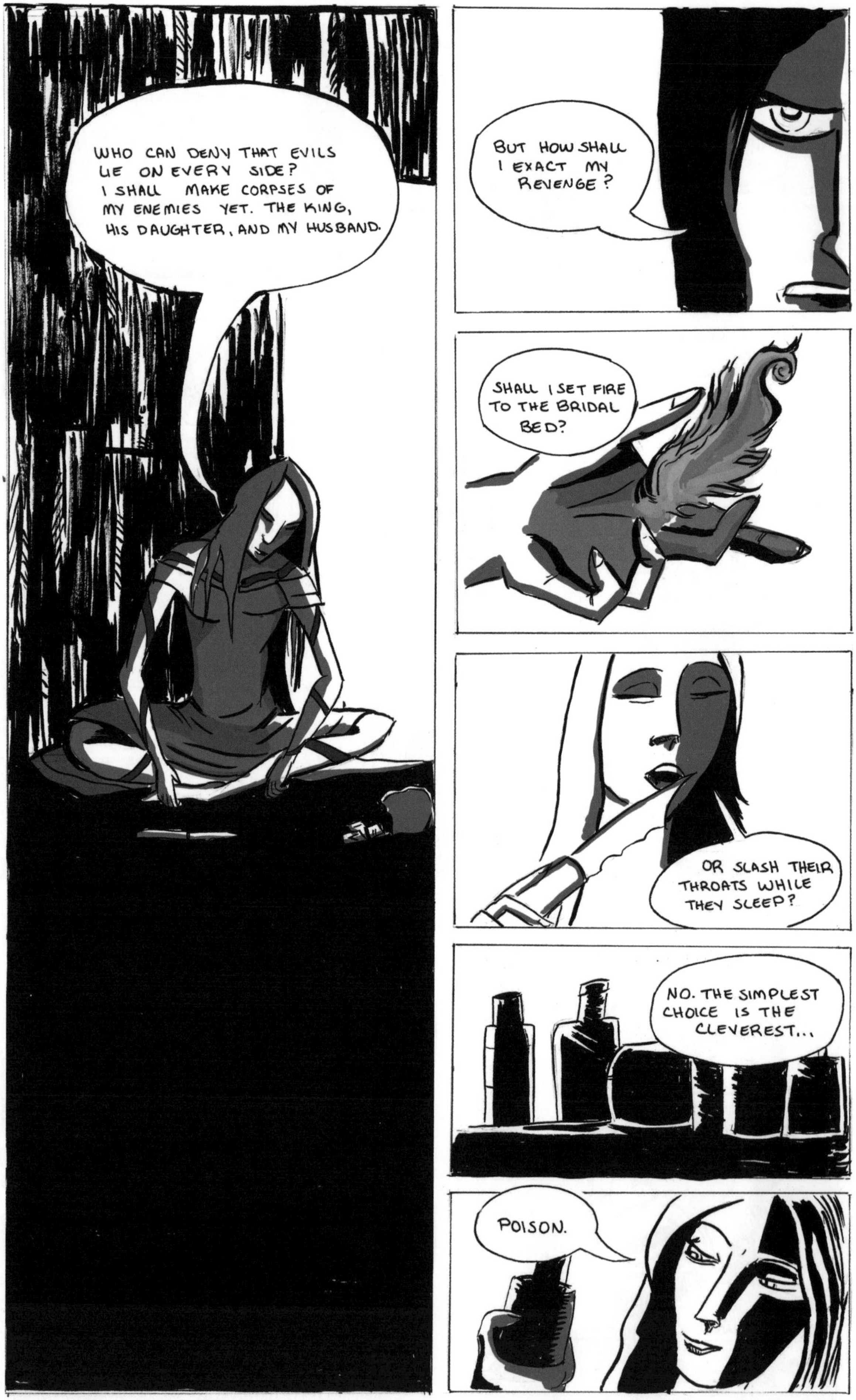
WHO CAN DENY THAT EVILS LIE ON EVERY SIDE? I SHALL MAKE CORPSES OF MY ENEMIES YET. THE KING, HIS DAUGHTER, AND MY HUSBAND.
BUT HOW SHALL I EXACT MY REVENGE?
SHALL I SET FIRE TO THE BRIDAL BED?
OR SLASH THEIR THROATS WHILE THEY SLEEP?
NO. THE SIMPLEST CHOICE IS THE CLEVEREST...
POISON.

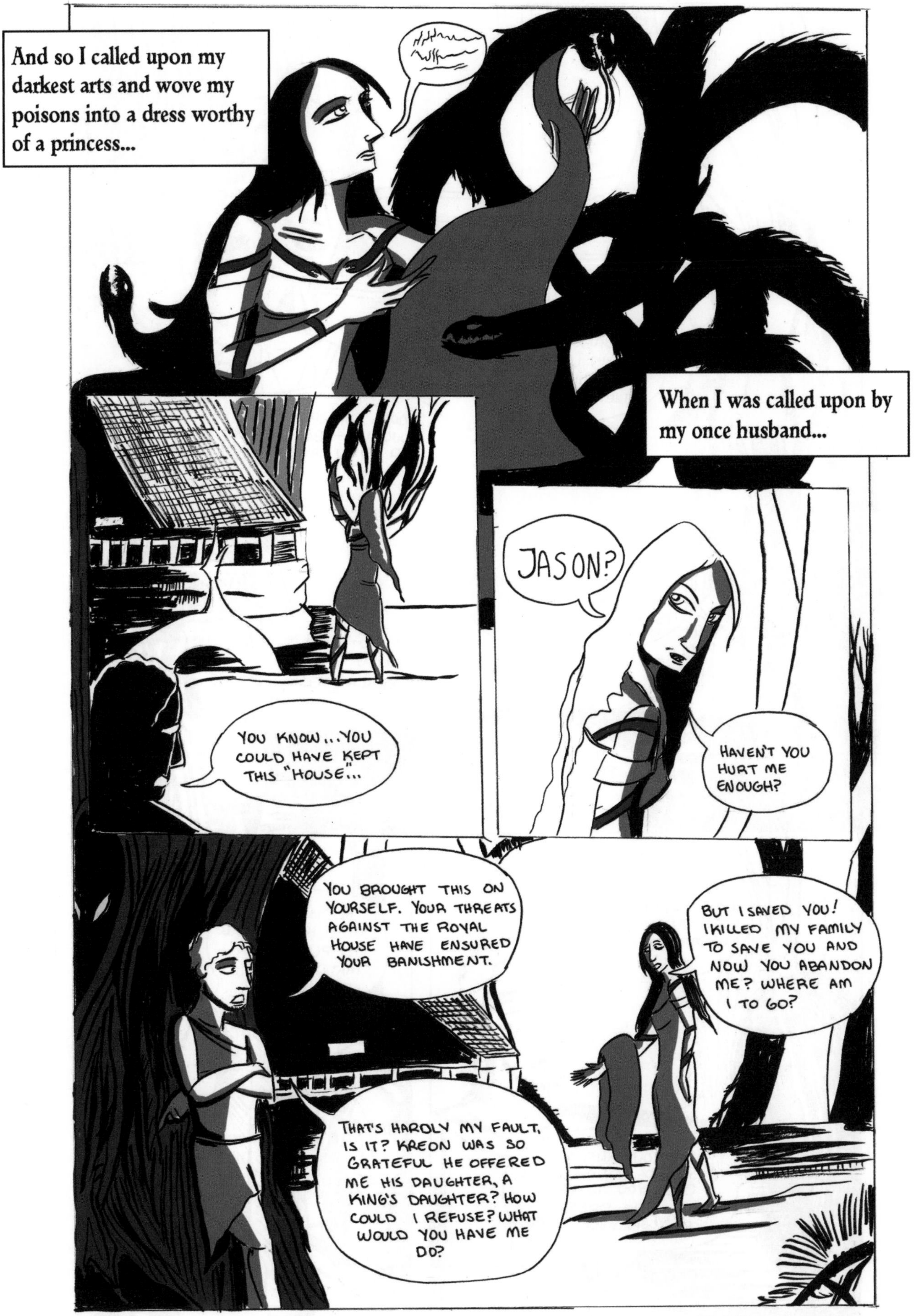
And so I called upon my darkest arts and wove my poisons into a dress worthy of a princess...
When I was called upon by my once husband...
JASON?
YOU KNOW...YOU COULD HAVE KEPT THIS "HOUSE"...
HAVEN'T YOU HURT ME ENOUGH?
YOU BROUGHT THIS ON YOURSELF. YOUR THREATS AGAINST THE ROYAL HOUSE HAVE ENSURED YOUR BANISHMENT.
BUT I SAVED YOU! I KILLED MY FAMILY TO SAVE YOU AND NOW YOU ABANDON ME? WHERE AM I TO GO?
THAT'S HARDLY MY FAULT, IS IT? KREON WAS SO GRATEFUL HE OFFERED ME HIS DAUGHTER, A KING'S DAUGHTER? HOW COULD I REFUSE? WHAT WOULD YOU HAVE ME DO?

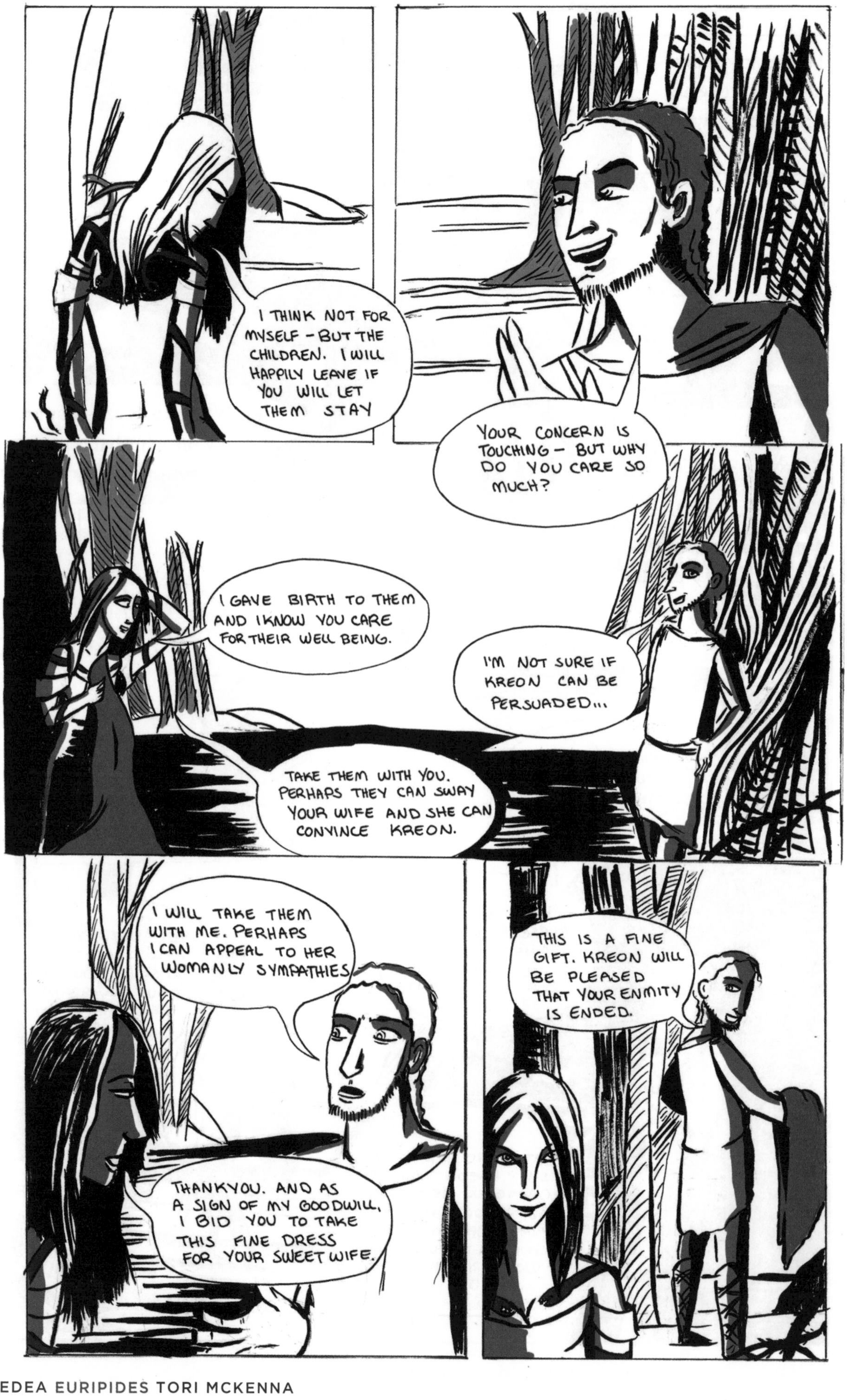
I THINK NOT FOR MYSELF - BUT THE CHILDREN. I WILL HAPPILY LEAVE IF YOU WILL LET THEM STAY
YOUR CONCERN IS TOUCHING - BUT WHY DO YOU CARE SO MUCH?
I GAVE BIRTH TO THEM AND I KNOW YOU CARE FOR THEIR WELL BEING.
I'M NOT SURE IF KREON CAN BE PERSUADED...
TAKE THEM WITH YOU. PERHAPS THEY CAN SWAY YOUR WIFE AND SHE CAN CONVINCE KREON.
I WILL TAKE THEM WITH ME. PERHAPS I CAN APPEAL TO HER WOMANLY SYMPATHIES.
THANKYOU. AND AS A SIGN OF MY GOODWILL, I BID YOU TO TAKE THIS FINE DRESS FOR YOUR SWEET WIFE.
THIS IS A FINE GIFT. KREON WILL BE PLEASED THAT YOUR ENMITY IS ENDED.

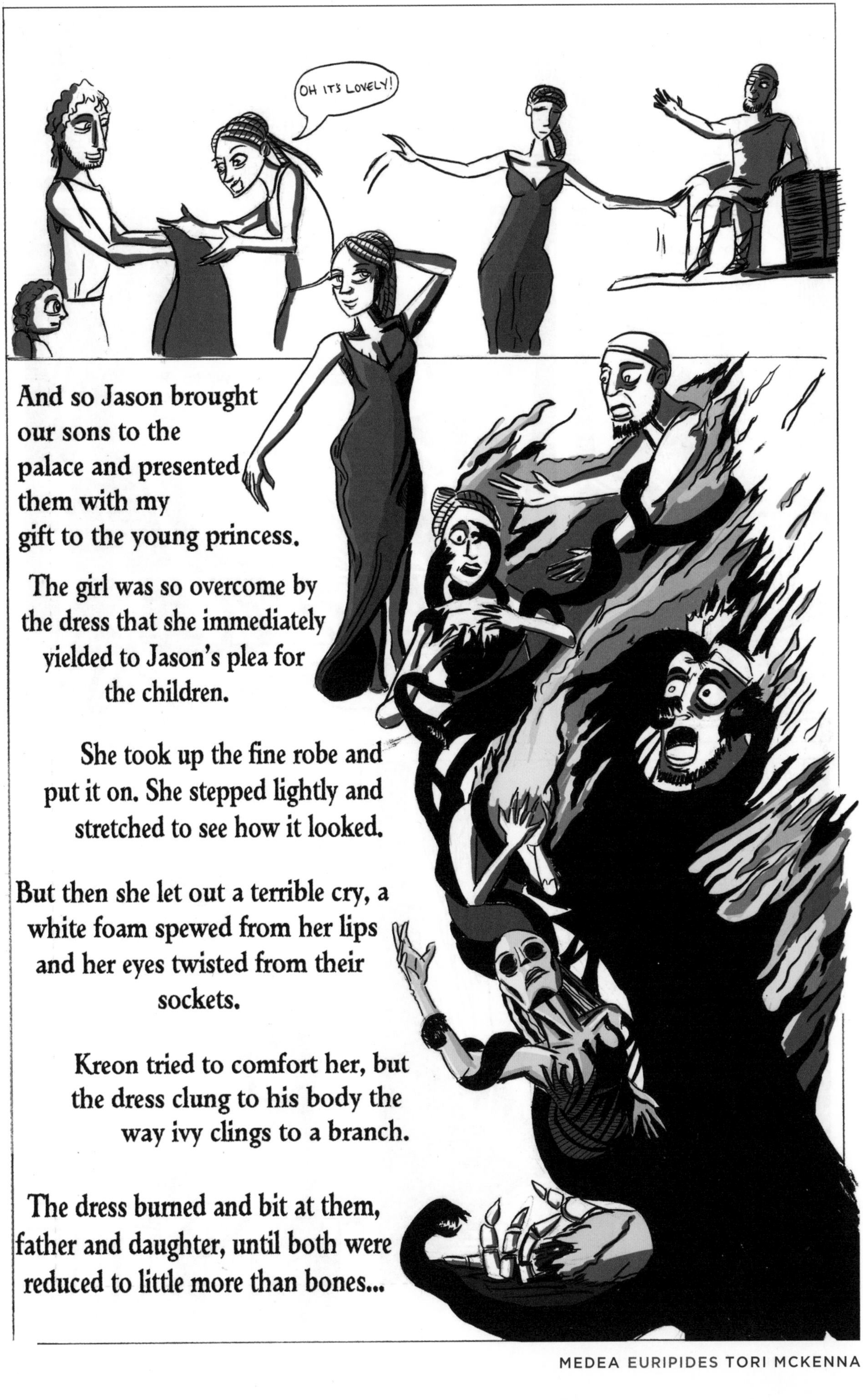
OH IT'S LOVELY!
And so Jason brought our sons to the palace and presented them with my gift to the young princess.
The girl was so overcome by the dress that she immediately yielded to Jason's plea for the children.
She took up the fine robe and put it on. She stepped lightly and stretched to see how it looked.
But then she let out a terrible cry, a white foam spewed from her lips and her eyes twisted from their sockets.
Kreon tried to comfort her, but the dress clung to his body the way ivy clings to a branch.
The dress burned and bit at them, father and daughter, until both were reduced to little more than bones...

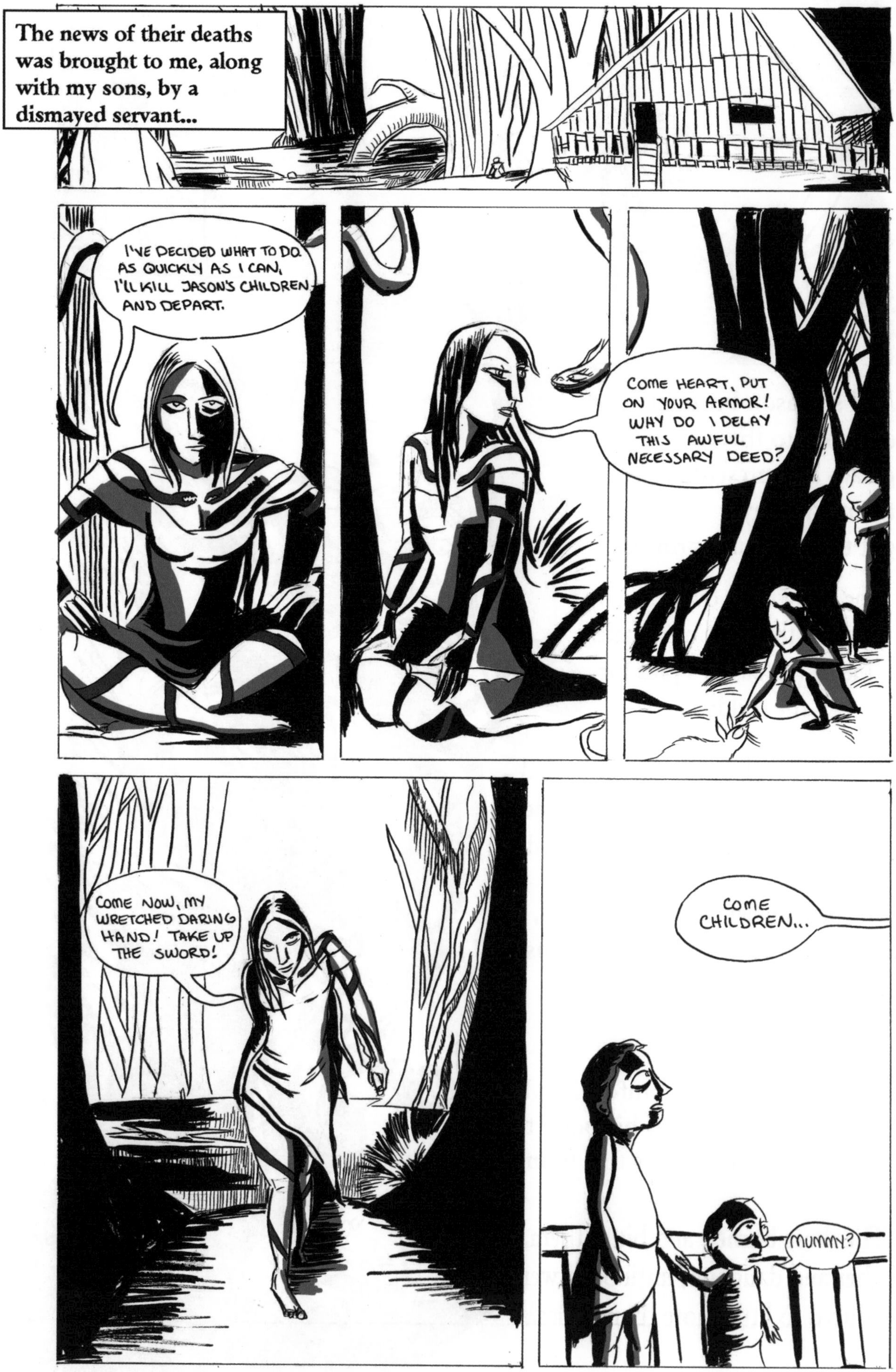
The news of their deaths was brought to me, along with my sons, by a dismayed servant...
I'VE DECIDED WHAT TO DO. AS QUICKLY AS I CAN, I'LL KILL JASON'S CHILDREN AND DEPART.
COME HEART, PUT ON YOUR ARMOR! WHY DO I DELAY THIS AWFUL NECESSARY DEED?
COME NOW, MY WRETCHED DARING HAND! TAKE UP THE SWORD!
COME CHILDREN...
MUMMY?

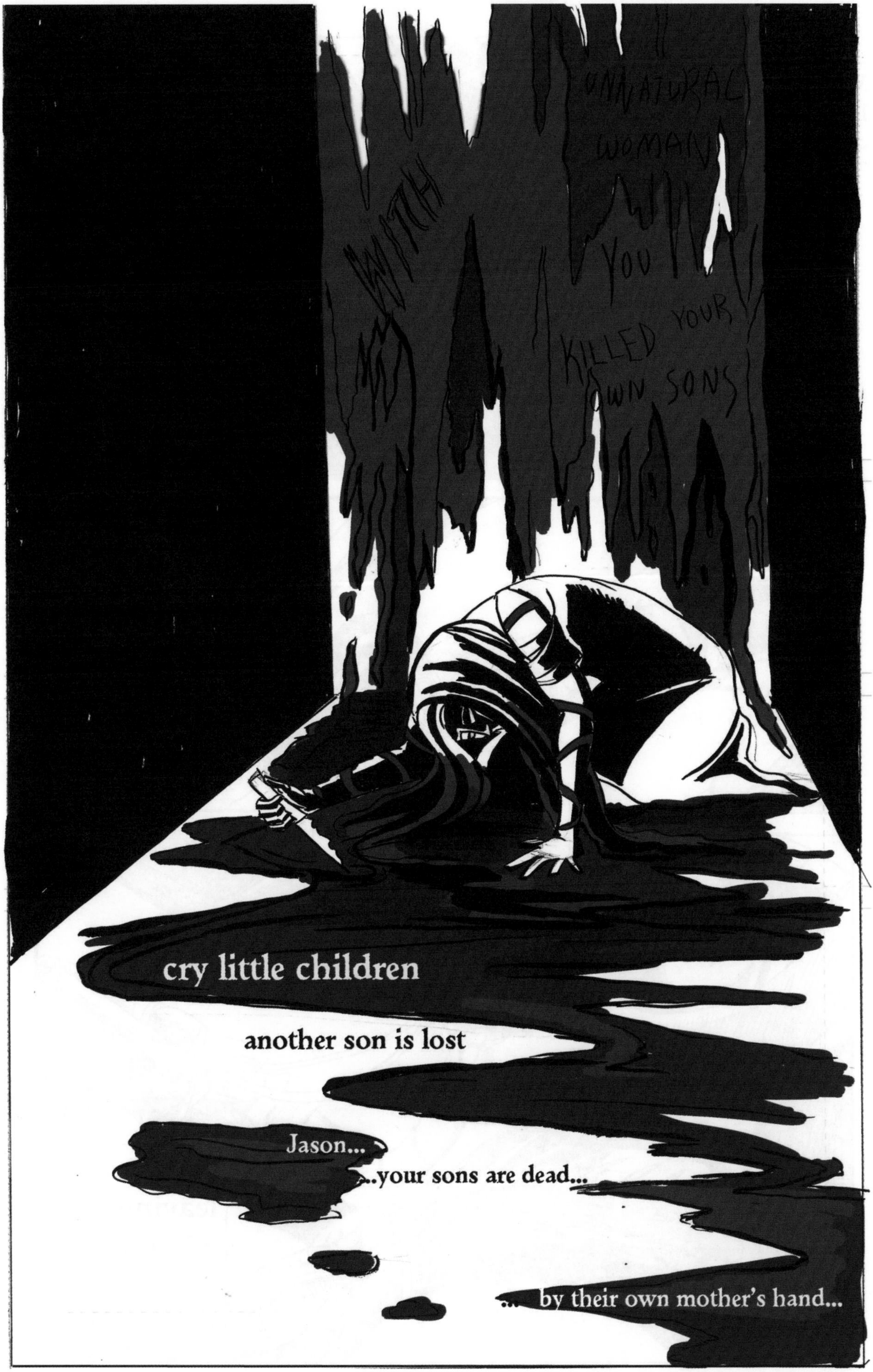

WITCH
UNNATURAL WOMAN
YOU KILLED YOUR OWN SONS
cry little children
another son is lost
Jason...
...your sons are dead...
... by their own mother's hand...

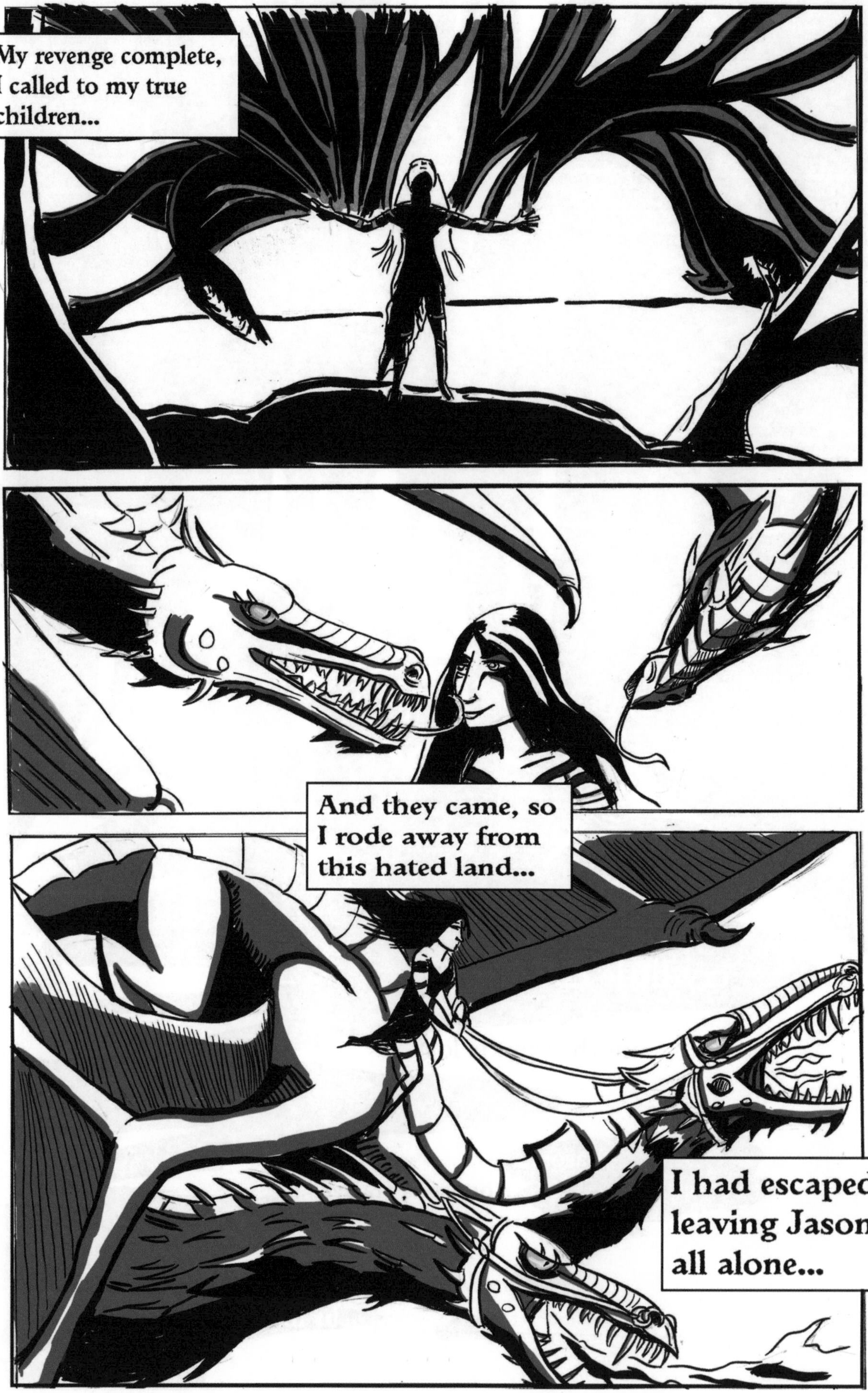
My revenge complete, I called to my true children...
And they came, so I rode away from this hated land...
I had escaped, leaving Jason all alone...

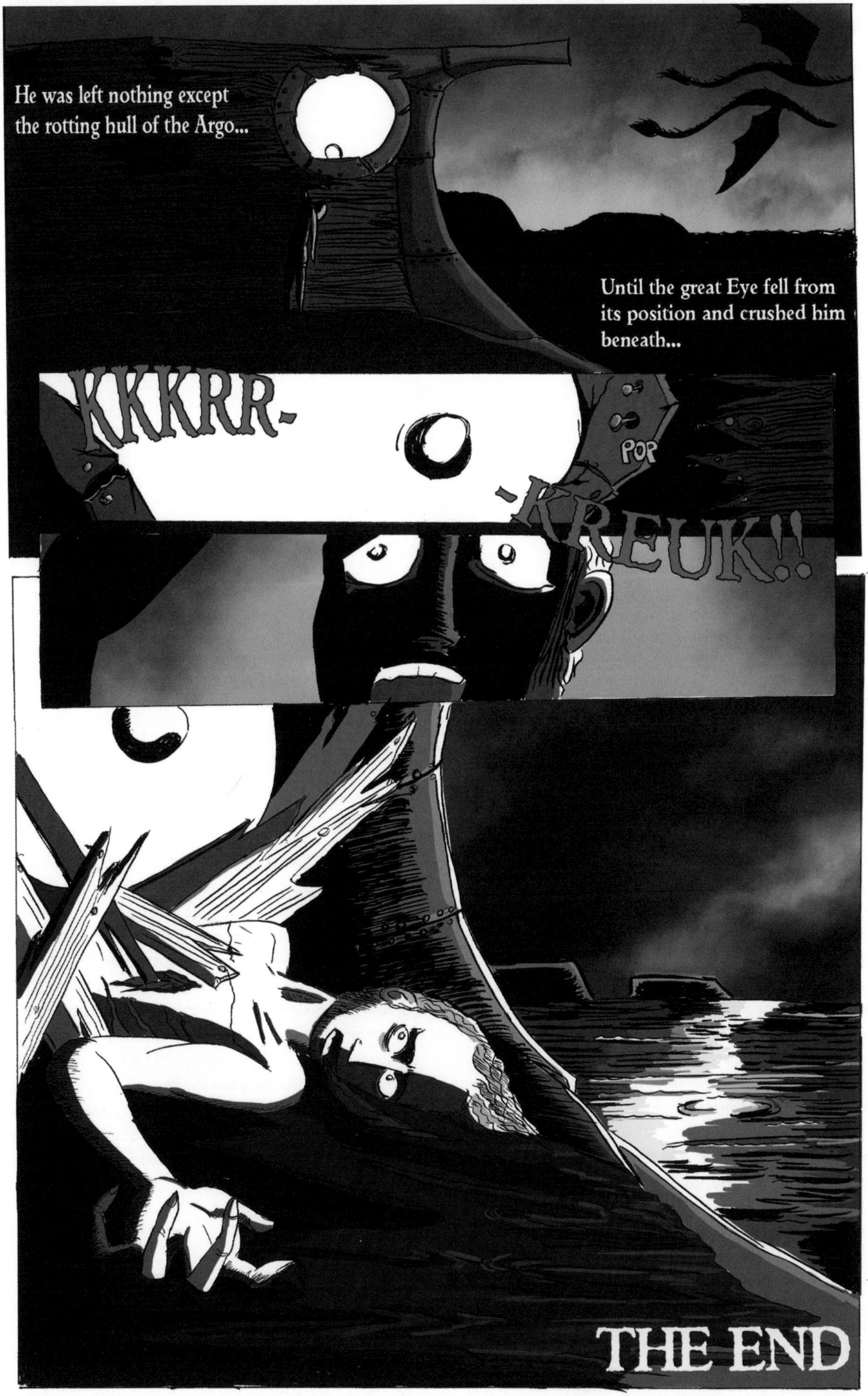
He was left nothing except the rotting hull of the Argo...
Until the great Eye fell from its position and crushed him beneath...
KKKRR-
POP
-KREUK!!
THE END

Lysistrata

Aristophanes

ART / ADAPTATION AND TRANSLATION BY **Valerie Schrag**

ARISTOPHANES WAS ONE OF THE GREAT PLAY-wrights of ancient Greece, but while Sophocles, Euripides, and the other titans of theater focused on tragedy, Aristophanes became the king of comedy. Of his eleven surviving plays (out of at least forty), *Lysistrata* is the best known.

Athens and a coalition of Greek city-states led by Sparta have been at war for years, and the women of Greece are tired of it. They want their husbands and sons back, so the Athenian woman Lysistrata devises a plan—the women will withhold sex from their husbands until they stop the war. This sex strike has potential, if only the women can stick with it. . . . (Less famously, the other part of Lysistrata's two-pronged approach is to cut the money supply to the Athenian war machine by having a group of old women occupy the Acropolis, which houses the treasury.)

The play is notoriously bawdy, even explicit. One famous passage—in which Lysistrata laments the lack not only of lovers but also of dildos—is almost never translated into English uncensored. Aristophanes actually used the Greek word for "dildo," but his translators almost always render it as "thing," "device," or otherwise bowdlerize the passage.

Aristophanes used the word for "penis," but even this is usually watered down (replaced with "man," "love," etc.). And then there's the fact that during the sex strike, the men onstage are sporting *highly* visible erections.

No need to worry about censorship in *The Graphic Canon*, though. Comics artist Valerie Schrag has given us a fully ribald, raunchy adaptation, exactly as Aristophanes intended it. She's even using her own translation from the ancient Greek, having been a classics major at the University of Chicago.

(P.S.: In reality, of course, there was no sex strike, and the Spartan-led coalition eventually defeated Athens in the Peloponnesian War. But in a case of life imitating art, in recent years local or nationwide sex strikes by women have been reported in Kenya, Liberia, Colombia, and the Philippines.)

SOURCE

Roberts, Deborah H. "Translation and the 'Surreptitious Classic': Obscenity and Translatability." In *Translation and the Classic: Identity as Change in the History of Culture*. Edited by Alexandra Lianeri and Vanda Zajko. Oxford University Press, 2008.

ARISTOPHANES
LYSISTRATA
Adapted from the Greek by
VALERIE SCHRAG

MM.XII.

HMMPH! IF I'D INVITED THE WOMEN TO A BACCHIC ORGY THEY'D ALL HAVE BEEN HERE AGES AGO!

LYSISTRATA!

KALONIKE! YOU CAME!

OF COURSE I DID, MY DEAR

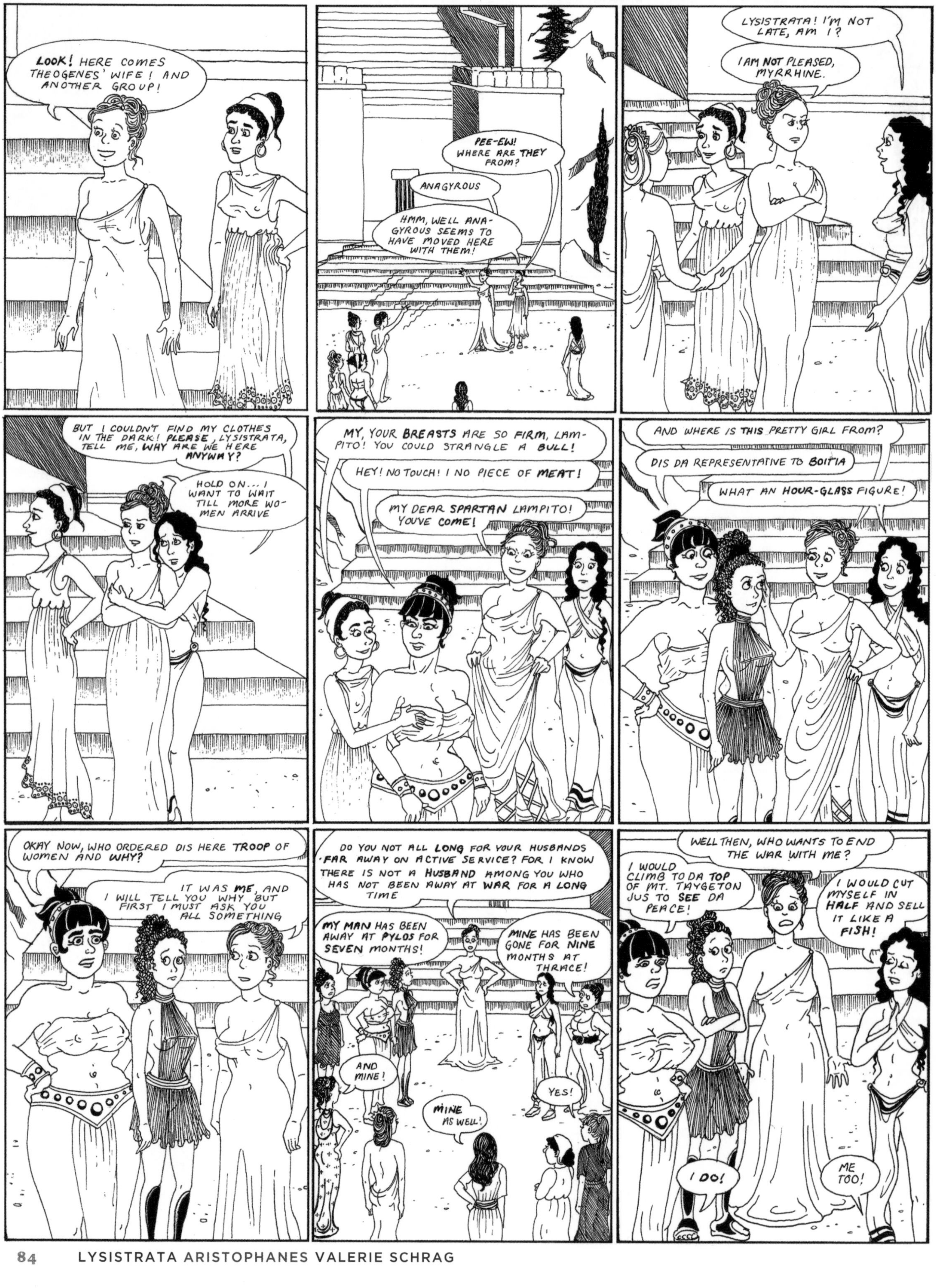
LOOK! HERE COMES THEOGENES' WIFE! AND ANOTHER GROUP!
PEE-EW! WHERE ARE THEY FROM?
ANAGYROUS
HMM, WELL ANAGYROUS SEEMS TO HAVE MOVED HERE WITH THEM!
LYSISTRATA! I'M NOT LATE, AM I?
I AM NOT PLEASED, MYRRHINE.
BUT I COULDN'T FIND MY CLOTHES IN THE DARK! PLEASE, LYSISTRATA, TELL ME, WHY ARE WE HERE ANYWAY?
HOLD ON... I WANT TO WAIT TILL MORE WOMEN ARRIVE
MY, YOUR BREASTS ARE SO FIRM, LAMPITO! YOU COULD STRANGLE A BULL!
HEY! NO TOUCH! I NO PIECE OF MEAT!
MY DEAR SPARTAN LAMPITO! YOU'VE COME!
AND WHERE IS THIS PRETTY GIRL FROM?
DIS DA REPRESENTATIVE TO BOITIA
WHAT AN HOUR-GLASS FIGURE!
OKAY NOW, WHO ORDERED DIS HERE TROOP OF WOMEN AND WHY?
IT WAS ME, AND I WILL TELL YOU WHY BUT FIRST I MUST ASK YOU ALL SOMETHING
DO YOU NOT ALL LONG FOR YOUR HUSBANDS FAR AWAY ON ACTIVE SERVICE? FOR I KNOW THERE IS NOT A HUSBAND AMONG YOU WHO HAS NOT BEEN AWAY AT WAR FOR A LONG TIME
MY MAN HAS BEEN AWAY AT PYLOS FOR SEVEN MONTHS!
MINE HAS BEEN GONE FOR NINE MONTHS AT THRACE!
AND MINE!
YES!
MINE AS WELL!
WELL THEN, WHO WANTS TO END THE WAR WITH ME?
I WOULD CLIMB TO DA TOP OF MT. TAYGETON JUS TO SEE DA PEACE!
I WOULD CUT MYSELF IN HALF AND SELL IT LIKE A FISH!
I DO!
ME TOO!

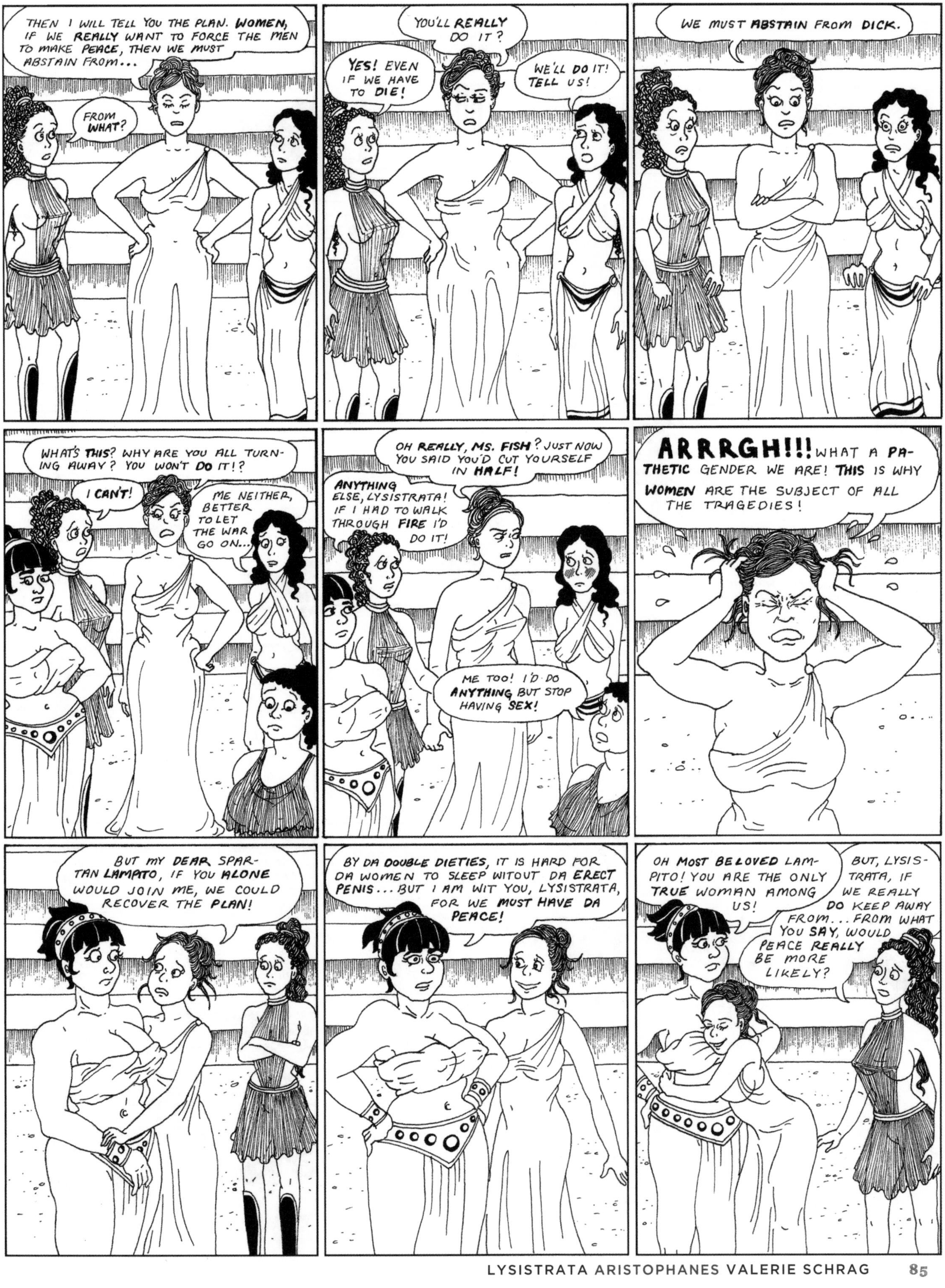
THEN I WILL TELL YOU THE PLAN. WOMEN, IF WE REALLY WANT TO FORCE THE MEN TO MAKE PEACE, THEN WE MUST ABSTAIN FROM...
FROM WHAT?
YOU'LL REALLY DO IT?
YES! EVEN IF WE HAVE TO DIE!
WE'LL DO IT! TELL US!
WE MUST ABSTAIN FROM DICK.
WHAT'S THIS? WHY ARE YOU ALL TURNING AWAY? YOU WON'T DO IT!?
I CAN'T!
ME NEITHER, BETTER TO LET THE WAR GO ON...
OH REALLY, MS. FISH? JUST NOW YOU SAID YOU'D CUT YOURSELF IN HALF!
ANYTHING ELSE, LYSISTRATA! IF I HAD TO WALK THROUGH FIRE I'D DO IT!
ME TOO! I'D DO ANYTHING BUT STOP HAVING SEX!
ARRRGH!!! WHAT A PATHETIC GENDER WE ARE! THIS IS WHY WOMEN ARE THE SUBJECT OF ALL THE TRAGEDIES!
BUT MY DEAR SPARTAN LAMPATO, IF YOU ALONE WOULD JOIN ME, WE COULD RECOVER THE PLAN!
BY DA DOUBLE DIETIES, IT IS HARD FOR DA WOMEN TO SLEEP WITOUT DA ERECT PENIS... BUT I AM WIT YOU, LYSISTRATA, FOR WE MUST HAVE DA PEACE!
OH MOST BELOVED LAMPITO! YOU ARE THE ONLY TRUE WOMAN AMONG US!
BUT, LYSISTRATA, IF WE REALLY DO KEEP AWAY FROM... FROM WHAT YOU SAY, WOULD PEACE REALLY BE MORE LIKELY?

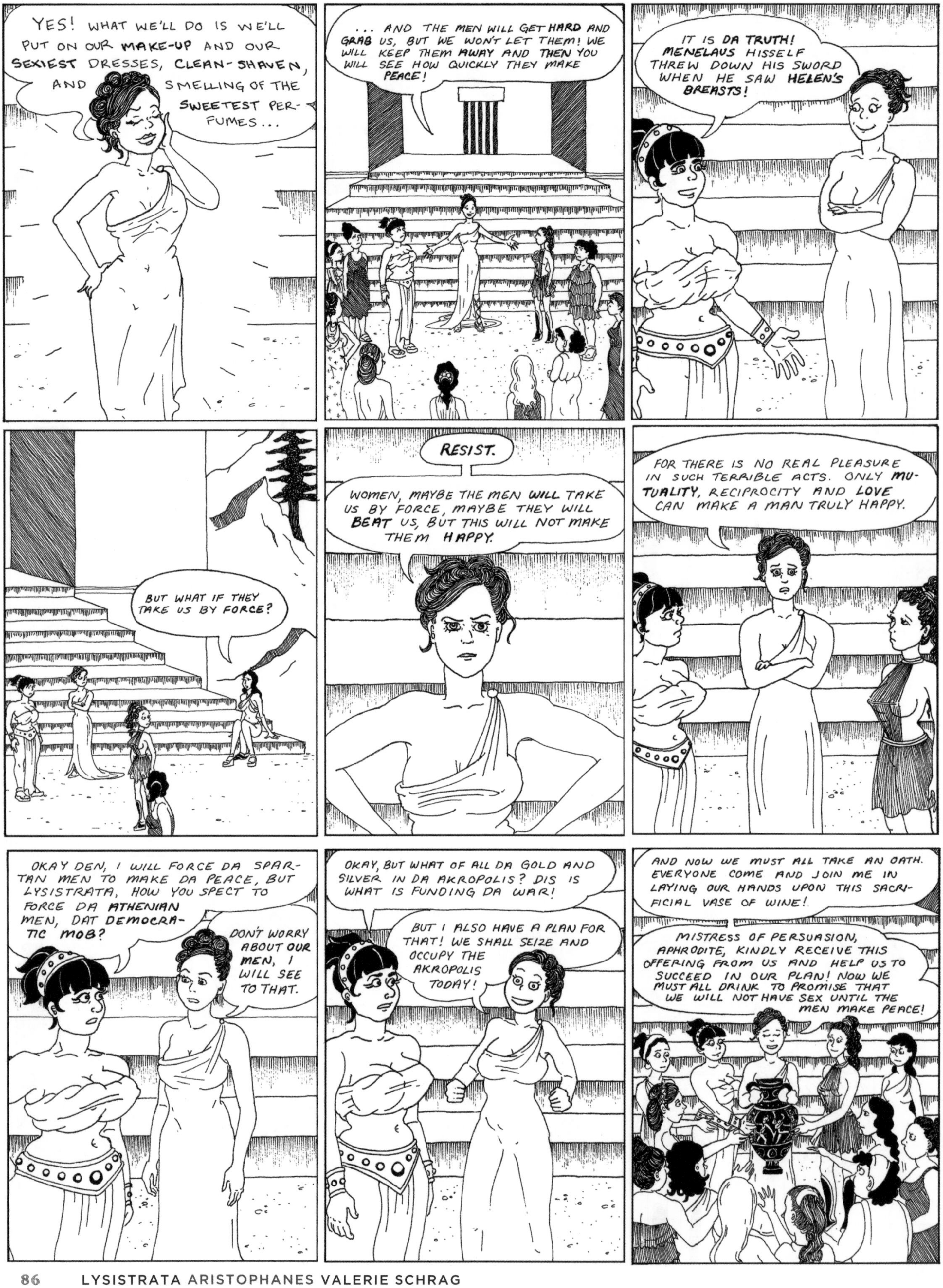
YES! WHAT WE'LL DO IS WE'LL PUT ON OUR MAKE-UP AND OUR SEXIEST DRESSES, CLEAN-SHAVEN, AND SMELLING OF THE SWEETEST PERFUMES...
... AND THE MEN WILL GET HARD AND GRAB US, BUT WE WON'T LET THEM! WE WILL KEEP THEM AWAY AND THEN YOU WILL SEE HOW QUICKLY THEY MAKE PEACE!
IT IS DA TRUTH! MENELAUS HISSELF THREW DOWN HIS SWORD WHEN HE SAW HELEN'S BREASTS!
BUT WHAT IF THEY TAKE US BY FORCE?
RESIST.
WOMEN, MAYBE THE MEN WILL TAKE US BY FORCE, MAYBE THEY WILL BEAT US, BUT THIS WILL NOT MAKE THEM HAPPY.
FOR THERE IS NO REAL PLEASURE IN SUCH TERRIBLE ACTS. ONLY MUTUALITY, RECIPROCITY AND LOVE CAN MAKE A MAN TRULY HAPPY.
OKAY DEN, I WILL FORCE DA SPARTAN MEN TO MAKE DA PEACE, BUT LYSISTRATA, HOW YOU SPECT TO FORCE DA ATHENIAN MEN, DAT DEMOCRATIC MOB?
DON'T WORRY ABOUT OUR MEN, I WILL SEE TO THAT.
OKAY, BUT WHAT OF ALL DA GOLD AND SILVER IN DA AKROPOLIS? DIS IS WHAT IS FUNDING DA WAR!
BUT I ALSO HAVE A PLAN FOR THAT! WE SHALL SEIZE AND OCCUPY THE AKROPOLIS TODAY!
AND NOW WE MUST ALL TAKE AN OATH. EVERYONE COME AND JOIN ME IN LAYING OUR HANDS UPON THIS SACRIFICIAL VASE OF WINE!
MISTRESS OF PERSUASION, APHRODITE, KINDLY RECEIVE THIS OFFERING FROM US AND HELP US TO SUCCEED IN OUR PLAN! NOW WE MUST ALL DRINK TO PROMISE THAT WE WILL NOT HAVE SEX UNTIL THE MEN MAKE PEACE!

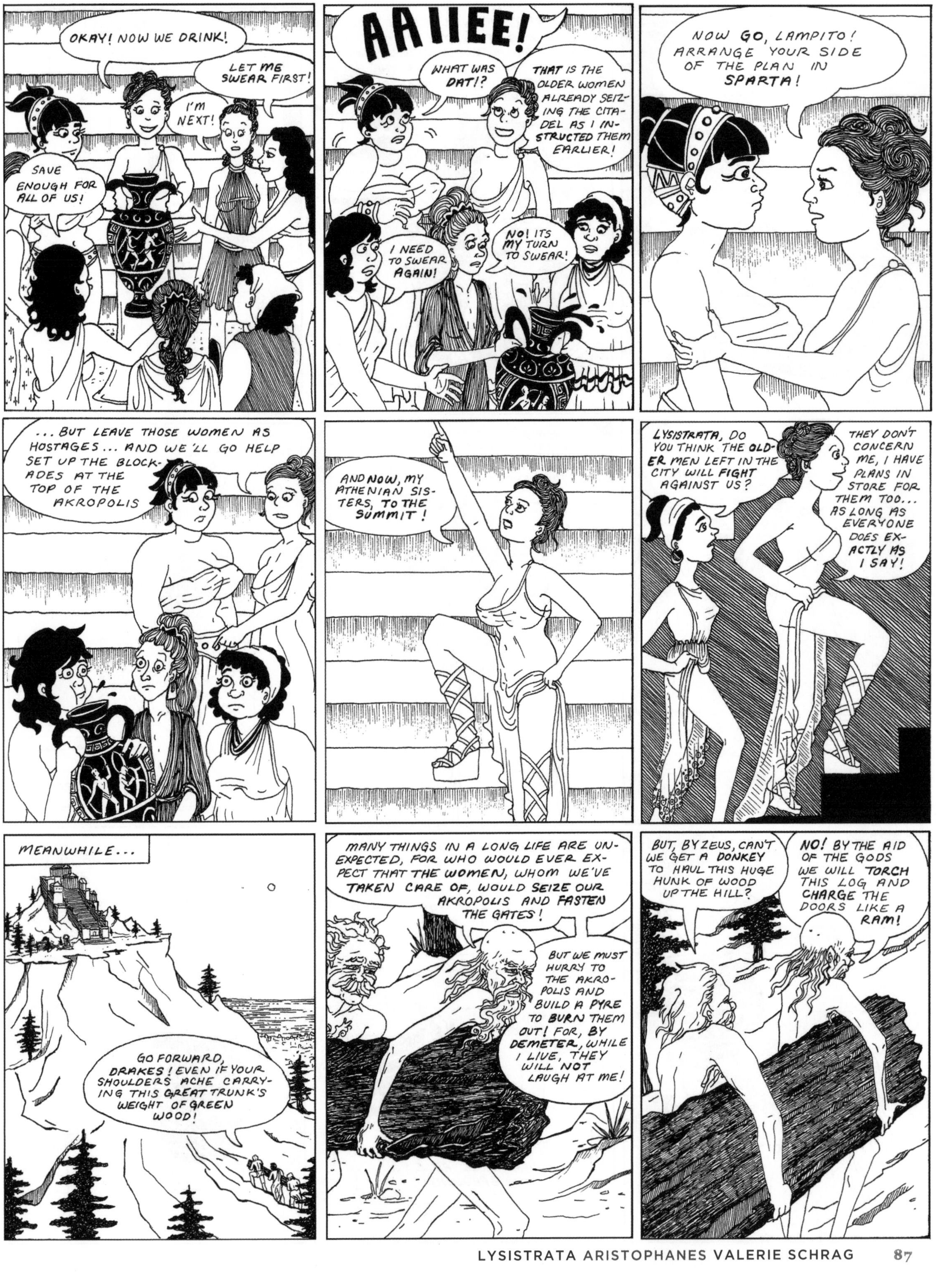
OKAY! NOW WE DRINK!
LET ME SWEAR FIRST!
I'M NEXT!
SAVE ENOUGH FOR ALL OF US!
AAIIEE!
WHAT WAS DAT!?
THAT IS THE OLDER WOMEN ALREADY SEIZING THE CITADEL AS I INSTRUCTED THEM EARLIER!
I NEED TO SWEAR AGAIN!
NO! ITS MY TURN TO SWEAR!
NOW GO, LAMPITO! ARRANGE YOUR SIDE OF THE PLAN IN SPARTA!
...BUT LEAVE THOSE WOMEN AS HOSTAGES... AND WE'LL GO HELP SET UP THE BLOCKADES AT THE TOP OF THE AKROPOLIS
AND NOW, MY ATHENIAN SISTERS, TO THE SUMMIT!
LYSISTRATA, DO YOU THINK THE OLDER MEN LEFT IN THE CITY WILL FIGHT AGAINST US?
THEY DON'T CONCERN ME, I HAVE PLANS IN STORE FOR THEM TOO... AS LONG AS EVERYONE DOES EXACTLY AS I SAY!
MEANWHILE...
GO FORWARD, DRAKES! EVEN IF YOUR SHOULDERS ACHE CARRYING THIS GREAT TRUNK'S WEIGHT OF GREEN WOOD!
MANY THINGS IN A LONG LIFE ARE UNEXPECTED, FOR WHO WOULD EVER EXPECT THAT THE WOMEN, WHOM WE'VE TAKEN CARE OF, WOULD SEIZE OUR AKROPOLIS AND FASTEN THE GATES!
BUT WE MUST HURRY TO THE AKROPOLIS AND BUILD A PYRE TO BURN THEM OUT! FOR, BY DEMETER, WHILE I LIVE, THEY WILL NOT LAUGH AT ME!
BUT, BY ZEUS, CAN'T WE GET A DONKEY TO HAUL THIS HUGE HUNK OF WOOD UP THE HILL?
NO! BY THE AID OF THE GODS WE WILL TORCH THIS LOG AND CHARGE THE DOORS LIKE A RAM!

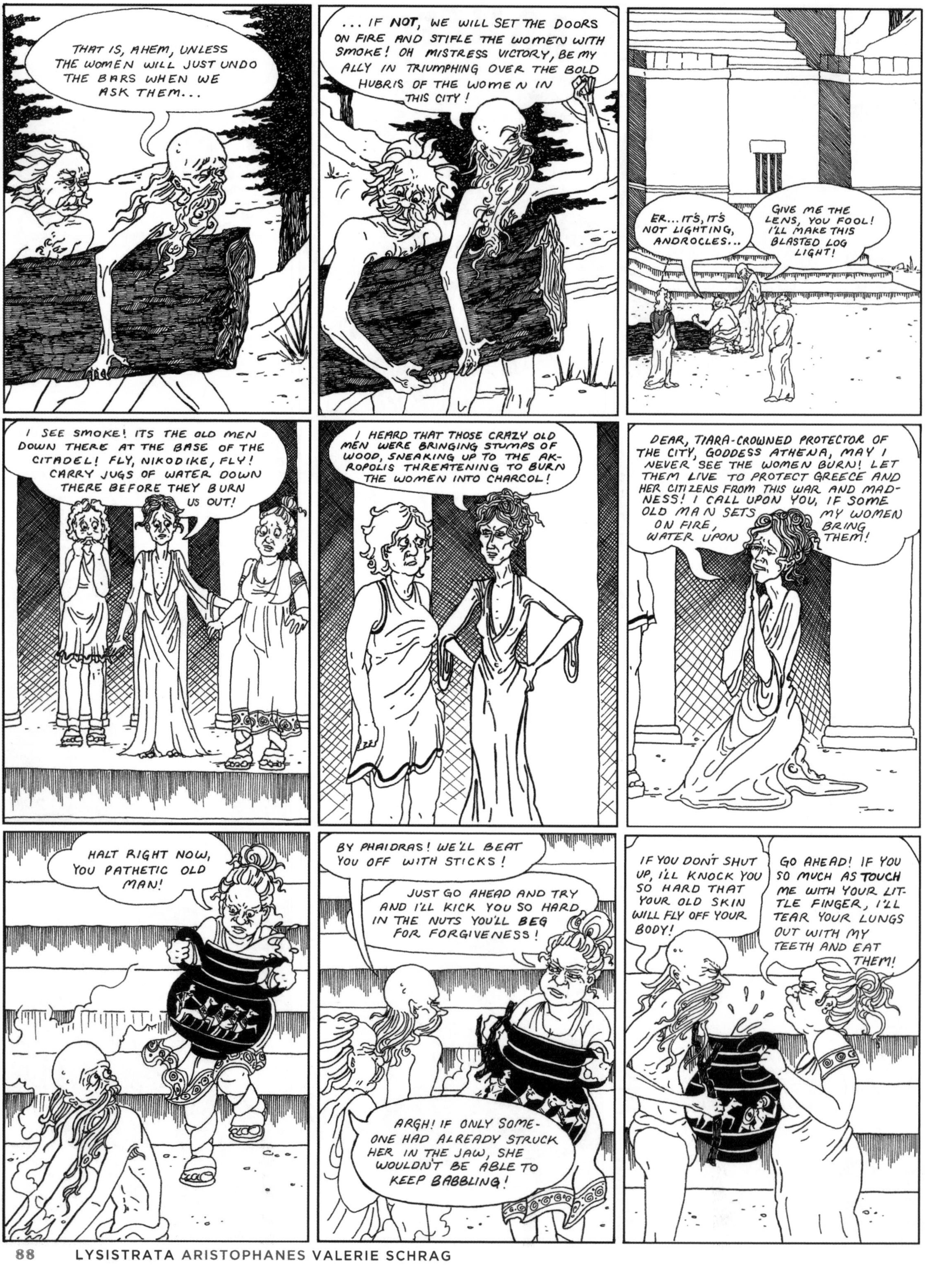
THAT IS, AHEM, UNLESS THE WOMEN WILL JUST UNDO THE BARS WHEN WE ASK THEM...
... IF NOT, WE WILL SET THE DOORS ON FIRE AND STIFLE THE WOMEN WITH SMOKE! OH MISTRESS VICTORY, BE MY ALLY IN TRIUMPHING OVER THE BOLD HUBRIS OF THE WOMEN IN THIS CITY!
ER... IT'S, IT'S NOT LIGHTING, ANDROCLES...
GIVE ME THE LENS, YOU FOOL! I'LL MAKE THIS BLASTED LOG LIGHT!
I SEE SMOKE! ITS THE OLD MEN DOWN THERE AT THE BASE OF THE CITADEL! FLY, NIKODIKE, FLY! CARRY JUGS OF WATER DOWN THERE BEFORE THEY BURN US OUT!
I HEARD THAT THOSE CRAZY OLD MEN WERE BRINGING STUMPS OF WOOD, SNEAKING UP TO THE AK-ROPOLIS THREATENING TO BURN THE WOMEN INTO CHARCOL!
DEAR, TIARA-CROWNED PROTECTOR OF THE CITY, GODDESS ATHENA, MAY I NEVER SEE THE WOMEN BURN! LET THEM LIVE TO PROTECT GREECE AND HER CITIZENS FROM THIS WAR AND MAD-NESS! I CALL UPON YOU, IF SOME OLD MAN SETS MY WOMEN ON FIRE, BRING WATER UPON THEM!
HALT RIGHT NOW, YOU PATHETIC OLD MAN!
BY PHAIDRAS! WE'LL BEAT YOU OFF WITH STICKS!
JUST GO AHEAD AND TRY AND I'LL KICK YOU SO HARD IN THE NUTS YOU'LL BEG FOR FORGIVENESS!
ARGH! IF ONLY SOME-ONE HAD ALREADY STRUCK HER IN THE JAW, SHE WOULDN'T BE ABLE TO KEEP BABBLING!
IF YOU DON'T SHUT UP, I'LL KNOCK YOU SO HARD THAT YOUR OLD SKIN WILL FLY OFF YOUR BODY!
GO AHEAD! IF YOU SO MUCH AS TOUCH ME WITH YOUR LIT-TLE FINGER, I'LL TEAR YOUR LUNGS OUT WITH MY TEETH AND EAT THEM!

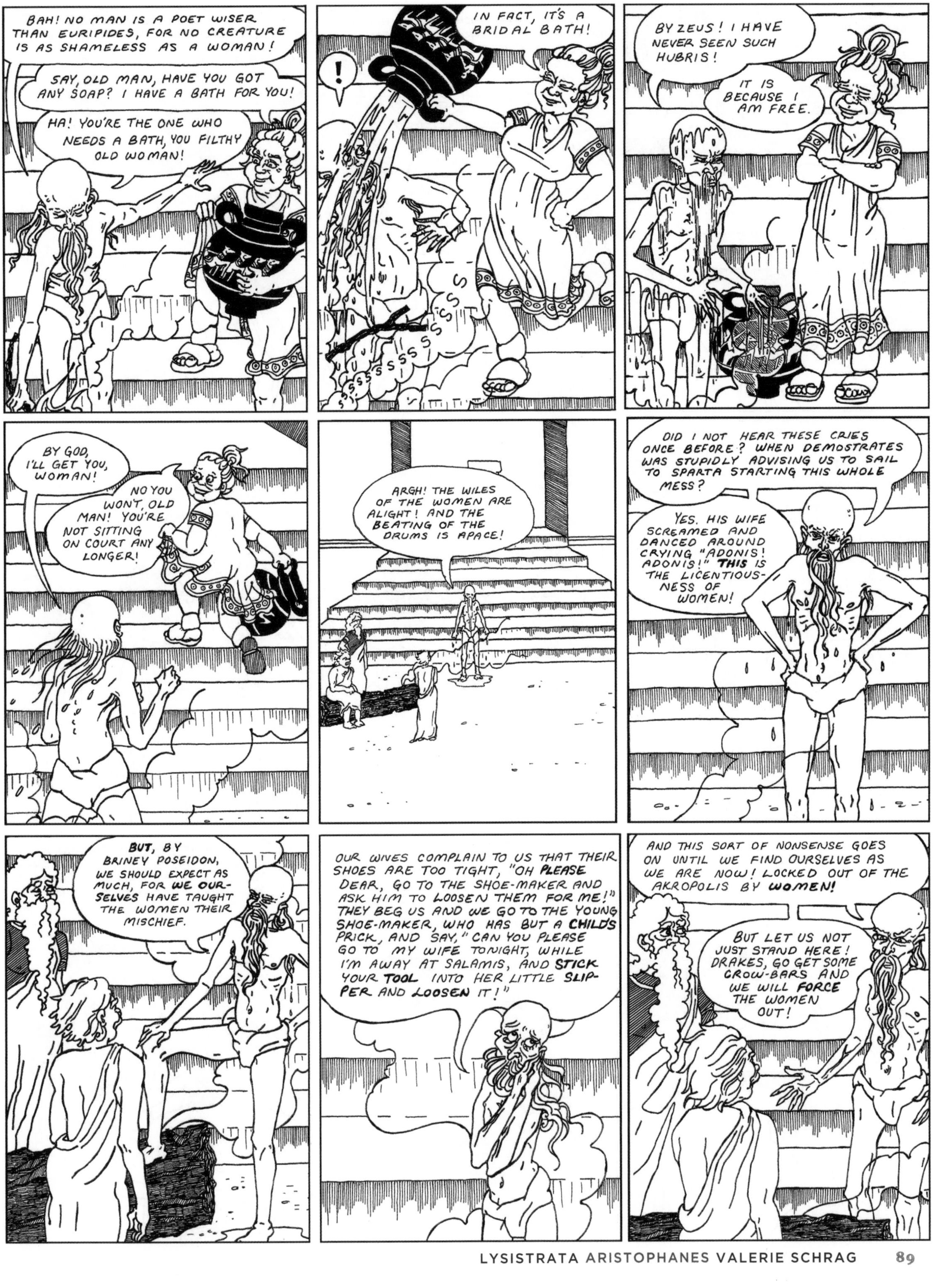
BAH! NO MAN IS A POET WISER THAN EURIPIDES, FOR NO CREATURE IS AS SHAMELESS AS A WOMAN!
SAY, OLD MAN, HAVE YOU GOT ANY SOAP? I HAVE A BATH FOR YOU!
HA! YOU'RE THE ONE WHO NEEDS A BATH, YOU FILTHY OLD WOMAN!
!
IN FACT, IT'S A BRIDAL BATH!
SSSSSSSSSSSSSSSS
BY ZEUS! I HAVE NEVER SEEN SUCH HUBRIS!
IT IS BECAUSE I AM FREE.
BY GOD, I'LL GET YOU, WOMAN!
NO YOU WON'T, OLD MAN! YOU'RE NOT SITTING ON COURT ANY LONGER!
ARGH! THE WILES OF THE WOMEN ARE ALIGHT! AND THE BEATING OF THE DRUMS IS APACE!
DID I NOT HEAR THESE CRIES ONCE BEFORE? WHEN DEMOSTRATES WAS STUPIDLY ADVISING US TO SAIL TO SPARTA STARTING THIS WHOLE MESS?
YES. HIS WIFE SCREAMED AND DANCED AROUND CRYING "ADONIS! ADONIS!" THIS IS THE LICENTIOUS-NESS OF WOMEN!
BUT, BY BRINEY POSEIDON, WE SHOULD EXPECT AS MUCH, FOR WE OURSELVES HAVE TAUGHT THE WOMEN THEIR MISCHIEF.
OUR WIVES COMPLAIN TO US THAT THEIR SHOES ARE TOO TIGHT, "OH PLEASE DEAR, GO TO THE SHOE-MAKER AND ASK HIM TO LOOSEN THEM FOR ME!" THEY BEG US AND WE GO TO THE YOUNG SHOE-MAKER, WHO HAS BUT A CHILD'S PRICK, AND SAY, "CAN YOU PLEASE GO TO MY WIFE TONIGHT, WHILE I'M AWAY AT SALAMIS, AND STICK YOUR TOOL INTO HER LITTLE SLIP-PER AND LOOSEN IT!"
AND THIS SORT OF NONSENSE GOES ON UNTIL WE FIND OURSELVES AS WE ARE NOW! LOCKED OUT OF THE AKROPOLIS BY WOMEN!
BUT LET US NOT JUST STAND HERE! DRAKES, GO GET SOME CROW-BARS AND WE WILL FORCE THE WOMEN OUT!

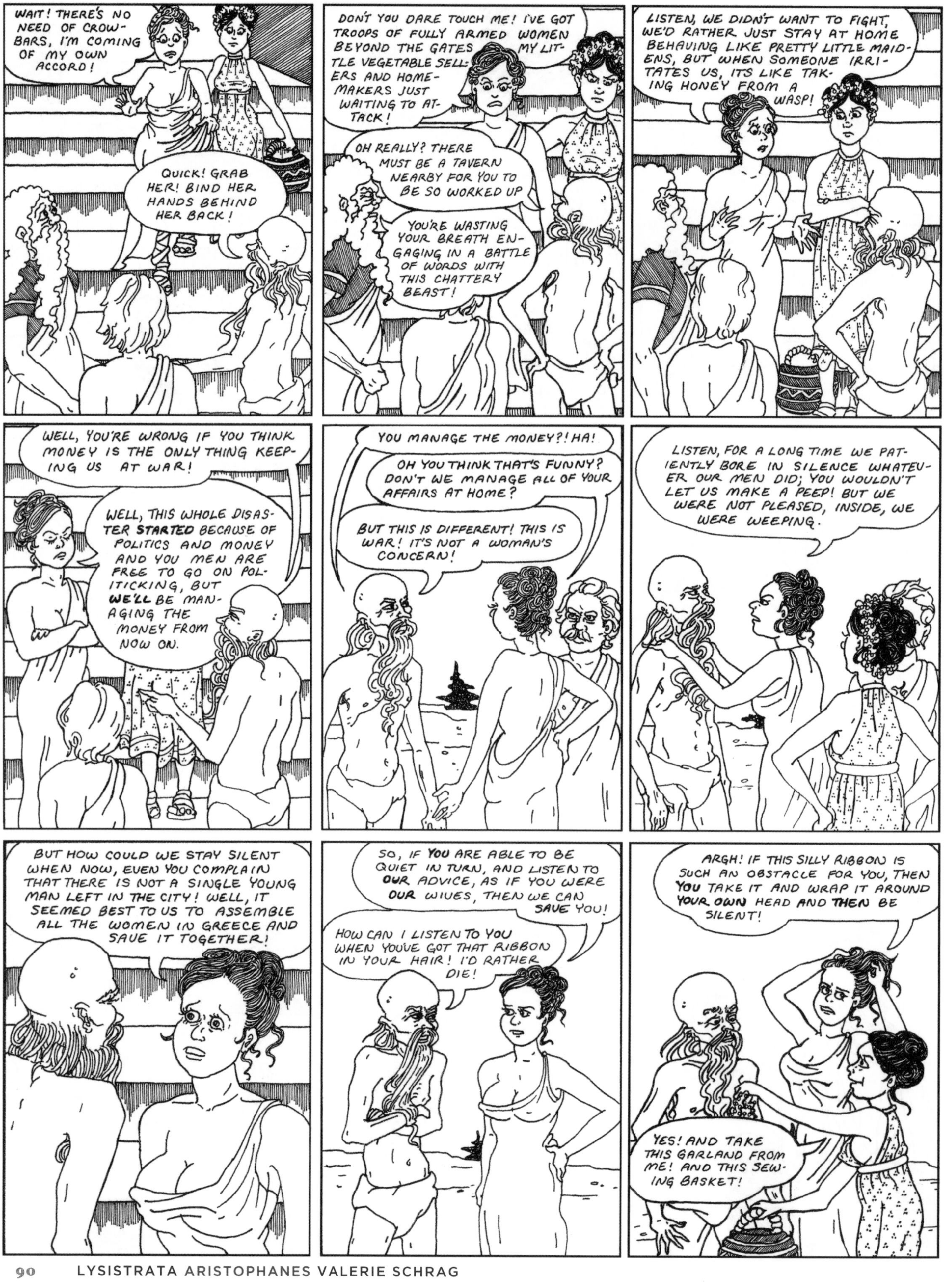
WAIT! THERE'S NO NEED OF CROW-BARS, I'M COMING OF MY OWN ACCORD!
QUICK! GRAB HER! BIND HER HANDS BEHIND HER BACK!
DON'T YOU DARE TOUCH ME! I'VE GOT TROOPS OF FULLY ARMED WOMEN BEYOND THE GATES MY LITTLE VEGETABLE SELLERS AND HOMEMAKERS JUST WAITING TO ATTACK!
OH REALLY? THERE MUST BE A TAVERN NEARBY FOR YOU TO BE SO WORKED UP
YOU'RE WASTING YOUR BREATH ENGAGING IN A BATTLE OF WORDS WITH THIS CHATTERY BEAST!
LISTEN, WE DIDN'T WANT TO FIGHT, WE'D RATHER JUST STAY AT HOME BEHAVING LIKE PRETTY LITTLE MAIDENS, BUT WHEN SOMEONE IRRITATES US, ITS LIKE TAKING HONEY FROM A WASP!
WELL, YOU'RE WRONG IF YOU THINK MONEY IS THE ONLY THING KEEPING US AT WAR!
WELL, THIS WHOLE DISASTER STARTED BECAUSE OF POLITICS AND MONEY AND YOU MEN ARE FREE TO GO ON POLITICKING, BUT WE'LL BE MANAGING THE MONEY FROM NOW ON.
YOU MANAGE THE MONEY?! HA!
OH YOU THINK THAT'S FUNNY? DON'T WE MANAGE ALL OF YOUR AFFAIRS AT HOME?
BUT THIS IS DIFFERENT! THIS IS WAR! IT'S NOT A WOMAN'S CONCERN!
LISTEN, FOR A LONG TIME WE PATIENTLY BORE IN SILENCE WHATEVER OUR MEN DID; YOU WOULDN'T LET US MAKE A PEEP! BUT WE WERE NOT PLEASED, INSIDE, WE WERE WEEPING.
BUT HOW COULD WE STAY SILENT WHEN NOW, EVEN YOU COMPLAIN THAT THERE IS NOT A SINGLE YOUNG MAN LEFT IN THE CITY! WELL, IT SEEMED BEST TO US TO ASSEMBLE ALL THE WOMEN IN GREECE AND SAVE IT TOGETHER!
SO, IF YOU ARE ABLE TO BE QUIET IN TURN, AND LISTEN TO OUR ADVICE, AS IF YOU WERE OUR WIVES, THEN WE CAN SAVE YOU!
HOW CAN I LISTEN TO YOU WHEN YOU'VE GOT THAT RIBBON IN YOUR HAIR! I'D RATHER DIE!
ARGH! IF THIS SILLY RIBBON IS SUCH AN OBSTACLE FOR YOU, THEN YOU TAKE IT AND WRAP IT AROUND YOUR OWN HEAD AND THEN BE SILENT!
YES! AND TAKE THIS GARLAND FROM ME! AND THIS SEWING BASKET!

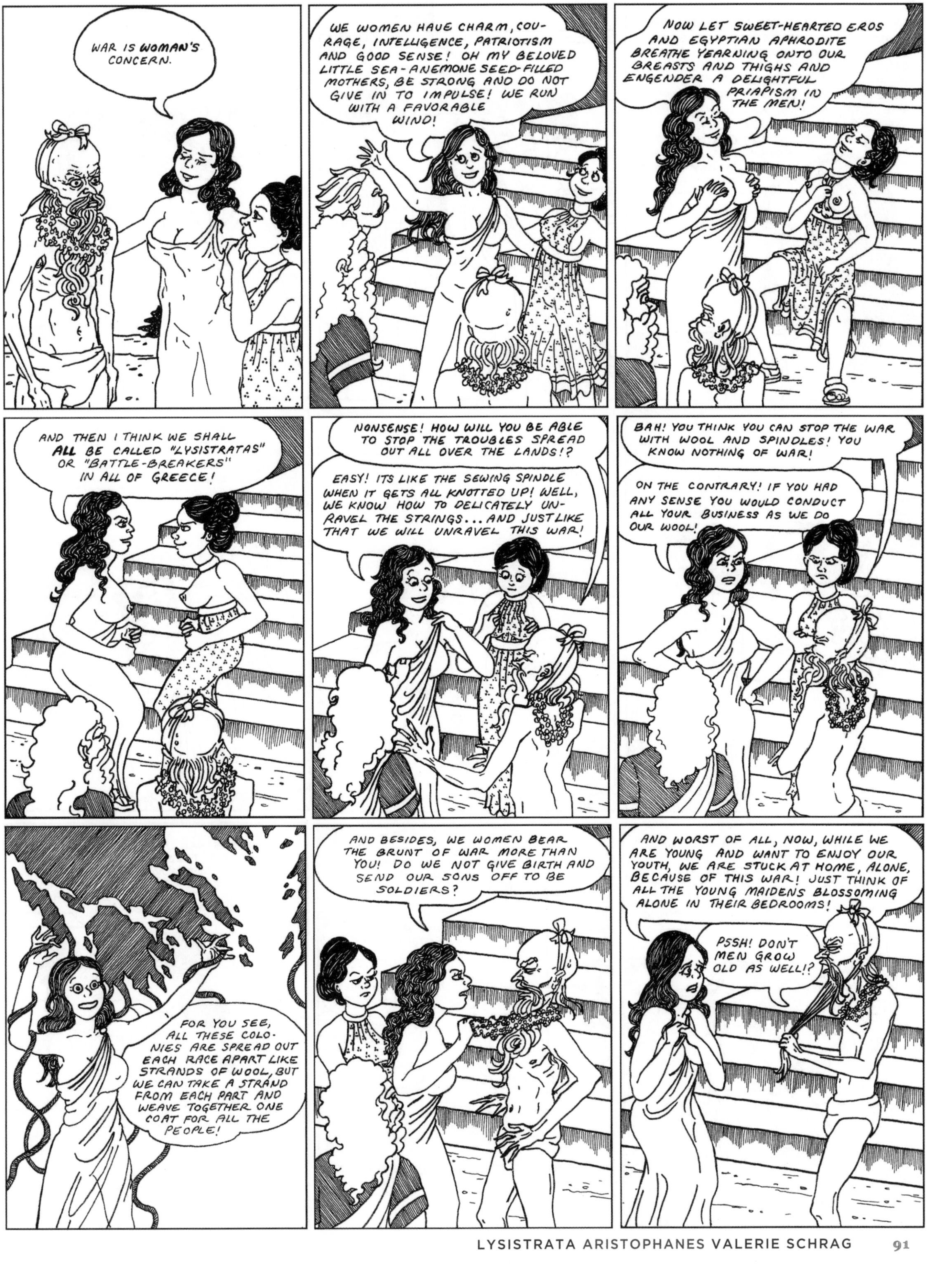
WAR IS **WOMAN'S** CONCERN.
WE WOMEN HAVE CHARM, COURAGE, INTELLIGENCE, PATRIOTISM AND GOOD SENSE! OH MY BELOVED LITTLE SEA-ANEMONE SEED-FILLED MOTHERS, BE STRONG AND DO NOT GIVE IN TO IMPULSE! WE RUN WITH A FAVORABLE WIND!
NOW LET SWEET-HEARTED EROS AND EGYPTIAN APHRODITE BREATHE YEARNING ONTO OUR BREASTS AND THIGHS AND ENGENDER A DELIGHTFUL PRIAPISM IN THE MEN!
AND THEN I THINK WE SHALL **ALL** BE CALLED "LYSISTRATAS" OR "BATTLE-BREAKERS" IN ALL OF GREECE!
NONSENSE! HOW WILL YOU BE ABLE TO STOP THE TROUBLES SPREAD OUT ALL OVER THE LANDS!?
EASY! ITS LIKE THE SEWING SPINDLE WHEN IT GETS ALL KNOTTED UP! WELL, WE KNOW HOW TO DELICATELY UNRAVEL THE STRINGS... AND JUST LIKE THAT WE WILL UNRAVEL THIS WAR!
BAH! YOU THINK YOU CAN STOP THE WAR WITH WOOL AND SPINDLES! YOU KNOW NOTHING OF WAR!
ON THE CONTRARY! IF YOU HAD ANY SENSE YOU WOULD CONDUCT ALL YOUR BUSINESS AS WE DO OUR WOOL!
FOR YOU SEE, ALL THESE COLONIES ARE SPREAD OUT EACH RACE APART LIKE STRANDS OF WOOL, BUT WE CAN TAKE A STRAND FROM EACH PART AND WEAVE TOGETHER ONE COAT FOR ALL THE PEOPLE!
AND BESIDES, WE WOMEN BEAR THE BRUNT OF WAR MORE THAN YOU! DO WE NOT GIVE BIRTH AND SEND OUR SONS OFF TO BE SOLDIERS?
AND WORST OF ALL, NOW, WHILE WE ARE YOUNG AND WANT TO ENJOY OUR YOUTH, WE ARE STUCK AT HOME, ALONE, BECAUSE OF THIS WAR! JUST THINK OF ALL THE YOUNG MAIDENS BLOSSOMING ALONE IN THEIR BEDROOMS!
PSSH! DON'T MEN GROW OLD AS WELL!?

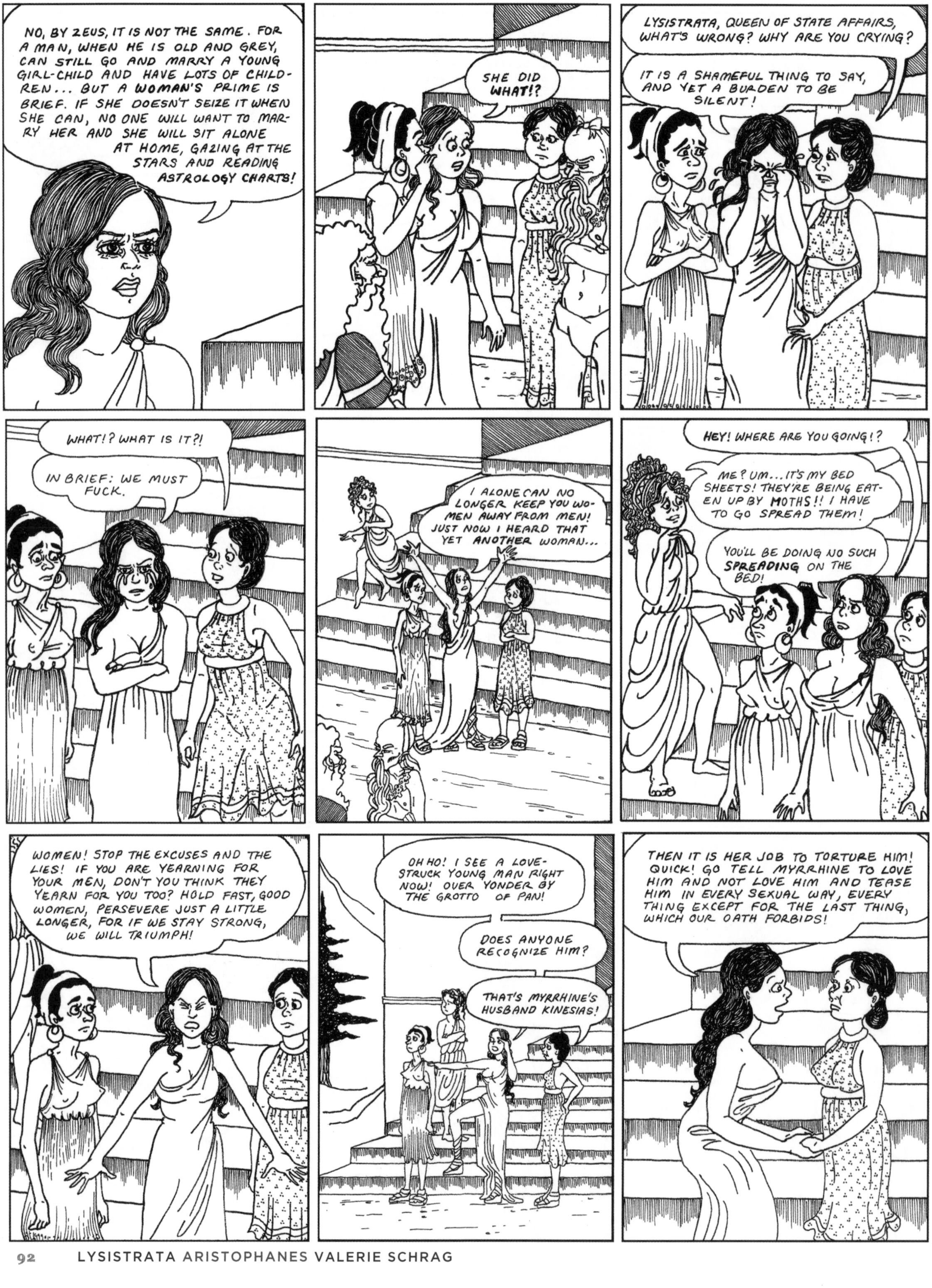
NO, BY ZEUS, IT IS NOT THE SAME. FOR A MAN, WHEN HE IS OLD AND GREY, CAN STILL GO AND MARRY A YOUNG GIRL-CHILD AND HAVE LOTS OF CHILDREN... BUT A WOMAN'S PRIME IS BRIEF. IF SHE DOESN'T SEIZE IT WHEN SHE CAN, NO ONE WILL WANT TO MARRY HER AND SHE WILL SIT ALONE AT HOME, GAZING AT THE STARS AND READING ASTROLOGY CHARTS!
SHE DID WHAT!?
LYSISTRATA, QUEEN OF STATE AFFAIRS, WHAT'S WRONG? WHY ARE YOU CRYING?
IT IS A SHAMEFUL THING TO SAY, AND YET A BURDEN TO BE SILENT!
WHAT!? WHAT IS IT?!
IN BRIEF: WE MUST FUCK.
I ALONE CAN NO LONGER KEEP YOU WOMEN AWAY FROM MEN! JUST NOW I HEARD THAT YET ANOTHER WOMAN...
HEY! WHERE ARE YOU GOING!?
ME? UM... IT'S MY BED SHEETS! THEY'RE BEING EATEN UP BY MOTHS!! I HAVE TO GO SPREAD THEM!
YOU'LL BE DOING NO SUCH SPREADING ON THE BED!
WOMEN! STOP THE EXCUSES AND THE LIES! IF YOU ARE YEARNING FOR YOUR MEN, DON'T YOU THINK THEY YEARN FOR YOU TOO? HOLD FAST, GOOD WOMEN, PERSEVERE JUST A LITTLE LONGER, FOR IF WE STAY STRONG, WE WILL TRIUMPH!
OH HO! I SEE A LOVE-STRUCK YOUNG MAN RIGHT NOW! OVER YONDER BY THE GROTTO OF PAN!
DOES ANYONE RECOGNIZE HIM?
THAT'S MYRRHINE'S HUSBAND KINESIAS!
THEN IT IS HER JOB TO TORTURE HIM! QUICK! GO TELL MYRRHINE TO LOVE HIM AND NOT LOVE HIM AND TEASE HIM IN EVERY SEXUAL WAY, EVERY THING EXCEPT FOR THE LAST THING, WHICH OUR OATH FORBIDS!

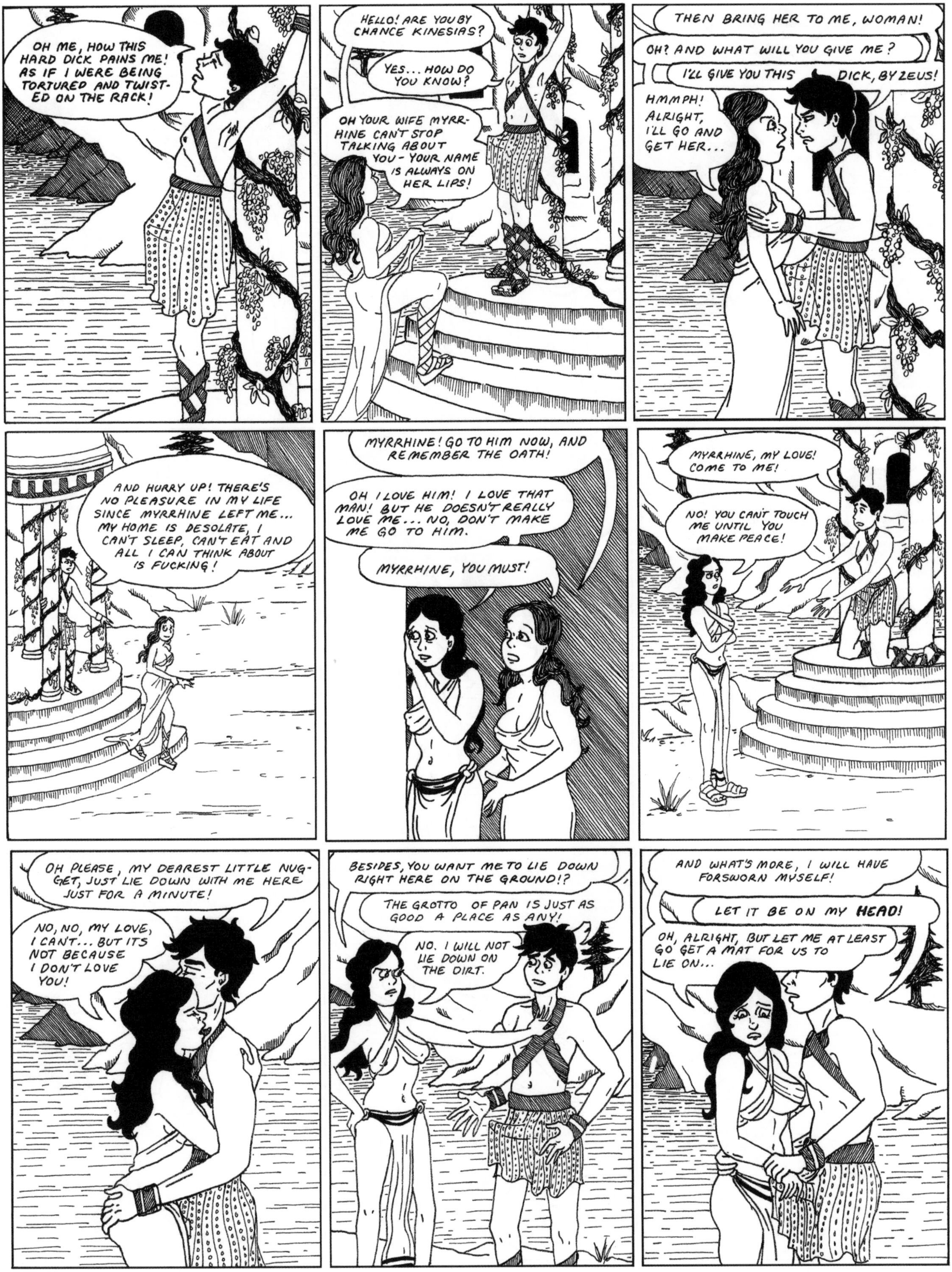
OH ME, HOW THIS HARD DICK PAINS ME! AS IF I WERE BEING TORTURED AND TWISTED ON THE RACK!
HELLO! ARE YOU BY CHANCE KINESIAS?
YES... HOW DO YOU KNOW?
OH YOUR WIFE MYRRHINE CAN'T STOP TALKING ABOUT YOU - YOUR NAME IS ALWAYS ON HER LIPS!
THEN BRING HER TO ME, WOMAN!
OH? AND WHAT WILL YOU GIVE ME?
I'LL GIVE YOU THIS DICK, BY ZEUS!
HMMPH! ALRIGHT, I'LL GO AND GET HER...
AND HURRY UP! THERE'S NO PLEASURE IN MY LIFE SINCE MYRRHINE LEFT ME... MY HOME IS DESOLATE, I CAN'T SLEEP, CAN'T EAT AND ALL I CAN THINK ABOUT IS FUCKING!
MYRRHINE! GO TO HIM NOW, AND REMEMBER THE OATH!
OH I LOVE HIM! I LOVE THAT MAN! BUT HE DOESN'T REALLY LOVE ME... NO, DON'T MAKE ME GO TO HIM.
MYRRHINE, YOU MUST!
MYRRHINE, MY LOVE! COME TO ME!
NO! YOU CAN'T TOUCH ME UNTIL YOU MAKE PEACE!
OH PLEASE, MY DEAREST LITTLE NUGGET, JUST LIE DOWN WITH ME HERE JUST FOR A MINUTE!
NO, NO, MY LOVE, I CAN'T... BUT ITS NOT BECAUSE I DON'T LOVE YOU!
BESIDES, YOU WANT ME TO LIE DOWN RIGHT HERE ON THE GROUND!?
THE GROTTO OF PAN IS JUST AS GOOD A PLACE AS ANY!
NO. I WILL NOT LIE DOWN ON THE DIRT.
AND WHAT'S MORE, I WILL HAVE FORSWORN MYSELF!
LET IT BE ON MY **HEAD**!
OH, ALRIGHT, BUT LET ME AT LEAST GO GET A MAT FOR US TO LIE ON...

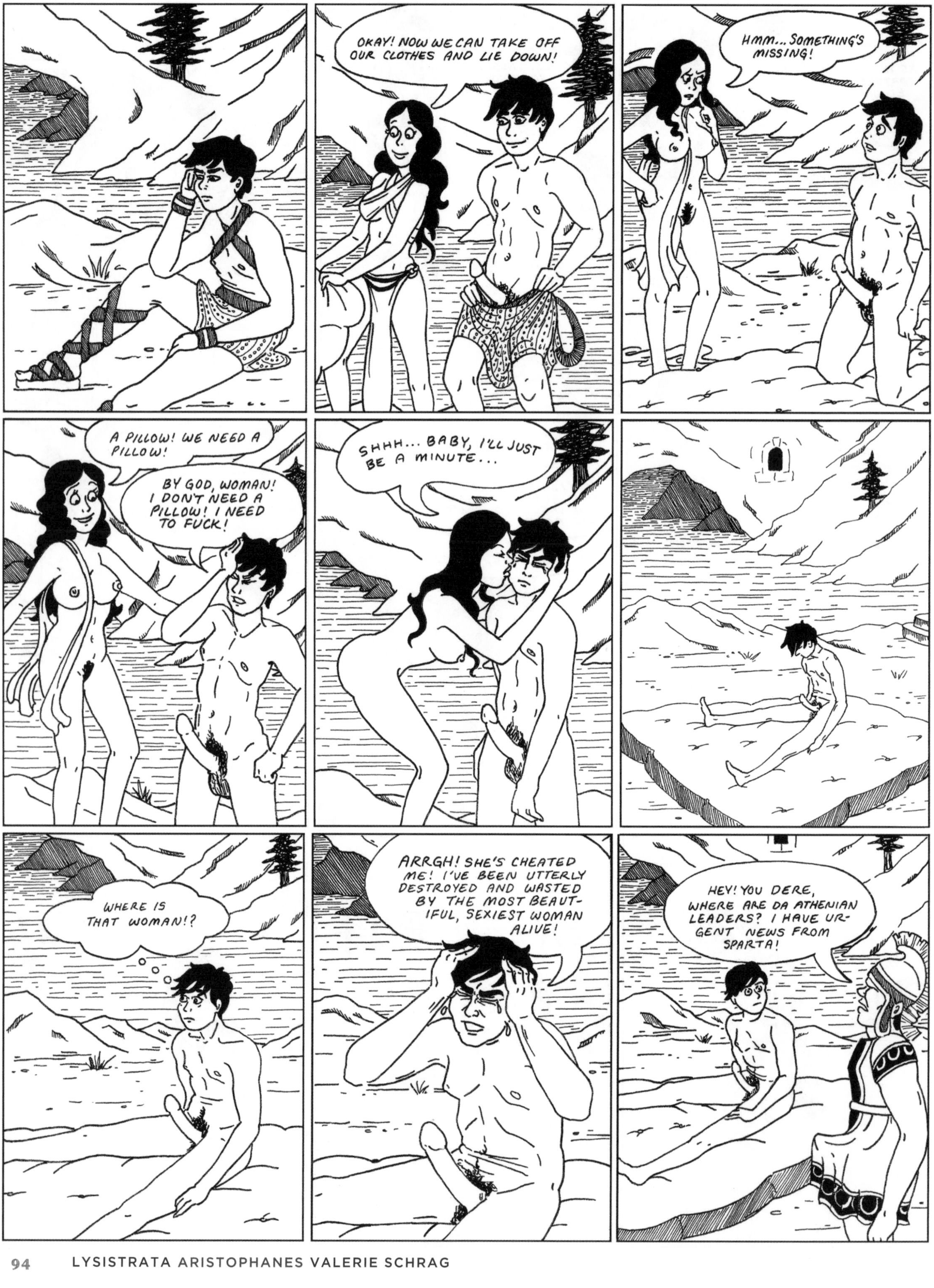
OKAY! NOW WE CAN TAKE OFF OUR CLOTHES AND LIE DOWN!
HMM... SOMETHING'S MISSING!
A PILLOW! WE NEED A PILLOW!
BY GOD, WOMAN! I DON'T NEED A PILLOW! I NEED TO FUCK!
SHHH... BABY, I'LL JUST BE A MINUTE...
WHERE IS THAT WOMAN!?
ARRGH! SHE'S CHEATED ME! I'VE BEEN UTTERLY DESTROYED AND WASTED BY THE MOST BEAUT-IFUL, SEXIEST WOMAN ALIVE!
HEY! YOU DERE, WHERE ARE DA ATHENIAN LEADERS? I HAVE UR-GENT NEWS FROM SPARTA!

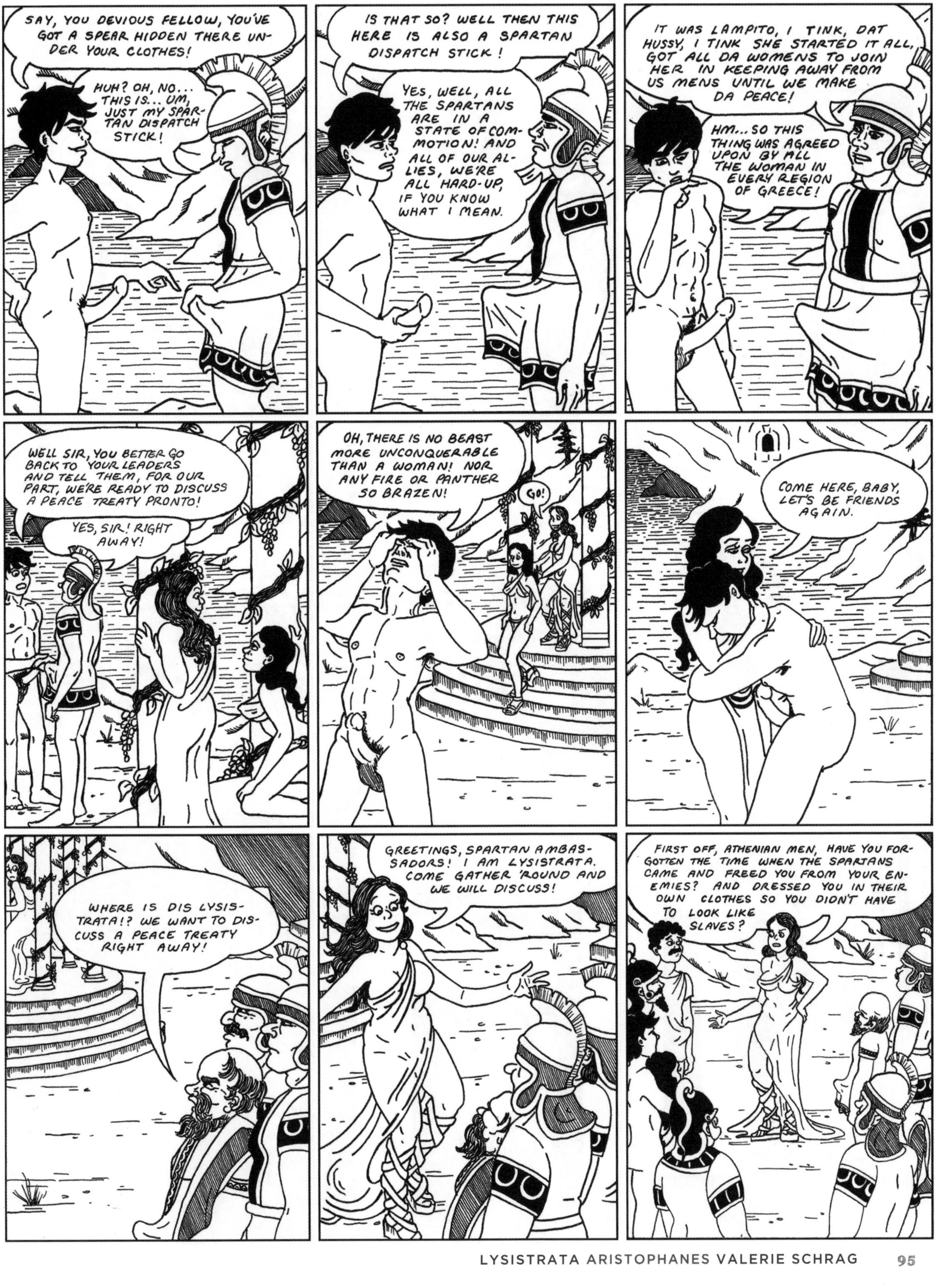
SAY, YOU DEVIOUS FELLOW, YOU'VE GOT A SPEAR HIDDEN THERE UNDER YOUR CLOTHES!
HUH? OH, NO... THIS IS... UM, JUST MY SPARTAN DISPATCH STICK!
IS THAT SO? WELL THEN THIS HERE IS ALSO A SPARTAN DISPATCH STICK!
YES, WELL, ALL THE SPARTANS ARE IN A STATE OF COMMOTION! AND ALL OF OUR ALLIES, WE'RE ALL HARD-UP, IF YOU KNOW WHAT I MEAN.
IT WAS LAMPITO, I TINK, DAT HUSSY, I TINK SHE STARTED IT ALL, GOT ALL DA WOMENS TO JOIN HER IN KEEPING AWAY FROM US MENS UNTIL WE MAKE DA PEACE!
HM... SO THIS THING WAS AGREED UPON BY ALL THE WOMAN IN EVERY REGION OF GREECE!
WELL SIR, YOU BETTER GO BACK TO YOUR LEADERS AND TELL THEM, FOR OUR PART, WE'RE READY TO DISCUSS A PEACE TREATY PRONTO!
YES, SIR! RIGHT AWAY!
OH, THERE IS NO BEAST MORE UNCONQUERABLE THAN A WOMAN! NOR ANY FIRE OR PANTHER SO BRAZEN!
GO!
COME HERE, BABY, LET'S BE FRIENDS AGAIN.
WHERE IS DIS LYSISTRATA!? WE WANT TO DISCUSS A PEACE TREATY RIGHT AWAY!
GREETINGS, SPARTAN AMBASSADORS! I AM LYSISTRATA. COME GATHER 'ROUND AND WE WILL DISCUSS!
FIRST OFF, ATHENIAN MEN, HAVE YOU FORGOTTEN THE TIME WHEN THE SPARTANS CAME AND FREED YOU FROM YOUR ENEMIES? AND DRESSED YOU IN THEIR OWN CLOTHES SO YOU DIDN'T HAVE TO LOOK LIKE SLAVES?

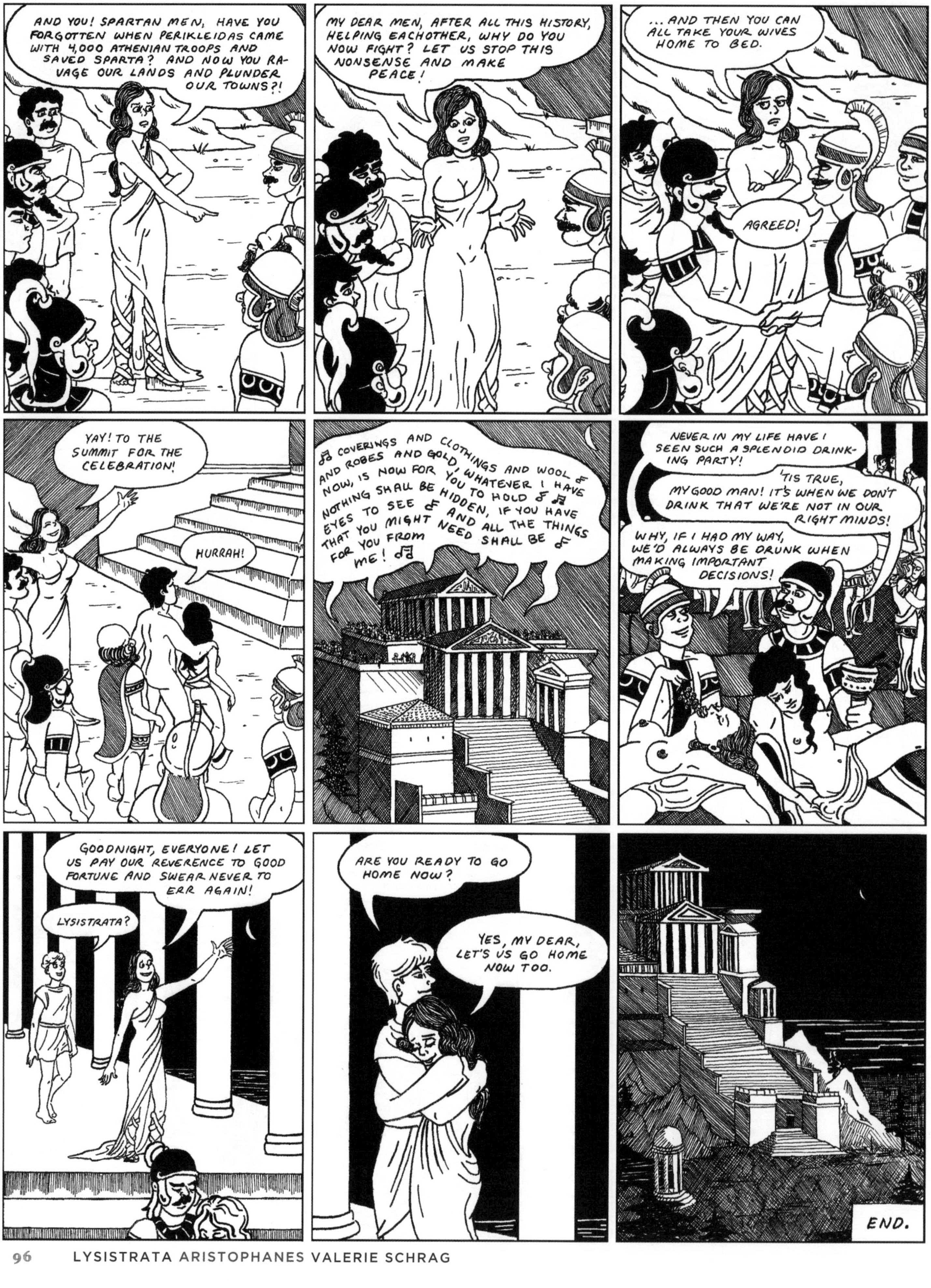
AND YOU! SPARTAN MEN, HAVE YOU FORGOTTEN WHEN PERIKLEIDAS CAME WITH 4,000 ATHENIAN TROOPS AND SAVED SPARTA? AND NOW YOU RAVAGE OUR LANDS AND PLUNDER OUR TOWNS?!
MY DEAR MEN, AFTER ALL THIS HISTORY, HELPING EACHOTHER, WHY DO YOU NOW FIGHT? LET US STOP THIS NONSENSE AND MAKE PEACE!
...AND THEN YOU CAN ALL TAKE YOUR WIVES HOME TO BED.
AGREED!
YAY! TO THE SUMMIT FOR THE CELEBRATION!
HURRAH!
♫ COVERINGS AND CLOTHINGS AND ROBES AND GOLD, WHATEVER I HAVE NOW, IS NOW FOR YOU TO HOLD ♫ ♫ NOTHING SHALL BE HIDDEN, IF YOU HAVE EYES TO SEE ♫ AND ALL THE THINGS THAT YOU MIGHT NEED SHALL BE ♫ FOR YOU FROM ME! ♫
NEVER IN MY LIFE HAVE I SEEN SUCH A SPLENDID DRINKING PARTY!
'TIS TRUE, MY GOOD MAN! IT'S WHEN WE DON'T DRINK THAT WE'RE NOT IN OUR RIGHT MINDS!
WHY, IF I HAD MY WAY, WE'D ALWAYS BE DRUNK WHEN MAKING IMPORTANT DECISIONS!
GOODNIGHT, EVERYONE! LET US PAY OUR REVERENCE TO GOOD FORTUNE AND SWEAR NEVER TO ERR AGAIN!
LYSISTRATA?
ARE YOU READY TO GO HOME NOW?
YES, MY DEAR, LET'S US GO HOME NOW TOO.
END.

The Book of Esther

from the Hebrew Bible

ART / ADAPTATION AND TRANSLATION BY **J. T. Waldman**

ONE OF THE UNJUSTLY OVERLOOKED BOOKS OF the Hebrew Bible (what Christians call the Old Testament), the Book of Esther—thought to have been written in the fourth century BCE—features two of the Bible's strongest female characters. When King Ahasuerus of Persia holds an elaborate celebration, he drunkenly orders Queen Vashti brought naked (except for her crown) to the feast, so that he may show her off. She refuses and for her insolence is stripped of her rank. After spending a year test-driving the most beautiful virgins from throughout his empire, Ahasuerus chooses Esther as his new queen. She disguises the fact that she's Jewish, but when Ahasuerus' prime minister starts a campaign of terror and execution against Jews throughout the land, Esther risks her own life to step up and save the day. The Hebrew holiday Purim celebrates this deliverance.

Surprisingly few biblical books have been made into full-length graphic adaptations. Philadelphia artist J. T. Waldman gave us one of this rare breed with 2005's *Megillat Esther*, featuring bold, intricate artwork; subplots and added layers of meaning based on rabbinic commentary (such as the Talmud); and the full text in ancient Hebrew, gorgeously hand-lettered, woven throughout every single page. The following pages contain the first part of the tale.

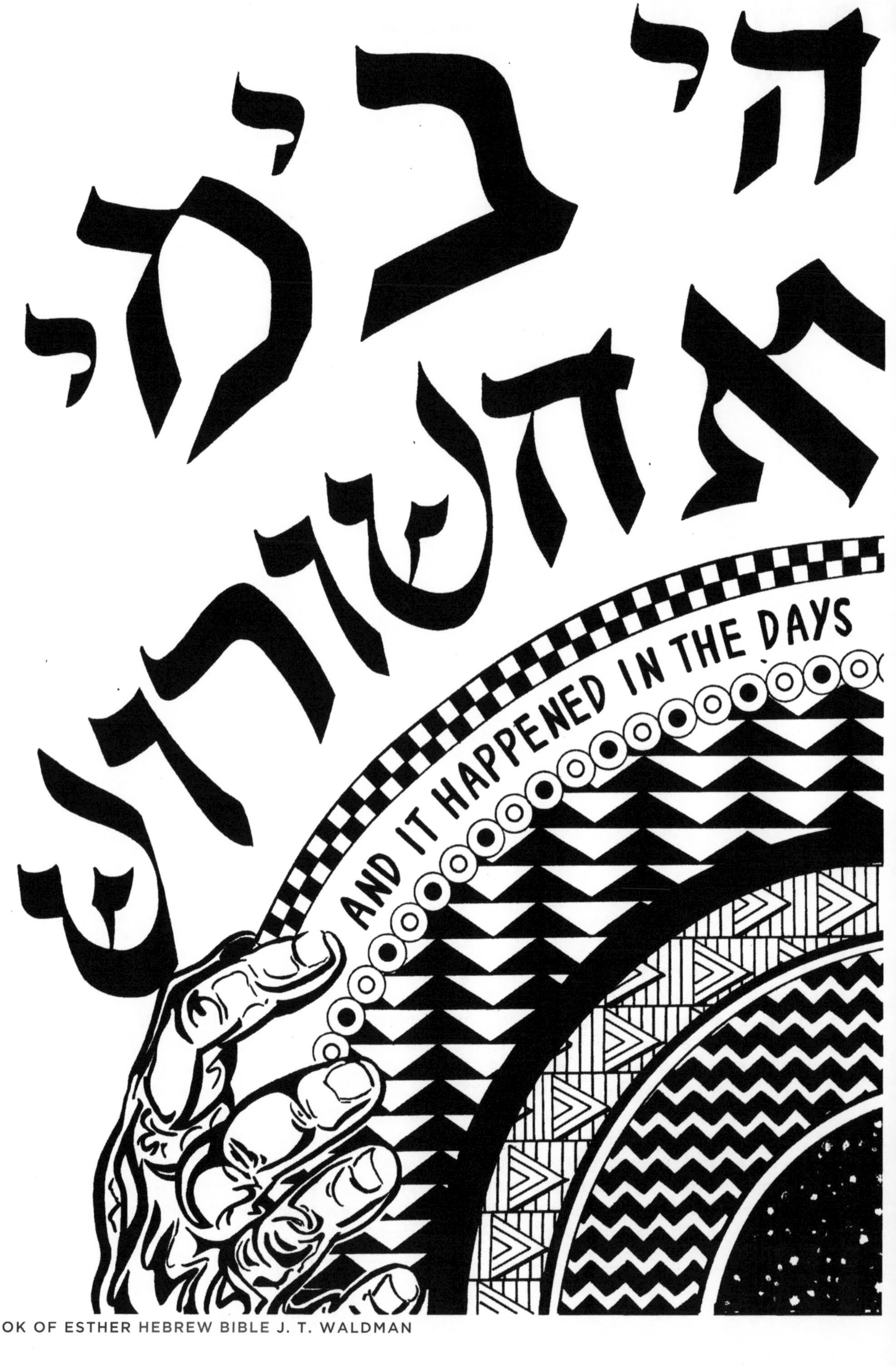
ויהי בימי אחשורוש
AND IT HAPPENED IN THE DAYS

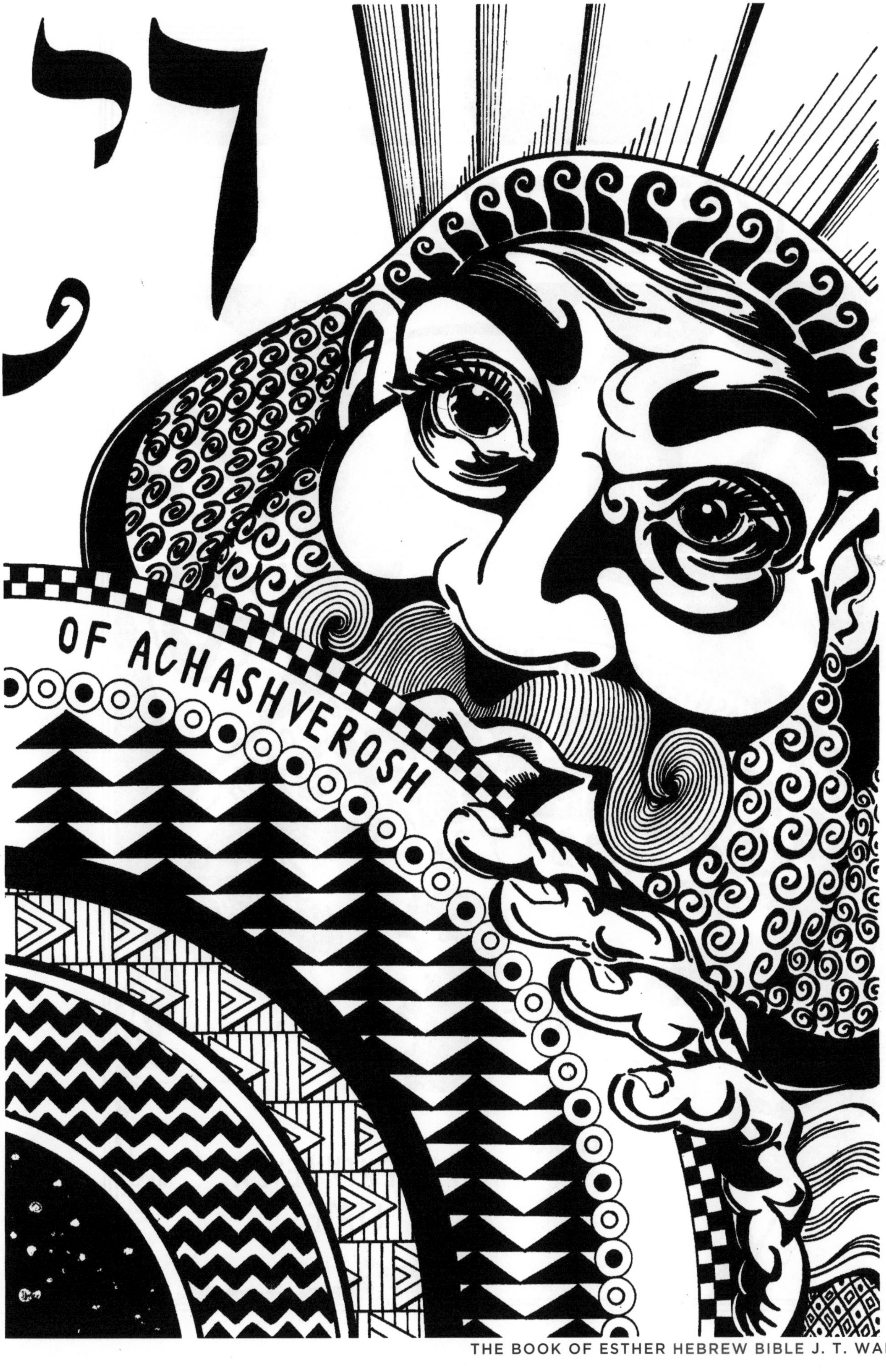

די
OF ACHASHVEROSH

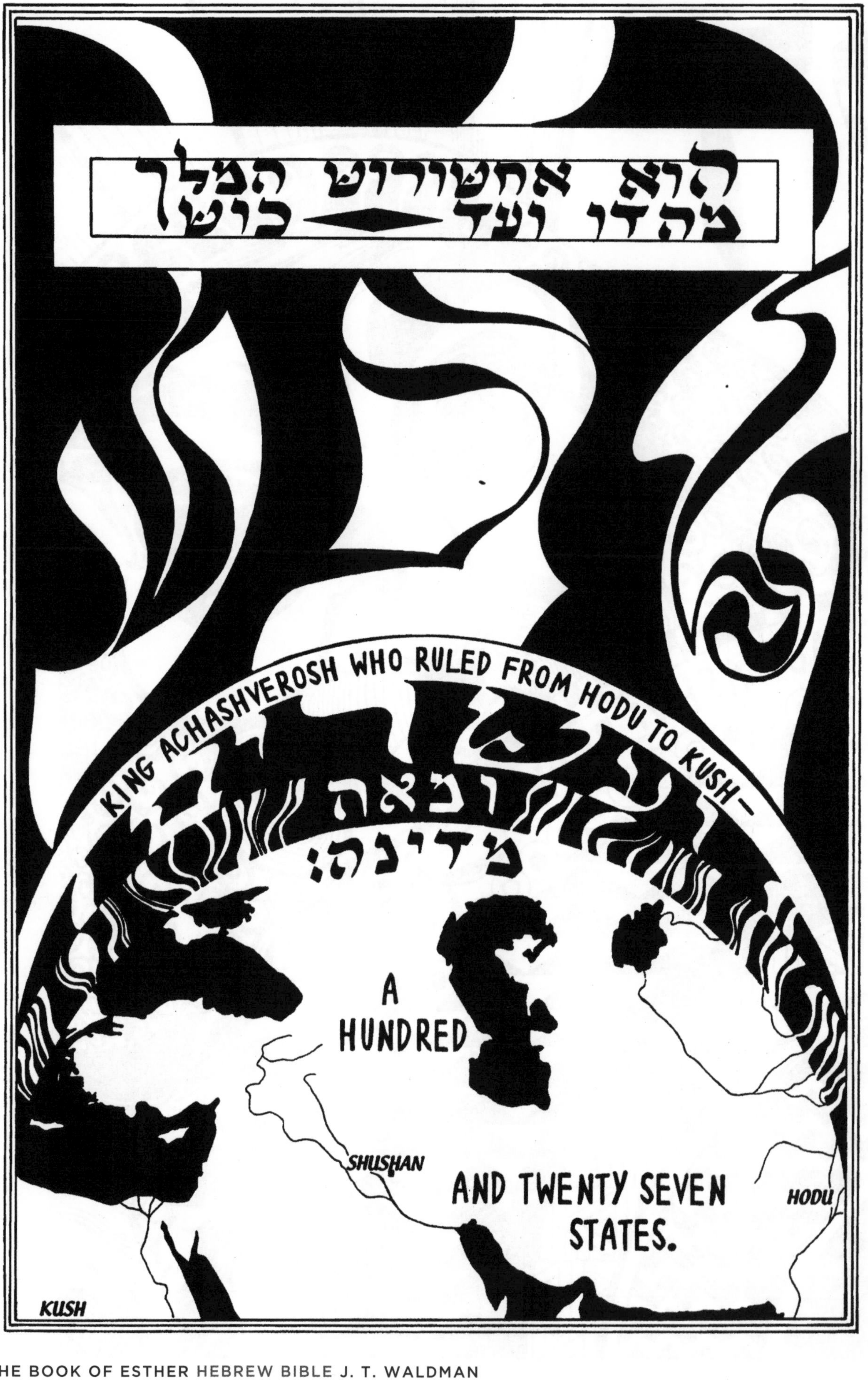

הוא אחשורוש המלך
מהדו ועד כוש
KING ACHASHVEROSH WHO RULED FROM HODU TO KUSH–
ומאה
מדינה:
A
HUNDRED
SHUSHAN
AND TWENTY SEVEN
STATES.
HODU
KUSH

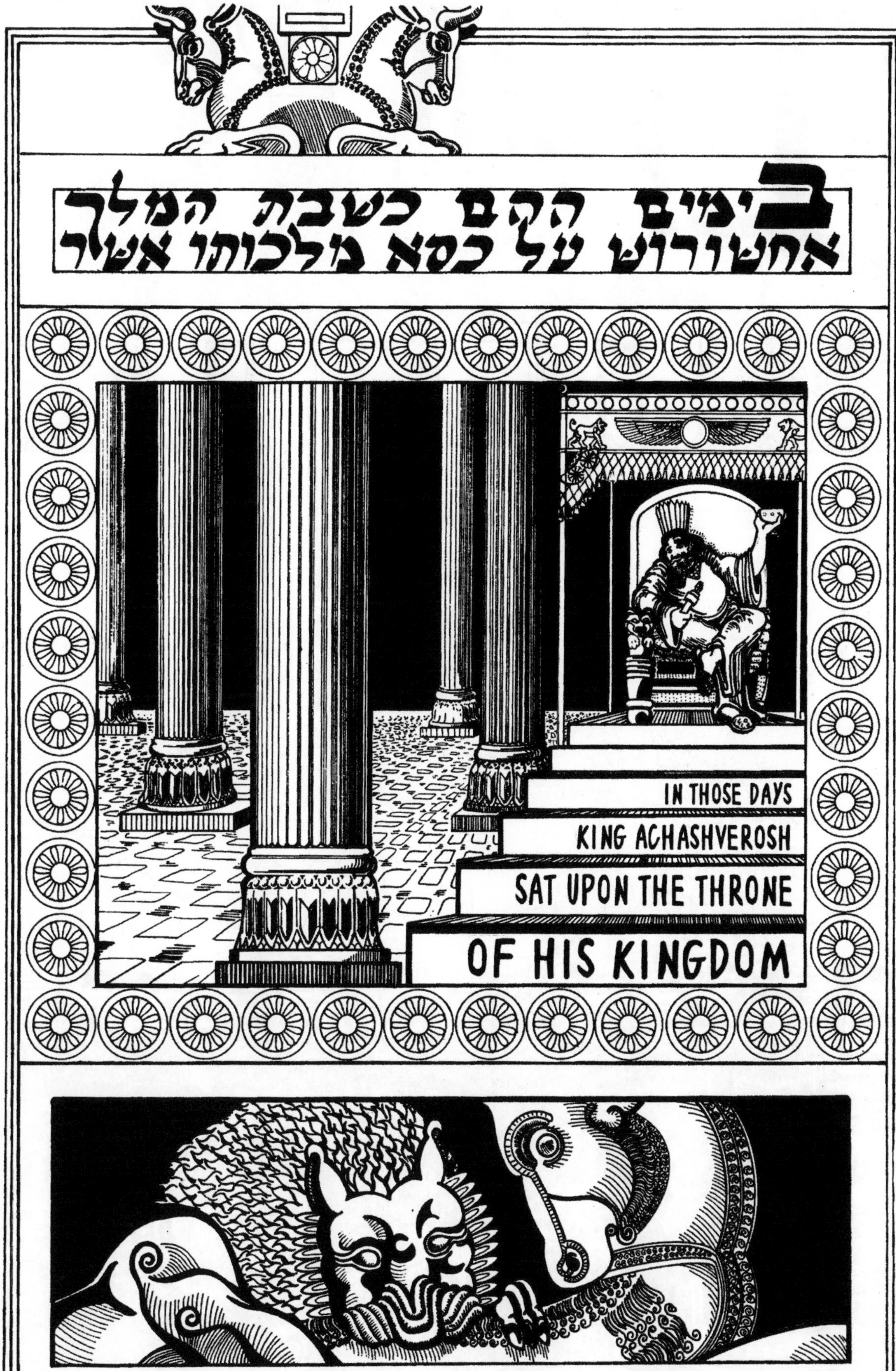
בימים ההם כשבת המלך
אחשורוש על כסא מלכותו אשר
IN THOSE DAYS
KING ACHASHVEROSH
SAT UPON THE THRONE
OF HIS KINGDOM

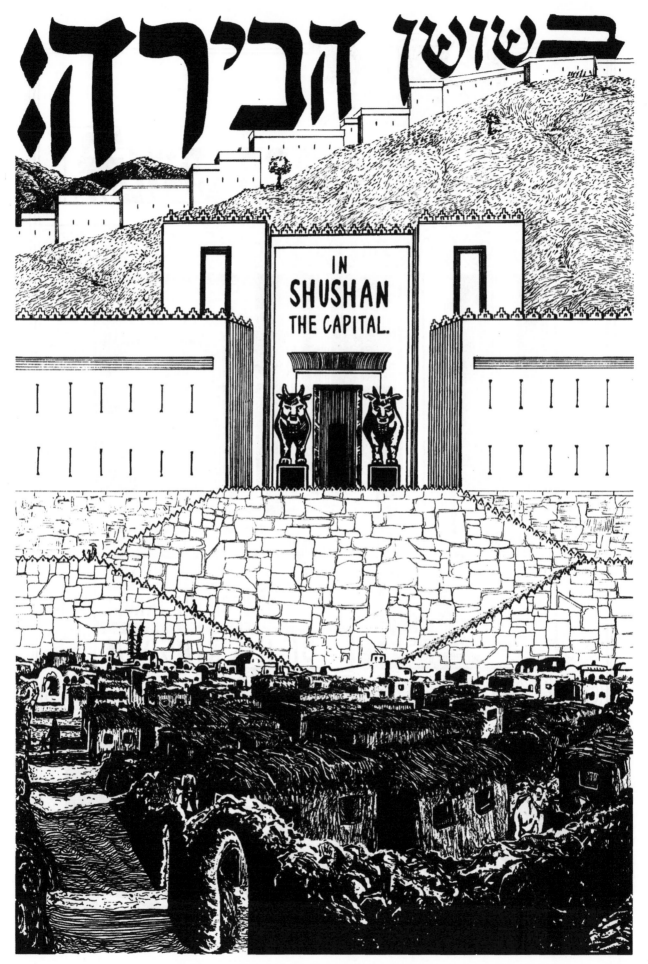

THE BOOK OF ESTHER HEBREW BIBLE J. T. WALDMAN

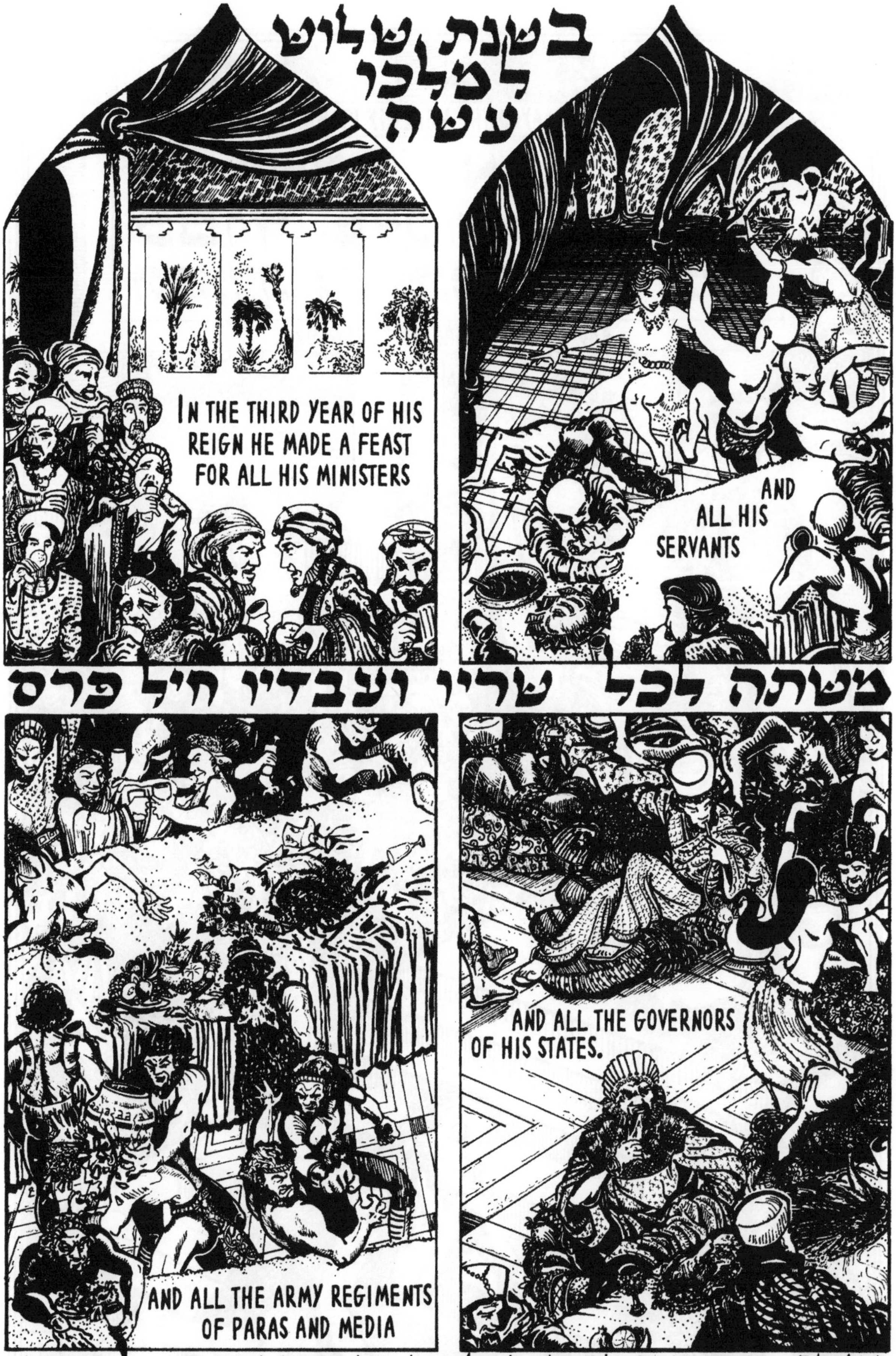

בשנת שלוש למלכו עשה
IN THE THIRD YEAR OF HIS REIGN HE MADE A FEAST FOR ALL HIS MINISTERS
AND ALL HIS SERVANTS
משתה לכל שריו ועבדיו חיל פרס
AND ALL THE ARMY REGIMENTS OF PARAS AND MEDIA
AND ALL THE GOVERNORS OF HIS STATES.
ומדי הפרתמים ושרי המדינות לפניו:

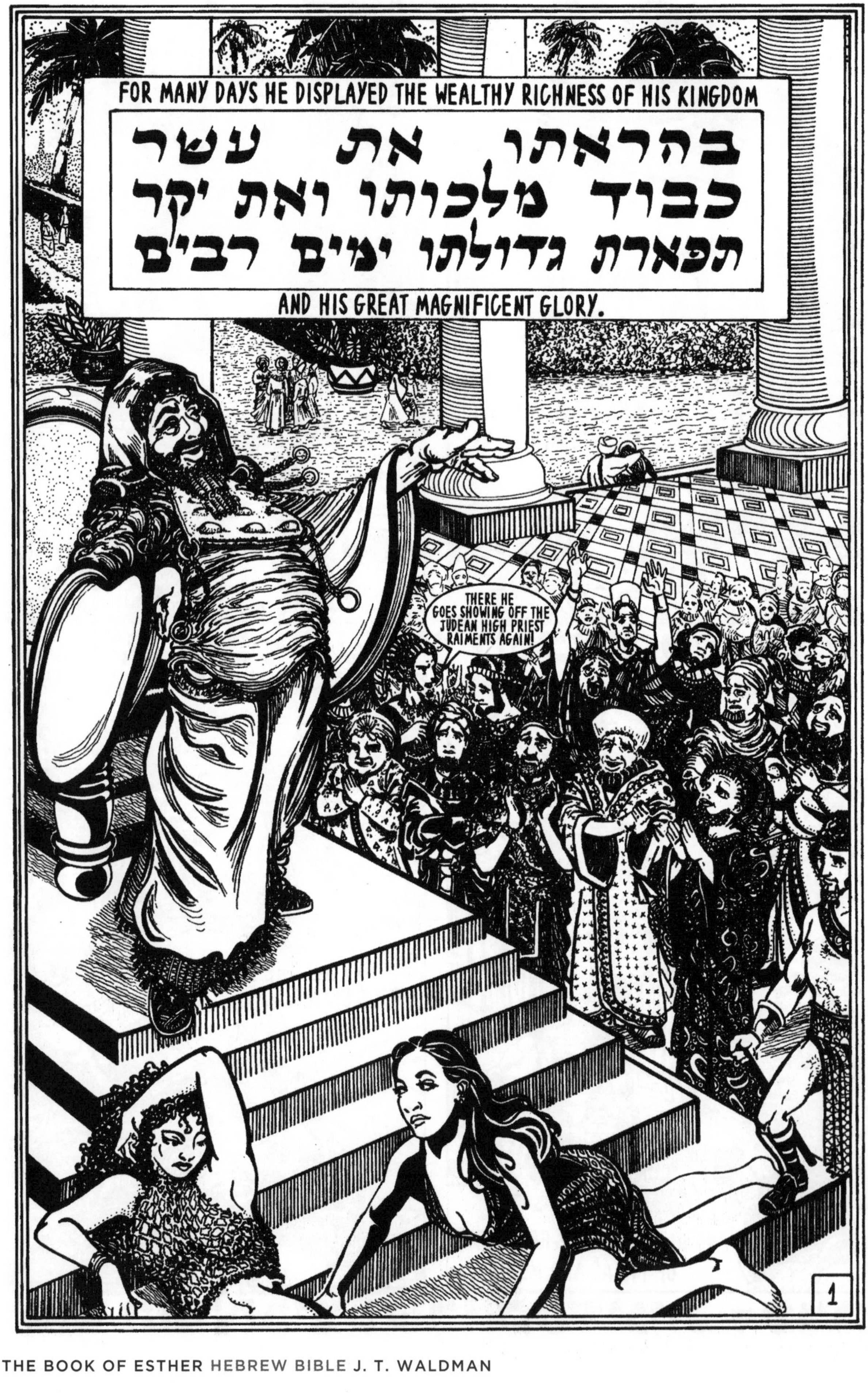
FOR MANY DAYS HE DISPLAYED THE WEALTHY RICHNESS OF HIS KINGDOM
בהראתו את עשר
כבוד מלכותו ואת יקר
תפארת גדולתו ימים רבים
AND HIS GREAT MAGNIFICENT GLORY.
THERE HE GOES SHOWING OFF THE JUDEAN HIGH PRIEST RAIMENTS AGAIN!
1

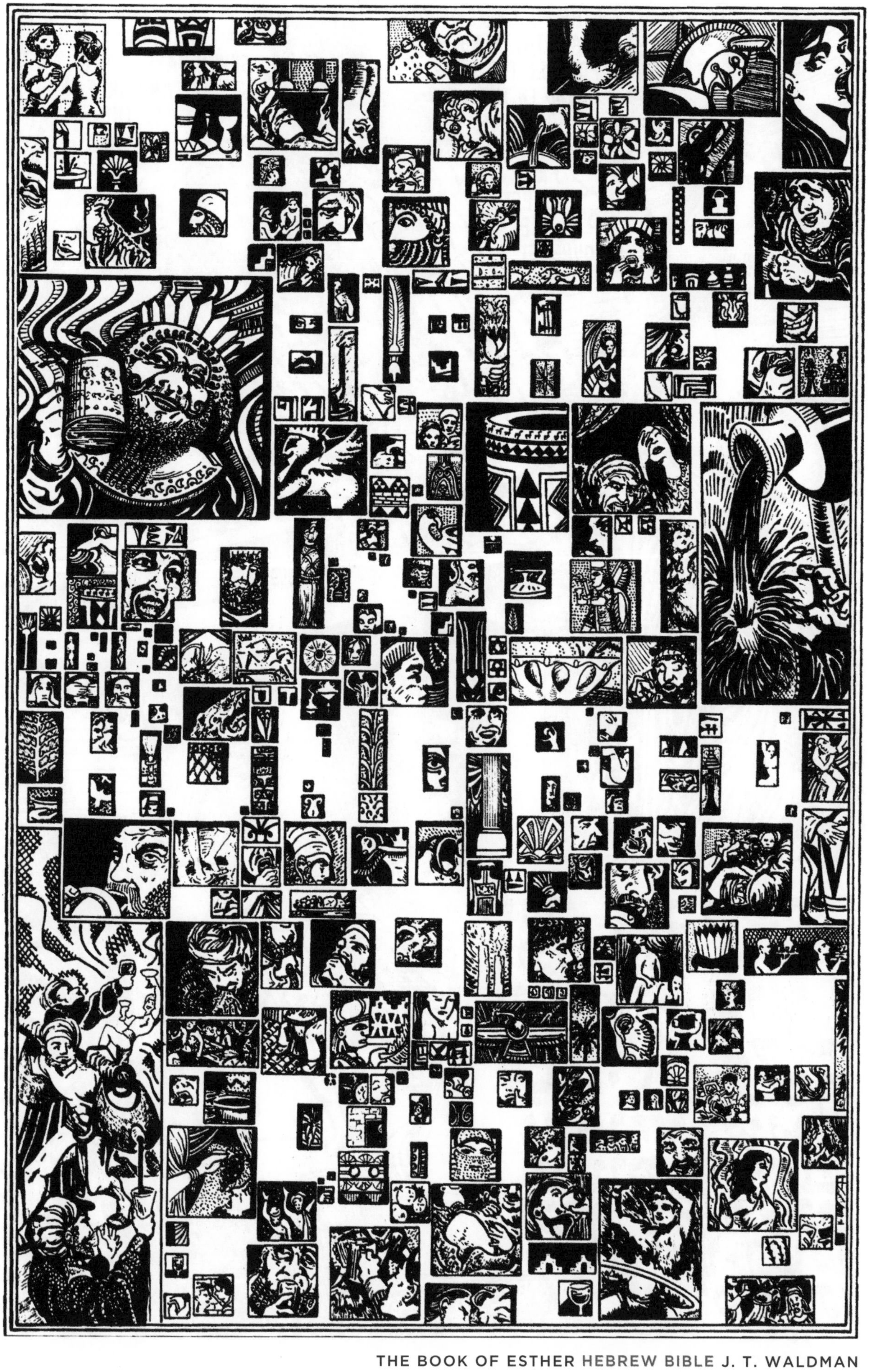

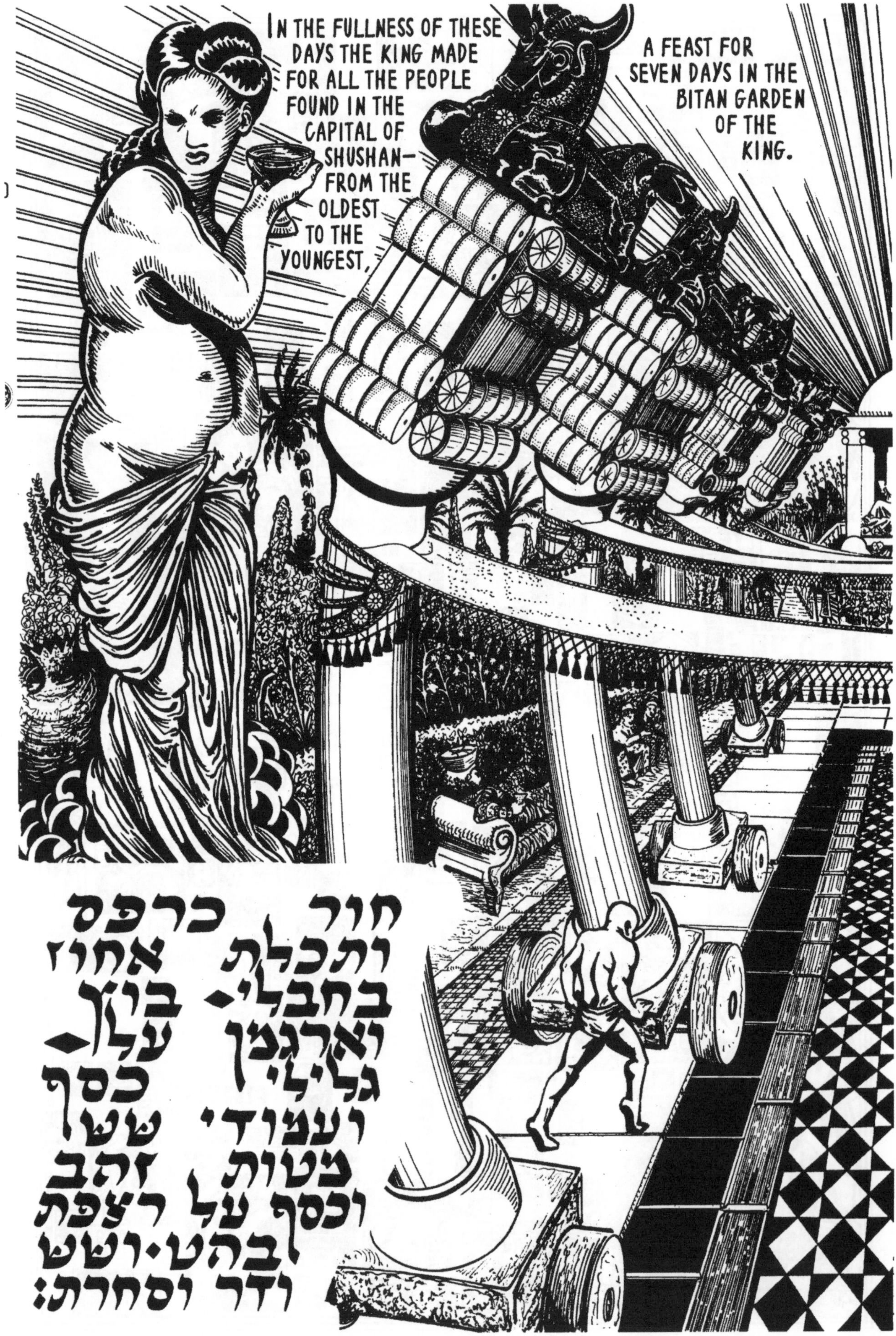
IN THE FULLNESS OF THESE DAYS THE KING MADE FOR ALL THE PEOPLE FOUND IN THE CAPITAL OF SHUSHAN— FROM THE OLDEST TO THE YOUNGEST,
A FEAST FOR SEVEN DAYS IN THE BITAN GARDEN OF THE KING.
חור כרפס
ותכלת אחוז
בחבלי בוץ
וארגמן על
גלילי כסף
ועמודי שש
מטות זהב
וכסף על רצפת
בהט ושש
ודר וסחרת:

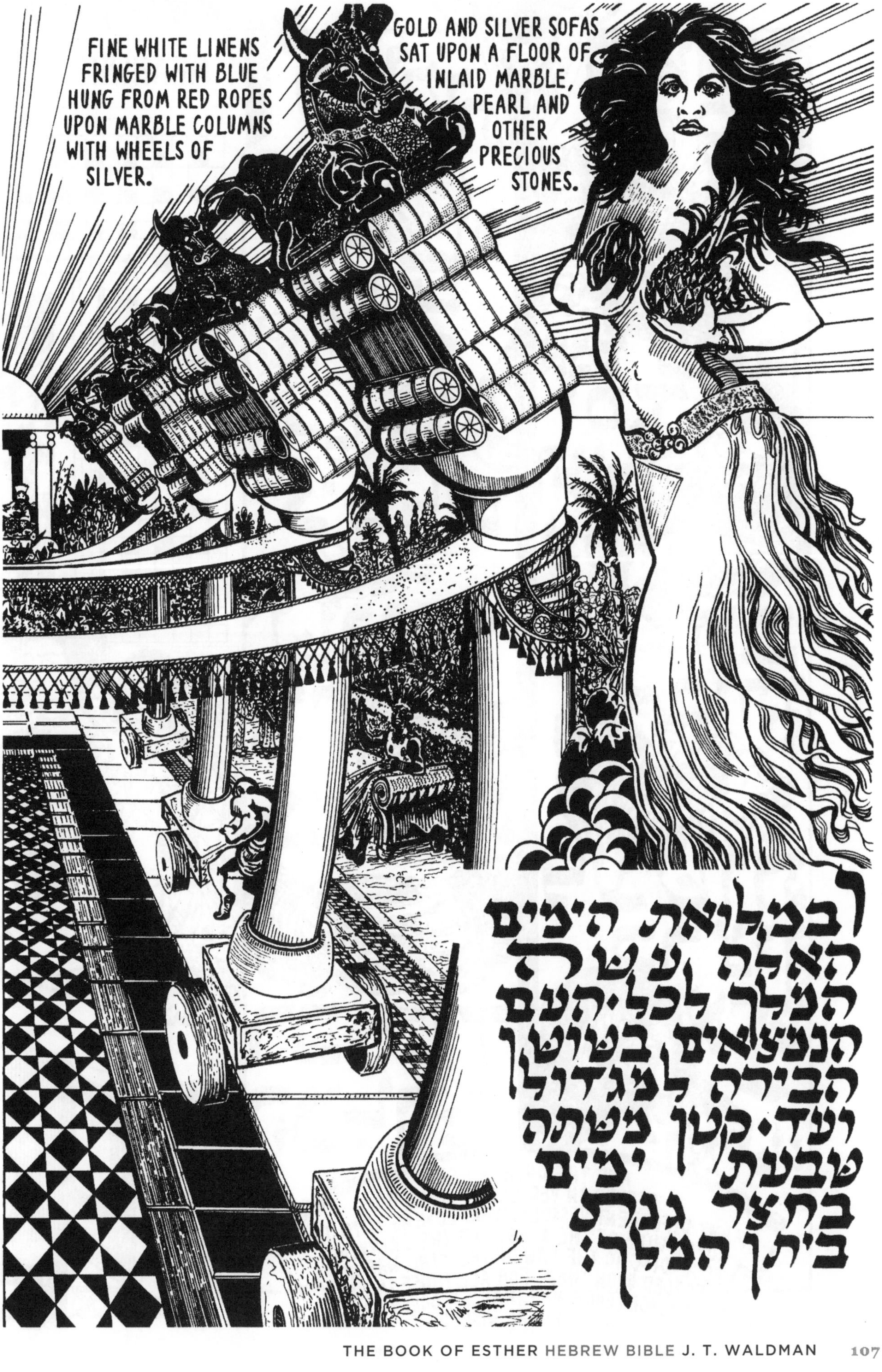
FINE WHITE LINENS FRINGED WITH BLUE HUNG FROM RED ROPES UPON MARBLE COLUMNS WITH WHEELS OF SILVER.
GOLD AND SILVER SOFAS SAT UPON A FLOOR OF INLAID MARBLE, PEARL AND OTHER PRECIOUS STONES.
ובמלואת הימים
האלה עשה
המלך לכל־העם
הנמצאים בשושן
הבירה למגדול
ועד־קטן משתה
שבעת ימים
בחצר גנת
ביתן המלך:

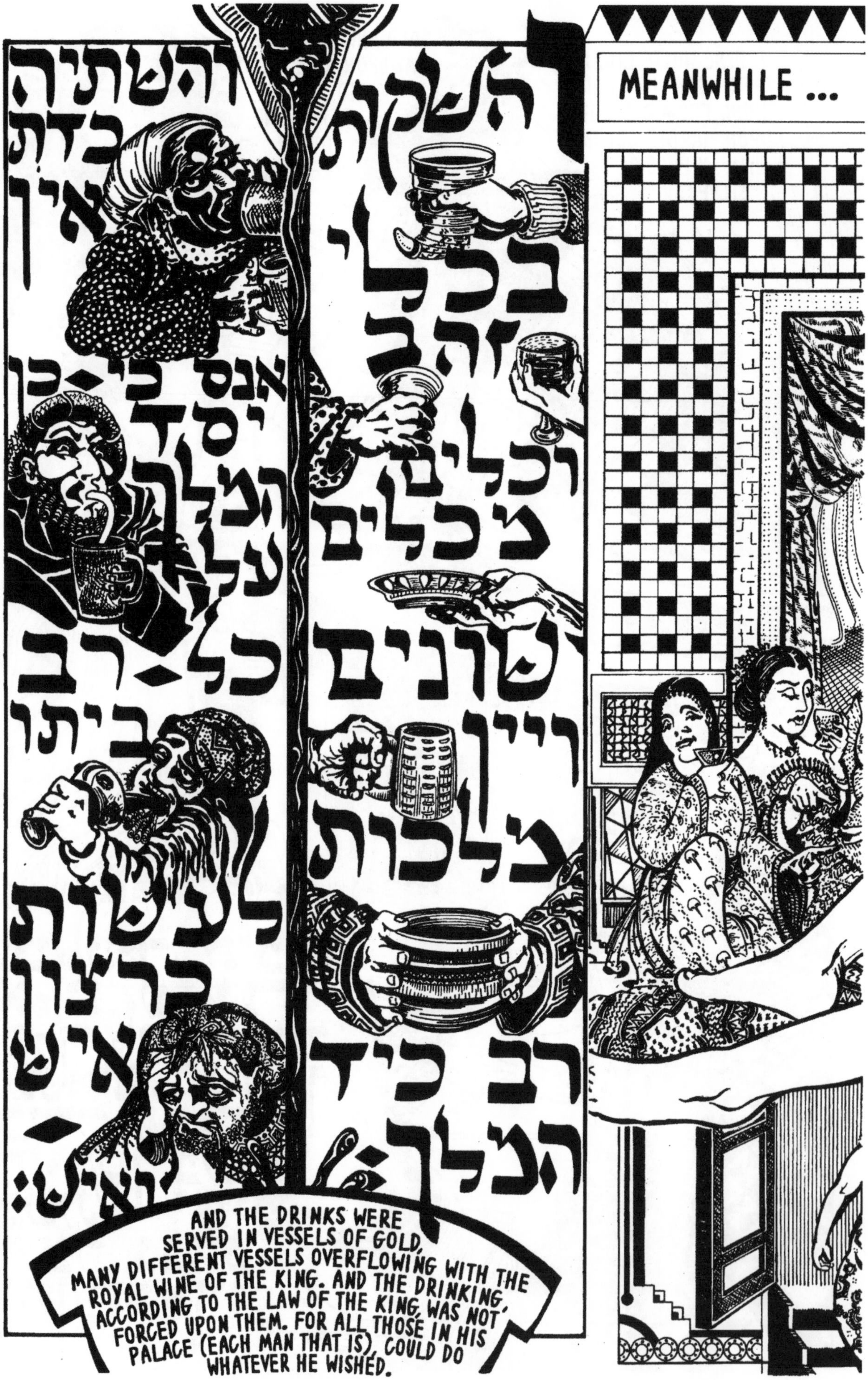
והשקות בכלי זהב וכלים מכלים שונים ויין מלכות רב כיד המלך:
והשתיה כדת אין אנס כי־כן יסד המלך על כל־רב ביתו לעשות כרצון איש־ואיש:
AND THE DRINKS WERE SERVED IN VESSELS OF GOLD, MANY DIFFERENT VESSELS OVERFLOWING WITH THE ROYAL WINE OF THE KING. AND THE DRINKING, ACCORDING TO THE LAW OF THE KING, WAS NOT FORCED UPON THEM. FOR ALL THOSE IN HIS PALACE (EACH MAN THAT IS), COULD DO WHATEVER HE WISHED.
MEANWHILE ...

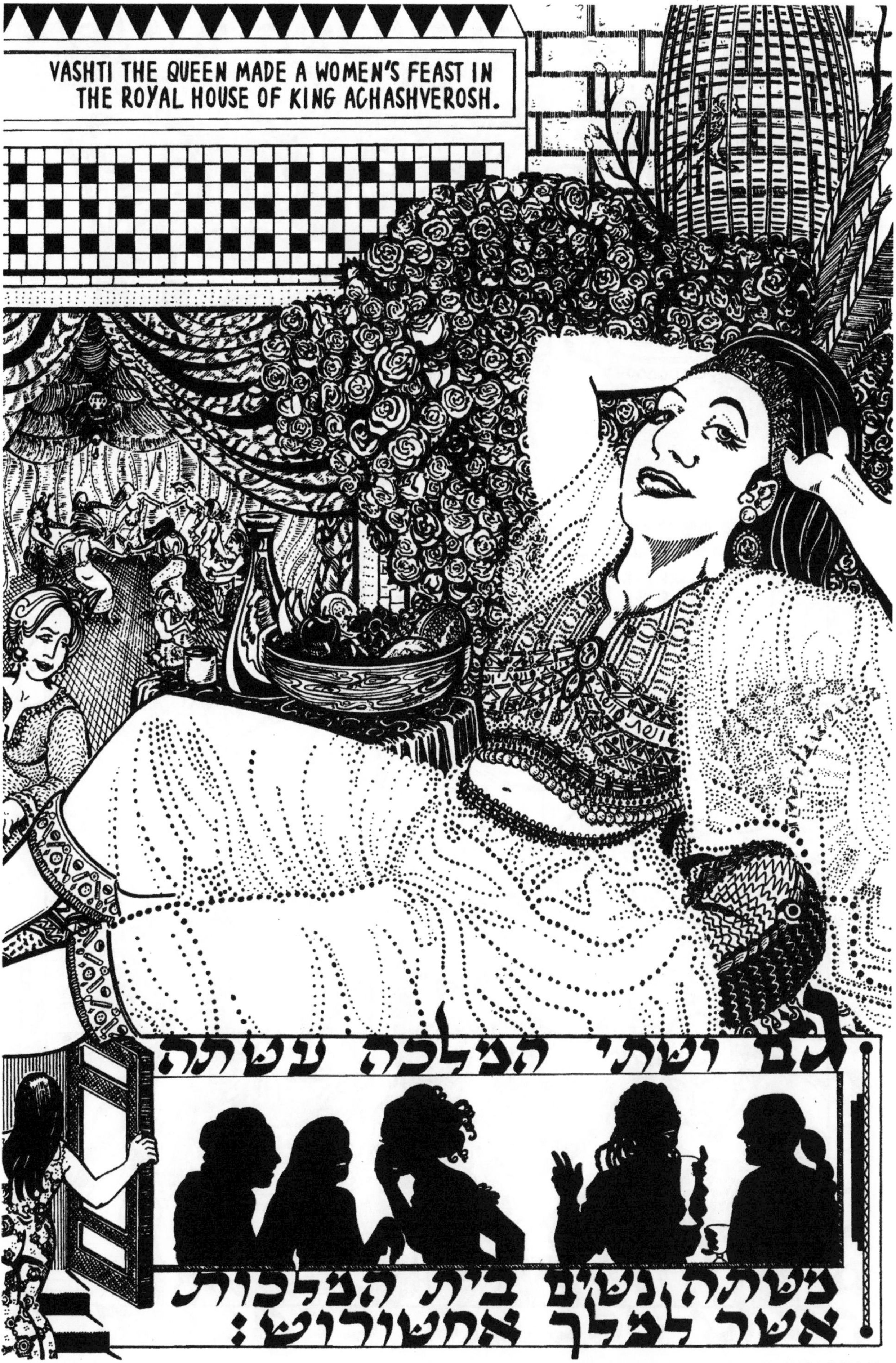
VASHTI THE QUEEN MADE A WOMEN'S FEAST IN THE ROYAL HOUSE OF KING ACHASHVEROSH.
גם ושתי המלכה עשתה
משתה נשים בית המלכות
אשר למלך אחשורוש:

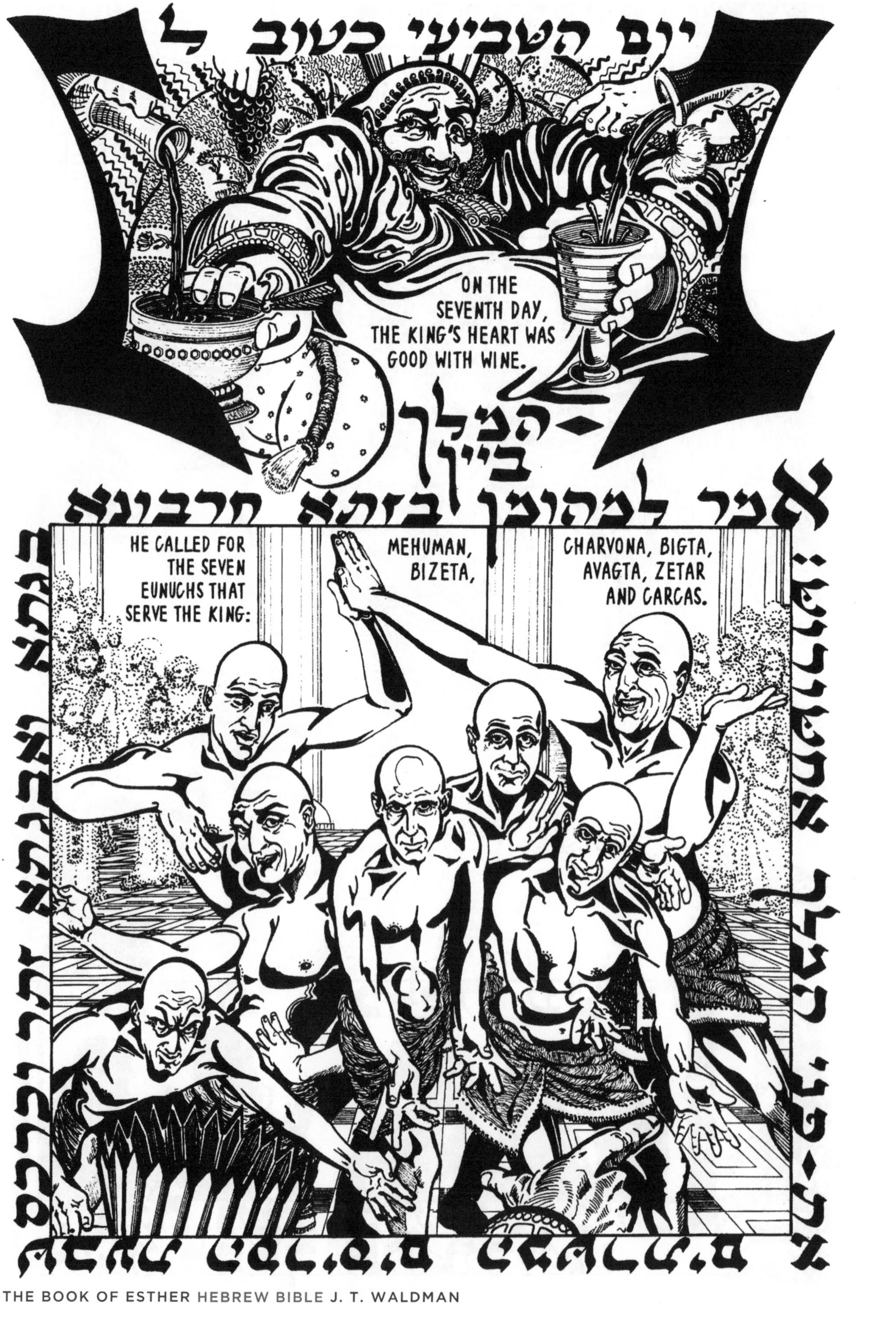

יום השביעי כטוב ל
ON THE SEVENTH DAY, THE KING'S HEART WAS GOOD WITH WINE.
המלך ביין
אמר למהומן בזתא חרבונא
HE CALLED FOR THE SEVEN EUNUCHS THAT SERVE THE KING:
MEHUMAN, BIZETA,
CHARVONA, BIGTA, AVAGTA, ZETAR AND CARCAS.

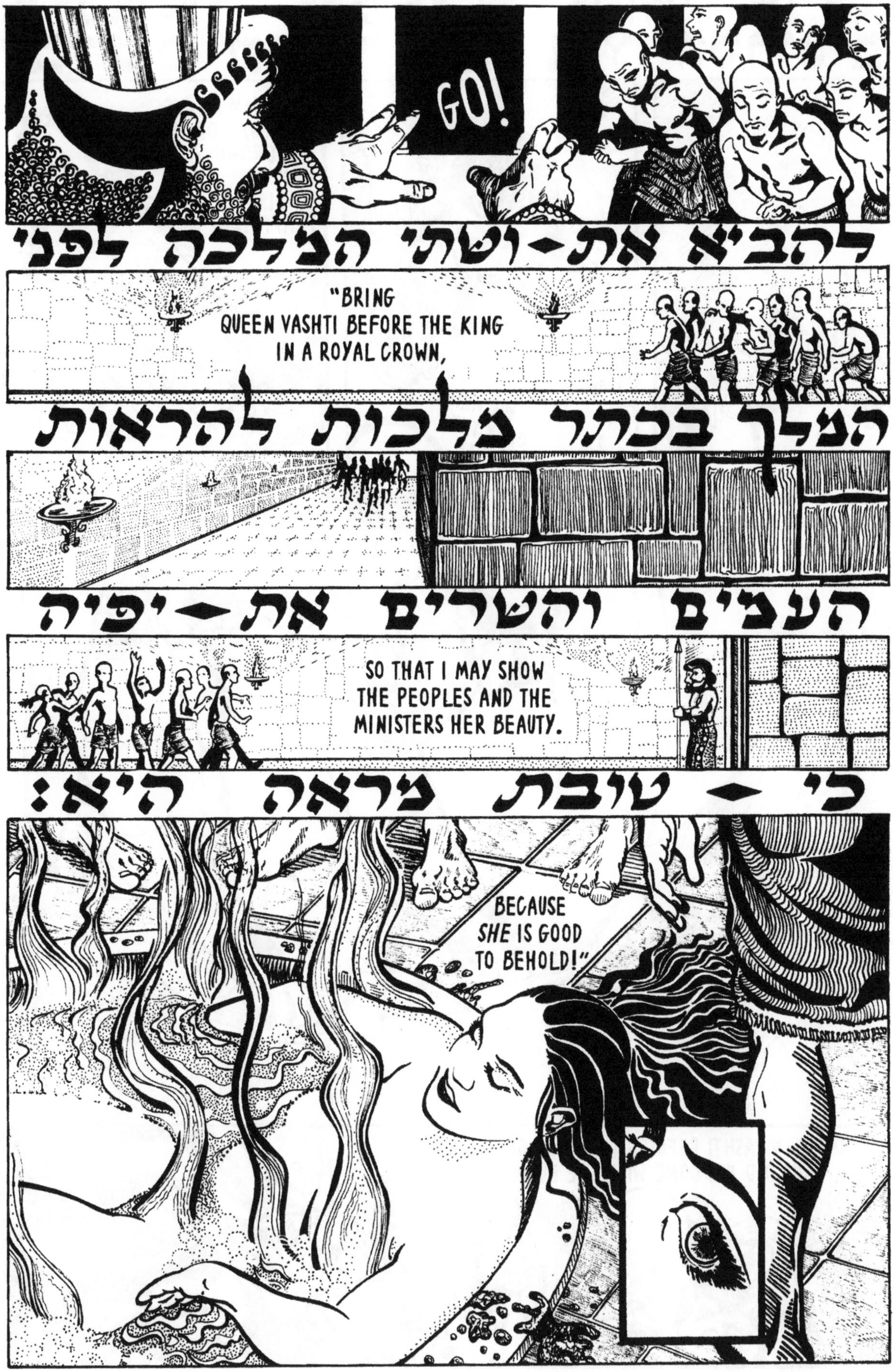
GO!
להביא את-ושתי המלכה לפני
"BRING QUEEN VASHTI BEFORE THE KING IN A ROYAL CROWN,
המלך בכתר מלכות להראות
העמים והשרים את-יפיה
SO THAT I MAY SHOW THE PEOPLES AND THE MINISTERS HER BEAUTY.
כי-טובת מראה היא:
BECAUSE *SHE* IS GOOD TO BEHOLD!"

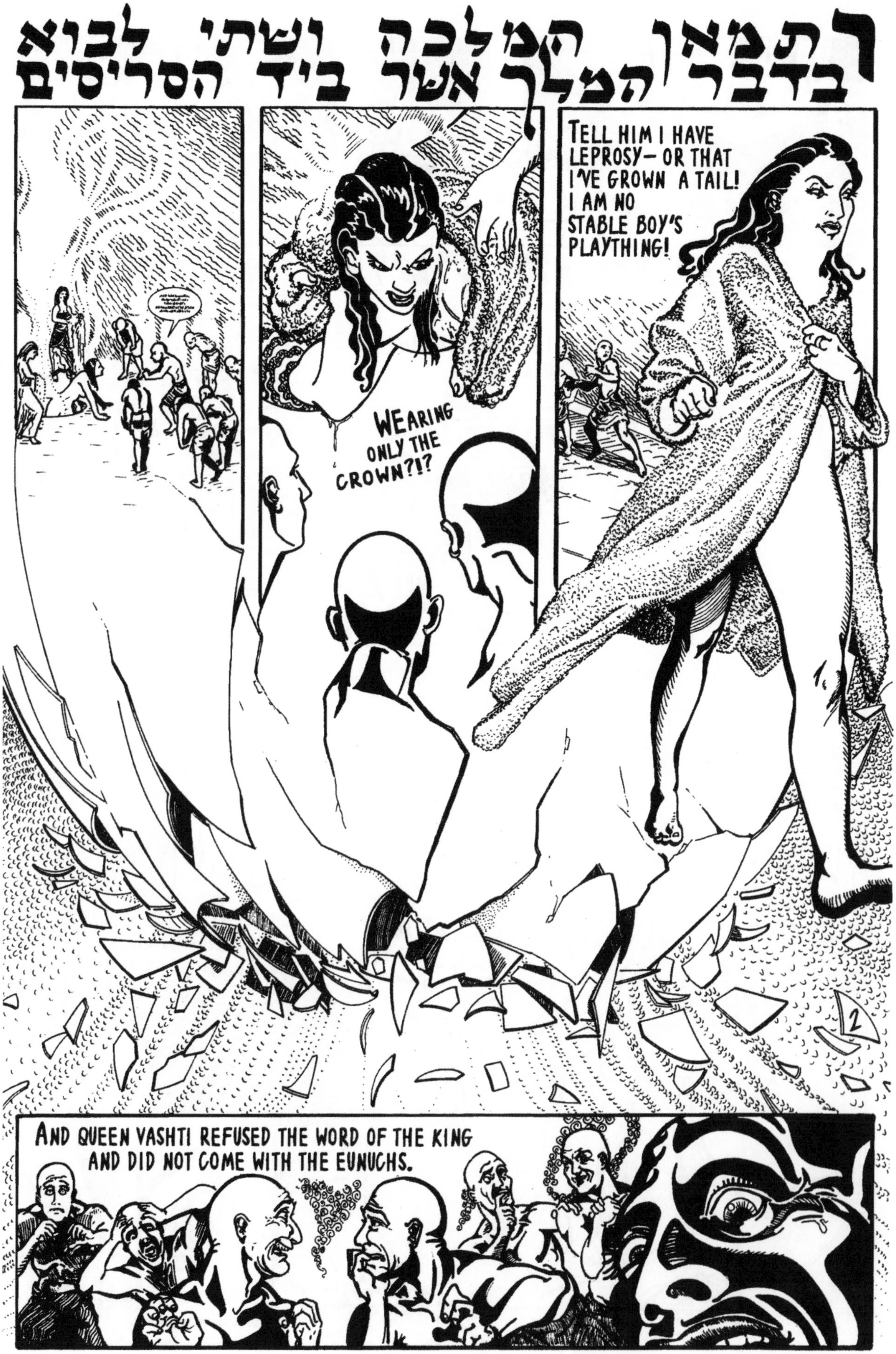
ותמאן המלכה ושתי לבוא
בדבר המלך אשר ביד הסריסים
TELL HIM I HAVE LEPROSY— OR THAT I'VE GROWN A TAIL! I AM NO STABLE BOY'S PLAYTHING!
WEARING ONLY THE CROWN?!?
AND QUEEN VASHTI REFUSED THE WORD OF THE KING AND DID NOT COME WITH THE EUNUCHS.

Symposium

Plato

ART / ADAPTATION BY **Yeji Yun**

SYMPOSIUM IS ONE OF THE GREATEST PHILO-
sophical and literary statements on love ever written. One
of Plato's thirty or so dialogs, dating probably from the
380s BCE, it takes place in the home of an Athenian poet,
Agathon, who is holding a symposium, an all-male dinner
party in which the elaborate meal is followed by ritualized
drinking of lots of wine while engaging in spirited debate
and speech-making. Seven prominent intellectuals—including a physician and Socrates himself—are in attendance,
each agreeing to speechify in praise of the god Eros (a.k.a.
Love, the Greek equivalent of the Roman Cupid). Love,
desire, and sex are praised, dissected, and debated. The
playwright Aristophanes (he of the sex comedy *Lysistrata*)
misses his turn because of hiccups but eventually gives
Symposium's most famous speech, a hilarious yet strangely
plausible creation myth that explains why human beings
are attracted to one another.

In the beginning, Aristophanes tells us, each human being
was essentially two humans welded together—four arms,
four legs, two heads, and two sets of genitals. Our ancestors,
who were very strong and fast, attempted to storm Mount
Olympus and usurp the gods. Upset, and a little worried,
Zeus smote these early humans, splitting them in half, each
individual now having two arms, two legs, a head, and one
set of genitals. Since then, we have all sensed that we have
a missing half and spend our lives searching for him or her
in order to temporarily reunite. (Most of the original four-
legged humans had mismatched genitals, but some had the
same type—two penises or two vulvas—thus explaining why
some people are attracted to the same sex.)

Illustrator Yeji Yun—born in Seoul, now in London—word-
lessly depicts these events in a series of three spreads,
which she calls *The Origins of Love.*

SOURCE

Plato. *The Symposium*. Edited, translated, and introduced by
 Christopher Gill. Penguin Classics, 2003.

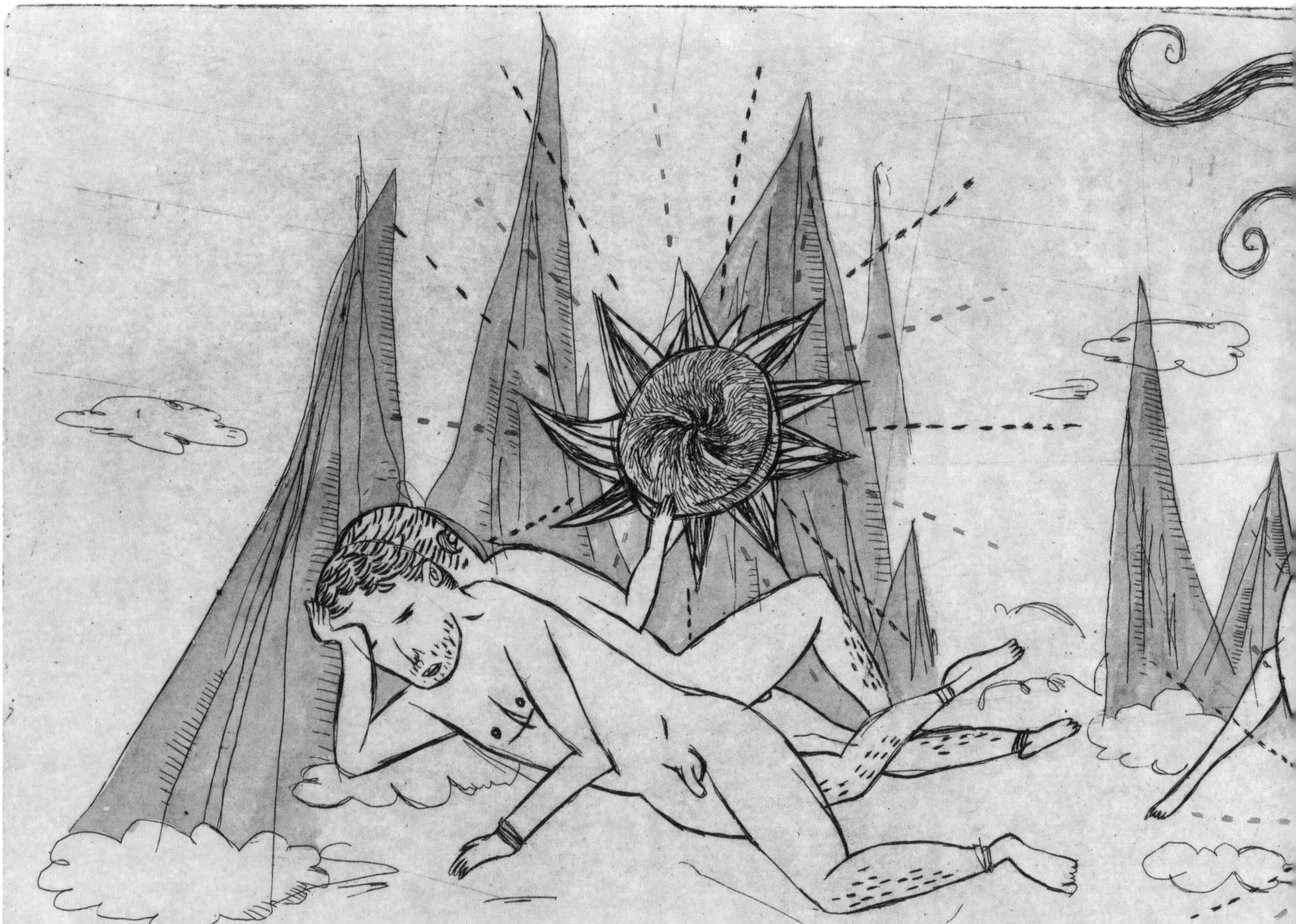

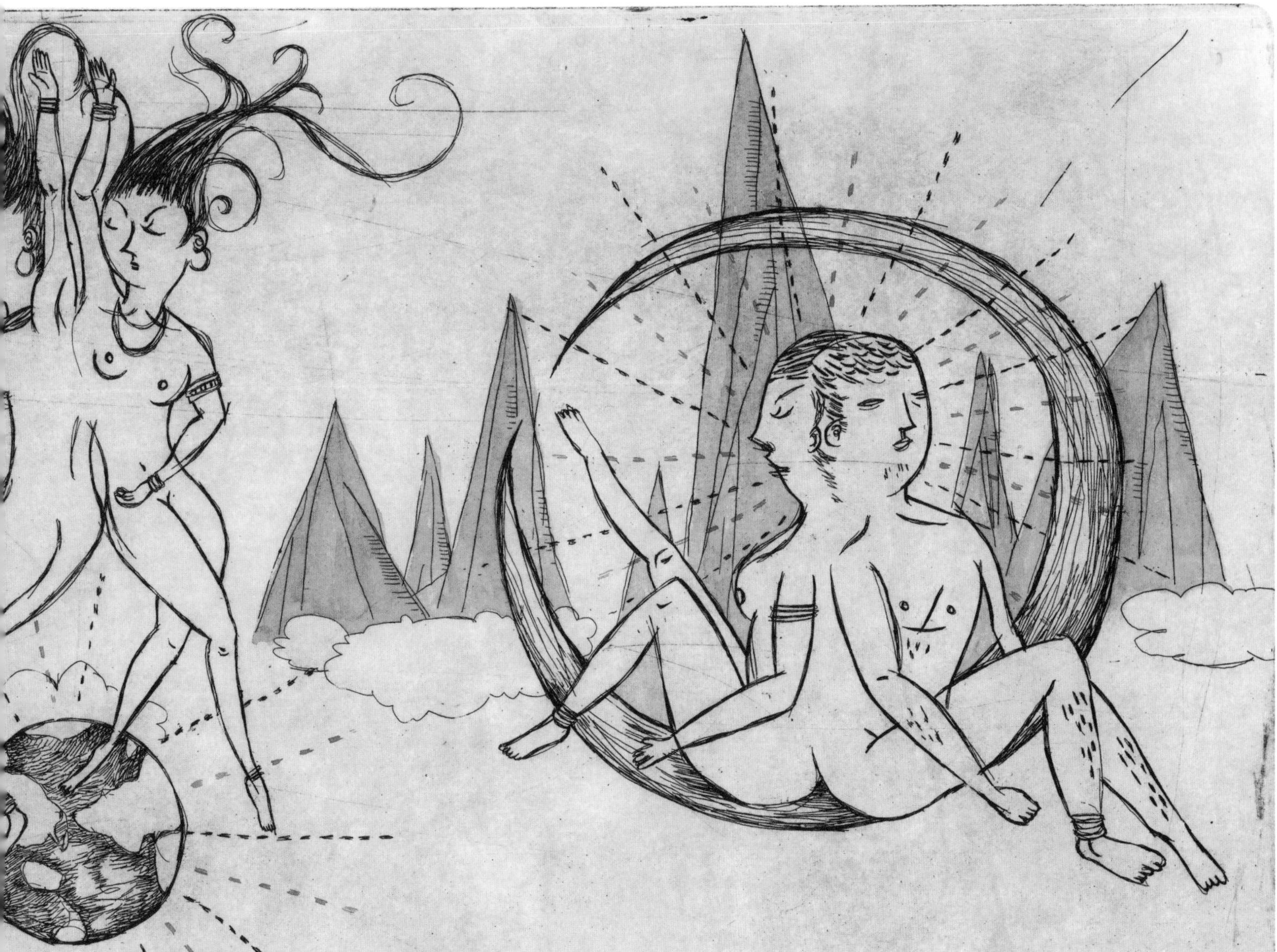

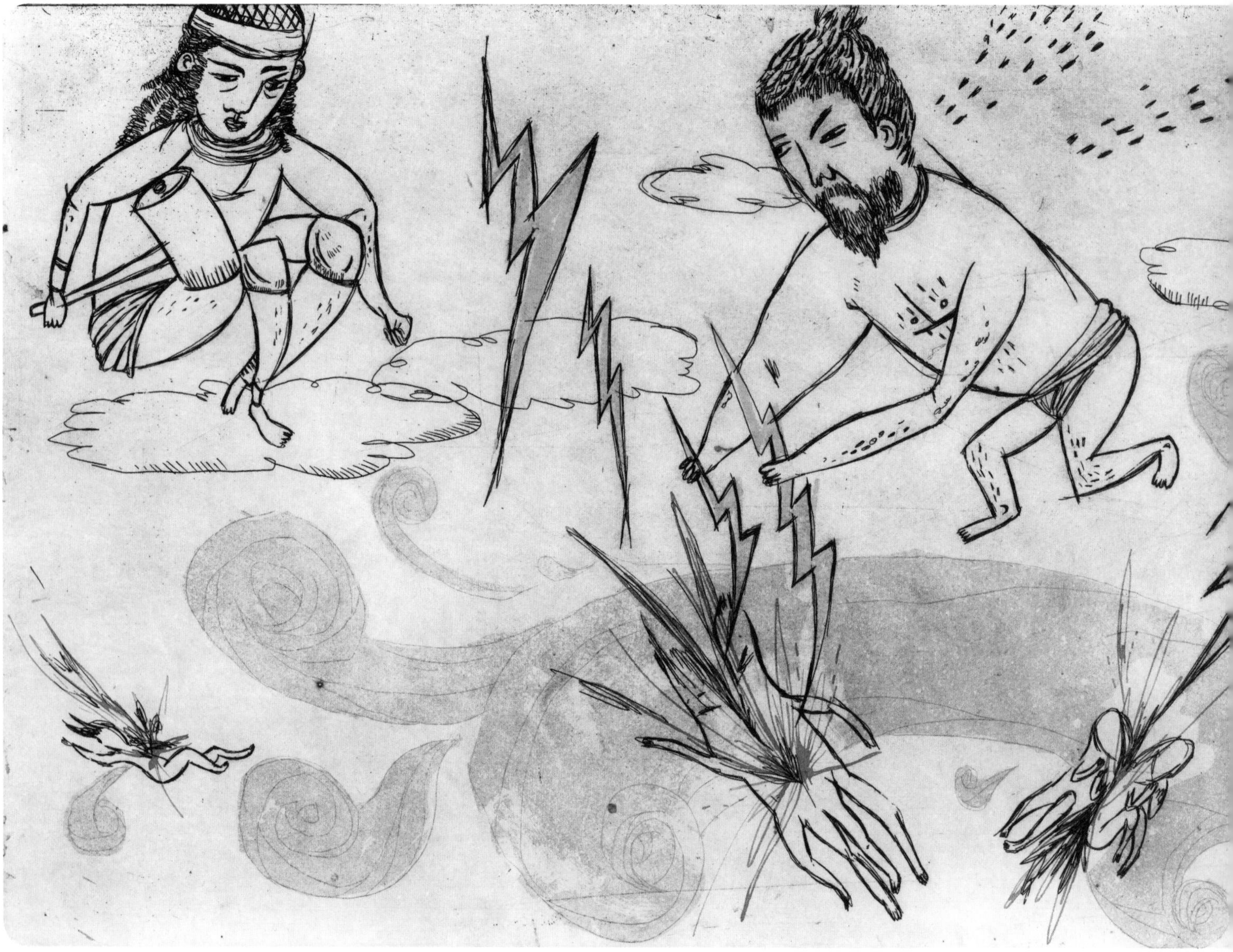

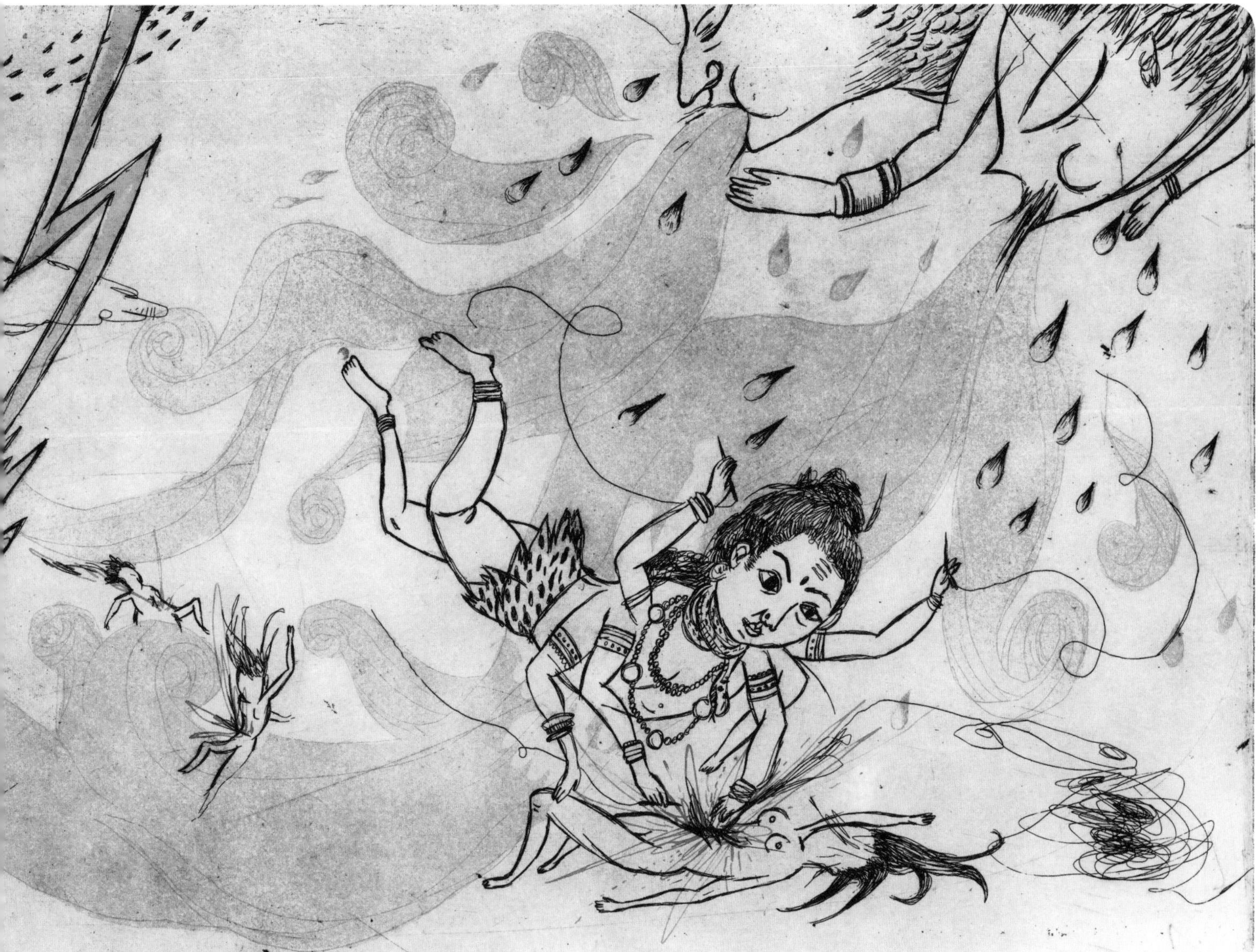

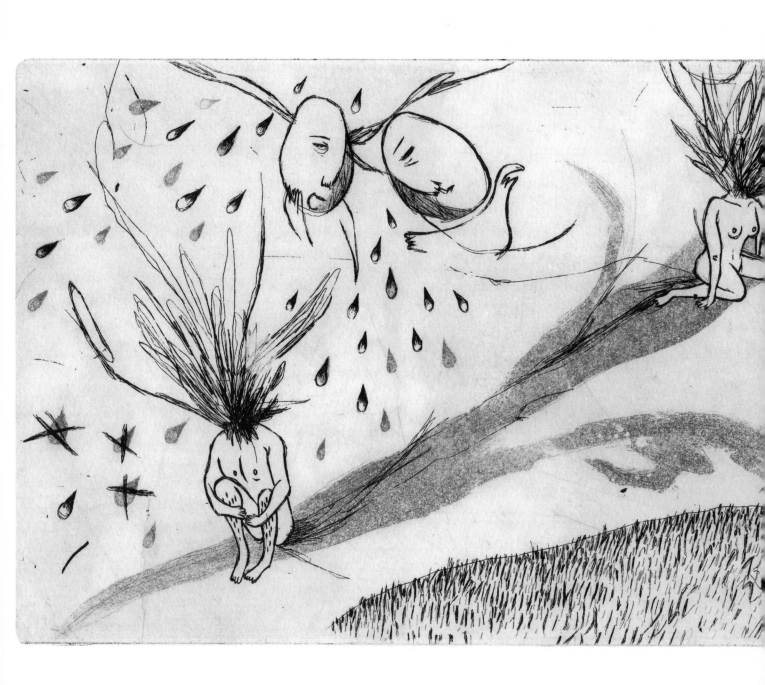

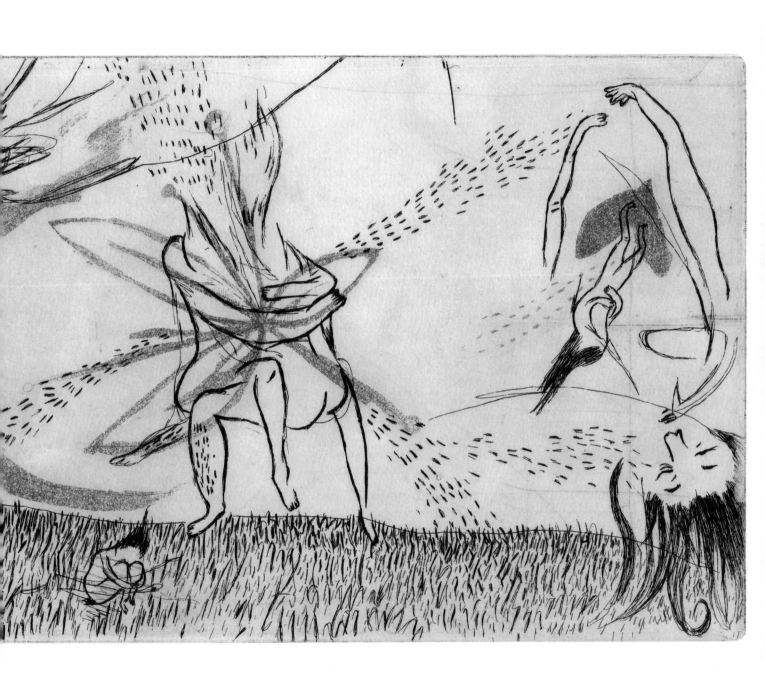

Tao Te Ching

Lao Tzu

ADAPTATION BY **Fred Van Lente**

ART BY **Ryan Dunlavey**

THE *TAO TE CHING* WAS WRITTEN AROUND 2,500 years ago, supposedly by a spiritual philosopher in China, Lao Tzu (which simply means "Old Master"), who may or may not have existed. Regardless of its misty origins, this collection of 81 brief, poetic statements on the ultimate nature of reality is the founding document of Taoism; it influenced other Eastern religious systems and has become a world classic of spirituality, translated into English possibly as many as 200 times.

In his famed series of essays on the classics, Kenneth Rexroth wrote that "the best way to understand the book [is] as a collection of subjects for meditation, catalysts for contemplation. It is certainly not a philosophical treatise or a religious one, either, in our sense of the words religion, philosophy, or treatise."

Striking a similar note, Lama Surya Das has written:

A little Tao goes a long way. The *Tao Te Ching* should be savored leaf by leaf, line by line, like haiku poetry—read and enjoyed, pondered, and reread again. These finely wrought, provocative, ultimate utterances are chock full of one-sentence sermons encapsulating universal wisdom in a charming, poetic form that leaves room for more interpretation than a Rorschach inkblot.

This cheeky take on the *Tao Te Ching* comes from Fred Van Lente and Ryan Dunlavey's *Action Philosophers!* comic series, which cleverly encapsulates the world's greatest thinkers, from Plato, Aquinas, and Bacon to Schopenhauer, Jung, and Derrida.

SOURCE

Lao Tzu. Trans. Derek Lin. *Tao Te Ching: Annotated and Explained.* Woodstock, Vermont: SkyLight Paths Publishing, 2006.

Rexroth, Kenneth. *More Classics Revisited.* New Directions Publishing, 1989.

LAO TZU

MM MMOW MEH MAH ME MAMMH ME MAH ME MEMER-NAL MOW.*

MMO MMEH MMRE-EMEMM MEREM MERMPMP MOM MIM MMOW MEH MMIM MMOUT MMOMMEM-MEM!*

*: "...THE TAO (CHINESE="PATH" OR "WAY") THAT *CAN BE NAMED* IS NOT THE *ETERNAL TAO.*"

says...

*: "SO WE PRESENT THE FOLLOWING *EXCERPTS* FROM THIS LEGENDARY SAGE'S SPIRITUAL MASTERPIECE, THE *TAO TE CHING* ("THE BOOK OF THE WAY AND ITS VIRTUE," C. 600 B.C.), *WITHOUT* COMMENTARY!"

UNDER HEAVEN ALL CAN SEE BEAUTY *AS* BEAUTY ONLY BECAUSE THERE IS *UGLINESS.*

ALL CAN KNOW GOOD *AS* GOOD ONLY BECAUSE THERE IS *EVIL.*

THEREFORE HAVING AND *NOT* HAVING ARISE *TOGETHER.*

DIFFICULT AND EASY *COMPLEMENT* EACH OTHER.

THEREFORE, THE SAGE GOES ABOUT DOING *NOTHING,* TEACHING *NO-TALKING.*

WORK IS *DONE,* THEN *FORGOTTEN.*

THEREFORE, IT LASTS *FOREVER.*

WHY DO HEAVEN AND EARTH LAST FOREVER?

THEY ARE *UNBORN,* SO EVER *LIVING.*

DO YOU THINK YOU CAN *IMPROVE* THE UNIVERSE?

I DO NOT BELIEVE IT CAN BE DONE.

THE UNIVERSE IS *SACRED.* IF YOU TRY TO CHANGE IT, YOU WILL *RUIN* IT. IF YOU TRY TO *HOLD* IT, YOU WILL *LOSE* IT.

THIRTY SPOKES SHARE THE WHEEL'S HUB; IT IS THE *CENTER HOLE* THAT MAKES IT *USEFUL.*

SHAPE CLAY INTO A *VESSEL*; IT IS THE SPACE *WITHIN* THAT MAKES IT *USEFUL.*

EMPTY YOURSELF OF *EVERYTHING.*

LET THE MIND REST AT *PEACE.*

RETURNING TO THE SOURCE IS *STILLNESS,* WHICH IS THE WAY OF *NATURE.*

THE WAY OF NATURE IS *UNCHANGING.*

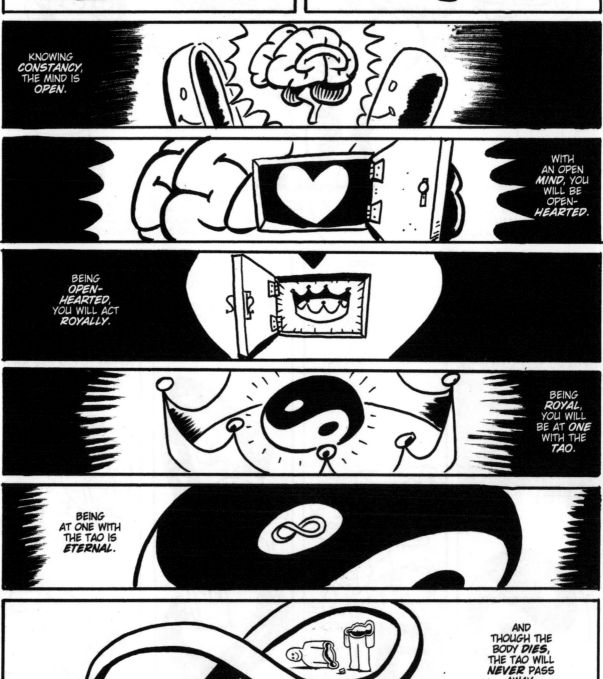

KNOWING *CONSTANCY,* THE MIND IS *OPEN.*

WITH AN OPEN *MIND,* YOU WILL BE OPEN-HEARTED.

BEING *OPEN-HEARTED,* YOU WILL ACT *ROYALLY.*

BEING *ROYAL,* YOU WILL BE AT *ONE* WITH THE *TAO.*

BEING AT ONE WITH THE TAO IS *ETERNAL.*

AND THOUGH THE BODY *DIES,* THE TAO WILL *NEVER* PASS AWAY.

TAO TE CHING LAO TZU FRED VAN LENTE & RYAN DUNLAVEY

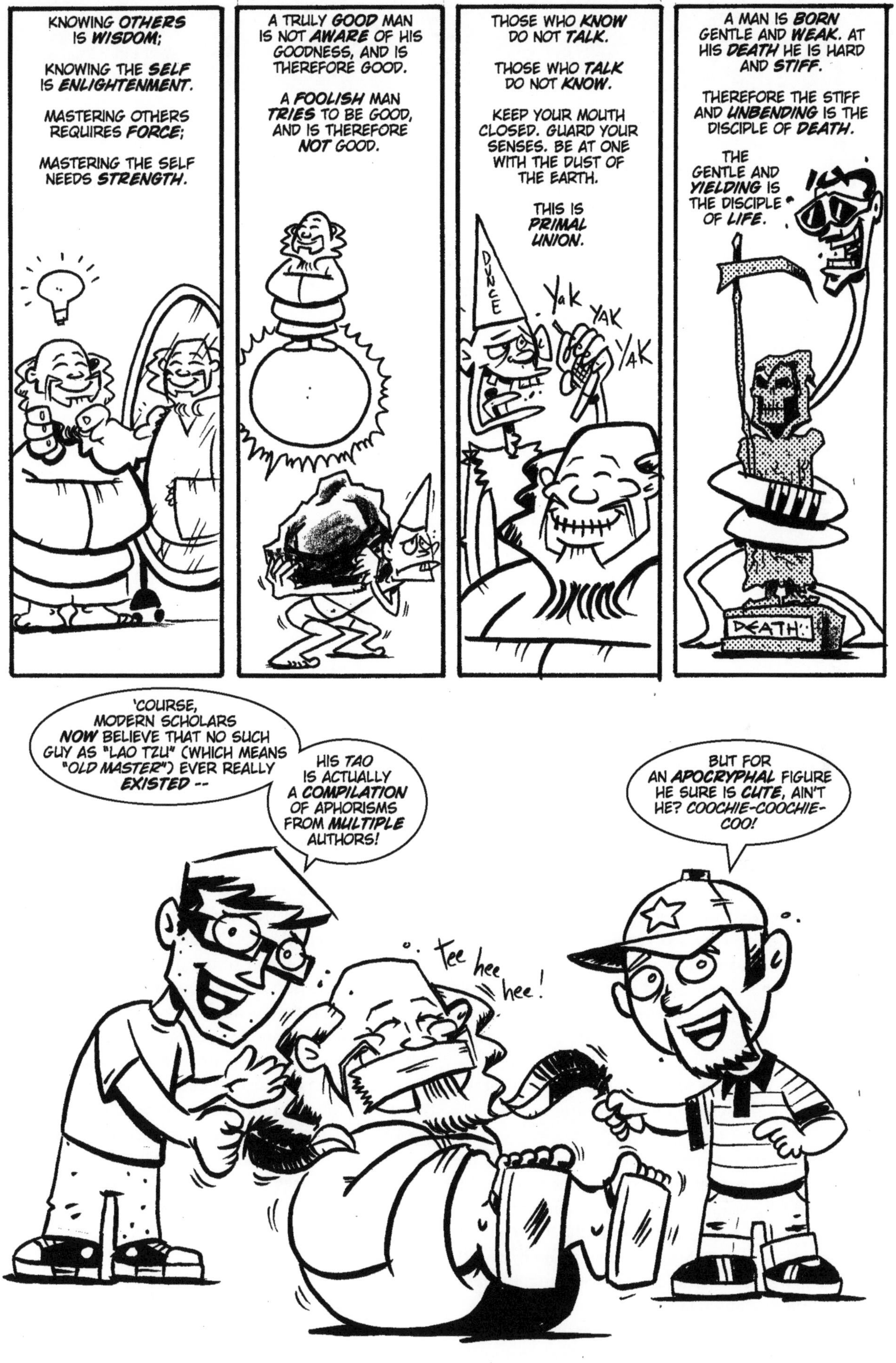

KNOWING OTHERS IS WISDOM;
KNOWING THE SELF IS ENLIGHTENMENT.
MASTERING OTHERS REQUIRES FORCE;
MASTERING THE SELF NEEDS STRENGTH.
A TRULY GOOD MAN IS NOT AWARE OF HIS GOODNESS, AND IS THEREFORE GOOD.
A FOOLISH MAN TRIES TO BE GOOD, AND IS THEREFORE NOT GOOD.
THOSE WHO KNOW DO NOT TALK.
THOSE WHO TALK DO NOT KNOW.
KEEP YOUR MOUTH CLOSED. GUARD YOUR SENSES. BE AT ONE WITH THE DUST OF THE EARTH.
THIS IS PRIMAL UNION.
DUNCE
YAK YAK YAK
A MAN IS BORN GENTLE AND WEAK. AT HIS DEATH HE IS HARD AND STIFF.
THEREFORE THE STIFF AND UNBENDING IS THE DISCIPLE OF DEATH.
THE GENTLE AND YIELDING IS THE DISCIPLE OF LIFE.
DEATH:
'COURSE, MODERN SCHOLARS NOW BELIEVE THAT NO SUCH GUY AS "LAO TZU" (WHICH MEANS "OLD MASTER") EVER REALLY EXISTED --
HIS TAO IS ACTUALLY A COMPILATION OF APHORISMS FROM MULTIPLE AUTHORS!
BUT FOR AN APOCRYPHAL FIGURE HE SURE IS CUTE, AIN'T HE? COOCHIE-COOCHIE-COO!
Tee hee hee!

Mahabharata

Vyasa

ART / ADAPTATION BY **Matt Wiegle**

***MAHABHARATA* IS ONE OF THE TWO MAIN EPIC** poems from ancient India. And when I say "epic," I mean it. This is the world's longest poem, easily outdoing *The Odyssey*, *Beowulf*, *The Faerie Queene*, and *Paradise Lost*. More than 200,000 lines of verse burst with over 1.8 million words.

Like so much ancient literature, it started as shorter, unwritten works recited by storytellers and holy men. Sometime after 350 CE, the puzzle pieces were assembled, codified, and written down in Sanskrit. (The authorship of *Mahabharata* is traditionally ascribed to the Hindu sage Vyasa, who also appears in the poem.) Professor James L. Fitzgerald of Brown University—who is editing an English-language translation of the entire *Mahabharata* directly from Sanskrit—summarizes the titanic work:

> The innermost narrative kernel of the *Mahābhārata* tells the story of two sets of paternal first cousins—the five sons of the deceased King Pāṇḍu (the five Pāṇḍavas) and the one hundred sons of blind King Dhṛtarāṣṭra (the 100 hundred Dhārtarāṣṭras)—who became bitter rivals, and opposed each other in war for possession of the ancestral Bharata kingdom with its capital in the "City of the Elephant," Hāstinapura, on the Gaṅgā river in north central India. What is dramatically interesting within this simple opposition is

the large number of individual agendas the many characters pursue, and the numerous personal conflicts, ethical puzzles, subplots, and plot twists that give the story a strikingly powerful development.

Adding to the weight of the events, the Pāṇḍavas were actually fathered by gods, while the Dhārtarāṣṭras are demon-spawn, and then there's the presence of the blue-skinned Lord Krishna, an avatar of the god Vishnu. *Mahabharata* is one of the backbones of Hinduism and greatly influenced other Eastern religions as well.

A few pages is enough room to present just a slice of a sliver of this sprawling story. Matt Wiegle zeroes in on an episode ("The House of Lac") taking place well before the climactic eighteen-day war, during the years when the Dhārtarāṣṭras relentlessly persecuted and abused the Pāṇḍavas. The 2010 Ignatz Award–winner for Promising New Talent, Wiegle uses color and panel structure ingeniously in this tale of a planned massacre.

SOURCE

The Mahābhārata: The Great Epic of India (website). Maintained by James L. Fitzgerald, Ph.D. [www.brown.edu/Departments/Sanskrit_in_Classics_at_Brown/Mahabharata/]

The House of Lac

FROM THE MAHABHARATA, ATTRIBUTED TO VYASA; ADAPTED BY MATT WIEGLE

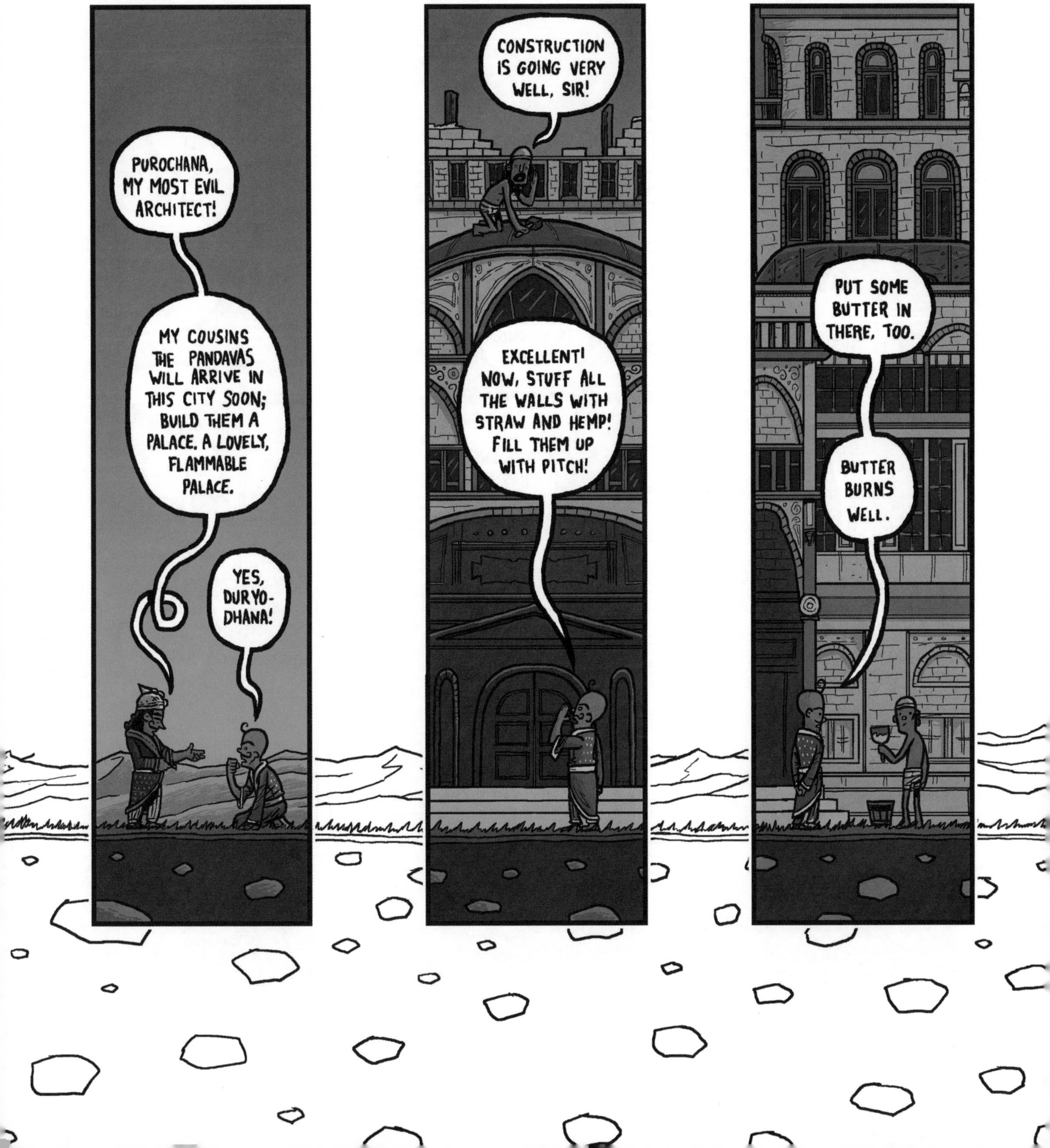
PUROCHANA, MY MOST EVIL ARCHITECT!
MY COUSINS THE PANDAVAS WILL ARRIVE IN THIS CITY SOON; BUILD THEM A PALACE. A LOVELY, FLAMMABLE PALACE.
YES, DURYO-DHANA!
CONSTRUCTION IS GOING VERY WELL, SIR!
EXCELLENT! NOW, STUFF ALL THE WALLS WITH STRAW AND HEMP! FILL THEM UP WITH PITCH!
PUT SOME BUTTER IN THERE, TOO.
BUTTER BURNS WELL.

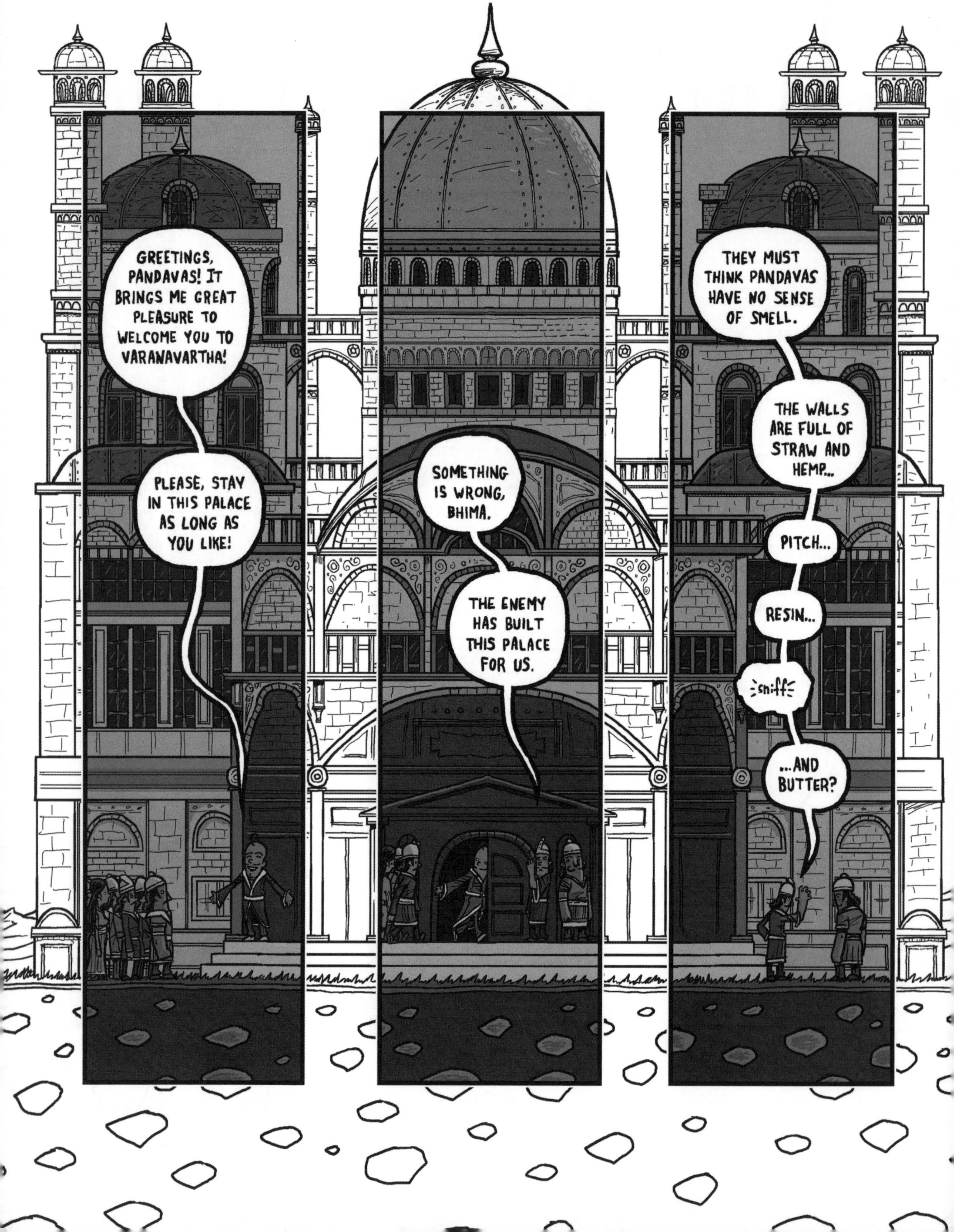
GREETINGS, PANDAVAS! IT BRINGS ME GREAT PLEASURE TO WELCOME YOU TO VARANAVARTHA!
PLEASE, STAY IN THIS PALACE AS LONG AS YOU LIKE!
SOMETHING IS WRONG, BHIMA.
THE ENEMY HAS BUILT THIS PALACE FOR US.
THEY MUST THINK PANDAVAS HAVE NO SENSE OF SMELL.
THE WALLS ARE FULL OF STRAW AND HEMP...
PITCH...
RESIN...
sniff
...AND BUTTER?

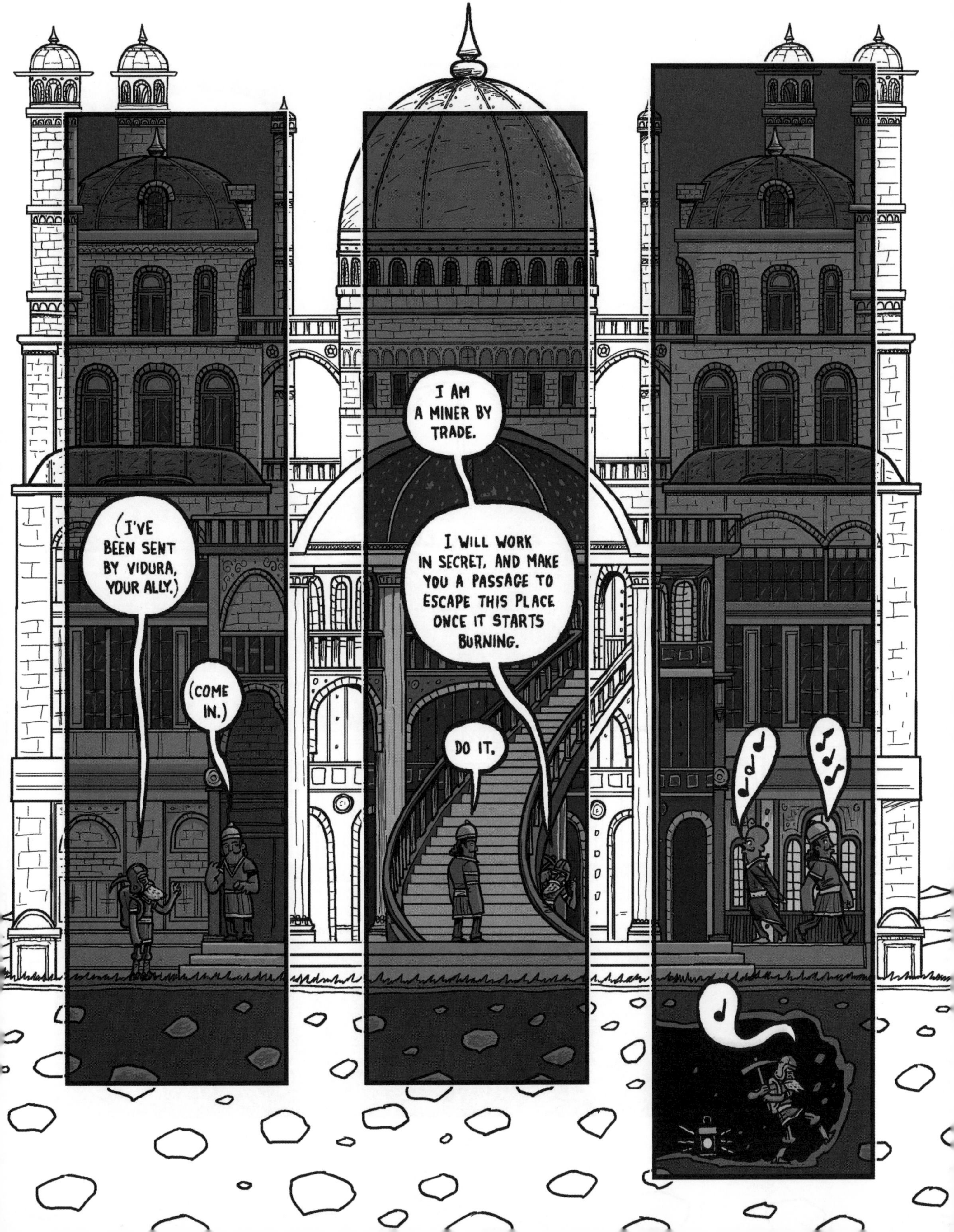
(I'VE BEEN SENT BY VIDURA, YOUR ALLY.)
(COME IN.)
I AM A MINER BY TRADE.
I WILL WORK IN SECRET, AND MAKE YOU A PASSAGE TO ESCAPE THIS PLACE ONCE IT STARTS BURNING.
DO IT.

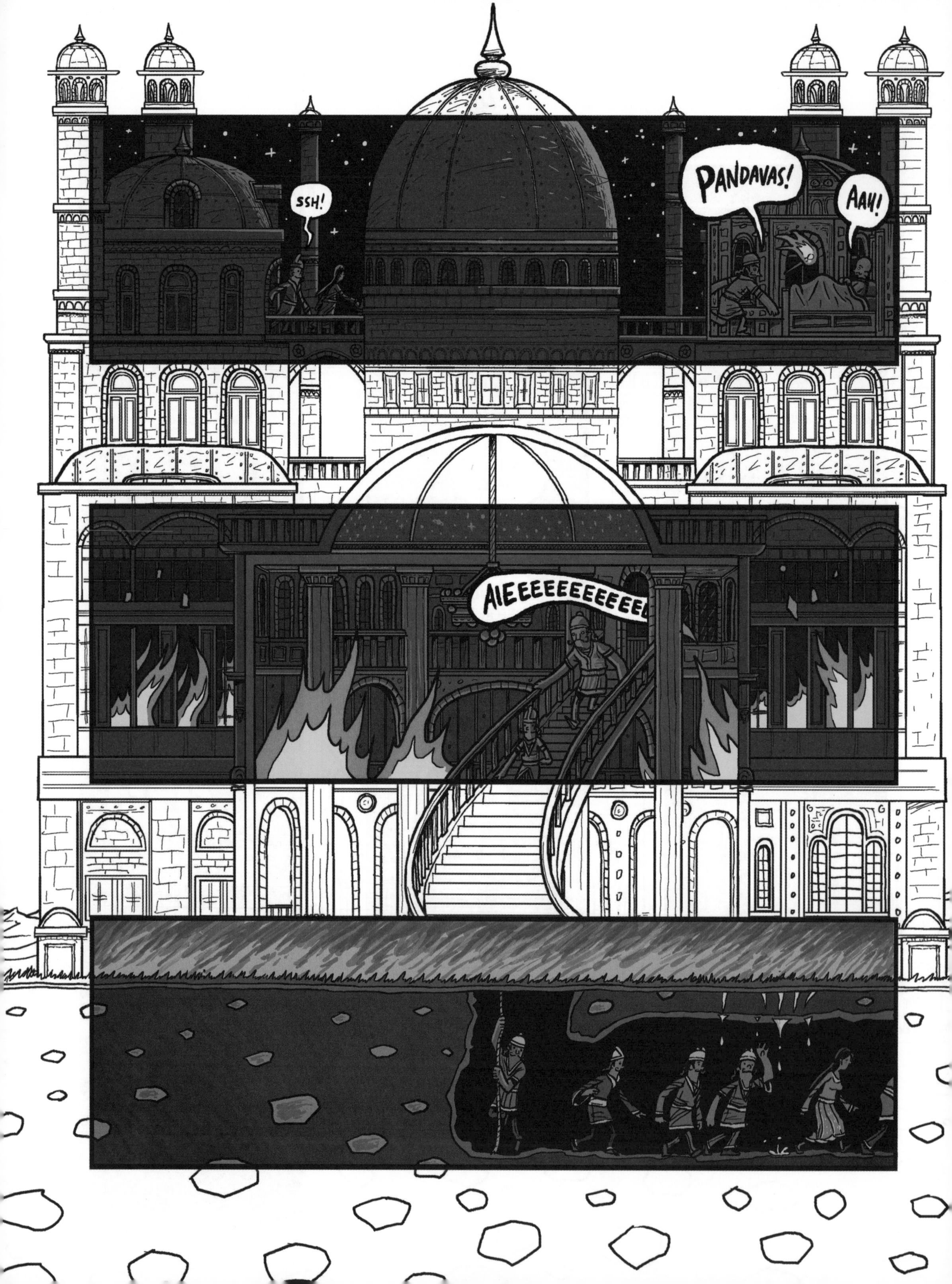
SSH!
PANDAVAS!
AAH!
AIEEEEEEEEEEEE

Analects and Other Writings

Confucius

ADAPTATION BY **Fred Van Lente**

ART BY **Ryan Dunlavey**

LIKE OTHER ANCIENT WRITERS SUCH AS HOMER and Lao Tzu, Confucius may or may not have actually existed. He's traditionally said to have been born in 551 BCE to a family of the lowest-ranking nobility. Regardless of his flesh-and-blood reality, though, the works ascribed to him and his pupils (as authors or compilers) are the most influential books in the history of China. History professor Michael Nylan writes that Confucianism's Five Classics "once occupied in East Asia a position roughly analogous to the Bible in the West."

The *Analects* is a record of the pithy sayings Confucius rained upon his disciples during their conversations concerning right, virtuous action in regard to learning, ruling, teaching, dealing with one's parents, and living in general. Meanwhile, the works known as the Five Classics (which Confucius and his disciples *may* have had a hand in compiling and editing) incorporate folksongs, hymns, myths, a court diary, philosophical statements, rules of conduct, tips on government, and, most famously, the *I Ching* (*The Book of Changes*), a divination manual.

As part of their indispensable *Action Philosophers!* series, Fred Van Lente and Ryan Dunlavey introduce us to Master Kong (the literal meaning of the name "Confucius").

THOUGH KNOWN IN THE WEST AS *CONFUCIUS* (551-479 B.C.), THIS LEGENDARY CHINESE THINKER IS BETTER KNOWN IN HIS NATIVE LAND AS *KONGZI*, WHICH LITERALLY TRANSLATES TO...

MASTER KONG

WHAT LITTLE IS KNOWN OF CONFUCIUS'S LIFE SUGGESTS HE SERVED AS A *SHI*, OR MIDDLE-CLASS *RETAINER*, DURING CHINA'S "DAYS OF SPRING AND AUTUMN" (800-400 B.C.) ...

...WHEN PETTY *TRIBAL KINGS* WARRED OVER THE FRAGMENTS OF THE COLLAPSED *ZHOU* DYNASTY.

THESE *FEUDAL THUGS* WERE EAGER TO ADD LEGITIMACY AND RESPECTABILITY TO THEIR REIGNS BY LEARNING THE COURT ETIQUETTE AND DIPLOMATIC PROTOCOL OF THE *ZHOUS* FROM ITERANT SCHOLARS LIKE CONFUCIUS.

CONFUCIUS'S TEACHINGS WERE COLLECTED IN THE *"FIVE CLASSICS"*, WHICH ULTIMATELY BECAME THE NATIONAL STANDARD OF TRADITIONAL *CHINESE ETHICS*.

AS EARLY AS 136 B.C., THE *FIVE CLASSICS* WERE *MANDATORY* READING FOR *ALL* WOULD-BE CIVIL SERVANTS.

CENTRAL TO CONFUCIAN THOUGHT IS THE IDEA THAT THE MANDATE OF *TIAN* ("HEAVEN") IS THE SAME AS MORAL GOOD...

...BUT ONLY THROUGH *HUMAN AGENCY* MAY THAT MANDATE BE ACTUALIZED HERE ON EARTH!

THUS, CONFUCIANISM IS FUNDAMENTALLY *DIDACTIC*, REINFORCING AESTHETIC, MORAL AND SOCIAL *ORDER* VIA *LI*, OR RITUAL PROPRIETY.

GOOD *MANNERS*, FOR INSTANCE, SATISFY ALL THREE FORMS OF ORDER: THEY *LOOK* GOOD (AESTHETIC), AND THEY MAKE YOU *FEEL* GOOD (MORAL) BECAUSE THEY MAKE *OTHERS* FEEL GOOD (SOCIAL).

KEEPING IN MIND THIS IDEA OF *CONTINUITY* OF *ORDER*, THEN, IT SHOULD COME AS NO SURPRISE TO LEARN THAT CONFUCIUS UPHELD *OBEDIENCE* TO ONE'S *ELDERS* (*XIAO*, OR "FILIAL PIETY") AS THE *HIGHEST* VIRTUE.

IN THE FIRST BOOK OF HIS *ANALECTS* CONFUCIUS WRITES, "OBSERVE WHAT A PERSON HAS IN MIND TO DO WHEN HIS FATHER IS *ALIVE*, AND THEN OBSERVE WHAT HE DOES WHEN HIS FATHER IS *DEAD*."

"IF, FOR *THREE YEARS*, HE MAKES *NO* CHANGES TO HIS FATHER'S WAYS, HE CAN BE SAID TO BE A *GOOD SON*."

THERE'S A *TRICKLE-DOWN* EFFECT TO ALL THIS FILIAL PIETY: A GOOD SON WILL BE A GOOD FATHER AND LIKEWISE RAISE A GOOD SON.

A GOOD *MONARCH* WILL ALLOW HIS *GOODNESS* TO FLOW OUT TO HIS *SUBJECTS*.

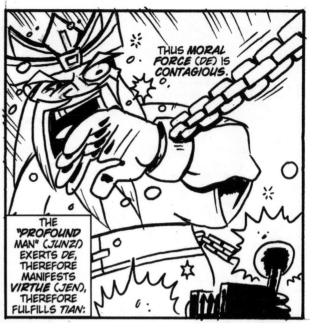

THUS *MORAL FORCE* (DE) IS CONTAGIOUS.

THE "*PROFOUND MAN*" (JUNZI) EXERTS DE, THEREFORE MANIFESTS *VIRTUE* (JEN), THEREFORE FULFILLS *TIAN*:

"THE PROFOUND MAN ... DOES NOT SET HIS MIND EITHER *FOR* ANYTHING, OR *AGAINST* ANYTHING; WHAT IS *RIGHT* HE WILL FOLLOW," WRITES CONFUCIUS.

BUT THE *XIAOREN*, THE *SMALL* MAN, HE'S NOT WITH THE PROGRAM:

"THE PROFOUND MAN UNDERSTANDS WHAT IS *MORAL*; THE SMALL MAN UNDERSTANDS WHAT IS *PROFITABLE*." (ANALECTS 4:16)

"WHAT THE PROFOUND MAN SEEKS IS IN *HIMSELF*. WHAT THE SMALL MAN SEEKS IS IN *OTHERS*." (15:20)

SO WHAT'S THE *MORAL* OF MASTER KONG'S STORY? THAT'S RIGHT:

THE SMALL MAN *SUCKS*.

The Book of Daniel
from the Hebrew Bible
ART / ADAPTATION BY **Benjamin Frisch**

THE BOOK OF DANIEL IS A PART OF THE HEBREW Bible / Old Testament / Holy Bible, and, as such, it is considered sacred by Jews, Christians, and, less famously, Muslims. It's an anonymous work of ancient Israelite literature that most scholars date to 165/164 BCE, though believers say it's much older, from the sixth century BCE, written by Daniel himself during the events it describes. The first half relates the adventures of Daniel and three other royal Israelites from the Kingdom of Judah when King Nebuchadnezzar of Babylon conquers the land and forces them to serve in his court. Daniel is able to interpret the king's dreams, which earns him high standing. The second half of the book relates four prophetic visions from Daniel, making it the Old Testament precursor of the Book of Revelation.

The adaptation here is a self-contained episode from chapter three: Daniel's three young companions—Shadrach, Meshach, and Abednego—show the pagan Nebuchadnezzar the power of faith in the god of the Israelites. (In a parallel tale later in the book, Daniel is famously forced into a lion's den but walks out unhurt the next day, thanks again to divine intervention.) Benjamin Frisch—whose graphic novel *Ayn Rand's Adventures in Wonderland* was first published as a serial on the website Wonkette—has created a highly stylized adaptation with a luscious color scheme. Through the centuries, many illustrators of this story have depicted the young men as feminine (sometimes startlingly so), and Benjamin chose to keep this intriguing, androgynous convention.

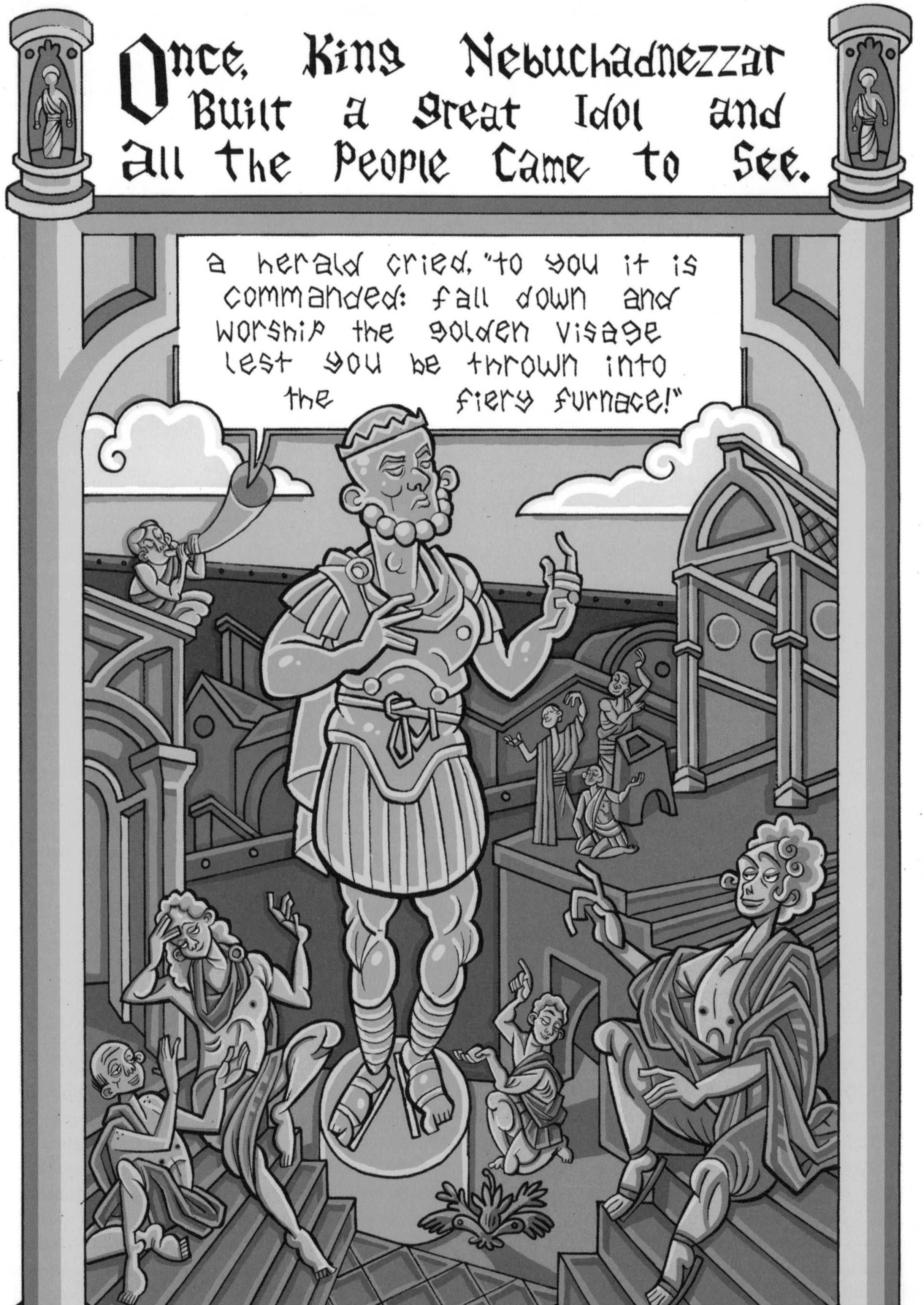
Once, King Nebuchadnezzar Built a Great Idol and All the People Came to See.
a herald cried, "to you it is commanded: fall down and worship the golden visage lest you be thrown into the fiery furnace!"
and all did fall down and worship.

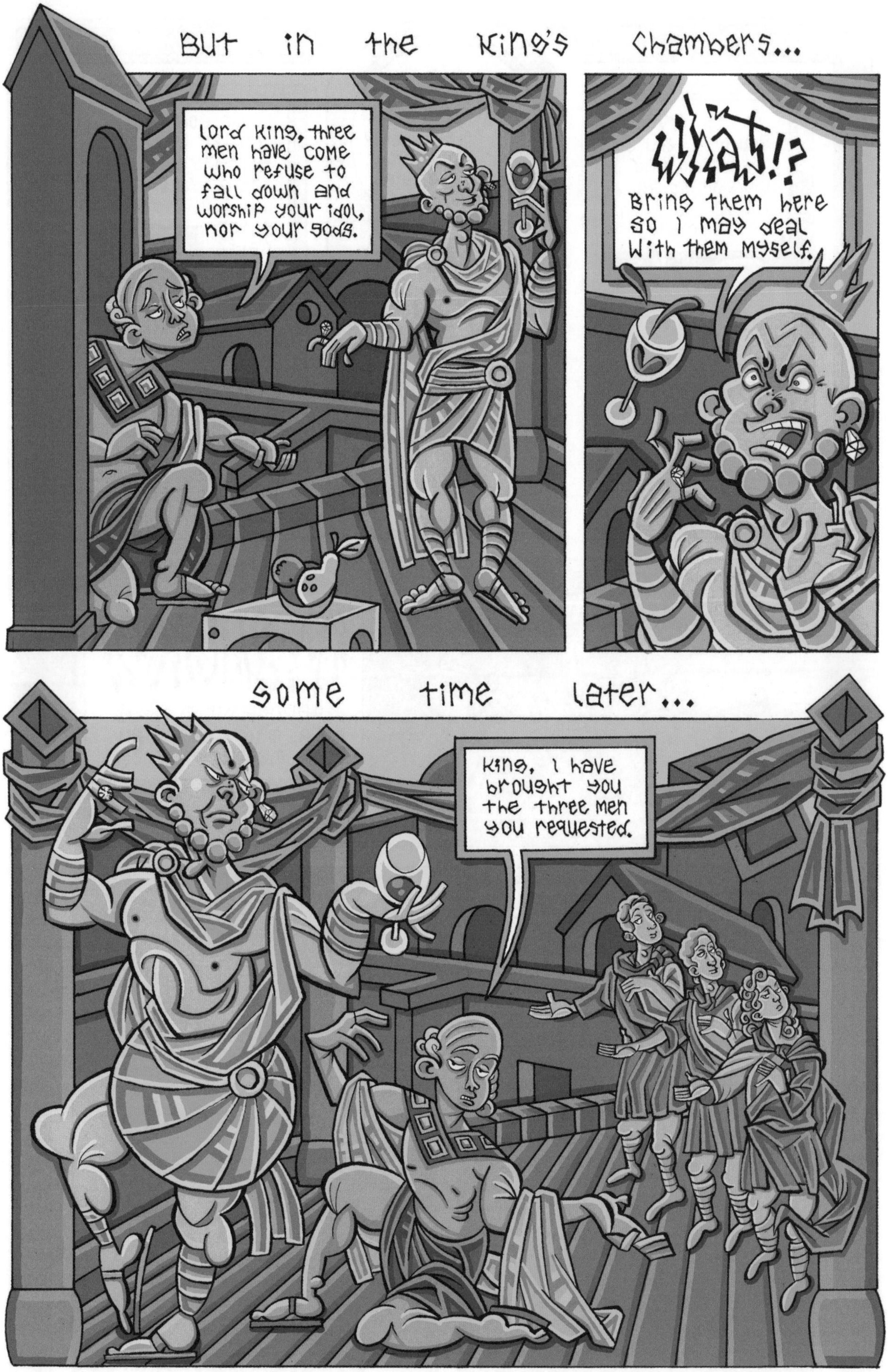
But in the King's Chambers...
Lord King, three men have come who refuse to fall down and worship your idol, nor your gods.
WHAT!?
Bring them here so I may deal With them Myself.
Some time later...
King, I have brought you the three men you requested.

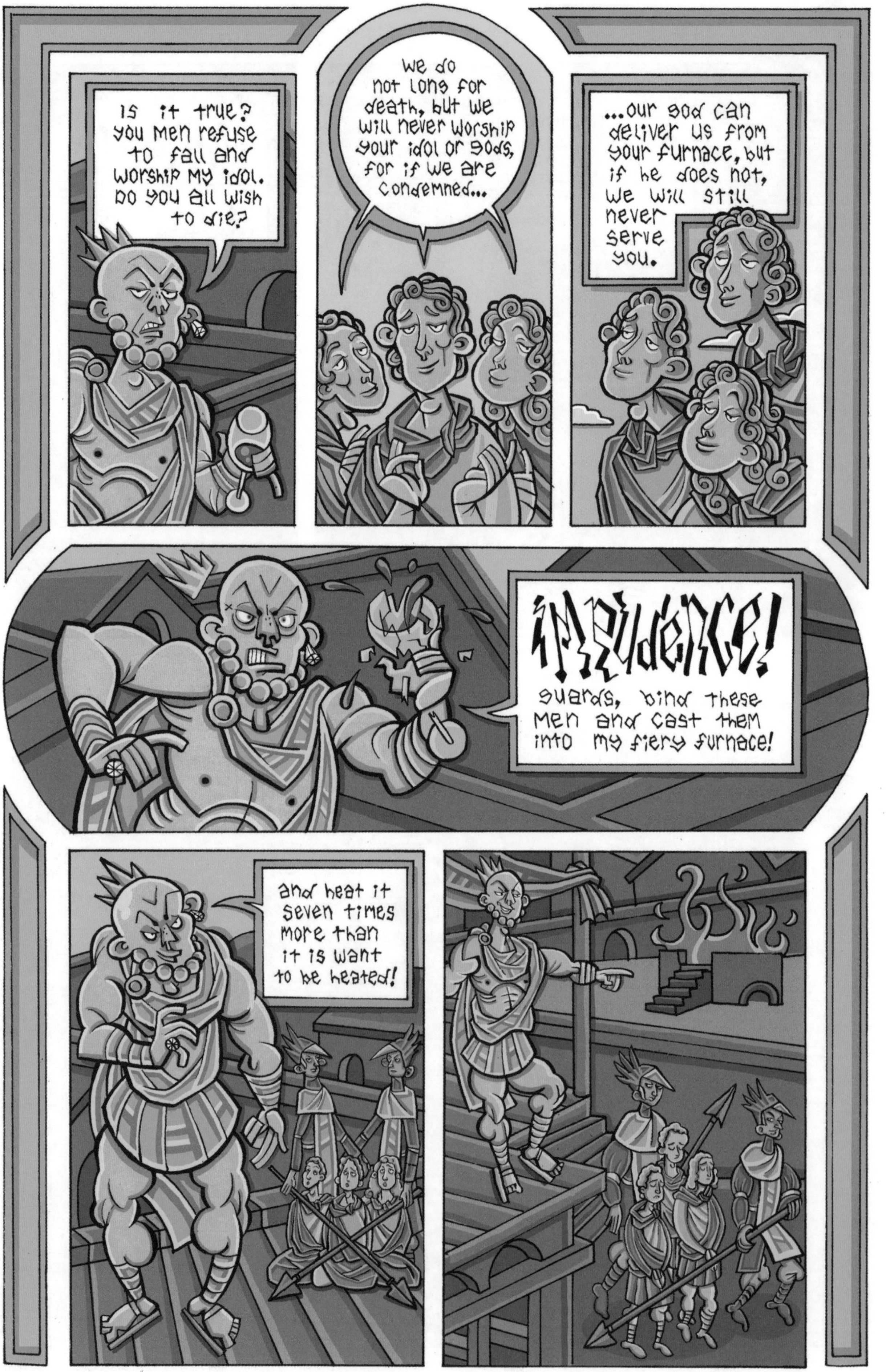
Is it true? You men refuse to fall and worship my idol. Do you all wish to die?
We do not long for death, but we will never worship your idol or gods, for if we are condemned...
...our God can deliver us from your furnace, but if he does not, we will still never serve you.
IMPUDENCE!
Guards, bind these men and cast them into my fiery furnace!
And heat it seven times more than it is want to be heated!

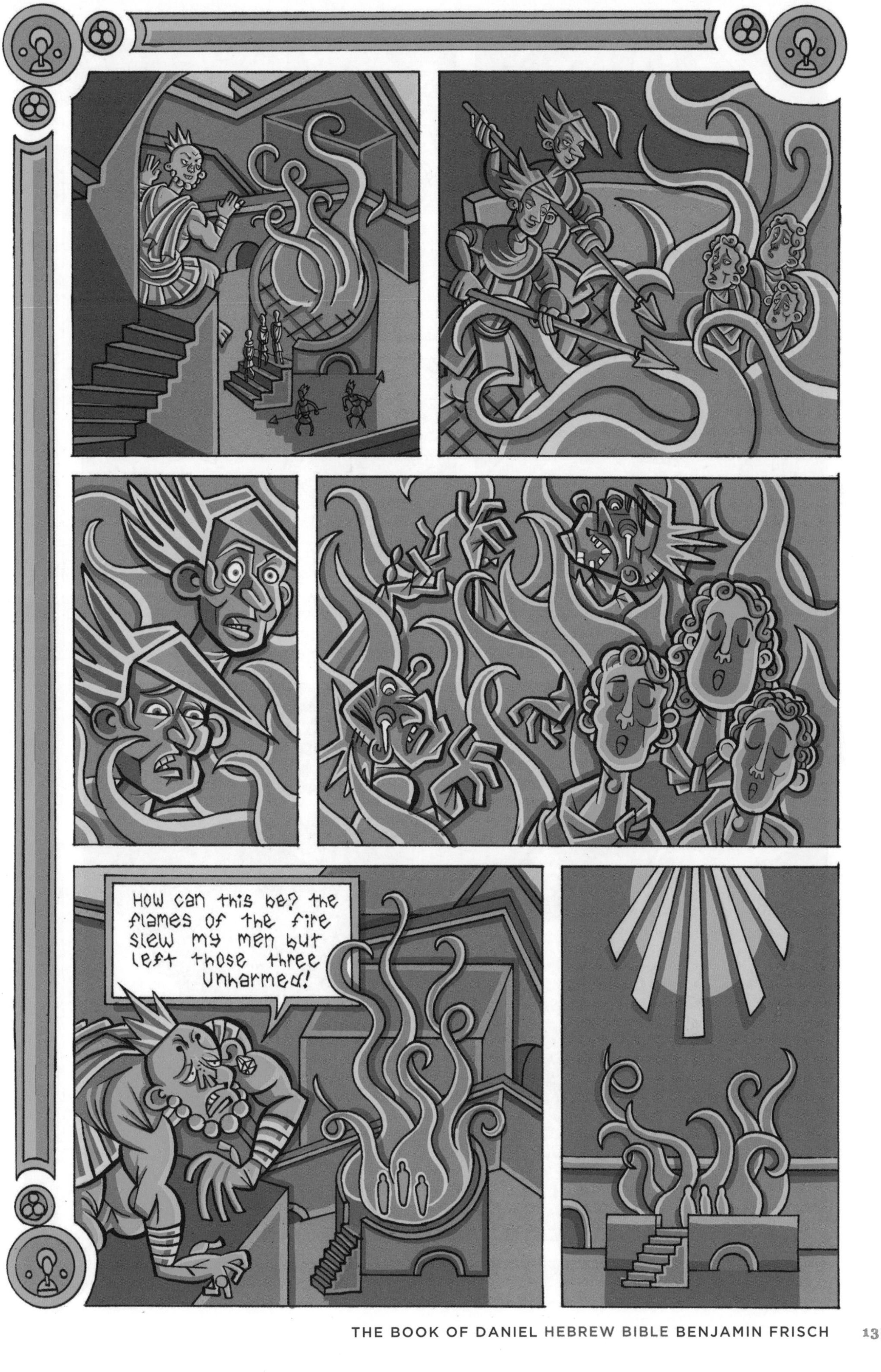
How can this be? the flames of the fire slew my men but left those three unharmed!

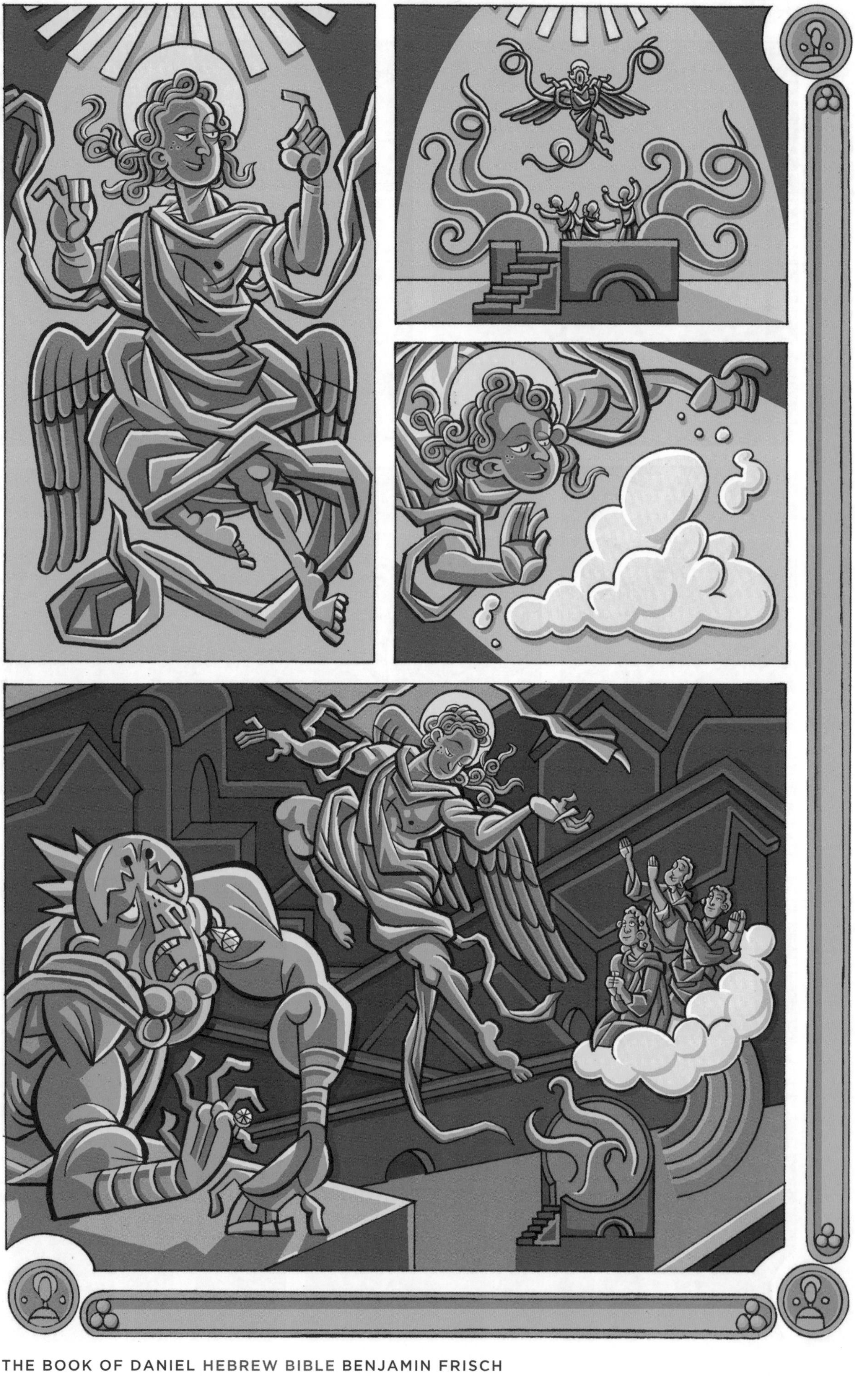

and all the people being gathered together saw these men, upon whose bodies the fire had no power. The King was astonished, and he made a great decree.

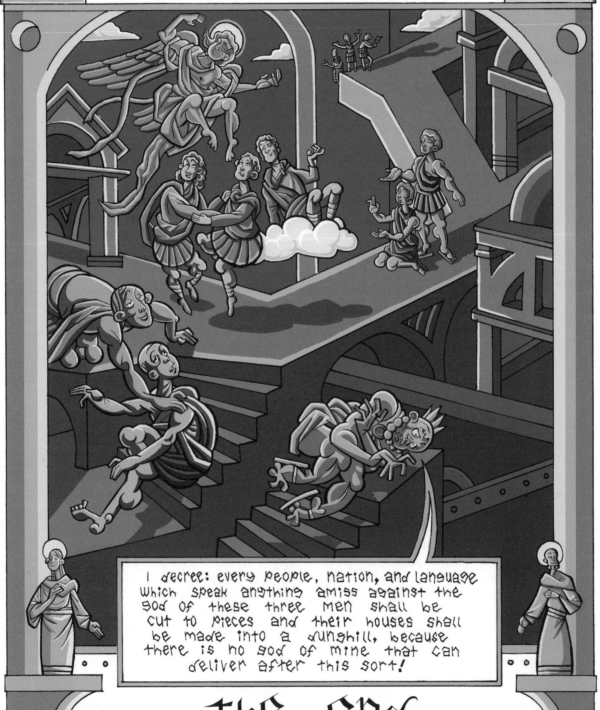

I decree: every people, nation, and language which speak anything amiss against the god of these three men shall be cut to pieces and their houses shall be made into a dunghill, because there is no god of mine that can deliver after this sort!

the end.

◆ The Three Youths and the Fiery Furnace ◆
By Benjamin Frisch

On the Nature of Things

Lucretius

ART / ADAPTATION BY **Tom Biby**

AND **Jonathan Fetter-Vorm**

(A.K.A. **Two Fine Chaps**)

IT'S NOT EVERY MAJOR PHILOSOPHICAL WORK that's written as an epic poem. In fact, it's not many at all. Some people shoehorn the *Tao Te Ching*, *The Divine Comedy*, and *Faust* into this category, but really, if we're talking about long expository essays on philosophy, written in verse, there's only *On the Nature of Things* (*De rerum natura*) and a small number of extremely obscure works.

Lucretius—a Roman living in the first century BCE—wrote his 7,400-line poem to explain Epicurianism, the philosophy that advocates minimizing physical pain and emotional strife and maximizing an easygoing tranquility. But Lucretius focuses less on how life should be lived and more on the physics espoused by Epicureanism, its explanation of the structure of the universe, the earth, the human body, and so on. He discusses atoms and evolution, the soul and death, storms and earthquakes, love and friendship, language and the physical senses, and a whole lot more, painting vivid pictures of the human condition and of natural phenomena at all levels.

Tom Biby and Jonathan Fetter-Vorm, working as Two Fine Chaps, create and publish beautiful illustrated versions of classic literature printed in very small runs. Their exquisite oblong booklet for *On the Nature of Things* opens to a two-panel spread, then unfolds to a jaw-dropping four-panel spread. A mere 200 individually numbered copies were produced, and I'm delighted to be able to reproduce the artwork in full here. The artists chose to work with the final part of Book Two, explaining that they "have framed the ancient poet's text with modern imagery and metaphors. Here is Lucretius' tale of the earth overtaxed and of lands too choked to bear fruit, retold with a twist: from the perspective of American farmers during the Great Depression."

SOURCE

Sedley, David. "Lucretius." *The Stanford Encyclopedia of Philosophy (Fall 2008 Edition)*. Edward N. Zalta (ed.) http://plato.stanford.edu/archives/fall2008/entries/lucretius/

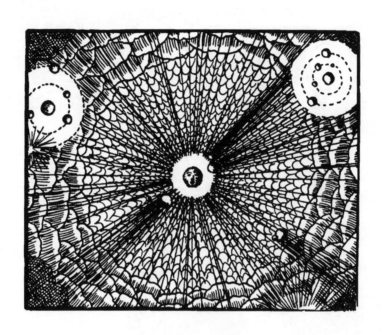

AND SINCE THAT TIME

when the world was born, since the day that birthed both sea and earth, & since the sun first rose, many bodies have been added from outside, many seeds added all around, a knot of bodies tossed together by the great expanse . . .

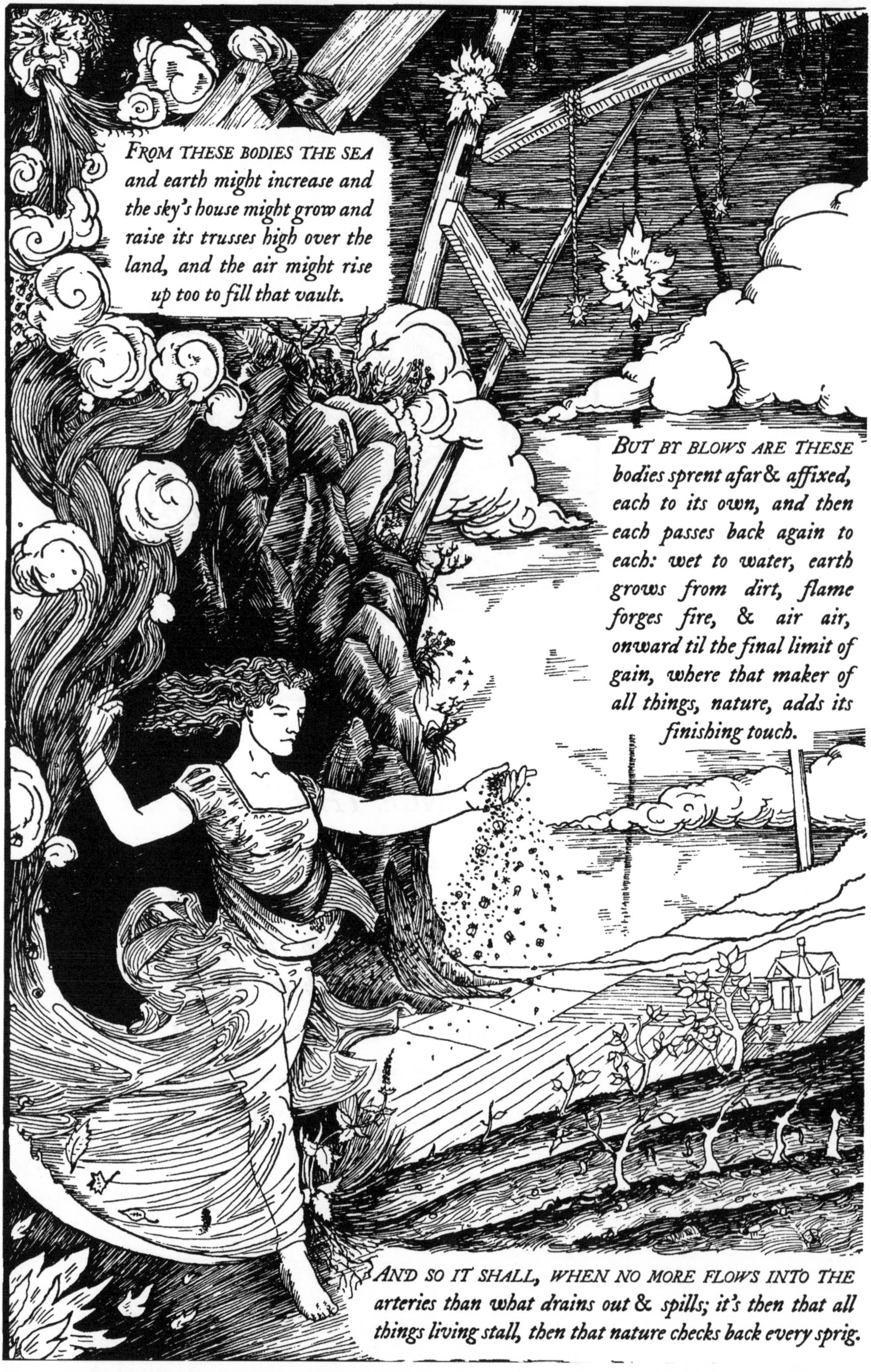
FROM THESE BODIES THE SEA and earth might increase and the sky's house might grow and raise its trusses high over the land, and the air might rise up too to fill that vault.
BUT BY BLOWS ARE THESE bodies sprent afar & affixed, each to its own, and then each passes back again to each: wet to water, earth grows from dirt, flame forges fire, & air air, onward til the final limit of gain, where that maker of all things, nature, adds its finishing touch.
AND SO IT SHALL, WHEN NO MORE FLOWS INTO THE arteries than what drains out & spills; it's then that all things living stall, then that nature checks back every sprig.

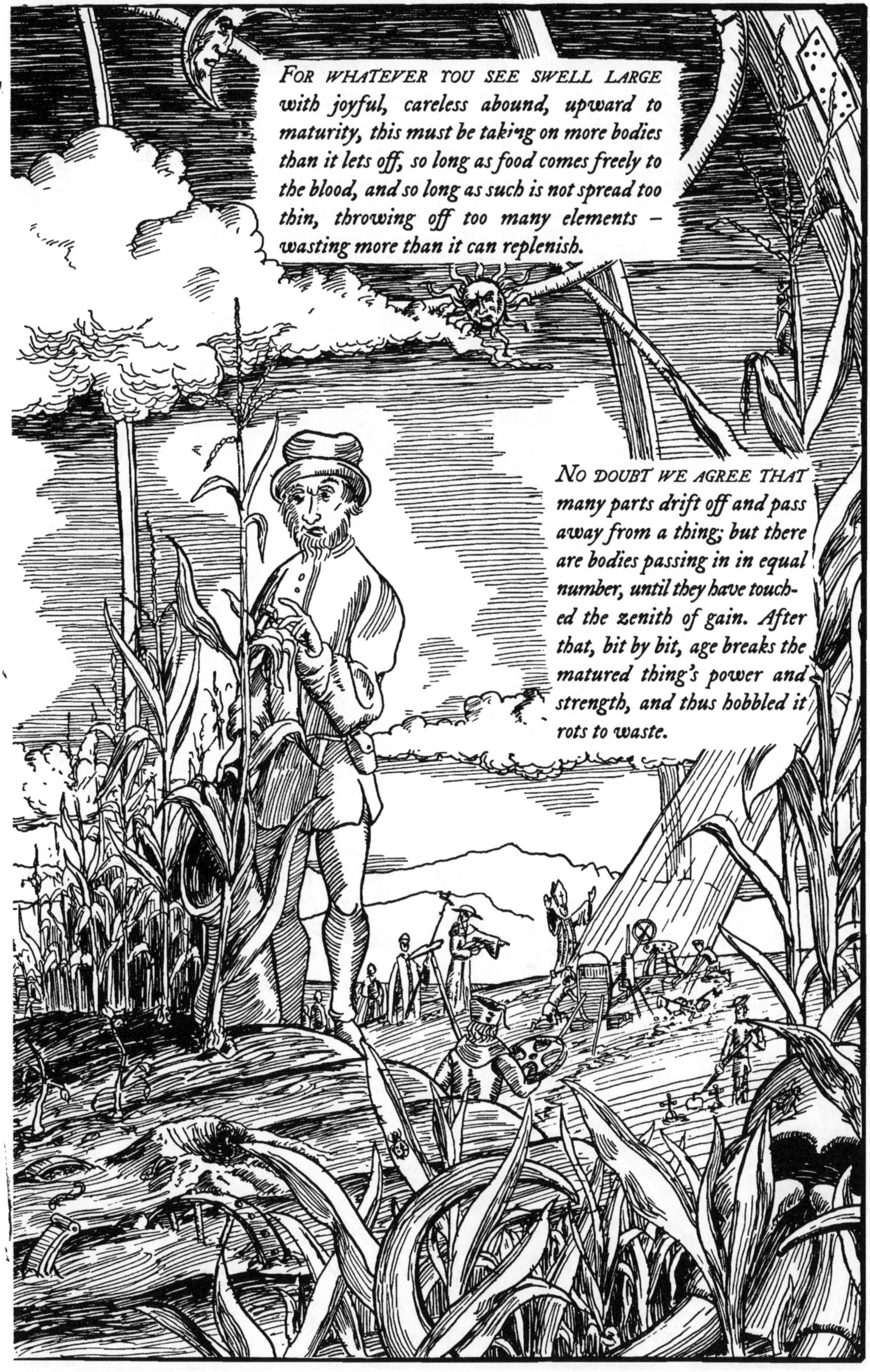
FOR WHATEVER YOU SEE SWELL LARGE with joyful, careless abound, upward to maturity, this must be taking on more bodies than it lets off, so long as food comes freely to the blood, and so long as such is not spread too thin, throwing off too many elements – wasting more than it can replenish.
NO DOUBT WE AGREE THAT many parts drift off and pass away from a thing; but there are bodies passing in in equal number, until they have touched the zenith of gain. After that, bit by bit, age breaks the matured thing's power and strength, and thus hobbled it rots to waste.

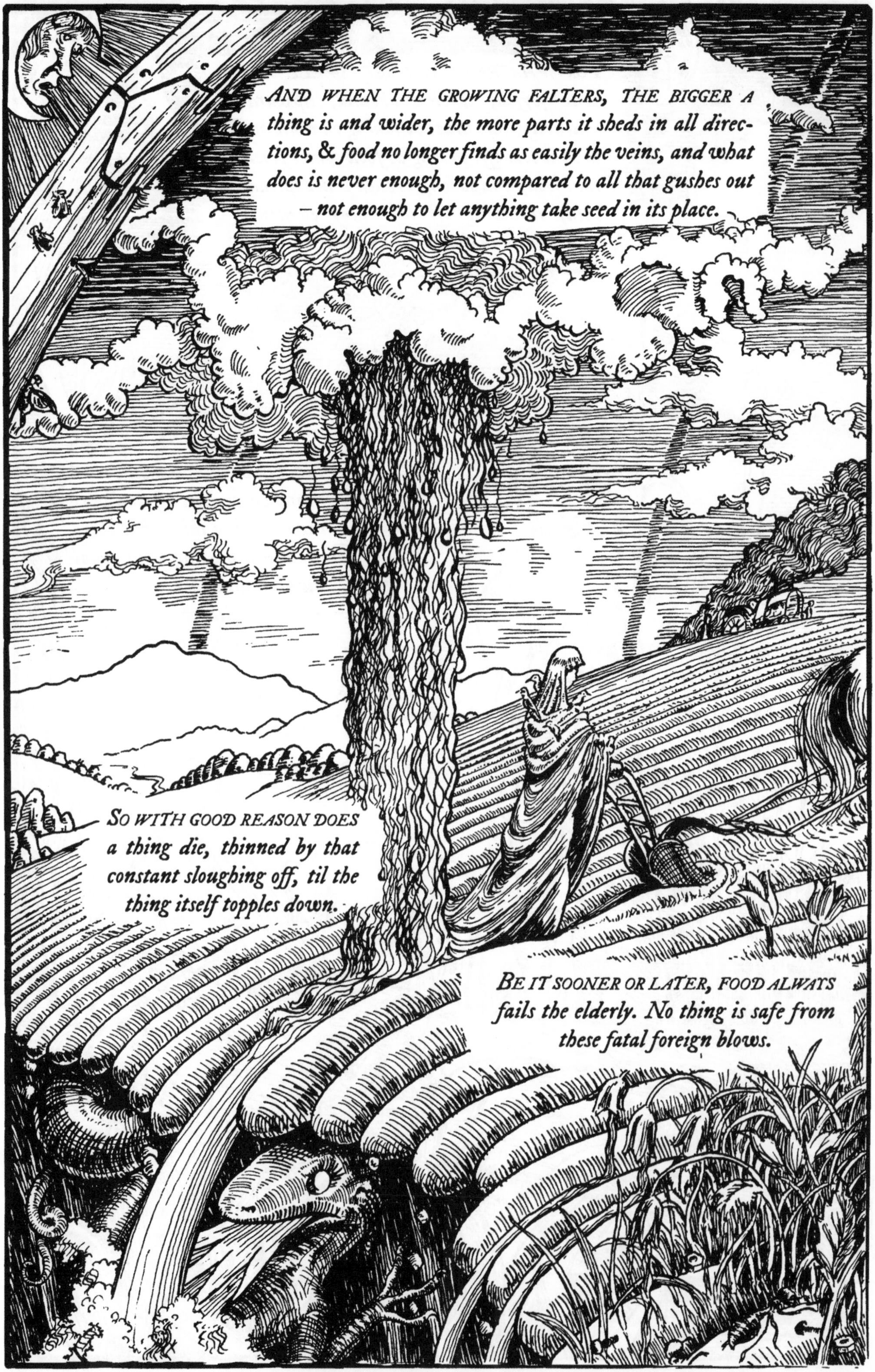
AND WHEN THE GROWING FALTERS, THE BIGGER A thing is and wider, the more parts it sheds in all directions, & food no longer finds as easily the veins, and what does is never enough, not compared to all that gushes out – not enough to let anything take seed in its place.
SO WITH GOOD REASON DOES a thing die, thinned by that constant sloughing off, til the thing itself topples down.
BE IT SOONER OR LATER, FOOD ALWAYS fails the elderly. No thing is safe from these fatal foreign blows.

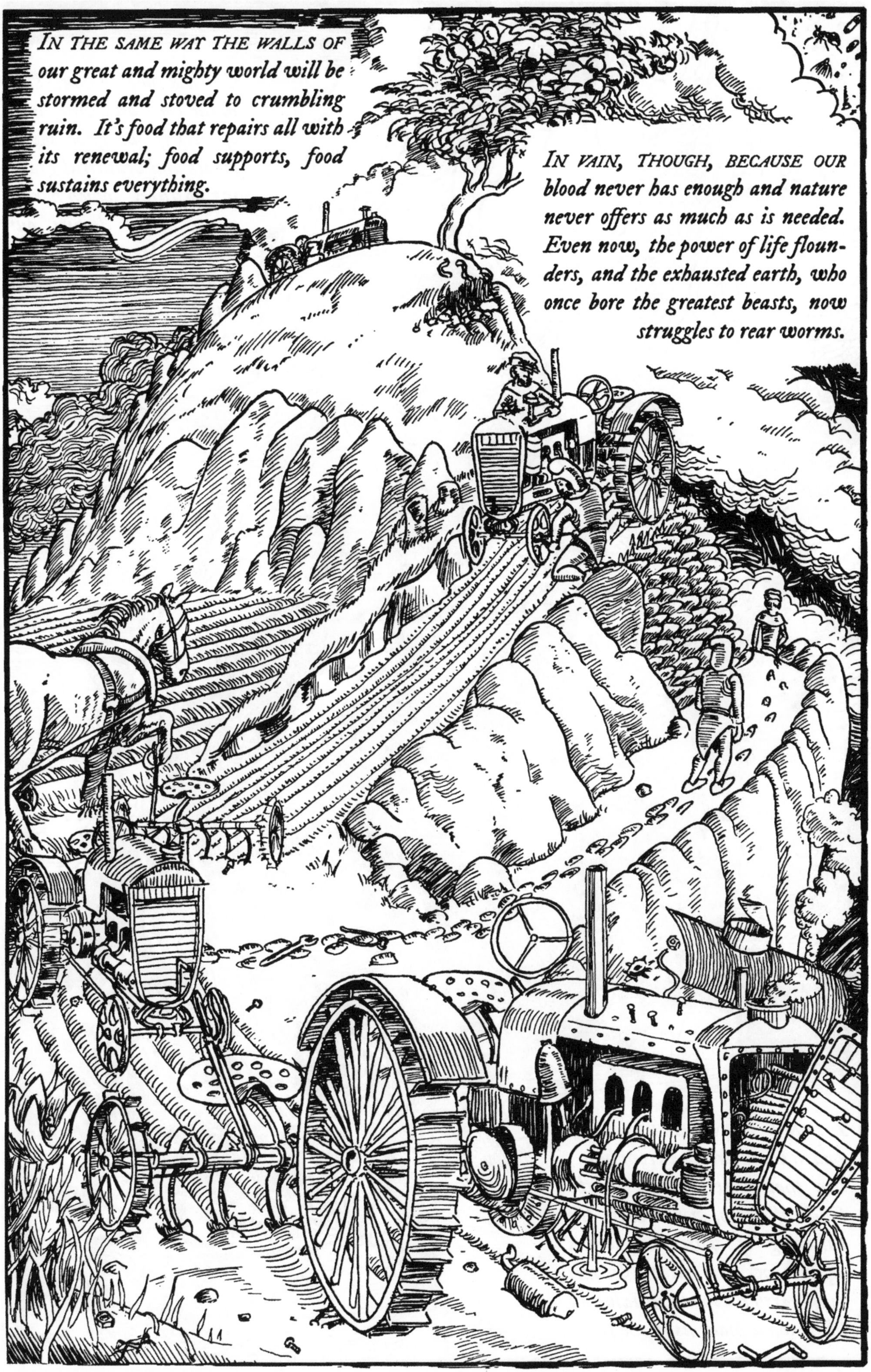
In the same way the walls of our great and mighty world will be stormed and stoved to crumbling ruin. It's food that repairs all with its renewal; food supports, food sustains everything.
In vain, though, because our blood never has enough and nature never offers as much as is needed. Even now, the power of life flounders, and the exhausted earth, who once bore the greatest beasts, now struggles to rear worms.

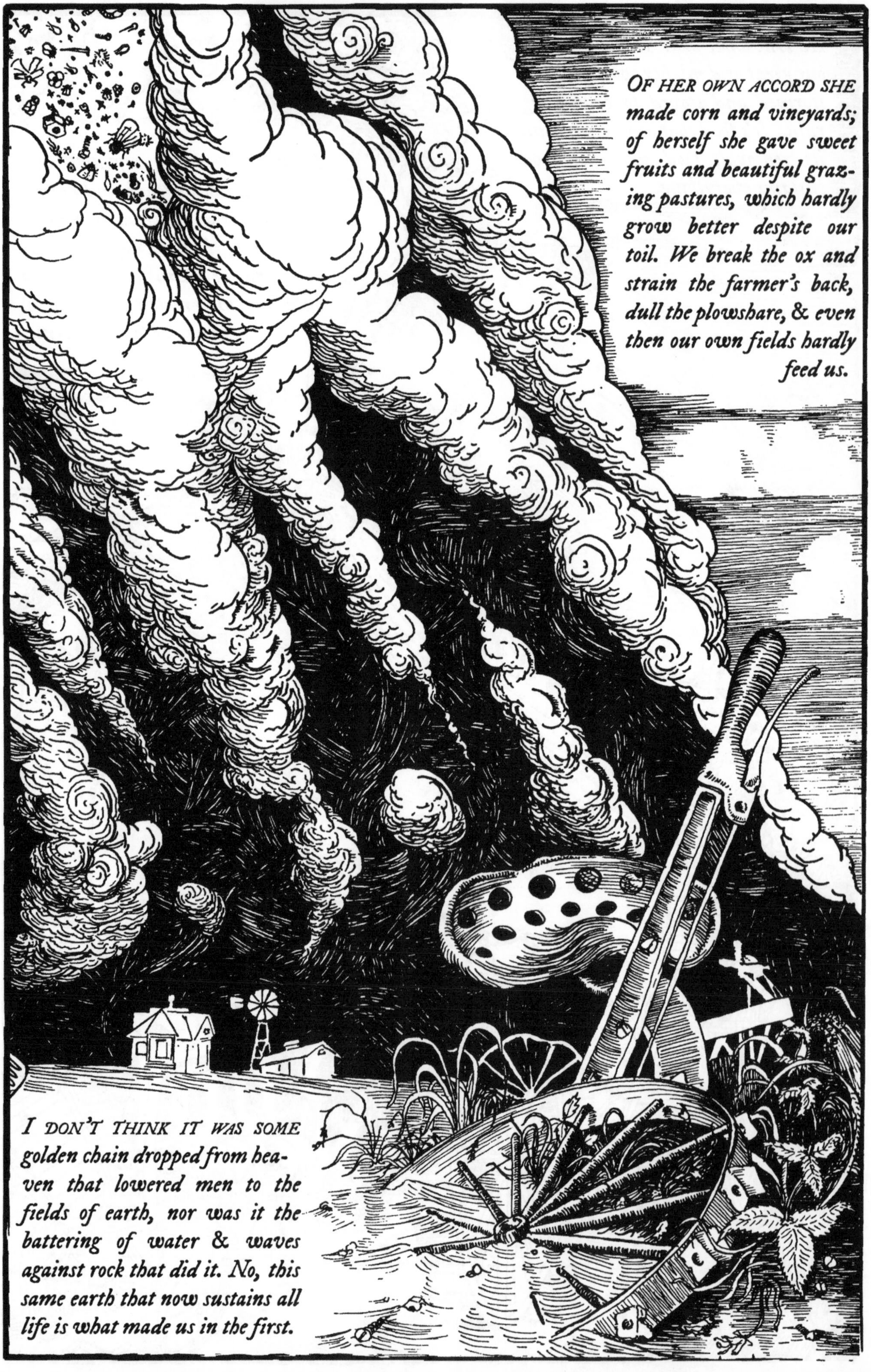
OF HER OWN ACCORD SHE made corn and vineyards; of herself she gave sweet fruits and beautiful grazing pastures, which hardly grow better despite our toil. We break the ox and strain the farmer's back, dull the plowshare, & even then our own fields hardly feed us.
I DON'T THINK IT WAS SOME golden chain dropped from heaven that lowered men to the fields of earth, nor was it the battering of water & waves against rock that did it. No, this same earth that now sustains all life is what made us in the first.

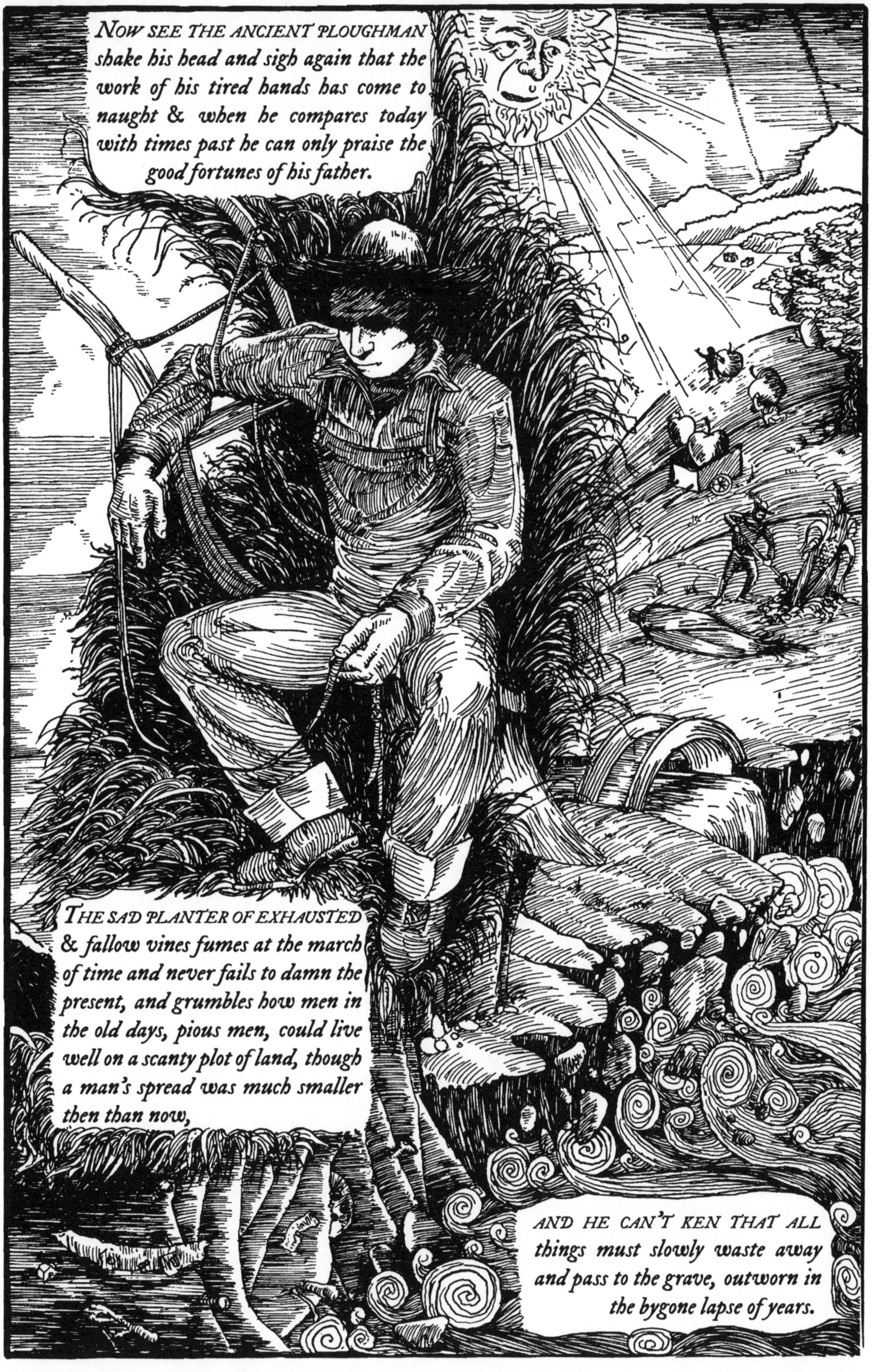
NOW SEE THE ANCIENT PLOUGHMAN shake his head and sigh again that the work of his tired hands has come to naught & when he compares today with times past he can only praise the good fortunes of his father.
THE SAD PLANTER OF EXHAUSTED & fallow vines fumes at the march of time and never fails to damn the present, and grumbles how men in the old days, pious men, could live well on a scanty plot of land, though a man's spread was much smaller then than now,
AND HE CAN'T KEN THAT ALL things must slowly waste away and pass to the grave, outworn in the bygone lapse of years.

Aeneid

Virgil

ART / ADAPTATION BY **Michael Lagocki**

AENEID **WAS COMMISSIONED BY EMPEROR** Augustus, who wanted an epic heroic poem based on Rome's founding myth. Whatever he paid, he ended up getting more than his money's worth. He gave the task to Virgil, who was already highly lauded for two book-length poems he had written. Virgil worked for ten years (29–19 BCE) on the 10,000-line poem; he had completed it but felt it still needed substantial revising when he fell ill. As he lay dying, he demanded that the manuscript be burned. Luckily, Augustus stepped in and rescued what is universally considered the supreme work of ancient Roman literature.

Aeneid picks up after *The Iliad* ends. As Troy burns—thanks to the Greek soldiers hidden in the wooden horse—the pious Trojan warrior Aeneas escapes the flames with his father, son, and some other citizens. Their perilous journey by sea to Italy (with other stops en route) is described in the first half of *Aeneid*. Along the way, ghosts, goddesses, and prophets tell Aeneas that he is destined to found a great city, a new Troy. Aeneas and a much smaller crew finally reach Italy, and their adventures there form the second half of *Aeneid*.

When I approached Dallas–Fort Worth artist Michael Lagocki specifically about adapting *Aeneid*, he had just returned from a trip the day before. He had been in *Rome*! I do love synchronicity. Michael managed to supercondense the long, complex tale into nine pages. The first three pages are essentially an overview of the sea voyage, while the remaining pages zoom in on the war between Aeneas' forces and those of the Italian chieftain Turnus, which eventually ends (as does *Aeneid* itself) with a duel between the two men. The spilling of Turnus' blood is the act that symbolically fertilizes the ground on which Rome will grow.

SOURCE

Perkell, Christine (editor). *Reading Vergil's Aeneid: An Interpretive Guide*. University of Oklahoma Press, 1999.

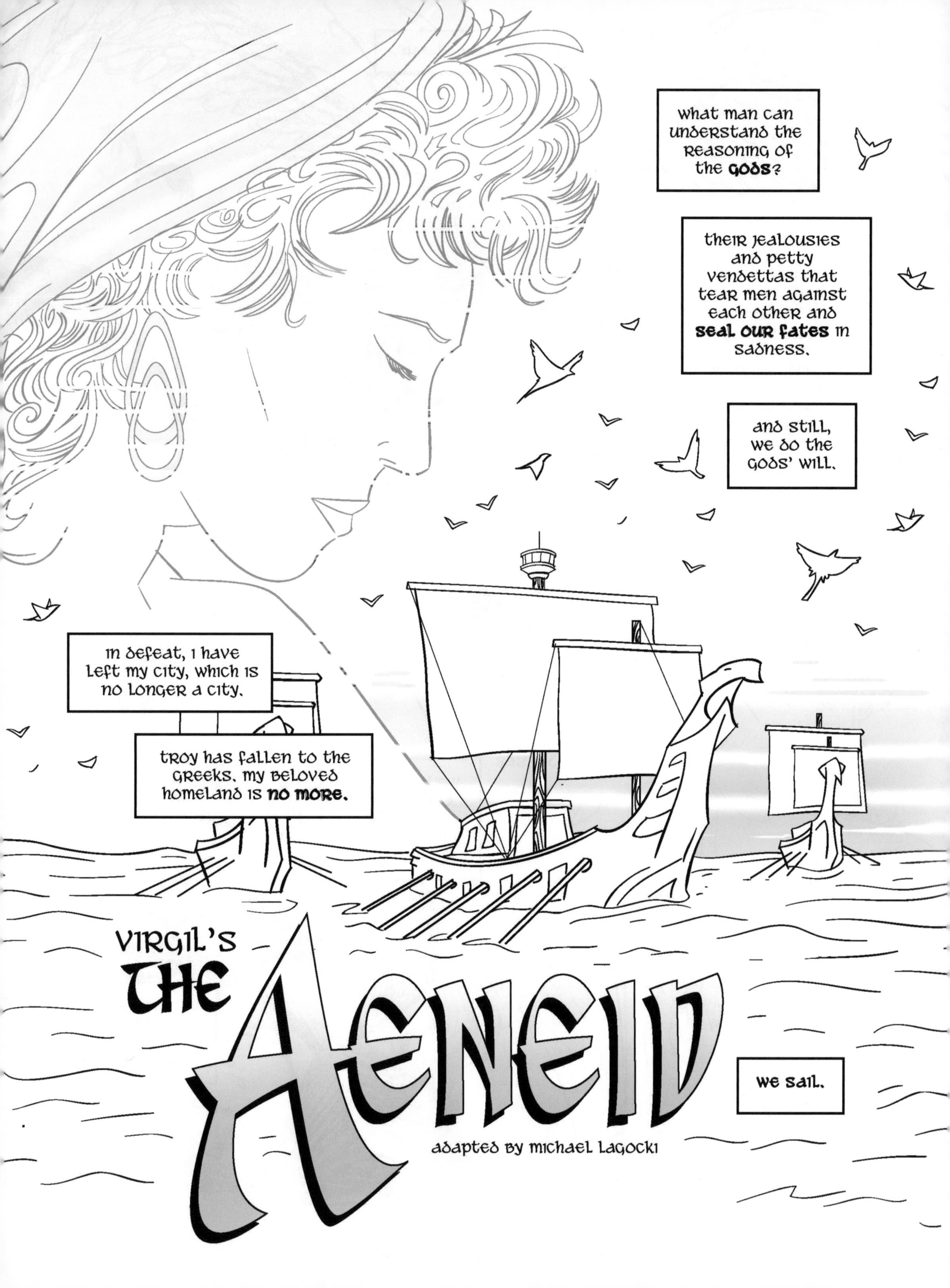
what man can understand the reasoning of the **gods**?
their jealousies and petty vendettas that tear men against each other and **seal our fates** in sadness.
and still, we do the gods' will.
in defeat, I have left my city, which is no longer a city.
troy has fallen to the greeks. my beloved homeland is **no more.**
VIRGIL'S
THE
AENEID
adapted by michael lagocki
we sail.

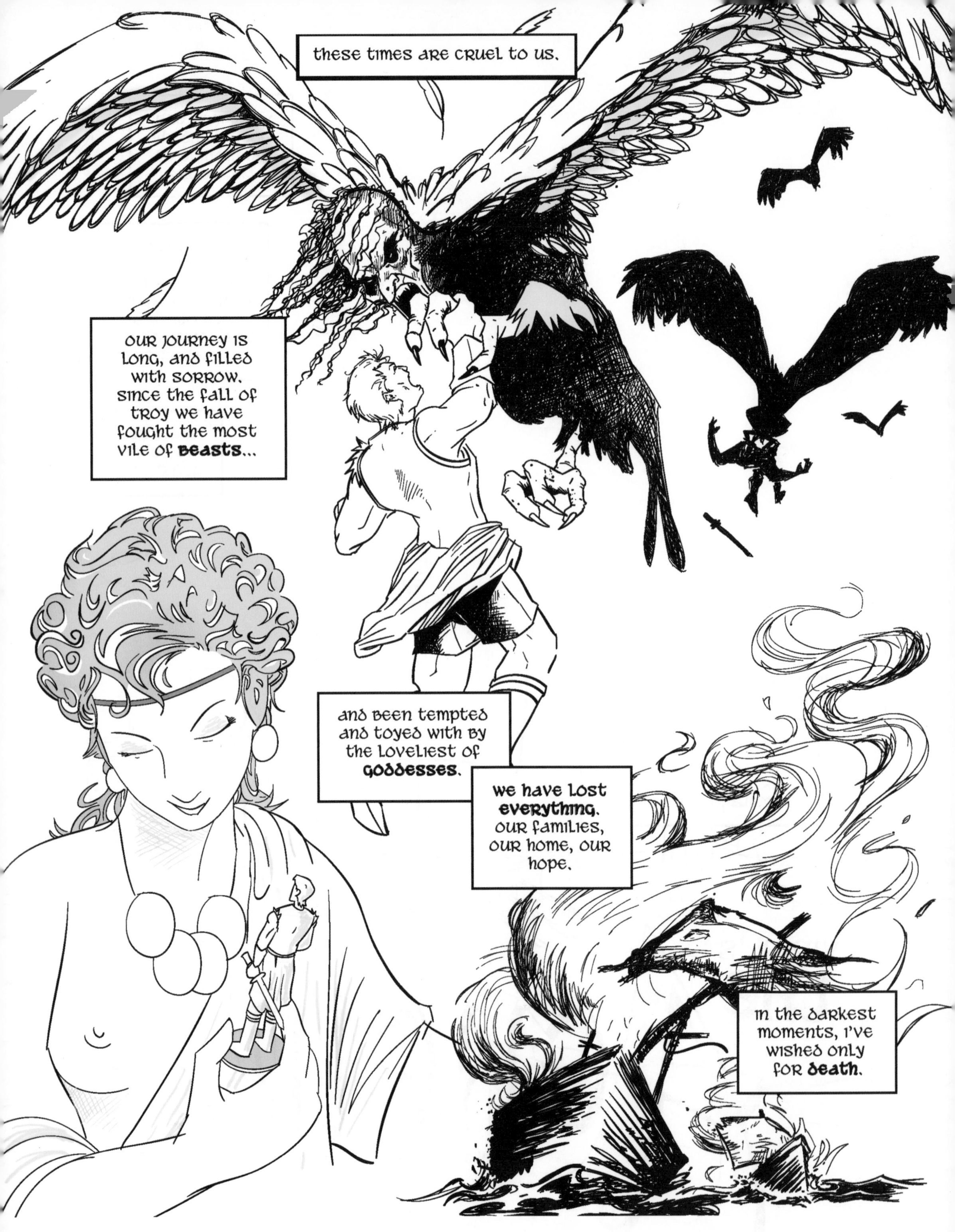
these times are cruel to us.
our journey is long, and filled with sorrow. since the fall of troy we have fought the most vile of **beasts**...
and been tempted and toyed with by the loveliest of **goddesses**.
we have lost **everything**. our families, our home, our hope.
in the darkest moments, i've wished only for **death**.

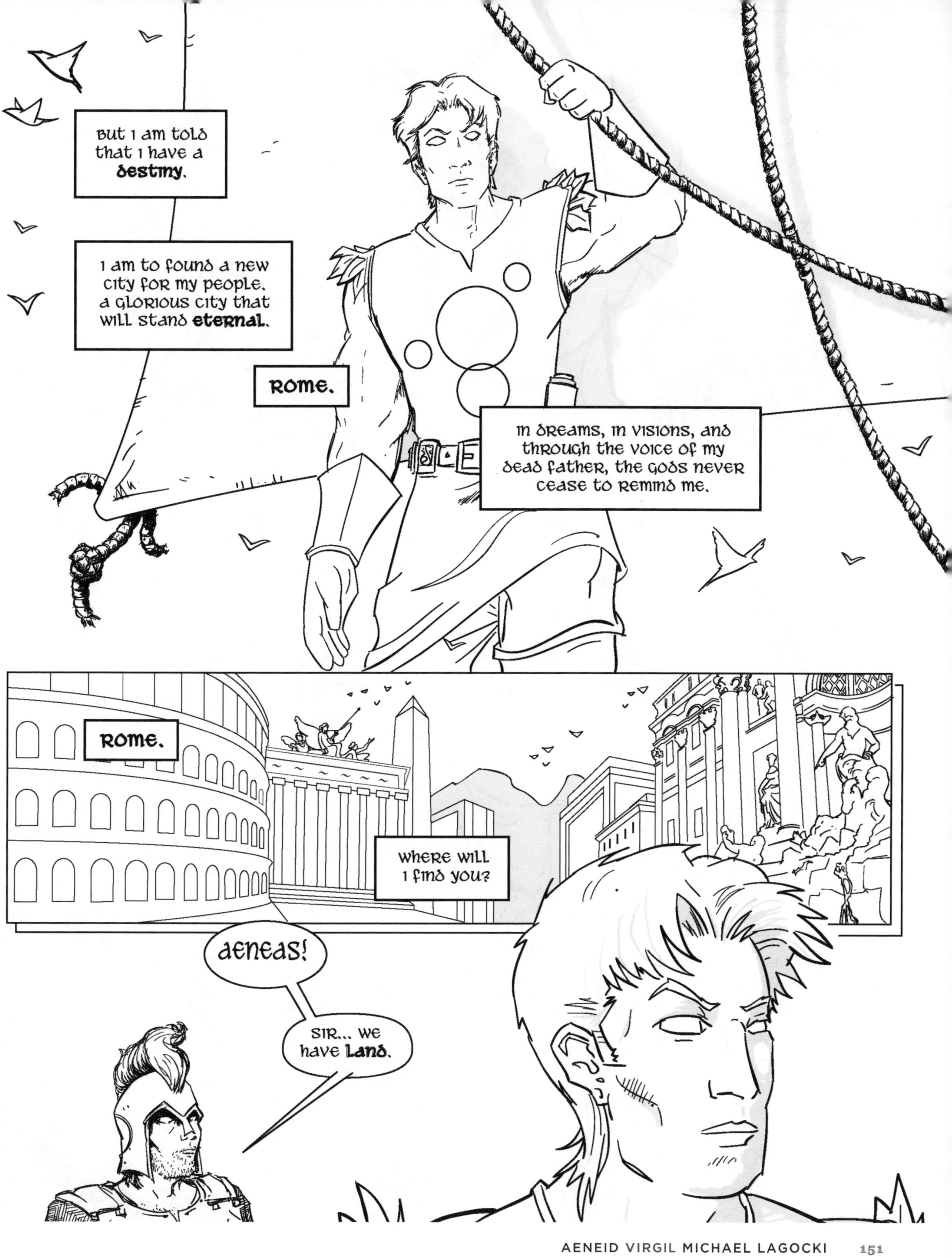
But I am told that I have a destiny.
I am to found a new city for my people, a glorious city that will stand eternal.
Rome.
In dreams, in visions, and through the voice of my dead father, the gods never cease to remind me.
Rome.
Where will I find you?
Aeneas!
Sir... we have land.

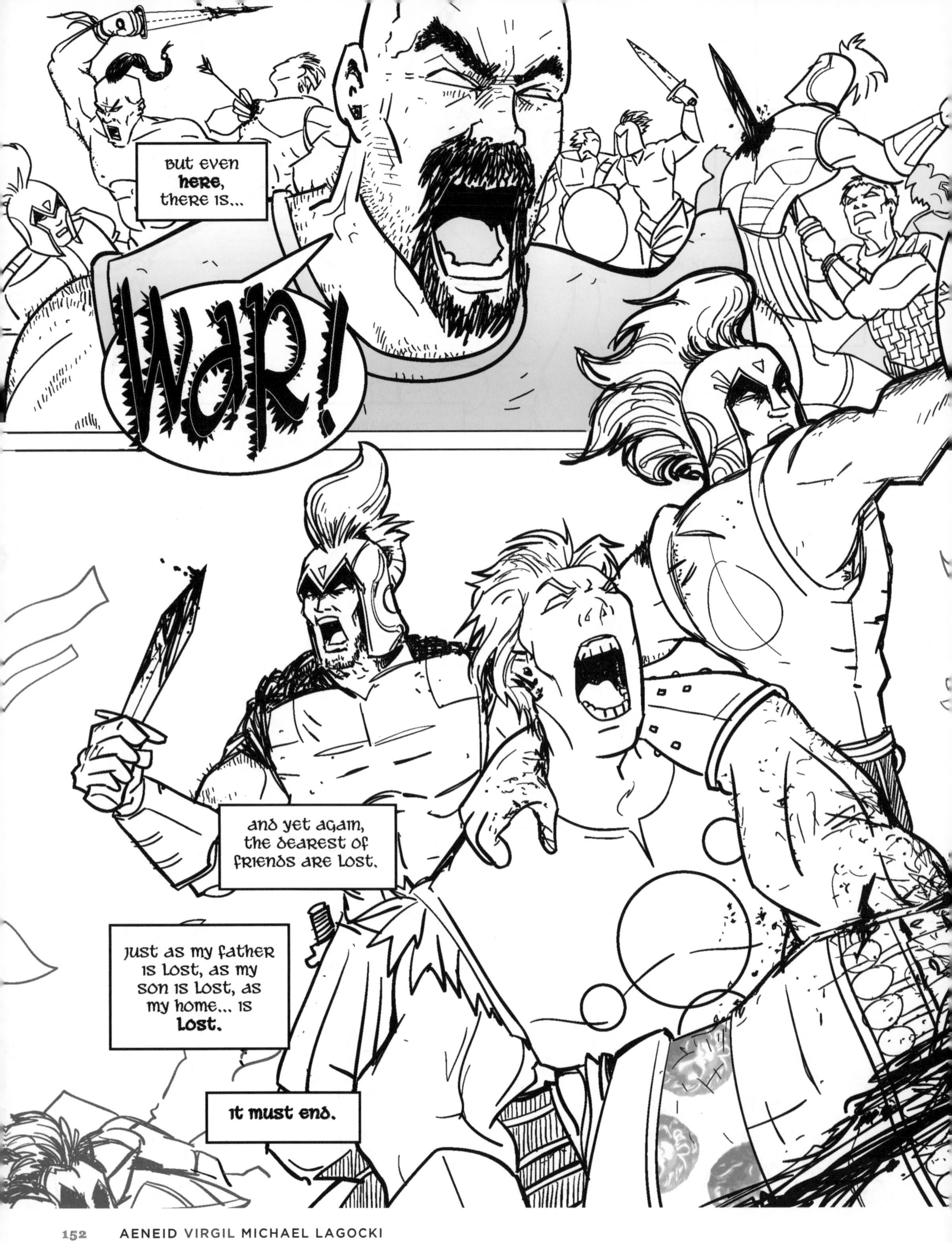
But even **here**, there is...
WAR!
and yet again, the dearest of friends are lost.
Just as my father is lost, as my son is lost, as my home... is **lost.**
It must end.

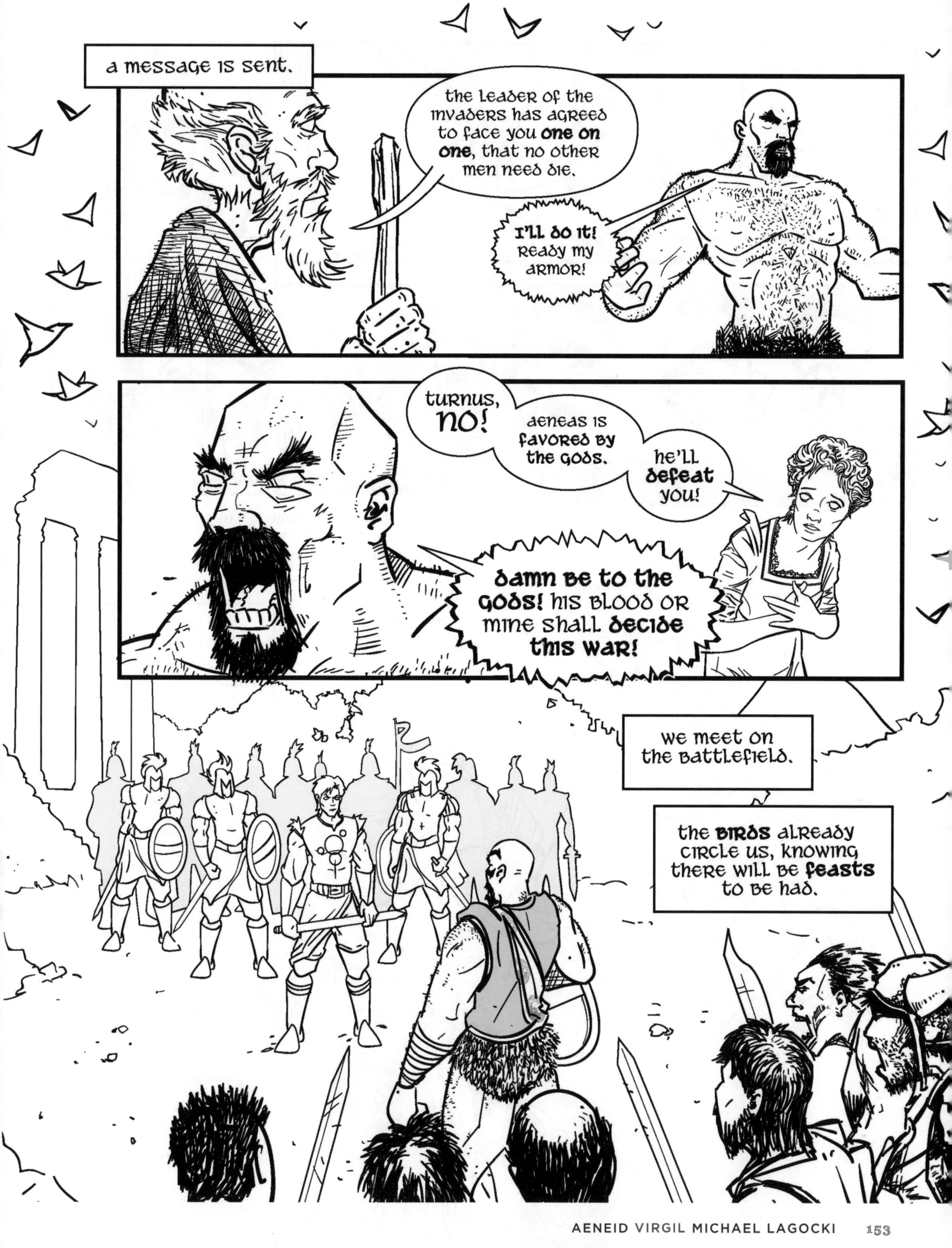
a message is sent.
the leader of the invaders has agreed to face you one on one, that no other men need die.
I'll do it! Ready my armor!
turnus, no!
aeneas is favored by the gods.
he'll defeat you!
damn be to the gods! his blood or mine shall decide this war!
we meet on the battlefield.
the birds already circle us, knowing there will be feasts to be had.

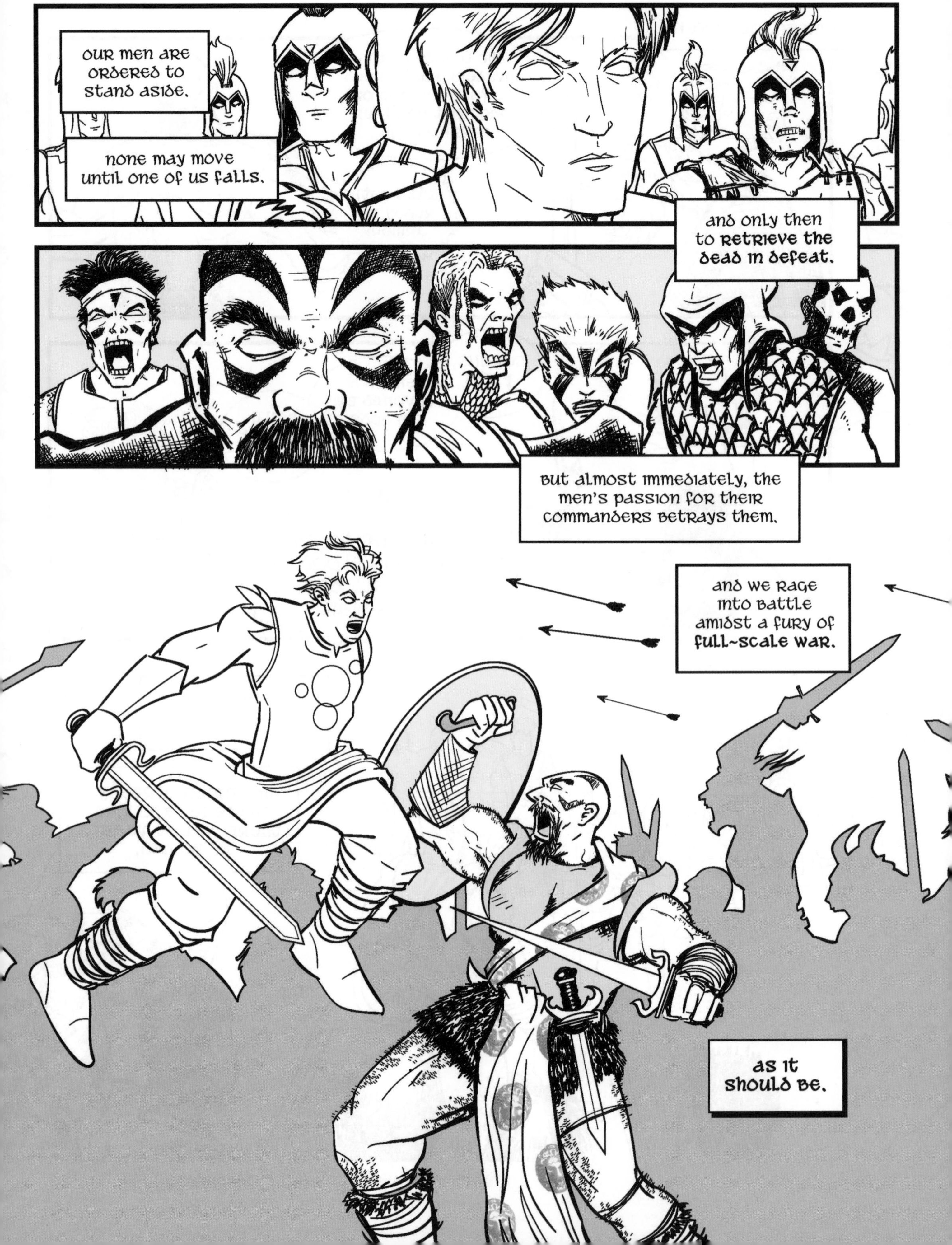
our men are ordered to stand aside.
none may move until one of us falls.
and only then to retrieve the dead in defeat.
but almost immediately, the men's passion for their commanders betrays them.
and we rage into battle amidst a fury of full~scale war.
as it should be.

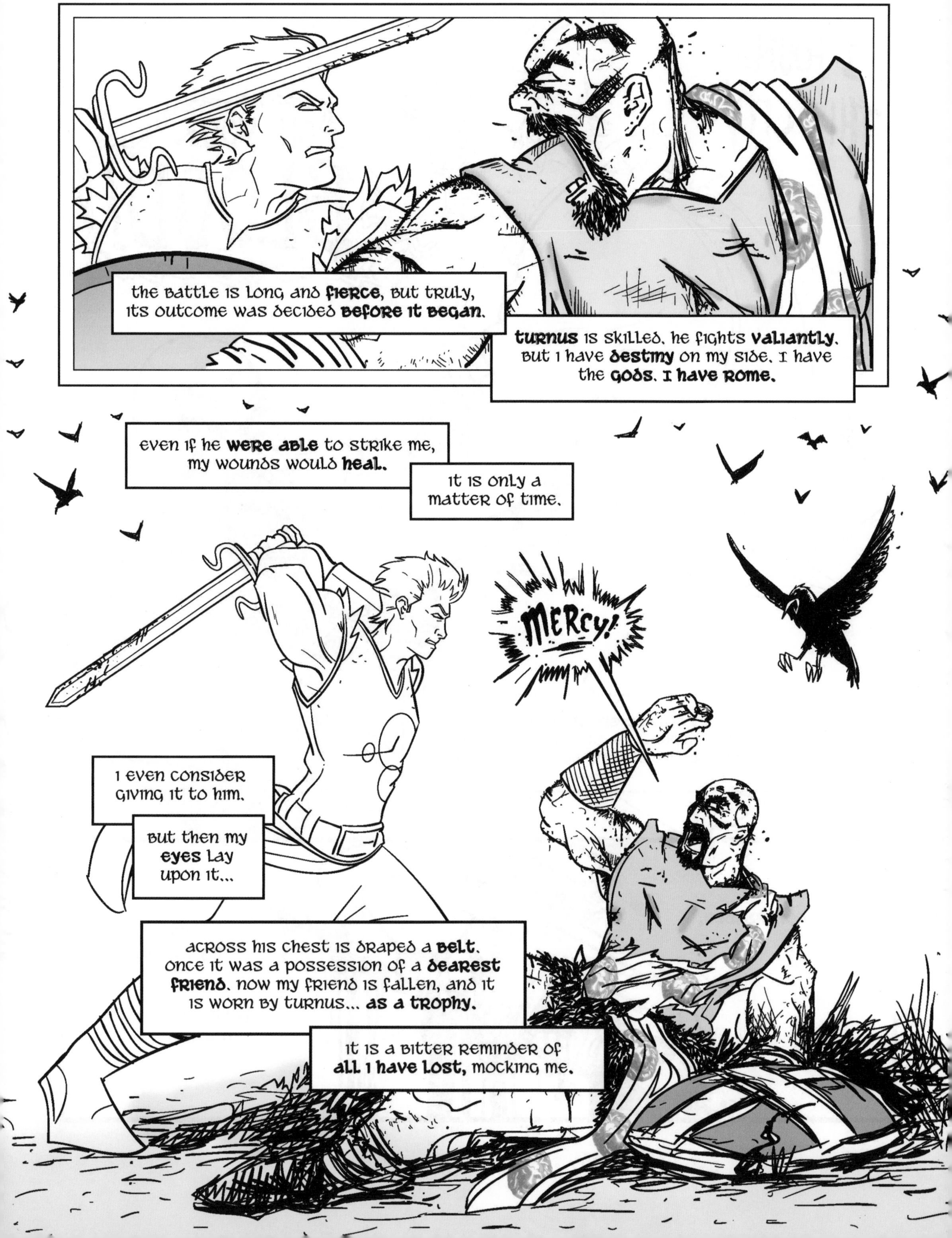

the battle is long and fierce, but truly, its outcome was decided before it began.
turnus is skilled, he fights valiantly, but I have destiny on my side. I have the gods. I have Rome.
even if he were able to strike me, my wounds would heal.
it is only a matter of time.
MERCY!
I even consider giving it to him.
but then my eyes lay upon it...
across his chest is draped a belt. once it was a possession of a dearest friend. now my friend is fallen, and it is worn by turnus... as a trophy.
it is a bitter reminder of all I have lost, mocking me.

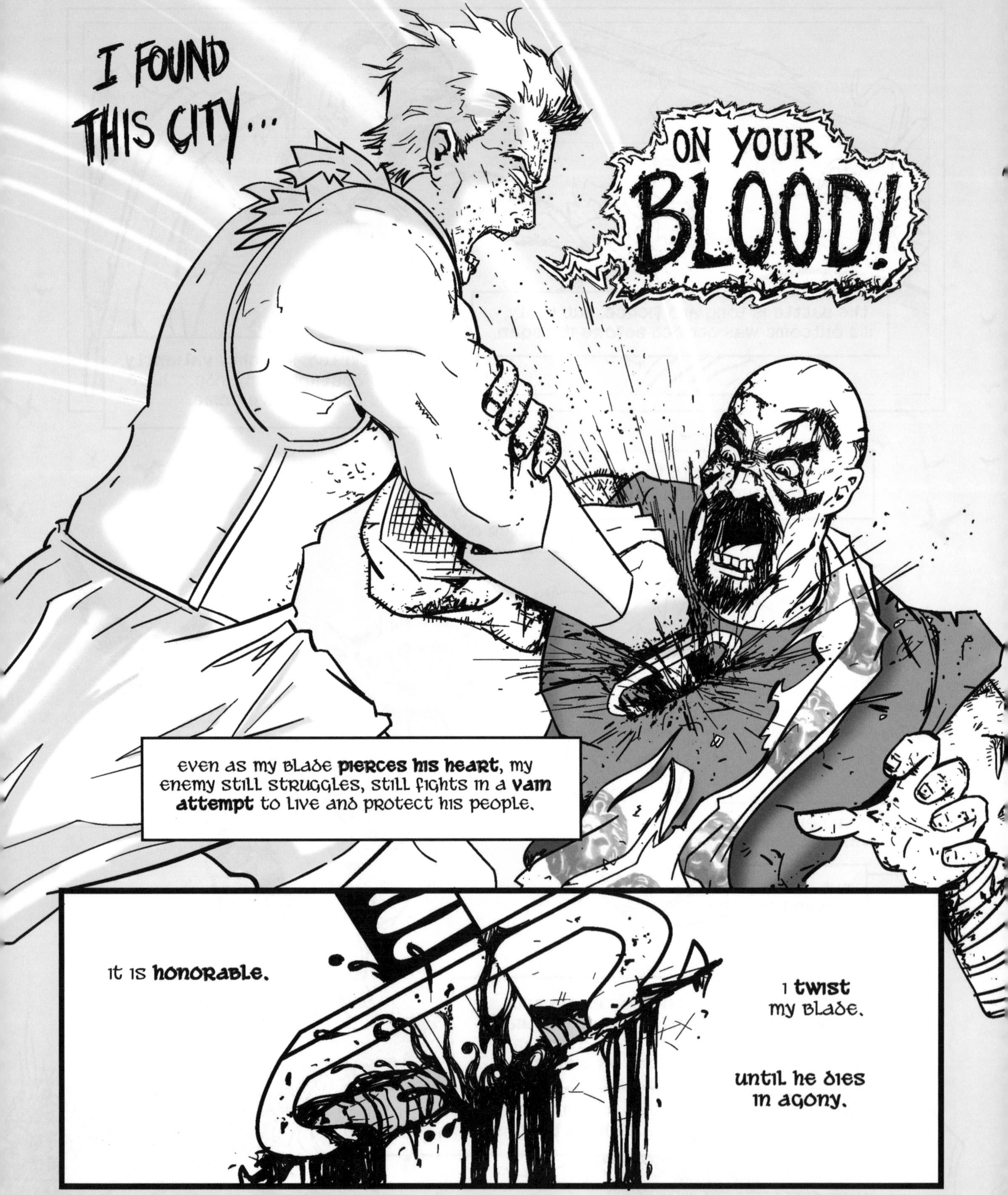
I FOUND THIS CITY...
ON YOUR BLOOD!
even as my blade pierces his heart, my enemy still struggles, still fights in a vain attempt to live and protect his people.
it is honorable.
i twist my blade.
until he dies in agony.

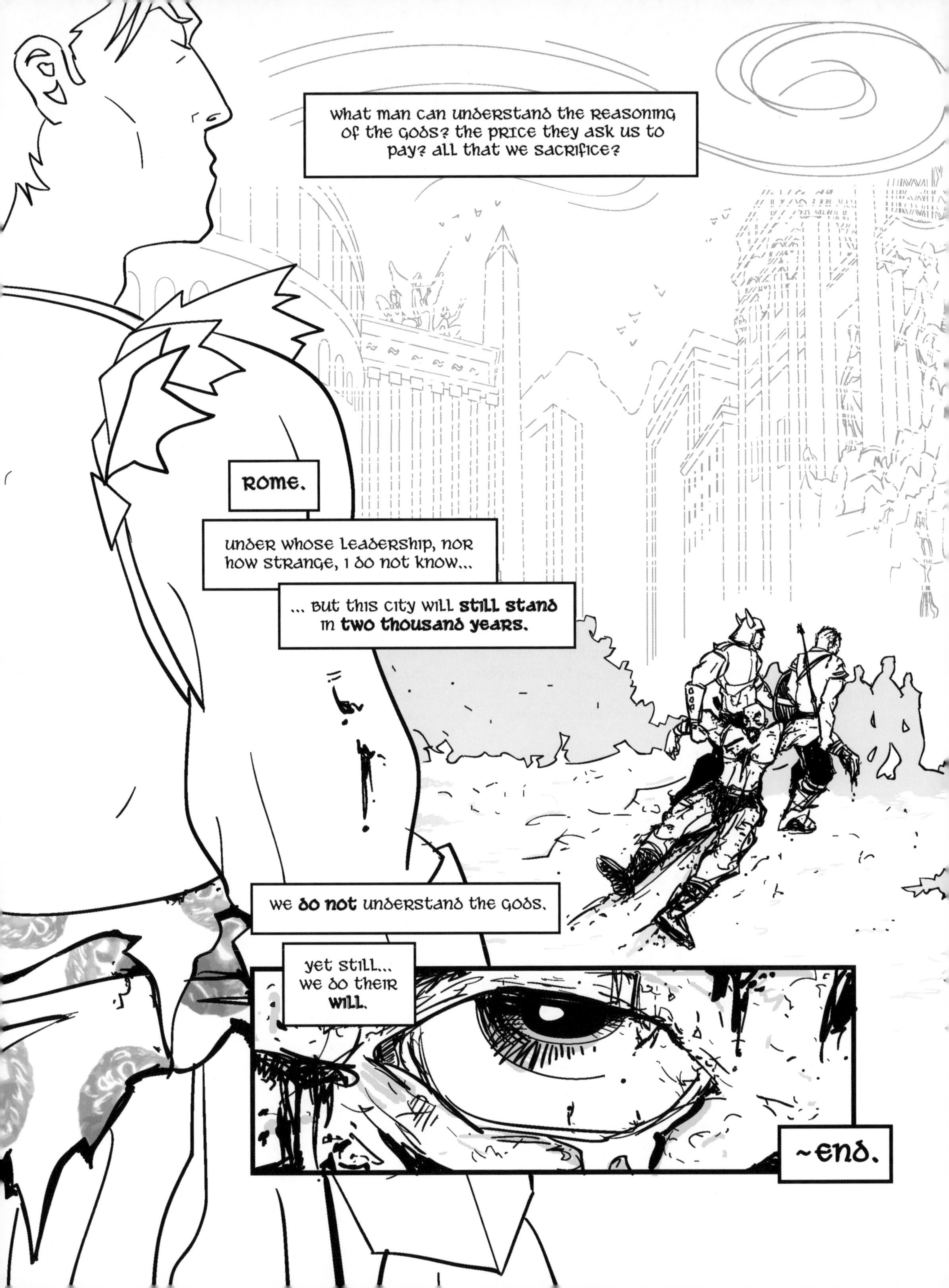
what man can understand the reasoning of the gods? the price they ask us to pay? all that we sacrifice?
ROME.
under whose leadership, nor how strange, I do not know...
... but this city will **still stand** in **two thousand years.**
we **do not** understand the gods.
yet still... we do their **will**.
~END.

The Book of Revelation

from the New Testament

ART / ADAPTATION BY **Rick Geary**

THE FINAL BOOK OF THE NEW TESTAMENT, AND thus the Christian Bible as a whole, the Book of Revelation just might be the strangest work in the entire literary canon. Populated by the Whore of Babylon, the Four Horsemen of the Apocalypse, the Beast, a lamb with seven horns and seven eyes, locusts with human faces, a seven-headed dragon, a false prophet, Satan, angels blowing trumpets of destruction, and other bizarre characters, this series of four visions has been interpreted as a literal guide to the fiery, blood-soaked end of the world as we know it and the establishment of Christ's 1,000-year kingdom on Earth, as a coded guide to spiritual development, and as an intense mushroom trip.

In his book on Revelation, Jonathan Kirsch writes:

> For anyone who reads the book of Revelation from beginning to end, the experience resembles a fever-dream or a nightmare: strange figures and objects appear and disappear and reappear, and the author himself flashes back and forth in time and place, sometimes finding himself in heaven and sometimes on earth, sometimes in the here and now and sometimes in the end-times, sometimes watching from afar and sometimes caught up in the events he describes. The author refers to the same characters by different names and titles, and he describes the same incidents from different vantage points. All the while, the characters and incidents, the words and phrases, even the letters and numbers of Revelation seem to shimmer with symbolic meanings that always float just out of reach.

Believers say the book was written by the Apostle John, but most scholars contend that it was written around 92–96 CE by an otherwise unknown early Christian prophet named John. Kirsch notes that the Book of Revelation is

> deeply woven into the fabric of Western civilization, both in high culture and in pop culture, starting in distant bibli-

cal antiquity and continuing into our own age. The Battle of Armageddon, the Four Horsemen of the Apocalypse, the Seventh Seal, the Great Whore of Babylon, and, more obliquely, the Antichrist, the Grim Reaper, and the Grapes of Wrath have migrated from the pages of Revelation to some of our most exalted works of literature, art, and music as well as the sports pages, the movie screen, and the paperback best seller.

> . . . The conquest of Jerusalem by medieval crusaders, the Bonfire of the Vanities in Florence during the Renaissance, the naming of the newly discovered Americas as the New World, and the thousand-year Reich promised by Adolf Hitler are all examples of the unlikely and unsettling ways that the book of Revelation has resonated through history.

Revelation has been called "the one great poem which the first Christian age produced." Thomas Jefferson said that it's "merely the ravings of a maniac."

When I approached Rick Geary—for many years, a regular contributor to *National Lampoon* and *MAD magazine*—about doing an adaptation for this anthology, I expected that he would choose a work of Victorian literature. He had already done the eight-volume, nonfiction graphic-novel series *A Treasury of Victorian Murder* (Jack the Ripper, Lizzie Borden, Abraham Lincoln . . .) and had adapted works from Dickens, Twain, Poe, and others from the 1800s. I was surprised and excited that he chose Revelation, managing to condense the chaotic work into twelve dense pages and delivering one extraordinary visual after another.

SOURCE

Kirsch, Jonathan. *A History of the End of the World: How the Most Controversial Book in the Bible Changed the Course of Western Civilization.* HarperOne, 2007.

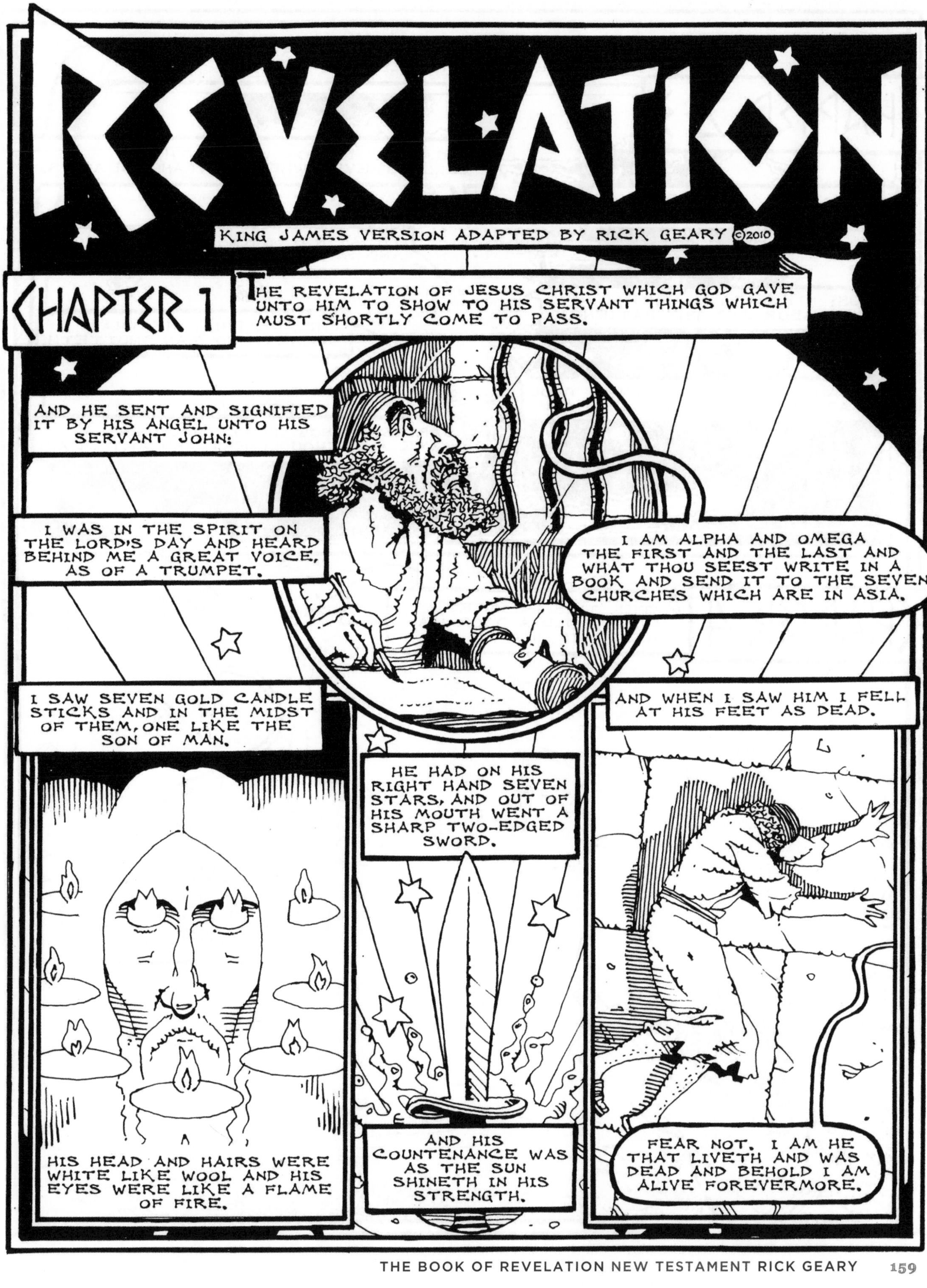
REVELATION
KING JAMES VERSION ADAPTED BY RICK GEARY ©2010
CHAPTER 1
THE REVELATION OF JESUS CHRIST WHICH GOD GAVE UNTO HIM TO SHOW TO HIS SERVANT THINGS WHICH MUST SHORTLY COME TO PASS.
AND HE SENT AND SIGNIFIED IT BY HIS ANGEL UNTO HIS SERVANT JOHN:
I WAS IN THE SPIRIT ON THE LORD'S DAY AND HEARD BEHIND ME A GREAT VOICE, AS OF A TRUMPET.
I AM ALPHA AND OMEGA THE FIRST AND THE LAST AND WHAT THOU SEEST WRITE IN A BOOK AND SEND IT TO THE SEVEN CHURCHES WHICH ARE IN ASIA.
I SAW SEVEN GOLD CANDLE STICKS AND IN THE MIDST OF THEM, ONE LIKE THE SON OF MAN.
HIS HEAD AND HAIRS WERE WHITE LIKE WOOL AND HIS EYES WERE LIKE A FLAME OF FIRE.
HE HAD ON HIS RIGHT HAND SEVEN STARS, AND OUT OF HIS MOUTH WENT A SHARP TWO-EDGED SWORD.
AND HIS COUNTENANCE WAS AS THE SUN SHINETH IN HIS STRENGTH.
AND WHEN I SAW HIM I FELL AT HIS FEET AS DEAD.
FEAR NOT. I AM HE THAT LIVETH AND WAS DEAD AND BEHOLD I AM ALIVE FOREVERMORE.

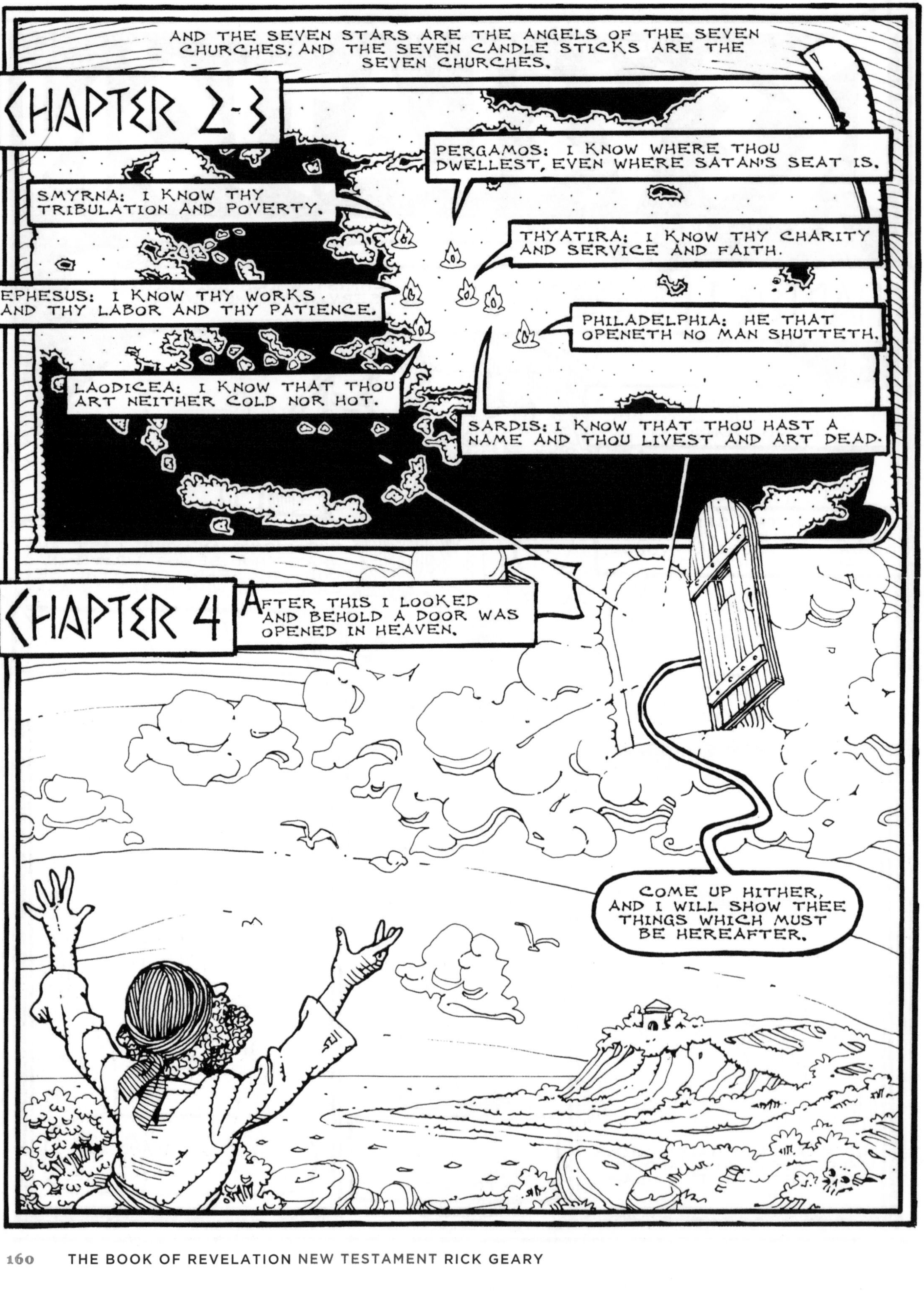
AND THE SEVEN STARS ARE THE ANGELS OF THE SEVEN CHURCHES; AND THE SEVEN CANDLE STICKS ARE THE SEVEN CHURCHES.
CHAPTER 2-3
PERGAMOS: I KNOW WHERE THOU DWELLEST, EVEN WHERE SATAN'S SEAT IS.
SMYRNA: I KNOW THY TRIBULATION AND POVERTY.
THYATIRA: I KNOW THY CHARITY AND SERVICE AND FAITH.
EPHESUS: I KNOW THY WORKS AND THY LABOR AND THY PATIENCE.
PHILADELPHIA: HE THAT OPENETH NO MAN SHUTTETH.
LAODICEA: I KNOW THAT THOU ART NEITHER COLD NOR HOT.
SARDIS: I KNOW THAT THOU HAST A NAME AND THOU LIVEST AND ART DEAD.
CHAPTER 4
AFTER THIS I LOOKED AND BEHOLD A DOOR WAS OPENED IN HEAVEN.
COME UP HITHER, AND I WILL SHOW THEE THINGS WHICH MUST BE HEREAFTER.

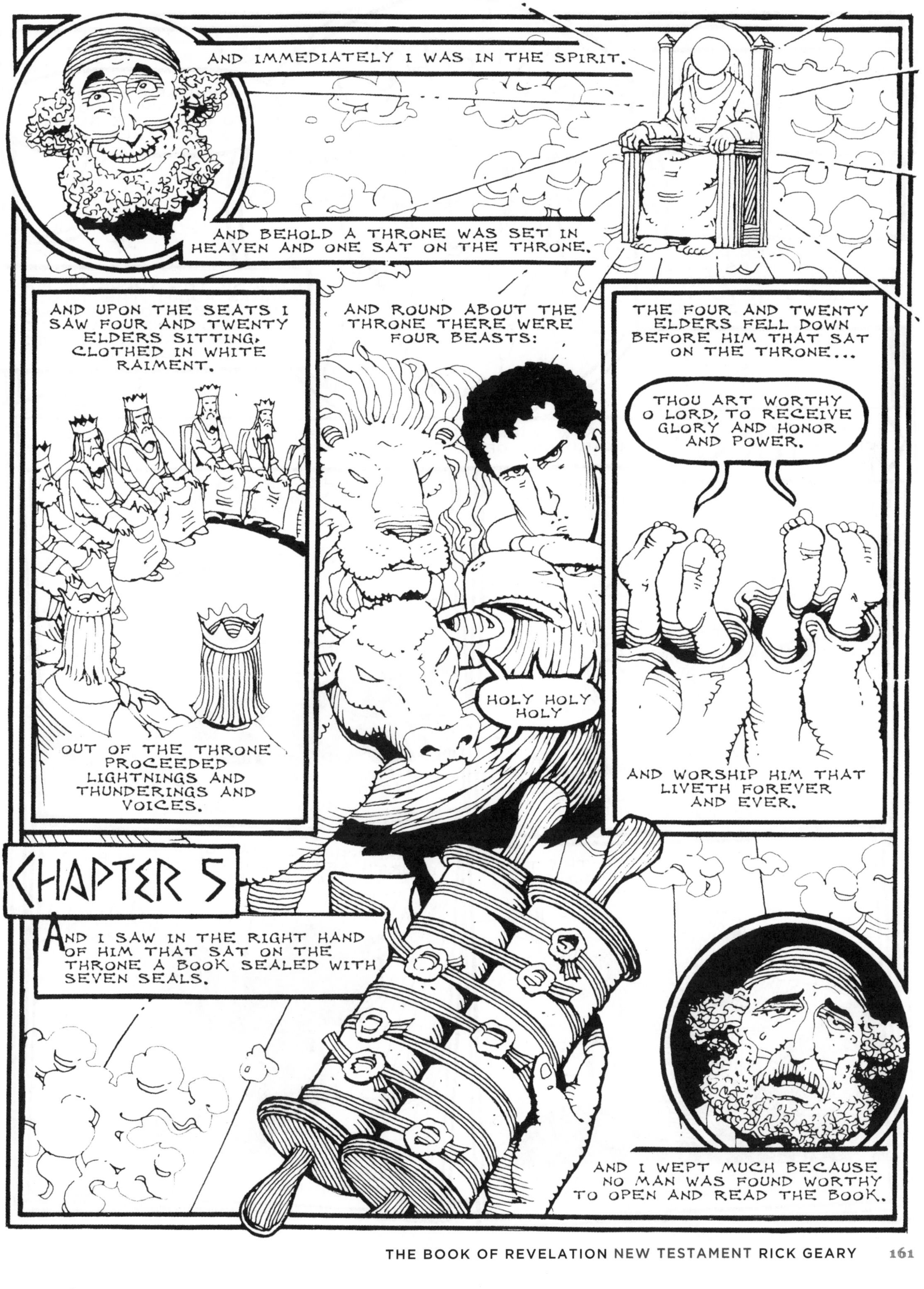

AND IMMEDIATELY I WAS IN THE SPIRIT.
AND BEHOLD A THRONE WAS SET IN HEAVEN AND ONE SAT ON THE THRONE.
AND UPON THE SEATS I SAW FOUR AND TWENTY ELDERS SITTING, CLOTHED IN WHITE RAIMENT.
OUT OF THE THRONE PROCEEDED LIGHTNINGS AND THUNDERINGS AND VOICES.
AND ROUND ABOUT THE THRONE THERE WERE FOUR BEASTS:
HOLY HOLY HOLY
THE FOUR AND TWENTY ELDERS FELL DOWN BEFORE HIM THAT SAT ON THE THRONE...
THOU ART WORTHY O LORD, TO RECEIVE GLORY AND HONOR AND POWER.
AND WORSHIP HIM THAT LIVETH FOREVER AND EVER.
CHAPTER 5
AND I SAW IN THE RIGHT HAND OF HIM THAT SAT ON THE THRONE A BOOK SEALED WITH SEVEN SEALS.
AND I WEPT MUCH BECAUSE NO MAN WAS FOUND WORTHY TO OPEN AND READ THE BOOK.

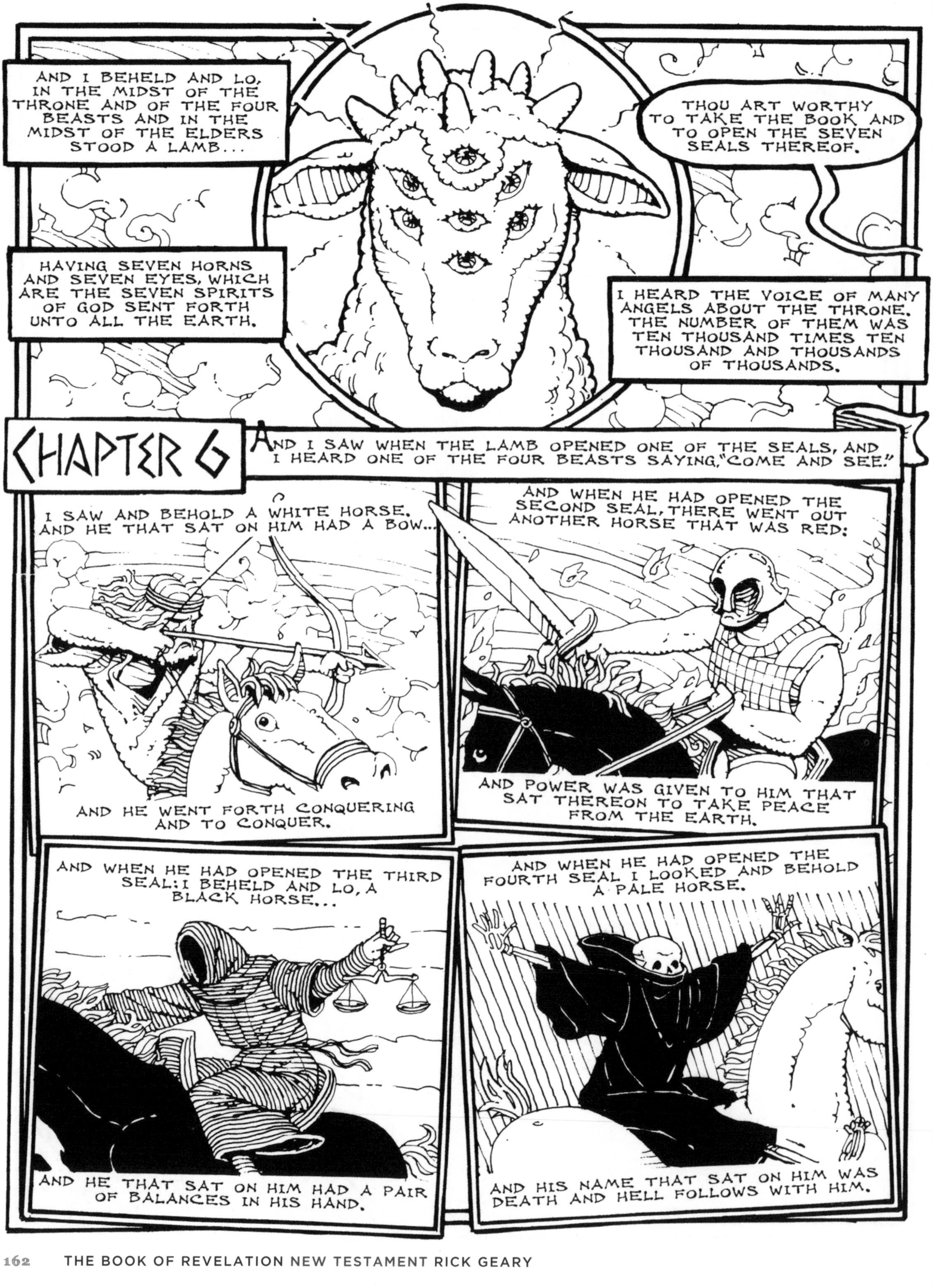

AND I BEHELD AND LO, IN THE MIDST OF THE THRONE AND OF THE FOUR BEASTS AND IN THE MIDST OF THE ELDERS STOOD A LAMB...
THOU ART WORTHY TO TAKE THE BOOK AND TO OPEN THE SEVEN SEALS THEREOF.
HAVING SEVEN HORNS AND SEVEN EYES, WHICH ARE THE SEVEN SPIRITS OF GOD SENT FORTH UNTO ALL THE EARTH.
I HEARD THE VOICE OF MANY ANGELS ABOUT THE THRONE. THE NUMBER OF THEM WAS TEN THOUSAND TIMES TEN THOUSAND AND THOUSANDS OF THOUSANDS.
CHAPTER 6
AND I SAW WHEN THE LAMB OPENED ONE OF THE SEALS, AND I HEARD ONE OF THE FOUR BEASTS SAYING, "COME AND SEE."
I SAW AND BEHOLD A WHITE HORSE. AND HE THAT SAT ON HIM HAD A BOW...
AND HE WENT FORTH CONQUERING AND TO CONQUER.
AND WHEN HE HAD OPENED THE SECOND SEAL, THERE WENT OUT ANOTHER HORSE THAT WAS RED:
AND POWER WAS GIVEN TO HIM THAT SAT THEREON TO TAKE PEACE FROM THE EARTH.
AND WHEN HE HAD OPENED THE THIRD SEAL: I BEHELD AND LO, A BLACK HORSE...
AND HE THAT SAT ON HIM HAD A PAIR OF BALANCES IN HIS HAND.
AND WHEN HE HAD OPENED THE FOURTH SEAL I LOOKED AND BEHOLD A PALE HORSE.
AND HIS NAME THAT SAT ON HIM WAS DEATH AND HELL FOLLOWS WITH HIM.

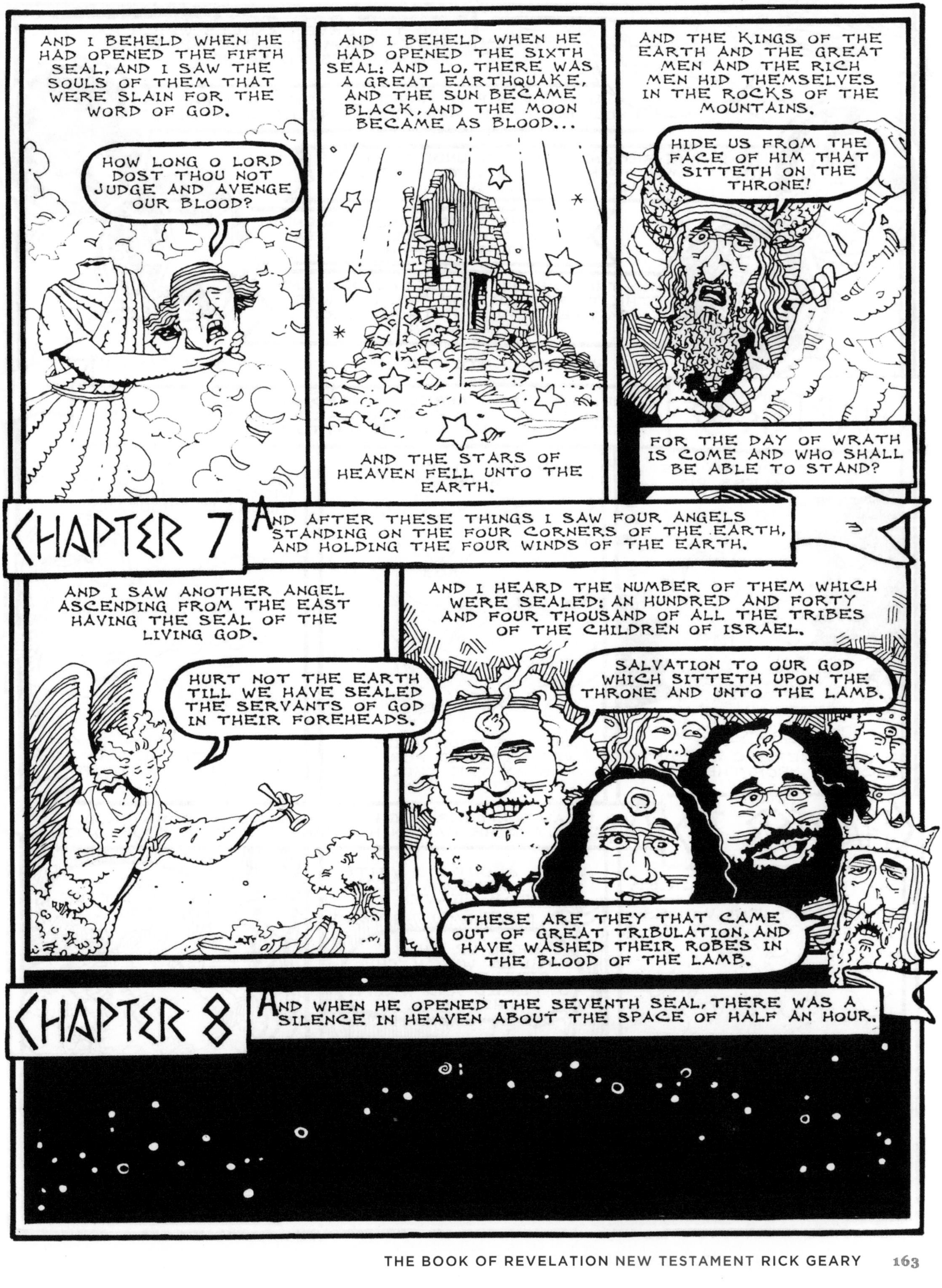

AND I BEHELD WHEN HE HAD OPENED THE FIFTH SEAL, AND I SAW THE SOULS OF THEM THAT WERE SLAIN FOR THE WORD OF GOD.
HOW LONG O LORD DOST THOU NOT JUDGE AND AVENGE OUR BLOOD?
AND I BEHELD WHEN HE HAD OPENED THE SIXTH SEAL: AND LO, THERE WAS A GREAT EARTHQUAKE, AND THE SUN BECAME BLACK, AND THE MOON BECAME AS BLOOD...
AND THE STARS OF HEAVEN FELL UNTO THE EARTH.
AND THE KINGS OF THE EARTH AND THE GREAT MEN AND THE RICH MEN HID THEMSELVES IN THE ROCKS OF THE MOUNTAINS.
HIDE US FROM THE FACE OF HIM THAT SITTETH ON THE THRONE!
FOR THE DAY OF WRATH IS COME AND WHO SHALL BE ABLE TO STAND?
CHAPTER 7
AND AFTER THESE THINGS I SAW FOUR ANGELS STANDING ON THE FOUR CORNERS OF THE EARTH, AND HOLDING THE FOUR WINDS OF THE EARTH.
AND I SAW ANOTHER ANGEL ASCENDING FROM THE EAST HAVING THE SEAL OF THE LIVING GOD.
HURT NOT THE EARTH TILL WE HAVE SEALED THE SERVANTS OF GOD IN THEIR FOREHEADS.
AND I HEARD THE NUMBER OF THEM WHICH WERE SEALED: AN HUNDRED AND FORTY AND FOUR THOUSAND OF ALL THE TRIBES OF THE CHILDREN OF ISRAEL.
SALVATION TO OUR GOD WHICH SITTETH UPON THE THRONE AND UNTO THE LAMB.
THESE ARE THEY THAT CAME OUT OF GREAT TRIBULATION, AND HAVE WASHED THEIR ROBES IN THE BLOOD OF THE LAMB.
CHAPTER 8
AND WHEN HE OPENED THE SEVENTH SEAL, THERE WAS A SILENCE IN HEAVEN ABOUT THE SPACE OF HALF AN HOUR.

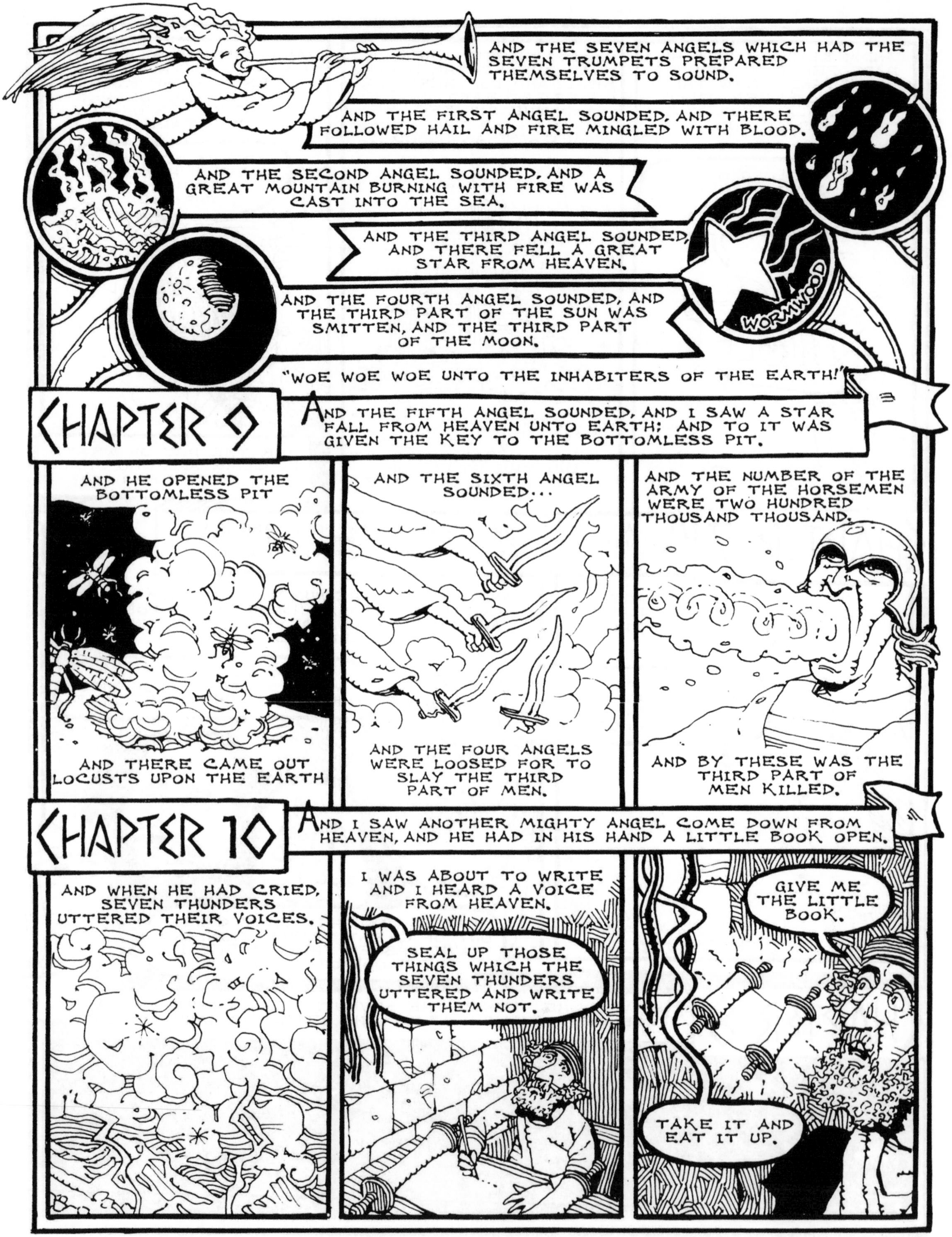

AND THE SEVEN ANGELS WHICH HAD THE SEVEN TRUMPETS PREPARED THEMSELVES TO SOUND.
AND THE FIRST ANGEL SOUNDED, AND THERE FOLLOWED HAIL AND FIRE MINGLED WITH BLOOD.
AND THE SECOND ANGEL SOUNDED, AND A GREAT MOUNTAIN BURNING WITH FIRE WAS CAST INTO THE SEA.
AND THE THIRD ANGEL SOUNDED, AND THERE FELL A GREAT STAR FROM HEAVEN.
WORMWOOD
AND THE FOURTH ANGEL SOUNDED, AND THE THIRD PART OF THE SUN WAS SMITTEN, AND THE THIRD PART OF THE MOON.
"WOE WOE WOE UNTO THE INHABITERS OF THE EARTH!"
CHAPTER 9
AND THE FIFTH ANGEL SOUNDED, AND I SAW A STAR FALL FROM HEAVEN UNTO EARTH; AND TO IT WAS GIVEN THE KEY TO THE BOTTOMLESS PIT.
AND HE OPENED THE BOTTOMLESS PIT
AND THERE CAME OUT LOCUSTS UPON THE EARTH
AND THE SIXTH ANGEL SOUNDED...
AND THE FOUR ANGELS WERE LOOSED FOR TO SLAY THE THIRD PART OF MEN.
AND THE NUMBER OF THE ARMY OF THE HORSEMEN WERE TWO HUNDRED THOUSAND THOUSAND.
AND BY THESE WAS THE THIRD PART OF MEN KILLED.
CHAPTER 10
AND I SAW ANOTHER MIGHTY ANGEL COME DOWN FROM HEAVEN, AND HE HAD IN HIS HAND A LITTLE BOOK OPEN.
AND WHEN HE HAD CRIED, SEVEN THUNDERS UTTERED THEIR VOICES.
I WAS ABOUT TO WRITE AND I HEARD A VOICE FROM HEAVEN.
SEAL UP THOSE THINGS WHICH THE SEVEN THUNDERS UTTERED AND WRITE THEM NOT.
GIVE ME THE LITTLE BOOK.
TAKE IT AND EAT IT UP.

CHAPTER 11

AND THERE WAS GIVEN TO ME A REED LIKE UNTO A ROD: AND THE ANGEL STOOD SAYING RISE AND MEASURE THE TEMPLE OF GOD AND THEM THAT WORSHIP THEREIN.

BUT THE COURT WHICH IS WITHOUT THE TEMPLE MEASURE IT NOT FOR IT IS GIVEN UNTO THE GENTILES."

AND THE HOLY CITY THEY SHALL TREAD UNDER FOOT FORTY AND TWO MONTHS.

AND THE SAME HOUR THERE WAS A GREAT EARTHQUAKE AND WERE SLAIN OF MEN SEVEN THOUSAND.

AND THE SECOND WOE IS PAST AND BEHOLD THE THIRD WOE COMETH QUICKLY.

AND THE SEVENTH ANGEL SOUNDED: AND THE TEMPLE OF GOD WAS OPENED IN HEAVEN...

AND THERE WERE LIGHTNINGS AND VOICES AND THUNDERINGS AND AN EARTHQUAKE AND GREAT HAIL.

CHAPTER 12

AND THERE APPEARED ANOTHER WONDER IN HEAVEN: A WOMAN CLOTHED WITH THE SUN. AND SHE BEING WITH CHILD CRIED, TRAVAILING IN BIRTH.

AND THERE APPEARED ANOTHER WONDER IN HEAVEN: AND BEHOLD A GREAT RED DRAGON.

AND THE DRAGON STOOD BEFORE THE WOMAN TO DEVOUR THE CHILD AS SOON AS IT WAS BORN.

AND SHE BROUGHT FORTH A MAN CHILD, WHO WAS TO RULE ALL NATIONS WITH A ROD OF IRON.

AND THERE WAS A WAR IN HEAVEN: MICHAEL AND HIS ANGELS FOUGHT AGAINST THE DRAGON.

AND THE GREAT DRAGON, CALLED THE DEVIL AND SATAN, WAS CAST OUT INTO THE EARTH.

AND THE DRAGON WAS WROTH WITH THE WOMAN, AND WENT TO MAKE WAR WITH THE REMNANT OF HER SEED.

CHAPTER 13

AND I SAW A BEAST RISE UP OUT OF THE SEA, HAVING SEVEN HEADS, TEN HORNS, AND UPON HIS HORNS TEN CROWNS, AND UPON HIS HEADS THE NAME OF BLASPHEMY.

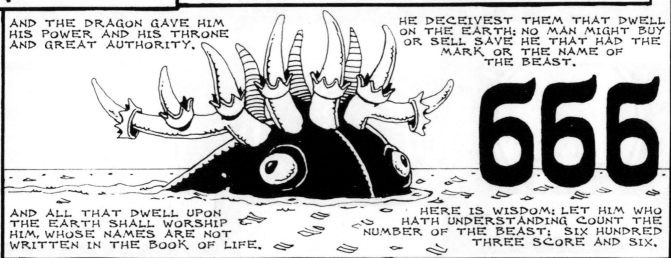

AND THE DRAGON GAVE HIM HIS POWER AND HIS THRONE AND GREAT AUTHORITY.

HE DECEIVEST THEM THAT DWELL ON THE EARTH: NO MAN MIGHT BUY OR SELL SAVE HE THAT HAD THE MARK OR THE NAME OF THE BEAST.

666

AND ALL THAT DWELL UPON THE EARTH SHALL WORSHIP HIM, WHOSE NAMES ARE NOT WRITTEN IN THE BOOK OF LIFE.

HERE IS WISDOM: LET HIM WHO HATH UNDERSTANDING COUNT THE NUMBER OF THE BEAST: SIX HUNDRED THREE SCORE AND SIX.

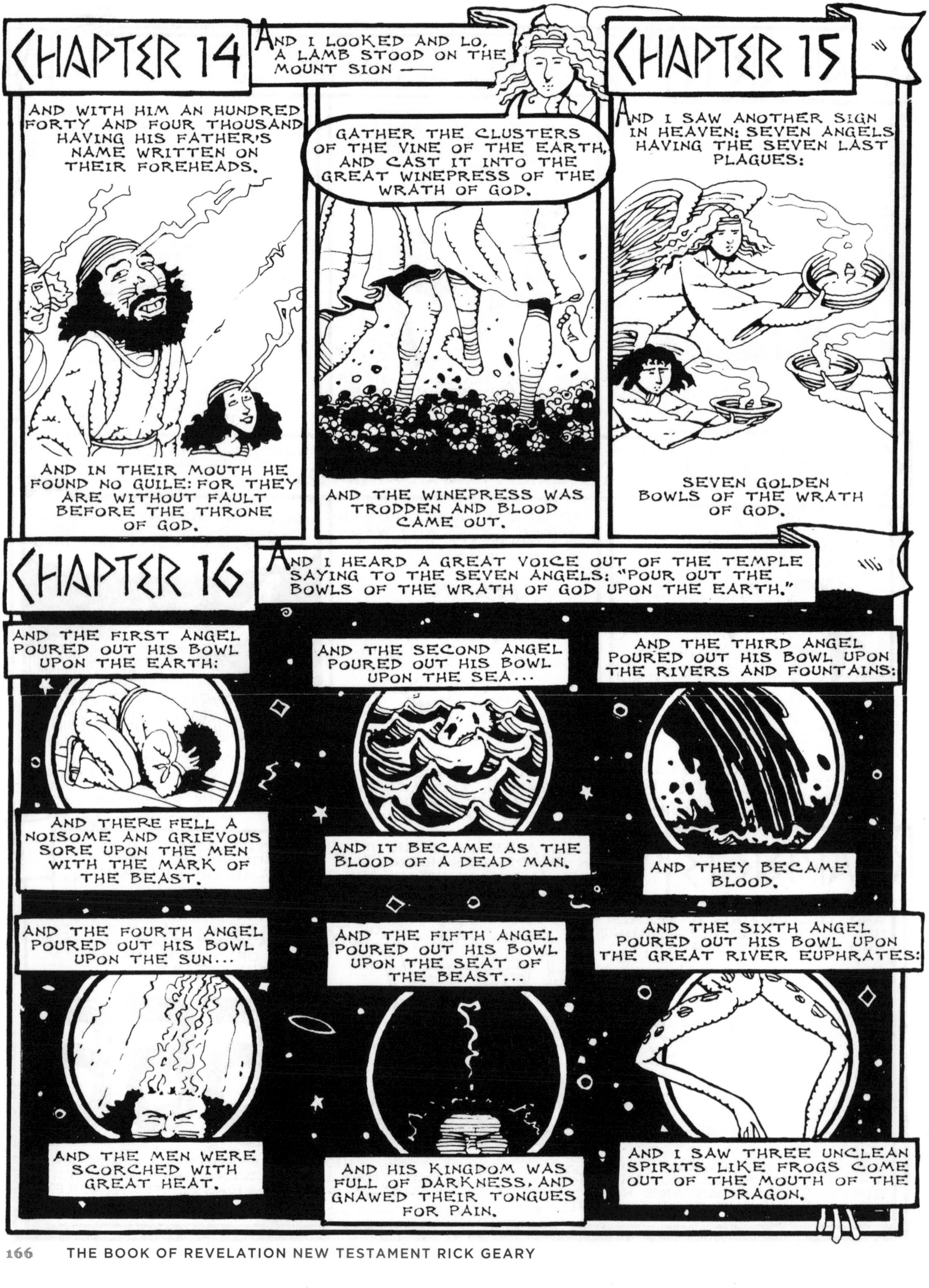
CHAPTER 14
AND I LOOKED AND LO, A LAMB STOOD ON THE MOUNT SION —
AND WITH HIM AN HUNDRED FORTY AND FOUR THOUSAND HAVING HIS FATHER'S NAME WRITTEN ON THEIR FOREHEADS.
AND IN THEIR MOUTH HE FOUND NO GUILE: FOR THEY ARE WITHOUT FAULT BEFORE THE THRONE OF GOD.
GATHER THE CLUSTERS OF THE VINE OF THE EARTH, AND CAST IT INTO THE GREAT WINEPRESS OF THE WRATH OF GOD.
AND THE WINEPRESS WAS TRODDEN AND BLOOD CAME OUT.
CHAPTER 15
AND I SAW ANOTHER SIGN IN HEAVEN: SEVEN ANGELS HAVING THE SEVEN LAST PLAGUES:
SEVEN GOLDEN BOWLS OF THE WRATH OF GOD.
CHAPTER 16
AND I HEARD A GREAT VOICE OUT OF THE TEMPLE SAYING TO THE SEVEN ANGELS: "POUR OUT THE BOWLS OF THE WRATH OF GOD UPON THE EARTH."
AND THE FIRST ANGEL POURED OUT HIS BOWL UPON THE EARTH:
AND THERE FELL A NOISOME AND GRIEVOUS SORE UPON THE MEN WITH THE MARK OF THE BEAST.
AND THE SECOND ANGEL POURED OUT HIS BOWL UPON THE SEA...
AND IT BECAME AS THE BLOOD OF A DEAD MAN.
AND THE THIRD ANGEL POURED OUT HIS BOWL UPON THE RIVERS AND FOUNTAINS:
AND THEY BECAME BLOOD.
AND THE FOURTH ANGEL POURED OUT HIS BOWL UPON THE SUN...
AND THE MEN WERE SCORCHED WITH GREAT HEAT.
AND THE FIFTH ANGEL POURED OUT HIS BOWL UPON THE SEAT OF THE BEAST...
AND HIS KINGDOM WAS FULL OF DARKNESS, AND GNAWED THEIR TONGUES FOR PAIN.
AND THE SIXTH ANGEL POURED OUT HIS BOWL UPON THE GREAT RIVER EUPHRATES:
AND I SAW THREE UNCLEAN SPIRITS LIKE FROGS COME OUT OF THE MOUTH OF THE DRAGON.

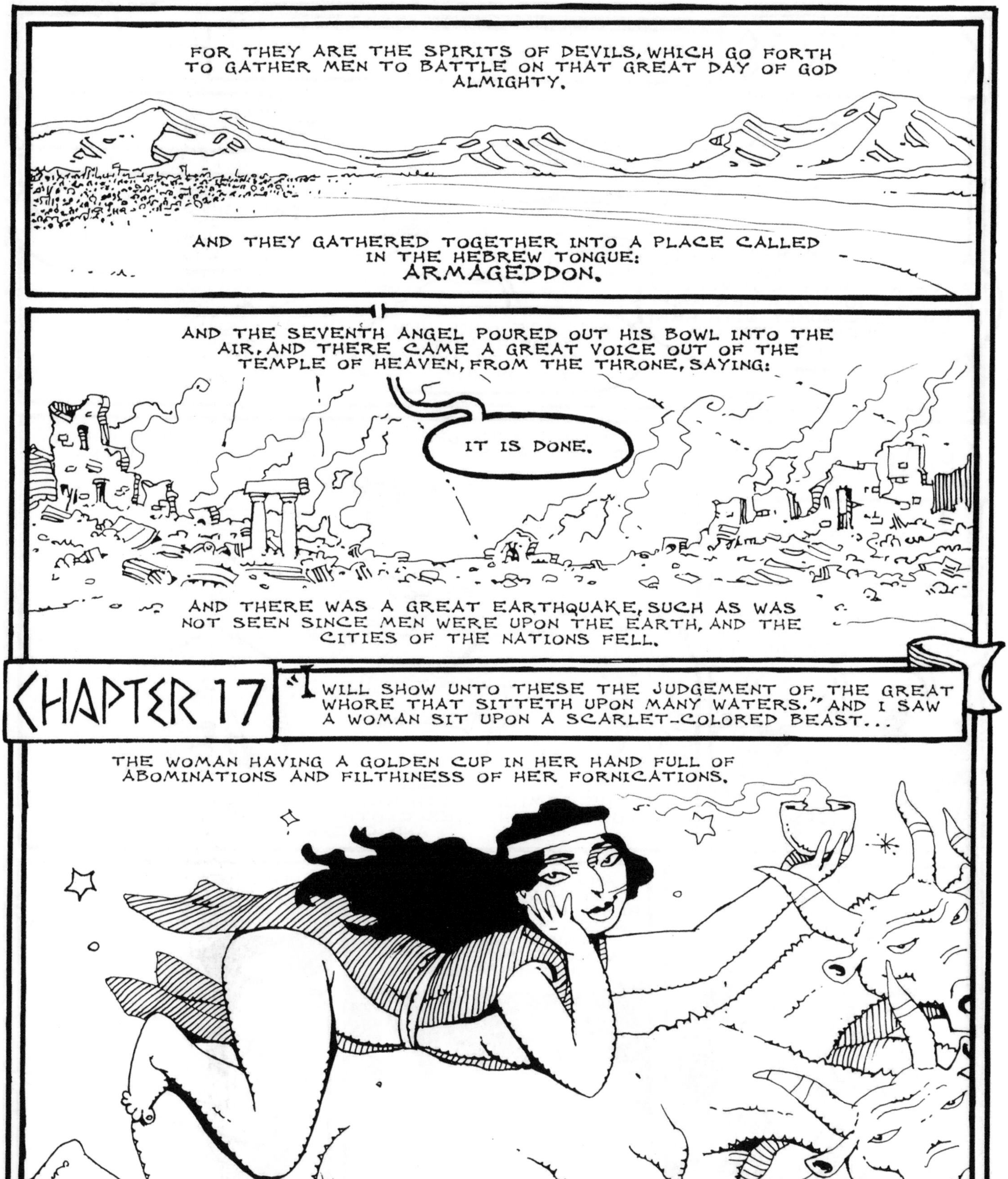
FOR THEY ARE THE SPIRITS OF DEVILS, WHICH GO FORTH TO GATHER MEN TO BATTLE ON THAT GREAT DAY OF GOD ALMIGHTY.
AND THEY GATHERED TOGETHER INTO A PLACE CALLED IN THE HEBREW TONGUE: ARMAGEDDON.
AND THE SEVENTH ANGEL POURED OUT HIS BOWL INTO THE AIR, AND THERE CAME A GREAT VOICE OUT OF THE TEMPLE OF HEAVEN, FROM THE THRONE, SAYING:
IT IS DONE.
AND THERE WAS A GREAT EARTHQUAKE, SUCH AS WAS NOT SEEN SINCE MEN WERE UPON THE EARTH, AND THE CITIES OF THE NATIONS FELL.
CHAPTER 17
"I WILL SHOW UNTO THESE THE JUDGEMENT OF THE GREAT WHORE THAT SITTETH UPON MANY WATERS." AND I SAW A WOMAN SIT UPON A SCARLET-COLORED BEAST...
THE WOMAN HAVING A GOLDEN CUP IN HER HAND FULL OF ABOMINATIONS AND FILTHINESS OF HER FORNICATIONS.
"AND UPON HER FOREHEAD WAS THE NAME WRITTEN: MYSTERY, BABYLON THE GREAT, MOTHER OF HARLOTS AND ABOMINATIONS OF THE EARTH."

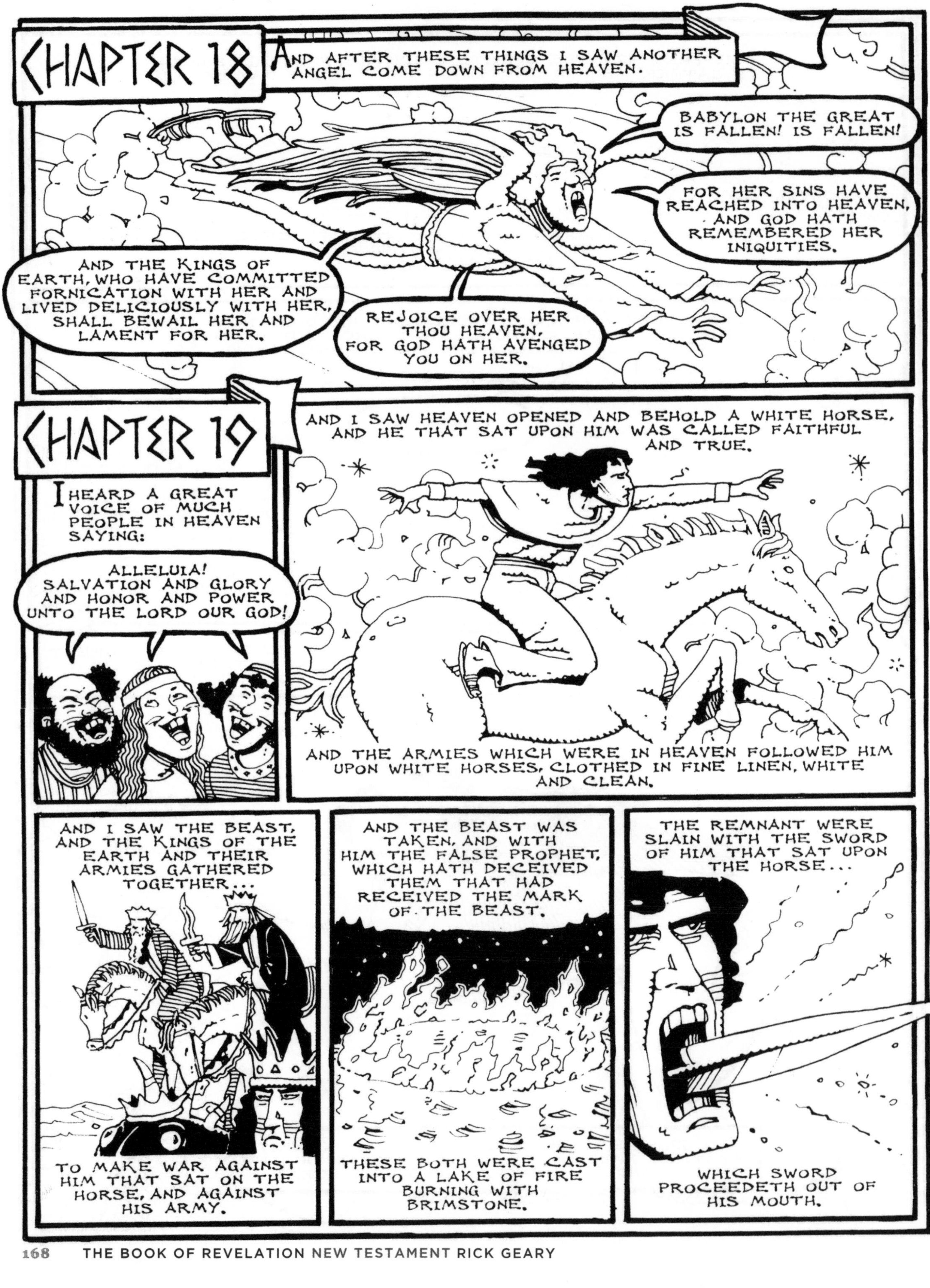
CHAPTER 18
AND AFTER THESE THINGS I SAW ANOTHER ANGEL COME DOWN FROM HEAVEN.
BABYLON THE GREAT IS FALLEN! IS FALLEN!
FOR HER SINS HAVE REACHED INTO HEAVEN, AND GOD HATH REMEMBERED HER INIQUITIES.
AND THE KINGS OF EARTH, WHO HAVE COMMITTED FORNICATION WITH HER AND LIVED DELICIOUSLY WITH HER, SHALL BEWAIL HER AND LAMENT FOR HER.
REJOICE OVER HER THOU HEAVEN, FOR GOD HATH AVENGED YOU ON HER.
CHAPTER 19
I HEARD A GREAT VOICE OF MUCH PEOPLE IN HEAVEN SAYING:
ALLELUIA! SALVATION AND GLORY AND HONOR AND POWER UNTO THE LORD OUR GOD!
AND I SAW HEAVEN OPENED AND BEHOLD A WHITE HORSE, AND HE THAT SAT UPON HIM WAS CALLED FAITHFUL AND TRUE.
AND THE ARMIES WHICH WERE IN HEAVEN FOLLOWED HIM UPON WHITE HORSES, CLOTHED IN FINE LINEN, WHITE AND CLEAN.
AND I SAW THE BEAST, AND THE KINGS OF THE EARTH AND THEIR ARMIES GATHERED TOGETHER...
TO MAKE WAR AGAINST HIM THAT SAT ON THE HORSE, AND AGAINST HIS ARMY.
AND THE BEAST WAS TAKEN, AND WITH HIM THE FALSE PROPHET, WHICH HATH DECEIVED THEM THAT HAD RECEIVED THE MARK OF THE BEAST.
THESE BOTH WERE CAST INTO A LAKE OF FIRE BURNING WITH BRIMSTONE.
THE REMNANT WERE SLAIN WITH THE SWORD OF HIM THAT SAT UPON THE HORSE...
WHICH SWORD PROCEEDETH OUT OF HIS MOUTH.

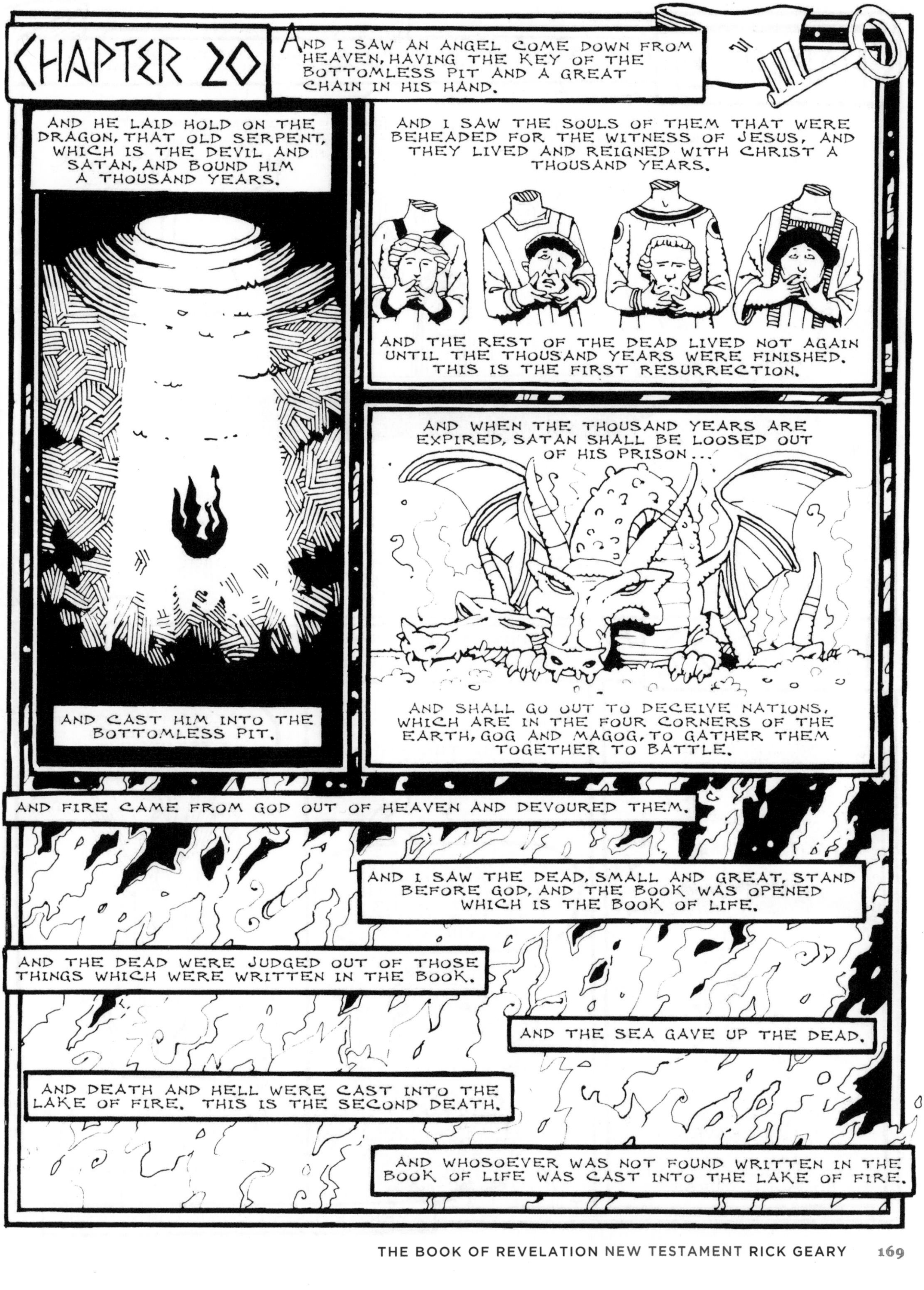
CHAPTER 20
AND I SAW AN ANGEL COME DOWN FROM HEAVEN, HAVING THE KEY OF THE BOTTOMLESS PIT AND A GREAT CHAIN IN HIS HAND.
AND HE LAID HOLD ON THE DRAGON, THAT OLD SERPENT, WHICH IS THE DEVIL AND SATAN, AND BOUND HIM A THOUSAND YEARS.
AND CAST HIM INTO THE BOTTOMLESS PIT.
AND I SAW THE SOULS OF THEM THAT WERE BEHEADED FOR THE WITNESS OF JESUS, AND THEY LIVED AND REIGNED WITH CHRIST A THOUSAND YEARS.
AND THE REST OF THE DEAD LIVED NOT AGAIN UNTIL THE THOUSAND YEARS WERE FINISHED. THIS IS THE FIRST RESURRECTION.
AND WHEN THE THOUSAND YEARS ARE EXPIRED, SATAN SHALL BE LOOSED OUT OF HIS PRISON...
AND SHALL GO OUT TO DECEIVE NATIONS, WHICH ARE IN THE FOUR CORNERS OF THE EARTH, GOG AND MAGOG, TO GATHER THEM TOGETHER TO BATTLE.
AND FIRE CAME FROM GOD OUT OF HEAVEN AND DEVOURED THEM.
AND I SAW THE DEAD, SMALL AND GREAT, STAND BEFORE GOD, AND THE BOOK WAS OPENED WHICH IS THE BOOK OF LIFE.
AND THE DEAD WERE JUDGED OUT OF THOSE THINGS WHICH WERE WRITTEN IN THE BOOK.
AND THE SEA GAVE UP THE DEAD.
AND DEATH AND HELL WERE CAST INTO THE LAKE OF FIRE. THIS IS THE SECOND DEATH.
AND WHOSOEVER WAS NOT FOUND WRITTEN IN THE BOOK OF LIFE WAS CAST INTO THE LAKE OF FIRE.

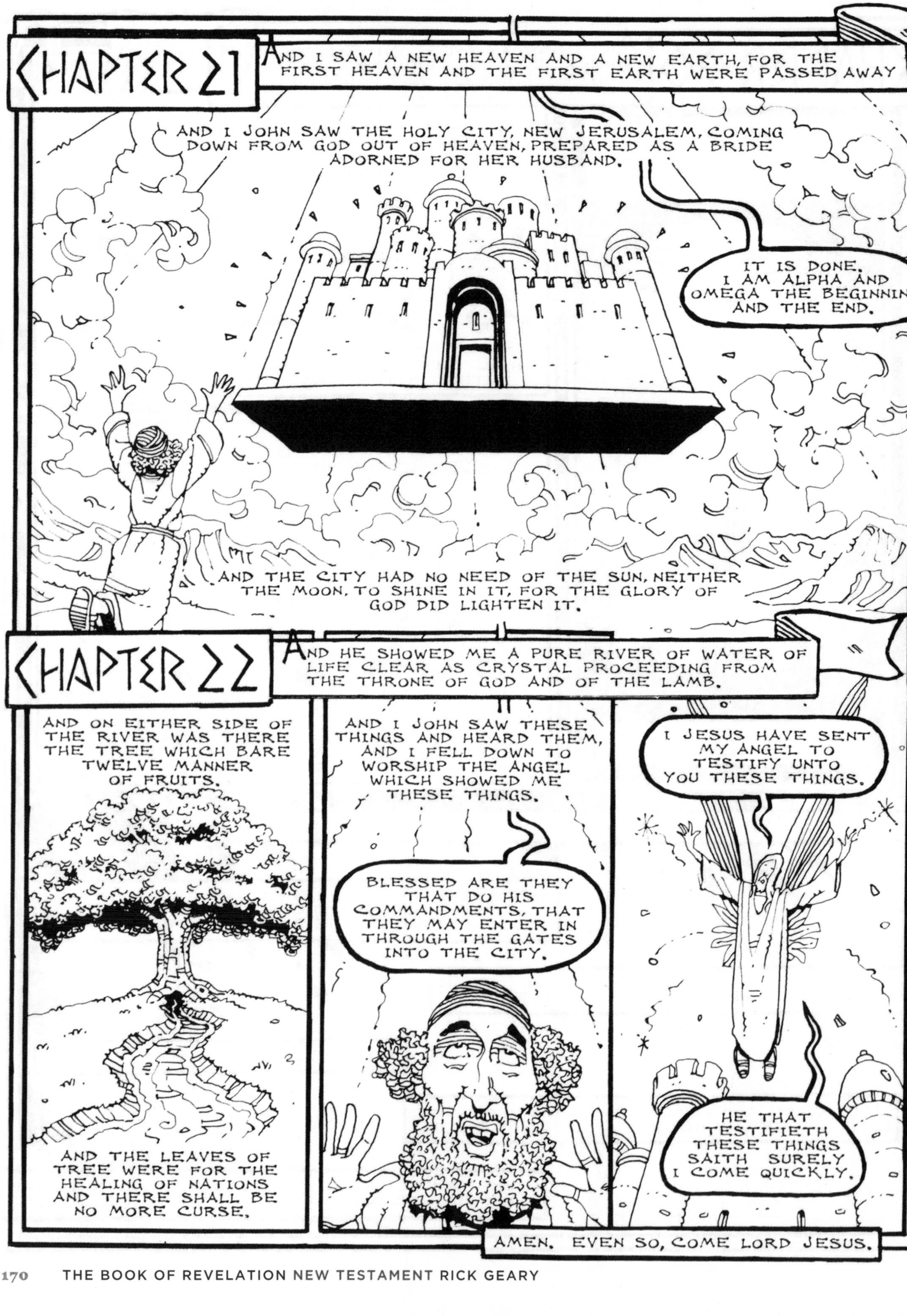
CHAPTER 21
AND I SAW A NEW HEAVEN AND A NEW EARTH, FOR THE FIRST HEAVEN AND THE FIRST EARTH WERE PASSED AWAY
AND I JOHN SAW THE HOLY CITY, NEW JERUSALEM, COMING DOWN FROM GOD OUT OF HEAVEN, PREPARED AS A BRIDE ADORNED FOR HER HUSBAND.
IT IS DONE. I AM ALPHA AND OMEGA THE BEGINNING AND THE END.
AND THE CITY HAD NO NEED OF THE SUN, NEITHER THE MOON, TO SHINE IN IT, FOR THE GLORY OF GOD DID LIGHTEN IT.
CHAPTER 22
AND HE SHOWED ME A PURE RIVER OF WATER OF LIFE CLEAR AS CRYSTAL PROCEEDING FROM THE THRONE OF GOD AND OF THE LAMB.
AND ON EITHER SIDE OF THE RIVER WAS THERE THE TREE WHICH BARE TWELVE MANNER OF FRUITS.
AND THE LEAVES OF TREE WERE FOR THE HEALING OF NATIONS AND THERE SHALL BE NO MORE CURSE.
AND I JOHN SAW THESE THINGS AND HEARD THEM, AND I FELL DOWN TO WORSHIP THE ANGEL WHICH SHOWED ME THESE THINGS.
BLESSED ARE THEY THAT DO HIS COMMANDMENTS, THAT THEY MAY ENTER IN THROUGH THE GATES INTO THE CITY.
I JESUS HAVE SENT MY ANGEL TO TESTIFY UNTO YOU THESE THINGS.
HE THAT TESTIFIETH THESE THINGS SAITH SURELY I COME QUICKLY.
AMEN. EVEN SO, COME LORD JESUS.

Three Tang poems

Wang Han, Cui Hu, and Li Bai

ART / ADAPTATION AND TRANSLATION BY **Sharon Rudahl**

WHEN YOU READ ABOUT CHINESE POETRY during the Tang Dynasty (618–907 CE), you'll see the phrase "golden age" a lot. The greatest verse in the nation's history was written during these three centuries, and it's often said that the three or four supreme Chinese poets lived during this period. Not that they were the only ones; an astonishing 49,000 poems by 2,200 poets from the Tang Dynasty have survived to the present. The most famous ones are those collected in Sun Zhu's 1763 anthology, *Tang Shi San Bai Shou* [*300 Tang Poems*], which includes the three found here.

Essentially nothing is known of Wang Han, writer of "Frontier Song." However, there is a story, possibly apocryphal, behind Cui Hu and his poem, "A Village South of the Capital." It's said that Cui Hu was a dashing scholar who went to the capital to take his civil servant exam. While walking in the countryside, he knocked on the door of a farmer's house to ask for a drink of water. He was greeted by the stunningly beautiful daughter of the farmer. The next year, when taking the annual exam, he called again on the house, but no one was there. Despondent, he left his poem on the door. A few days later, he went back, and the agitated farmer said that his daughter had collapsed upon finding the verse. Hearing her dreamboat at the door, she recovered, and the two soon married.

Li Bai (also known as Li Po), author of "Drinking Alone Beneath the Moon," is one of the aforementioned greatest Chinese poets in history, practically deified in his homeland. According to translator David Hinton, "[H]e spent some time as a 'knight-errant,' which involved avenging injustices suffered by the helpless, and it is said that in this role he killed several people with his sword. He also spent several years as a Taoist recluse in the mountains near his home. These two occupations are emblematic of Li Po's temperament: a deep and quiet spirituality on the one hand, and on the other, a swaggering brashness."

Sharon Rudahl is a pioneer of underground comics, part of the generation that created the medium. Among many other things, she cofounded and drew for the pathbreaking *Wimmen's Comix* in the early 1970s. Here, she gives us what are apparently the first graphic adaptations of Tang poems, complete with her own English translations and beautiful calligraphy of the original Chinese.

SOURCES

Po, Li. *The Selected Poems of Li Po.* Translated by David Hinton. New Directions, 1996.

Gill, John, and Susan Tidwell (editors). *After Many Autumns: A Collection of Chinese Buddhist Literature.* Buddha's Light Publishing, 2011.

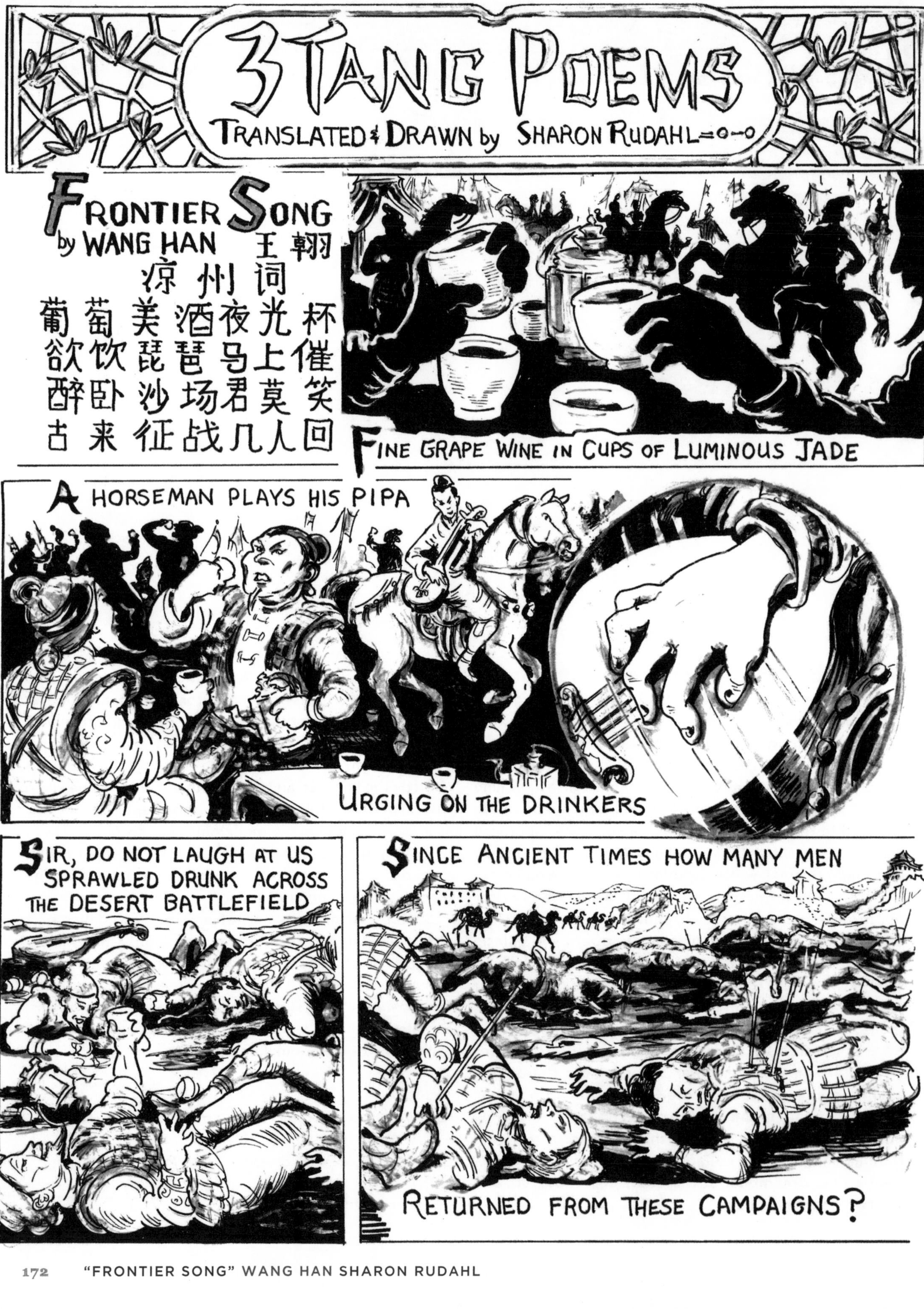
3 TANG POEMS
TRANSLATED & DRAWN by SHARON RUDAHL
FRONTIER SONG
by WANG HAN 王翰
凉州词
葡萄美酒夜光杯
欲饮琵琶马上催
醉卧沙场君莫笑
古来征战几人回
FINE GRAPE WINE IN CUPS OF LUMINOUS JADE
A HORSEMAN PLAYS HIS PIPA
URGING ON THE DRINKERS
SIR, DO NOT LAUGH AT US SPRAWLED DRUNK ACROSS THE DESERT BATTLEFIELD
SINCE ANCIENT TIMES HOW MANY MEN
RETURNED FROM THESE CAMPAIGNS?

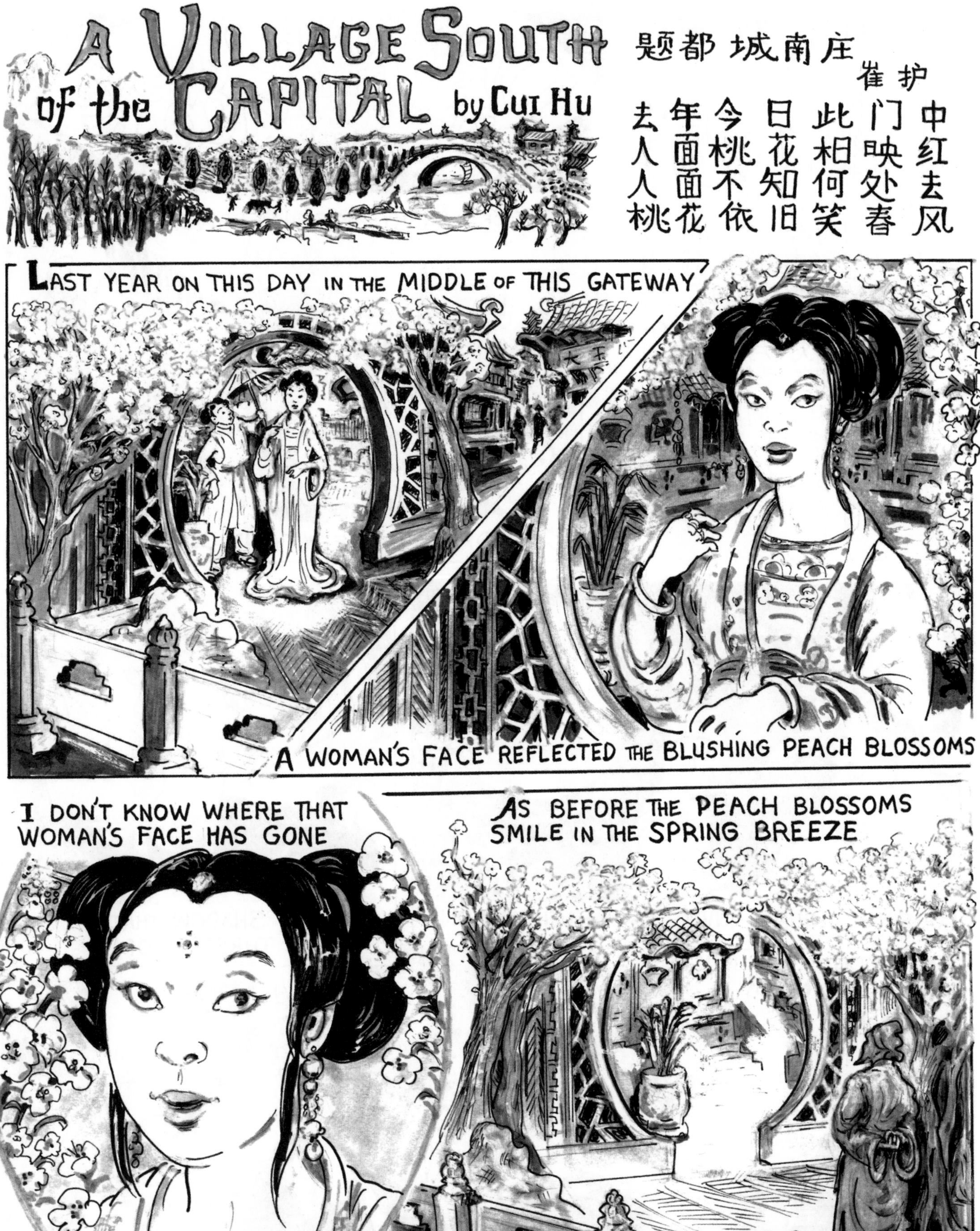
A VILLAGE SOUTH of the CAPITAL
by CUI HU
题都城南庄
崔护
去年今日此门中
人面桃花相映红
人面不知何处去
桃花依旧笑春风
LAST YEAR ON THIS DAY IN THE MIDDLE OF THIS GATEWAY
A WOMAN'S FACE REFLECTED THE BLUSHING PEACH BLOSSOMS
I DON'T KNOW WHERE THAT WOMAN'S FACE HAS GONE
AS BEFORE THE PEACH BLOSSOMS SMILE IN THE SPRING BREEZE
SHARON RUDAHL '16

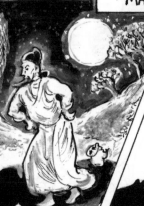

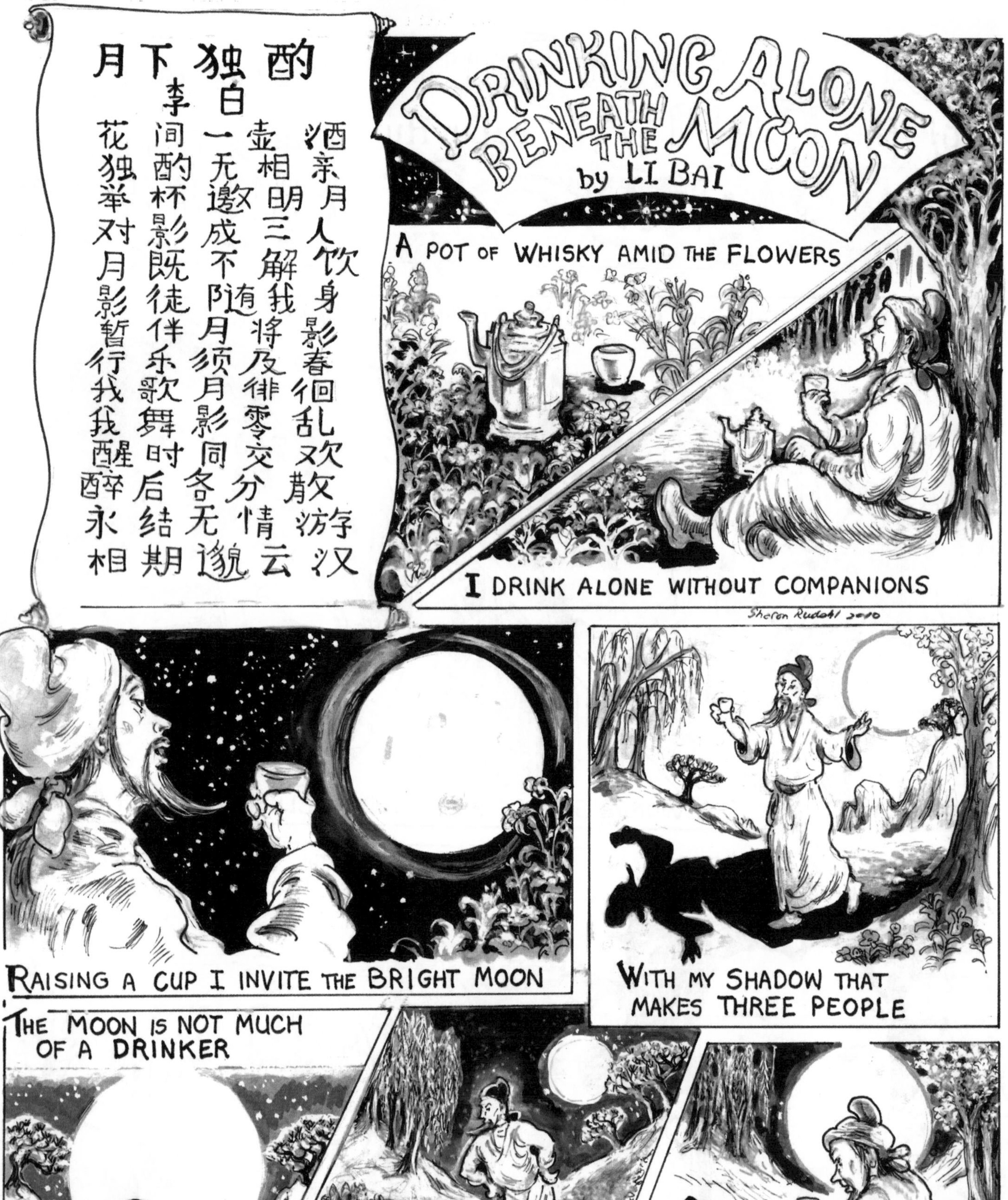
月下独酌
李白
花间一壶酒
独酌无相亲
举杯邀明月
对影成三人
月既不解饮
影徒随我身
暂伴月将影
行乐须及春
我歌月徘徊
我舞影零乱
醒时同交欢
醉后各分散
永结无情游
相期邈云汉
DRINKING ALONE BENEATH THE MOON
by LI BAI
A POT OF WHISKY AMID THE FLOWERS
I DRINK ALONE WITHOUT COMPANIONS
Sharon Rudahl 2010
RAISING A CUP I INVITE THE BRIGHT MOON
WITH MY SHADOW THAT MAKES THREE PEOPLE
THE MOON IS NOT MUCH OF A DRINKER
THE SHADOW PERSISTENTLY TAGS AFTER ME
BUT FOR NOW I'LL KEEP MOON AND SHADOW COMPANY

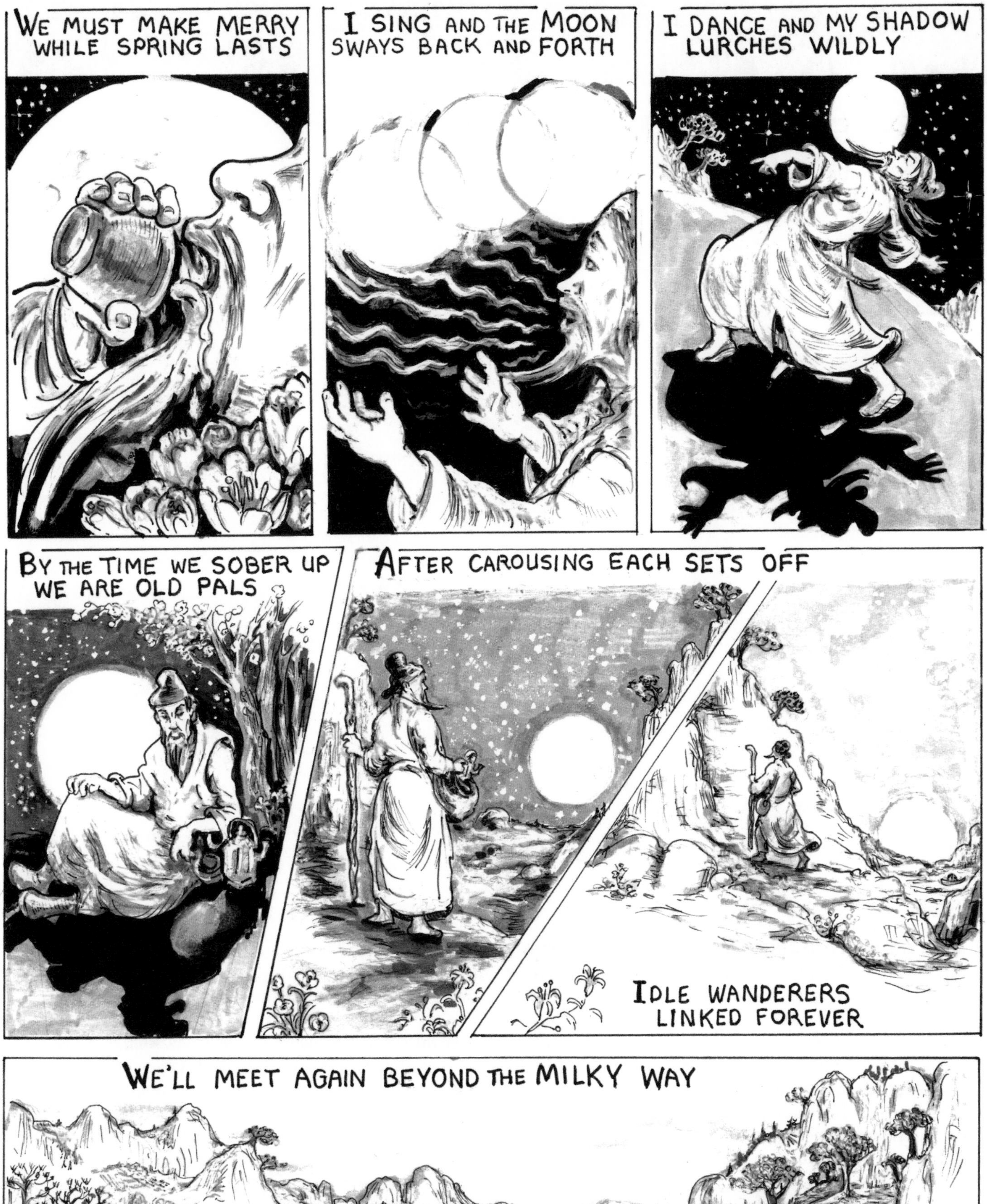
WE MUST MAKE MERRY WHILE SPRING LASTS
I SING AND THE MOON SWAYS BACK AND FORTH
I DANCE AND MY SHADOW LURCHES WILDLY
BY THE TIME WE SOBER UP WE ARE OLD PALS
AFTER CAROUSING EACH SETS OFF
IDLE WANDERERS LINKED FOREVER
WE'LL MEET AGAIN BEYOND THE MILKY WAY
SHARON RUDAHL 2010

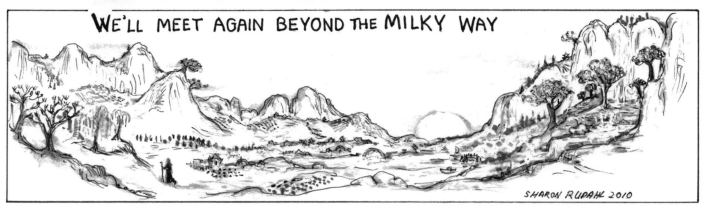

Beowulf

Anglo-Saxon epic poem

ART / ADAPTATION BY **Gareth Hinds**

LIKE SO MANY WORKS OF ANCIENT LITERATURE, the origins of the great Anglo-Saxon epic poem *Beowulf* are hopelessly cloudy. Was it originally an oral poem that was eventually set down by a scribe, or did a poet write an original work, albeit one based on legends? Was it created in the 700s CE (as J. R. R. Tolkien believed) or around the year 1000, or sometime in between? If you crave certainty, literature is not a field that will give you comfort.

This poem of almost 3,200 lines, written in Old English, is set in Scandinavia in the fifth century CE. In the first part, the King of the Danes (a Germanic tribe in what is now Denmark) has a pest-control problem—the monstrous Grendel is invading his huge mead hall and slaughtering his warriors. Beowulf, a hero from another Germanic tribe (the Geats, in what is now Sweden), offers himself as the exterminator, leading to one of the most epic fight scenes in all of literature.

In part two, Beowulf battles Grendel's infuriated mother in her underwater lair. The third, final part of the tale takes place fifty years later, when Beowulf, now King of the Geats, squares off with a dragon; the two kill each other.

Gareth Hinds—who also contributed adaptations of *The Odyssey* and *Gulliver's Travels* to this volume—self-published a series of comics adapting the epic in all its gory glory, with each of the three parts done in a different style using various media, including ink, paints, wood panels, white charcoal, and digital coloring. These were later collected into a graphic novel by Candlewick Press. In the pages that follow, you'll find a shortened version of part one, as abridged by Gareth for *The Graphic Canon*.

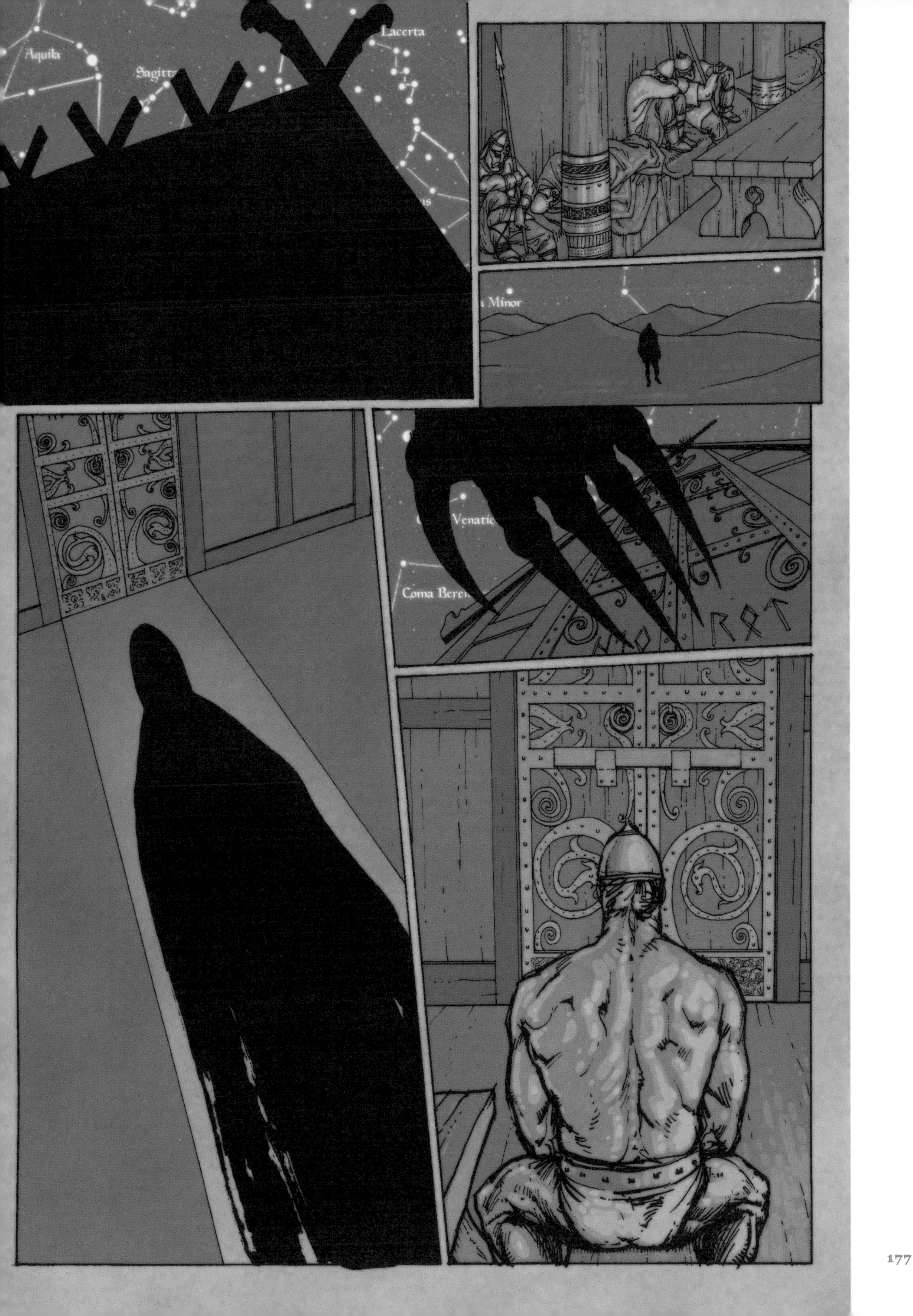
Aquila
Lacerta

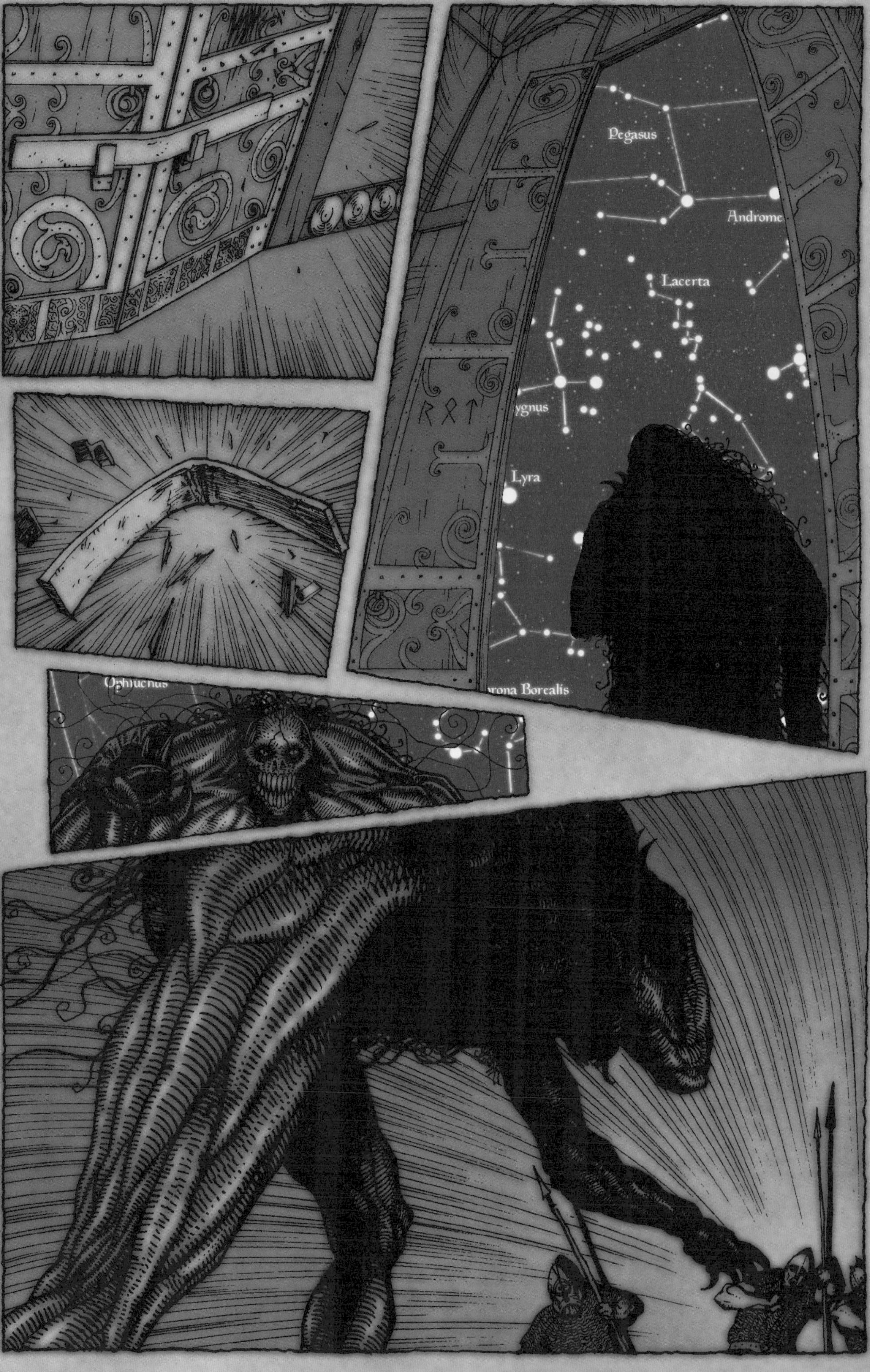
Pegasus
Androme
Lacerta
ygnus
Lyra
rona Borealis
Ophiuchus

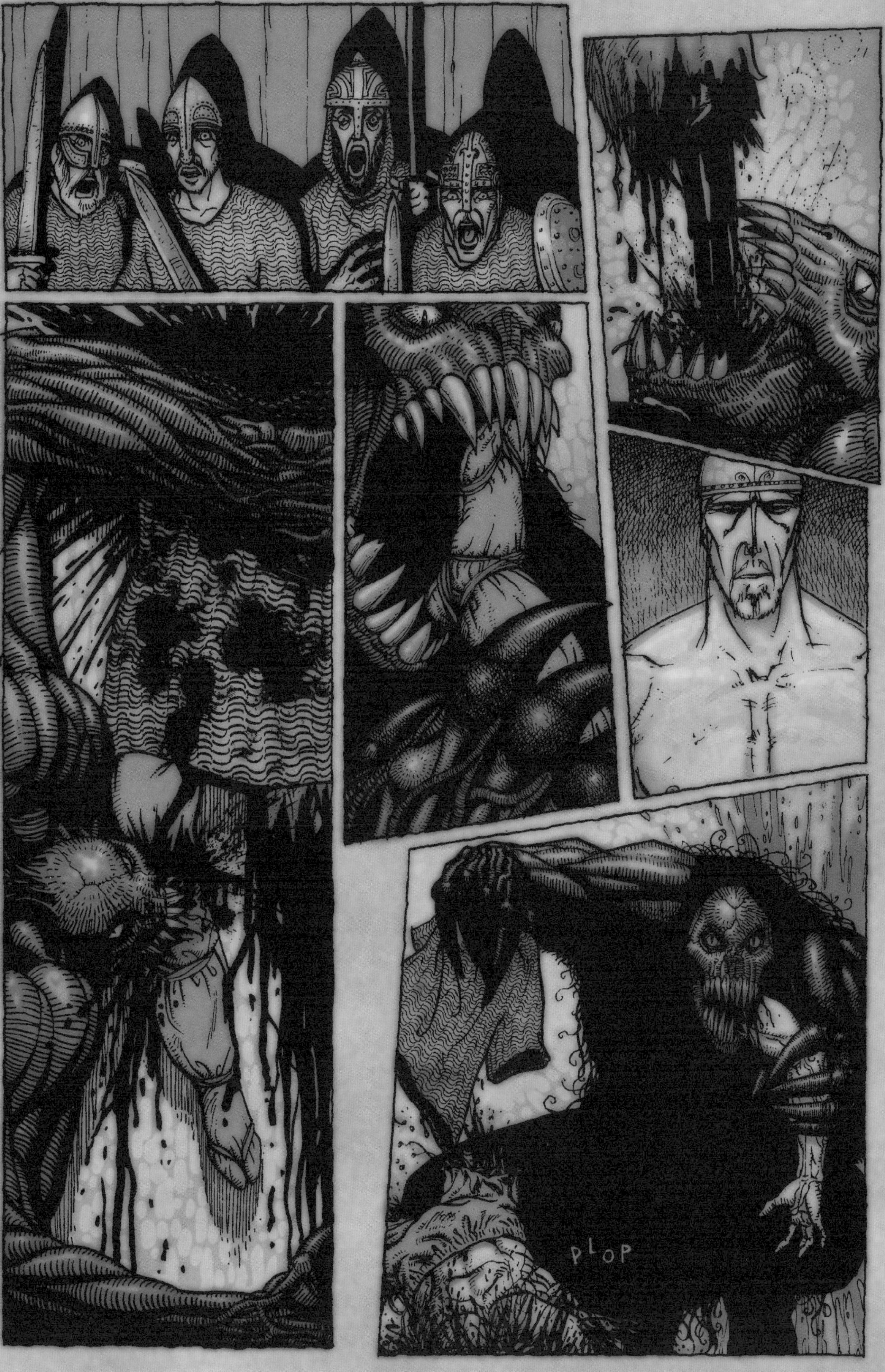
PLOP

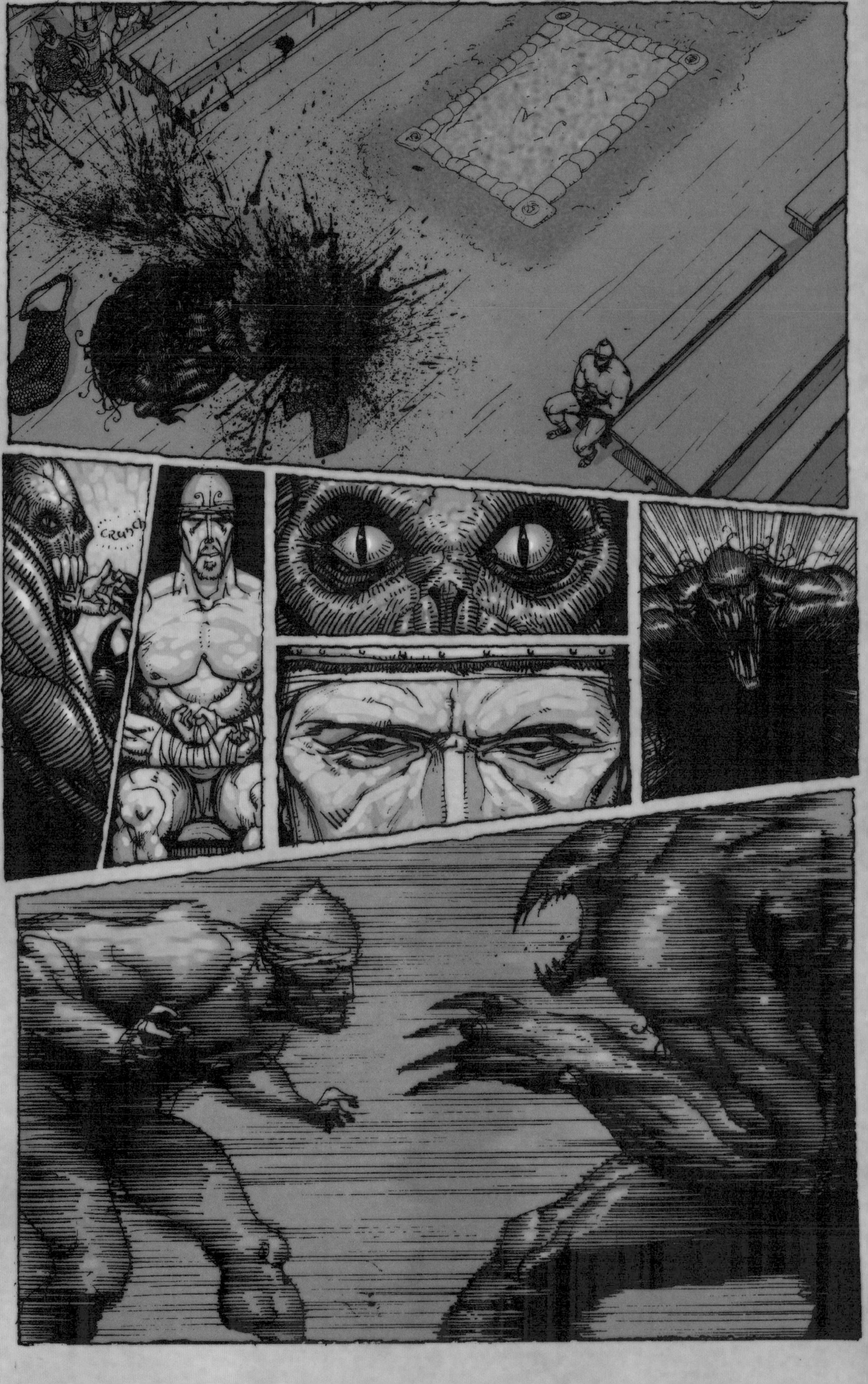
CRUNCH

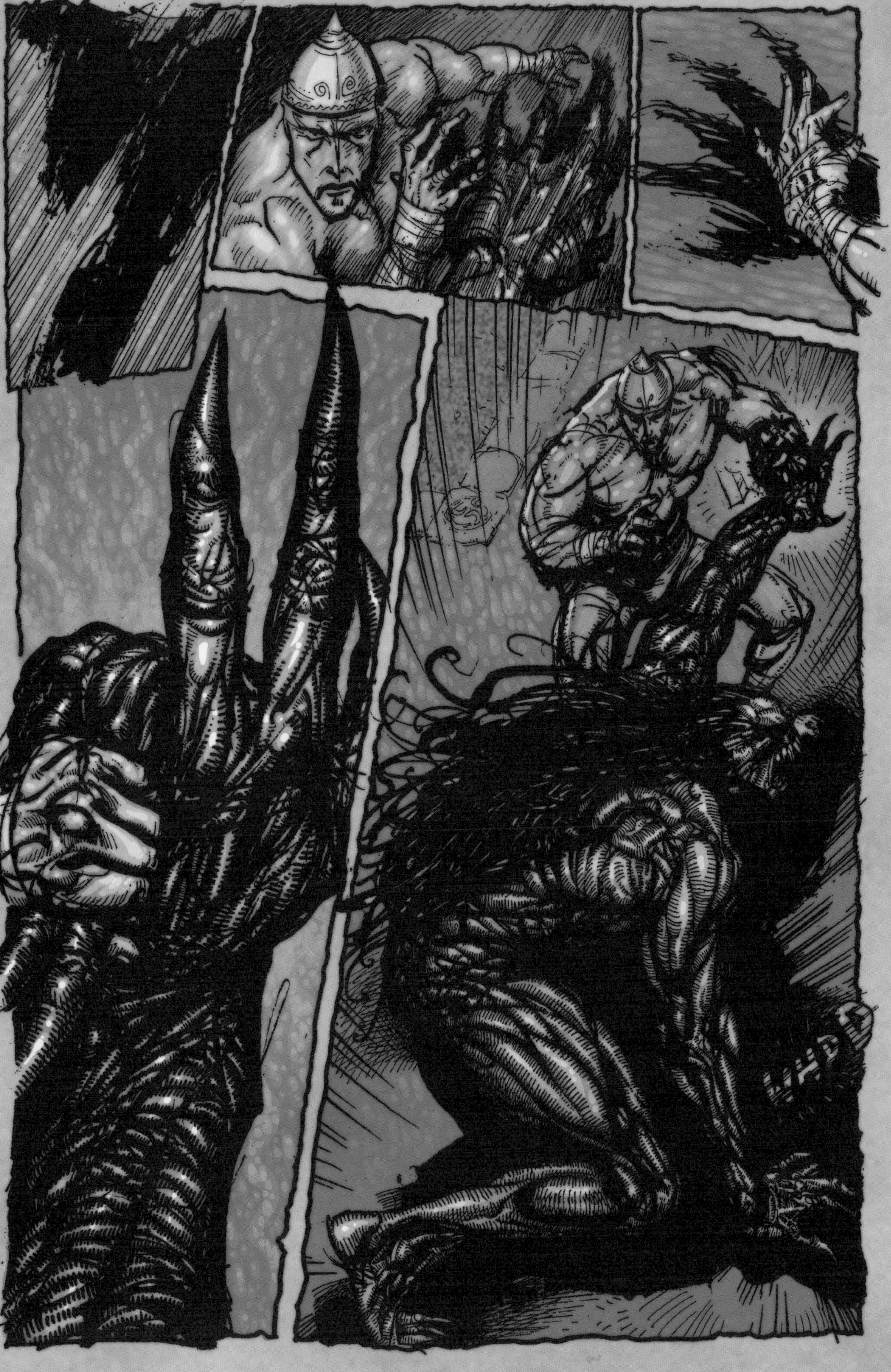

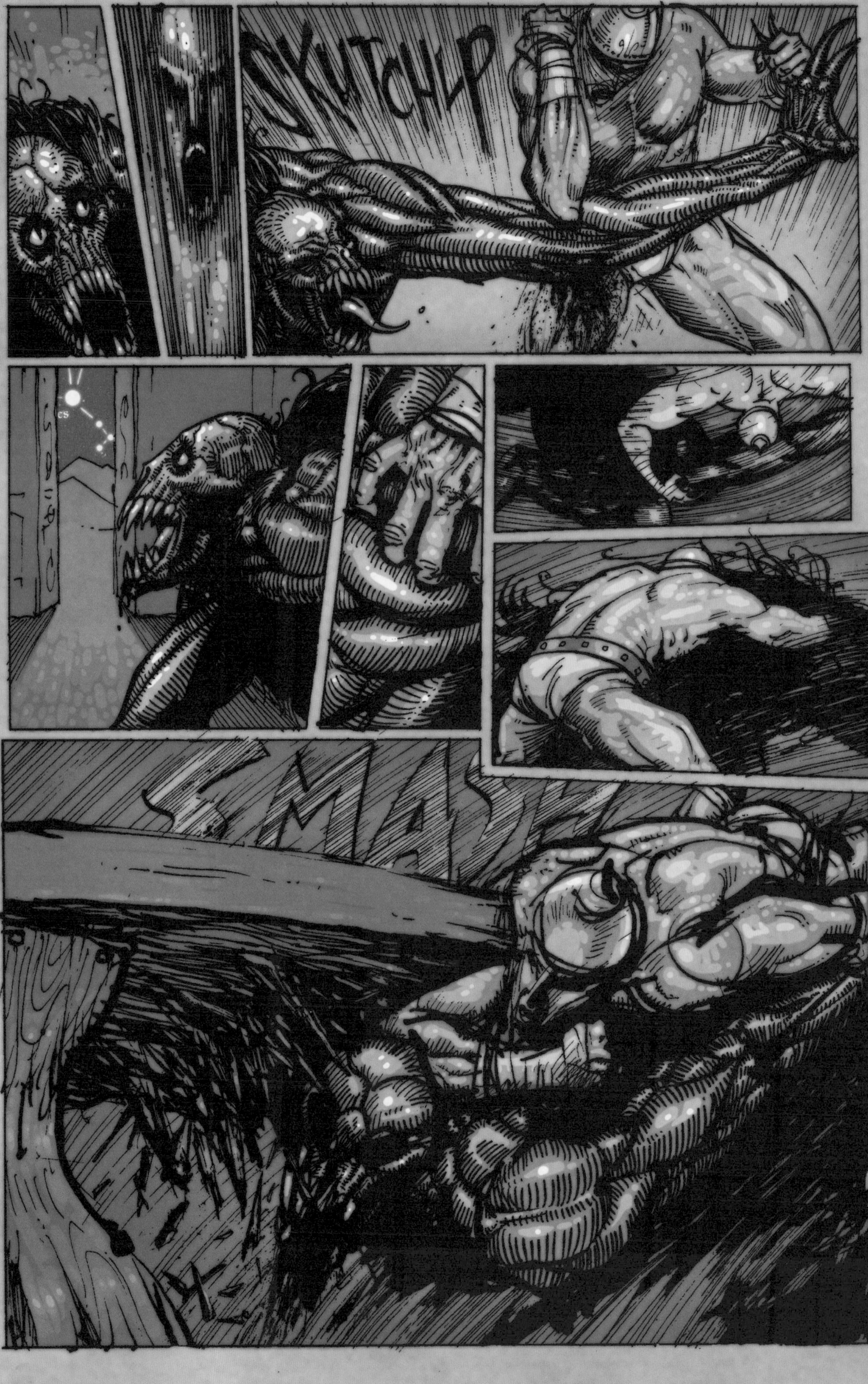
SKUTCHLP

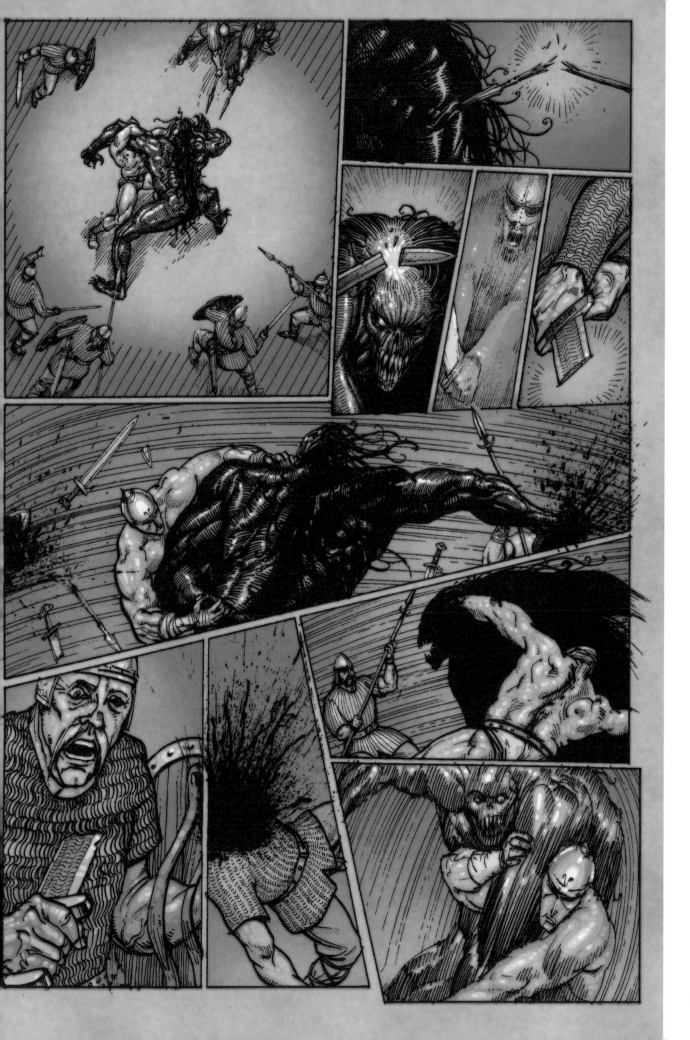

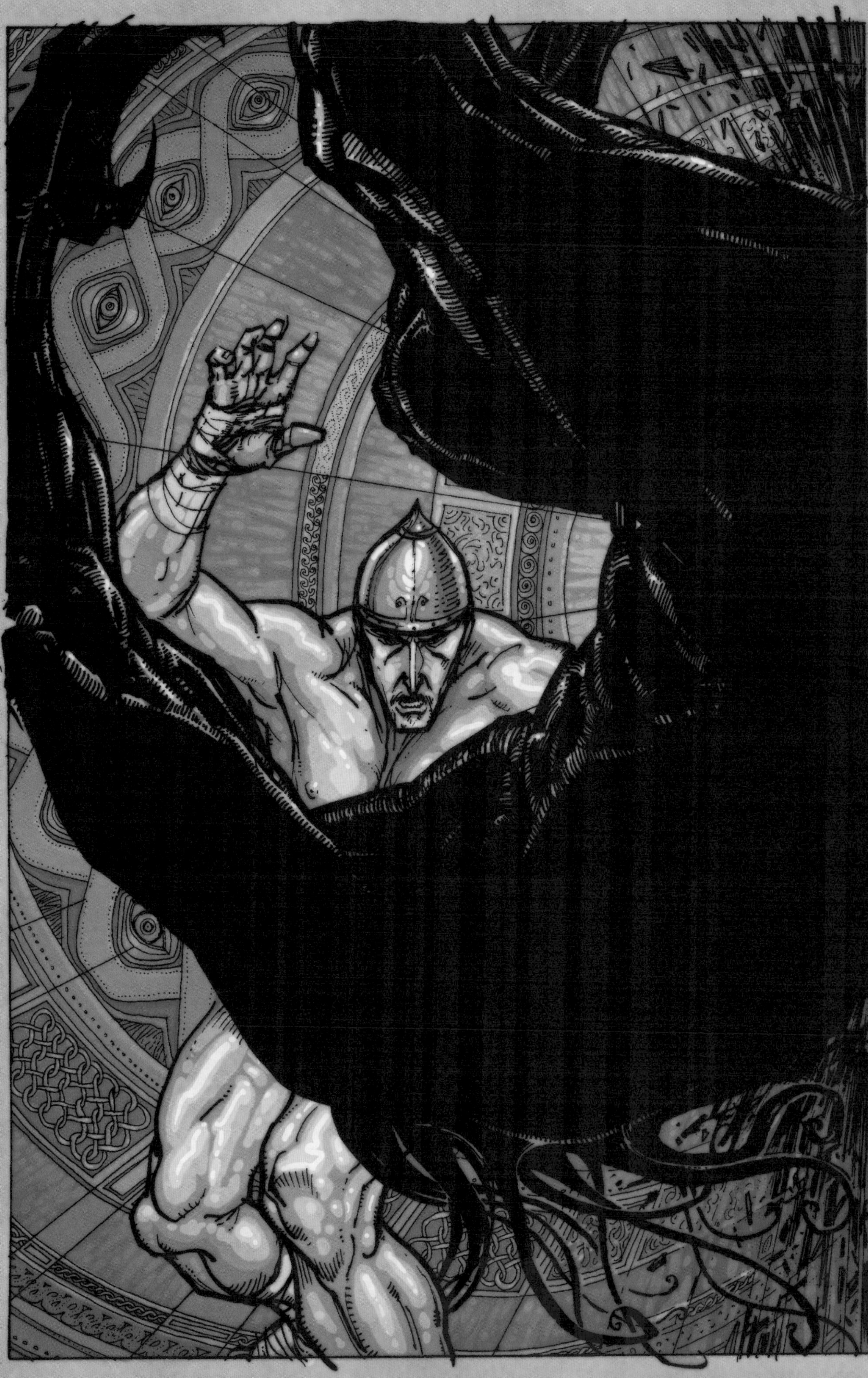

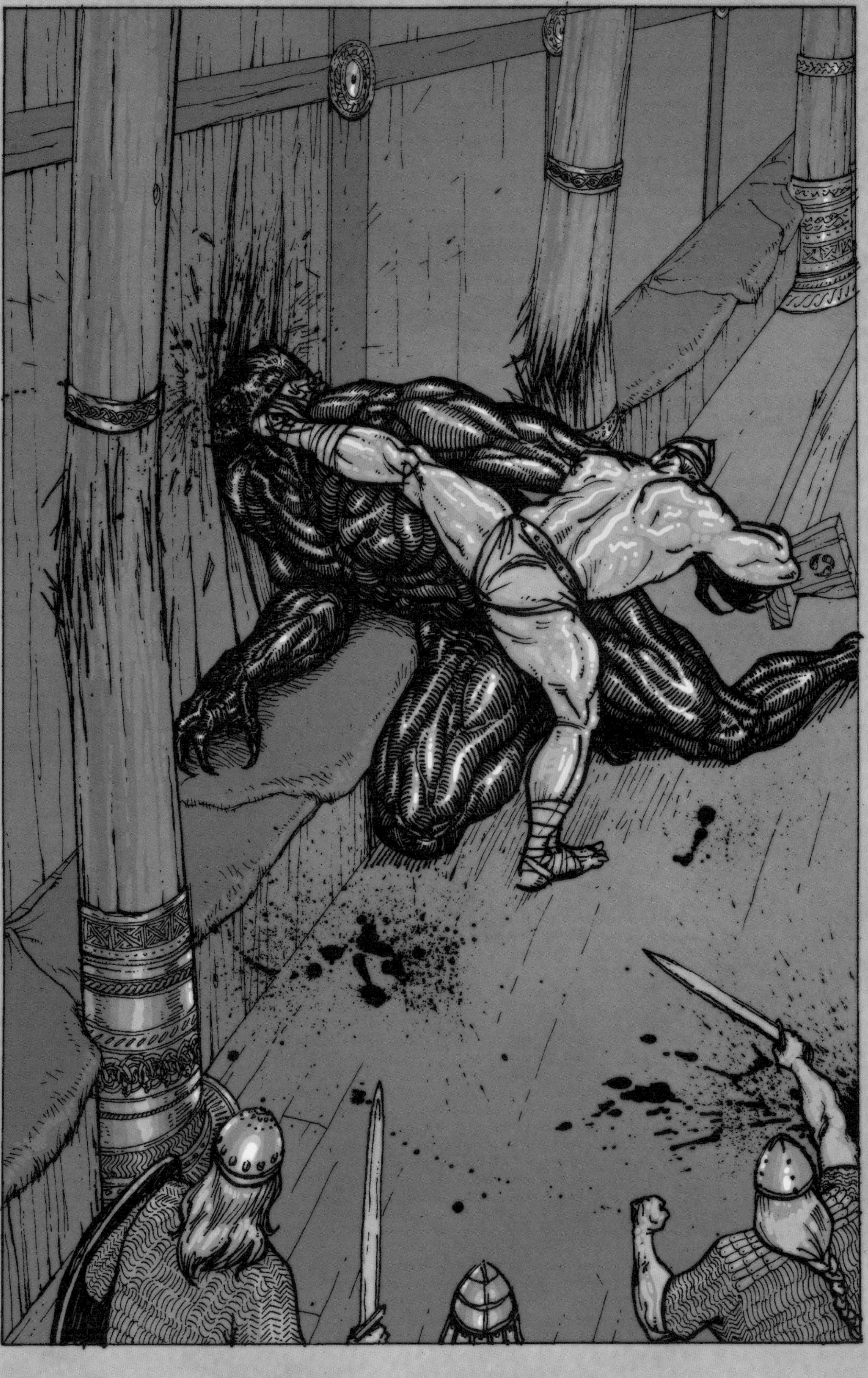

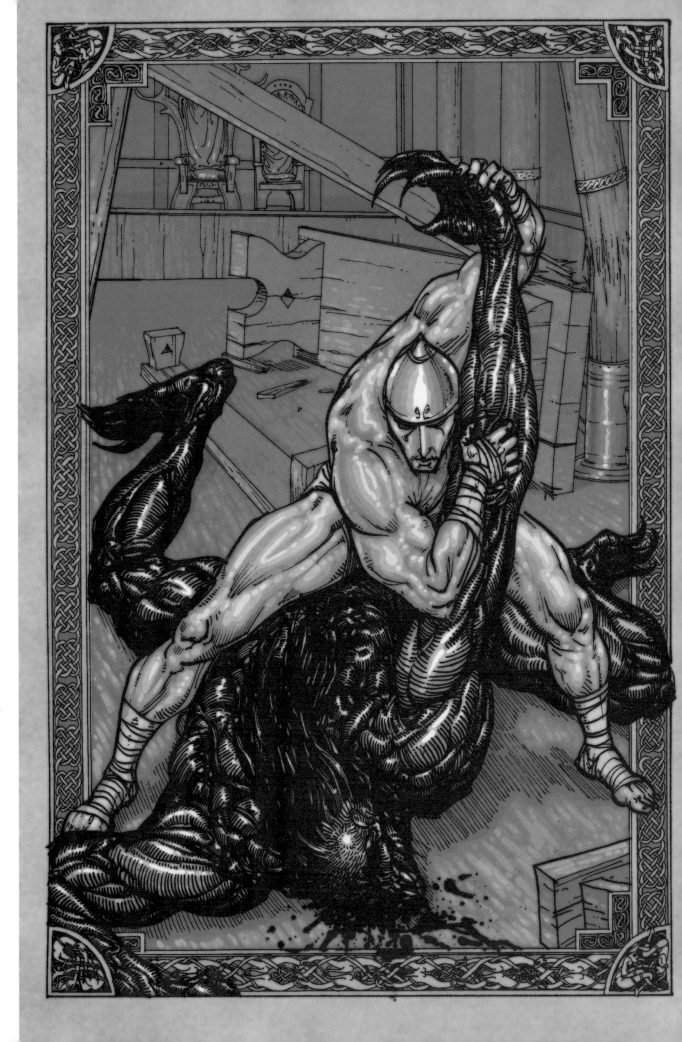

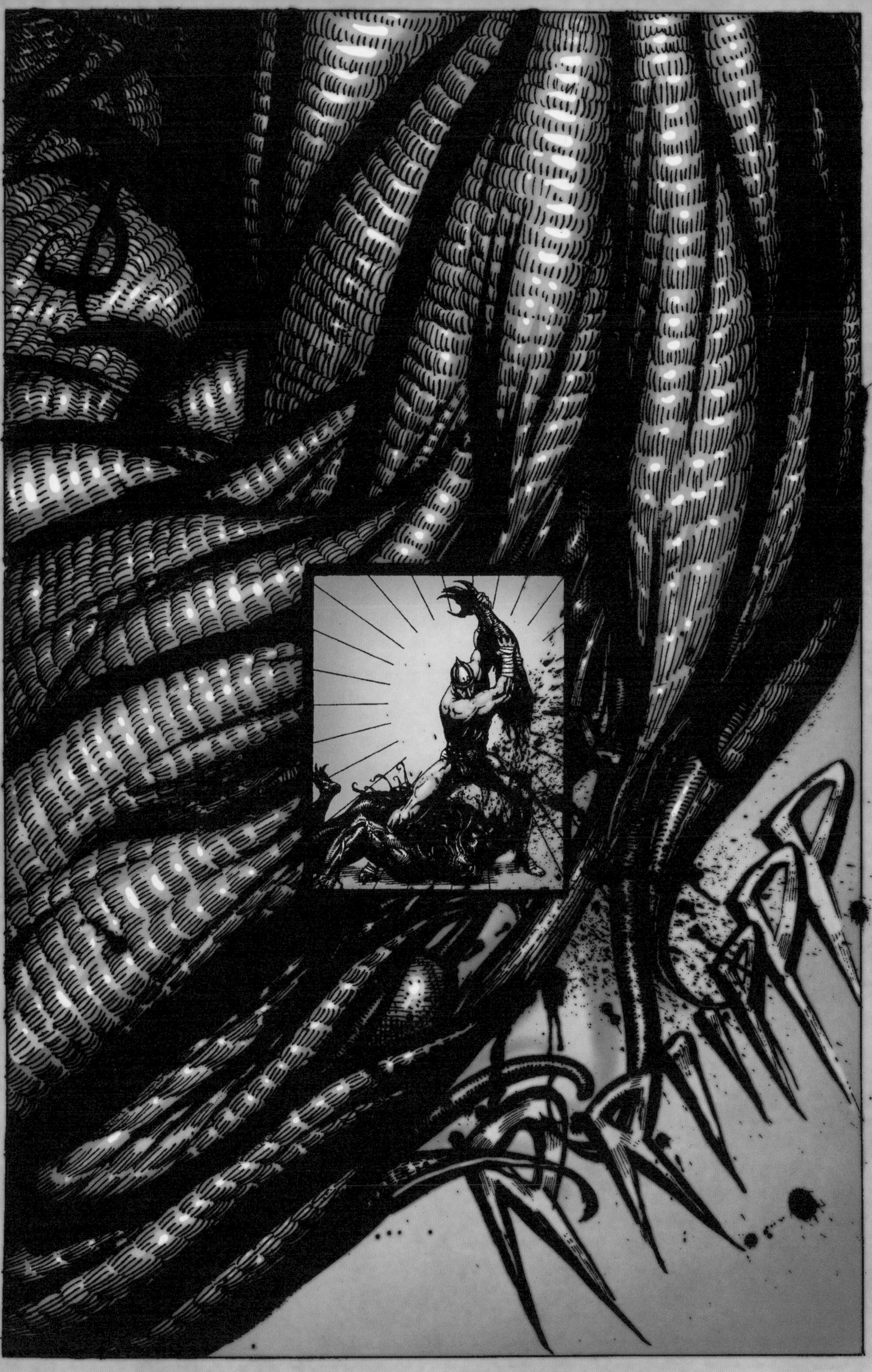

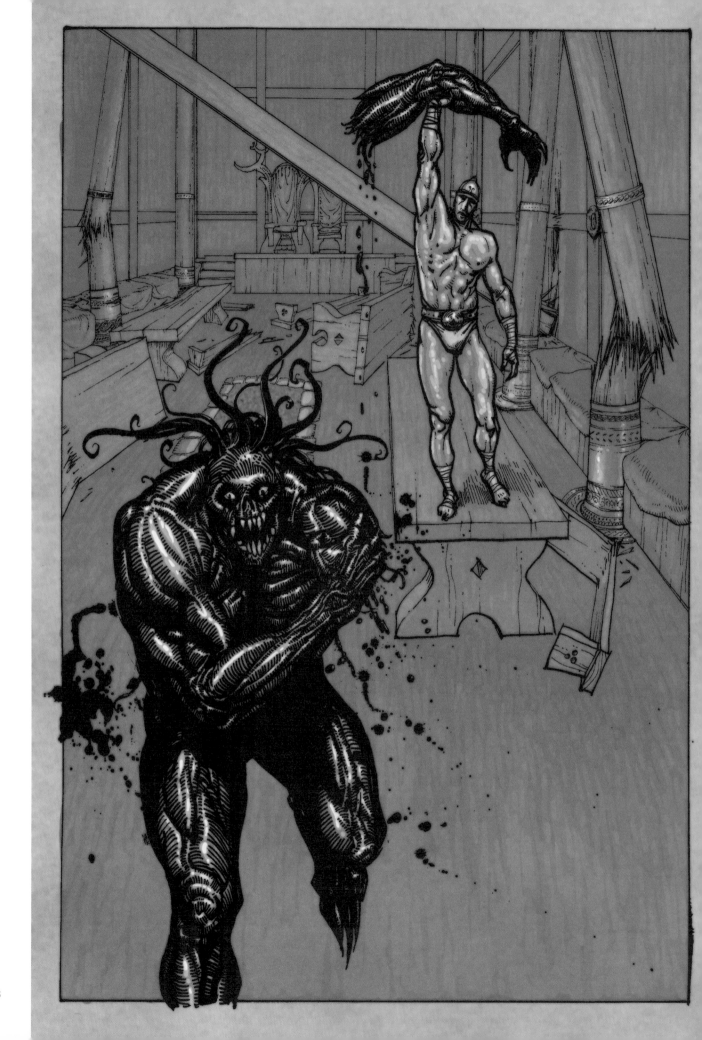

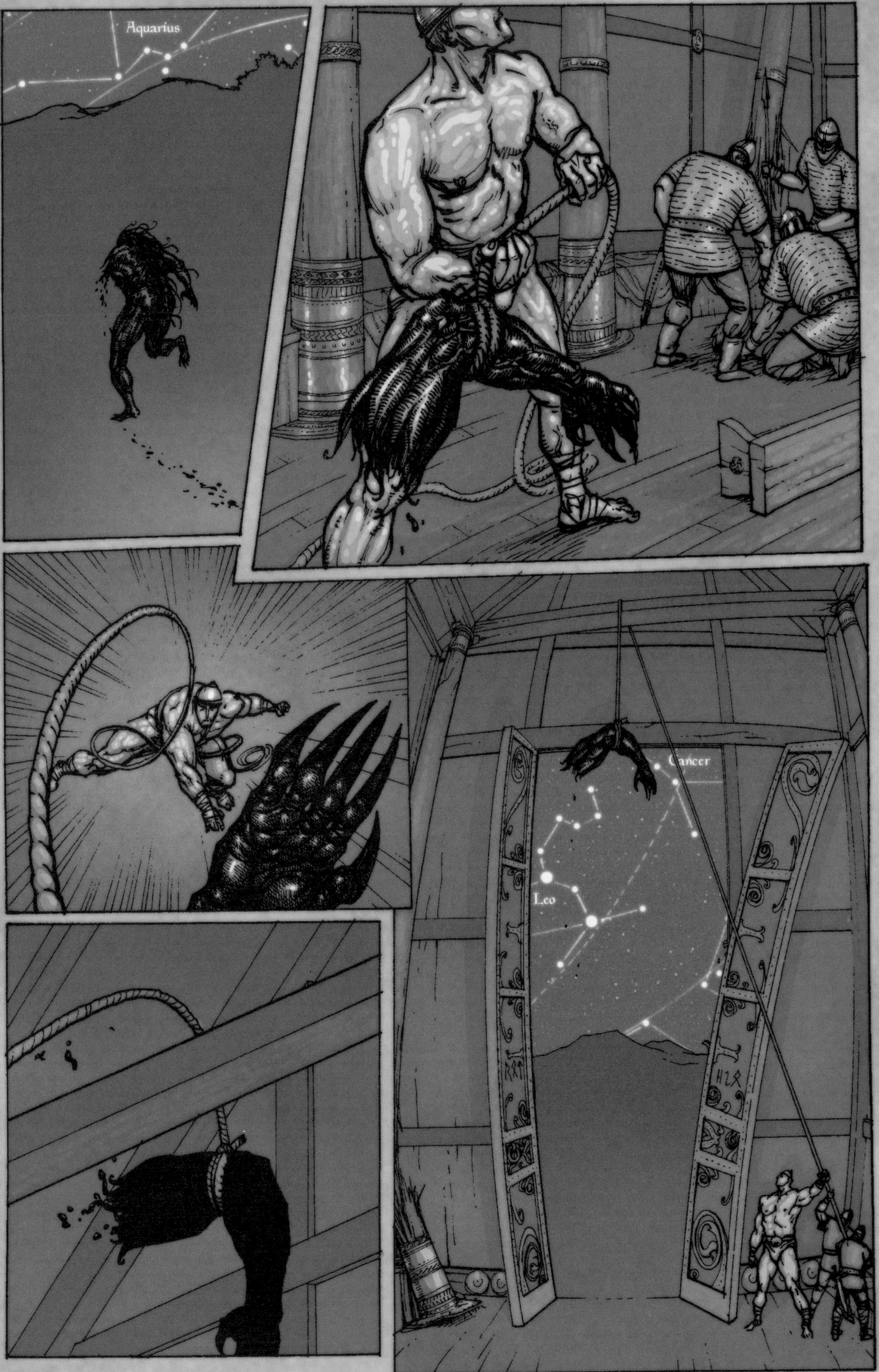
Aquarius
Cancer
Leo

The Tale of Genji

Murasaki Shikibu

ART / ADAPTATION BY **Molly Kiely**

THE TALE OF GENJI **IS WIDELY CONSIDERED THE** world's first novel and remains Japan's crowning work of literature. Written about a thousand years ago by Murasaki Shikibu, a lady of the Japanese court, it's a monster— unabridged English-language translations usually top 1,100 pages. It chiefly follows the romantic exploits of its title character, a son of the Emperor and one of his concubines of low rank, as he woos, pursues, and sometimes coerces various women and girls, usually of the aristocratic variety, all the while negotiating the political landscape of the imperial Heian period. When he dies, Genji's alleged son (who isn't really his) and Genji's grandson become the protagonists of the book's last part, wherein they chase various women, sometimes competing for the same one. *Genji* has been adapted umpteen times into manga, including a 13-volume version that has sold in excess of 14 million copies.

Molly Kiely is best known as one of the *very* few female artists creating erotic comics. Her sequential stories and one-page pinups are still remembered by fans not only for their exultant sexiness but also for their pervasive humor—in every flavor from the sly and the extremely clever to the charmingly silly—and for their *joie de vivre.* Having put out two graphic novels, two series, and two one-shots (among other works) under Fantagraphics' Eros imprint, Molly put her career on hold to start a family. Her adaptations in all three volumes of *The Graphic Canon* mark her blazing return to comics and illustration, with *The Tale of Genji*'s large cast of beautiful women allowing her to apply her pinup approach and Beardsleyesque style to a work from medieval Japan, giving identities to the women who remained literally shut inside the court, hidden behind screens, seldom glimpsed by anyone but their attendants.

SOURCE

Puette, William J. *The Tale of Genji: A Reader's Guide.* Tokyo and North Clarendon, VT: Tuttle Publishing (1983).

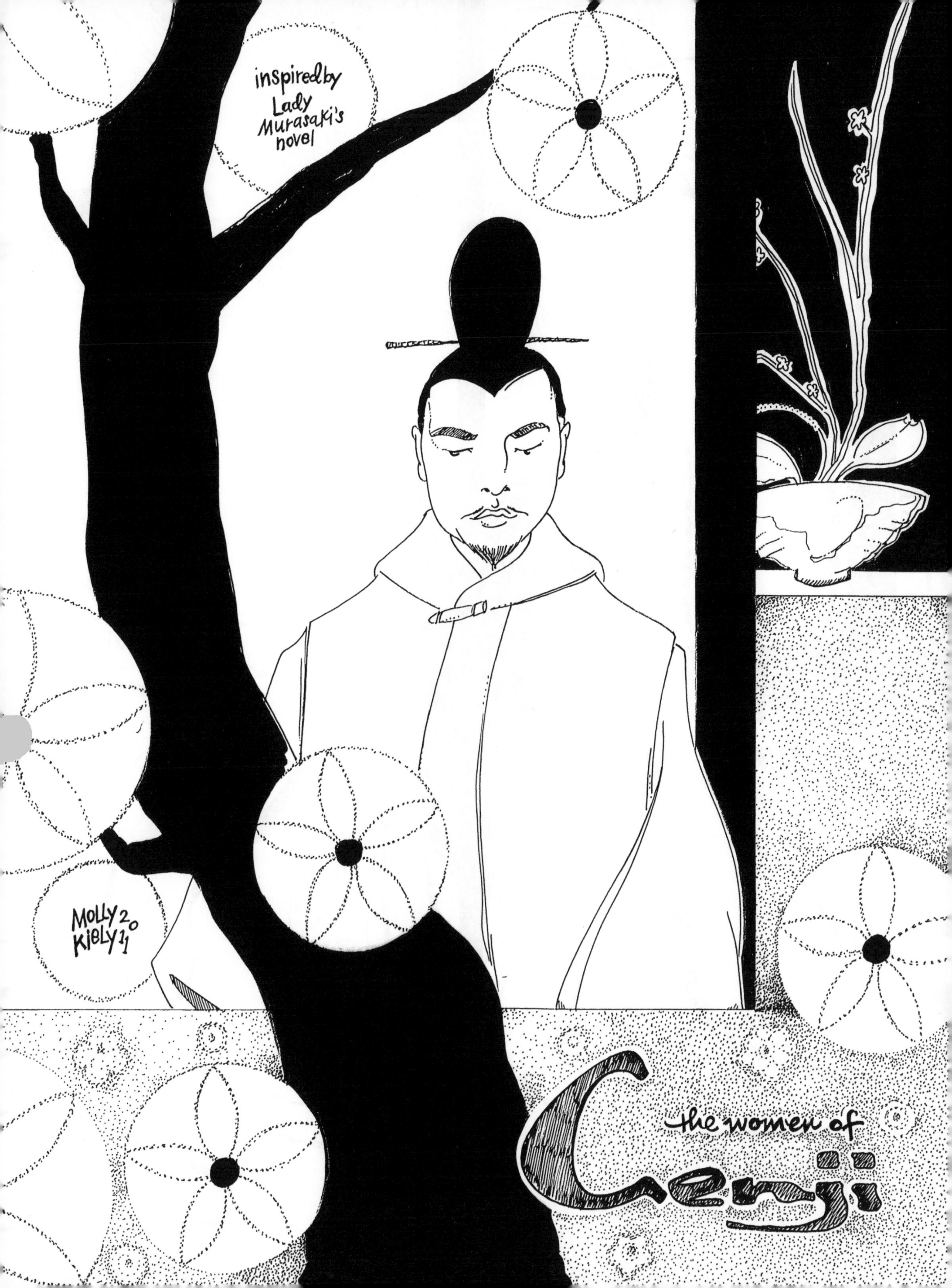
inspired by Lady Murasaki's novel
Molly Kiely 2011
the women of Genji

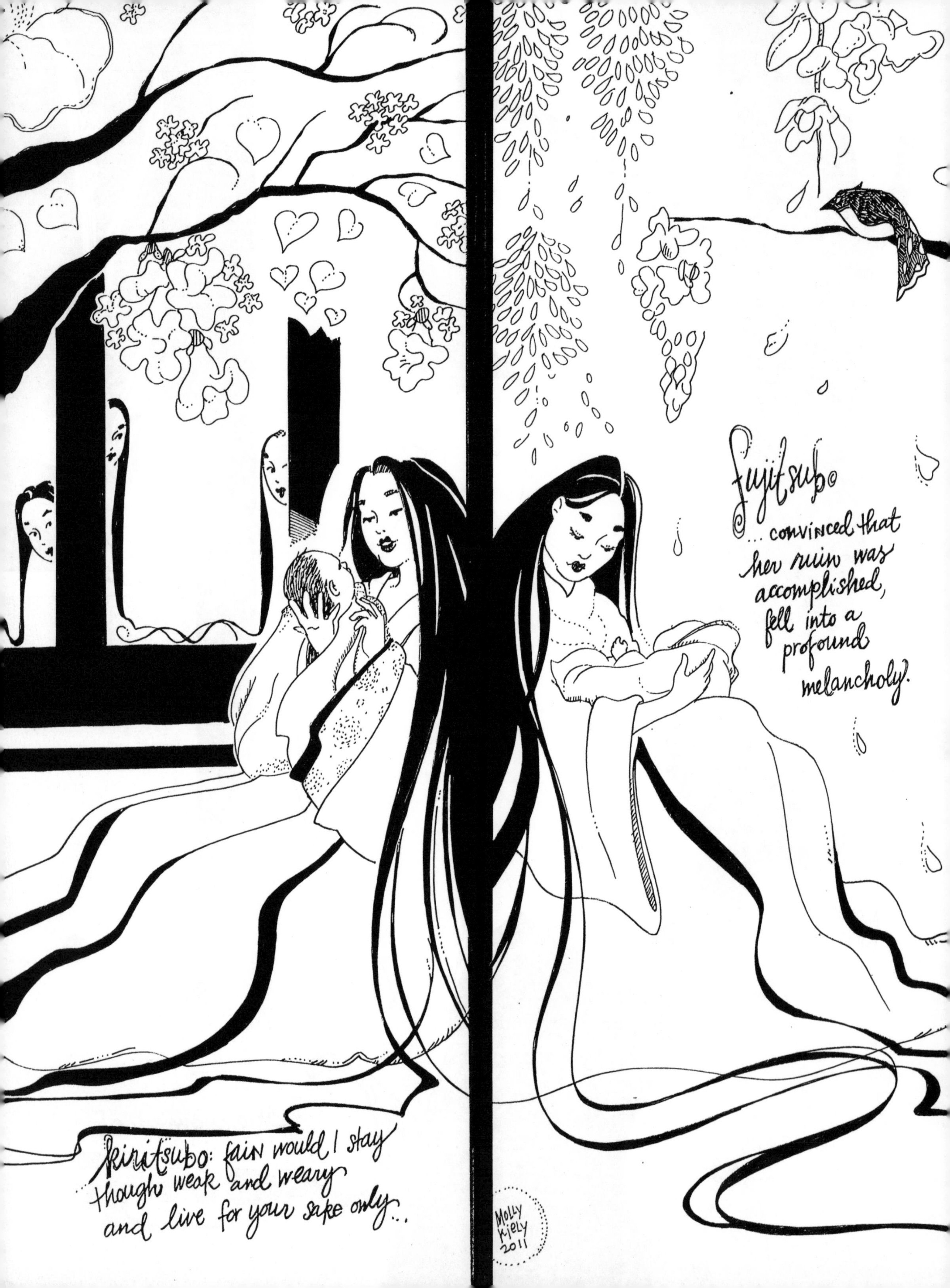
Fujitsubo
... convinced that her ruin was accomplished, fell into a profound melancholy.
Kiritsubo: fain would I stay though weak and weary and live for your sake only...
Molly Kiely 2011

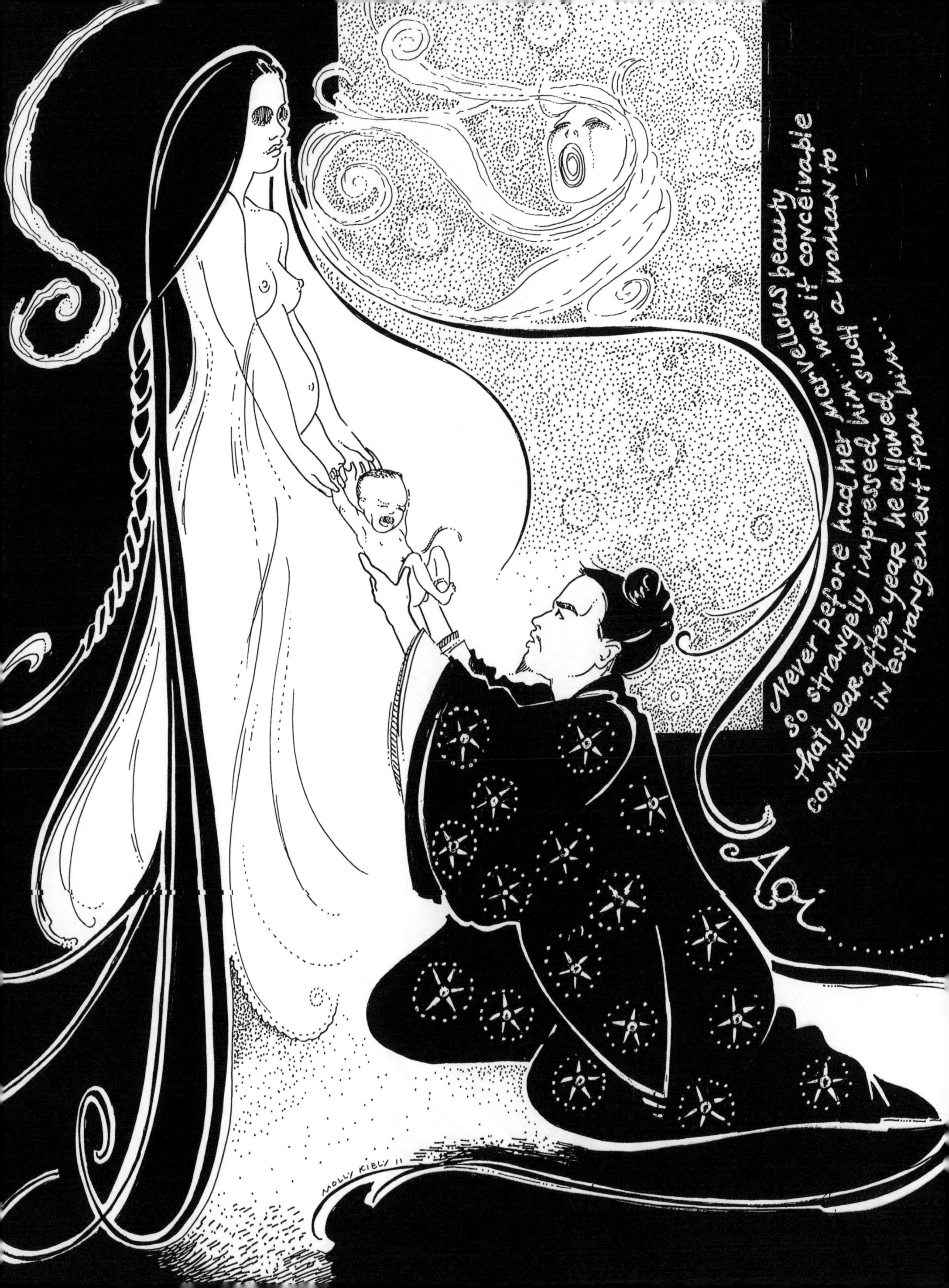
Never before had her marvellous beauty
so strangely impressed him... was it conceivable
that year after year he allowed such a woman to
continue in estrangement from him....
Aoi....
MOLLY KIELY 11

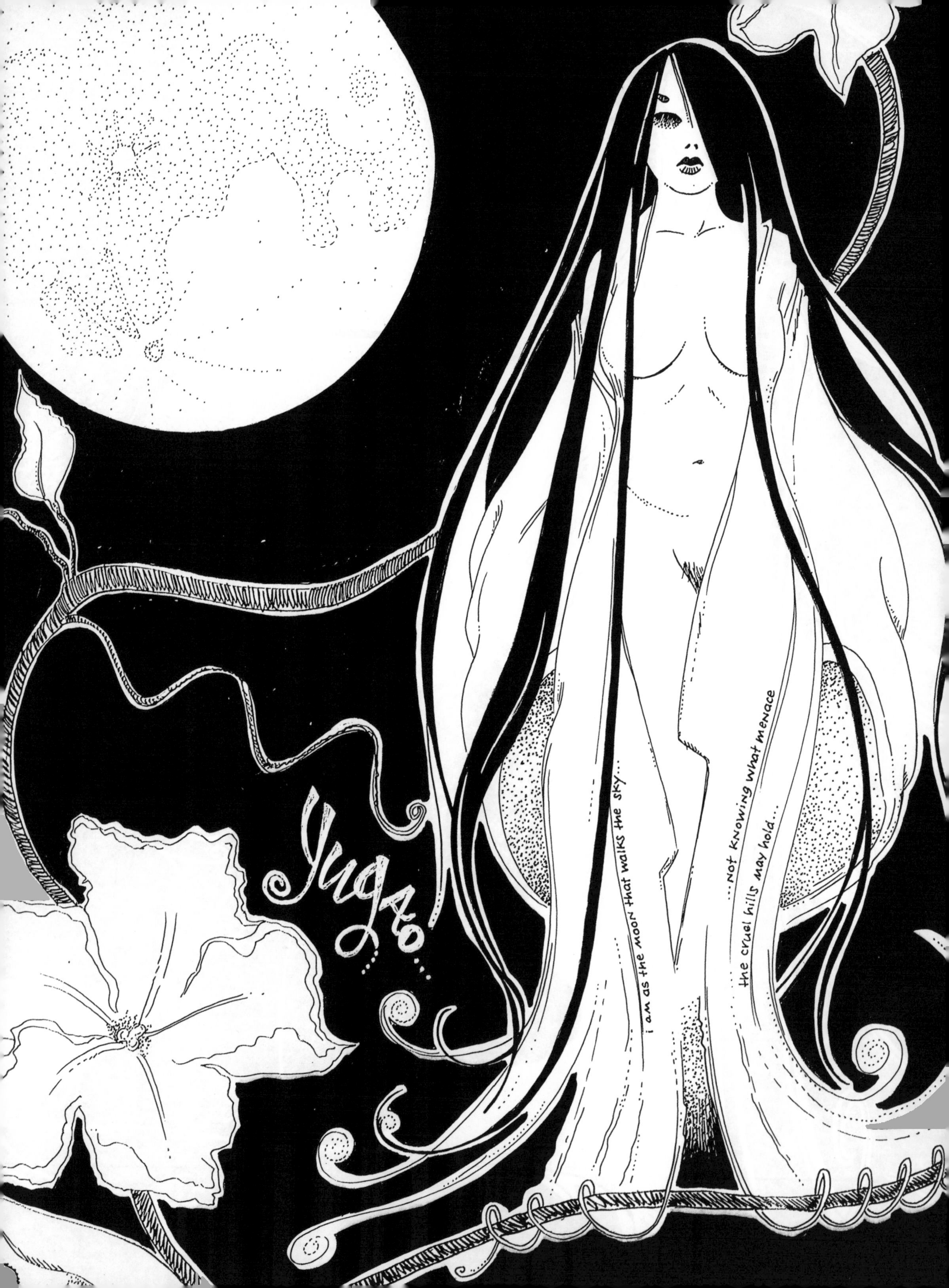
Yugao...
i am as the moon that walks the sky...
...not knowing what menace
the cruel hills may hold...

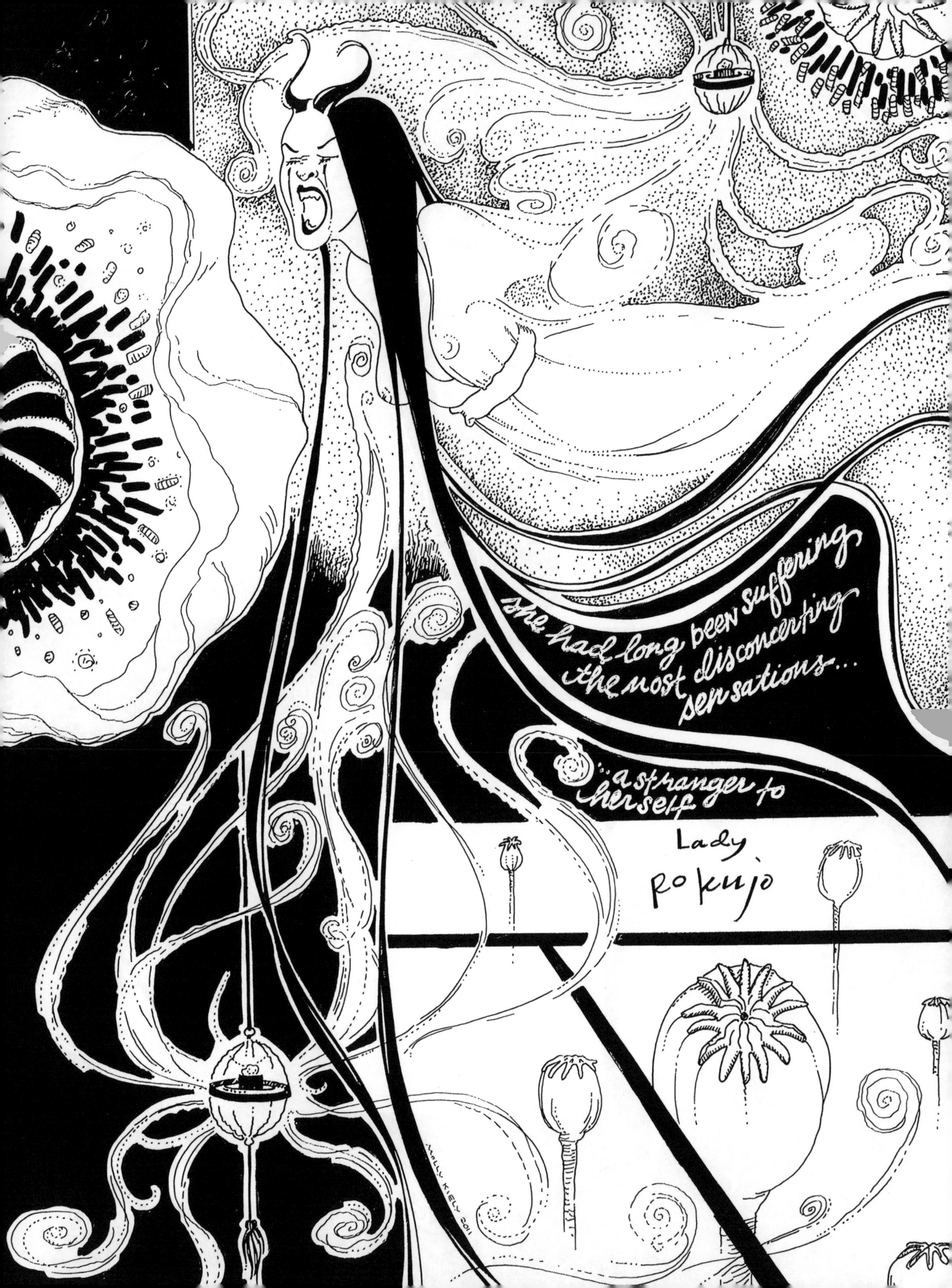
she had long been suffering the most disconcerting sensations...
...a stranger to herself
Lady Rokujo
MOLLY KIELY 2011

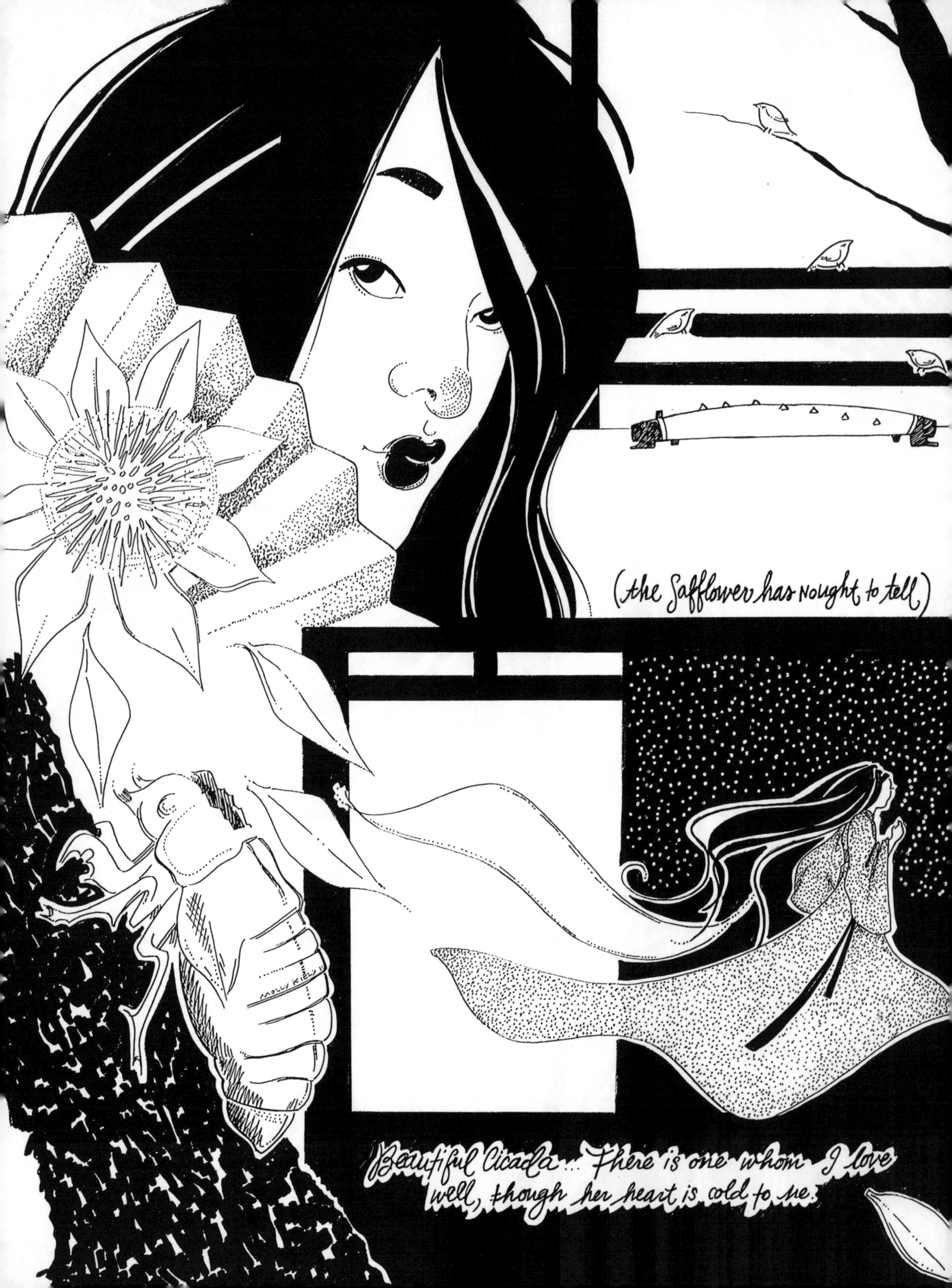
(the safflower has nought to tell)
MOLLY KIELY
Beautiful Cicada... There is one whom I love well, though her heart is cold to me.

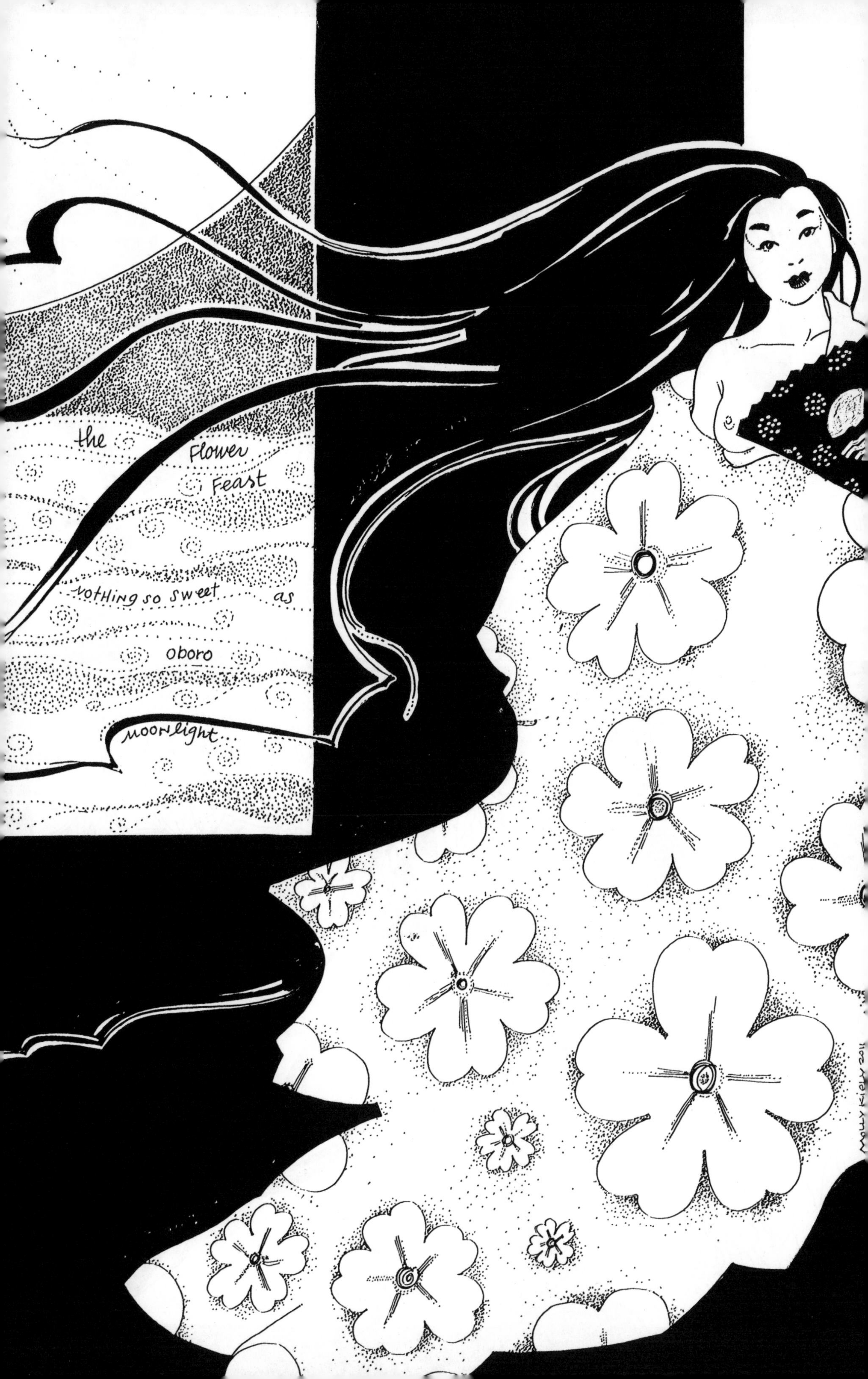
the Flower Feast
nothing so sweet as
oboro
moonlight
Molly Kiely 2011

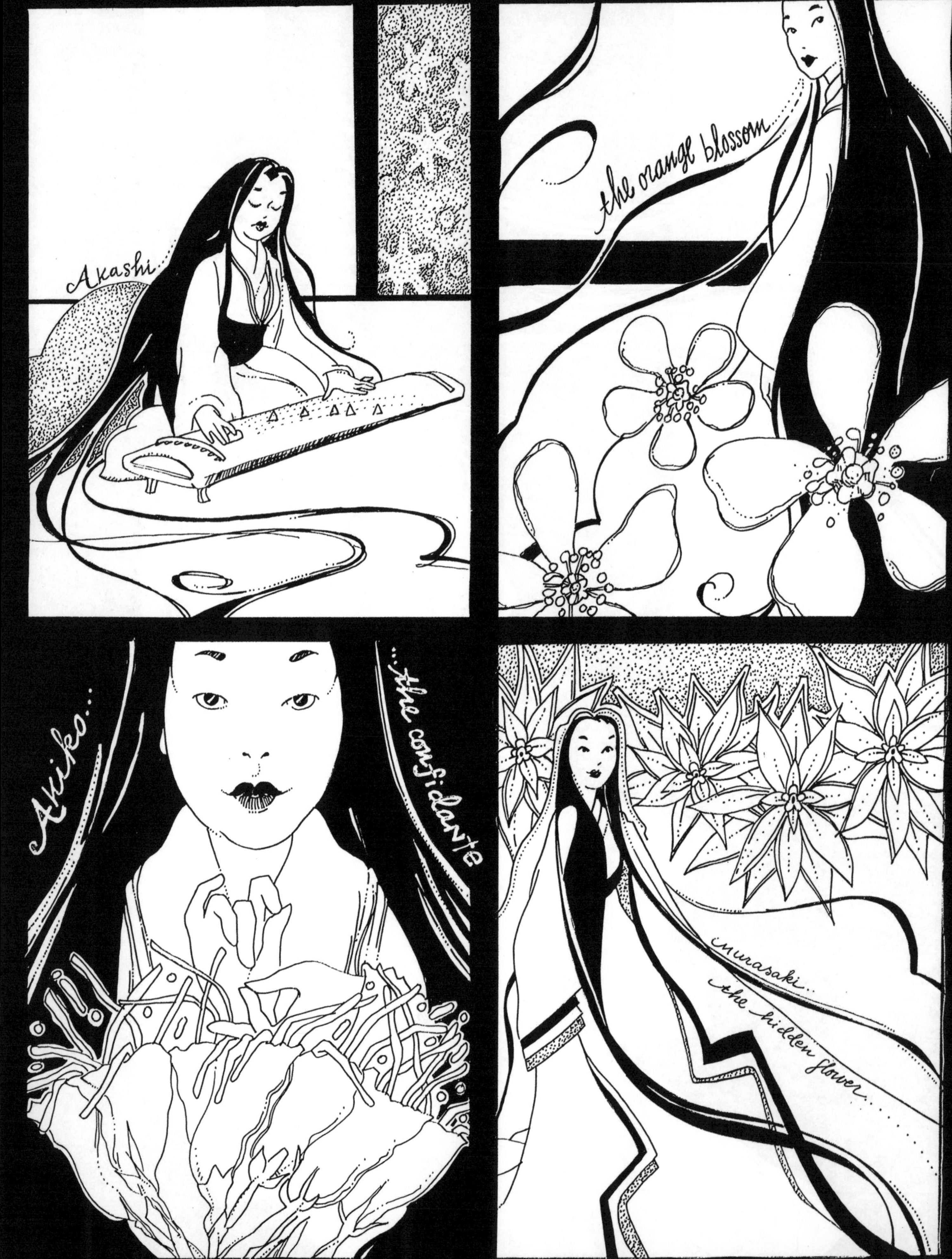
Akashi...
...the orange blossom...
Akiiko...
...the confidante
murasaki...
...the hidden flower...

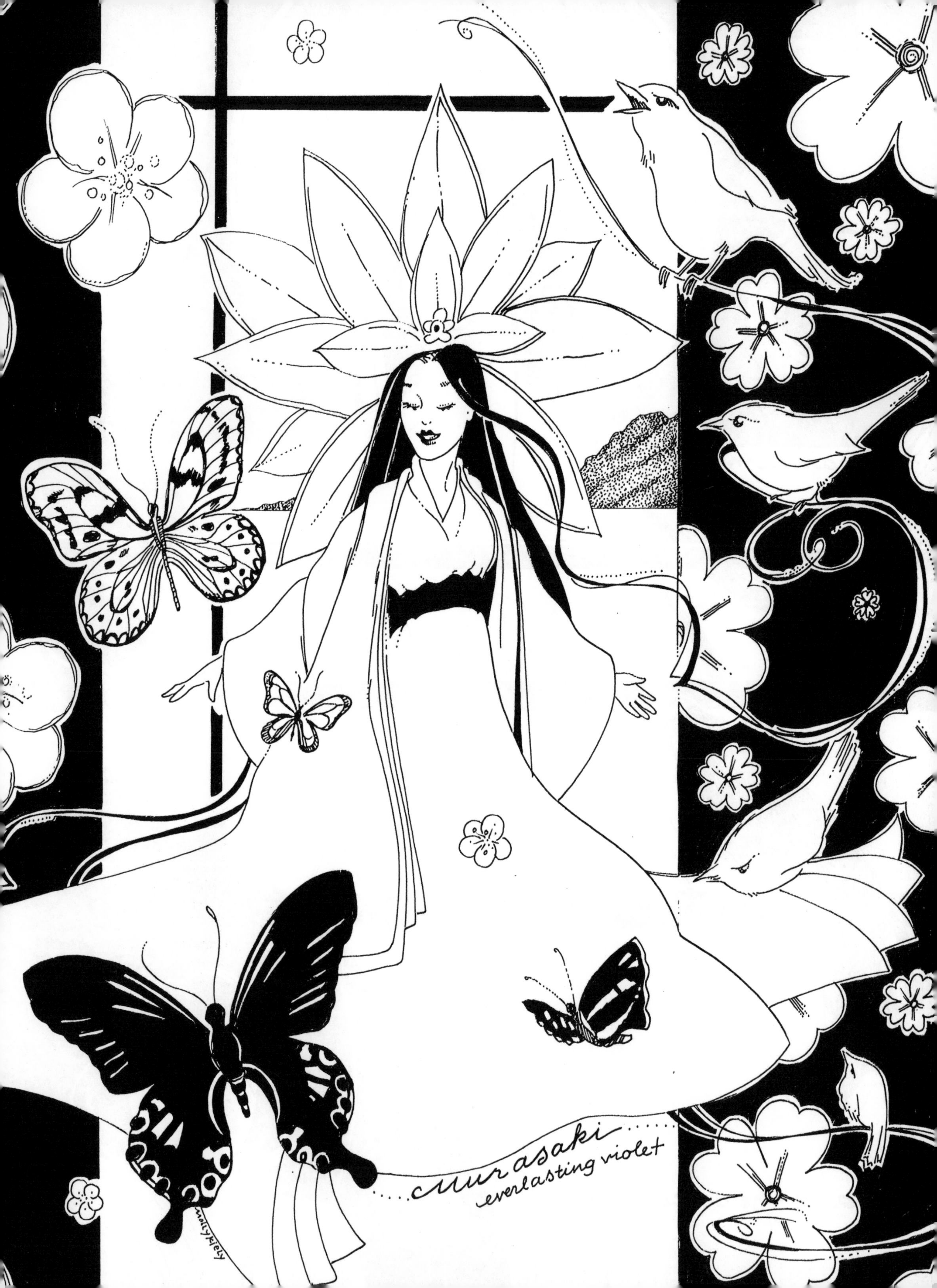
Murasaki
everlasting violet
mollykiely

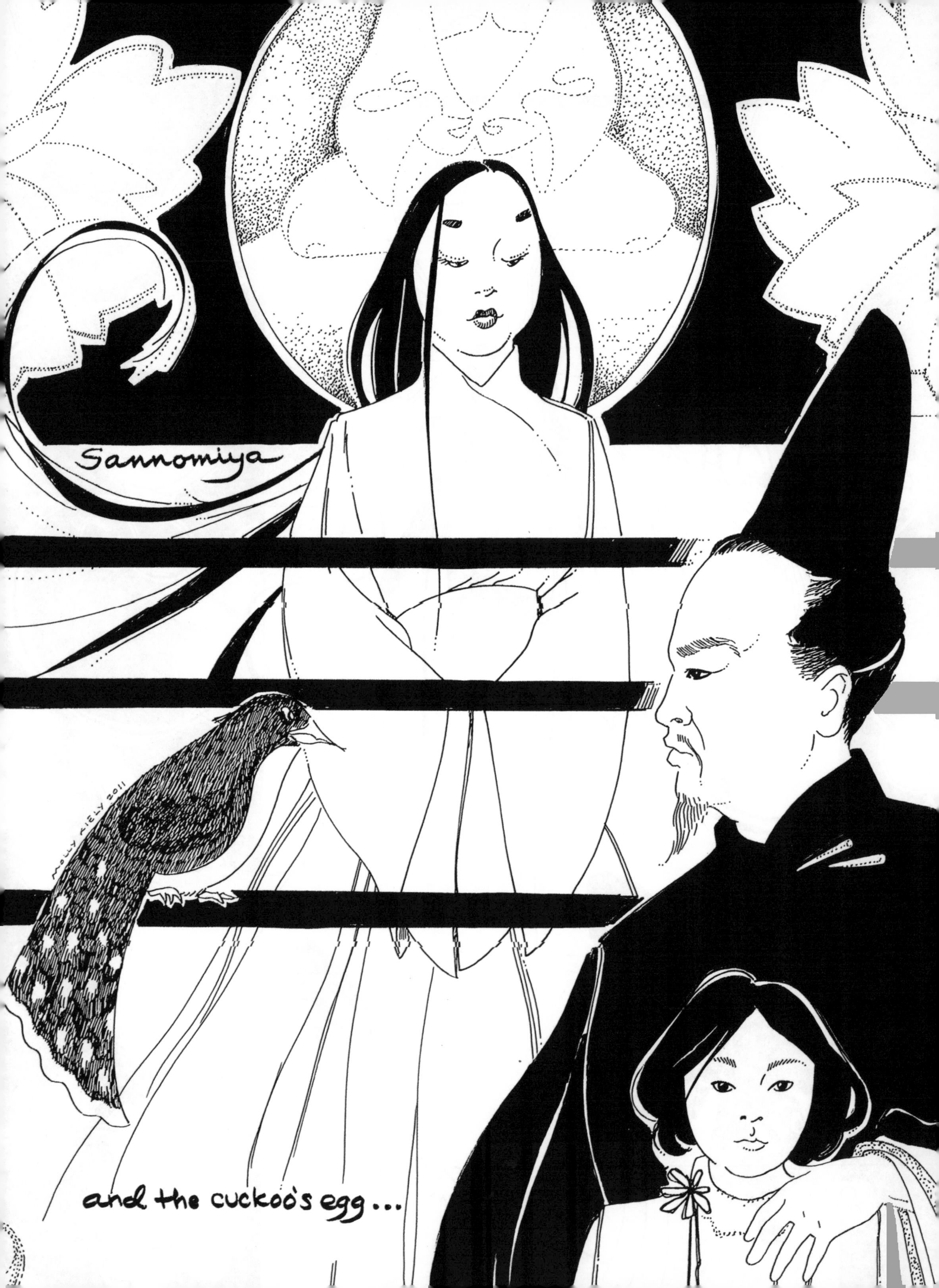
Sannomiya
MOLLY KIELY 2011
and the cuckoo's egg...

The Letters of Heloise and Abelard

ART / ADAPTATION BY **Ellen Lindner**

THE QUINTESSENTIAL STAR-CROSSED LOVERS, the much-mythologized medieval French couple Pierre Abelard and Heloise d'Argenteuil have given literature a beautiful, complex set of seven love letters. Though Abelard is mostly overlooked now, he was the greatest French philosopher of his day (the early 1100s), a veritable rock star who attracted throngs wherever he went. Heloise, a young noblewoman living with her uncle, was known "as the most learned woman in the France of her time." Abelard volunteered to tutor the lass while living in her uncle's home, his plan being to seduce her. Mission accomplished. (We don't know exactly when Heloise was born, nor when the two met, so estimates of her age at the time of their tutoring range from mid-teens to late twenties, with Abelard in his late thirties.)

Heloise's uncle was extremely displeased when he learned of these unauthorized lessons, forcing the two to part. When Héloïse wrote to Abelard that she was pregnant, they hid out at his sister's house. (His sister would be entrusted with the resulting son, unbelievably named Astralabe, after the scientific instrument.) To placate Heloise's uncle—and despite her extreme misgivings—the two were secretly married, though she continued living with her uncle. When Heloise's uncle began physically abusing her, Abelard had her entered into a convent outside of Paris. Furious at this move, Heloise's kinsmen broke into Abelard's house one night and castrated him. He soon joined a monastery. They both would become the leaders of their cloisters. They never saw each other again.

Some fifteen years later, Abelard wrote a long, autobiographical letter to a monk, which somehow got into Heloise's hands. She hadn't known of the vicious mutilation of Abelard, nor of his subsequent run-ins with Church authorities (he had some unorthodox theological positions), and in response, she wrote an anguished, love-filled letter to her husband, their first communication since the tumultuous events. Abelard responded, and the exchange resulted in three letters from her, four from him. He would live another ten years after the writing of these letters, Heloise another thirty, and true to his request, her remains were buried next to his.

Using warm autumnal colors, Ellen Lindner—a coeditor/publisher of the all-female *Whores of Mensa* and *The Strumpet* comics anthology series—excerpts and illuminates the first letter from each of them in the style of a medieval manuscript. If you can reach the final line of this adaptation with dry eyes, you're a colder brute than I.

SOURCES

Levitan, William (translator). *Abelard & Heloise: The Letters and Other Writings*. Indianapolis, Indiana: Hackett Publishing Company, 2007.

Translation from *The Love Letters of Abelard and Heloise*. London: J.M. Dent & Co: Aldine House, 1904.

FROM HELOISE TO ABELARD

EXCERPTS FROM HER FIRST LETTER

To her Lord, her Father, her husband, her Brother, his Servant, his Child, his Wife, his Sister and to express all that is humble, respectful and loving to her Abelard, Heloise writes this.

A consolatory letter of yours to a friend happened to fall into my hands; my knowledge of the writing and my love of the hand gave me the curiosity to read it. But how dear did my curiosity cost me! I met with my name a hundred times; some heavy calamity always followed it. I saw yours too, equally unhappy.

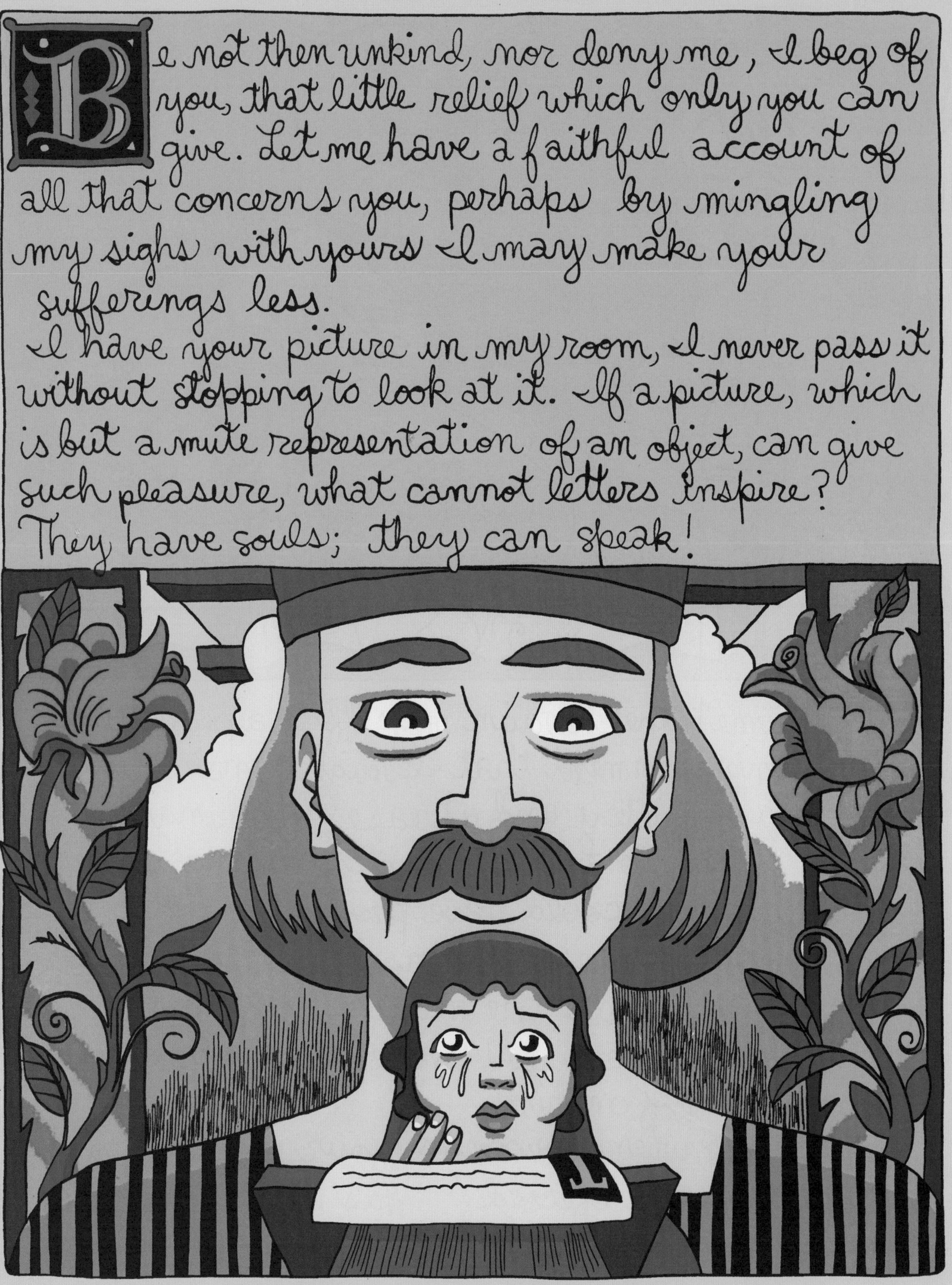
Be not then unkind, nor deny me, I beg of you, that little relief which only you can give. Let me have a faithful account of all that concerns you, perhaps by mingling my sighs with yours I may make your sufferings less.
I have your picture in my room, I never pass it without stopping to look at it. If a picture, which is but a mute representation of an object, can give such pleasure, what cannot letters inspire? They have souls; they can speak!

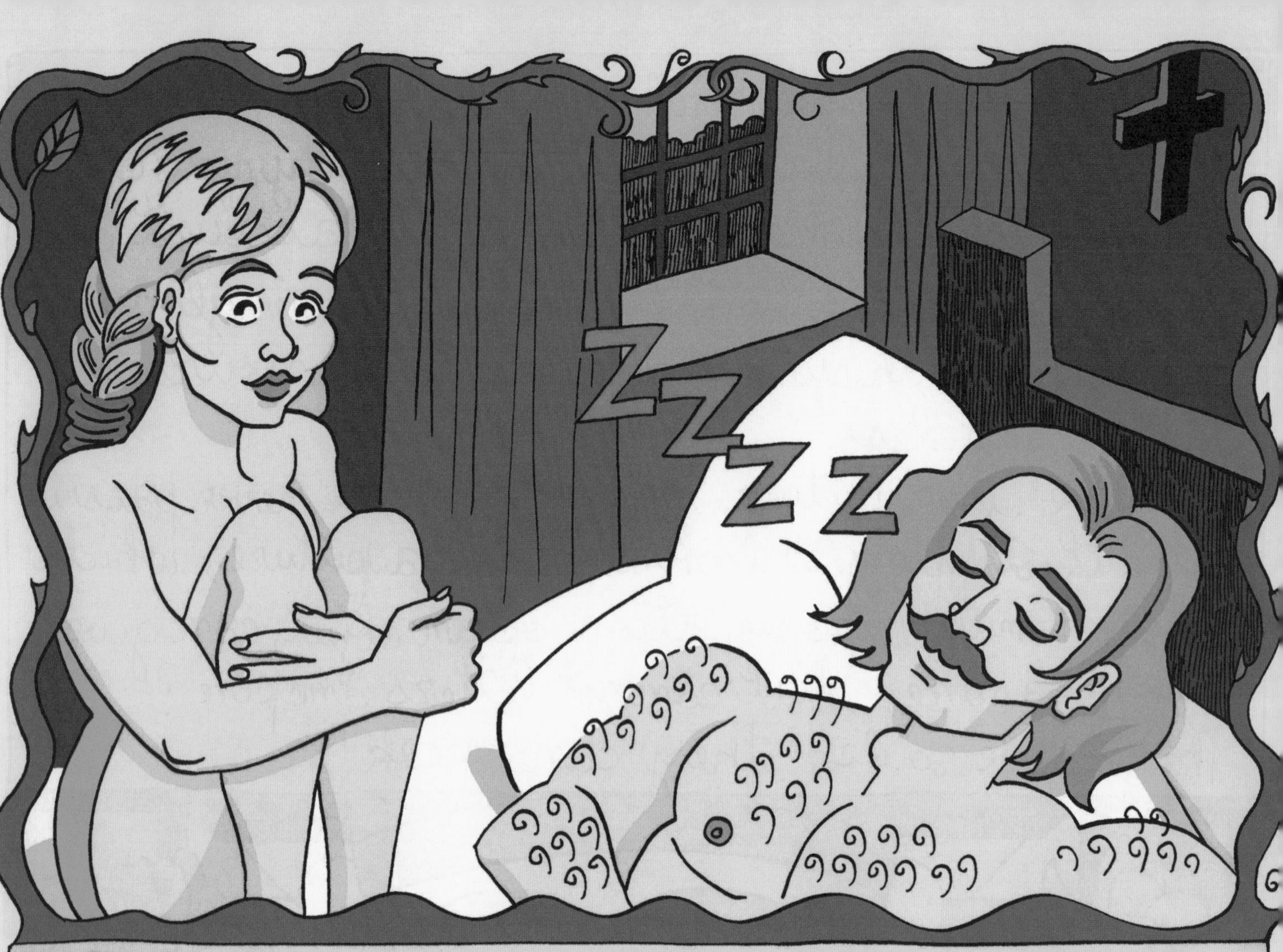
ZZZZ

I came hitherto ruin myself in a perpetual imprisonment that I might make you live quietly and at ease. Nothing but virtue, joined to a love perfectly disengaged from the senses, could have produced such effects. Vice never inspires anything like this... my cruel Uncle.. thought it was the man and not the person I loved. But I love you more than ever and so revenge myself on him.

But tell me ~ whence proceeds your neglect of me since my being professed? Was it not the sole thought of pleasure which engaged you to me?

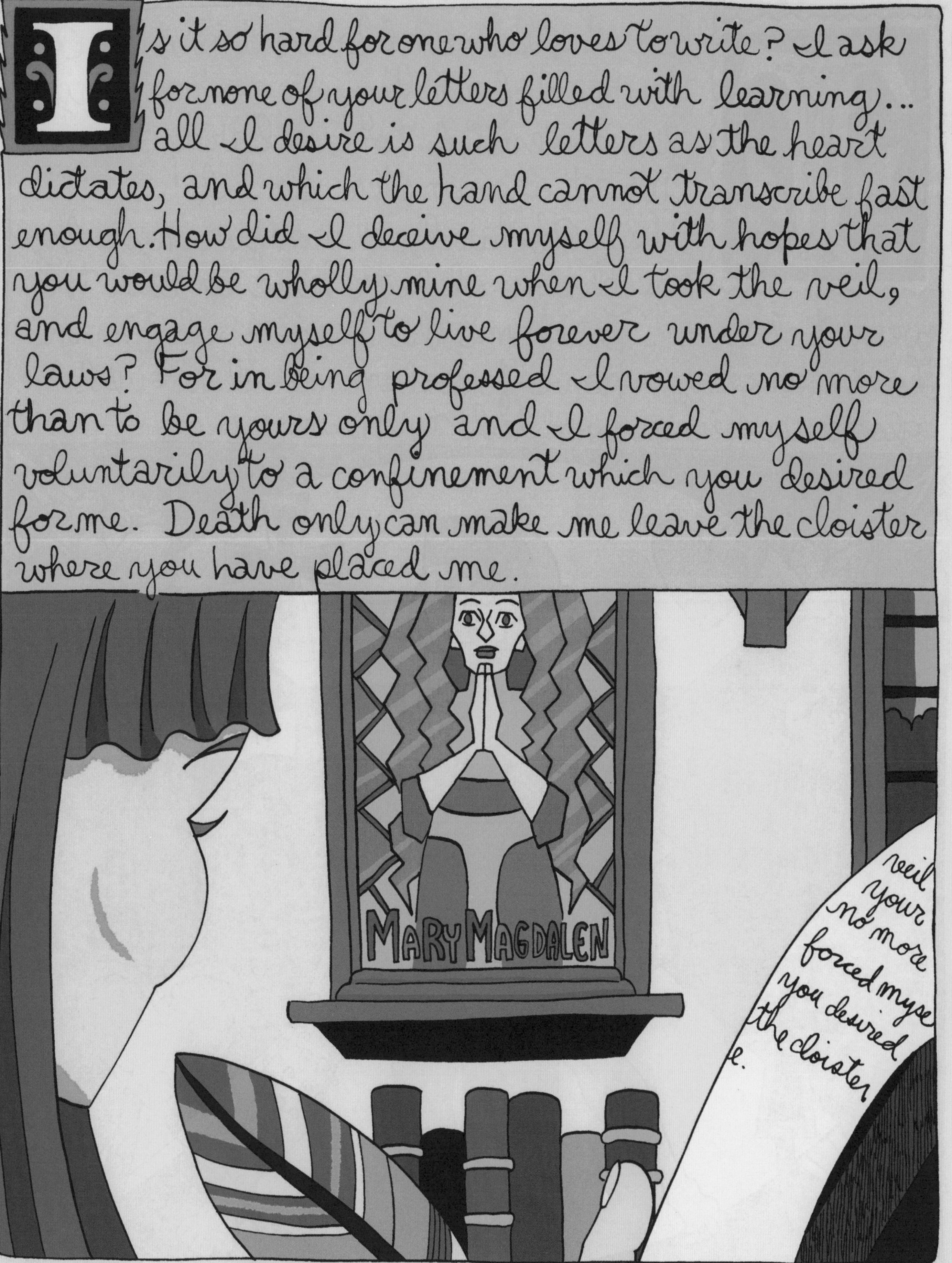
Is it so hard for one who loves to write? I ask for none of your letters filled with learning... all I desire is such letters as the heart dictates, and which the hand cannot transcribe fast enough. How did I deceive myself with hopes that you would be wholly mine when I took the veil, and engage myself to live forever under your laws? For in being professed I vowed no more than to be yours only and I forced myself voluntarily to a confinement which you desired for me. Death only can make me leave the cloister where you have placed me.
MARY MAGDALEN
veil
your
no more
forced myse
you desired
the cloister
e.

Thus I strive and labor in vain. At the head of a religious community I am devoted to Abelard alone. What a monster am I!

Yes, Abelard, I conjure you by the chains I bear here to ease the weight of them. Teach me the maxim of Divine Love; since you have forsaken me I would glory in being wedded to Heaven.

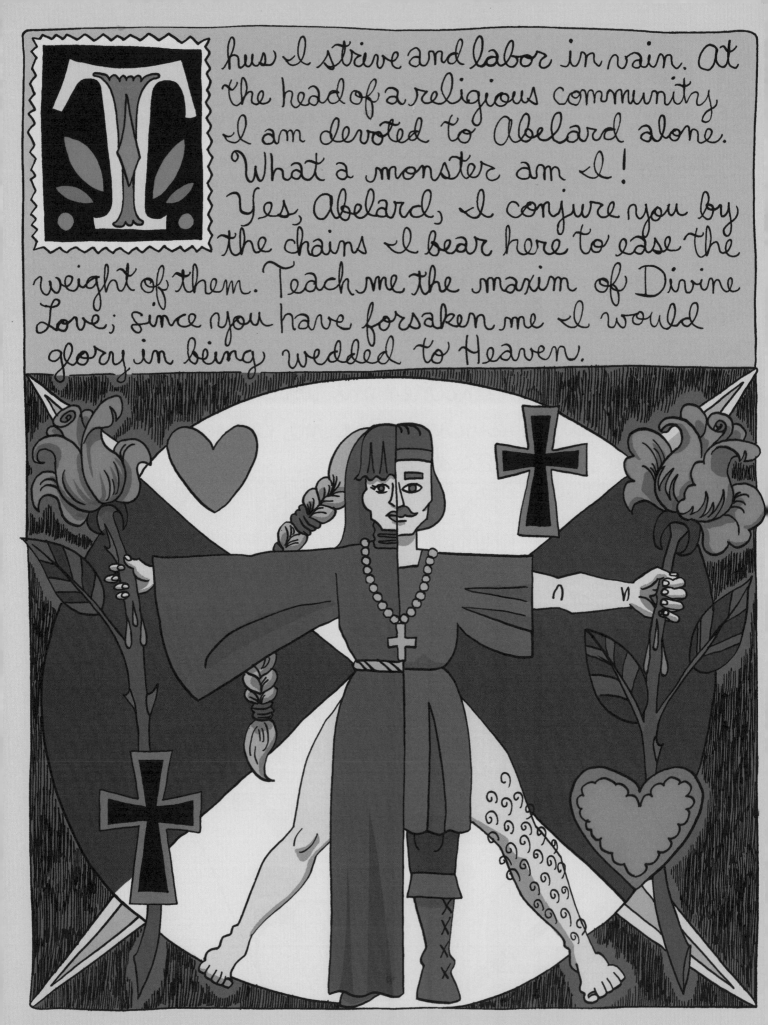

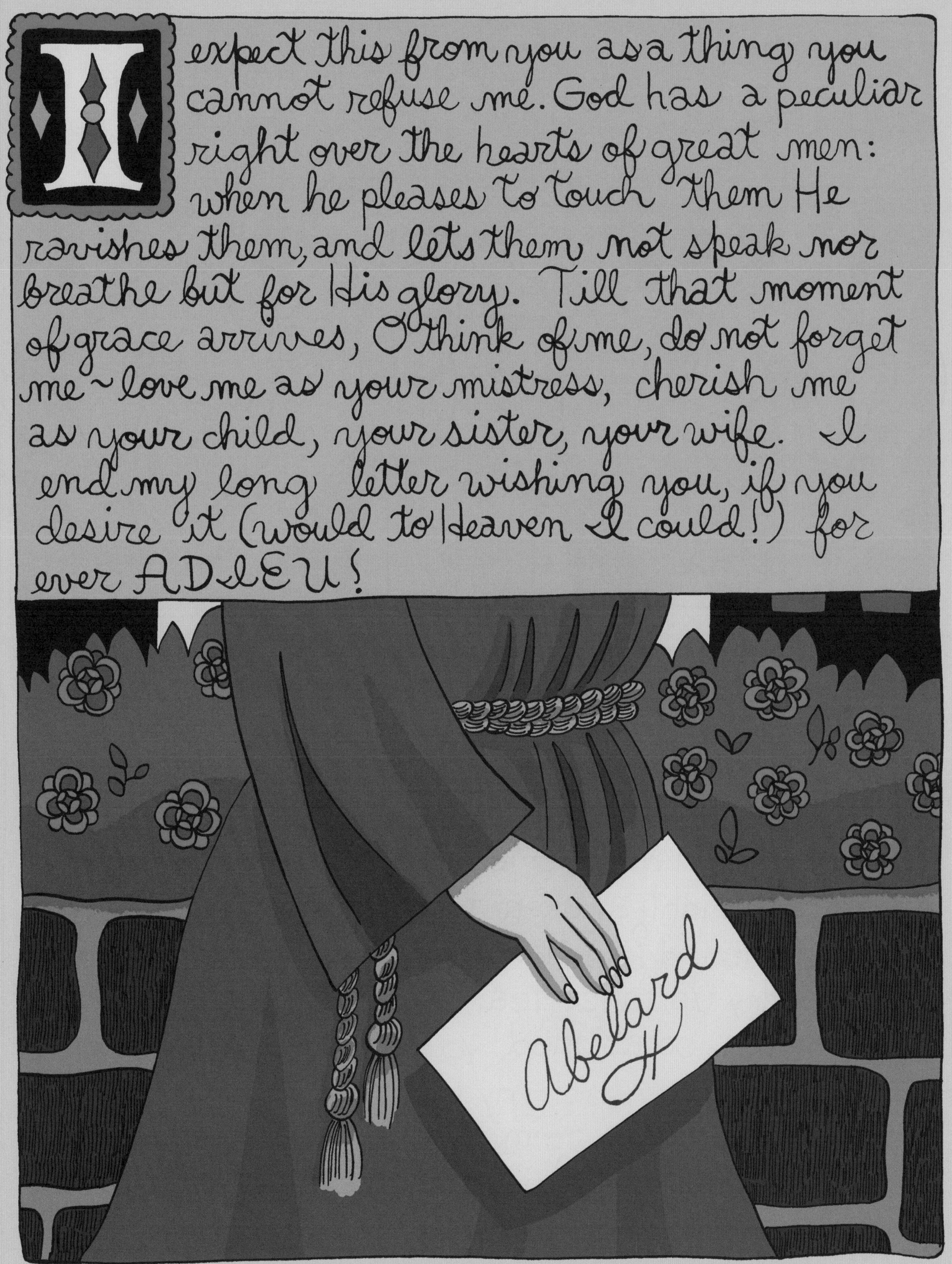
I expect this from you as a thing you cannot refuse me. God has a peculiar right over the hearts of great men: when he pleases to touch them He ravishes them, and lets them not speak nor breathe but for His glory. Till that moment of grace arrives, O think of me, do not forget me~love me as your mistress, cherish me as your child, your sister, your wife. I end my long letter wishing you, if you desire it (would to Heaven I could!) for ever ADIEU!
Abelard
H

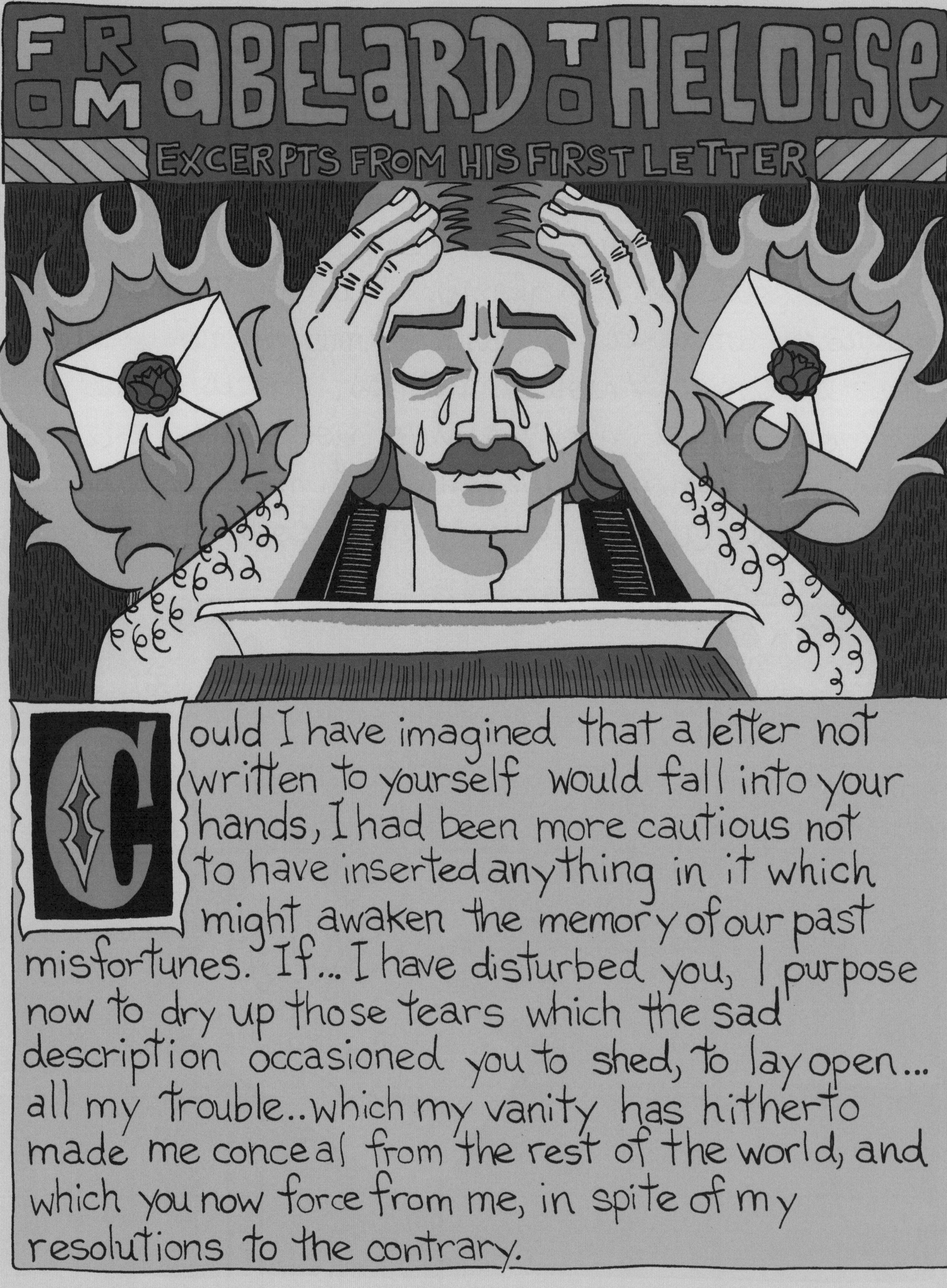
FROM ABELARD TO HELOISE
EXCERPTS FROM HIS FIRST LETTER
Could I have imagined that a letter not written to yourself would fall into your hands, I had been more cautious not to have inserted anything in it which might awaken the memory of our past misfortunes. If... I have disturbed you, I purpose now to dry up those tears which the sad description occasioned you to shed, to lay open... all my trouble..which my vanity has hitherto made me conceal from the rest of the world, and which you now force from me, in spite of my resolutions to the contrary.

I had wished to find in philosophy and religion a remedy for my disgrace, and I searched out an asylum to free me from love. But what have I gained from this? If my passion has been put under a restraint, my thoughts yet run free. I promise myself I will forget you, and yet cannot think of it without loving you.

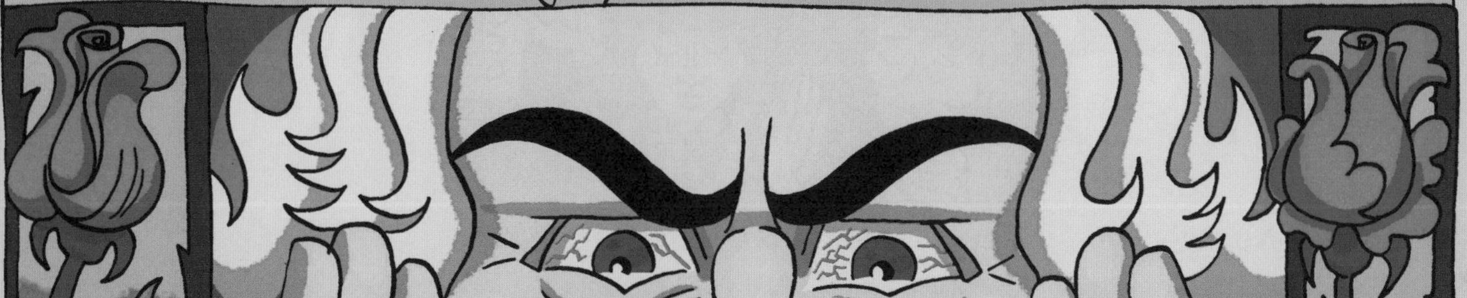

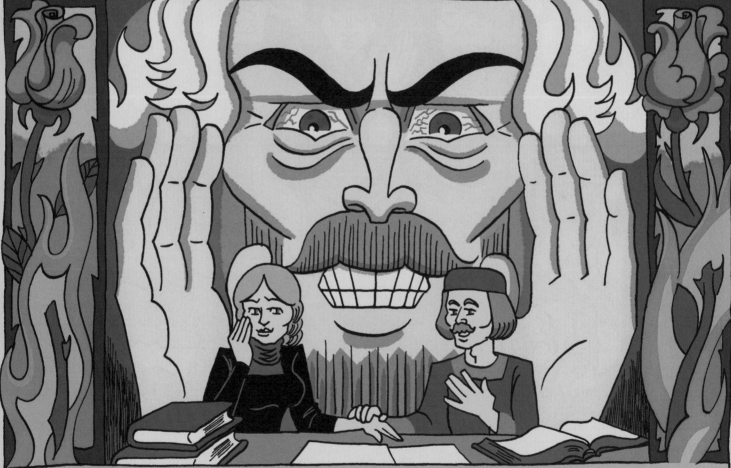

You call me your Master; it is true you were entrusted to my care. I was earnest to teach you vain sciences ~ it cost you your innocence and me my liberty. Your Uncle, who was fond of you, became my enemy and revenged himself on me.

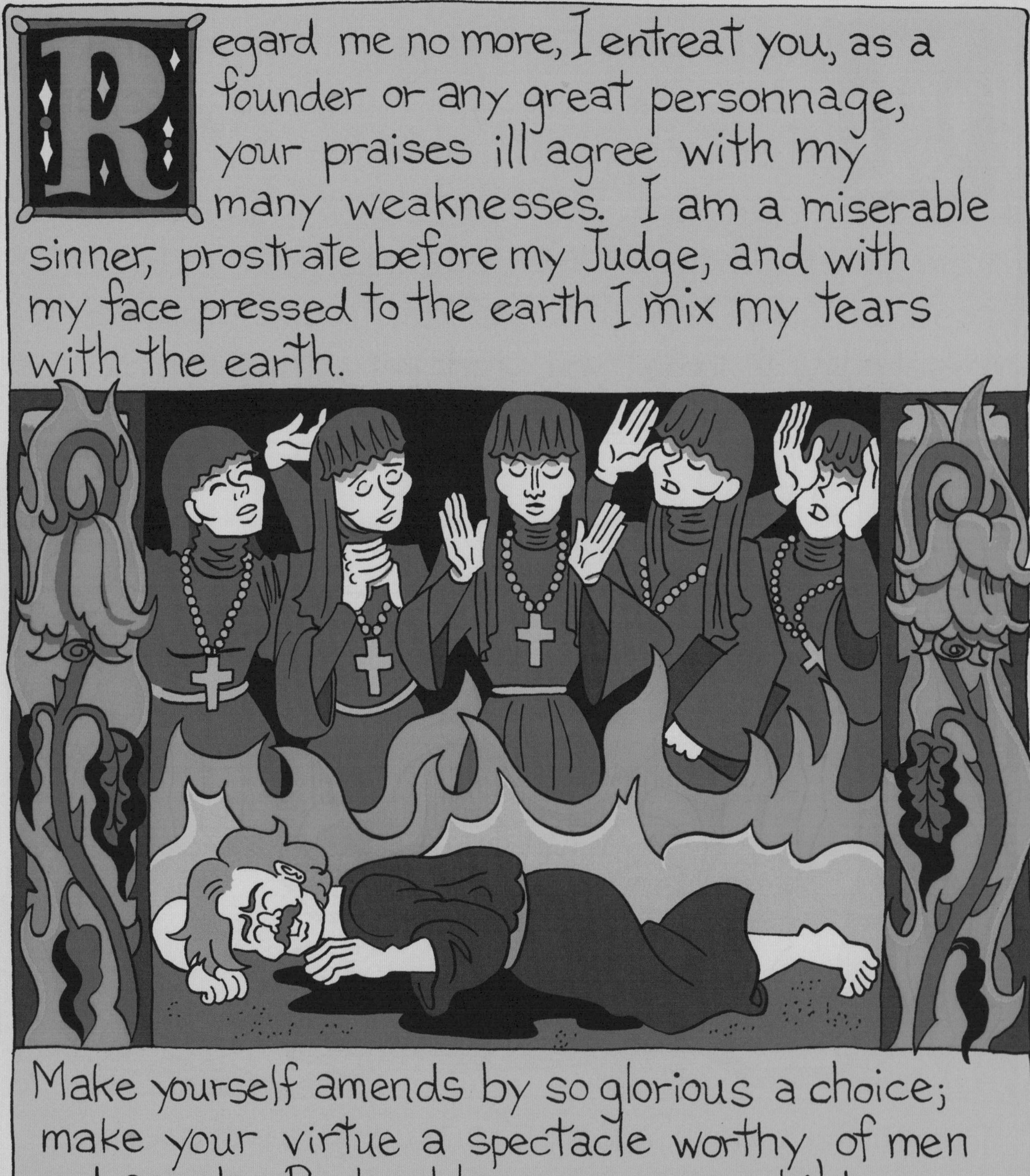
Regard me no more, I entreat you, as a founder or any great personnage, your praises ill agree with my many weaknesses. I am a miserable sinner, prostrate before my Judge, and with my face pressed to the earth I mix my tears with the earth.
Make yourself amends by so glorious a choice; make your virtue a spectacle worthy of men and angels. Be humble among your children, assiduous in your choice; exact in your discipline; diligent in your reading; make even your recreations useful.

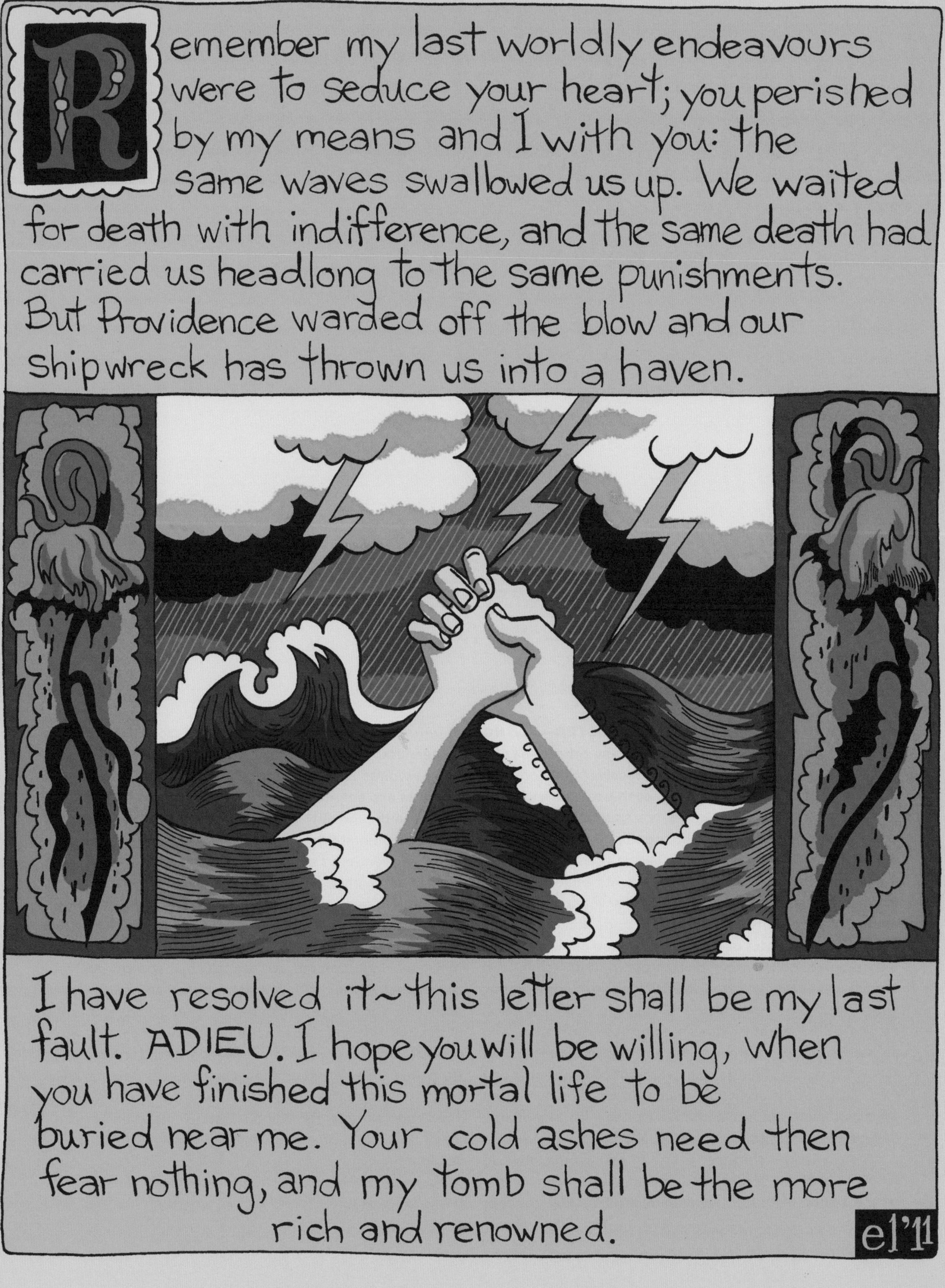
Remember my last worldly endeavours were to seduce your heart; you perished by my means and I with you: the same waves swallowed us up. We waited for death with indifference, and the same death had carried us headlong to the same punishments. But Providence warded off the blow and our shipwreck has thrown us into a haven.
I have resolved it~this letter shall be my last fault. ADIEU. I hope you will be willing, when you have finished this mortal life to be buried near me. Your cold ashes need then fear nothing, and my tomb shall be the more rich and renowned.
el'11

"O nobilissima viriditas"

Hildegard of Bingen

ART / ADAPTATION BY **Molly Kiely**

HILDEGARD OF BINGEN IS ALWAYS LISTED—ALONG with Teresa of Ávila, Julian of Norwich, and others—as one of the great mystical nuns, a lifelong receiver of visions and trances. (She describes and analyzes these visions in three books, the first of which, *Scivias*, is a spiritual classic.) But there's much more to this twelfth-century German nun than her visions; she was the very definition of a "Renaissance man," founding and running two convents while engaging in studies, first-hand research, and observations of plants, animals, the heavens, and the human body that qualify her as a medieval scientist and physician. On top of that, she was a theologian, philosopher, poet, biographer of saints, and composer of seventy-seven chants plus one musical drama, which are still being recorded. (She's universally regarded as one of the greatest female composers in history and as perhaps the first great composer of either gender.) All this while writing the first fully wrought morality play and two classic works on herbal healing (*Causae et Curae* and *Physica*), inventing an alternative alphabet and language, and corresponding with emperors and popes.

"O nobilissima viriditas" is one of her hymns, notable for its lack of direct reference to God, Jesus, Mary, or any of the saints. Instead it invokes Hildegard's key concept of *viriditas*, which, literally translated from Latin, means "greenness." But it's not that simple. In Hildegard's world-view, *viriditas* is the mysterious, wondrous life force that animates and energizes nature; it's carried into this world by the Sun, although as Hildegard makes clear elsewhere in her works, its ultimate origin is God. Vexing her translators, it's also been rendered as "greenery," "evergreen," "greening power," and "greening force." (And this is just in the natural world—*viriditas* is a force in the spiritual realm, as well.)

Molly Kiely—whom we met during *The Tale of Genji* a few pages ago—gives us a vibrant interpretation of this hymn to nature, richly colored, not digitally but, appropriately for the subject matter, with raw plant-based and earth-based pigments. She says that Hildegard's "unabashed celebration of the feminine and nature appealed to me, especially when considering how completely male-dominated and removed from the natural world religion in general has become." The translation from the original Latin was done especially for *The Graphic Canon* by Quintus' Latin Translation Service.

SOURCE

Flanagan, Sabina. *Hildegard of Bingen: A Visionary Life.* London: Routledge, 1989.

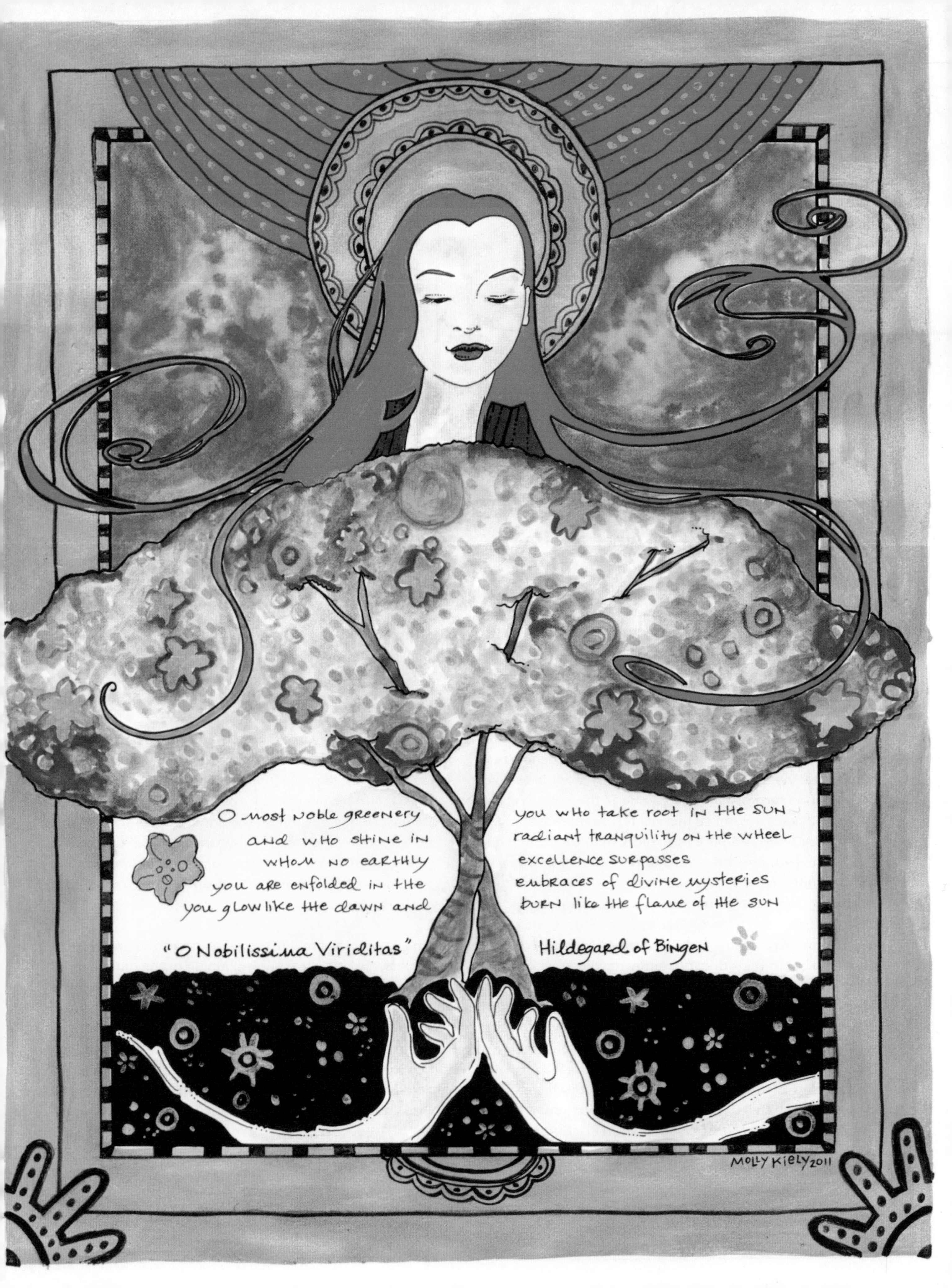
O most noble greenery
and who shine in
whom no earthly
you are enfolded in the
you glow like the dawn and
you who take root in the sun
radiant tranquility on the wheel
excellence surpasses
embraces of divine mysteries
burn like the flame of the sun
"O Nobilissima Viriditas"
Hildegard of Bingen
MOLLY KIELY 2011

"The Fisherman and the Genie"

from *The Arabian Nights*

ART / ADAPTATION BY **Andrice Arp**

THE ARABIAN NIGHTS (OR *THE 1,001 NIGHTS*) contains hundreds of individual stories told within a larger framework. King Shahryar is in the habit of marrying a beautiful young woman, enormously enjoying their wedding night, and having her executed in the morning. He repeats the cycle again and again. In order to avoid this fate (and save subsequent women), his new wife Scheherazade hatches a scheme—she tells him a nightly story but leaves it unfinished, promising to continue it the next evening. Often, a character within a tale will tell a separate tale, and sometimes there will be a tale told within that one. Thus, she keeps avoiding the executioner's blade, and on the 1,001st night Shahryar, being so pleased with Scheherazade, magnanimously spares her life on a permanent basis.

As a large collection of stories from Persia, India, and other countries in the region, *The Arabian Nights* has a complex history, but the work apparently reached recognizable form in the first half of the 1300s, when someone in Cairo had the various tales and manuscripts consolidated and set down into one work, with some local flavor mixed in. Tales would continue to be added to later Arabic versions, while the stories most famous in the West—those of Ali Baba, Sinbad, and Aladdin—were much later additions stuck in by European translators (although they are actual Middle Eastern tales). The *Nights* first appeared in a European language, French, in an edition published from 1704 to 1717. Sir Richard Burton's legendary English translation—complete and uncensored—was privately published in the 1880s.

In his *Companion* to the work, historian Robert Irwin explains:

> It is commonly regarded as a collection of Arab fairy tales, the oriental equivalent of the *Marchen* (fairy tales or household tales) of the Brothers Grimm. But, while it is true that there are items in the *Nights* which might pass as fairy tales, the collection's compass is much wider than this. It also includes long heroic epics, wisdom literature, fables, cosmological fantasy, pornography, scatological jokes, mystical devotional tales, chronicles of low life, rhetorical debates and masses of poetry. A few tales are hundreds of pages long; others amount to no more than a short paragraph.

"The Fisherman and the Genie" is one of the first tales of the *Nights*, and it's a textbook example of the multilayered format—the fisherman tells the genie a story involving a king, who tells a story involving a parrot, who has a little story of its own to relate. Andrice Arp—a coeditor of the *Hi-Horse* comics anthology series—visualizes this Russian doll approach with the panels of each nested tale getting smaller and smaller, until, as the tales begin concluding, the panels step back up in size until we're at the main tale again.

SOURCE

Irwin, Robert. *The Arabian Nights: A Companion.* London & New York: J.B. Tauris & Co Ltd, 2004.

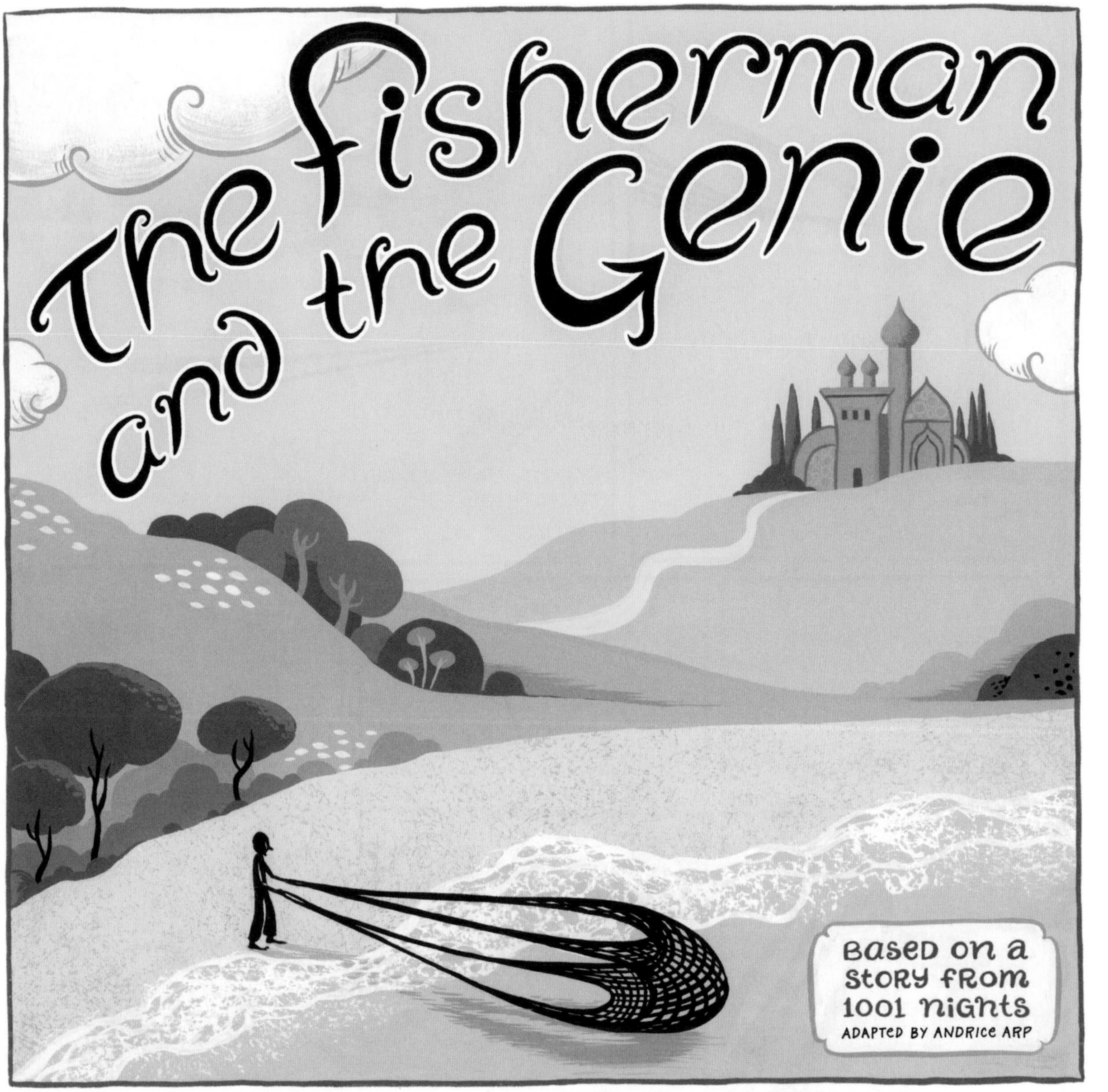
The Fisherman and the Genie
Based on a story from 1001 Nights
ADAPTED BY ANDRICE ARP

Every day, a poor fisherman went down to the shore to cast his net.

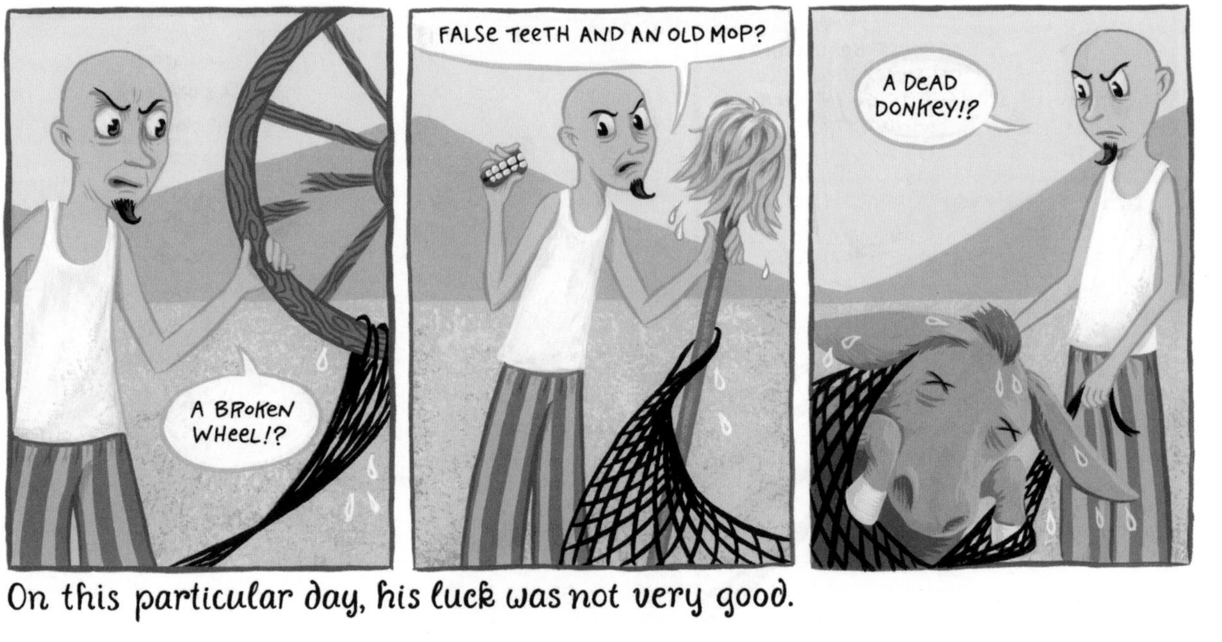
A BROKEN WHEEL!?
FALSE TEETH AND AN OLD MOP?
A DEAD DONKEY!?

On this particular day, his luck was not very good.

LAST TIME...
THIS BETTER BE GOOD
NNNG
IT MUST BE CAUGHT ON SOMETHING. I'LL HAVE TO GO IN THERE AND GET IT.

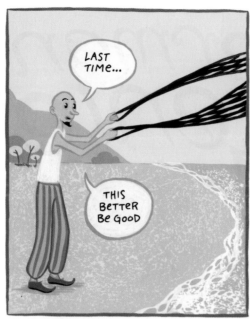

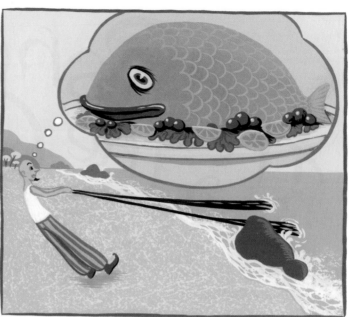

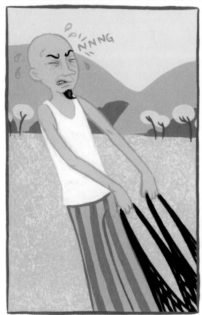

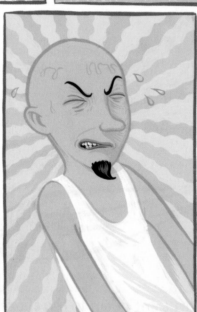

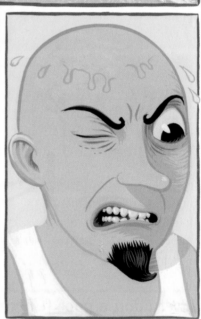

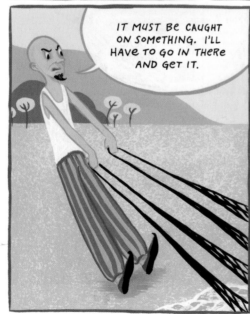

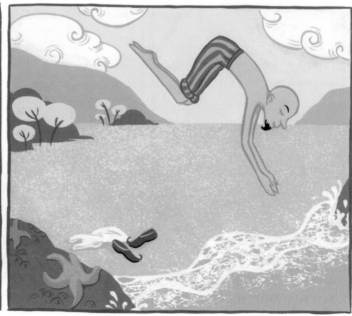

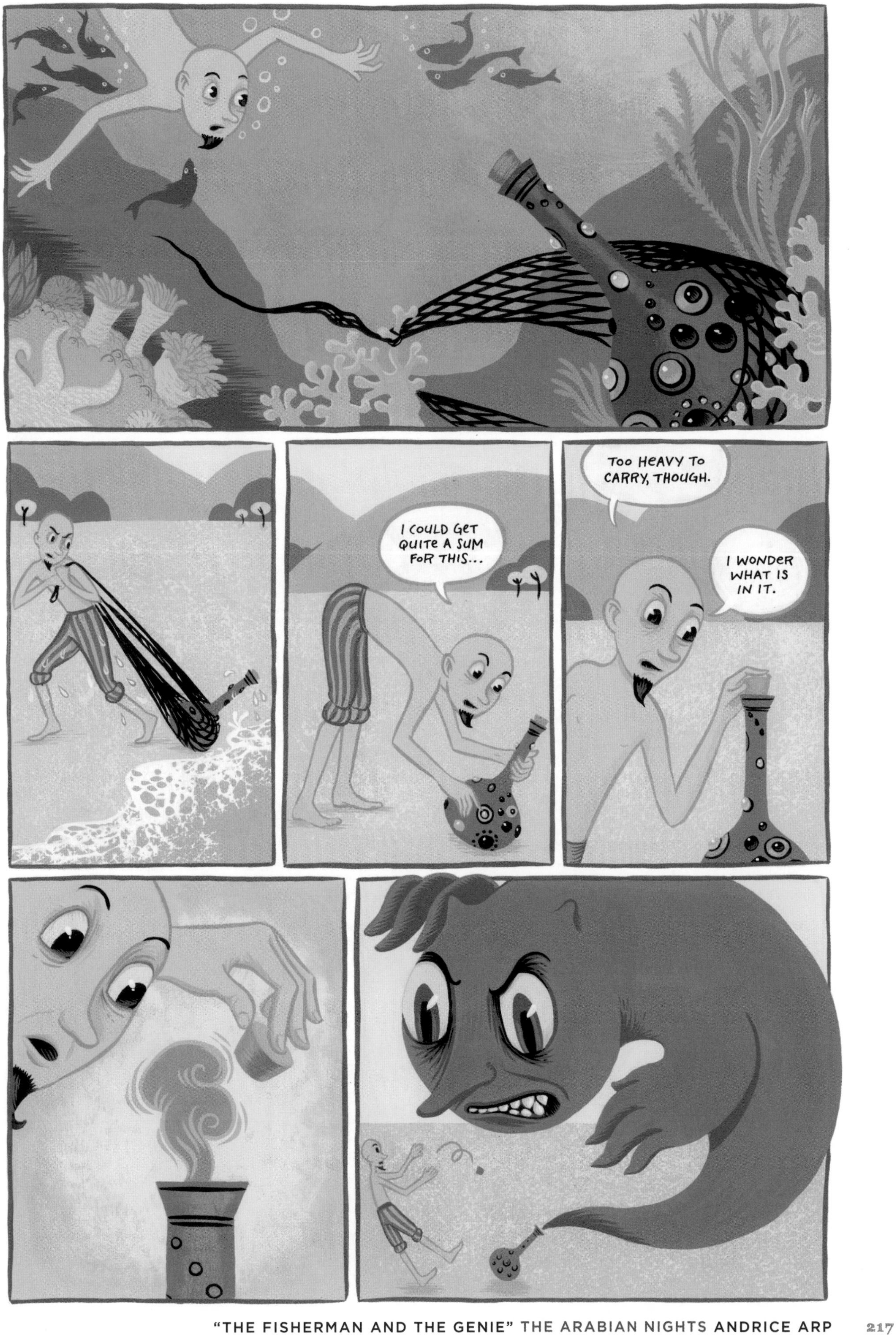
I COULD GET QUITE A SUM FOR THIS...
TOO HEAVY TO CARRY, THOUGH.
I WONDER WHAT IS IN IT.

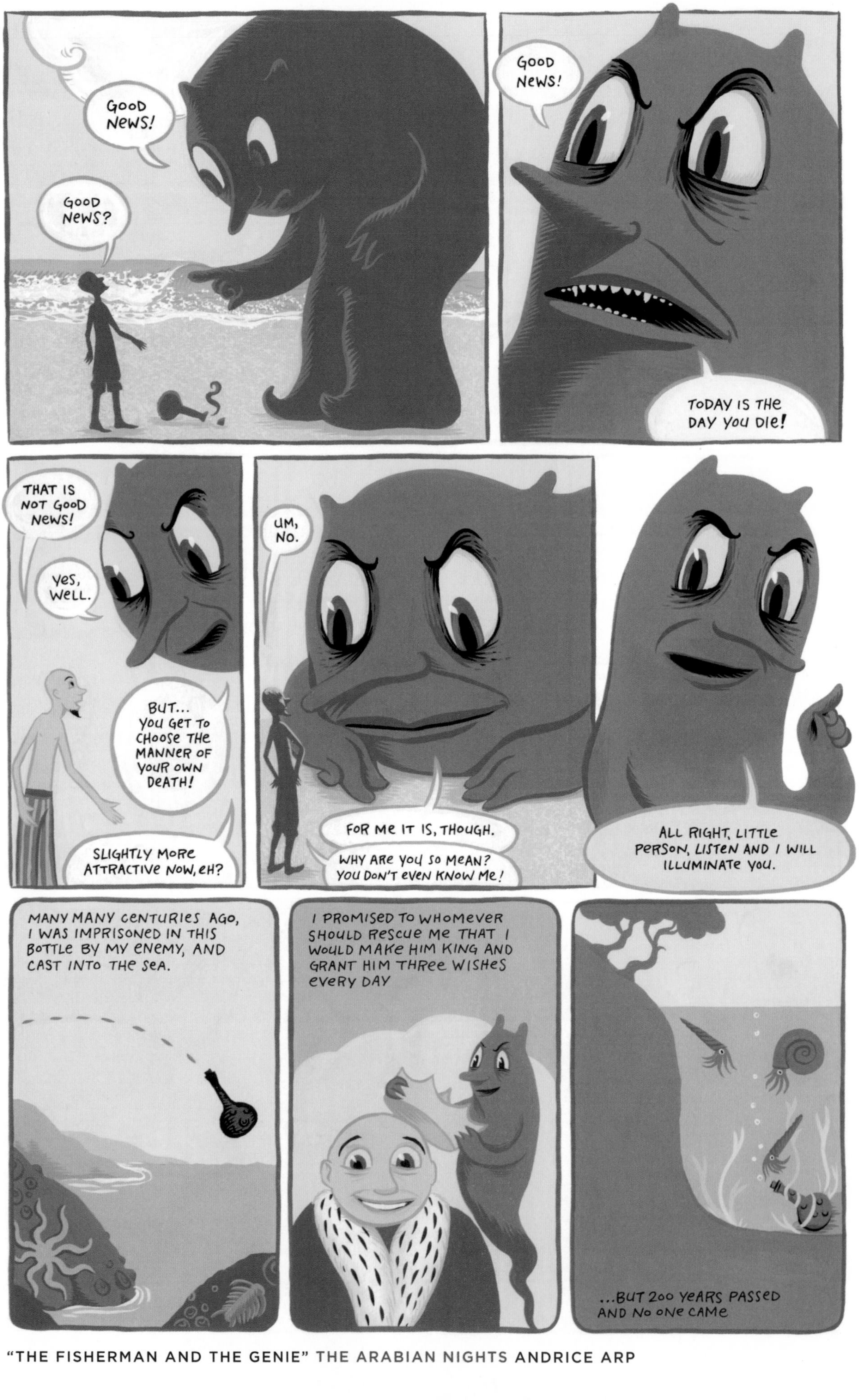
GOOD NEWS!
GOOD NEWS?
GOOD NEWS!
TODAY IS THE DAY YOU DIE!
THAT IS NOT GOOD NEWS!
YES, WELL.
BUT... YOU GET TO CHOOSE THE MANNER OF YOUR OWN DEATH!
SLIGHTLY MORE ATTRACTIVE NOW, EH?
UM, NO.
FOR ME IT IS, THOUGH.
WHY ARE YOU SO MEAN? YOU DON'T EVEN KNOW ME!
ALL RIGHT, LITTLE PERSON, LISTEN AND I WILL ILLUMINATE YOU.
MANY MANY CENTURIES AGO, I WAS IMPRISONED IN THIS BOTTLE BY MY ENEMY, AND CAST INTO THE SEA.
I PROMISED TO WHOMEVER SHOULD RESCUE ME THAT I WOULD MAKE HIM KING AND GRANT HIM THREE WISHES EVERY DAY
...BUT 200 YEARS PASSED AND NO ONE CAME

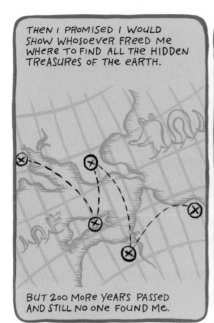

THEN I PROMISED I WOULD SHOW WHOSOEVER FREED ME WHERE TO FIND ALL THE HIDDEN TREASURES OF THE EARTH.

BUT 200 MORE YEARS PASSED AND STILL NO ONE FOUND ME.

SO THEN I PROCLAIMED THAT IF ANYONE LET ME OUT I WOULD GRANT HIM ONE WISH.

ANOTHER 200 YEARS – AND STILL I REMAINED TRAPPED ON THE OCEAN FLOOR.

THEN I PROMISED THAT IF SOMEONE DISCOVERED ME AND OPENED THIS BOTTLE, I WOULD THANK HIM SINCERELY AND GO ON MY WAY.

STILL NOTHING, FOR ANOTHER 200 YEARS!

FINALLY I SWORE THAT I WOULD SIMPLY LET MY RESCUER CHOOSE THE MANNER OF HIS OWN DEATH

SO... HOW DO YOU WISH TO DIE?

...

MM-HM, THAT'S RIGHT.

JUST BE GLAD YOU DID NOT COME ALONG 200 YEARS **LATER!**

NOW.

WHAT WILL IT BE?

IF YOU ARE HAVING TROUBLE DECIDING I COULD OFFER SOME SUGGESTIONS

BOILED IN OIL? TORN APART BY GIBBONS...?

UM...

WHAT!?

CAN I ASK YOU A QUESTION?

FINE, BUT HURRY.

WERE YOU REALLY IN THIS LI'L BOTTLE?

DUH!

YOU LIE! IT IS TINY AND YOU ARE HUGE!

=SIGH= DO I HAVE TO SHOW YOU?

"THE FISHERMAN AND THE GENIE" THE ARABIAN NIGHTS ANDRICE ARP   219

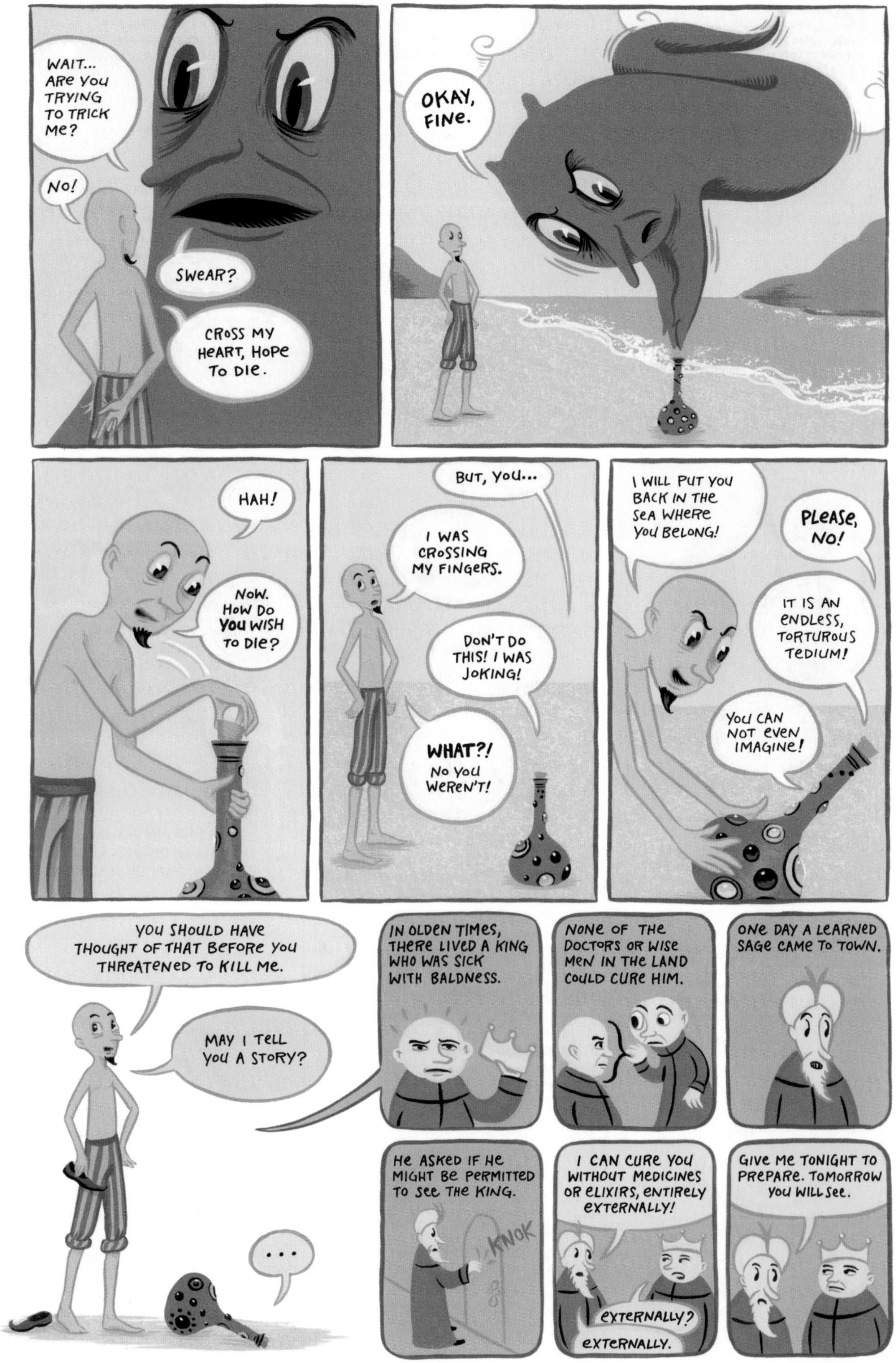
WAIT... ARE YOU TRYING TO TRICK ME?
NO!
SWEAR?
CROSS MY HEART, HOPE TO DIE.
OKAY, FINE.
HAH!
NOW. HOW DO YOU WISH TO DIE?
BUT, YOU...
I WAS CROSSING MY FINGERS.
DON'T DO THIS! I WAS JOKING!
WHAT?! NO YOU WEREN'T!
I WILL PUT YOU BACK IN THE SEA WHERE YOU BELONG!
PLEASE, NO!
IT IS AN ENDLESS, TORTUROUS TEDIUM!
YOU CAN NOT EVEN IMAGINE!
YOU SHOULD HAVE THOUGHT OF THAT BEFORE YOU THREATENED TO KILL ME.
MAY I TELL YOU A STORY?
...
IN OLDEN TIMES, THERE LIVED A KING WHO WAS SICK WITH BALDNESS.
NONE OF THE DOCTORS OR WISE MEN IN THE LAND COULD CURE HIM.
ONE DAY A LEARNED SAGE CAME TO TOWN.
HE ASKED IF HE MIGHT BE PERMITTED TO SEE THE KING.
KNOK
I CAN CURE YOU WITHOUT MEDICINES OR ELIXIRS, ENTIRELY EXTERNALLY!
EXTERNALLY?
EXTERNALLY.
GIVE ME TONIGHT TO PREPARE. TOMORROW YOU WILL SEE.

THE SAGE SPENT THE NIGHT DISTILLING MEDICINES WHICH HE PLACED INSIDE A RAG DOLL.

SLEEP TONIGHT CLUTCHING THIS DOLLY, AND COVER YOURSELF WITH TWENTY BLANKETS. THE MEDICINE IN THE DOLL WILL MIX WITH YOUR SWEAT

AND BE ABSORBED INTO YOUR BODY.

THE NEXT MORNING, THE KING LOOKED IN THE MIRROR AND HIS BALDNESS WAS GONE!

THE KING WAS OVER-JOYED, AND BESTOWED ROBES OF HONOR ON THE SAGE AND GAVE HIM A POSITION IN THE COURT.

BUT THE KING'S ENVIOUS VIZIER HAD OTHER PLANS...

YOUR HIGHNESS, I HAVE REASON TO BELIEVE THAT THIS SAGE INTENDS TO KILL YOU.

WHAT!?

WHAT IS THIS NONSENSE?

I THINK YOU ARE JEALOUS! AND I DO NOT WISH TO DO SOMETHING I WILL REGRET. MAY I TELL YOU A STORY?

YES, YOUR HIGHNESS.

ONCE THERE WAS A JEALOUS MAN WHO HAD A VERY BEAUTIFUL WIFE.

HE HATED TO LET HER OUT OF HIS SIGHT, BUT EVENTUALLY HE HAD TO LEAVE TOWN ON BUS-INESS, SO HE BOUGHT A PARROT

WHO WOULD REPORT TO HIM WHAT WENT ON WHILE HE WAS AWAY.

WHEN THE MAN RETURNED...

SO?

THE PARROT GAVE A DETAILED ACCOUNT OF THE WIFE'S UNFAITHFULNESS

THE HUSBAND WAS VERY ANGRY.

THE WIFE QUESTIONED HER SERVANTS, AND FINALLY DETERMINED THAT IT WAS THE PARROT WHO HAD TOLD.

THE NEXT TIME HER HUSBAND WENT AWAY, SHE HAD HER MAIDS BANG POTS AND PANS, FLASH BRIGHT LIGHTS, AND THROW WATER ON THE CAGE ALL NIGHT LONG.

THE NEXT DAY:

MASTER, I COULD NOT SEE OR HEAR ANYTHING LAST NIGHT DUE TO THE CRAZY THUNDERSTORM!

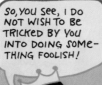
? ! ?

IT HAS NOT RAINED IN MONTHS!

AND HE KILLED THE PARROT.

YOU LIE!

LATER HE LEARNED FROM NEIGHBORS THAT WHAT THE BIRD REPORTED WAS TRUE

AND HE WAS FILLED WITH REGRET.

WHY?

SO, YOU SEE, I DO NOT WISH TO BE TRICKED BY YOU INTO DOING SOME-THING FOOLISH!

BUT DON'T YOU SEE? HE CURED YOU BY GIVING YOU SOMETHING TO HOLD IN YOUR HANDS.

HE COULD JUST AS EASILY KILL YOU BY GIVING YOU SOMETHING TO SMELL!

OR LOOK AT!

AND GRADUALLY THE VIZIER PLANTED THE SEEDS OF DOUBT IN THE KING'S MIND.

SEND FOR THE SAGE!

DO YOU KNOW WHY I HAVE CALLED YOU HERE?

NO

I AM GOING TO CHOP OFF YOUR HEAD.

B...BUT... WHY!?

I AM GOING TO KILL YOU BEFORE YOU KILL ME.

WHAT!? WHAT REASON COULD YOU HAVE? HAVE I NOT BEEN—

STRIKE OFF HIS HEAD!

"THE FISHERMAN AND THE GENIE" THE ARABIAN NIGHTS ANDRICE ARP   221

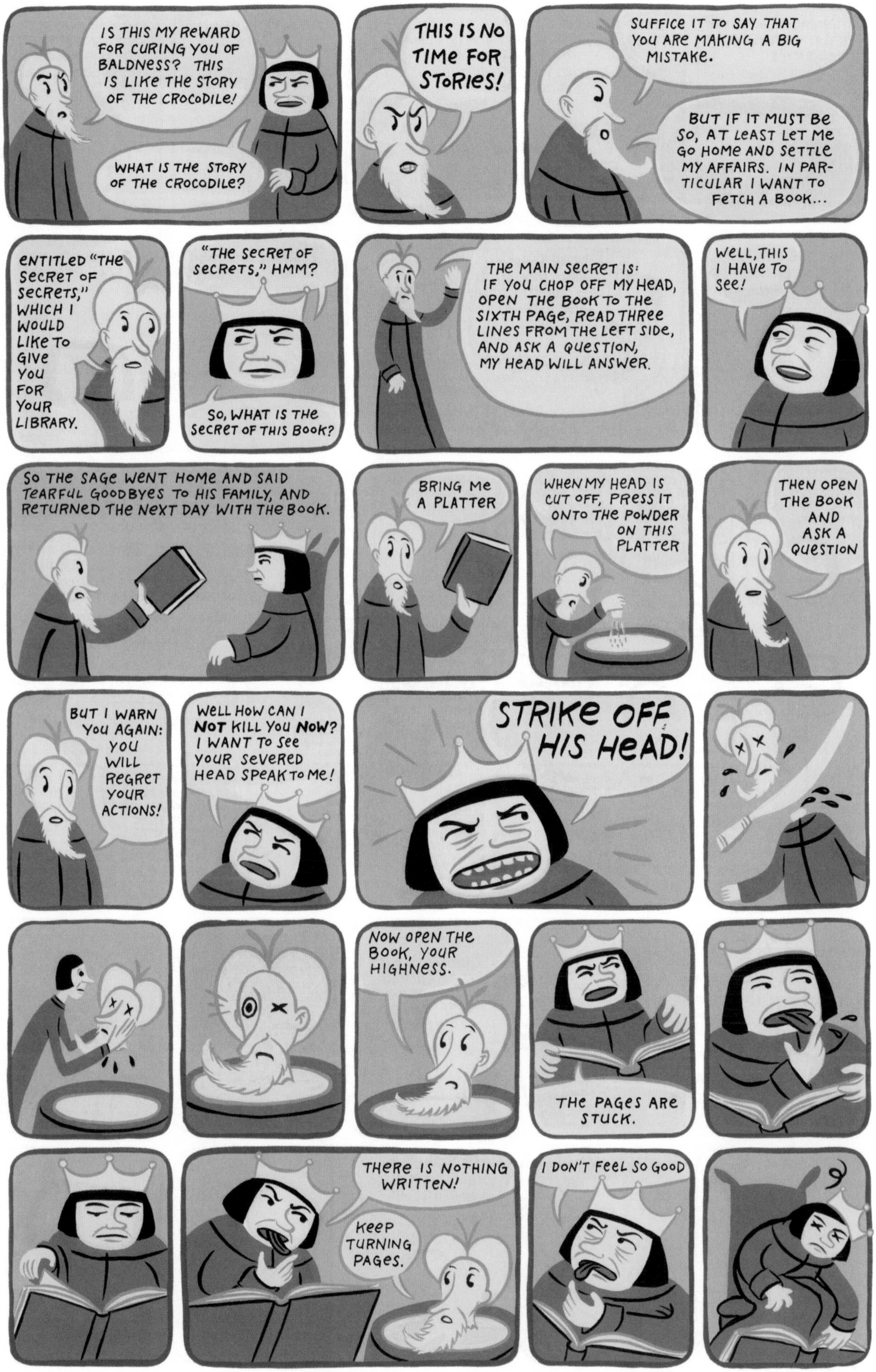
IS THIS MY REWARD FOR CURING YOU OF BALDNESS? THIS IS LIKE THE STORY OF THE CROCODILE!
WHAT IS THE STORY OF THE CROCODILE?
THIS IS NO TIME FOR STORIES!
SUFFICE IT TO SAY THAT YOU ARE MAKING A BIG MISTAKE.
BUT IF IT MUST BE SO, AT LEAST LET ME GO HOME AND SETTLE MY AFFAIRS. IN PARTICULAR I WANT TO FETCH A BOOK...
ENTITLED "THE SECRET OF SECRETS," WHICH I WOULD LIKE TO GIVE YOU FOR YOUR LIBRARY.
"THE SECRET OF SECRETS," HMM?
SO, WHAT IS THE SECRET OF THIS BOOK?
THE MAIN SECRET IS: IF YOU CHOP OFF MY HEAD, OPEN THE BOOK TO THE SIXTH PAGE, READ THREE LINES FROM THE LEFT SIDE, AND ASK A QUESTION, MY HEAD WILL ANSWER.
WELL, THIS I HAVE TO SEE!
SO THE SAGE WENT HOME AND SAID TEARFUL GOODBYES TO HIS FAMILY, AND RETURNED THE NEXT DAY WITH THE BOOK.
BRING ME A PLATTER
WHEN MY HEAD IS CUT OFF, PRESS IT ONTO THE POWDER ON THIS PLATTER
THEN OPEN THE BOOK AND ASK A QUESTION
BUT I WARN YOU AGAIN: YOU WILL REGRET YOUR ACTIONS!
WELL HOW CAN I NOT KILL YOU NOW? I WANT TO SEE YOUR SEVERED HEAD SPEAK TO ME!
STRIKE OFF HIS HEAD!
NOW OPEN THE BOOK, YOUR HIGHNESS.
THE PAGES ARE STUCK.
THERE IS NOTHING WRITTEN!
KEEP TURNING PAGES.
I DON'T FEEL SO GOOD

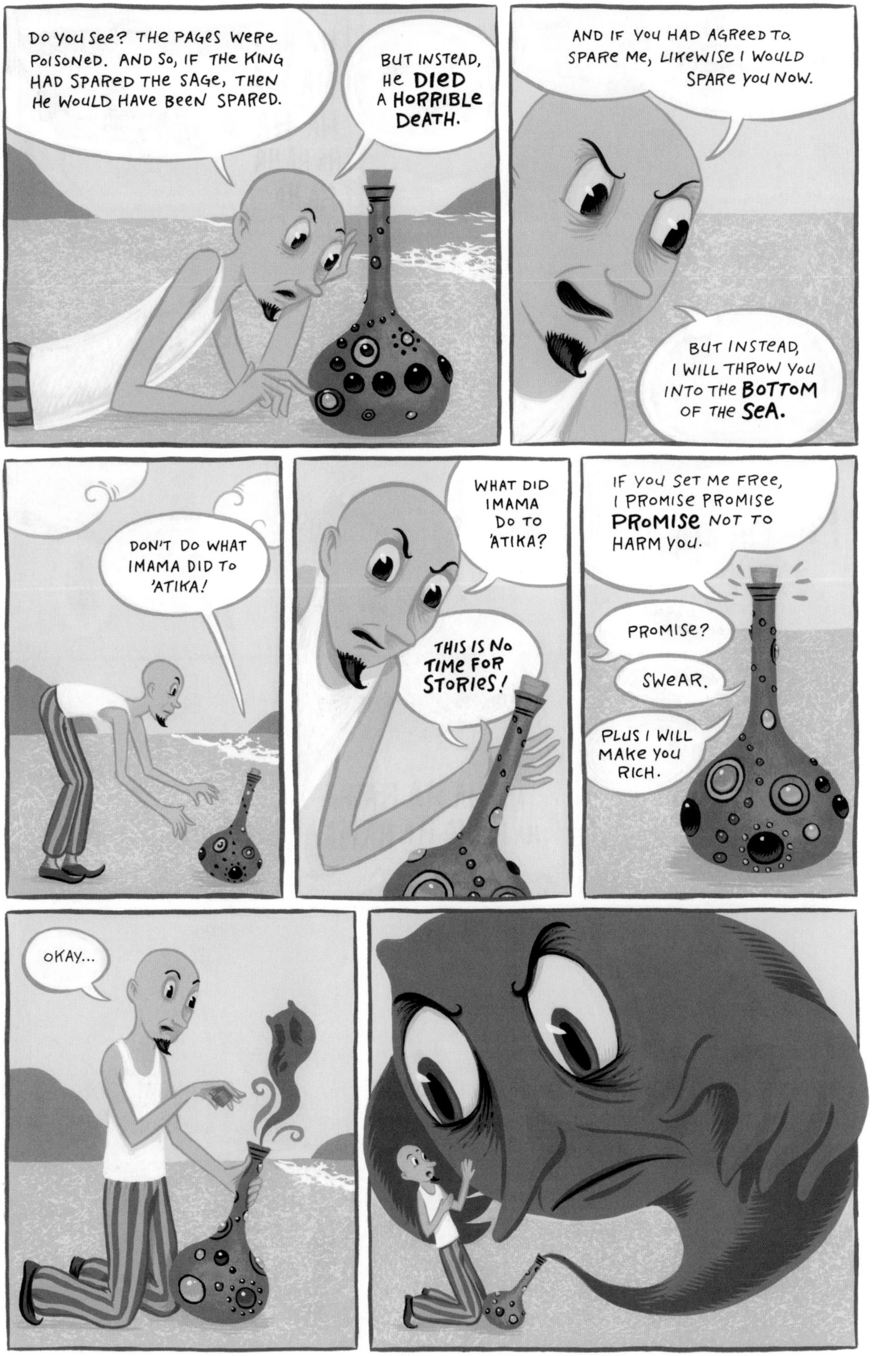
Do you see? THE PAGES WERE POISONED. AND SO, IF THE KING HAD SPARED THE SAGE, THEN HE WOULD HAVE BEEN SPARED.
BUT INSTEAD, HE DIED A HORRIBLE DEATH.
AND IF YOU HAD AGREED TO SPARE ME, LIKEWISE I WOULD SPARE YOU NOW.
BUT INSTEAD, I WILL THROW YOU INTO THE BOTTOM OF THE SEA.
DON'T DO WHAT IMAMA DID TO 'ATIKA!
WHAT DID IMAMA DO TO 'ATIKA?
THIS IS NO TIME FOR STORIES!
IF YOU SET ME FREE, I PROMISE PROMISE PROMISE NOT TO HARM YOU.
PROMISE?
SWEAR.
PLUS I WILL MAKE YOU RICH.
OKAY...

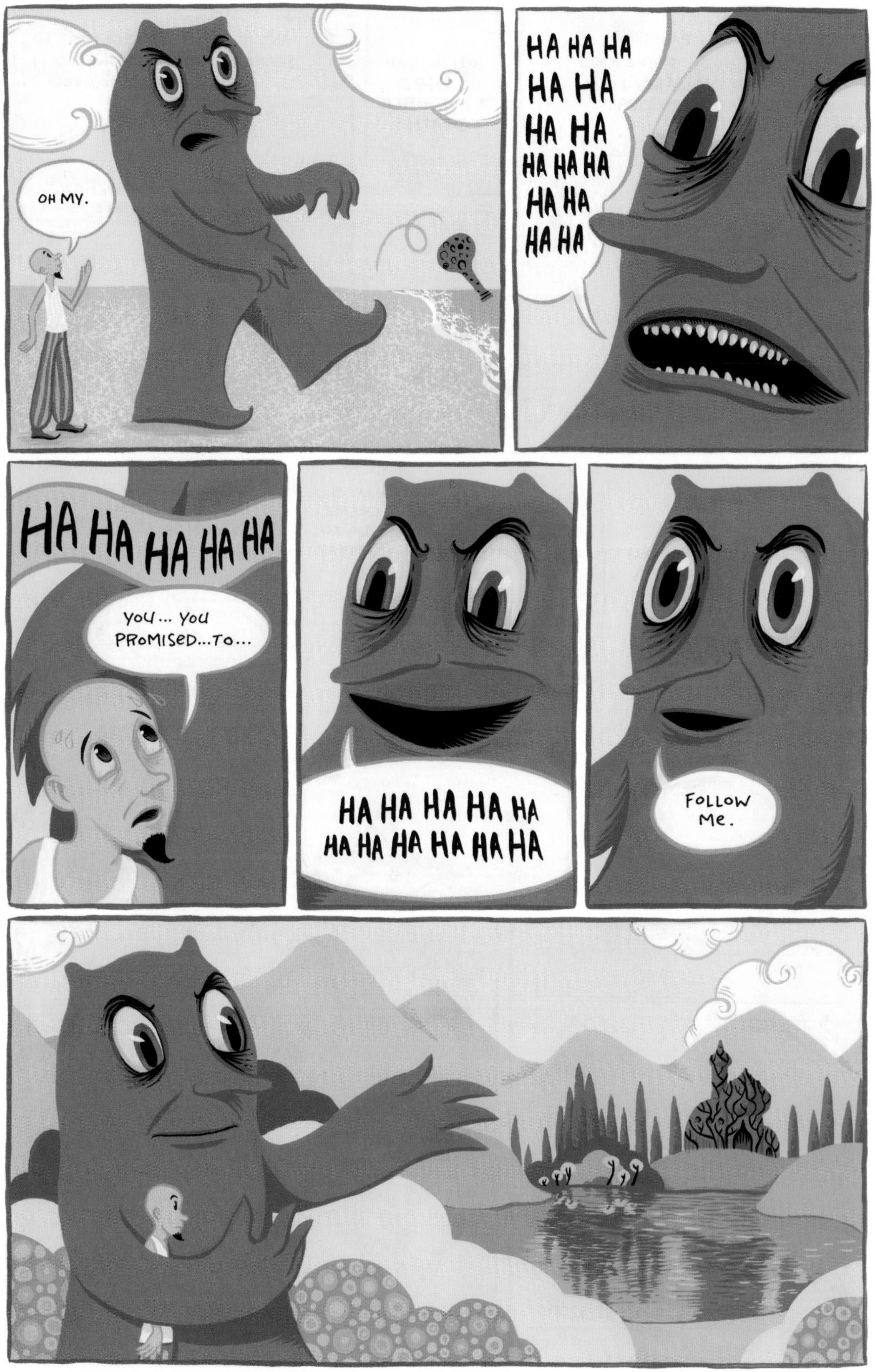
OH MY.
HA HA HA
HA HA
HA HA
HA HA HA
HA HA
HA HA
HA HA HA HA HA
YOU... YOU
PROMISED...TO...
HA HA HA HA HA
HA HA HA HA HA HA
FOLLOW
ME.

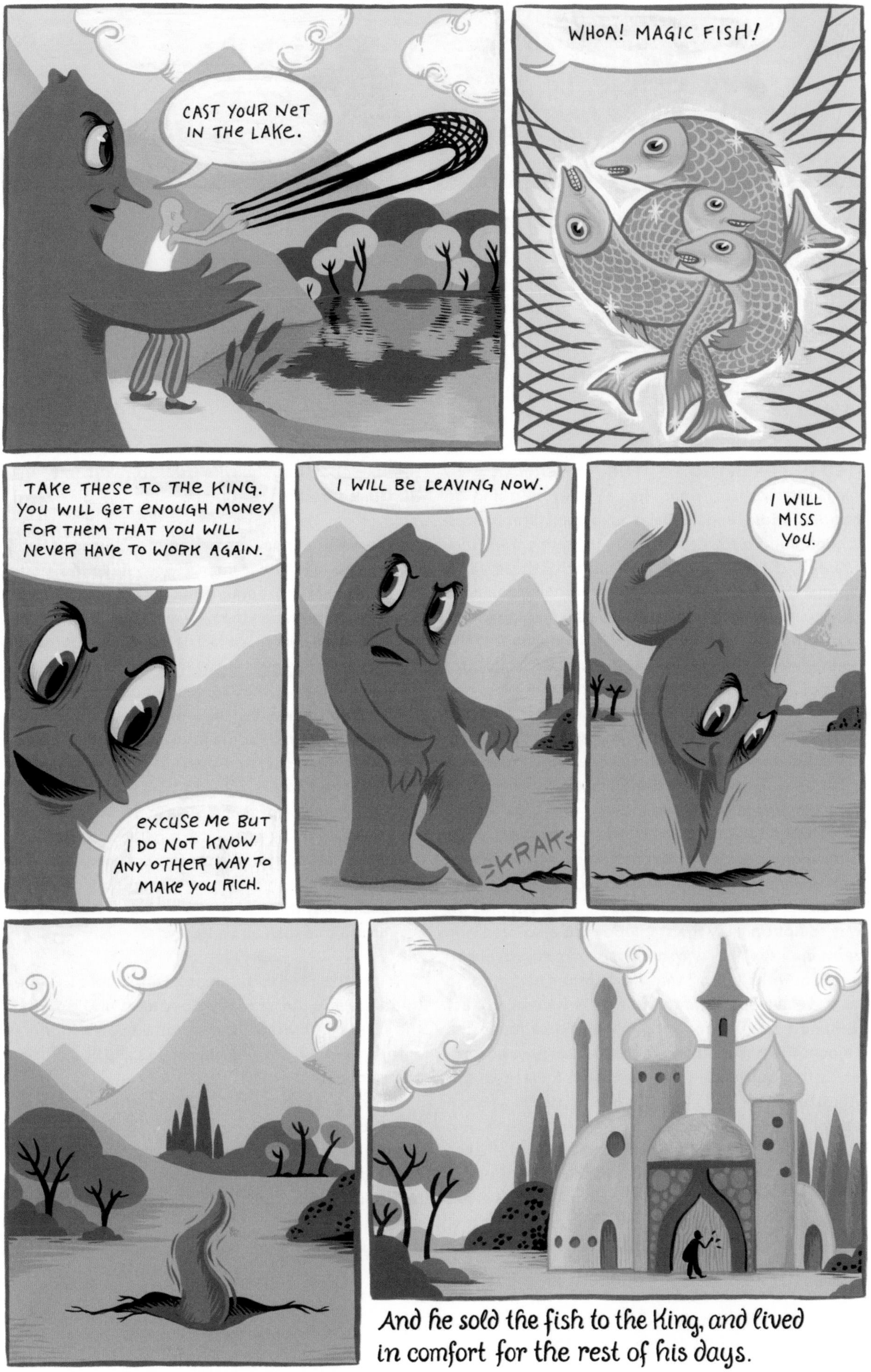
CAST YOUR NET IN THE LAKE.
WHOA! MAGIC FISH!
TAKE THESE TO THE KING. YOU WILL GET ENOUGH MONEY FOR THEM THAT YOU WILL NEVER HAVE TO WORK AGAIN.
EXCUSE ME BUT I DO NOT KNOW ANY OTHER WAY TO MAKE YOU RICH.
I WILL BE LEAVING NOW.
KRAK
I WILL MISS YOU.
And he sold the fish to the King, and lived in comfort for the rest of his days.

"The Woman with Two Coyntes"

from *The Arabian Nights*

ART / ADAPTATION BY **Vicki Nerino**

AS NOTED IN THE INTRO TO "THE FISHERMAN AND the Genie," *The Arabian Nights* has a lot more going on than Sinbad, Aladdin, and Ali Baba. Like many literary collections containing a lot of folktales—including *The Canterbury Tales* and *The Decameron*—a bunch of these yarns explicitly deal with sex. Most often, adultery. Or—to narrow it down further—neglected, crafty wives who find ingenious ways to cheat on their unsatisfying, doltish husbands. "The Woman with Two Coyntes" is the most perfect, most outrageous example of this huge genre. You won't find it in any of the abridged selections of *The Arabian Nights* at bookstores, but yes, this over-the-top tale is really in there, in the unabridged, unexpurgated versions, including Sir Richard Burton's legendary sixteen-volume translation from the 1880s (where it is tale 9 in volume 15).

Called "The Lady with Two Coyntes" in his version, it features a government official (possibly the governor of Constantinople), his wife, and a stableboy. The wife is frustrated by her husband's lack of interest, so she comes up with a way to not only lay the stableboy but also keep him as her permanent boy toy *with* her husband's approval and assistance. She tells hubby that her mother has died so she must travel several days to attend the funeral, collect her inheritance, and so on, but she's afraid to make the journey alone. The husband orders the stableboy to accompany her. So far, so good—this gives them a week to get it on in the stableboy's house and a nearby garden. When they "return," the wife has a surprise for her husband: Her mother bequeathed her vagina to her daughter, and she has attached it behind her own. Standing naked in front of her husband, she points to her vulva, telling him that this is her original one and, therefore, the one he may access (not that he will). She then turns around and bends over, telling him that this alleged second vulva is her mother's. It would be unseemly for him to have sex with it, so it needs a husband of its own, someone known and trustworthy who won't dare have sex with the husband's coynte. The husband suggests the stableboy, and the wife pseudo-reluctantly agrees. The Burton translation continues:

> Hereat the man summoned his servant before him and said to him, "Hear me, O Syce; verily the mother of my wife to her hath bequeathed her Coynte, and 'tis our intent to bestow it upon thee in lawful wedlock; yet beware lest thou draw near that which is our own property." The horsekeeper answered, "No, O my lord, I never will." Now after they arrived at that agreement concerning the matter in question, whenever the wife waxed hot with heat of lust she would send for the Syce and take him and repair with him, he and she, to a place of privacy within the Harem, whilst her mate remained sitting thoroughly satisfied, and they would enjoy themselves to the uttermost, after which the twain would come forth together. And the Kaim-makam never ceased saying on such occasions, "Beware, O Syce, lest thou poach upon that which is my property;" and at such times the wife would exclaim, "By Allah, O my lord, he is a true man and a trusty."

(I feel the need to summarize and quote the tale in order to assure you that it really does exist and is part of one of the classics of world literature! Burton's *Nights* is online in its entirety in several places, in case you'd like to verify independently.)

Canadian comics artist and illustrator Vicki Nerino brings her charmingly grotesque style to the tale, keeping its original setting but updating the language to reflect twenty-first-century sensibilities (with smidgens of the Victorian rendering). This is perfectly in order, since this is a folktale, which will always be told in the language of the folk. For those of a certain age, I offer the following brief glossary: totes = totally, OMG = Oh my God, WTF = What the fuck, aaight = all right.

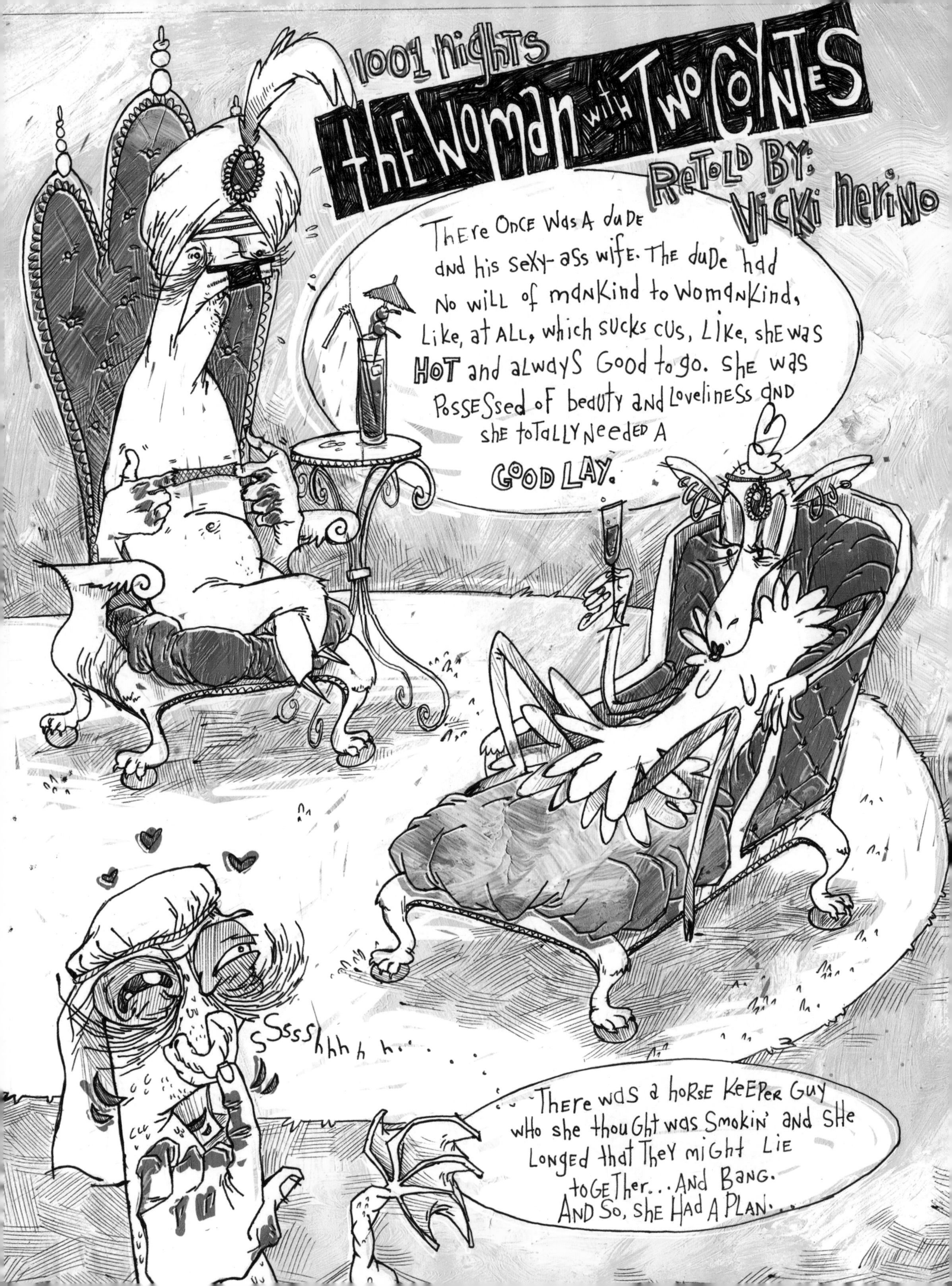
1001 nights
The Woman with Two Coyntes
Retold By: Vicki Nerino
There Once Was A dude and his sexy-ass wife. The dude had No will of mankind to womankind, Like, at ALL, which sucks cus, Like, she was HOT and always Good to go. She was Possessed of beauty and Loveliness and she totally needed A GOOD LAY.
Sssssshhhh h h...
...There was a horse keeper Guy who she thought was Smokin' and She Longed that They might Lie together... And Bang. And So, she Had A Plan...

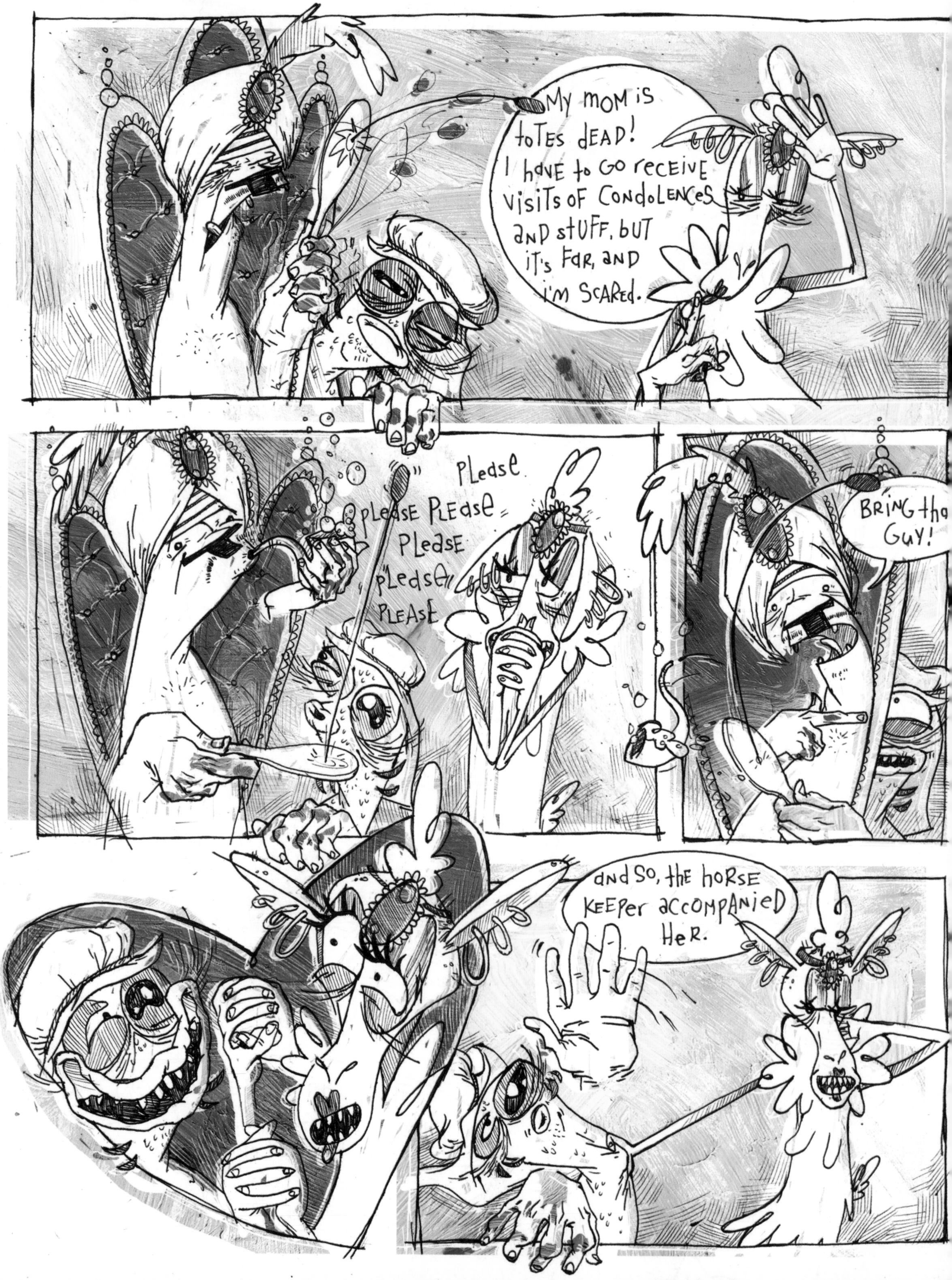
My mom is totes dead! I have to go receive visits of condolences and stuff, but it's far, and i'm scared.
Please please please Please please PLEASE
Bring tha Guy!
and so, the horse keeper accompanied her.

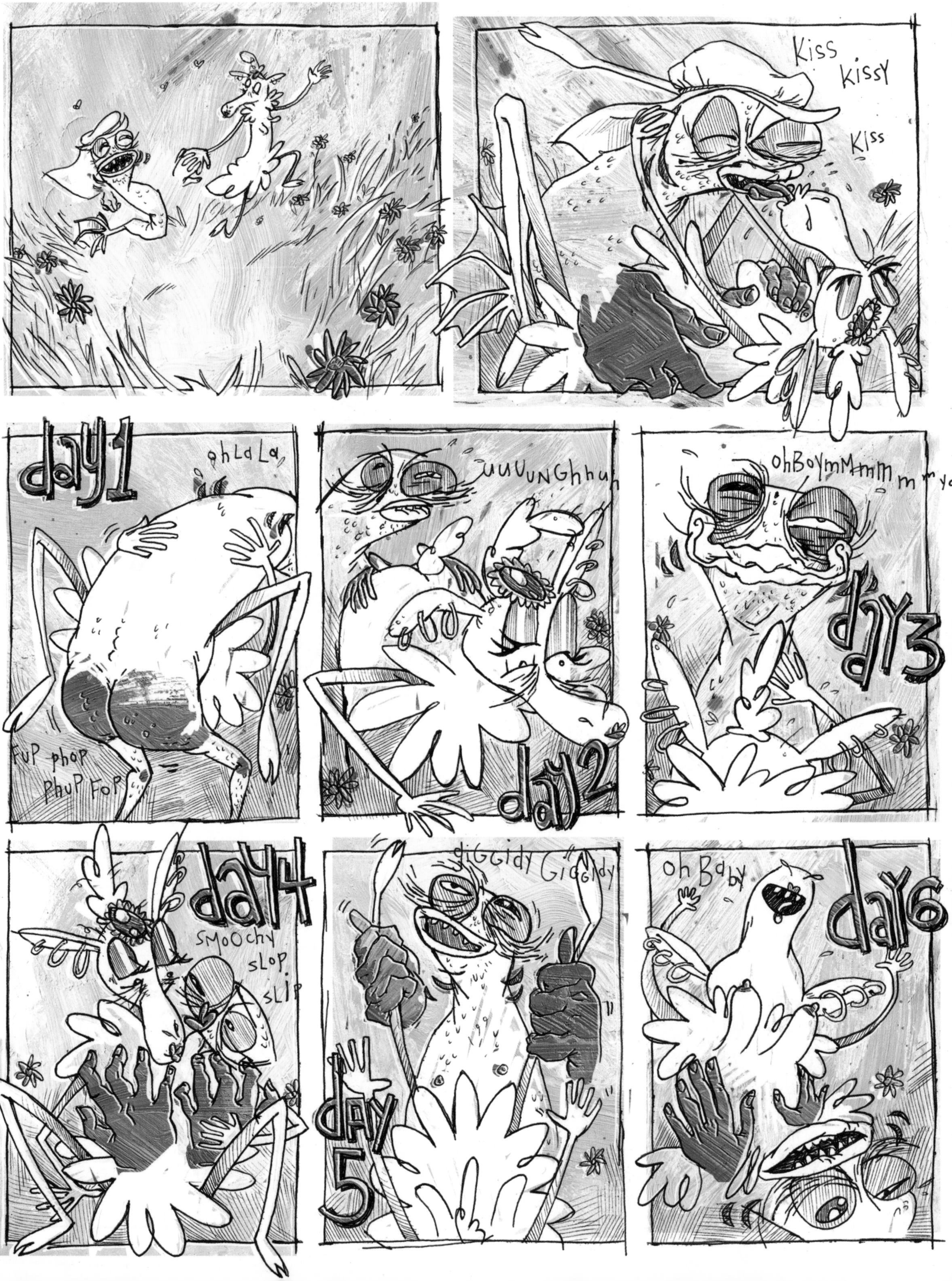

Kiss kissy
Kiss
day1
ohLaLa
FUP phop PHUP FOP
UUUUNGhhuh
day2
ohBoymmmmmm
day3
day4
SMOOChy slop sLIP
giGGidy GiGGidy
day5
Oh Baby
day6

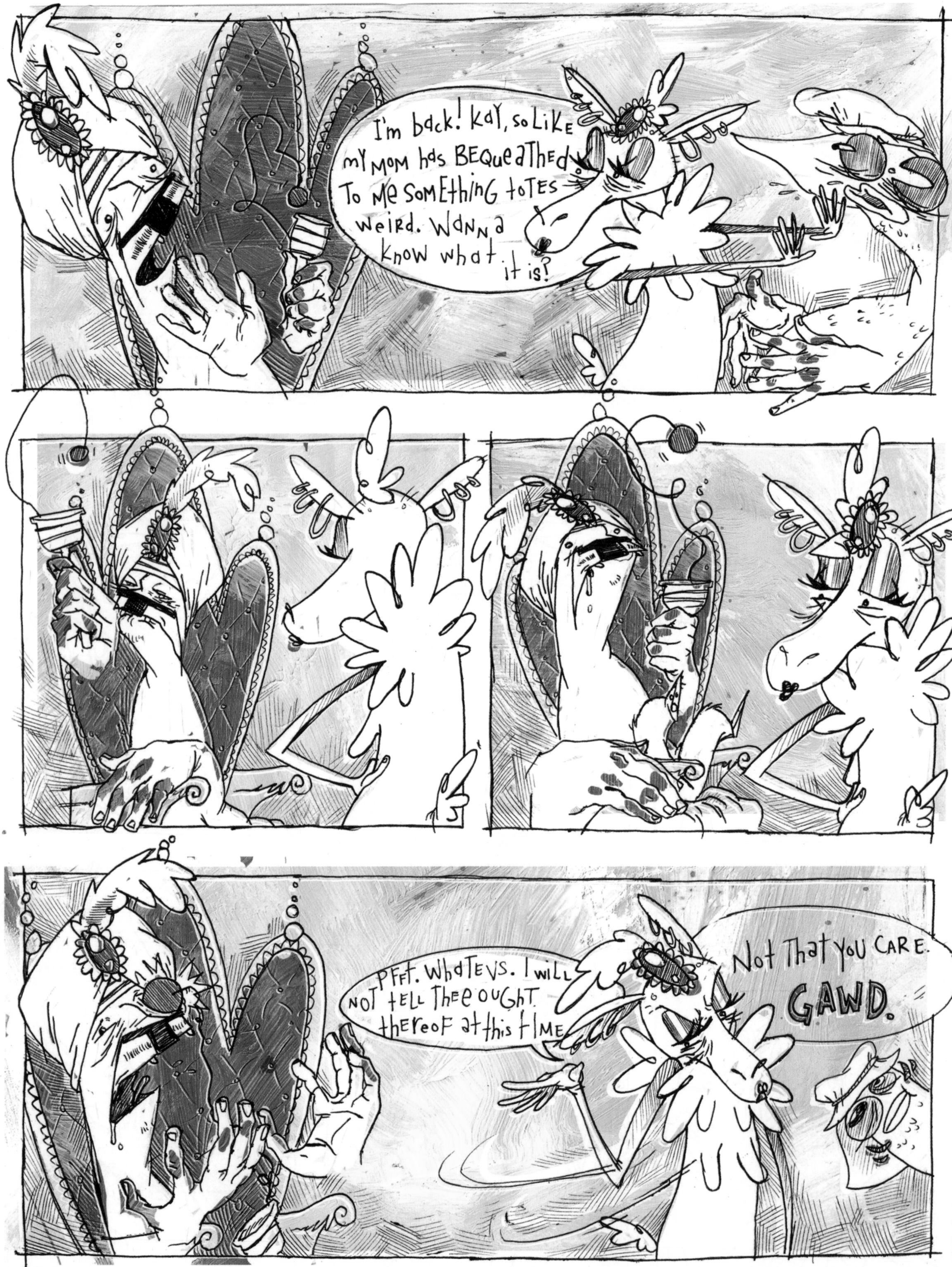
I'm back! kay, so LIKE my MOM has BEQUEaTHED To ME SOMEThing totes weird. Wanna know what it is?
PFft. WhaTEVS. I WILL NOT tELL ThEE OUGhT thereof at this tIME
Not That You CARE.
GAWD.

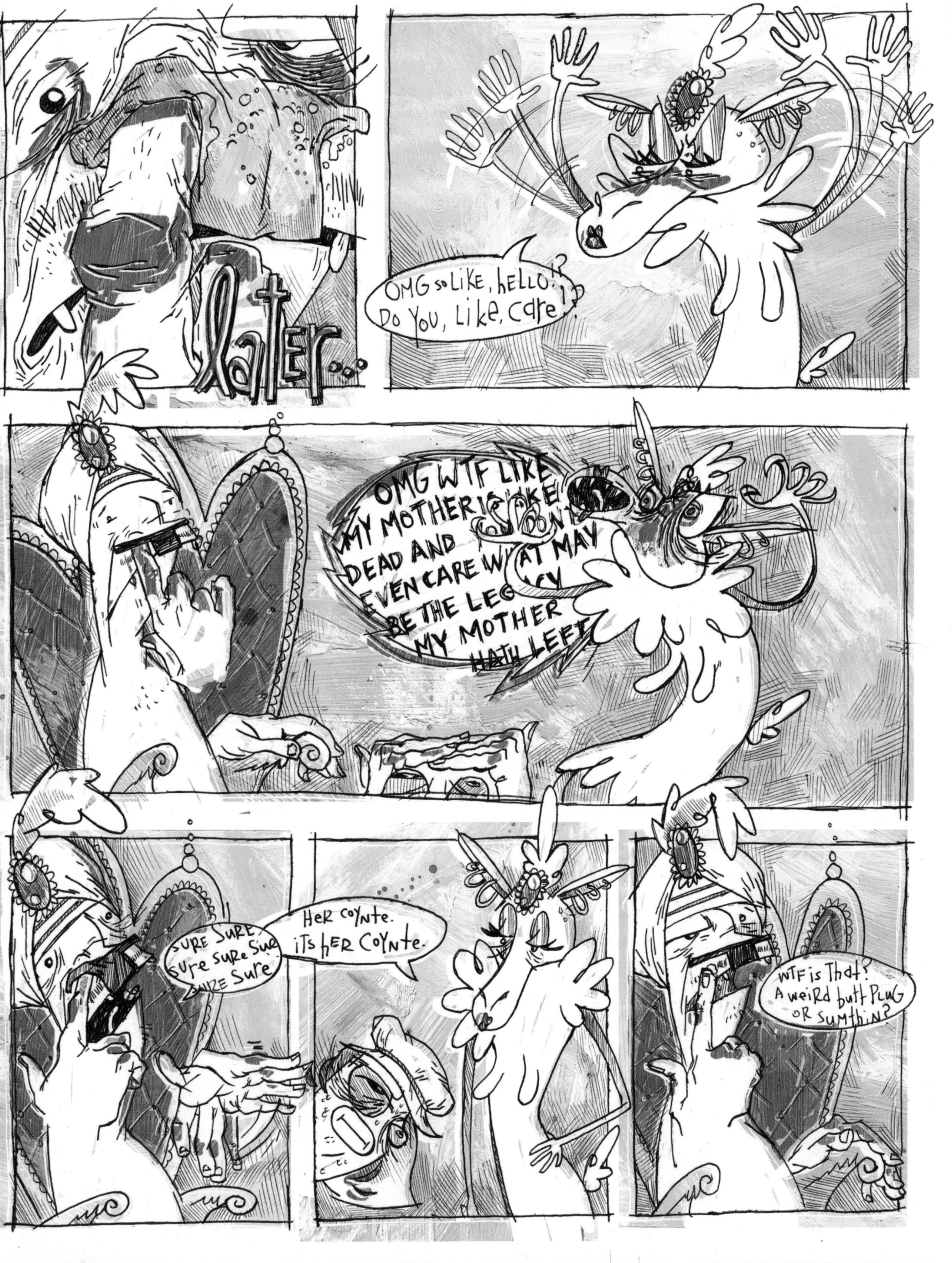
later...
OMG so Like, hello!? Do you, Like, care!?
OMG WTF LIKE MY MOTHER IS LIKE DEAD AND YOU DON'T EVEN CARE WHAT MAY BE THE LEGACY MY MOTHER HATH LEFT
SURE SURE SURE SURE SURE SURE SURE SURE
HER coynte. its HER coynte.
WTF is That? A weird butt PLUG OR SUMTHIN?

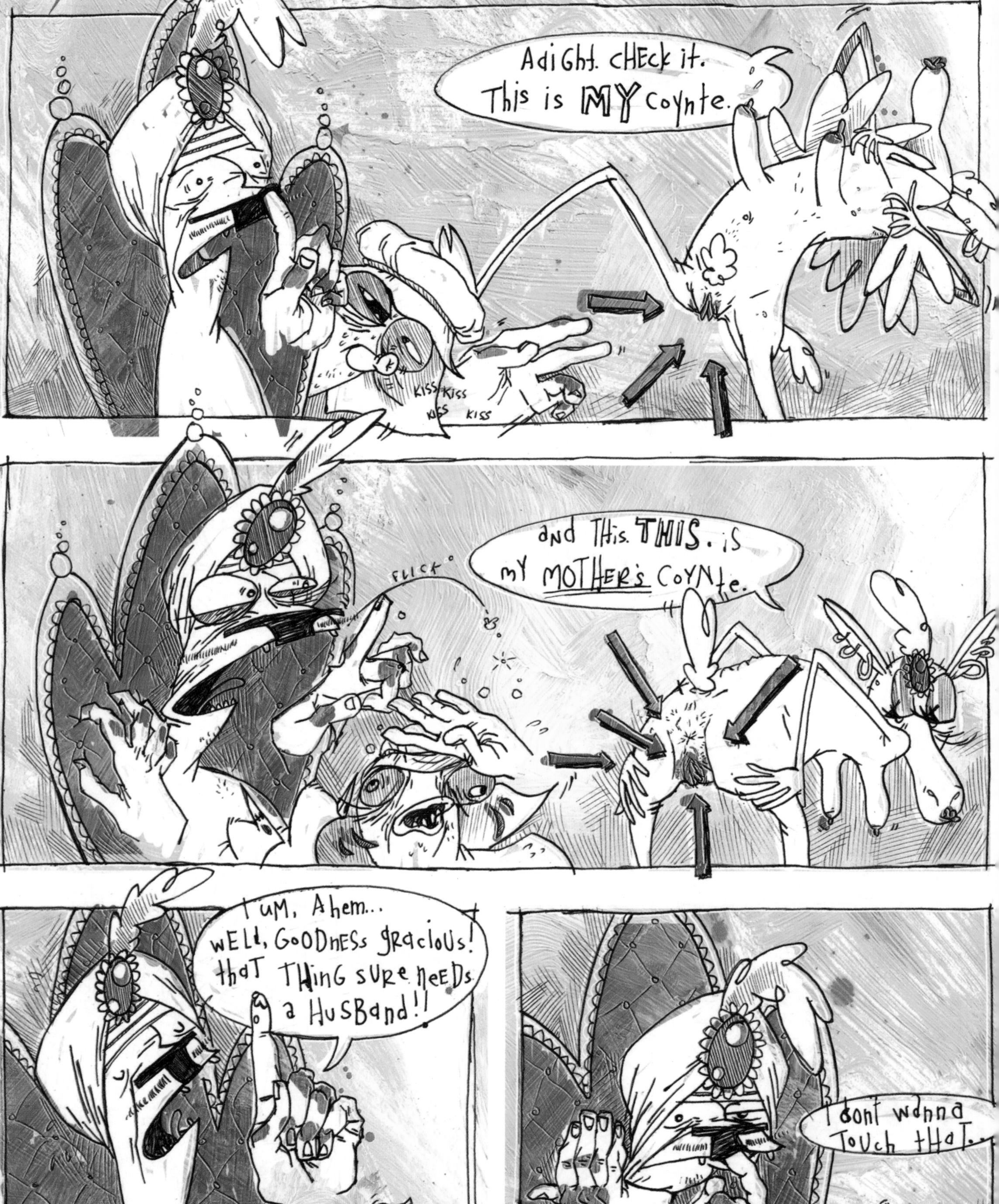
AdiGht. CHECK it. This is MY coynte.
KISS KISS KISS KISS
FLICK
and THis. THIS. is my MOTHER's COYNte.
um, Ahem... WELL, GOODness gracious! that THING sure needs a HUSBand!!
I dont wanna Touch thaT...

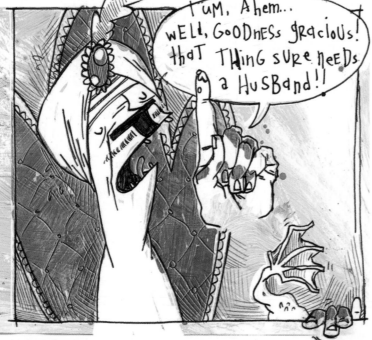

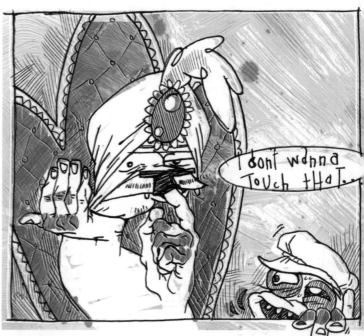

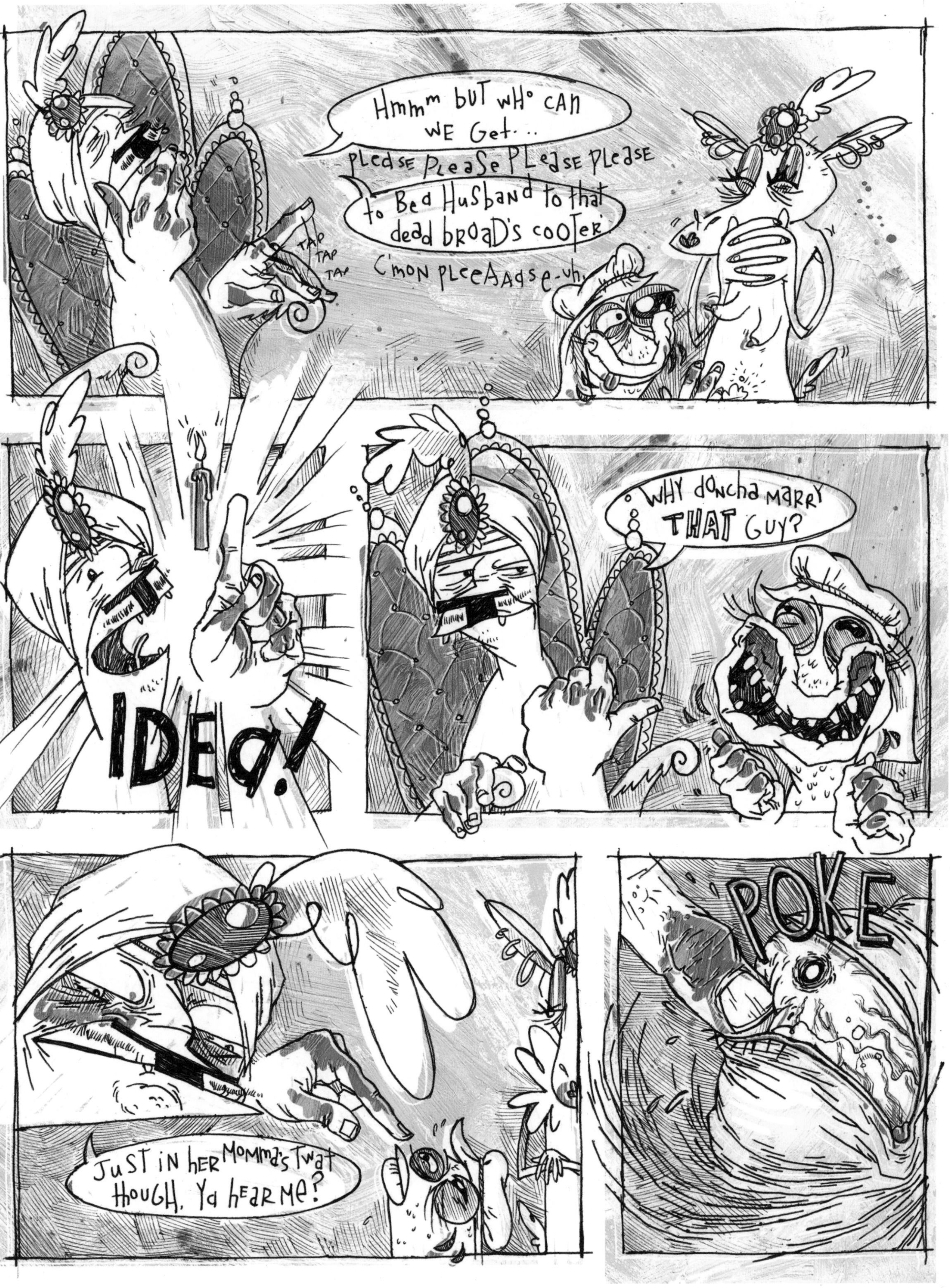
Hmmm but who can we Get...
please please please please
to Be a Husband to that dead broad's cooter
C'mon pleeaaase-uh
TAP TAP TAP
IDEA!
WHY doncha marry THAT guy?
Just in her Momma's Twat though, Ya hear me?
POKE

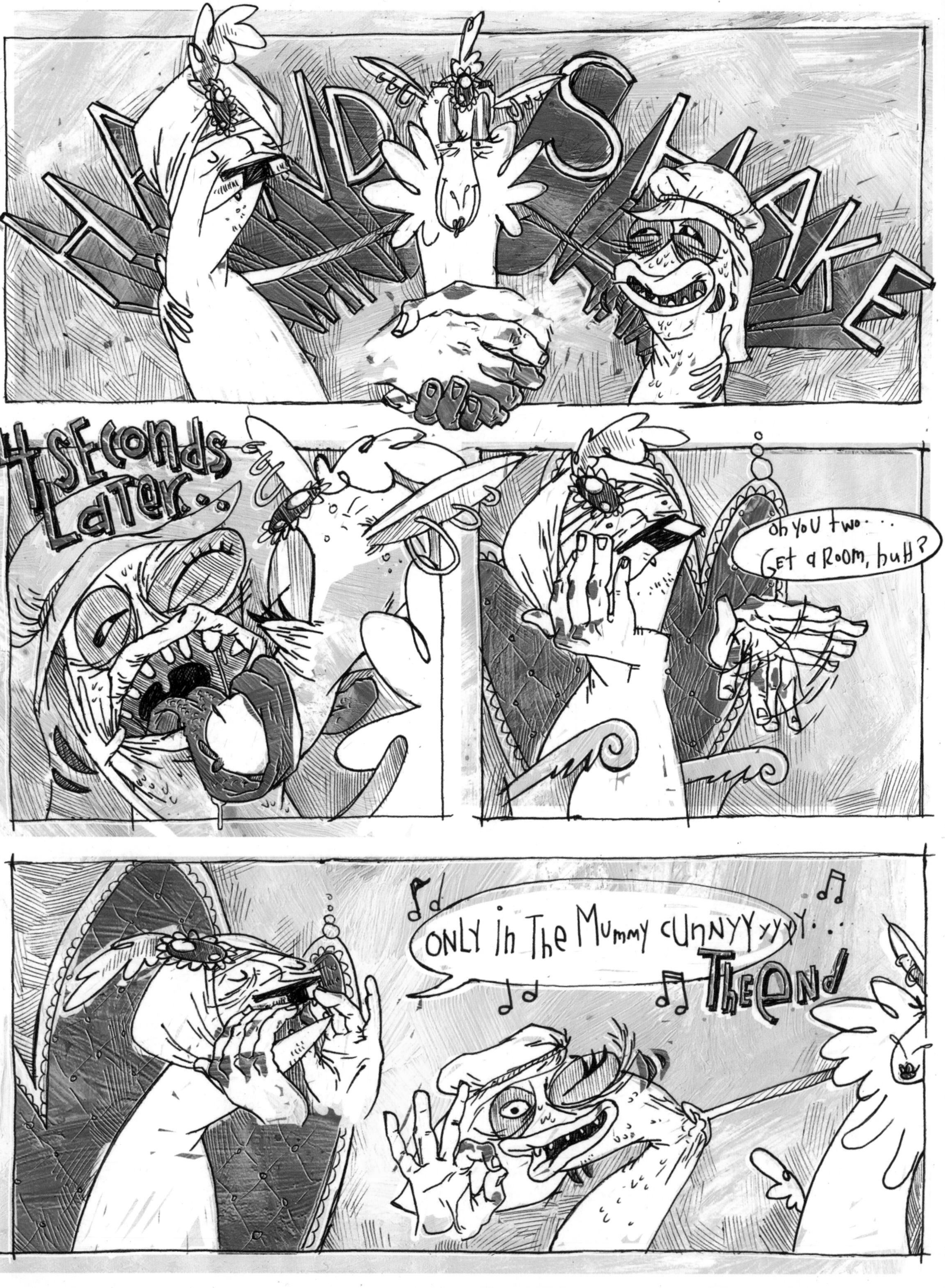
HANDSHAKE
4 SEconds Later...
oh you two...
Get a Room, huH?
ONLY in The Mummy cUNNYYyyyy...
TheEnd

Poems

Rumi

ART / ADAPTATION BY **Michael Green**

TRANSLATIONS BY **Coleman Barks**

THE MYSTICAL BRANCH OF ISLAM IS SUFISM, AND the Sufis created a huge body of beautiful poetry about the joyous, drunken, love-filled union with the Divine. The best known of these poets is Rumi, who was a Muslim religious teacher, theologian, sermonizer, and juror (i.e., he made rulings on matters according to Islamic law) in what is now Turkey during the 1200s. He had great book-knowledge, but a new world opened to him when he met the wandering mystic Shams, who apparently triggered some sort of enlightenment experience in Rumi.

The two were inseparable for several months, as Shams taught Rumi through words and in more subtle, ineffable ways. Rumi's students were intensely jealous of this relationship, and when Shams started receiving death threats, he left. Rumi was devastated, but it's also at this point that he started composing his poetry, which would eventually total more than 70,000 verses. Shams returned months later, but soon disappeared for good, and it's widely believed that he was murdered by one of Rumi's students or even Rumi's son. Rumi was again devastated and wandered in search of his beloved Shams, though stopped when he realized that he was Shams, that he carried his friend/teacher within him.

Like many of the Sufis, Rumi wrote about the rapture of merging back into one's true self, into the divine oneness (which can be referred to as Allah, God, and many other names), and this was often accomplished by a love-based, though nonphysical, merging with a beloved human being. (For, since we're all part of the oneness, merging with any person *is* merging with the Divine.) Love plays a central role in the Sufi worldview, being the basic force that draws us back to the oneness. God is often referred to as "the Beloved," and this merging is sometimes portrayed in ways indistinguishable from intense love for another person. Some of the wisest things ever said about love come from Rumi. ("Our task is not to seek love, but to uncover all obstacles to it that we have built within ourselves." "It is nobler to die on love's rocks than to live a life of death.")

Rumi is widely cited as the best-selling poet in the US. This remarkable achievement for a Persian mystic from 800 years ago is largely due to Coleman Barks, whose life's work has been, to a large extent, the rendering of various translations of Rumi into charming, moving, lucid yet profound versions that speak to a wide variety of people. Coleman's renditions were visualized by artist Michael Green in the best-selling instaclassic *The Illuminated Rumi* and its sequel, *One Song*. The following pages contain the chapter on love from *One Song*.

O AMAZING LOVE

O AMAZING LOVE,
LET ME SING OF YOUR WONDERS
WITH THESE WORDS
LET ME OPEN
A DOOR
INTO LIGHT

At one time or another, I believe everyone gets the Call. The shutters open for an instant and perfection tumbles through. Maybe it is a rainy day, and you are eleven years old, watching a drop of water slowly slide down the windowpane–into eternity. Or maybe one sunrise, losing yourself you become a flight of birds. But after the Call there's a whole lot of forgetting. Or, if not forgetting, a reluctance to accept its full consequences, which is to become obsessed with regaining your true identity. Rumi says the only thing that can drive this great quest is a *special kind of love*. It's not infatuation or sensual excitement, though these agitations sometimes work as coming attractions. This love, this oceanic love, is really dangerous: one sip can send you spinning forever. Rumi is a change-agent, and he wants nothing more than to shake us to the roots and turn us around forever. Can we trust this man as a spiritual friend? Real trust doesn't arise from persuasive arguments, but it might from a taste of Amazing Love. There's more than a taste around Rumi; there's a flowing heart-river. *Faith, hope, and love*, the Bible says, *these three, but the foremost is love*. I would follow him anywhere. If we can stand for even one moment on the shore of his heart, we may catch a small glimpse of what he sees and how he knows things. Implicit in all these poems, these love poems, is his poignant invitation: *Will you join me?* All the heavens will be decorated, and all the angels will sing, on the day his call and our response become one and the same song.

If you can't wrap this love
around you like a cloak at midnight,
don't put on something else,
go back to bed.

Let THIS LOVE run spinning
through your brain.
It's what holds everything together,
and it's the everything too!

Without a little dancing,
there is no disappearing.

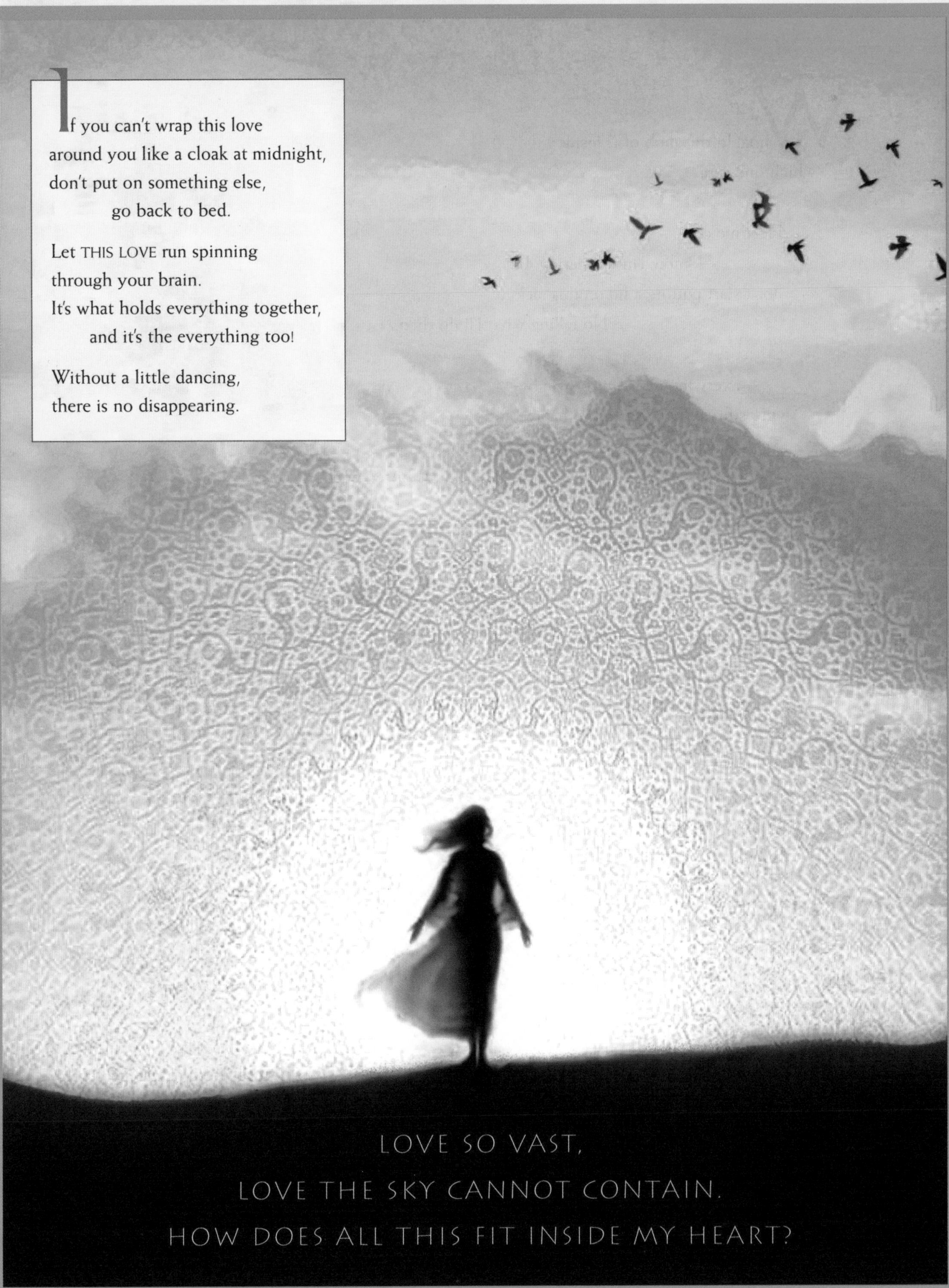

LOVE SO VAST,
LOVE THE SKY CANNOT CONTAIN.
HOW DOES ALL THIS FIT INSIDE MY HEART?

Whoa! In this mob of *I*'s inside,

which one is *me*?

Hear me out.

I know I'm wandering, but

don't start putting a lid on this racket.

No telling what I'll do then.

Every moment I'm thrown by

your story. One moment it's happy, and

I'm singing. One moment it's sad, and

I'm weeping. It turns bitter; and

I pull away.

But then you spill a little grace, and just like that,

I'm all light.

It's not so bad,

this arrangement,

actually.

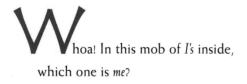

Good, old-time monotheism has managed to churn up some pretty heavy-handed versions of Yahweh in its day. When God the Dominator glowers down from some Byzantine church, better dive for cover. Not much love radiating there. But with Rumi we're privy to real contact with sacredness, and the living presence is quite different. Fear-based boundaries and mental certainties dissolve when mystical love starts flowing. Ramakrishna (the Hindu saint who embraced Christianity and then Islam just to see if GOD, ALLAH, and TRUTH-CONSCIOUSNESS-BLISS were identical*) used to say that this contact was like "a salt doll exploring the sea." Dispatches from such a front are bound to be a little diffused, as we see in the shape-shifting, divine *You* that Rumi is always addressing. Sometimes *You* is a stupendous overarching Divine Presence. Then it is the intimacy of the Friend, as when he experiences that vastness through the person of Shams. Sometimes *You* is a Beloved, all feminine and alluring, and Rumi is whispering *I would love to kiss You*. Altogether, it's a charged, slightly scandalous situation, and his genius is to make us accomplices, guilty as charged.

Diving into the ocean deeps, or waving *this way* from the shore, there's a big secret Rumi has to pass on: *At some point, the salt doll becomes the sea.* When the smoke-and-mirrors ego surrenders to Vastness, there's nothing left but *holy holy holy*, and ecstatic, total identification with Godhead. This is over the edge for most folk, something to put off to the Rapture. But we still want Rumi to tell us, again and again, *holy holy is what you really are*, right now. He liked to invoke the legendary Hallaj, a Sufi who was constantly drawn into union, then unable to stop himself from exclaiming inside the streaming galactic whirl, "I am Light! I am Truth!"

*He concluded they were.

Last night I took a vow, by your life this time,
that I would never again turn my eyes from your face.
Pierce me with a sword, I will not look away from you.

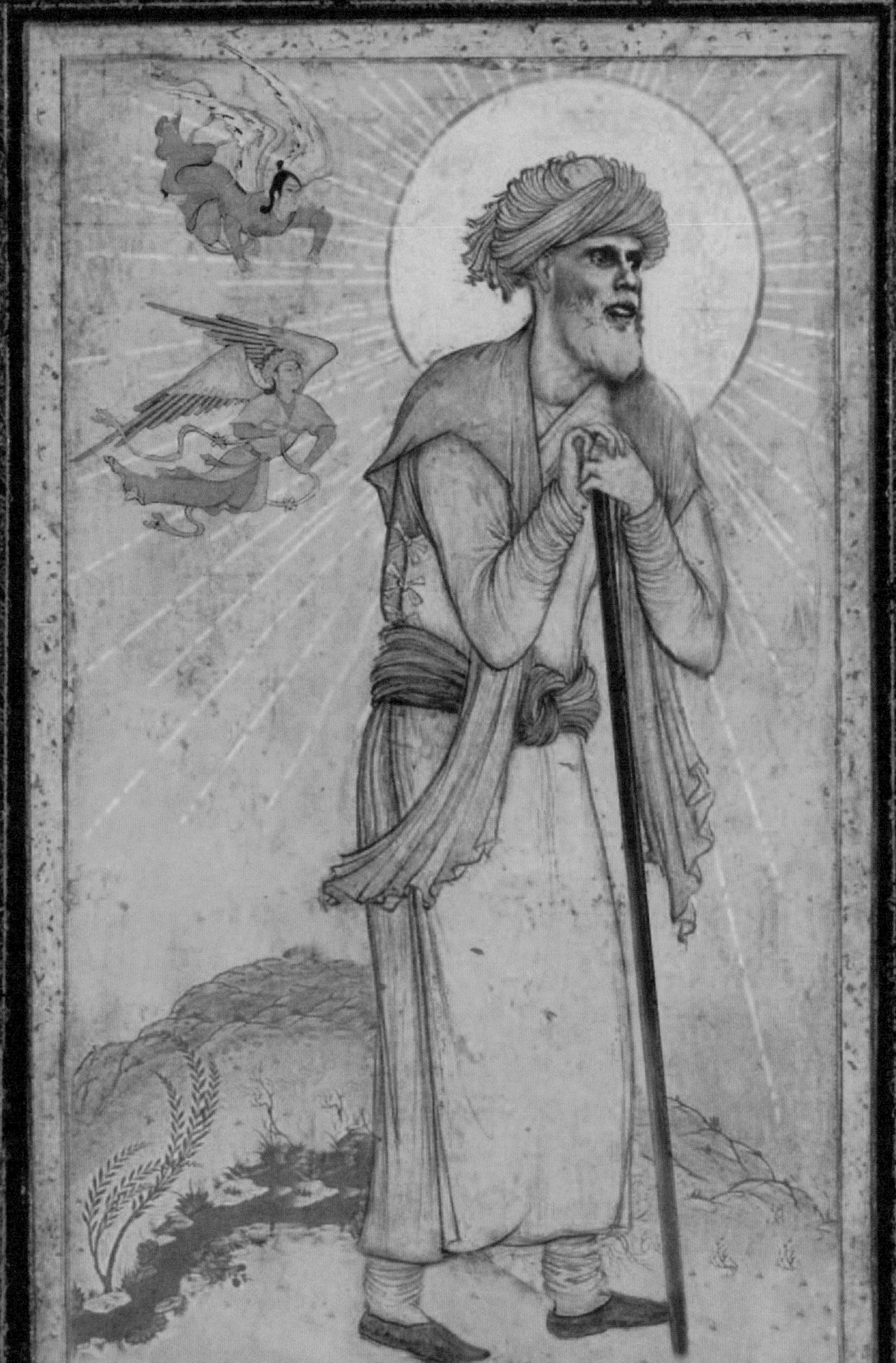

Cast me into a fire, I won't even sigh.
You pass, and I rise from your path like dust.
Now, like dust, I settle back to earth.

COME!

JUST LISTEN.

We know a way from
your scene
to the Unseen. You've

lived too long in that
gloomy house. This
path leads to a garden

that will lift you
right out of yourself.
The gardener is an

old friend, the cypress
and jasmine too.
Every day

we come and gather
a hundred blossoms
here to scatter

among you.
Don't worry, there are
no hidden motives,

just too much
love blooming
to keep for ourselves.

These words
are a fragrance escaping
from this garden. See

how the world
is softened by their
sweetness. Hear

them whisper,
Come! Come! It
really is like this!

When we first caught
the scent, it
swept us away, then

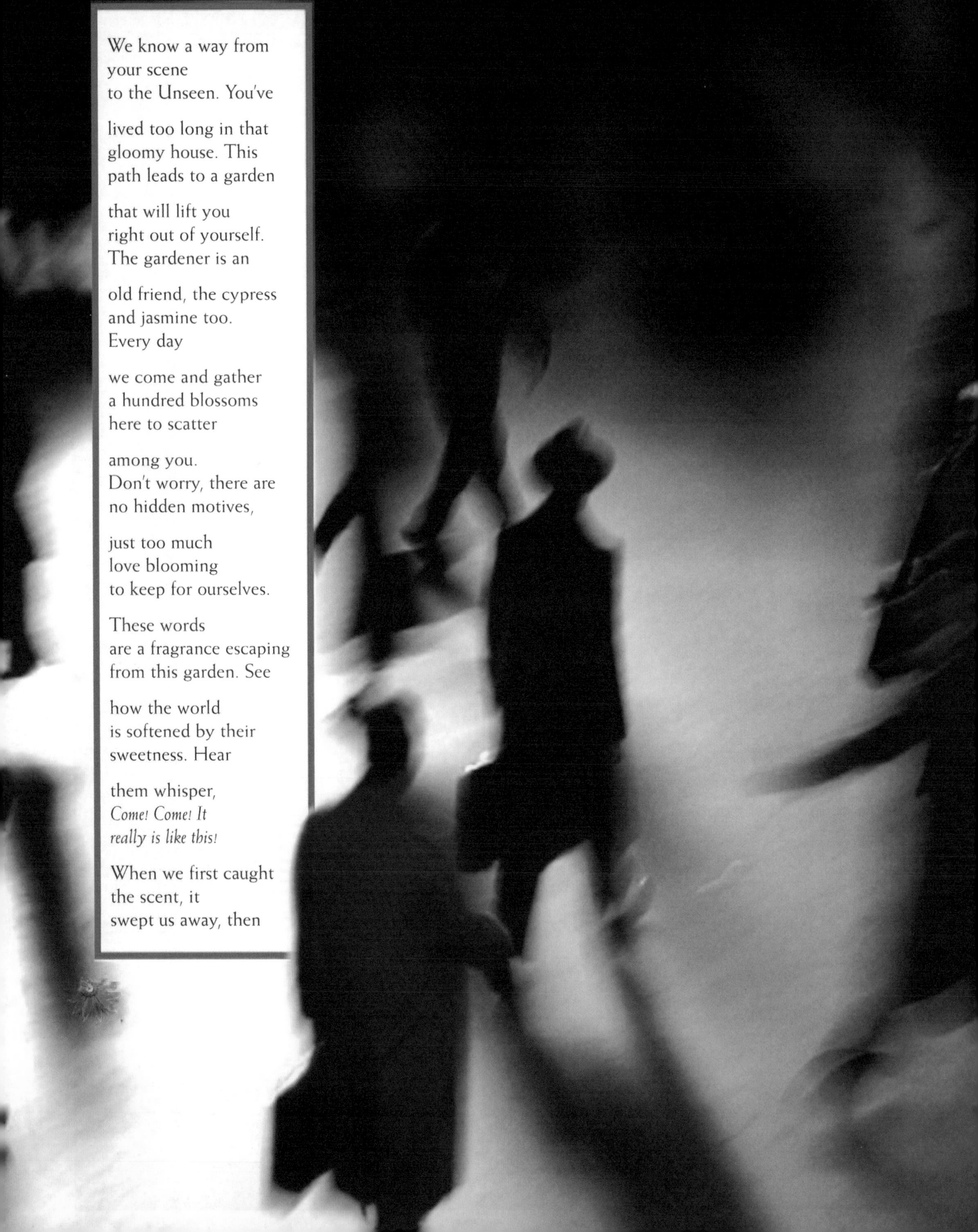

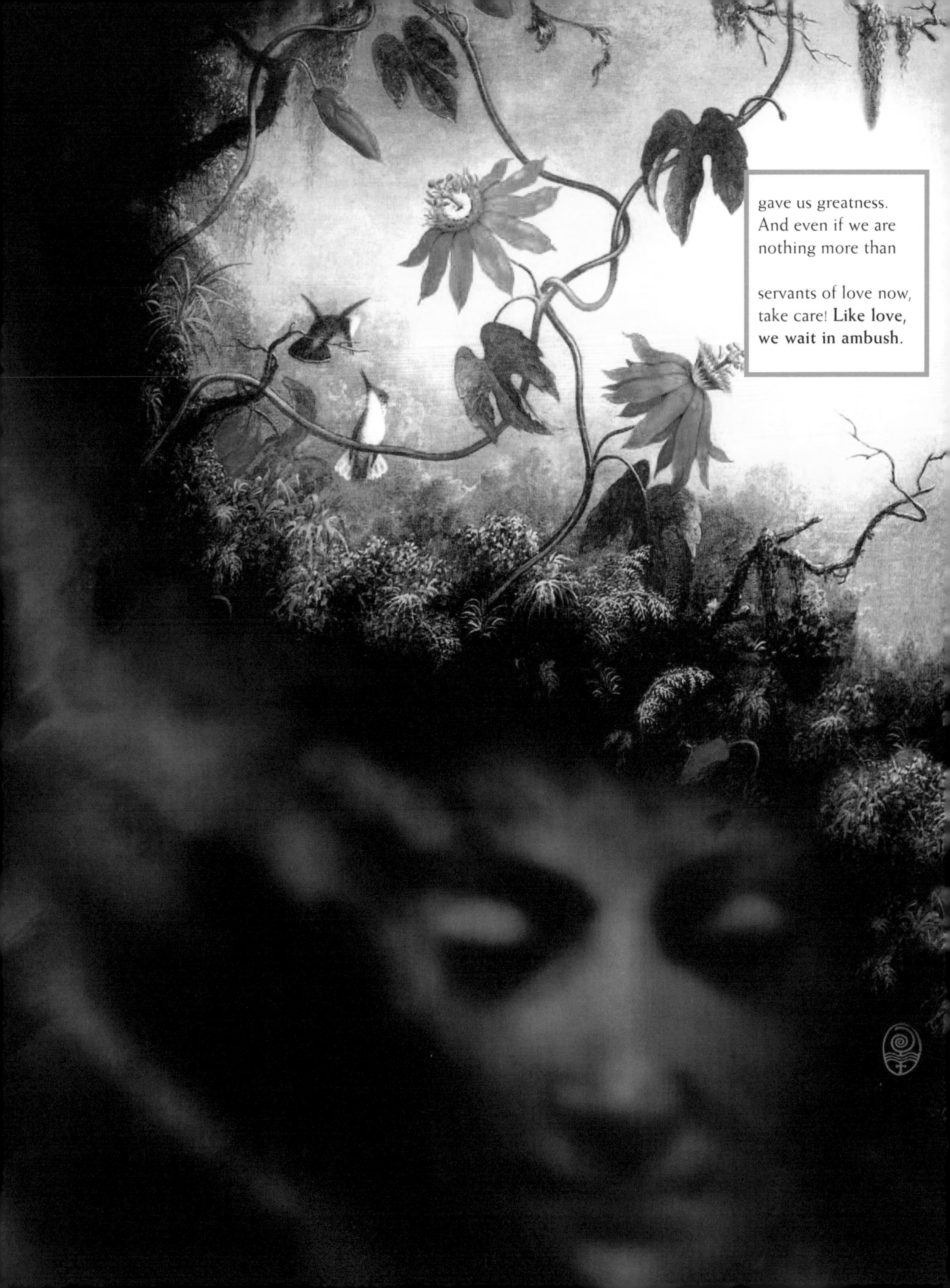

gave us greatness.
And even if we are
nothing more than

servants of love now,
take care! **Like love,
we wait in ambush.**

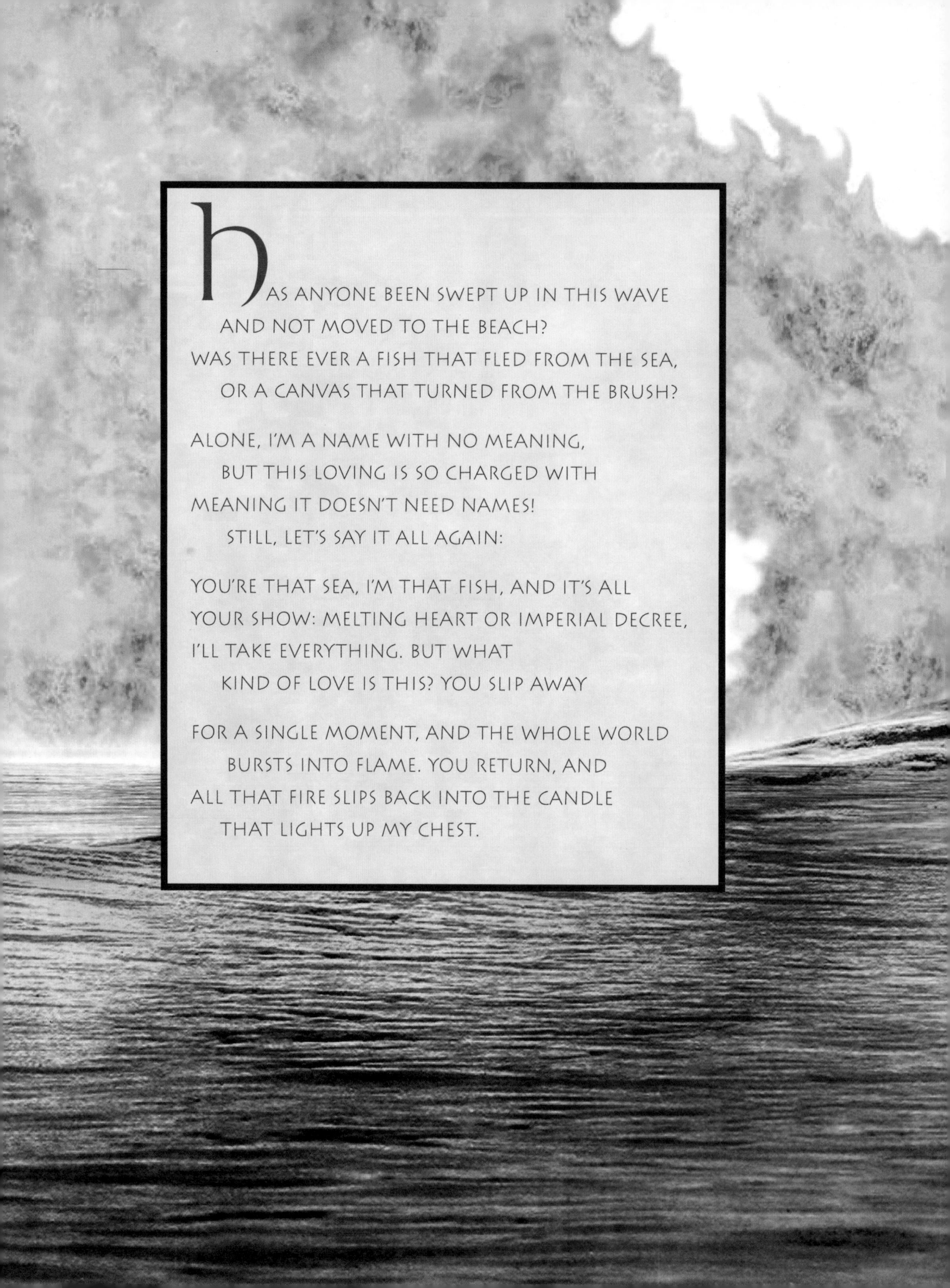

HAS ANYONE BEEN SWEPT UP IN THIS WAVE
    AND NOT MOVED TO THE BEACH?
WAS THERE EVER A FISH THAT FLED FROM THE SEA,
    OR A CANVAS THAT TURNED FROM THE BRUSH?

ALONE, I'M A NAME WITH NO MEANING,
    BUT THIS LOVING IS SO CHARGED WITH
MEANING IT DOESN'T NEED NAMES!
    STILL, LET'S SAY IT ALL AGAIN:

YOU'RE THAT SEA, I'M THAT FISH, AND IT'S ALL
YOUR SHOW: MELTING HEART OR IMPERIAL DECREE,
I'LL TAKE EVERYTHING. BUT WHAT
    KIND OF LOVE IS THIS? YOU SLIP AWAY

FOR A SINGLE MOMENT, AND THE WHOLE WORLD
    BURSTS INTO FLAME. YOU RETURN, AND
ALL THAT FIRE SLIPS BACK INTO THE CANDLE
    THAT LIGHTS UP MY CHEST.

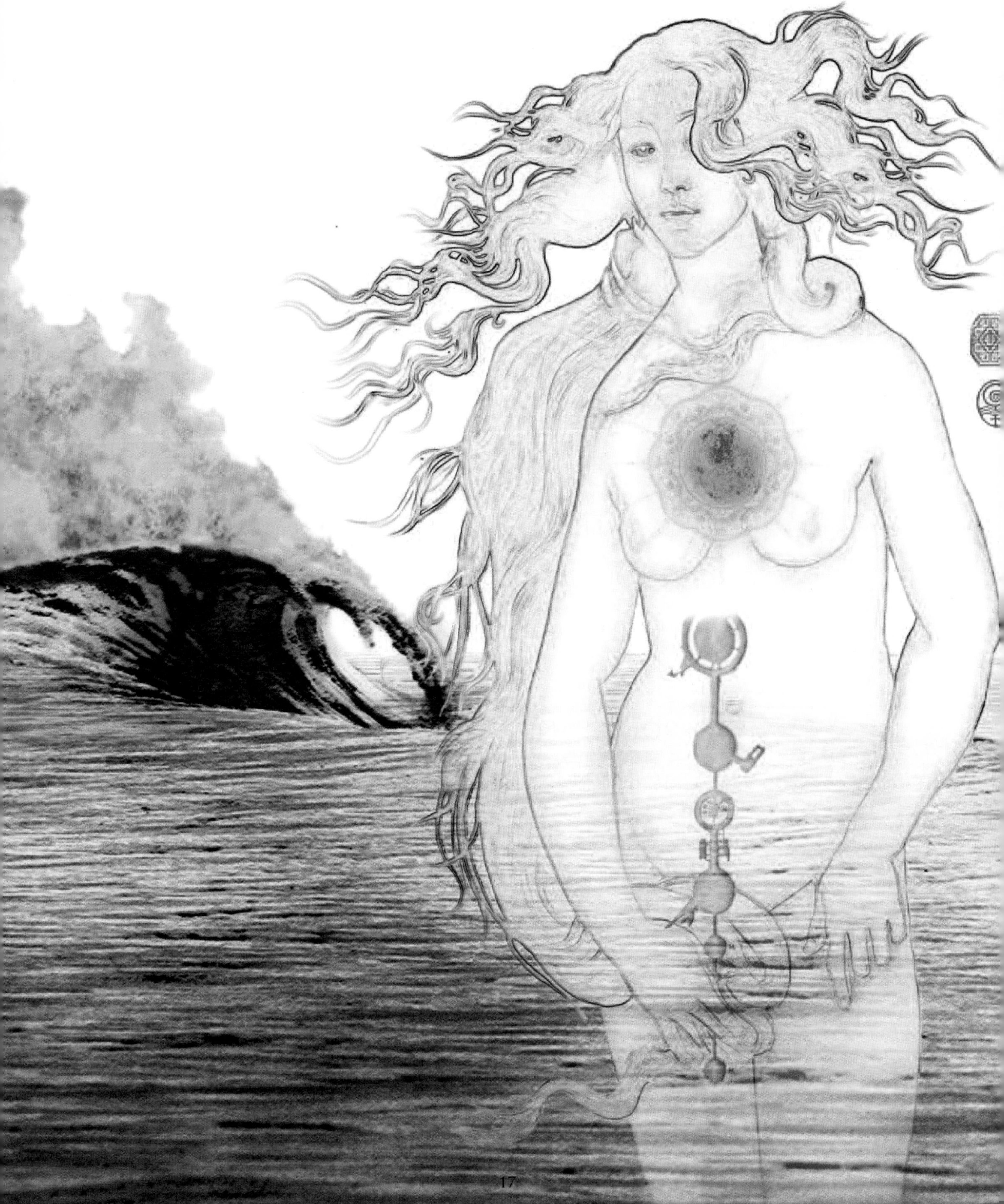

I

F SOMEONE ASKS,
"WHAT KIND OF LOVE IS THIS?" SAY,
LET GO YOUR TILLER AND SEE! THOSE
WHO HAVEN'T ABANDONED FREE WILL
    WILL NEVER KNOW.

DIVE INTO THIS LOVE
AND THE WORLD PARTS BEFORE YOU.
THIS LOVE AND YOU ARE
CIRCLING OUTSIDE OF TIME.
    EVERYTHING ELSE

IS BORROWED AND CRUMBLING.
WHAT IS BORN IN THE SPRING FADES
IN THE FALL. DON'T PINE FOR A
BEAUTIFUL CORPSE. THIS LOVE
    IS THE ROSE

                        THAT

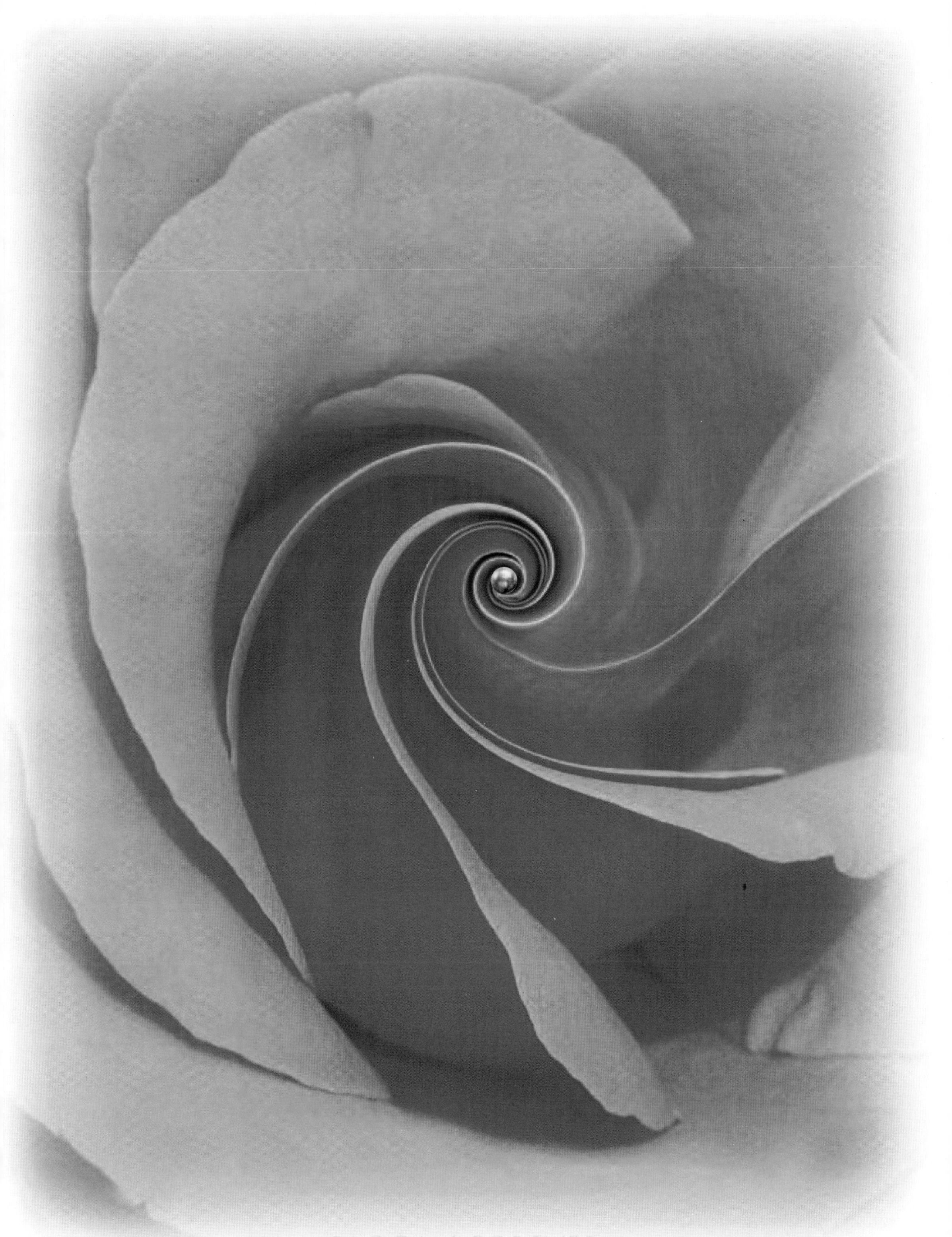

BLOOMS FOREVER.

WHEN THIS KIND OF LOVE FINALLY

MELTS THE HEART

THERE'S
NO SHORTAGE OF
CRITICS AND USELESS ADVICE!

DOGS BARK AT THE MOON & WHAT'S THE HARM?

THIS KIND OF LOVE

MAKES YOU A MOUNTAIN, NOT SOME FLUFF IN THE WIND.

There's blame.
a rule some-
where that **This**
Kind of Love
gathers blame,
another that it turns
a deaf ear to

Cultivate this
garden, and
everywhere
else is going
to seem like
desolation row.

"Welcome!"
JESUS CALLS

"Come wash at the fountains,
Come sit at the table."

• IT'S THE TAVERN OF ANNIHILATION! •

GO AHEAD. YOU'VE SPENT TOO MUCH TIME ALREADY, CALL-
ING FOR JUSTICE IN THE DECEIVER'S COURTHOUSE.
JUST GET TO THAT TABLE. THERE'S A DRINK WAIT-
ING THERE THAT WILL STILL ALL YOUR JUSTICE
CHATTER. AFTER ALL, YOU'RE A LOVER,
AND
THIS KIND OF LOVE
IS
BEST SIPPED IN SILENCE

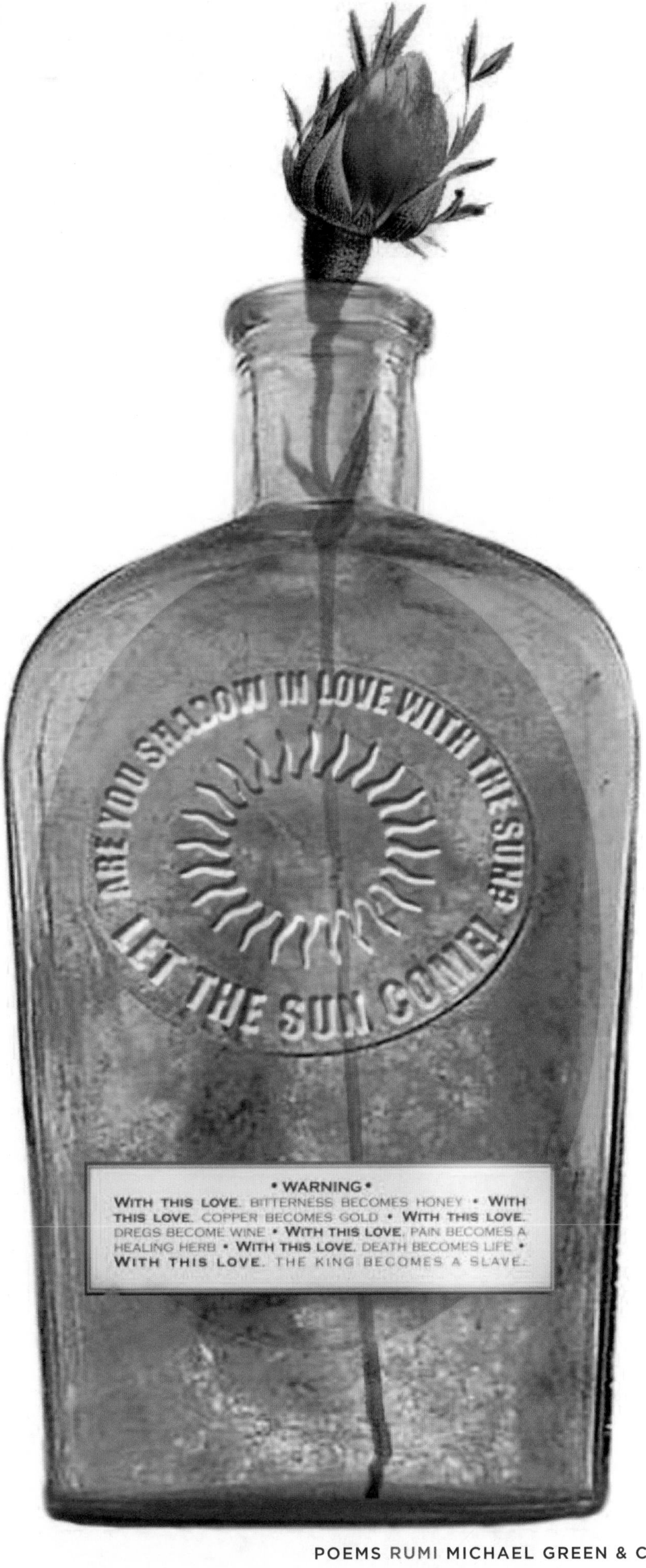
ARE YOU SHADOW IN LOVE WITH THE SUN?
LET THE SUN COME!
• WARNING •
WITH THIS LOVE, BITTERNESS BECOMES HONEY • WITH THIS LOVE, COPPER BECOMES GOLD • WITH THIS LOVE, DREGS BECOME WINE • WITH THIS LOVE, PAIN BECOMES A HEALING HERB • WITH THIS LOVE, DEATH BECOMES LIFE • WITH THIS LOVE, THE KING BECOMES A SLAVE.

fig. 2

THE REED SONG

For Rumi, the beauty of *union* is tied to the longing for it. The plaintive music of the reed flute reflects its yearning to return to its original home in the riverbank. This is the opening poem in his great work the *Mathnavi*, and by happy coincidence, the first we put to song.

Listen to a simple story
Told by a reed taken from its home.
Here's a tale for all you people
Who've wandered lost and all alone.

Since I was cut from out the reed-bed
I have made this crying sound.
Anyone parted from a true love
Knows the sorrow that I have found.

Anyone pulled from Source and center
And taken far from house and home
longs to return to where the roots are,
longs to rest, no more to roam.

Now if you gather I too will be there,
In the laughter and the grief,
A friend to one and to the other
Above, behind, before, beneath.

But few will hear the deepest secrets
hidden in my trembling air.
There are no ears can hear these secrets,
Only a heart that's stripped and bare.

Body flows from out of Spirit.
Spirit flows from out our form.
We can't conceal that mystic mixing,
Nor see the soul when it's never been born.

This flute is filled with God's own fire,
No earthly wind can play its tune.
Just be that empty, and be that hollow,
Reflect the light like the full moon.

Hear the love-fire full of yearning
Tangled with each note in space,
As bewilderment and my heart's sorrow
Turns into wine of amazing grace.

The reed is friend to every pilgrim
Who prays the veil be torn away.
The reed is hurt and salve combining.
Darkest night and brightest day.

Intimacy, and the longing for it,
A single song they have become.
A disastrous, complete surrender,
And finest love, becoming one.

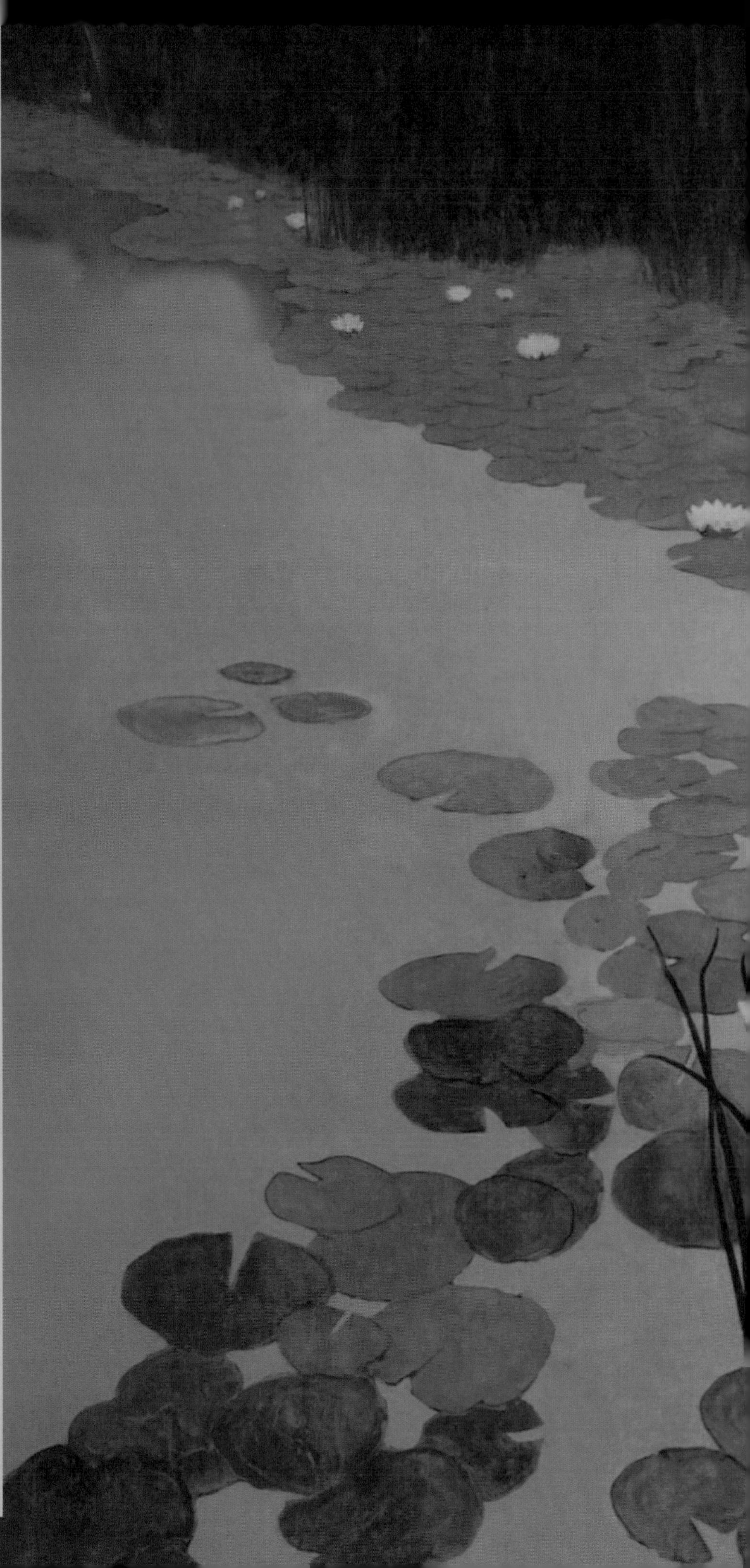

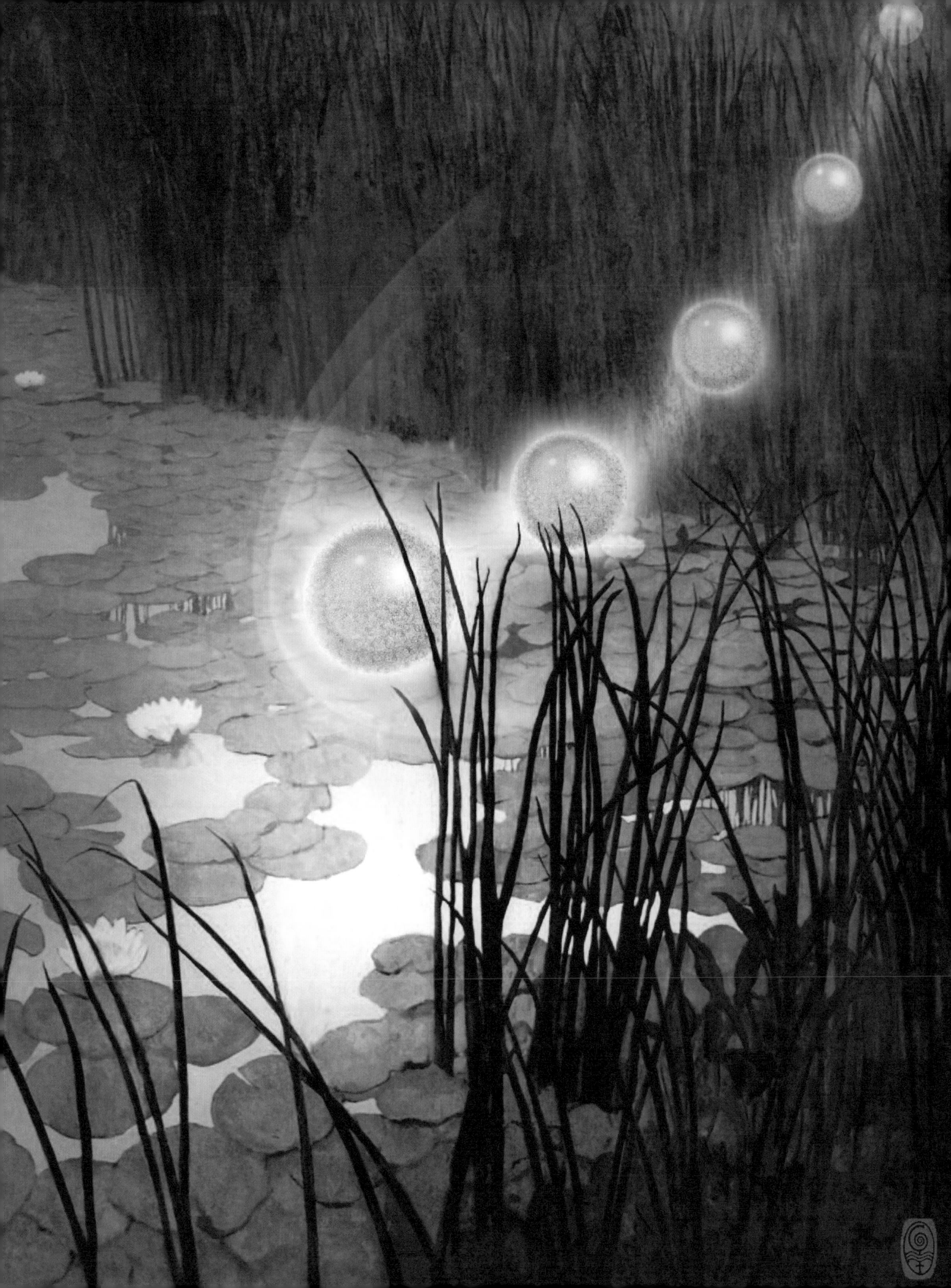

The Divine Comedy

Dante Alighieri

ART / ADAPTATION BY **Seymour Chwast**

ONE OF THE ABSOLUTE A-LIST WORKS OF WORLD literature, and the pride of Italy, *The Divine Comedy* is what happened when a prominent city councilman and lyric poet in medieval Florence got exiled for repeatedly opposing the Pope's wishes. He then had the time to write an epic poem of over 14,000 lines in which he himself would take a tour of Hell, Purgatory, and Heaven (in the cantos *The Inferno*, *Purgatory*, and *Paradise*). In the first two treks, he's guided by the greatest ancient Roman poet, Virgil. The journey through Heaven is led by Beatrice, a woman whom Dante loved intensely from the time they were both children despite the fact that they were never involved and had not even communicated at any length. The work is heavy on Catholic theology and spiritual journeying, although Dante manages to work in potshots at his political enemies, including the Pope.

The Inferno is the best-known, most-referenced part of the work. People can't seem to get enough of the extremely creative, grotesque, and appropriate punishments meted out to sinners in the infamous Nine Circles of Hell. *Purgatory* also contains vivid descriptions of sinners being tortured in imaginative ways, but it hasn't gotten as much

play. (I wonder if that's because most people don't grasp the concept of Purgatory, which contains punishments as bad as those in Hell, the difference being that the sinners eventually are purified and allowed into Heaven.) The final part, *Paradise*, gets the least notice of all, although it contains one gorgeous, mystical scene after another as Dante progresses through the Nine Spheres to ultimate union with God and love.

Strangely, despite its abundance of jaw-dropping visuals, *The Divine Comedy* had never been the subject of a graphic novel until Seymour Chwast took up the challenge in 2010. Seymour is legendary for his design work and his illustrations, both of which use an immediately recognizable, stripped-down, diagram-like approach infused with wit and dry humor. Through the decades, he's done covers for *Time*, ads for IBM and AT&T, and antiwar posters, has been exhibited at the Louvre, and is in the permanent collection of the Museum of Modern Art. Here, he cheekily gives Dante's masterpiece a Roaring Twenties look. The following selection contains excerpts from all three parts of the *Comedy*.

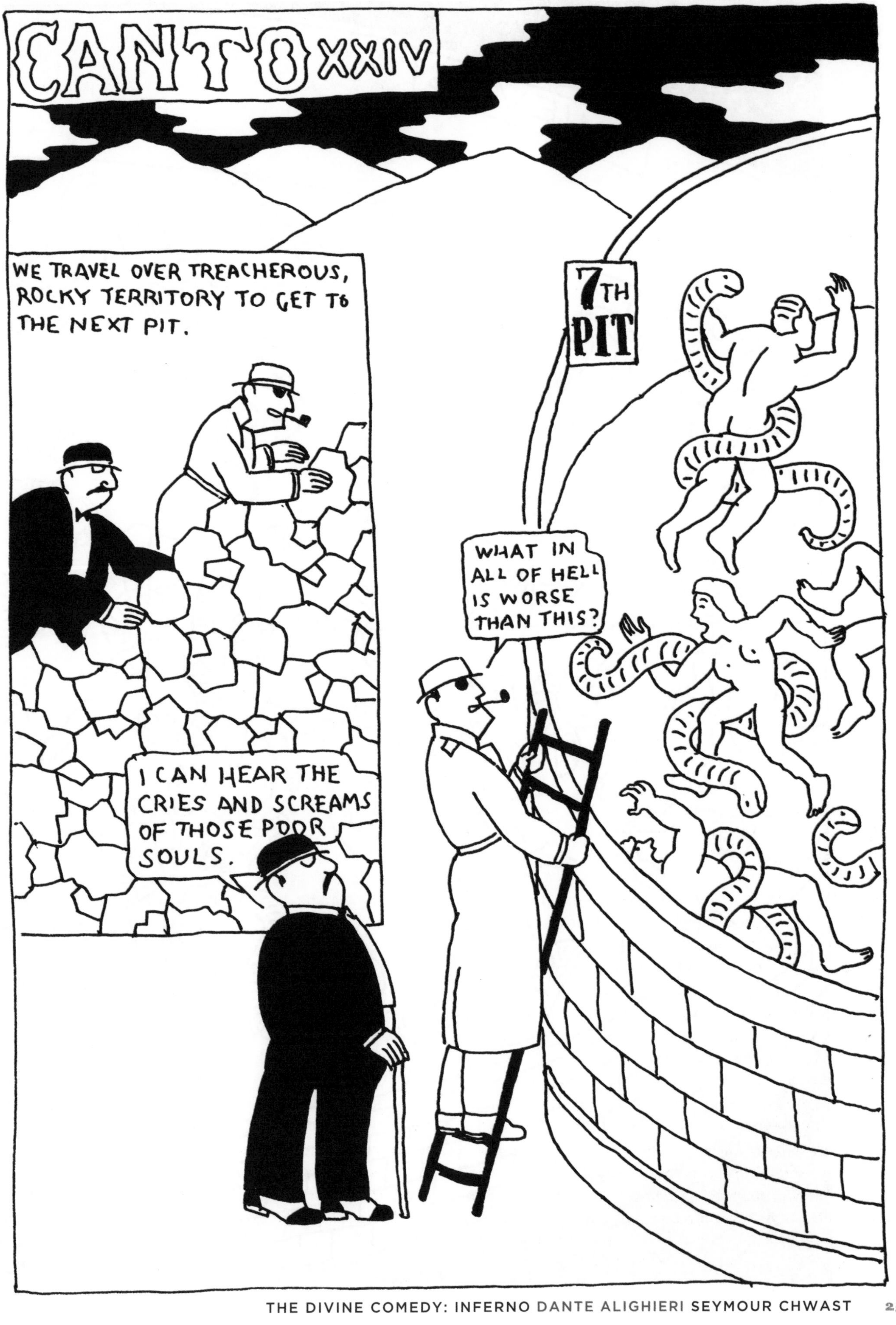
CANTO XXIV
WE TRAVEL OVER TREACHEROUS, ROCKY TERRITORY TO GET TO THE NEXT PIT.
7TH PIT
WHAT IN ALL OF HELL IS WORSE THAN THIS?
I CAN HEAR THE CRIES AND SCREAMS OF THOSE POOR SOULS.

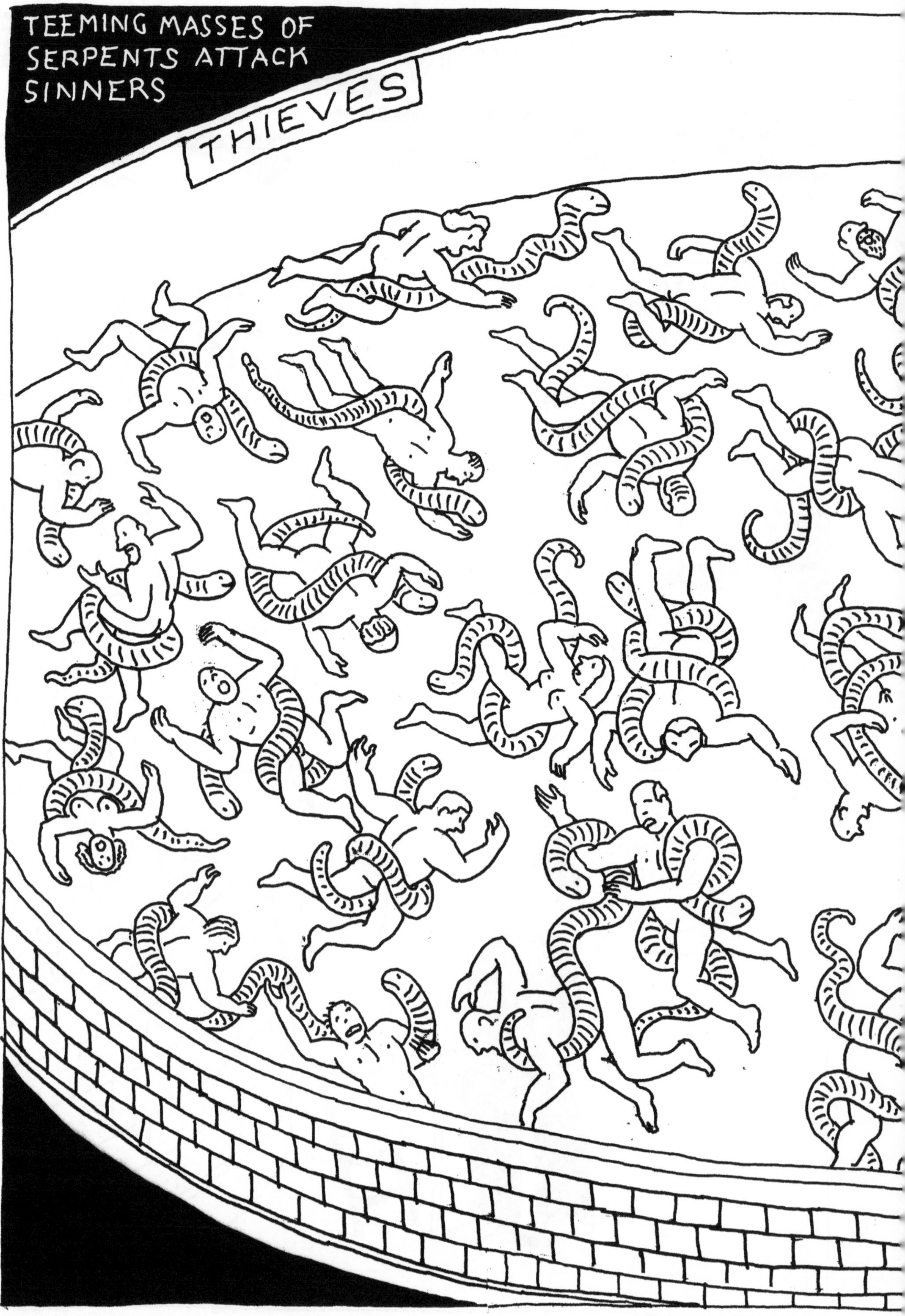
TEEMING MASSES OF SERPENTS ATTACK SINNERS
THIEVES

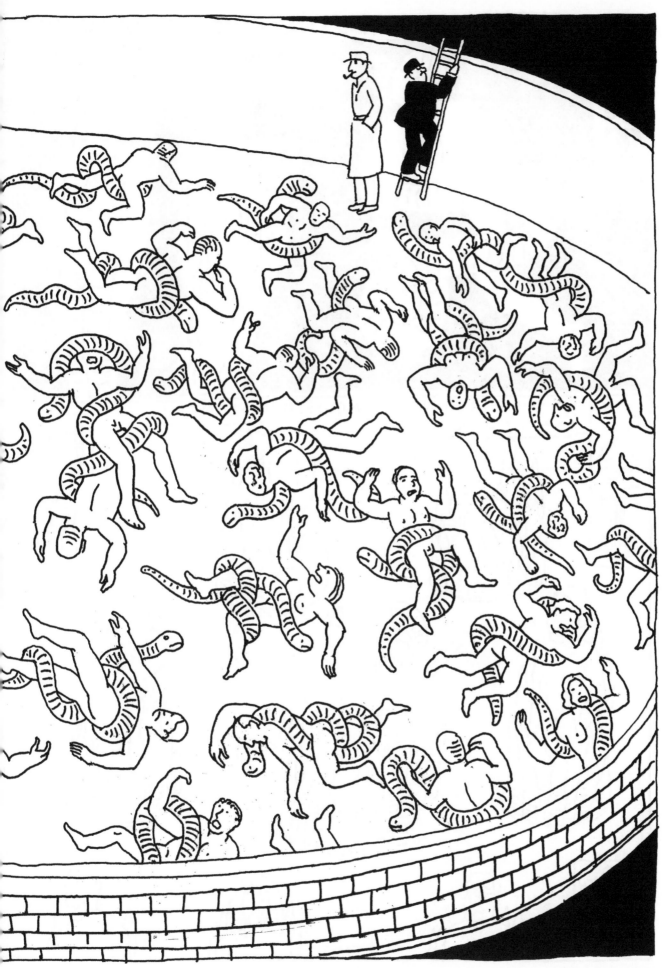

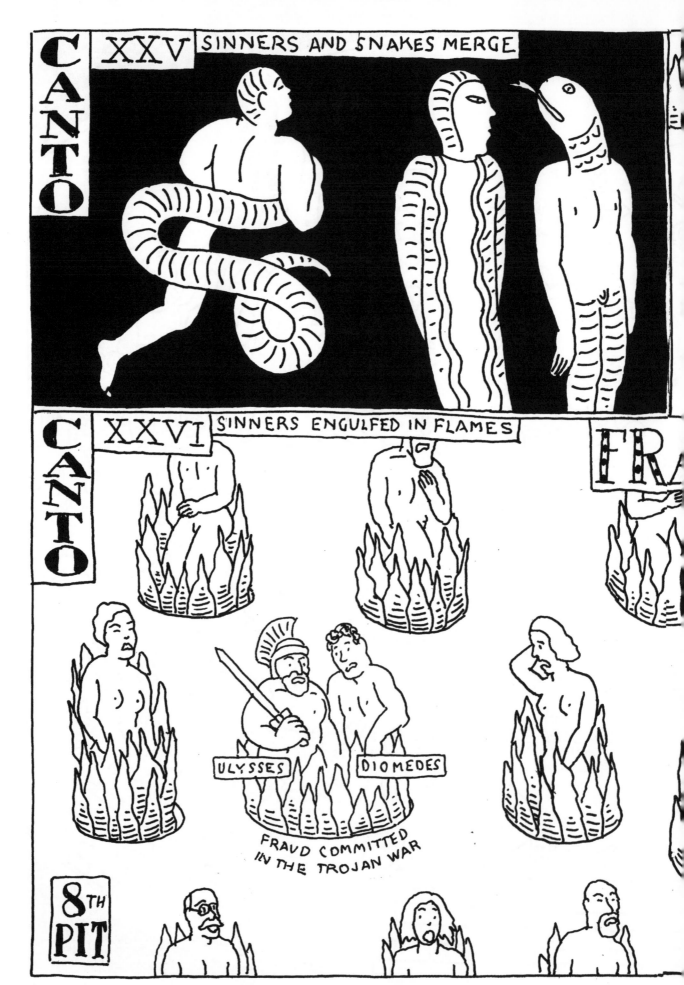

CANTO XXV SINNERS AND SNAKES MERGE

CANTO XXVI SINNERS ENGULFED IN FLAMES

FRA

ULYSSES DIOMEDES

FRAUD COMMITTED IN THE TROJAN WAR

8TH PIT

THE DIVINE COMEDY: INFERNO DANTE ALIGHIERI SEYMOUR CHWAST

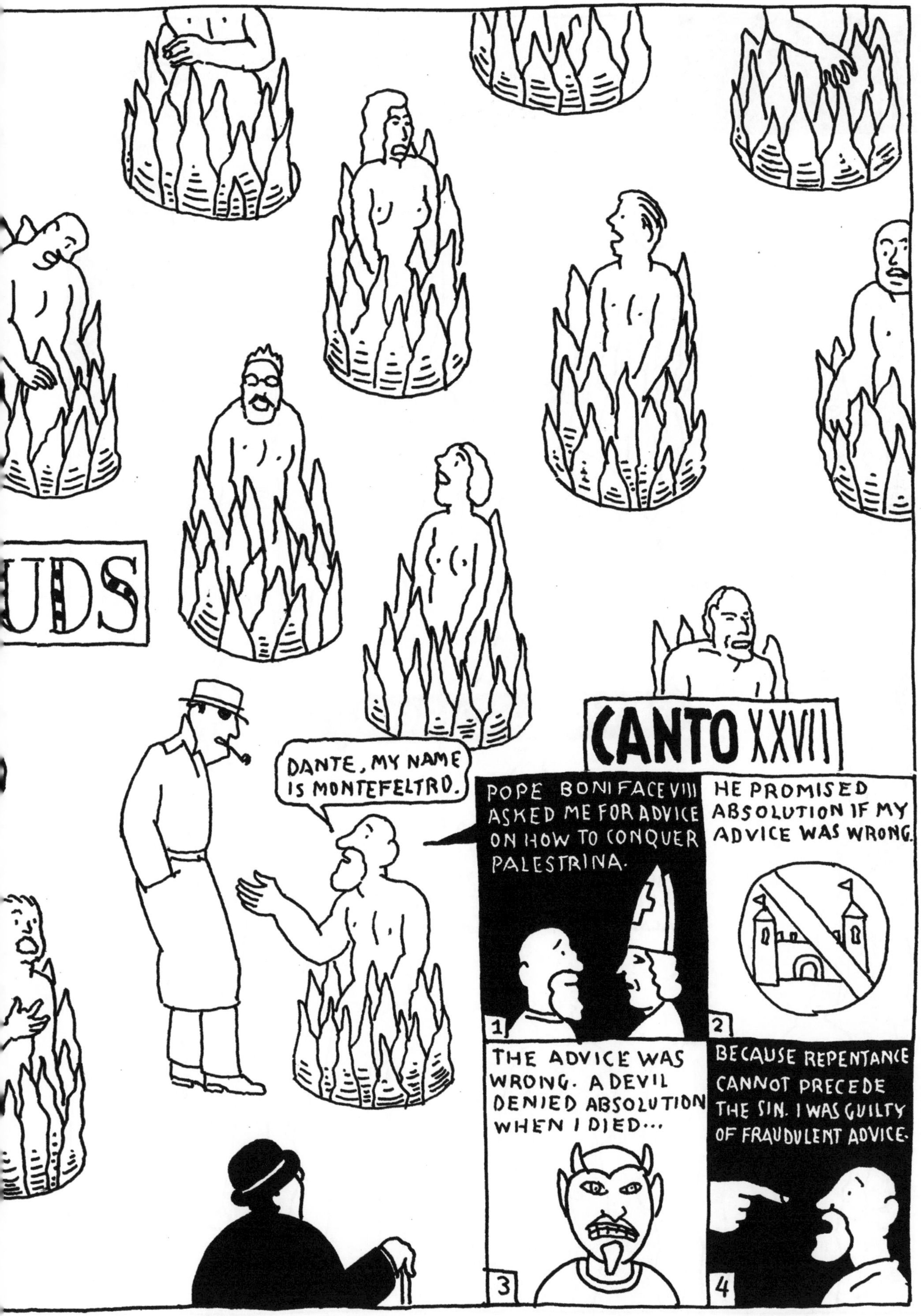
UDS
CANTO XXVII
DANTE, MY NAME IS MONTEFELTRO.
POPE BONIFACE VIII ASKED ME FOR ADVICE ON HOW TO CONQUER PALESTRINA.
HE PROMISED ABSOLUTION IF MY ADVICE WAS WRONG.
THE ADVICE WAS WRONG. A DEVIL DENIED ABSOLUTION WHEN I DIED...
BECAUSE REPENTANCE CANNOT PRECEDE THE SIN. I WAS GUILTY OF FRAUDULENT ADVICE.
1
2
3
4

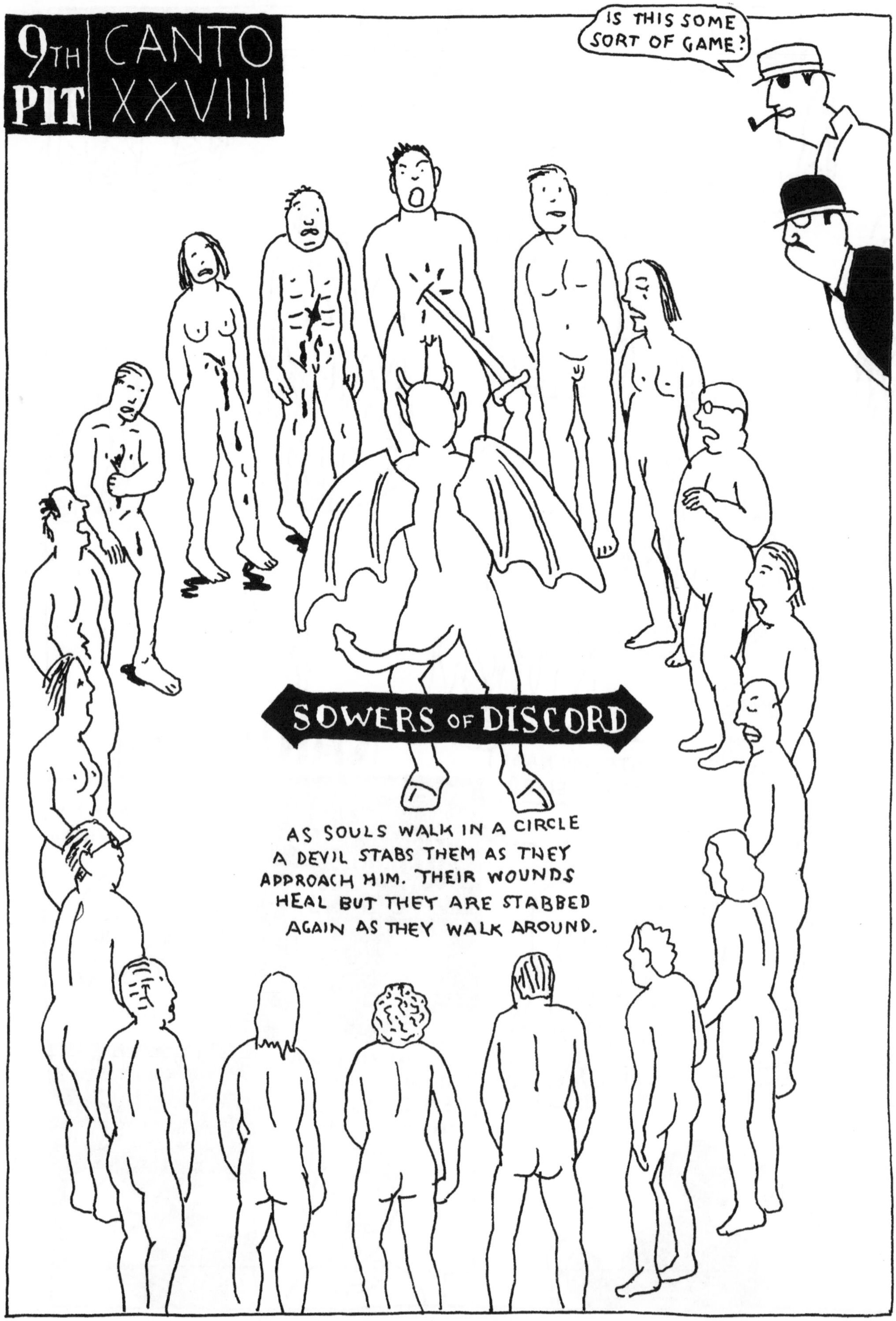
9TH PIT
CANTO XXVIII
IS THIS SOME SORT OF GAME?
SOWERS OF DISCORD
AS SOULS WALK IN A CIRCLE A DEVIL STABS THEM AS THEY APPROACH HIM. THEIR WOUNDS HEAL BUT THEY ARE STABBED AGAIN AS THEY WALK AROUND.

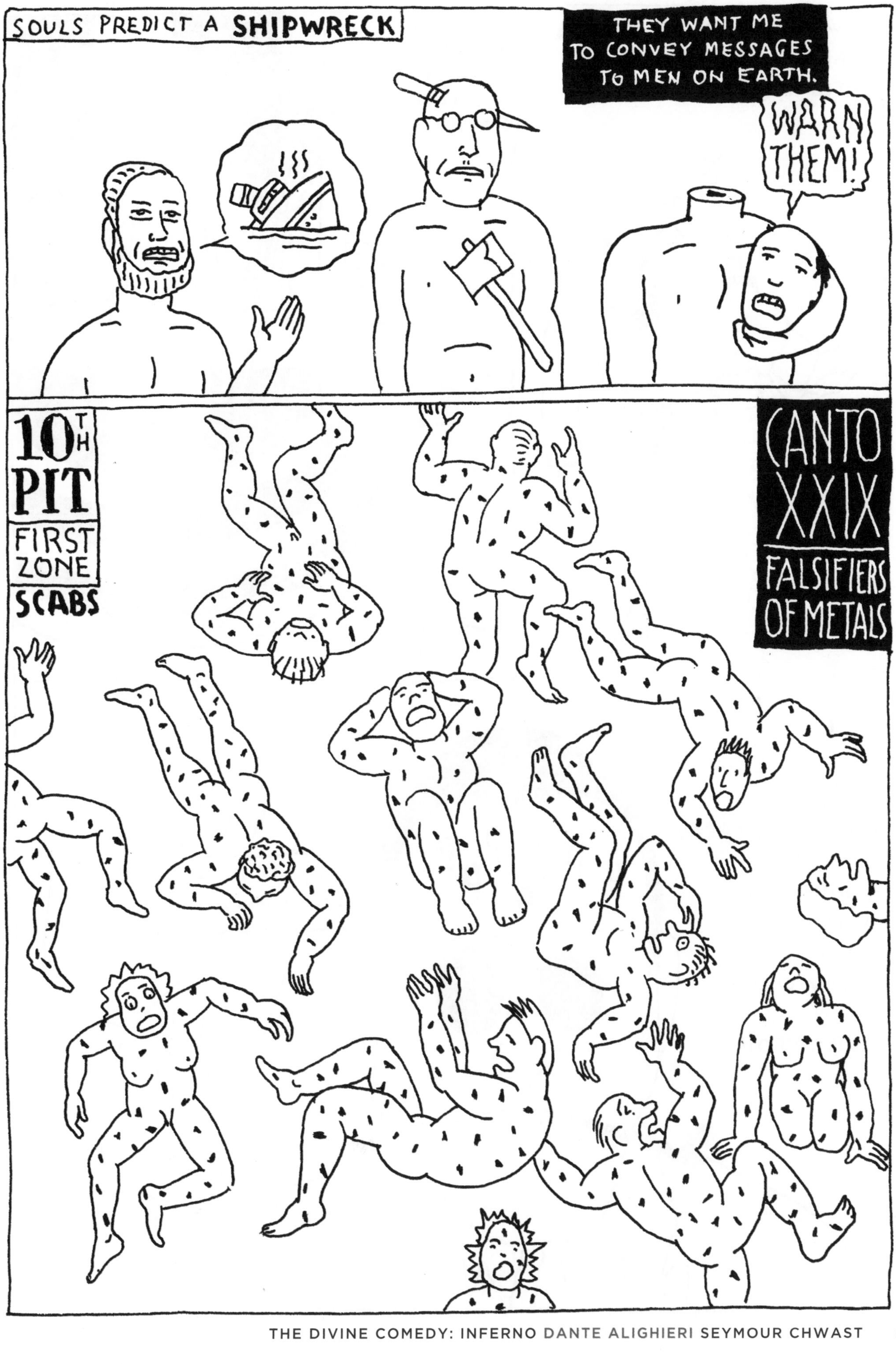
SOULS PREDICT A SHIPWRECK
THEY WANT ME TO CONVEY MESSAGES TO MEN ON EARTH.
WARN THEM!
10TH PIT
FIRST ZONE
SCABS
CANTO XXIX
FALSIFIERS OF METALS

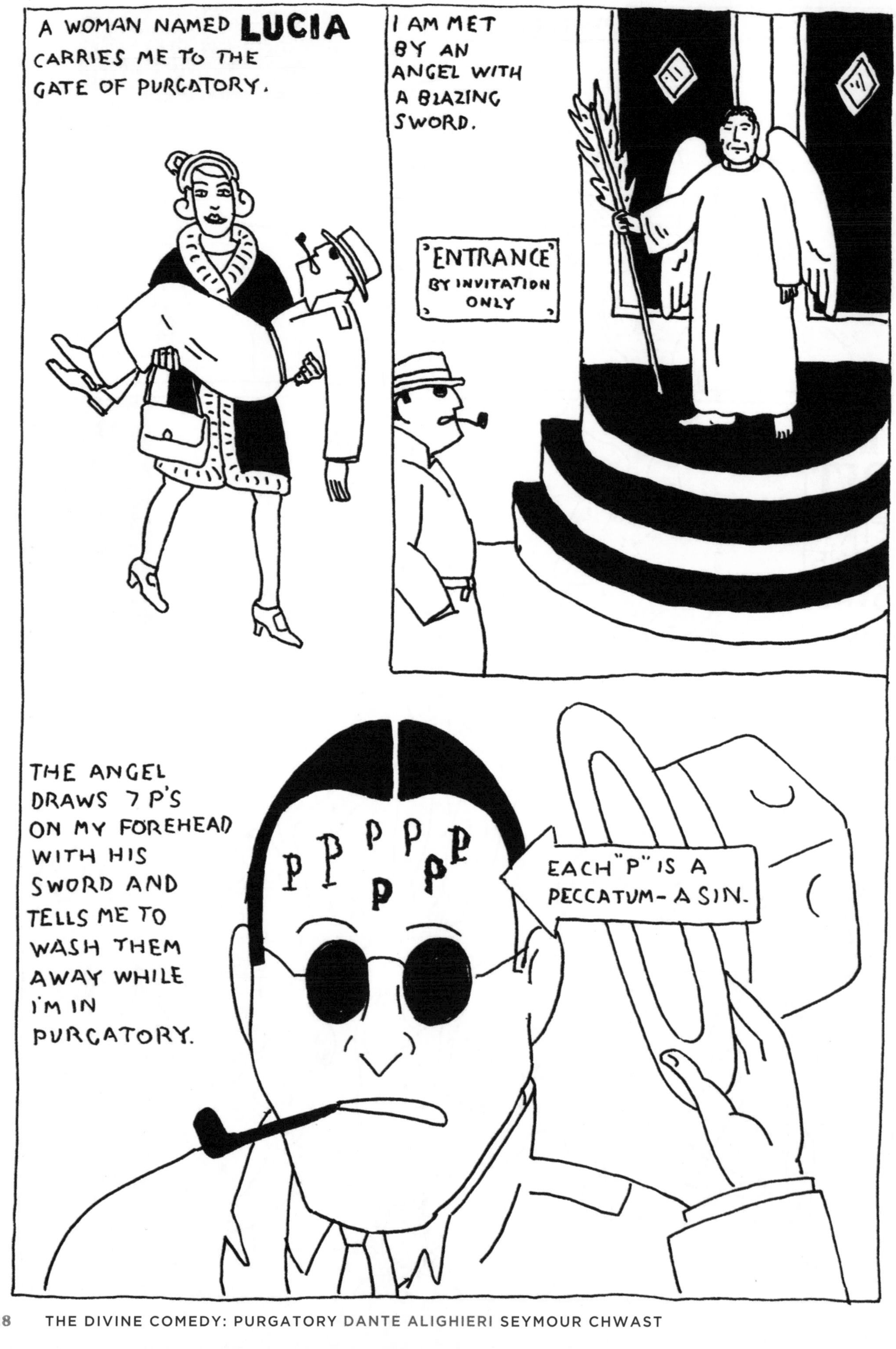
A WOMAN NAMED LUCIA CARRIES ME TO THE GATE OF PURGATORY.
I AM MET BY AN ANGEL WITH A BLAZING SWORD.
ENTRANCE BY INVITATION ONLY
THE ANGEL DRAWS 7 P'S ON MY FOREHEAD WITH HIS SWORD AND TELLS ME TO WASH THEM AWAY WHILE I'M IN PURGATORY.
P P P P P P P
EACH "P" IS A PECCATUM- A SIN.

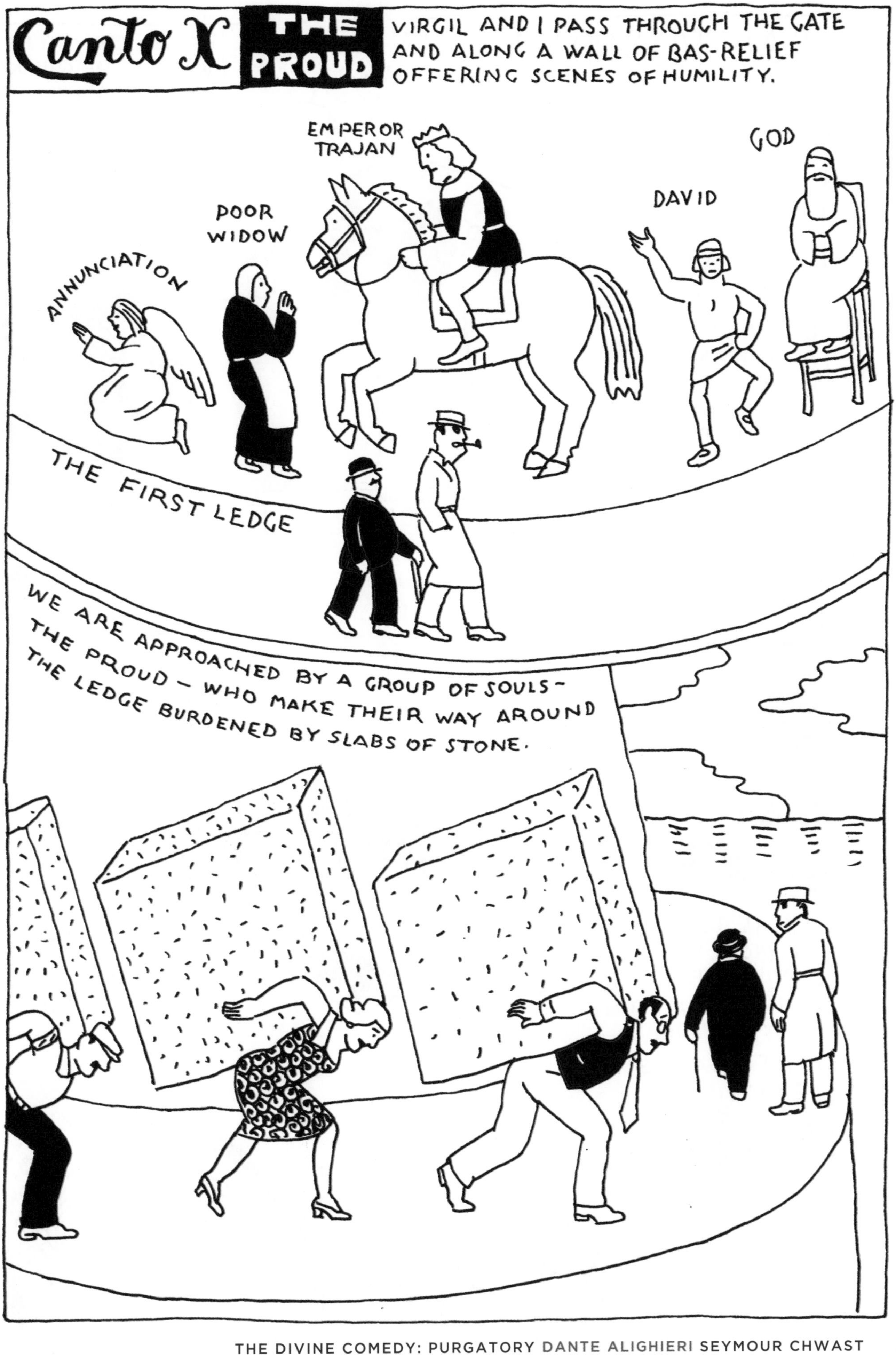
Canto X
THE PROUD
VIRGIL AND I PASS THROUGH THE GATE AND ALONG A WALL OF BAS-RELIEF OFFERING SCENES OF HUMILITY.
EMPEROR TRAJAN
GOD
POOR WIDOW
DAVID
ANNUNCIATION
THE FIRST LEDGE
WE ARE APPROACHED BY A GROUP OF SOULS - THE PROUD - WHO MAKE THEIR WAY AROUND THE LEDGE BURDENED BY SLABS OF STONE.

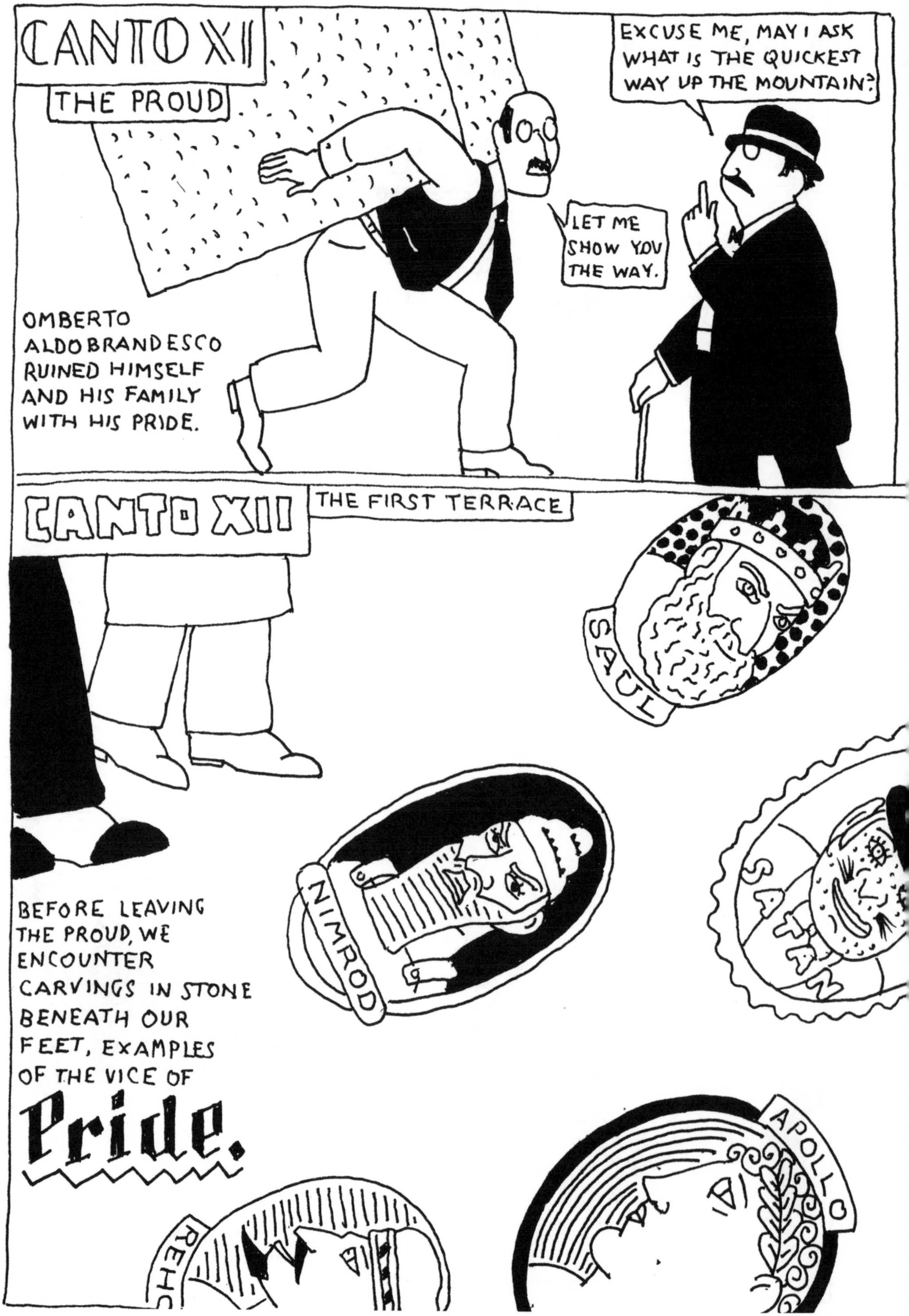
CANTO XI
THE PROUD
EXCUSE ME, MAY I ASK WHAT IS THE QUICKEST WAY UP THE MOUNTAIN?
LET ME SHOW YOU THE WAY.
OMBERTO ALDOBRANDESCO RUINED HIMSELF AND HIS FAMILY WITH HIS PRIDE.
CANTO XII
THE FIRST TERRACE
SAUL
NIMROD
SATAN
BEFORE LEAVING THE PROUD, WE ENCOUNTER CARVINGS IN STONE BENEATH OUR FEET, EXAMPLES OF THE VICE OF
Pride.
APOLLO

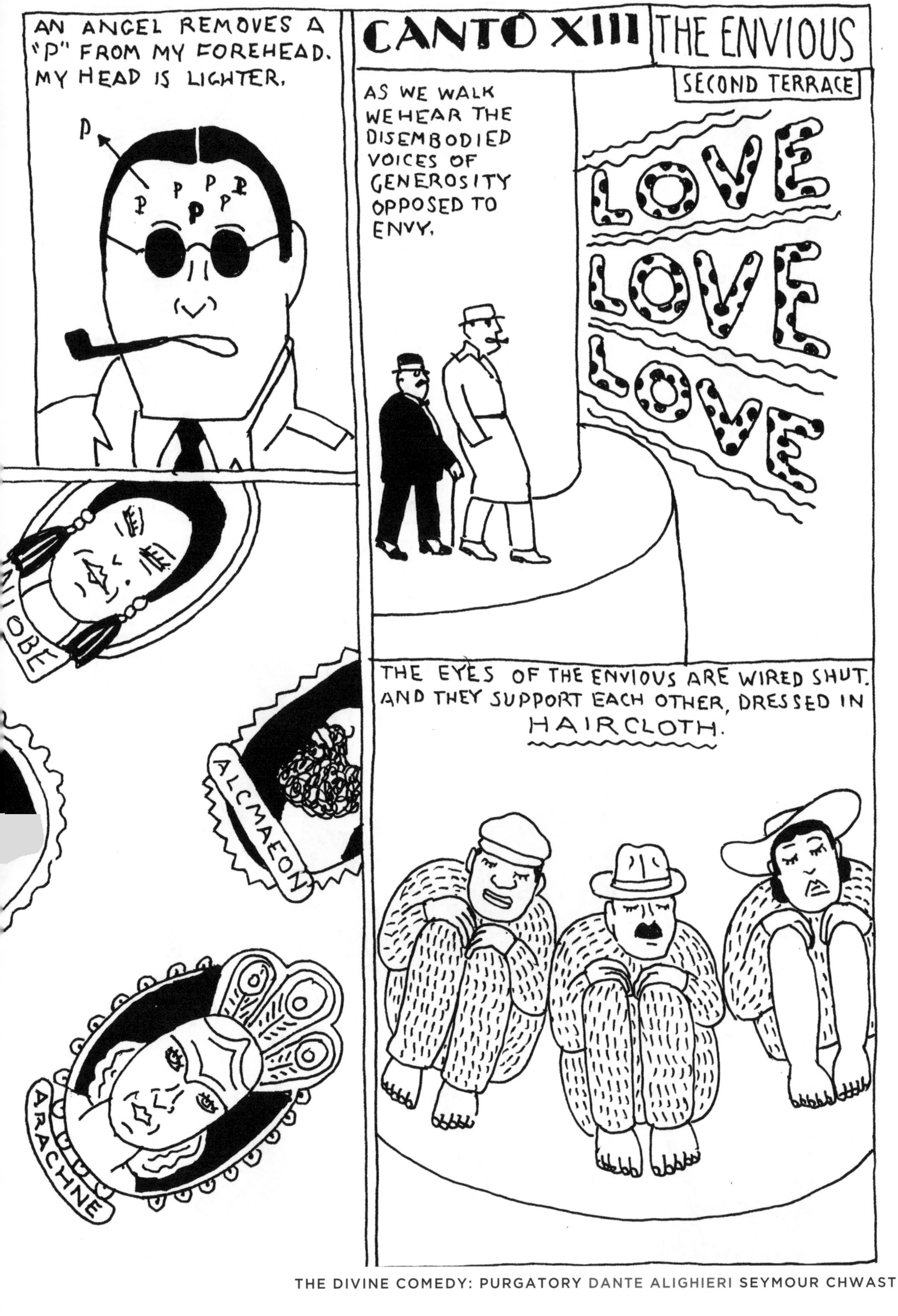
AN ANGEL REMOVES A "P" FROM MY FOREHEAD. MY HEAD IS LIGHTER.
CANTO XIII
THE ENVIOUS
SECOND TERRACE
AS WE WALK WE HEAR THE DISEMBODIED VOICES OF GENEROSITY OPPOSED TO ENVY.
LOVE
LOVE
LOVE
NIOBE
ALCMAEON
ARACHNE
THE EYES OF THE ENVIOUS ARE WIRED SHUT. AND THEY SUPPORT EACH OTHER, DRESSED IN HAIRCLOTH.

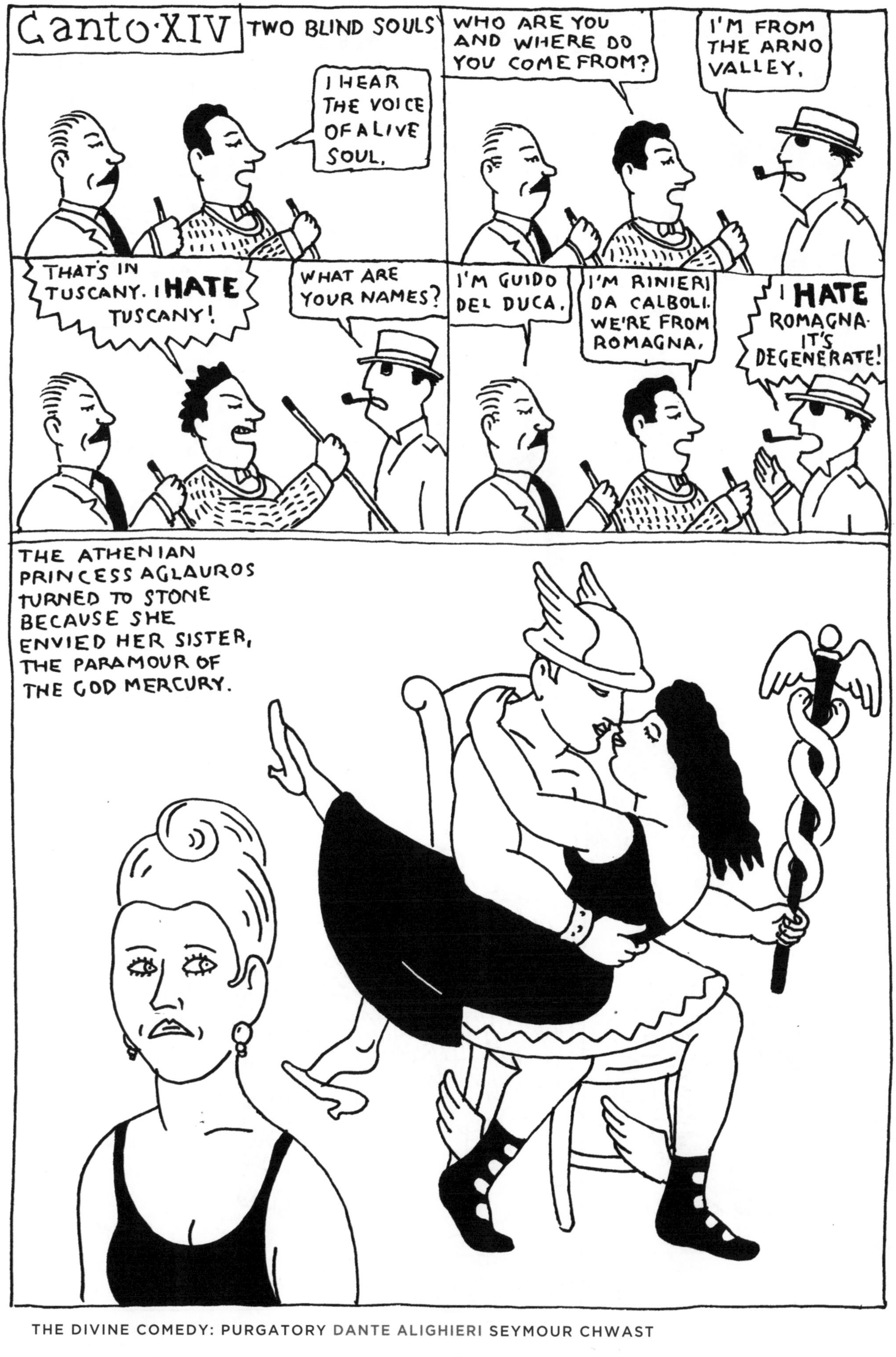
Canto·XIV
TWO BLIND SOULS
I HEAR THE VOICE OF A LIVE SOUL.
WHO ARE YOU AND WHERE DO YOU COME FROM?
I'M FROM THE ARNO VALLEY.
THAT'S IN TUSCANY. I HATE TUSCANY!
WHAT ARE YOUR NAMES?
I'M GUIDO DEL DUCA.
I'M RINIERI DA CALBOLI. WE'RE FROM ROMAGNA.
I HATE ROMAGNA. IT'S DEGENERATE!
THE ATHENIAN PRINCESS AGLAUROS TURNED TO STONE BECAUSE SHE ENVIED HER SISTER, THE PARAMOUR OF THE GOD MERCURY.

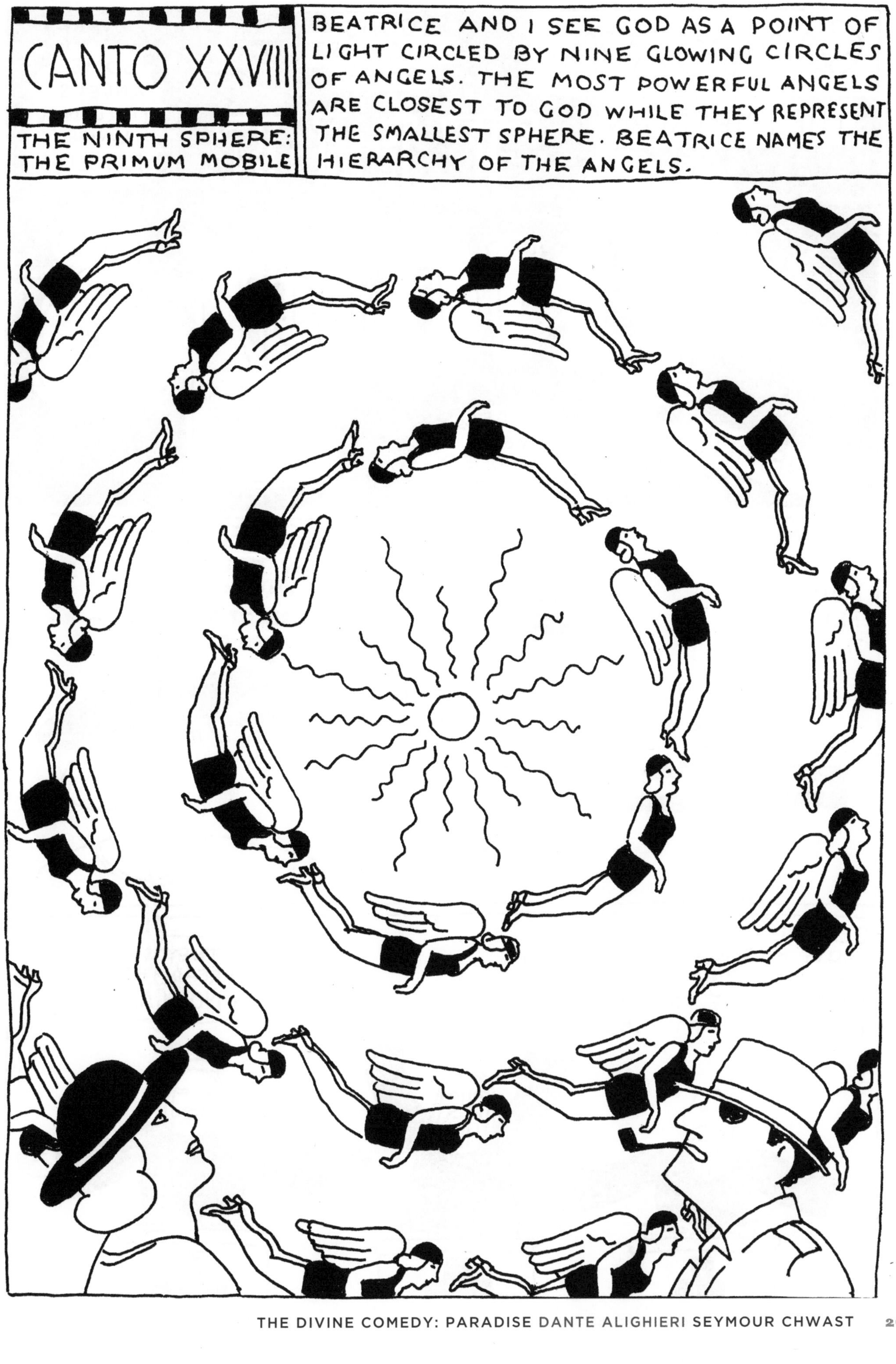
CANTO XXVIII
THE NINTH SPHERE: THE PRIMUM MOBILE
BEATRICE AND I SEE GOD AS A POINT OF LIGHT CIRCLED BY NINE GLOWING CIRCLES OF ANGELS. THE MOST POWERFUL ANGELS ARE CLOSEST TO GOD WHILE THEY REPRESENT THE SMALLEST SPHERE. BEATRICE NAMES THE HIERARCHY OF THE ANGELS.

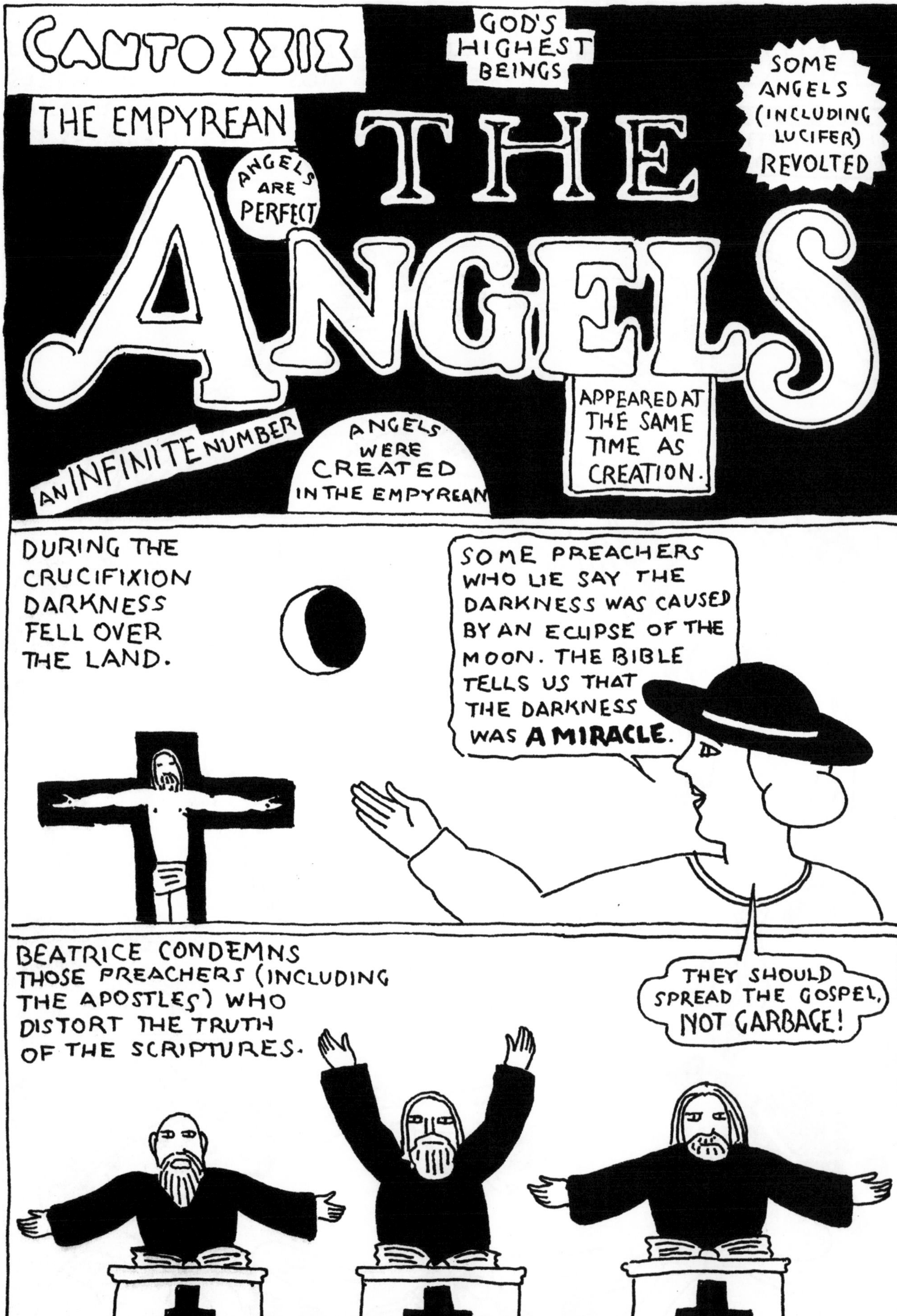
CANTO XXIX
THE EMPYREAN
GOD'S HIGHEST BEINGS
THE ANGELS
ANGELS ARE PERFECT
SOME ANGELS (INCLUDING LUCIFER) REVOLTED
AN INFINITE NUMBER
ANGELS WERE CREATED IN THE EMPYREAN
APPEARED AT THE SAME TIME AS CREATION.
DURING THE CRUCIFIXION DARKNESS FELL OVER THE LAND.
SOME PREACHERS WHO LIE SAY THE DARKNESS WAS CAUSED BY AN ECLIPSE OF THE MOON. THE BIBLE TELLS US THAT THE DARKNESS WAS A MIRACLE.
BEATRICE CONDEMNS THOSE PREACHERS (INCLUDING THE APOSTLES) WHO DISTORT THE TRUTH OF THE SCRIPTURES.
THEY SHOULD SPREAD THE GOSPEL, NOT GARBAGE!

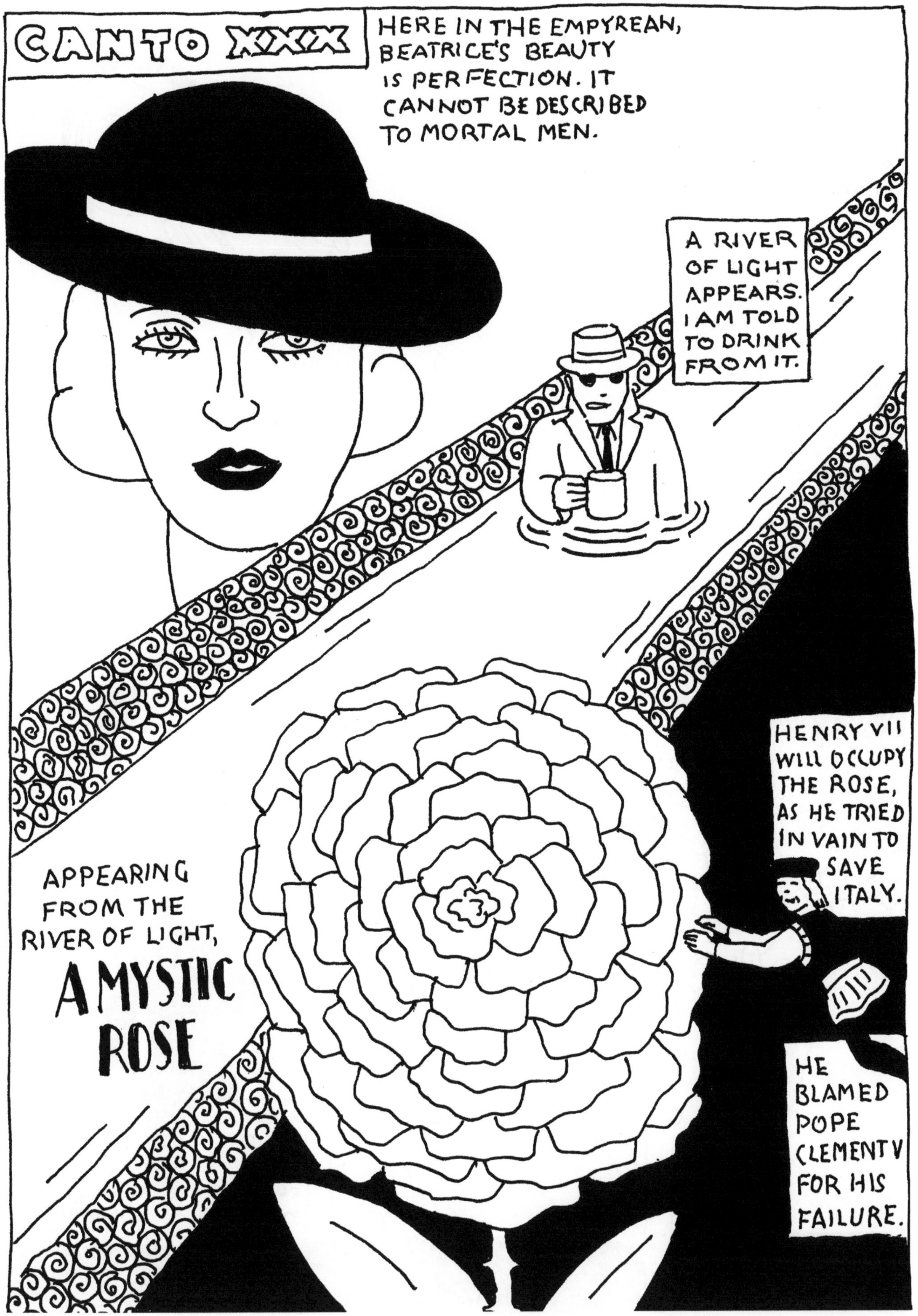
CANTO XXX
HERE IN THE EMPYREAN, BEATRICE'S BEAUTY IS PERFECTION. IT CANNOT BE DESCRIBED TO MORTAL MEN.
A RIVER OF LIGHT APPEARS. I AM TOLD TO DRINK FROM IT.
APPEARING FROM THE RIVER OF LIGHT,
A MYSTIC ROSE
HENRY VII WILL OCCUPY THE ROSE, AS HE TRIED IN VAIN TO SAVE ITALY.
HE BLAMED POPE CLEMENT V FOR HIS FAILURE.

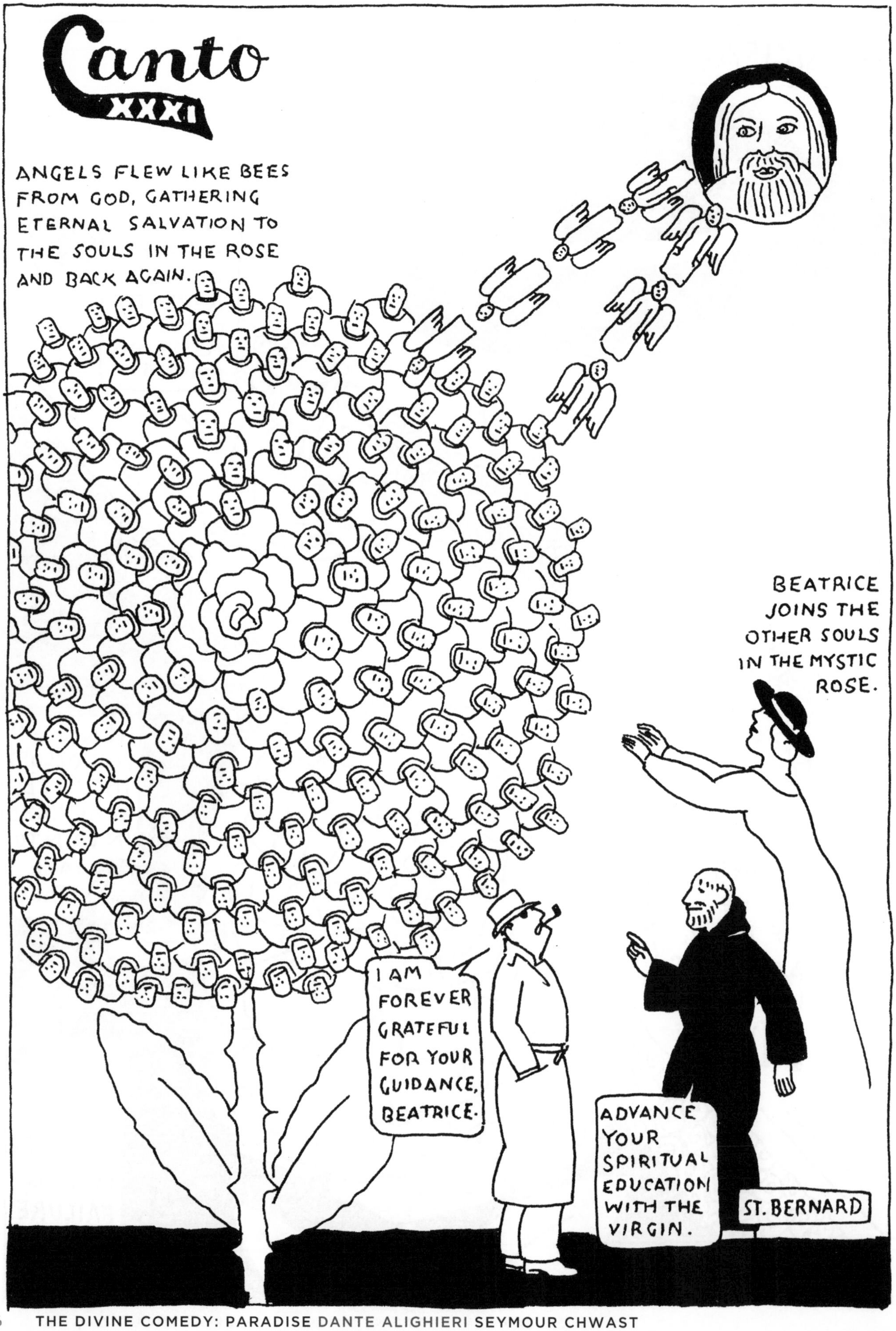

Canto XXXI
ANGELS FLEW LIKE BEES FROM GOD, GATHERING ETERNAL SALVATION TO THE SOULS IN THE ROSE AND BACK AGAIN.
BEATRICE JOINS THE OTHER SOULS IN THE MYSTIC ROSE.
I AM FOREVER GRATEFUL FOR YOUR GUIDANCE, BEATRICE.
ADVANCE YOUR SPIRITUAL EDUCATION WITH THE VIRGIN.
ST. BERNARD

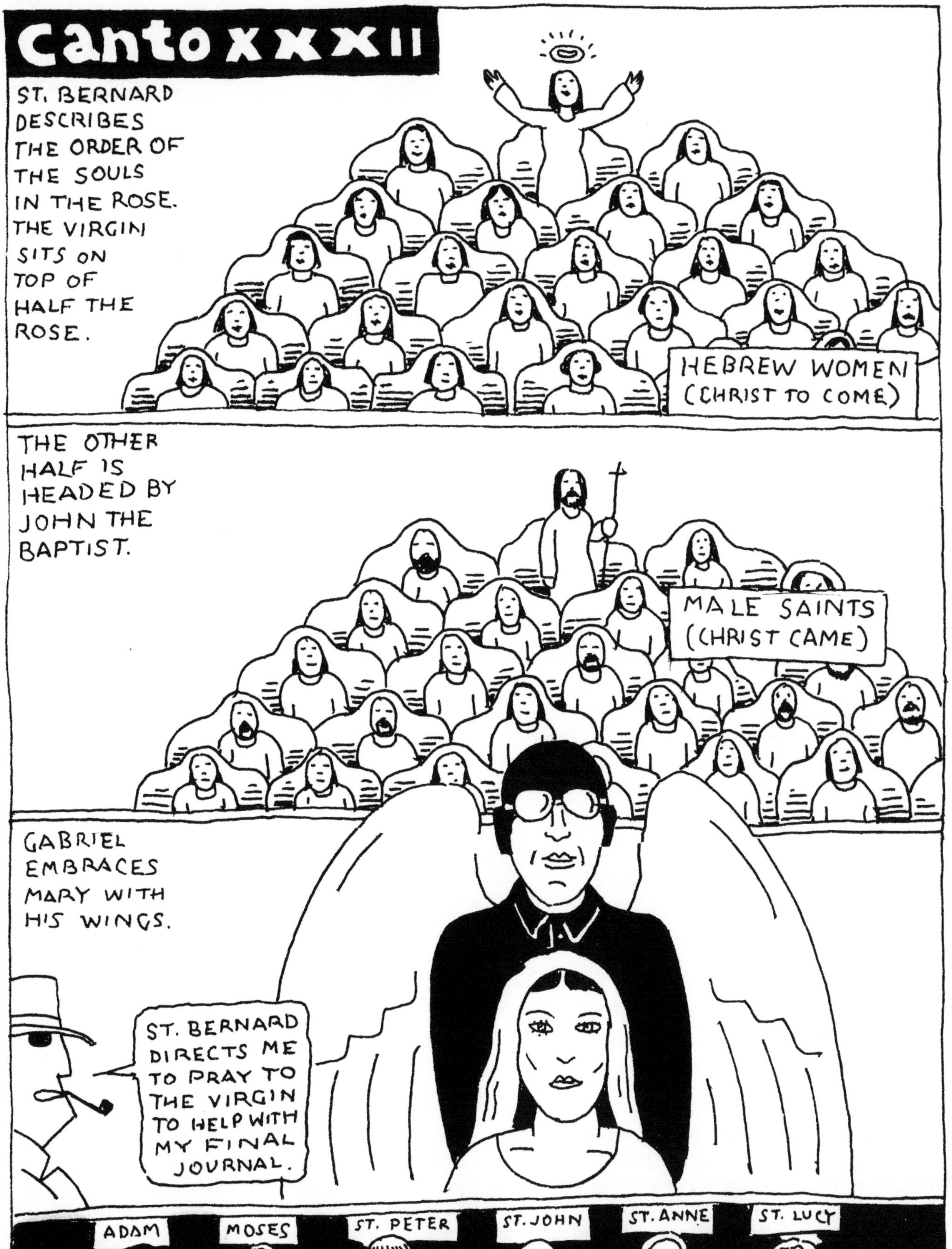
Canto XXXII
ST. BERNARD DESCRIBES THE ORDER OF THE SOULS IN THE ROSE. THE VIRGIN SITS ON TOP OF HALF THE ROSE.
HEBREW WOMEN (CHRIST TO COME)
THE OTHER HALF IS HEADED BY JOHN THE BAPTIST.
MALE SAINTS (CHRIST CAME)
GABRIEL EMBRACES MARY WITH HIS WINGS.
ST. BERNARD DIRECTS ME TO PRAY TO THE VIRGIN TO HELP WITH MY FINAL JOURNAL.
ADAM
MOSES
ST. PETER
ST. JOHN
ST. ANNE
ST. LUCY
ST. BERNARD POINTS TO THE OTHER IMPORTANT SOULS IN THE ROSE.

The Inferno

Dante Alighieri

ART / ADAPTATION BY **Hunt Emerson**

AS NOTED IN THE INTRODUCTION TO THE previous piece, *The Inferno* is far and away the most well-known, influential part of *The Divine Comedy*. No one can resist the inventiveness and appropriateness of the punishments suffered by sinners. Hypocrites wear outwardly beautiful cloaks that are lined with lead. Fortune-tellers have their heads on backward. Gluttons lie in putrid mud like pigs. Those who were violent against others boil in a river of blood. Flatterers, meanwhile, spend eternity submerged in shit.

Such material could make for an extremely gruesome and morbid visual adaptation, but Hunt Emerson manages to find the humor in Hell. Often called "the dean of British comics artists," Hunt adds quirkiness and levity to everything he's touched over the last three decades, including other works of classic lit (look for his takes on Coleridge and Keats in Volume Two of *The Graphic Canon*). His adaptation of the complete *Inferno* will be published at some point in the future. For now, here is Hunt's tour of the Eighth Circle of Hell, home to those who committed various kinds of fraud.

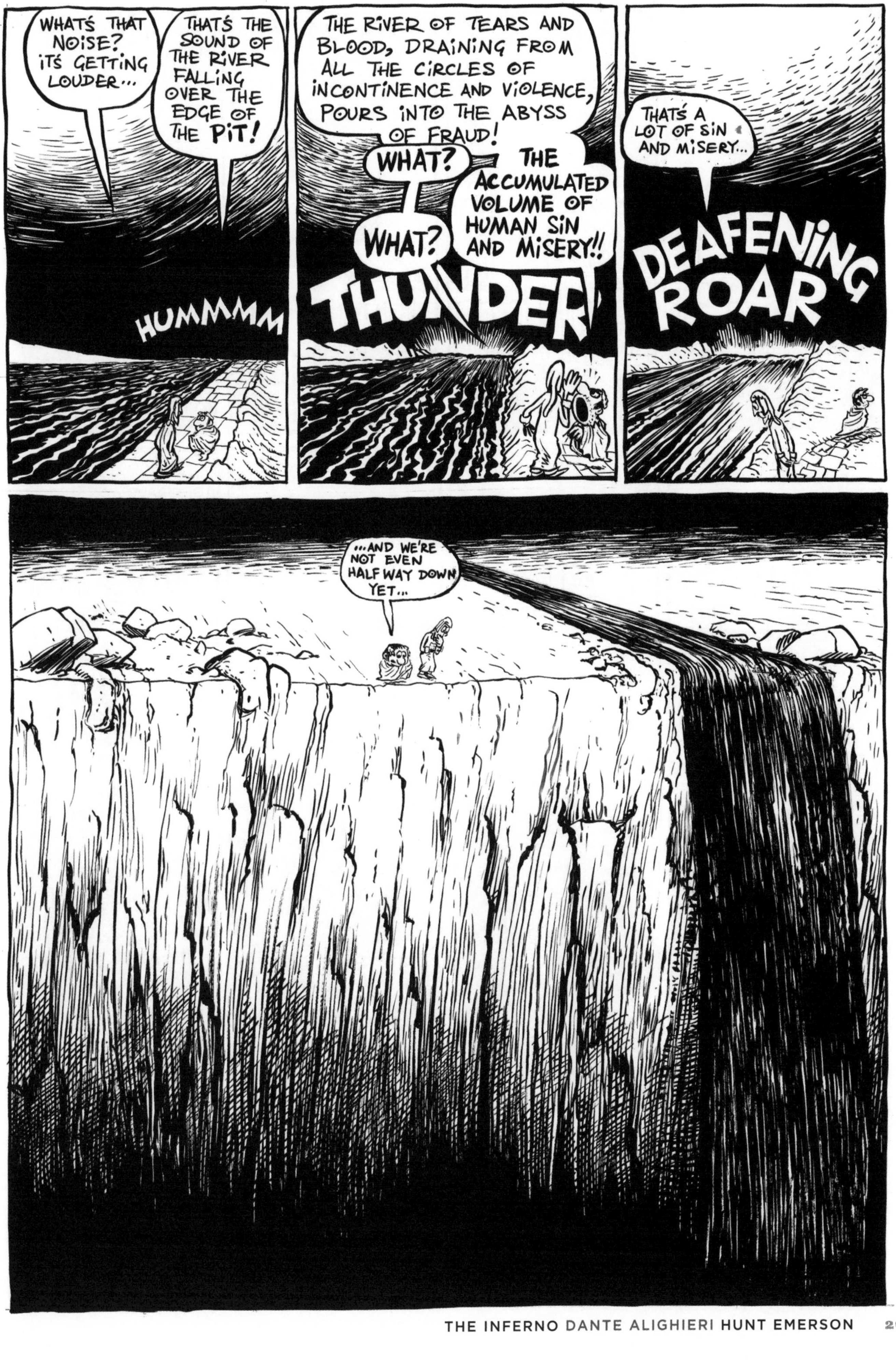
WHAT'S THAT NOISE? IT'S GETTING LOUDER...
THAT'S THE SOUND OF THE RIVER FALLING OVER THE EDGE OF THE PIT!
HUMMMMM
THE RIVER OF TEARS AND BLOOD, DRAINING FROM ALL THE CIRCLES OF INCONTINENCE AND VIOLENCE, POURS INTO THE ABYSS OF FRAUD!
WHAT?
THE ACCUMULATED VOLUME OF HUMAN SIN AND MISERY!!
WHAT?
THUNDER
THAT'S A LOT OF SIN AND MISERY...
DEAFENING ROAR
...AND WE'RE NOT EVEN HALF WAY DOWN YET...

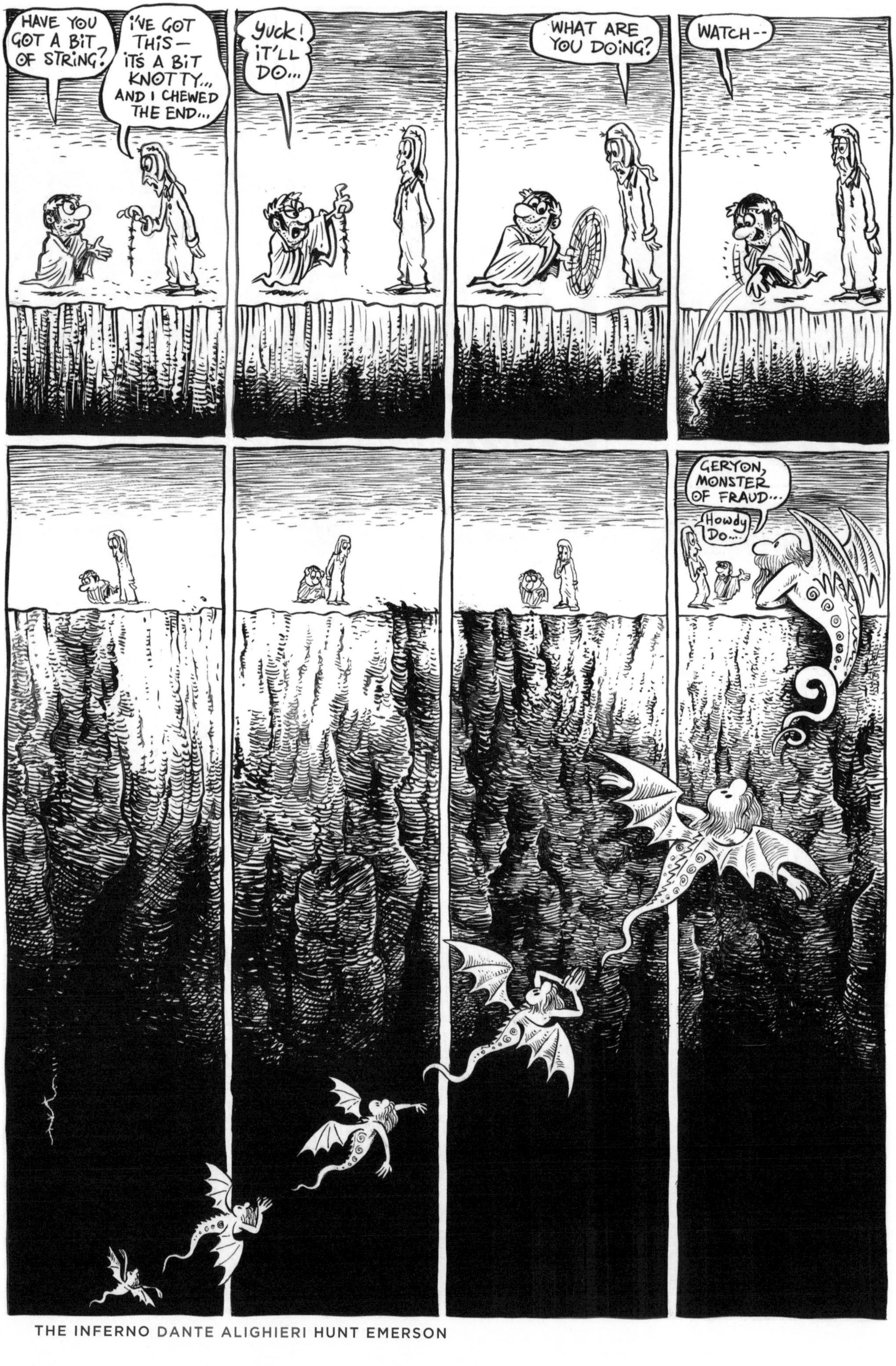
HAVE YOU GOT A BIT OF STRING?
I'VE GOT THIS— ITS A BIT KNOTTY... AND I CHEWED THE END...
YUCK! IT'LL DO...
WHAT ARE YOU DOING?
WATCH--
GERYON, MONSTER OF FRAUD...
Howdy Do...

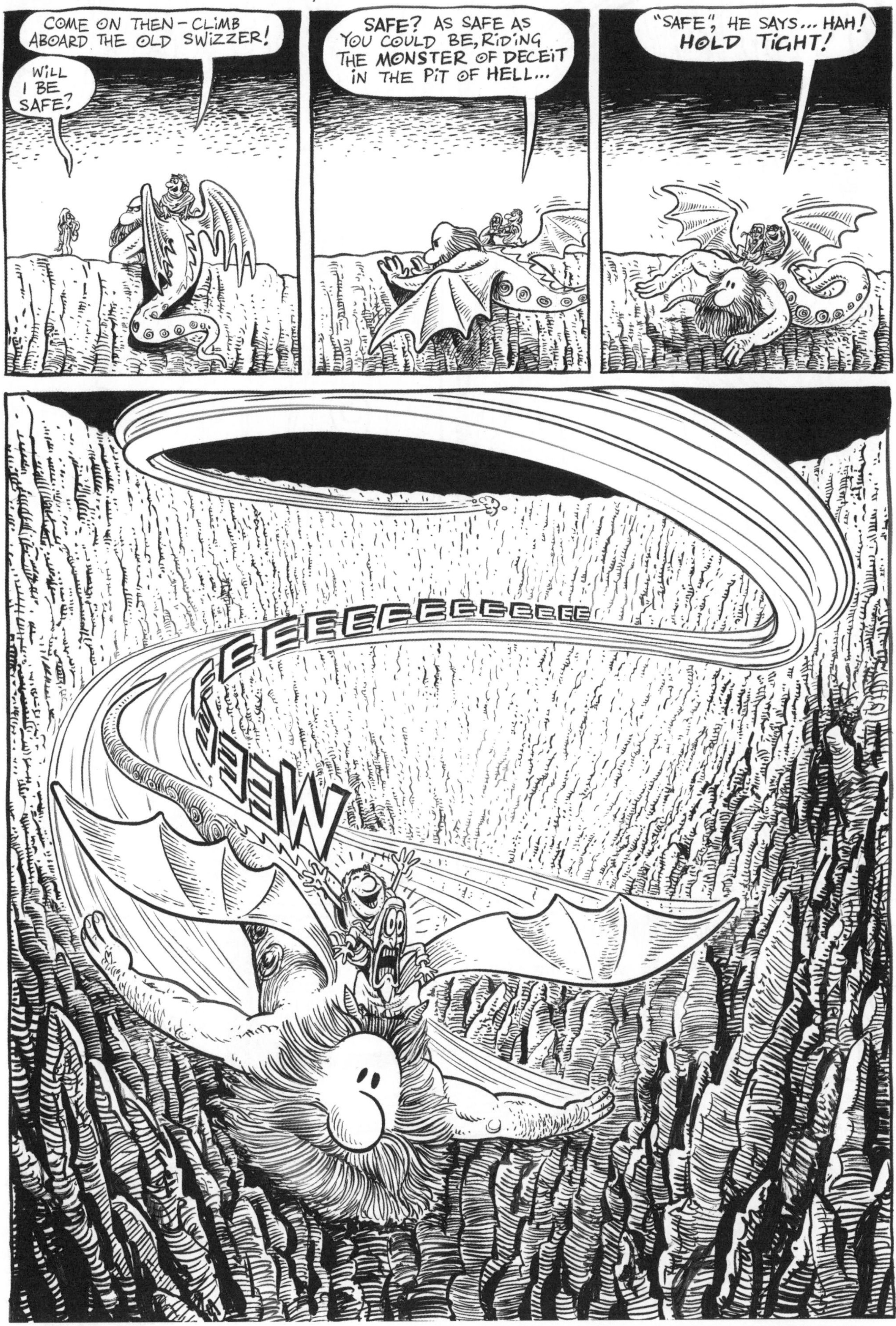
COME ON THEN – CLIMB ABOARD THE OLD SWIZZER!
WILL I BE SAFE?
SAFE? AS SAFE AS YOU COULD BE, RIDING THE MONSTER OF DECEIT IN THE PIT OF HELL...
"SAFE", HE SAYS... HAH! HOLD TIGHT!
WEEEEEEEEEEEEEEEEEEEE

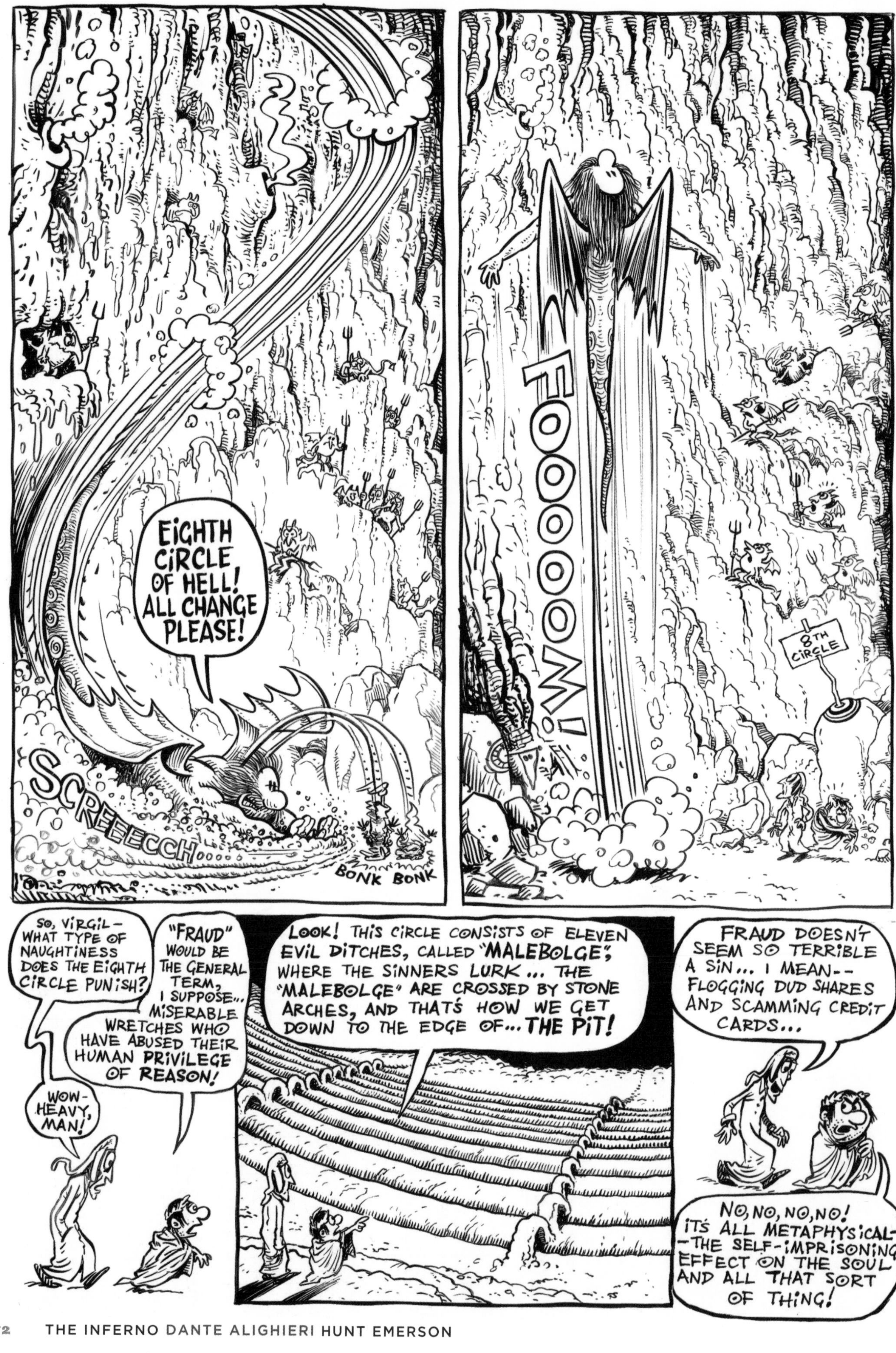
EIGHTH CIRCLE OF HELL! ALL CHANGE PLEASE!
SCREEECCH
BONK BONK
FOOOOOOM!
8TH CIRCLE
SO, VIRGIL - WHAT TYPE OF NAUGHTINESS DOES THE EIGHTH CIRCLE PUNISH?
"FRAUD" WOULD BE THE GENERAL TERM, I SUPPOSE... MISERABLE WRETCHES WHO HAVE ABUSED THEIR HUMAN PRIVILEGE OF REASON!
WOW - HEAVY, MAN!
LOOK! THIS CIRCLE CONSISTS OF ELEVEN EVIL DITCHES, CALLED "MALEBOLGE", WHERE THE SINNERS LURK... THE "MALEBOLGE" ARE CROSSED BY STONE ARCHES, AND THAT'S HOW WE GET DOWN TO THE EDGE OF... THE PIT!
FRAUD DOESN'T SEEM SO TERRIBLE A SIN... I MEAN-- FLOGGING DUD SHARES AND SCAMMING CREDIT CARDS...
NO, NO, NO, NO! IT'S ALL METAPHYSICAL --THE SELF-IMPRISONING EFFECT ON THE SOUL AND ALL THAT SORT OF THING!

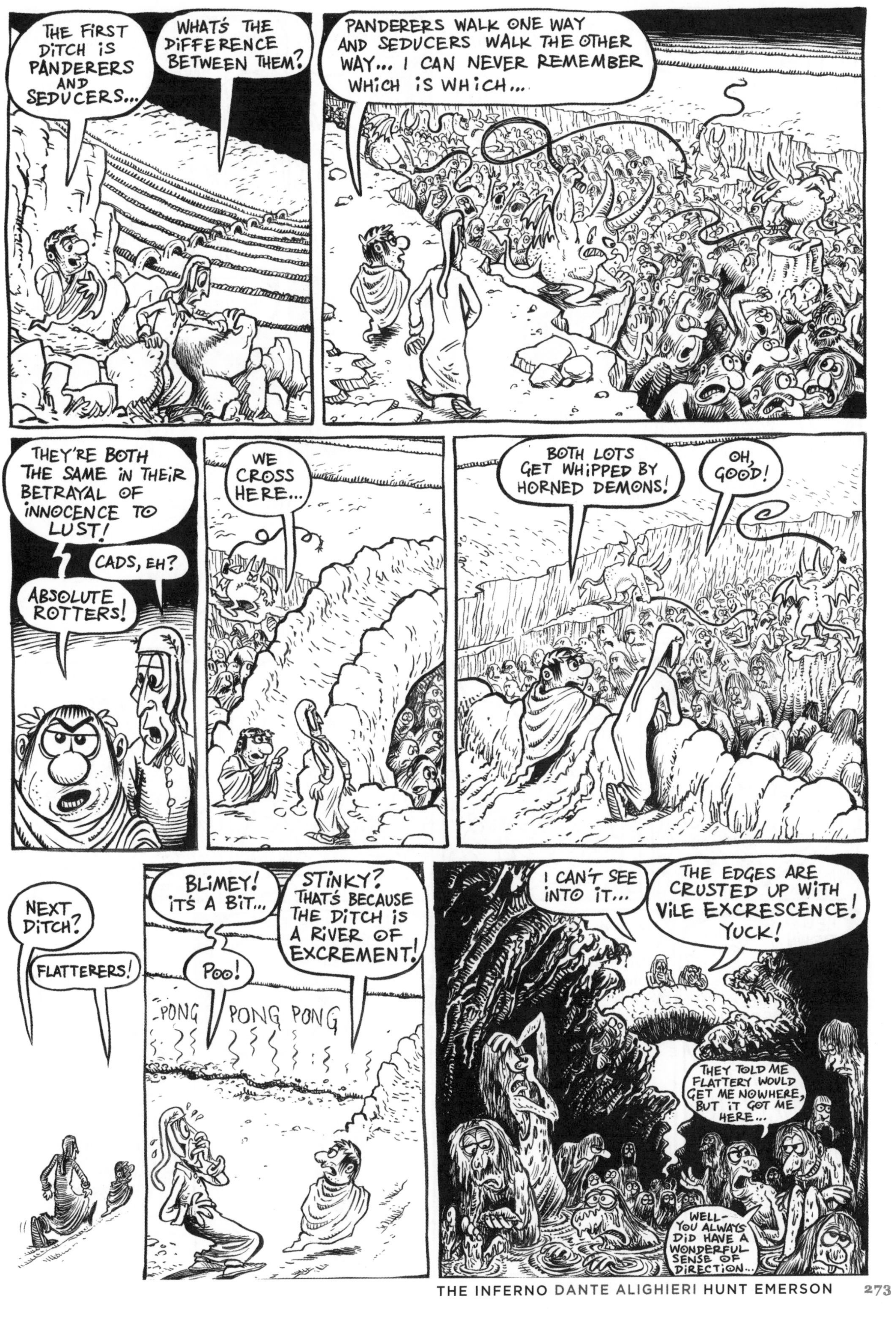

THE FIRST DITCH IS PANDERERS AND SEDUCERS...
WHAT'S THE DIFFERENCE BETWEEN THEM?
PANDERERS WALK ONE WAY AND SEDUCERS WALK THE OTHER WAY... I CAN NEVER REMEMBER WHICH IS WHICH...
THEY'RE BOTH THE SAME IN THEIR BETRAYAL OF INNOCENCE TO LUST!
CADS, EH?
ABSOLUTE ROTTERS!
WE CROSS HERE...
BOTH LOTS GET WHIPPED BY HORNED DEMONS!
OH, GOOD!
NEXT DITCH?
FLATTERERS!
BLIMEY! IT'S A BIT...
POO!
STINKY? THAT'S BECAUSE THE DITCH IS A RIVER OF EXCREMENT!
PONG PONG PONG
I CAN'T SEE INTO IT...
THE EDGES ARE CRUSTED UP WITH VILE EXCRESCENCE! YUCK!
THEY TOLD ME FLATTERY WOULD GET ME NOWHERE, BUT IT GOT ME HERE...
WELL- YOU ALWAYS DID HAVE A WONDERFUL SENSE OF DIRECTION...

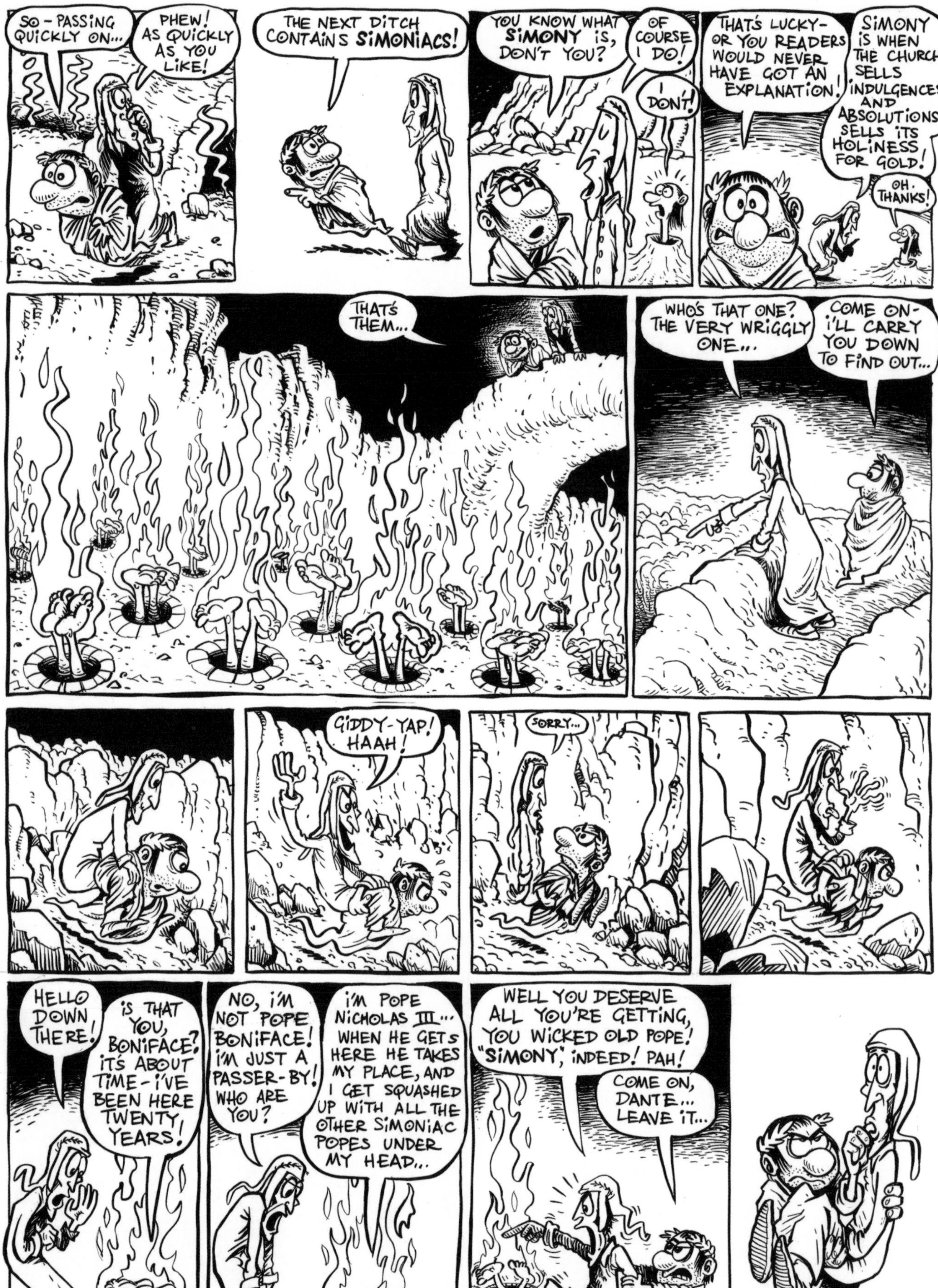
SO - PASSING QUICKLY ON...
PHEW! AS QUICKLY AS YOU LIKE!
THE NEXT DITCH CONTAINS SIMONIACS!
YOU KNOW WHAT SIMONY IS, DON'T YOU?
OF COURSE I DO!
I DON'T!
THAT'S LUCKY- OR YOU READERS WOULD NEVER HAVE GOT AN EXPLANATION!
SIMONY IS WHEN THE CHURCH SELLS INDULGENCES AND ABSOLUTIONS- SELLS ITS HOLINESS FOR GOLD!
OH. THANKS!
THAT'S THEM...
WHO'S THAT ONE? THE VERY WRIGGLY ONE...
COME ON- I'LL CARRY YOU DOWN TO FIND OUT...
GIDDY-YAP! HAAH!
SORRY...
HELLO DOWN THERE!
IS THAT YOU, BONIFACE? IT'S ABOUT TIME- I'VE BEEN HERE TWENTY YEARS!
NO, I'M NOT POPE BONIFACE! I'M JUST A PASSER-BY! WHO ARE YOU?
I'M POPE NICHOLAS III... WHEN HE GETS HERE HE TAKES MY PLACE, AND I GET SQUASHED UP WITH ALL THE OTHER SIMONIAC POPES UNDER MY HEAD...
WELL YOU DESERVE ALL YOU'RE GETTING, YOU WICKED OLD POPE! "SIMONY," INDEED! PAH!
COME ON, DANTE... LEAVE IT...

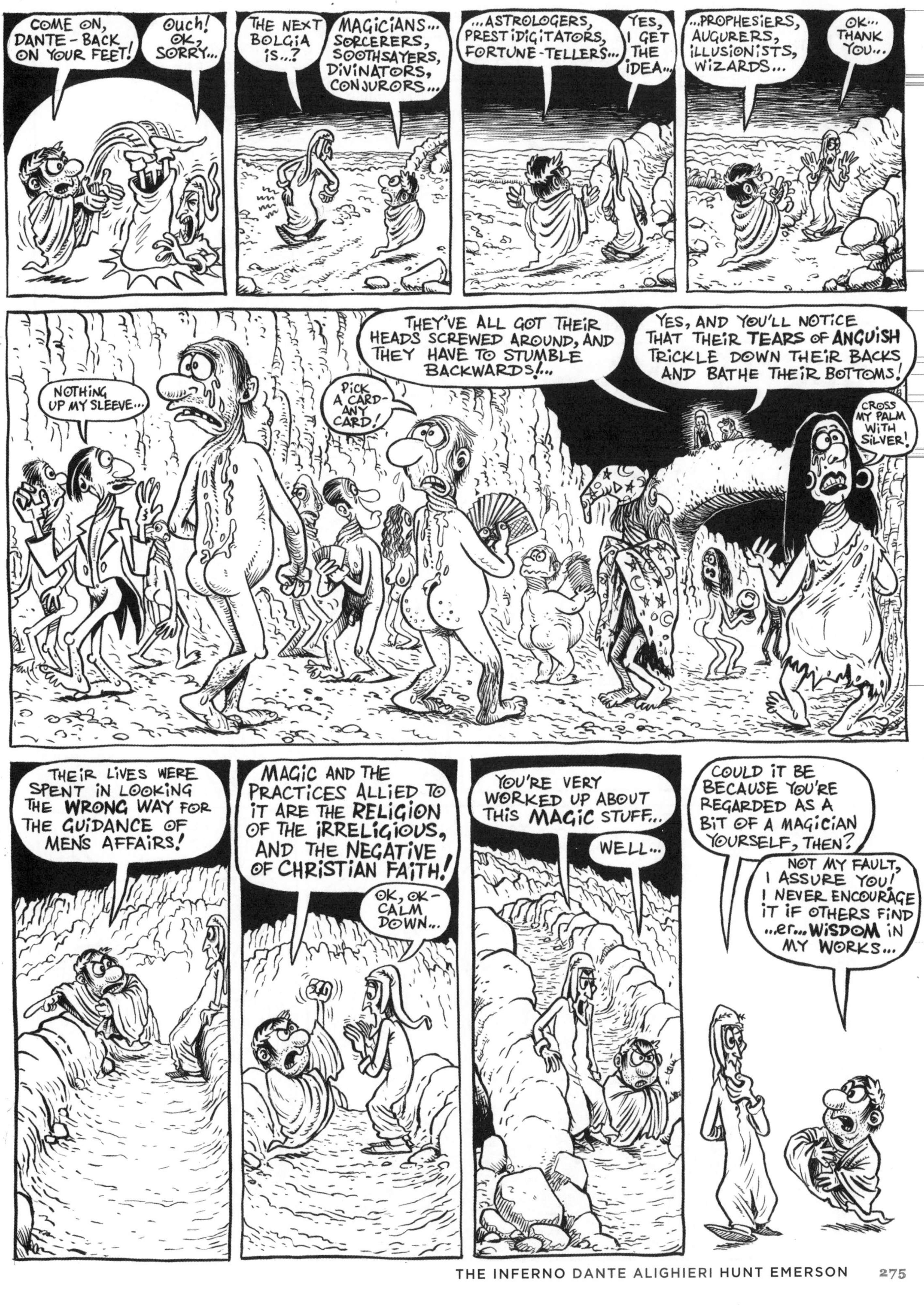
COME ON, DANTE - BACK ON YOUR FEET!
Ouch! OK, SORRY...
THE NEXT BOLGIA IS...?
MAGICIANS... SORCERERS, SOOTHSAYERS, DIVINATORS, CONJURORS...
...ASTROLOGERS, PRESTIDIGITATORS, FORTUNE-TELLERS...
YES, I GET THE IDEA...
...PROPHESIERS, AUGURERS, ILLUSIONISTS, WIZARDS...
OK... THANK YOU...
THEY'VE ALL GOT THEIR HEADS SCREWED AROUND, AND THEY HAVE TO STUMBLE BACKWARDS!...
YES, AND YOU'LL NOTICE THAT THEIR TEARS OF ANGUISH TRICKLE DOWN THEIR BACKS AND BATHE THEIR BOTTOMS!
NOTHING UP MY SLEEVE...
PICK A CARD-ANY CARD!
CROSS MY PALM WITH SILVER!
THEIR LIVES WERE SPENT IN LOOKING THE WRONG WAY FOR THE GUIDANCE OF MEN'S AFFAIRS!
MAGIC AND THE PRACTICES ALLIED TO IT ARE THE RELIGION OF THE IRRELIGIOUS, AND THE NEGATIVE OF CHRISTIAN FAITH!
OK, OK-CALM DOWN...
YOU'RE VERY WORKED UP ABOUT THIS MAGIC STUFF...
WELL...
COULD IT BE BECAUSE YOU'RE REGARDED AS A BIT OF A MAGICIAN YOURSELF, THEN?
NOT MY FAULT, I ASSURE YOU! I NEVER ENCOURAGE IT IF OTHERS FIND ...er... WISDOM IN MY WORKS...

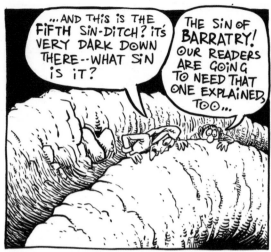

...AND THIS IS THE FIFTH SIN-DITCH? IT'S VERY DARK DOWN THERE--WHAT SIN IS IT?

THE SIN OF BARRATRY! OUR READERS ARE GOING TO NEED THAT ONE EXPLAINED TOO...

A BARRATOR IS A SWINDLER IN PUBLIC OFFICE! THEY SPEND THEIR ETERNITY COOKING IN BOILING PITCH!

OH-OH... GET BEHIND THESE ROCKS--THERE'S A DEMON COMING!

EEKEEK EEK EEK EEKEEK EEK EEK EEK

AHOY, DEMONS! HERE'S A TOWN COUNCILLOR FROM LUCCA, WHERE THE WHOLE CREW OF THEM ARE A BUNCH OF BARRATORS! COOK HIM WELL, WHILE I GO FOR MORE!

AAAAGH

YAHAHAHAHAAAAA

STAY HERE WHILE I GO AND PARLEY WITH THEM...

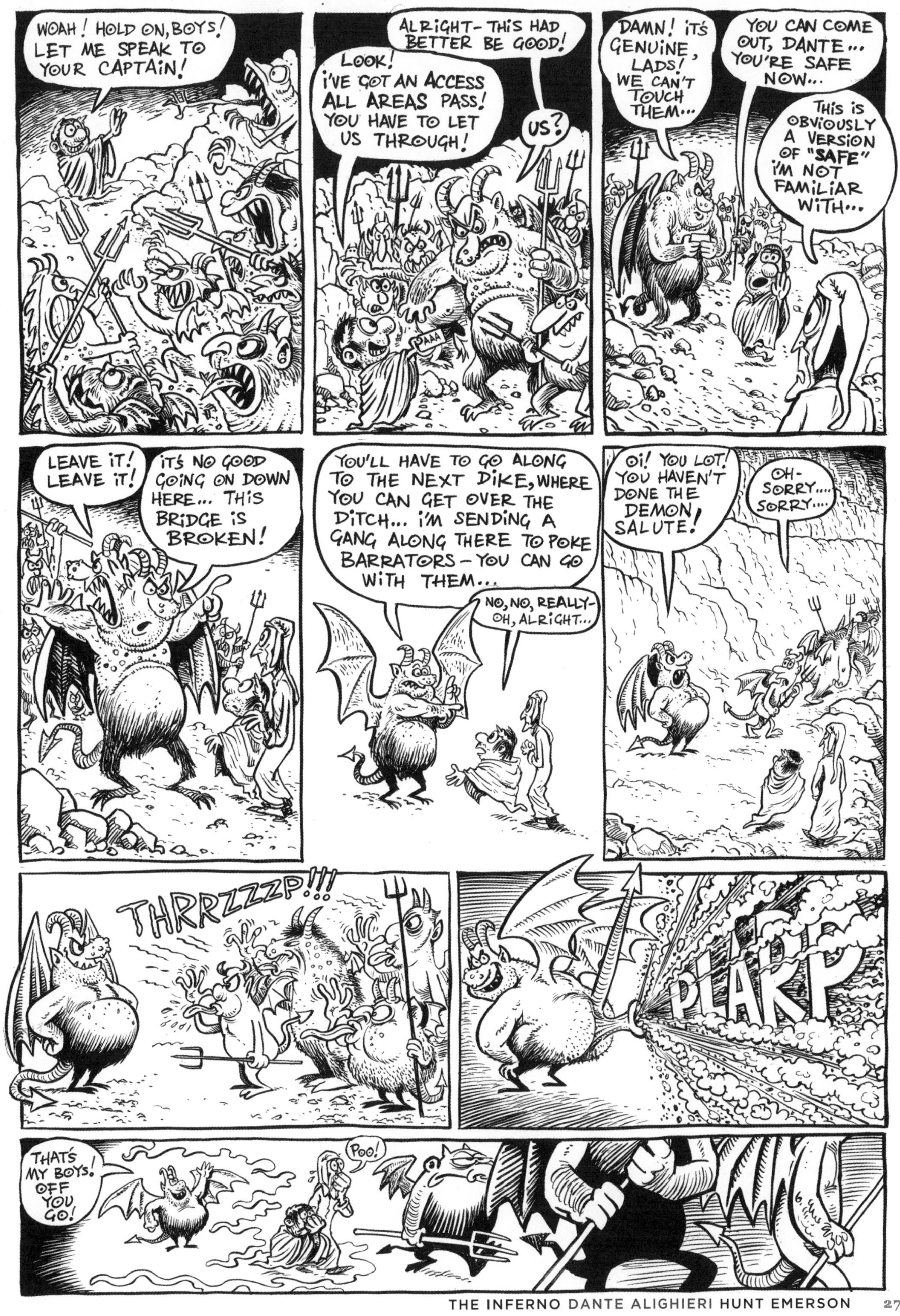

WOAH! HOLD ON, BOYS! LET ME SPEAK TO YOUR CAPTAIN!
LOOK! I'VE GOT AN ACCESS ALL AREAS PASS! YOU HAVE TO LET US THROUGH!
ALRIGHT- THIS HAD BETTER BE GOOD!
US?
PAAA
DAMN! IT'S GENUINE, LADS! WE CAN'T TOUCH THEM...
YOU CAN COME OUT, DANTE... YOU'RE SAFE NOW...
THIS IS OBVIOUSLY A VERSION OF "SAFE" I'M NOT FAMILIAR WITH...
LEAVE IT! LEAVE IT!
IT'S NO GOOD GOING ON DOWN HERE... THIS BRIDGE IS BROKEN!
YOU'LL HAVE TO GO ALONG TO THE NEXT DIKE, WHERE YOU CAN GET OVER THE DITCH... I'M SENDING A GANG ALONG THERE TO POKE BARRATORS - YOU CAN GO WITH THEM...
NO, NO, REALLY- OH, ALRIGHT...
OI! YOU LOT! YOU HAVEN'T DONE THE DEMON SALUTE!
OH- SORRY.... SORRY....
THRRZZZP!!!
PLARP
THAT'S MY BOYS! OFF YOU GO!
POO!

The Tibetan Book of the Dead (Bardo Thodol)

Padmasambhava and Karma Lingpa

ART / ADAPTATION BY **Sanya Glisic**

THE TIBETAN BOOK OF THE DEAD IS THE NAME given to a series of Buddhist texts meant to be read to people during and in the days immediately after their deaths, guiding them as they experience the "in-between" state before being reborn (or, occasionally, achieving liberation/ enlightenment, thus ending the cycle of reincarnation). The entire cycle is known as *Liberation Through Hearing in the Bardo* (or: *Bardo Thodol*), and the English translations (called *The Tibetan Book of the Dead*) usually contain just three sections of this work.

The original documents were said to have been written in a secret language by Padmasambhava, a ninth-century Indian Buddhist master who brought Buddhism to Tibet. Knowing that the time wasn't right for Tibet to receive these texts (and thousands of others), he had them buried and otherwise hidden throughout the country. When the people are ready for a particular teaching, he appears in a dream to one of his reincarnated disciples and tells them where to find the document, which they are able to translate into Tibetan.

According to tradition, the *Bardo Thodol* was found by Karma Lingpa at the top of Mount Gampodar in the mid-1300s. A widely traveled American anthropologist, Walter Evans-Wentz, encountered a rare copy while in the Himalayas in 1919 and arranged to have it translated into English by the Lama Kazi Dawa-Samdup. Illustrator and silk-screener Sanya Glisic used a number of traditional and experimental techniques in creating her astounding images of the beings and experiences of the *bardo*, the in-between state.

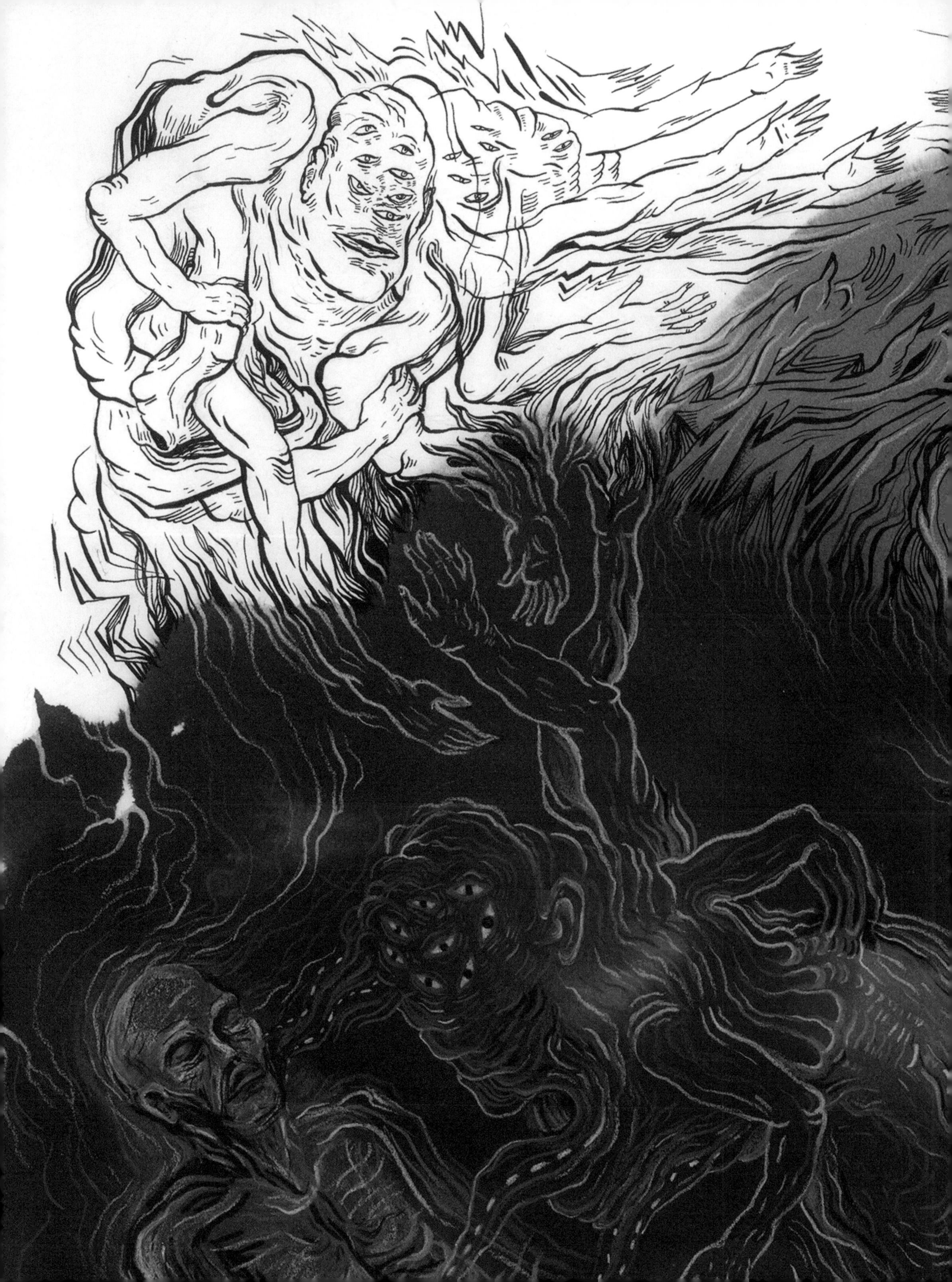

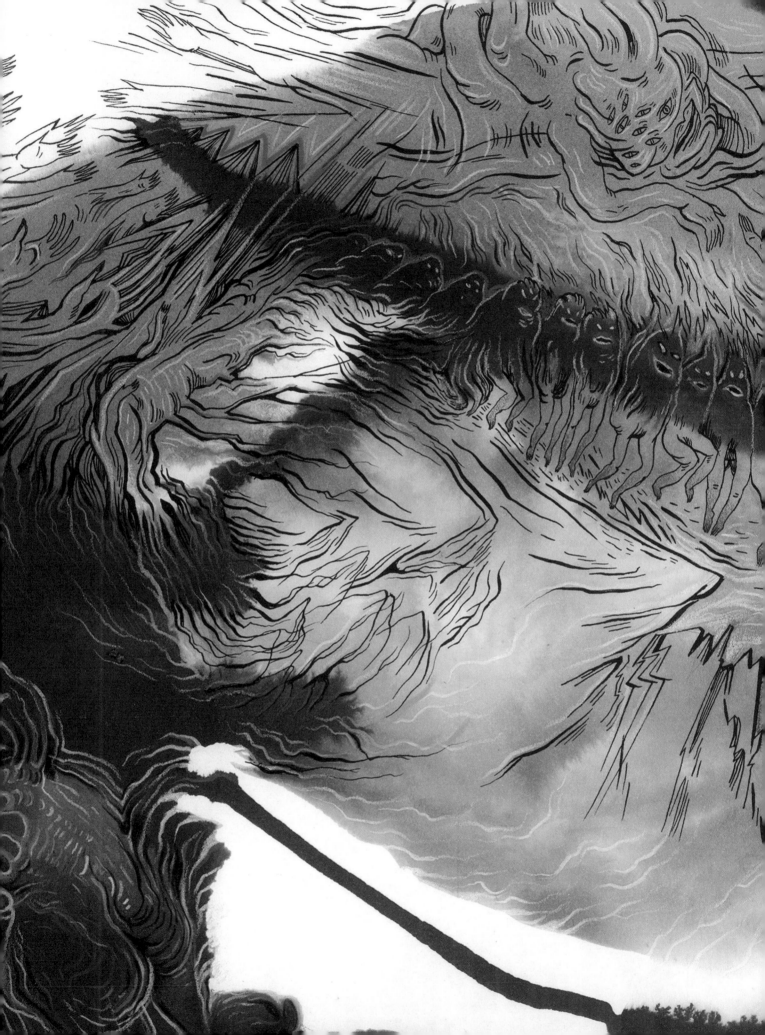

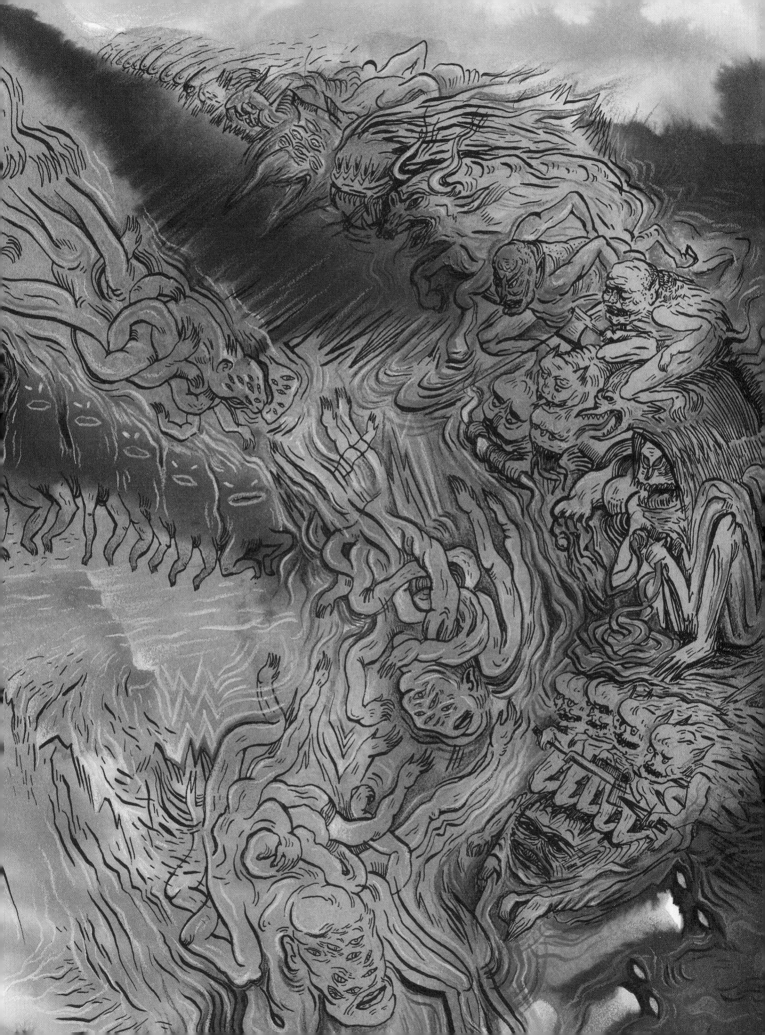

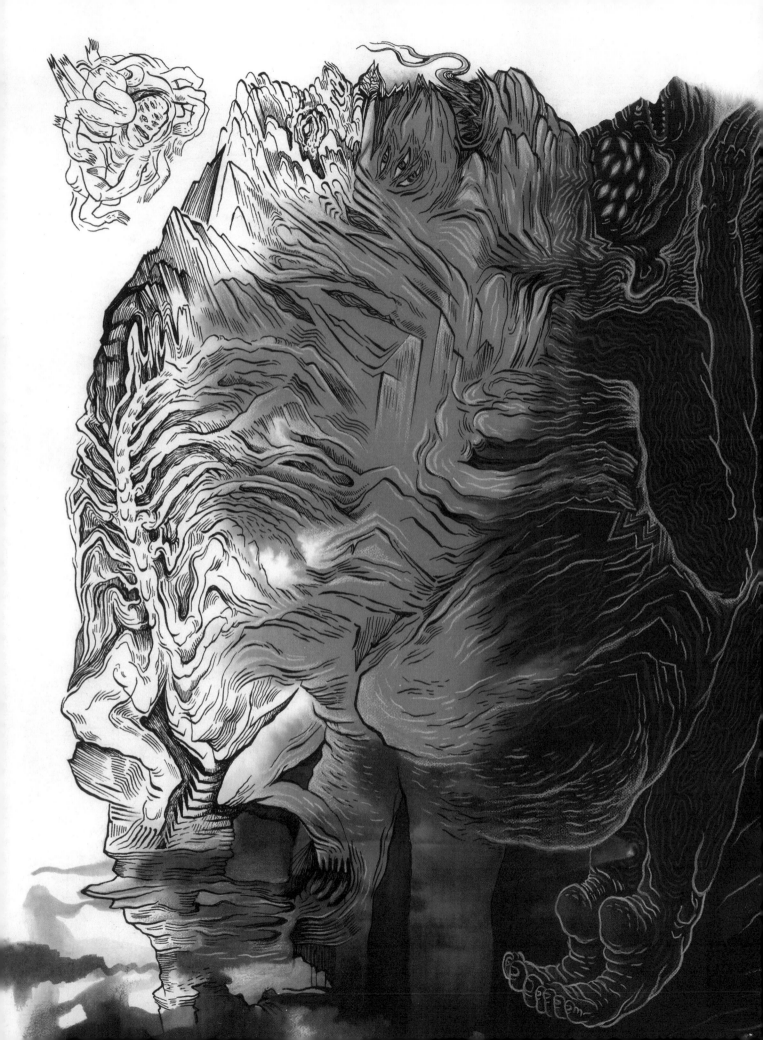

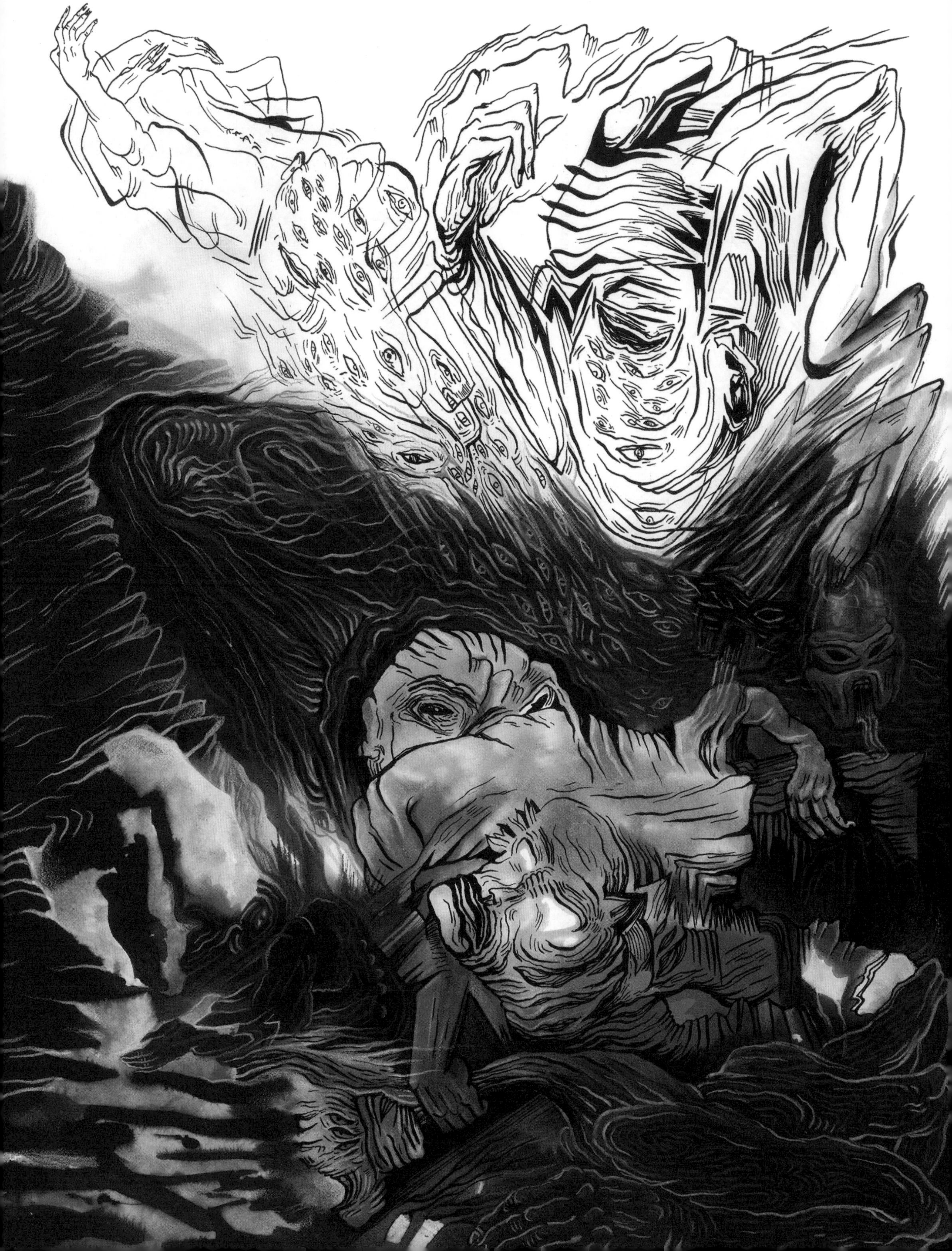

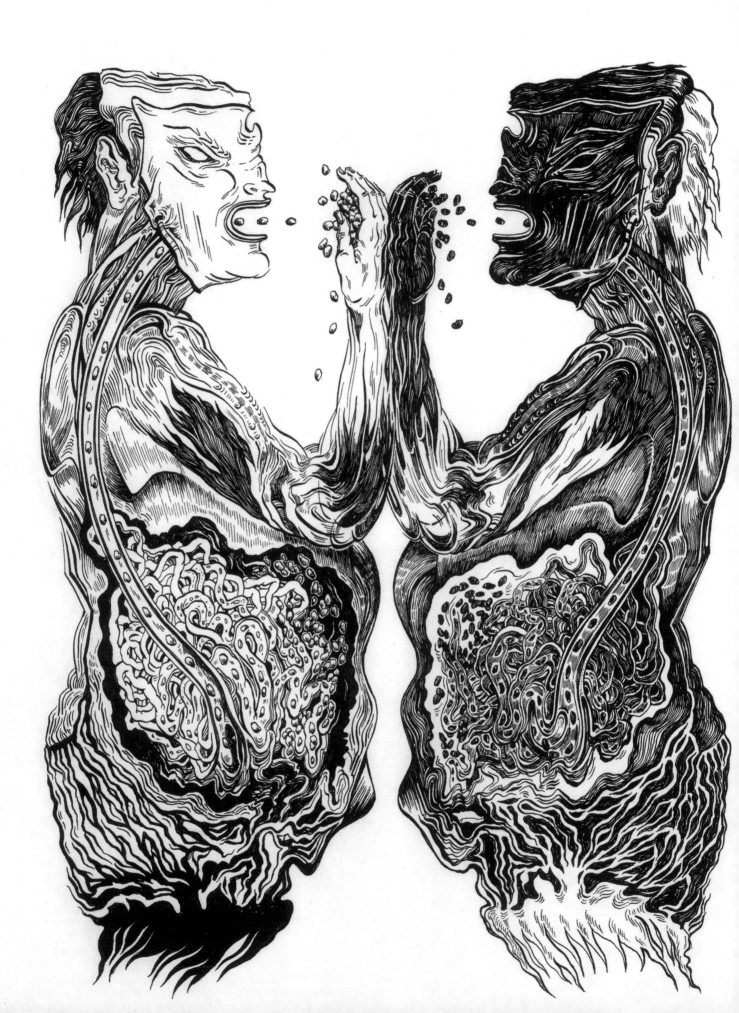

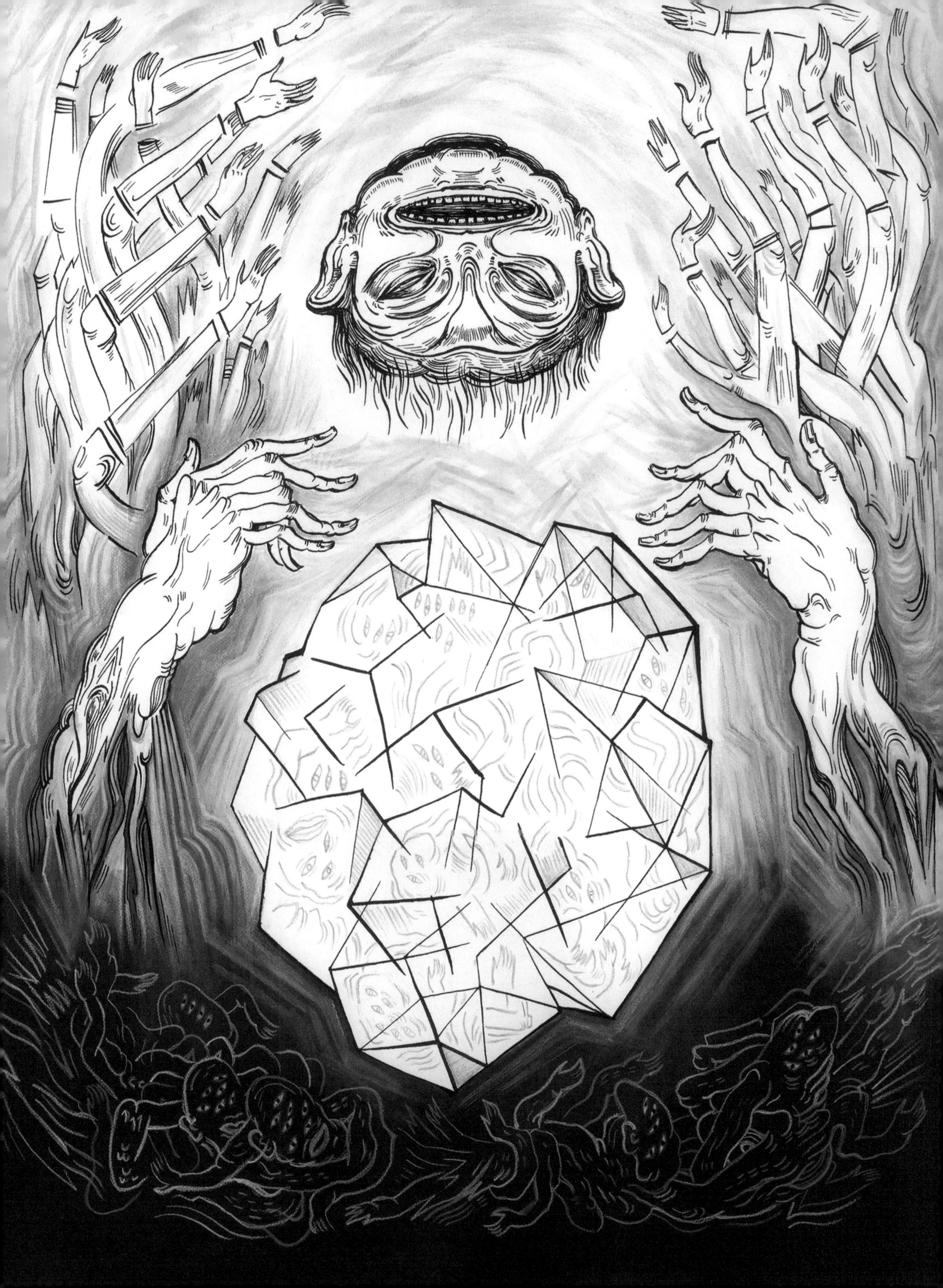

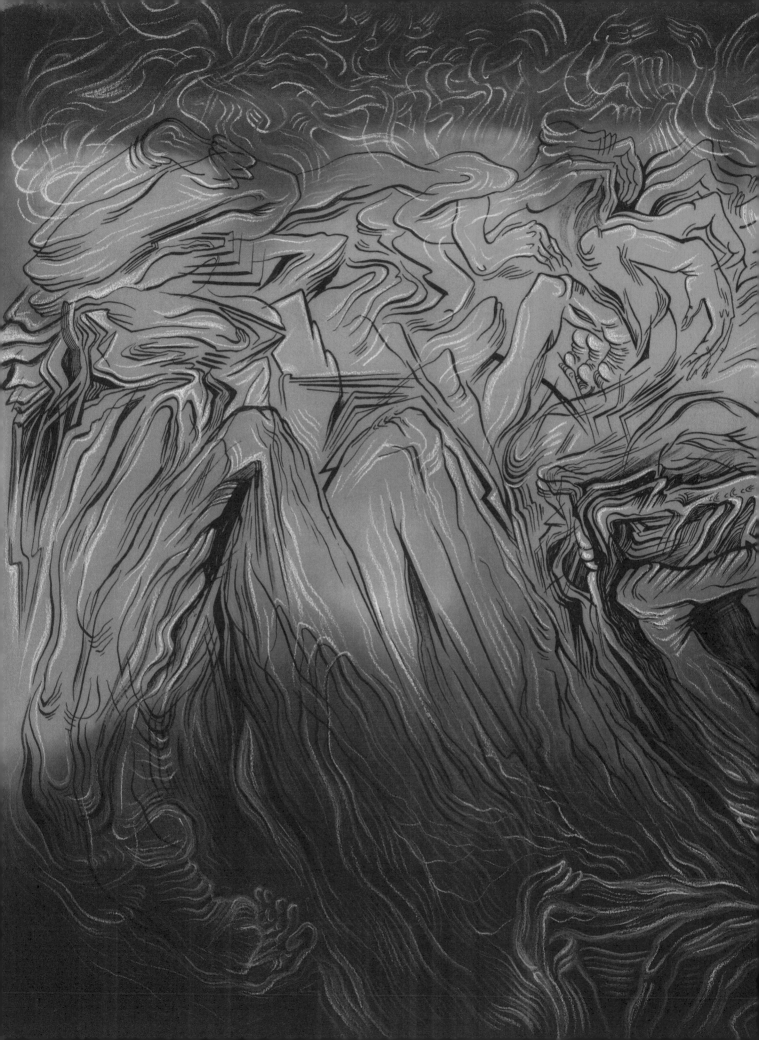

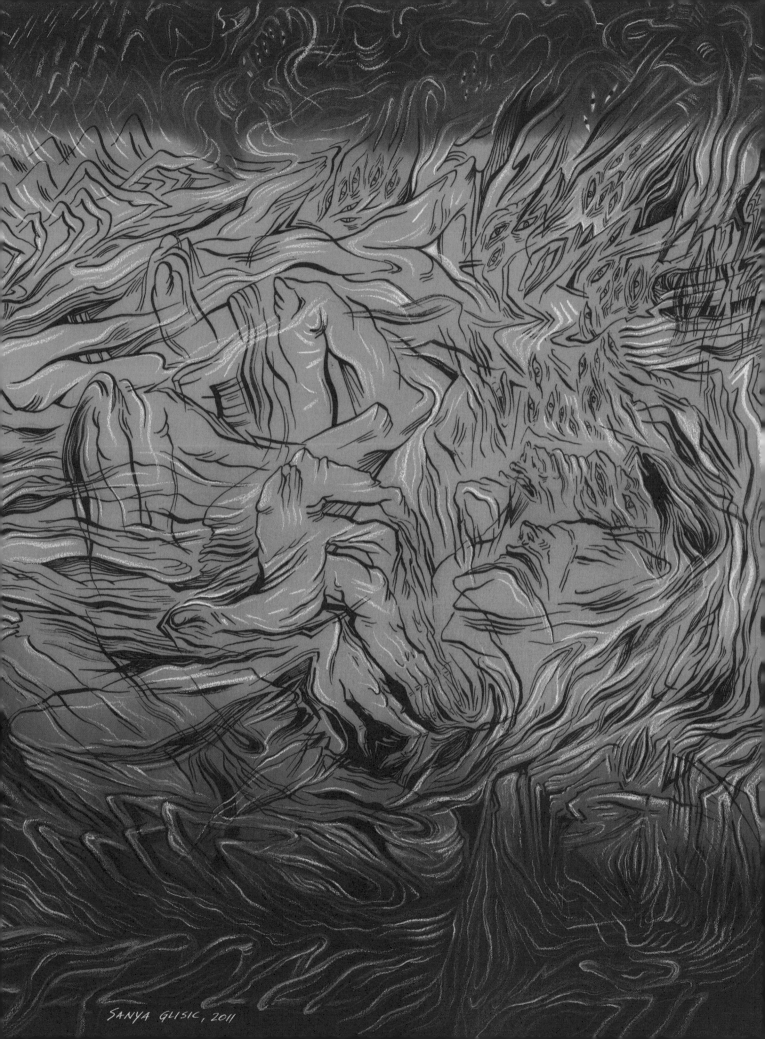

SANYA GLISIC, 2011

"The Last Ballad"

François Villon

ART / ADAPTATION BY **Julian Peters**

THOUGH HE'S NOT PUBLISHED OR ANTHOLOGIZED much in English, François Villon is one of France's greatest lyric poets. Born into poverty at a tumultuous time in France's history, the middle 1400s, Villon led a rapscallion's life, doing lots of time in jail or in exile for various crimes (including killing a priest in a bar fight, though he was pardoned by the king when it was found to be self-defense), and eventually disappearing for good while exiled from Paris.

After being imprisoned for three months in a filthy pit so deep that light couldn't reach the bottom, Villon poured forth a blazing masterpiece of poetry, *Le Grand Testament*, over 2,000 verses, largely autobiographical, encompassing ribaldry, love, piety, regret, *carpe diem*, criminality and lowlife, aging, and a zest for life. "The Last Ballad" is literally the final poem of the work. At least once, Villon had been under a death sentence, and this poem recounts that time and the thoughts running through his head. Now, if you think that someone about to be hanged might have more pressing matters on his mind than failed love, well, you've never really had a broken heart.

Montreal illustrator Julian Peters uses a style inspired by *fumetti* (photo-comics), and with "The Last Ballad" he says, "I tried to capture the poem's particular sense of humour (the very definition, I suppose, of gallows humour), while at the same time hopefully eliciting a certain measure of real empathy for the considerable human suffering that provides its inspiration."

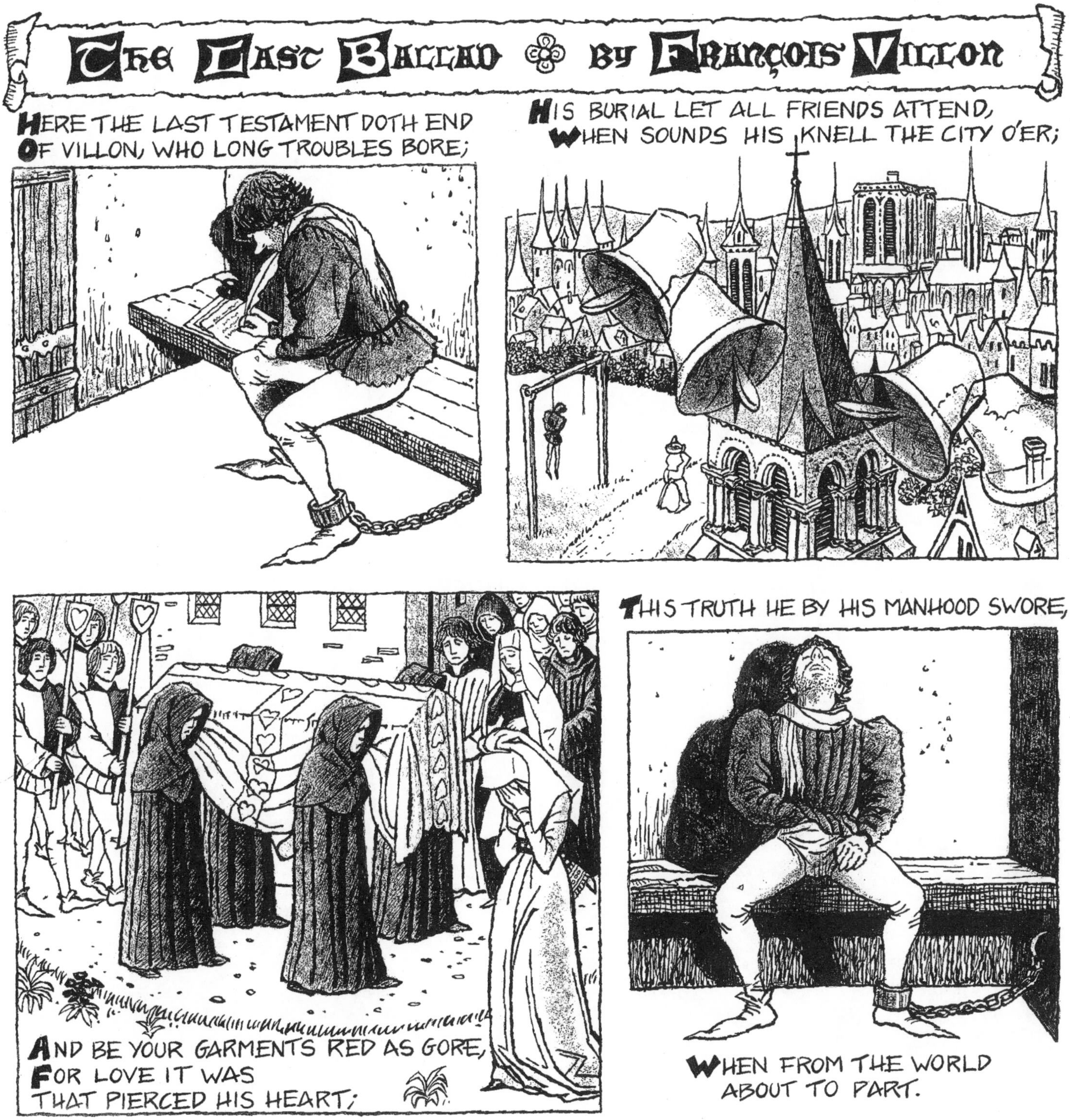

THE LAST BALLAD BY FRANÇOIS VILLON
HERE THE LAST TESTAMENT DOTH END
OF VILLON, WHO LONG TROUBLES BORE;
HIS BURIAL LET ALL FRIENDS ATTEND,
WHEN SOUNDS HIS KNELL THE CITY O'ER;
AND BE YOUR GARMENTS RED AS GORE,
FOR LOVE IT WAS
THAT PIERCED HIS HEART;
THIS TRUTH HE BY HIS MANHOOD SWORE,
WHEN FROM THE WORLD
ABOUT TO PART.

NOR THINK I THIS DOTH TRUTH OFFEND,
FOR HE WAS DRIVEN FROM THEIR DOOR

WHOM HE HAD DEEMED HIS LOVES AND FRIENDS.

FROM HENCE TO ROUSSILLON EXPLORE.

BRAMBLES AND THORNS YOU MEET GOOD STORE,
AND NONE YOU FIND YOUR PATH ATHWART,

BUT ALL HIS CLOTHES TO TATTERS TORE,

WHEN FROM THE WORLD ABOUT TO PART.

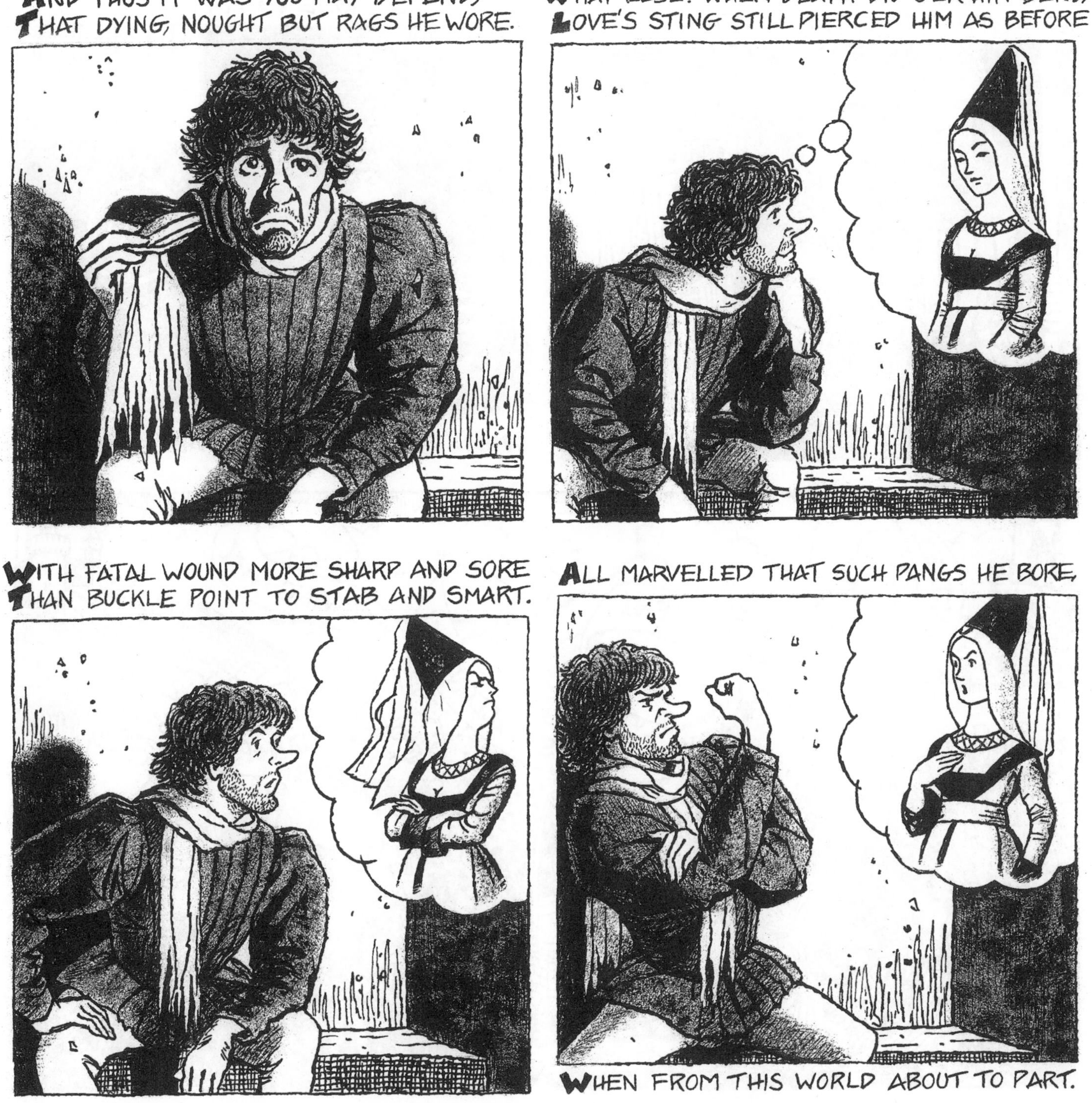
AND THUS IT WAS YOU MAY DEPEND,
THAT DYING, NOUGHT BUT RAGS HE WORE.
WHAT ELSE? WHEN DEATH DID O'ER HIM BEND,
LOVE'S STING STILL PIERCED HIM AS BEFORE
WITH FATAL WOUND MORE SHARP AND SORE
THAN BUCKLE POINT TO STAB AND SMART.
ALL MARVELLED THAT SUCH PANGS HE BORE,
WHEN FROM THIS WORLD ABOUT TO PART.

PRINCE, BLITHE AS HAWK ALOFT TO SOAR,
KNOW THAT TO CHEER HIS FINAL START

LARGE DRAUGHTS OF WINE
HE CHOSE TO POUR,

WHEN FROM THIS WORLD ABOUT TO PART.

TAKEN + FROM + "LE + TESTAMENT"
BY + FRANÇOIS + VILLON + 1461
DRAWINGS + BY
JULIAN + PETERS + 2009

The Canterbury Tales

Geoffrey Chaucer

ART / ADAPTATION BY **Seymour Chwast**

ALMOST EVERYONE READ PORTIONS OF *THE Canterbury Tales* in school. Looking back, it's amazing that such a bawdy, scatological work became a staple of the high school classroom. Although not every one of the tales is saucy, this is certainly the raciest of the works on literature's A-list. For those who slept through that part of English class, *The Canterbury Tales* is a collection of self-contained stories told within the framework of a religious pilgrimage. Twenty-nine people and the narrator are heading to Thomas Becket's shrine, and to pass the time they have a tale-telling contest. Geoffrey Chaucer was a well-educated man of the world, and he poured all his knowledge and experience of life in medieval England into this book-length poem. In a radical move, he wrote his epic in English, establishing it as a literary language equal to Latin and French.

Part of the work's genius is that not only are most of the widely varied tales interesting, but the pilgrims are vividly drawn individuals, and the way they interact, often sniping at each other, adds greatly to the work. They come from a variety of backgrounds, socioeconomic classes, and professions. A knight and a miller. A doctor and a carpenter. A monk and a cook. A nun and a shipman.

The Wife of Bath is widely regarded as one of the greatest literary characters ever created. Earthy, lustful, and frank, she has outlived four husbands, is planning to outlive the current one, and is already looking for number six. She enjoys sex but also uses it to get what she wants. Her long prologue is one of the highlights of the work, though her tale itself is a bit anticlimactic.

After adapting *The Divine Comedy* (also excerpted in this volume), the illustrious designer/illustrator Seymour Chwast turned his sights on *The Canterbury Tales*, adding touches like motorcycles for the pilgrims.

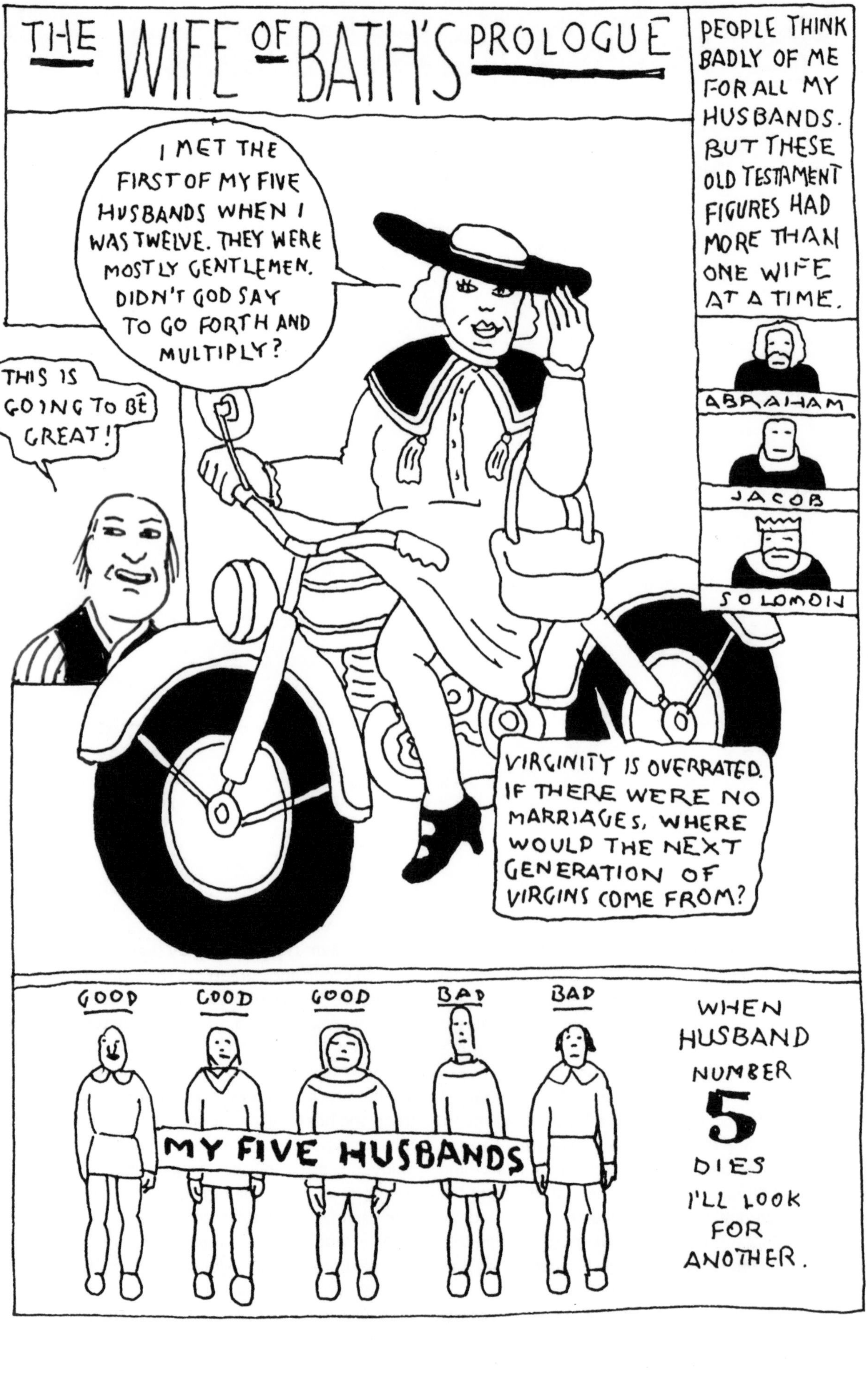
THE WIFE OF BATH'S PROLOGUE
PEOPLE THINK BADLY OF ME FOR ALL MY HUSBANDS. BUT THESE OLD TESTAMENT FIGURES HAD MORE THAN ONE WIFE AT A TIME.
ABRAHAM
JACOB
SOLOMON
I MET THE FIRST OF MY FIVE HUSBANDS WHEN I WAS TWELVE. THEY WERE MOSTLY GENTLEMEN. DIDN'T GOD SAY TO GO FORTH AND MULTIPLY?
THIS IS GOING TO BE GREAT!
VIRGINITY IS OVERRATED. IF THERE WERE NO MARRIAGES, WHERE WOULD THE NEXT GENERATION OF VIRGINS COME FROM?
GOOD
GOOD
GOOD
BAD
BAD
MY FIVE HUSBANDS
WHEN HUSBAND NUMBER 5 DIES I'LL LOOK FOR ANOTHER.

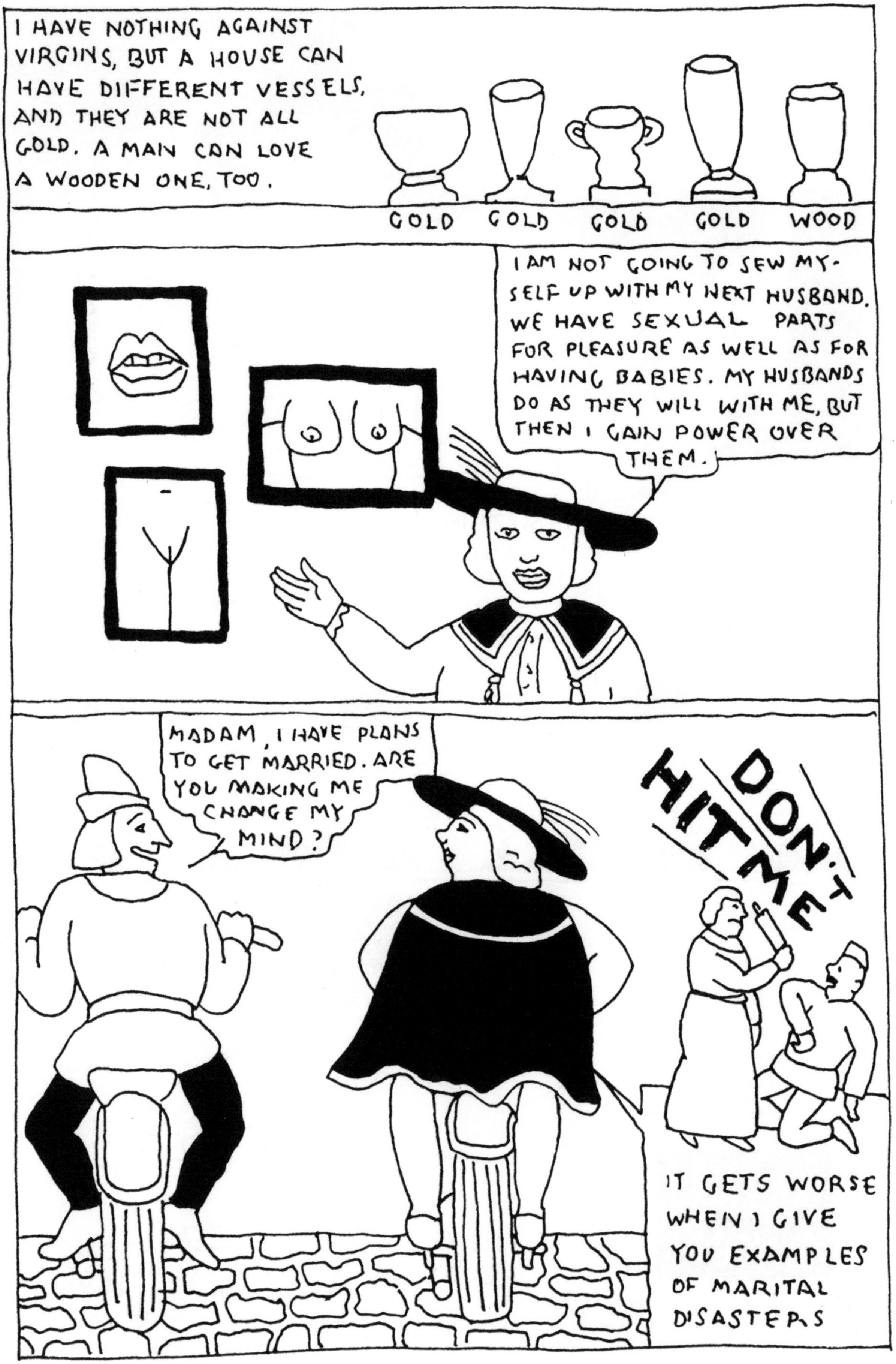
I HAVE NOTHING AGAINST VIRGINS, BUT A HOUSE CAN HAVE DIFFERENT VESSELS, AND THEY ARE NOT ALL GOLD. A MAN CAN LOVE A WOODEN ONE, TOO.
GOLD
GOLD
GOLD
GOLD
WOOD
I AM NOT GOING TO SEW MYSELF UP WITH MY NEXT HUSBAND. WE HAVE SEXUAL PARTS FOR PLEASURE AS WELL AS FOR HAVING BABIES. MY HUSBANDS DO AS THEY WILL WITH ME, BUT THEN I GAIN POWER OVER THEM.
MADAM, I HAVE PLANS TO GET MARRIED. ARE YOU MAKING ME CHANGE MY MIND?
DON'T HIT ME
IT GETS WORSE WHEN I GIVE YOU EXAMPLES OF MARITAL DISASTERS

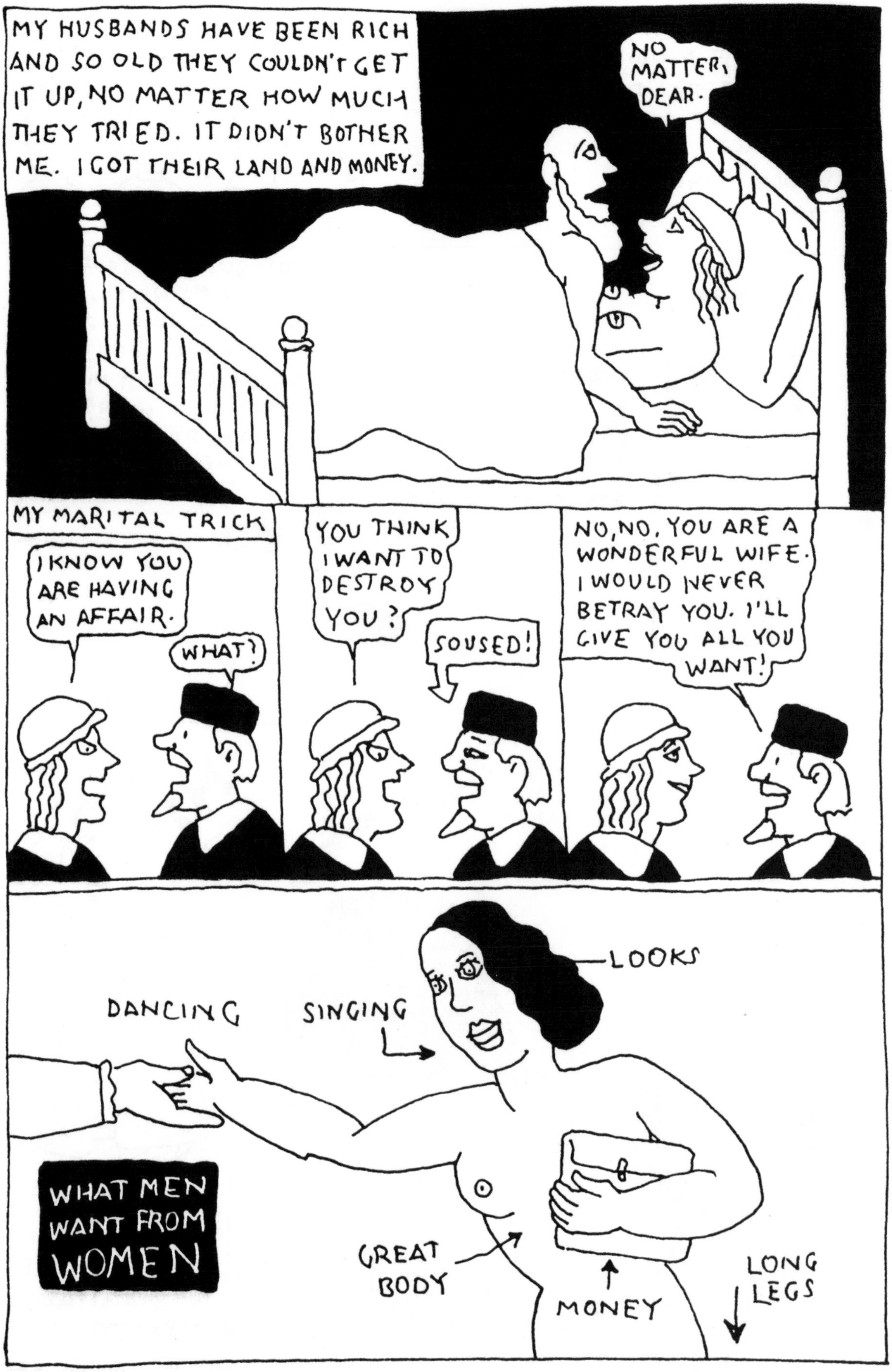
MY HUSBANDS HAVE BEEN RICH AND SO OLD THEY COULDN'T GET IT UP, NO MATTER HOW MUCH THEY TRIED. IT DIDN'T BOTHER ME. I GOT THEIR LAND AND MONEY.
NO MATTER, DEAR.
MY MARITAL TRICK
I KNOW YOU ARE HAVING AN AFFAIR.
WHAT?
YOU THINK I WANT TO DESTROY YOU?
SOUSED!
NO, NO, YOU ARE A WONDERFUL WIFE. I WOULD NEVER BETRAY YOU. I'LL GIVE YOU ALL YOU WANT!
LOOKS
DANCING
SINGING
WHAT MEN WANT FROM WOMEN
GREAT BODY
MONEY
LONG LEGS

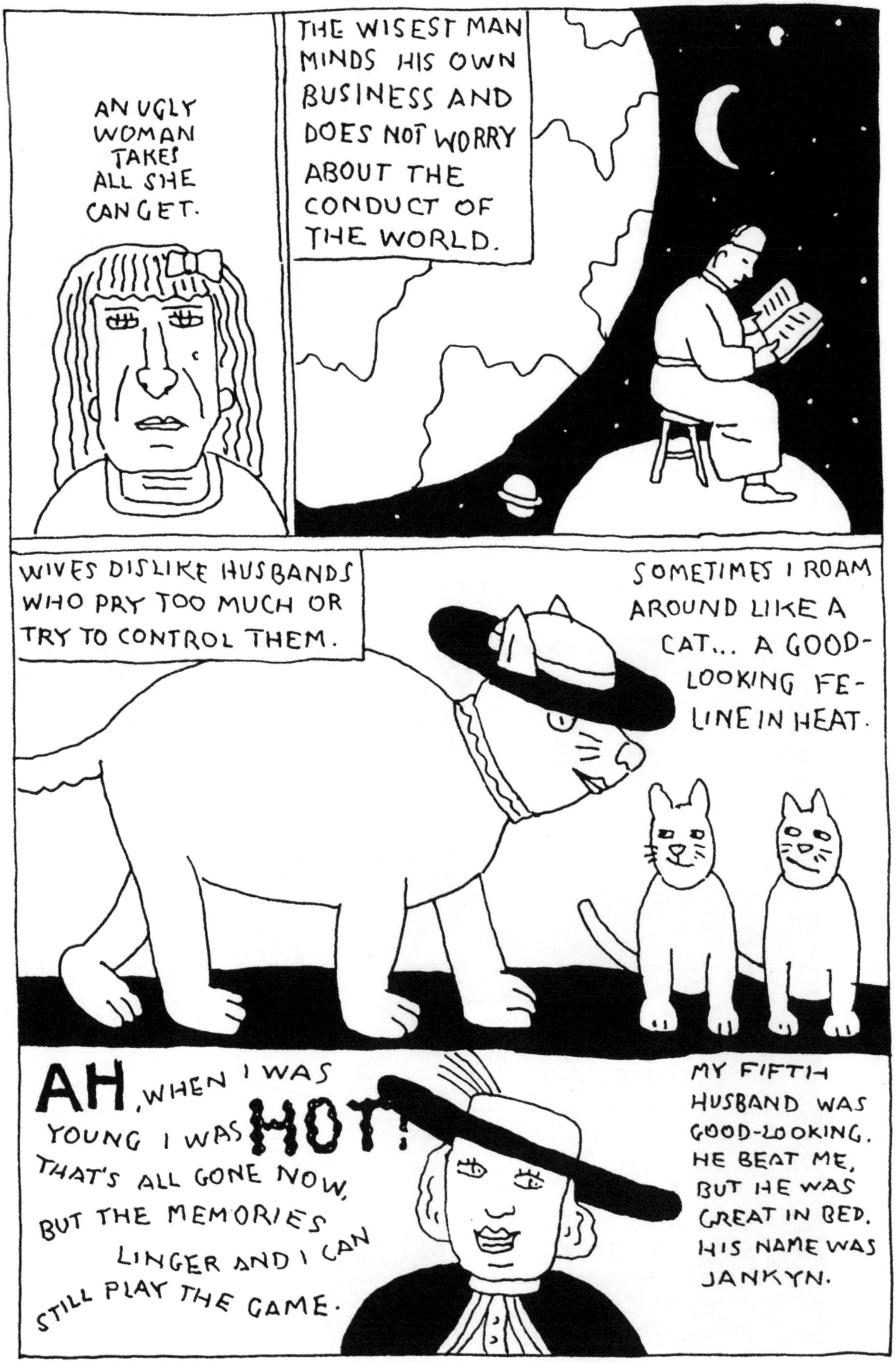
AN UGLY WOMAN TAKES ALL SHE CAN GET.
THE WISEST MAN MINDS HIS OWN BUSINESS AND DOES NOT WORRY ABOUT THE CONDUCT OF THE WORLD.
WIVES DISLIKE HUSBANDS WHO PRY TOO MUCH OR TRY TO CONTROL THEM.
SOMETIMES I ROAM AROUND LIKE A CAT... A GOOD-LOOKING FE-LINE IN HEAT.
AH, WHEN I WAS YOUNG I WAS HOT! THAT'S ALL GONE NOW, BUT THE MEMORIES LINGER AND I CAN STILL PLAY THE GAME.
MY FIFTH HUSBAND WAS GOOD-LOOKING. HE BEAT ME, BUT HE WAS GREAT IN BED. HIS NAME WAS JANKYN.

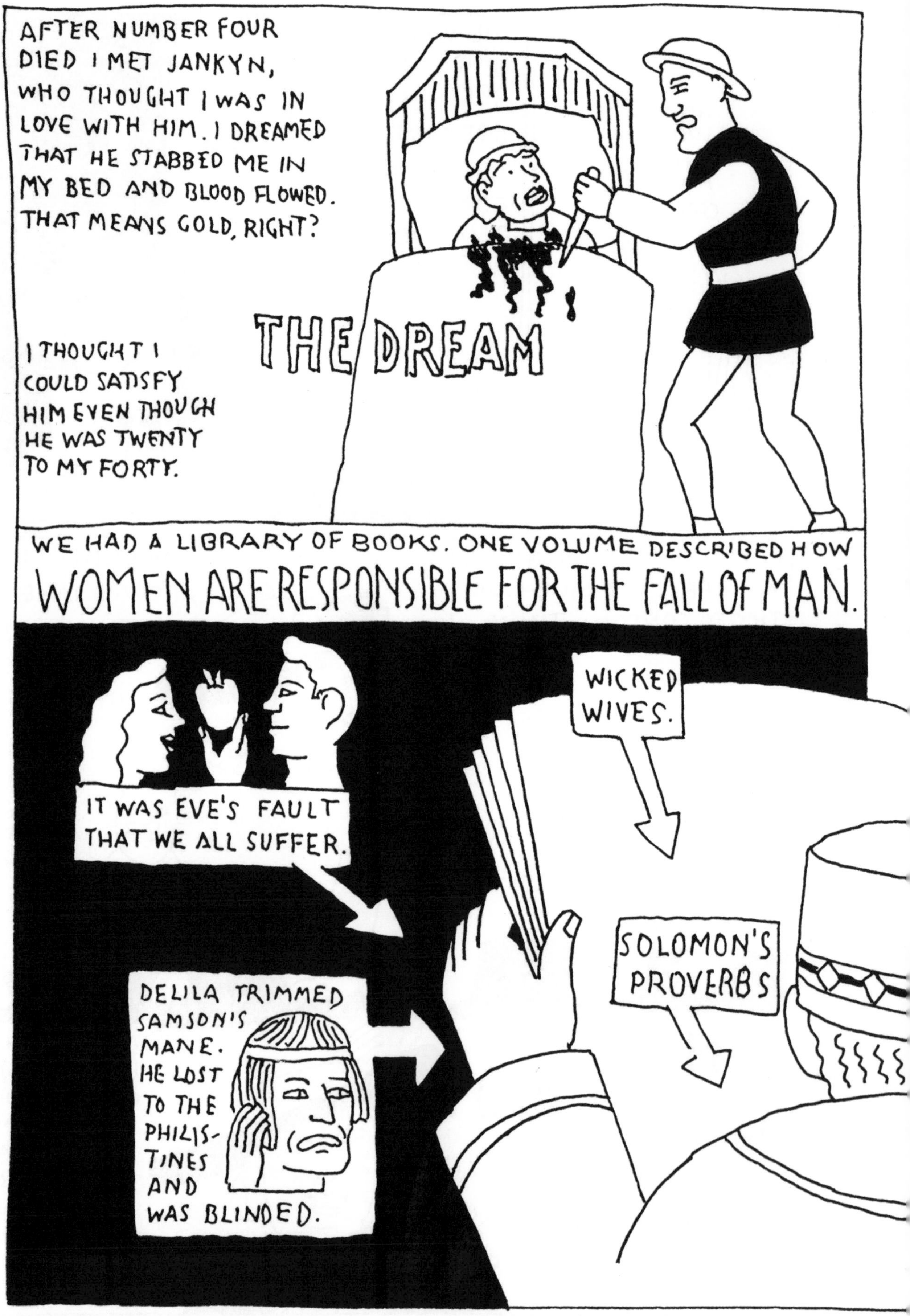
AFTER NUMBER FOUR DIED I MET JANKYN, WHO THOUGHT I WAS IN LOVE WITH HIM. I DREAMED THAT HE STABBED ME IN MY BED AND BLOOD FLOWED. THAT MEANS GOLD, RIGHT?
THE DREAM
I THOUGHT I COULD SATISFY HIM EVEN THOUGH HE WAS TWENTY TO MY FORTY.
WE HAD A LIBRARY OF BOOKS. ONE VOLUME DESCRIBED HOW
WOMEN ARE RESPONSIBLE FOR THE FALL OF MAN.
IT WAS EVE'S FAULT THAT WE ALL SUFFER.
WICKED WIVES.
SOLOMON'S PROVERBS
DELILA TRIMMED SAMSON'S MANE. HE LOST TO THE PHILIS-TINES AND WAS BLINDED.

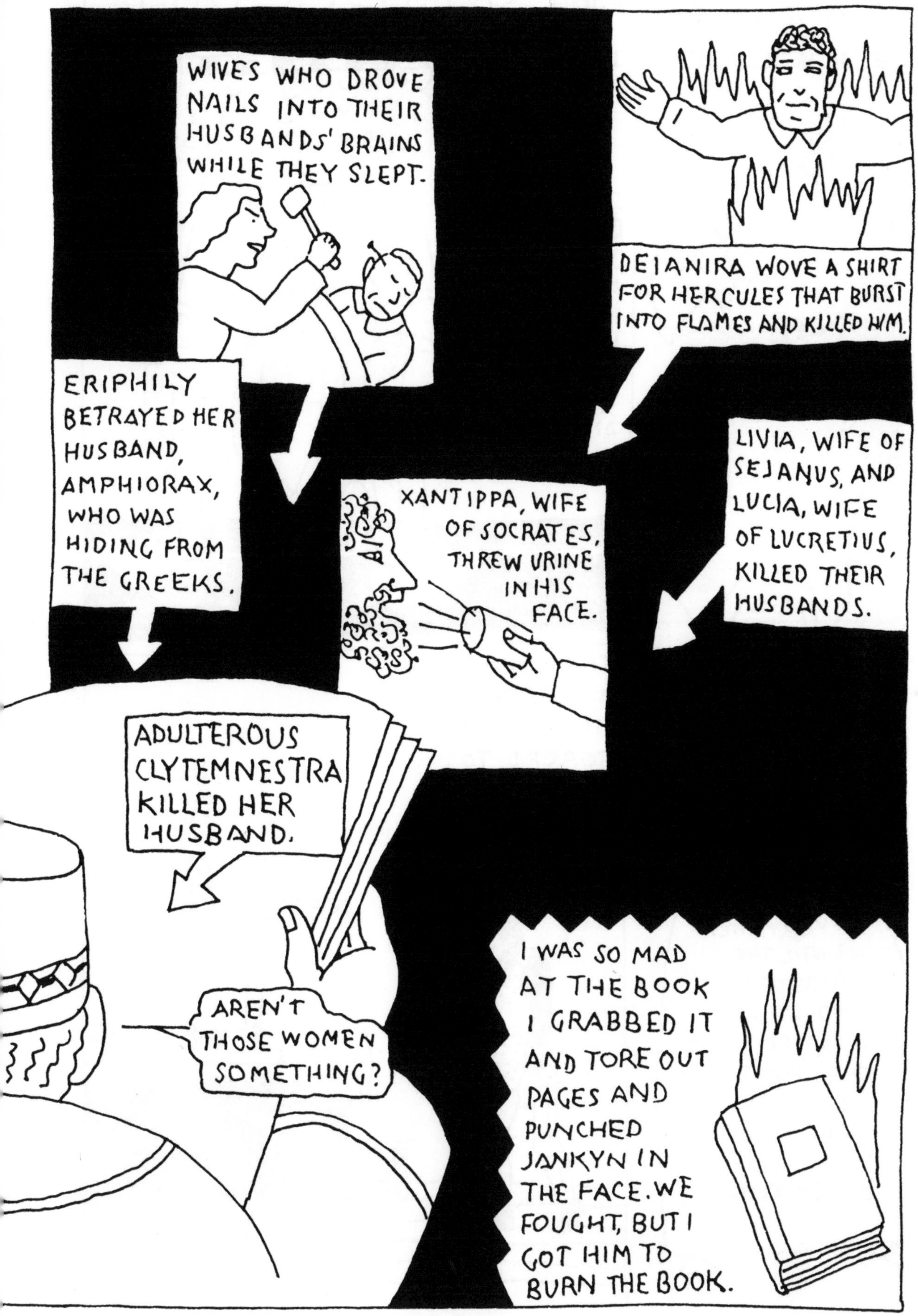
WIVES WHO DROVE NAILS INTO THEIR HUSBANDS' BRAINS WHILE THEY SLEPT.
DEIANIRA WOVE A SHIRT FOR HERCULES THAT BURST INTO FLAMES AND KILLED HIM.
ERIPHILY BETRAYED HER HUSBAND, AMPHIORAX, WHO WAS HIDING FROM THE GREEKS.
XANTIPPA, WIFE OF SOCRATES, THREW URINE IN HIS FACE.
LIVIA, WIFE OF SEJANUS, AND LUCIA, WIFE OF LUCRETIUS, KILLED THEIR HUSBANDS.
ADULTEROUS CLYTEMNESTRA KILLED HER HUSBAND.
AREN'T THOSE WOMEN SOMETHING?
I WAS SO MAD AT THE BOOK I GRABBED IT AND TORE OUT PAGES AND PUNCHED JANKYN IN THE FACE. WE FOUGHT, BUT I GOT HIM TO BURN THE BOOK.

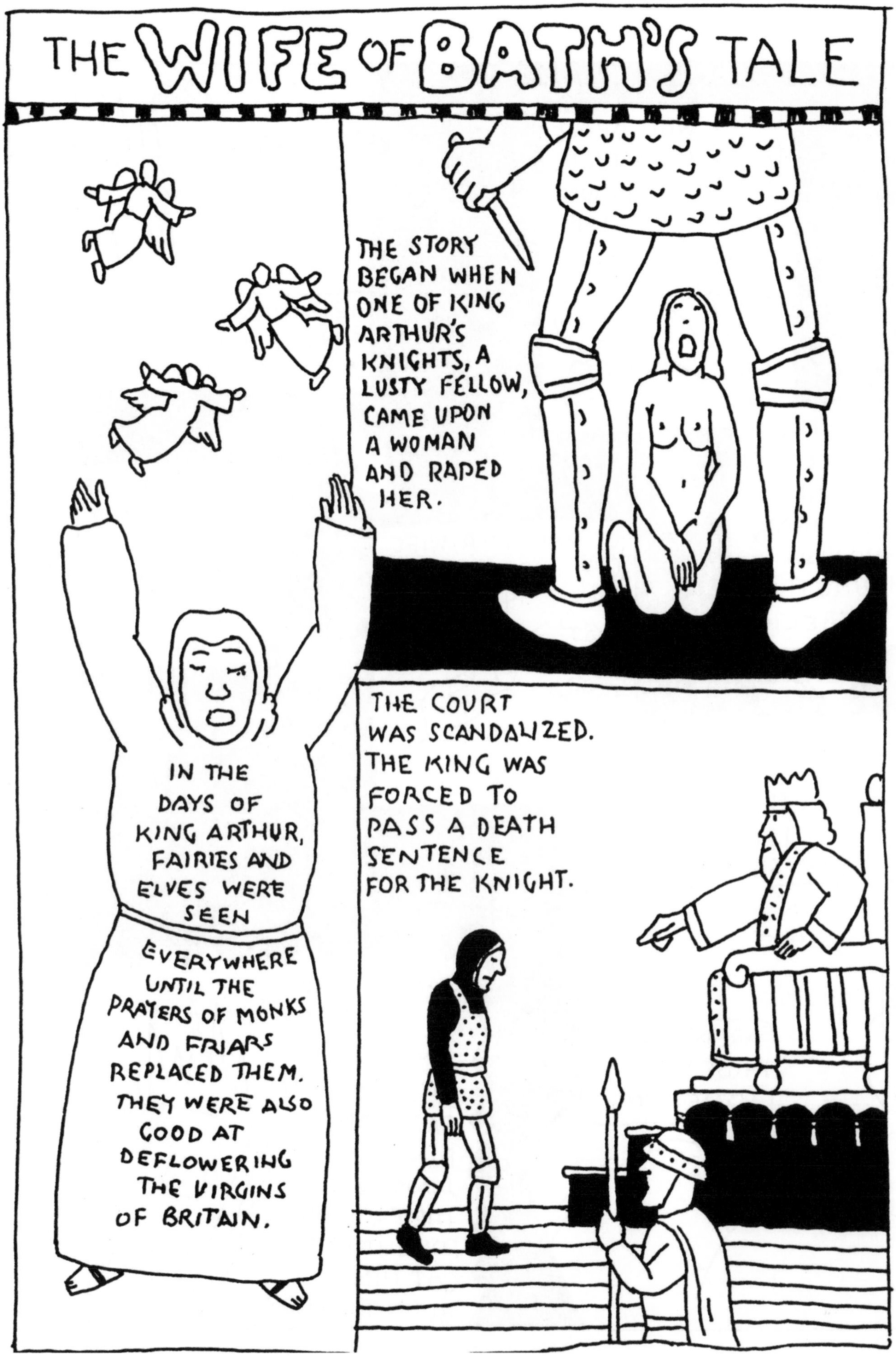
THE WIFE OF BATH'S TALE
IN THE DAYS OF KING ARTHUR, FAIRIES AND ELVES WERE SEEN
EVERYWHERE UNTIL THE PRAYERS OF MONKS AND FRIARS REPLACED THEM. THEY WERE ALSO GOOD AT DEFLOWERING THE VIRGINS OF BRITAIN.
THE STORY BEGAN WHEN ONE OF KING ARTHUR'S KNIGHTS, A LUSTY FELLOW, CAME UPON A WOMAN AND RAPED HER.
THE COURT WAS SCANDALIZED. THE KING WAS FORCED TO PASS A DEATH SENTENCE FOR THE KNIGHT.

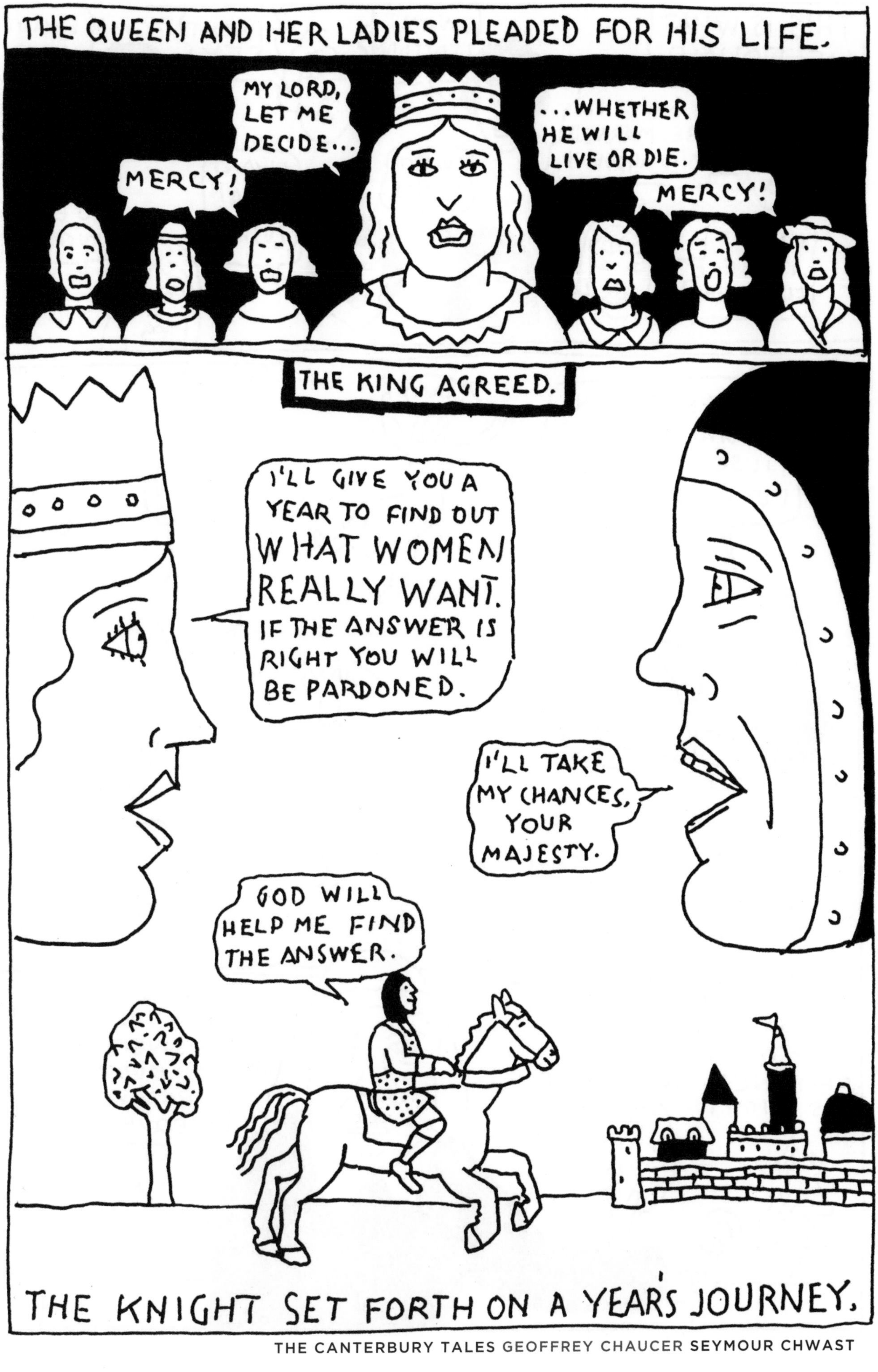
THE QUEEN AND HER LADIES PLEADED FOR HIS LIFE.
MERCY!
MY LORD, LET ME DECIDE...
...WHETHER HE WILL LIVE OR DIE.
MERCY!
THE KING AGREED.
I'LL GIVE YOU A YEAR TO FIND OUT WHAT WOMEN REALLY WANT. IF THE ANSWER IS RIGHT YOU WILL BE PARDONED.
I'LL TAKE MY CHANCES, YOUR MAJESTY.
GOD WILL HELP ME FIND THE ANSWER.
THE KNIGHT SET FORTH ON A YEAR'S JOURNEY.

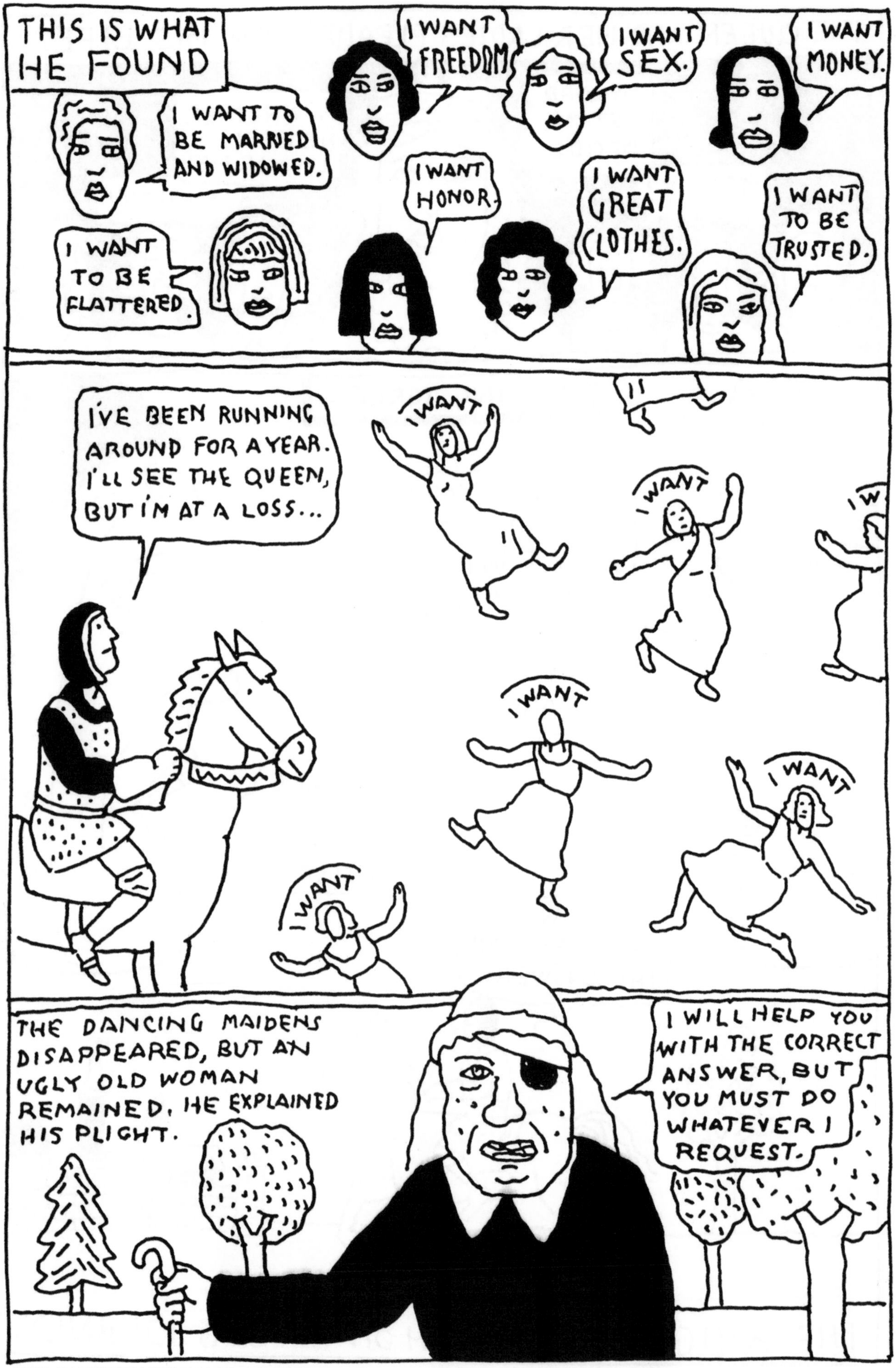
THIS IS WHAT HE FOUND
I WANT FREEDOM
I WANT SEX.
I WANT MONEY.
I WANT TO BE MARRIED AND WIDOWED.
I WANT HONOR.
I WANT GREAT CLOTHES.
I WANT TO BE TRUSTED.
I WANT TO BE FLATTERED.
I'VE BEEN RUNNING AROUND FOR A YEAR. I'LL SEE THE QUEEN, BUT I'M AT A LOSS...
I WANT
I WANT
I WANT
I WANT
I WANT
THE DANCING MAIDENS DISAPPEARED, BUT AN UGLY OLD WOMAN REMAINED. HE EXPLAINED HIS PLIGHT.
I WILL HELP YOU WITH THE CORRECT ANSWER, BUT YOU MUST DO WHATEVER I REQUEST.

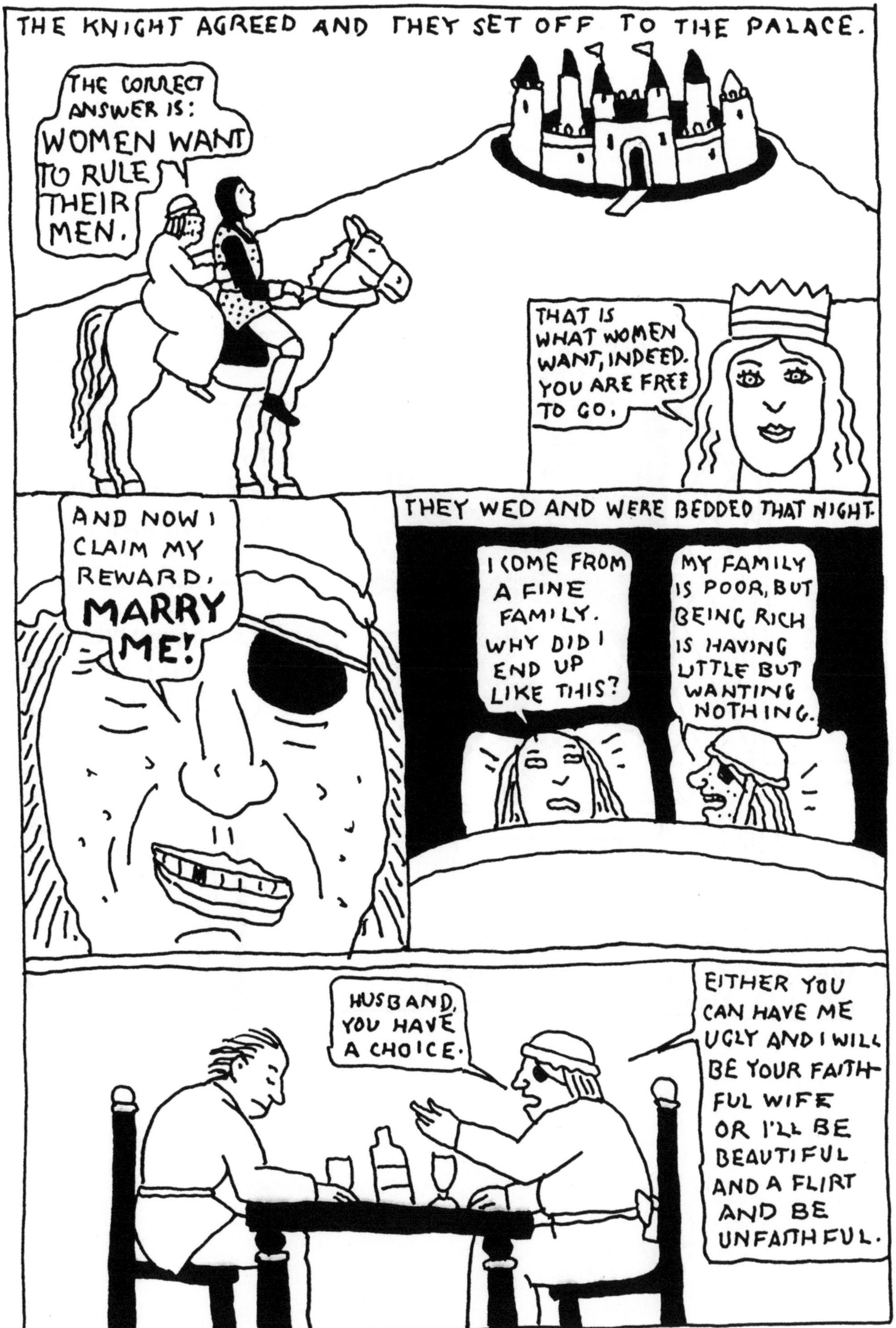

THE KNIGHT AGREED AND THEY SET OFF TO THE PALACE.
THE CORRECT ANSWER IS: WOMEN WANT TO RULE THEIR MEN.
THAT IS WHAT WOMEN WANT, INDEED. YOU ARE FREE TO GO.
AND NOW I CLAIM MY REWARD. MARRY ME!
THEY WED AND WERE BEDDED THAT NIGHT.
I COME FROM A FINE FAMILY. WHY DID I END UP LIKE THIS?
MY FAMILY IS POOR, BUT BEING RICH IS HAVING LITTLE BUT WANTING NOTHING.
HUSBAND, YOU HAVE A CHOICE.
EITHER YOU CAN HAVE ME UGLY AND I WILL BE YOUR FAITHFUL WIFE OR I'LL BE BEAUTIFUL AND A FLIRT AND BE UNFAITHFUL.

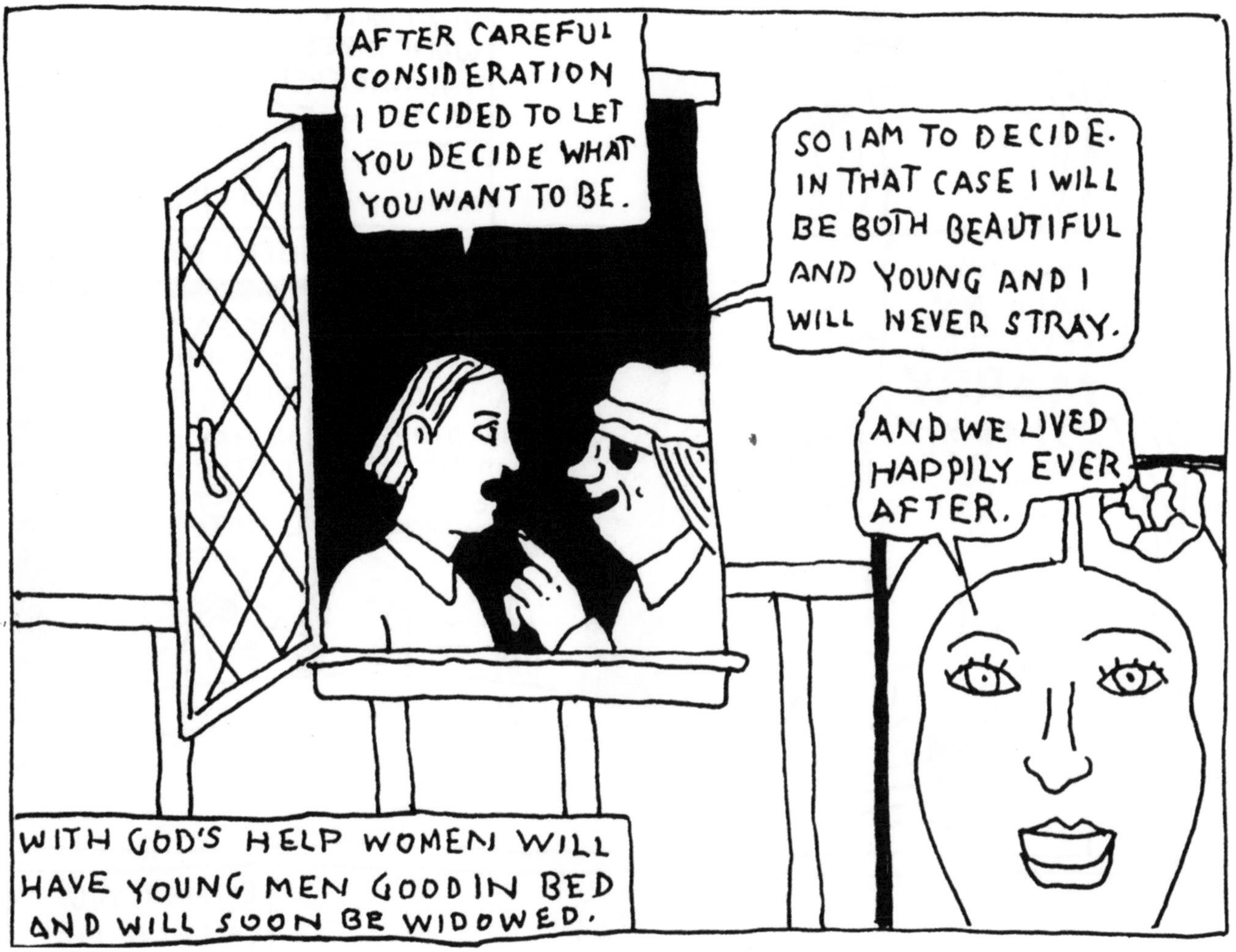
AFTER CAREFUL CONSIDERATION I DECIDED TO LET YOU DECIDE WHAT YOU WANT TO BE.
SO I AM TO DECIDE. IN THAT CASE I WILL BE BOTH BEAUTIFUL AND YOUNG AND I WILL NEVER STRAY.
AND WE LIVED HAPPILY EVER AFTER.
WITH GOD'S HELP WOMEN WILL HAVE YOUNG MEN GOOD IN BED AND WILL SOON BE WIDOWED.

Le Morte d'Arthur

Sir Thomas Malory

ART / ADAPTATION BY **Omaha Perez**

ALMOST ALL ENGLISH-LANGUAGE LITERATURE ON King Arthur flows from the 1,000-page *Le Morte d'Arthur* that Sir Thomas Malory completed in 1470 (it was published fifteen years later, after his death). He gathered and translated the best of the many Norman-French tales that had appeared over the prior two centuries, added some Old English material, and perhaps created some of his own tales, then arranged them to form a mostly coherent storyline. Pretty much everything you expect from the genre is here: the sword in the stone, the Round Table, the Holy Grail, the Lady of the Lake, Merlin, Lancelot, Guinevere. . . .

Interesting backstory: Malory was able to complete this behemoth only because he spent so much time in various jails, which gave him plenty of free time. Despite being born into a well-to-do family and serving as a distinguished soldier and a Member of Parliament, he became a rampant criminal, doing time for robbery, extortion, rape, attempted murder, and a host of other crimes.

Omaha Perez, who ventured into literary territory before with Sherlock Holmes, has adapted the tale of unfortunate Sir Gawain(e), told in chapters seven and eight of Book Three. (Just so you know, at the very end of this tale, which Omaha omitted because it's so anticlimactic, King Arthur and Queen Guinevere decree that Gawaine must go on lots of missions for ladies, must be courteous, and must give mercy to those who ask for it.)

SOURCE

Graves, Robert. "Introduction." In *Malory's Le Morte d'Arthur: King Arthur and the Legends of the Round Table*. Signet Classic, 2001.

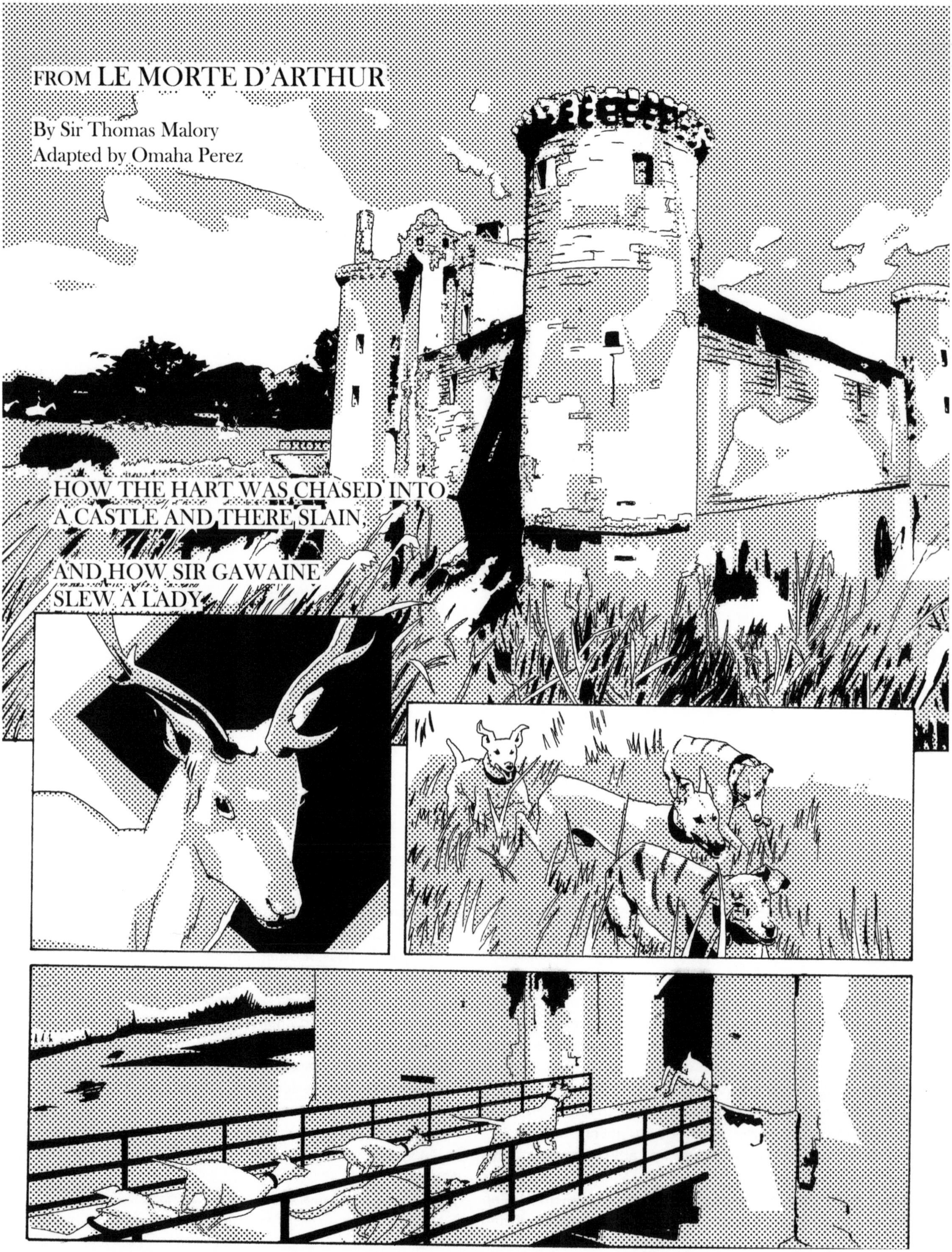
FROM LE MORTE D'ARTHUR
By Sir Thomas Malory
Adapted by Omaha Perez
HOW THE HART WAS CHASED INTO A CASTLE AND THERE SLAIN,
AND HOW SIR GAWAINE SLEW A LADY

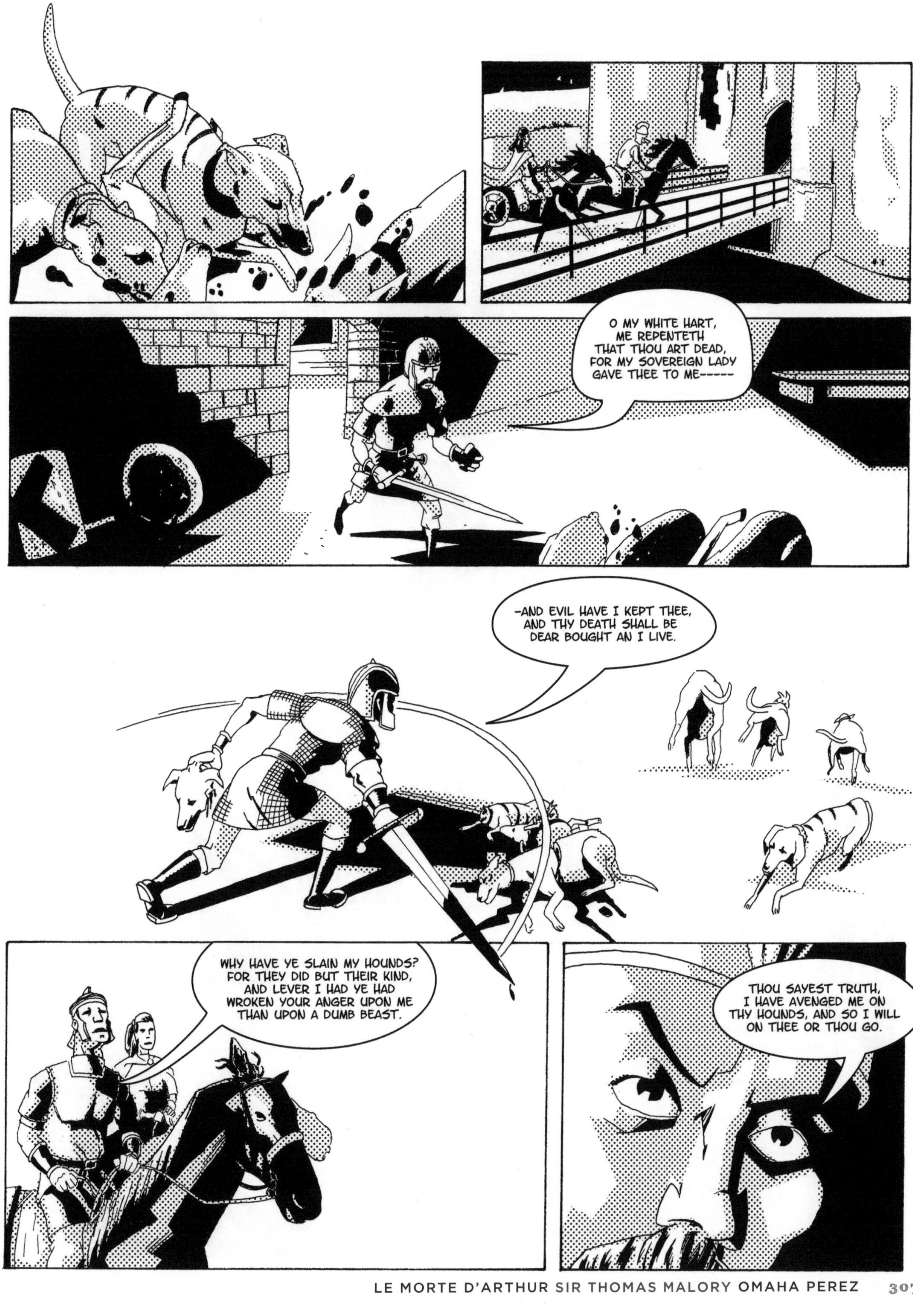
O MY WHITE HART, ME REPENTETH THAT THOU ART DEAD, FOR MY SOVEREIGN LADY GAVE THEE TO ME-----
-AND EVIL HAVE I KEPT THEE, AND THY DEATH SHALL BE DEAR BOUGHT AN I LIVE.
WHY HAVE YE SLAIN MY HOUNDS? FOR THEY DID BUT THEIR KIND, AND LEVER I HAD YE HAD WROKEN YOUR ANGER UPON ME THAN UPON A DUMB BEAST.
THOU SAYEST TRUTH, I HAVE AVENGED ME ON THY HOUNDS, AND SO I WILL ON THEE OR THOU GO.

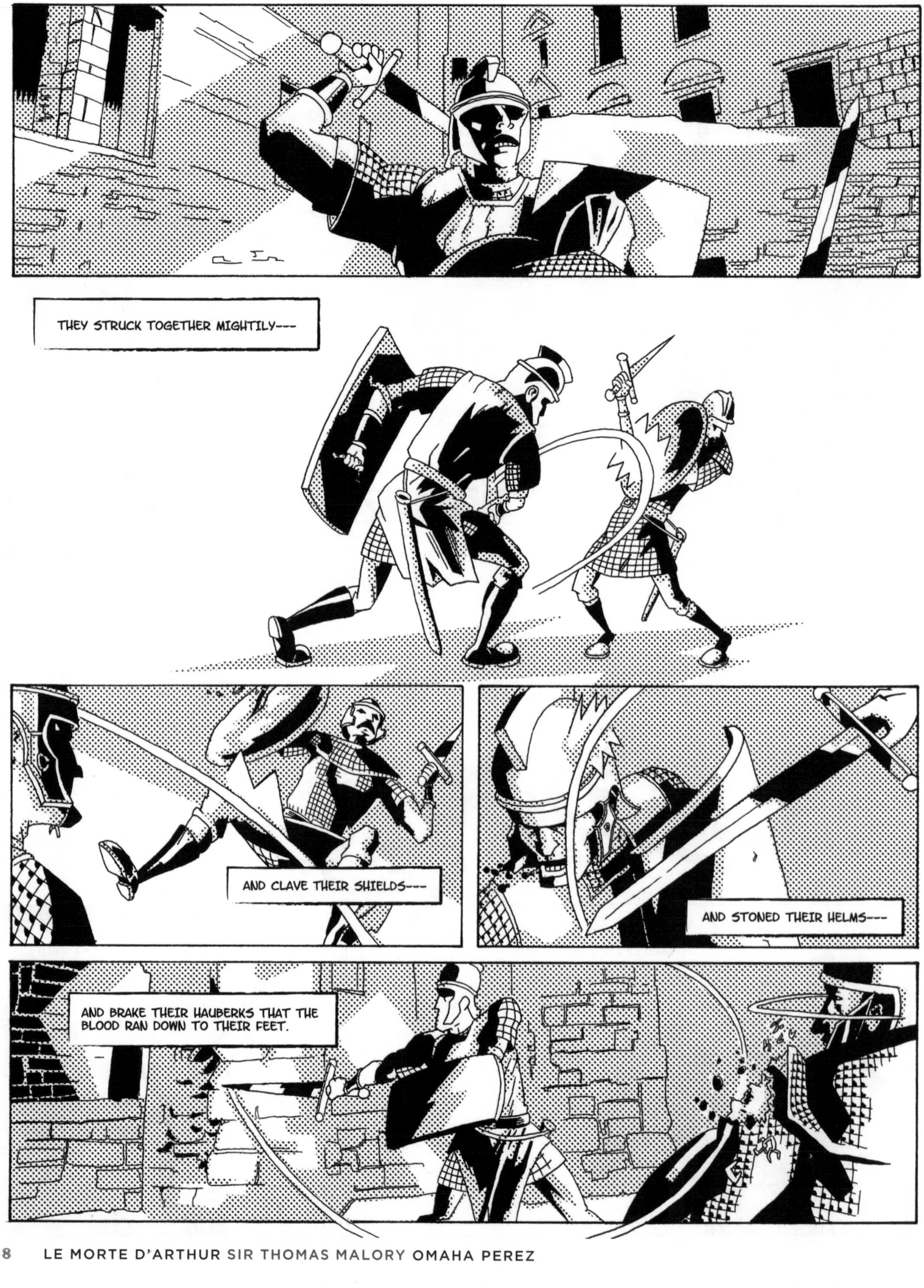
THEY STRUCK TOGETHER MIGHTILY---
AND CLAVE THEIR SHIELDS---
AND STONED THEIR HELMS---
AND BRAKE THEIR HAUBERKS THAT THE BLOOD RAN DOWN TO THEIR FEET.

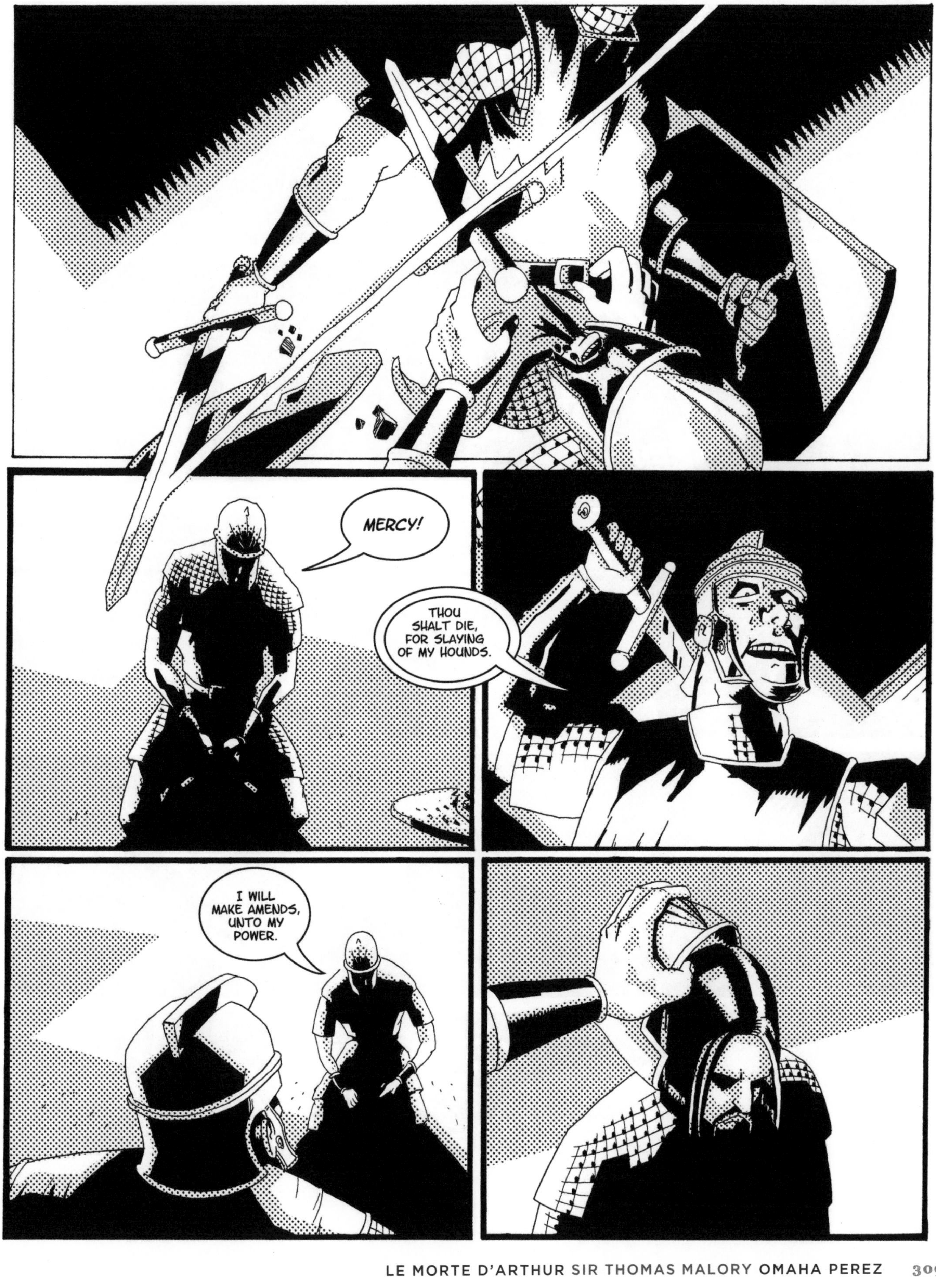
MERCY!
THOU SHALT DIE, FOR SLAYING OF MY HOUNDS.
I WILL MAKE AMENDS, UNTO MY POWER.

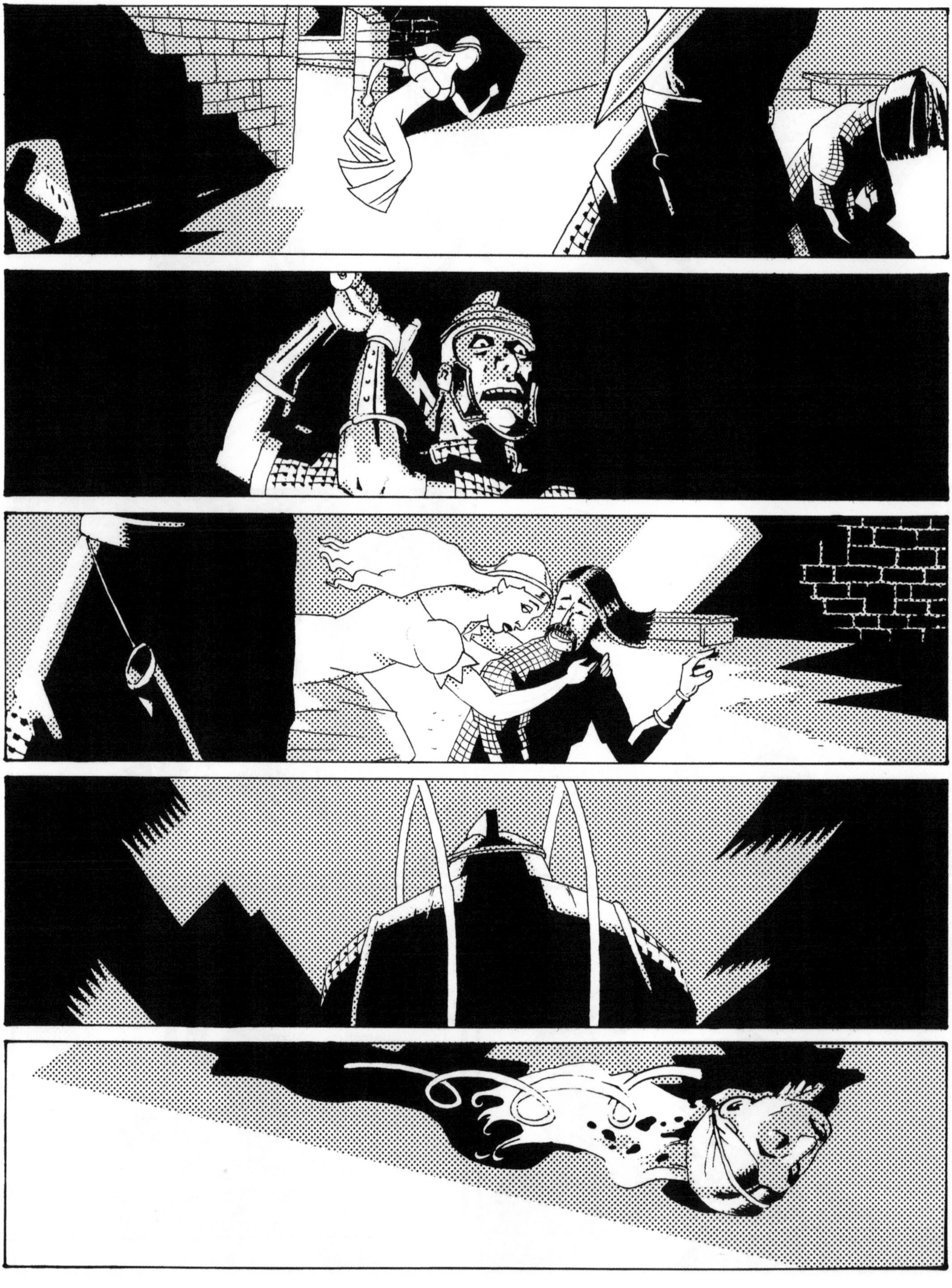

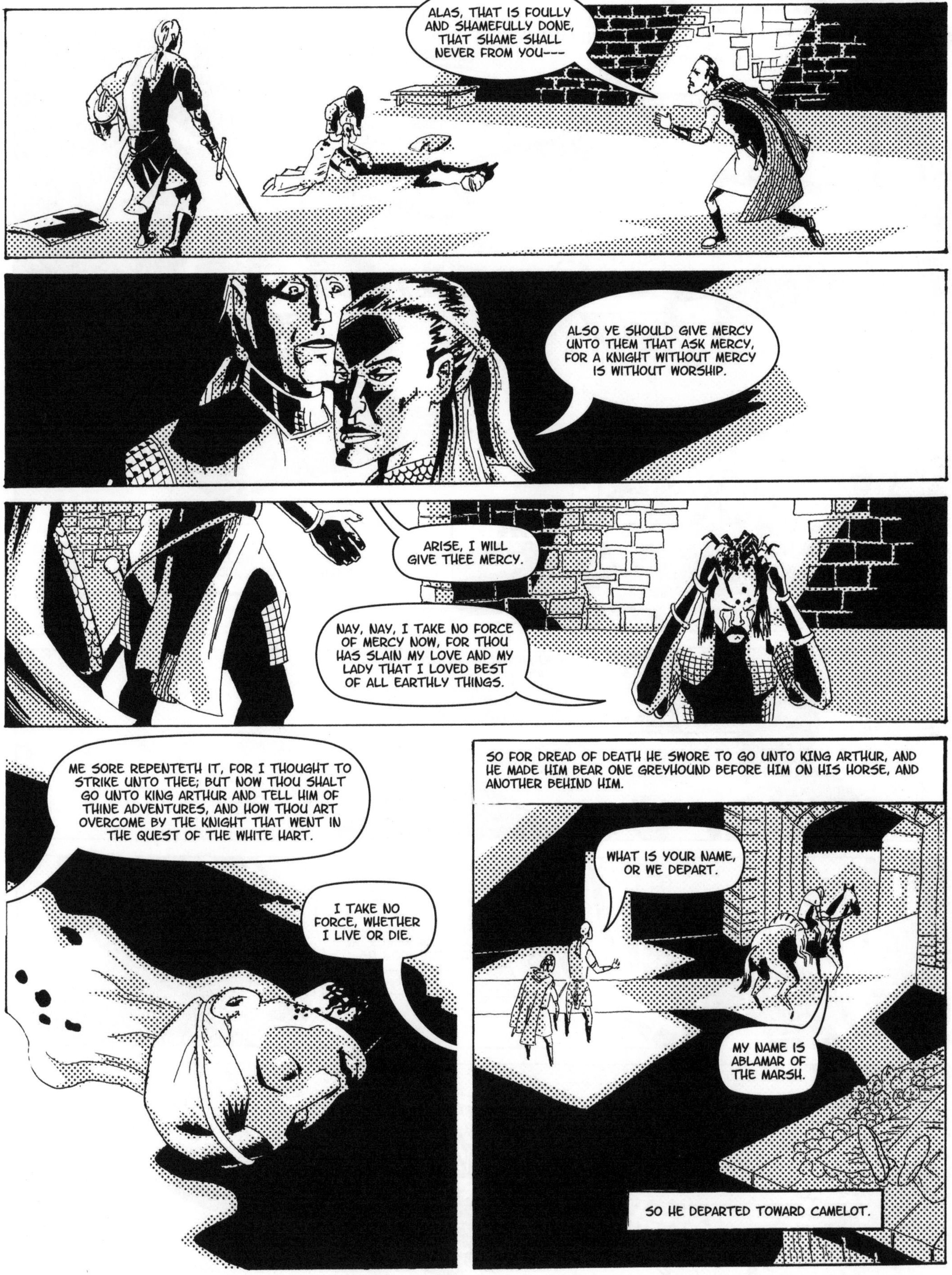
ALAS, THAT IS FOULLY AND SHAMEFULLY DONE, THAT SHAME SHALL NEVER FROM YOU---
ALSO YE SHOULD GIVE MERCY UNTO THEM THAT ASK MERCY, FOR A KNIGHT WITHOUT MERCY IS WITHOUT WORSHIP.
ARISE, I WILL GIVE THEE MERCY.
NAY, NAY, I TAKE NO FORCE OF MERCY NOW, FOR THOU HAS SLAIN MY LOVE AND MY LADY THAT I LOVED BEST OF ALL EARTHLY THINGS.
ME SORE REPENTETH IT, FOR I THOUGHT TO STRIKE UNTO THEE; BUT NOW THOU SHALT GO UNTO KING ARTHUR AND TELL HIM OF THINE ADVENTURES, AND HOW THOU ART OVERCOME BY THE KNIGHT THAT WENT IN THE QUEST OF THE WHITE HART.
I TAKE NO FORCE, WHETHER I LIVE OR DIE.
SO FOR DREAD OF DEATH HE SWORE TO GO UNTO KING ARTHUR, AND HE MADE HIM BEAR ONE GREYHOUND BEFORE HIM ON HIS HORSE, AND ANOTHER BEHIND HIM.
WHAT IS YOUR NAME, OR WE DEPART.
MY NAME IS ABLAMAR OF THE MARSH.
SO HE DEPARTED TOWARD CAMELOT.

HOW FOUR KNIGHTS FOUGHT AGAINST GAWAINE AND GAHERIS, AND HOW THEY WERE OVERCOME, AND THEIR LIVES SAVED AT REQUEST OF FOUR LADIES

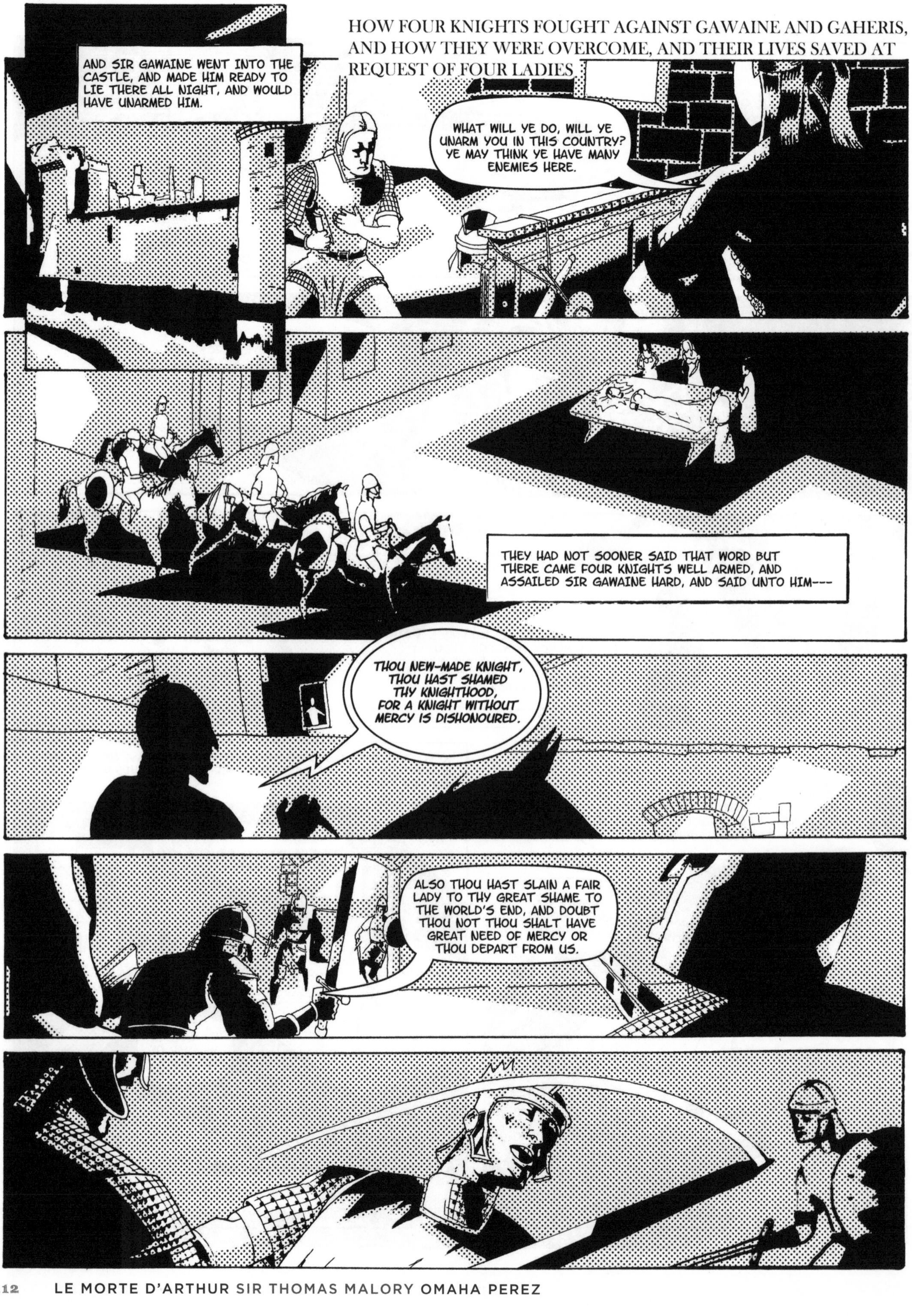
AND SIR GAWAINE WENT INTO THE CASTLE, AND MADE HIM READY TO LIE THERE ALL NIGHT, AND WOULD HAVE UNARMED HIM.
WHAT WILL YE DO, WILL YE UNARM YOU IN THIS COUNTRY? YE MAY THINK YE HAVE MANY ENEMIES HERE.
THEY HAD NOT SOONER SAID THAT WORD BUT THERE CAME FOUR KNIGHTS WELL ARMED, AND ASSAILED SIR GAWAINE HARD, AND SAID UNTO HIM---
THOU NEW-MADE KNIGHT, THOU HAST SHAMED THY KNIGHTHOOD, FOR A KNIGHT WITHOUT MERCY IS DISHONOURED.
ALSO THOU HAST SLAIN A FAIR LADY TO THY GREAT SHAME TO THE WORLD'S END, AND DOUBT THOU NOT THOU SHALT HAVE GREAT NEED OF MERCY OR THOU DEPART FROM US.

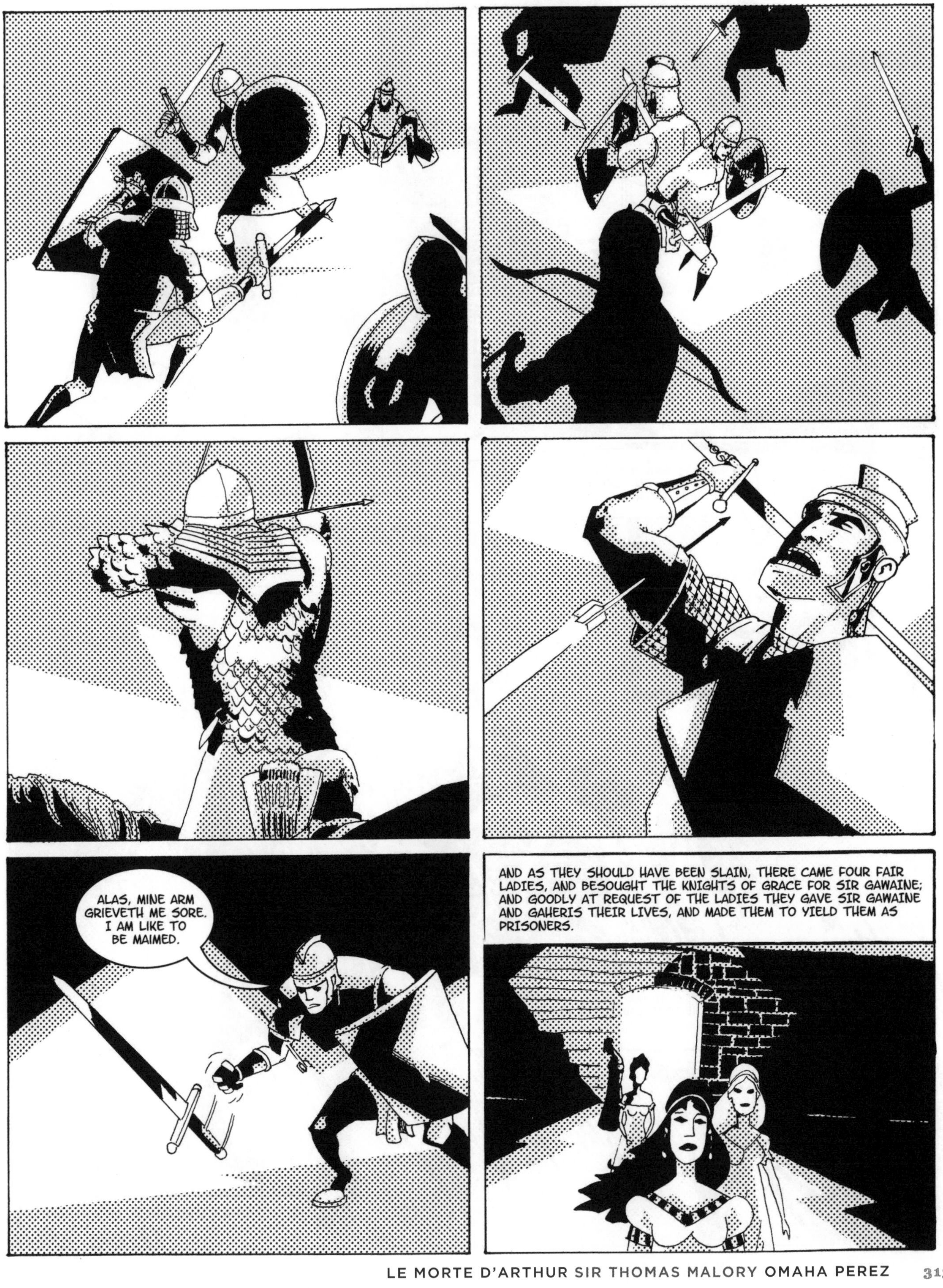
ALAS, MINE ARM GRIEVETH ME SORE. I AM LIKE TO BE MAIMED.
AND AS THEY SHOULD HAVE BEEN SLAIN, THERE CAME FOUR FAIR LADIES, AND BESOUGHT THE KNIGHTS OF GRACE FOR SIR GAWAINE; AND GOODLY AT REQUEST OF THE LADIES THEY GAVE SIR GAWAINE AND GAHERIS THEIR LIVES, AND MADE THEM TO YIELD THEM AS PRISONERS.

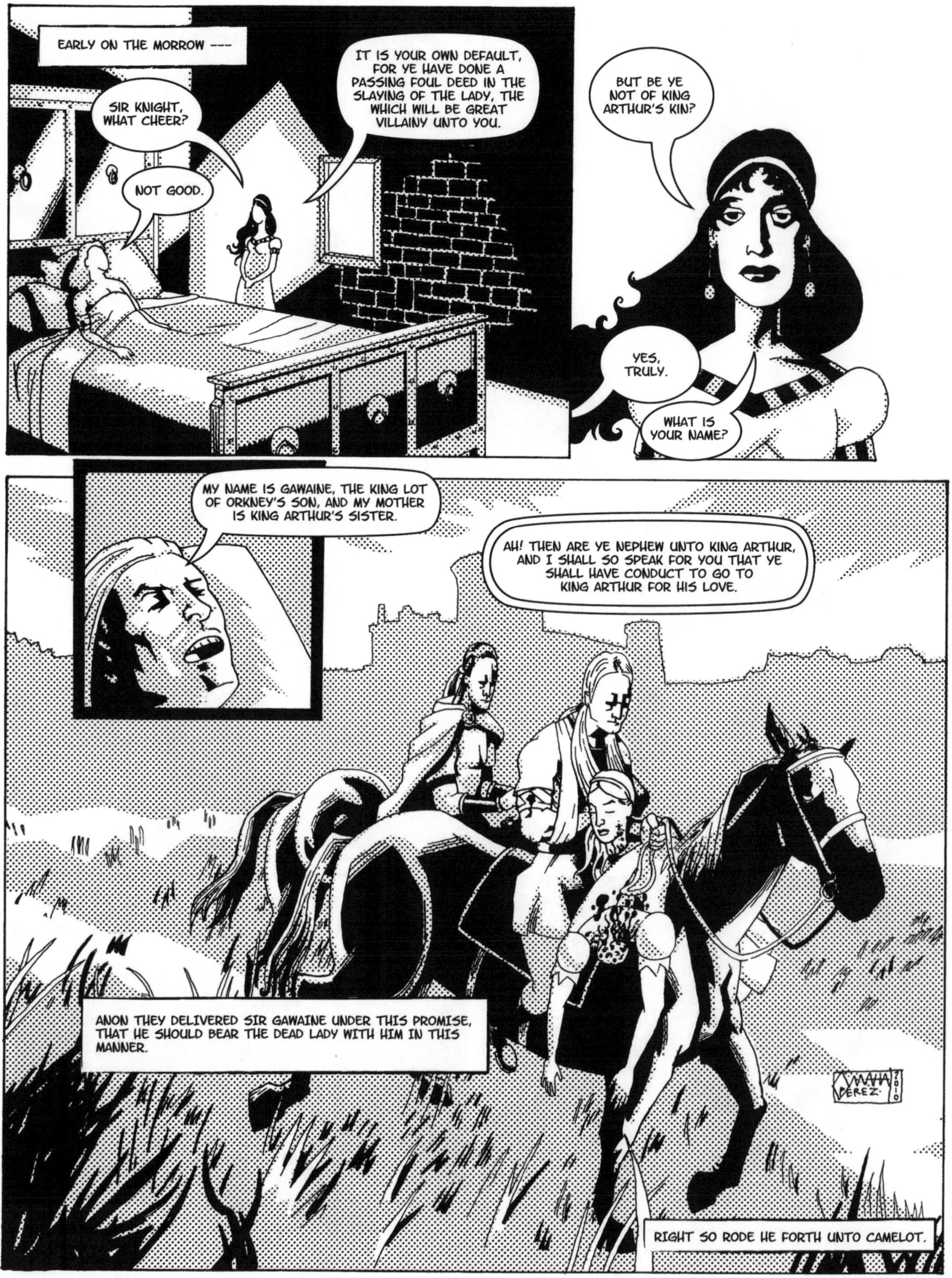
EARLY ON THE MORROW ---
SIR KNIGHT, WHAT CHEER?
NOT GOOD.
IT IS YOUR OWN DEFAULT, FOR YE HAVE DONE A PASSING FOUL DEED IN THE SLAYING OF THE LADY, THE WHICH WILL BE GREAT VILLAINY UNTO YOU.
BUT BE YE NOT OF KING ARTHUR'S KIN?
YES, TRULY.
WHAT IS YOUR NAME?
MY NAME IS GAWAINE, THE KING LOT OF ORKNEY'S SON, AND MY MOTHER IS KING ARTHUR'S SISTER.
AH! THEN ARE YE NEPHEW UNTO KING ARTHUR, AND I SHALL SO SPEAK FOR YOU THAT YE SHALL HAVE CONDUCT TO GO TO KING ARTHUR FOR HIS LOVE.
ANON THEY DELIVERED SIR GAWAINE UNDER THIS PROMISE, THAT HE SHOULD BEAR THE DEAD LADY WITH HIM IN THIS MANNER.
OMAHA PEREZ 2010
RIGHT SO RODE HE FORTH UNTO CAMELOT.

Apu Ollantay
an Incan play
ART / ADAPTATION BY **Caroline Picard**

THE ANCIENT INCAS HAD A STRONG PENCHANT for theater. The Spanish invasion all but wiped out this facet—along with every other facet—of their culture, but a single play survives. *Apu Ollantay* remained in the memories of some of the Incas (like most indigenous peoples, they had a mainly oral culture, rather than a written one), and a Spanish priest had it transcribed. It appears to be the only full play from pre-Columbian Native Americans to have survived. Given this unique and important status, you'd think that it would be better known, yet it languishes in obscurity in the English-speaking world—almost never performed or anthologized, ignored in every history of theater I've checked. (It does fare better in the Spanish-speaking world.)

It's an old-fashioned love story, the kind that appears in every age and culture. The great chieftain and warrior, Apu Ollantay, and the emperor's daughter, Cusi Coyllur, are in love, but there's a star-crossed problem—only someone of royal blood may marry the princess. The two secretly wed and she becomes pregnant. Trouble, including civil war, ensues. . . .

Chicago artist and writer Caroline Picard creates highly inventive comics. Pushing the form forward, she arranges and integrates images and words to create a unique, sinuous flow. Panels as such don't exist. Everything blends seamlessly, and each page seems like a single work of art even though it contains a sequential narrative. Caroline has adapted the entire play here, abridging it somewhat, mainly by condensing the military action.

SOURCE

Apu Ollantay: A Drama of the Time of the Incas. Translated by Sir Clements Markham, K. C. B. [No publisher], 1910.

315

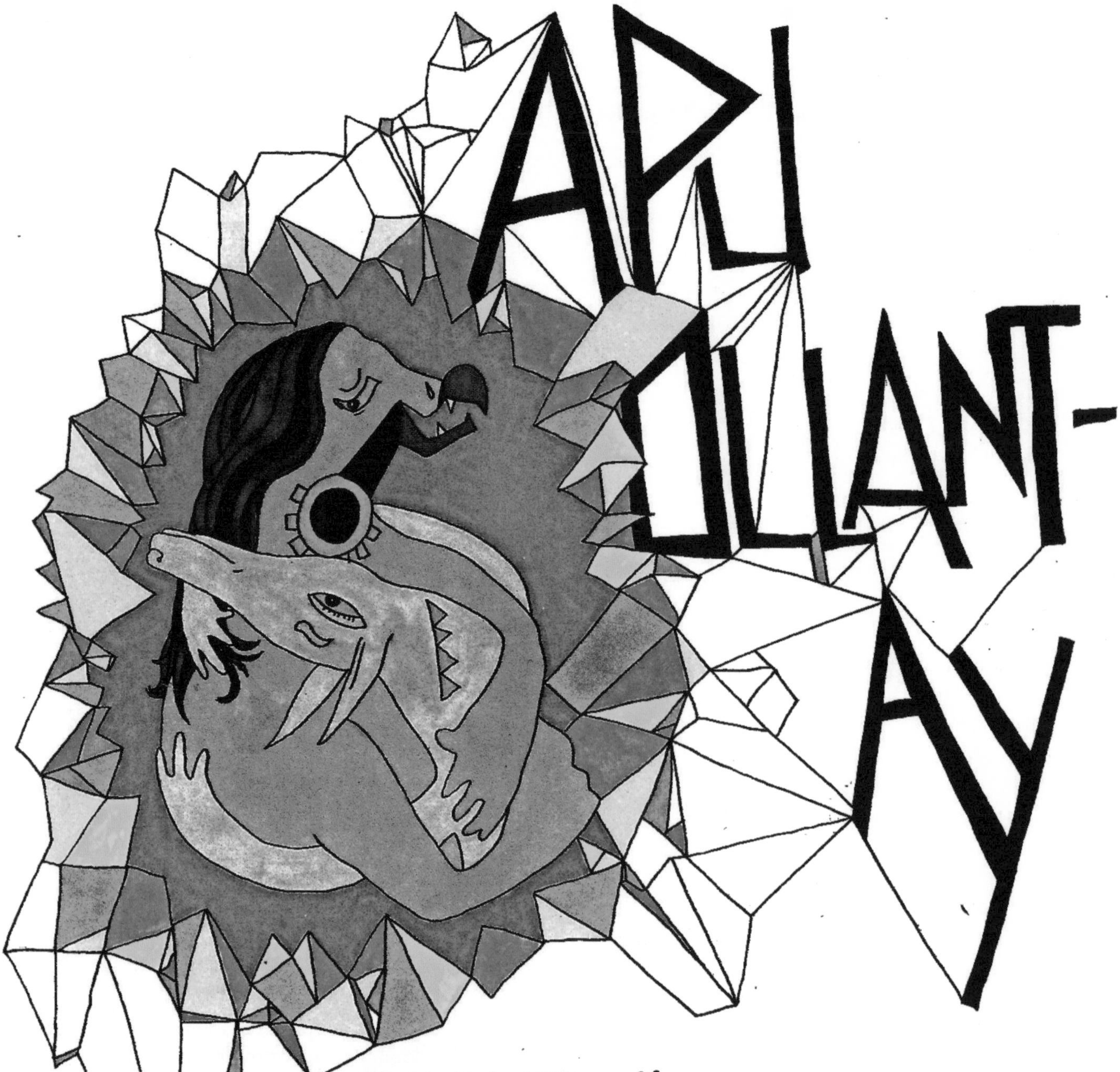
APU OLLANTAY

TRANSLATED BY

SIR CLEMENTS R. MARKHAM

ABRIDGED & ILLUSTRATED BY CAROLINE PICARD

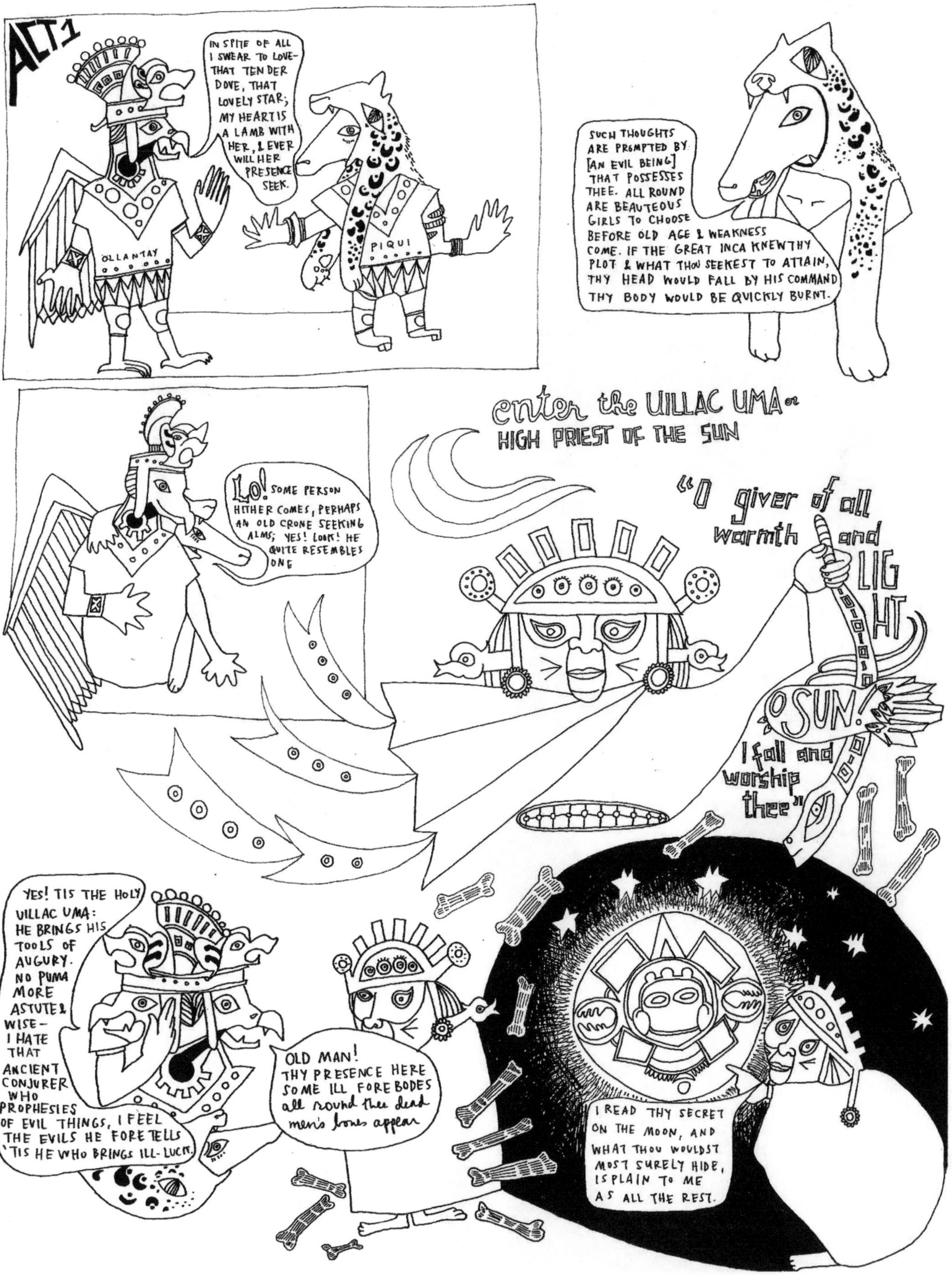
ACT 1
IN SPITE OF ALL I SWEAR TO LOVE-THAT TENDER DOVE, THAT LOVELY STAR; MY HEART IS A LAMB WITH HER, & EVER WILL HER PRESENCE SEEK.
OLLANTAY
PIQUI
SUCH THOUGHTS ARE PROMPTED BY [AN EVIL BEING] THAT POSSESSES THEE. ALL ROUND ARE BEAUTEOUS GIRLS TO CHOOSE BEFORE OLD AGE & WEAKNESS COME. IF THE GREAT INCA KNEW THY PLOT & WHAT THOU SEEKEST TO ATTAIN, THY HEAD WOULD FALL BY HIS COMMAND THY BODY WOULD BE QUICKLY BURNT.
enter the UILLAC UMA or HIGH PRIEST OF THE SUN
LO! SOME PERSON HITHER COMES, PERHAPS AN OLD CRONE SEEKING ALMS; YES! LOOK! HE QUITE RESEMBLES ONE
"O giver of all warmth and LIGHT
O SUN!
I fall and worship thee"
YES! TIS THE HOLY UILLAC UMA: HE BRINGS HIS TOOLS OF AUGURY. NO PUMA MORE ASTUTE & WISE- I HATE THAT ANCIENT CONJURER WHO PROPHESIES OF EVIL THINGS, I FEEL THE EVILS HE FORETELLS 'TIS HE WHO BRINGS ILL-LUCK.
OLD MAN! THY PRESENCE HERE SOME ILL FOREBODES all round thee dead men's bones appear
I READ THY SECRET ON THE MOON, AND WHAT THOU WOULDST MOST SURELY HIDE, IS PLAIN TO ME AS ALL THE REST.

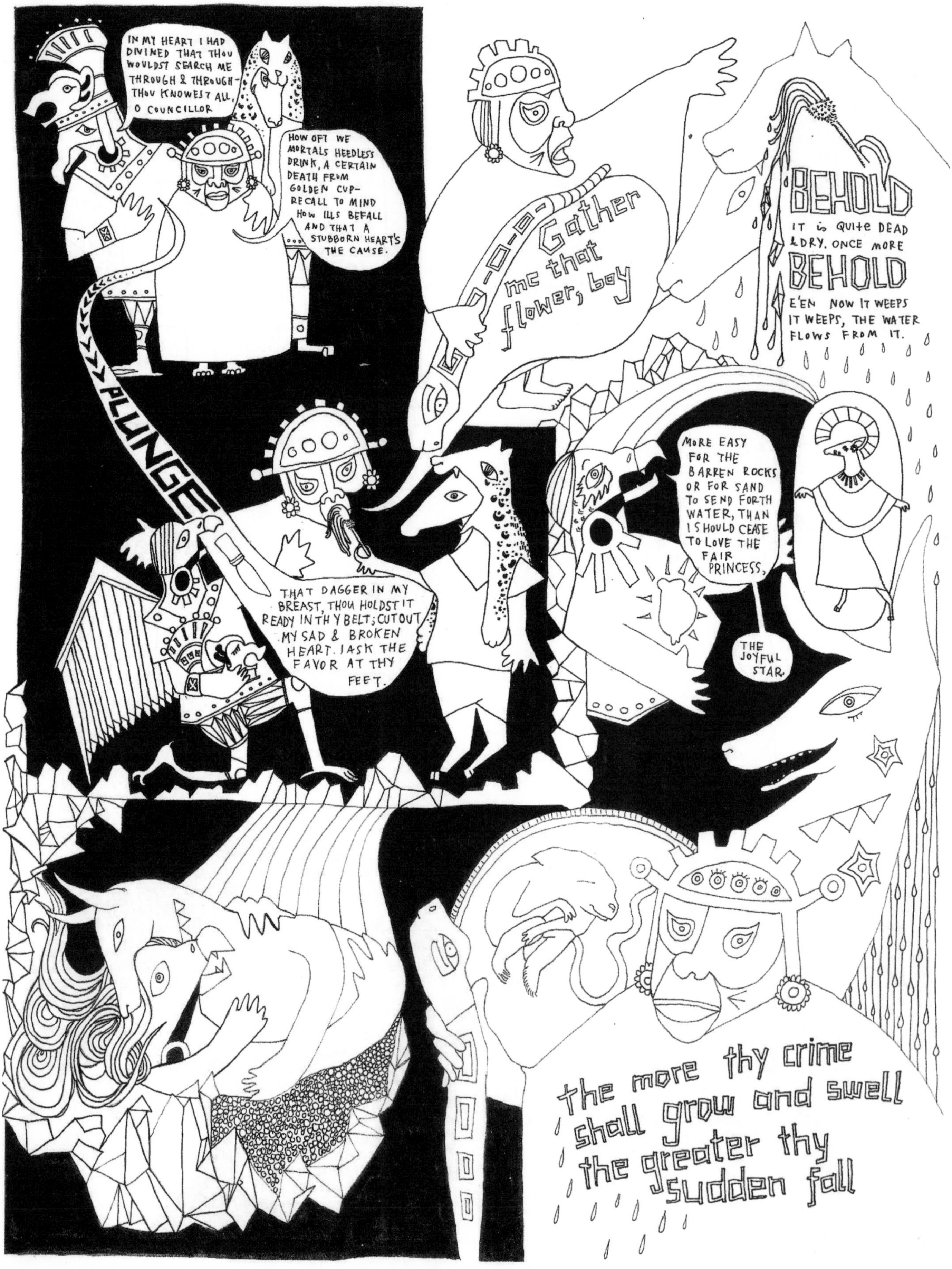
IN MY HEART I HAD DIVINED THAT THOU WOULDST SEARCH ME THROUGH & THROUGH - THOU KNOWEST ALL, O COUNCILLOR
HOW OFT WE MORTALS HEEDLESS DRINK, A CERTAIN DEATH FROM GOLDEN CUP - RECALL TO MIND HOW ILLS BEFALL AND THAT A STUBBORN HEART'S THE CAUSE.
O-O-O-Gather me that flower, boy
BEHOLD
IT is Quite DEAD & DRY. ONCE MORE
BEHOLD
E'EN NOW IT WEEPS IT WEEPS, THE WATER FLOWS FROM IT.
PLUNGE
THAT DAGGER IN MY BREAST, THOU HOLDST IT READY IN THY BELT; CUT OUT MY SAD & BROKEN HEART. I ASK THE FAVOR AT THY FEET.
MORE EASY FOR THE BARREN ROCKS OR FOR SAND TO SEND FORTH WATER, THAN I SHOULD CEASE TO LOVE THE FAIR PRINCESS,
THE JOYFUL STAR.
the more thy crime shall grow and swell the greater thy sudden fall

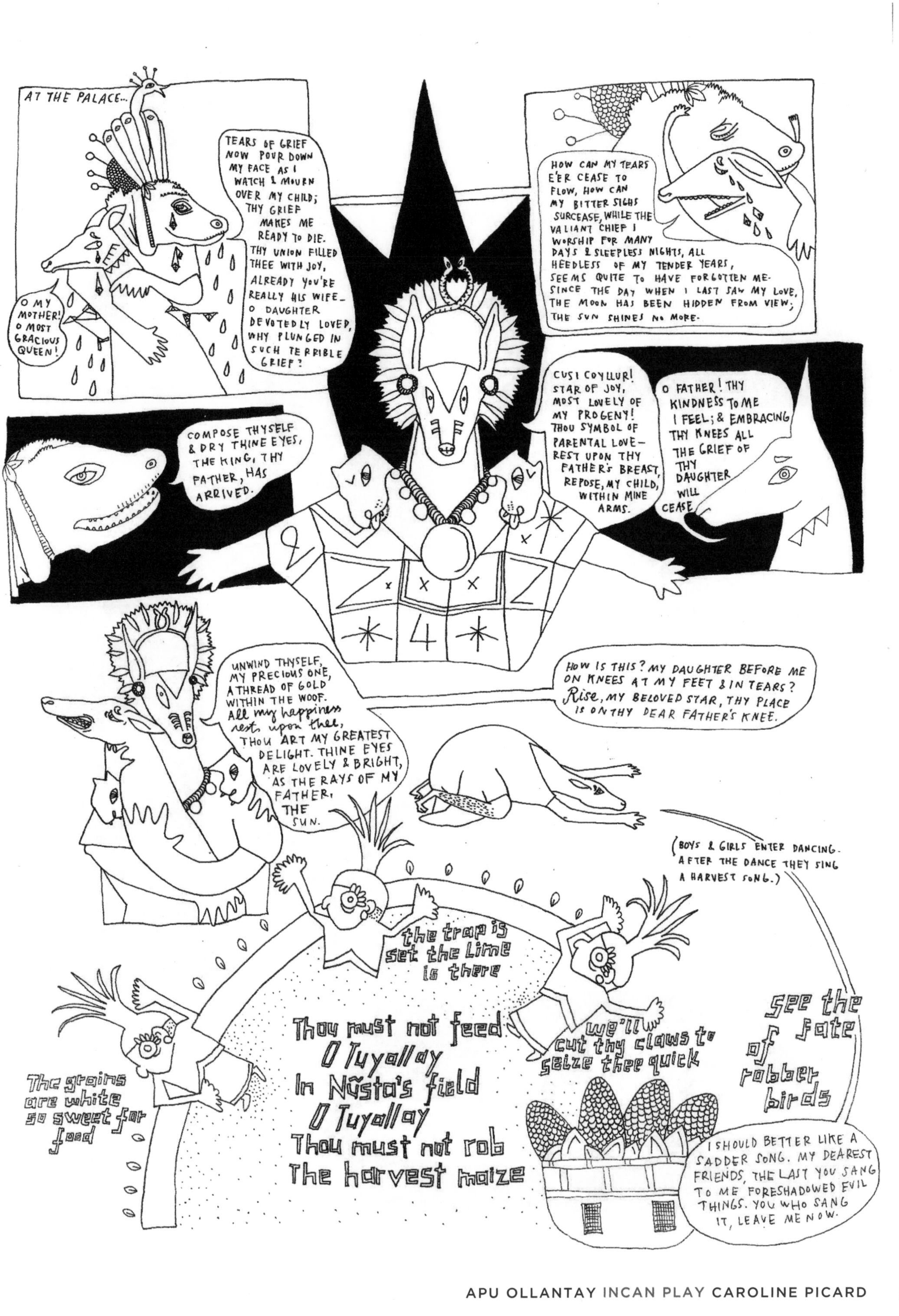
AT THE PALACE...
TEARS OF GRIEF NOW POUR DOWN MY FACE AS I WATCH & MOURN OVER MY CHILD; THY GRIEF MAKES ME READY TO DIE. THY UNION FILLED THEE WITH JOY, ALREADY YOU'RE REALLY HIS WIFE_ O DAUGHTER DEVOTEDLY LOVED, WHY PLUNGED IN SUCH TERRIBLE GRIEF?
O MY MOTHER! O MOST GRACIOUS QUEEN!
HOW CAN MY TEARS E'ER CEASE TO FLOW, HOW CAN MY BITTER SIGHS SURCEASE, WHILE THE VALIANT CHIEF I WORSHIP FOR MANY DAYS & SLEEPLESS NIGHTS, ALL HEEDLESS OF MY TENDER YEARS, SEEMS QUITE TO HAVE FORGOTTEN ME-SINCE THE DAY WHEN I LAST SAW MY LOVE, THE MOON HAS BEEN HIDDEN FROM VIEW; THE SUN SHINES NO MORE.
COMPOSE THYSELF & DRY THINE EYES, THE KING, THY FATHER, HAS ARRIVED.
CUSI COYLLUR! STAR OF JOY, MOST LOVELY OF MY PROGENY! THOU SYMBOL OF PARENTAL LOVE—REST UPON THY FATHER'S BREAST, REPOSE, MY CHILD, WITHIN MINE ARMS.
O FATHER! THY KINDNESS TO ME I FEEL; & EMBRACING THY KNEES ALL THE GRIEF OF THY DAUGHTER WILL CEASE.
HOW IS THIS? MY DAUGHTER BEFORE ME ON KNEES AT MY FEET & IN TEARS? Rise, MY BELOVED STAR, THY PLACE IS ON THY DEAR FATHER'S KNEE.
UNWIND THYSELF, MY PRECIOUS ONE, A THREAD OF GOLD WITHIN THE WOOF. All my happiness rests upon thee, THOU ART MY GREATEST DELIGHT. THINE EYES ARE LOVELY & BRIGHT, AS THE RAYS OF MY FATHER, THE SUN.
(BOYS & GIRLS ENTER DANCING. AFTER THE DANCE THEY SING A HARVEST SONG.)
the trap is set the Lime is there
Thou must not feed O Tuyallay In Ñusta's field O Tuyallay Thou must not rob The harvest maize
we'll cut thy claws to seize thee quick
See the fate of robber birds
The grains are white so sweet for food
I SHOULD BETTER LIKE A SADDER SONG. MY DEAREST FRIENDS, THE LAST YOU SANG TO ME FORESHADOWED EVIL THINGS. YOU WHO SANG IT, LEAVE ME NOW.

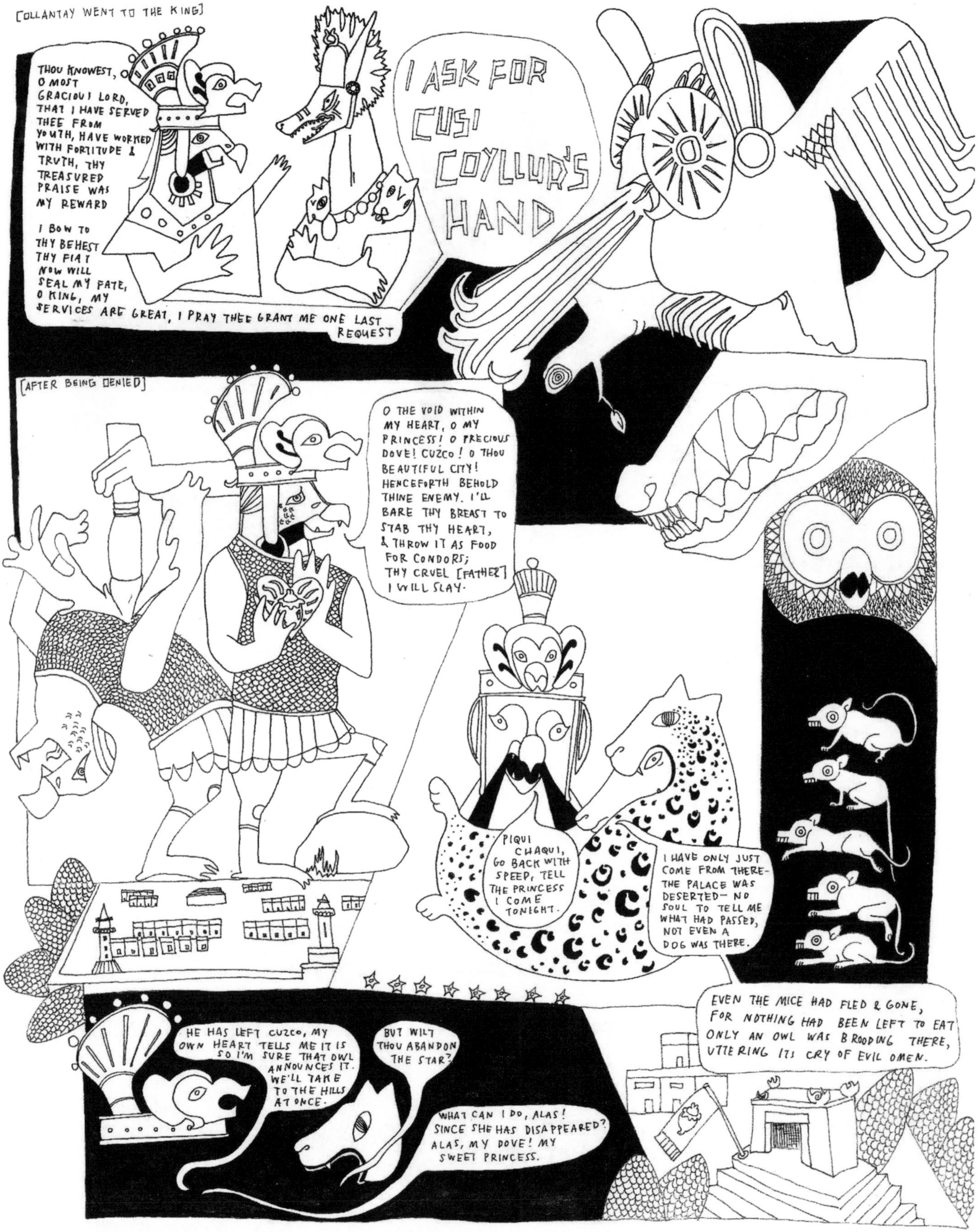

[OLLANTAY WENT TO THE KING]
THOU KNOWEST, O MOST GRACIOUS LORD, THAT I HAVE SERVED THEE FROM YOUTH, HAVE WORKED WITH FORTITUDE & TRUTH, THY TREASURED PRAISE WAS MY REWARD
I BOW TO THY BEHEST THY FIAT NOW WILL SEAL MY FATE, O KING, MY SERVICES ARE GREAT, I PRAY THEE GRANT ME ONE LAST REQUEST
I ASK FOR CUSI COYLLUR'S HAND
[AFTER BEING DENIED]
O THE VOID WITHIN MY HEART, O MY PRINCESS! O PRECIOUS DOVE! CUZCO! O THOU BEAUTIFUL CITY! HENCEFORTH BEHOLD THINE ENEMY. I'LL BARE THY BREAST TO STAB THY HEART, & THROW IT AS FOOD FOR CONDORS; THY CRUEL [FATHER] I WILL SLAY.
PIQUI CHAQUI, GO BACK WITH SPEED, TELL THE PRINCESS I COME TONIGHT.
I HAVE ONLY JUST COME FROM THERE- THE PALACE WAS DESERTED- NO SOUL TO TELL ME WHAT HAD PASSED, NOT EVEN A DOG WAS THERE.
EVEN THE MICE HAD FLED & GONE, FOR NOTHING HAD BEEN LEFT TO EAT ONLY AN OWL WAS BROODING THERE, UTTERING ITS CRY OF EVIL OMEN.
HE HAS LEFT CUZCO, MY OWN HEART TELLS ME IT IS SO I'M SURE THAT OWL ANNOUNCES IT. WE'LL TAKE TO THE HILLS AT ONCE.
BUT WILT THOU ABANDON THE STAR?
WHAT CAN I DO, ALAS! SINCE SHE HAS DISAPPEARED? ALAS, MY DOVE! MY SWEET PRINCESS.

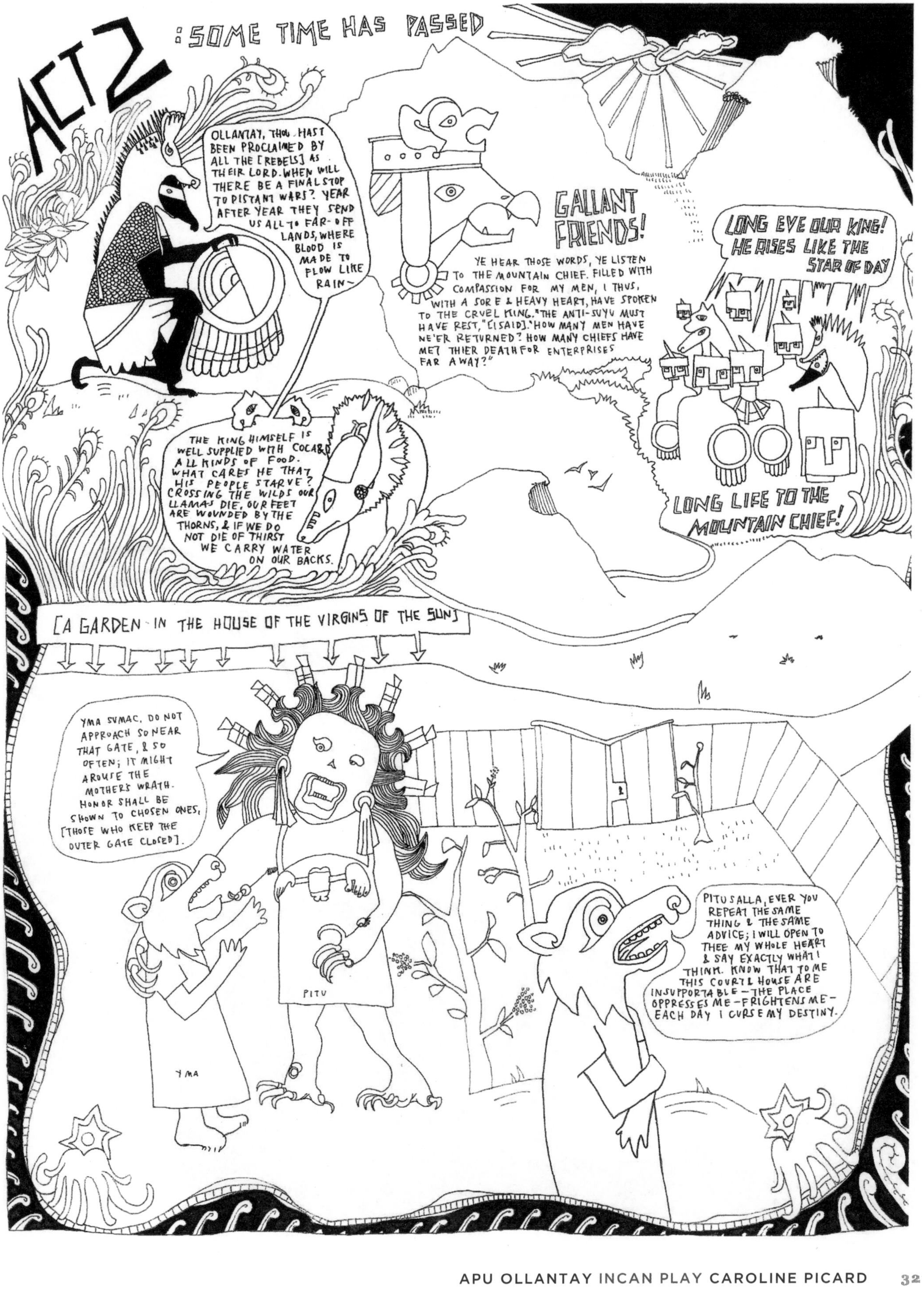
ACT 2 : SOME TIME HAS PASSED
OLLANTAY, THOU HAST BEEN PROCLAIMED BY ALL THE [REBELS] AS THEIR LORD. WHEN WILL THERE BE A FINAL STOP TO DISTANT WARS? YEAR AFTER YEAR THEY SEND US ALL TO FAR-OFF LANDS, WHERE BLOOD IS MADE TO FLOW LIKE RAIN~
GALLANT FRIENDS!
YE HEAR THOSE WORDS, YE LISTEN TO THE MOUNTAIN CHIEF. FILLED WITH COMPASSION FOR MY MEN, I THUS, WITH A SORE & HEAVY HEART, HAVE SPOKEN TO THE CRUEL KING. "THE ANTI-SUYU MUST HAVE REST," [I SAID]. "HOW MANY MEN HAVE NE'ER RETURNED? HOW MANY CHIEFS HAVE MET THIER DEATH FOR ENTERPRISES FAR AWAY?"
LONG EVE OUR KING! HE RISES LIKE THE STAR OF DAY
THE KING HIMSELF IS WELL SUPPLIED WITH COCA & ALL KINDS OF FOOD. WHAT CARES HE THAT HIS PEOPLE STARVE? CROSSING THE WILDS OUR LLAMAS DIE, OUR FEET ARE WOUNDED BY THE THORNS, & IF WE DO NOT DIE OF THIRST WE CARRY WATER ON OUR BACKS.
LONG LIFE TO THE MOUNTAIN CHIEF!
[A GARDEN IN THE HOUSE OF THE VIRGINS OF THE SUN]
YMA SUMAC, DO NOT APPROACH SO NEAR THAT GATE, & SO OFTEN; IT MIGHT AROUSE THE MOTHER'S WRATH. HONOR SHALL BE SHOWN TO CHOSEN ONES, [THOSE WHO KEEP THE OUTER GATE CLOSED].
PITU
YMA
PITU SALLA, EVER YOU REPEAT THE SAME THING & THE SAME ADVICE; I WILL OPEN TO THEE MY WHOLE HEART & SAY EXACTLY WHAT I THINK. KNOW THAT TO ME THIS COURT & HOUSE ARE INSUPPORTABLE—THE PLACE OPPRESSES ME—FRIGHTENS ME—EACH DAY I CURSE MY DESTINY.

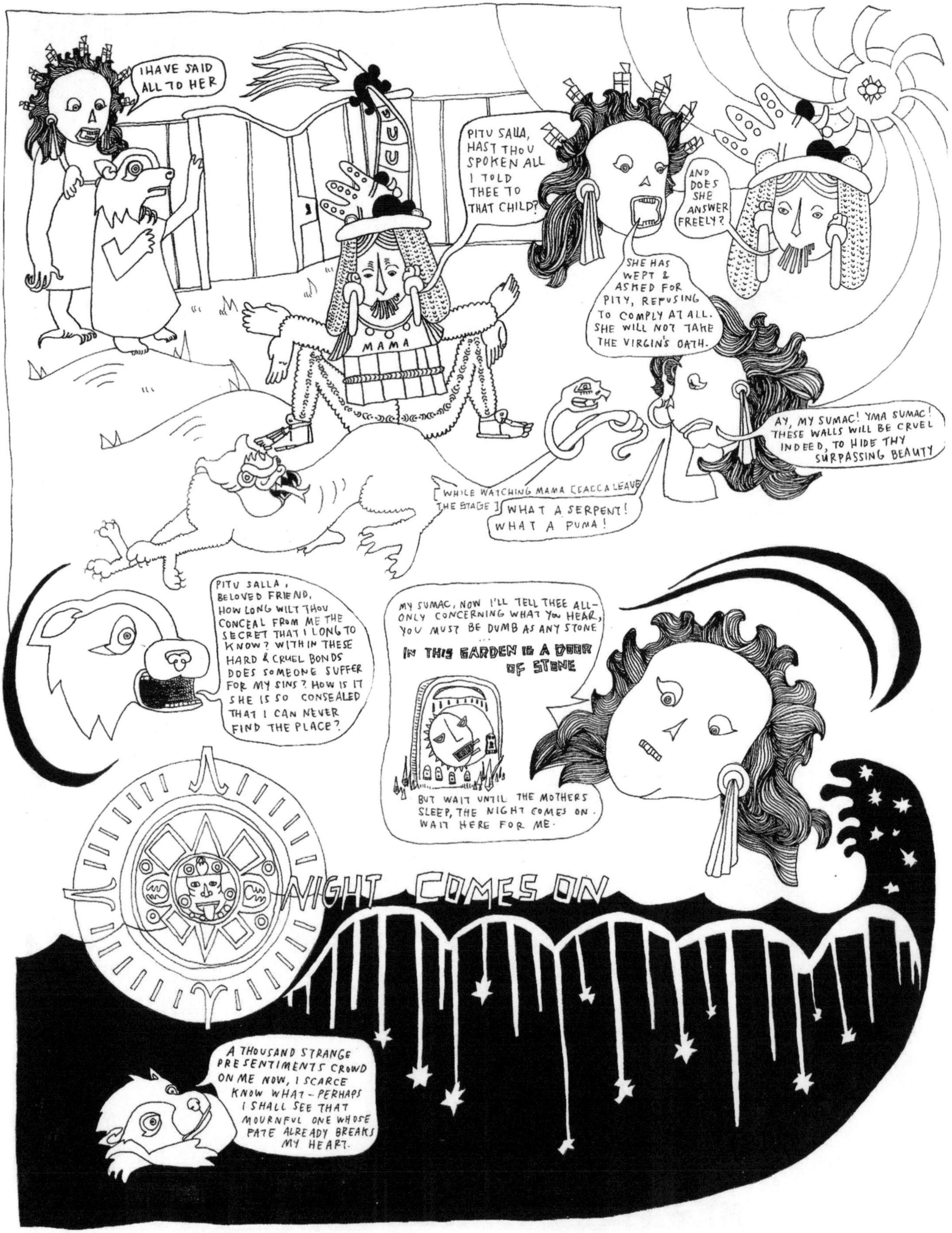
IHAVE SAID ALL TO HER
PITU SALLA, HAST THOU SPOKEN ALL I TOLD THEE TO THAT CHILD?
MAMA
AND DOES SHE ANSWER FREELY?
SHE HAS WEPT & ASKED FOR PITY, REFUSING TO COMPLY AT ALL. SHE WILL NOT TAKE THE VIRGIN'S OATH.
AY, MY SUMAC! YMA SUMAC! THESE WALLS WILL BE CRUEL INDEED, TO HIDE THY SURPASSING BEAUTY
[WHILE WATCHING MAMA CCACCA LEAVE THE STAGE]
WHAT A SERPENT! WHAT A PUMA!
PITU SALLA, BELOVED FRIEND, HOW LONG WILT THOU CONCEAL FROM ME THE SECRET THAT I LONG TO KNOW? WITHIN THESE HARD & CRUEL BONDS DOES SOMEONE SUFFER FOR MY SINS? HOW IS IT SHE IS SO CONSEALED THAT I CAN NEVER FIND THE PLACE?
MY SUMAC, NOW I'LL TELL THEE ALL - ONLY CONCERNING WHAT YOU HEAR, YOU MUST BE DUMB AS ANY STONE ...
IN THIS GARDEN IS A DOOR OF STONE
BUT WAIT UNTIL THE MOTHERS SLEEP, THE NIGHT COMES ON. WAIT HERE FOR ME.
NIGHT COMES ON
A THOUSAND STRANGE PRESENTIMENTS CROWD ON ME NOW, I SCARCE KNOW WHAT - PERHAPS I SHALL SEE THAT MOURNFUL ONE WHOSE FATE ALREADY BREAKS MY HEART.

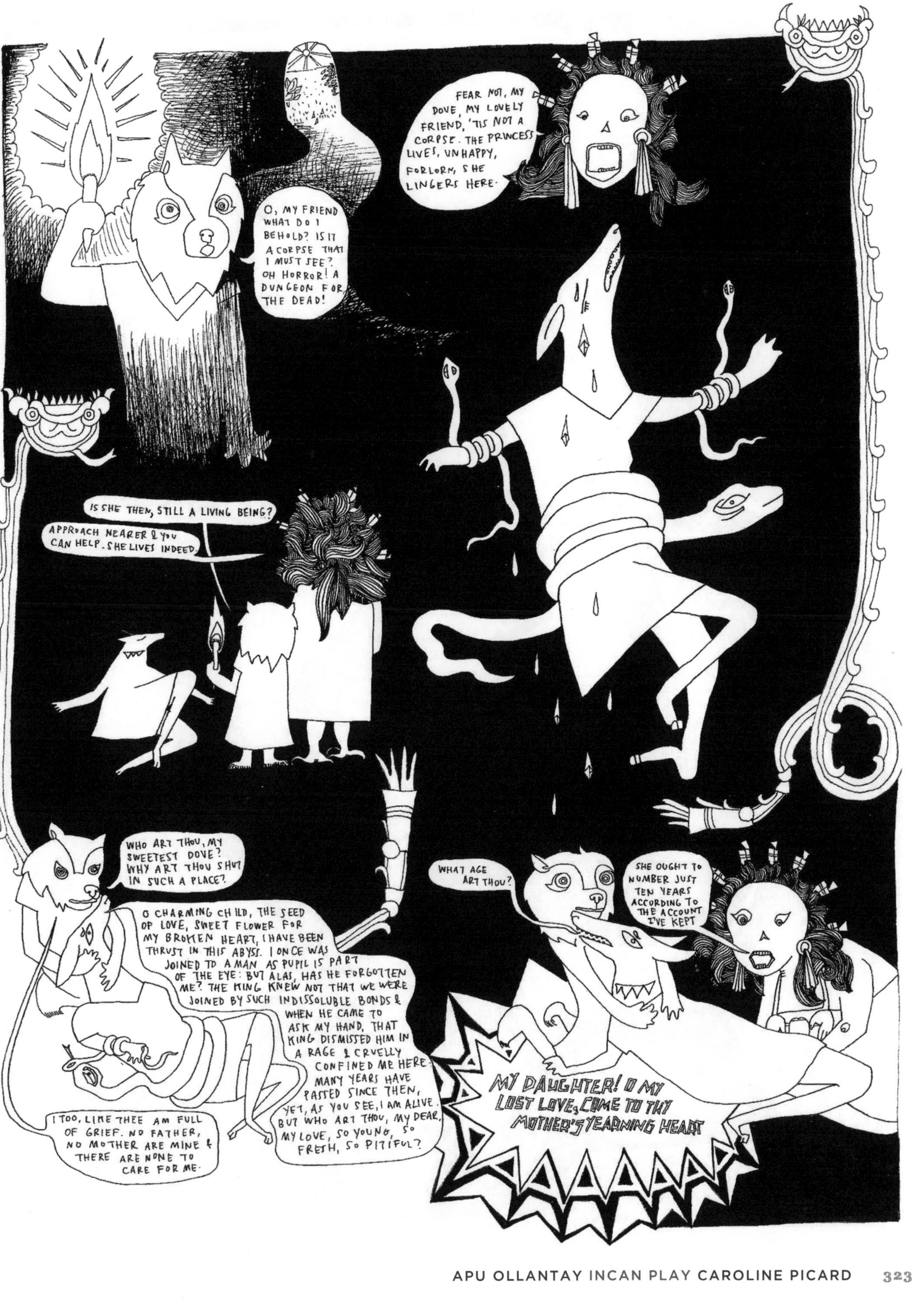
O, MY FRIEND WHAT DO I BEHOLD? IS IT A CORPSE THAT I MUST SEE? OH HORROR! A DUNGEON FOR THE DEAD!
FEAR NOT, MY DOVE, MY LOVELY FRIEND, 'TIS NOT A CORPSE. THE PRINCESS LIVES, UNHAPPY, FORLORN, SHE LINGERS HERE.
IS SHE THEN, STILL A LIVING BEING?
APPROACH NEARER & YOU CAN HELP. SHE LIVES INDEED.
WHO ART THOU, MY SWEETEST DOVE? WHY ART THOU SHUT IN SUCH A PLACE?
O CHARMING CHILD, THE SEED OF LOVE, SWEET FLOWER FOR MY BROKEN HEART, I HAVE BEEN THRUST IN THIS ABYSS. I ONCE WAS JOINED TO A MAN AS PUPIL IS PART OF THE EYE: BUT ALAS, HAS HE FORGOTTEN ME? THE KING KNEW NOT THAT WE WERE JOINED BY SUCH INDISSOLUBLE BONDS & WHEN HE CAME TO ASK MY HAND, THAT KING DISMISSED HIM IN A RAGE & CRUELLY CONFINED ME HERE. MANY YEARS HAVE PASSED SINCE THEN, YET, AS YOU SEE, I AM ALIVE. BUT WHO ART THOU, MY DEAR, MY LOVE, SO YOUNG, SO FRESH, SO PITIFUL?
I TOO, LIKE THEE AM FULL OF GRIEF. NO FATHER, NO MOTHER ARE MINE & THERE ARE NONE TO CARE FOR ME.
WHAT AGE ART THOU?
SHE OUGHT TO NUMBER JUST TEN YEARS ACCORDING TO THE ACCOUNT I'VE KEPT
MY DAUGHTER! O MY LOST LOVE, COME TO THY MOTHER'S YEARNING HEART

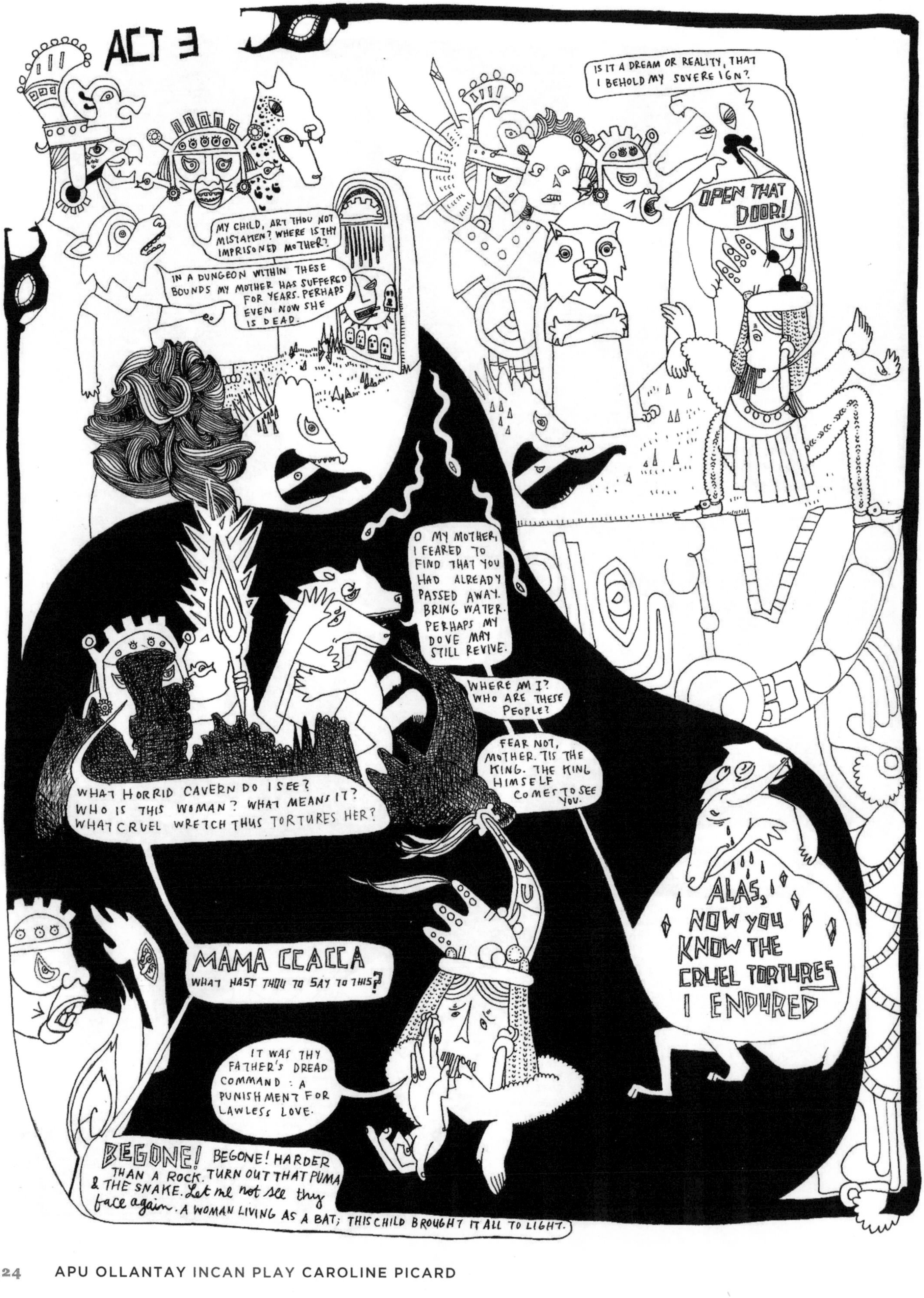
ACT 3
MY CHILD, ART THOU NOT MISTAKEN? WHERE IS THY IMPRISONED MOTHER?
IN A DUNGEON WITHIN THESE BOUNDS MY MOTHER HAS SUFFERED FOR YEARS. PERHAPS EVEN NOW SHE IS DEAD.
IS IT A DREAM OR REALITY, THAT I BEHOLD MY SOVEREIGN?
OPEN THAT DOOR!
O MY MOTHER, I FEARED TO FIND THAT YOU HAD ALREADY PASSED AWAY. BRING WATER. PERHAPS MY DOVE MAY STILL REVIVE.
WHERE AM I? WHO ARE THESE PEOPLE?
FEAR NOT, MOTHER. TIS THE KING. THE KING HIMSELF COMES TO SEE YOU.
WHAT HORRID CAVERN DO I SEE? WHO IS THIS WOMAN? WHAT MEANS IT? WHAT CRUEL WRETCH THUS TORTURES HER?
ALAS, NOW YOU KNOW THE CRUEL TORTURES I ENDURED
MAMA CCACCA WHAT HAST THOU TO SAY TO THIS?
IT WAS THY FATHER'S DREAD COMMAND: A PUNISHMENT FOR LAWLESS LOVE.
BEGONE! BEGONE! HARDER THAN A ROCK. TURN OUT THAT PUMA & THE SNAKE. Let me not see thy face again. A WOMAN LIVING AS A BAT; THIS CHILD BROUGHT IT ALL TO LIGHT.

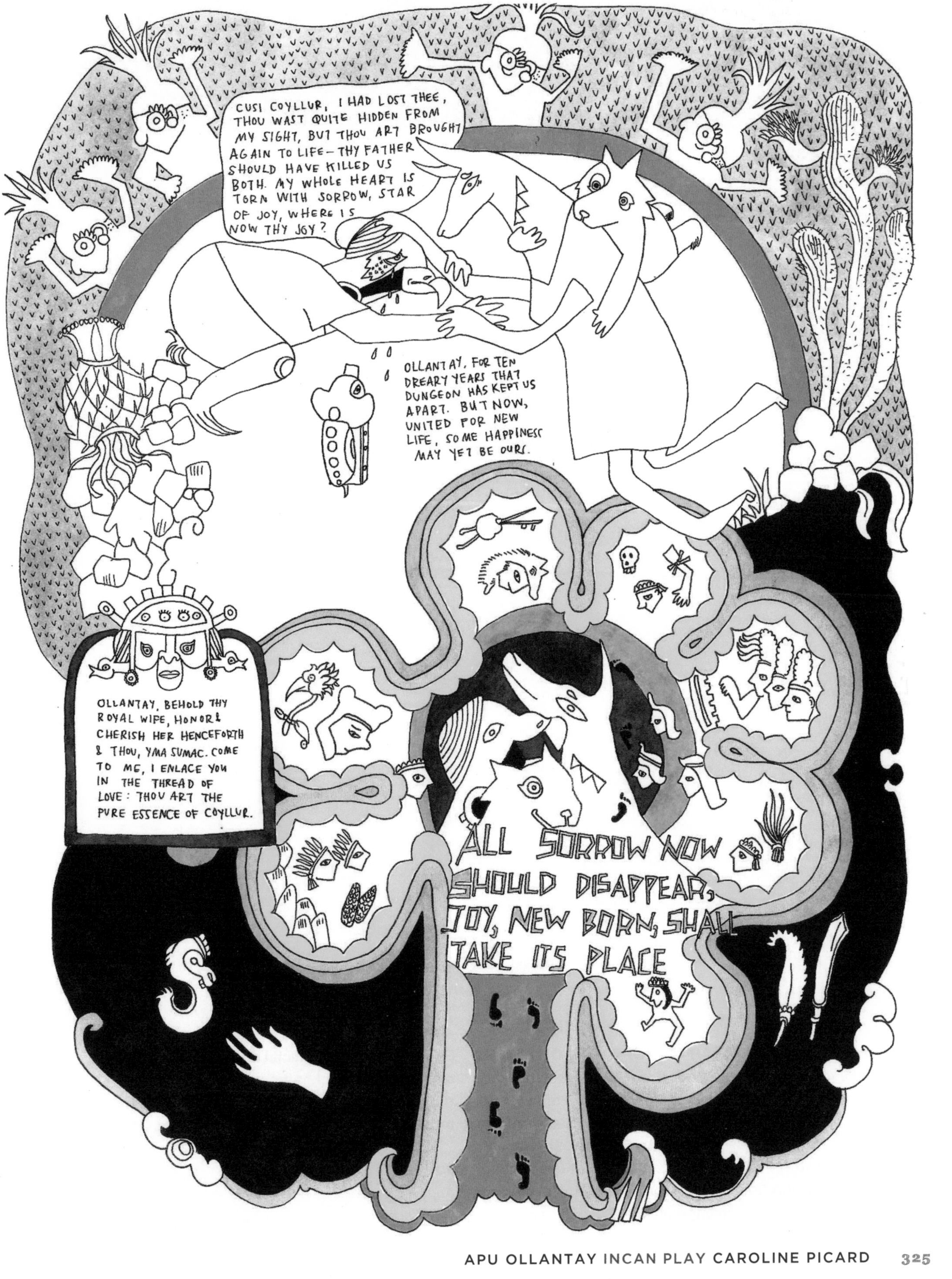
CUSI COYLLUR, I HAD LOST THEE, THOU WAST QUITE HIDDEN FROM MY SIGHT, BUT THOU ART BROUGHT AGAIN TO LIFE—THY FATHER SHOULD HAVE KILLED US BOTH. MY WHOLE HEART IS TORN WITH SORROW, STAR OF JOY, WHERE IS NOW THY JOY?
OLLANTAY, FOR TEN DREARY YEARS THAT DUNGEON HAS KEPT US APART. BUT NOW, UNITED FOR NEW LIFE, SOME HAPPINESS MAY YET BE OURS.
OLLANTAY, BEHOLD THY ROYAL WIFE, HONOR & CHERISH HER HENCEFORTH & THOU, YMA SUMAC. COME TO ME, I ENLACE YOU IN THE THREAD OF LOVE: THOU ART THE PURE ESSENCE OF COYLLUR.
ALL SORROW NOW SHOULD DISAPPEAR, JOY, NEW BORN, SHALL TAKE ITS PLACE

Outlaws of the Water Margin

Shi Nai'an

ILLUSTRATIONS BY **Shawn Cheng**

OUTLAWS OF THE WATER MARGIN (OR, OUTLAWS *of the Marsh*) is one of the Four Great Classical Novels of China, and is often compared to the tales of Robin Hood. Based on the embroidered exploits of an actual group of brigands during the time of the Song Dynsaty, Shi Nai'an's huge, fourteenth-century novel is an action-packed tale of 108 antiheroes who fight against corrupt tyrannical government officials from their stronghold in the Liangshan Marsh.

Each of them has special capabilities, a preferred weapon, and a colorful nickname, giving artist Shawn Cheng prime material for a rogues' gallery. He has illustrated eight of the most important and interesting of the rebels.

SOURCE

Anonymous. *China: Five Thousand Years of History and Civilization.* City University of Hong Kong Press, 2007.

水浒传

Outlaws of the Water Margin by Shi Nai'an

Illustrations by Shawn Cheng

In the twilight years of the Northern Song Dynasty (c. 1121–1127), the Chinese empire is ruled by corruption and vice. In this unjust world, righteous men are forced to become outlaws. Eventually, 108 such men (and women) will gather in the mountains at Liangshan Marsh.

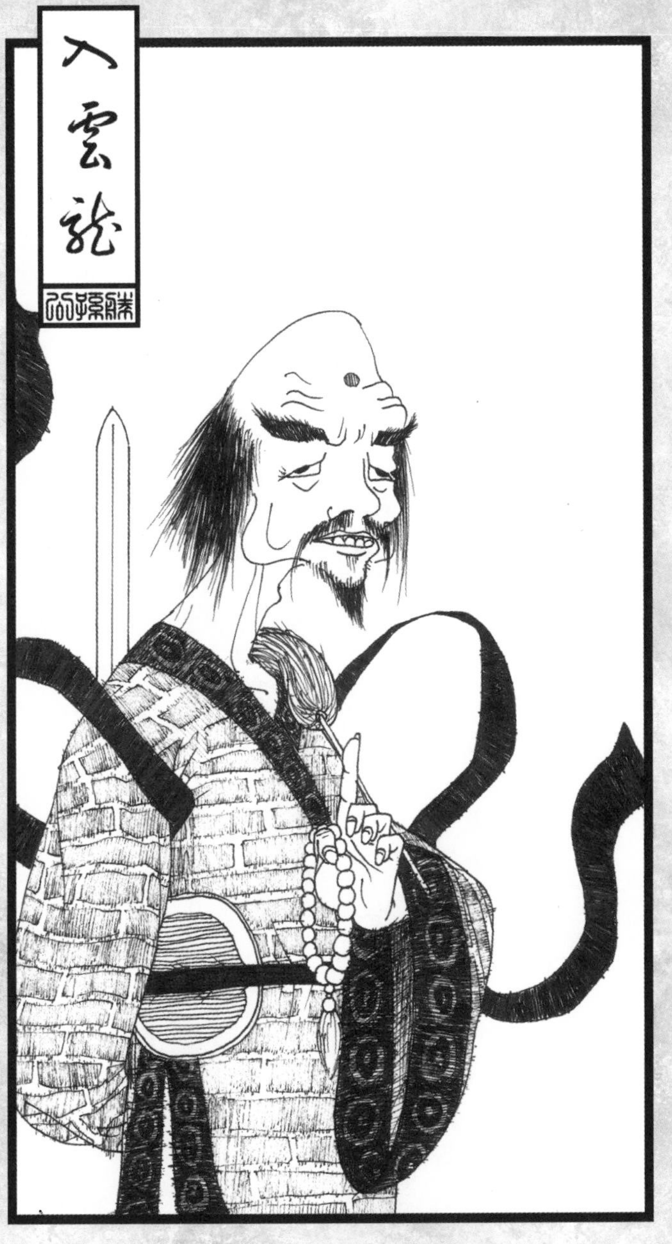
入雲龍

Dragon in the Clouds
Gongsun Sheng

Gongsun, a Taoist priest with powers over wind and rain, comes to the Liangshan Marsh after taking part in the "Righteous Seven" robbery of imperial birthday gifts.

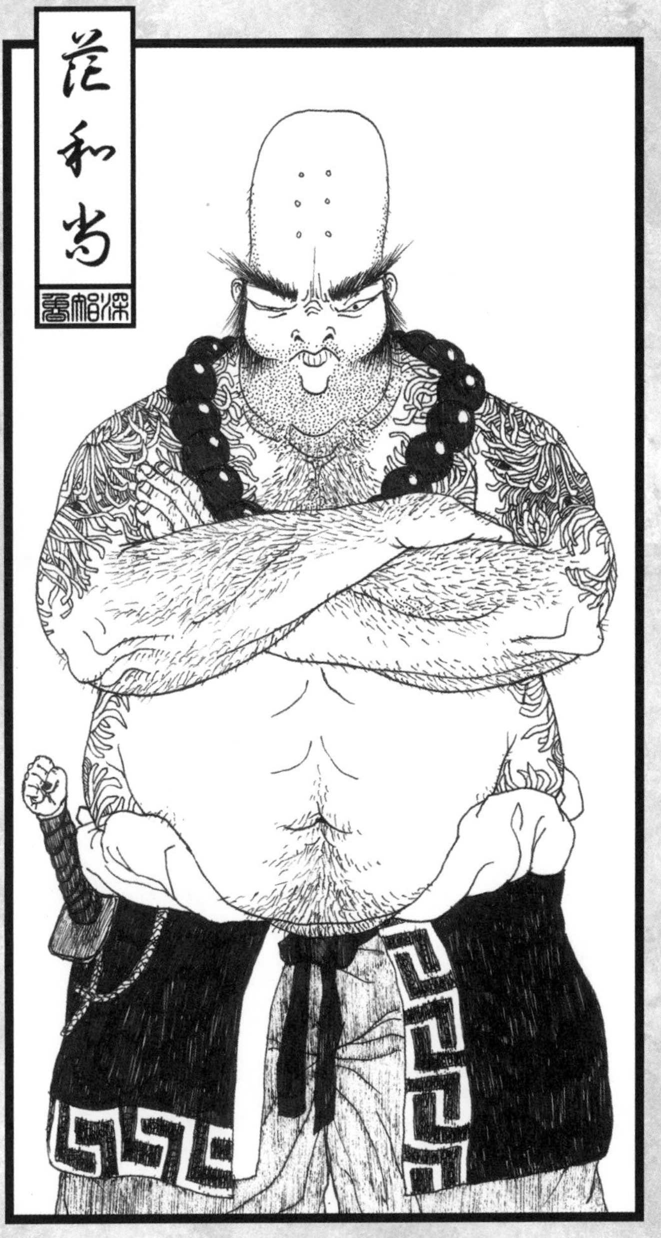
花和尚

Tattooed Monk
Lu Zhishen

Lu is brutish and brash, but with a strong sense of justice. He becomes a monk after killing a local strongman who was terrorizing a singer and her father.

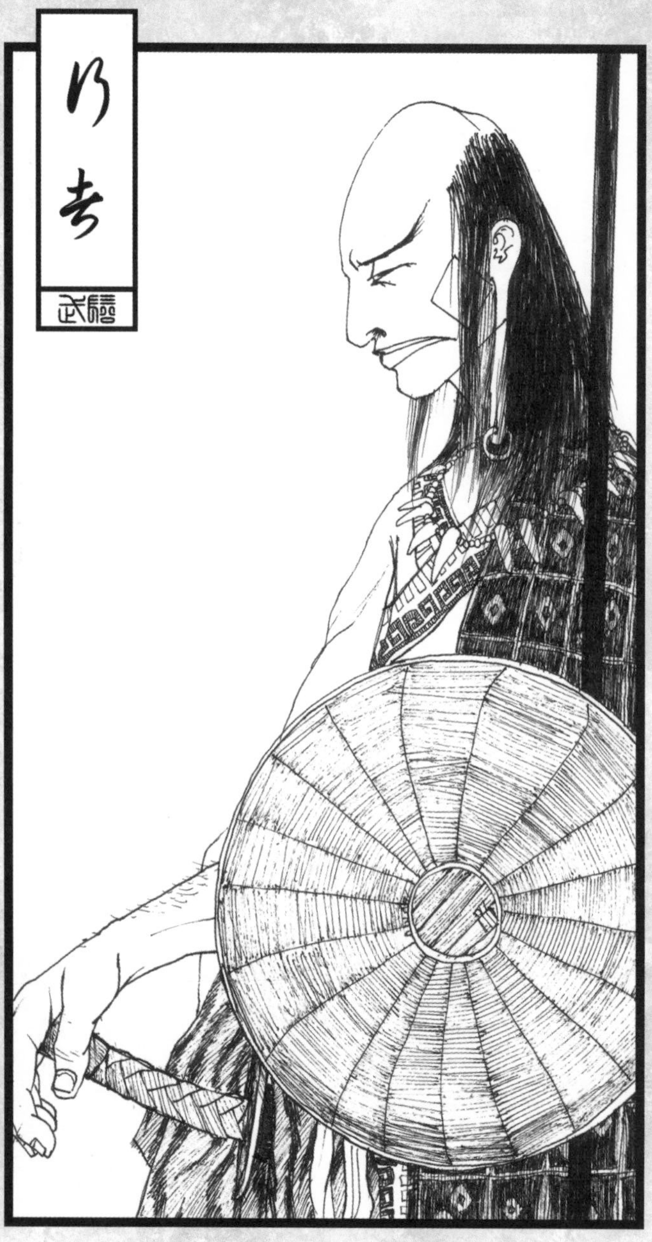

Wandering Priest

Wu Song

Wu discovers that his adulterous sister-in-law had killed his brother. After extracting a confession, he kills her and turns himself in to the authorities.

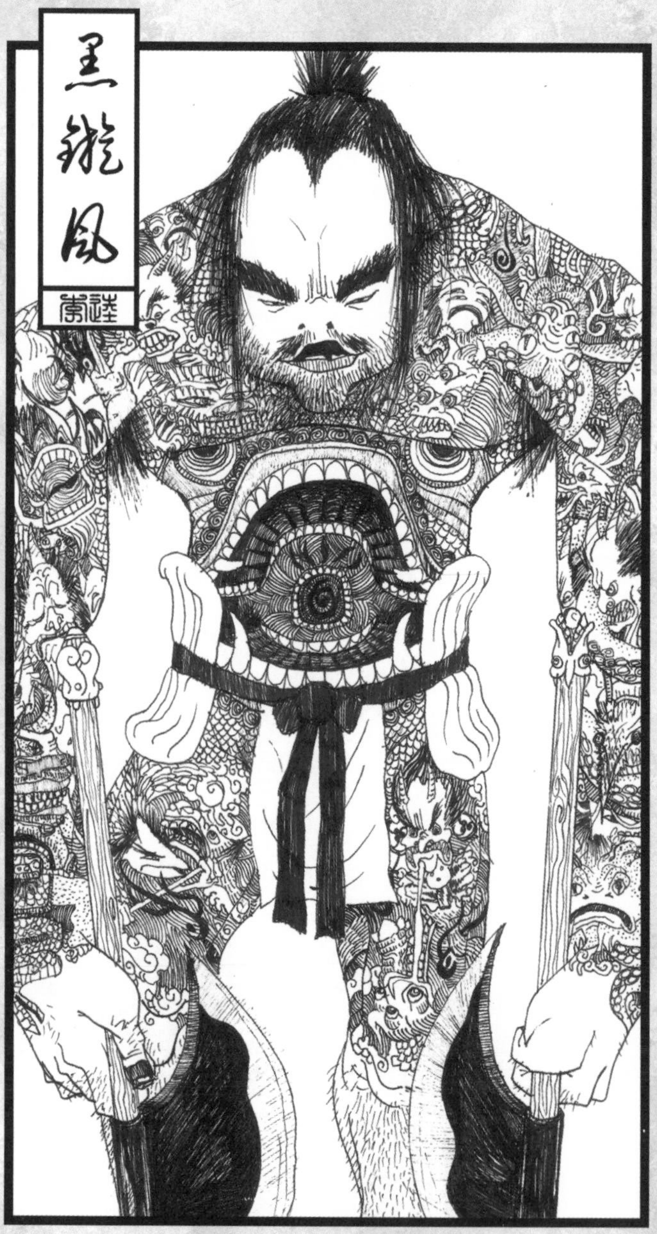

Black Whirlwind

Li Kui

Ill-tempered and given to drink, Li is an unpredictable force of nature. He plays an important role in rescuing the leaders of Liangshan Marsh from execution.

Heavenly General on the Ground
Ruan Xiaoer

One of the "Righteous Seven" who intercepted a convoy of imperial birthday presents, Ruan becomes an important naval commander of the Liangshan Marsh outlaws.

Heaven-Shaking Thunder
Ling Zhen

An imperial general skilled in artillery, Ling proves to be a formidable foe before being captured at Liangshan Marsh. He is then persuaded to join the outlaws.

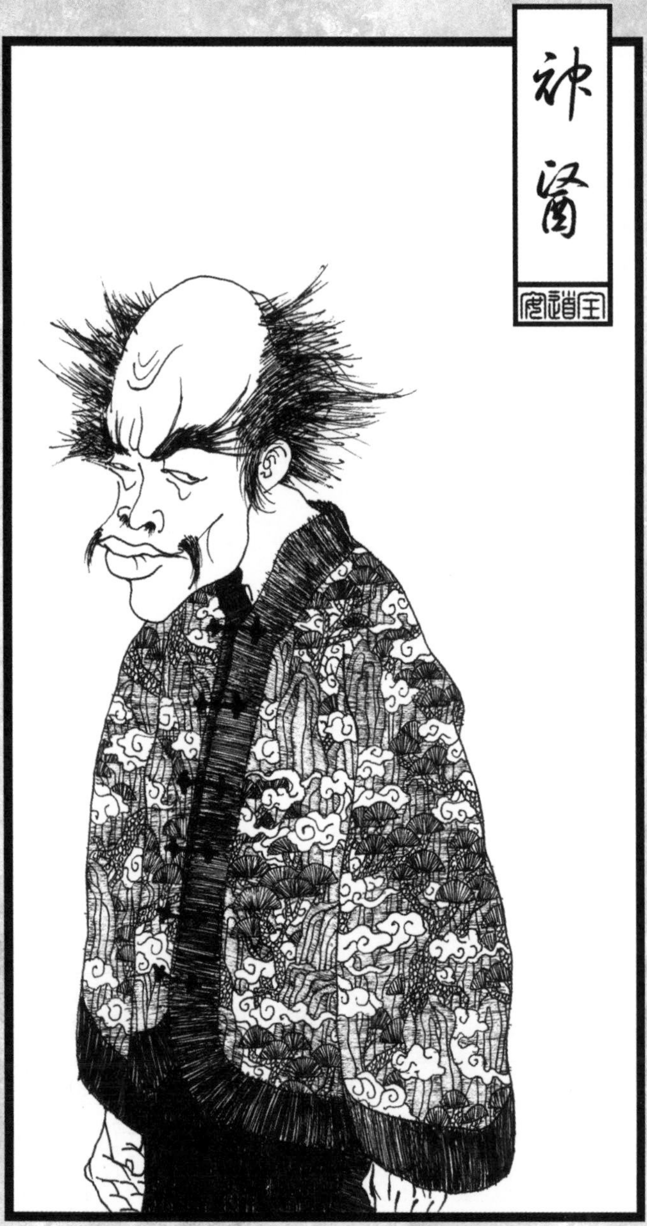
神醫

Divine Physician
An Daoquan

An is sympathetic to, but refuses to join, the outlaws of Liangshan Marsh. One of the outlaws kills An's lover and frames him for the murder, leaving him no other choice.

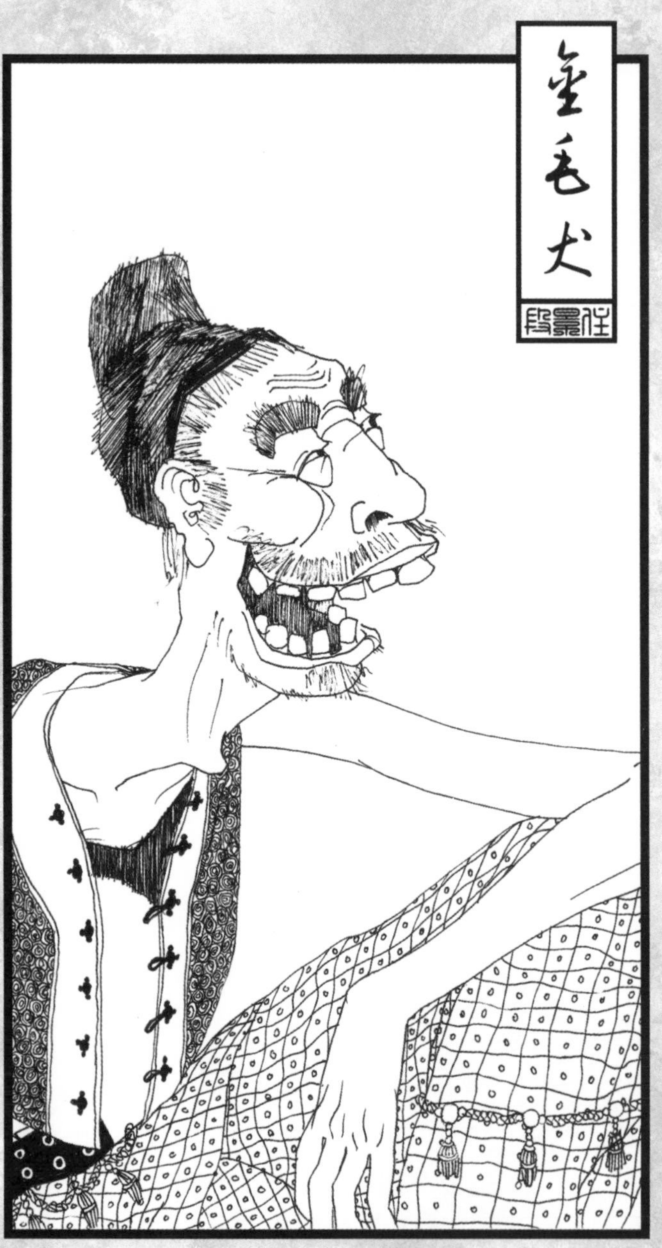
金毛犬

Golden-Haired Dog
Duan Jingzhu

Duan, a horse thief from the north, acquires the royal steed "Moonlight Jade Lion" and intends to present it at Liangshan Marsh. He is waylaid en route and loses the horse.

Hagoromo (Celestial Feather Robe)

a Japanese Noh play

ART / ADAPTATION BY **Isabel Greenberg**

NOH IS A FORM OF JAPANESE DRAMA DEVELOPED for the aristocracy in the 1300s. By 1500, the entire Noh canon (around 300 plays) had been written, although they have been performed more or less continuously since then. The poetic text is half-sung or chanted on a bare stage whose sole decoration is a pine tree painted on the back wall. The elaborate costumes and masks make up for the austerity of the stage. *The Dictionary of World Literature* says:

> The technique of action is a miracle of delicacy and charm. Understatement is the keynote; "art hidden by its own perfection." The plots of the plays are simple; the poetical construction and ring appeal to the emotions and supply the charm.

Hagoromo, by an unknown author, is one of the most popular and lasting of the plays. (The title is often translated as *Feather Mantle*, but I prefer the more poetic *Celestial Feather Robe*.) A fisherman finds a *hagoromo* that has been accidentally dropped by a *tennin*, a being described in various English translations as an angel, an aerial spirit, or a celestial dancer.

Isabel Greenberg, who won the London *Observer*'s 2011 graphic short story prize, brings understatement and delicateness to this tale of an ordinary man's brief encounter with the divine.

SOURCE

Shipley, Joseph Twadell. *Dictionary of World Literature: Criticism, Forms, Technique*. Taylor & Francis, 1964.

HAGOROMO

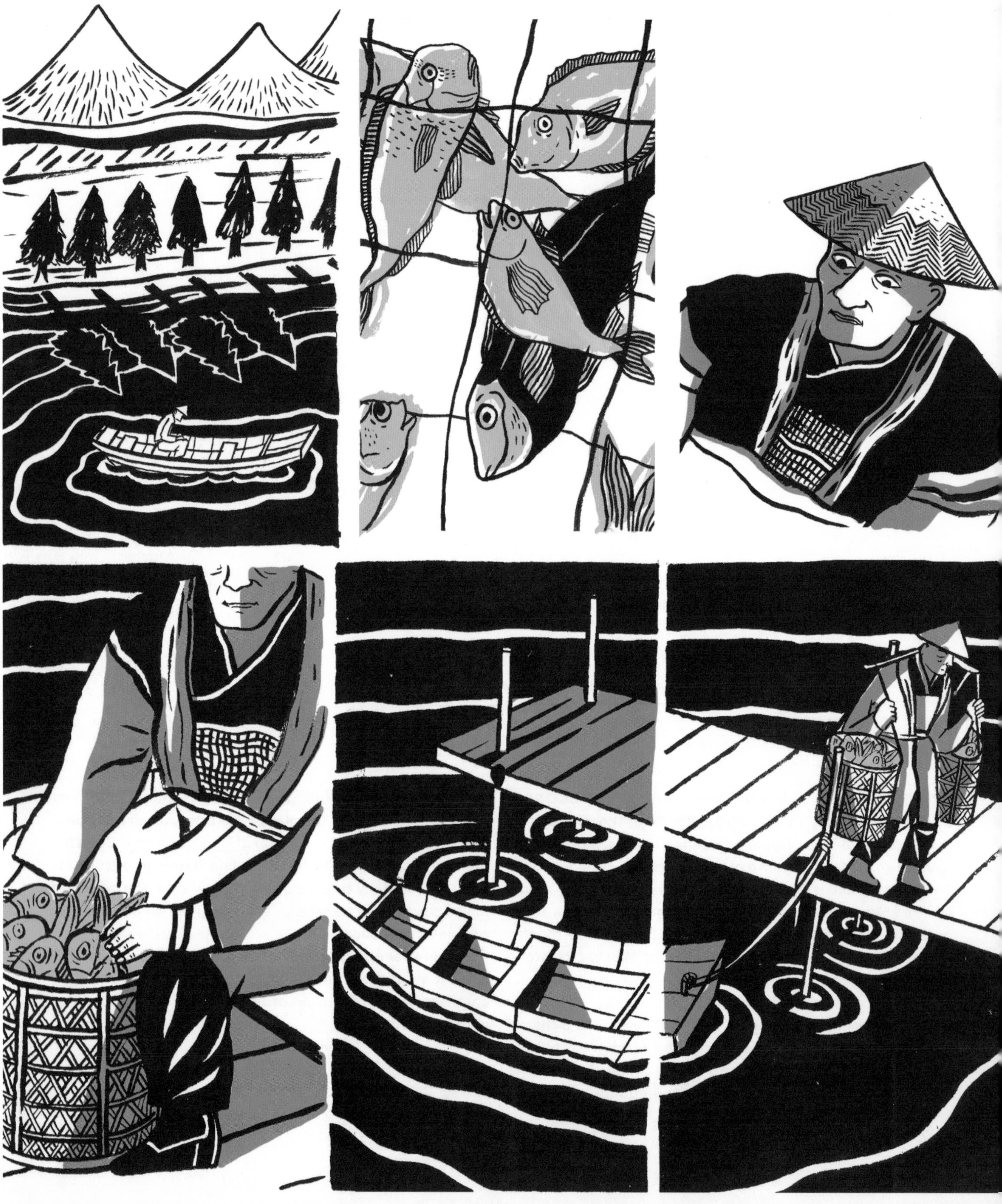

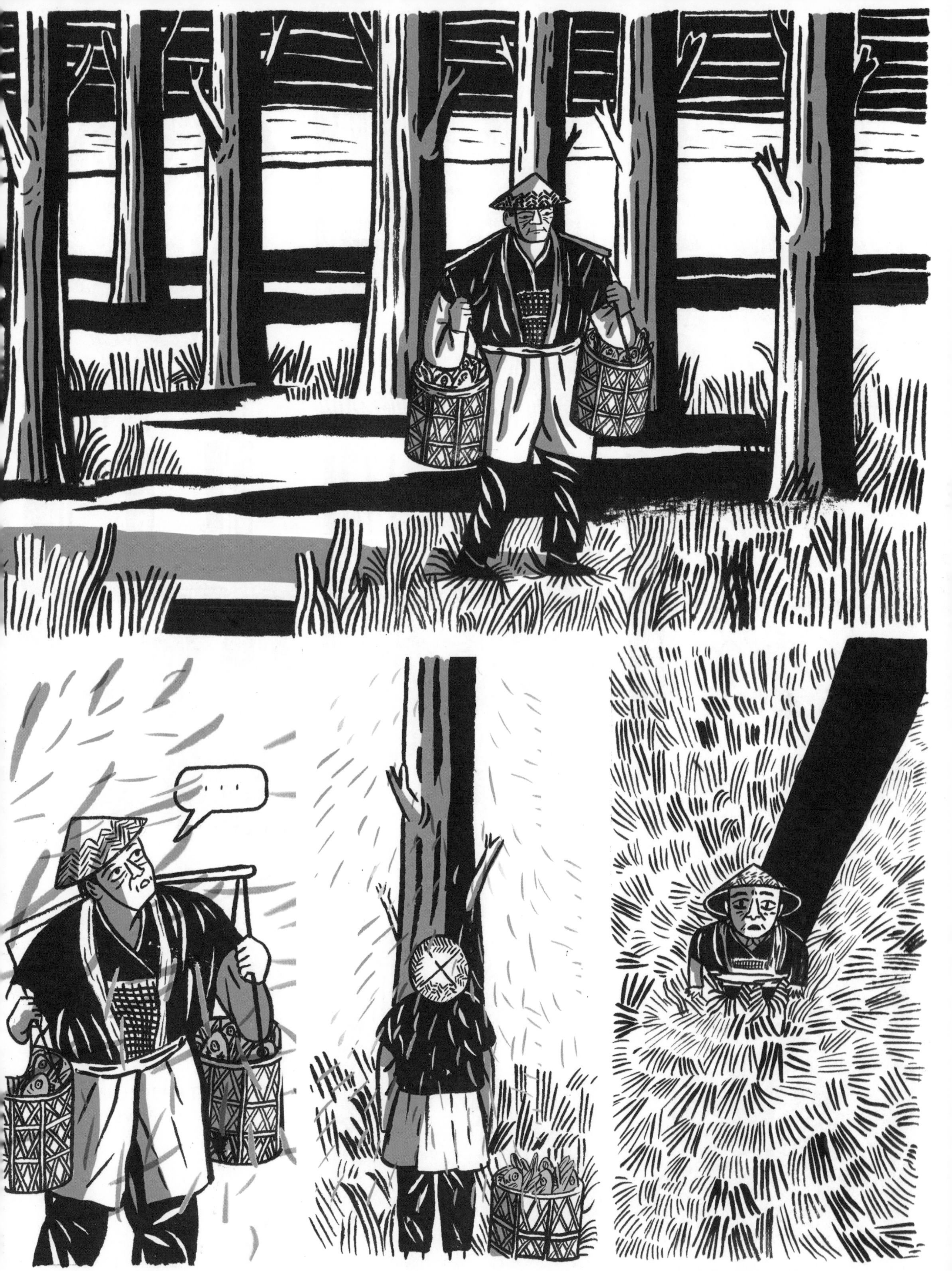
. . .

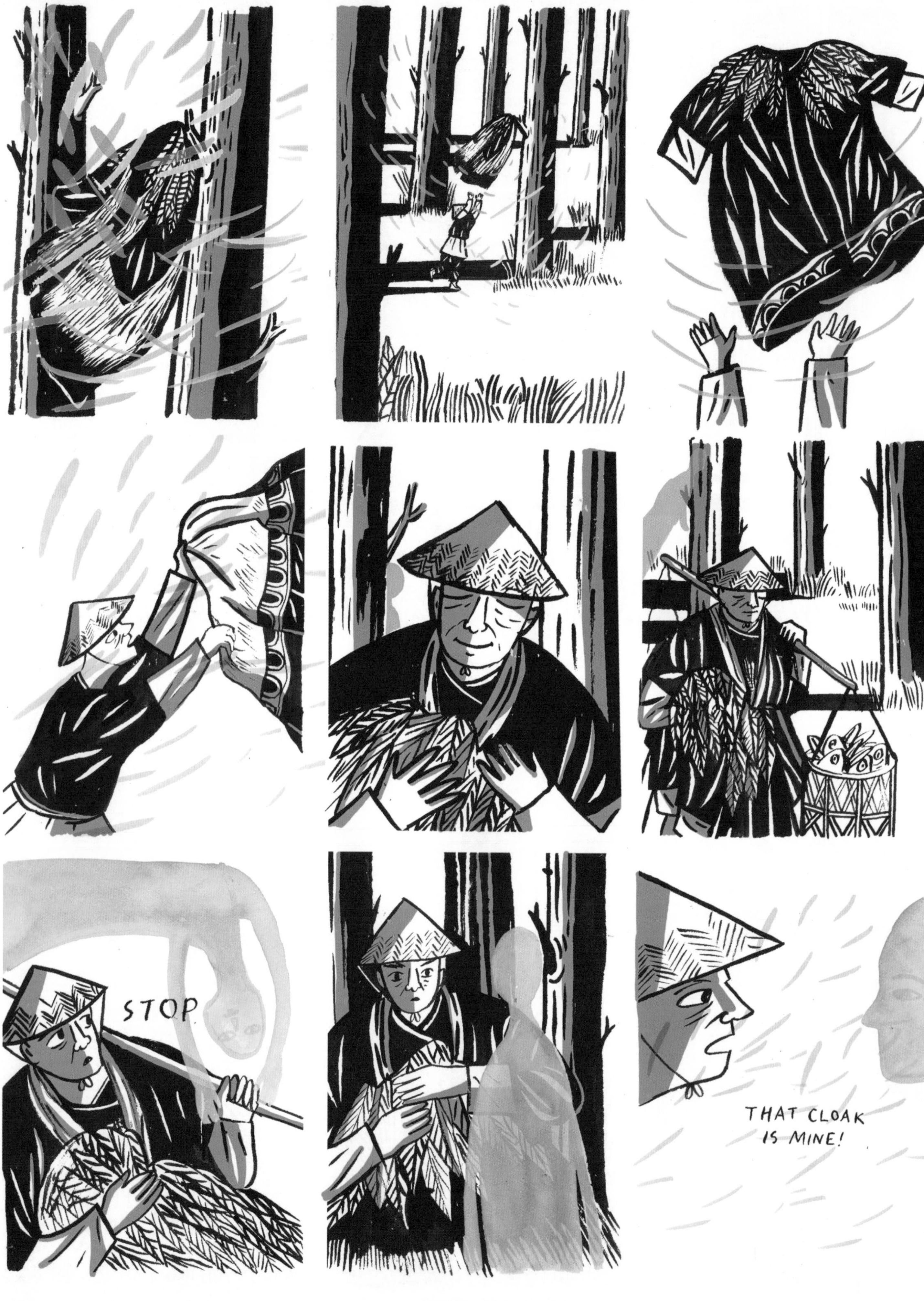
STOP
THAT CLOAK IS MINE!

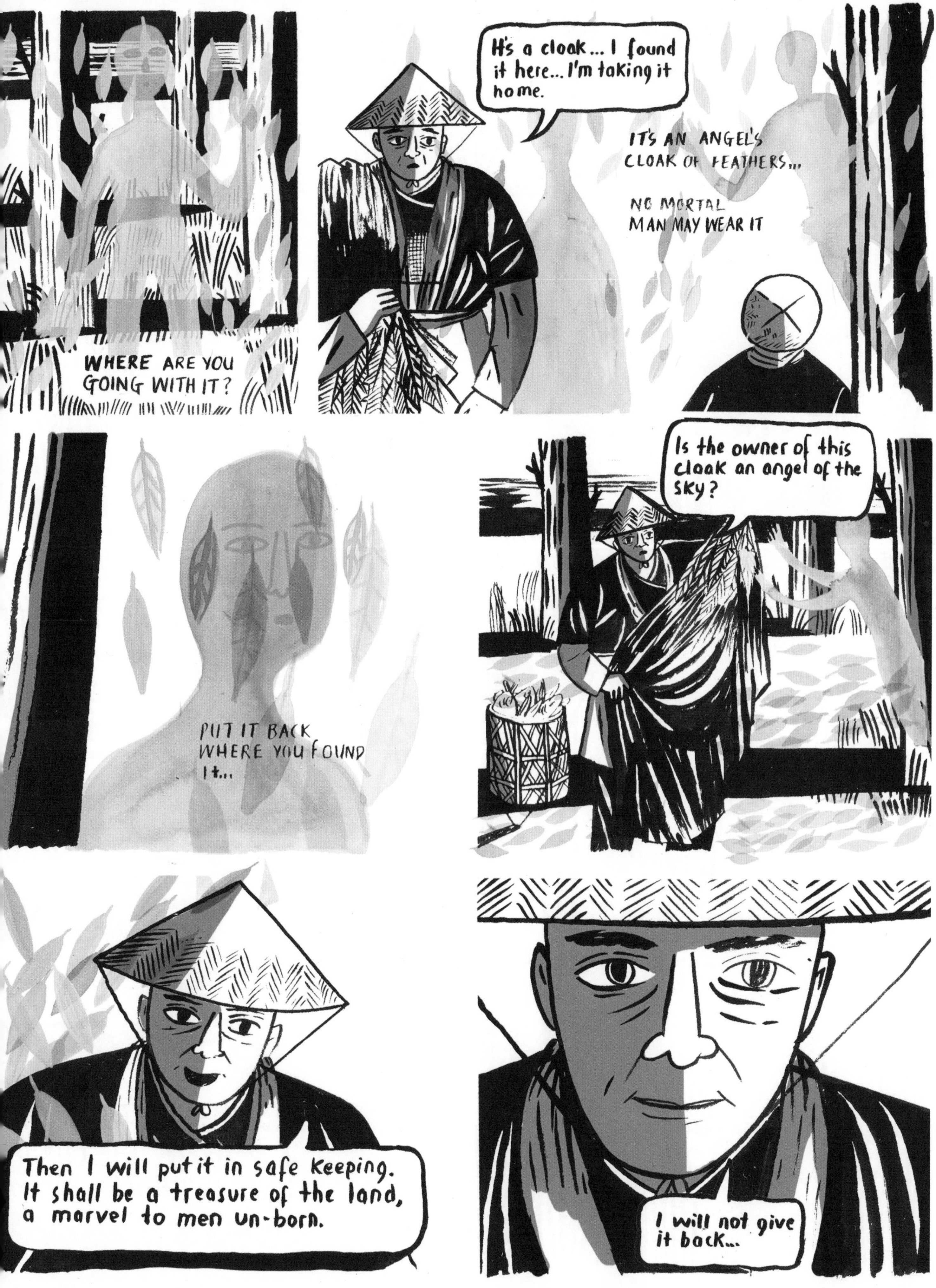
WHERE ARE YOU GOING WITH IT?
It's a cloak... I found it here... I'm taking it home.
IT'S AN ANGEL'S CLOAK OF FEATHERS...
NO MORTAL MAN MAY WEAR IT
PUT IT BACK WHERE YOU FOUND IT...
Is the owner of this cloak an angel of the sky?
Then I will put it in safe keeping. It shall be a treasure of the land, a marvel to men un-born.
I will not give it back...

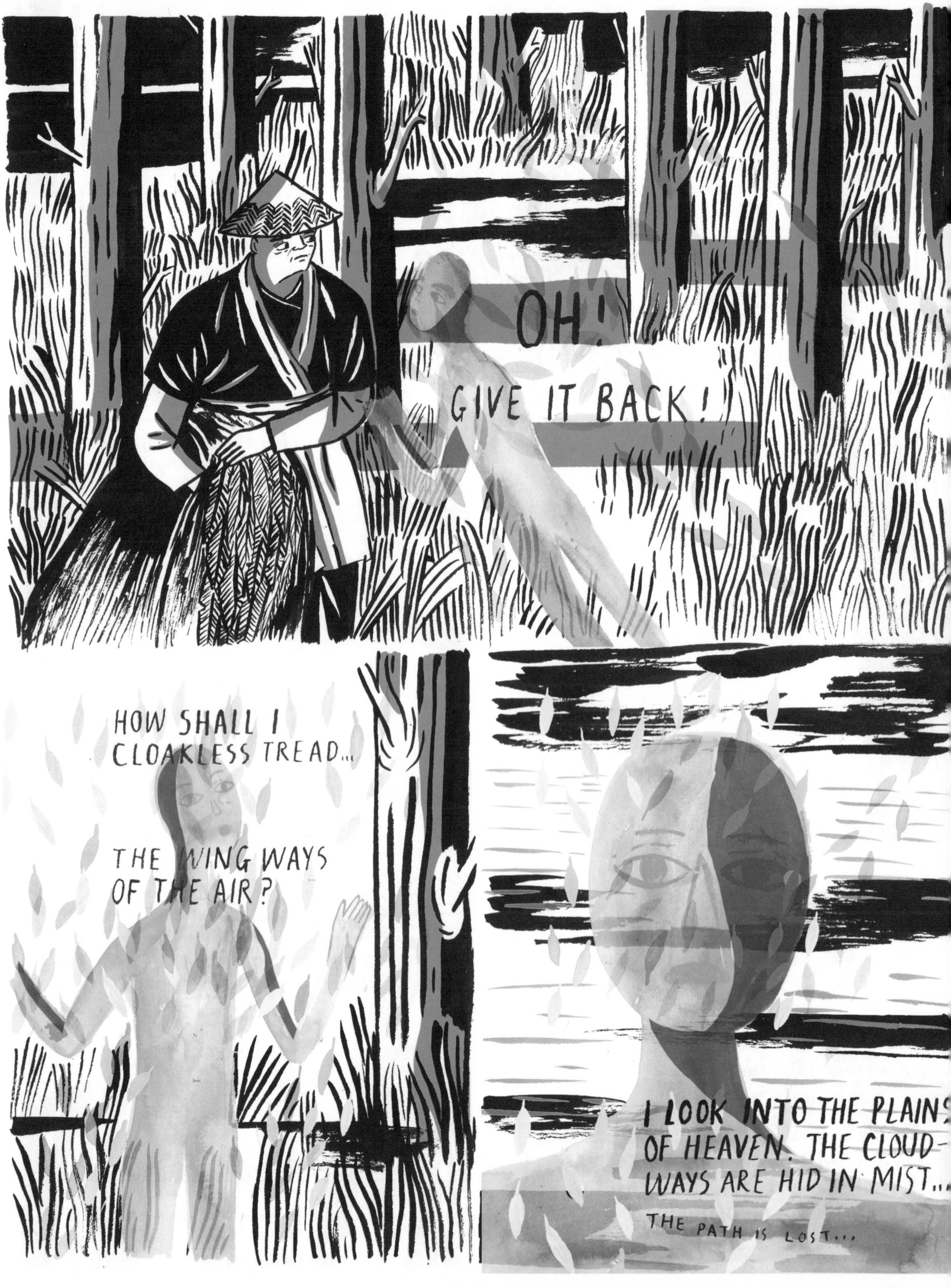
OH!
GIVE IT BACK!
HOW SHALL I CLOAKLESS TREAD...
THE WING WAYS OF THE AIR?
I LOOK INTO THE PLAINS OF HEAVEN. THE CLOUD-WAYS ARE HID IN MIST...
THE PATH IS LOST...

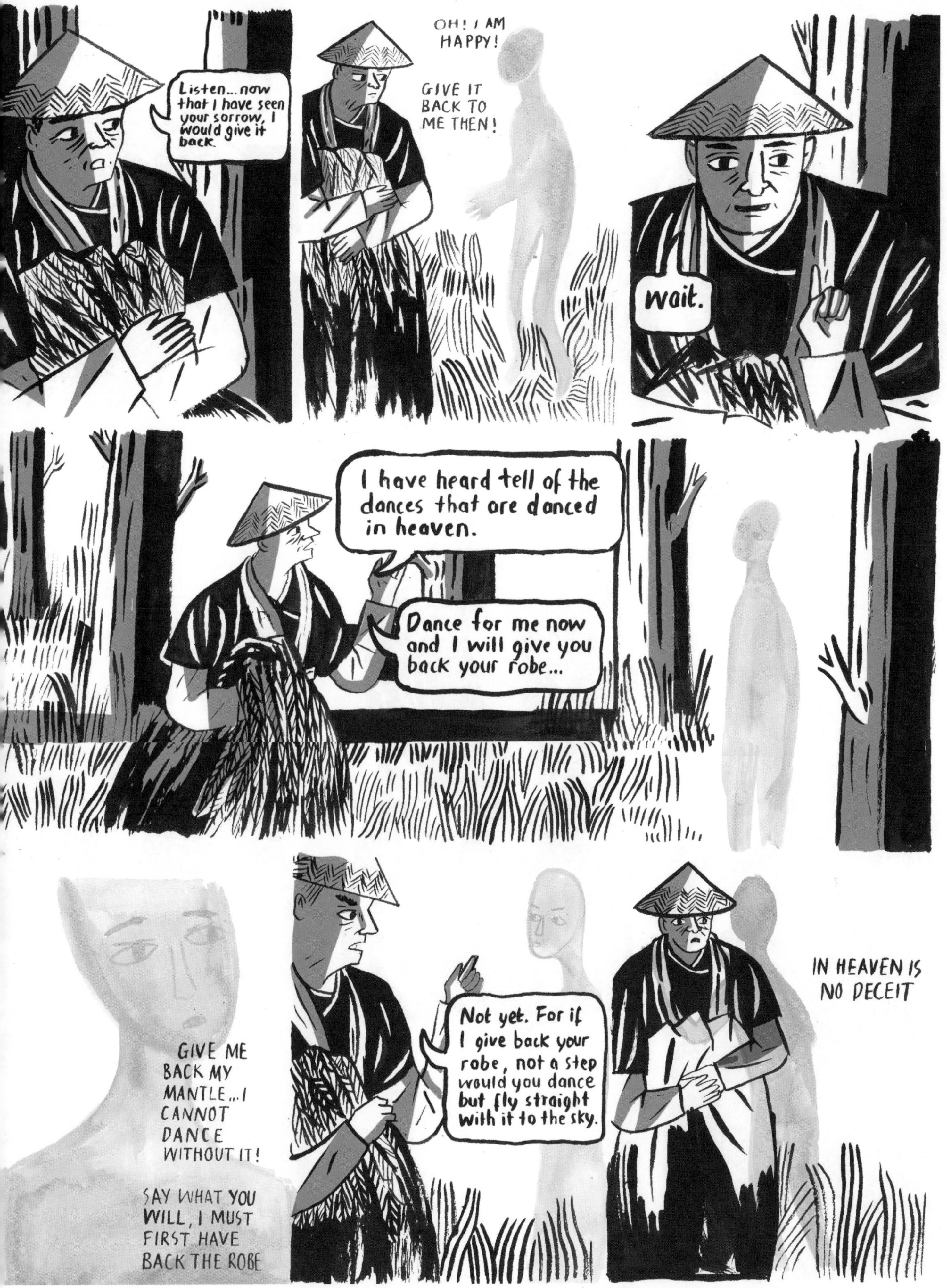
Listen... now that I have seen your sorrow, I would give it back.
OH! I AM HAPPY!
GIVE IT BACK TO ME THEN!
wait.
I have heard tell of the dances that are danced in heaven.
Dance for me now and I will give you back your robe...
GIVE ME BACK MY MANTLE... I CANNOT DANCE WITHOUT IT!
SAY WHAT YOU WILL, I MUST FIRST HAVE BACK THE ROBE
Not yet. For if I give back your robe, not a step would you dance but fly straight with it to the sky.
IN HEAVEN IS NO DECEIT

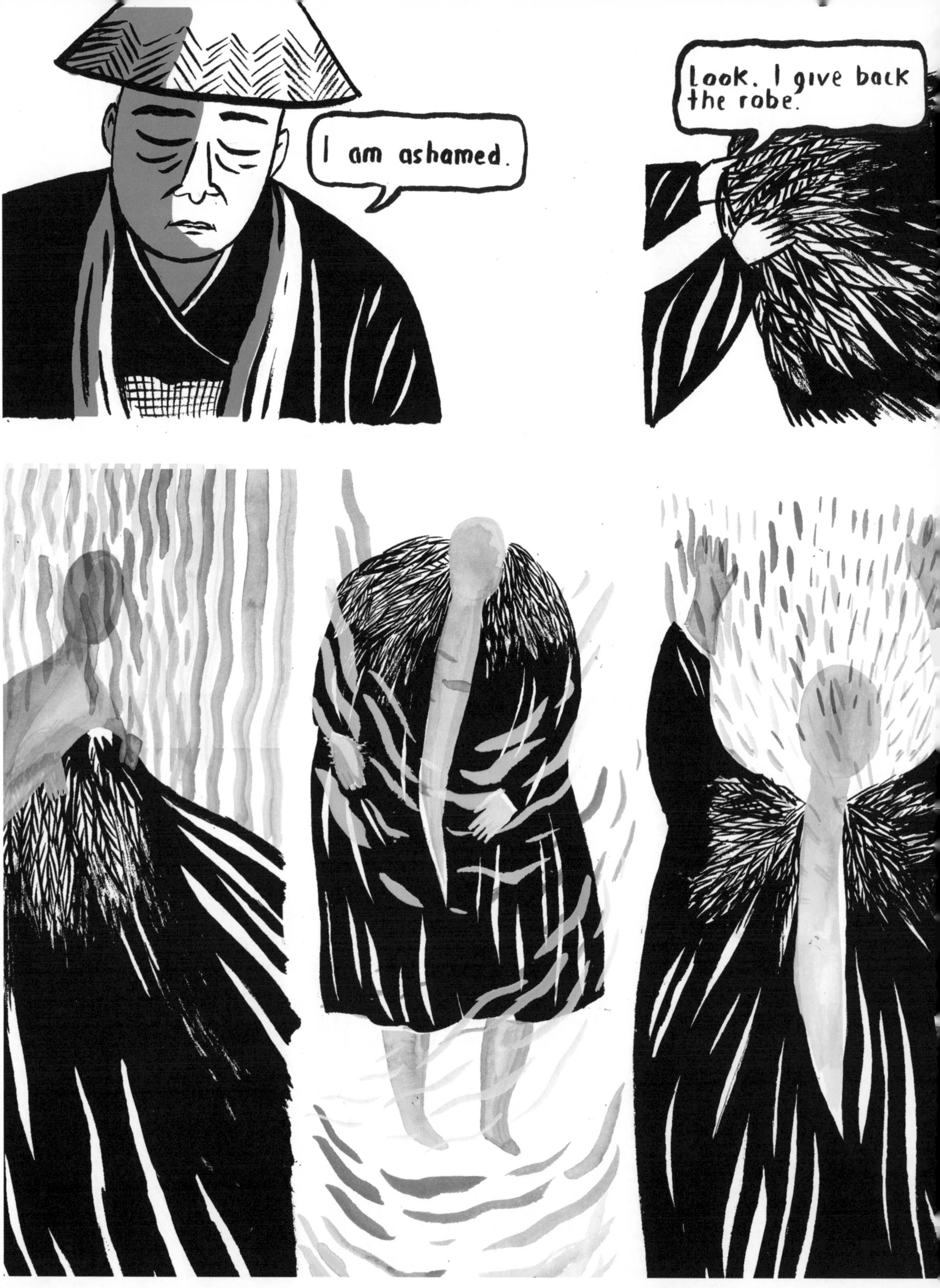
I am ashamed.
Look. I give back the robe.

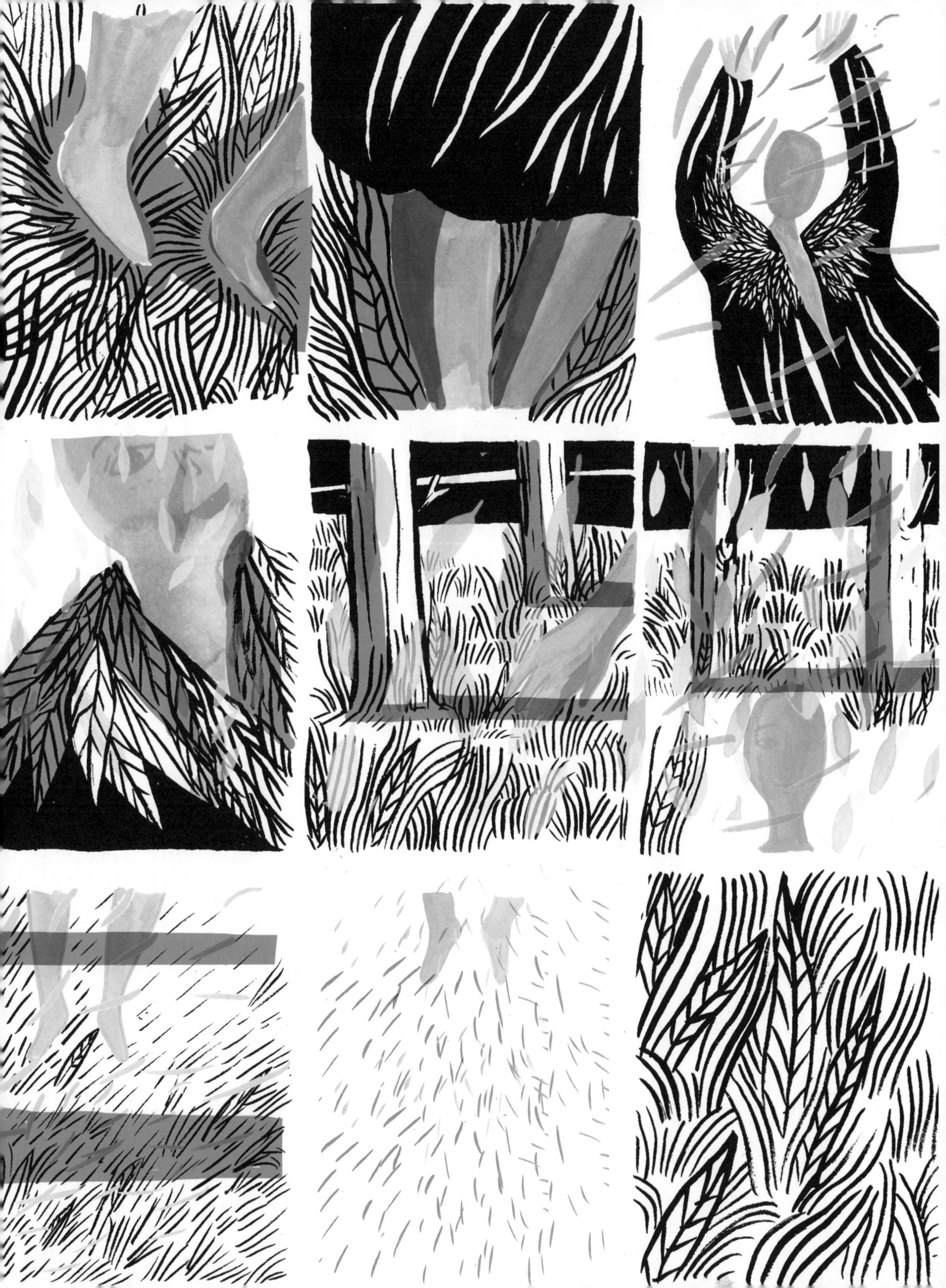

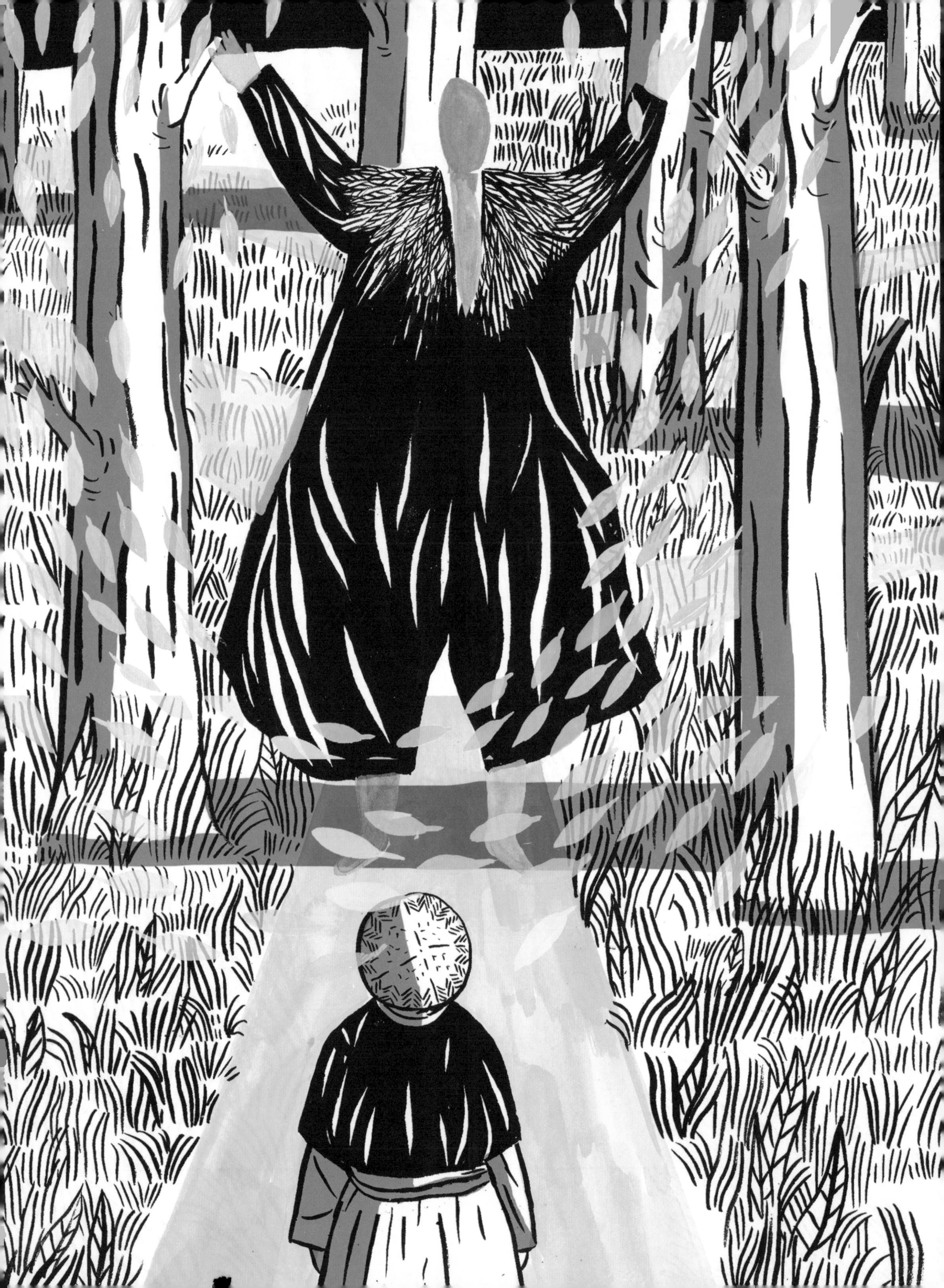

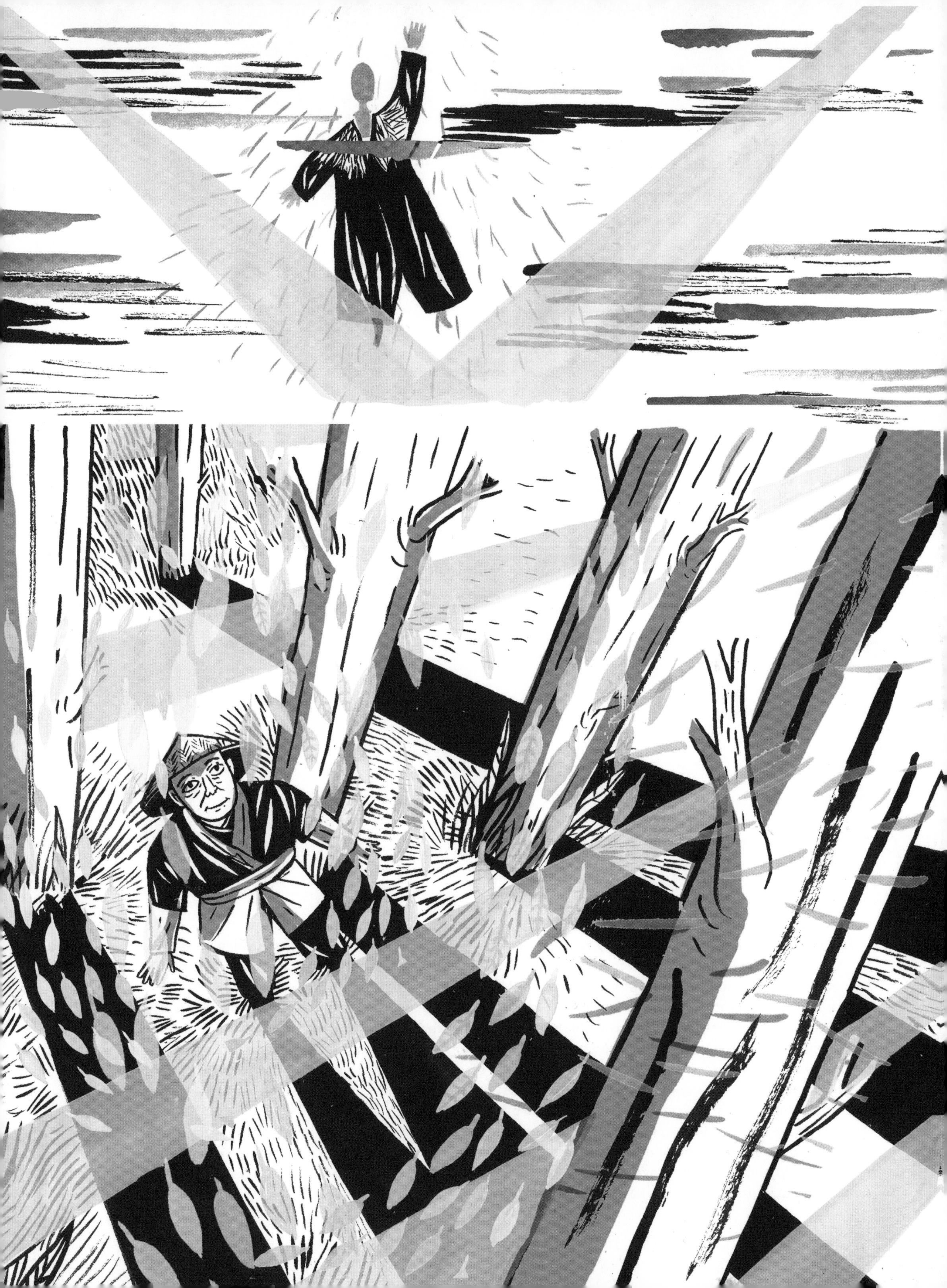

Popol Vuh

sacred book of the Quiché Maya

ART / ADAPTATION BY **Roberta Gregory**

POPOL VUH (I.E., COUNCIL BOOK) IS THE SACRED book of the Quiché Maya of Guatemala. It contains their wonderful creation story, an epic adventure tale of heroic twin brothers, a mythological history of the Quiché Maya, and a genealogy of their rulers. It is the only such book of any Native American tribe to survive and thus has a unique place in world literature.

The invading and occupying Spaniards burned most but not all of the Mayans' hieroglyphic books; only four are known to have survived to the present. Missionaries created a Roman alphabet version of the native language so the Mayans could write Catholic prayers and such in their own language, but, putting this new writing system to unauthor-

ized use, members of the royal lineages translated several ancient hieroglyphic works and assembled them into *Popol Vuh* in the mid-1500s.

Legendary underground comics artist Roberta Gregory—creator of the character Bitchy Bitch and the *Feminist Funnies* comic strip—gives us the first graphic adaptation from *Popol Vuh*: the story of the creation of humans.

SOURCE

Tedlock, Dennis (translator). *Popol Vuh: The Definitive Edition of the Mayan Book of the Dawn of Life and the Glories of Gods and Kings* (revised and expanded edition). Touchstone/Simon & Schuster, 1996.

How the gods peopled the earth: a story from: Popol Vuh*

* The Quiché Mayan book of creation

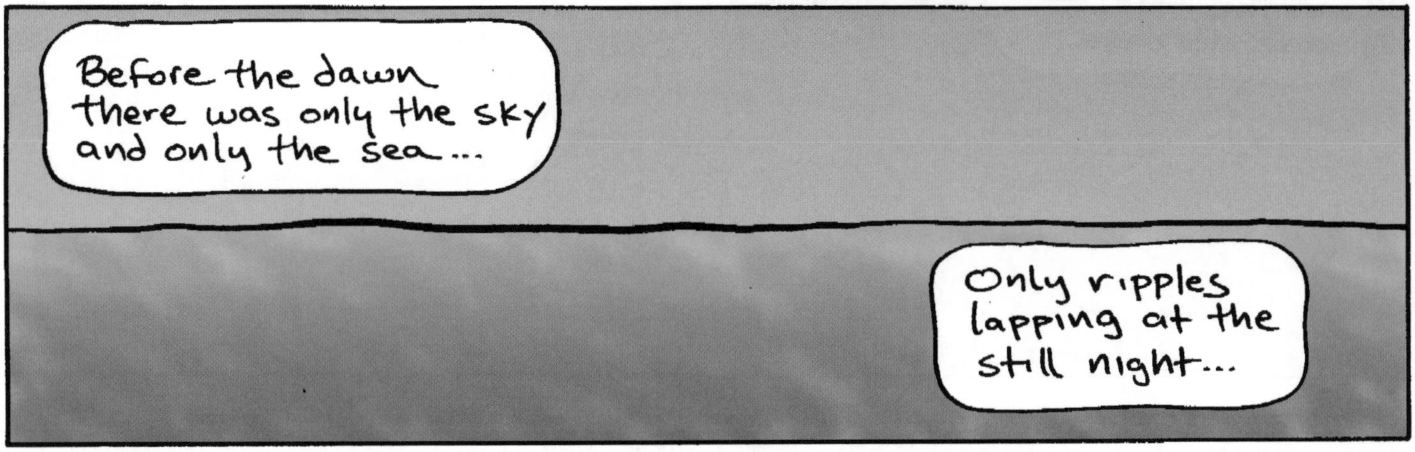
Before the dawn there was only the sky and only the sea...
Only ripples lapping at the still night...

And the gods spoke: Maker, Modeler, Bearer, Begetter:

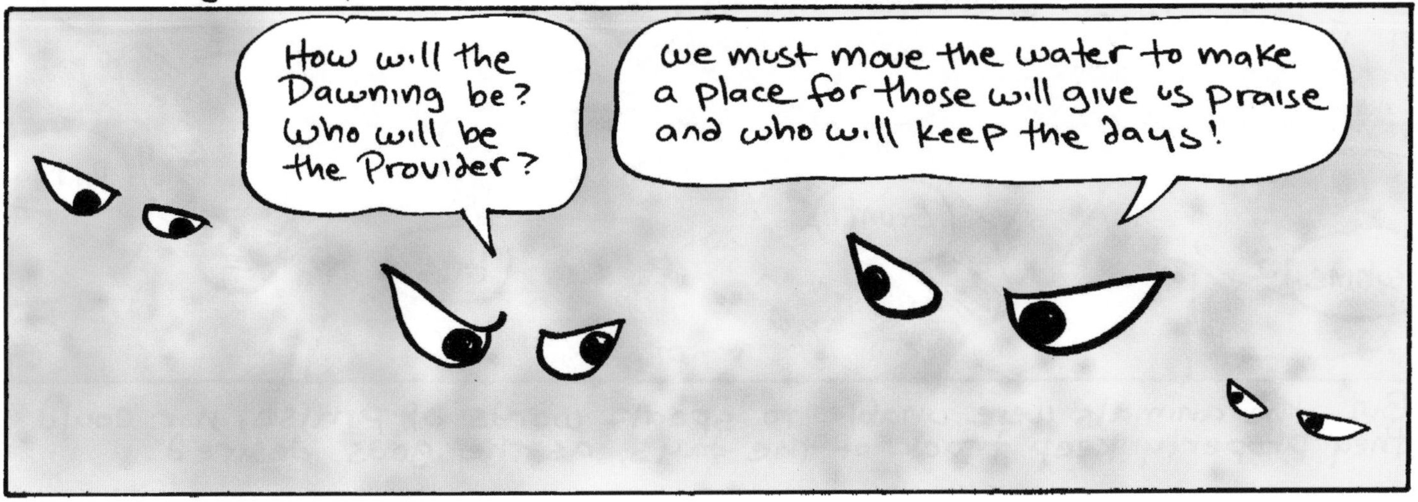
How will the Dawning be? Who will be the Provider?
We must move the water to make a place for those will give us praise and who will keep the days!

At their words, the land arose: Mountains, plains, forests, and rivers. But...

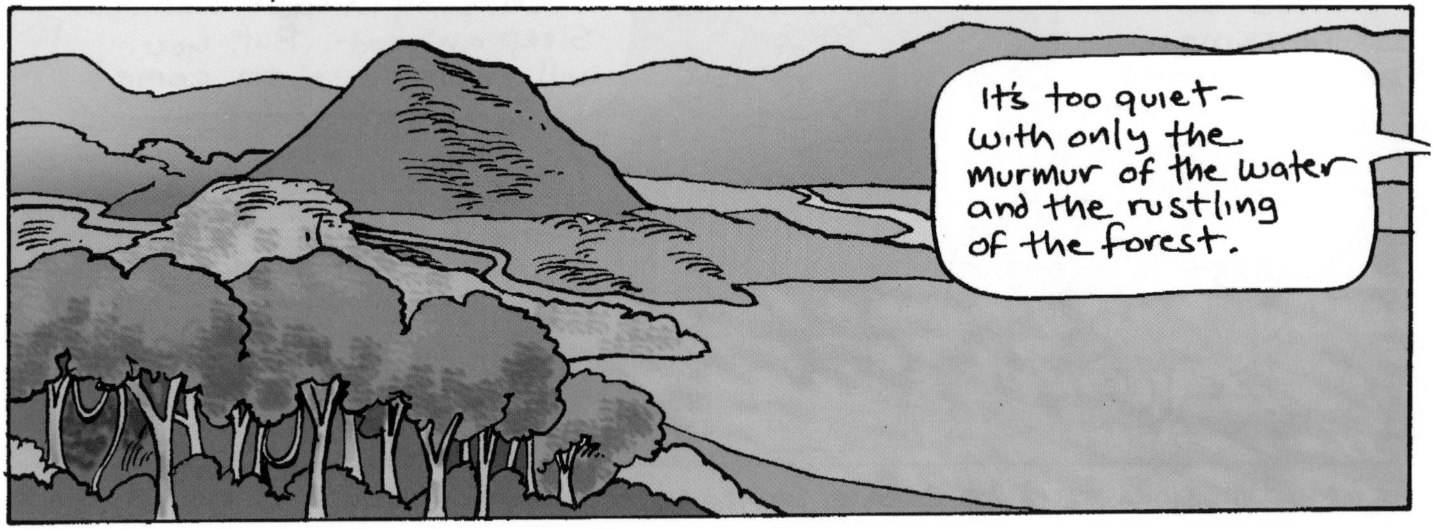
It's too quiet— with only the murmur of the water and the rustling of the forest.

And so came the animals, the guardians, deer and birds, to the land.

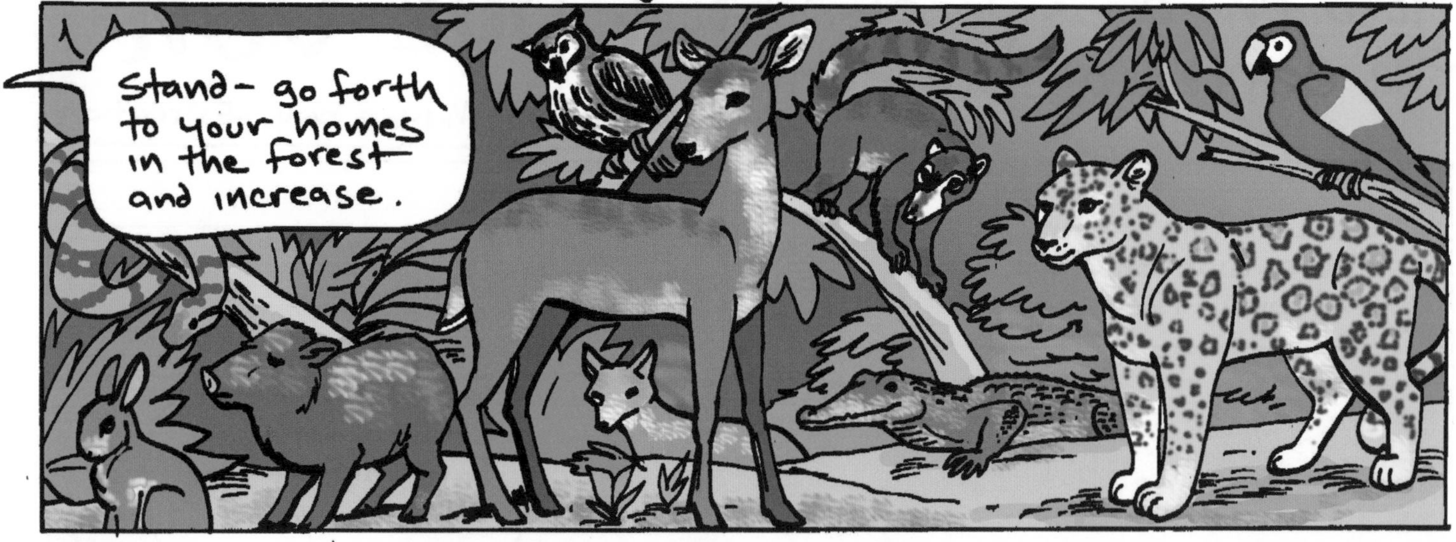
Stand- go forth to your homes in the forest and increase.

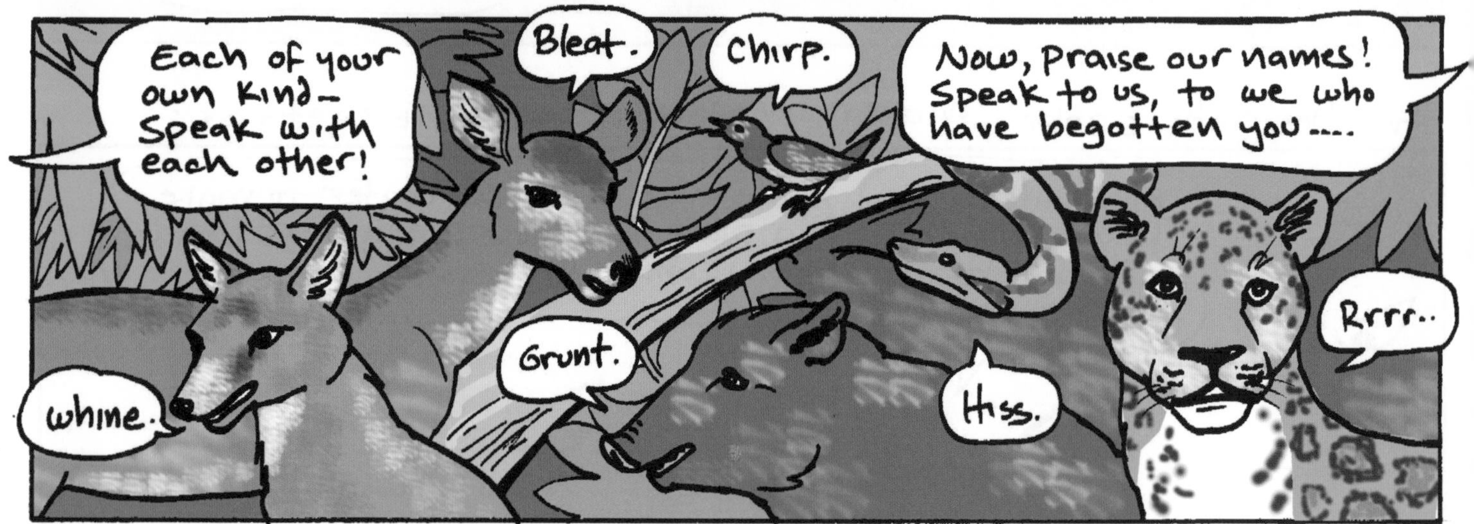
Each of your own kind- Speak with each other!
Bleat.
Chirp.
Now, praise our names! Speak to us, to we who have begotten you....
Rrrr..
Grunt.
whine.
Hiss.

But, the animals were unable to speak words of praise, nor could they properly keep track of the days, as the gods desired.

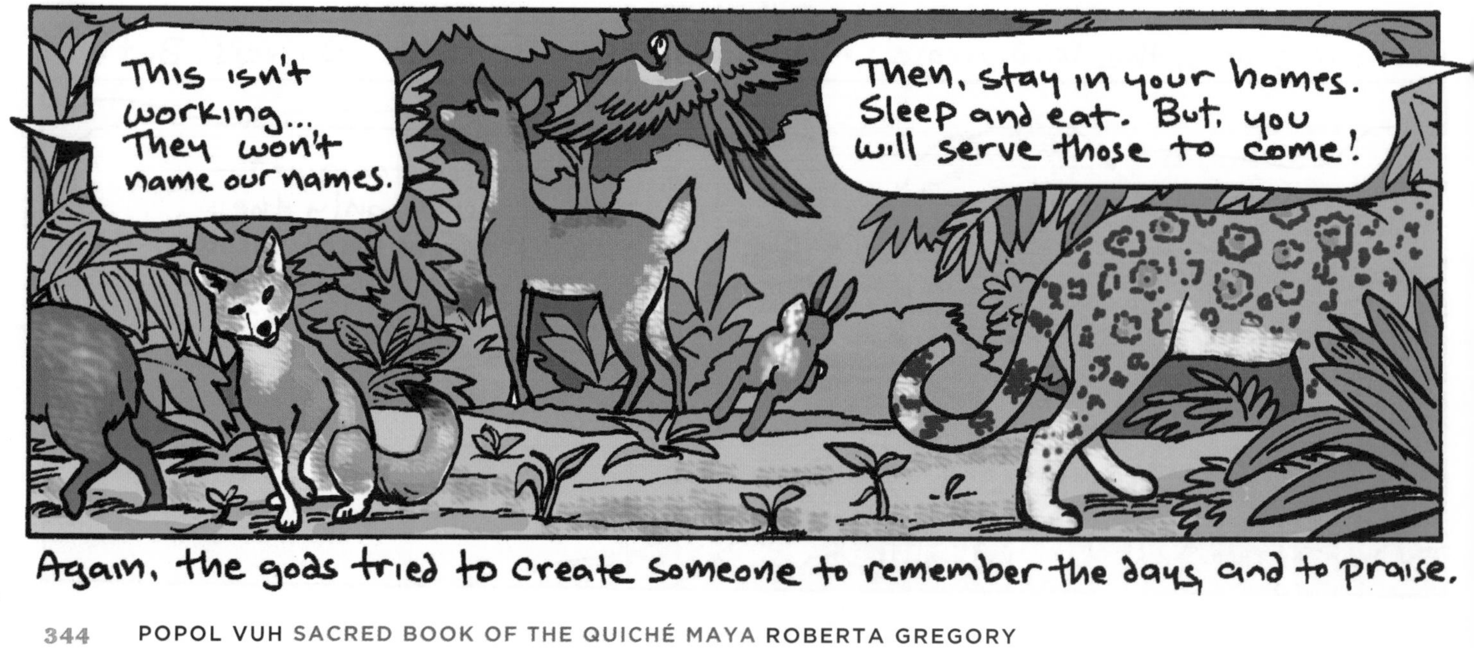
This isn't working... They won't name our names.
Then, stay in your homes. Sleep and eat. But, you will serve those to come!

Again, the gods tried to create someone to remember the days, and to praise.

Out of the mud of the earth itself, the gods modeled humankind. But...

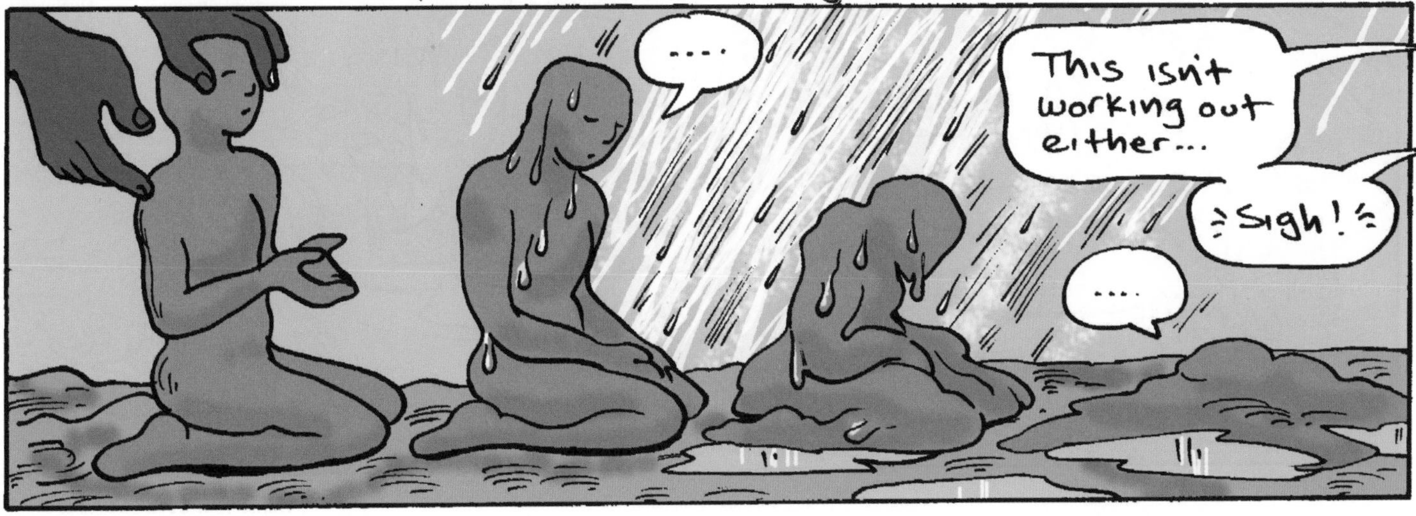
....
This isn't working out either...
Sigh!
....

The gods consulted the daykeepers: Xpiyacoc and Xmucane.

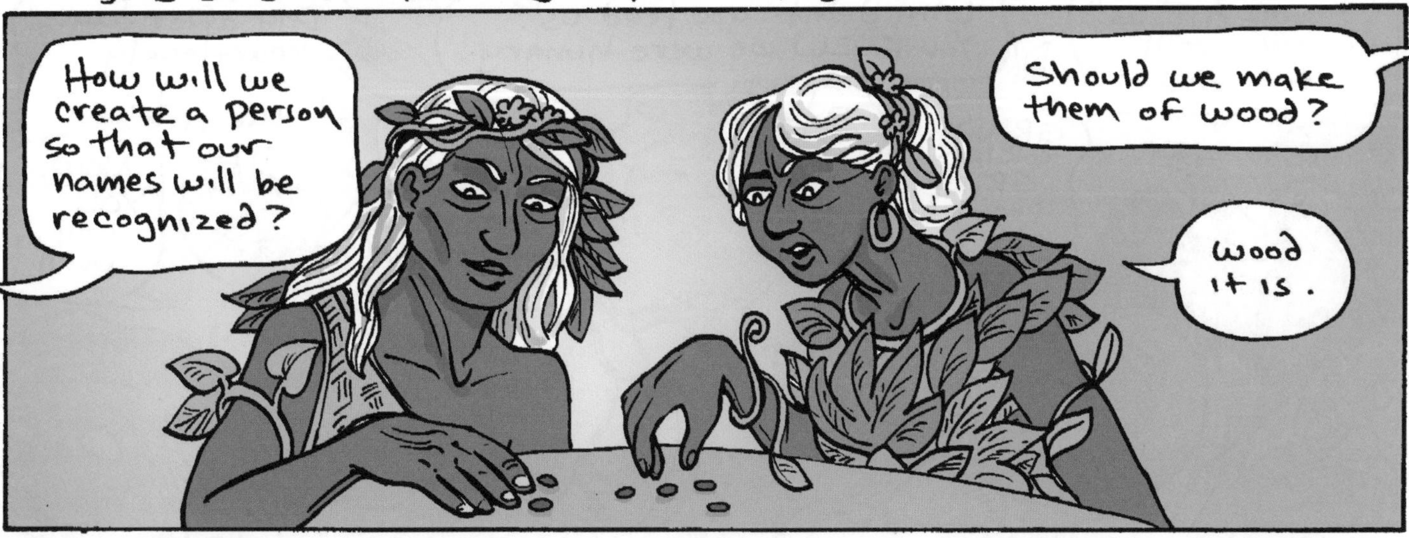
How will we create a person so that our names will be recognized?
Should we make them of wood?
Wood it is.

And, the people of wood came, to build homes and fill the land with children.

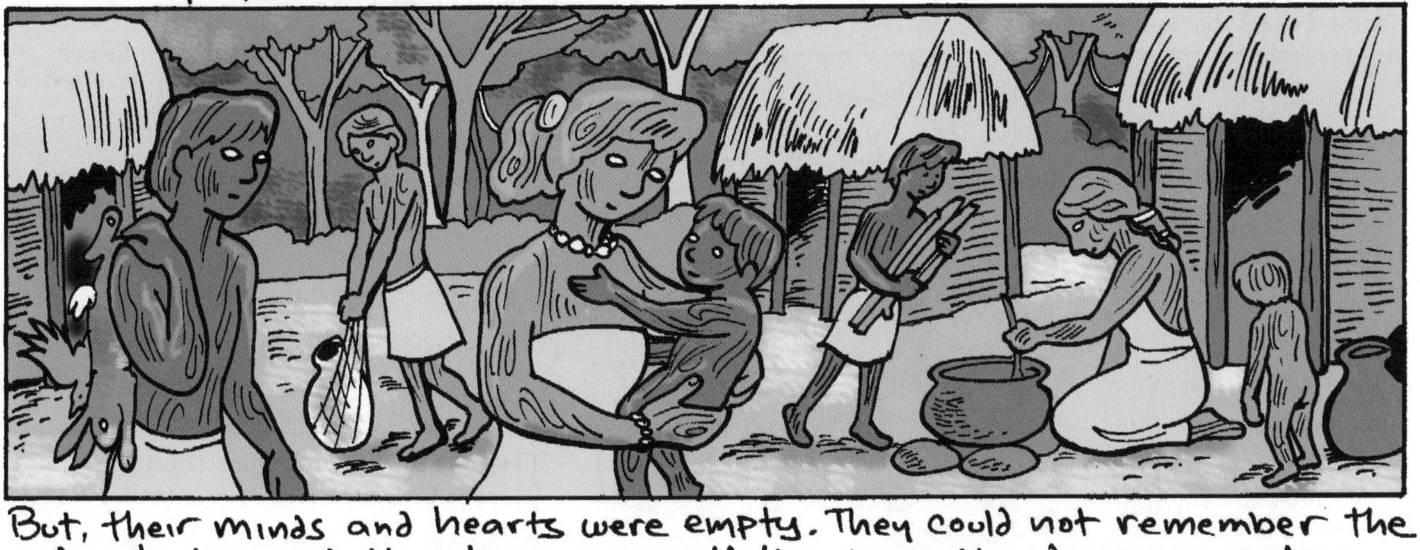

But, their minds and hearts were empty. They could not remember the gods who brought them here, nor could they keep the days in order.

This time the gods themselves destroyed their badly-flawed creations.

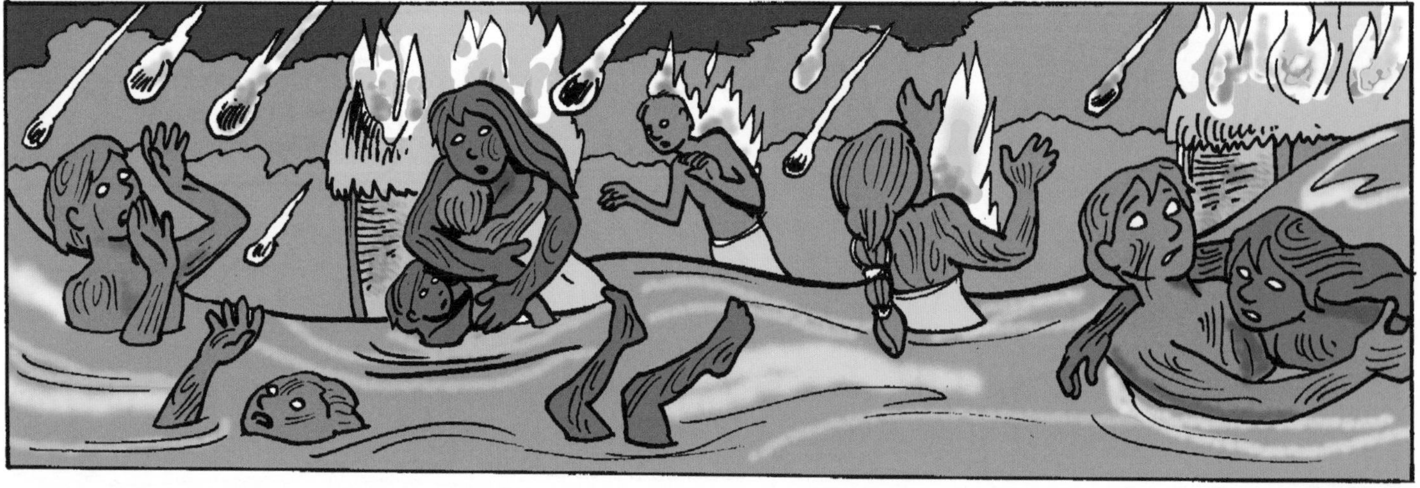

Their dogs and turkeys, cookpots and grinding stones spoke of vengeance.

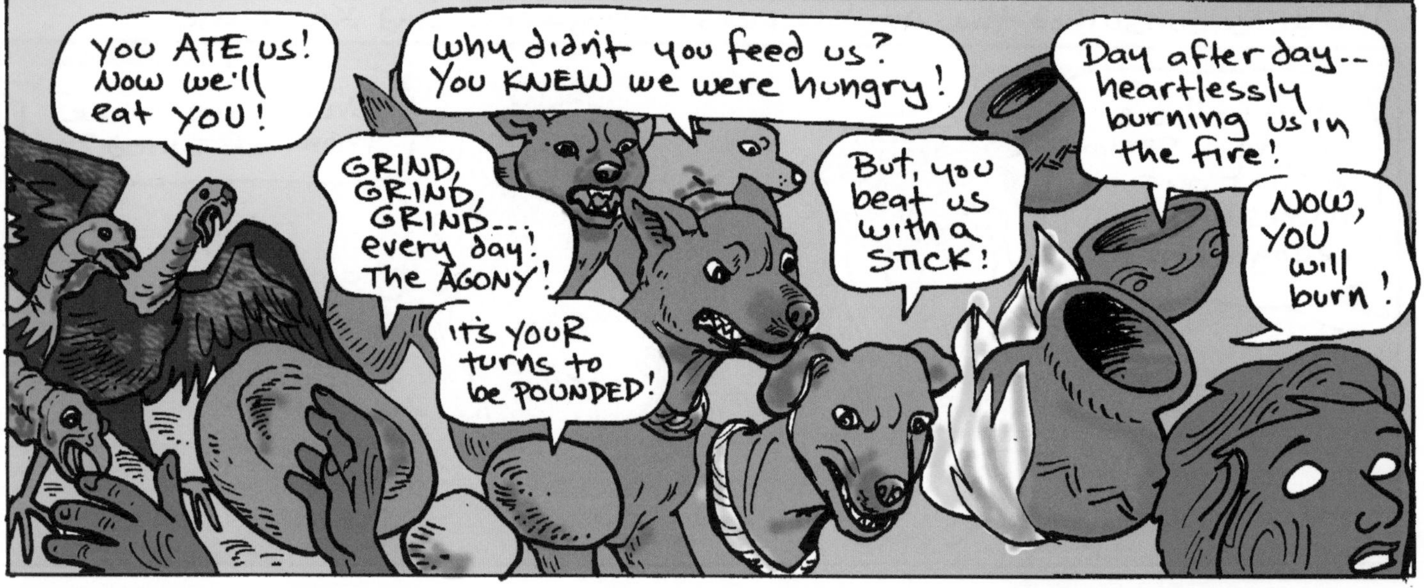

You ATE us! Now we'll eat YOU!
Why didn't you feed us? You KNEW we were hungry!
Day after day.. heartlessly burning us in the fire!
GRIND, GRIND, GRIND... every day! The AGONY!
But, you beat us with a STICK!
NOW, YOU will burn!
It's YOUR turns to be POUNDED!

The people tried to climb trees, but were thrown off.
They tried to hide in caves, but the caves closed up.

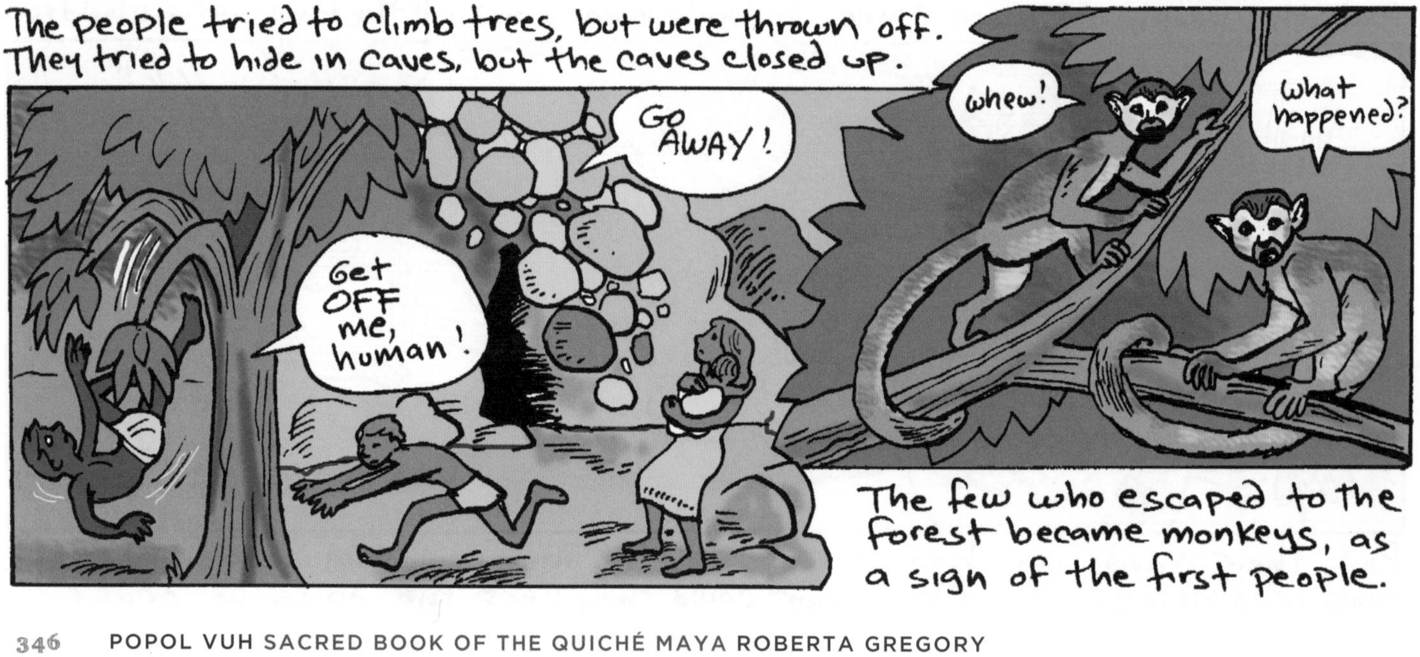

whew!
What happened?
GO AWAY!
Get OFF me, human!

The few who escaped to the forest became monkeys, as a sign of the first people.

At last, the animals showed the way. Coyote, fox, Parrot and Crow came to the mountain called Split Place, and discovered the good foods:

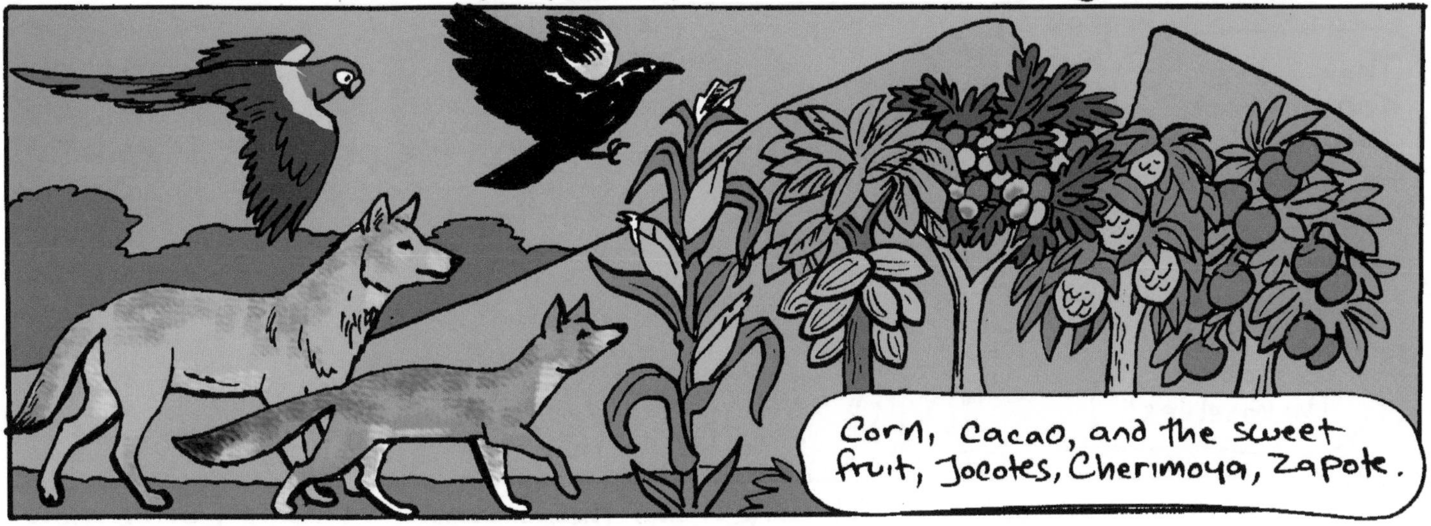
Corn, Cacao, and the sweet fruit, Jocotes, Cherimoya, Zapote.

Grandmother Xmucane ground the corn finely, nine times, and modeled four men. These were true humans, the very first mother-fathers.

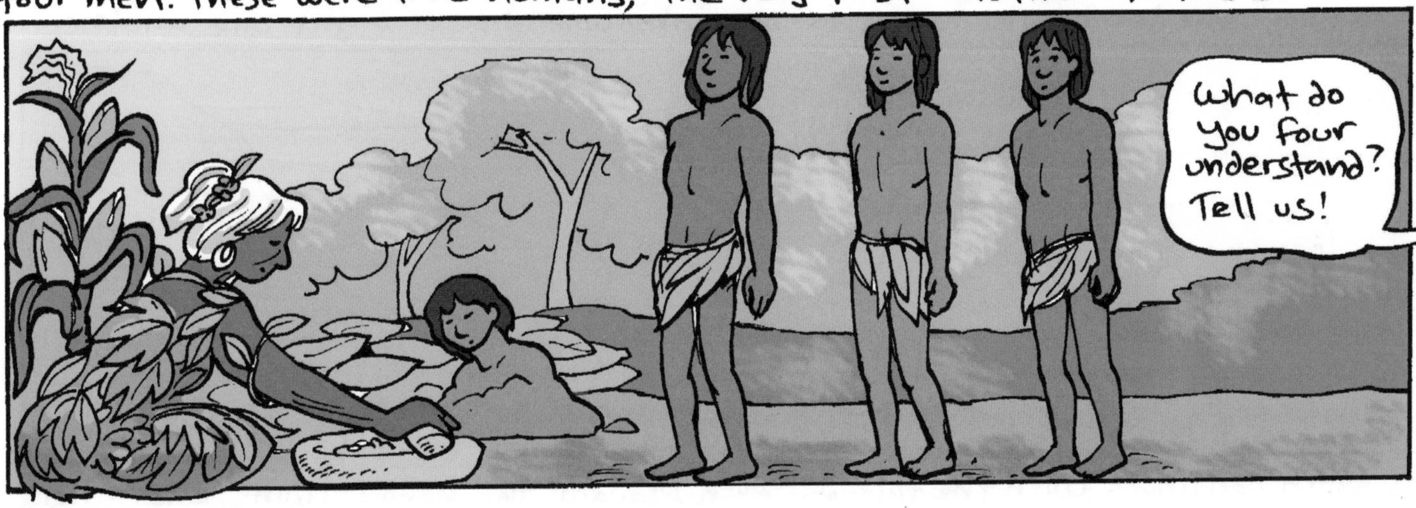
What do you four understand? Tell us!

They were all-knowing. They could see everything and they gave thanks.

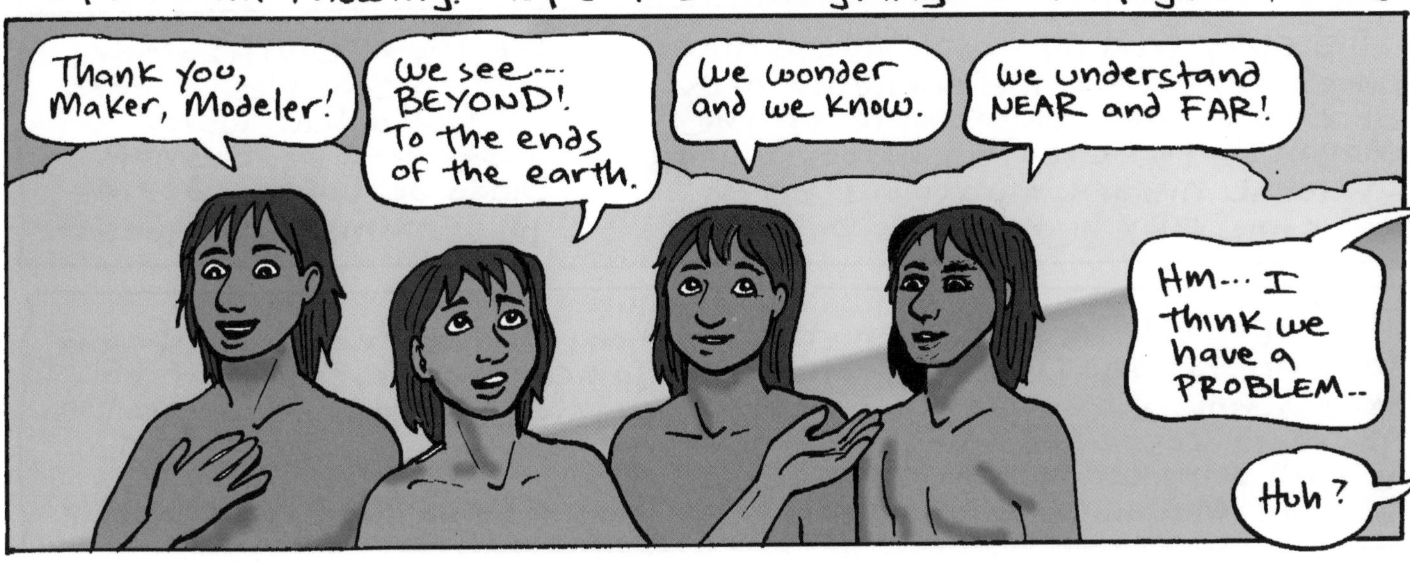
Thank you, Maker, Modeler!
We see... BEYOND! To the ends of the earth.
We wonder and we know.
We understand NEAR and FAR!
Hm... I think we have a PROBLEM..
Huh?

So, the gods took away knowledge...clouded their vision, as a mirror is fogged.

Hm?

They were too perfect! They can't see to eternity!

I...?

They'd be as great as gods themselves!

But they gave each man a beautiful wife... and they were very happy once more.

And so, the new age began. The people grew in number and spread throughout the land, into many tribes who would soon fight one another...

But, this is only the... beginning!

The story continues with the tale of Seven Macaw, the heroic Twins, and others.

This story from the Popol Vuh is just an excerpt from the surviving copy of one version of the epic of the Mayan People. Creation, heroes, villains, cultural history, miraculous birth and some VERY high-stakes ball games!

The Maya Civilization created countless books. All but a few were destroyed by Bishop Diego de Landa during the Spanish conquest.

The Popol Vuh is still open to interpretation. Dennis Tedlock's translation is considered one of the more respected, but the story is still being written in the lives of the Mayan People today!

Many thanks to my good friend Janice Van Cleve, author of Eighteen Rabbit, for suggestions and additional information.

Thanx to Donna Barr for color help!

The visions of St. Teresa of Ávila

from her autobiography

ART / ADAPTATION BY **Edie Fake**

ST. TERESA OF ÁVILA IS CERTAINLY THE MOST well-known of the Catholic Church's mystical nuns. Her autobiography (*The Life of St. Teresa of Jesus*) and *The Interior Castle* are all-time classics of spiritual literature, and both contain numerous accounts of her mystical visions and transcendent experiences. (She's also a highly regarded part of Spain's literary canon in general.) Teresa's most famous vision—of an angel who pierced her heart with a burning spear, sending her into paroxysms of divine love—is depicted by one of the world's greatest statues, Bernini's *The Ecstasy of Saint Teresa.*

Teresa engaged the earthly world as well, actively reforming the Carmelite order in the 1500s by founding over a dozen convents based on simplicity, poverty, and prayer, thus incurring the wrath of the Inquisition. The Pope eventually called off the persecution of Teresa, though many of her comrades weren't so fortunate.

I was delighted when Edie Fake decided to illustrate Teresa's visions. All of his highly stylized artwork already seems like it's depicting mystical visions, so applying it to Teresa's vividly described experiences from her autobiography results in a perfect pairing.

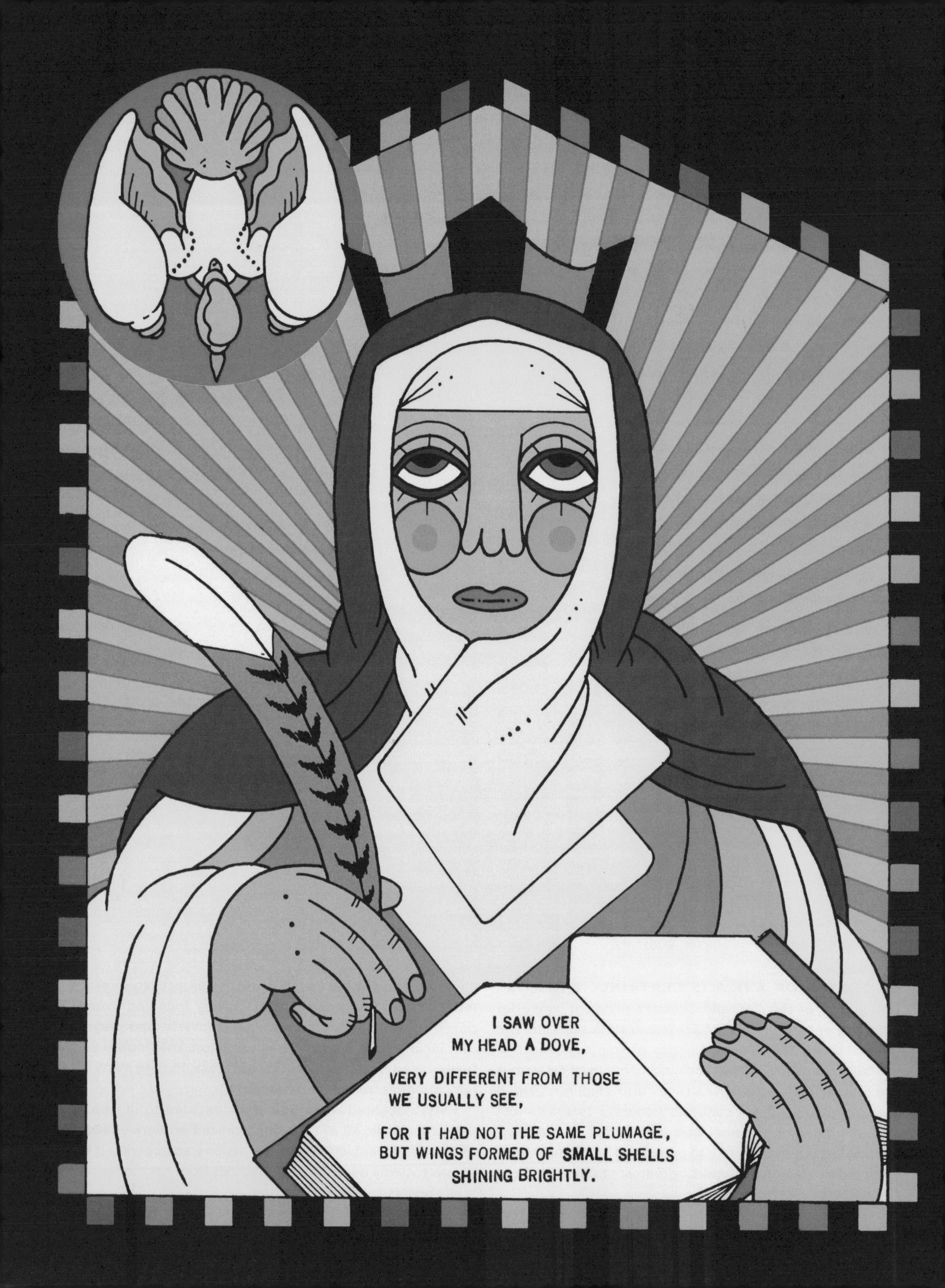
I SAW OVER
MY HEAD A DOVE,
VERY DIFFERENT FROM THOSE
WE USUALLY SEE,
FOR IT HAD NOT THE SAME PLUMAGE,
BUT WINGS FORMED OF SMALL SHELLS
SHINING BRIGHTLY.

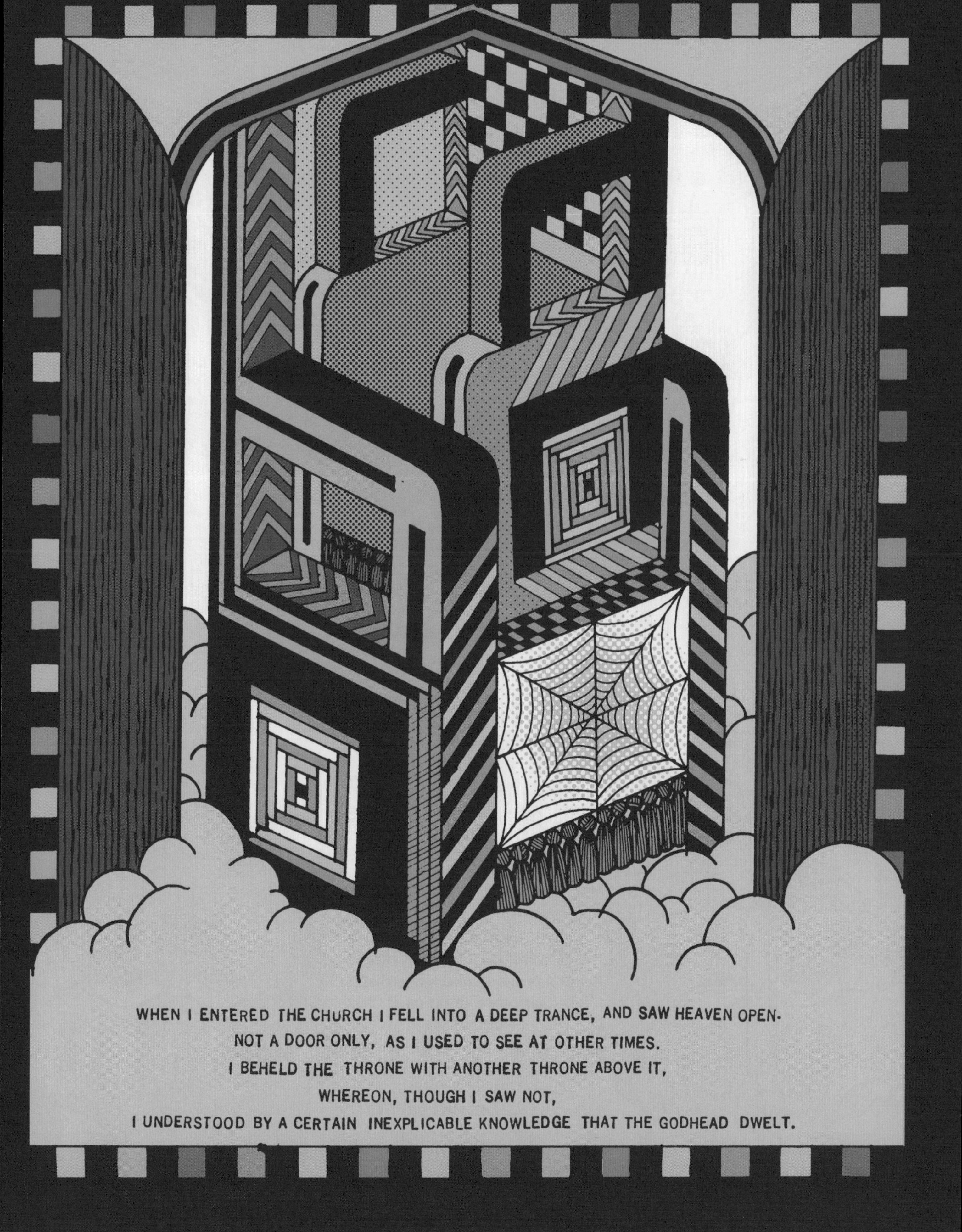
WHEN I ENTERED THE CHURCH I FELL INTO A DEEP TRANCE, AND SAW HEAVEN OPEN-
NOT A DOOR ONLY, AS I USED TO SEE AT OTHER TIMES.
I BEHELD THE THRONE WITH ANOTHER THRONE ABOVE IT,
WHEREON, THOUGH I SAW NOT,
I UNDERSTOOD BY A CERTAIN INEXPLICABLE KNOWLEDGE THAT THE GODHEAD DWELT.

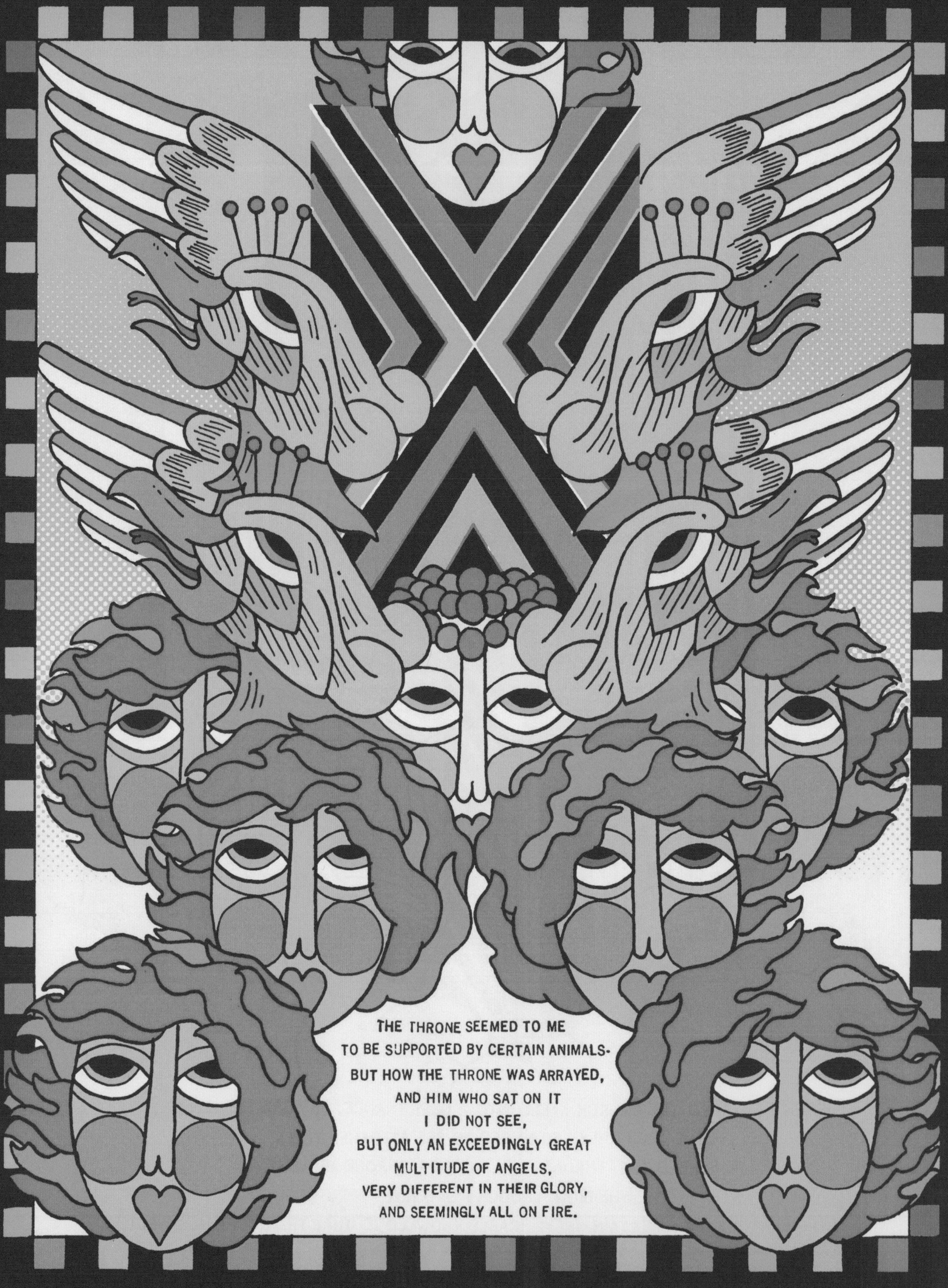
THE THRONE SEEMED TO ME
TO BE SUPPORTED BY CERTAIN ANIMALS-
BUT HOW THE THRONE WAS ARRAYED,
AND HIM WHO SAT ON IT
I DID NOT SEE,
BUT ONLY AN EXCEEDINGLY GREAT
MULTITUDE OF ANGELS,
VERY DIFFERENT IN THEIR GLORY,
AND SEEMINGLY ALL ON FIRE.

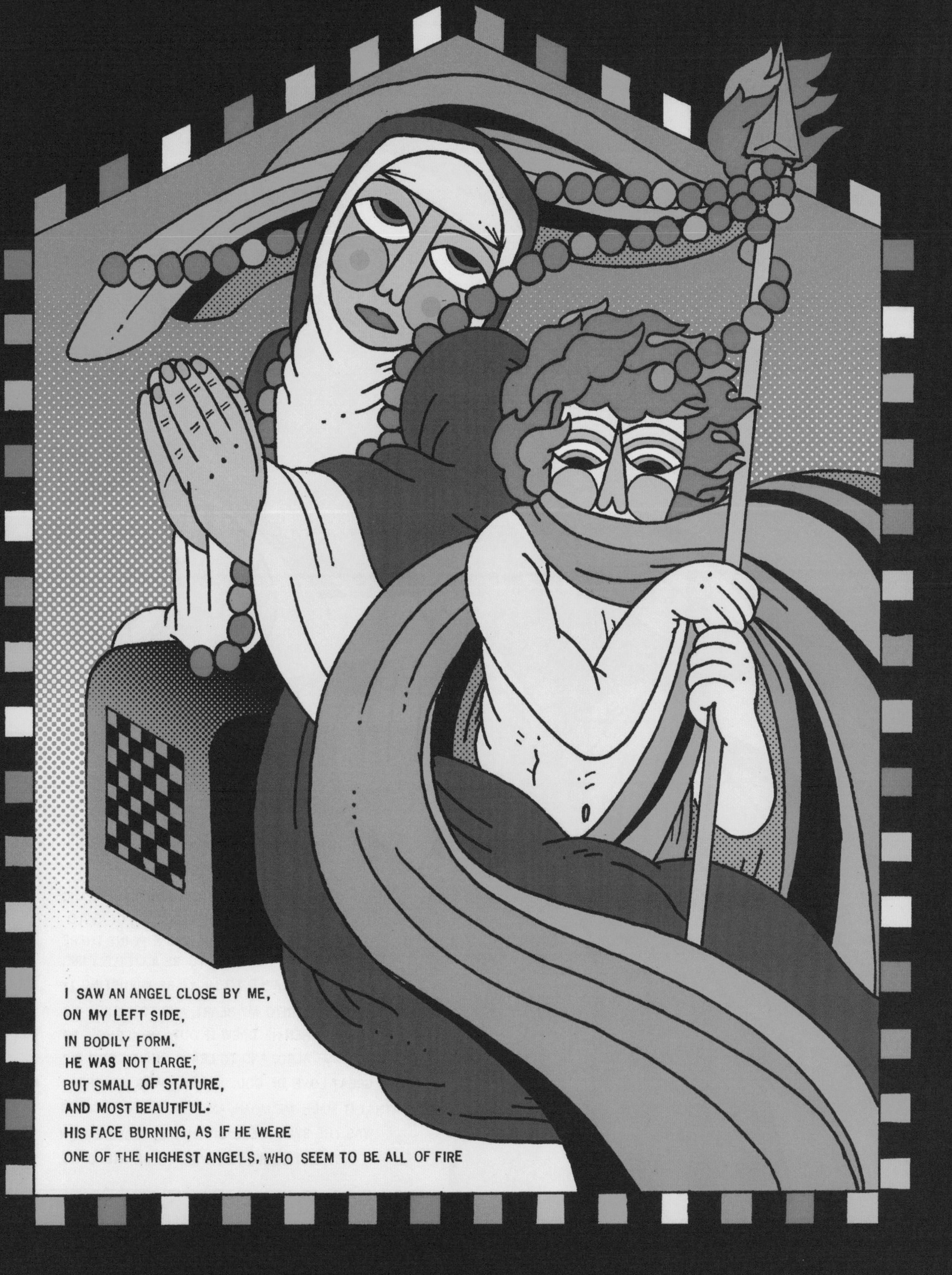
I SAW AN ANGEL CLOSE BY ME,
ON MY LEFT SIDE,
IN BODILY FORM.
HE WAS NOT LARGE,
BUT SMALL OF STATURE,
AND MOST BEAUTIFUL.
HIS FACE BURNING, AS IF HE WERE
ONE OF THE HIGHEST ANGELS, WHO SEEM TO BE ALL OF FIRE

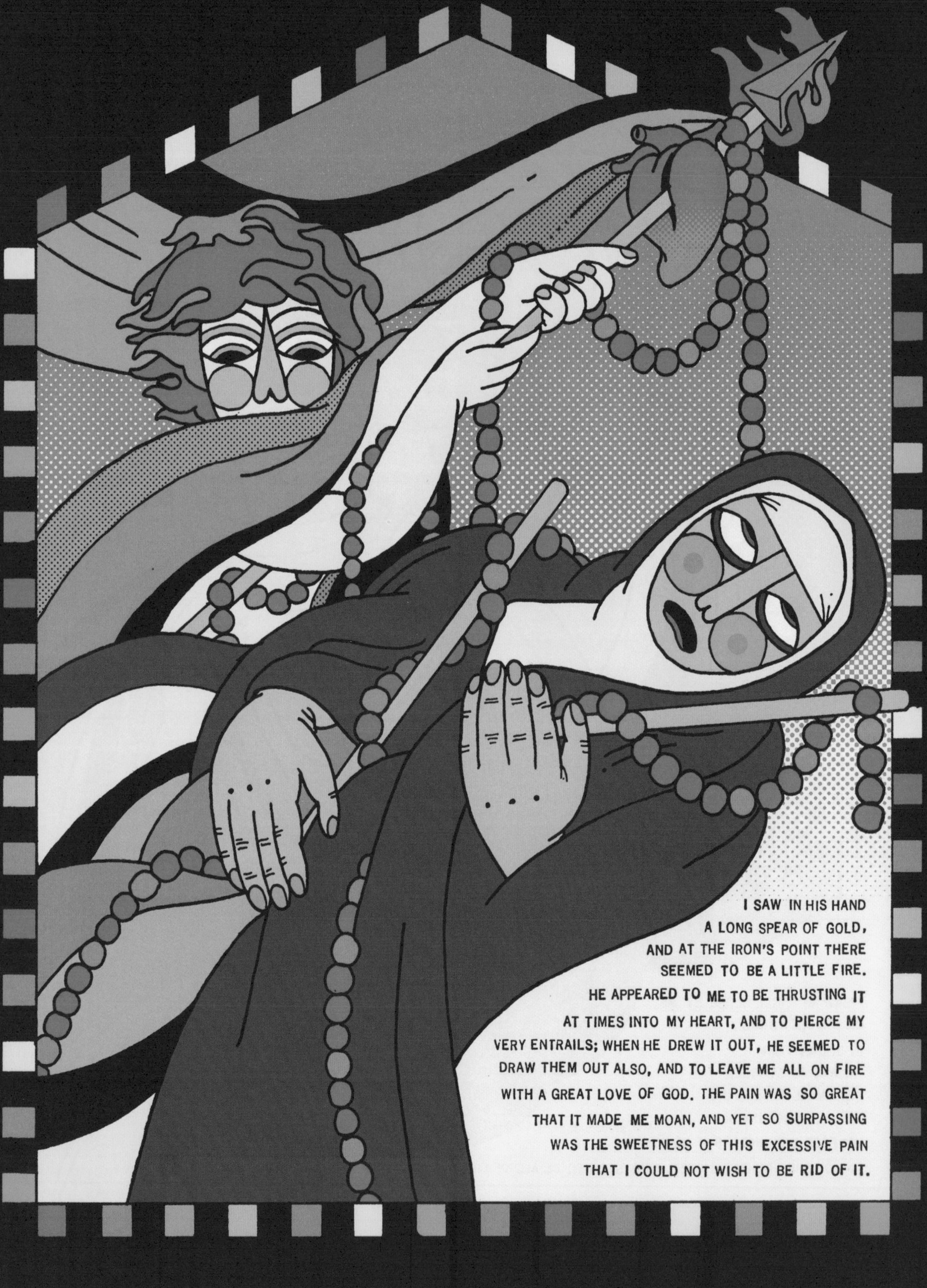
I SAW IN HIS HAND
A LONG SPEAR OF GOLD,
AND AT THE IRON'S POINT THERE
SEEMED TO BE A LITTLE FIRE.
HE APPEARED TO ME TO BE THRUSTING IT
AT TIMES INTO MY HEART, AND TO PIERCE MY
VERY ENTRAILS; WHEN HE DREW IT OUT, HE SEEMED TO
DRAW THEM OUT ALSO, AND TO LEAVE ME ALL ON FIRE
WITH A GREAT LOVE OF GOD. THE PAIN WAS SO GREAT
THAT IT MADE ME MOAN, AND YET SO SURPASSING
WAS THE SWEETNESS OF THIS EXCESSIVE PAIN
THAT I COULD NOT WISH TO BE RID OF IT.

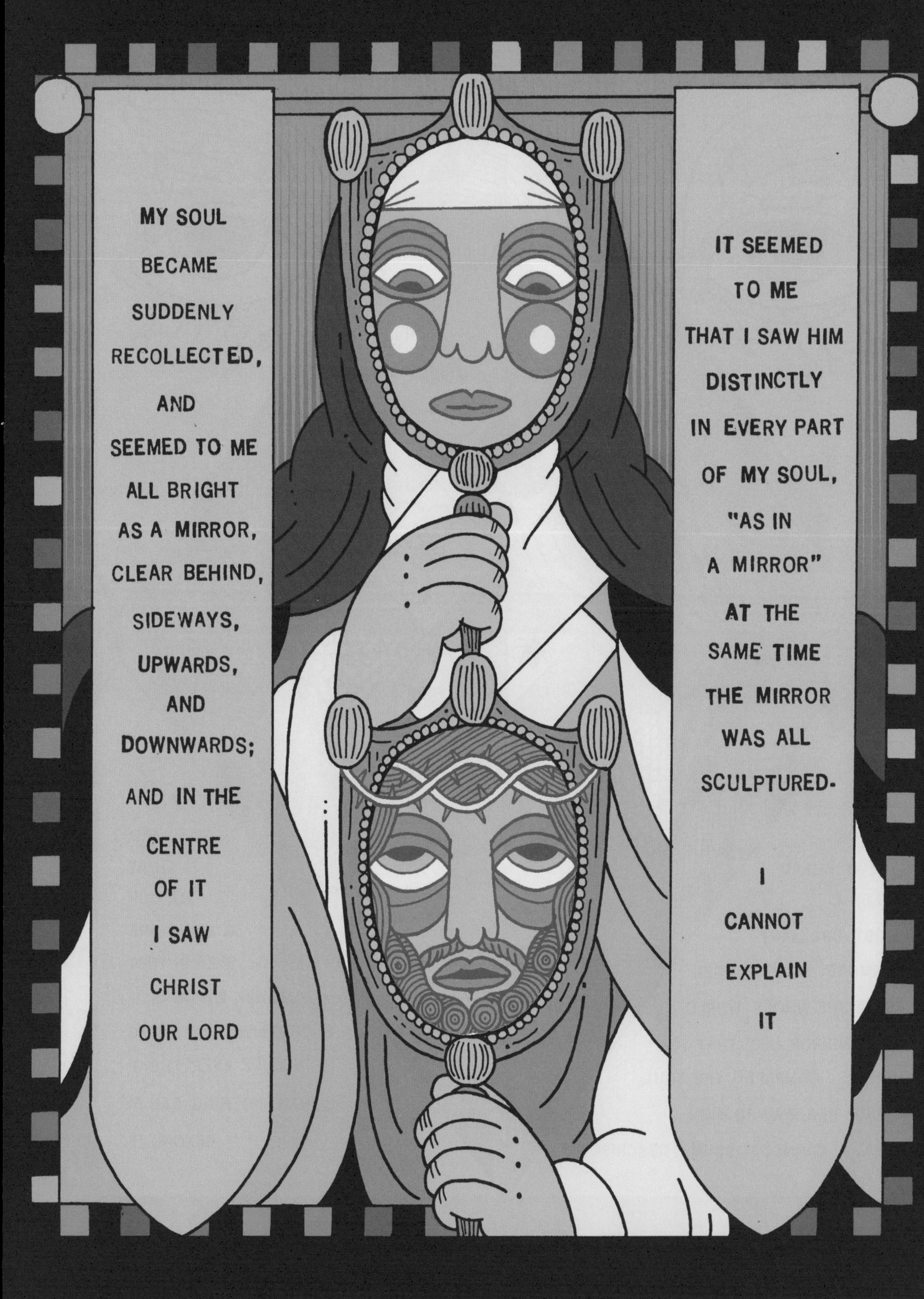
MY SOUL BECAME SUDDENLY RECOLLECTED, AND SEEMED TO ME ALL BRIGHT AS A MIRROR, CLEAR BEHIND, SIDEWAYS, UPWARDS, AND DOWNWARDS; AND IN THE CENTRE OF IT I SAW CHRIST OUR LORD
IT SEEMED TO ME THAT I SAW HIM DISTINCTLY IN EVERY PART OF MY SOUL, "AS IN A MIRROR" AT THE SAME TIME THE MIRROR WAS ALL SCULPTURED-
I CANNOT EXPLAIN IT

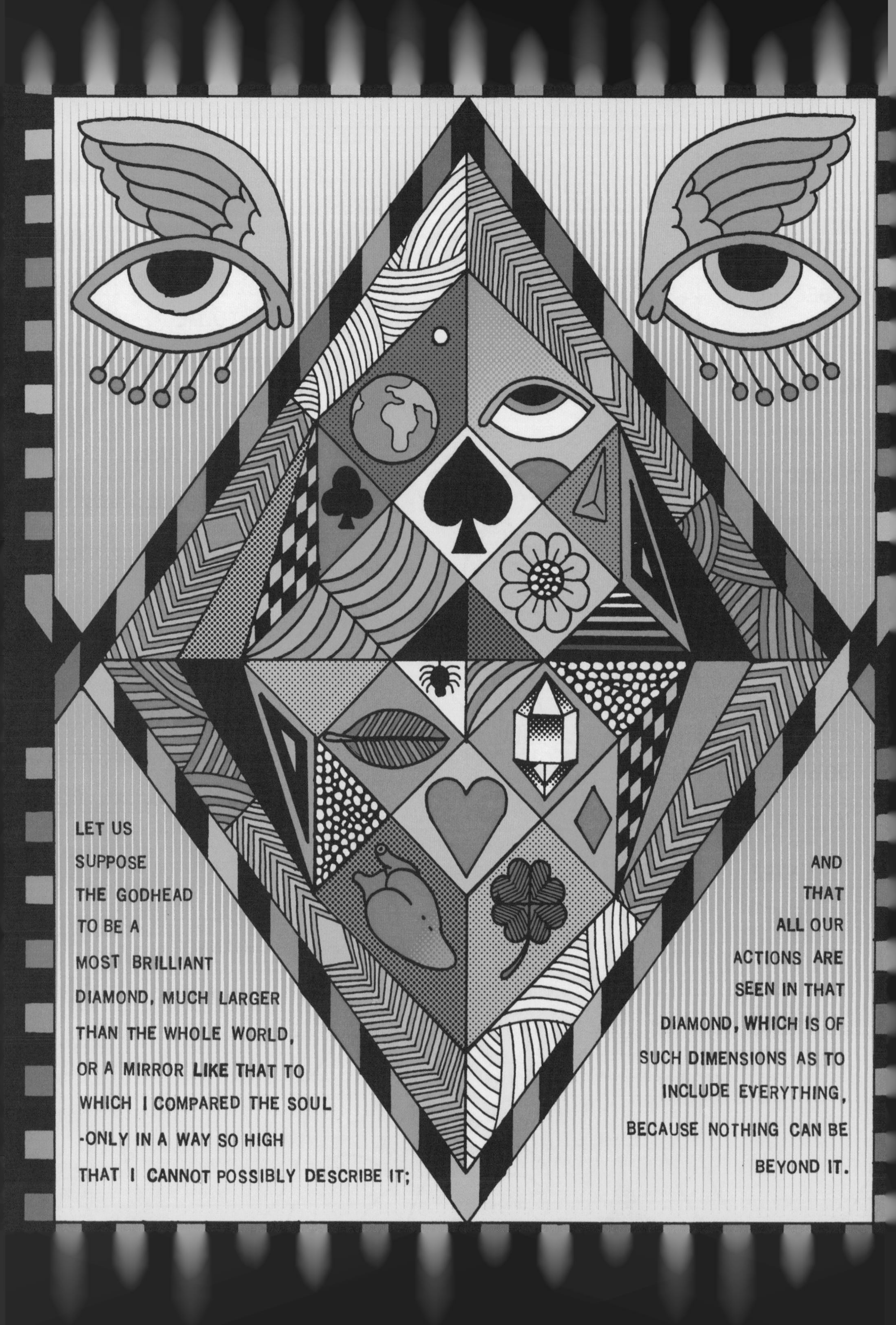
LET US SUPPOSE THE GODHEAD TO BE A MOST BRILLIANT DIAMOND, MUCH LARGER THAN THE WHOLE WORLD, OR A MIRROR LIKE THAT TO WHICH I COMPARED THE SOUL -ONLY IN A WAY SO HIGH THAT I CANNOT POSSIBLY DESCRIBE IT;
AND THAT ALL OUR ACTIONS ARE SEEN IN THAT DIAMOND, WHICH IS OF SUCH DIMENSIONS AS TO INCLUDE EVERYTHING, BECAUSE NOTHING CAN BE BEYOND IT.

"Hot Sun, Cool Fire"

George Peele

ART / ADAPTATION BY **Dave Morice**

THOUGH POPULAR IN HIS DAY—THE SECOND HALF of the 1500s—English dramatist and poet George Peele is mostly forgotten now. This lovely though ominous verse comes from the beginning of his play *The Love of King David and Fair Bethsabe.* David, you may recall, saw the beautiful Bathsheba bathing outside, and ended up arranging for her husband to die in battle so that he could marry the new widow, who was already pregnant with David's child. At the risk of oversimplifying this surprisingly complex little poem, in the first half, fair Bathsheba is asking her attendant to keep her from being burned by the Sun, perhaps by standing so that the attendant's shadow "shrouds" her. Things take a dark, foreshadowing turn in line six, as Bathsheba compares herself to the Sun in that she inflames (desire) and pierces the eye of anyone who might be spying upon her, which could (and does) end up causing mourning.

Dave Morice is a pioneer of visually adapting poems. From 1979 to 1982, his self-published zine *Poetry Comics* contained his takes on Shakespeare, Keats, Blake, Dickinson, Plath, Ginsberg, and dozens of others, leading to three anthologies, including an eponymous collection from Simon and Schuster. His visually arresting op art version of "Hot Sun, Cool Fire" almost singes our eyeballs, which makes clear the powerful energy—radiating from the Sun and from Bathsheba—contained in the poem.

SOURCE

Rumens, Carol. "Poem of the week: Bethsabe's Song by George Peele." London *Guardian* website, October 11, 2010.

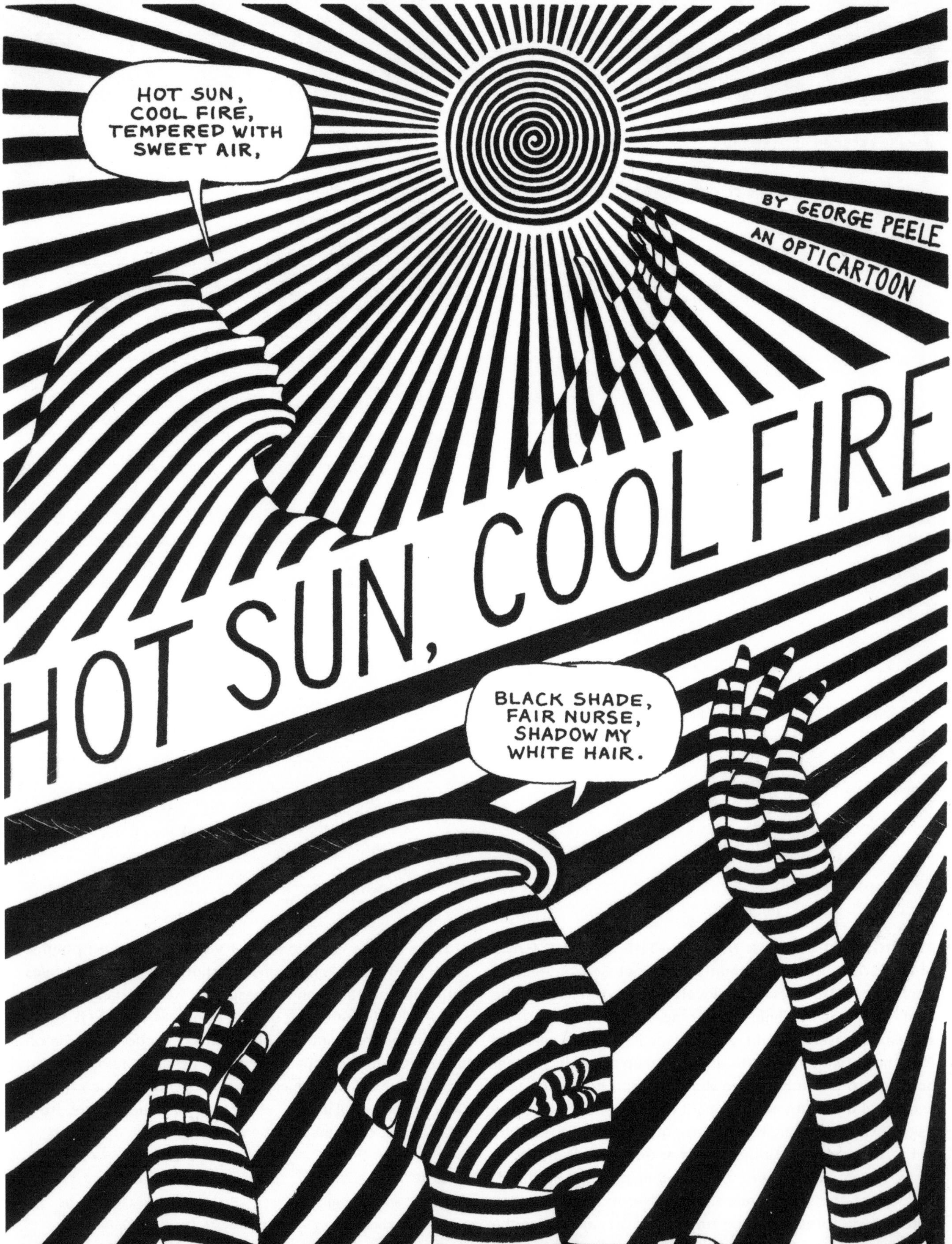
HOT SUN, COOL FIRE, TEMPERED WITH SWEET AIR,
BY GEORGE PEELE
AN OPTICARTOON
HOT SUN, COOL FIRE
BLACK SHADE, FAIR NURSE, SHADOW MY WHITE HAIR.

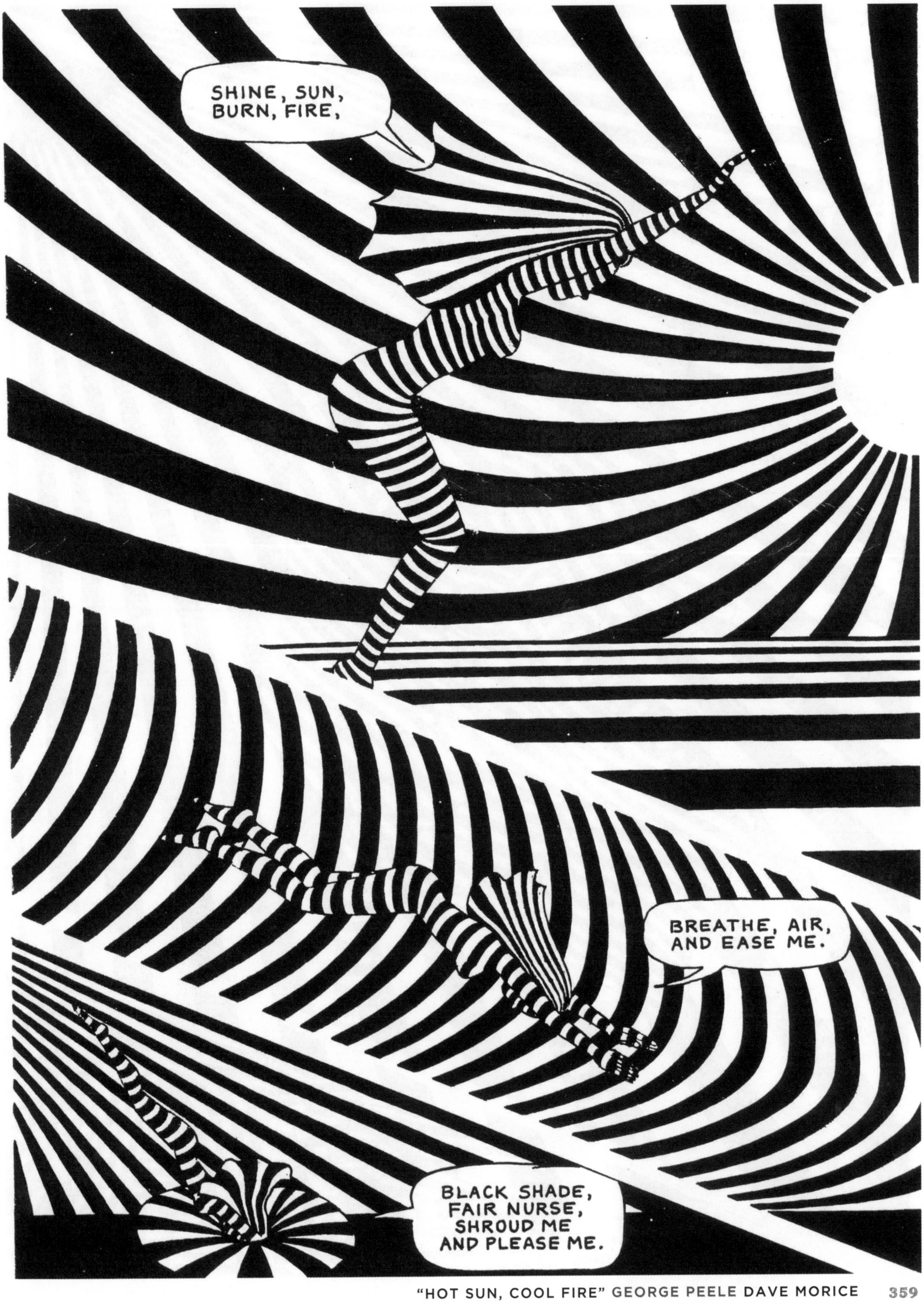
SHINE, SUN,
BURN, FIRE,
BREATHE, AIR,
AND EASE ME.
BLACK SHADE,
FAIR NURSE,
SHROUD ME
AND PLEASE ME.

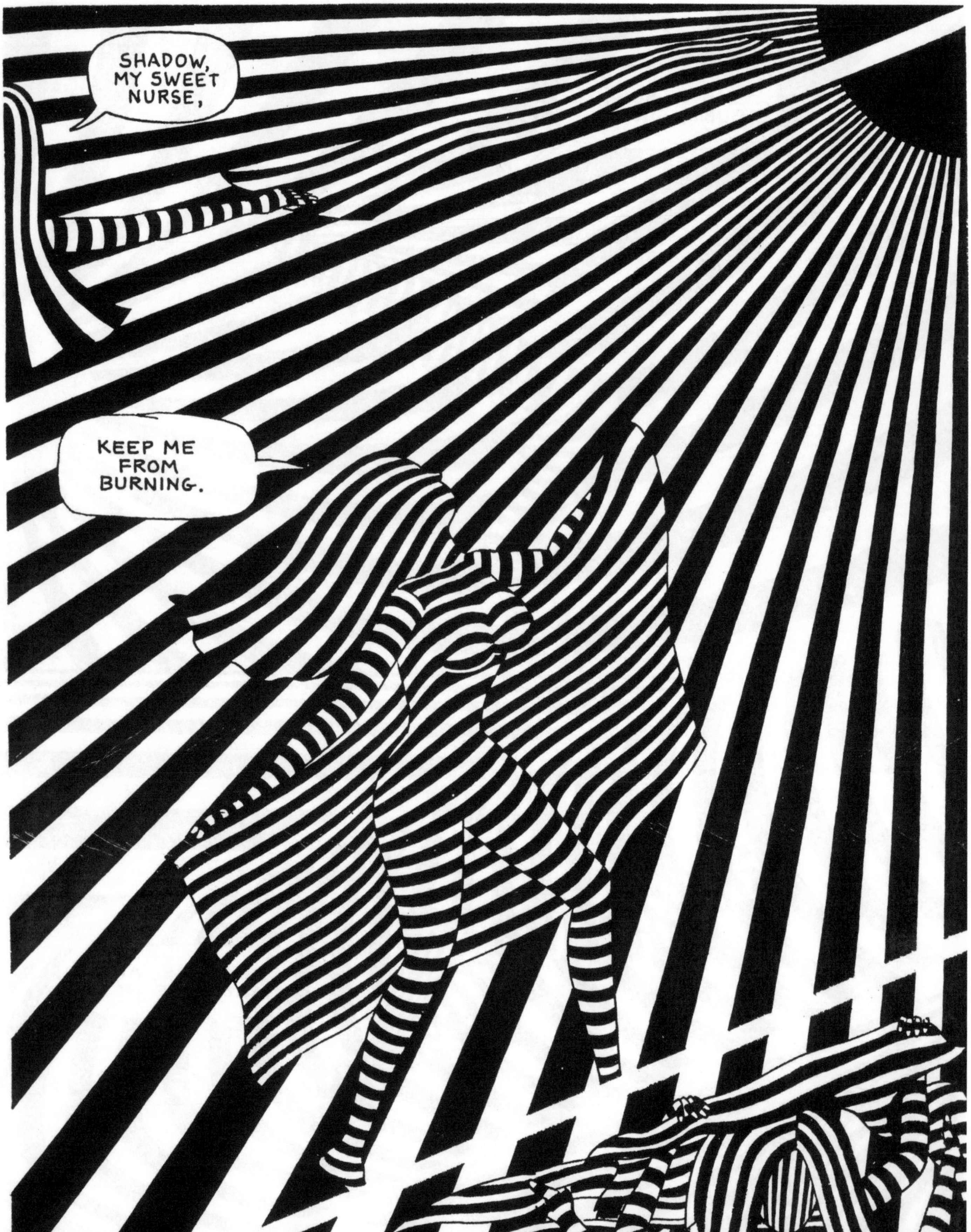
SHADOW, MY SWEET NURSE,
KEEP ME FROM BURNING.
MAKE NOT MY GLAD CAUSE CAUSE FOR MOURNING.

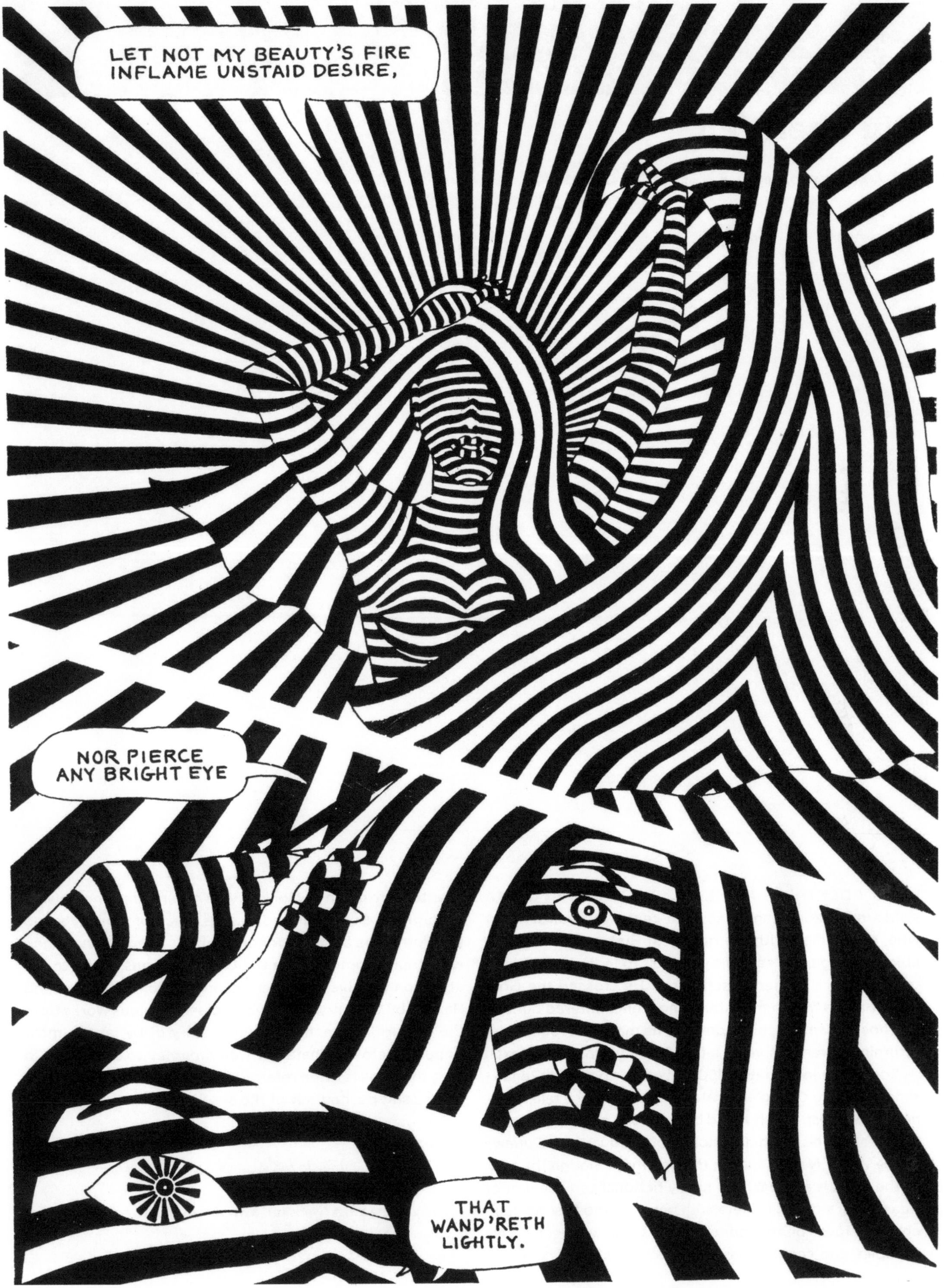
LET NOT MY BEAUTY'S FIRE
INFLAME UNSTAID DESIRE,
NOR PIERCE
ANY BRIGHT EYE
THAT
WAND'RETH
LIGHTLY.

Journey to the West

Wu Cheng'en

ART / ADAPTATION BY **Conor Hughes**

MANY FOLKTALES AND EARLY WRITINGS IN CHINA swirl around Xuan Zang, a seventh-century Buddhist priest who, dissatisfied with the quality of Buddhist texts available in his country, set off by himself to India, determined to bring back authentic scriptures. He crossed the Gobi Desert and a frozen mountain range, encountered bandits and hostile sentries, but incredibly he made the round-trip, returning seventeen years later with more than 600 texts.

Sometime in the latter 1500s, writer, poet, and Renaissance man Wu Cheng'en wrote his version of the tale, *Journey to the West*, which would become one of the Four Great Classical Novels of China (another of the quartet is *Outlaws of the Water Margin,* also in this volume). Though the bulk of the book is a fantastical, highly fictionalized account of Xuan Zang's quest, replete with demons, the first thirteen chapters focus on the four characters who will become his disciples and companions on the journey. The first seven chapters are given to Monkey, who attains amazing powers through his Buddhist studies. It is much of Monkey's tale that forms the basis of Conor Hughes's adaptation. Conor, who creates graphics for the United Nations, came to my attention with his pitch-perfect adaptation of "Hearts and Hands" by O. Henry. After we discussed various works from the Eastern canon, he chose the story of by far the most popular, beloved character from *Journey to the West* (in fact, the book is often referred to as *The Monkey King*, with Xuan Zang pushed out of the spotlight).

SOURCES

Cheng'en, Wu. *Journey to the West* (Volume 1). Beijing: Foreign Languages Press, 1993.

Journey to the West (website): www.vbtutor.net/xiyouji/journeyto thewest.htm

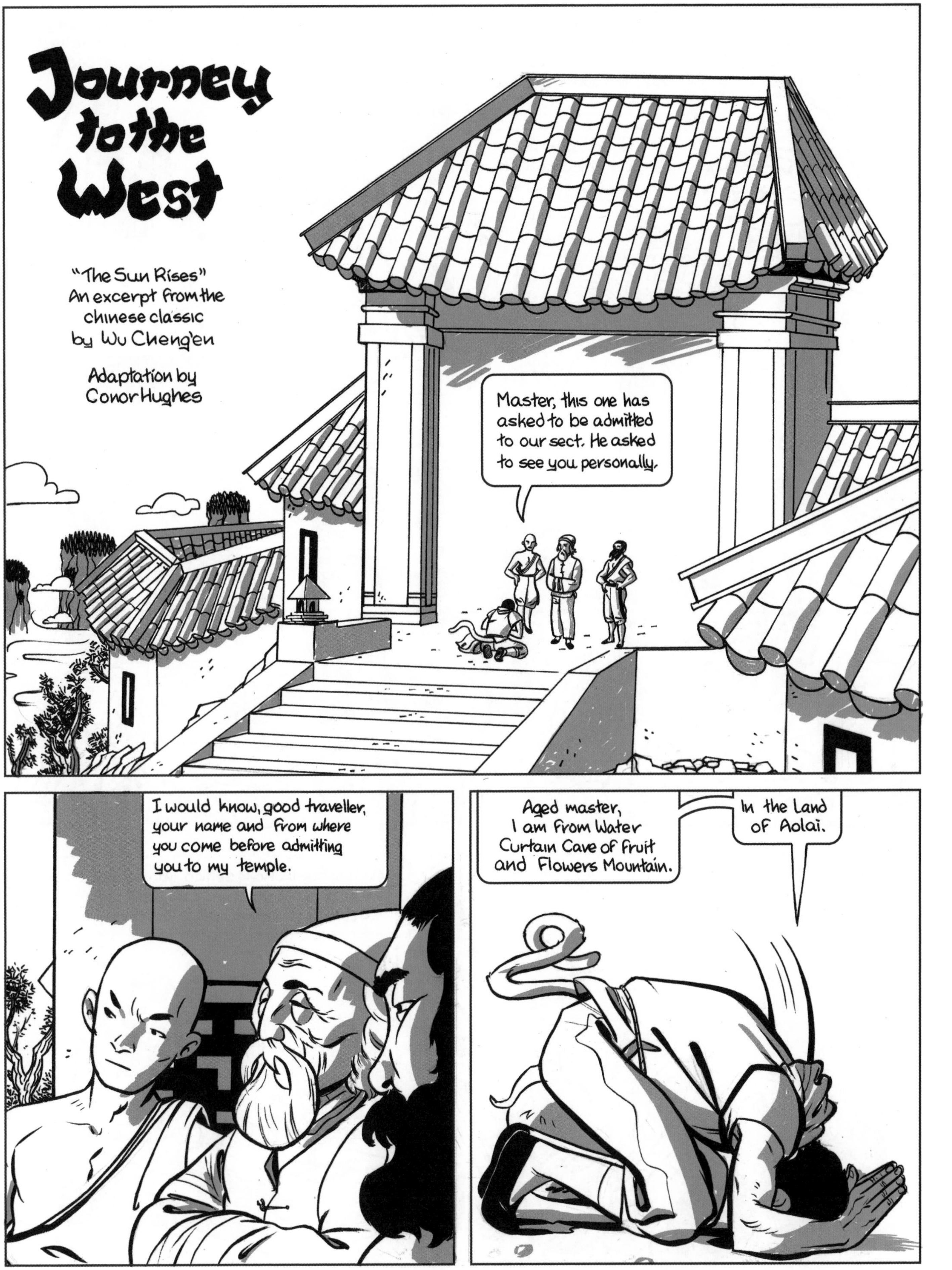
Journey to the West
"The Sun Rises"
An excerpt from the chinese classic by Wu Cheng'en
Adaptation by Conor Hughes
Master, this one has asked to be admitted to our sect. He asked to see you personally.
I would know, good traveller, your name and from where you come before admitting you to my temple.
Aged master, I am from Water Curtain Cave of fruit and Flowers Mountain.
In the Land of Aolai.

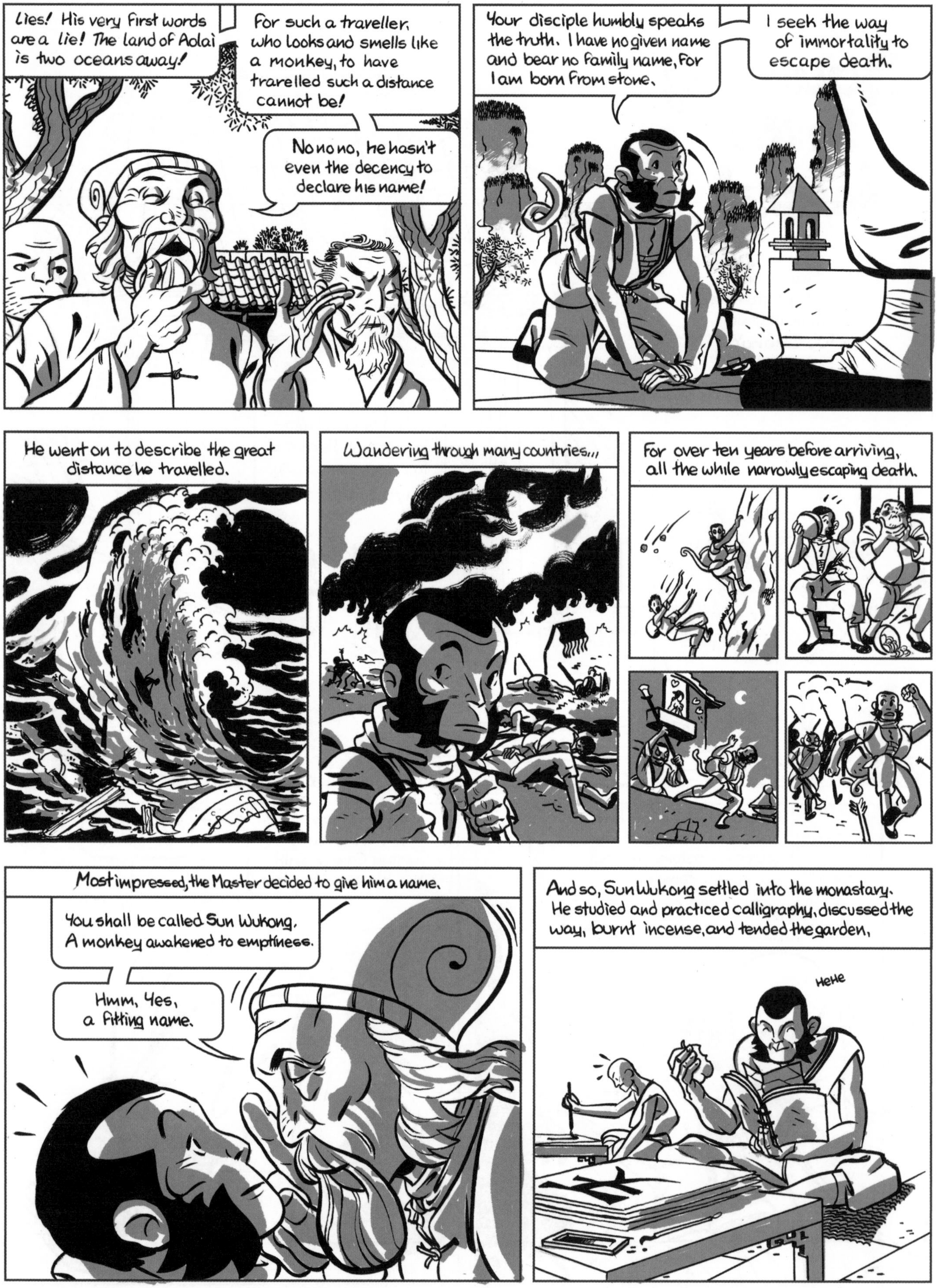

Lies! His very first words are a lie! The land of Aolai is two oceans away!
For such a traveller, who looks and smells like a monkey, to have travelled such a distance cannot be!
No no no, he hasn't even the decency to declare his name!
Your disciple humbly speaks the truth. I have no given name and bear no family name, for I am born from stone.
I seek the way of immortality to escape death.
He went on to describe the great distance he travelled.
Wandering through many countries...
For over ten years before arriving, all the while narrowly escaping death.
Most impressed, the Master decided to give him a name.
You shall be called Sun Wukong. A monkey awakened to emptiness.
Hmm, Yes, a fitting name.
And so, Sun Wukong settled into the monastary. He studied and practiced calligraphy, discussed the way, burnt incense, and tended the garden,
HeHe

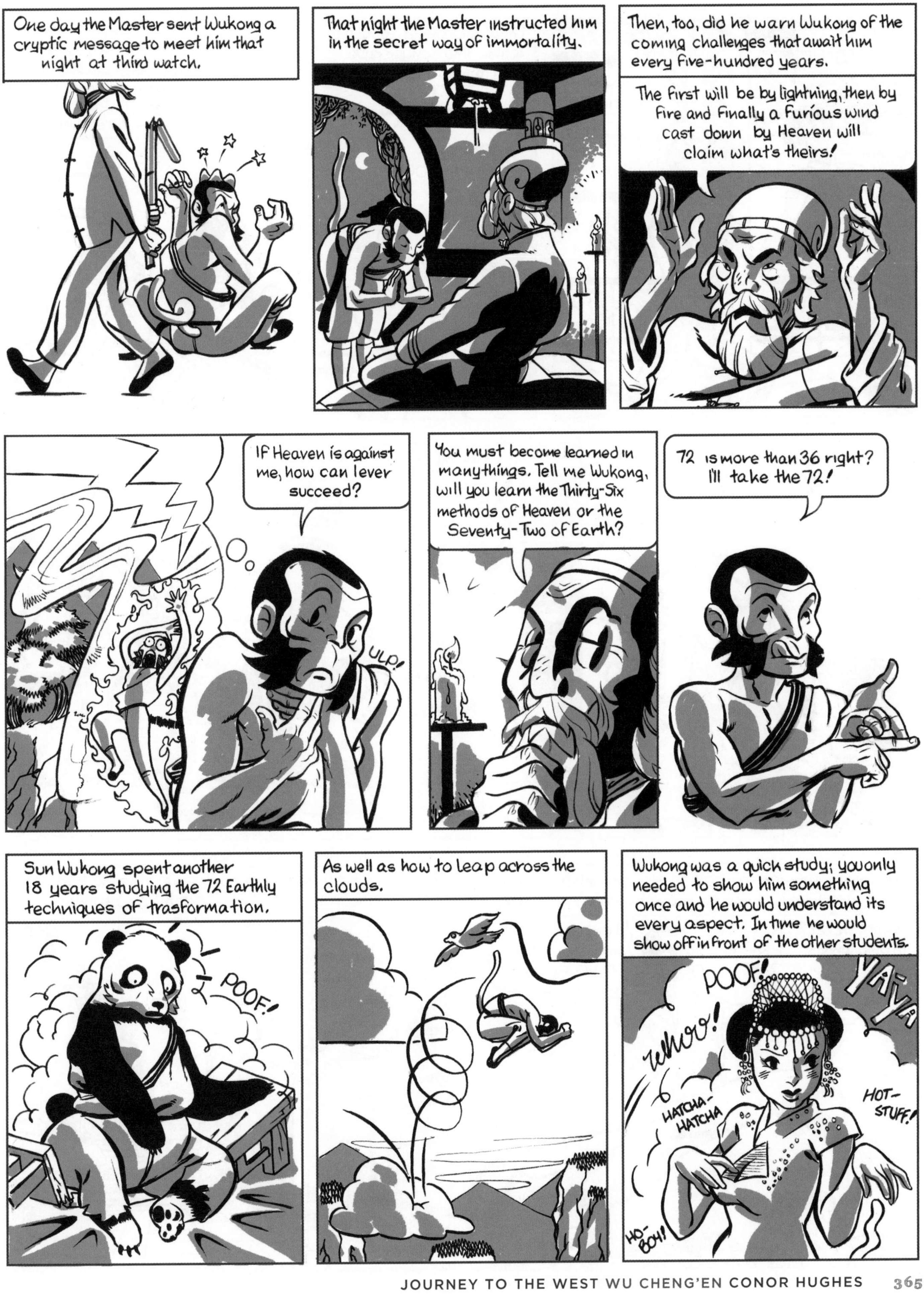

One day the Master sent Wukong a cryptic message to meet him that night at third watch.
That night the Master instructed him in the secret way of immortality.
Then, too, did he warn Wukong of the coming challenges that await him every five-hundred years.
The first will be by lightning, then by fire and finally a furious wind cast down by Heaven will claim what's theirs!
If Heaven is against me, how can I ever succeed?
ULP!
You must become learned in many things. Tell me Wukong, will you learn the Thirty-Six methods of Heaven or the Seventy-Two of Earth?
72 is more than 36 right? I'll take the 72!
Sun Wukong spent another 18 years studying the 72 Earthly techniques of trasformation.
POOF!
As well as how to leap across the clouds.
Wukong was a quick study; you only needed to show him something once and he would understand its every aspect. In time he would show off in front of the other students.
POOF!
YAYA
WHOO!
HATCHA-HATCHA
HOT-STUFF!
HO-BOY!

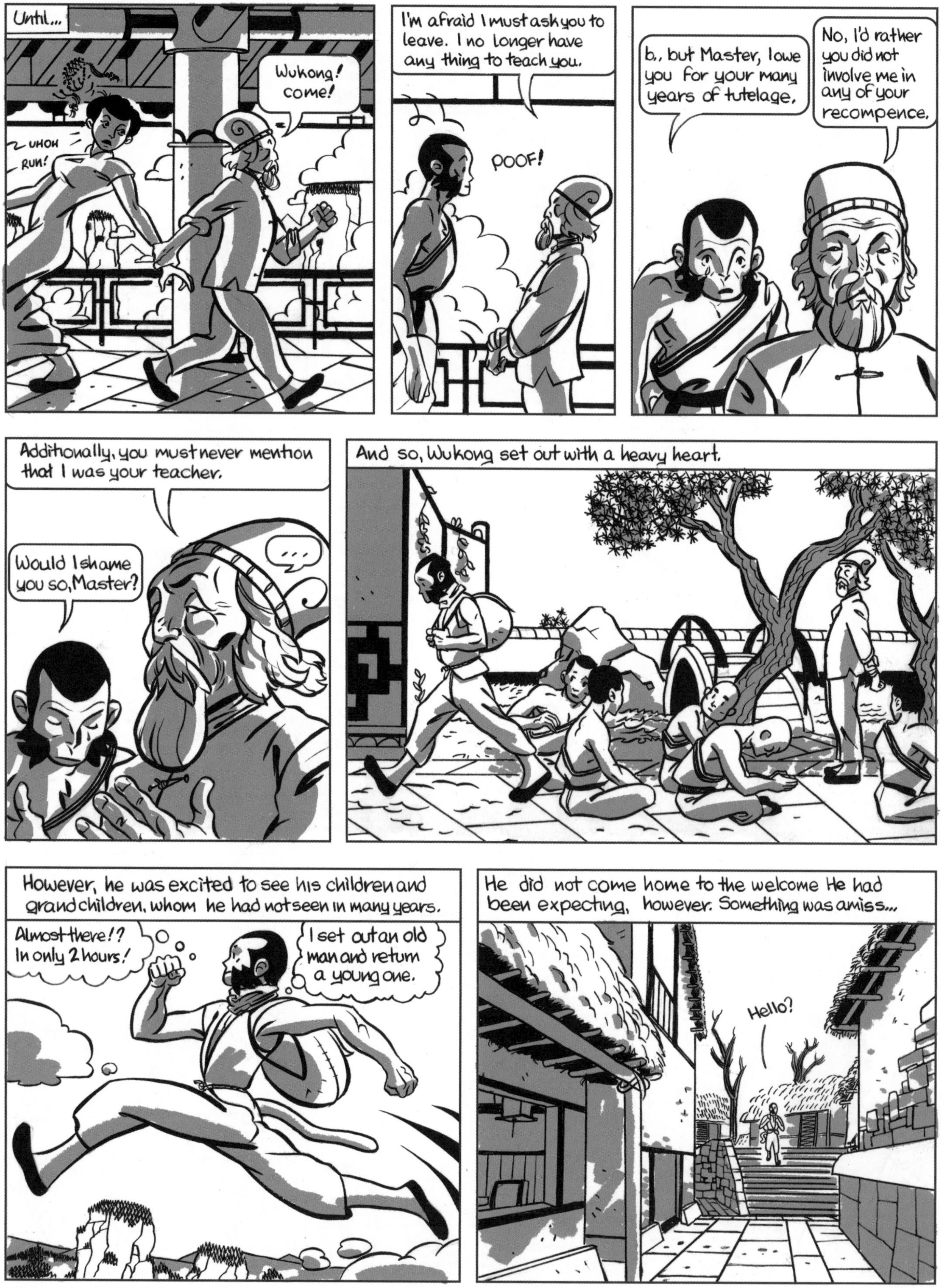
Until...
UHOH
RUN!
Wukong! come!
I'm afraid I must ask you to leave. I no longer have any thing to teach you.
POOF!
b., but Master, I owe you for your many years of tutelage.
No, I'd rather you did not involve me in any of your recompence.
Additionally, you must never mention that I was your teacher.
Would I shame you so, Master?
...
And so, Wukong set out with a heavy heart.
However, he was excited to see his children and grandchildren, whom he had not seen in many years.
Almost there!? In only 2 hours!
I set out an old man and return a young one.
He did not come home to the welcome He had been expecting, however. Something was amiss...
Hello?

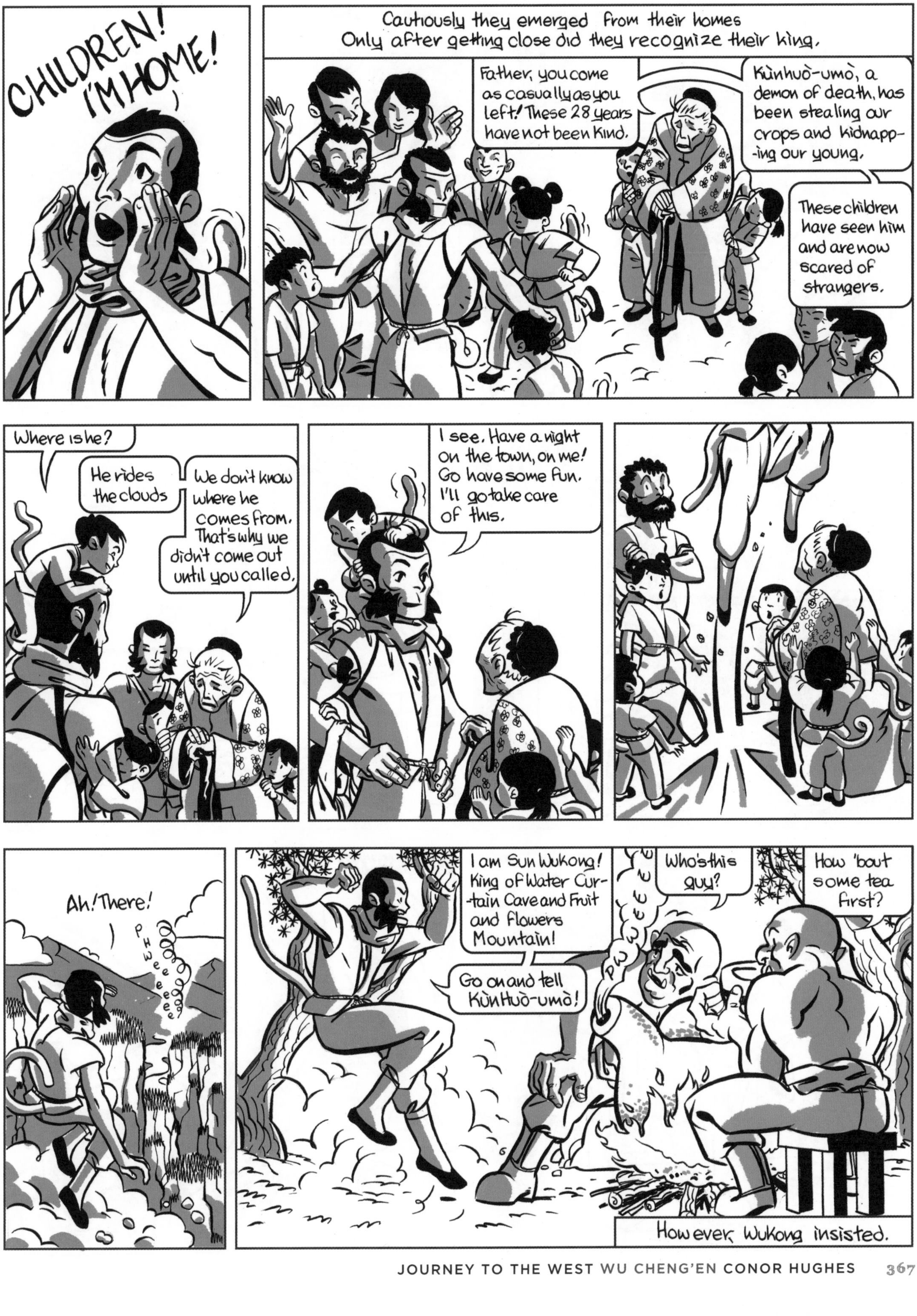
CHILDREN! I'M HOME!
Cautiously they emerged from their homes
Only after getting close did they recognize their king.
Father, you come as casually as you left! These 28 years have not been kind.
Kùnhuò-umò, a demon of death, has been stealing our crops and kidnapp--ing our young.
These children have seen him and are now scared of strangers.
Where is he?
He rides the clouds
We don't know where he comes from. That's why we didn't come out until you called.
I see. Have a night on the town, on me! Go have some fun. I'll go take care of this.
Ah! There!
PHWeeeeee
I am Sun Wukong! King of Water Cur--tain Cave and Fruit and Flowers Mountain!
Go on and tell Kùn Huò-umò!
PWeeeee
Who's this guy?
How 'bout some tea first?
However, Wukong insisted.

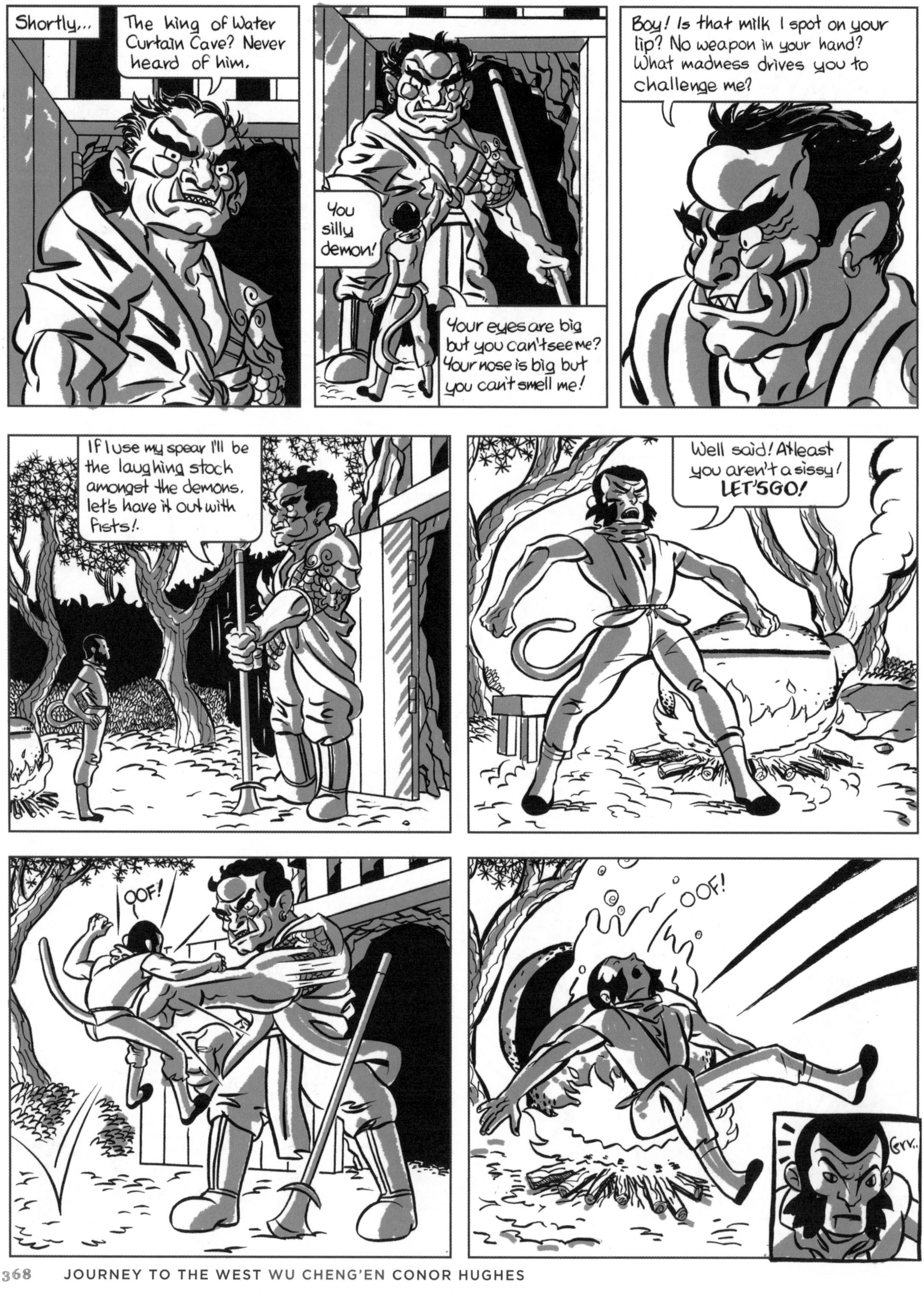
Shortly...
The king of Water Curtain Cave? Never heard of him.
You silly demon!
Your eyes are big but you can't see me? Your nose is big but you can't smell me!
Boy! Is that milk I spot on your lip? No weapon in your hand? What madness drives you to challenge me?
If I use my spear I'll be the laughing stock amongst the demons. let's have it out with fists!.
Well said! At least you aren't a sissy! LET'S GO!
OOF!
OOF!
Grr..

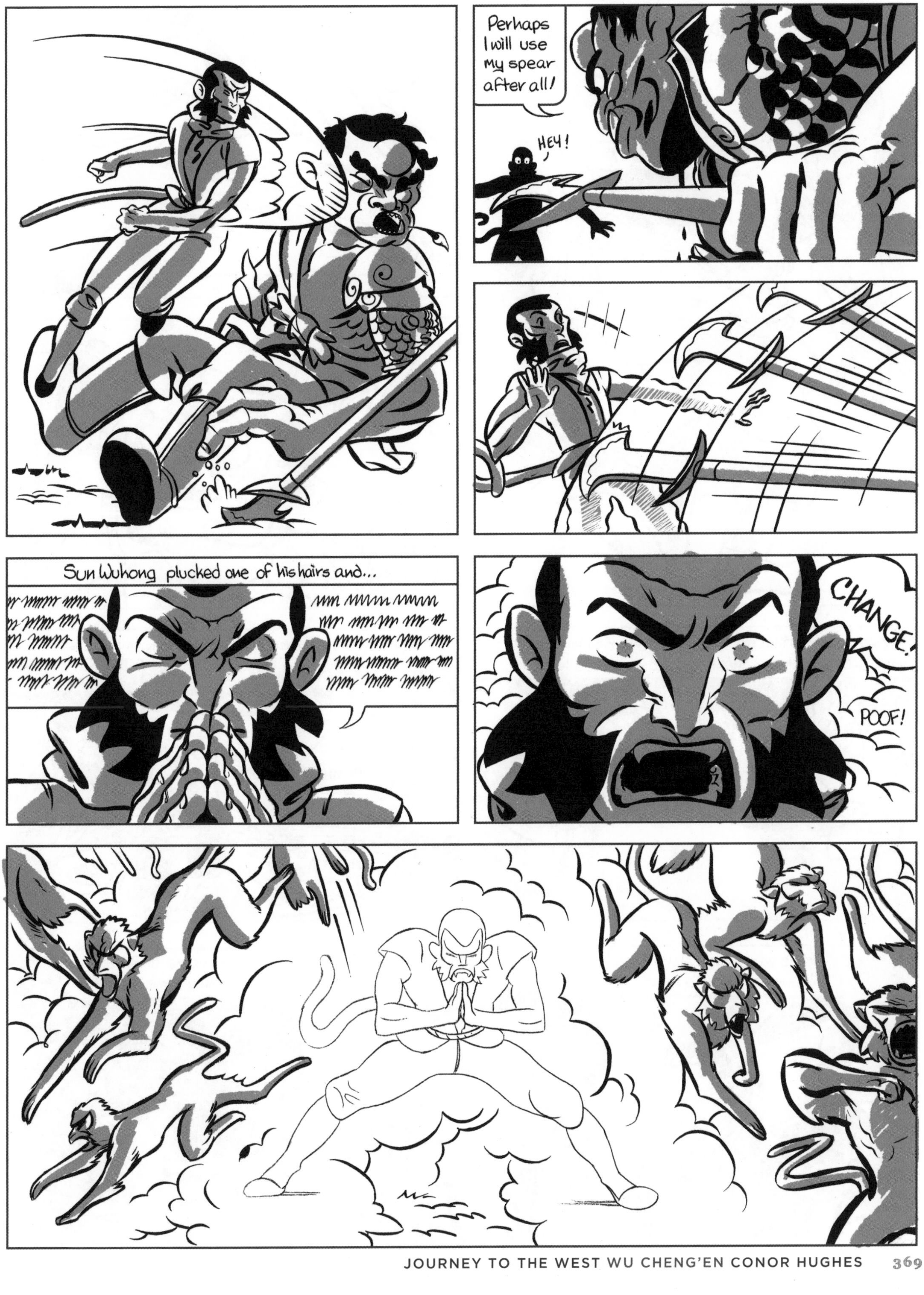
Perhaps I will use my spear after all!
HEY!
Sun Wuhong plucked one of his hairs and...
CHANGE!
POOF!

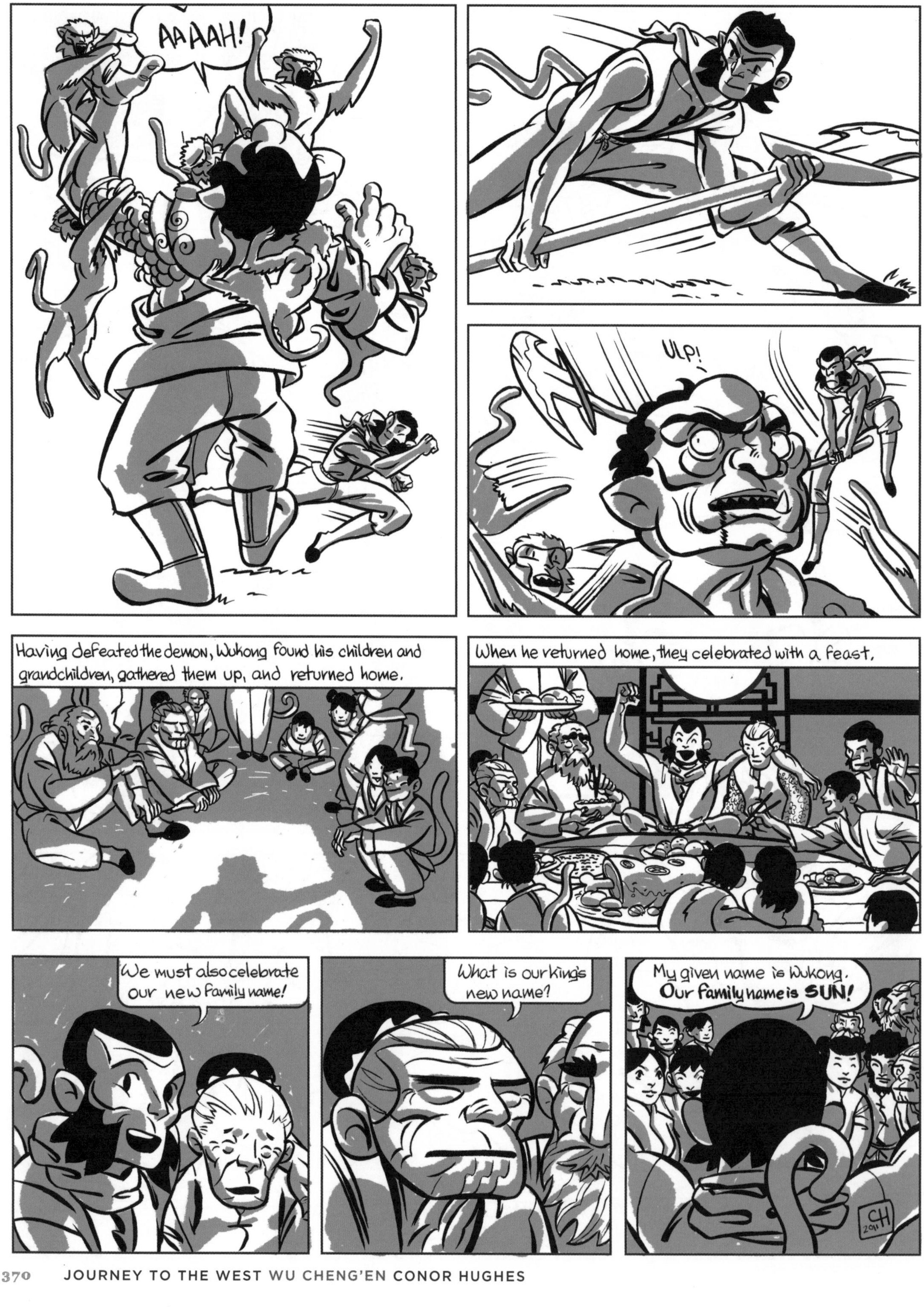
AAAAH!
ULP!
Having defeated the demon, Wukong found his children and grandchildren, gathered them up, and returned home.
When he returned home, they celebrated with a feast.
We must also celebrate our new family name!
What is our king's new name?
My given name is Wukong.
Our family name is SUN!
CH 2011

The Faerie Queene

Edmund Spenser

ADAPTATION BY **Michael Stanyer**

ART BY **Eric Johnson**

WHAT TO SAY ABOUT THE LONGEST POEM IN THE English language? First of all, it's actually only half as long as it was meant to be; Spenser died before writing Books 7 through 12. With the first six books, published in the 1590s, he created a complex Arthurian epic, fairy fantasy, and Christian (specifically, Protestant) allegory. Each book sees a different knight being sent on a quest by the Faerie Queene, with the six knights personifying Christian virtues: Holiness, Temperance, Chastity, Friendship, Justice, and Courtesy. Interestingly, the knight of Book Three, Britomart, is female, and it is from this book that the adaptation comes—we witness the creation of False Florimell. The adaptation's writer and artist explain:

> Our in-progress project, *The Counterfet* (Spenserian spelling), follows the creation and destruction of a minor character, False Florimell. Florimell, in Spenser's original work, is the most beautiful woman in all of Faerie Land, and False Florimell is her evil twin; created from snow and wax by a twisted witch, and animated with a deceitful spirit borrowed from the Devil, she is made to be a Florimell replacement for the witch's slovenly son. But False Florimell is stolen by a greedy knight and turned loose into the world.

She disrupts order in Faerie Land by using her beauty and promiscuity to turn noble knights against one another.

> False Florimell is a very minor character in *The Faerie Queene*, but she is interesting because she breaks character at times. Despite being a construct of snow, wax, and various other inanimate components, and despite being operated by a male spirit released from the underworld, "she" sometimes thinks she's the real Florimell. By centering our project around False Florimell, we can introduce Faerie Land and plenty of the original work's main characters without having to deal with its sprawling, unfinished state.

> The pages appearing here are selected from early in the story. They depict the Devil inspecting the partially constructed False Florimell in the Witch's workshop. This workshop scene is a frame for the backstory: Everything that happens before False Florimell's awakening is narrated in a series of vignettes as the Witch haggles with the Devil over a soul for her new creation. For example, the segment shown here ends with the Witch's line: "on the ocean's edge, a young man hoards treasure from the sea." It serves as a transition to the story of the knight Marinell. More information on *The Counterfet* can be found at www.counterfet.com.

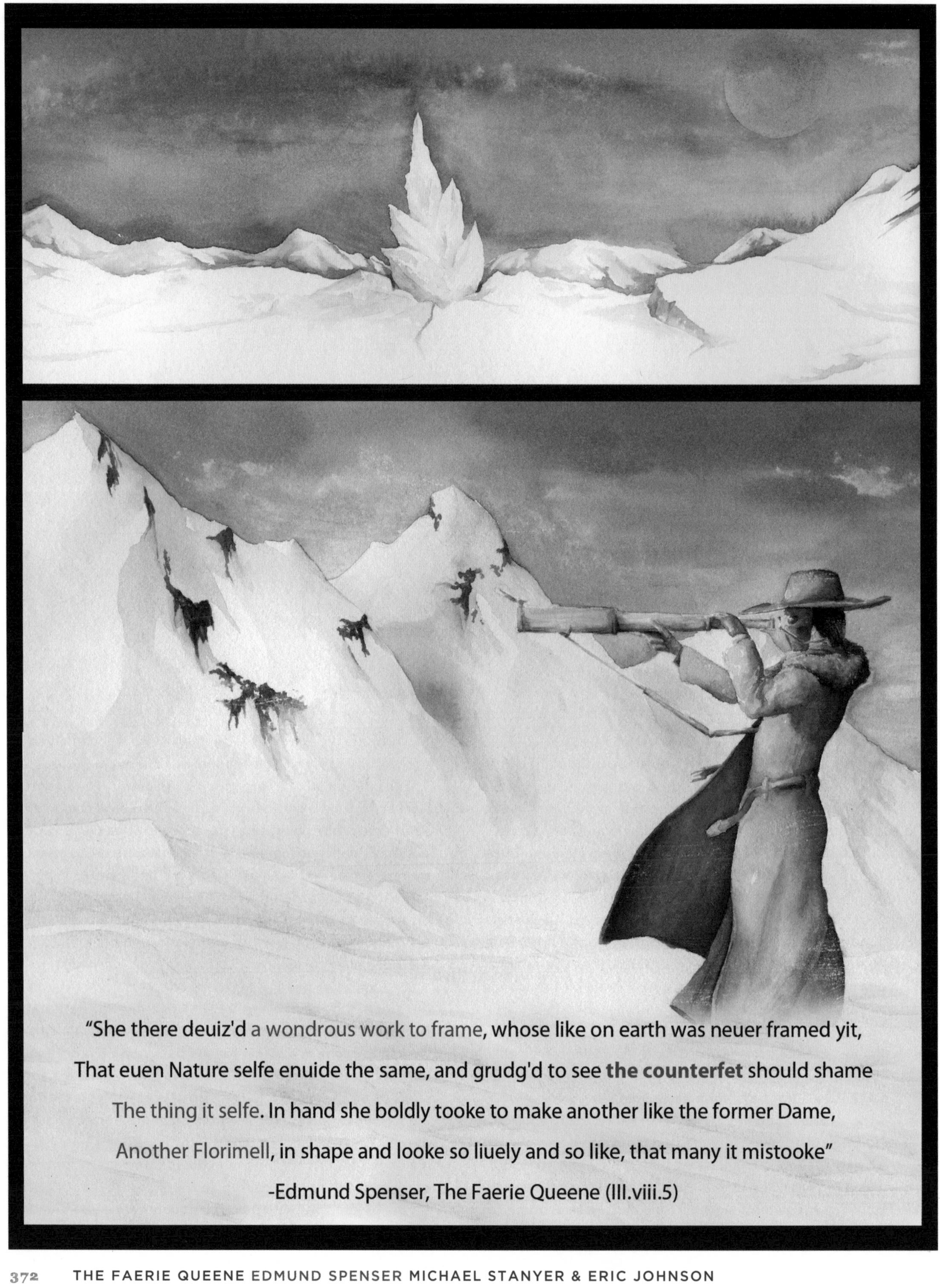
"She there deuiz'd a wondrous work to frame, whose like on earth was neuer framed yit,
That euen Nature selfe enuide the same, and grudg'd to see the counterfet should shame
The thing it selfe. In hand she boldly tooke to make another like the former Dame,
Another Florimell, in shape and looke so liuely and so like, that many it mistooke"
-Edmund Spenser, The Faerie Queene (III.viii.5)

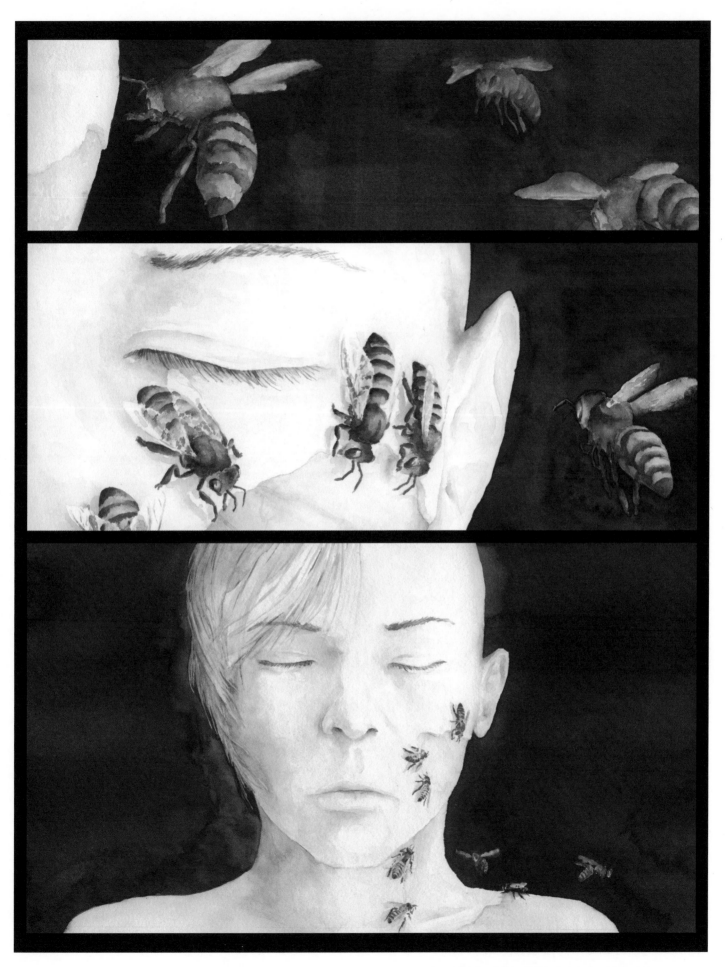

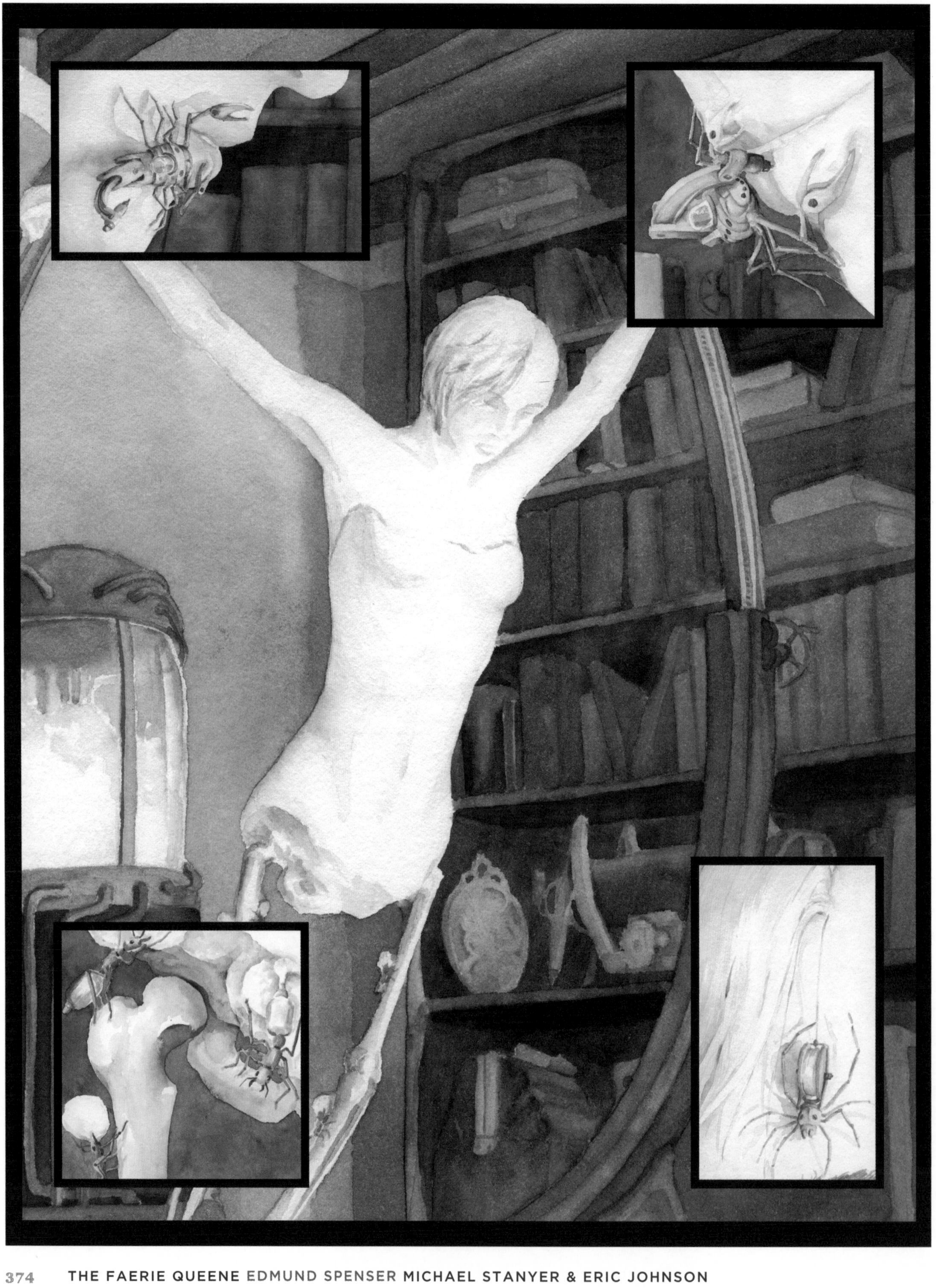

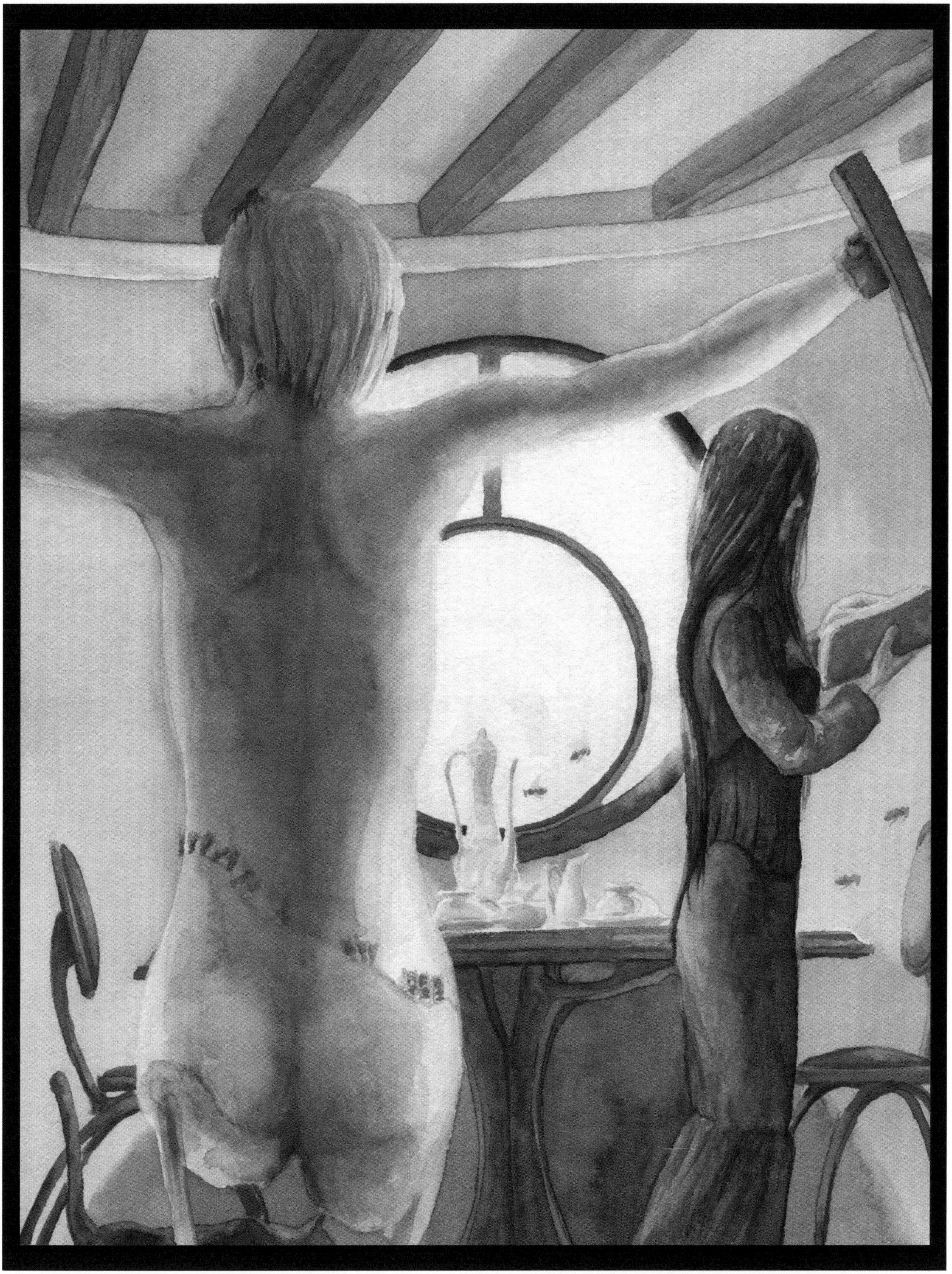

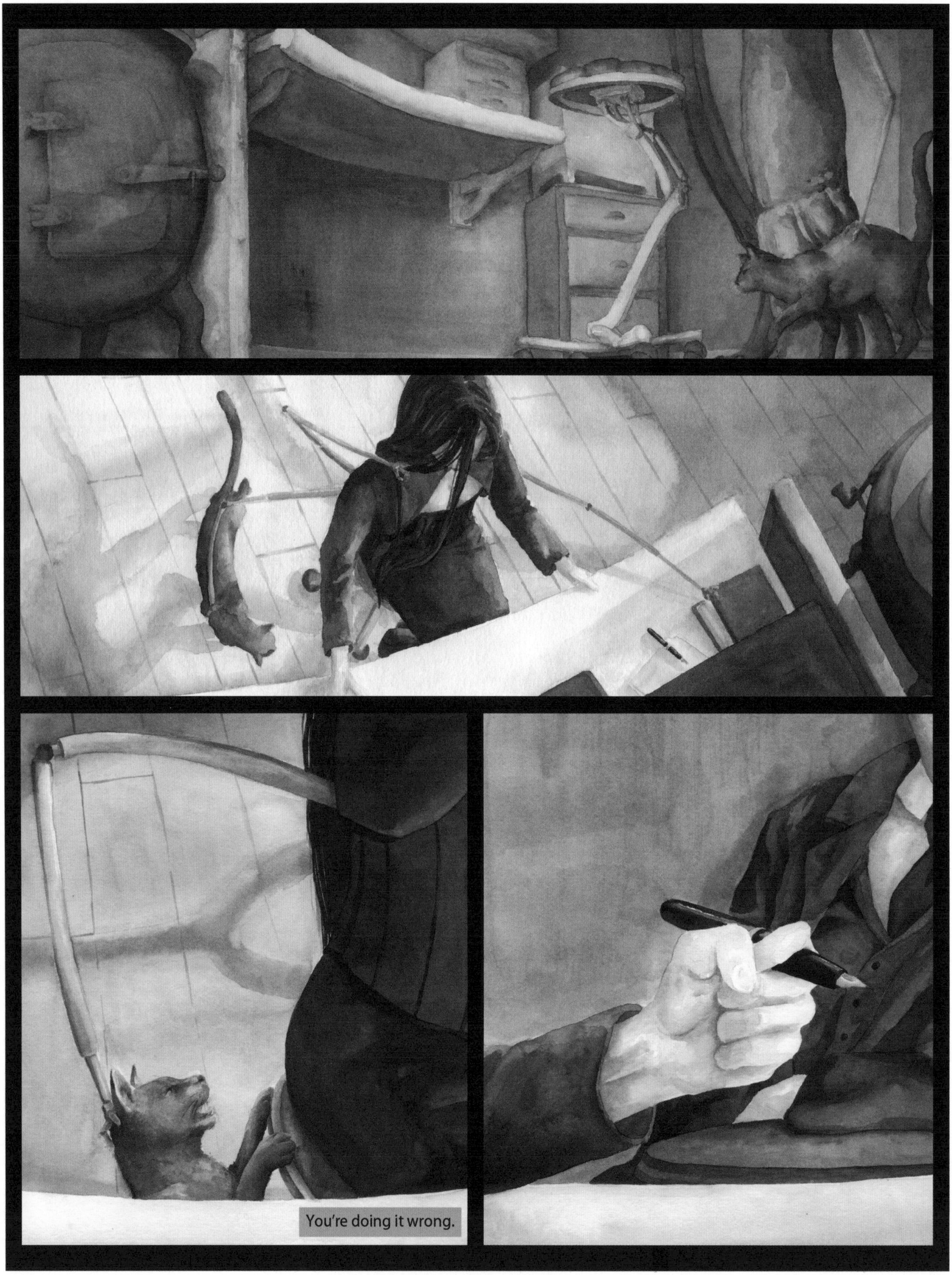
You're doing it wrong.

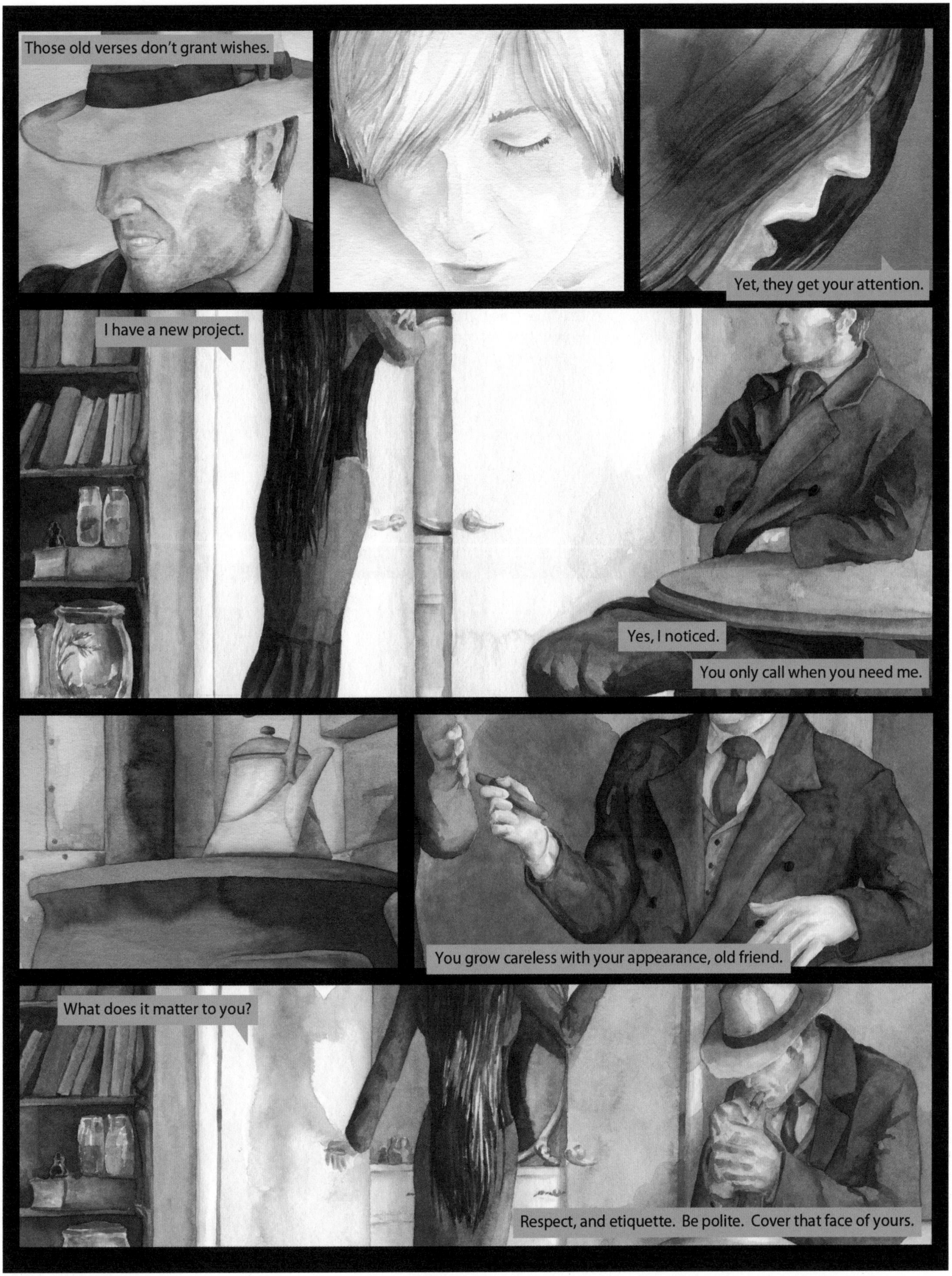
Those old verses don't grant wishes.
Yet, they get your attention.
I have a new project.
Yes, I noticed.
You only call when you need me.
You grow careless with your appearance, old friend.
What does it matter to you?
Respect, and etiquette. Be polite. Cover that face of yours.

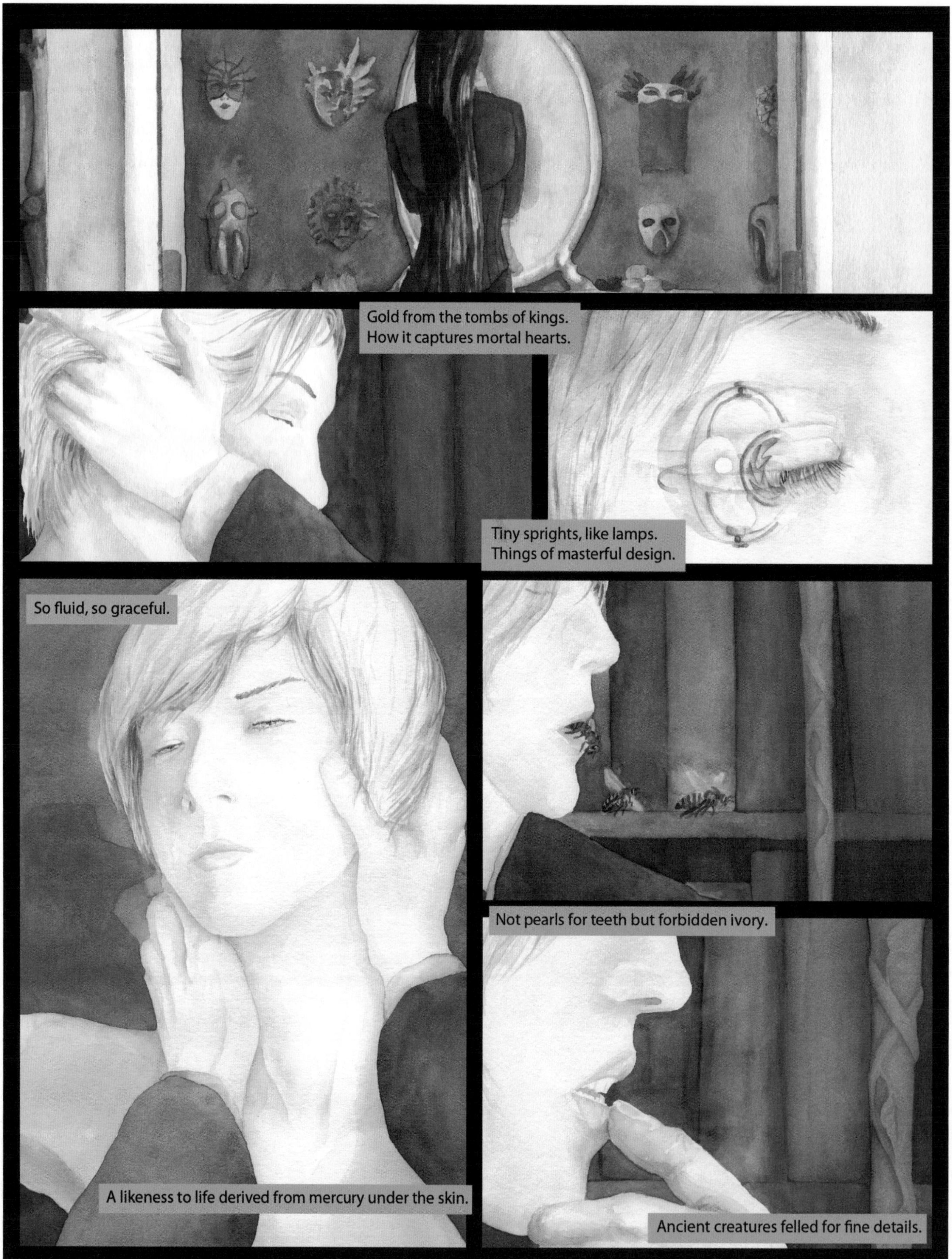
Gold from the tombs of kings.
How it captures mortal hearts.
Tiny sprights, like lamps.
Things of masterful design.
So fluid, so graceful.
A likeness to life derived from mercury under the skin.
Not pearls for teeth but forbidden ivory.
Ancient creatures felled for fine details.

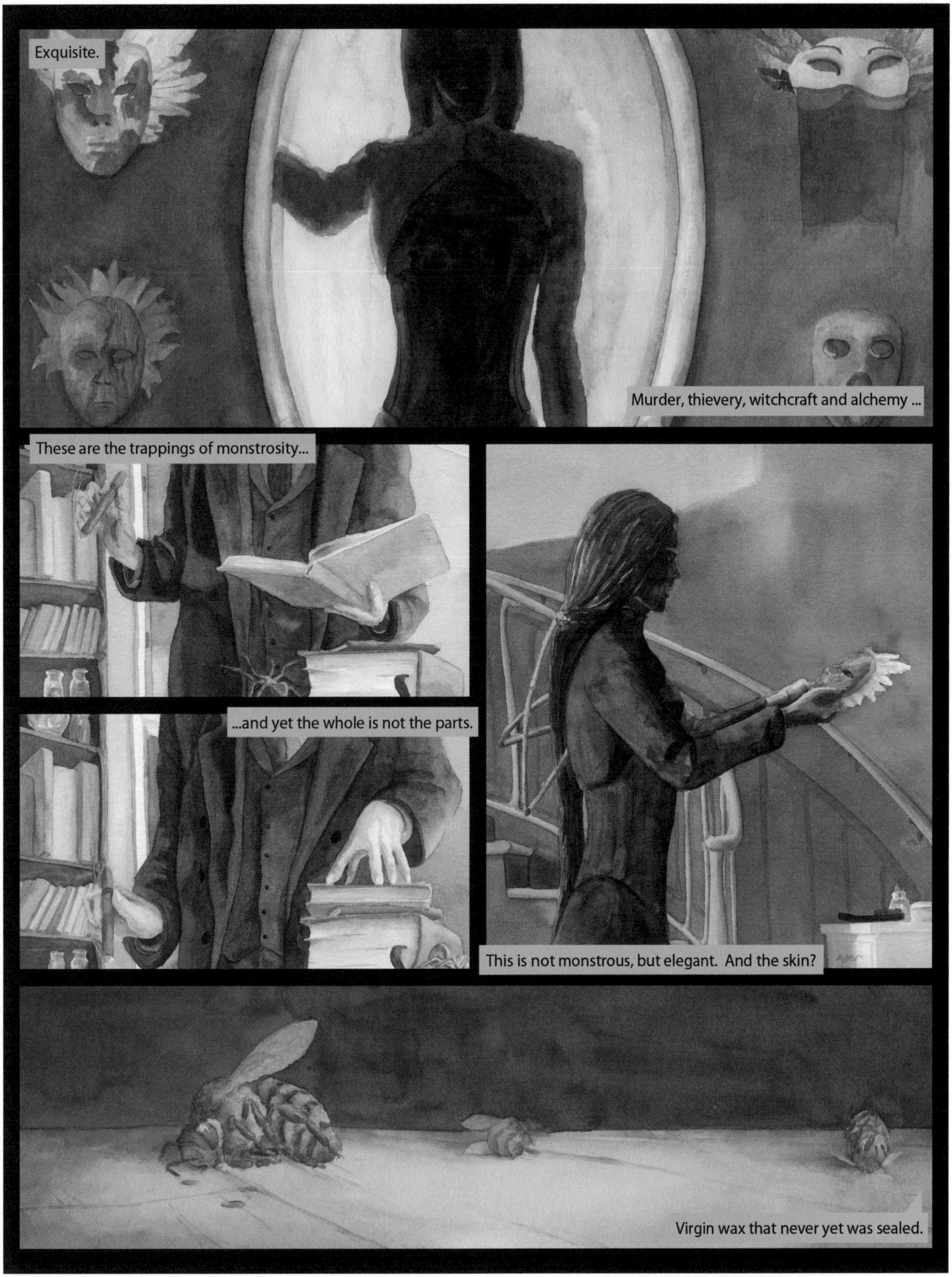
Exquisite.
Murder, thievery, witchcraft and alchemy ...
These are the trappings of monstrosity...
...and yet the whole is not the parts.
This is not monstrous, but elegant. And the skin?
Virgin wax that never yet was sealed.

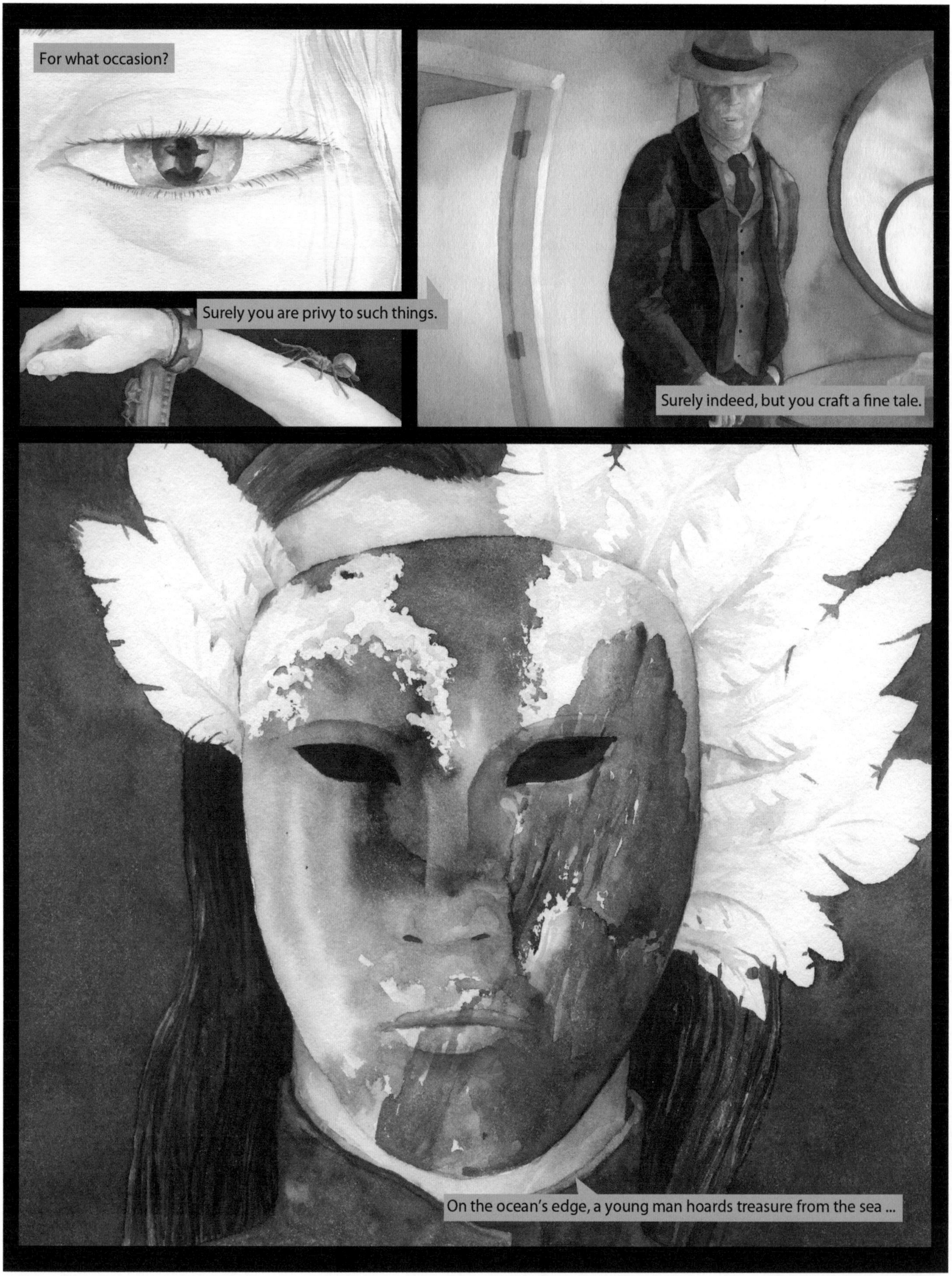
For what occasion?
Surely you are privy to such things.
Surely indeed, but you craft a fine tale.
On the ocean's edge, a young man hoards treasure from the sea ...

A Midsummer Night's Dream

William Shakespeare

ART /ADAPTATION BY **Maxx Kelly** WITH **Huxley King**

SHAKESPEARE WAS THIS GUY IN A SMALL ENGLISH town who was having a hard time earning a living, so he left his family behind and moved to London. We don't know what the greatest writer of all time did for the next seven years (just like we don't know much about him at all, such as the day he was born or how he died), but at some point he obviously caught the theater bug. So he wrote *Hamlet*. And *King Lear*. And *Macbeth*. And *Othello*. And *Romeo and Juliet*. And *A Midsummer Night's Dream*. And *Julius Caesar*. In all, thirty-eight of the greatest plays—nay, the greatest works of literature—ever written, in the space of twenty-three years, with most of the greatest ones written within a ten-year period. While he was at it, he also cranked out the greatest sonnet sequence in the English language, perhaps in any language. In his spare time, he helped create and run England's greatest theater, the Globe, and its highly acclaimed troupe, the King's Men. Oh, and since he was a member of the troupe, he acted in many of their productions. Quite a guy, that Shakespeare.

A Midsummer Night's Dream—undoubtedly the most beloved of Shakespeare's comedies (no one can resist love, magic, and fairies!)—was originally performed circa 1595–6. Three interlocking subplots revolve around the upcoming nuptials of Theseus, the Duke of Athens, and the Amazon Queen Hippolyta: the misadventures of four entangled lovers, the attempts of a band of craftsmen to rehearse and perform a play at the royal wedding, and the feud between the king and queen of the fairies, Oberon and Titania.

The excerpt being adapted in this volume—from the first scene of Act Two—concerns this last storyline. One of Titania's worshippers died giving birth to a son of a ruler in India, and Titania took the boy (as fairies are known for kidnapping human children). Oberon wants the prince in his retinue, but Titania vehemently refuses to give him up. (This may have something to do with the fact that the bride-to-be was one of Oberon's conquests.)

Maxx Kelly—an artist of my acquaintance in Nashville—gives us a rich glimpse into the fairies' world, with giant, floating seahorses pulling Titania's carriage, and the unexpectedly androgynous, golden Hindu god-child at the center of the couple's dispute.

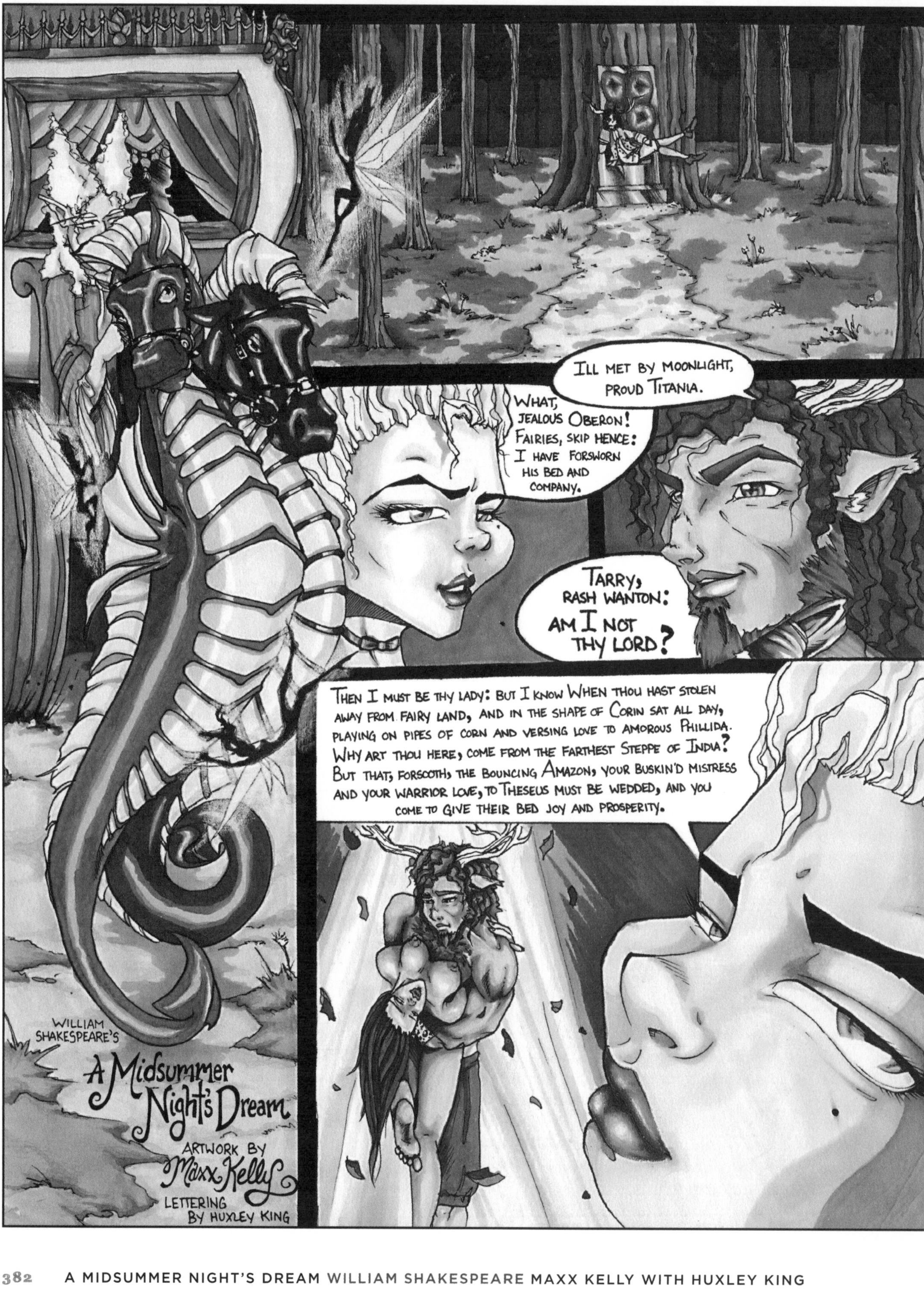

Ill met by moonlight, proud Titania.
What, jealous Oberon! Fairies, skip hence: I have forsworn his bed and company.
Tarry, rash wanton: am I not thy lord?
Then I must be thy lady: but I know when thou hast stolen away from fairy land, and in the shape of Corin sat all day, playing on pipes of corn and versing love to amorous Phillida. Why art thou here, come from the farthest steppe of India? But that, forsooth, the bouncing Amazon, your buskin'd mistress and your warrior love, to Theseus must be wedded, and you come to give their bed joy and prosperity.
William Shakespeare's
A Midsummer Night's Dream
Artwork by Maxx Kelly
Lettering by Huxley King

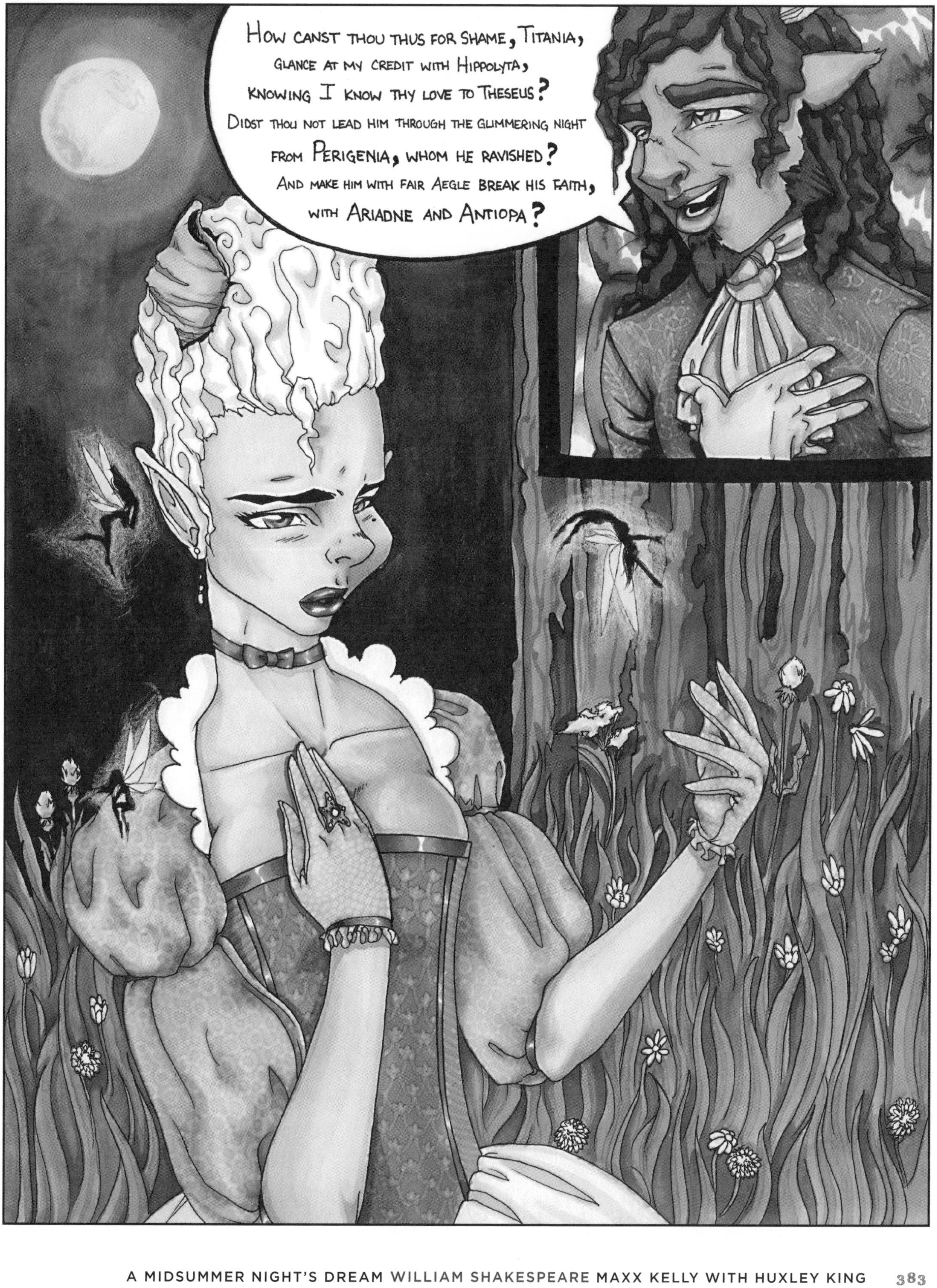
HOW CANST THOU THUS FOR SHAME, TITANIA, GLANCE AT MY CREDIT WITH HIPPOLYTA, KNOWING I KNOW THY LOVE TO THESEUS? DIDST THOU NOT LEAD HIM THROUGH THE GLIMMERING NIGHT FROM PERIGENIA, WHOM HE RAVISHED? AND MAKE HIM WITH FAIR AEGLE BREAK HIS FAITH, WITH ARIADNE AND ANTIOPA?

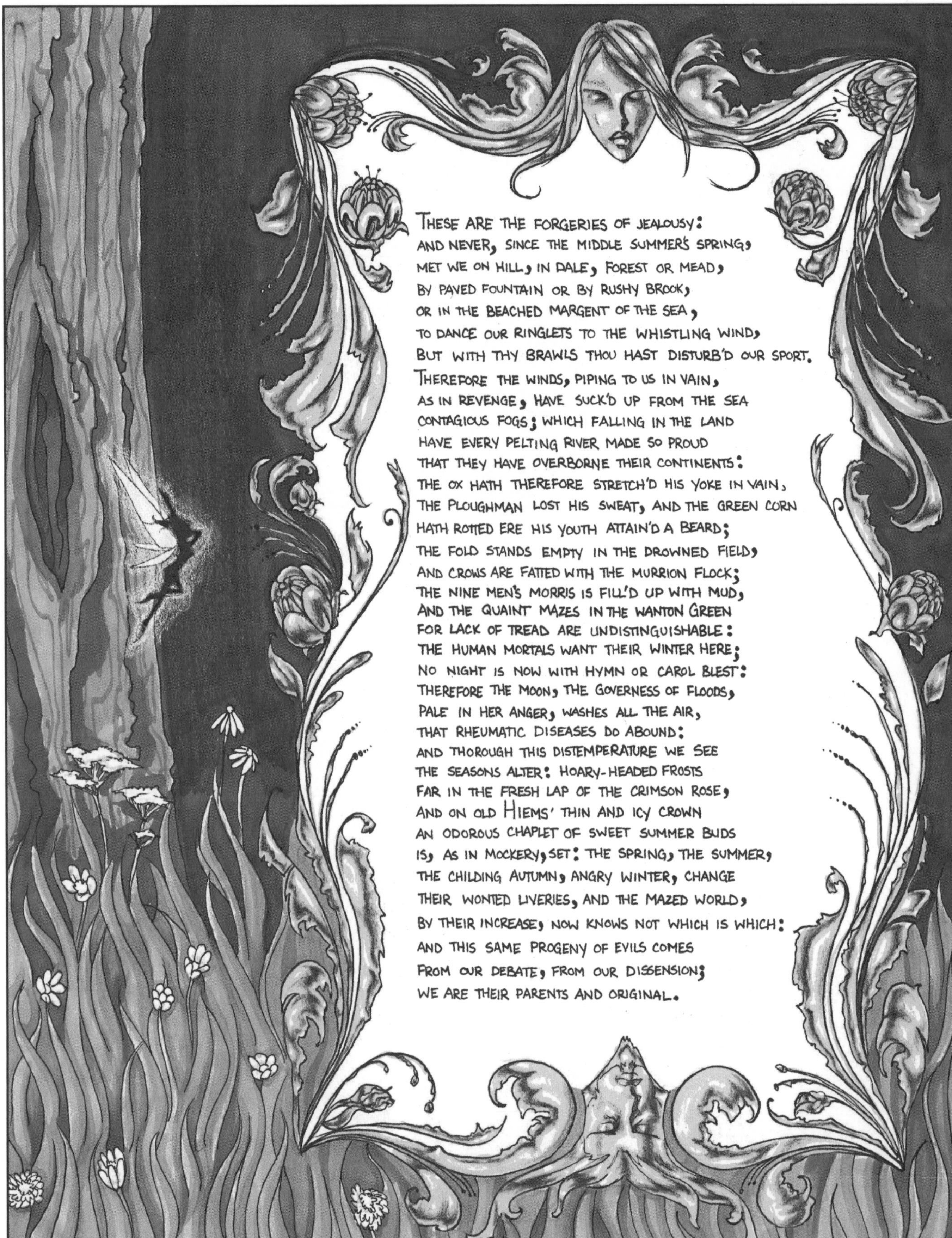
These are the forgeries of jealousy:
And never, since the middle summer's spring,
Met we on hill, in dale, forest or mead,
By paved fountain or by rushy brook,
Or in the beached margent of the sea,
To dance our ringlets to the whistling wind,
But with thy brawls thou hast disturb'd our sport.
Therefore the winds, piping to us in vain,
As in revenge, have suck'd up from the sea
Contagious fogs; which falling in the land
Have every pelting river made so proud
That they have overborne their continents:
The ox hath therefore stretch'd his yoke in vain,
The ploughman lost his sweat, and the green corn
Hath rotted ere his youth attain'd a beard;
The fold stands empty in the drowned field,
And crows are fatted with the murrion flock;
The nine men's morris is fill'd up with mud,
And the quaint mazes in the wanton green
For lack of tread are undistinguishable:
The human mortals want their winter here;
No night is now with hymn or carol blest:
Therefore the moon, the governess of floods,
Pale in her anger, washes all the air,
That rheumatic diseases do abound:
And thorough this distemperature we see
The seasons alter: hoary-headed frosts
Far in the fresh lap of the crimson rose,
And on old Hiems' thin and icy crown
An odorous chaplet of sweet summer buds
Is, as in mockery, set: the spring, the summer,
The childing autumn, angry winter, change
Their wonted liveries, and the mazed world,
By their increase, now knows not which is which:
And this same progeny of evils comes
From our debate, from our dissension;
We are their parents and original.

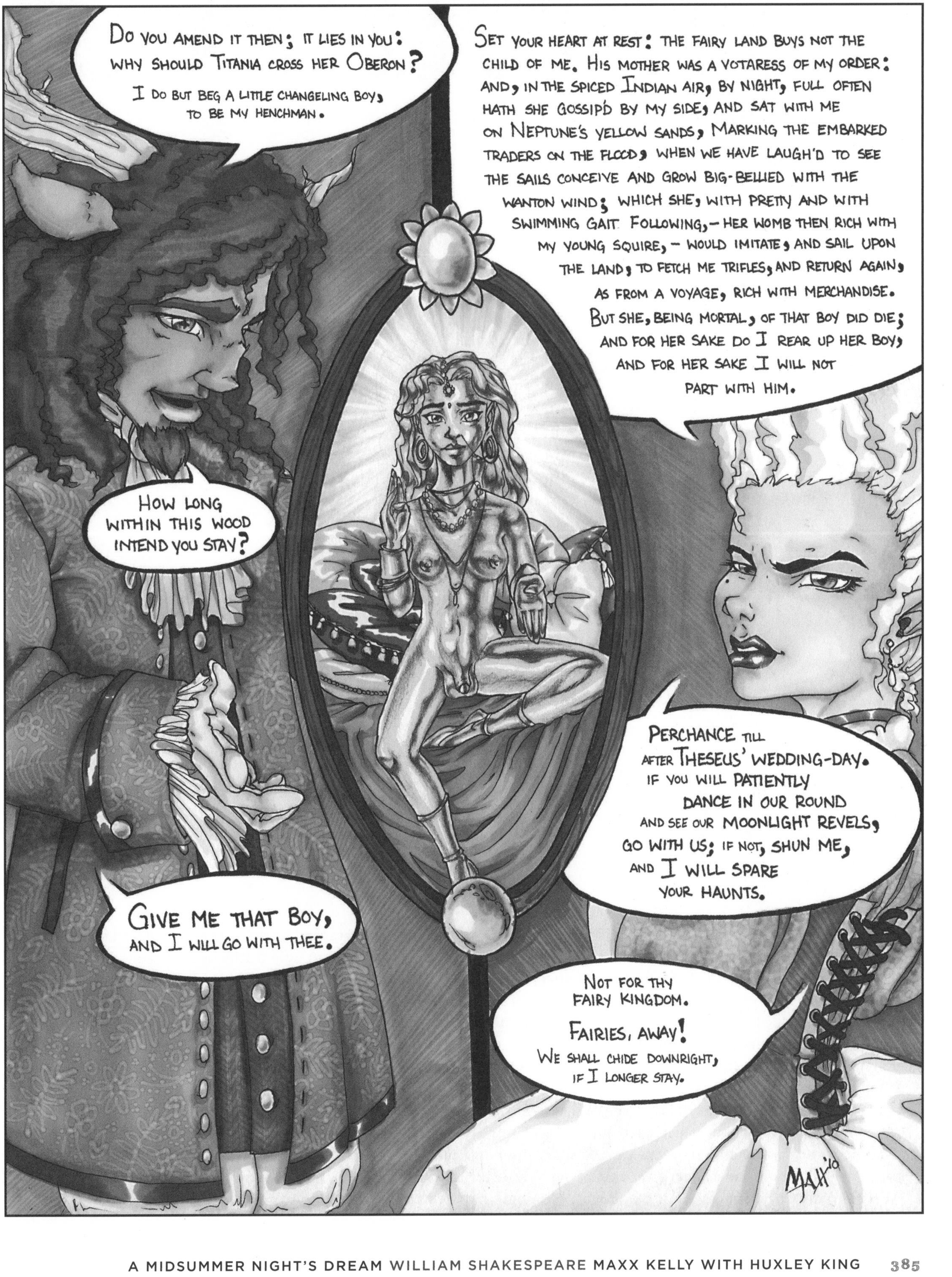
Do you amend it then; it lies in you: why should Titania cross her Oberon? I do but beg a little changeling boy, to be my henchman.
Set your heart at rest: the fairy land buys not the child of me. His mother was a votaress of my order: and, in the spiced Indian air, by night, full often hath she gossip'd by my side, and sat with me on Neptune's yellow sands, marking the embarked traders on the flood, when we have laugh'd to see the sails conceive and grow big-bellied with the wanton wind; which she, with pretty and with swimming gait following,— her womb then rich with my young squire,— would imitate, and sail upon the land, to fetch me trifles, and return again, as from a voyage, rich with merchandise. But she, being mortal, of that boy did die; and for her sake do I rear up her boy, and for her sake I will not part with him.
How long within this wood intend you stay?
Perchance till after Theseus' wedding-day. If you will patiently dance in our round and see our moonlight revels, go with us; if not, shun me, and I will spare your haunts.
Give me that boy, and I will go with thee.
Not for thy fairy kingdom. Fairies, away! We shall chide downright, if I longer stay.
Maxx '10

King Lear

William Shakespeare

ART / ADAPTATION BY **Ian Pollock**

OFTEN NAMED WITH HAMLET AS THE GREATEST OF Shakespeare's plays, the unrelentingly tragic *King Lear* was probably written in 1605–06. It opens with the aging King of Britain making what can be charitably described as a stupid move: he will divide his kingdom among his three daughters based on how profusely they profess their love for him. Goneril and Regan pander to the old man, but Cordelia refuses to take part in the ego-stroking. Enraged, Lear disinherits her. Once given the kingdom, the two daughters treat their father cruelly, causing him to lose his mind.

In the parallel secondary plot, the Earl of Gloucester has two sons—one loyal, one a back-stabber—and he too trusts the wrong child. Things end in a bloodbath. Throughout it all, Lear's jester, the Fool (one of Shakespeare's most fascinating characters), criticizes and advises Lear, getting away with speaking ugly truths because he couches them in humor.

Ian Pollock—whose work includes four British postage stamps—employed ink and watercolor to create a stunning full-length adaptation of this great tragedy. In the excerpt here, we see what finally causes Lear to snap. Regan and her husband, the Duke of Cornwall, have already arrived at Gloucester's castle and put Kent—a nobleman loyal to Lear—in stocks for a minor offense. Lear arrives—accompanied by the Fool and a knight—and Regan treats him badly. Goneril shows up and piles on the disrespect. Lear runs off into the encroaching storm. . . .

ACT II, SCENE IV

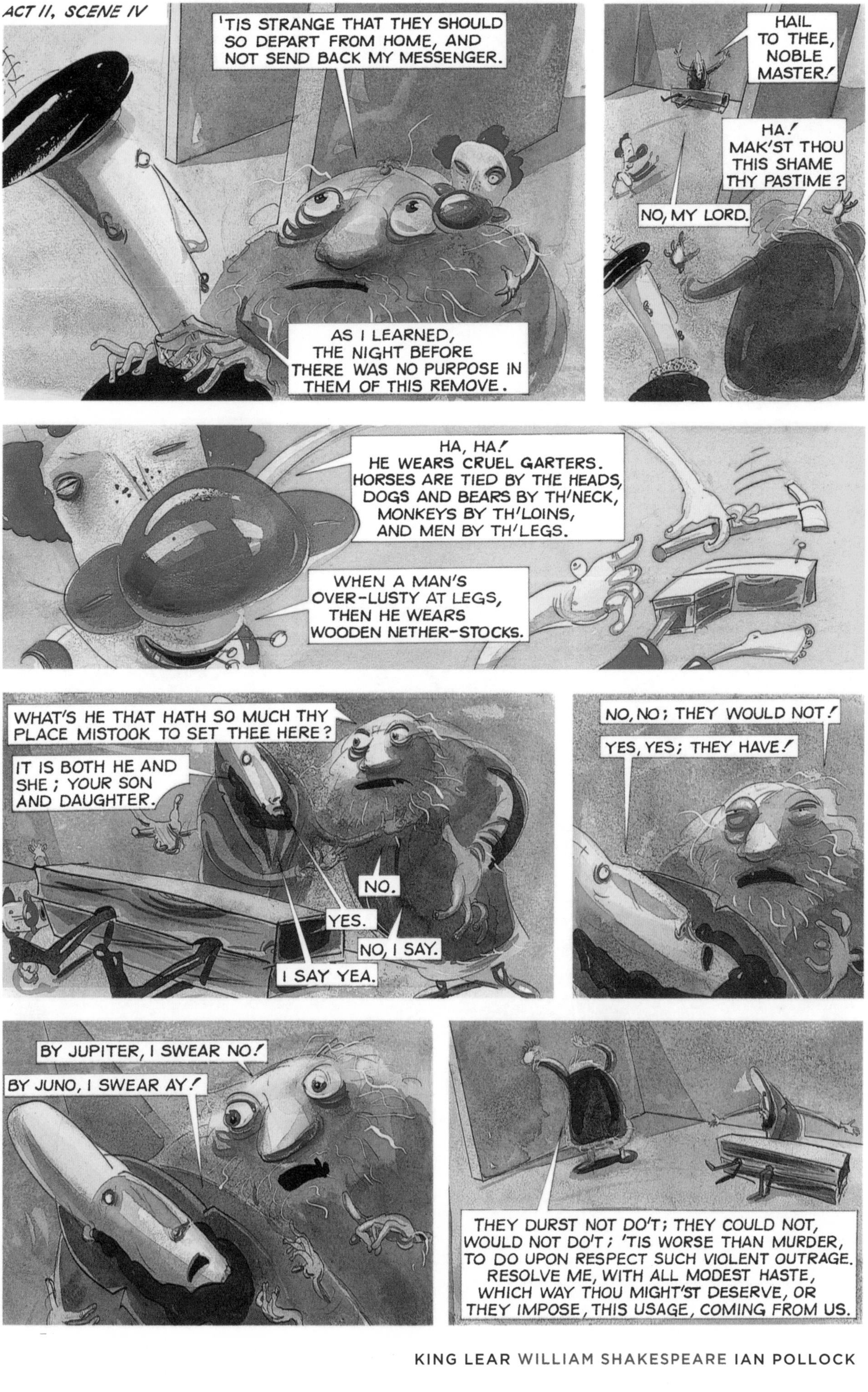

'TIS STRANGE THAT THEY SHOULD SO DEPART FROM HOME, AND NOT SEND BACK MY MESSENGER.
AS I LEARNED, THE NIGHT BEFORE THERE WAS NO PURPOSE IN THEM OF THIS REMOVE.
HAIL TO THEE, NOBLE MASTER!
HA! MAK'ST THOU THIS SHAME THY PASTIME?
NO, MY LORD.
HA, HA! HE WEARS CRUEL GARTERS. HORSES ARE TIED BY THE HEADS, DOGS AND BEARS BY TH'NECK, MONKEYS BY TH'LOINS, AND MEN BY TH'LEGS.
WHEN A MAN'S OVER-LUSTY AT LEGS, THEN HE WEARS WOODEN NETHER-STOCKS.
WHAT'S HE THAT HATH SO MUCH THY PLACE MISTOOK TO SET THEE HERE?
IT IS BOTH HE AND SHE; YOUR SON AND DAUGHTER.
NO.
YES.
NO, I SAY.
I SAY YEA.
NO, NO; THEY WOULD NOT!
YES, YES; THEY HAVE!
BY JUPITER, I SWEAR NO!
BY JUNO, I SWEAR AY!
THEY DURST NOT DO'T; THEY COULD NOT, WOULD NOT DO'T; 'TIS WORSE THAN MURDER, TO DO UPON RESPECT SUCH VIOLENT OUTRAGE. RESOLVE ME, WITH ALL MODEST HASTE, WHICH WAY THOU MIGHT'ST DESERVE, OR THEY IMPOSE, THIS USAGE, COMING FROM US.

MY LORD, WHEN AT THEIR HOME I DID COMMEND YOUR HIGHNESS' LETTERS TO THEM, ERE I WAS RISEN FROM THE PLACE THAT SHOWED MY DUTY KNEELING,

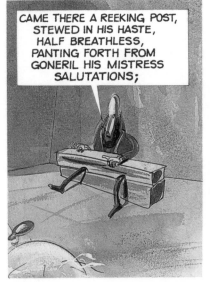

CAME THERE A REEKING POST, STEWED IN HIS HASTE, HALF BREATHLESS, PANTING FORTH FROM GONERIL HIS MISTRESS SALUTATIONS;

DELIVERED LETTERS, SPITE OF INTERMISSION, WHICH PRESENTLY THEY READ: ON WHOSE CONTENTS THEY SUMMONED UP THEIR MEINY, STRAIGHT TOOK HORSE; COMMANDED ME TO FOLLOW,

AND ATTEND THE LEISURE OF THEIR ANSWER; GAVE ME COLD LOOKS. AND MEETING HERE THE OTHER MESSENGER, WHOSE WELCOME, I PERCEIVED, HAD POISONED MINE —

BEING THE VERY FELLOW WHICH OF LATE DISPLAYED SO SAUCILY AGAINST YOUR HIGHNESS — HAVING MORE MAN THAN WIT ABOUT ME, DREW. HE RAISED THE HOUSE WITH LOUD AND COWARD CRIES.

YOUR SON AND DAUGHTER FOUND THIS TRESPASS WORTH THE SHAME WHICH HERE IT SUFFERS.

WINTER'S NOT GONE YET, IF THE WILD GEESE FLY THAT WAY.

FATHERS THAT WEAR RAGS DO MAKE THEIR CHILDREN BLIND, BUT FATHERS THAT BEAR BAGS SHALL SEE THEIR CHILDREN KIND. FORTUNE, THAT ARRANT WHORE, NE'ER TURNS THE KEY TO TH'POOR.

BUT FOR ALL THIS, THOU SHALT HAVE AS MANY DOLOURS FOR THY DAUGHTERS AS THOU CANST TELL IN A YEAR.

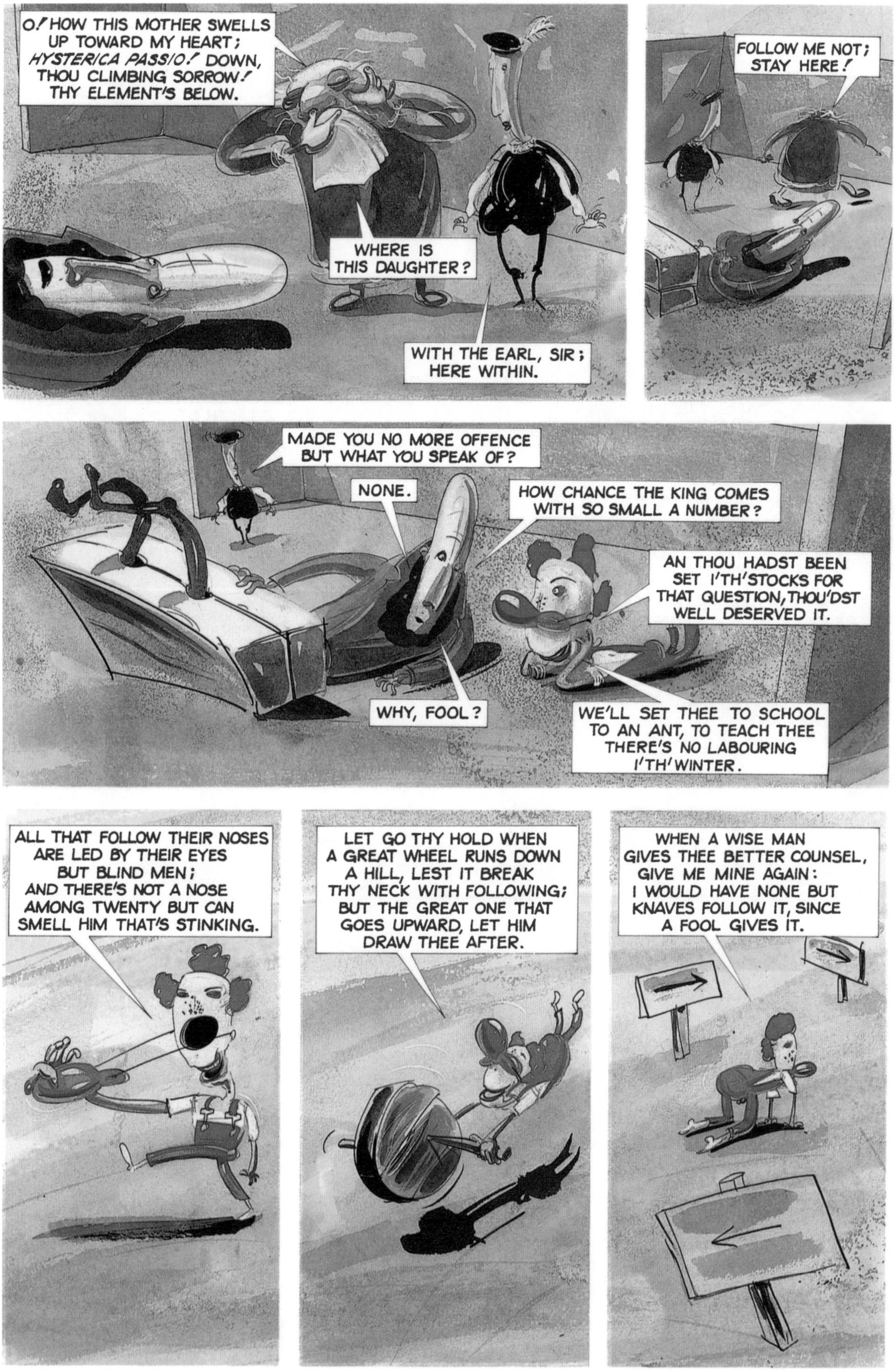
O! HOW THIS MOTHER SWELLS UP TOWARD MY HEART; HYSTERICA PASSIO! DOWN, THOU CLIMBING SORROW! THY ELEMENT'S BELOW.
WHERE IS THIS DAUGHTER?
WITH THE EARL, SIR; HERE WITHIN.
FOLLOW ME NOT; STAY HERE!
MADE YOU NO MORE OFFENCE BUT WHAT YOU SPEAK OF?
NONE.
HOW CHANCE THE KING COMES WITH SO SMALL A NUMBER?
AN THOU HADST BEEN SET I'TH'STOCKS FOR THAT QUESTION, THOU'DST WELL DESERVED IT.
WHY, FOOL?
WE'LL SET THEE TO SCHOOL TO AN ANT, TO TEACH THEE THERE'S NO LABOURING I'TH'WINTER.
ALL THAT FOLLOW THEIR NOSES ARE LED BY THEIR EYES BUT BLIND MEN; AND THERE'S NOT A NOSE AMONG TWENTY BUT CAN SMELL HIM THAT'S STINKING.
LET GO THY HOLD WHEN A GREAT WHEEL RUNS DOWN A HILL, LEST IT BREAK THY NECK WITH FOLLOWING; BUT THE GREAT ONE THAT GOES UPWARD, LET HIM DRAW THEE AFTER.
WHEN A WISE MAN GIVES THEE BETTER COUNSEL, GIVE ME MINE AGAIN: I WOULD HAVE NONE BUT KNAVES FOLLOW IT, SINCE A FOOL GIVES IT.

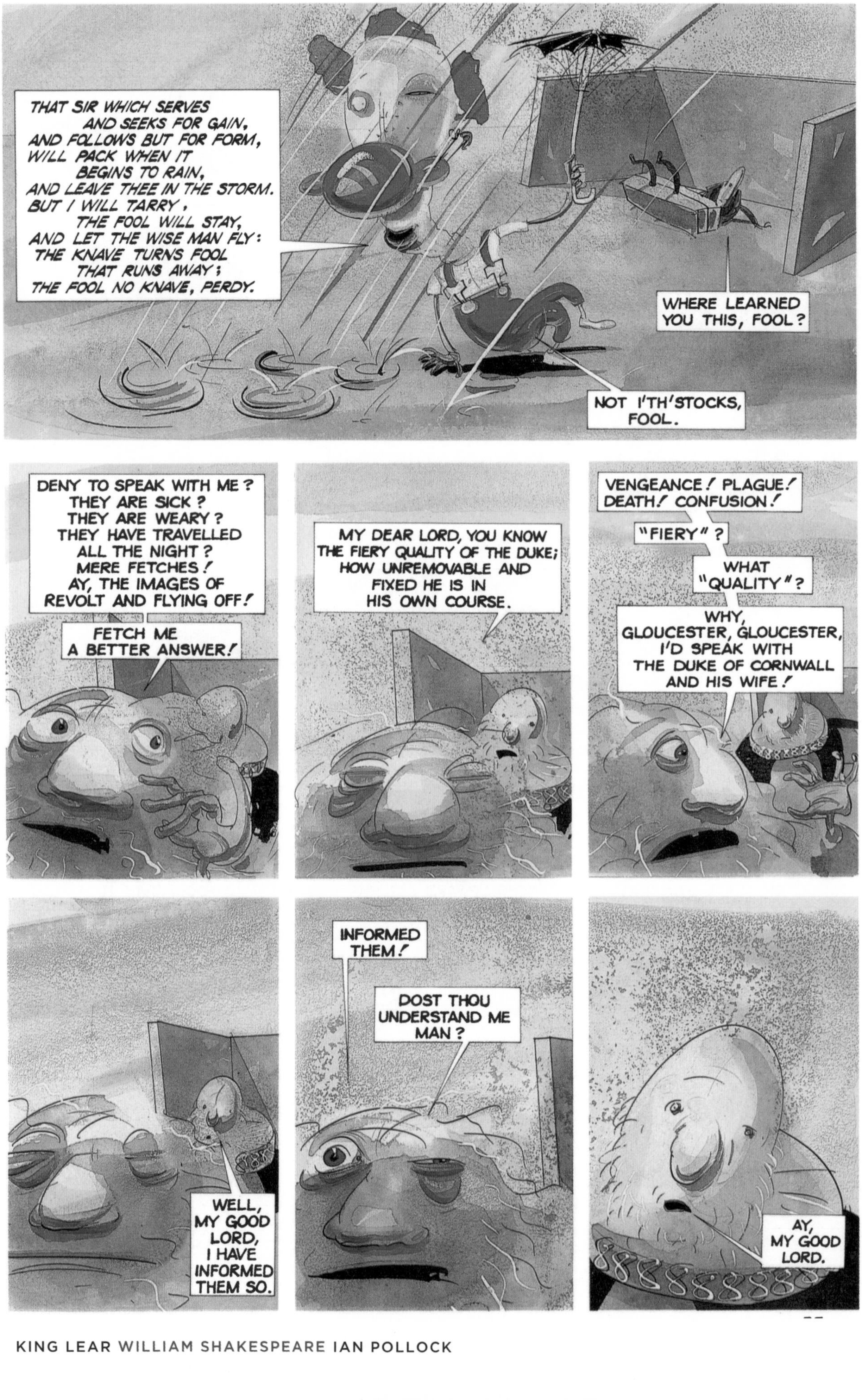
THAT SIR WHICH SERVES AND SEEKS FOR GAIN, AND FOLLOWS BUT FOR FORM, WILL PACK WHEN IT BEGINS TO RAIN, AND LEAVE THEE IN THE STORM. BUT I WILL TARRY, THE FOOL WILL STAY, AND LET THE WISE MAN FLY: THE KNAVE TURNS FOOL THAT RUNS AWAY; THE FOOL NO KNAVE, PERDY.
WHERE LEARNED YOU THIS, FOOL?
NOT I'TH'STOCKS, FOOL.
DENY TO SPEAK WITH ME? THEY ARE SICK? THEY ARE WEARY? THEY HAVE TRAVELLED ALL THE NIGHT? MERE FETCHES! AY, THE IMAGES OF REVOLT AND FLYING OFF!
FETCH ME A BETTER ANSWER!
MY DEAR LORD, YOU KNOW THE FIERY QUALITY OF THE DUKE; HOW UNREMOVABLE AND FIXED HE IS IN HIS OWN COURSE.
VENGEANCE! PLAGUE! DEATH! CONFUSION!
"FIERY"?
WHAT "QUALITY"?
WHY, GLOUCESTER, GLOUCESTER, I'D SPEAK WITH THE DUKE OF CORNWALL AND HIS WIFE!
WELL, MY GOOD LORD, I HAVE INFORMED THEM SO.
INFORMED THEM!
DOST THOU UNDERSTAND ME MAN?
AY, MY GOOD LORD.

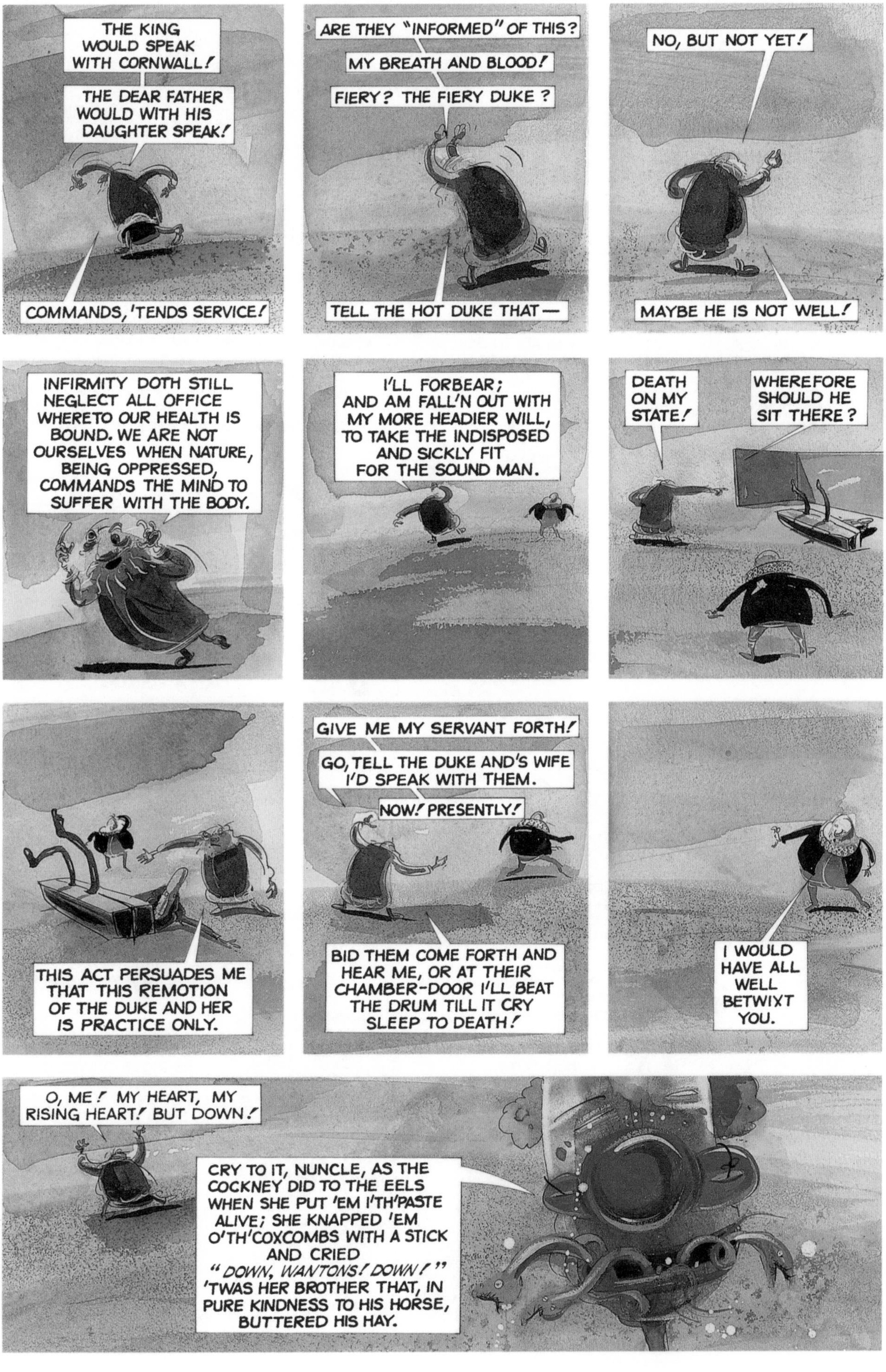
THE KING WOULD SPEAK WITH CORNWALL!
THE DEAR FATHER WOULD WITH HIS DAUGHTER SPEAK!
COMMANDS, 'TENDS SERVICE!
ARE THEY "INFORMED" OF THIS?
MY BREATH AND BLOOD!
FIERY? THE FIERY DUKE?
TELL THE HOT DUKE THAT—
NO, BUT NOT YET!
MAYBE HE IS NOT WELL!
INFIRMITY DOTH STILL NEGLECT ALL OFFICE WHERETO OUR HEALTH IS BOUND. WE ARE NOT OURSELVES WHEN NATURE, BEING OPPRESSED, COMMANDS THE MIND TO SUFFER WITH THE BODY.
I'LL FORBEAR; AND AM FALL'N OUT WITH MY MORE HEADIER WILL, TO TAKE THE INDISPOSED AND SICKLY FIT FOR THE SOUND MAN.
DEATH ON MY STATE!
WHEREFORE SHOULD HE SIT THERE?
THIS ACT PERSUADES ME THAT THIS REMOTION OF THE DUKE AND HER IS PRACTICE ONLY.
GIVE ME MY SERVANT FORTH!
GO, TELL THE DUKE AND'S WIFE I'D SPEAK WITH THEM.
NOW! PRESENTLY!
BID THEM COME FORTH AND HEAR ME, OR AT THEIR CHAMBER-DOOR I'LL BEAT THE DRUM TILL IT CRY SLEEP TO DEATH!
I WOULD HAVE ALL WELL BETWIXT YOU.
O, ME! MY HEART, MY RISING HEART! BUT DOWN!
CRY TO IT, NUNCLE, AS THE COCKNEY DID TO THE EELS WHEN SHE PUT 'EM I'TH'PASTE ALIVE; SHE KNAPPED 'EM O'TH'COXCOMBS WITH A STICK AND CRIED "DOWN, WANTONS! DOWN!" 'TWAS HER BROTHER THAT, IN PURE KINDNESS TO HIS HORSE, BUTTERED HIS HAY.

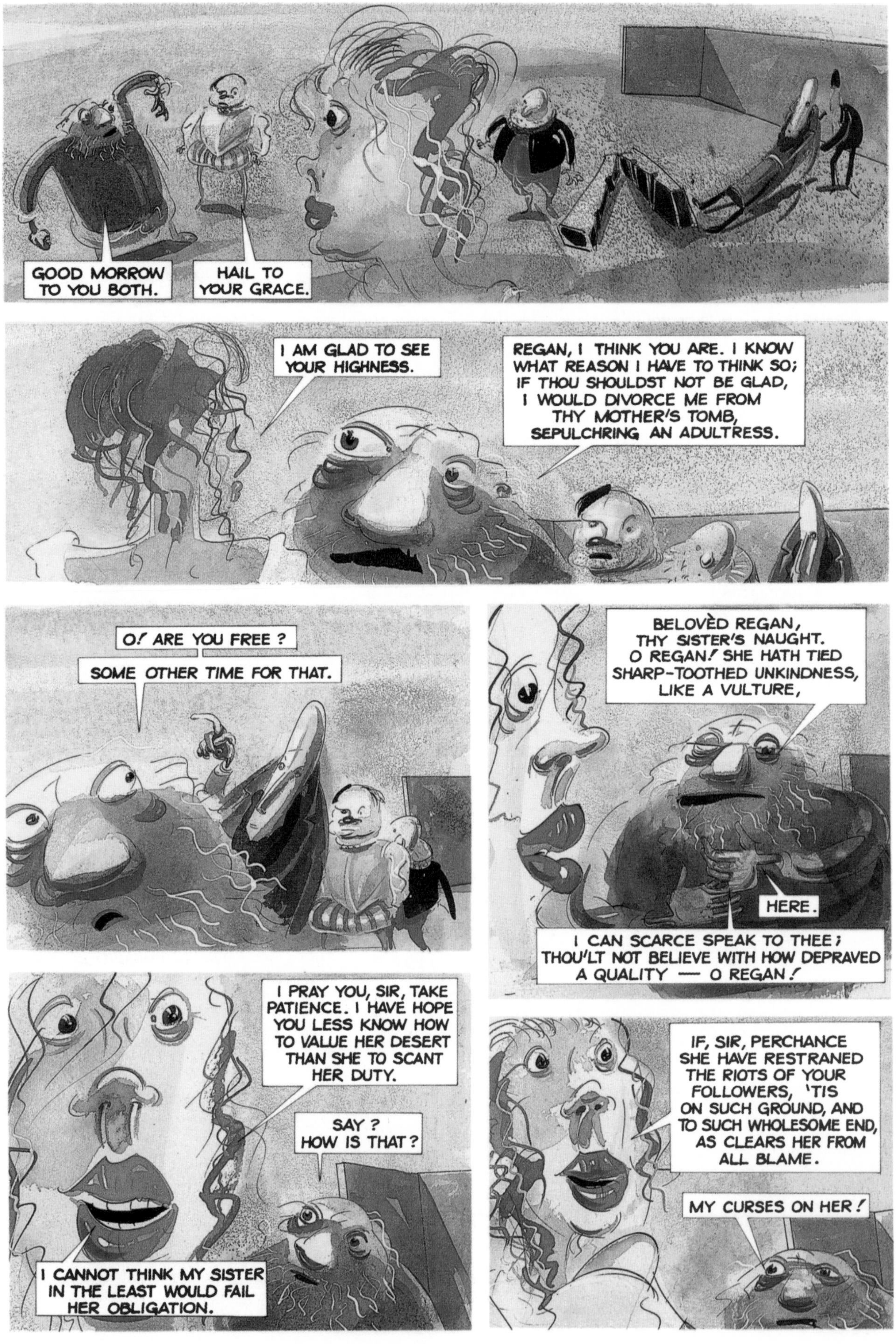
GOOD MORROW TO YOU BOTH.
HAIL TO YOUR GRACE.
I AM GLAD TO SEE YOUR HIGHNESS.
REGAN, I THINK YOU ARE. I KNOW WHAT REASON I HAVE TO THINK SO; IF THOU SHOULDST NOT BE GLAD, I WOULD DIVORCE ME FROM THY MOTHER'S TOMB, SEPULCHRING AN ADULTRESS.
O! ARE YOU FREE ?
SOME OTHER TIME FOR THAT.
BELOVÈD REGAN, THY SISTER'S NAUGHT. O REGAN! SHE HATH TIED SHARP-TOOTHED UNKINDNESS, LIKE A VULTURE,
HERE.
I CAN SCARCE SPEAK TO THEE; THOU'LT NOT BELIEVE WITH HOW DEPRAVED A QUALITY — O REGAN!
I PRAY YOU, SIR, TAKE PATIENCE. I HAVE HOPE YOU LESS KNOW HOW TO VALUE HER DESERT THAN SHE TO SCANT HER DUTY.
SAY ? HOW IS THAT ?
I CANNOT THINK MY SISTER IN THE LEAST WOULD FAIL HER OBLIGATION.
IF, SIR, PERCHANCE SHE HAVE RESTRANED THE RIOTS OF YOUR FOLLOWERS, 'TIS ON SUCH GROUND, AND TO SUCH WHOLESOME END, AS CLEARS HER FROM ALL BLAME.
MY CURSES ON HER!

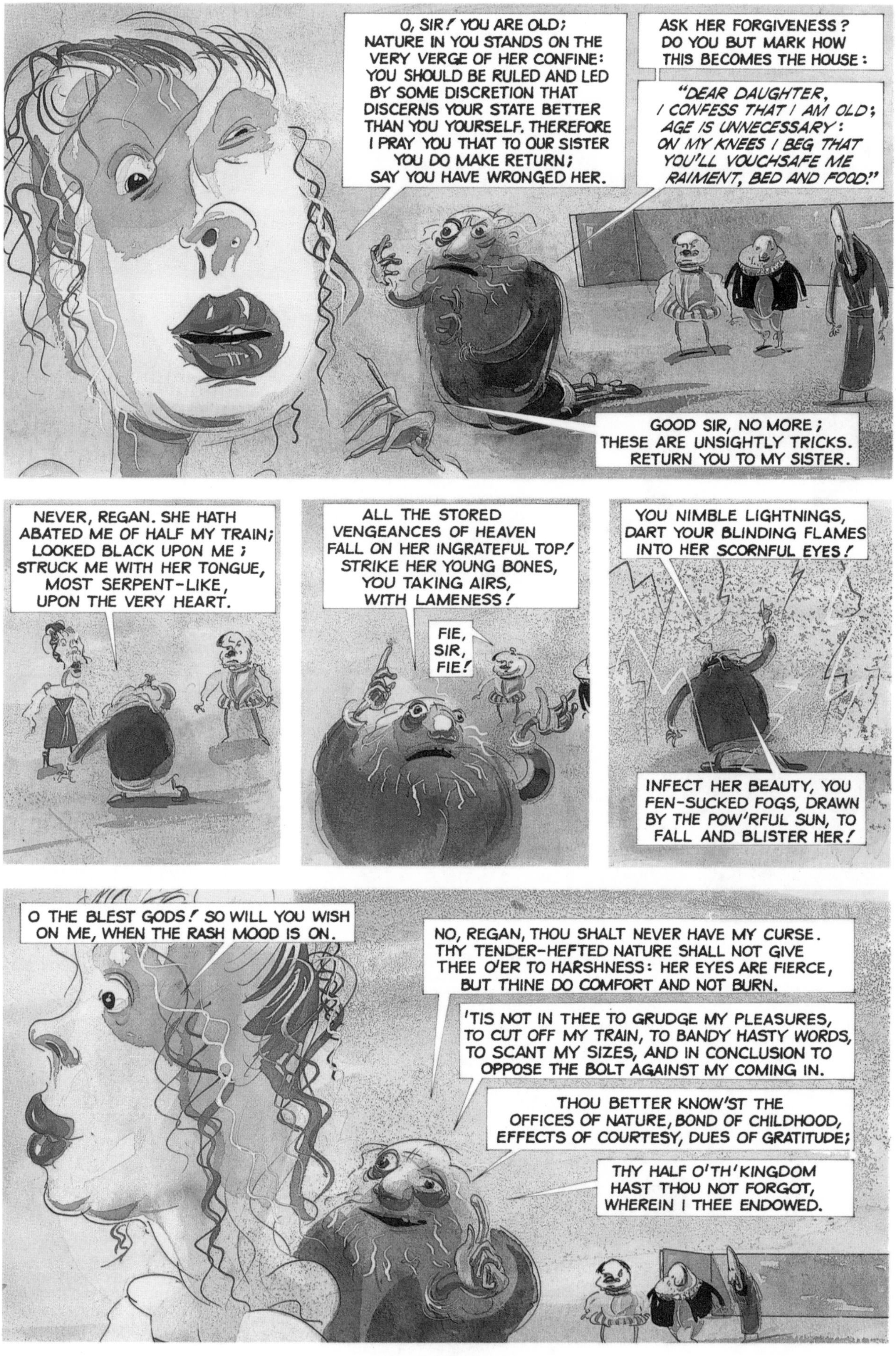

O, SIR! YOU ARE OLD; NATURE IN YOU STANDS ON THE VERY VERGE OF HER CONFINE: YOU SHOULD BE RULED AND LED BY SOME DISCRETION THAT DISCERNS YOUR STATE BETTER THAN YOU YOURSELF. THEREFORE I PRAY YOU THAT TO OUR SISTER YOU DO MAKE RETURN; SAY YOU HAVE WRONGED HER.
ASK HER FORGIVENESS? DO YOU BUT MARK HOW THIS BECOMES THE HOUSE:
"DEAR DAUGHTER, I CONFESS THAT I AM OLD; AGE IS UNNECESSARY: ON MY KNEES I BEG THAT YOU'LL VOUCHSAFE ME RAIMENT, BED AND FOOD."
GOOD SIR, NO MORE; THESE ARE UNSIGHTLY TRICKS. RETURN YOU TO MY SISTER.
NEVER, REGAN. SHE HATH ABATED ME OF HALF MY TRAIN; LOOKED BLACK UPON ME; STRUCK ME WITH HER TONGUE, MOST SERPENT-LIKE, UPON THE VERY HEART.
ALL THE STORED VENGEANCES OF HEAVEN FALL ON HER INGRATEFUL TOP! STRIKE HER YOUNG BONES, YOU TAKING AIRS, WITH LAMENESS!
FIE, SIR, FIE!
YOU NIMBLE LIGHTNINGS, DART YOUR BLINDING FLAMES INTO HER SCORNFUL EYES!
INFECT HER BEAUTY, YOU FEN-SUCKED FOGS, DRAWN BY THE POW'RFUL SUN, TO FALL AND BLISTER HER!
O THE BLEST GODS! SO WILL YOU WISH ON ME, WHEN THE RASH MOOD IS ON.
NO, REGAN, THOU SHALT NEVER HAVE MY CURSE. THY TENDER-HEFTED NATURE SHALL NOT GIVE THEE O'ER TO HARSHNESS: HER EYES ARE FIERCE, BUT THINE DO COMFORT AND NOT BURN.
'TIS NOT IN THEE TO GRUDGE MY PLEASURES, TO CUT OFF MY TRAIN, TO BANDY HASTY WORDS, TO SCANT MY SIZES, AND IN CONCLUSION TO OPPOSE THE BOLT AGAINST MY COMING IN.
THOU BETTER KNOW'ST THE OFFICES OF NATURE, BOND OF CHILDHOOD, EFFECTS OF COURTESY, DUES OF GRATITUDE;
THY HALF O'TH'KINGDOM HAST THOU NOT FORGOT, WHEREIN I THEE ENDOWED.

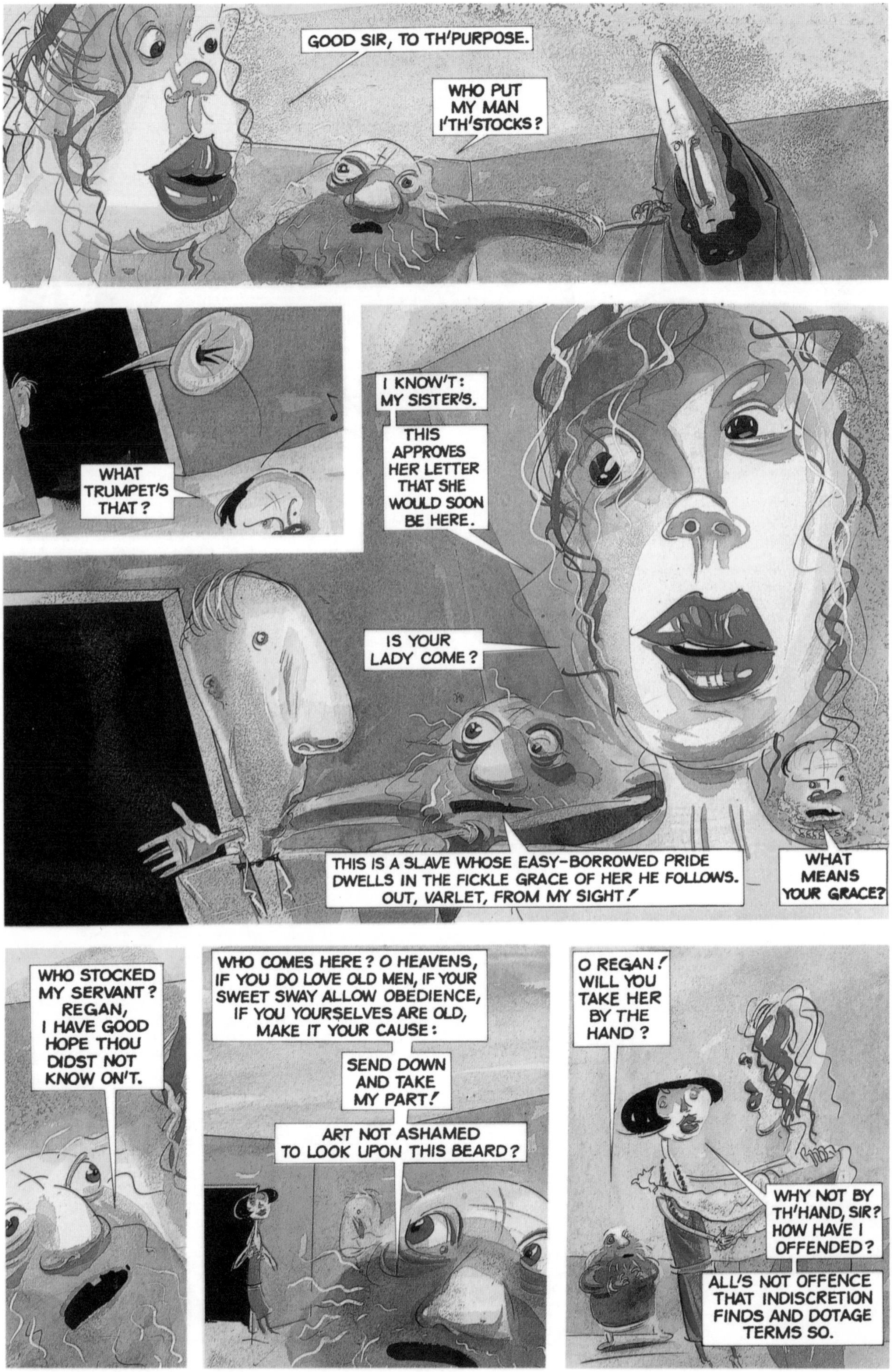
GOOD SIR, TO TH'PURPOSE.
WHO PUT MY MAN I'TH'STOCKS?
WHAT TRUMPET'S THAT?
I KNOW'T: MY SISTER'S.
THIS APPROVES HER LETTER THAT SHE WOULD SOON BE HERE.
IS YOUR LADY COME?
THIS IS A SLAVE WHOSE EASY-BORROWED PRIDE DWELLS IN THE FICKLE GRACE OF HER HE FOLLOWS. OUT, VARLET, FROM MY SIGHT!
WHAT MEANS YOUR GRACE?
WHO STOCKED MY SERVANT? REGAN, I HAVE GOOD HOPE THOU DIDST NOT KNOW ON'T.
WHO COMES HERE? O HEAVENS, IF YOU DO LOVE OLD MEN, IF YOUR SWEET SWAY ALLOW OBEDIENCE, IF YOU YOURSELVES ARE OLD, MAKE IT YOUR CAUSE:
SEND DOWN AND TAKE MY PART!
ART NOT ASHAMED TO LOOK UPON THIS BEARD?
O REGAN! WILL YOU TAKE HER BY THE HAND?
WHY NOT BY TH'HAND, SIR? HOW HAVE I OFFENDED?
ALL'S NOT OFFENCE THAT INDISCRETION FINDS AND DOTAGE TERMS SO.

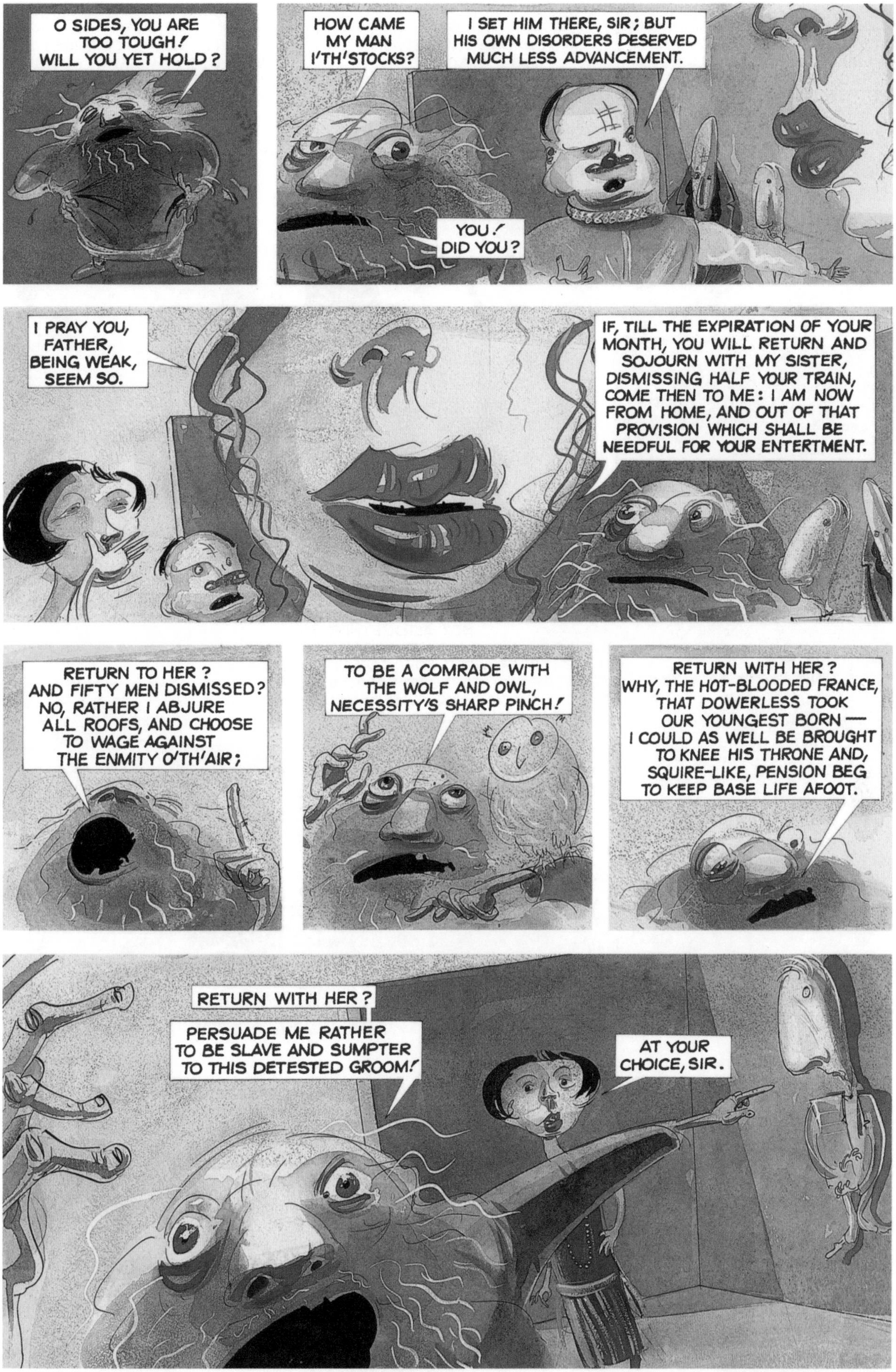
O SIDES, YOU ARE TOO TOUGH! WILL YOU YET HOLD?
HOW CAME MY MAN I'TH'STOCKS?
I SET HIM THERE, SIR; BUT HIS OWN DISORDERS DESERVED MUCH LESS ADVANCEMENT.
YOU! DID YOU?
I PRAY YOU, FATHER, BEING WEAK, SEEM SO.
IF, TILL THE EXPIRATION OF YOUR MONTH, YOU WILL RETURN AND SOJOURN WITH MY SISTER, DISMISSING HALF YOUR TRAIN, COME THEN TO ME: I AM NOW FROM HOME, AND OUT OF THAT PROVISION WHICH SHALL BE NEEDFUL FOR YOUR ENTERTMENT.
RETURN TO HER? AND FIFTY MEN DISMISSED? NO, RATHER I ABJURE ALL ROOFS, AND CHOOSE TO WAGE AGAINST THE ENMITY O'TH'AIR;
TO BE A COMRADE WITH THE WOLF AND OWL, NECESSITY'S SHARP PINCH!
RETURN WITH HER? WHY, THE HOT-BLOODED FRANCE, THAT DOWERLESS TOOK OUR YOUNGEST BORN— I COULD AS WELL BE BROUGHT TO KNEE HIS THRONE AND, SQUIRE-LIKE, PENSION BEG TO KEEP BASE LIFE AFOOT.
RETURN WITH HER?
PERSUADE ME RATHER TO BE SLAVE AND SUMPTER TO THIS DETESTED GROOM!
AT YOUR CHOICE, SIR.

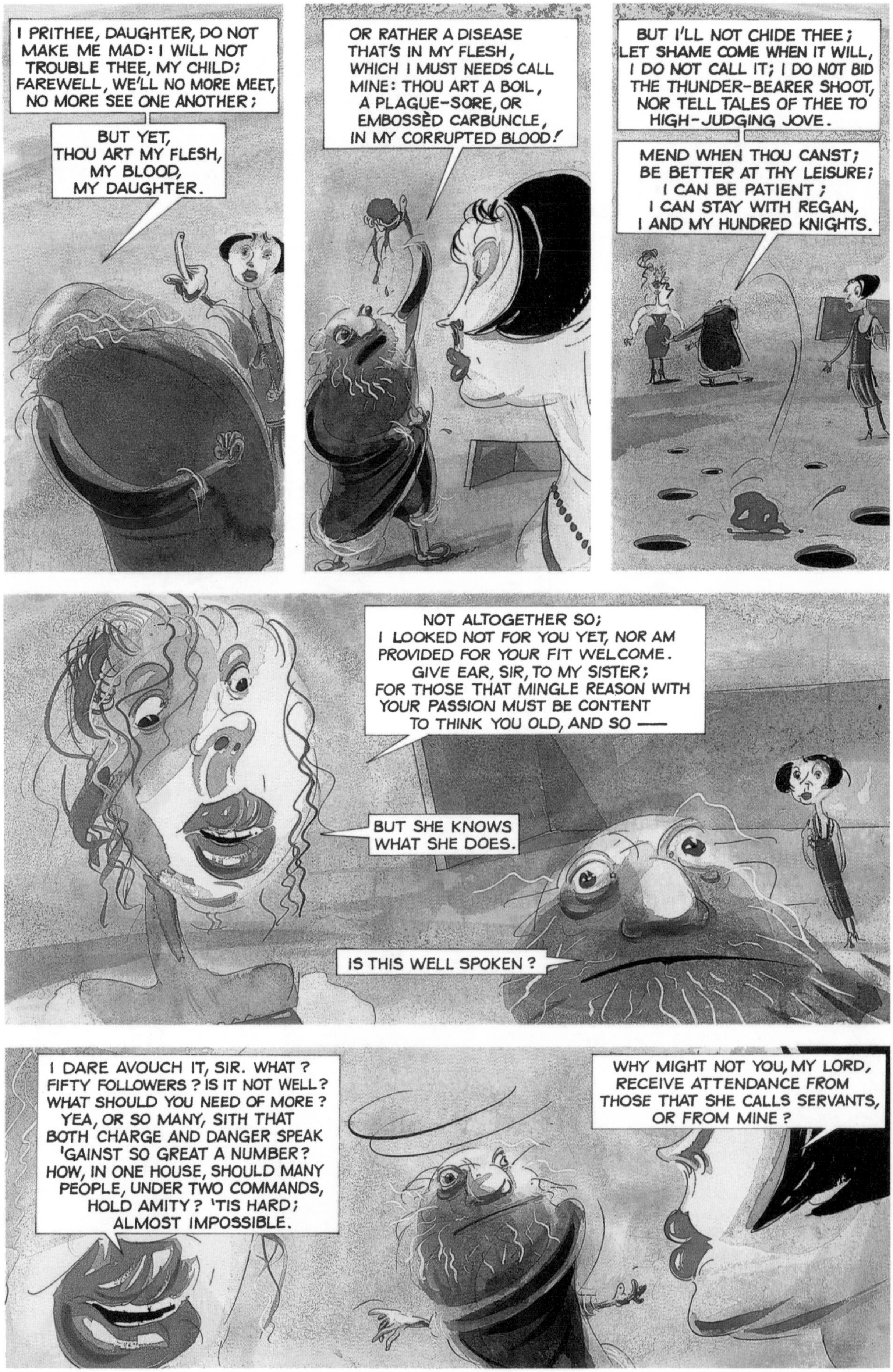
I PRITHEE, DAUGHTER, DO NOT MAKE ME MAD: I WILL NOT TROUBLE THEE, MY CHILD; FAREWELL, WE'LL NO MORE MEET, NO MORE SEE ONE ANOTHER;
BUT YET, THOU ART MY FLESH, MY BLOOD, MY DAUGHTER.
OR RATHER A DISEASE THAT'S IN MY FLESH, WHICH I MUST NEEDS CALL MINE: THOU ART A BOIL, A PLAGUE-SORE, OR EMBOSSÈD CARBUNCLE, IN MY CORRUPTED BLOOD!
BUT I'LL NOT CHIDE THEE; LET SHAME COME WHEN IT WILL, I DO NOT CALL IT; I DO NOT BID THE THUNDER-BEARER SHOOT, NOR TELL TALES OF THEE TO HIGH-JUDGING JOVE.
MEND WHEN THOU CANST; BE BETTER AT THY LEISURE; I CAN BE PATIENT; I CAN STAY WITH REGAN, I AND MY HUNDRED KNIGHTS.
NOT ALTOGETHER SO; I LOOKED NOT FOR YOU YET, NOR AM PROVIDED FOR YOUR FIT WELCOME. GIVE EAR, SIR, TO MY SISTER; FOR THOSE THAT MINGLE REASON WITH YOUR PASSION MUST BE CONTENT TO THINK YOU OLD, AND SO —
BUT SHE KNOWS WHAT SHE DOES.
IS THIS WELL SPOKEN?
I DARE AVOUCH IT, SIR. WHAT? FIFTY FOLLOWERS? IS IT NOT WELL? WHAT SHOULD YOU NEED OF MORE? YEA, OR SO MANY, SITH THAT BOTH CHARGE AND DANGER SPEAK 'GAINST SO GREAT A NUMBER? HOW, IN ONE HOUSE, SHOULD MANY PEOPLE, UNDER TWO COMMANDS, HOLD AMITY? 'TIS HARD; ALMOST IMPOSSIBLE.
WHY MIGHT NOT YOU, MY LORD, RECEIVE ATTENDANCE FROM THOSE THAT SHE CALLS SERVANTS, OR FROM MINE?

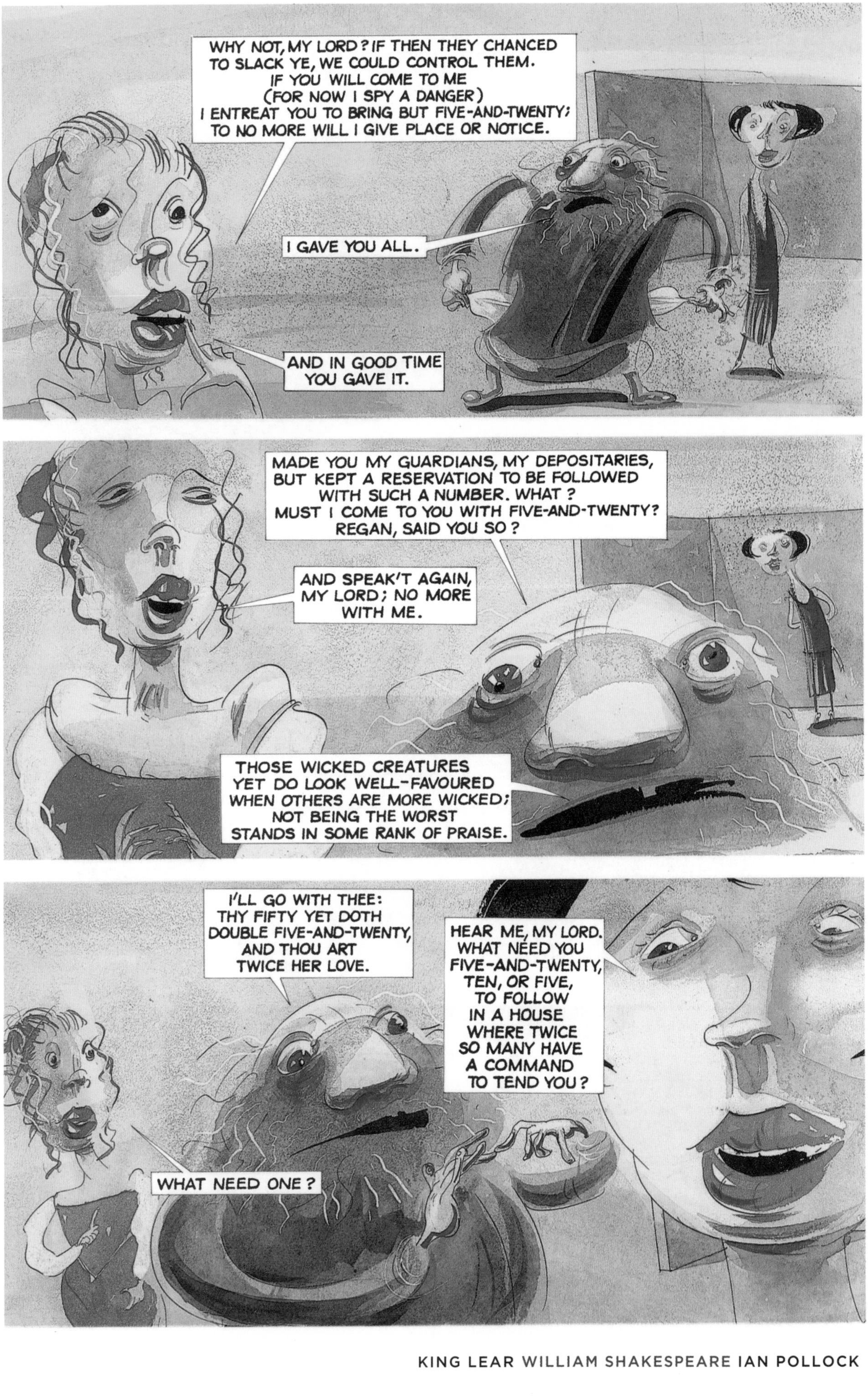
WHY NOT, MY LORD? IF THEN THEY CHANCED TO SLACK YE, WE COULD CONTROL THEM. IF YOU WILL COME TO ME (FOR NOW I SPY A DANGER) I ENTREAT YOU TO BRING BUT FIVE-AND-TWENTY; TO NO MORE WILL I GIVE PLACE OR NOTICE.
I GAVE YOU ALL.
AND IN GOOD TIME YOU GAVE IT.
MADE YOU MY GUARDIANS, MY DEPOSITARIES, BUT KEPT A RESERVATION TO BE FOLLOWED WITH SUCH A NUMBER. WHAT? MUST I COME TO YOU WITH FIVE-AND-TWENTY? REGAN, SAID YOU SO?
AND SPEAK'T AGAIN, MY LORD; NO MORE WITH ME.
THOSE WICKED CREATURES YET DO LOOK WELL-FAVOURED WHEN OTHERS ARE MORE WICKED; NOT BEING THE WORST STANDS IN SOME RANK OF PRAISE.
I'LL GO WITH THEE: THY FIFTY YET DOTH DOUBLE FIVE-AND-TWENTY, AND THOU ART TWICE HER LOVE.
HEAR ME, MY LORD. WHAT NEED YOU FIVE-AND-TWENTY, TEN, OR FIVE, TO FOLLOW IN A HOUSE WHERE TWICE SO MANY HAVE A COMMAND TO TEND YOU?
WHAT NEED ONE?

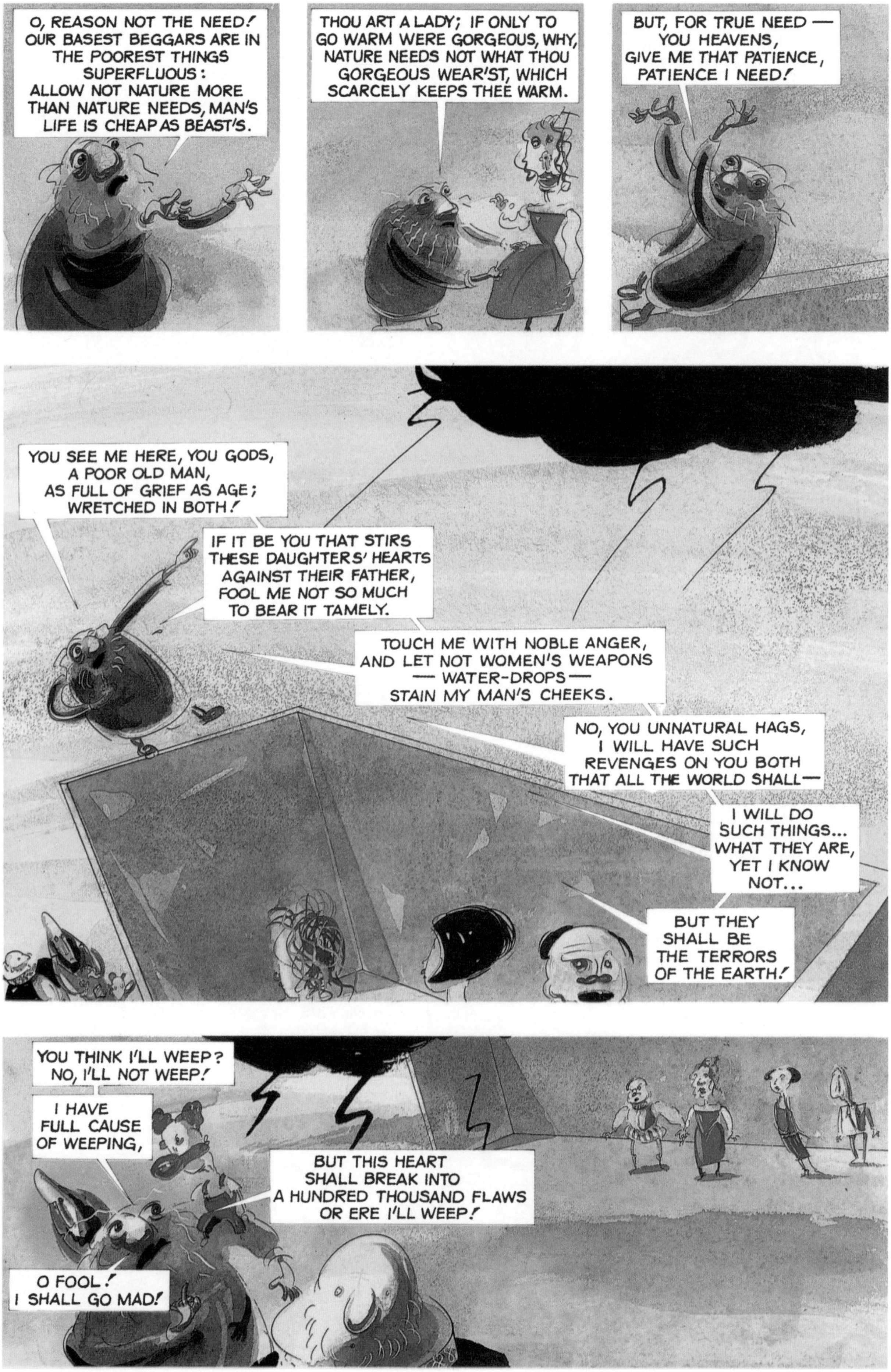

O, REASON NOT THE NEED! OUR BASEST BEGGARS ARE IN THE POOREST THINGS SUPERFLUOUS: ALLOW NOT NATURE MORE THAN NATURE NEEDS, MAN'S LIFE IS CHEAP AS BEAST'S.
THOU ART A LADY; IF ONLY TO GO WARM WERE GORGEOUS, WHY, NATURE NEEDS NOT WHAT THOU GORGEOUS WEAR'ST, WHICH SCARCELY KEEPS THEE WARM.
BUT, FOR TRUE NEED — YOU HEAVENS, GIVE ME THAT PATIENCE, PATIENCE I NEED!
YOU SEE ME HERE, YOU GODS, A POOR OLD MAN, AS FULL OF GRIEF AS AGE; WRETCHED IN BOTH!
IF IT BE YOU THAT STIRS THESE DAUGHTERS' HEARTS AGAINST THEIR FATHER, FOOL ME NOT SO MUCH TO BEAR IT TAMELY.
TOUCH ME WITH NOBLE ANGER, AND LET NOT WOMEN'S WEAPONS — WATER-DROPS — STAIN MY MAN'S CHEEKS.
NO, YOU UNNATURAL HAGS, I WILL HAVE SUCH REVENGES ON YOU BOTH THAT ALL THE WORLD SHALL—
I WILL DO SUCH THINGS... WHAT THEY ARE, YET I KNOW NOT...
BUT THEY SHALL BE THE TERRORS OF THE EARTH!
YOU THINK I'LL WEEP? NO, I'LL NOT WEEP!
I HAVE FULL CAUSE OF WEEPING,
BUT THIS HEART SHALL BREAK INTO A HUNDRED THOUSAND FLAWS OR ERE I'LL WEEP!
O FOOL! I SHALL GO MAD!

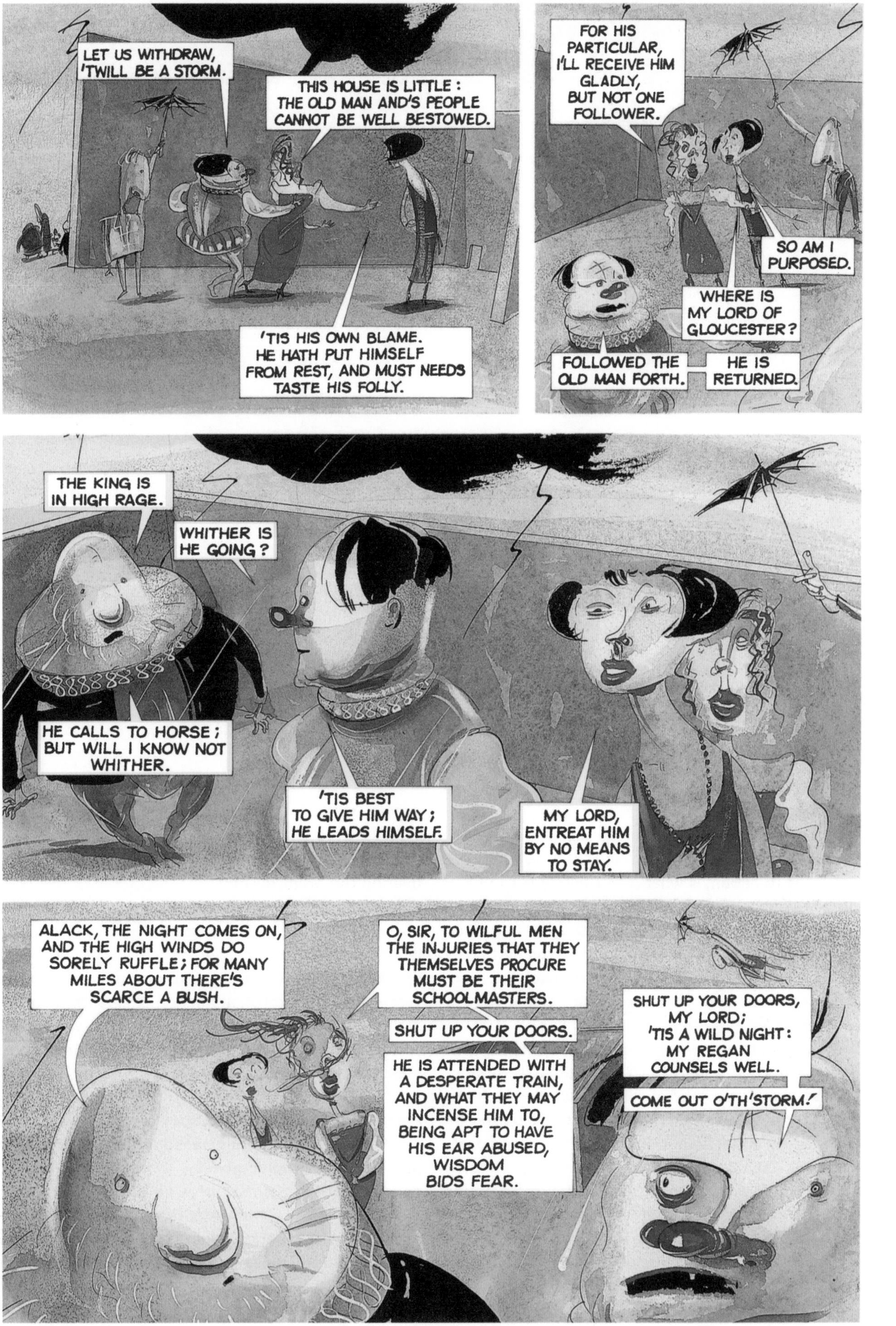
LET US WITHDRAW, 'TWILL BE A STORM.
THIS HOUSE IS LITTLE : THE OLD MAN AND'S PEOPLE CANNOT BE WELL BESTOWED.
'TIS HIS OWN BLAME. HE HATH PUT HIMSELF FROM REST, AND MUST NEEDS TASTE HIS FOLLY.
FOR HIS PARTICULAR, I'LL RECEIVE HIM GLADLY, BUT NOT ONE FOLLOWER.
SO AM I PURPOSED.
WHERE IS MY LORD OF GLOUCESTER?
FOLLOWED THE OLD MAN FORTH.
HE IS RETURNED.
THE KING IS IN HIGH RAGE.
WHITHER IS HE GOING?
HE CALLS TO HORSE; BUT WILL I KNOW NOT WHITHER.
'TIS BEST TO GIVE HIM WAY; HE LEADS HIMSELF.
MY LORD, ENTREAT HIM BY NO MEANS TO STAY.
ALACK, THE NIGHT COMES ON, AND THE HIGH WINDS DO SORELY RUFFLE; FOR MANY MILES ABOUT THERE'S SCARCE A BUSH.
O, SIR, TO WILFUL MEN THE INJURIES THAT THEY THEMSELVES PROCURE MUST BE THEIR SCHOOLMASTERS.
SHUT UP YOUR DOORS.
HE IS ATTENDED WITH A DESPERATE TRAIN, AND WHAT THEY MAY INCENSE HIM TO, BEING APT TO HAVE HIS EAR ABUSED, WISDOM BIDS FEAR.
SHUT UP YOUR DOORS, MY LORD; 'TIS A WILD NIGHT: MY REGAN COUNSELS WELL.
COME OUT O'TH'STORM!

Don Quixote

Miguel Cervantes

ART / ADAPTATION BY **Will Eisner**

WHAT *THE DIVINE COMEDY* IS TO ITALY, WHAT *THE Tale of Genji* is to Japan, is what *Don Quixote* is to Spain: that country's eminent work of literature. And while *Genji* is considered the world's first novel, *Don Quixote* is dubbed the first modern novel, and sometimes even the first postmodern novel, as it's filled with self-references, multiple layers of authorship, and characters who realize they're being written about.

Miguel Cervantes was writing a parody of the tales of chivalrous knights that were popular at the time. He thought they were so much hokey, brain-rotting fluff, so he developed a character whose mind really did get clouded by incessant reading about knights in shining armor and damsels in distress. Don Quixote is a land-owning gentleman who puts on an old suit of armor (a family heirloom), hops on an old nag he believes to be a steed, and rides around the countryside living out his chivalric delusions. He famously tilts at windmills he believes to be giants, as well as attacking random passers-by, including sheep, and getting beat down by ruffians. His down-to-earth foil, Sancho Panza,

tries to keep his friend out of trouble but often ends up bearing the brunt for him.

What is called *Don Quixote* is actually two books—the original novel of 1605 and its sequel, published ten years later. They're now published as a single volume. After the first book of *Don Quixote* instantly became a huge success—indeed, a total phenomenon—Cervantes wrote a more high-minded sequel. Quixote is less of a violent maniac, and in this more complex tale, it gets difficult to tell his delusions from reality.

The late Will Eisner needs little introduction. One of the grandaddies of comic books and graphic novels, he created the 1940s comic sensation *The Spirit*, the early, pathbreaking graphic novel *A Contract With God* (1978), and the term *sequential art*. One of the two most prestigious awards for comic art is named after him. Never one to sit still, in his eighties Eisner produced a thirty-two-page, highly anecdotal take on *Don Quixote*, heavy on the humor, called *The Last Knight*. The novel's iconic early scenes are excerpted here.

400

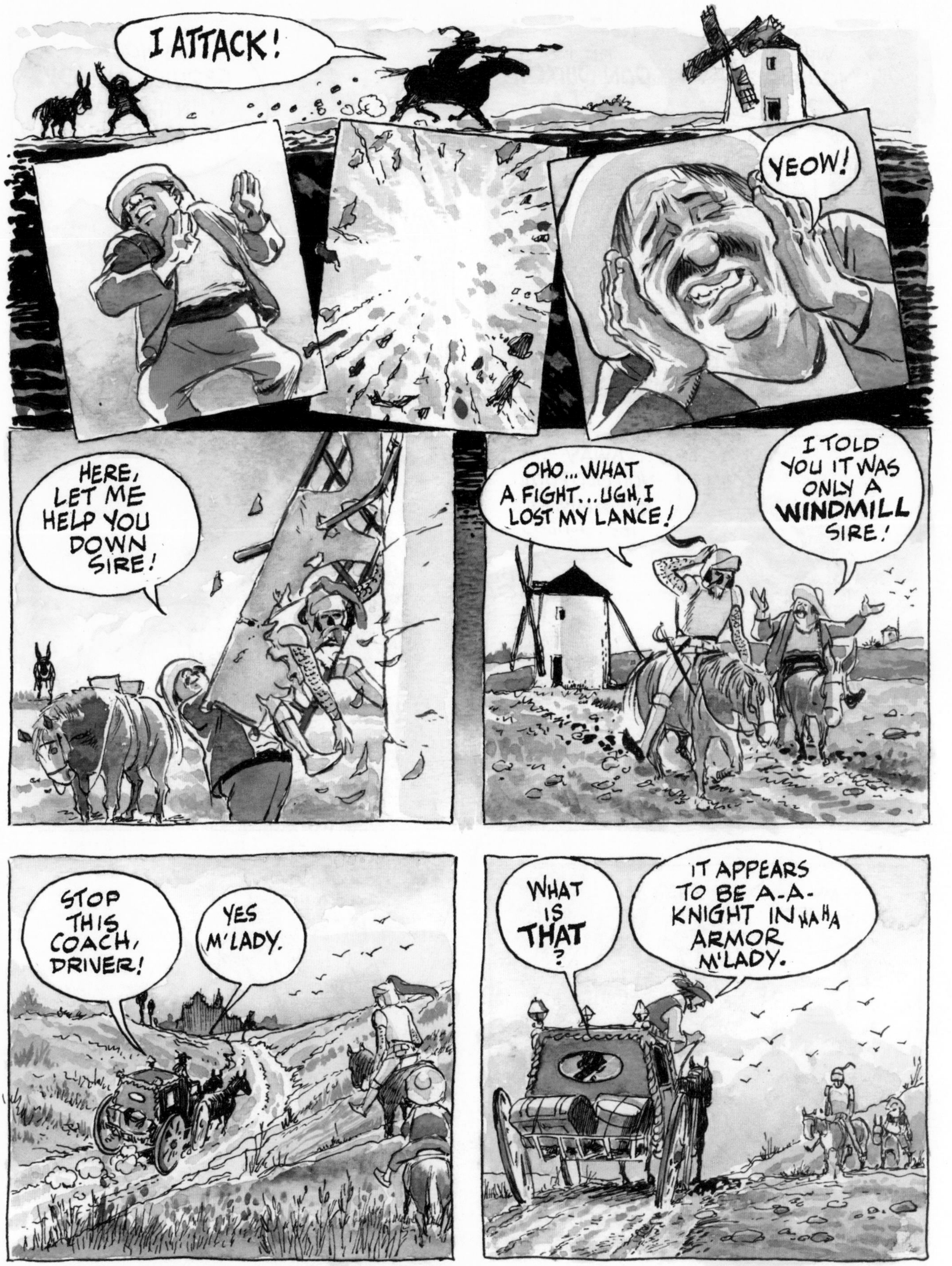
I ATTACK!
YEOW!
HERE, LET ME HELP YOU DOWN SIRE!
OHO... WHAT A FIGHT... UGH, I LOST MY LANCE!
I TOLD YOU IT WAS ONLY A WINDMILL SIRE!
STOP THIS COACH, DRIVER!
YES M'LADY.
WHAT IS THAT ?
IT APPEARS TO BE A-A- KNIGHT IN HA HA ARMOR M'LADY.

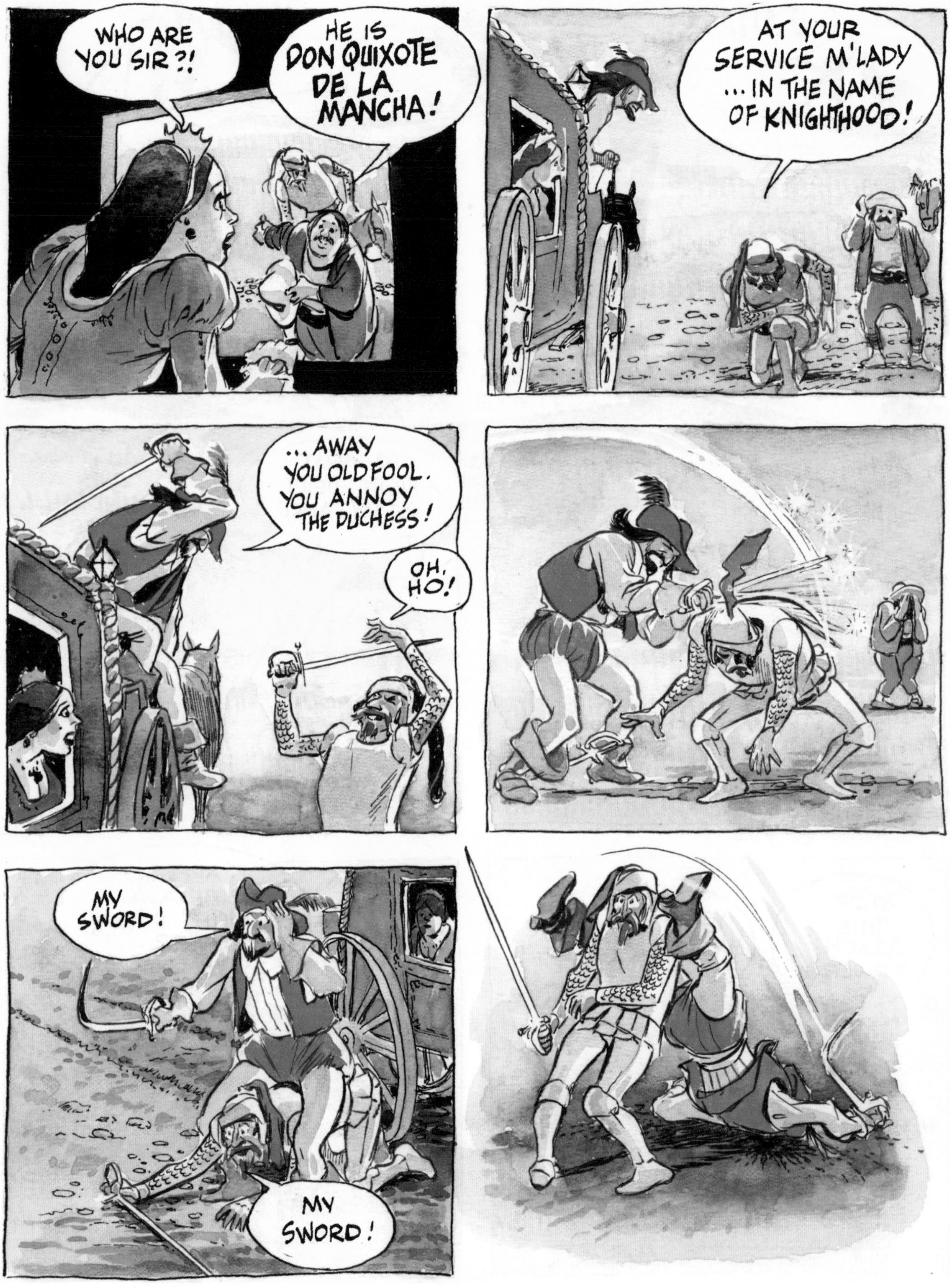
WHO ARE YOU SIR?!
HE IS DON QUIXOTE DE LA MANCHA!
AT YOUR SERVICE M'LADY ...IN THE NAME OF KNIGHTHOOD!
...AWAY YOU OLD FOOL. YOU ANNOY THE DUCHESS!
OH, HO!
MY SWORD!
MY SWORD!

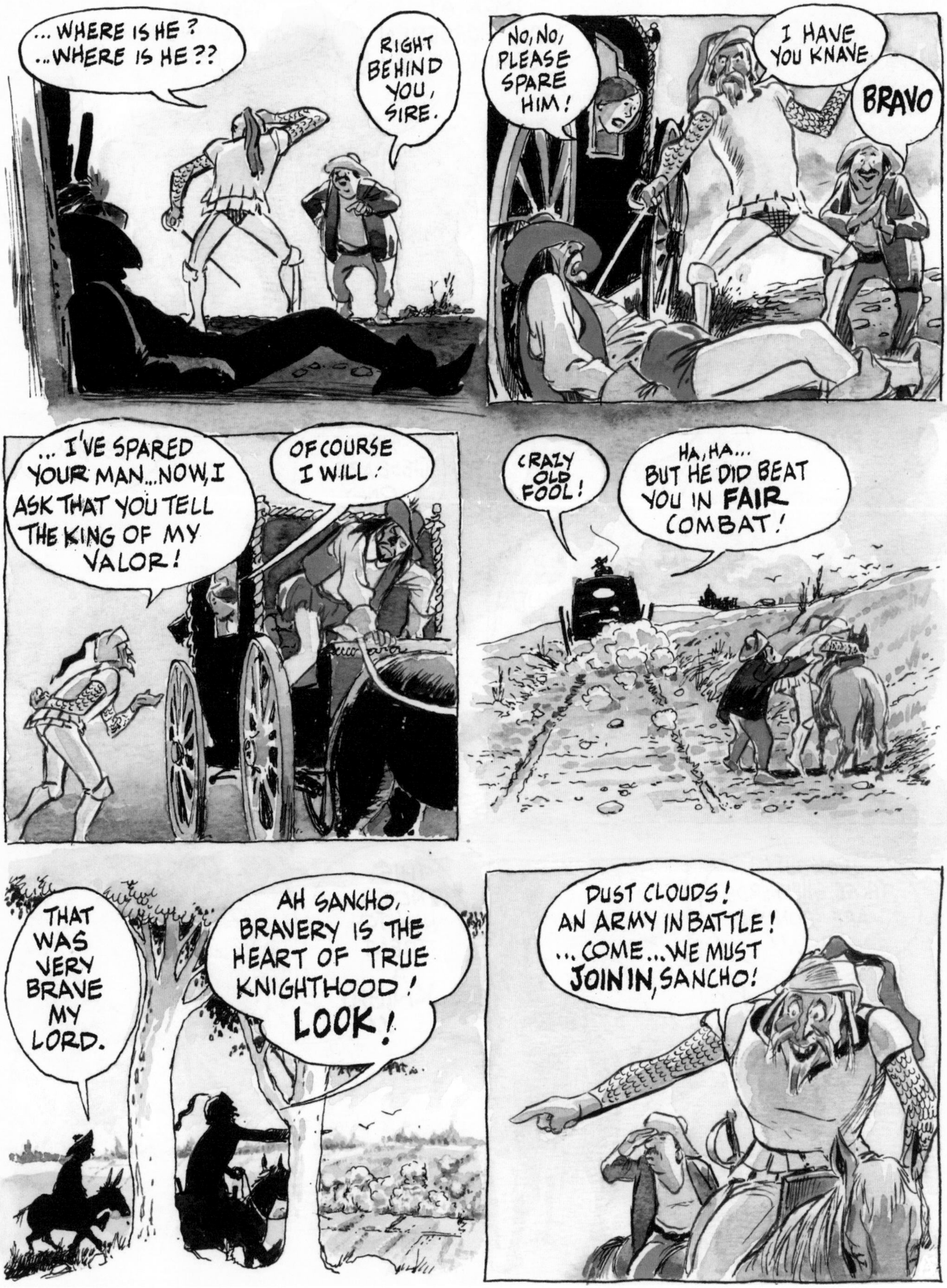
...WHERE IS HE? ...WHERE IS HE??
RIGHT BEHIND YOU, SIRE.
NO, NO, PLEASE SPARE HIM!
I HAVE YOU KNAVE
BRAVO
... I'VE SPARED YOUR MAN...NOW, I ASK THAT YOU TELL THE KING OF MY VALOR!
OF COURSE I WILL!
CRAZY OLD FOOL!
HA, HA... BUT HE DID BEAT YOU IN FAIR COMBAT!
THAT WAS VERY BRAVE MY LORD.
AH SANCHO, BRAVERY IS THE HEART OF TRUE KNIGHTHOOD! LOOK!
DUST CLOUDS! AN ARMY IN BATTLE! ...COME...WE MUST JOIN IN, SANCHO!

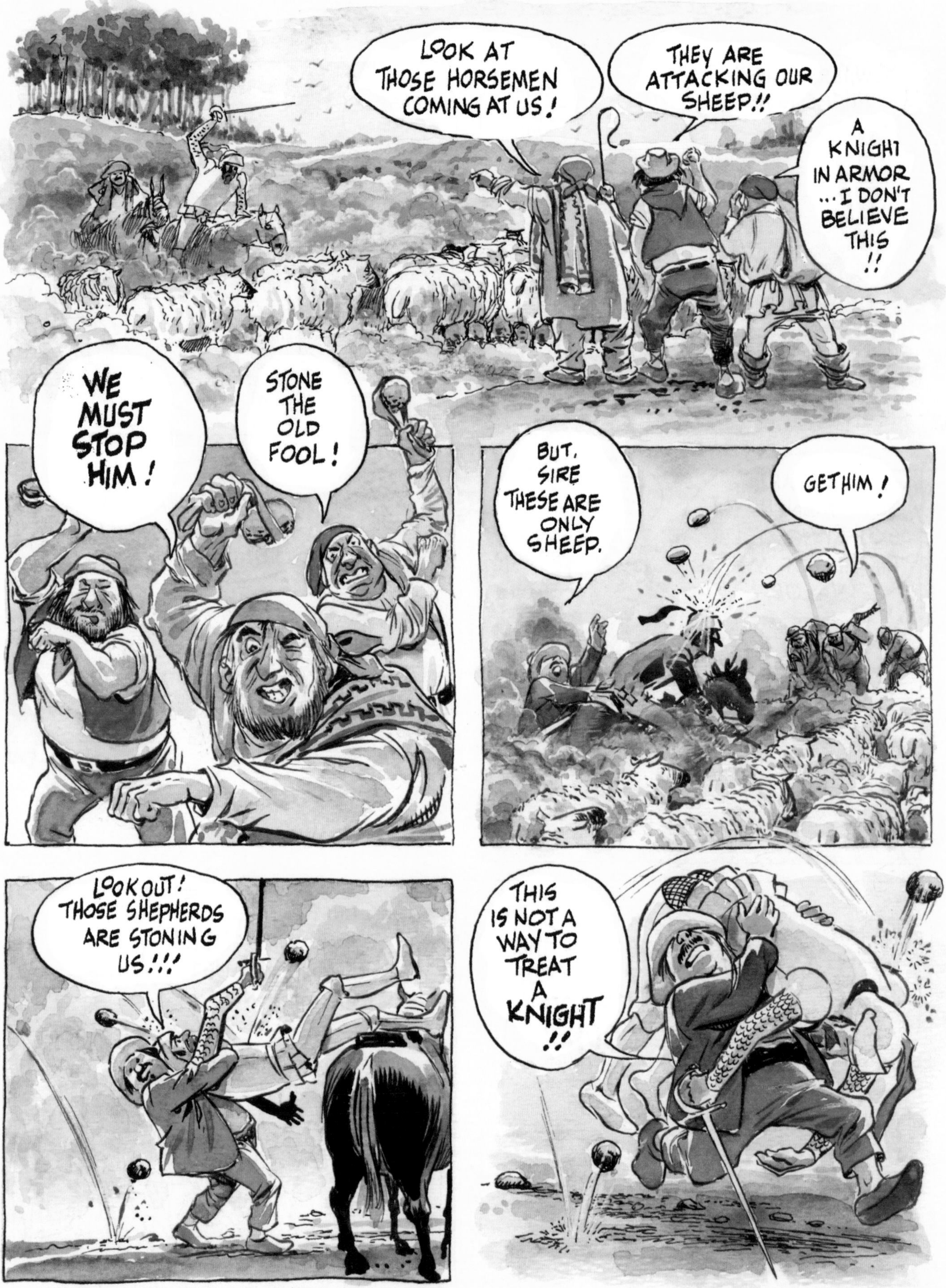
LOOK AT THOSE HORSEMEN COMING AT US!
THEY ARE ATTACKING OUR SHEEP!!
A KNIGHT IN ARMOR ... I DON'T BELIEVE THIS!!
WE MUST STOP HIM!
STONE THE OLD FOOL!
BUT, SIRE THESE ARE ONLY SHEEP.
GET HIM!
LOOK OUT! THOSE SHEPHERDS ARE STONING US!!!
THIS IS NOT A WAY TO TREAT A KNIGHT!!

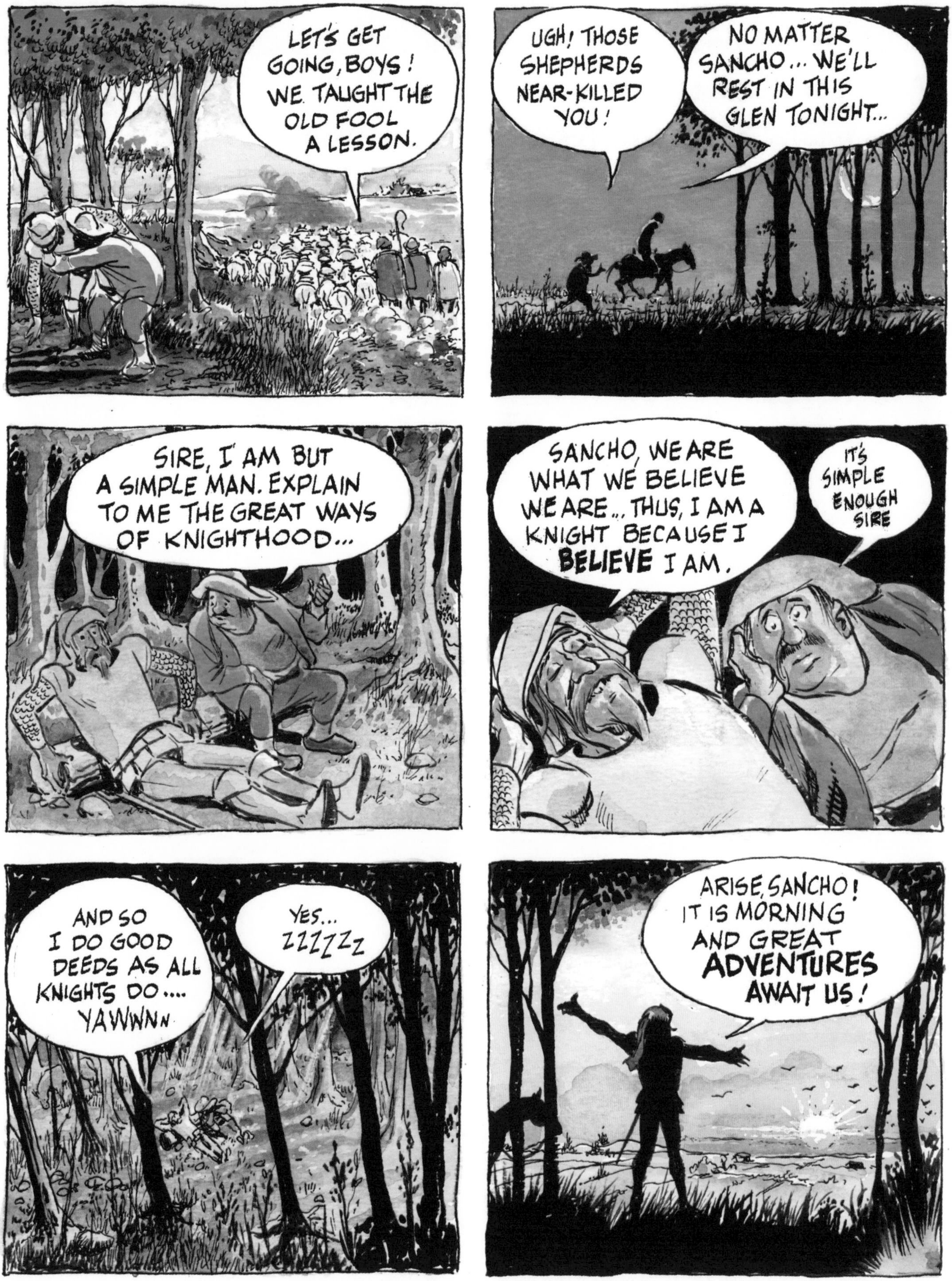
LET'S GET GOING, BOYS! WE TAUGHT THE OLD FOOL A LESSON.
UGH! THOSE SHEPHERDS NEAR-KILLED YOU!
NO MATTER SANCHO... WE'LL REST IN THIS GLEN TONIGHT...
SIRE, I AM BUT A SIMPLE MAN. EXPLAIN TO ME THE GREAT WAYS OF KNIGHTHOOD...
SANCHO, WE ARE WHAT WE BELIEVE WE ARE... THUS, I AM A KNIGHT BECAUSE I **BELIEVE** I AM.
IT'S SIMPLE ENOUGH SIRE
AND SO I DO GOOD DEEDS AS ALL KNIGHTS DO.... YAWWNN
YES... ZZZZZz
ARISE, SANCHO! IT IS MORNING AND GREAT **ADVENTURES** AWAIT US!

Sonnet 18

William Shakespeare

ART / ADAPTATION BY **Robert Berry** WITH **Josh Levitas**

ONE OF SHAKESPEARE'S MOST FAMOUS sonnets—"Shall I compare thee to a summer's day?"—gets an unexpected twist from Robert Berry, the artist behind *Ulysses "Seen,"* the ambitious online project to graphically adapt every bit of James Joyce's masterpiece. This ode to a beloved is always cast as a romantic poem, so much so that we see it that way without realizing it, but Robert shows us another meaning, a different type of love. Josh Levitas handles the coloring, bringing in beautiful, sunshiney yellows that magnify the emotional warmth (and tie in nicely with the mention of the Sun in lines 5–6).

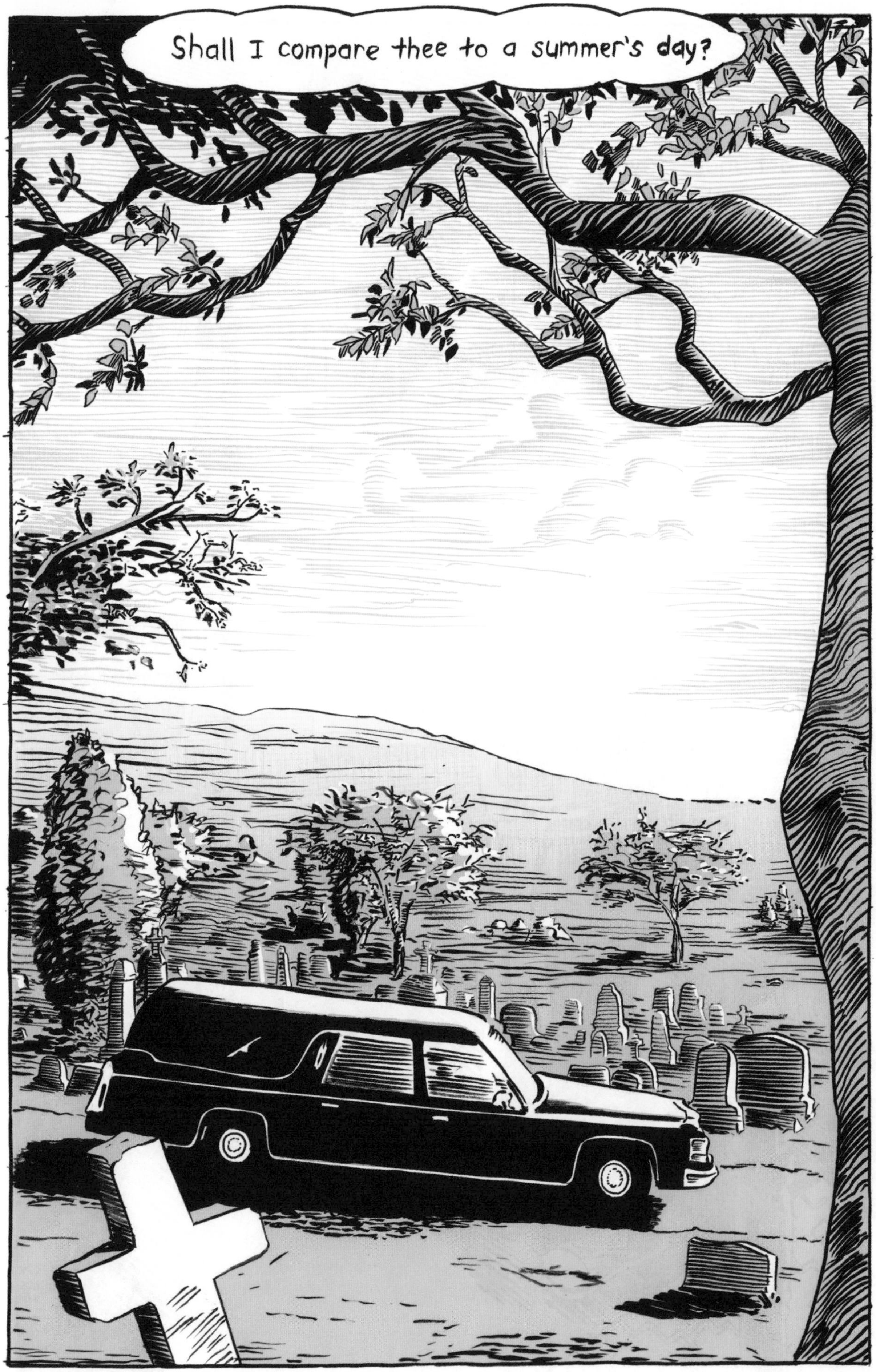
Shall I compare thee to a summer's day?

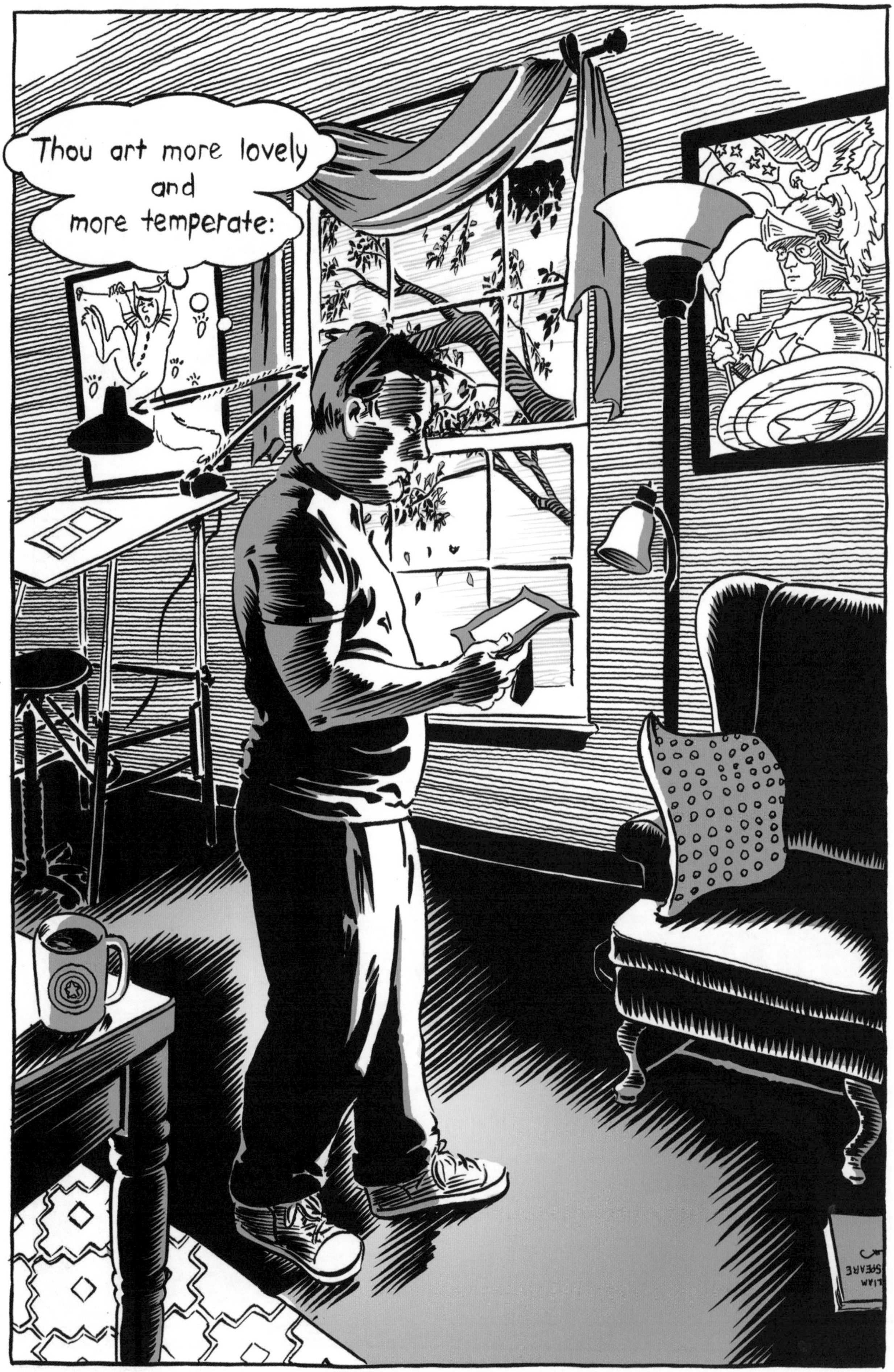
Thou art more lovely and more temperate:

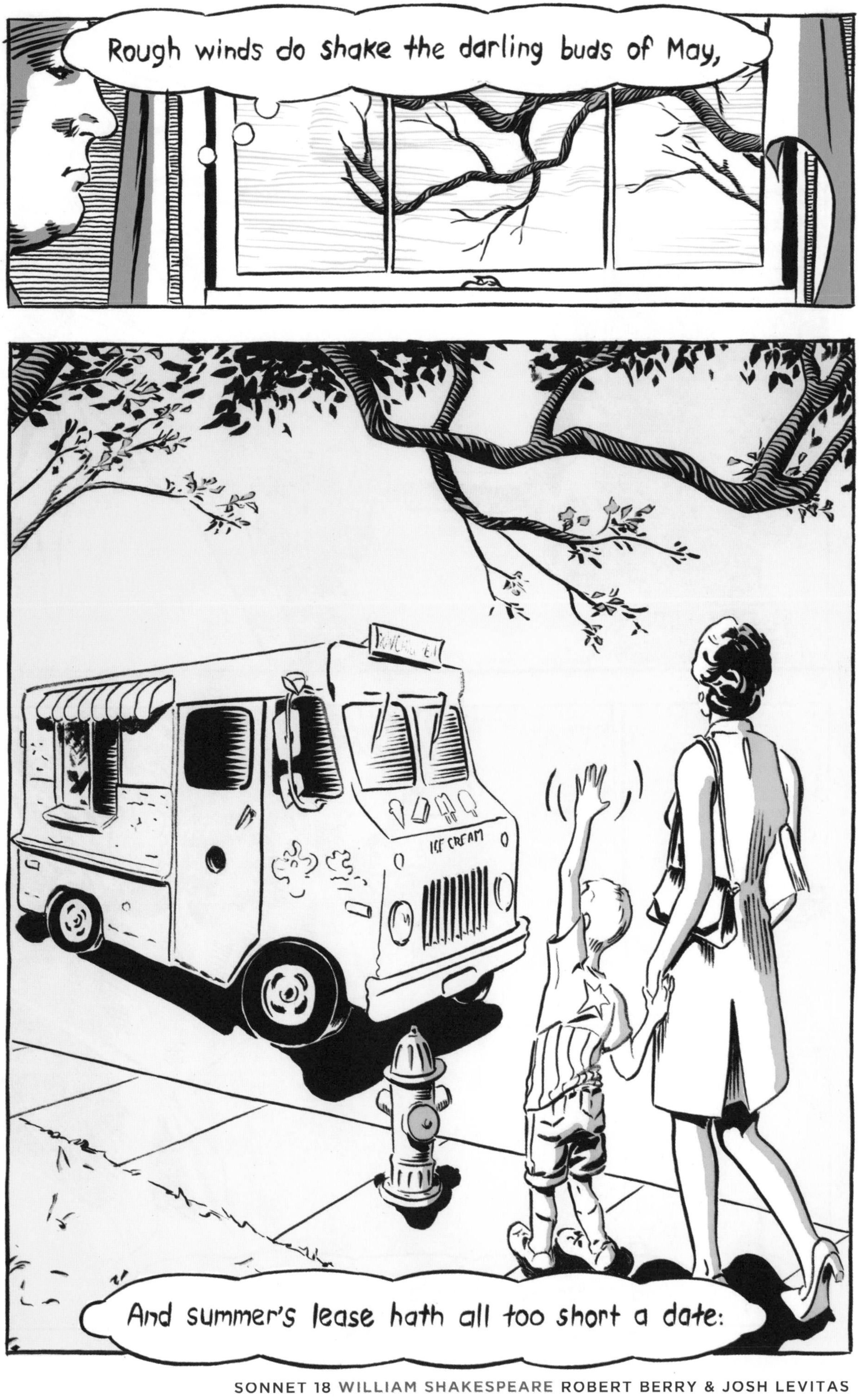
Rough winds do shake the darling buds of May,
ICE CREAM
And summer's lease hath all too short a date:

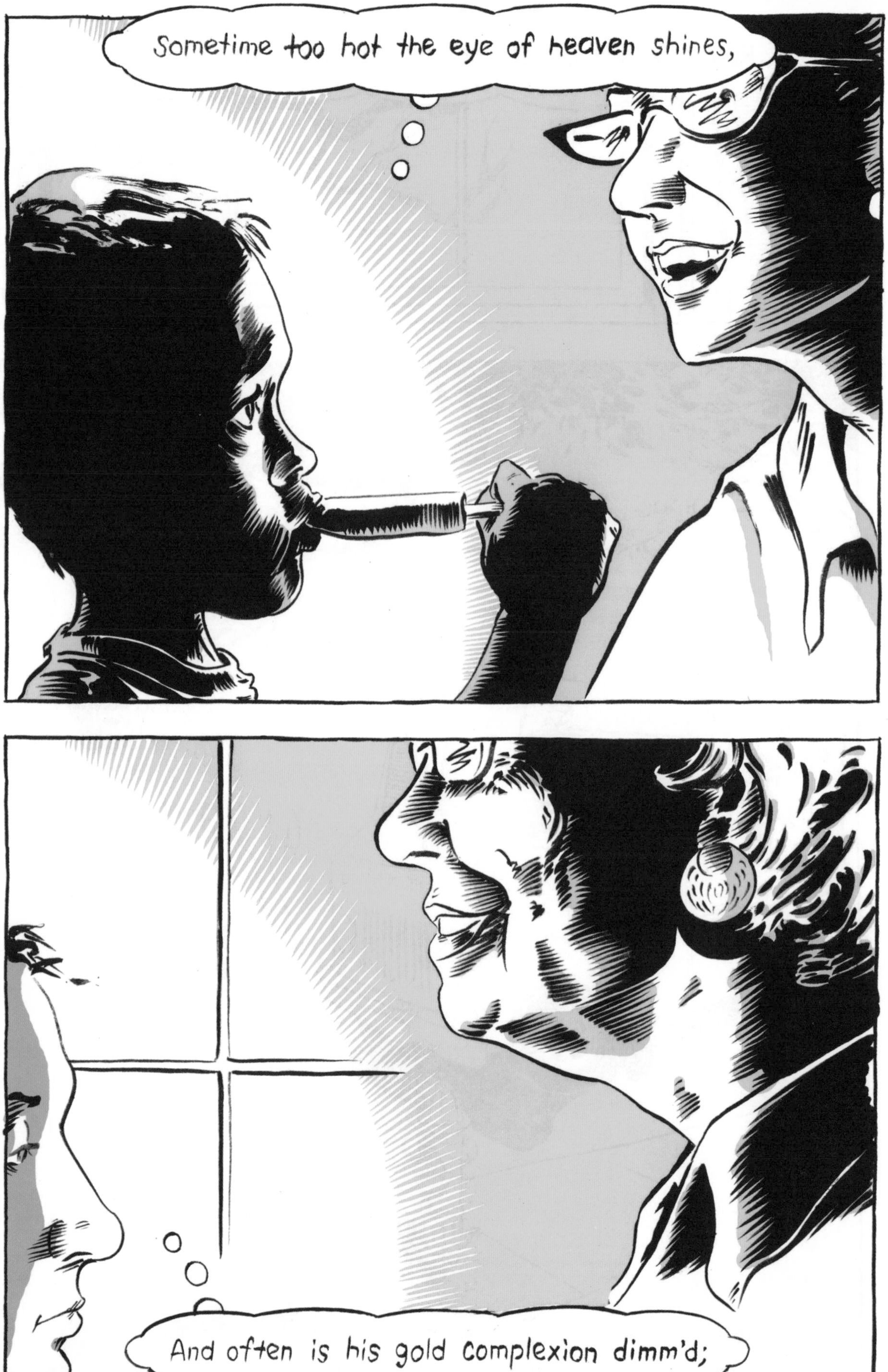
Sometime too hot the eye of heaven shines,
And often is his gold complexion dimm'd;

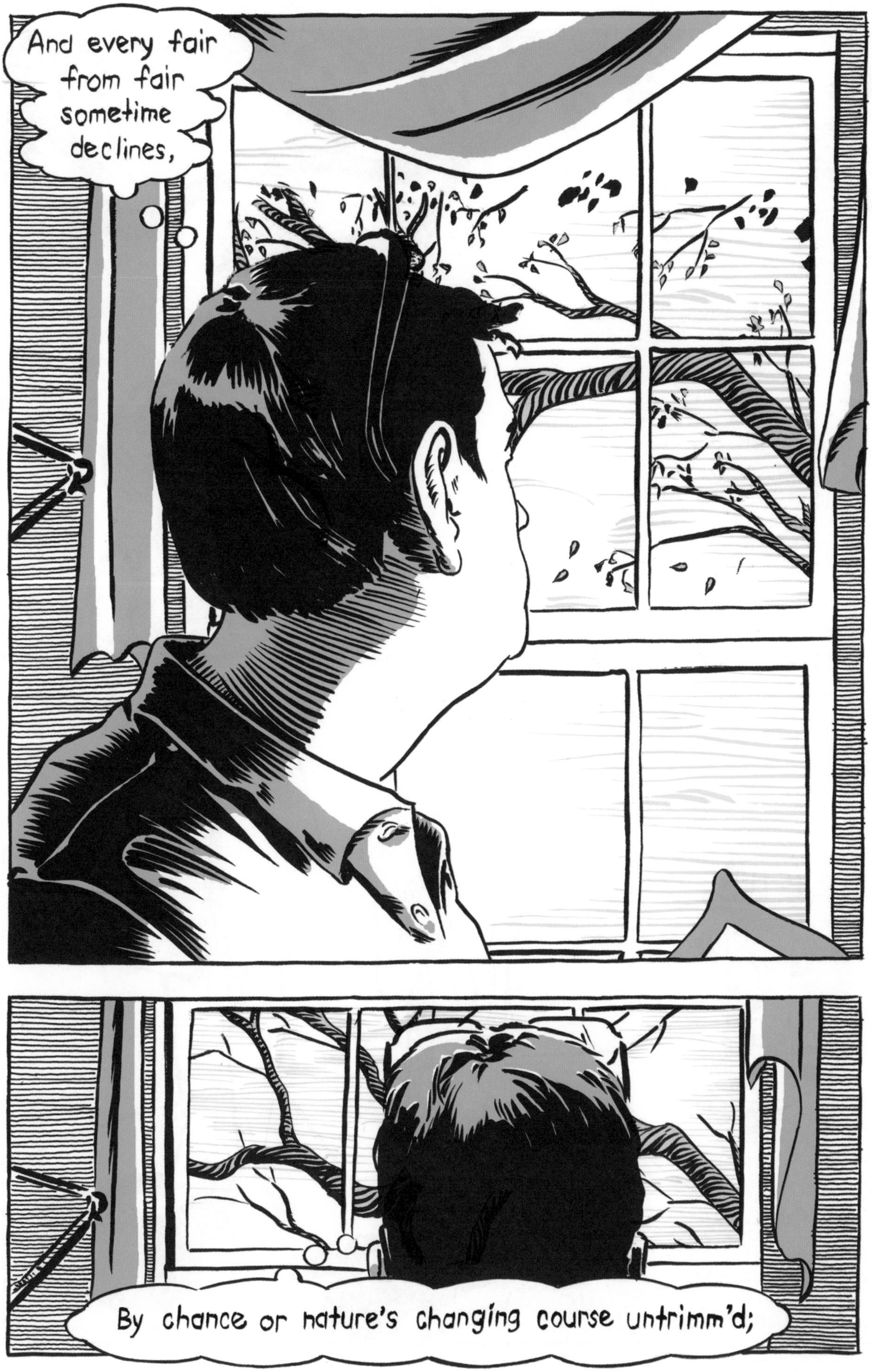
And every fair from fair sometime declines,
By chance or nature's changing course untrimm'd;

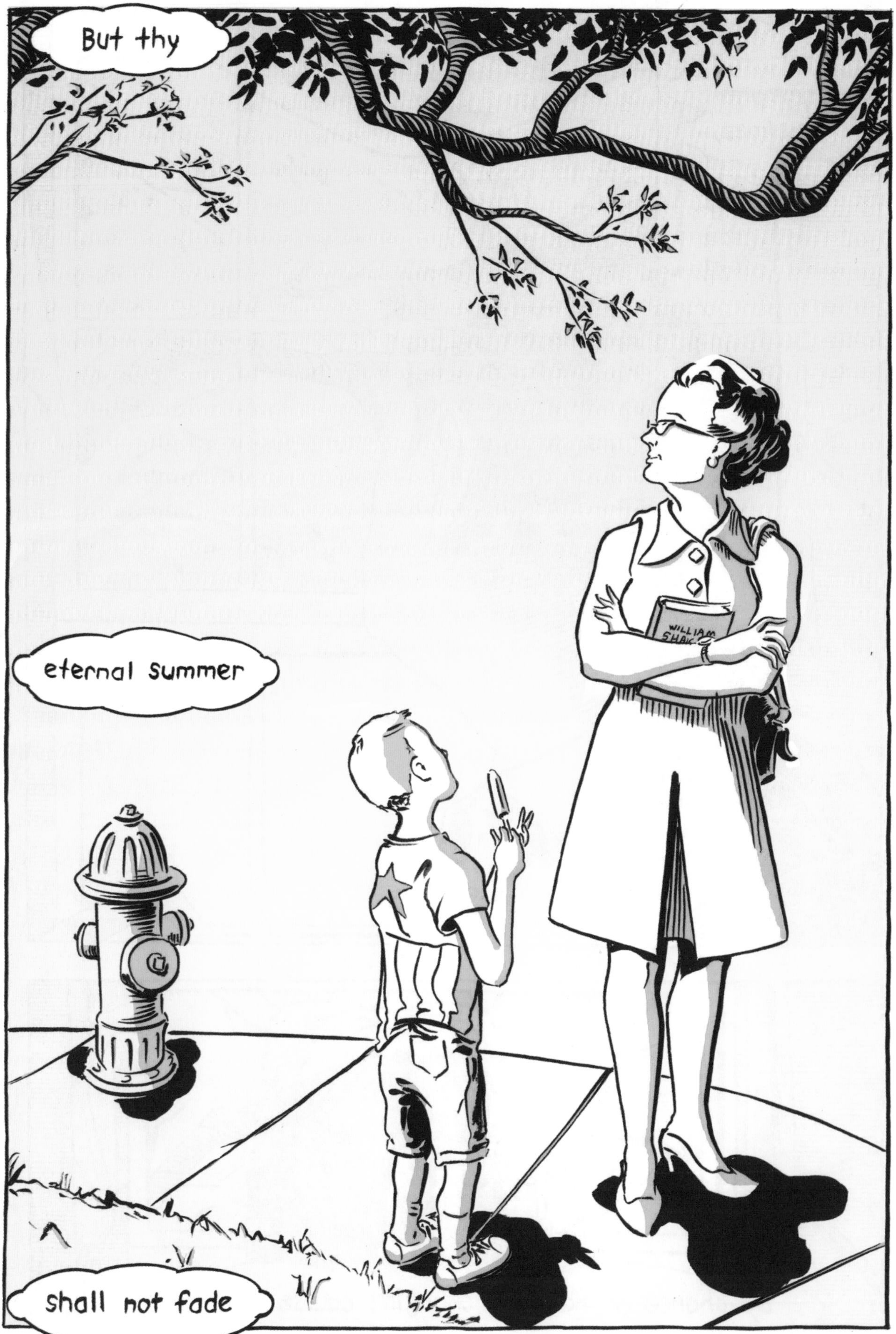
But thy
eternal summer
shall not fade
WILLIAM SHAK

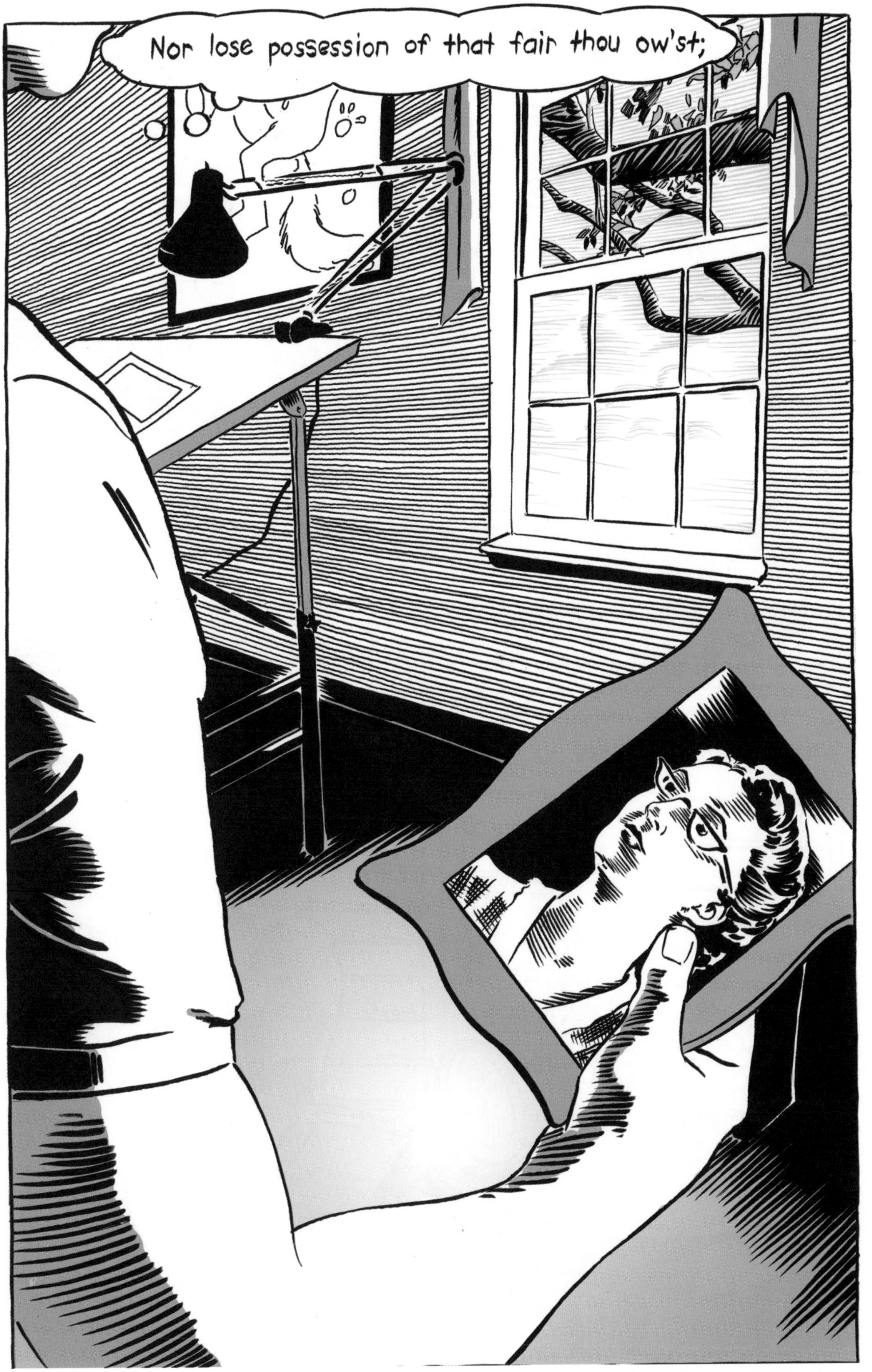
Nor lose possession of that fair thou ow'st;

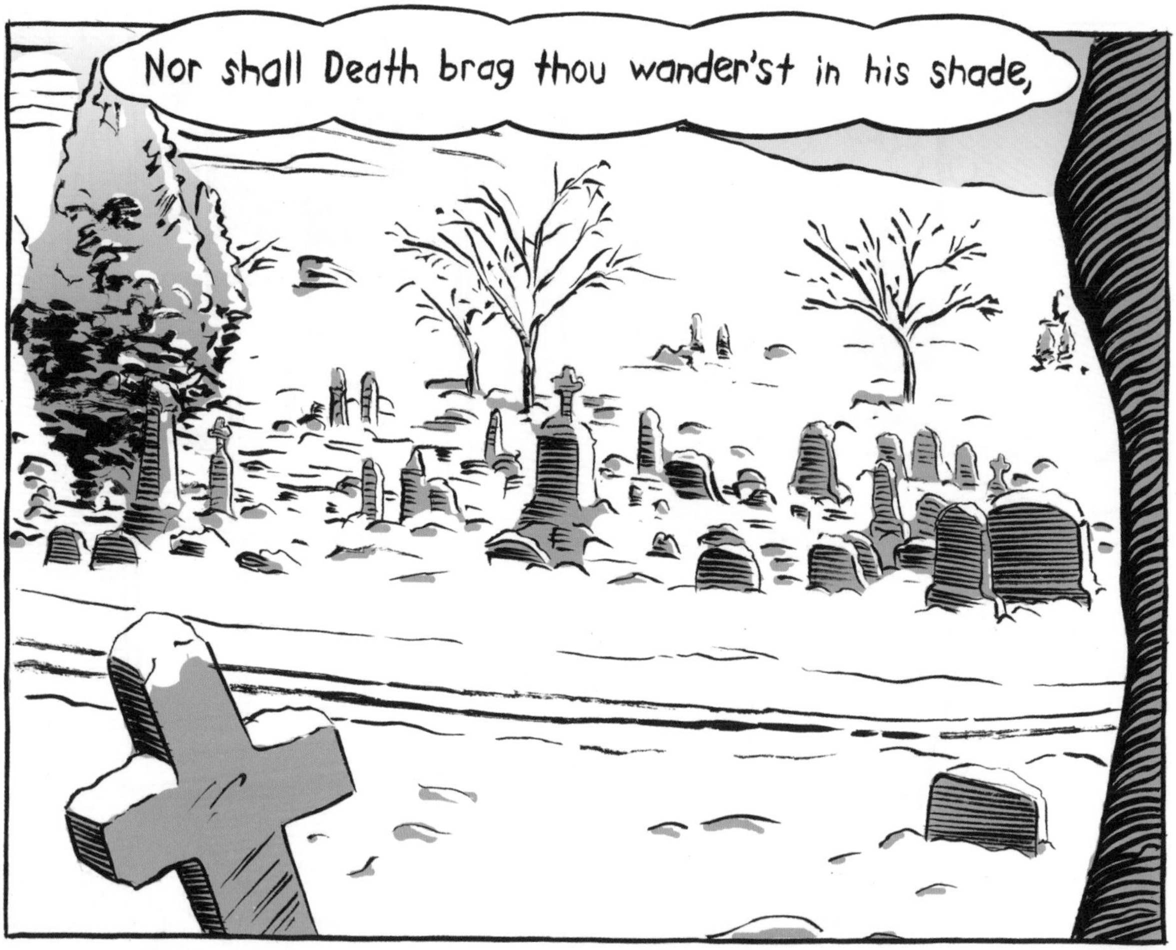
Nor shall Death brag thou wander'st in his shade,

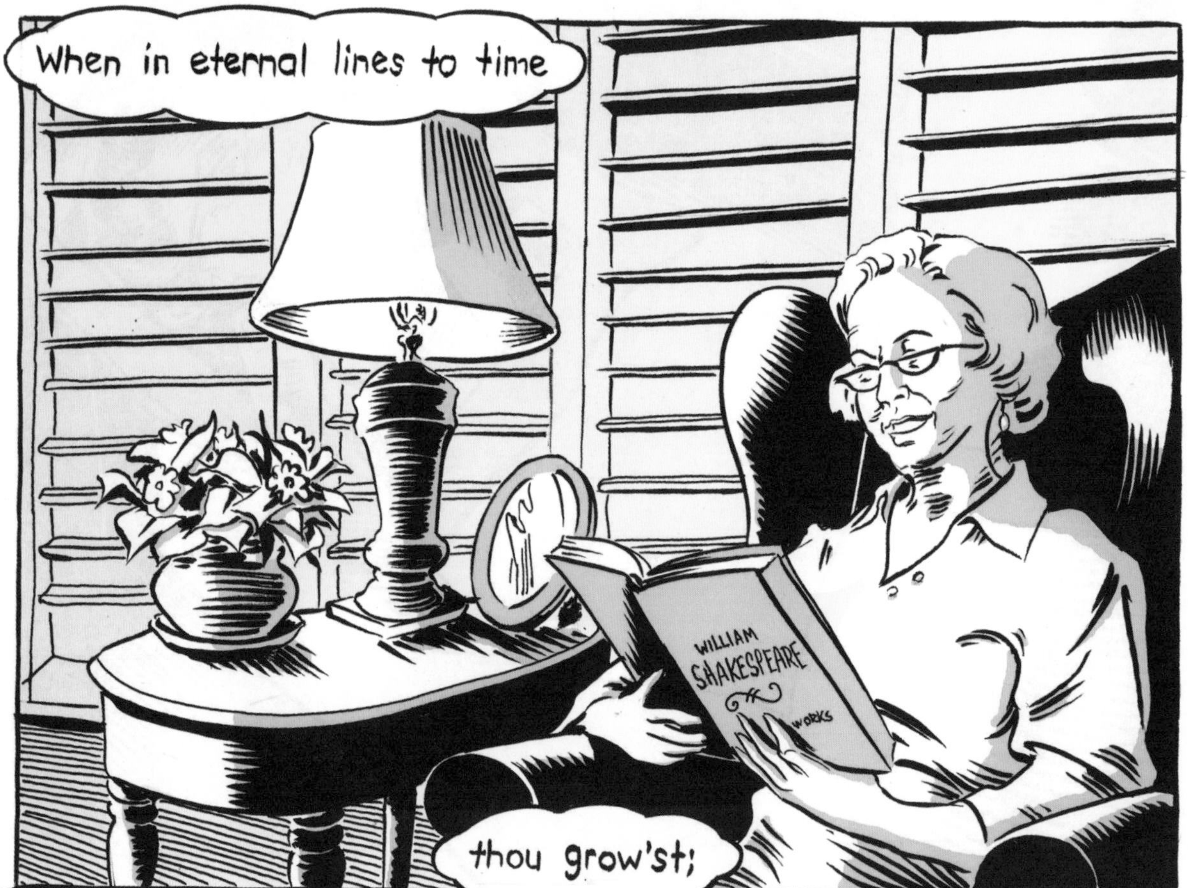
When in eternal lines to time
WILLIAM SHAKESPEARE
WORKS
thou grow'st;

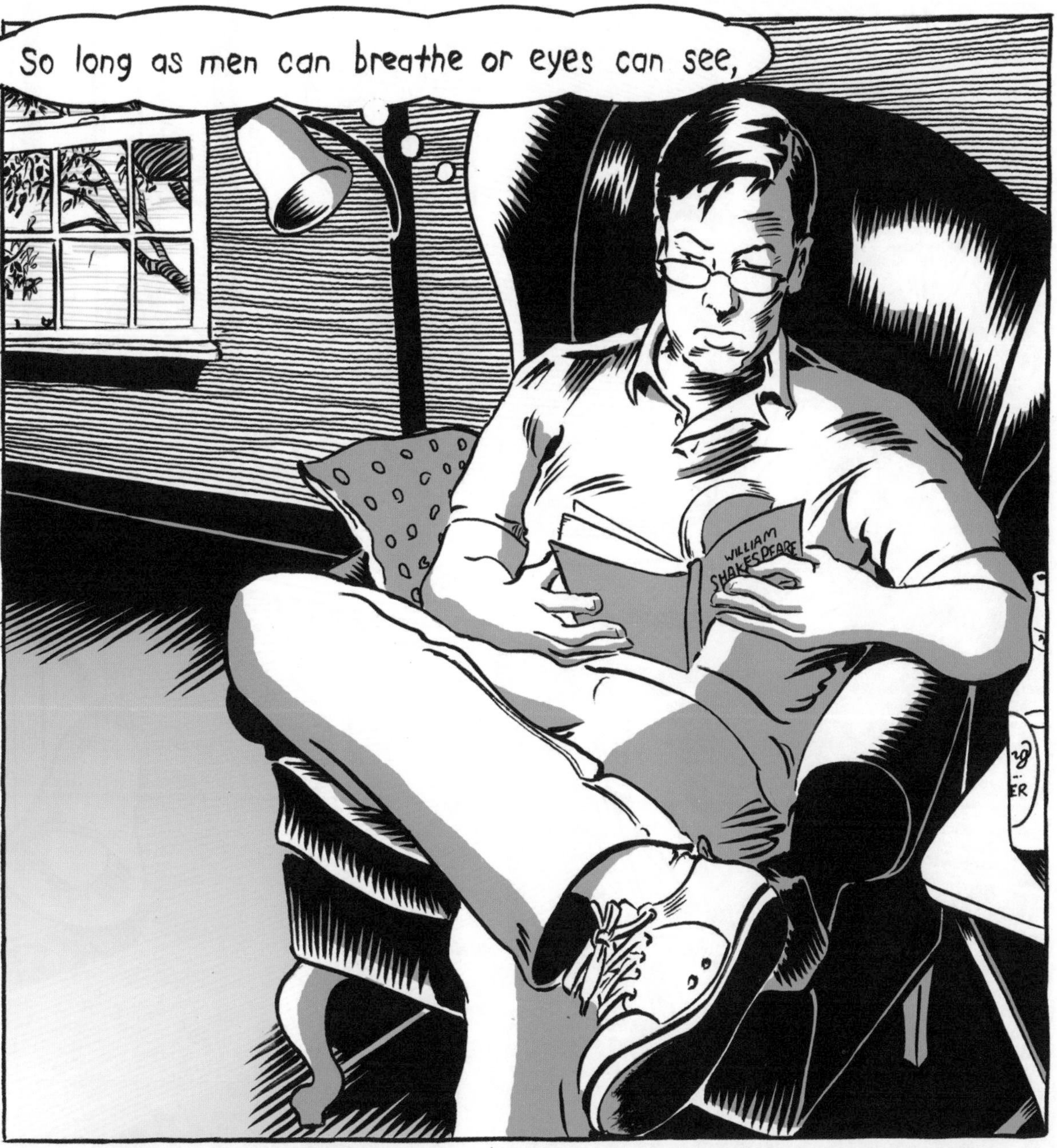
So long as men can breathe or eyes can see,
WILLIAM SHAKESPEARE

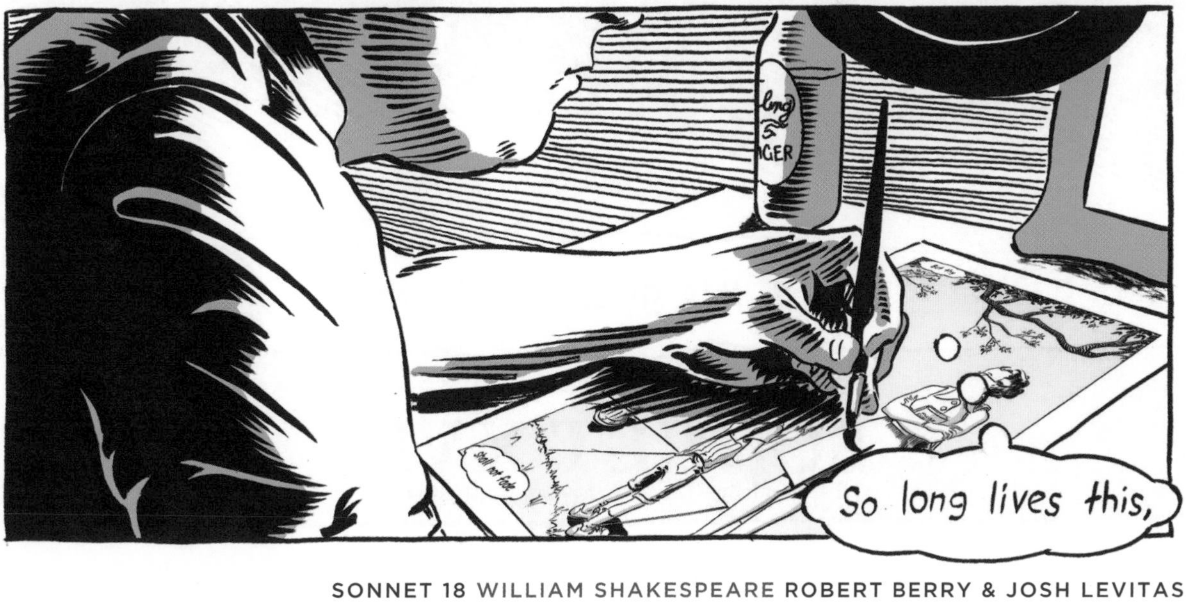
Shall not fade
So long lives this,

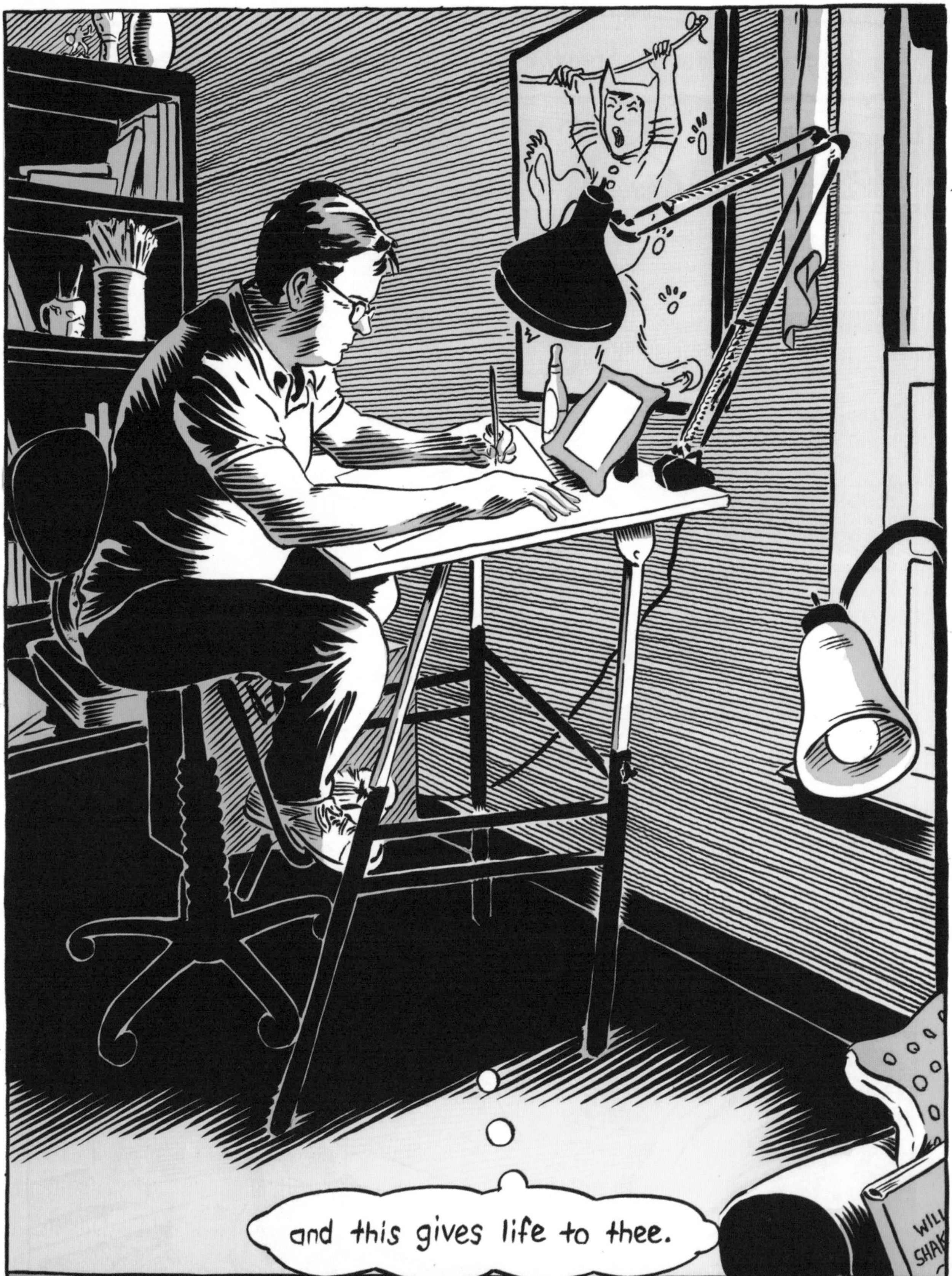
and this gives life to thee.
WILLIAM SHAKESPEARE'S
SONNET XVIII
ADAPTED BY ROBERT BERRY WITH JOSH LEVITAS

Sonnet 20

William Shakespeare

ART / ADAPTATION BY **Aidan Koch**

SHAKESPEARE'S TWENTIETH SONNET MAY HAVE invoked more debate than any other. Like many of his sonnets, its tone is affectionate and romantically admiring while being directed at a man, fueling endless speculation about Shakespeare's sexual preferences. Surprisingly for a poem published in 1609 (and probably written in the early 1590s), the sonnet plays with notions of gender. It gushes that the man in question was created as beautiful as any woman, referring to him as "the Master-Mistress of my passion." In fact, the lines go on, he easily could have been a woman except that nature got carried away and as the final touch gave him a penis, "adding one thing to my purpose nothing." This gives Shakespeare the opportunity to bring in one of his beloved sexual puns, saying that nature "prick'd thee out for women's pleasure." Closing with an ambiguous note, the poem's narrator says that while women can get enjoyable use from the man in question, the narrator will still have the man's "love." Make of that what you will. Aidan Koch brings her checkerboard layout filled with hand-lettering and drawings to the sonnet, combining masculine and feminine imagery.

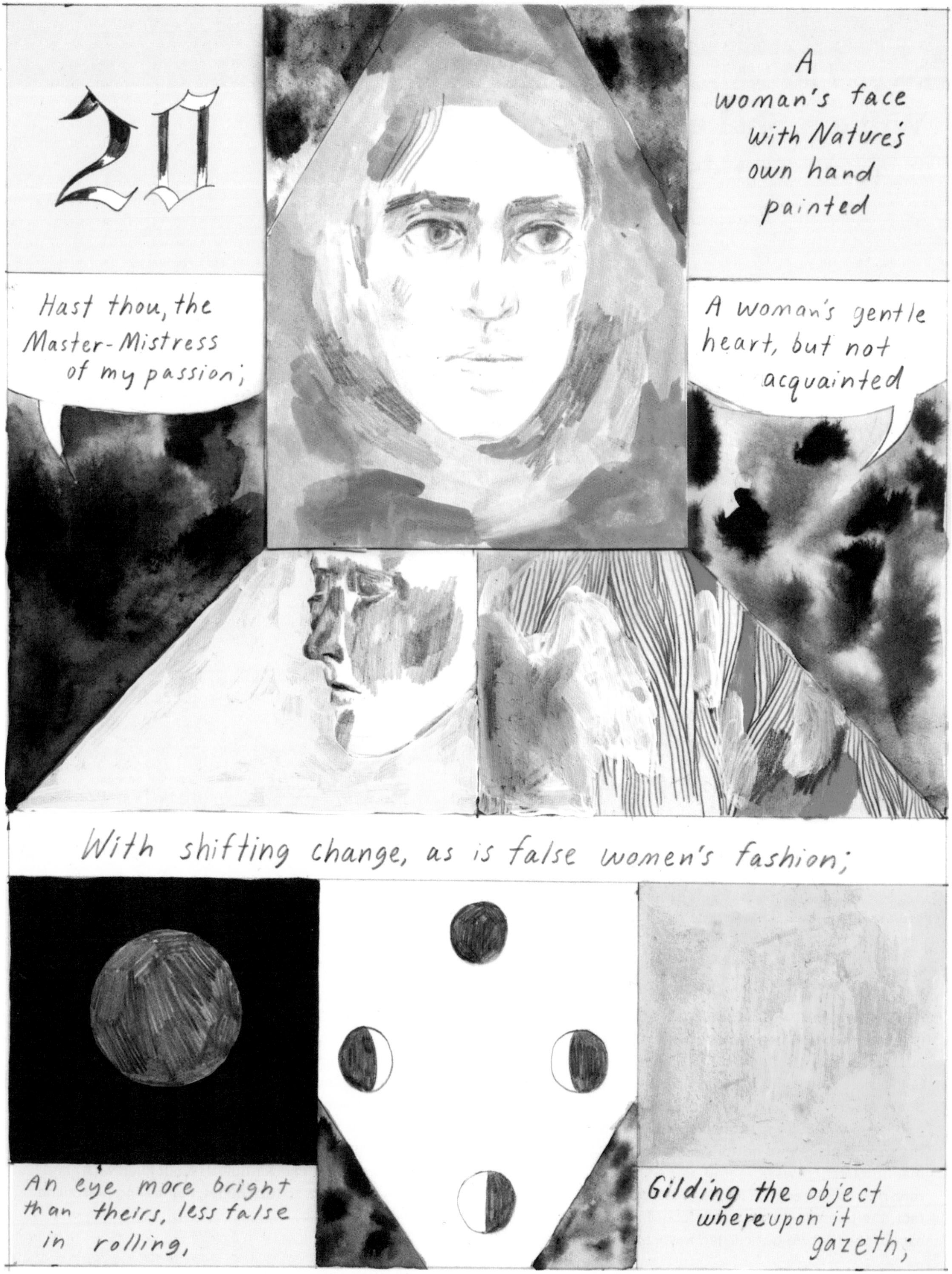
20
A woman's face with Nature's own hand painted
Hast thou, the Master-Mistress of my passion;
A woman's gentle heart, but not acquainted
With shifting change, as is false women's fashion;
An eye more bright than theirs, less false in rolling,
Gilding the object whereupon it gazeth;

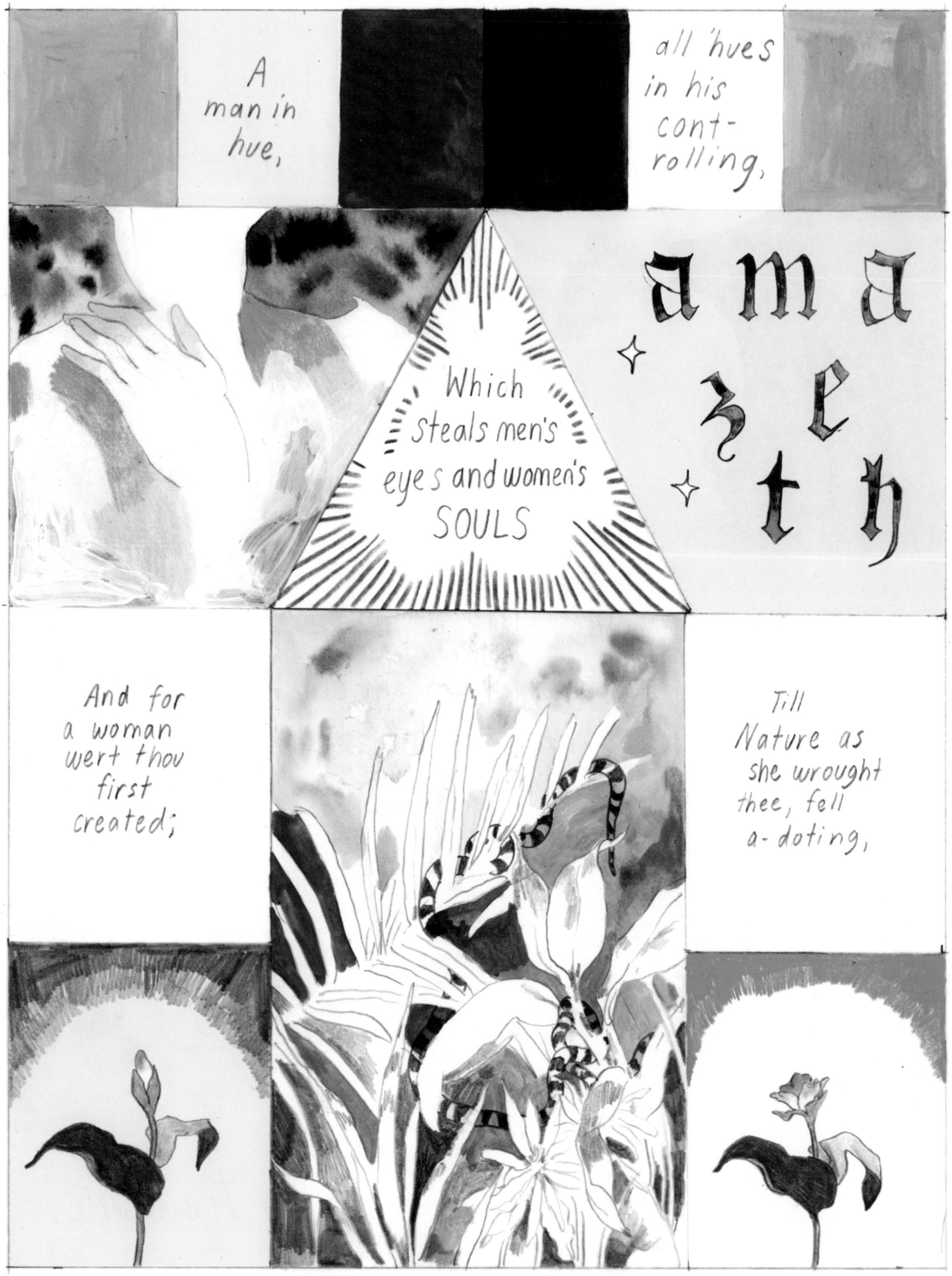
A man in hue,
all 'hues in his cont-rolling,
Which steals men's eyes and women's SOULS
amazeth
And for a woman wert thou first created;
Till Nature as she wrought thee, fell a-doting,

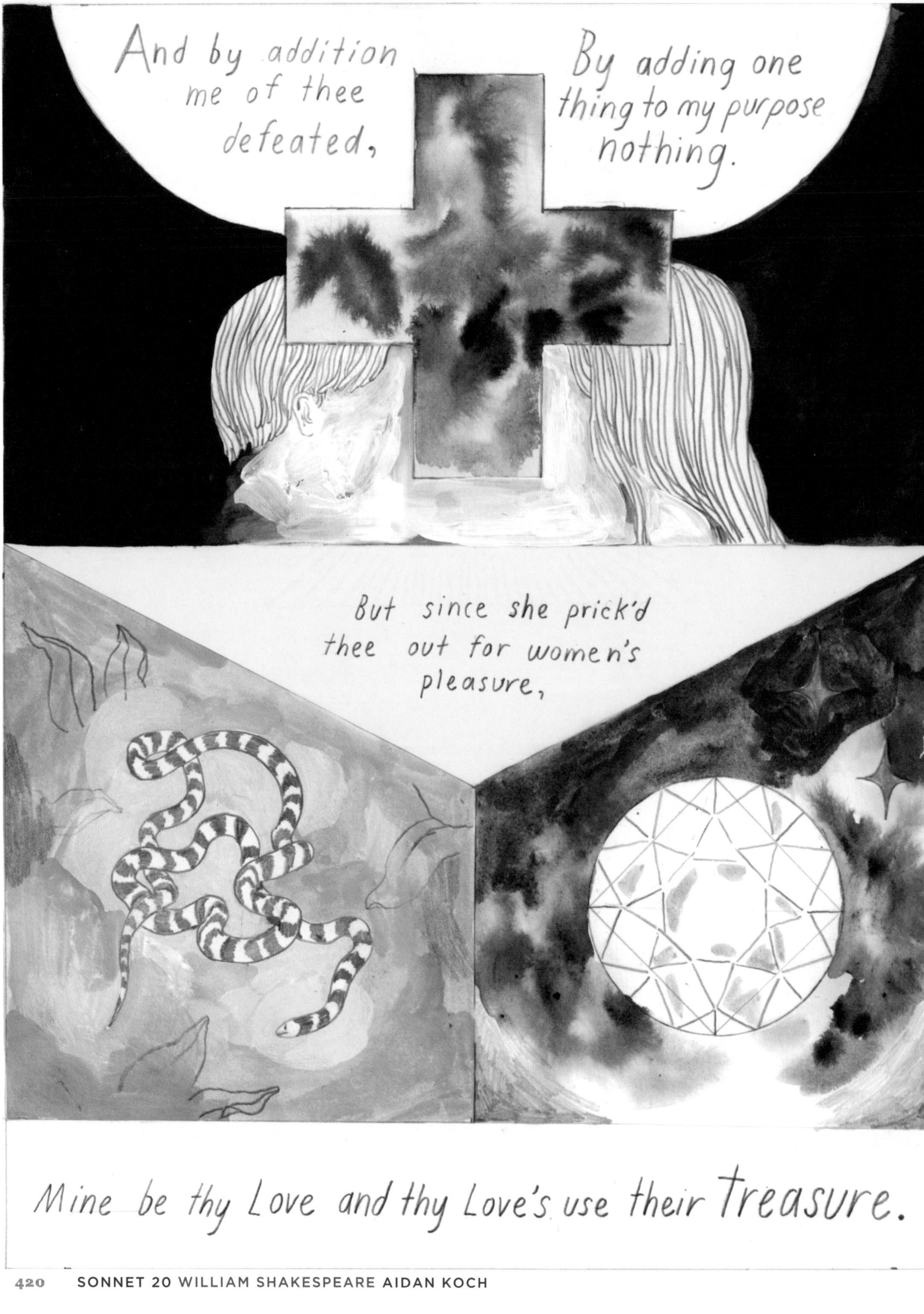
And by addition me of thee defeated,
By adding one thing to my purpose nothing.
But since she prick'd thee out for women's pleasure,
Mine be thy Love and thy Love's use their treasure.

"The Flea"

John Donne

ART / ADAPTATION BY **Noah Patrick Pfarr**

A LUSTY YET SPIRITUAL MAN, JOHN DONNE (1572–1631) was a dazzling poet, able to beautifully convey elaborate, clever metaphors (called conceits) in such a way that, though completely unexpected, they seem obvious in the end. His poetic output can be clearly divided into various types—the social and political satires, the early verses on romantic love and sex, and the later religious poems. (He was an Anglican priest for the last sixteen years of his life, churning out sermons containing well over one million words total.) Though densely written, his poetry remains continuously in print, and it has given the world the phrases "Death, be not proud," "No man is an island," and "For whom the bell tolls."

In one of his best-known poems, "The Flea," the narrator is trying to convince a woman to have sex with him. You may think you know every possible way to cajole someone into giving it up, but Donne has come up with the most outlandish one ever, and he did it 400 years ago. A flea has feasted on the narrator's blood and has now leaped to the woman in question, where it is sucking out her corpuscles. See, the narrator says, our blood has mingled—we have been united—inside this flea. We've thus been physically joined, our fluids mixed, and we're as good as married, maybe even better than married. So we might as well have sex.

Apparently with tongue in cheek, he asks her not to kill the flea, which now contains both their life forces. She does anyway, and in the final stanza he mock-chastises her for it. The poem ends when he tells her that the minuscule amount of blood the flea took from her is the same immeasurably tiny amount of honor she'll lose by submitting to his wishes. We never do find out if his playfully far-fetched approach has the desired effect.

Now, I've been using the masculine pronoun "he" to refer to the narrator because everyone assumes that a man is wheedling this woman. (We know the intended object of the narrator's affections is female because of the reference to her maidenhead.) But Noah Patrick Pfarr picked up on the fact that nothing in the poem absolutely says that the narrator is a man. Donne probably didn't intend it this way, but based strictly on the poem itself, we can't rule out that this is a woman trying to convince another woman to take that plunge. And this unexpected twist on a poem about an unexpected twist on a flea is exactly what Noah gives us.

SOURCES

Edwards, David L. *John Donne: Man of Flesh and Spirit.* London and New York: Continuum, 2001.

Paglia, Camille. *Break Burn Blow: Camille Paglia Reads Forty-Three of the World's Best Poems.* Vintage Books, 2005.

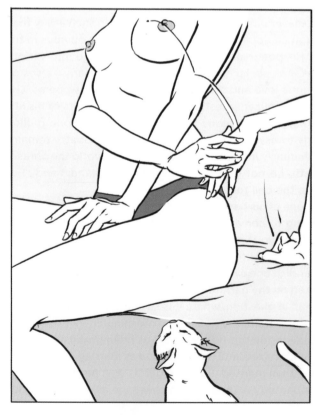

"THE FLEA" JOHN DONNE NOAH PATRICK PFARR

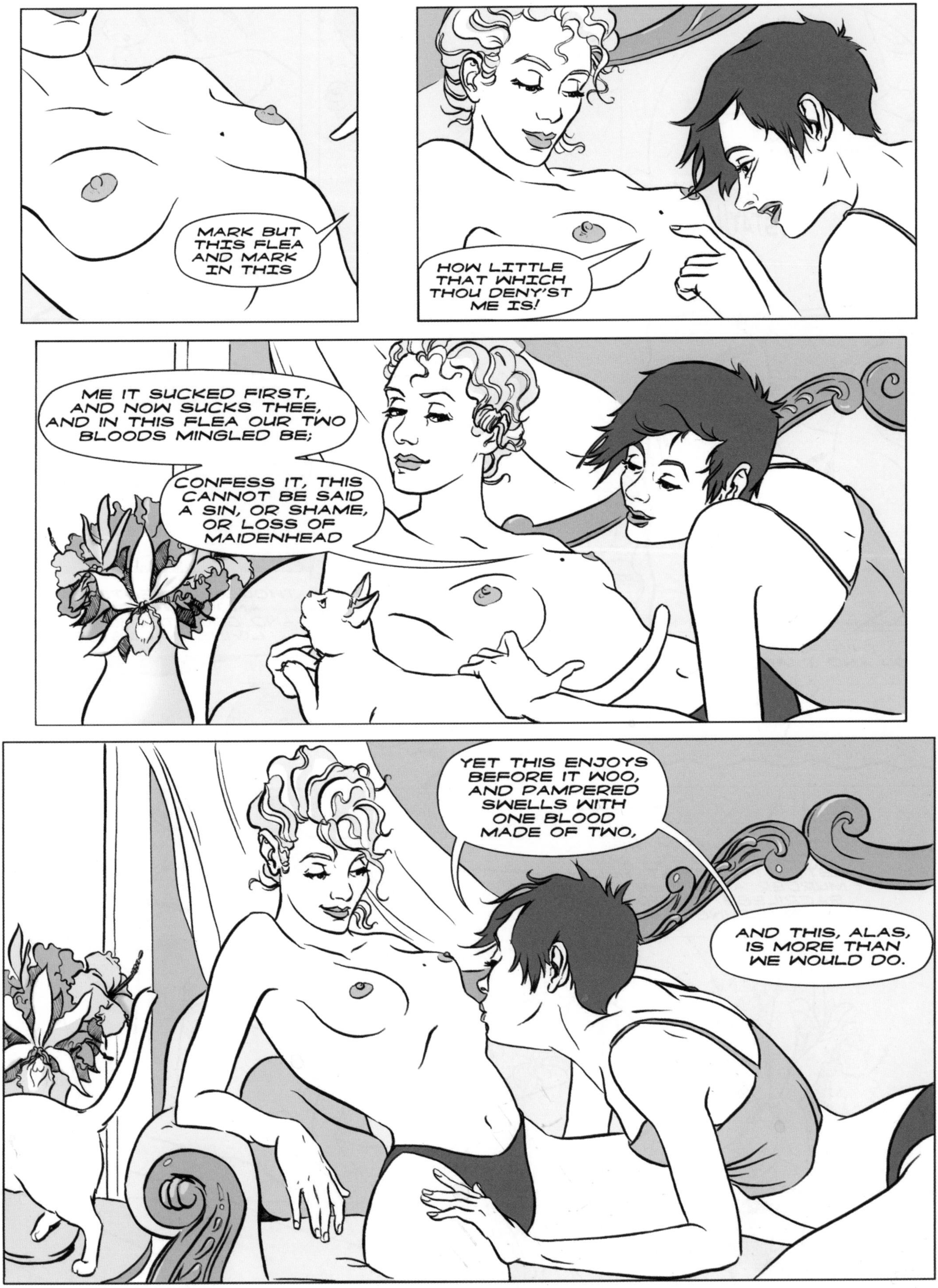
MARK BUT THIS FLEA AND MARK IN THIS
HOW LITTLE THAT WHICH THOU DENY'ST ME IS!
ME IT SUCKED FIRST, AND NOW SUCKS THEE, AND IN THIS FLEA OUR TWO BLOODS MINGLED BE;
CONFESS IT, THIS CANNOT BE SAID A SIN, OR SHAME, OR LOSS OF MAIDENHEAD
YET THIS ENJOYS BEFORE IT WOO, AND PAMPERED SWELLS WITH ONE BLOOD MADE OF TWO,
AND THIS, ALAS, IS MORE THAN WE WOULD DO.

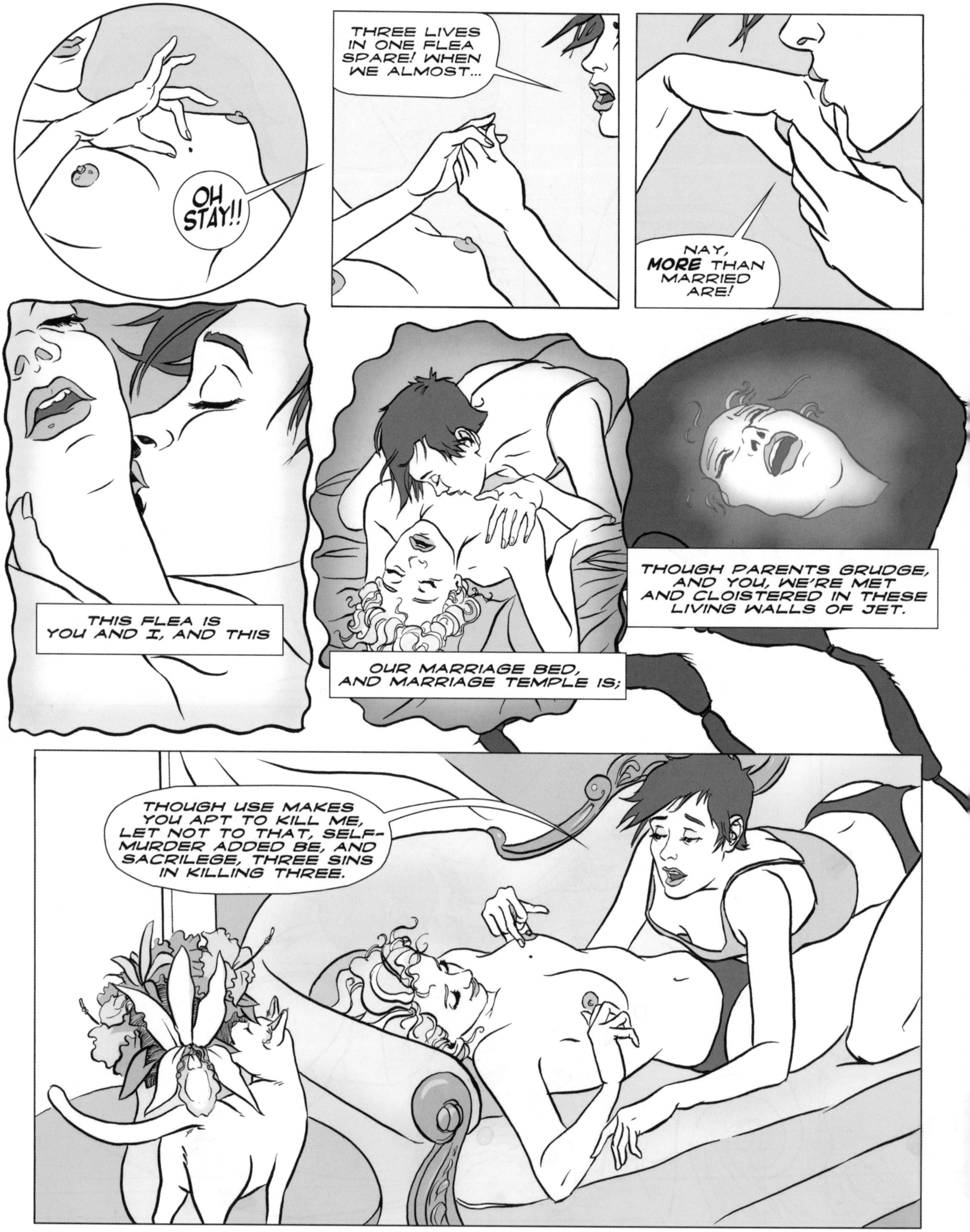
OH STAY!!
THREE LIVES IN ONE FLEA SPARE! WHEN WE ALMOST...
NAY, MORE THAN MARRIED ARE!
THIS FLEA IS YOU AND I, AND THIS
OUR MARRIAGE BED, AND MARRIAGE TEMPLE IS;
THOUGH PARENTS GRUDGE, AND YOU, WE'RE MET AND CLOISTERED IN THESE LIVING WALLS OF JET.
THOUGH USE MAKES YOU APT TO KILL ME, LET NOT TO THAT, SELF-MURDER ADDED BE, AND SACRILEGE, THREE SINS IN KILLING THREE.

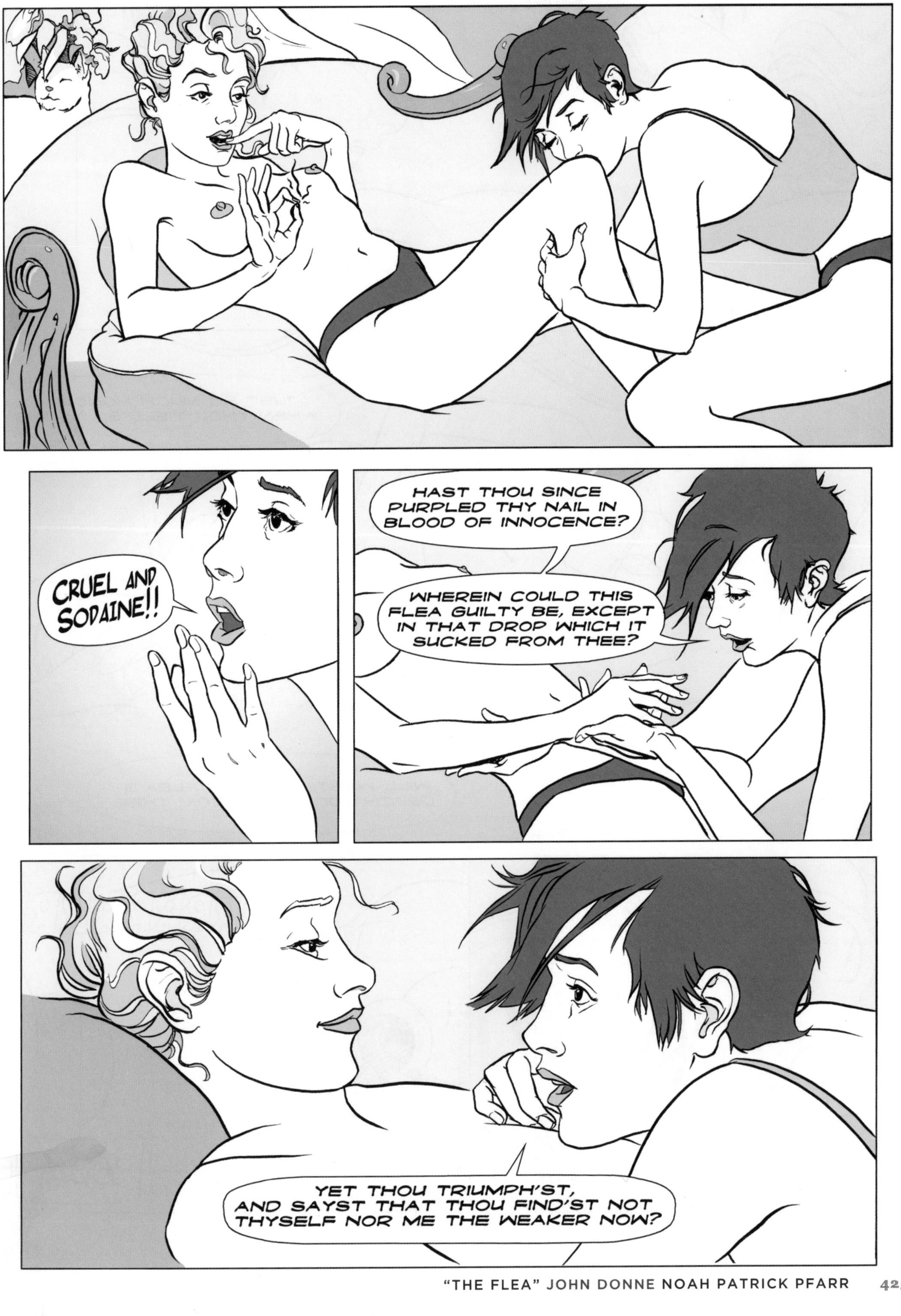
CRUEL AND SODAINE!!
HAST THOU SINCE PURPLED THY NAIL IN BLOOD OF INNOCENCE?
WHEREIN COULD THIS FLEA GUILTY BE, EXCEPT IN THAT DROP WHICH IT SUCKED FROM THEE?
YET THOU TRIUMPH'ST, AND SAYST THAT THOU FIND'ST NOT THYSELF NOR ME THE WEAKER NOW?

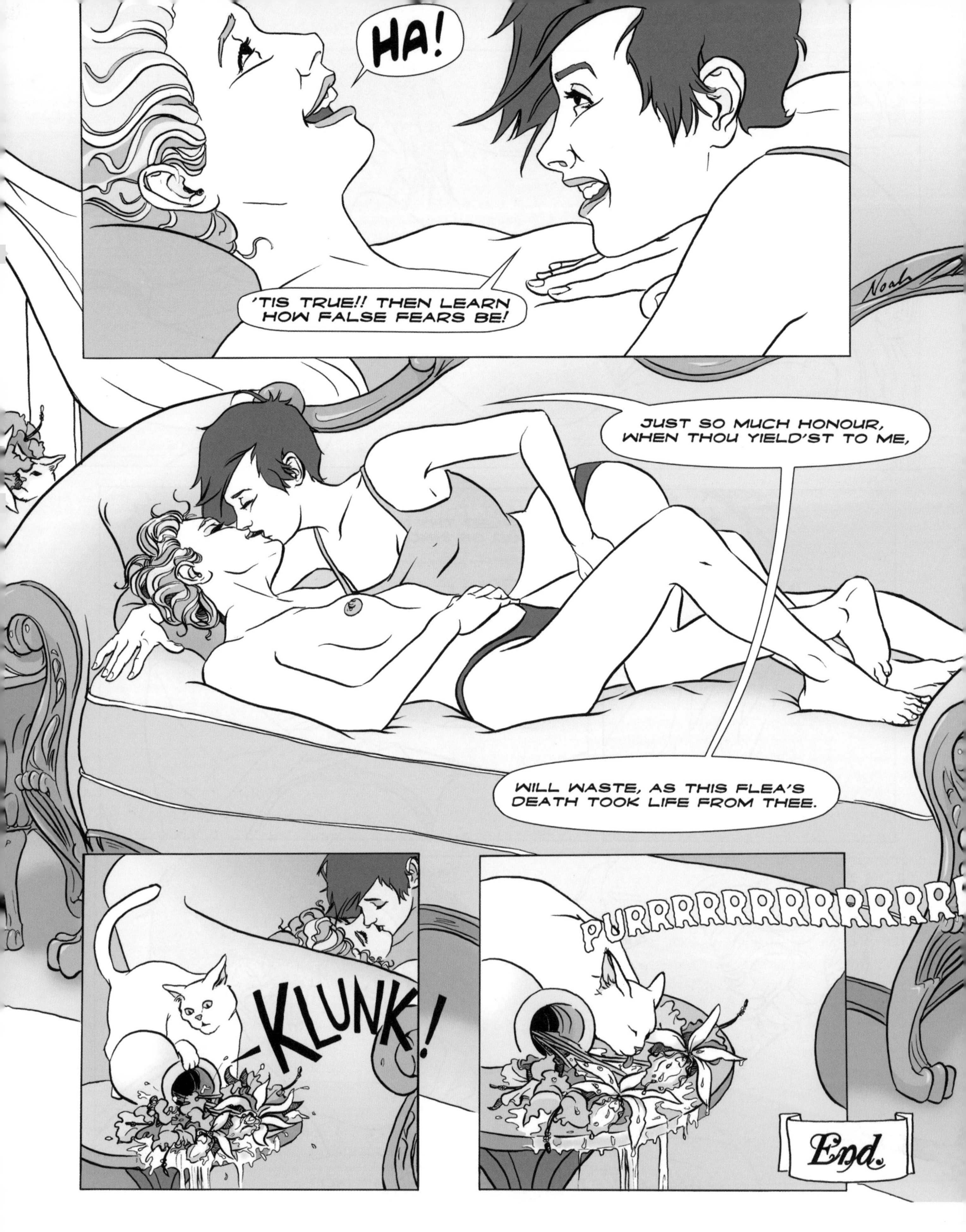
HA!
'TIS TRUE!! THEN LEARN HOW FALSE FEARS BE!
Noah
JUST SO MUCH HONOUR, WHEN THOU YIELD'ST TO ME,
WILL WASTE, AS THIS FLEA'S DEATH TOOK LIFE FROM THEE.
KLUNK!
PURRRRRRRRRRRRRR
End.

"To His Coy Mistress"

Andrew Marvell

ART / ADAPTATION BY **Yien Yip**

THE SON OF A MINISTER AT HOLY TRINITY CHURCH in Hull, England, Andrew Marvell was best known for being a civil servant and government official, and for his political satires skewering both the monarchy and Oliver Cromwell's Commonwealth (he also supported both institutions at different times and somehow managed to avoid execution throughout). Little of Marvell's incandescent lyric poetry was published in his lifetime. It was only after his death that his housekeeper found a manuscript of his poems and, posing as his wife, had it published, thus establishing him as one of the greatest poets of the seventeenth century. (Chalk this up as yet another instance of great literature almost being lost to us forever.)

"To His Coy Mistress" is Marvell's most famous, most anthologized poem, and one of the greatest *carpe diem* statements ever penned. In it, a man is trying to talk a woman into bed. ("Mistress" didn't have the same meaning as it now has—it could refer to a girlfriend or simply to a lady in general.) She's probably interested but has definitely been putting him off, perhaps playfully, perhaps out of a sense of decorum. Taking it slow and jumping through hoops is all well and good, he says, if we had eternity to pussyfoot around, but like all people we're careening toward death, so we need to get our pleasure now. The poem hums with powerful lines:

> But at my back I always hear
> Time's wingèd chariot hurrying near;
> . . .
> The grave's a fine and private place,
> But none, I think, do there embrace.

A finer, more inarguable case for jumping into the sack has never been made (although John Donne's "The Flea" presents probably the cleverest and most unexpected). Illustrator and textile artist Yien Yip places her adaptation in the 1800s, some two centuries after the poem was likely written (the early 1650s), and it could also easily have been set in the present. Seizing the day never goes out of style.

SOURCE

Wilcher, Robert. *Andrew Marvell.* Cambridge University Press, 1985.

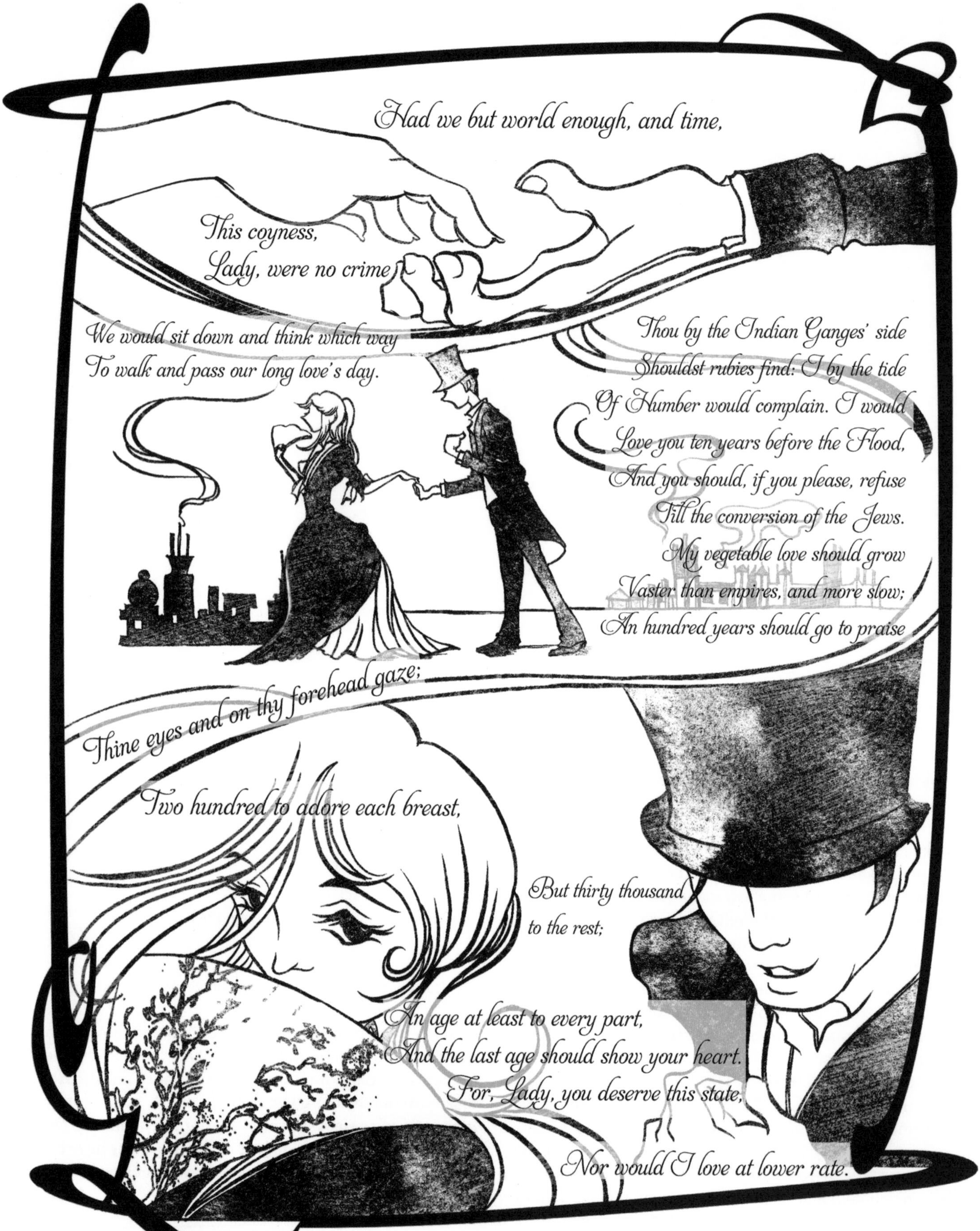
Had we but world enough, and time,
This coyness,
Lady, were no crime
We would sit down and think which way
To walk and pass our long love's day.
Thou by the Indian Ganges' side
Shouldst rubies find: I by the tide
Of Humber would complain. I would
Love you ten years before the Flood,
And you should, if you please, refuse
Till the conversion of the Jews.
My vegetable love should grow
Vaster than empires, and more slow;
An hundred years should go to praise
Thine eyes and on thy forehead gaze;
Two hundred to adore each breast,
But thirty thousand
to the rest;
An age at least to every part,
And the last age should show your heart.
For, Lady, you deserve this state,
Nor would I love at lower rate.

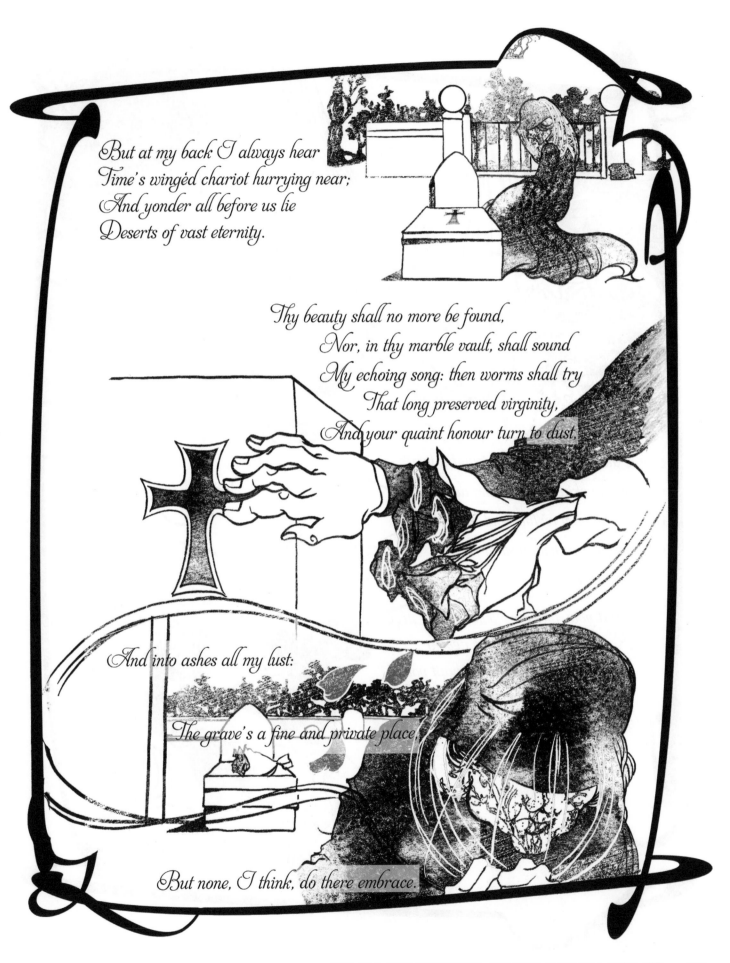

But at my back I always hear
Time's wingèd chariot hurrying near;
And yonder all before us lie
Deserts of vast eternity.

Thy beauty shall no more be found,
Nor, in thy marble vault, shall sound
My echoing song: then worms shall try
That long preserved virginity,
And your quaint honour turn to dust,

And into ashes all my lust:

The grave's a fine and private place,

But none, I think, do there embrace.

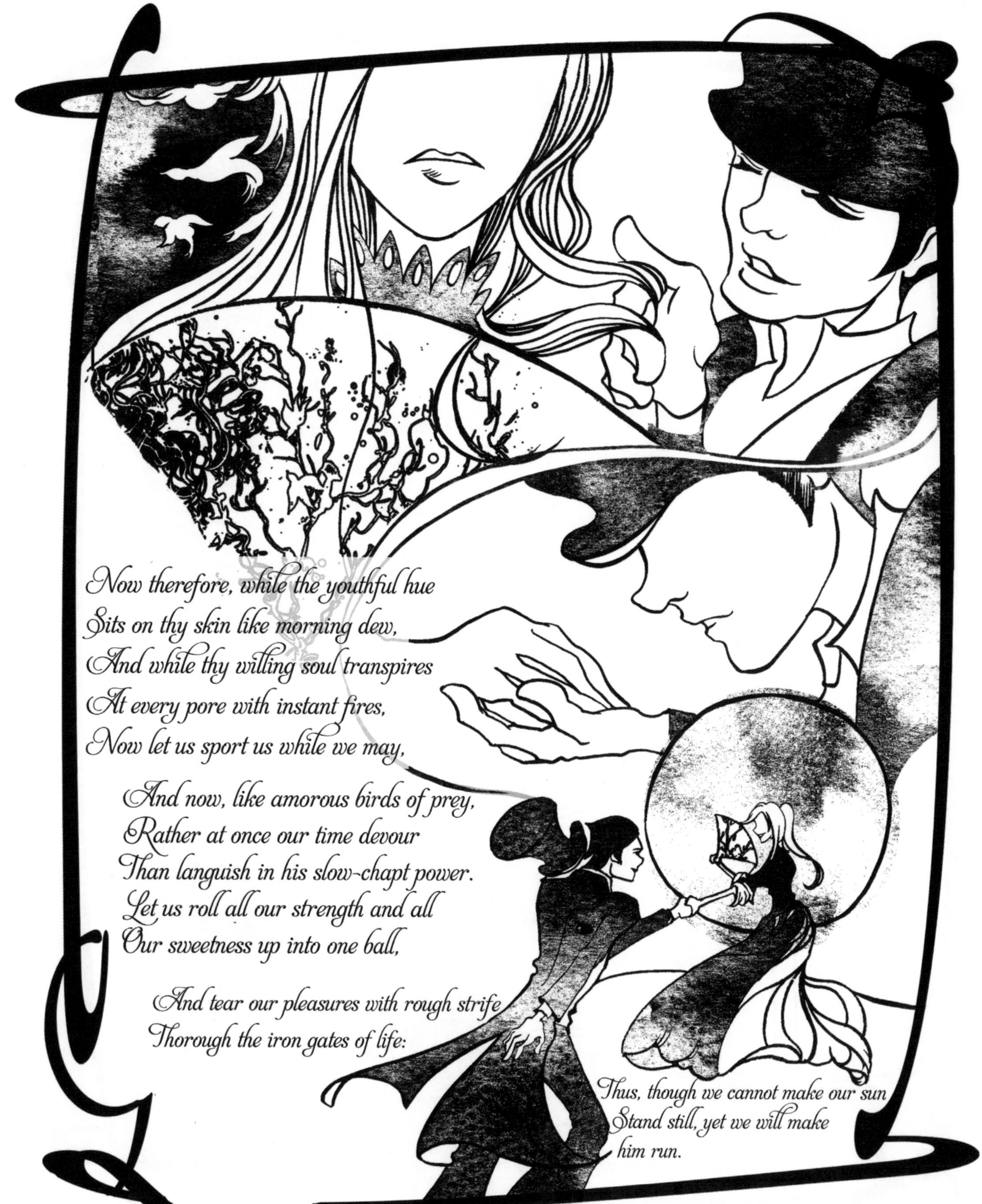
Now therefore, while the youthful hue
Sits on thy skin like morning dew,
And while thy willing soul transpires
At every pore with instant fires,
Now let us sport us while we may,
And now, like amorous birds of prey,
Rather at once our time devour
Than languish in his slow-chapt power.
Let us roll all our strength and all
Our sweetness up into one ball,
And tear our pleasures with rough strife
Thorough the iron gates of life:
Thus, though we cannot make our sun
Stand still, yet we will make
him run.

"Forgive Us Our Trespasses"

Aphra Behn

ART / ADAPTATION BY **Alex Eckman-Lawn**

APHRA BEHN IS TYPICALLY REGARDED AS THE first professional female writer in the English language. After serving as a spy for England while in Antwerp, she was thrown into debtors' prison in 1668 when Charles II didn't pay her for her services. Upon her release a short while later, she wrote a large number of plays that were performed, as well as short stories, well-received poems, and some of the earliest British novels. Her work often deals with sexual themes, making her even more of a pioneer. Her poem "Forgive Us Our Trespasses" can be read as a defense of her sexually liberated attitudes, which she is rumored to have put into practice in her personal life. It contains one of my favorite passages of love poetry:

Of all my crimes, the breach of all thy laws,
Love, soft bewitching love, has been the cause.

Alex Eckman-Lawn, who has done album art for many extreme and avant-garde metal bands (among other work), provides a dark, complex, yet ultimately hopeful interpretation: Has her heart ensnared him? Or is he trying to rip her heart out of her chest? They both have knives, so they could cut the cords if they wanted to, yet they aren't.

SOURCE

Woodcock, George. *Aphra Behn: The English Sappho*. Montreal: Black Rose Books, 1989.

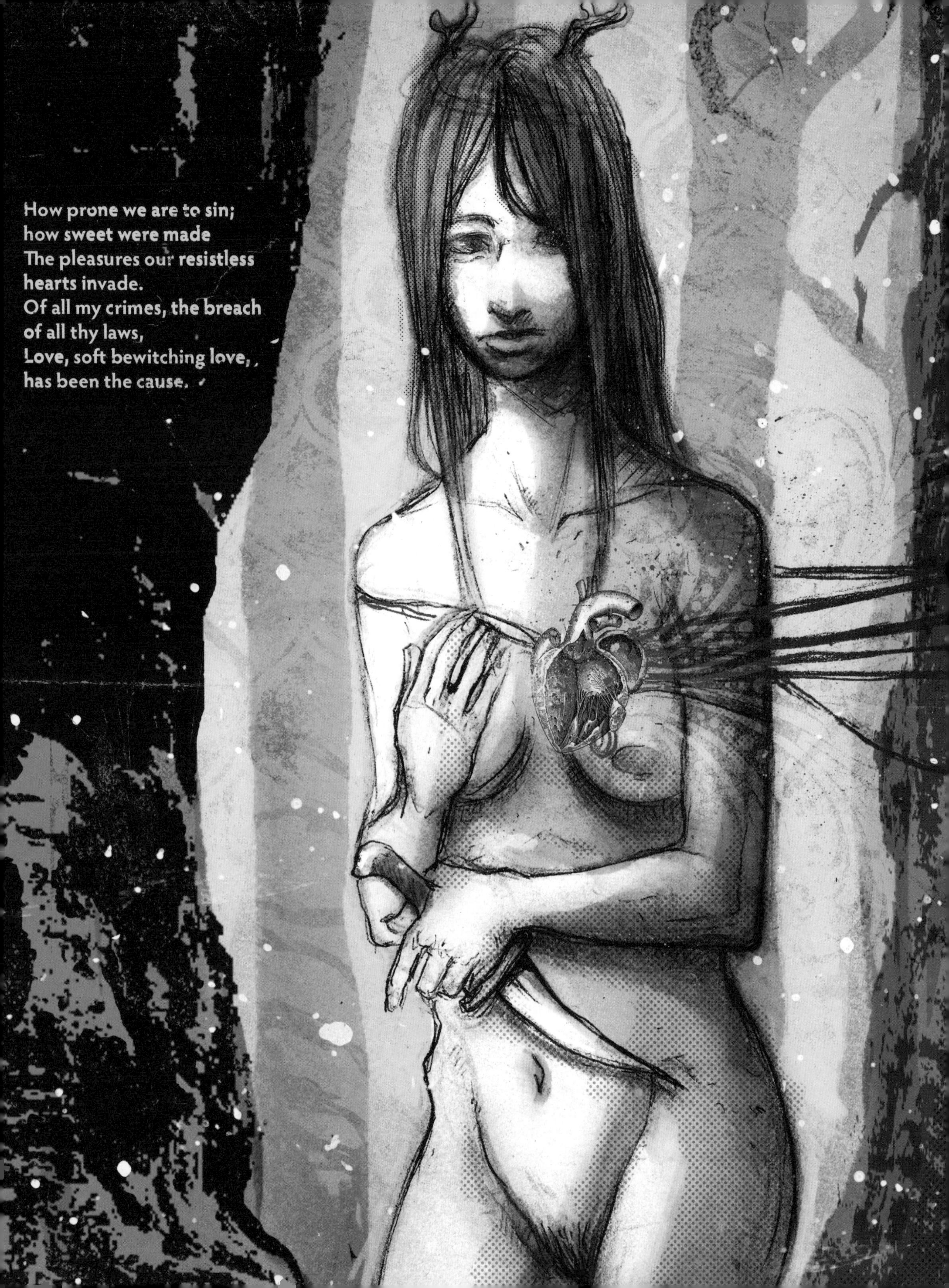
How prone we are to sin;
how sweet were made
The pleasures our resistless
hearts invade.
Of all my crimes, the breach
of all thy laws,
Love, soft bewitching love,
has been the cause.

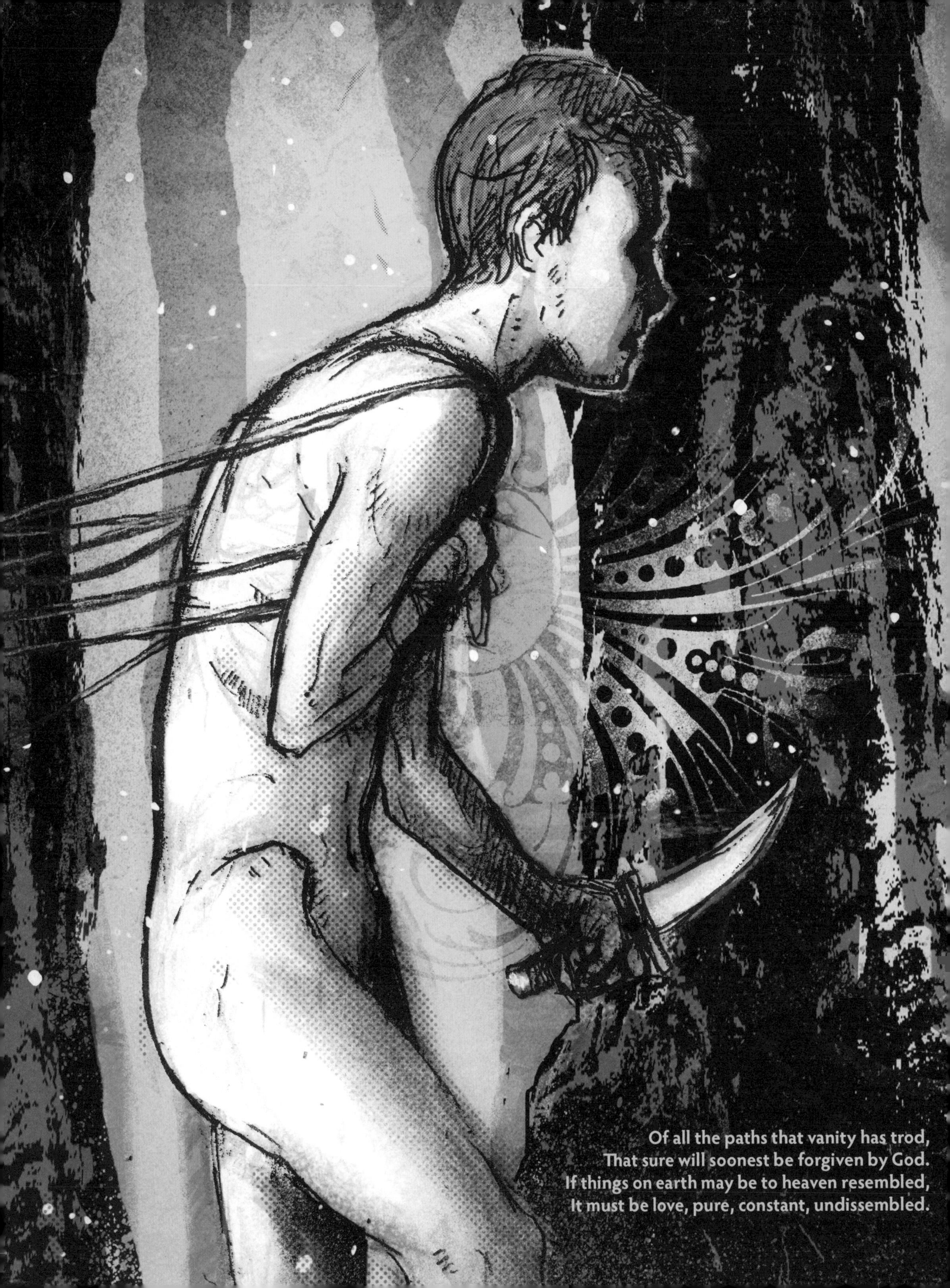
Of all the paths that vanity has trod,
That sure will soonest be forgiven by God.
If things on earth may be to heaven resembled,
It must be love, pure, constant, undissembled.

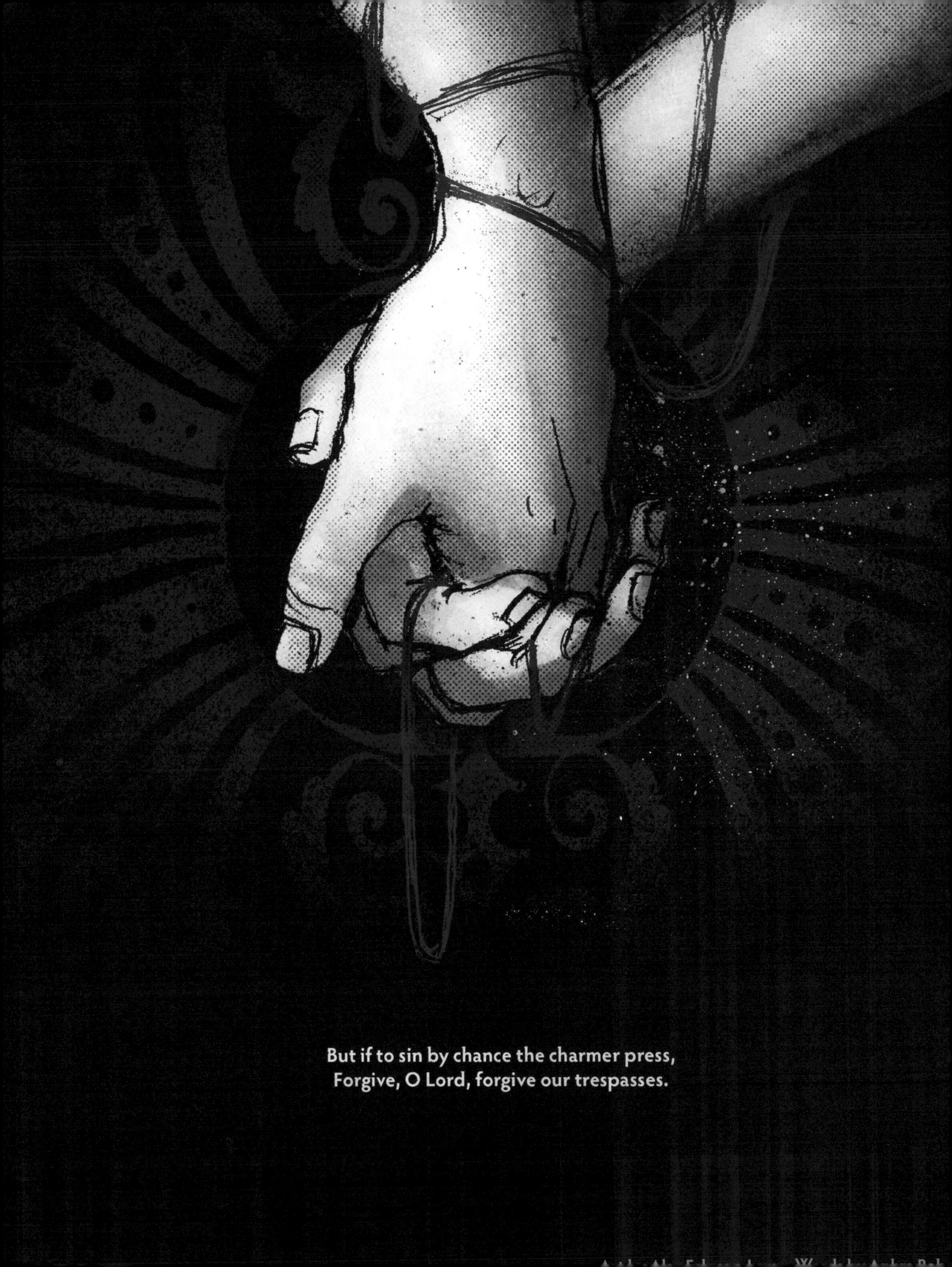
But if to sin by chance the charmer press,
Forgive, O Lord, forgive our trespasses.

Paradise Lost

John Milton

ART / ADAPTATION BY **Rebecca Dart**

CONSIDERED A SUPREME MASTERWORK OF English-language literature, nearly or on par with Shakespeare's greatest plays, *Paradise Lost* features an awesome cast of characters: God, Satan, Adam and Eve, Jesus (referred to as the Son), demons, and angels. A poet of some renown—and an essayist/pamphleteer with sharp, controversial political, religious, and social opinions—the British public servant John Milton had already gone blind by age fifty when he decided on a topic for his long-planned epic poem: the biblical fall of the human race via Adam and Eve, with assistance from Satan. From 1658 to 1664, Milton dictated the 10,000-line poem to his aides. It was published three years later to immediate hosannas.

Milton isn't telling this sprawling tale of war in Heaven and temptation in Paradise simply as a ripping good yarn; he means it. A hardcore nondenominational Christian, he penned *Paradise Lost* as a way to theologically and philosophically explain why these events happened. In fact, as a number of scholars have pointed out, he does such a good job describing Satan's actions and explaining his motivations that it is actually Satan, not God, who is the protagonist here. At the very least, Satan comes across as an antihero, rebelling against a tyrannical leader, first through outright violent revolution, then by monkeywrenching God's creation by tricking Eve into eating from the Tree of Knowledge.

In many aspects, Milton modeled *Paradise Lost* on *The Iliad*, *The Odyssey*, and *Aeneid*, but his wordsmithing prow-ess goes way beyond this. Professor Francis C. Blessington gives us an idea of the density contained here:

> Built into the poem are . . . verbal echoes from Greek, Latin, Hebrew, Italian, and English poetry. There are discussions of concepts: music, poetry, political liberty, the nature of God, the nature of nature, free will, sex, domestic happiness and domestic hell, human history and divine love, the nature of power and the pretexts of rebellion, the interpretation of dreams, the tragedy and naturalness of death, and the longing for immortality, to name a few.

I should have known that Vancouver artist Rebecca Dart would turn in a radically original adaptation of *Paradise Lost*. Her twenty-four-page oversized comic *RabbitHead* wowed everyone in 2004, with its branching, parallel storylines that literally run alongside each other as the action keeps forking before collapsing back to a single thread. Saying that it had been "a dream of mine to illustrate Milton's *Paradise Lost*," she encapsulates the epic with twelve magnificent full-page, hand-lettered illustrations in which the characters are geometric objects—glyphs and symbols come to life.

SOURCE

Blessington, Francis C. *Paradise Lost: A Student's Companion to the Poem*. iUniverse, 2004.

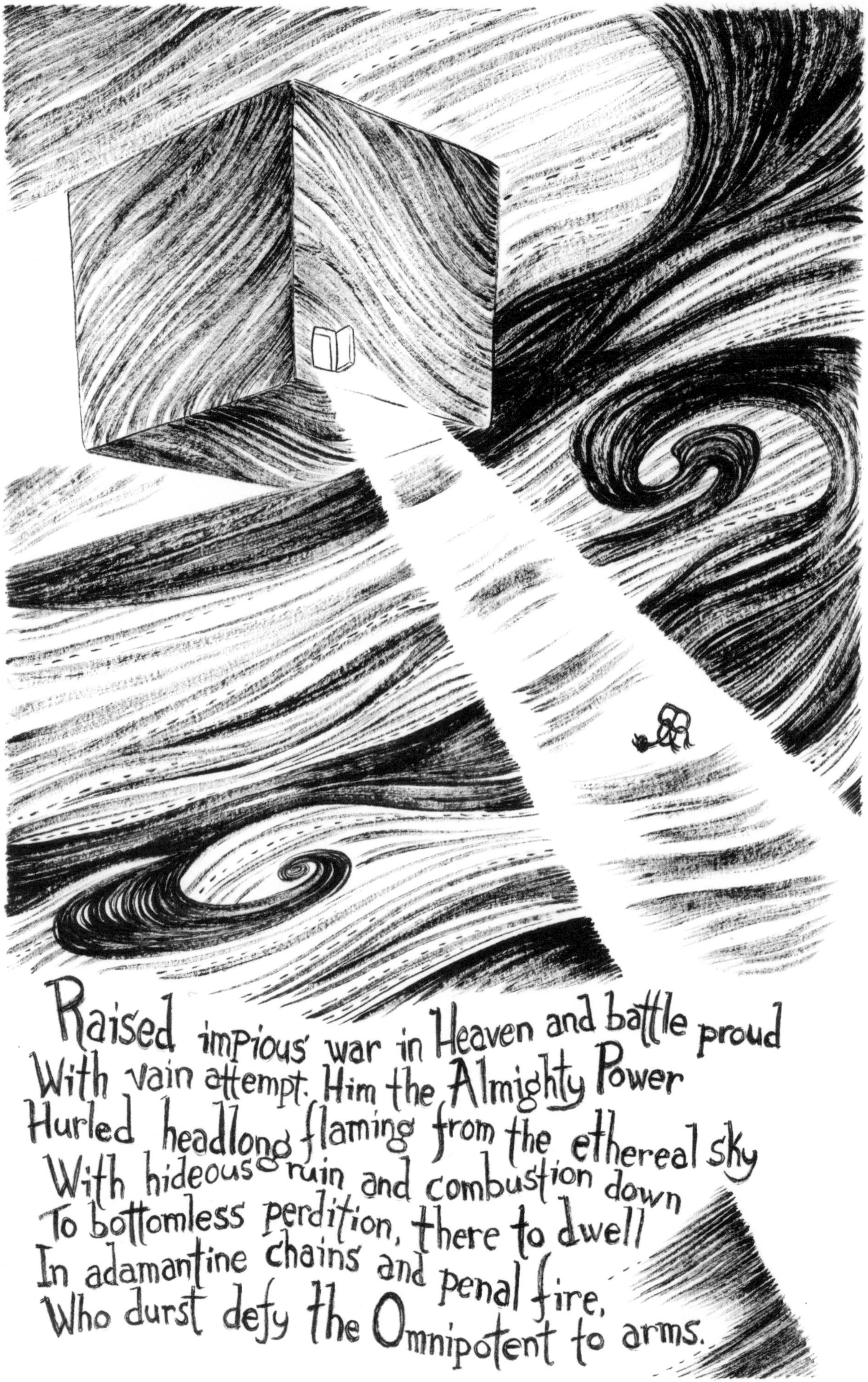
Raised impious war in Heaven and battle proud
With vain attempt. Him the Almighty Power
Hurled headlong flaming from the ethereal sky
With hideous ruin and combustion down
To bottomless perdition, there to dwell
In adamantine chains and penal fire,
Who durst defy the Omnipotent to arms.

A solemn council forthwith to be held
At Pandemonium, the high capital
Of Satan and his peers; their summons called
From every band and squared regiment
By place or choice the worthiest; they anon
With hundreds and with thousands
Trooping came attended.

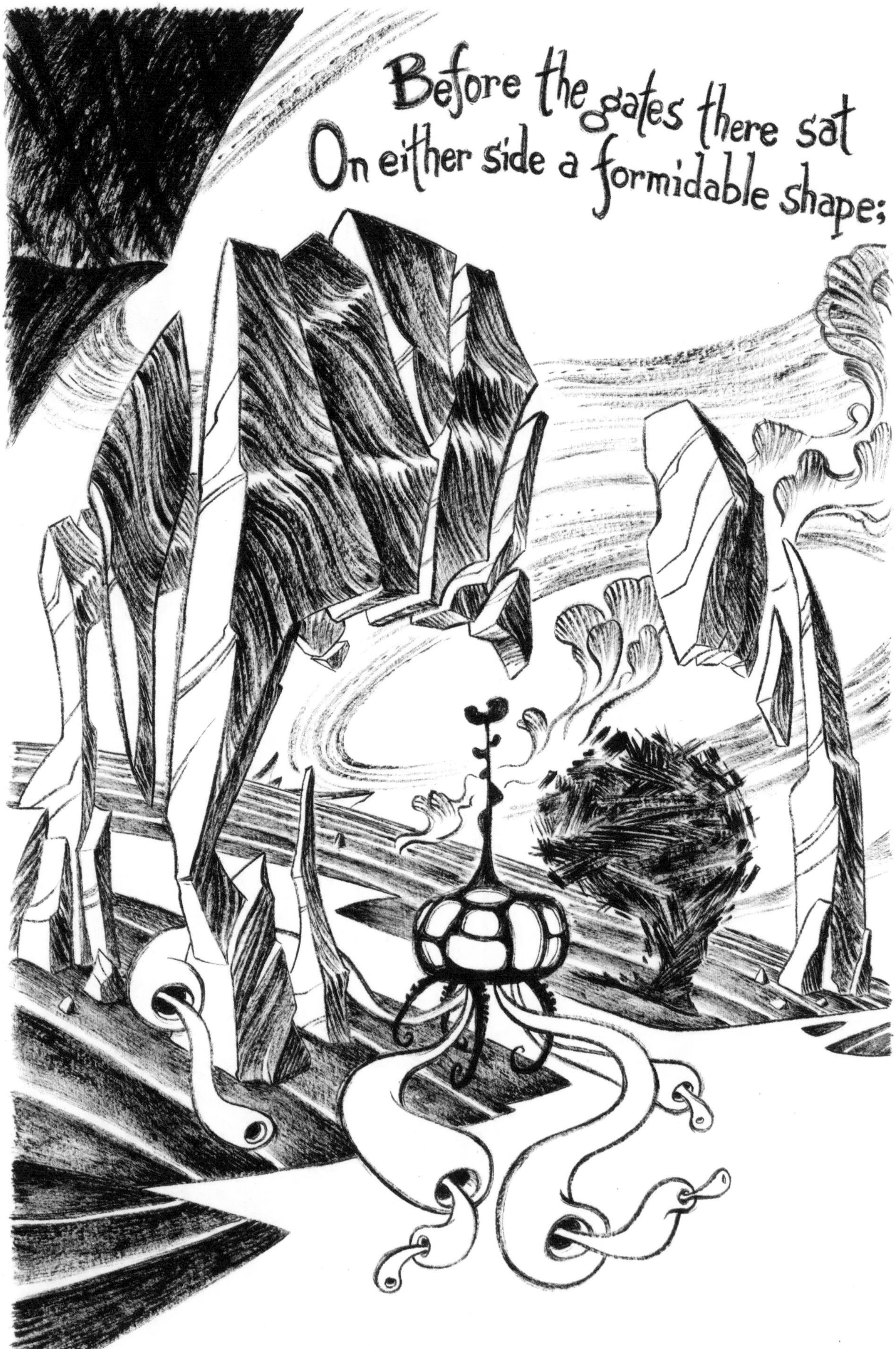
Before the gates there sat
On either side a formidable shape;

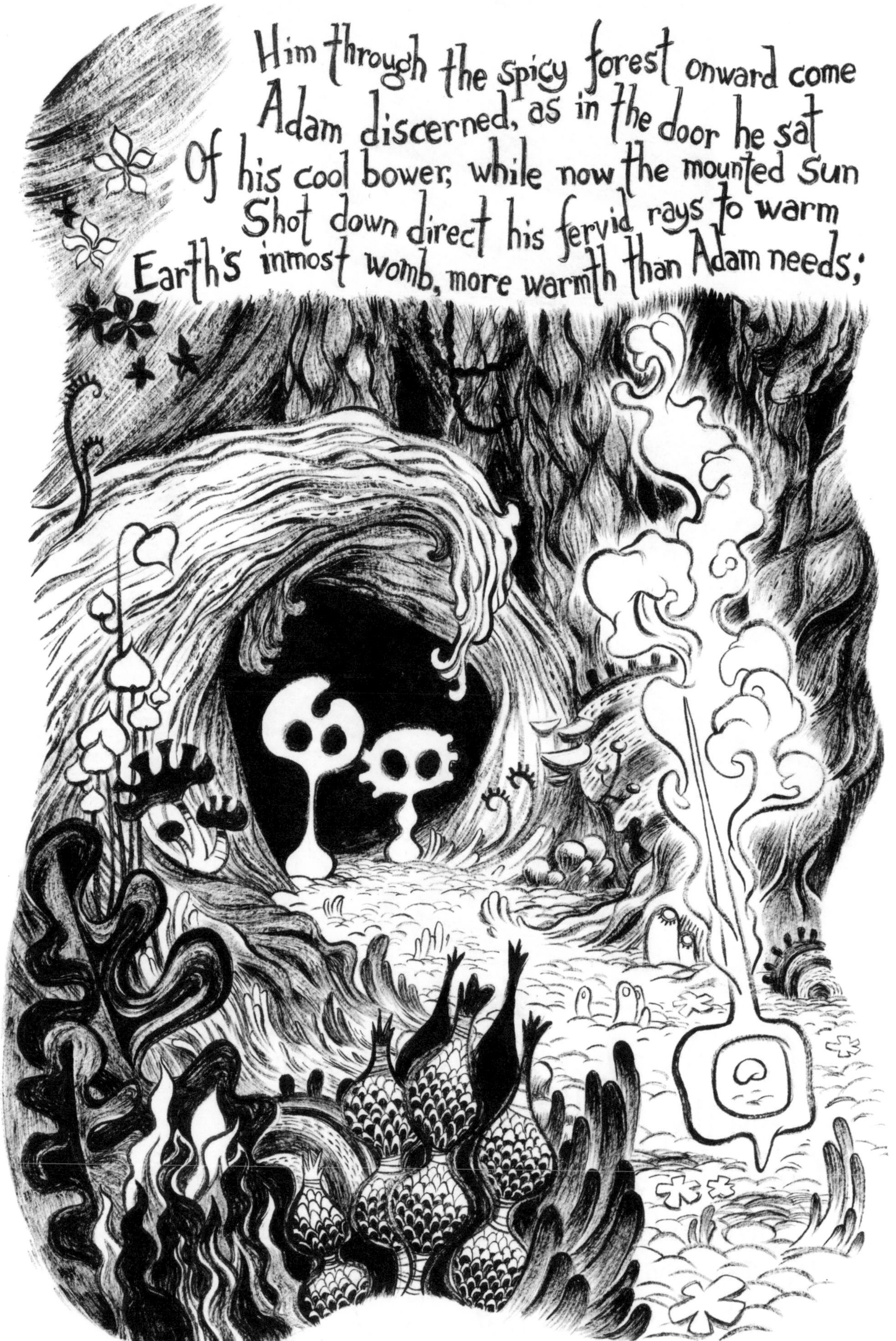
Him through the spicy forest onward come
Adam discerned, as in the door he sat
Of his cool bower, while now the mounted Sun
Shot down direct his fervid rays to warm
Earth's inmost womb, more warmth than Adam needs;

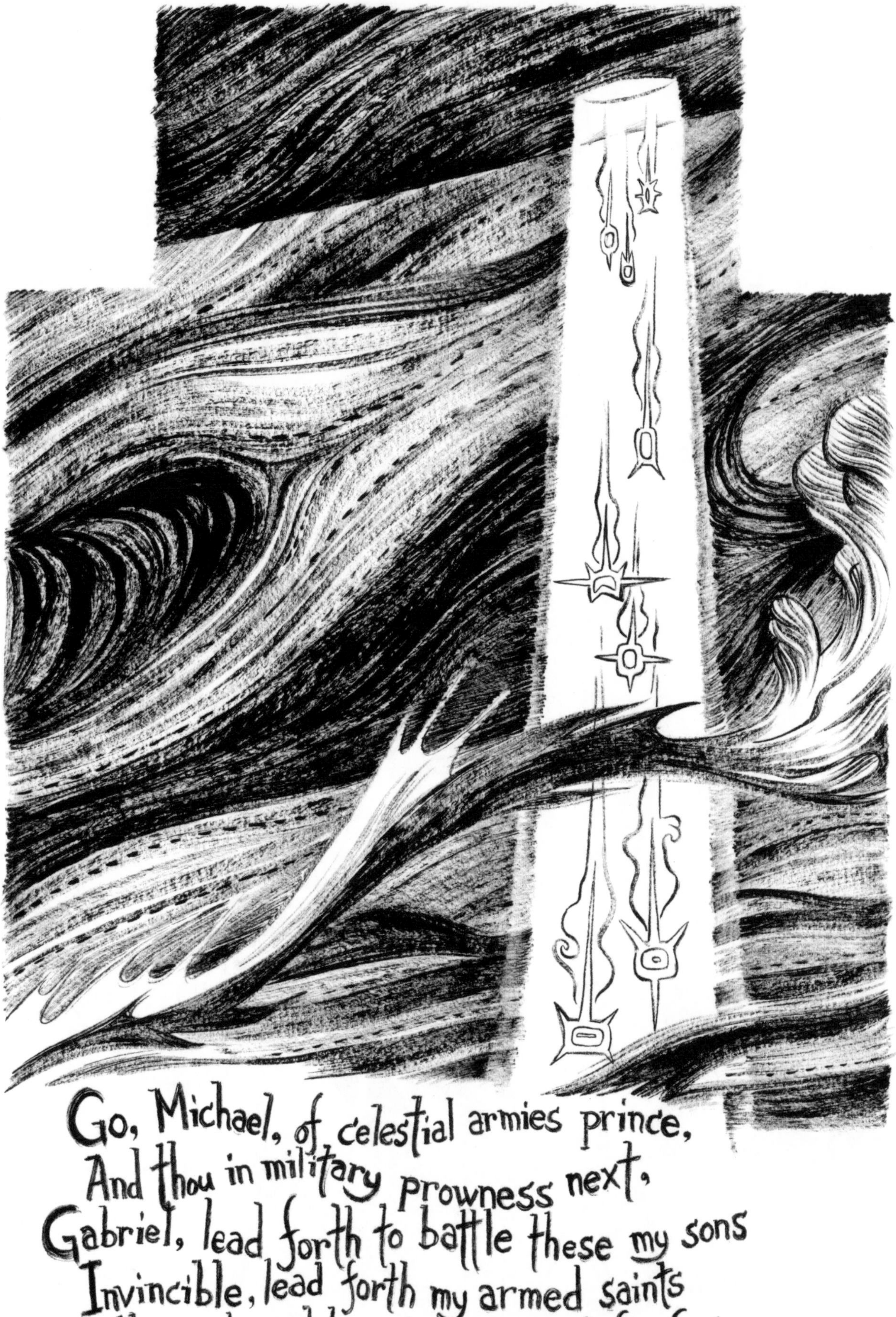

Go, Michael, of celestial armies prince,
And thou in military prowness next,
Gabriel, lead forth to battle these my sons
Invincible, lead forth my armed saints
By thousands and by millions ranged for fight,
Equal in number to that godless crew

Then Satan first knew pain,
And writhed him to and fro convolved; so sore
The griding sword with discontinuous wound
Passed through him; but the ethereal substance
closed

Not long divisible, and from the gash
A stream of nectarous humor issuing flowed
Sanguine, such as celestial spirits may bleed,

Yet haply of thy race
In future days, if malice should abound,
Some one intent on mischief, or inspired
With devilish machination, might devise,
Like instrument to plague the sons of men
For sin, on war and mutual slaughter bent.

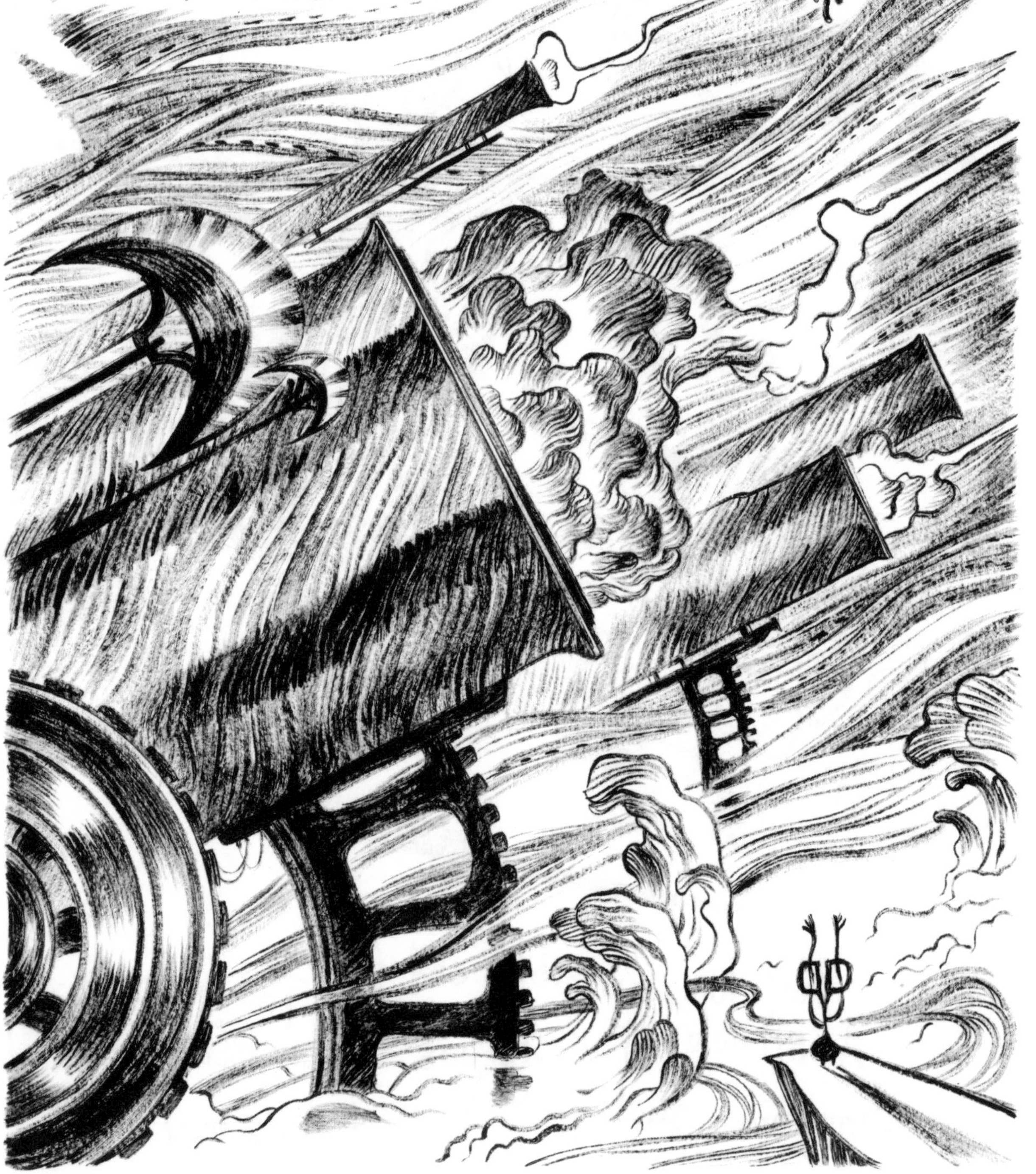

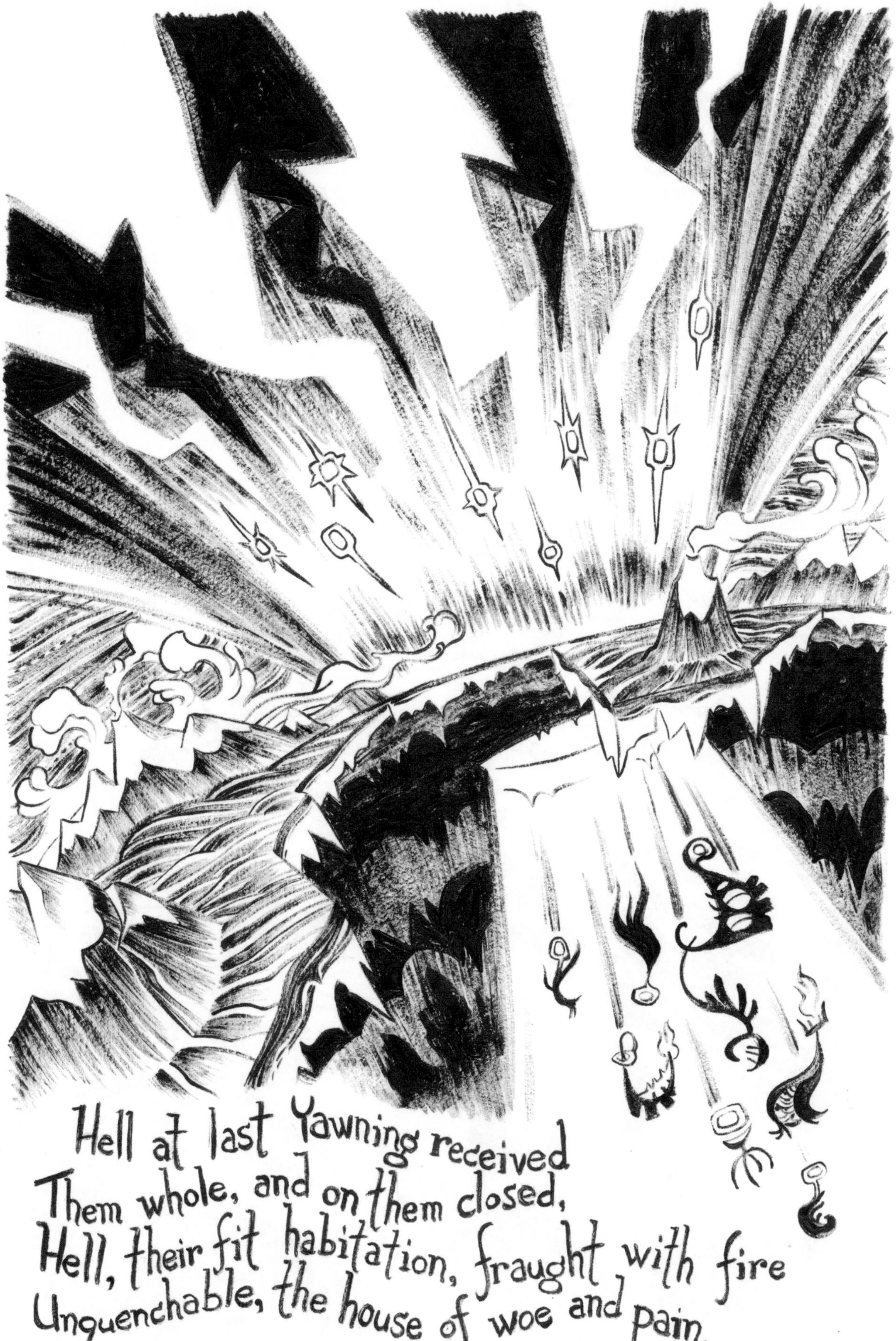
Hell at last Yawning received
Them whole, and on them closed,
Hell, their fit habitation, fraught with fire
Unquenchable, the house of woe and pain.

"Of these the vigilance
I dread, and to elude, thus wrapped in mist
Of midnight vapor glide obscure, and pry
In every bush and brake, where hap may find
The serpent sleeping, in whose mazy folds
To hide me, and the dark intent I bring."

"Here grows the cure of all, this fruit divine,
Fair to the eye, inviting to the taste,
Of virtue to make wise; what hinders then
To reach, and feed at once both body and mind?"

So saying her rash hand in evil hour
Forth reaching to the fruit, she plucked, she eat.
Earth felt the wound, and Nature from her seat
Sighing through all her works gave signs of woe,
That all was lost.

She gave him of that fair enticing fruit
With liberal hand. He scrupled not to eat
Against his better knowledge, not deceived,
But fondly overcome with female charm.

Earth trembled from her entrails, as again
In pangs, and Nature gave a second groan;
Sky lowr'd, and, muttering thunder, some sad drops
Wept at completing of the mortal sin.

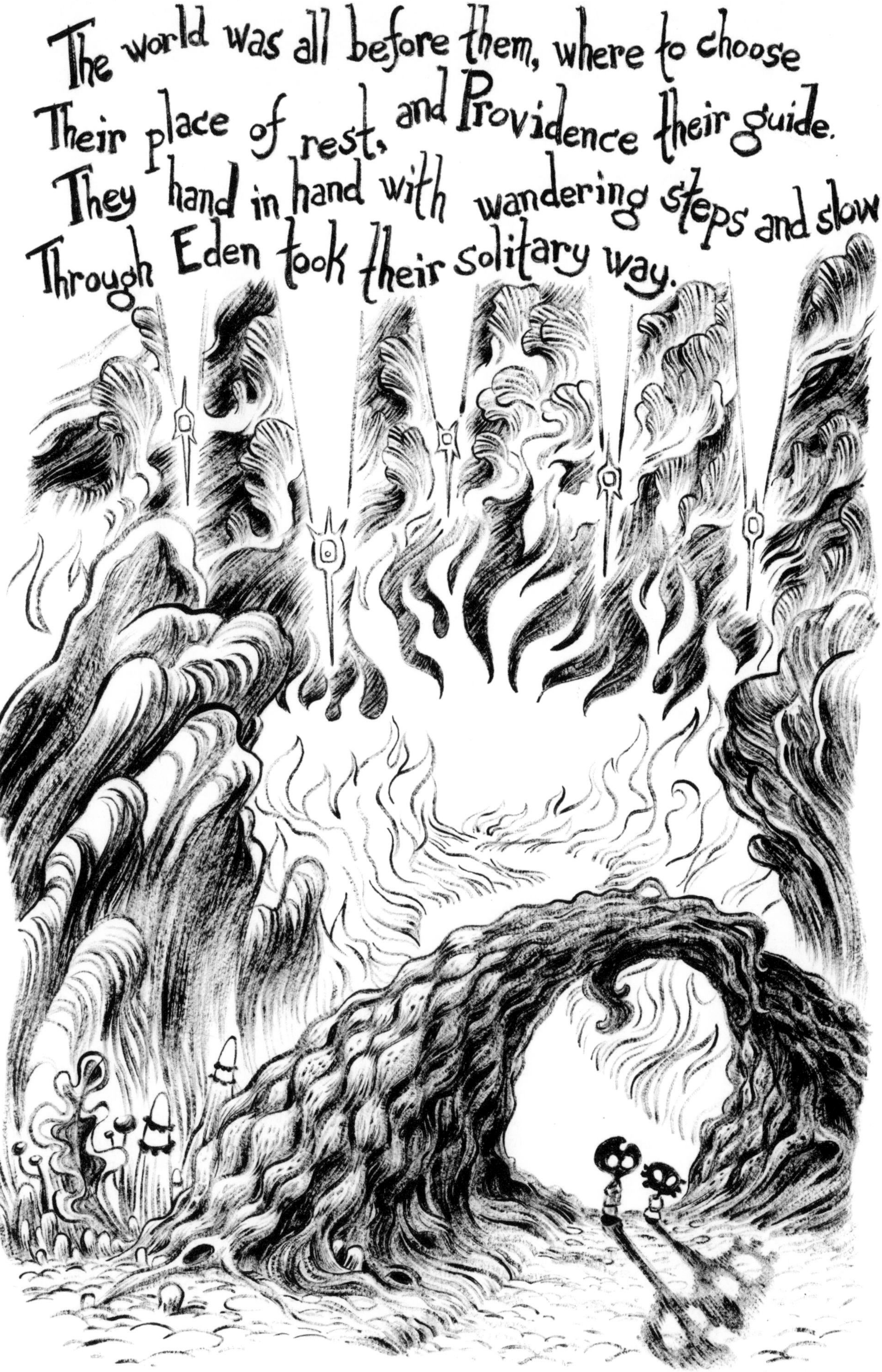
The world was all before them, where to choose
Their place of rest, and Providence their guide.
They hand in hand with wandering steps and slow
Through Eden took their solitary way.

Gulliver's Travels

Jonathan Swift

ART / ADAPTATION BY **Gareth Hinds**

***GULLIVER'S TRAVELS* IS THE PREEMINENT**
Enlightenment satire on politics, religion, and human nature in general. Jonathan Swift's tale of the seagoing surgeon (and later, captain) Lemuel Gulliver is best known for its first part, in which he washes up on the shore of Lilliput, a land inhabited by tiny people. They want Gulliver to be their super-weapon in conquering a neighboring land, but he refuses to conquer the other country, leading to an order of execution against him. (The two countries are at war because they disagree over how to break an egg—on the little end or on the big end. Swift is mocking the similarly trivial differences that lead to bloody religious strife between Catholics and Protestants.)

The further parts of the novel—the other lands and their inhabitants—get short shrift, so it's most welcome to see full-time literature-adapter Gareth Hinds turn his attention to part two, set in Brobdingnag, the land of giants. Gulliver's attempt to impress the king regarding England doesn't exactly have its desired effect. When reading this part of the piece, be amazed and saddened that this Anglo-Irish novel from 1726 could be describing the US or UK in the present day, proving that 1) great literature is timeless and 2) politics is always a cesspool, no matter where or when it's practiced.

GULLIVER'S TRAVELS

PART II: A VOYAGE TO BROBDINGNAG

by JONATHAN SWIFT, 1726 - Adaptation by Gareth Hinds, 2003

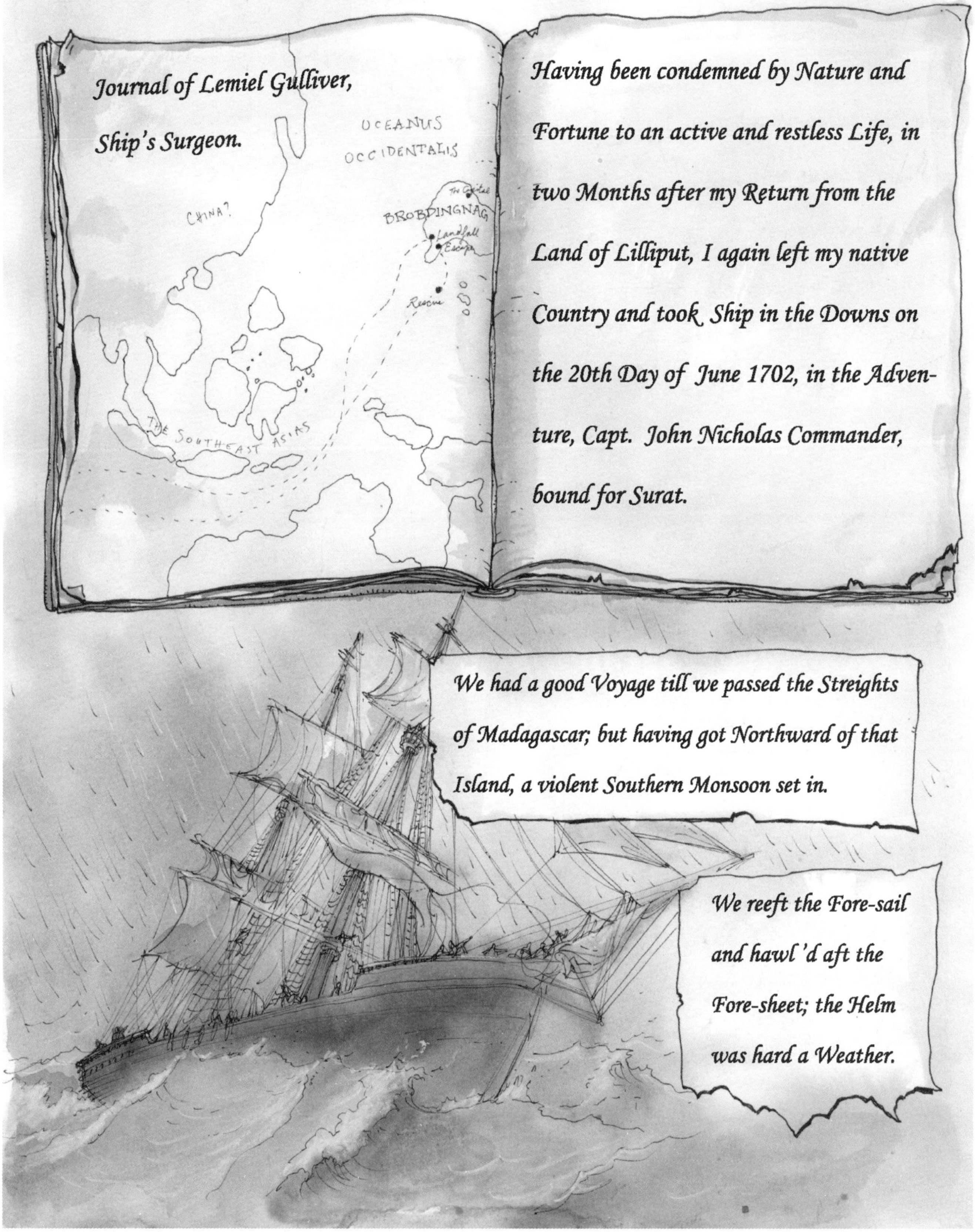

Journal of Lemiel Gulliver,
Ship's Surgeon.
OCEANUS OCCIDENTALIS
CHINA?
BROBDINGNAG
Landfall
Escape
Rescue
THE SOUTHEAST ASIAS
Having been condemned by Nature and Fortune to an active and restless Life, in two Months after my Return from the Land of Lilliput, I again left my native Country and took Ship in the Downs on the 20th Day of June 1702, in the Adventure, Capt. John Nicholas Commander, bound for Surat.
We had a good Voyage till we passed the Streights of Madagascar; but having got Northward of that Island, a violent Southern Monsoon set in.
We reeft the Fore-sail and hawl'd aft the Fore-sheet; the Helm was hard a Weather.

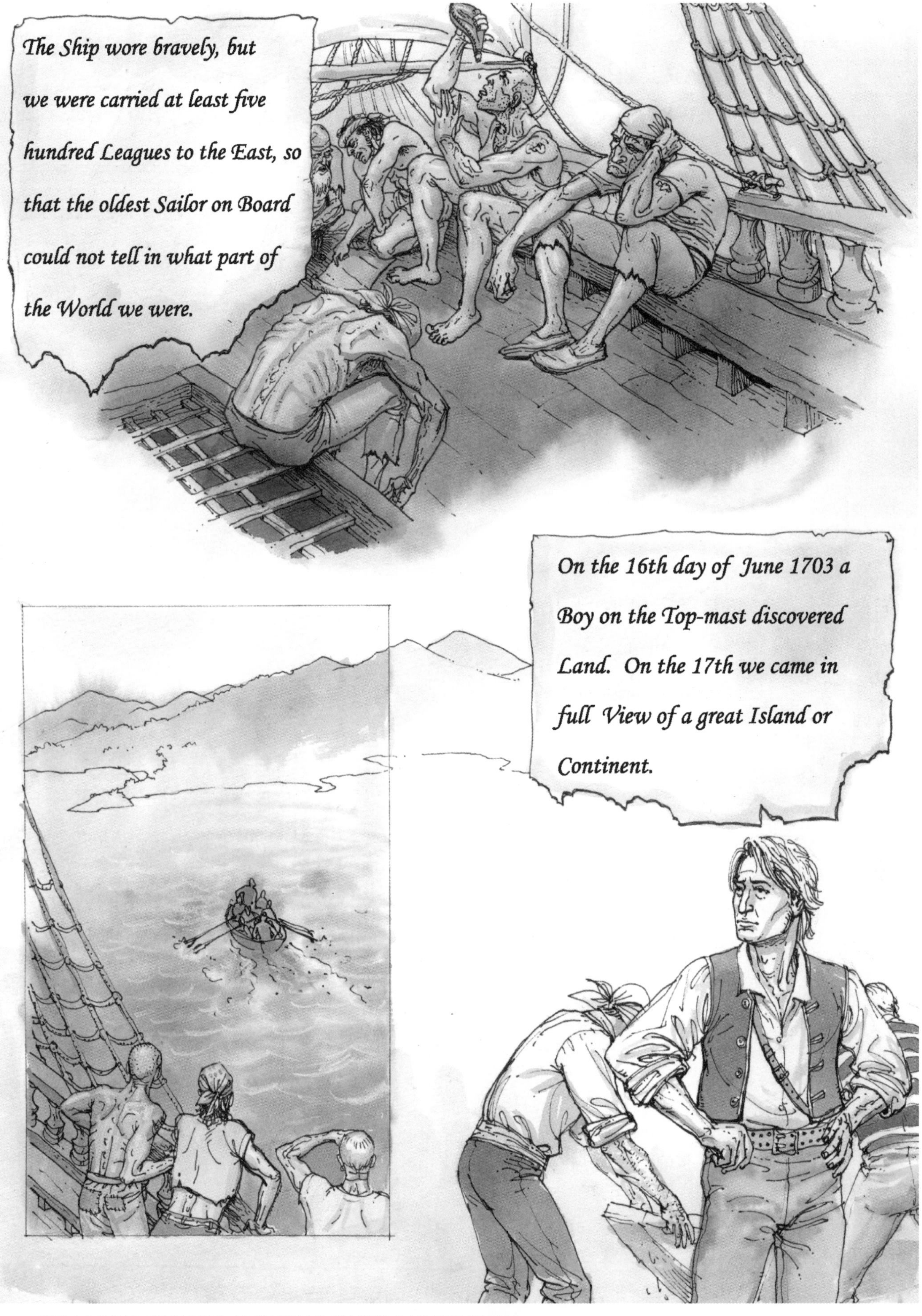
The Ship wore bravely, but we were carried at least five hundred Leagues to the East, so that the oldest Sailor on Board could not tell in what part of the World we were.
On the 16th day of June 1703 a Boy on the Top-mast discovered Land. On the 17th we came in full View of a great Island or Continent.

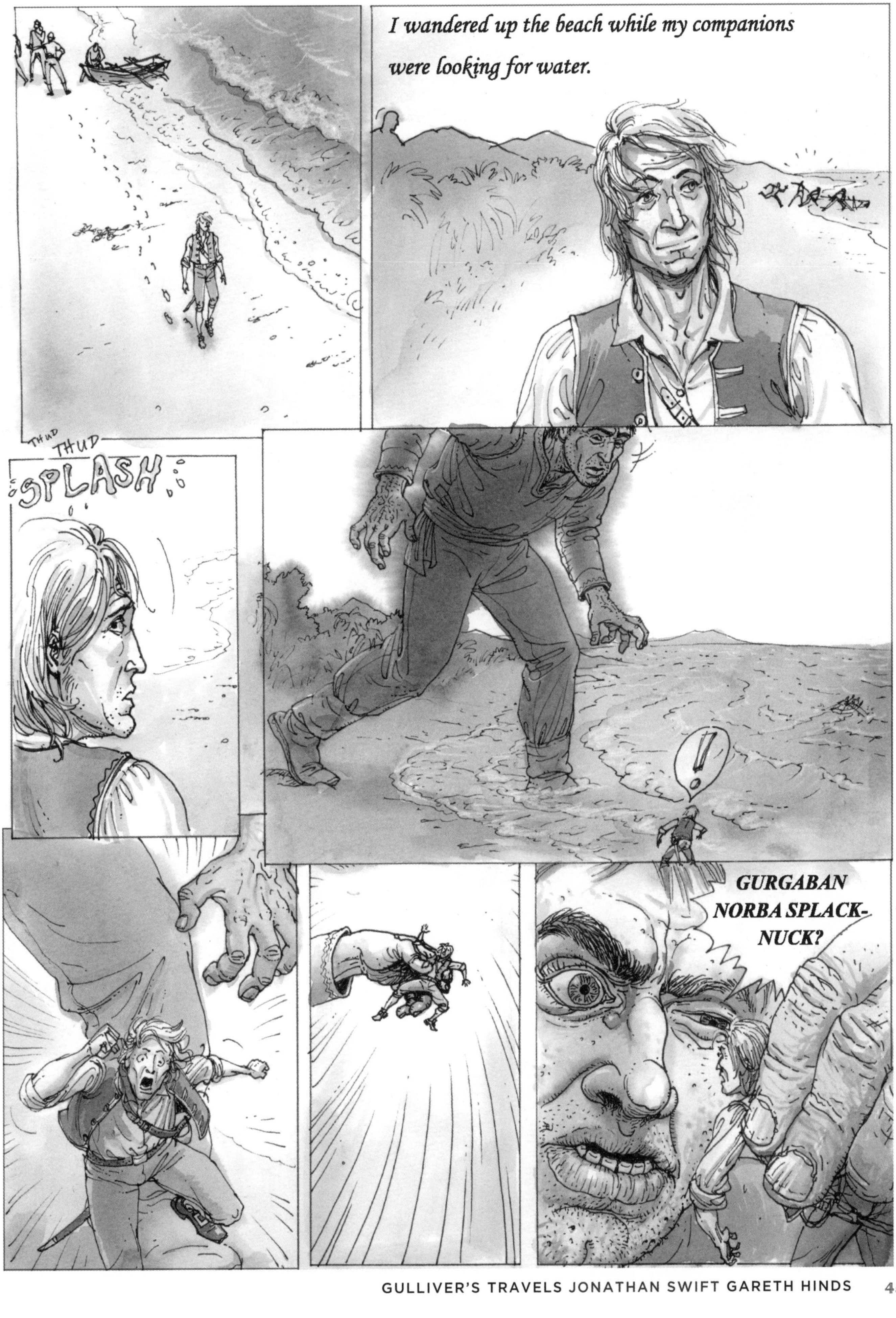
I wandered up the beach while my companions were looking for water.
THUD THUD
SPLASH
!
GURGABAN NORBA SPLACK-NUCK?

The giant and I did not comprehend each other's words, but by my speach and gestures he was convinced that I was a rational being. He then undertook to bring me to the ruler of his country.

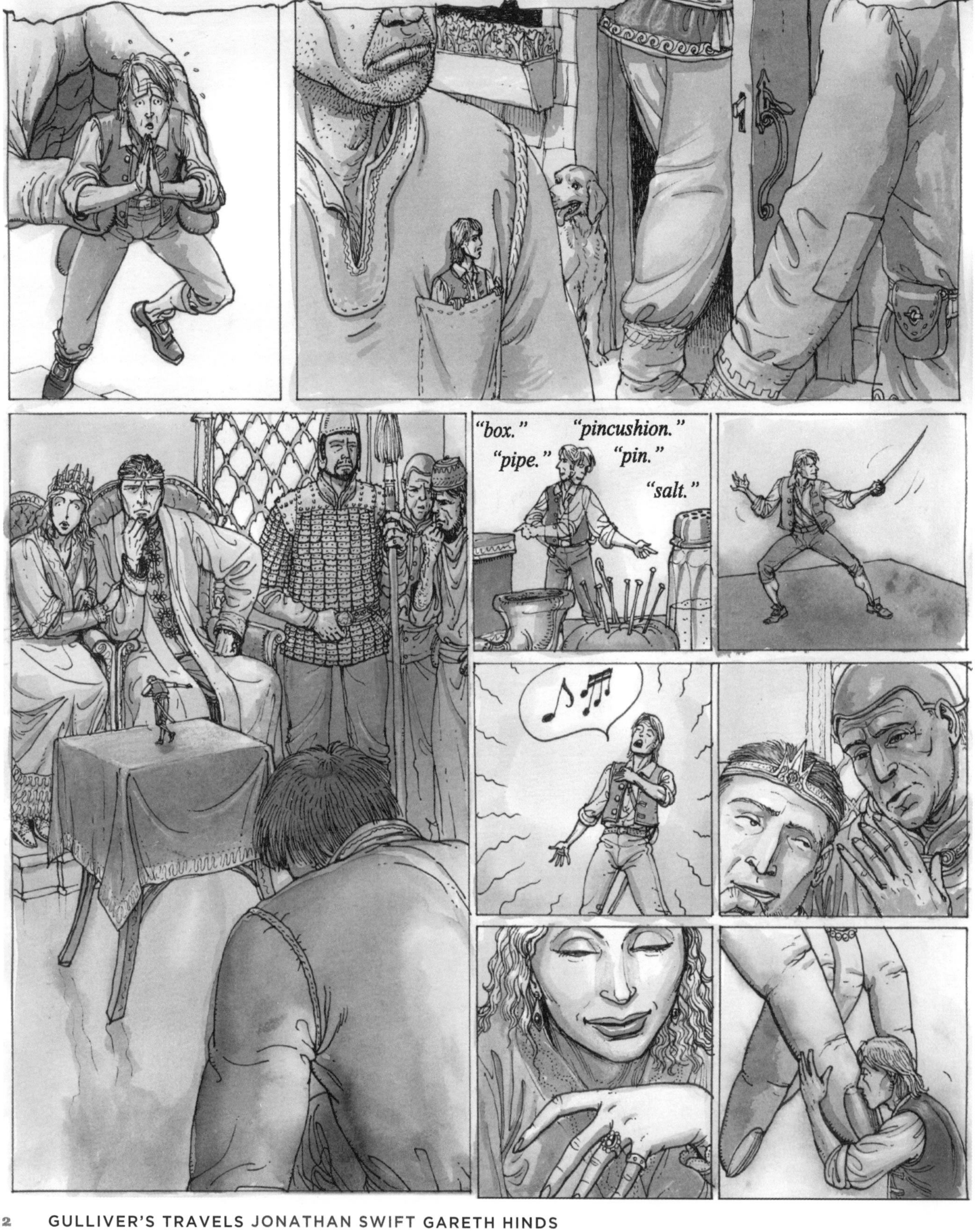
"box."
"pincushion."
"pipe."
"pin."
"salt."

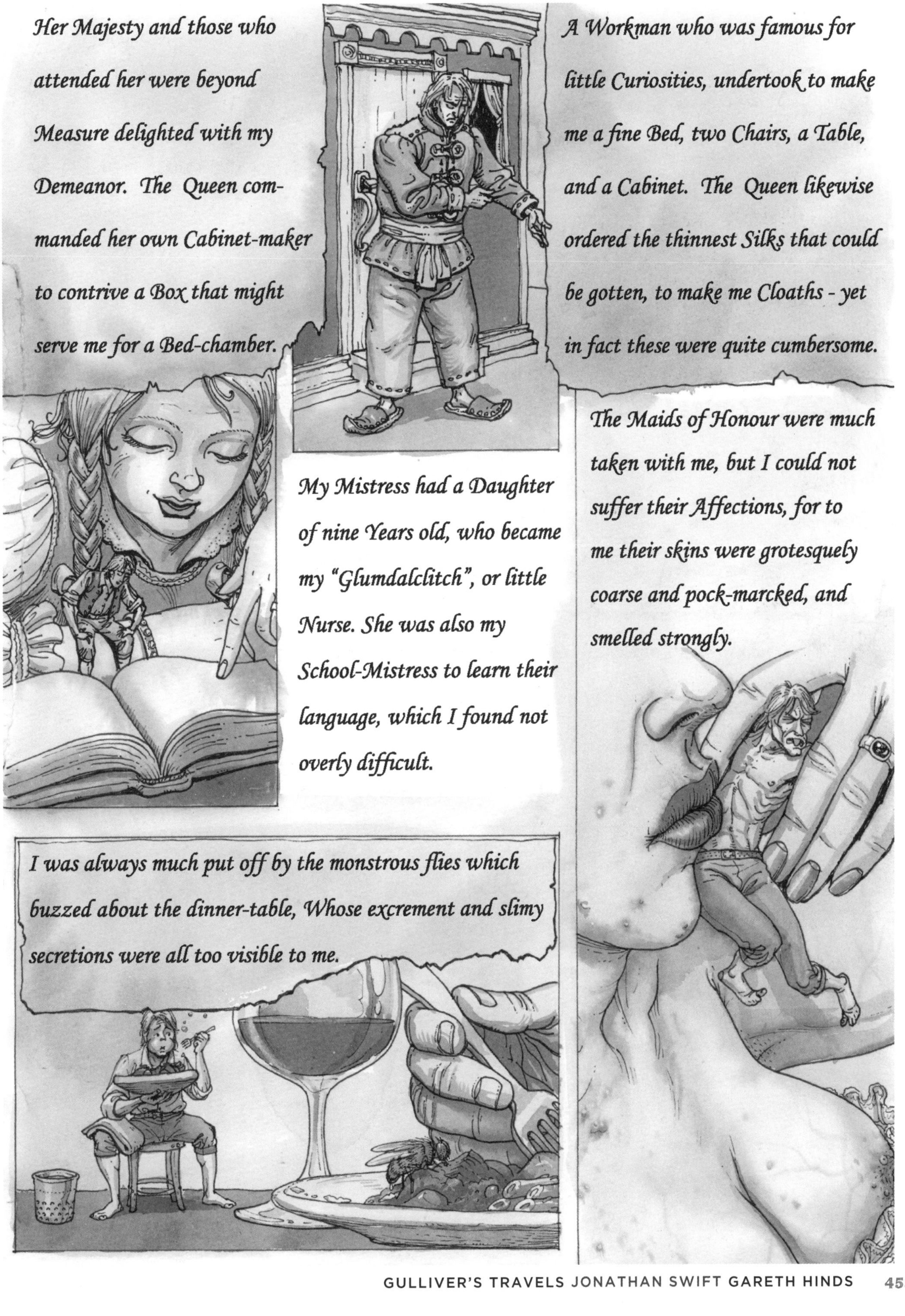
Her Majesty and those who attended her were beyond Measure delighted with my Demeanor. The Queen commanded her own Cabinet-maker to contrive a Box that might serve me for a Bed-chamber.
A Workman who was famous for little Curiosities, undertook to make me a fine Bed, two Chairs, a Table, and a Cabinet. The Queen likewise ordered the thinnest Silks that could be gotten, to make me Cloaths - yet in fact these were quite cumbersome.
My Mistress had a Daughter of nine Years old, who became my "Glumdalclitch", or little Nurse. She was also my School-Mistress to learn their language, which I found not overly difficult.
The Maids of Honour were much taken with me, but I could not suffer their Affections, for to me their skins were grotesquely coarse and pock-marcked, and smelled strongly.
I was always much put off by the monstrous flies which buzzed about the dinner-table, Whose excrement and slimy secretions were all too visible to me.

Indeed, as most everything in this land was of a size proportional to the Inhabitants, I found myself on several occasions in great Danger from the local Creatures.

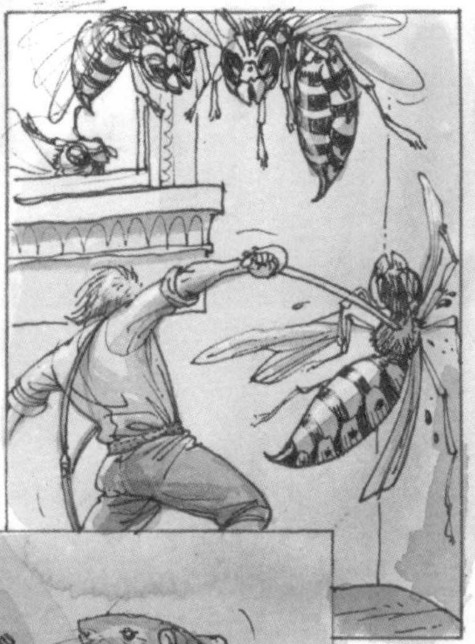

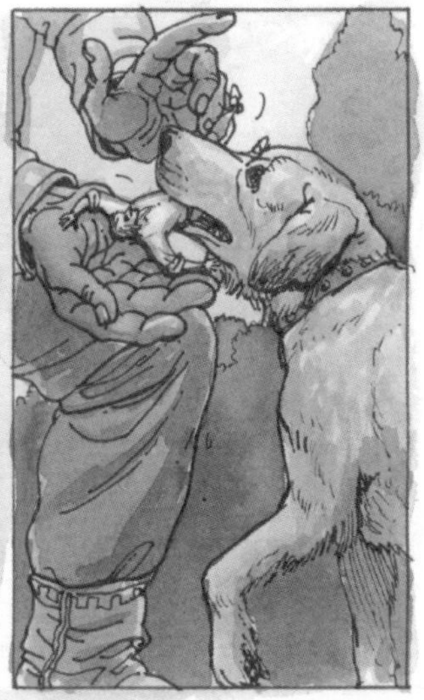

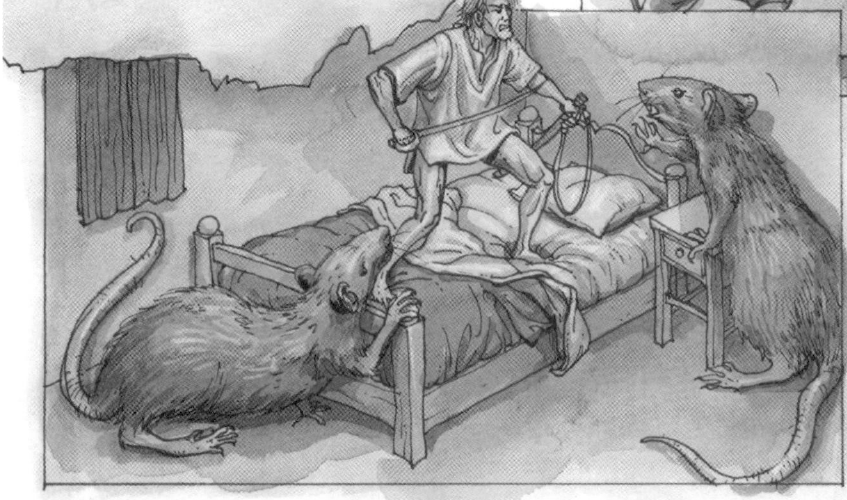

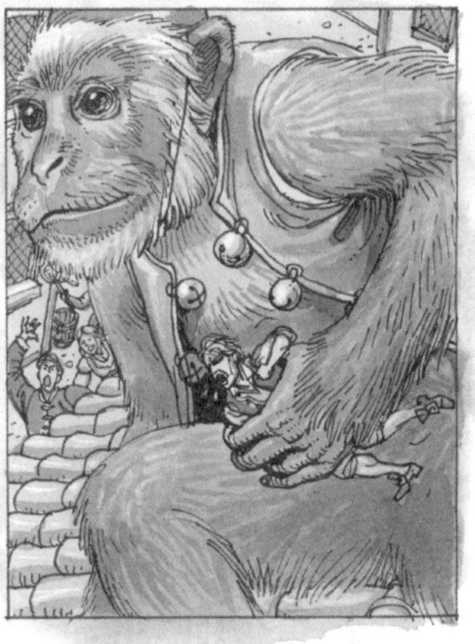

The King, who was a Lord of excellent Understanding, would frequently order that I should be brought in my Box, and set upon his Table. He desired that I should give him an exact Account of my Homeland, and the manner in which it was Governed.

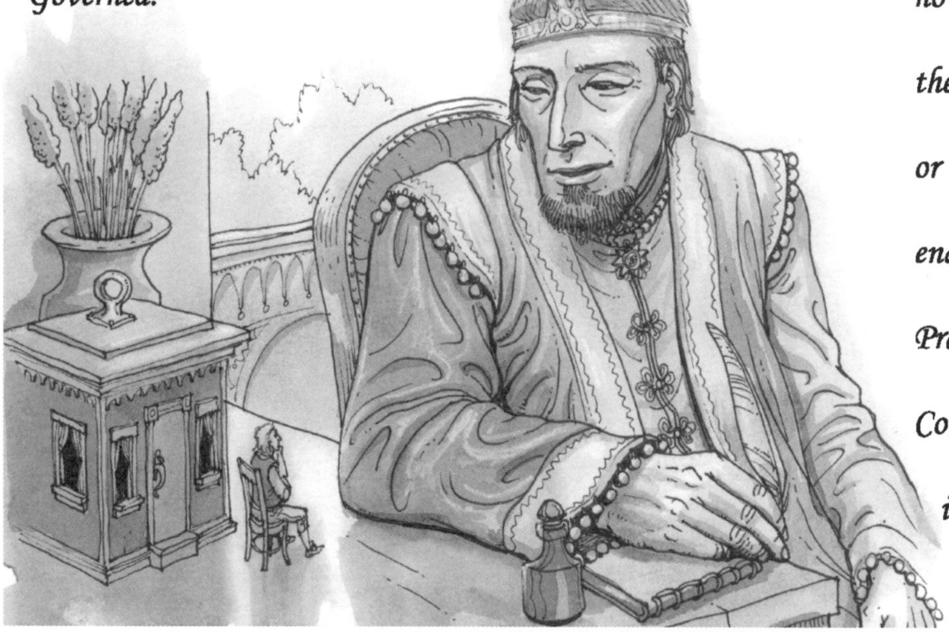

Imagine, courteous Reader, how often I then wished for the Tongue of Demosthenes or Cicero, that might have enabled me to celebrate the Praise of my own dear native Country in a Stile equal to its Merits and Felicity.

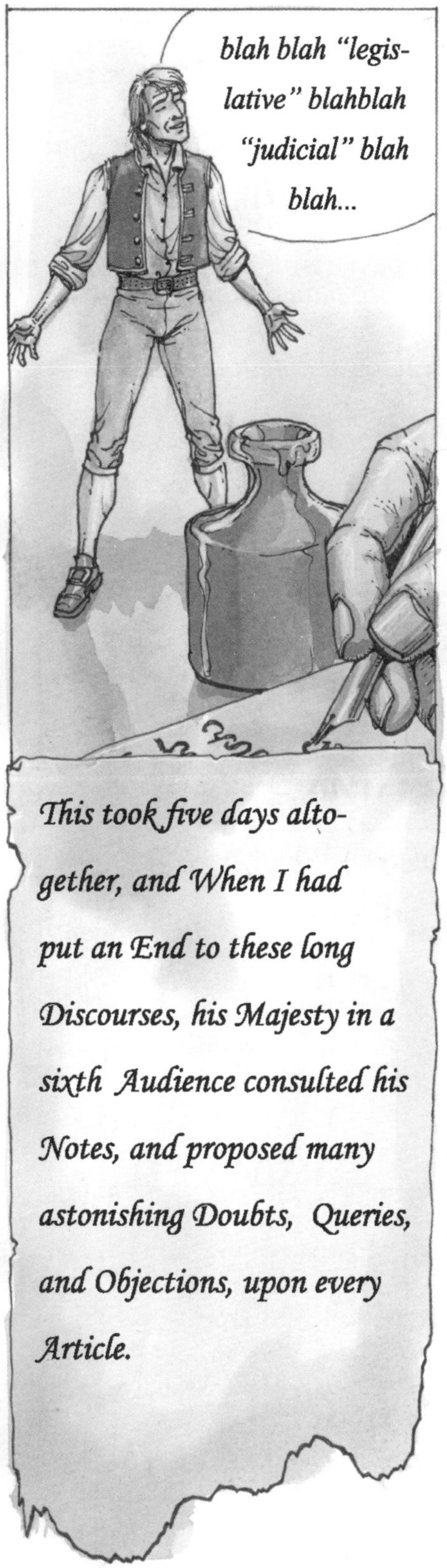
blah blah "legislative" blahblah "judicial" blah blah...
This took five days altogether, and When I had put an End to these long Discourses, his Majesty in a sixth Audience consulted his Notes, and proposed many astonishing Doubts, Queries, and Objections, upon every Article.

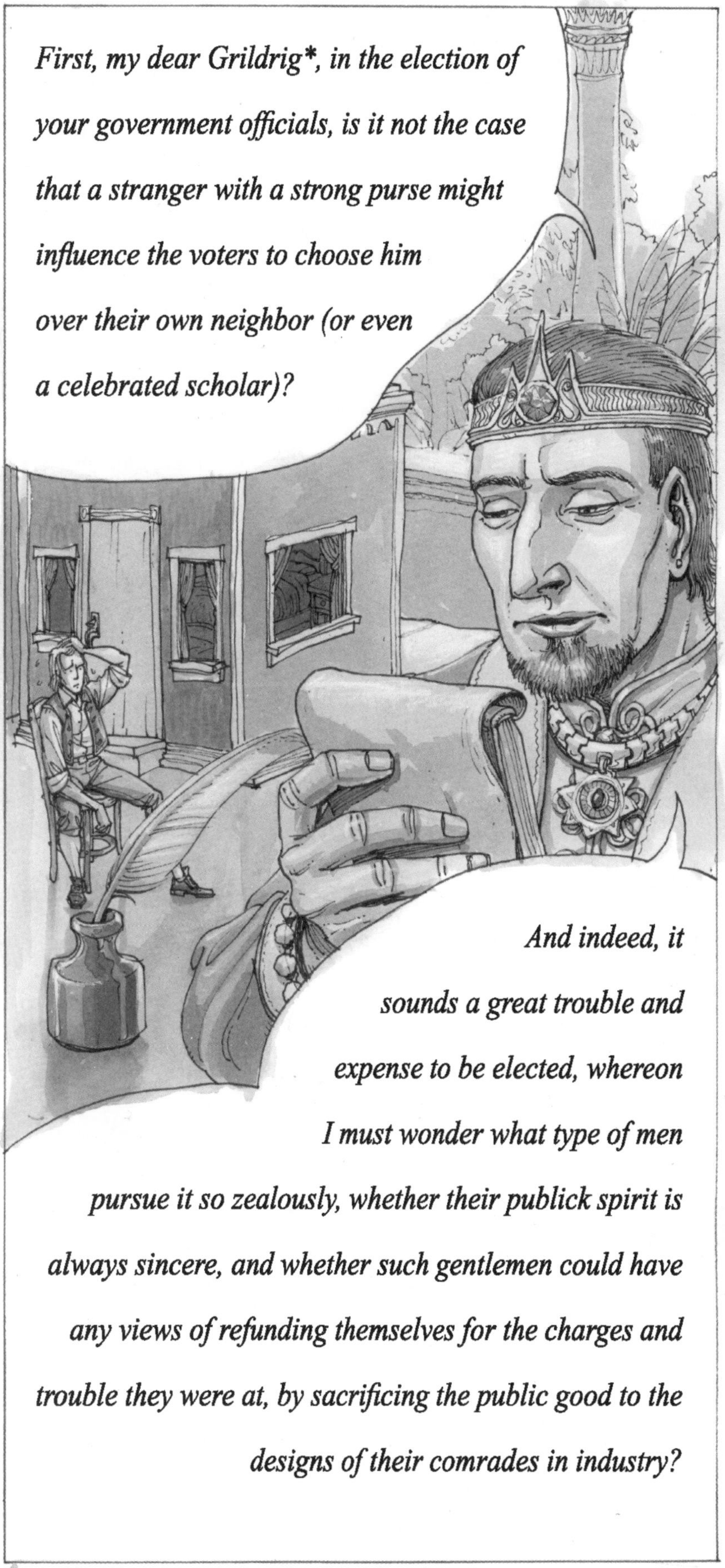
First, my dear Grildrig*, in the election of your government officials, is it not the case that a stranger with a strong purse might influence the voters to choose him over their own neighbor (or even a celebrated scholar)?
And indeed, it sounds a great trouble and expense to be elected, whereon I must wonder what type of men pursue it so zealously, whether their publick spirit is always sincere, and whether such gentlemen could have any views of refunding themselves for the charges and trouble they were at, by sacrificing the public good to the designs of their comrades in industry?

***Grildrig**, as they called me, imports what the Latins call "Nanunculus", and the English "Mannikin".*

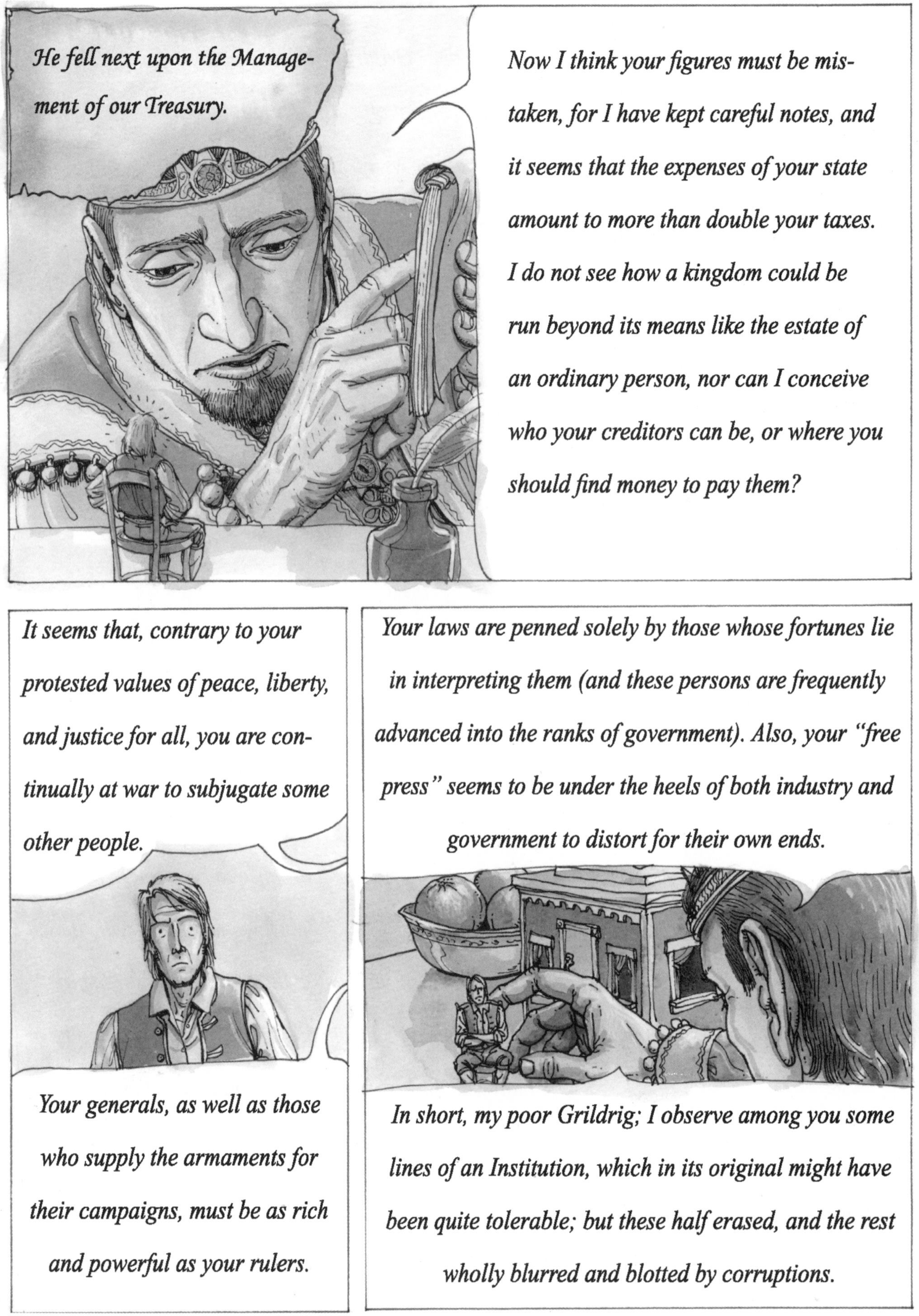

He fell next upon the Management of our Treasury.

Now I think your figures must be mistaken, for I have kept careful notes, and it seems that the expenses of your state amount to more than double your taxes. I do not see how a kingdom could be run beyond its means like the estate of an ordinary person, nor can I conceive who your creditors can be, or where you should find money to pay them?

It seems that, contrary to your protested values of peace, liberty, and justice for all, you are continually at war to subjugate some other people.

Your generals, as well as those who supply the armaments for their campaigns, must be as rich and powerful as your rulers.

Your laws are penned solely by those whose fortunes lie in interpreting them (and these persons are frequently advanced into the ranks of government). Also, your "free press" seems to be under the heels of both industry and government to distort for their own ends.

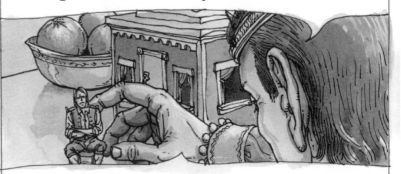

In short, my poor Grildrig; I observe among you some lines of an Institution, which in its original might have been quite tolerable; but these half erased, and the rest wholly blurred and blotted by corruptions.

I was forced to rest with Patience while my noble and most beloved Country was so injuriously treated. Yet I may be allowed to say in my own defense, that I artfully eluded many of his Questions, and gave to every Point a more favourable Turn by many Degrees than the Strictness of Truth would allow.

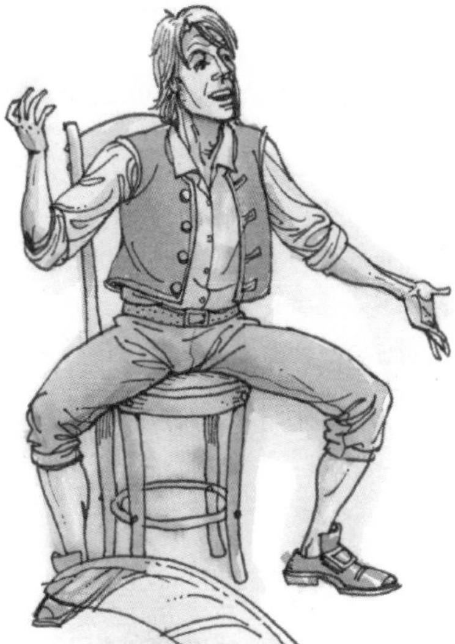

For I have always borne that laudable Partiality to my own Country, so necessary to the Historian : I would hide the Frailties and Deformities of my political Mother, and place her Virtues and Beauties in the most advantageous Light.

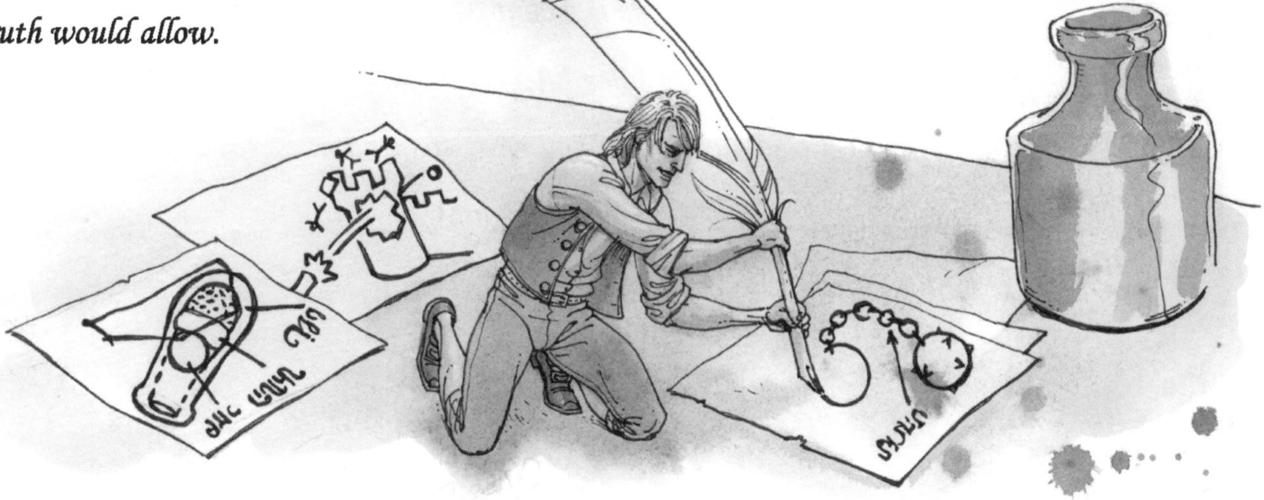

In hopes to ingratiate my self farther into his Majesty's Favour, I described to him the invention of gunpowder. I explained that a proper Quantity of this Powder rammed into a hollow Tube of Brass or Iron, according to its Bigness, would drive a Ball of Iron or Lead with such Violence and Speed, as nothing was able to sustain its Force. That the largest Balls thus discharged, would not only destroy whole Ranks of an Army at once, but batter the strongest Walls to the Ground, sink down Ships, with a Thousand Men in each, to the Bottom of the Sea; and, when linked together by a Chain, would cut through Masts and Rigging, divide hundreds of Bodies in the Middle, and lay all waste before them.

I explained that we often put this Powder into large hollow Balls of Iron, and discharged them by an Engine into some City we were besieging, which would burst and throw Shards on every Side, rip up the Pavements, tear the Houses to pieces, and dash out the Brains of all who were nearby.

I offered that I could easily direct his Engineers how to make --

Stop! This is a contrivance of some Enemy of Mankind. I command you never to mention it to anyone again!

A strange Effect of narrow Principles and short Views! But I ta this Defect among them to have risen from their ignorance, they not having ... ced Politicks int ... ... more acute ... ... ve done

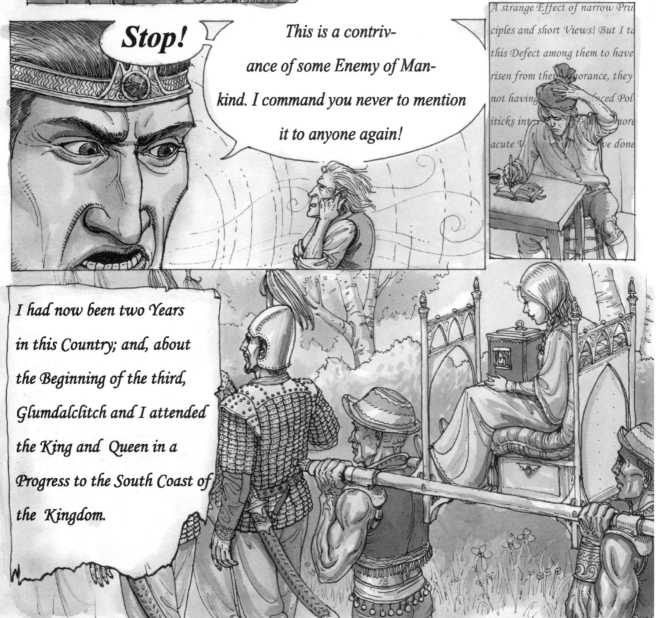

I had now been two Years in this Country; and, about the Beginning of the third, Glumdalclitch and I attended the King and Queen in a Progress to the South Coast of the Kingdom.

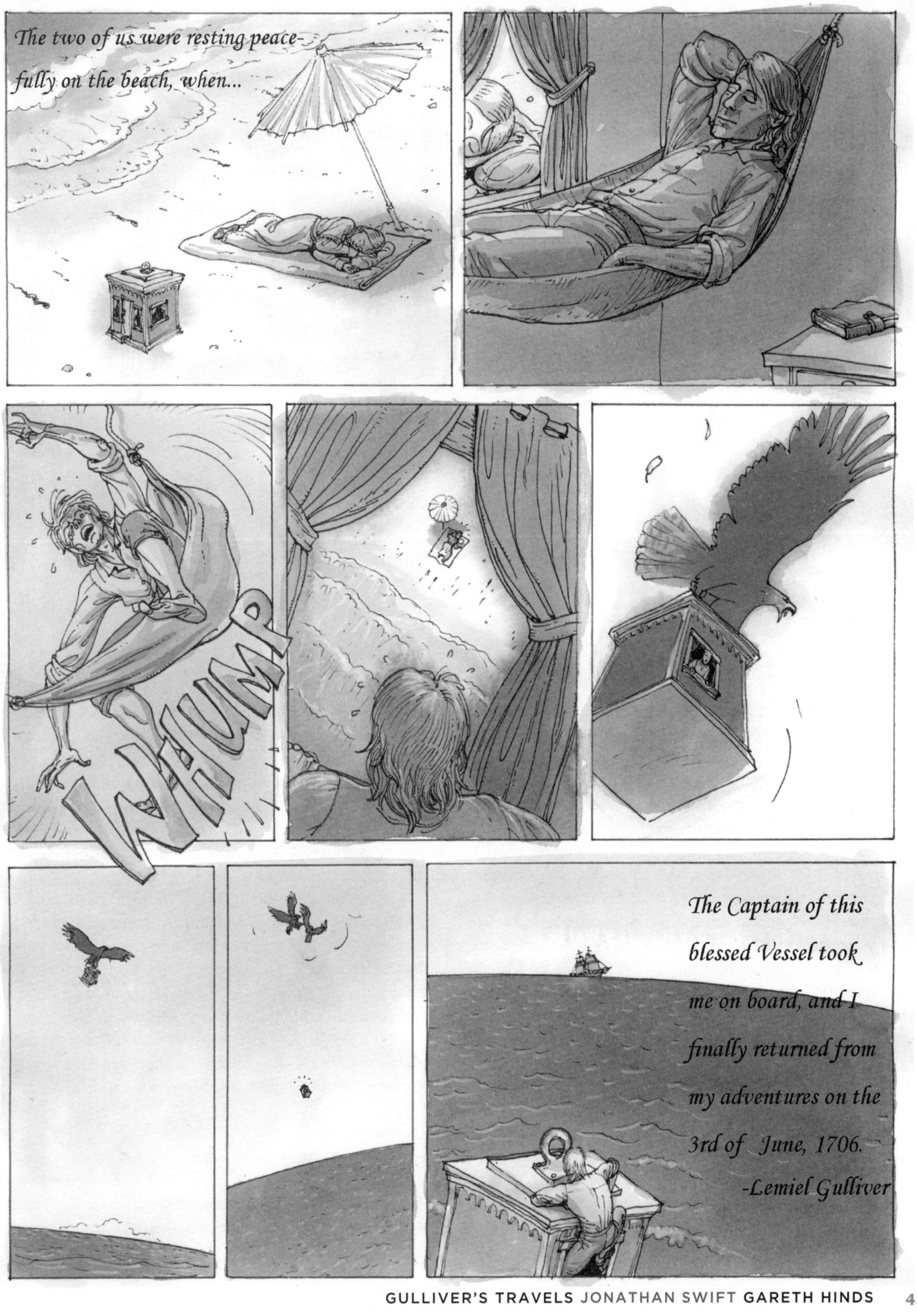
The two of us were resting peace-fully on the beach, when...
WHUMP
The Captain of this blessed Vessel took me on board, and I finally returned from my adventures on the 3rd of June, 1706.
-Lemiel Gulliver

Candide

Voltaire

ILLUSTRATIONS BY **Ian Ball**

VOLTAIRE CRANKED OUT AN ASTONISHING AMOUNT of writing—philosophical and scientific works, histories, over fifty plays, loads of pamphlets, the first epic poem written in French, and over 20,000 letters. You might picture a pale figure, crouched over a desk, locked away from the world as he writes millions of words with a quill pen, but Voltaire was a man of the world. His biting views on religion and politics got him thrown into the Bastille. His work was sometimes banned and was burned at least once. He had to flee Paris, and at another point was forced to leave France altogether. Like so many Enlightenment bigwigs, he was well laid, with the twist being that he was probably bisexual and is said to have counted his own niece and Frederick the Great of Prussia among his lovers. He agitated for human rights, including religious freedom. He swindled the French lottery. He loved to get his hands dirty gardening and farming his land.

He was obviously a complex person, and the same goes for his best-known work, the slender 1759 novella *Candide*. It's usually characterized as an all-out attack on and refutation of optimism (particularly as espoused by the German philosopher Leibniz), the idea that "this is the best of all possible worlds" because it had been created by a perfect God. Our hapless hero Candide starts as a Pollyannaish opti-

mist, but he and the other characters experience a nonstop series of ridiculously over-the-top disasters and misfortunes, and the character Pangloss (a caricature of Leibniz) always puts a positive spin on them. Candide eventually changes his outlook, but he doesn't become a pessimist. That would be far too easy. He ends up with a much more nuanced, harder to define worldview. As philosophy professor A. C. Grayling puts it, Candide becomes a quietist: "accepting things as they are, keeping out of the line of fire, and getting on with life quietly . . . no longer fretting over questions (still less endeavours) concerning the best and the worst of things."

In the following illustrations, Ian Ball captures with panache two of the novella's most famous moments: the natural disasters that befall Lisbon as Candide and Pangloss arrive by boat, and the passage in which Pangloss traces the lineage of his syphilis, from the chambermaid who gave it to him, back to Columbus's crew.

SOURCES

Grayling, A. C. "Voltaire's *Candide, or Optimism*." Penguin Classics UK website.

Voltaire. *Candide and Related Texts*. Translated and introduced by David Wootton. Indianapolis, IN: Hackett Publishing Company, 2000.

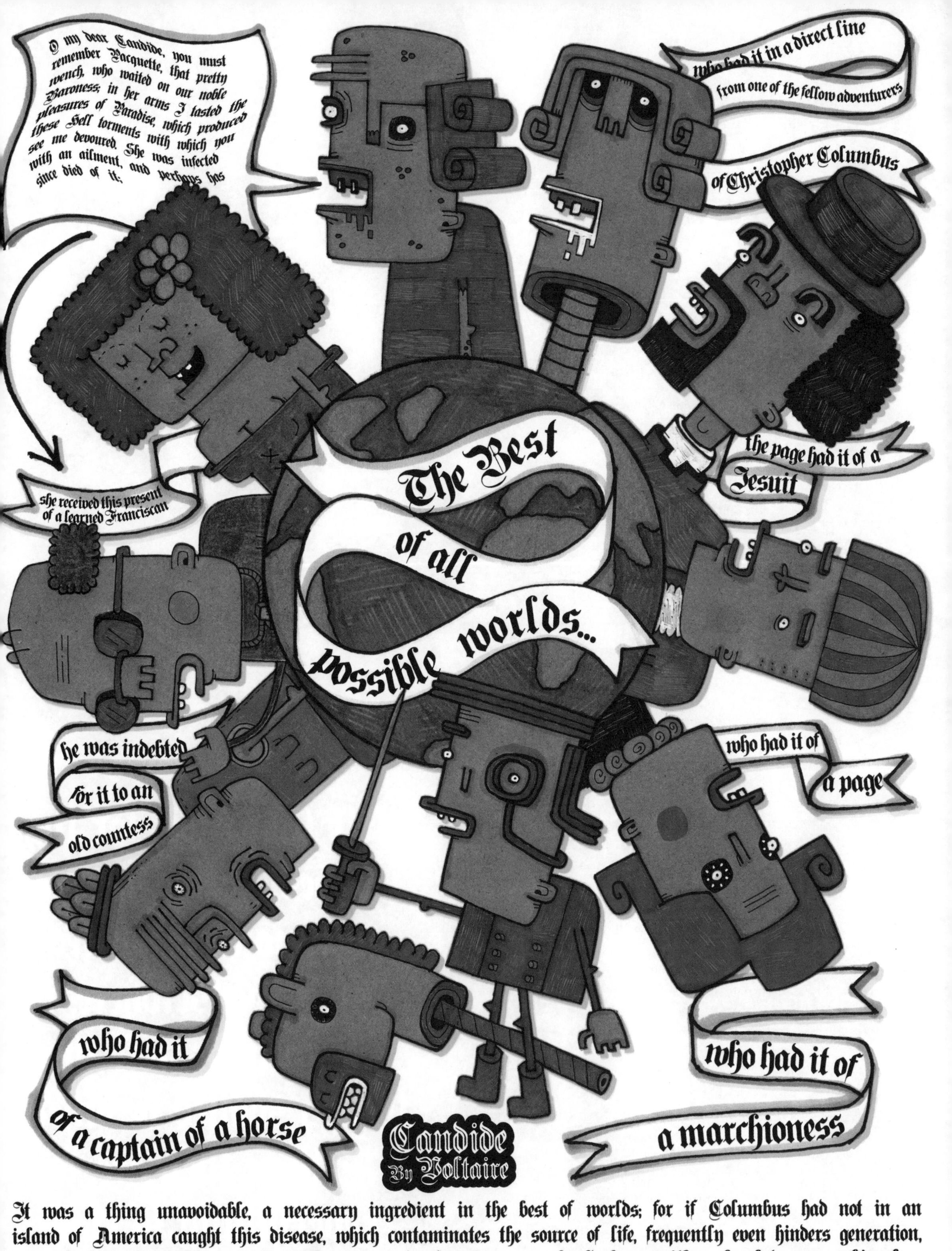

O my dear Candide, you must remember Pacquette, that pretty wench, who waited on our noble Baroness; in her arms I tasted the pleasures of Paradise, which produced these Hell torments with which you see me devoured. She was infected with an ailment, and perhaps has since died of it;
The Best of all possible worlds...
she received this present of a learned Franciscan
he was indebted for it to an old countess
who had it of a captain of a horse
who had it of a marchioness
who had it of a page
the page had it of a Jesuit
who had it in a direct line from one of the fellow adventurers of Christopher Columbus
Candide By Voltaire

It was a thing unavoidable, a necessary ingredient in the best of worlds; for if Columbus had not in an island of America caught this disease, which contaminates the source of life, frequently even hinders generation, and which is evidently opposed to the great end of nature, we should have neither chocolate nor cochineal.

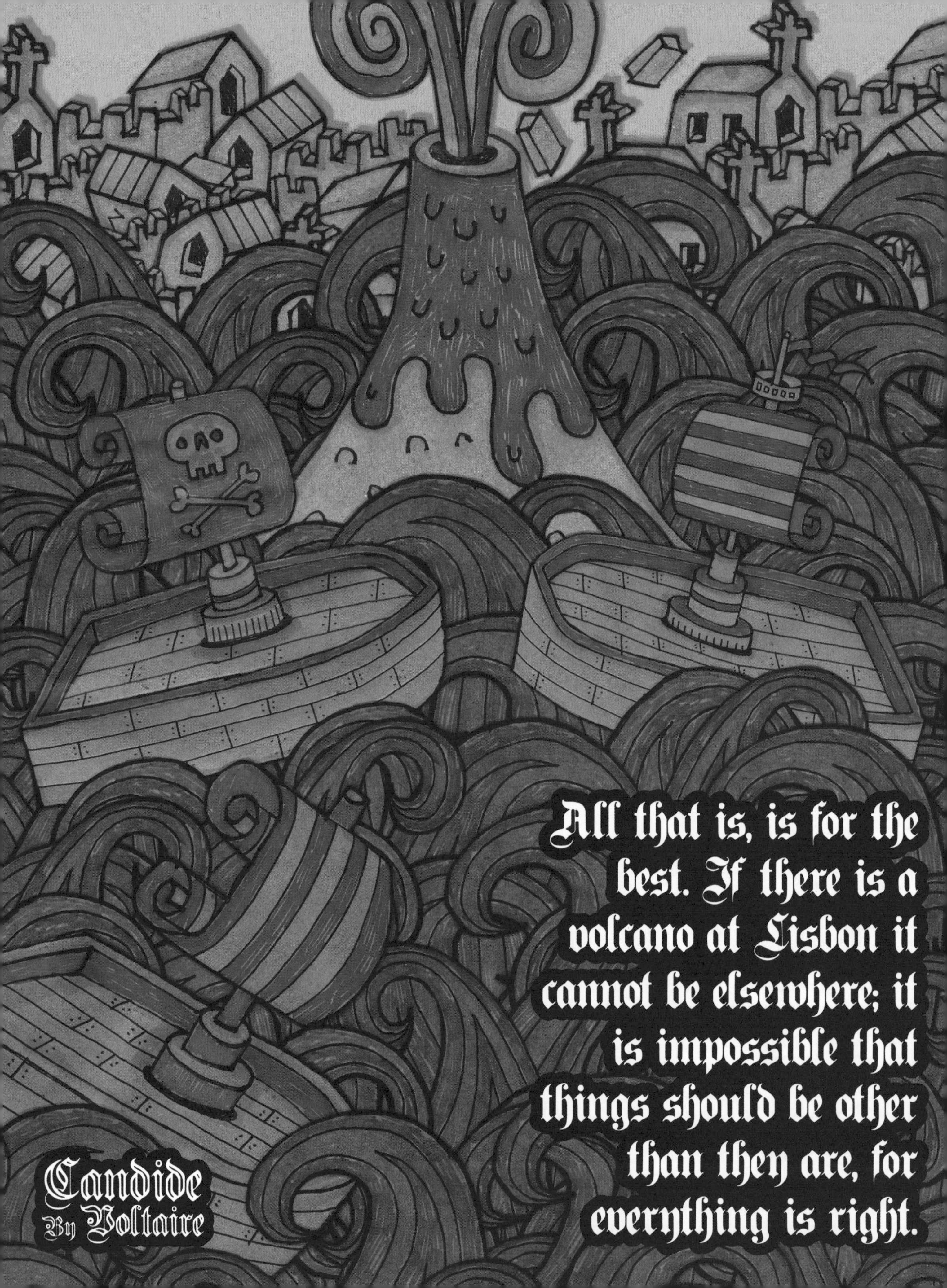
All that is, is for the best. If there is a volcano at Lisbon it cannot be elsewhere; it is impossible that things should be other than they are, for everything is right.
Candide
By Voltaire

"A Modest Proposal"

Jonathan Swift

ART / ADAPTATION BY **Peter Kuper**

IN 1729, AMONG THE MANY PAMPHLETS OFFERED for sale in the book stalls of London and elsewhere, was one titled "A Modest Proposal for Preventing the Children of Poor People in Ireland From Being a Burden on Their Parents or Country, and for Making Them Beneficial to the Publick." The anonymous author suggested that the destitute people of Ireland sell their infants as food to rich people in Britain.

There was very little, if any, intimation that the pamphleteer was joking. He presented culinary, financial, and moral details about his plan. The British government had subjected the people of Ireland to inhumane economic deprivation and political oppression. This pamphlet simply took the situation to its logical extreme.

As the world now knows, the writer was Enlightenment wit Jonathan Swift, the master of satire, and his essay is now a staple of undergrad literature courses teaching irony. Like most of Swift's scathing writing, "A Modest Proposal" still stings today. He may have been focusing on Ireland and Britain in the early eighteenth century, but his overall message applies to the US and many other countries in the twenty-first. Indeed, Peter Kuper—himself a specialist in using his art to make withering sociopolitical commentary—has brought the proposal into the present.

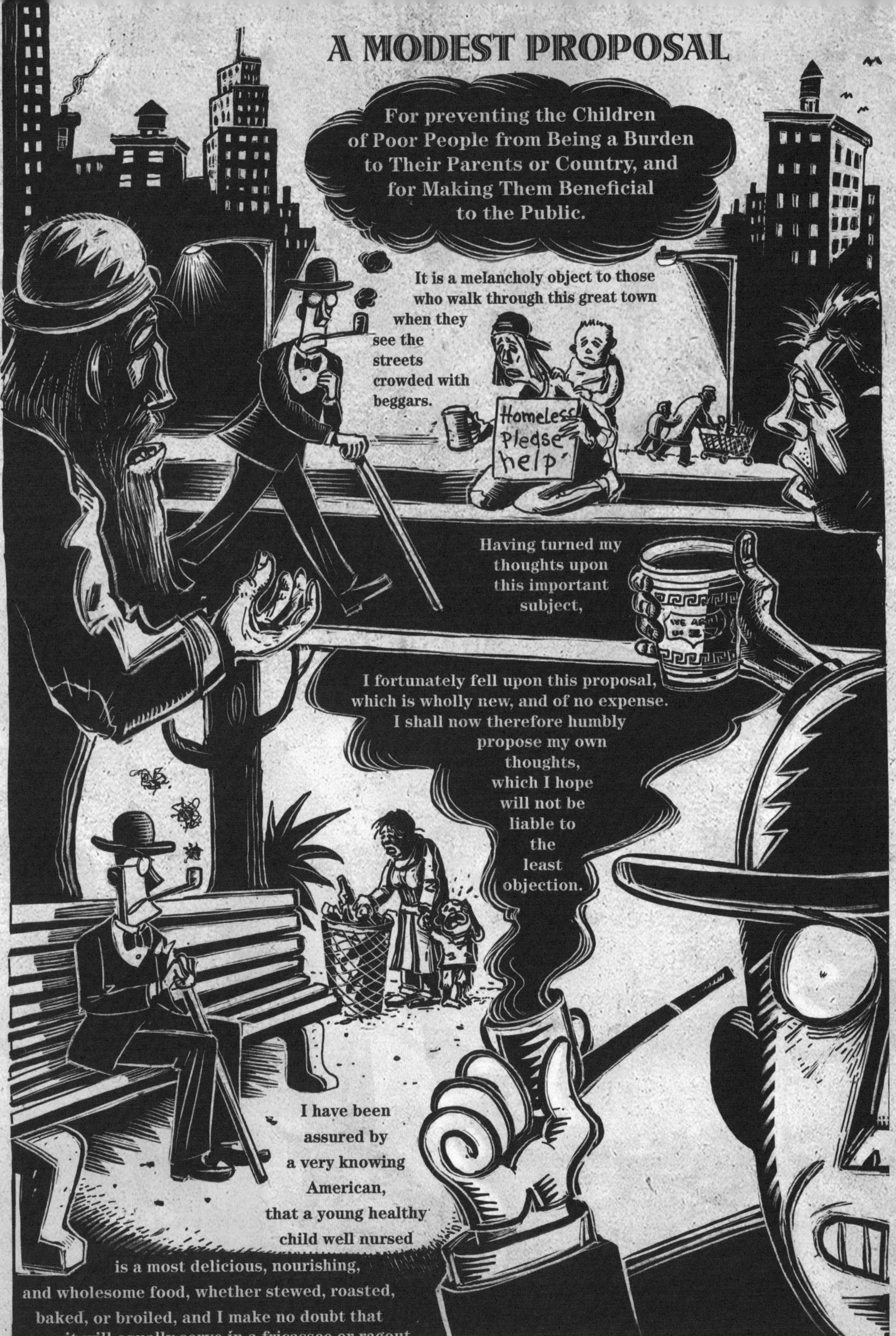
A MODEST PROPOSAL
For preventing the Children of Poor People from Being a Burden to Their Parents or Country, and for Making Them Beneficial to the Public.
It is a melancholy object to those who walk through this great town when they see the streets crowded with beggars.
Homeless Please help
Having turned my thoughts upon this important subject,
I fortunately fell upon this proposal, which is wholly new, and of no expense. I shall now therefore humbly propose my own thoughts, which I hope will not be liable to the least objection.
I have been assured by a very knowing American, that a young healthy child well nursed is a most delicious, nourishing, and wholesome food, whether stewed, roasted, baked, or broiled, and I make no doubt that it will equally serve in a fricassee or ragout.

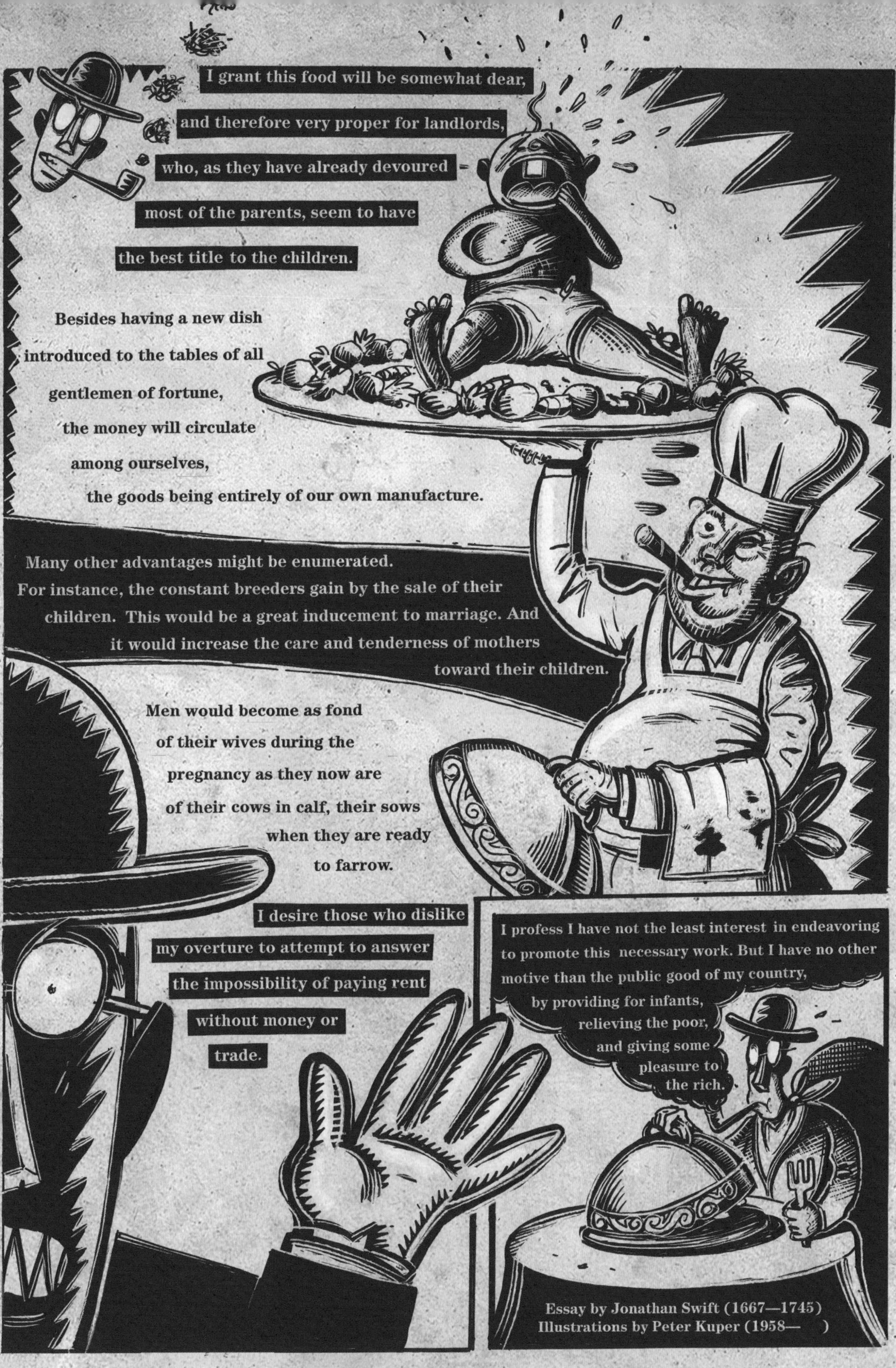

I grant this food will be somewhat dear,
and therefore very proper for landlords,
who, as they have already devoured
most of the parents, seem to have
the best title to the children.
Besides having a new dish
introduced to the tables of all
gentlemen of fortune,
the money will circulate
among ourselves,
the goods being entirely of our own manufacture.
Many other advantages might be enumerated.
For instance, the constant breeders gain by the sale of their
children. This would be a great inducement to marriage. And
it would increase the care and tenderness of mothers
toward their children.
Men would become as fond
of their wives during the
pregnancy as they now are
of their cows in calf, their sows
when they are ready
to farrow.
I desire those who dislike
my overture to attempt to answer
the impossibility of paying rent
without money or
trade.
I profess I have not the least interest in endeavoring
to promote this necessary work. But I have no other
motive than the public good of my country,
by providing for infants,
relieving the poor,
and giving some
pleasure to
the rich.
Essay by Jonathan Swift (1667—1745)
Illustrations by Peter Kuper (1958—)

"Advice to a Young Man on the Choice of a Mistress"

Benjamin Franklin

PAINTING BY **Cortney Skinner**

DOES BENJAMIN FRANKLIN NEED INTRODUCING? In some ways, yes. The image we have of him from our schooling is incomplete. Not surprising when you consider that he was a polymath, a Renaissance man, the United States' main contributor to the Enlightenment (along with Thomas Jefferson), a scientist-inventor-philosopher-publisher-ambassador-Lothario whose collected papers will fill *forty-seven* chunky volumes when Yale University Press finally publishes them all (they started in 1959 and still aren't done).

Like so many of his Enlightenment brethren (such as Swift, Voltaire, and Boswell), Franklin had a bawdy side, and *The Graphic Canon* is here to present it. In 1745, he wrote a mock letter meant for circulation among the dudes he knew, in which he enumerates the virtues of sex with older women. The letter made the rounds through surreptitious channels for 180 years before being openly published in 1926. Yale has included it in volume three of Franklin's *Papers*.

Cortney Skinner is no stranger to painting historical subjects, as well as landscapes, military, horror, and sci-fi. Here he gives us a faithful, meticulously detailed (each of those bricks was painted by hand!) vision of a young man of the times putting Franklin's advice into practice. Or at least that's the plan. . . .

My dear Friend,

I know of no Medicine fit to diminish the violent natural Inclinations you mention; and if I did, I think I should not communicate it to you. Marriage is the proper Remedy. It is the most natural State of Man, and therefore the State in which you are most likely to find solid Happiness. Your Reasons against entring into it at present, appear to me not well-founded. The cirmcumstantial Advantages you have in View by postponing it, are not only uncertain, but they are small in comparison with that of the Thing itself, the being *married and settled*. It is the Man and Woman united that make the compleat human Being. Separate, she wants his Force of Body and Strength of Reason; he, her Softness, Sensibility and acute Discernment. Together they are more likely to succeed in the World. A single Man has not nearly the Value he would have in that State of Union. He is an incomplete Animal. He resembles the odd Half of a Pair of Scissars. If you get a prudent healthy Wife, your Industry in your Profession, with her good Oeconomy, will be a Fortune sufficient.

But if you will not take this Counsel, and persist in thinking a Commerce with the Sex inevitable, then I repeat my former Advice, that in all your Amours you should *prefer old Women to young ones*. You call this a Paradox, and demand my Reasons. They are these:

1. Because as they have more Knowledge of the World and their Minds are better stor'd with Observations, their Conversation is more improving and more lastingly agreable.

2. Because when Women cease to be handsome, they study to be good. To maintain their Influence over Men, they supply the Diminution of Beauty by an Augmentation of Utility. They learn to do a 1000 Services small and great, and are the most tender and useful of all Friends when you are sick. Thus they continue amiable. And hence there is hardly such a thing to be found as an old Woman who is not a good Woman.

3. Because there is no hazard of Children, which irregularly produc'd may be attended with much Inconvenience.

4. Because thro' more Experience, they are more prudent and discreet in conducting an Intrigue to prevent Suspicion. The Commerce with them is therefore safer with regard to your Reputation. And with regard to theirs, if the Affair should happen to be known, considerate People might be rather inclin'd to excuse an old Woman who would kindly take care of a young Man, form his Manners by her good Counsels, and prevent his ruining his Health and Fortune among mercenary Prostitutes.

5. Because in every Animal that walks upright, the Deficiency of the Fluids that fill the Muscles appears first in the highest Part: The Face first grows lank and wrinkled; then the Neck; then the Breast and Arms; the lower Parts continuing to the last as plump as ever: So that covering all above with a Basket, and regarding only what is below the Girdle, it is impossible of two Women to know an old from a young one. And as in the dark all Cats are grey, the Pleasure of corporal Enjoyment with an old Woman is at least equal, and frequently superior, every Knack being by Practice capable of Improvement.

6. Because the Sin is less. The debauching a Virgin may be her Ruin, and make her for Life unhappy.

7. Because the Compunction is less. The having made a young Girl *miserable* may give you frequent bitter Reflections; none of which can attend the making an old Woman happy.

8thly and Lastly. They are *so grateful!!* Thus much for my Paradox. But still I advise you to marry directly; being sincerely Your affectionate Friend.

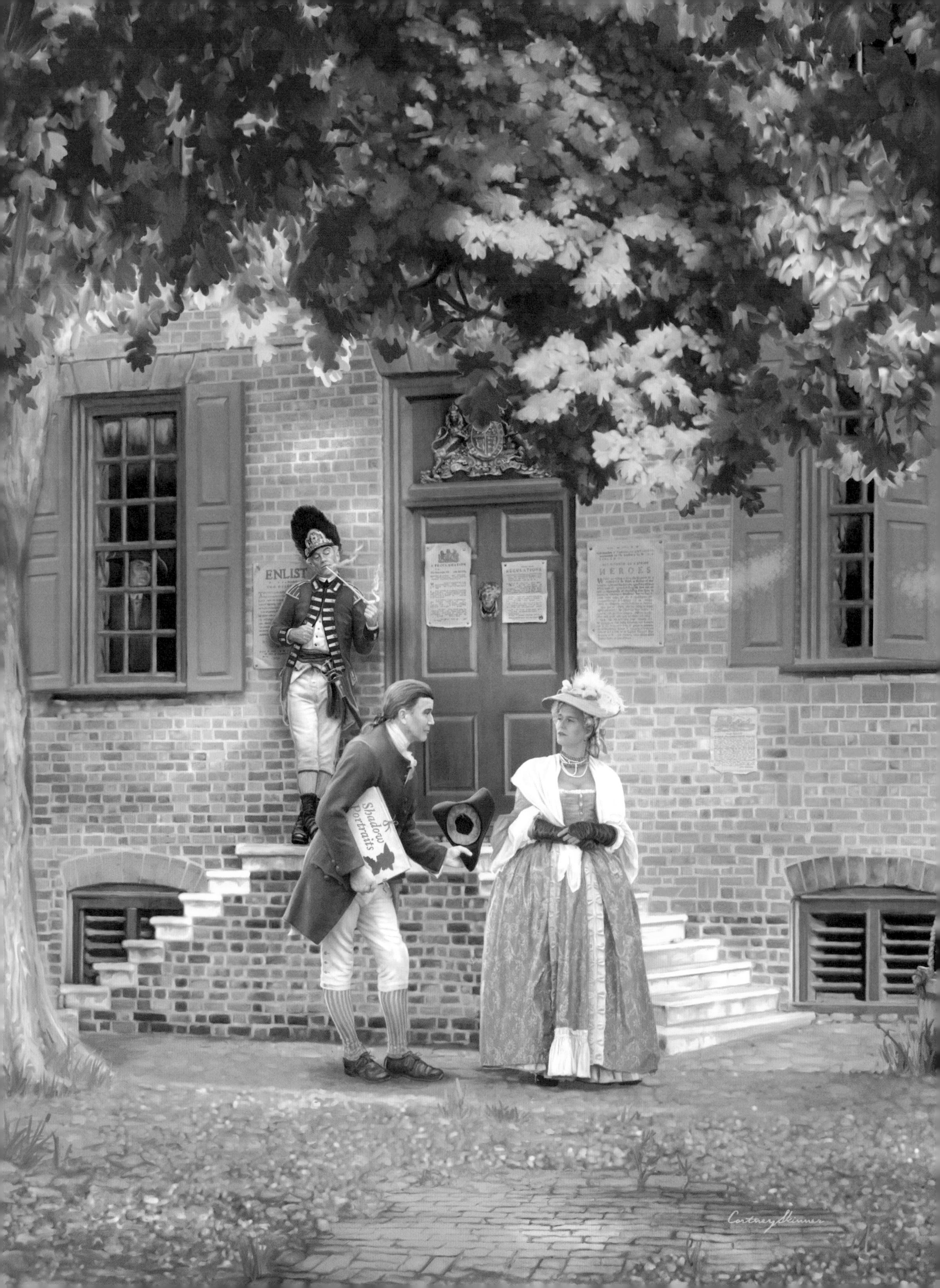
ENLIST
A PROCLAMATION
REGULATIONS
HEROES
Shadow Portraits
CortneySkinner

London Journal

James Boswell

ART / ADAPTATION BY **Robert Crumb**

THE EIGHTEENTH-CENTURY SCOTSMAN JAMES Boswell was a lawyer, writer, intellectual, and libertine with a lifelong habit of overindulging in wine, sex, and gambling. He penned what is widely considered the greatest biography in literature, *Life of Johnson*, about his friend Samuel Johnson, one of Britain's greatest literary lights and creator of one of the most important dictionaries of the English language.

Boswell also kept extensive journals/diaries throughout his life. Because he included his dissolute activities, along with his interactions with leading intellectuals of the day, his heirs refused to allow their publication. They were considered a family embarrassment, yet, luckily, Boswell's various descendants couldn't bring themselves to destroy what they knew was a literary treasure trove. The voluminous papers spent around 130 years in dresser drawers, trunks in an abandoned outhouse, and—in the case of the *London Journal*—a croquet box. It was only in the 1920s that Boswell's life's work was rescued by outsiders and preserved at Yale.

London Journal covers the period from November 1762 to the following August, and includes perhaps the most significant event of his life, his meeting Samuel Johnson.

I would assume that Robert Crumb needs no introduction to most readers of this anthology. Literally a legend in his own time, he's the most prominent of the first generation of underground comics artists, and his popularity and output show no signs of flagging. (How many people could buy a house in the South of France in exchange for one of his own sketchbooks?) He has adapted several classic works of literature (Sartre's *Nausea* will be in Volume Three of this collection), and with Boswell he has found a subject who alternates sexual and intellectual pursuits.

SOURCES

Boswell, James. *Boswell's London Journal*, 1762–1763. Frederick Pottle (editor). Preface by Christopher Morley. Yale University Press, 1992.

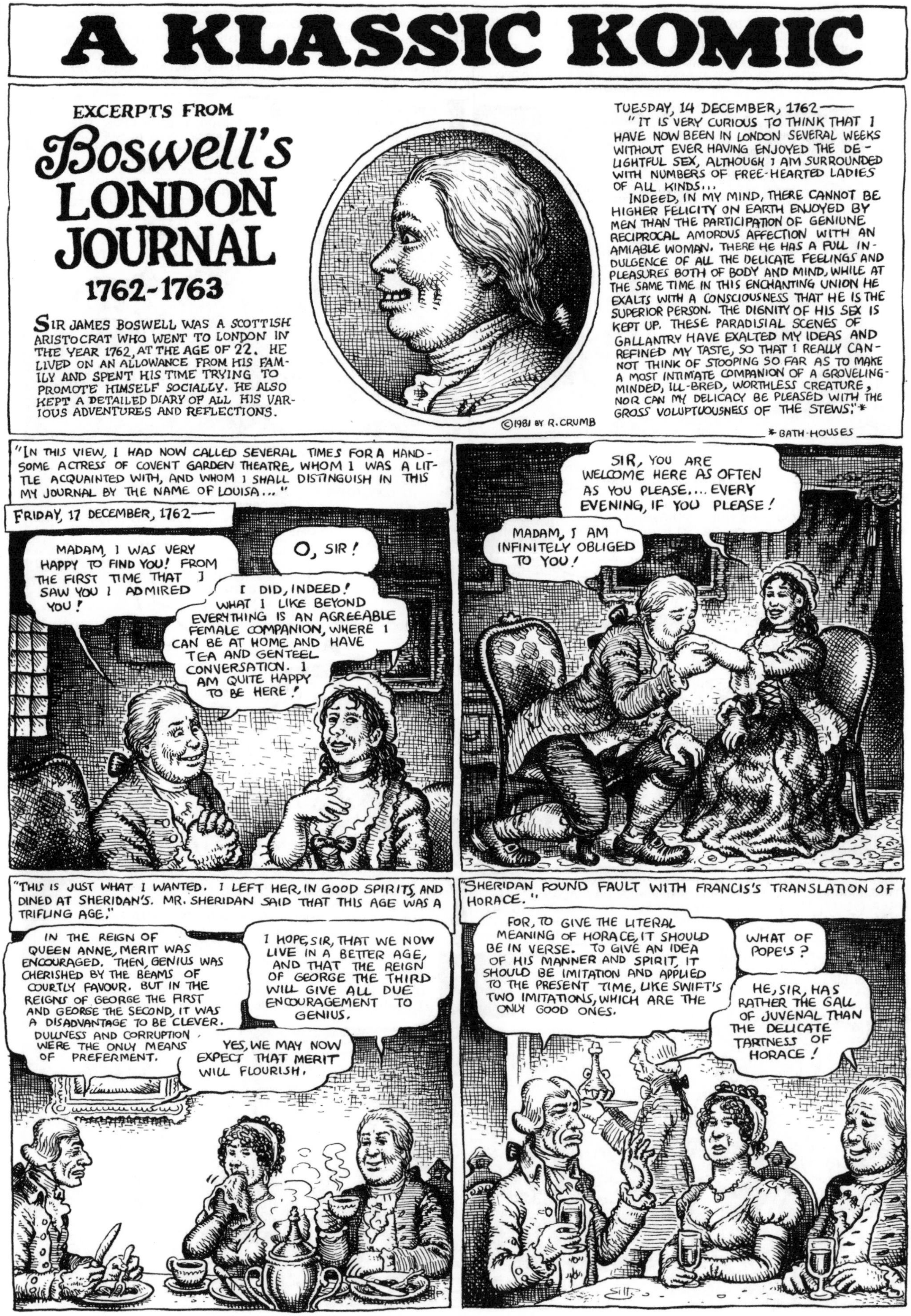

A KLASSIC KOMIC
EXCERPTS FROM
Boswell's LONDON JOURNAL
1762-1763
SIR JAMES BOSWELL WAS A SCOTTISH ARISTOCRAT WHO WENT TO LONDON IN THE YEAR 1762, AT THE AGE OF 22. HE LIVED ON AN ALLOWANCE FROM HIS FAMILY AND SPENT HIS TIME TRYING TO PROMOTE HIMSELF SOCIALLY. HE ALSO KEPT A DETAILED DIARY OF ALL HIS VARIOUS ADVENTURES AND REFLECTIONS.
©1981 BY R. CRUMB
TUESDAY, 14 DECEMBER, 1762—
"IT IS VERY CURIOUS TO THINK THAT I HAVE NOW BEEN IN LONDON SEVERAL WEEKS WITHOUT EVER HAVING ENJOYED THE DELIGHTFUL SEX, ALTHOUGH I AM SURROUNDED WITH NUMBERS OF FREE-HEARTED LADIES OF ALL KINDS...
INDEED, IN MY MIND, THERE CANNOT BE HIGHER FELICITY ON EARTH ENJOYED BY MEN THAN THE PARTICIPATION OF GENUINE RECIPROCAL AMOROUS AFFECTION WITH AN AMIABLE WOMAN. THERE HE HAS A FULL INDULGENCE OF ALL THE DELICATE FEELINGS AND PLEASURES BOTH OF BODY AND MIND, WHILE AT THE SAME TIME IN THIS ENCHANTING UNION HE EXALTS WITH A CONSCIOUSNESS THAT HE IS THE SUPERIOR PERSON. THE DIGNITY OF HIS SEX IS KEPT UP. THESE PARADISIAL SCENES OF GALLANTRY HAVE EXALTED MY IDEAS AND REFINED MY TASTE, SO THAT I REALLY CANNOT THINK OF STOOPING SO FAR AS TO MAKE A MOST INTIMATE COMPANION OF A GROVELING-MINDED, ILL-BRED, WORTHLESS CREATURE, NOR CAN MY DELICACY BE PLEASED WITH THE GROSS VOLUPTUOUSNESS OF THE STEWS."*
* BATH-HOUSES
"IN THIS VIEW, I HAD NOW CALLED SEVERAL TIMES FOR A HANDSOME ACTRESS OF COVENT GARDEN THEATRE, WHOM I WAS A LITTLE ACQUAINTED WITH, AND WHOM I SHALL DISTINGUISH IN THIS MY JOURNAL BY THE NAME OF LOUISA..."
FRIDAY, 17 DECEMBER, 1762—
MADAM, I WAS VERY HAPPY TO FIND YOU! FROM THE FIRST TIME THAT I SAW YOU I ADMIRED YOU!
O, SIR!
I DID, INDEED! WHAT I LIKE BEYOND EVERYTHING IS AN AGREEABLE FEMALE COMPANION, WHERE I CAN BE AT HOME AND HAVE TEA AND GENTEEL CONVERSATION. I AM QUITE HAPPY TO BE HERE!
SIR, YOU ARE WELCOME HERE AS OFTEN AS YOU PLEASE.... EVERY EVENING, IF YOU PLEASE!
MADAM, I AM INFINITELY OBLIGED TO YOU!
"THIS IS JUST WHAT I WANTED. I LEFT HER IN GOOD SPIRITS, AND DINED AT SHERIDAN'S. MR. SHERIDAN SAID THAT THIS AGE WAS A TRIFLING AGE."
IN THE REIGN OF QUEEN ANNE, MERIT WAS ENCOURAGED. THEN, GENIUS WAS CHERISHED BY THE BEAMS OF COURTLY FAVOUR. BUT IN THE REIGNS OF GEORGE THE FIRST AND GEORGE THE SECOND, IT WAS A DISADVANTAGE TO BE CLEVER. DULLNESS AND CORRUPTION WERE THE ONLY MEANS OF PREFERMENT.
I HOPE, SIR, THAT WE NOW LIVE IN A BETTER AGE, AND THAT THE REIGN OF GEORGE THE THIRD WILL GIVE ALL DUE ENCOURAGEMENT TO GENIUS.
YES, WE MAY NOW EXPECT THAT MERIT WILL FLOURISH.
"SHERIDAN FOUND FAULT WITH FRANCIS'S TRANSLATION OF HORACE."
FOR, TO GIVE THE LITERAL MEANING OF HORACE, IT SHOULD BE IN VERSE. TO GIVE AN IDEA OF HIS MANNER AND SPIRIT, IT SHOULD BE IMITATION AND APPLIED TO THE PRESENT TIME, LIKE SWIFT'S TWO IMITATIONS, WHICH ARE THE ONLY GOOD ONES.
WHAT OF POPE'S?
HE, SIR, HAS RATHER THE GALL OF JUVENAL THAN THE DELICATE TARTNESS OF HORACE!

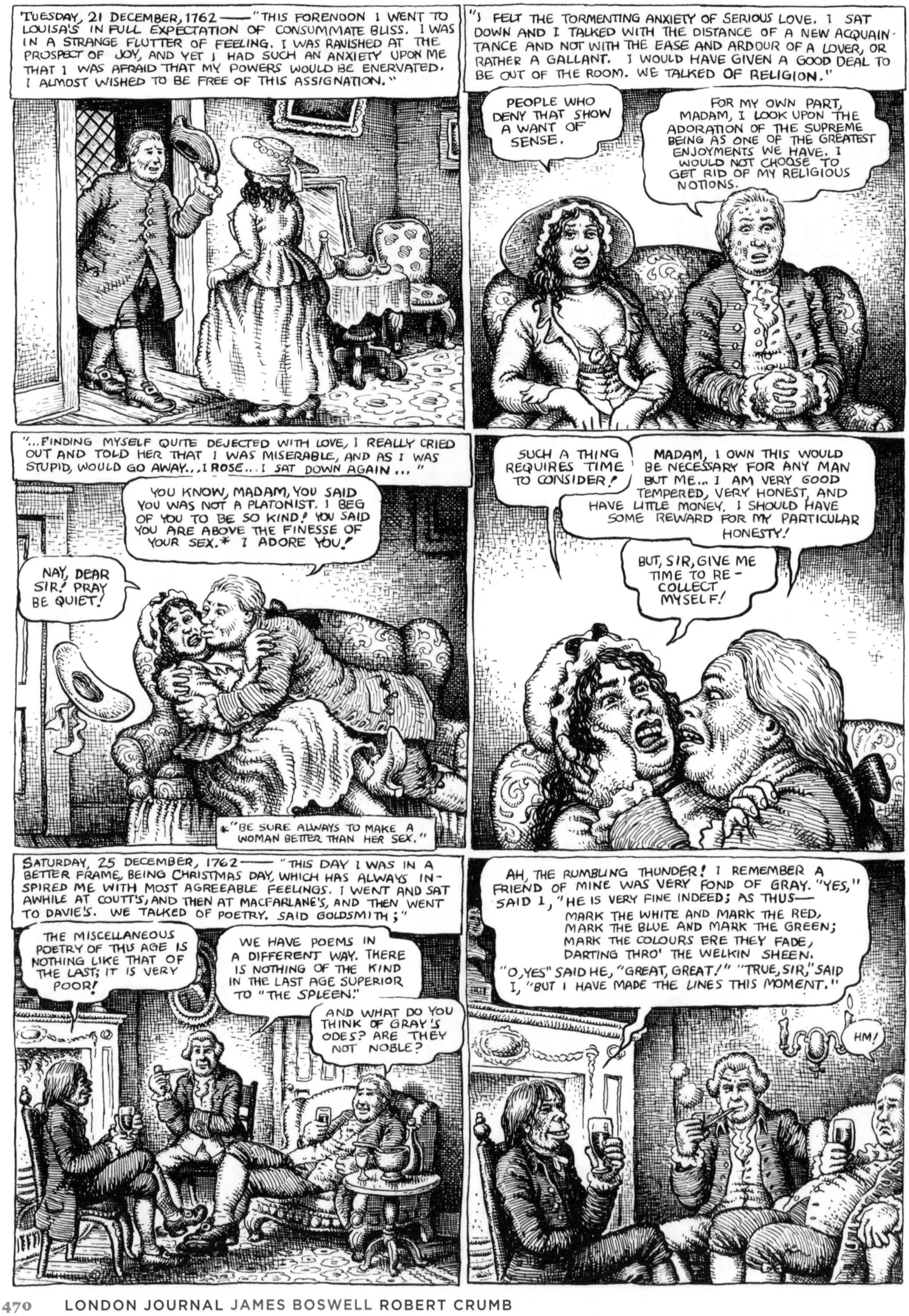
TUESDAY, 21 DECEMBER, 1762 —— "THIS FORENOON I WENT TO LOUISA'S IN FULL EXPECTATION OF CONSUMMATE BLISS. I WAS IN A STRANGE FLUTTER OF FEELING. I WAS RAVISHED AT THE PROSPECT OF JOY, AND YET I HAD SUCH AN ANXIETY UPON ME THAT I WAS AFRAID THAT MY POWERS WOULD BE ENERVATED. I ALMOST WISHED TO BE FREE OF THIS ASSIGNATION."
"I FELT THE TORMENTING ANXIETY OF SERIOUS LOVE. I SAT DOWN AND I TALKED WITH THE DISTANCE OF A NEW ACQUAINTANCE AND NOT WITH THE EASE AND ARDOUR OF A LOVER, OR RATHER A GALLANT. I WOULD HAVE GIVEN A GOOD DEAL TO BE OUT OF THE ROOM. WE TALKED OF RELIGION."
PEOPLE WHO DENY THAT SHOW A WANT OF SENSE.
FOR MY OWN PART, MADAM, I LOOK UPON THE ADORATION OF THE SUPREME BEING AS ONE OF THE GREATEST ENJOYMENTS WE HAVE. I WOULD NOT CHOOSE TO GET RID OF MY RELIGIOUS NOTIONS.
"...FINDING MYSELF QUITE DEJECTED WITH LOVE, I REALLY CRIED OUT AND TOLD HER THAT I WAS MISERABLE, AND AS I WAS STUPID, WOULD GO AWAY... I ROSE... I SAT DOWN AGAIN..."
YOU KNOW, MADAM, YOU SAID YOU WAS NOT A PLATONIST. I BEG OF YOU TO BE SO KIND! YOU SAID YOU ARE ABOVE THE FINESSE OF YOUR SEX.* I ADORE YOU!
NAY, DEAR SIR! PRAY BE QUIET!
*"BE SURE ALWAYS TO MAKE A WOMAN BETTER THAN HER SEX."
SUCH A THING REQUIRES TIME TO CONSIDER!
MADAM, I OWN THIS WOULD BE NECESSARY FOR ANY MAN BUT ME... I AM VERY GOOD TEMPERED, VERY HONEST, AND HAVE LITTLE MONEY. I SHOULD HAVE SOME REWARD FOR MY PARTICULAR HONESTY!
BUT, SIR, GIVE ME TIME TO RE-COLLECT MYSELF!
SATURDAY, 25 DECEMBER, 1762 —— "THIS DAY I WAS IN A BETTER FRAME, BEING CHRISTMAS DAY, WHICH HAS ALWAYS INSPIRED ME WITH MOST AGREEABLE FEELINGS. I WENT AND SAT AWHILE AT COUTT'S, AND THEN AT MACFARLANE'S, AND THEN WENT TO DAVIE'S. WE TALKED OF POETRY. SAID GOLDSMITH;"
THE MISCELLANEOUS POETRY OF THIS AGE IS NOTHING LIKE THAT OF THE LAST; IT IS VERY POOR!
WE HAVE POEMS IN A DIFFERENT WAY. THERE IS NOTHING OF THE KIND IN THE LAST AGE SUPERIOR TO "THE SPLEEN."
AND WHAT DO YOU THINK OF GRAY'S ODES? ARE THEY NOT NOBLE?
AH, THE RUMBLING THUNDER! I REMEMBER A FRIEND OF MINE WAS VERY FOND OF GRAY. "YES," SAID I, "HE IS VERY FINE INDEED; AS THUS—
MARK THE WHITE AND MARK THE RED,
MARK THE BLUE AND MARK THE GREEN;
MARK THE COLOURS ERE THEY FADE,
DARTING THRO' THE WELKIN SHEEN.
"O, YES" SAID HE, "GREAT, GREAT!" "TRUE, SIR," SAID I, "BUT I HAVE MADE THE LINES THIS MOMENT."
HM!

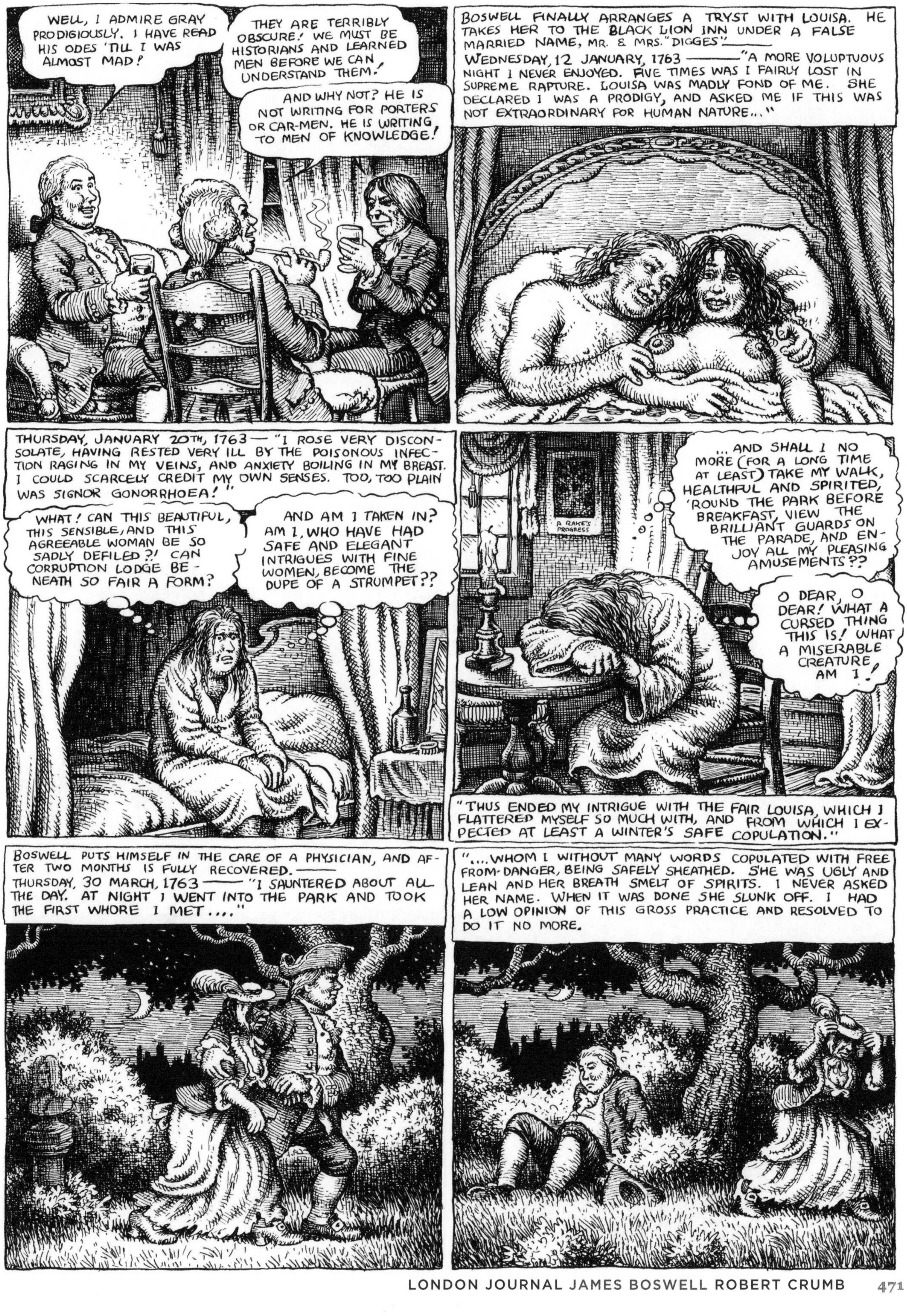
WELL, I ADMIRE GRAY PRODIGIOUSLY. I HAVE READ HIS ODES 'TILL I WAS ALMOST MAD!
THEY ARE TERRIBLY OBSCURE! WE MUST BE HISTORIANS AND LEARNED MEN BEFORE WE CAN UNDERSTAND THEM!
AND WHY NOT? HE IS NOT WRITING FOR PORTERS OR CAR-MEN. HE IS WRITING TO MEN OF KNOWLEDGE!
BOSWELL FINALLY ARRANGES A TRYST WITH LOUISA. HE TAKES HER TO THE BLACK LION INN UNDER A FALSE MARRIED NAME, MR. & MRS. "DIGGES"——
WEDNESDAY, 12 JANUARY, 1763 ——— "A MORE VOLUPTUOUS NIGHT I NEVER ENJOYED. FIVE TIMES WAS I FAIRLY LOST IN SUPREME RAPTURE. LOUISA WAS MADLY FOND OF ME. SHE DECLARED I WAS A PRODIGY, AND ASKED ME IF THIS WAS NOT EXTRAORDINARY FOR HUMAN NATURE..."
THURSDAY, JANUARY 20TH, 1763— "I ROSE VERY DISCONSOLATE, HAVING RESTED VERY ILL BY THE POISONOUS INFECTION RAGING IN MY VEINS, AND ANXIETY BOILING IN MY BREAST. I COULD SCARCELY CREDIT MY OWN SENSES. TOO, TOO PLAIN WAS SIGNOR GONORRHOEA!"
WHAT! CAN THIS BEAUTIFUL, THIS SENSIBLE, AND THIS AGREEABLE WOMAN BE SO SADLY DEFILED?! CAN CORRUPTION LODGE BENEATH SO FAIR A FORM?
AND AM I TAKEN IN? AM I, WHO HAVE HAD SAFE AND ELEGANT INTRIGUES WITH FINE WOMEN, BECOME THE DUPE OF A STRUMPET??
A RAKE'S PROGRESS
... AND SHALL I NO MORE (FOR A LONG TIME AT LEAST) TAKE MY WALK, HEALTHFUL AND SPIRITED, 'ROUND THE PARK BEFORE BREAKFAST, VIEW THE BRILLIANT GUARDS ON THE PARADE, AND ENJOY ALL MY PLEASING AMUSEMENTS??
O DEAR, O DEAR! WHAT A CURSED THING THIS IS! WHAT A MISERABLE CREATURE AM I!
"THUS ENDED MY INTRIGUE WITH THE FAIR LOUISA, WHICH I FLATTERED MYSELF SO MUCH WITH, AND FROM WHICH I EXPECTED AT LEAST A WINTER'S SAFE COPULATION."
BOSWELL PUTS HIMSELF IN THE CARE OF A PHYSICIAN, AND AFTER TWO MONTHS IS FULLY RECOVERED.——
THURSDAY, 30 MARCH, 1763 —— "I SAUNTERED ABOUT ALL THE DAY. AT NIGHT I WENT INTO THE PARK AND TOOK THE FIRST WHORE I MET...."
"....WHOM I WITHOUT MANY WORDS COPULATED WITH FREE FROM DANGER, BEING SAFELY SHEATHED. SHE WAS UGLY AND LEAN AND HER BREATH SMELT OF SPIRITS. I NEVER ASKED HER NAME. WHEN IT WAS DONE SHE SLUNK OFF. I HAD A LOW OPINION OF THIS GROSS PRACTICE AND RESOLVED TO DO IT NO MORE.

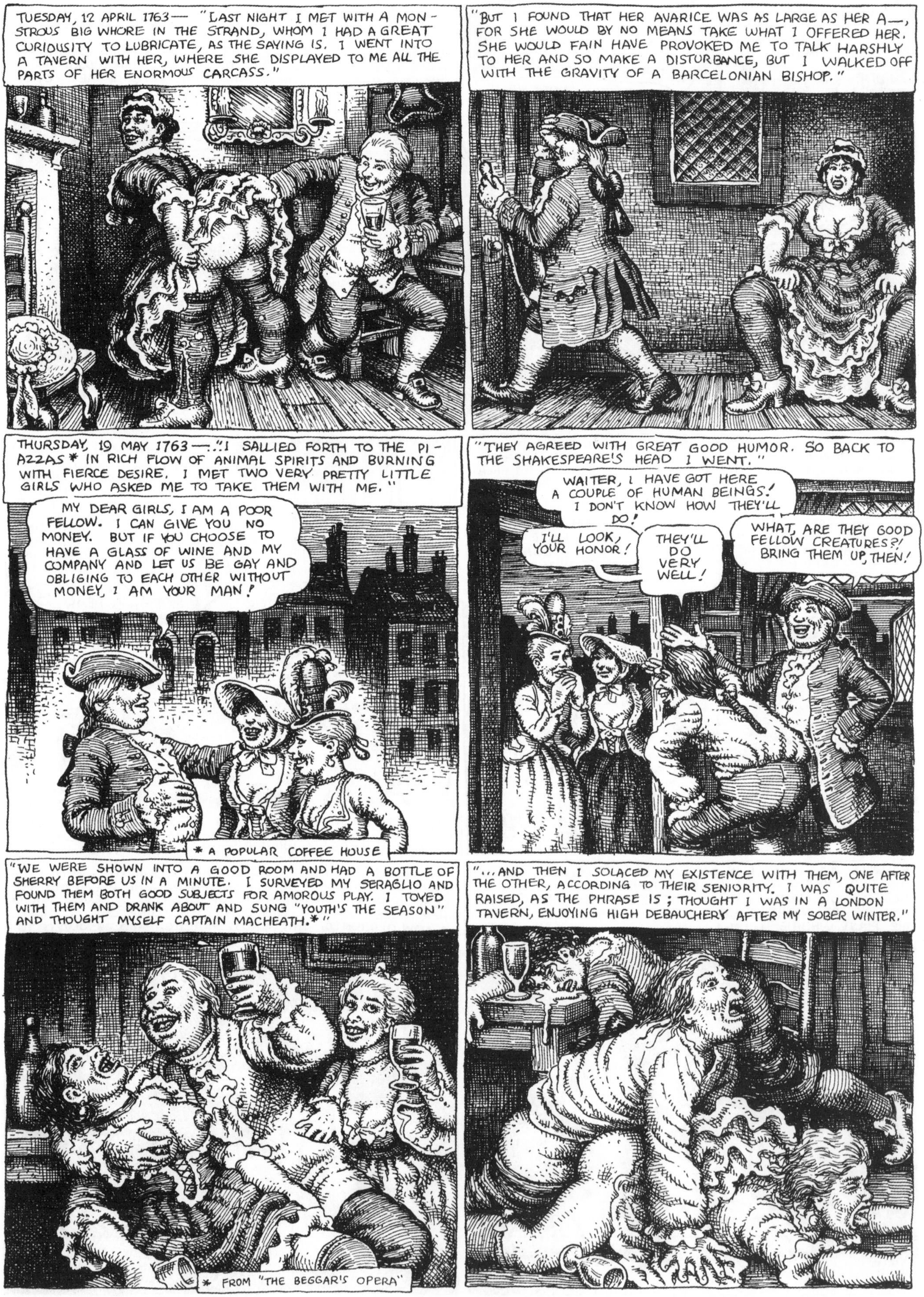
TUESDAY, 12 APRIL 1763— "LAST NIGHT I MET WITH A MONSTROUS BIG WHORE IN THE STRAND, WHOM I HAD A GREAT CURIOUSITY TO LUBRICATE, AS THE SAYING IS. I WENT INTO A TAVERN WITH HER, WHERE SHE DISPLAYED TO ME ALL THE PARTS OF HER ENORMOUS CARCASS."
"BUT I FOUND THAT HER AVARICE WAS AS LARGE AS HER A—, FOR SHE WOULD BY NO MEANS TAKE WHAT I OFFERED HER. SHE WOULD FAIN HAVE PROVOKED ME TO TALK HARSHLY TO HER AND SO MAKE A DISTURBANCE, BUT I WALKED OFF WITH THE GRAVITY OF A BARCELONIAN BISHOP."
THURSDAY, 19 MAY 1763—"I SALLIED FORTH TO THE PIAZZAS* IN RICH FLOW OF ANIMAL SPIRITS AND BURNING WITH FIERCE DESIRE. I MET TWO VERY PRETTY LITTLE GIRLS WHO ASKED ME TO TAKE THEM WITH ME."
MY DEAR GIRLS, I AM A POOR FELLOW. I CAN GIVE YOU NO MONEY. BUT IF YOU CHOOSE TO HAVE A GLASS OF WINE AND MY COMPANY AND LET US BE GAY AND OBLIGING TO EACH OTHER WITHOUT MONEY, I AM YOUR MAN!
* A POPULAR COFFEE HOUSE
"THEY AGREED WITH GREAT GOOD HUMOR. SO BACK TO THE SHAKESPEARE'S HEAD I WENT."
WAITER, I HAVE GOT HERE A COUPLE OF HUMAN BEINGS! I DON'T KNOW HOW THEY'LL DO!
I'LL LOOK, YOUR HONOR!
THEY'LL DO VERY WELL!
WHAT, ARE THEY GOOD FELLOW CREATURES?! BRING THEM UP, THEN!
"WE WERE SHOWN INTO A GOOD ROOM AND HAD A BOTTLE OF SHERRY BEFORE US IN A MINUTE. I SURVEYED MY SERAGLIO AND FOUND THEM BOTH GOOD SUBJECTS FOR AMOROUS PLAY. I TOYED WITH THEM AND DRANK ABOUT AND SUNG "YOUTH'S THE SEASON" AND THOUGHT MYSELF CAPTAIN MACHEATH.*"
* FROM "THE BEGGAR'S OPERA"
"...AND THEN I SOLACED MY EXISTENCE WITH THEM, ONE AFTER THE OTHER, ACCORDING TO THEIR SENIORITY. I WAS QUITE RAISED, AS THE PHRASE IS; THOUGHT I WAS IN A LONDON TAVERN, ENJOYING HIGH DEBAUCHERY AFTER MY SOBER WINTER."

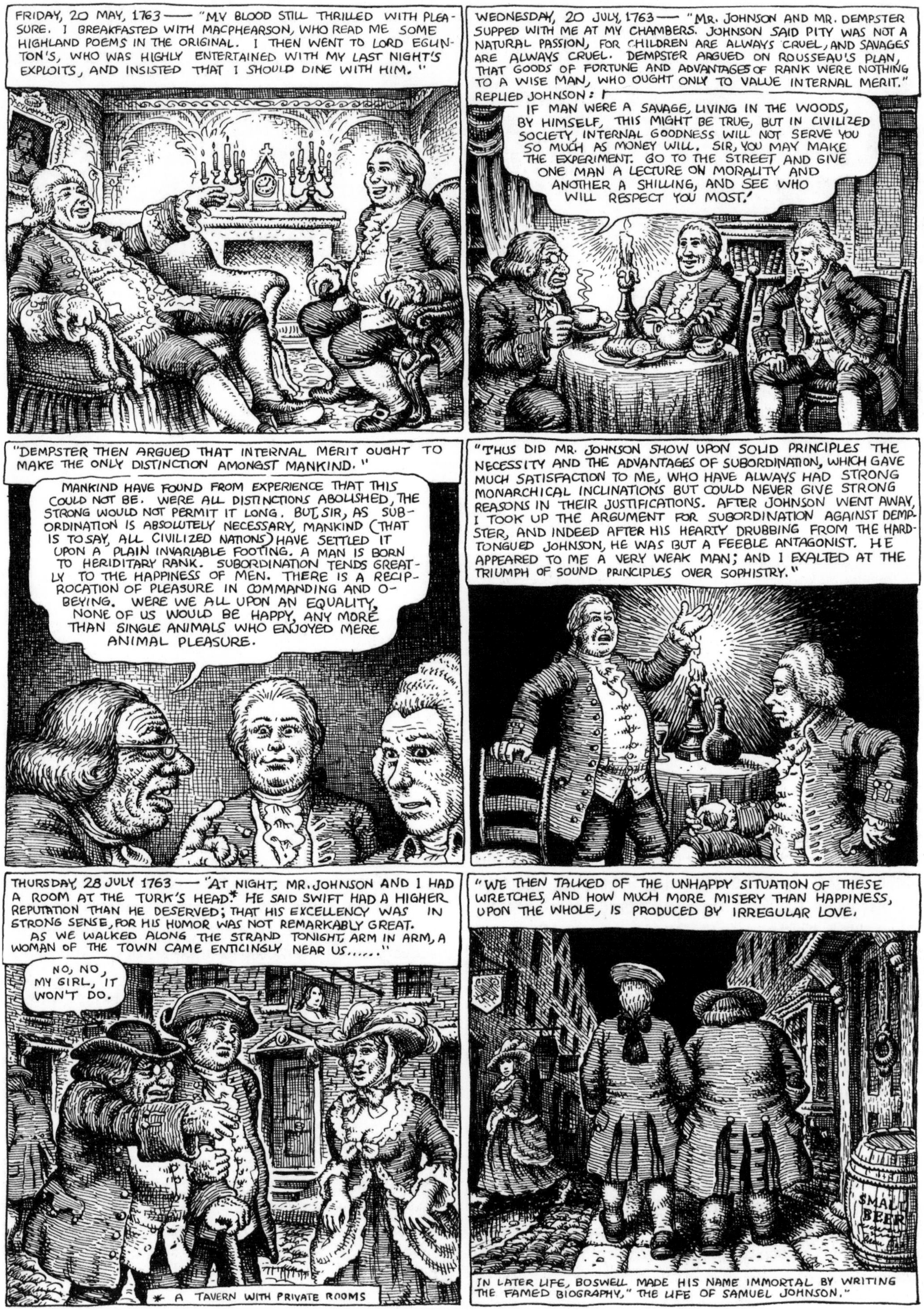

FRIDAY, 20 MAY, 1763 —— "MY BLOOD STILL THRILLED WITH PLEASURE. I BREAKFASTED WITH MACPHEARSON, WHO READ ME SOME HIGHLAND POEMS IN THE ORIGINAL. I THEN WENT TO LORD EGLINTON'S, WHO WAS HIGHLY ENTERTAINED WITH MY LAST NIGHT'S EXPLOITS, AND INSISTED THAT I SHOULD DINE WITH HIM."
WEDNESDAY, 20 JULY, 1763 —— "MR. JOHNSON AND MR. DEMPSTER SUPPED WITH ME AT MY CHAMBERS. JOHNSON SAID PITY WAS NOT A NATURAL PASSION, FOR CHILDREN ARE ALWAYS CRUEL, AND SAVAGES ARE ALWAYS CRUEL. DEMPSTER ARGUED ON ROUSSEAU'S PLAN, THAT GOODS OF FORTUNE AND ADVANTAGES OF RANK WERE NOTHING TO A WISE MAN, WHO OUGHT ONLY TO VALUE INTERNAL MERIT." REPLIED JOHNSON:
'IF MAN WERE A SAVAGE, LIVING IN THE WOODS, BY HIMSELF, THIS MIGHT BE TRUE, BUT IN CIVILIZED SOCIETY, INTERNAL GOODNESS WILL NOT SERVE YOU SO MUCH AS MONEY WILL. SIR, YOU MAY MAKE THE EXPERIMENT. GO TO THE STREET AND GIVE ONE MAN A LECTURE ON MORALITY AND ANOTHER A SHILLING, AND SEE WHO WILL RESPECT YOU MOST.'
"DEMPSTER THEN ARGUED THAT INTERNAL MERIT OUGHT TO MAKE THE ONLY DISTINCTION AMONGST MANKIND."
MANKIND HAVE FOUND FROM EXPERIENCE THAT THIS COULD NOT BE. WERE ALL DISTINCTIONS ABOLISHED, THE STRONG WOULD NOT PERMIT IT LONG. BUT, SIR, AS SUBORDINATION IS ABSOLUTELY NECESSARY, MANKIND (THAT IS TO SAY, ALL CIVILIZED NATIONS) HAVE SETTLED IT UPON A PLAIN INVARIABLE FOOTING. A MAN IS BORN TO HERIDITARY RANK. SUBORDINATION TENDS GREATLY TO THE HAPPINESS OF MEN. THERE IS A RECIPROCATION OF PLEASURE IN COMMANDING AND OBEYING. WERE WE ALL UPON AN EQUALITY, NONE OF US WOULD BE HAPPY, ANY MORE THAN SINGLE ANIMALS WHO ENJOYED MERE ANIMAL PLEASURE.
"THUS DID MR. JOHNSON SHOW UPON SOLID PRINCIPLES THE NECESSITY AND THE ADVANTAGES OF SUBORDINATION, WHICH GAVE MUCH SATISFACTION TO ME, WHO HAVE ALWAYS HAD STRONG MONARCHICAL INCLINATIONS BUT COULD NEVER GIVE STRONG REASONS IN THEIR JUSTIFICATIONS. AFTER JOHNSON WENT AWAY, I TOOK UP THE ARGUMENT FOR SUBORDINATION AGAINST DEMPSTER, AND INDEED AFTER HIS HEARTY DRUBBING FROM THE HARD-TONGUED JOHNSON, HE WAS BUT A FEEBLE ANTAGONIST. HE APPEARED TO ME A VERY WEAK MAN; AND I EXALTED AT THE TRIUMPH OF SOUND PRINCIPLES OVER SOPHISTRY."
THURSDAY, 28 JULY 1763 —— "AT NIGHT, MR. JOHNSON AND I HAD A ROOM AT THE TURK'S HEAD.* HE SAID SWIFT HAD A HIGHER REPUTATION THAN HE DESERVED; THAT HIS EXCELLENCY WAS IN STRONG SENSE, FOR HIS HUMOR WAS NOT REMARKABLY GREAT. AS WE WALKED ALONG THE STRAND TONIGHT, ARM IN ARM, A WOMAN OF THE TOWN CAME ENTICINGLY NEAR US......"
NO, NO, MY GIRL, IT WON'T DO.
* A TAVERN WITH PRIVATE ROOMS
"WE THEN TALKED OF THE UNHAPPY SITUATION OF THESE WRETCHES, AND HOW MUCH MORE MISERY THAN HAPPINESS, UPON THE WHOLE, IS PRODUCED BY IRREGULAR LOVE.
SMALL BEER
IN LATER LIFE, BOSWELL MADE HIS NAME IMMORTAL BY WRITING THE FAMED BIOGRAPHY, "THE LIFE OF SAMUEL JOHNSON."

"Letter to the Royal Academy of Brussels" (a.k.a. "Fart Proudly")

Benjamin Franklin

ART / ADAPTATION BY **Stan Shaw**

THERE'S A LONG BUT NEGLECTED TRADITION OF scatology in literature—poop, pee, and farts show up in *Gilgamesh*, the Bible, Rabelais, Chaucer, Martin Luther (his sermons), Shakespeare, Swift, Hugo, Twain, Joyce, Pynchon, and elsewhere. Benjamin Franklin is a part of this excretory canon, due to his "Letter to the Royal Academy of Brussels." Though this essay is informally known as "Fart Proudly," those words don't actually appear in it; rather, that was the title of the small-press anthology of Franklin's scurrilous writings that popularized the essay.

While residing in Paris as the US ambassador to France, Franklin used his press to privately print his little, humorous essays (*bagatelles*, "trifles") for the enjoyment of his circle of acquaintances (especially the ladies). Topics included drinking, chess, moving to America, and, well, farting. The purpose of this last one was to ridicule the Royal Academy of Brussels, a prestigious scientific society, which Franklin believed was wasting its massive collective brainpower on inane, meaningless problems. He proposes the group put its talents to use dealing with a much more pressing, practical concern.

(The French text quoted in the first paragraph is the Academy's actual mathematical challenge for its members. The translation of the first French sentence, as given in *Fart Proudly*: "Given any single figure, inscribe therein a smaller figure, which is also given, as many times as possible." The second sentence: "The academy has judged that this discovery, by widening the boundaries of our knowledge, will not be without utility.")

Stan Shaw includes the full text of this essay (with the spelling made contemporary) in this visual tribute to *The Daily Show with Jon Stewart*. Which makes you realize that Franklin really would be the ideal correspondent—if not host—of the political humor / news parody show.

SOURCES

Franklin, Benjamin. *The Bagatelles From Passy*. New York: Eakins Press, 1967.

Franklin, Benjamin. *Fart Proudly: Writings of Benjamin Franklin You Never Read in School*. Carl Japikse (editor). Enthea Press and Frog Ltd.: 1993, 2003.

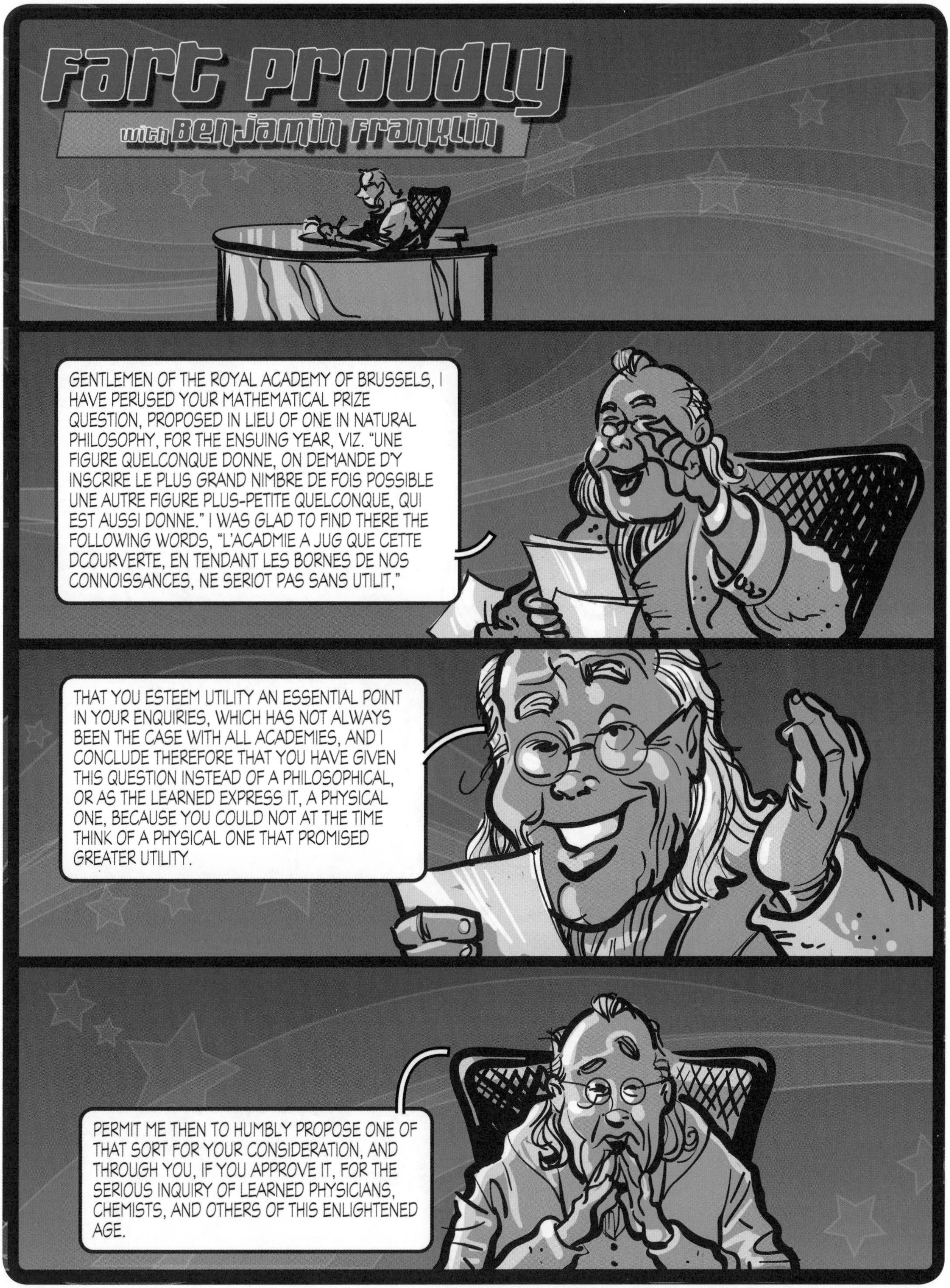
FART PROUDLY
WITH BENJAMIN FRANKLIN
GENTLEMEN OF THE ROYAL ACADEMY OF BRUSSELS, I HAVE PERUSED YOUR MATHEMATICAL PRIZE QUESTION, PROPOSED IN LIEU OF ONE IN NATURAL PHILOSOPHY, FOR THE ENSUING YEAR, VIZ. "UNE FIGURE QUELCONQUE DONNE, ON DEMANDE D'Y INSCRIRE LE PLUS GRAND NIMBRE DE FOIS POSSIBLE UNE AUTRE FIGURE PLUS-PETITE QUELCONQUE, QUI EST AUSSI DONNE." I WAS GLAD TO FIND THERE THE FOLLOWING WORDS, "L'ACADMIE A JUG QUE CETTE DCOURVERTE, EN TENDANT LES BORNES DE NOS CONNOISSANCES, NE SERIOT PAS SANS UTILIT,"
THAT YOU ESTEEM UTILITY AN ESSENTIAL POINT IN YOUR ENQUIRIES, WHICH HAS NOT ALWAYS BEEN THE CASE WITH ALL ACADEMIES, AND I CONCLUDE THEREFORE THAT YOU HAVE GIVEN THIS QUESTION INSTEAD OF A PHILOSOPHICAL, OR AS THE LEARNED EXPRESS IT, A PHYSICAL ONE, BECAUSE YOU COULD NOT AT THE TIME THINK OF A PHYSICAL ONE THAT PROMISED GREATER UTILITY.
PERMIT ME THEN TO HUMBLY PROPOSE ONE OF THAT SORT FOR YOUR CONSIDERATION, AND THROUGH YOU, IF YOU APPROVE IT, FOR THE SERIOUS INQUIRY OF LEARNED PHYSICIANS, CHEMISTS, AND OTHERS OF THIS ENLIGHTENED AGE.

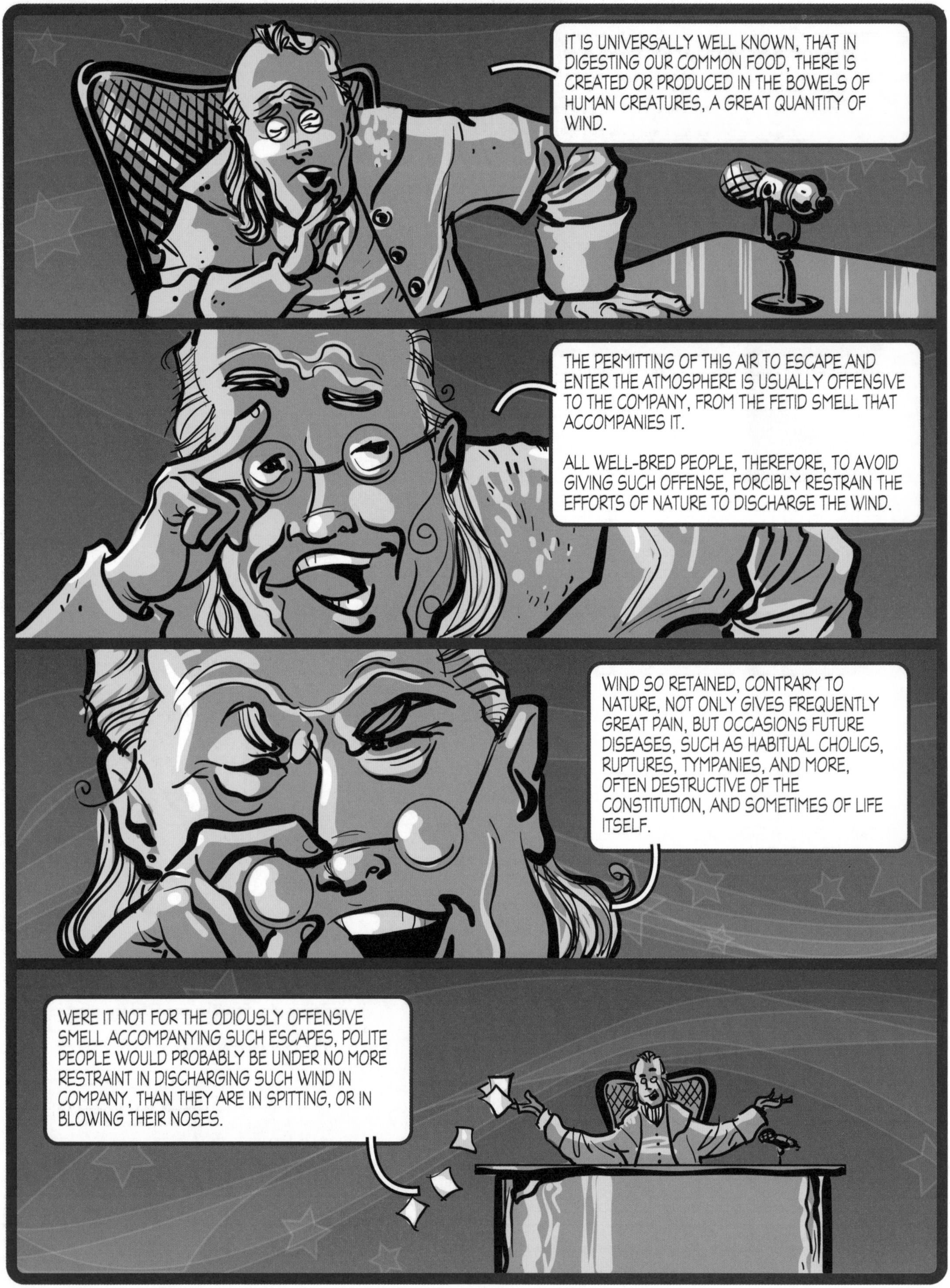
IT IS UNIVERSALLY WELL KNOWN, THAT IN DIGESTING OUR COMMON FOOD, THERE IS CREATED OR PRODUCED IN THE BOWELS OF HUMAN CREATURES, A GREAT QUANTITY OF WIND.
THE PERMITTING OF THIS AIR TO ESCAPE AND ENTER THE ATMOSPHERE IS USUALLY OFFENSIVE TO THE COMPANY, FROM THE FETID SMELL THAT ACCOMPANIES IT.
ALL WELL-BRED PEOPLE, THEREFORE, TO AVOID GIVING SUCH OFFENSE, FORCIBLY RESTRAIN THE EFFORTS OF NATURE TO DISCHARGE THE WIND.
WIND SO RETAINED, CONTRARY TO NATURE, NOT ONLY GIVES FREQUENTLY GREAT PAIN, BUT OCCASIONS FUTURE DISEASES, SUCH AS HABITUAL CHOLICS, RUPTURES, TYMPANIES, AND MORE, OFTEN DESTRUCTIVE OF THE CONSTITUTION, AND SOMETIMES OF LIFE ITSELF.
WERE IT NOT FOR THE ODIOUSLY OFFENSIVE SMELL ACCOMPANYING SUCH ESCAPES, POLITE PEOPLE WOULD PROBABLY BE UNDER NO MORE RESTRAINT IN DISCHARGING SUCH WIND IN COMPANY, THAN THEY ARE IN SPITTING, OR IN BLOWING THEIR NOSES.

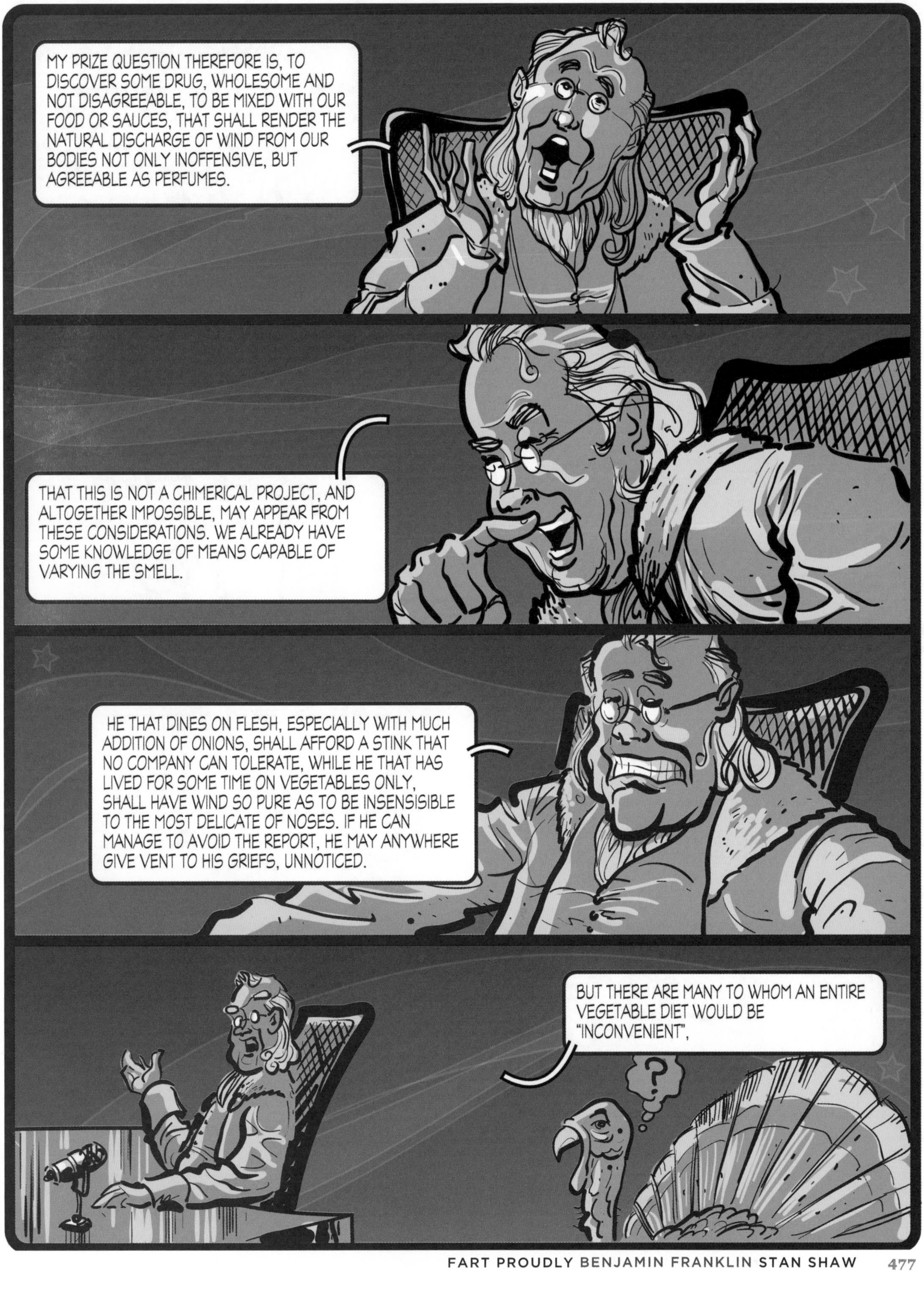
MY PRIZE QUESTION THEREFORE IS, TO DISCOVER SOME DRUG, WHOLESOME AND NOT DISAGREEABLE, TO BE MIXED WITH OUR FOOD OR SAUCES, THAT SHALL RENDER THE NATURAL DISCHARGE OF WIND FROM OUR BODIES NOT ONLY INOFFENSIVE, BUT AGREEABLE AS PERFUMES.
THAT THIS IS NOT A CHIMERICAL PROJECT, AND ALTOGETHER IMPOSSIBLE, MAY APPEAR FROM THESE CONSIDERATIONS. WE ALREADY HAVE SOME KNOWLEDGE OF MEANS CAPABLE OF VARYING THE SMELL.
HE THAT DINES ON FLESH, ESPECIALLY WITH MUCH ADDITION OF ONIONS, SHALL AFFORD A STINK THAT NO COMPANY CAN TOLERATE, WHILE HE THAT HAS LIVED FOR SOME TIME ON VEGETABLES ONLY, SHALL HAVE WIND SO PURE AS TO BE INSENSIBLE TO THE MOST DELICATE OF NOSES. IF HE CAN MANAGE TO AVOID THE REPORT, HE MAY ANYWHERE GIVE VENT TO HIS GRIEFS, UNNOTICED.
BUT THERE ARE MANY TO WHOM AN ENTIRE VEGETABLE DIET WOULD BE "INCONVENIENT",
?

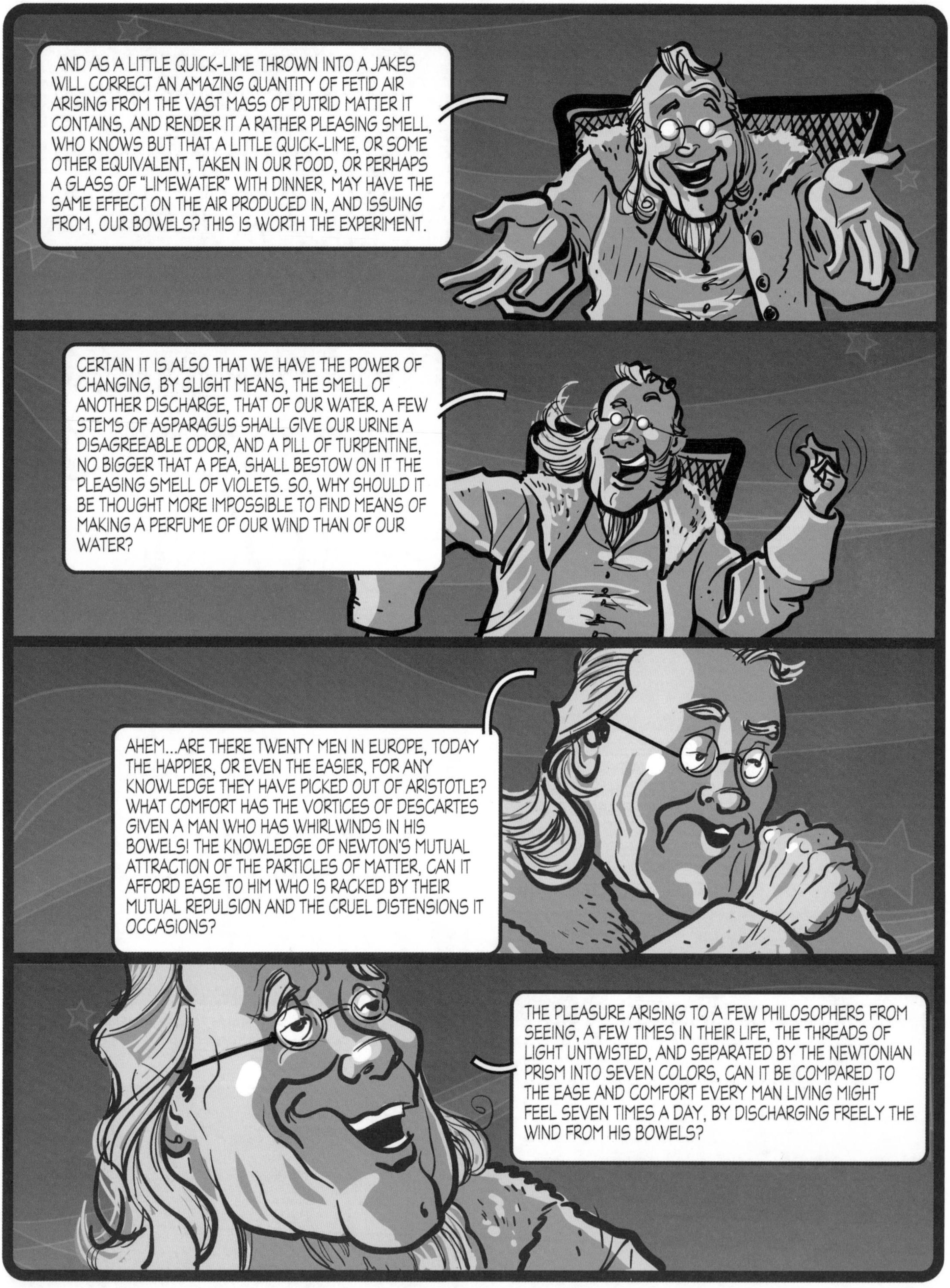

AND AS A LITTLE QUICK-LIME THROWN INTO A JAKES WILL CORRECT AN AMAZING QUANTITY OF FETID AIR ARISING FROM THE VAST MASS OF PUTRID MATTER IT CONTAINS, AND RENDER IT A RATHER PLEASING SMELL, WHO KNOWS BUT THAT A LITTLE QUICK-LIME, OR SOME OTHER EQUIVALENT, TAKEN IN OUR FOOD, OR PERHAPS A GLASS OF "LIMEWATER" WITH DINNER, MAY HAVE THE SAME EFFECT ON THE AIR PRODUCED IN, AND ISSUING FROM, OUR BOWELS? THIS IS WORTH THE EXPERIMENT.
CERTAIN IT IS ALSO THAT WE HAVE THE POWER OF CHANGING, BY SLIGHT MEANS, THE SMELL OF ANOTHER DISCHARGE, THAT OF OUR WATER. A FEW STEMS OF ASPARAGUS SHALL GIVE OUR URINE A DISAGREEABLE ODOR, AND A PILL OF TURPENTINE, NO BIGGER THAT A PEA, SHALL BESTOW ON IT THE PLEASING SMELL OF VIOLETS. SO, WHY SHOULD IT BE THOUGHT MORE IMPOSSIBLE TO FIND MEANS OF MAKING A PERFUME OF OUR WIND THAN OF OUR WATER?
AHEM...ARE THERE TWENTY MEN IN EUROPE, TODAY THE HAPPIER, OR EVEN THE EASIER, FOR ANY KNOWLEDGE THEY HAVE PICKED OUT OF ARISTOTLE? WHAT COMFORT HAS THE VORTICES OF DESCARTES GIVEN A MAN WHO HAS WHIRLWINDS IN HIS BOWELS! THE KNOWLEDGE OF NEWTON'S MUTUAL ATTRACTION OF THE PARTICLES OF MATTER, CAN IT AFFORD EASE TO HIM WHO IS RACKED BY THEIR MUTUAL REPULSION AND THE CRUEL DISTENSIONS IT OCCASIONS?
THE PLEASURE ARISING TO A FEW PHILOSOPHERS FROM SEEING, A FEW TIMES IN THEIR LIFE, THE THREADS OF LIGHT UNTWISTED, AND SEPARATED BY THE NEWTONIAN PRISM INTO SEVEN COLORS, CAN IT BE COMPARED TO THE EASE AND COMFORT EVERY MAN LIVING MIGHT FEEL SEVEN TIMES A DAY, BY DISCHARGING FREELY THE WIND FROM HIS BOWELS?

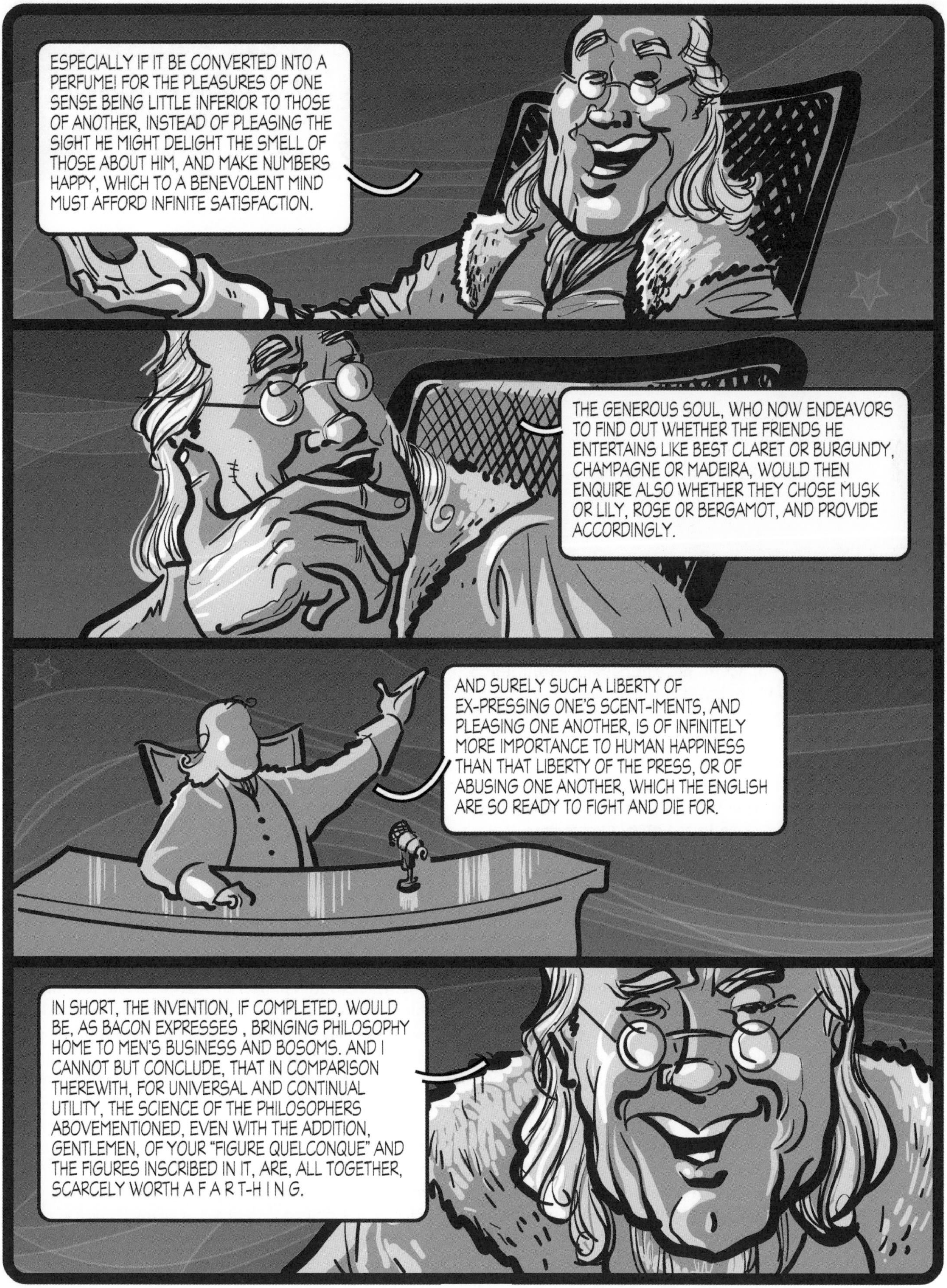
ESPECIALLY IF IT BE CONVERTED INTO A PERFUME! FOR THE PLEASURES OF ONE SENSE BEING LITTLE INFERIOR TO THOSE OF ANOTHER, INSTEAD OF PLEASING THE SIGHT HE MIGHT DELIGHT THE SMELL OF THOSE ABOUT HIM, AND MAKE NUMBERS HAPPY, WHICH TO A BENEVOLENT MIND MUST AFFORD INFINITE SATISFACTION.
THE GENEROUS SOUL, WHO NOW ENDEAVORS TO FIND OUT WHETHER THE FRIENDS HE ENTERTAINS LIKE BEST CLARET OR BURGUNDY, CHAMPAGNE OR MADEIRA, WOULD THEN ENQUIRE ALSO WHETHER THEY CHOSE MUSK OR LILY, ROSE OR BERGAMOT, AND PROVIDE ACCORDINGLY.
AND SURELY SUCH A LIBERTY OF EX-PRESSING ONE'S SCENT-IMENTS, AND PLEASING ONE ANOTHER, IS OF INFINITELY MORE IMPORTANCE TO HUMAN HAPPINESS THAN THAT LIBERTY OF THE PRESS, OR OF ABUSING ONE ANOTHER, WHICH THE ENGLISH ARE SO READY TO FIGHT AND DIE FOR.
IN SHORT, THE INVENTION, IF COMPLETED, WOULD BE, AS BACON EXPRESSES , BRINGING PHILOSOPHY HOME TO MEN'S BUSINESS AND BOSOMS. AND I CANNOT BUT CONCLUDE, THAT IN COMPARISON THEREWITH, FOR UNIVERSAL AND CONTINUAL UTILITY, THE SCIENCE OF THE PHILOSOPHERS ABOVEMENTIONED, EVEN WITH THE ADDITION, GENTLEMEN, OF YOUR "FIGURE QUELCONQUE" AND THE FIGURES INSCRIBED IN IT, ARE, ALL TOGETHER, SCARCELY WORTH A F A R T-H I N G.

A Vindication of the Rights of Woman

Mary Wollstonecraft

ADAPTATION BY **Fred Van Lente**

ART BY **Ryan Dunlavey**

THIS ONE-PAGER FROM FRED VAN LENTE AND RYAN Dunlavey's wonderful *Action Philosophers!* series acts as an introduction to Mary Wollstonecraft and her most enduring work, so I'll use this space to present passages from the introduction that Wollstonecraft wrote for her courageous proto-feminist tract:

After considering the historic page, and viewing the living world with anxious solicitude, the most melancholy emotions of sorrowful indignation have depressed my spirits, and I have sighed when obliged to confess, that either nature has made a great difference between man and man, or that the civilization which has hitherto taken place in the world has been very partial. I have turned over various books written on the subject of education, and patiently observed the conduct of parents and the management of schools; but what has been the result?—a profound conviction that the neglected education of my fellow-creatures is the grand source of the misery I deplore; and that women, in particular, are rendered weak and wretched by a variety of concurring causes, originating from one hasty conclusion. The conduct and manners of women, in fact, evidently prove that their minds are not in a healthy state; for, like the flowers which are planted in too rich a soil, strength and usefulness are sacrificed to beauty; and the flaunting leaves, after having pleased a fastidious eye, fade, disregarded on the stalk, long before the season when they ought to have arrived at maturity.

One cause of this barren blooming I attribute to a false system of education, gathered from the books written on this subject by men who, considering females rather as women than human creatures, have been more anxious to make them alluring mistresses than wives; and the understanding of the sex has been so bubbled by this specious homage, that the civilized women of the present century, with a few exceptions, are only anxious to inspire love, when they ought to cherish a nobler ambition, and by their abilities and virtues exact respect.

My own sex, I hope, will excuse me, if I treat them like rational creatures, instead of flattering their *fascinating* graces, and viewing them as if they were in a state of perpetual childhood, unable to stand alone. I earnestly wish to point out in what true dignity and human happiness consists—I wish to persuade women to endeavour to acquire strength, both of mind and body, and to convince them that the soft phrases, susceptibility of heart, delicacy of sentiment, and refinement of taste, are almost synonymous with epithets of weakness, and that those beings who are only the objects of pity and that kind of love, which has been termed its sister, will soon become objects of contempt.

Dismissing then those pretty feminine phrases, which the men condescendingly use to soften our slavish dependence, and despising that weak elegancy of mind, exquisite sensibility, and sweet docility of manners, supposed to be the sexual characteristics of the weaker vessel, I wish to show that elegance is inferior to virtue, that the first object of laudable ambition is to obtain a character as a human being, regardless of the distinction of sex; and that secondary views should be brought to this simple touchstone.

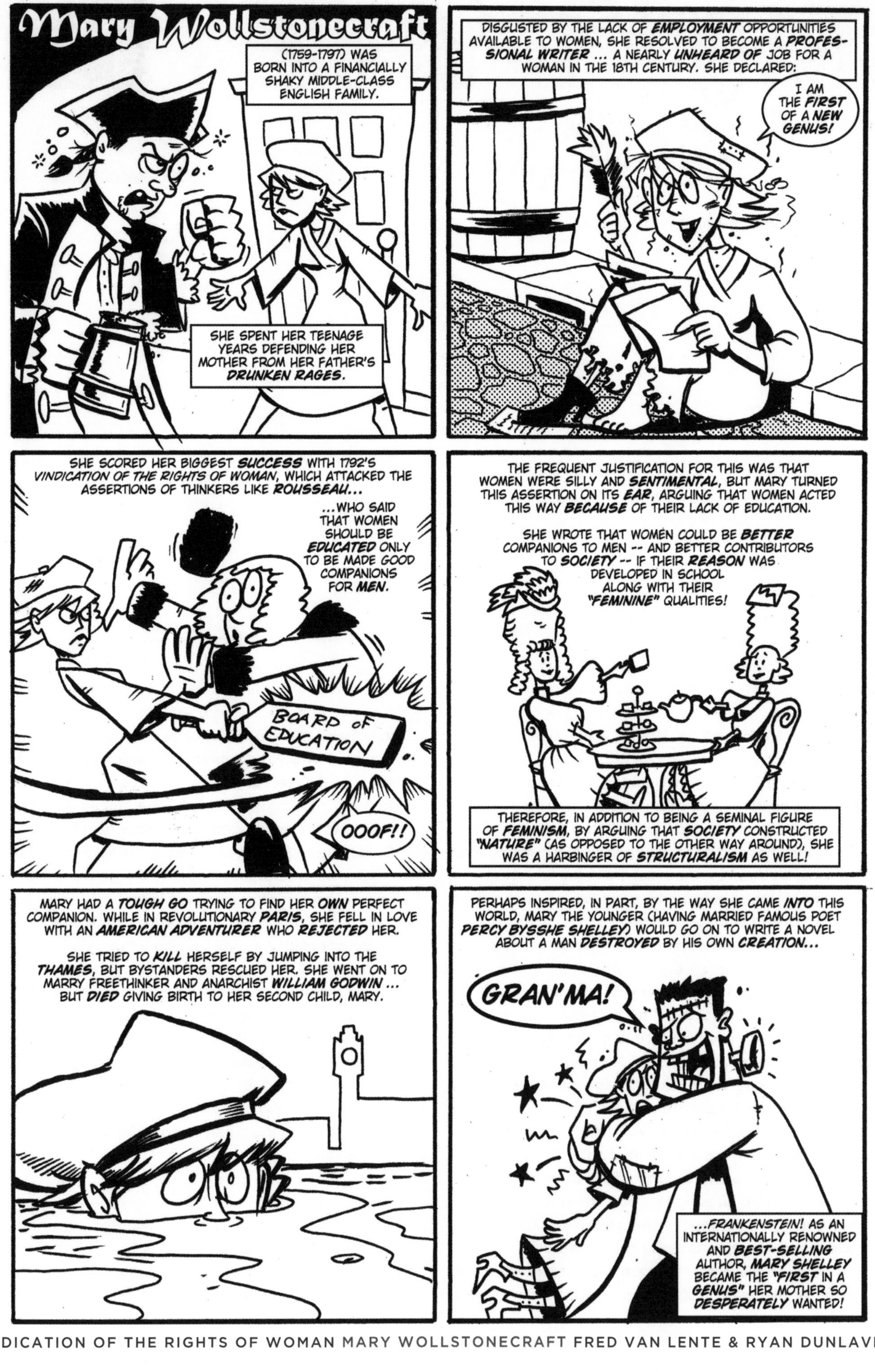

Mary Wollstonecraft
(1759-1797) WAS BORN INTO A FINANCIALLY SHAKY MIDDLE-CLASS ENGLISH FAMILY.
SHE SPENT HER TEENAGE YEARS DEFENDING HER MOTHER FROM HER FATHER'S DRUNKEN RAGES.
DISGUSTED BY THE LACK OF EMPLOYMENT OPPORTUNITIES AVAILABLE TO WOMEN, SHE RESOLVED TO BECOME A PROFESSIONAL WRITER ... A NEARLY UNHEARD OF JOB FOR A WOMAN IN THE 18TH CENTURY. SHE DECLARED:
I AM THE FIRST OF A NEW GENUS!
SHE SCORED HER BIGGEST SUCCESS WITH 1792'S VINDICATION OF THE RIGHTS OF WOMAN, WHICH ATTACKED THE ASSERTIONS OF THINKERS LIKE ROUSSEAU...
...WHO SAID THAT WOMEN SHOULD BE EDUCATED ONLY TO BE MADE GOOD COMPANIONS FOR MEN.
BOARD OF EDUCATION
OOOF!!
THE FREQUENT JUSTIFICATION FOR THIS WAS THAT WOMEN WERE SILLY AND SENTIMENTAL, BUT MARY TURNED THIS ASSERTION ON ITS EAR, ARGUING THAT WOMEN ACTED THIS WAY BECAUSE OF THEIR LACK OF EDUCATION.
SHE WROTE THAT WOMEN COULD BE BETTER COMPANIONS TO MEN -- AND BETTER CONTRIBUTORS TO SOCIETY -- IF THEIR REASON WAS DEVELOPED IN SCHOOL ALONG WITH THEIR "FEMININE" QUALITIES!
THEREFORE, IN ADDITION TO BEING A SEMINAL FIGURE OF FEMINISM, BY ARGUING THAT SOCIETY CONSTRUCTED "NATURE" (AS OPPOSED TO THE OTHER WAY AROUND), SHE WAS A HARBINGER OF STRUCTURALISM AS WELL!
MARY HAD A TOUGH GO TRYING TO FIND HER OWN PERFECT COMPANION. WHILE IN REVOLUTIONARY PARIS, SHE FELL IN LOVE WITH AN AMERICAN ADVENTURER WHO REJECTED HER.
SHE TRIED TO KILL HERSELF BY JUMPING INTO THE THAMES, BUT BYSTANDERS RESCUED HER. SHE WENT ON TO MARRY FREETHINKER AND ANARCHIST WILLIAM GODWIN ... BUT DIED GIVING BIRTH TO HER SECOND CHILD, MARY.
PERHAPS INSPIRED, IN PART, BY THE WAY SHE CAME INTO THIS WORLD, MARY THE YOUNGER (HAVING MARRIED FAMOUS POET PERCY BYSSHE SHELLEY) WOULD GO ON TO WRITE A NOVEL ABOUT A MAN DESTROYED BY HIS OWN CREATION...
GRAN'MA!
...FRANKENSTEIN! AS AN INTERNATIONALLY RENOWNED AND BEST-SELLING AUTHOR, MARY SHELLEY BECAME THE "FIRST IN A GENUS" HER MOTHER SO DESPERATELY WANTED!

Dangerous Liaisons

Choderlos de Laclos

ILLUSTRATIONS BY **Molly Crabapple**

DANGEROUS LIAISONS **"BURNS AS ICE DOES," SAID** Charles Baudelaire, one of France's greatest, darkest poets. This 1782 novel, the only one by military man and politician Choderlos de Laclos, lures you in with smooth, delicious prose that almost makes you forget that you're reading about two libertine sociopaths who are cruelly manipulating everyone around them for personal revenge. Told strictly as an exchange of letters among the various parties, the story seamlessly builds in intricacy as we see plots hatched, plans derailed, contingencies implemented, and events spinning out of control.

The Marquise de Merteuil's former flame dumped her for another woman a while back. That other woman was the Vicomte de Valmont's wife. Now Merteuil's ex has moved on again and is betrothed to the young, virginal Cécil de Volanges. But he's out of the country for the moment, and Merteuil has hatched a plot to ruin his life: she will enlist Valmont to debauch the nubile Cécil, then, after the wedding, will spread the word among Paris society that her ex's teenage trophy wife is not a virgin but rather a practiced devotee of cock. (Obviously this wouldn't raise an eyebrow now, but back in quainter times—even in decadent, pre-Revolutionary Paris—it was cause for suicide.)

Things get complicated from the very beginning when Valmont informs Merteuil that he's unable to participate because he's trying to debauch someone else, a prim married woman who would never dream of cheating on her husband. As we see, though, he's also upset at the marquise for no longer taking him as her lover. Meanwhile the frisson builds as Merteuil admits her attraction to the flowering Cécil, who is being pursued by the young Chevalier Danceny, who stealthily delivers mash notes to her in her harp case. This budding romance is craftily encouraged by Merteuil because if the vicomte won't deflower Cécil, this young Romeo will. . . .

Laclos said: "I resolved to write . . . a book which would continue to cause a stir and echo through the world after I have left it." Well done, sir.

Artist Molly Crabapple was born to illustrate *Dangerous Liaisons*. Debauched, cake-eating, powdered-wig aristocrats are among her core stable of characters, and she drew what is probably the first work of steampunk to be set in rococo France, rather than Victorian London (cf. the DC webcomic *Puppet Makers*).

SOURCES

Laclos, Choderlos de. (Helen Constantine, translator.) *Dangerous Liaisons*. New York: Penguin Classics, 2007.

Laclos, Choderlos de. (Ernest Dowson, translator.) *Les Liaisons Dangereuses*. Mineola, NY: Dover Publications, 2006.

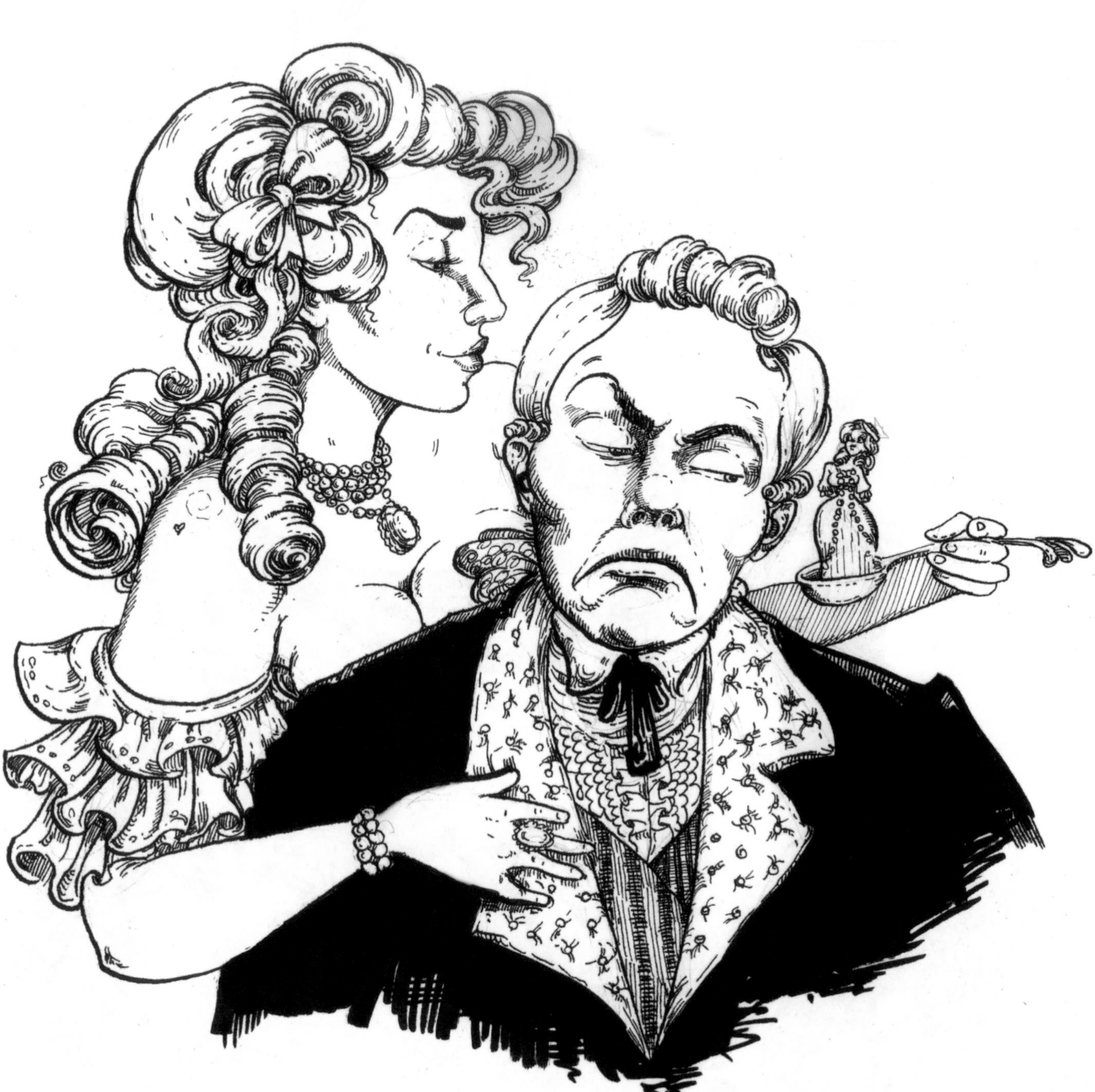

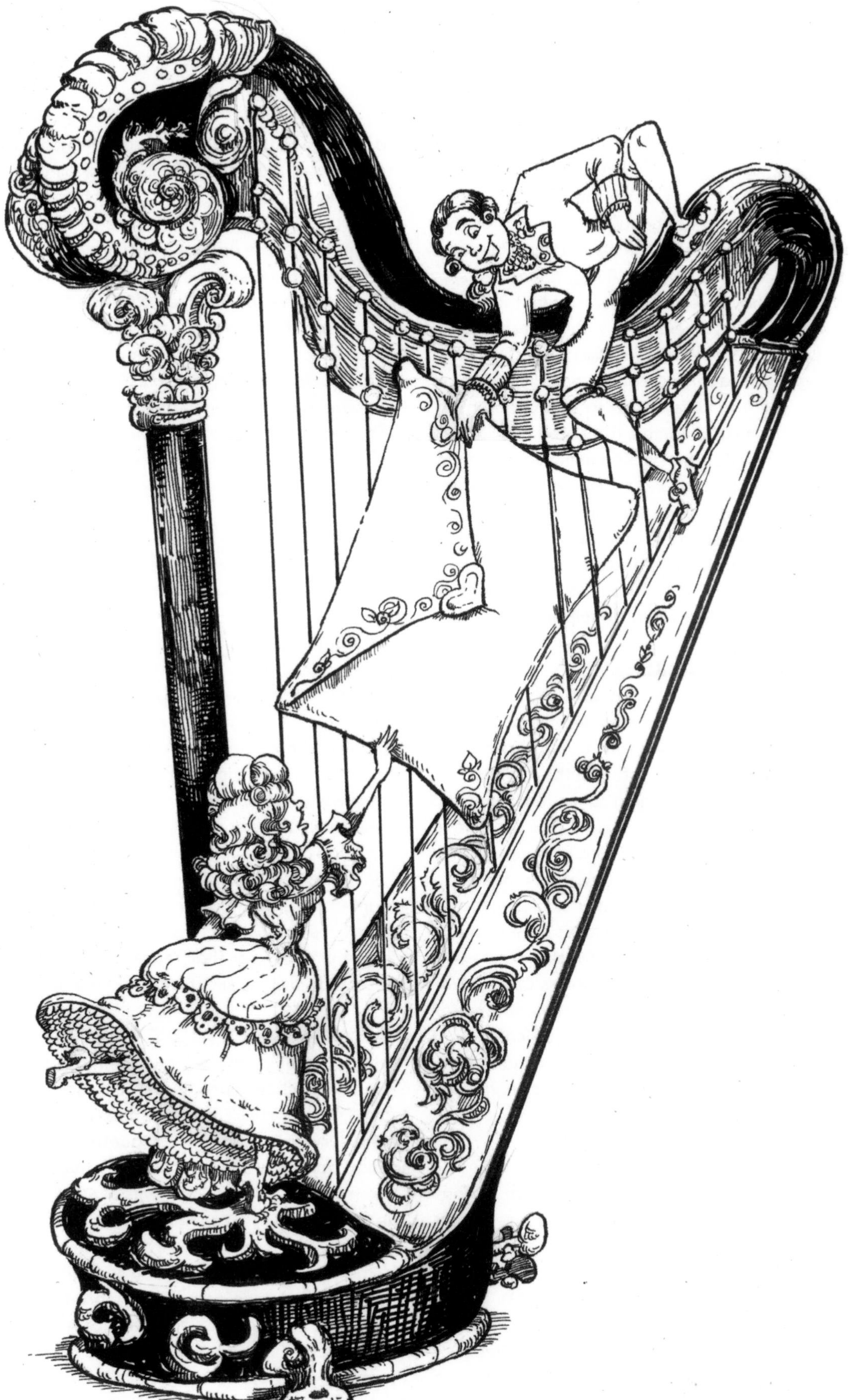

FURTHER READING
LIZ BYER

THE EPIC OF GILGAMESH

As *Gilgamesh* is among the oldest works of literature in existence, it is no surprise that there are a plethora of translations, renditions, and critical works on the subject. The version that has generated the most critical and academic buzz in recent years is Stephen Mitchell's *Gilgamesh: A New English Version* (Free Press, 2006), a highly readable literary adaptation that breathes fresh air into an ancient text, with extensive notes that provide much insight into the translation process. If you're looking for a slightly cheaper but equally engaging take on Gil's adventures, you can always turn to that old standby Penguin Classics. Their 2003 edition, translated and with an introduction by Andrew George, packs a punch for the price: the verse translation is spirited, and acclaimed Assyriologist George provides supplementary materials that help contextualize a work that can sometimes feel distant and dry to modern readers. And speaking of old standbys, you also can't go wrong with king-of-ancient-literature John Gardner and John Maier's breathtaking 1985 edition, published by Vintage.

"COYOTE AND THE PEBBLES"

Sad to say, but there is something of a dearth of books about Native American folklore, apart from children's books and academic and scholarly works. However, Micah Farritor and Dayton Edmonds' rendition of "Coyote and the Pebbles" for this volume was taken from a stunning collection of graphic reimaginings of Native American tales called *Trickster: Native American Tales* (Matt Dembicki, ed., Fulcrum Books, 2010). The twenty-one stories in the collection are each rendered in a unique and vibrant style, celebrating the trickster motif that is a common thread among so many folktales from so many different tribes. For more stories about Coyote, the arrogant scamp of trickster mythology, Mourning Dove's *Coyote Stories* (Bison Books, 1990) is an invaluable document. And for a more adult rendition of the trickster genre, which, though frequently sanitized for younger audiences, was traditionally rather racy, see Richard Erdoes and Alfonso Ortiz's enjoyable *American Indian Trickster Tales* (Penguin, 1999).

THE ILIAD

The list of the numerous translations and reinterpretations of Homer's *Iliad* runs so long that you could very well call it "epic." In terms of greatest hits, the standard among AP high school students and college classics intro classes these days is probably Robert Fagles' (Penguin Classics, 1998). Fagles renders the classic war epic in blank verse, with a fluidity and simplicity of language that feels true to the original Greek yet still familiar for contemporary readers. And the introduction by Bernard Knox is not to be missed for its depth and scholarship. Contemporary translations available in paperback that are excellent include Robert Fitzgerald's, Richmond Lattimore's,

and, most recently (2011), Stephen Mitchell's. For traditionalists, however, the likely contender for all-time greatest *Iliad* is Alexander Pope's 1715–1720 translation of the masterpiece into heroic couplets. Pope's verse retains all of the excitement and emotion of the original, while remaining more true to the musicality of the Greek oral tradition. The only edition currently in print, published by Aeterna in 2011, is a little pricey. Luckily for students and readers earning graphic-novelist-sized paychecks, you can access the entire text for free at Project Gutenberg (http://www.gutenberg.org/files/6130/6130-h/6130-h.html). For someone interested in getting a profound interpretation of the antiwar message of *The Iliad*, check out Simone Weil's *The Iliad or the Poem of Force*, a short essay available in various collections or as a stand-alone pamphlet.

THE ODYSSEY

Much like *The Iliad*, *The Odyssey* has been covered by everyone from Homer to James Joyce to Homer (Simpson). And again, as with *The Iliad*, the currently favored translation in most college programs is the Robert Fagles/Bernard Knox (Penguin Classics, 2006). Like the previous epic, Fagles' blank verse and straightforward language give the classic text a more modern feel. And again, there is an Alexander Pope version (though perhaps somewhat less celebrated than his *Iliad*) that, while difficult to find in print, is readily available for free online (http://www.gutenberg.org/ebooks/3160). Meanwhile, many scholars and classical geeks prefer Richmond Lattimore's 1965 translation (currently available from Harper Perennial Modern Classics in a very reasonably priced edition). His is a more literal interpretation of Homer's words, retaining the tropes used by the Greek oral poets ("resourceful Odysseus, circumspect Penelope," etc.) in all their repetition where Fagles opts for a more modern style, sacrificing tradition for variety.

POEM FRAGMENTS BY SAPPHO

Perhaps the classical poet with the most modern sensibility, Sappho left scholars precious little to go on when she died in the sixth century BC. There have been a number of translations of the surviving fragments of poetry from her nine books, though none more ambitious and breathtaking than Anne Carson's *If Not, Winter: Fragments of Sappho* (Vintage, 2003). The volume displays the original Greek alongside Carson's lithe and lyrical renderings of the fragments into English, allowing the fragments to read as poems in their own right by placing just one on each page. For a more traditional academic translation, try David A. Campbell's *Greek Lyric: Sappho and Alcaeus* (Loeb Classical Library, 1982), which also includes the testimonies of the other classical heavy-hitters on both poets. If you're looking to delve further into Greek lyric poetry, Kenneth Rexroth's 1962 *Poems from the Greek Anthology* (currently available from the University of Michigan Press) is a stunning introduction to some of the other Greek lyricists.

MEDEA

The themes of Euripides' *Medea*—passion, family, and ultimately vengeance—have a lot of appeal to contemporary readers, and variations on the play have been staged and filmed a lot in the last twenty-five years: Neil Labute's 1999 *Medea Redux*, Kristina Leach's 2004 *The Medea Project*, and even David Simon has said the themes from Euripides' tragedies were a large source of inspiration for *The Wire*. Of the few recent translations, the most notable is probably Robin Robertson's 2009 verse translation, available from the Free Press for a very reasonable price. The verse flows seamlessly: Robertson grasps the economy of language necessary for a good translation of Euripides, and he embraces the great tragedian's use of colloquial, idiomatic language.

LYSISTRATA

Lysistrata is a perennially popular play thanks to its humor and often-timely themes of war, sex, and (some would argue) feminism. Of the editions on the market, Sarah Ruden's 2003 rendition, available from Hackett, is readable, bawdy (teachers, be forewarned: Ruden is liberal in her use of F-bombs), and quite funny. The supplementary materials, which include some helpful historical essays and wonderfully detailed footnotes, make this edition that much more useful to those less familiar with classical literature. For a more scholarly, less profanity-laden take on the play, see Alan H. Sommerstein's translation (Penguin Classics, 2003). It still contains all the racy fun but in a more . . . subtle tone. For a more feminist take, check out Germaine Greer's 1972 *Lysistrata: The Sex Strike* (Samuel French, 2011) for a more radical, if somewhat dated, reading of the play.

SYMPOSIUM

Plato's *Symposium*, probably the most entertaining work of classical philosophy, is available for free literally hundreds of places on the web. However, if you care about translation, owning a physical copy you can hold in your hands, and/or supplemental materials, two books stand out among the dozens on the market. The first is the Seth Benardete translation (University of Chicago Press, 2001). Of all the more recent translations, this is probably the prettiest and the simplest to understand. Plus, it is coupled with Allan Bloom's thoughtful essay "The Ladder of Love," which gives additional background and insights that are particularly helpful to the first-time reader. The second translation is the version by Percy Bysshe Shelley, currently available from Pagan Press under the title *The Banquet* (2001). As one would expect, the writing is poetic and lyrical, and the text is coupled with Shelley's fascinating "A Discourse on the Manners of the Ancient Greeks Relative to the Subject of Love," an essay suppressed in his lifetime for its progressive stance on homosexuality.

THE BOOK OF ESTHER AND THE BOOK OF DANIEL

As you can imagine, there are countless editions of the Old Testament and even more works of scholarship on the subject. If you're looking for the text of many of the books of the Torah, but don't want a more traditional school version, check out David Rosenberg's *A Literary Bible* (Counterpoint, 2009). As a poet, Rosenberg's translations of eighteen of the books of the Hebrew Bible tell the familiar stories in a more personal, expressive voice than the drier King James language we're all used to. For a feminist perspective on biblical teachings and Jewish ritual, Vanessa L. Ochs' *Words on Fire: One Woman's Journey Into the Sacred* (Westview Press, 1999), though potentially a bit trickier to track down, is a fascinating book combining memoir with rigorous biblical scholarship.

TAO TE CHING

The cheapest and most readily available edition of the *Tao Te Ching* in English is Stephen Mitchell's 1988 translation, published by Harper Collins. It is beloved by many, though much maligned by many others, particularly Chinese academics and scholars who feel that Mitchell's version is too modern and personal, and that his outlook borders on that of a Western colonialist. For a more literal and scholarly translation, check out the edition translated by Red Pine (a.k.a. Bill Porter; Copper Canyon Press, 2009). The translation is spare and elegant, and the text features illuminating commentary by poets, monks, and scholars. Or, if you're looking to brush up on your Mandarin, Stanley Lombardo and Stephen Addiss' translation (Shambhala, 2007) gives one important line from each chapter in the original Mandarin and features an extensive glossary of Chinese characters in the back, allowing the reader to translate it herself so as to gain a deeper understanding of the variety of ways the text can be interpreted.

MAHABHARATA

Mahabharata is just about the most important work of Sanskrit literature; it is epic, exciting, violent, spiritual, and looooong. NYU Press is attempting a new English translation of the full text and is currently up to volume fifteen, of a projected thirty-two. (The first fifteen books will set you back a cool $264.) For most Western readers looking for an introduction to the story, an abridged version is probably the way to go. William Buck's translation from the sixties (University of California Press, 2000) clocks in at a mere 440 pages. It remains true to the spirit of the epic and preserves the overall story, but he does take some liberties and tweaks the plot in a few places, irking some traditionalists. For a briefer take on the text—with a wonderful introduction by the translator—see R. K. Narayan's version (University of Chicago Press, 2000). At just 192 pages, Narayan tells the story in a compact, accessible way.

ANALECTS AND OTHER WRITINGS

It is difficult to find a translation of all five books of *The Five Classics* in English, but of all of the books of *The Five Classics*, the *I Ching* is probably the most familiar to Western readers. Richard Wilhelm and Cary F. Baynes' *I Ching or Book of Changes* (Princeton University Press, 1967) is probably the most beloved version here in the US. *The Book of Songs: The Ancient Chinese Classic of Poetry* is readily available in a competent translation by Arthur Waley (Grove Press, 1996). More interesting, though a bit more expensive, is Ezra Pound's take on it, *Shih-ching: The Classic Anthology Defined by Confucius* (Harvard University Press, 1983). Pound's translations are as Modernist/crank-y as any of his poetry, but they retain the sparse beauty of the original poems. His reverence for, and fascination with, Chinese cultural history really shine through.

ON THE NATURE OF THINGS

Lucretius' classic classical poem, which has been so highly influential to modern philosophical thought, is available in a number of editions in English. The Martin Ferguson Smith translation from 1969 (Hackett, 2001) still holds up as one of the best of the lot. Vibrant and easy to read, it also features a fabulous introduction by Smith. The 2007 Penguin Classics edition, translated by A. E. Stallings, is a fantastic newer translation that will save you a few bucks. It has a bit more contemporary flair to it and features an instructive introduction by Oxford classics scholar Richard Jenkyns.

AENEID

If you were a classics major or attended a fancy East Coast prep school, chances are you have your own translation of *Aeneid* buried in a notebook somewhere in your mom's attic. For the rest of us, no one has yet to capture the tone and spirit of the tale of "pius Aeneas" as faithfully and beautifully as Robert Fitzgerald in his 1983 translation (Vintage, 1990). Robert Fagles, the current darling of classical translation, penned the Penguin Classics edition of 2010, a more readable version to those who feel uncomfortable stepping outside the realm of contemporary prose, with a Bernard Knox introduction that is enjoyable and informative, even to those already familiar with the story and historical context. The other top contender for the people's favorite translation is the Allen Mandelbaum version, currently in a thirty-fifth anniversary edition, featuring some awesome illustrations by Barry Moser, from University of California Press.

THE BOOK OF REVELATION

Revelation is the most fiery, contested, and downright weird books of the New Testament. If you want the text itself in a pretty package (ironically enough) Penguin's Great Ideas series features a beautifully designed edition of The Revelation of St. John the Divine and the Book of Job (2005). For a more scholarly look, Harry O. Maier's *Apocalypse Recalled* (Fortress Press, 2009) examines Revelation in religious, historical, and literary contexts.

THREE TANG POEMS

Three Hundred Tang Poems, the Chinese collection of poems from the Tang Dynasty (618–907 AD) compiled in the mid-eighteenth century by Sun Zhu, remains a classic in China but is difficult to find in English. Of the three poets featured here, Li Bai (or, more familiarly to Western audiences, Li Po) is the most readily available in English translation. One of the best collections of his work available right now is *The Selected Poems of Li Po* (translated by David Hinton; New Directions, 1996). The crisp, spare verses depicting tranquil natural scenes are a pleasure to read. Interested in delving further into Tang poetry? Check out the work of Cold Mountain (Han Shan), the reclusive, cave-dwelling poet who captured the hearts of the Beats. (Kerouac even dedicated *The Dharma Bums* to him.) The most complete, evocative translation of his work is probably *The Collected Songs of Cold Mountain*, by Red Pine (Copper Canyon Press, 2000).

BEOWULF

If you're looking for a bloody, exciting Old English text to read as you toss back a few at your local mead hall, you can't go wrong with *Beowulf*. When Irish poet Seamus Heaney released his translation for W.W. Norton & Company in 2001, medieval scholars and poetry buffs alike were wetting themselves in anticipation. Heaney's version of the poem is beautiful, though it adheres more to contemporary poetic aesthetics than those of medieval times. It does, however, contain the original Old English so readers can compare between the two. For a translation that feels more true to the clunky, ancient, nearly mystical sound of the untranslated version, Howell D. Chickering's *Beowulf* (Anchor, 2006) does the job and has extensive and informative notes. And any über-nerds out there would be well advised to take a look at J. R. R. Tolkien's fascinating and influential lecture on Beowulf, "The Monsters and the Critics" (available in *The Monsters and the Critics*, Grafton, 1997).

THE TALE OF GENJI

Considered by many to be the first novel, *Genji* has become a staple in many enlightened colleges' freshman literature classes. There are three well-known English translations. Arthur Waley, whose translations of Confucius remain the standard, wrote a translation in 1933 that, while very well received at the time, has since been superseded by versions more true to the original text. People are of differing opinions when it comes to the other two. Edward Seidensticker's 1976 translation (Everyman's Library, 1993) simplifies the prose and identifies the characters by name (in the original they are identified only with generic terms and honorifics), making it more readable for a contemporary audience. Royall Tyler's 2001 translation (Penguin Classics, 2006), though perhaps a bit more challenging for American readers, remains more true to the original Japanese and supplies copious notes that illuminate the text. Also worth checking out is Osamu Dezaki's epic eleven-part anime version from 2009.

THE LETTERS OF HELOISE AND ABELARD

You may already be familiar with the ill-fated love affair between Heloise and Abelard from John Cusack's creepy puppet show in the film *Being John Malkovich*. If that's as far as your knowledge of the story goes, though, consider reading William Levitan's translations in *Abelard & Heloise: The Letters and Other Writings* (Hackett, 2007). Levitan does a fine job making the Latin texts eminently accessible, and the edition includes many helpful supplementary materials, including additional writings and poems by Abelard, a chronology, and a map. For more historical and biographical context, read James Burge's fabulous *Heloise and Abelard: A New Biography* (HarperCollins, 2003).

"O NOBILISSIMA VIRIDITAS"

Hildegard's popularity with medieval music fans, feminists, and self-proclaimed mystics has been on the rise again since the 900th anniversary of her birth in 1998. For the perfect soundtrack to accompany Molly Kiely's lush graphic take on "O nobilissima," track down the version performed by Germany's Sequentia ensemble, available on their haunting *Canticles of Ecstasy* album. For a sampling of Hildegard's writings, see *Secrets of God: Writings of Hildegard of*

Bingen, translated by Sabina Flanagan (Shambhala, 1996). It contains excerpts from a great range of the works of the "Sibyl of the Rhine," including portions of her books of visions, her writings on healing plants, and the lyrics to a number of her songs. And Flanagan's biography *Hildegard of Bingen: A Visionary Life* (Routledge, 1989) is an excellent introduction to what we know of the mystic nun's biography and the historical context in which she lived.

"THE FISHERMAN AND THE GENIE" AND "THE WOMAN WITH TWO COYNTES" FROM *THE ARABIAN NIGHTS*

The frame of *The Arabian Nights* is this: clever Scheherazade prevents the evil king from killing her by leaving him hanging mid-story night after night. Unfortunately, of the tales she tells, the ones most of us are familiar with weren't even in the original. Most translations—even more accurate ones—have been sanitized so as not to include the bawdier stories like "The Woman with Two Coyntes." As mentioned in the introduction to the piece in this book, one of the only versions that retains all of the juicy stuff is the sprawling sixteen-volume Richard Burton translation, which, though out of print (except in an abridged version that doesn't include the story) is readily available for your perusal online (http://burtoniana.org/books/1885-Arabian%20 Nights/index.htm). The recent three-volume Penguin Classics edition, translated by Malcolm C. Lyons, is thorough and fast paced, keeping you glued to the page just as surely as King Shahryar was hooked. The general consensus, however, is that the best translation out there right now is Husain Haddaway's abridged 1990 selection. It is currently available in a reasonably priced critical edition from W.W. Norton, which includes the added bonus of historical text, related works from the twentieth century, and a number of critical essays, including a standout by Jorge Luis Borges.

POEMS OF RUMI

Rumi's poems have been around for 800 years, but interest in the great Sufi poet in the Western world has increased exponentially in the last twenty years, possibly due to increased awareness of and preoccupation with Islamic culture. Rumi is a veritable pop culture phenomenon, with dozens of collections in translation on the market, including a watered-down volume of love poems edited by Deepak Chopra. A good starting place for the interested reader is *The Essential Rumi*, translated by Coleman Barks and John Moyne (HarperOne, 2004). Barks and Moyne's translations of the poems in free verse are a wonder to behold—as elegantly simple and full of fiery passion as their author intended. Once you've whetted your appetite, you can move on to Shahram Shiva's stunning *Rending the Veil: Literal and Poetic Translations of Rumi* (Hohm, 1995). The edition is a bit spendy, but well worth the price for Rumi lovers who don't read Persian. Shiva gives us each of the 252 poems he has chosen in the original calligraphy, accompanied by a literal, word-for-word translation along with a more poetic translation, allowing the reader to both parse the full richness of meaning in the words and hear the music of the poems.

THE DIVINE COMEDY

Dante's journey through the afterlife in search of his lost love, Beatrice, ranks with Shakespeare in terms of literary weight and influence. While most of us had to read the first third of *The Divine Comedy*, *Inferno*, at some point in high school or college, fewer had to read *Purgatorio* or *Paradiso*. The first American to translate the whole thing was Henry Wadsworth Longfellow, and while the language may sound a bit clunky and stilted to the contemporary ear, it is an impressive translation that is available for free online in a number of places (http://www.everypoet. com/archive/poetry/dante/dante_contents.htm). A cheap, basic introduction to the work in its entirety is John Ciardi's translation (NAL, 2003). It is fluid, easy to read, and contains summaries before each Canto as well as many helpful notes elucidating the political and social commentaries on Renaissance Italy with which Dante peppered the text. For further Further Reading, *Dante in English*, edited by Eric Griffiths and Matthew Reynolds (Penguin, 2005), is a wonderful sort of compendium of various authors' translations of different passages and a selection of the many English-language poems inspired by the great Italian work.

THE INFERNO

Dante's *Inferno* has inspired everything from books to paintings to plays to films—and even a video game. The most widely read book of the three-part *Divine Comedy*, *The Inferno* is also the segment boasting the most translations in print. The most talked-about addition to the pile in the last twenty years would have to be former poet laureate Robert Pinsky's sizzling 1996 version (Farrar, Straus and Giroux). Pinsky took on the extremely daunting task of preserving Dante's intricately complex *terza rima* structure. He succeeded brilliantly, staying true to the original Italian rhyme scheme yet keeping the language fresh. You can sense the relish with which he artfully depicts Dante's nine horrific circles. Of the other translations of the last fifty years, Allen Mandelbaum's 1982 translation is a vigorous, free-verse rendering, available very inexpensively from Bantam Classics. And, more recently, husband-and-wife team Robert and Jean Hollander's 2002 translation, while perhaps not as singularly remarkable an achievement as Pinksky's, is nonetheless lovely, learned, and replete with informative notes.

THE TIBETAN BOOK OF THE DEAD (BARDO THODOL)

Probably the most well-known text of Tibetan Buddhism in the Western world, the *Bardo Thodol* instructs readers on how to prepare for and navigate the space between death and rebirth. If you're reading up to prepare for your transition into the great beyond, you're going to want an accurate translation. The oldest English translation, by W. Y. Evans-Wentz in 1927 (Oxford University Press, 2000), is still very well regarded and contains a neat intro by Carl Jung. America's favorite Buddhist scholar—no, not Richard Gere, I'm talking about Robert Thurman—published a thoughtful and rigorous translation (Bantam Books, 1993) that succeeded in getting a thumbs-up from the Dalai Lama. However, for all you completists out there, it wasn't until Gyurme Dorje's 2005 translation (Penguin Classics, 2007) that the English-speaking world had access to the unabridged text. Now considered the definitive version, this edition also contains an intro by the Dalai Lama. If the trip you're taking is less of the spiritual than of the chemical variety, Timothy Leary's classic psychedelic take on the book, *The Psychedelic Experience: A Manual Based on the Tibetan Book of the Dead* (Citadel, 2000), might be more your bag.

THE CANTERBURY TALES

Think Middle English is a snooze? Turn off that Judd Apatow movie and pick up a copy of Chaucer's *Canterbury Tales*, the Middle Ages' great repository of dick and fart jokes—and one of the most important works of early Western literature. David Wright's translation into modern English (Oxford University Press, 2008) preserves all of the raunchy fun of Chaucer's original without sanitizing his deliciously naughty language as many other editions have. And it's one of the least expensive editions available. Slightly more expensive but even more readable is Peter Ackroyd's recent adaptation (Penguin Classics, 2010). The fun and accessible prose catapults the pilgrims into a verbal landscape more easily understandable to contemporary readers, and Ted Stearn's hilarious cover and flap-comics are an added bonus. Feeling extra adventurous? Why not try reading the *Tales* in the original Middle English? It might take a few pages to get into the groove, but being able to interpret Chaucer for yourself is highly rewarding. The 2005 Penguin Classics edition, edited by Jill Mann, provides a wealth of explanatory notes to help you along the way.

"THE LAST BALLAD"

François Villon was the bad boy of the French Middle Ages; a punk rocker for the premodern age. Some of the most famous interpretations of his work include Dante Gabriel Rossetti's notorious—perhaps overly flowery—refrain "But where are the snows of yesteryear?" and Bertolt Brecht's translations of his ballads into German for *The Threepenny Opera*. There are a few collections of his translated work available in print. Pulitzer Prize–winner Louis Simpson's 2000 *François Villon's The Legacy and The Testament* (Story Line Press) is a skillful verse translation—no easy feat given the nuances of Villon's language. The 1977 *The Poems of François Villon* by Galway Kinnell (University Press of New England, 1982) remains an outstanding free-verse translation that captures the essence and soul of the ballads.

LE MORTE D'ARTHUR

Sir Thomas Malory's compilation of the tales of King Arthur and the Knights of the Round Table remains the standard to which all other Arthur stories adhere. Keith Baines' 1962 translation (Signet Classics, 2001) is a much loved and faithful—though somewhat abridged—retelling, featuring an introduction by celebrated classicist Robert Graves. Of further interest is John Steinbeck's reimagining, *The Acts of King Arthur and His Noble Knights* (Penguin Classics, 2008). Although not an exact translation, *Le Morte* was one of Steinbeck's most beloved books, and he considered his stab at reimagining it to be one of his life's great works. The (unfinished) book provides fresh insight into both the Arthurian legend and its influence on one of the great American writers of the twentieth century. An interesting sidebar for all of you as visual arts fans: the 1892 illustrated edition of Malory's classic launched the career of a young Aubrey Beardsley. Dover published a beautiful edition of some selections in 2001, which is well worth seeking out.

APU OLLANTAY

The Incans had a rich, dramatic culture, but when the Spaniards came and wiped them out, most of it was lost. *Ollantay* is one of the few remaining works of the Incan dramatic tradition available to us, and is considered to be the oldest work of indigenous American literature. The only English translation available is by nineteenth-century British historian Clements Markham (who added "Apu" to the title) and in print it is only available through Kessinger Publishing. You may just be better off downloading a free version at Project Gutenberg or another site where public domain works are available (http://www.gutenberg.org/ebooks/9068). For another Inca-related drama, about how and why this rich cultural history has mostly been lost, see Peter Shaffer's 1964 *The Royal Hunt of the Sun*. The play is out of print in the US, but used copies are fairly easy to find and worth digging up.

HAGOROMO

This timeless work of Noh theater about a fisherman and a heavenly beauty has inspired many artists and writers throughout the world. The first English-language interpretation of the story may have been W. B. Yeats' *At the Hawk's Well*, a one-act play written in 1916. Yeats penned the foreword to a seminal Modernist interpretation of Noh theater, essentially the introduction of Japanese drama to the West, first published by New Directions in 1959. The book, *The Classic Noh Theater of Japan*, features translations of many key works of Noh theater, by Ezra Pound and Ernest Fenollosa. The translations are poetic and precise, and the volume, which is still in print, contains extensive notes on traditional staging and costumes. Another, more recent collection of Noh plays in translation is Royall Tyler's thorough *Japanese No Dramas* (Penguin Classics, 1993). Tyler's translations are elegant, and he precedes each play with an introduction contextualizing it in terms of Japanese history and culture.

OUTLAWS OF THE WATER MARGIN

One of the great novels of classical Chinese literature, *Outlaws of the Water Margin* is rarely read in the United States these days. The tale of a band of outlaws and their eventual pardon and assimilation into the army enjoyed a spike in popularity here in the 1930s when novelist Pearl S. Buck published her (largely problematic and frequently inaccurate) translation under the title *All Men Are Brothers* (available from Moyer Bell Publishing, 2006). A more recent, and complete, translation, *The Marshes of Mount Liang*, was put together by father-son team John and Alex Dent-Young. Their five-volume version, available from the Chinese University Press, is fast-paced and entertaining, though occasionally clunky. But the general consensus is that the four-volume Sidney Shapiro translation, *Outlaws of the Marsh*, from 1980 (Foreign Languages Press, 2001), is the most vibrant, funny, and true to the spirit of the original.

POPOL VUH

Yes, Krautrockers Popol Vuh were cool. But the sacred book of the Mayan people of Guatemala, from which the band snagged its name, is even cooler. One of the few surviving Mesoamerican texts, this collection of mythology and folklore survived thanks to a Dominican Friar. Unfortunately, the one original manuscript has no organizing structure and has been difficult to translate and edit. The version that is largely considered the most authoritative is Dennis Tedlock's *Popol Vuh: The Definitive Edition of the Mayan Book of the Dawn of Life and the Glories of Gods and Kings* (Touchstone, 1996). Tedlock's comprehensive translation is aided by the fact that he spent years living with Mayan priests and wrote his edition in consultation with a K'iche' daykeeper, or calendar-priest. Barbara Tedlock (Dennis' wife, also a Mayan scholar) provides an illuminating companion to this text with her anthropological study of Mayan timekeeping, *Time and the Highland Maya* (University of New Mexico Press, 1992). Allen J. Christenson's 2004 translation (University of Oklahoma Press, 2007) is the most recent and updated, and allows the reader to compare his translation with the original K'iche' text.

THE VISIONS OF ST. TERESA OF ÁVILA

St. Teresa could very well be the patron saint of feminists, due to the number of liberated women who have cited her as an influence (Simone de Beauvoir, Jorie Graham, etc.). The most recent translation of this celebrated mystic saint's autobiography is also the first to have been written by a woman. Mirabai Starr's *Teresa of Ávila: The Book of My Life* (New Seeds, 2007) breathes passionate new life into the work, presenting us with a wholly relatable and three-dimensional version of Teresa. If the autobiography leaves you with a taste for more Teresa, her letters, collected in a two-volume edition translated by Kieran Kavanaugh (ICS Publications, 2001 and 2007), offer an even more candid look into the details of her daily life and relationships. And for an engaging recent biography of this eccentric, strong-willed, visionary saint, see Cathleen Medwick's *Teresa of Avila: The Progress of a Soul* (Image, 2001).

"HOT SUN, COOL FIRE"

Sixteenth-century bard George Peele is now mainly forgotten thanks to the enormous shadow cast by his near contemporary, Bill Shakespeare. Peele's three-volume collected works, put out by Yale University Press in the fifties and sixties, has long been out of print. In fact, most editions of everything Peele ever wrote have been out of print since the sixties, when he was still somewhat in academic vogue thanks to the controversy surrounding his possible authorship of Shakespeare's *Titus Andronicus*. A very short excerpt of Peele's poetry is available in *The Penguin Book of Renaissance Verse: 1509–1659* (Penguin Books, 2005). Algernon Charles Swinburne's *Contemporaries of Shakespeare*, also out of print, is worth digging up for some background information. Similarly, A. R. Braunmuller's 1983 biography, *George Peele*, is out of print but pops up in used bookstores every now and again and is worth keeping your eyes out for if you're interested in learning more about this Renaissance dramatist and poet.

JOURNEY TO THE WEST

One of the Four Great Classic Novels in Chinese (along with the previously discussed *Outlaws of the Water Margin*), *Journey to the West* is an epic Chinese story featuring a cast of hundreds. One of the most well-known early English transla-

tions is Arthur Waley's abridged *Monkey* (the title the book is frequently known by in the West) from 1943, still available in print (Grove Press, 1994). Waley's translation has aged fairly well, and is a rollicking, funny introduction to one of the great works of early Taoist literature. The unabridged, four-volume Anthony C. Yu translation is still in print (University of Chicago Press, 1977–1983). Yu's rendition is both more contemporary and more complete, and features a wealth of explanatory notes and an illuminating academic introduction.

THE FAERIE QUEENE

Edmund Spenser's epic allegorical poem in praise of Queen Elizabeth I may have scored him points with the Virgin Queen (she endowed him with a pension for life after its publication), but it certainly did nothing to endear him to the legions of college students who've since had to slog their way through his deliberately archaic verse. A heavily annotated version will help a lot if you aspire to get through the whole thing. Longman's 2006 edition, edited by A. C. Hamilton and expertly translated by Hiroshi Yamashita and Toshiyuki Suzuki, provides a whole slew of scholarly notes to help the reader along. Less pricey though more bare bones is the Penguin Classics edition from 1979, edited by Thomas P. Roche, providing no introduction and fewer notes than the Hamilton—if you're looking to spend less money and excited by the idea of decrypting antique English, this is the edition for you. Decided on the Penguin edition but then realized you were in over your head? Don't fret; just pick up a copy of *The Cambridge Companion to Spenser* (Cambridge University Press, 2001). The essays contained within this informative volume should help get you situated in the proper historical context and poetic aesthetic to get Spenser sorted out.

A MIDSUMMER NIGHT'S DREAM

This most beloved of Shakespeare's comedies reads like a teeny-bopper girl's dream (indeed, it was adapted into the 2001 teen sex comedy *Get Over It*) with its fairies and potions. The unbridled sexuality and humor of the original make this one of the most contemporary feeling of the Bard's plays. Shakespeare's language is so timeless and beautiful that even a simple edition with little or no annotation will generally do the job, although in the case of *Midsummer Night*, the romantic reconfigurings can become so convoluted that it helps to have an edition that makes sense of them. The Signet Classics edition (1998) is cheap, portable, and has some notes to help you make sense of some of the more outmoded language, but not so many that they distract from your own reading. The Pelican edition (2000) is also inexpensive, has an instructive introduction, and is more prettily designed. There have been countless reinterpretations of the story in literature, music, and film, but the most interesting to readers of this volume might be Neil Gaiman's *Dream Country* from the *Sandman* series (2010).

KING LEAR

Lear is probably Shakespeare's most tragic figure, and the play is among his most harrowing. As with *Midsummer Night*, a less expensive version with fewer additional embellishments is fine for most readers (Signet, Pelican, etc.). For a more scholarly look at the play, the Arden Shakespeare edition

(1997), edited by R. A. Foakes, provides plenty of informative notes and a useful introduction. It is one of the editions available that attempts to conflate the two different earliest surviving manuscripts of *King Lear*, rather than simply forcing the reader to make do with one version or the other. Another "conflated" Lear that is also quite good is the Folger Shakespeare Library edition, edited by Barbara A. Mowatt and Paul Werstine (2005). In addition to its fabulous supplementary material, the editors have chosen to print the notes side by side with the text, making for easier critical reading prompts.

DON QUIXOTE
Cervantes' knight errant has inspired countless reimaginings and spoofs, including a musical and the short-lived Hanna-Barbera cartoon *The Adventures of Don Coyote and Sancho Panda*. Though Cervantes wrote in Spanish, the book has enriched the English language with terms such as "tilting at windmills" and "quixotic." English translations have been appearing since the 1620s, so there are a LOT of editions to choose from out there. The most recent translation, by Tom Lathrop, has been heralded as a grand achievement and is available in a mass-market, pocket-sized paperback (Signet Classics, 2011) with detailed notes and an informative introduction detailing Lathrop's reasoning for throwing his hat into the ring. Another lauded recent addition is Edith Grossman's translation (Harper Perennial, 2005). Grossman's has been touted as the most simple, true-to-the-original-language version in English.

SONNET 18 AND SONNET 20
Shakespeare's sonnets are considered to be the precursors to the modern love poem, having inspired the Romantics considerably more than the older Petrarchan sonnets, a form the Bard played with and somewhat mocked. The most complete and scholarly edition of the sonnets available at the moment is the Oxford World's Classics edition, edited by Colin Burrow (2008), whose thorough introduction is one of the best studies of Shakespeare's poems around. For those who remain wary of slogging through the Elizabethan language, the Arden Shakespeare edition, edited by Katherine Duncan-Jones (1997) provides "translations" of the poems into more contemporary language side by side with the original text. Her notes and introduction also play up the racier aspect of the love poems, whose overt sexuality is often skirted by editors and critics.

"THE FLEA"
John Donne's metaphysical poems are the late Renaissance equivalent of *Penthouse Letters*: full of veiled sexuality and lust cleverly disguised, as in his most famous poem, "The Flea." For a good introduction to Donne's work, see the fabulous *The Complete Poetry and Selected Prose of John Donne* (Modern Library Classics, 2001). Expertly edited by Charles M. Coffin, and with a detailed introduction by Denis Donoghue, the collection features all of Donne's sonnets and poems, along with a sampling of his prose work. For a simple introduction to Donne's greatest hits at a budget price, the Dover Thrift edition (1993) is a serviceable and superlatively cheap collection. For those seeking further scholarly enlightenment on Donne's work, *The Cambridge Companion to John Donne* (Cambridge University Press, 2006) provides a number of insightful critical essays on the poet's work.

"TO HIS COY MISTRESS"
Most famous for his erotically charged "To His Coy Mistress," Andrew Marvell's poetry is by turns full of passionate lust and drily political. For a complete overview of his poems, check out *The Complete Poems*, edited by Elizabeth Story Donno (Penguin Classics, 2005). If you're just looking for a collection of Marvell's more engaging and notorious poems, the Dover Thrift edition *"To His Coy Mistress" and Other Poems* (1997) has what you're looking for at a low, low price. For more on the political and personal life of the intensely private poet, Nigel Smith's extensive *Andrew Marvell: The Chameleon* (Yale University Press, 2010) provides a thorough investigation into Marvell's life, poetry, and historical context.

PARADISE LOST
John Milton's most famous work is both the template for contemporary renderings of Eden and the devil and the bane of many a college freshman. Luckily, the notoriously dense and difficult-to-read classic is available in a number of editions meant to help engage with the English-language masterpiece. The most helpful for contemporary readers not so familiar with Milton is the Norton Critical edition (2004), edited by Gordon Teskey, who opts to modernize the spelling and syntax, and whose notes and selection of critical essays help to illuminate the text. For an even more simplified version, Dennis Danielson's *Paradise Lost: Parallel Prose Edition* (Broadview Press, 2012) gives a side-by-side, page-for-page translation of the poem into contemporary prose. And of particular interest to readers of this book, Dover has reproduced the fifty plates of illustrations by nineteenth-century artist Gustave Doré in a slim and attractive edition (1993).

"FORGIVE US OUR TRESPASSES"
Aphra Behn was an astounding figure of the English Restoration: playwright, poetess, spy, and proto-feminist. In *A Room of One's Own*, the great Virginia Woolf praises Behn as the woman who "earned [women] the right to speak their minds." More well known for her plays and novels, there are few collections devoted to Behn's poetry available to modern readers. *Selected Poems: Aphra Behn*, edited by Malcolm Hicks (Carcanet Press, 2006) is one of the (slim) volumes dedicated to her poems. For further works, the Penguin Classics editions of *Oroonoko, The Rover, and Other Works* (2003) provides a fine introduction to the feisty Ms. Behn, with a selection of novels, plays, and poems, edited and introduced by Behn scholar Janet Todd. Todd's meticulously researched *The Secret Life of Aphra Behn* (Rutgers University Press, 1996) is difficult to track down and quite expensive, while her Penguin edition of Behn's work provides the transgressive writer's own work, alongside Todd's keen critical insights, for a fraction of the price.

GULLIVER'S TRAVELS
Swift's classic satire was first published in 1726 and has remained in print ever since. It is easy to see why, given the novel's hilarious and largely cynical observations on human nature. In spite

of the universal themes, however, many of the in-jokes are commentaries on the specific time and cultural context in which it was written, so an annotated version can help to explain the full extent of Swift's humor here. The Norton Critical edition, edited by Albert J. Rivero (2001), contains notes, critical essays, and contextual materials galore. On the other hand, because this work is decidedly more modern feeling than, say, Shakespeare or Milton, and has graced the English language with such wonderfully rich and (now) commonplace terms as "gullible," "Lilliputian," and "Yahoo," a more bare-bones, less expensive version can be suitable, even if it means missing out on some of the jokes. The Dover Thrift edition (1996) is true to its name and supplies the text in its entirety, even if it is lacking in supplementary materials. If you're a sci-fi geek with a disposable income, the 1980 Clarkson N. Potter edition is annotated by Isaac Asimov, providing a unique and sci-fi–friendly reading of this prototypical spoof.

"A MODEST PROPOSAL"

Speaking of satire, Swift's short essay entitled "A Modest Proposal" is about as biting and nasty as satire gets, with its tongue-in-cheek advice that the hard-up Irish beat their plight by selling their children to the rich—as food. Reading like something straight out of the *Onion* newspaper circa 2010, this underappreciated masterpiece continues to make its mark on contemporary pop culture, appearing in Adult Swim cartoons and episodes of *The Colbert Report*. If you want an inexpensive edition with the text of both "A Modest Proposal" and Swift's more notorious novel, Simon & Schuster's 2005 *Gulliver's Travels and A Modest Proposal* is a cheap and portable way to go. The Barnes & Noble Library of Essential Reading edition is also unabridged and inexpensive, with an introduction by Lewis C. Daly.

"ADVICE TO A YOUNG MAN ON THE CHOICE OF A MISTRESS" AND "LETTER TO THE ROYAL ACADEMY OF BRUSSELS" (A.K.A. "FART PROUDLY")

Benjamin Franklin ranks with Mark Twain as one of the earliest and greatest American humorists. For many years "Advice to a Young Man" was censored, being completely omitted from the founding father's collected works. "Fart Proudly," when included, was glossed over and not much discussed. Neither work is available as an edition of its own, but both are collected in *Fart Proudly: Writings of Benjamin Franklin You Never Read in School* (Frog, Ltd., 2003). There are many more scholarly volumes of Franklin's collected writings. The two-volume Library of America set (2005), expertly edited by J. A. Leo Lemay, ranks among the most attractive and complete editions available. For a less expensive annotated version, the Oxford World's Classics *Autobiography and Other Writings* (2008), edited by Ormond Seavey, is a standout.

CANDIDE

Voltaire's classic dis to optimists got him in trouble with both the church and the French powers that be in the 1700s. It's still a marvelously fresh and funny tale today, with a number of different editions available to English readers. The best translation currently available is probably Theo Cuffe's lively version published by Penguin Classics (2005). The introduction by Michael Wood provides an excellent context for the philosophical and historical background. For a budget edition that contains even more of Voltaire's writings, check out *Candide, Zadig, and Selected Stories* (Signet Classics, 2009), translated by Donald M. Frame, with an informative intro by John Iverson. And for you Francophiles out there: while it may not be the best translation on the market, Dover's *Candide: A Dual Language Book* (1993) allows you to read the original alongside the translation.

LONDON JOURNAL

James Boswell's racy *London Journal* is a lot more fun to read than that of any other eighteenth-century diarist. There are few editions currently in print, but one of the best remains the Yale University Press edition (2004), edited by Boswell scholar Frederick A. Pottle, which is skillfully annotated. Boswell's most famous work is his *The Life of Samuel Johnson*. Clocking in at more than 1,200 pages, you'll want a well-edited version if you're going to try to tackle this one. David Womersley does a fabulous job taming the text for Penguin Classics (2008). Alternately, the Oxford World's Classics edition (2008), while a bit more dense, contains a highly informative introduction.

A VINDICATION OF THE RIGHTS OF WOMAN

Mary Wollstonecraft's ur-feminist text remains a hugely important work for bluestockings and latter-day riot grrrls, not to mention history buffs and general readers. While the book is still (sadly) quite applicable to today's world, the eighteenth-century language can feel difficult and overwhelming to contemporary readers. For a thorough critical review, you can't beat the Norton Critical edition (2009), edited by Deidre Shauna Lynch. It's packed full of background information and critical works from various time periods highlighting how scholarly readings of Wollstonecraft's manifesto have changed over the years. For an introduction to Wollstonecraft's feminist fiction writing, her stories "Mary" and "Maria" are available in an edition that also includes her daughter Mary Shelley's scandalous "Matilda," from Penguin Classics (1992). Also worth seeking out: the detailed biography *Mary Wollstonecraft: A Revolutionary Life* (Columbia University Press, 2002), penned by Janet Todd, leading scholar of early-modern female writers.

DANGEROUS LIAISONS

Dangerous Liaisons is one of those rare books that simultaneously allows you to feel like you're reading one of the great classics of world literature and a fun, trashy gossip rag. It has inspired many interpretations on the stage and screen, most memorably in Stephen Frears' 1988 film *Dangerous Liaisons*, and least memorably in Roger Kumble's 1999 film *Cruel Intentions*. Of the translations available, Douglas Parmée's for Oxford World's Classics (2008) is beloved by some and loathed by others for its (admittedly somewhat affected) use of British idiom. But he captures the juvenile amorality of Valmont and Merteuil pitch-perfectly, and the introduction, supplied by David Coward, provides an amusing and fascinating look at the life of Choderlos de Laclos. If you find Parmée's syntax irksome, the more recent translation by Helen Constantine (Penguin Classics, 2007) has been lauded as faithful and readable.

CONTRIBUTORS

ANDRICE ARP makes comics, paintings, illustrations, and small objects in Portland, Oregon. She was the coeditor of the Hi-Horse comic book series, which ran from 2001 to 2004, and *Hi-Horse Omnibus*, which was published in 2004 by Alternative Comics. Since then, her comics and paintings have appeared semi-regularly in Fantagraphics' quarterly anthology *MOME*, among other places. Her paintings have been in group shows at Giant Robot and other galleries, and in a solo show at Secret Headquarters. She is currently working on trying to understand everything.

IAN "ALBINAL" BALL produces professional animation, illustration, and interactive awesomeness for people who want to do something marvelous with their messages. He has won awards for his web work, picked up prizes in prestigious competitions, and had his pictures published in proper books. Juggling his work, children (not literally), and personal projects keeps him busy enough, but he also tries regular running to "burn off a bit of blubber."

COLEMAN BARKS was born and raised in Chattanooga, Tennessee, and was educated at the University of North Carolina and the University of California at Berkeley. He taught poetry and creative writing at the University of Georgia for thirty years. He is the author of numerous Rumi translations and has been a student of Sufism since 1977. His work with Rumi was the subject of an hour-long segment in Bill Moyers' *Language of Life* series on PBS, and he is a featured poet and translator in Bill Moyers' poetry special, *Fooling with Words*. Coleman is the father of two grown children and the grandfather of four. He lives in Athens, Georgia.

ROBERT BERRY left behind a career as an easel painter in Detroit ten years ago and moved to Philadelphia to make comics and stories. With his production partner, Josh Levitas, he's the cartoonist of *Ulysses "Seen,"* an interactive comic book adaptation of Joyce's great novel. His work here is, of course, dedicated to his mother, who taught him everything he knows about Shakespeare, poetry, and the uncompromising drive it takes to make art.

TOM BIBY grew up in Montana and went to school for fine art in Missoula. He currently lives in San Francisco doing woodworking and carpentry, as well as writing and drawing graphic novels and illustrated books as one of the Two Fine Chaps. Their work can be seen at twofinechaps.com.

ALESSANDRO BONACCORSI is an illustrator and graphic designer from Tuscany. He has been working in different areas such as editorial, design, publishing, cultural, and corporate for several years, in a style that is a surrealistic and imaginific mix of painting, hand-lettering, and digital. He leaves realism to others, preferring the unimaginable, the absurd, the dreamt, the unexpected, the unusual, the bizarre, the exciting. You can view his portfolio at zuppassion.com or bonaccorsiart.com.

LISA BROWN is a *New York Times*–bestselling illustrator, author, and cartoonist. She lives in San Francisco. You can usually find her at americanchickens.com.

LIZ BYER is a freelance editor and writer living in Brooklyn, New York. Her editorial clients have included over a dozen presses, large and small, and her writing has appeared in *Get Ahead* magazine, *Worn* fashion journal, and a number of online publications.

SHAWN CHENG is an artist and cartoonist working in New York City. He creates handmade, limited-edition comic books as a member of the comics and art collective Partyka. His comics have appeared in the *SPX Anthology* and *Best American Comics*; his paintings and prints have been shown at Fredericks & Freiser Gallery in New York and the Giant Robot galleries in Los Angeles and San Francisco. Shawn was born in Taiwan and grew up on Long Island. He studied painting and printmaking at Yale University. Shawn currently lives in Astoria, Queens, with his wife and two daughters.

SEYMOUR CHWAST's award-winning work has influenced two generations of designers and illustrators. He cofounded Push Pin Studios, which rapidly gained an international reputation for innovative design and illustrations. Push Pin's visual language (which references culture and literature) arose from its passion for historical design movements and helped revolutionize the way people look at design. He is a recipient of the AIGA Medal, was inducted into the Art Directors Hall of Fame, and has an honorary PhD in fine art from the Parsons School of Design. His work is in the Museum of Modern Art, the Metropolitan Museum of Art, and other major museums around the world. Chwast has exhibited and lectured widely.

MOLLY CRABAPPLE is an artist, comics creator, and the founder of Dr. Sketchy's Anti-Art School, a chain of alt-drawing events that takes place in 140 cities around the world. She is the coauthor, with John Leavitt, of *Puppet Makers* (DC Comics) and *Straw House* (First Second Books).

For nearly four decades, **ROBERT CRUMB** has shocked, entertained, titillated, and challenged the imaginations (and the inhibitions) of comics fans the world over. In truth, alternative comics as we know them today might never have come about without R. Crumb's influence—the acknowledged "Father" of the underground comics could also be considered the

"Grandfather" of alternative comics. Mr. Natural, Angelfood McSpade, Flakey Foont, and most especially, the hedonistic anthropomorphic version of Crumb's childhood pet, Fritz (a cat), have become cult icons. His voluptuous, acid-inspired romps of the 1960s gave way to comparatively sober, introspective dialogues and biting indictments of American culture. In 2009 he published—to worldwide acclaim—a complete adaptation of the Book of Genesis.

REBECCA DART is an artist and animator living in Vancouver, British Columbia. She cohabitates with fellow artist Robin Bougie and a fat, asthmatic cat. Follow her artistic adventures at flickr.com/people/rebeccadart.

KENT H. DIXON has published work in all genres, predominantly fiction. He's won grants and awards for his fiction and nonfiction over the years, received Pushcart nominations, and made finalist and semifinalist at any number of competitions (*Sarabande*, Iowa Short Fiction, *Midwest Quarterly*). He has translations of Baudelaire and Mallarmé, Rilke, and Sappho online, and to do his rendition of *The Epic of Gilgamesh*, he took a Cuneiform by Mail course from the University of Chicago's Oriental Institute. He teaches creative writing and literature at Wittenberg University, in Springfield, Ohio, where with wife Mimi he raised four wonderful sons, one of whom is the graphic artist for the Bull of Heaven episode from *Gilgamesh*, in this anthology.

Using his father Kent Dixon's thoroughly researched rendition of the text, **KEVIN DIXON** has converted the world's oldest epic from cuneiform to comix. Kevin is also responsible for the autobiographical series *...And Then There Was Rock*, true stories about playing in a crappy loser band. With collaborator Eric Knisley, he produced *Tales of the Sinister Harvey, Mickey Death and the Winds of Impotence*, and the Xeric Award–winning *Flavor Contra Comix and Stories*. His latest non-Gilgamesh project is *Mkele Mbembe*, which has nothing to do with the legendary modern-day dinosaur of Kenya. You can contact him at ultrakevin@hotmail.com.

ALICE DUKE is an illustrator and sequential artist based in the UK. Her comics work has appeared in anthologies by publishers Self Made Hero (*Lovecraft Anthology Vol. 1* and *Nevermore*) and Blank Slate (*Nelson*). Her illustration work can be found on album covers, in magazines, inside video games, and tattooed on skin. More information is available at alice-duke.com.

Illustrator **RYAN DUNLAVEY** is best known as the artist and cocreator of the American Library Award–winning *Action Philosophers!* comic book series (with author Fred Van Lente). Some of Ryan's other comics include *MODOK* for Marvel Comics, *Tommy Atomic* for *Royal Flush* magazine, and the self-published *Comic Book Comics* (also with Van Lente), the first

ever cartoon history of the American comic book industry. His comics and illustrations have appeared in *MAD, Wizard, ToyFare*, the *Princeton Review, Time Out*, and *Disney Adventures*. He lives in New York City with his wife and son.

ALEX ECKMAN-LAWN graduated from the University of the Arts in 2007 with a BA in illustration and a lust for blood. Alex's work has appeared in comics, role-playing games, on CD covers, book covers, and in films, as well as several group and solo gallery shows.

From the Southern summer dance grounds of Oklahoma to the wildlife refuges of the snowy Northwest; from stories of ancestral circuits and stories of present-day struggles, **DAYTON EDMONDS**, a full-blooded Native American of the Caddo Nation, has developed a fine, diverse ministry, lifestyle, and artistry. Dayton is a commissioned United Methodist missionary, now retired. For twenty-five years he served as a professional community developer living in Southern Oregon and North Central Washington. He works ecumenically nationwide with church congregations, educational institutions, camps, community groups, libraries, and others, using storytelling, puppetry, clowning, positive imaging, and other skills to teach sensitivity and awareness. Dayton's art forms—drawing, painting, sculpture, printmaking—blend with his storytelling abilities and help him weave thought-provoking pictures for the mind's eye. See more at daytonedmonds.net

WILL EISNER was born William Erwin Eisner on March 6, 1917, in Brooklyn, New York. By the time of his death on January 3, 2005, following complications from open-heart surgery, Eisner was recognized internationally as one of the giants in the field of sequential art, a term he coined. In a career that spanned nearly seventy years and eight decades—from the dawn of the comic book to the advent of digital comics—he truly was the "Orson Welles of comics" and the "father of the graphic novel." He broke new ground in the development of visual narrative and the language of comics and was the creator of The Spirit, John Law, Lady Luck, Mr. Mystic, Uncle Sam, Blackhawk, Sheena, and countless others. One of the comic industry's most prestigious awards, the Eisner Award, is named after him. Recognized as the "Oscars" of the American comic book business, the Eisners are presented annually before a packed ballroom at Comic-Con International in San Diego, America's largest comics convention.

HUNT EMERSON has drawn cartoons and comic strips since the early 1970s. He has published around thirty comic books and albums, mainly with Knockabout Comics (London), including *Lady Chatterley's Lover, The Rime of the Ancient Mariner*, and *Casanova's Last Stand*. His characters include Firkin the Cat (a strip of sexual satire that has run in *Fiesta* magazine,

UK, since 1981), Calculus Cat (the cat that hates television), PussPuss (yes—another cat!), Max Zillion and Alto Ego (a jazz musician and his saxophone), Alan Rabbit, and many more. His comic strips have been translated into ten languages, he has been awarded several comic strip prizes, and in 2000 he was chosen for inclusion in the exhibition "Les Maîtres de la Bande Dessinée Européenne" by the Bibliothèque nationale de France and the CNBDI, Angoulême. You can see and buy his work on his website, largecow.com.

EDIE FAKE was born in Chicagoland in 1980 and has since clocked time in Providence, New York, Los Angeles, San Francisco, and Baltimore. He was one of the first recipients of Printed Matter's Awards for Artists, and his drawings have been included in *Hot and Cold, Creative Time Comics*, and *LTTR*. His first graphic novel, *Gaylord Phoenix*, was published by Secret Acres in 2010. He currently lives in Chicago and works as a small-press sommelier for Quimby's Books.

MICAH FARRITOR is an illustrator who has completed two graphic novels: *The Living and the Dead* by Todd Livingston and Robert Tinnell, and *Night Trippers* by Mark Ricketts. Other work can be seen in *Read Magazine,* a *Weekly Reader/Reader's Digest* publication; Ape Entertainment's *White Picket Fences* series; *Trickster: Native American Tales*; *Science Fiction Classics*, containing a rendition of *The War of the Worlds*; and *Christmas Classics*, with a version of *A Christmas Carol.*

JONATHAN FETTER-VORM studied history and art at Stanford University. After graduating, he apprenticed as a letterpress printer and hand-bookbinder. Together with childhood friend Tom Biby, he started the imprint Two Fine Chaps, dedicated to publishing handmade illustrated books. Jonathan is currently writing and drawing a graphic history of the Manhattan Project, to be published by Hill & Wang in 2012. He lives in Brooklyn, New York.

BENJAMIN FRISCH is a comic book artist, journalist, and satirist from Williamsburg, Virginia. His published works include the serialized graphic novel *Ayn Rand's Adventures in Wonderland*, published on the award-winning political satire site Wonkette, and a short-lived but beloved cross-dressing comic strip entitled *Maurice Antoinette.* His story "At the Concert Hall, a Symphony for Space Invaders" was featured on the National Public Radio program *Weekend Edition Sunday.* In 2011 Benjamin graduated first in his class with an MFA in sequential art from the Savannah College of Art and Design. Benjamin currently lives in Austin, Texas, where he is developing a graphic novel about a cartoon family, and where he eats tacos every day.

RICK GEARY has been a freelance cartoonist and illustrator for around forty years. His illustrations and graphic stories have appeared in *National Lampoon, MAD*, the *New York Times, Heavy Metal, Disney Adventures*, and many other publications. He has written and illustrated five children's books. His graphic novels include the biographies *J. Edgar Hoover* and *Trotsky*, as well as nine volumes in the series *A Treasury of Victorian Murder* and four volumes in *A Treasury of 20th Century Murder*, the latest of which is *The Lives of Sacco & Vanzetti.* In 2007, after thirty years in San Diego, Rick and his wife, Deborah, moved to Carrizozo, New Mexico. See his more of his work at rickgeary.com.

SANYA GLISIC is an illustrator and printmaker in Chicago, Illinois. She is originally from Bosnia. During her 2010 Artist Residency at Spudnik Press in Chicago, she illustrated, screenprinted, and hand-bound an edition of books based on Heinrich Hoffmann's nineteenth-century *Der Struwwelpeter*. She has contributed to several publications, including *Lumpen Magazine* and *Artifice*, and her work has appeared on the covers of *Newcity Magazine* and *KOSHKA* zine. Her work will appear in the upcoming anthology *BLACK EYE No.2*, published by Rotland Press. Her prints have been included in the Blaque Lyte exhibition at Hyde Park Art Center, as well as other galleries in Chicago. She was awarded the 2011–2012 Artist Residency at the Chicago Printmakers Collaborative. More of her work can be found at sanyaglisic.com.

MICHAEL GREEN has been a wandering artist-monk, householder, sign painter, landscaper, and television art director. His talent finally found an enduring place in books. Today there are over 2,500,000 copies of his illustrated books currently in print, including, *The Illuminated Prayer, Unicornis, Zen & the Art of the Macintosh*, and (most famously) *The Illuminated Rumi.* His signature blend of art and text has always pointed, like modern physics, to a mysterious unity underlying the apparent multiplicity of reality. The irony of this transcendent field is that the ardor it can arouse—religiosity—often divides the human family. It's an irony that threatens the entire planet right now. If politicians fail to find common ground, perhaps art can open hearts and minds. Such is the hope of his work.

ISABEL GREENBERG is an illustrator and storyteller. She graduated in 2010 from the University of Brighton with BA in illustration, and since then has been living and working in London. Among other things she has worked with an exhibition design company on a number of projects for clients, including the National Trust, and has had a comic appear in the Nobrow anthology *A Graphic Cosmogony.*

ROBERTA GREGORY has been creating her unique comics since the 1970s with appearances in "undergrounds" like *Wimmens' Comix* and her own title, *Dynamite Damsels*, through the 1990s with forty issues (and many collections) of her Fantagraphics solo title, *Naughty Bits.* Her notorious

Bitchy Bitch character, translated into several languages, has been a weekly strip, three live theater productions, and an animated series on cable television. Roberta was also responsible for the *Winging It* graphic novel, *Sheila and the Unicorn*, and *Artistic Licentiousness*, among other works. Her most recent book is a collection of her travel comics, *Follow Your Art*, and she is currently working on a "Bitchy" graphic novel, *True Cat Toons*, and *Mother Mountain*, a series of four prose novels (with a graphic novel)—and more, such as this *Popol Vuh* story. She's been busy. It's easier to just visit her website, robertagregory.com.

GARETH HINDS specializes in graphic adaptations of classic literature. His books include *Beowulf* (which *Publishers Weekly* called a "mixed-media gem"), *King Lear* (which *Booklist* named one of the top ten graphic novels for teens), *The Merchant of Venice* (which *Kirkus* called "the standard that all others will strive to meet" for Shakespeare adaptation), and *The Odyssey* (which received four-star reviews and appeared on numerous "Best of 2010" lists). His books are published by Candlewick Press and can be found in bookstores and English classrooms across the country. His artwork has also appeared in such diverse venues as the Society of Illustrators, the New York Historical Society, and over a dozen published video games. His website is garethhinds.com.

CONOR HUGHES was born in New York City in 1986, then raised in New Jersey. His influences range from Boroque to Jack Kirby to Mazzucchelli, and his work ranges from the mythological to the mundane, with few examples in between. He studied at the School of Visual Arts and currently works at the United Nations. He is working to develop a webcomic but is open to new challenges. Feel free to contact him at conorthecartoonist@gmail.com if you want to yak about art and comics.

Programmer by day and artist by night, **ERIC JOHNSON** divorces the two by employing traditional watermedia techniques in his art. A decidedly escapist fantasy and science fiction enthusiast, he strives to inject two parts wonder and whimsy per measure of detail and realism in his work and his play.

MAXX KELLY is a Canadian-American performance artist, graphic novelist, and graffiti enthusiast from Nashville, Tennessee. She can often be found at comic cons dressed as the most recent incarnation of the cult classic Thong Girl. Maxx is a founding member of the E Flat Dillingers art collective (eflatdillingers.com), and looks forward to leaving her artistic mark on Bonnaroo every year. She is currently working with her friend and creative collaborator Huxley King on a historical adventure set in 1890s Nashville. She can be reached through her website at maxxkelly.wordpress.com.

MOLLY KIELY is an artist, illustrator, underground cartoonist; Canadian-in-exile in Tucson, Arizona; and stay-at-home mom to a spitfire. She's been drawing erotic comix since 1991, including the *Diary of a Dominatrix* and *Saucy Little Tart* series, and graphic novels *That Kind of Girl* and *Tecopa Jane*. See more at mollykiely.com or mollykiely.tumblr.com.

HUXLEY KING is an editor, writer, and artist living in Nashville, Tennessee. Over the course of her varied career, she has edited everything from Bible commentaries to a tome on Hindu love goddesses; written everything from catalog copy to theater reviews; and illustrated everything from album covers to comic books that deal with the lighter side of substance abuse. Ms. King also dabbles in performance art and can occasionally be found trolling local art galleries in mime makeup or painting murals at Bonnaroo with her art collective, the E Flat Dillingers (eflatdillingers.com). She is currently working with her husband and frequent collaborator, Terrence Boyce, and her partner in creative crime, Maxx Kelly, on a historical adventure set in 1890s Nashville. You can contact her through her website, huxleyking.com.

AIDAN KOCH is an illustrator and comic artist working out of Portland, Oregon. Her first graphic novella, *The Whale*, was released in 2010. See more at aidankoch.com.

PETER KUPER is cofounder of the political graphics magazine *World War 3 Illustrated*. Since 1997, he has written and drawn *Spy vs. Spy* for every issue of *MAD*. Kuper has produced over twenty books, including *The System* and an adaptation of Franz Kafka's *The Metamorphosis*. He lived in Oaxaca, Mexico, July 2006–2008, during a major teachers' strike, and his work from that time can be seen in his book *Diario de Oaxaca*. Kuper has been teaching comics courses for twenty-five years in New York and is a visiting professor at Harvard University.

MICHAEL LAGOCKI is the founder of the art activist crew ArtLoveMagic, where he collaborates with hundreds of artists, poets, and musicians to benefit his community. He earns his professional living doing live art in corporate environments and with well-known authors and speakers. But his first love is comics. Michael was offered the opportunity to adapt *Aeneid* less than twenty-four hours after returning from Rome, a synchronicity he simply couldn't ignore. Many of his personal photos and memories from the trip influenced the work, and were used as references for the adaptation.

JOSH LEVITAS shares the byline for *Ulysses "Seen,"* an annotated comics adaptation of James Joyce's *Ulysses*, with Robert Berry, handling the graphic design, web design, production art, and hand-lettering duties. He also handles the graphic design and app interface design for Throwaway Horse's other iPad releases: Martin Rowson's *The Waste Land "Seen"* and Eric Shanower's *Age of Bronze "Seen."* Here he is playing the role of colorist in Berry's unique graphic take on Shakespeare's Sonnet 18.

Born on Long Island, illustrator **ELLEN LINDNER** now lives in London. She is the author of *Undertow*, a graphic novel about Coney Island in the early 1960s, and the editor of *The Strumpet*, a transatlantic comics magazine showcasing art by upcoming women cartoonists. See more of Ellen's comics and illustration online at littlewhitebird.com, or take a peek at her sketchbook at ellenlindner.livejournal.com.

TORI MCKENNA first brought Euripides' *Medea* to life in place of a final paper for a Greek tragedy class at Beloit College. She graduated from there in 2006 with a bachelor's degree in both classical civilizations and ecology, evolution & behavioral biology. After graduation she decided to pursue her love of art and furthered her education at both the Massachusetts College of Art and Design and the Center for Digital Imaging Arts at Boston University. She is well versed in a wide variety of art forms in both digital and traditional art, from 3D modeling and animation, to costume and prop creation, to illustration and sequential art. She brings her love of biology and classics to all of her artistic endeavors. She now returns to her true love of sequential art with this updated version of *Medea* created especially for this compilation. See more at torimckenna.com.

DAVE MORICE is a writer, visual artist, performance artist, and educator. He has written and published under the names Dave Morice, Joyce Holland, and Dr. Alphabet. His works include sixty poetry marathons, three anthologies of *Poetry Comics*, the Wooden Nickel Art Project, and other art and writing, including *The Great American Fortune Cookie Novel*, composed entirely of actual fortunes from fortune cookies. He is one of the founders of the Actualist Poetry Movement.

There's some dude named **VICKI NERINO**. She grew up in Northwestern Ontario amongst the cow pies, moose tracks, and bear logs, where she used to have farting contests with her father while her mother avoided them. Vicki makes weird comics about animals boinking and floppy boobies and awkward dates and stuff like that. She also draws and paints old people and naked stuff and that kind of thing. You probably shouldn't visit her website, vickinerino.com.

OMAHA PEREZ is the writer/artist of the graphic novels *Holmes* (2008) and *Bodhisattva* (2004). He has contributed work to the anthologies *Comic Book Tattoo* (2008), *Flash Gordon 75th Anniversary* (2009), and now *The Graphic Canon*. His illustration work has been recognized by the Society of Illustrators New York, the Society of Illustrators Los Angeles, *Spectrum*, and *3x3 Magazine*'s annual juried illustration book. A professional graphic artist for over fifteen years, Omaha owns and operates the Los Angeles design studio Drude Studios. His next major comics project is *The Drude*.

JULIAN PETERS is a comic book artist and illustrator living in Montreal. A good portion of his formative comic-book-reading years were spent in Italy, and the masters of the *fumetti* tradition continue to be his greatest sources of artistic inspiration. He has a longstanding passion for history, which he values mainly as a form of escapism; his comics are set in all kinds of different historical eras but never in the present. In the past couple of years, Julian has become particularly interested in exploring the possibilities of combining poetry—the most imagistic of literary forms—with comics—the wordiest of the visual arts—and he has created comic book adaptations of many classic poems from the canons of English, French, and Italian literature.

NOAH PATRICK PFARR is a freelance illustrator and artist out of Portland, Oregon. Although he likes comics, he is ashamed to admit that he doesn't read (or draw!) them very often. He is, however, quite fond of literature, so this project was a perfect match. His time is carefully distributed between obsessing over his work and raising his two daughters, who, despite their deceptively innocent looks, take much joy in psychologically torturing their father. You can view more examples of Noah's work at noahillustration.com.

CAROLINE PICARD is an artist and writer based out of Chicago. She is also the founding director and senior editor for the Green Lantern Press. Her work has been published in a handful of publications, most recently *Artifice Magazine*, *MAKE Magazine*, *Ampersand Review*, *Pinch*, and *Proximity Magazine*. She is a weekly contributor on the BadatSports blog and released her first collection of short stories, *Psycho Dream Factory*, in 2011. For more information visit cocopicard.com.

IAN POLLOCK has been freelancing for the last thirty-five years. He lived in London for twenty years, and now lives as a recluse in Macclesfield on the edge of the Peak District with his wife, painter Helen Clapcott. He works mostly for magazines and newspapers and appears regularly in the "quality press." He was commissioned to design "Tales of Terror"—four postage stamps for the Royal Mail that were issued in May 1997. "Work still finds me up 'ere . . ." says Pollock, dribbling along the stem of an old clay pipe. "Work for anyone," he says, "even the taxman." Now a bitter, pathetic creature, he says he's highly professional and underpaid and is worried his work is showing signs of Gilles de la Tourette Syndrome.

SHARON RUDAHL was born in Arlington, Virginia, in 1947. As a teenager, she marched with Martin Luther King. She studied art at the Cooper Union in New York City, living in the East Village in its heyday. Proceeds from her feminist erotic novel *Acid Temple Ball* paid for her art supplies. After college, she helped start the anti–Vietnam War underground newspaper *Take Over.* She worked on underground newspapers in San Francisco in the early 1970s and began drawing comics in the first *Wimmen's Comix*. Her major works include *A Danger-*

ous Woman: The Graphic Biography of Emma Goldman; the recently reprinted Adventures of Crystal Night; large portions of the graphic version of Studs Terkel's Working; and Harvey Pekar's 2011 Yiddishkeit. She is married to a professional chess player and has two adult sons. She lives in a 100-year-old Hollywood bungalow so overgrown with foliage it cannot be seen on Google Earth.

VALERIE SCHRAG was born in Berkeley, California. She graduated from the University of Chicago with a BA in classics and from New York University School of Law. In addition to acquiring useless degrees, Schrag spends her time writing and drawing comic books. She was first inspired to transform Aristophanes' bawdy and delightful feminist comedy Lysistrata into a comic when she translated the play in college. She is thrilled to fulfill this long-lived dream seven years later in this compilation. Other works by Schrag include "Snitch" in Stuck in the Middle (Viking Children's Books) and the following stories in progress: "The Autistic Lover" and "The Ufologist's Son." Schrag lives in Brooklyn, New York, with a small orange tabby by the name of Jewish Henry.

STAN SHAW is known as a comic book artist. This is only partially true, due to the fact that he has to buy groceries once in a while. Most of his time is spent on editorial illustration, advertising, animation, and storyboards, with a client list that includes the Village Voice, Esquire, Slate, Starbucks, the Seattle Mariners, Nintendo, Rhino Records, Microsoft, REI, BET, DC Comics, Wizards of the Coast, Hasbro, Lucas Film Licensing, MAD, and the Washington Post Sunday Magazine. His work has appeared in How, Communication Arts, Print, and Covers and Jackets by Steven Heller. He can be reached at drawstanley@harbornet.com or drawstanley.com.

CORTNEY SKINNER was born and raised in New England, where his appreciation for Rockwell, Wyeth, and other classic painters and illustrators influenced his own art. Comfortable in either traditional or digital media, he likes to work in many genres, including science fiction, fantasy, horror, pulp mystery, military aviation, and historic subjects. An accomplished freelance illustrator, he is regularly called upon to create artwork and concepts for magazines, books, and films. At the turn of the last century, he relocated further down the Appalachian chain into the Shenandoah Valley of Virginia, where he lives with author Elizabeth Massie and finds new inspiration for his illustration, still life, portrait, and landscape painting.

MICHAEL STANYER is a graduate student in English literature and marketing at the University of Northern British Columbia. His research focuses on monstrous character design for online video games. While performing research, he works part-time as a photographer and graphic designer. He loves to travel, but has a distrust for sea life.

FRED VAN LENTE is the New York Times–bestselling author of Incredible Hercules (with Greg Pak) and Marvel Zombies 3 & 4, as well as the American Library Association Award–winning Action Philosophers!. His original graphic novel Cowboys & Aliens (written with Andrew Foley) was made into a major motion picture starring Daniel Craig and directed by Jon Favreau. His other comics include Comic Book Comics, MODOK's 11, X-Men Noir, and Amazing Spider-Man. Wizard magazine nominated him for 2008 Breakout Talent (Writer). Comics Should Be Good named Fred one of the 365 Reasons to Love Comics. He's been called "one of the most idiosyncratic and insightful new voices in comics."

J. T. WALDMAN is a comix illustrator and interaction designer based in Philly. He is best known for the graphic novel Megillat Esther. See more at jtwaldman.com.

MATT WIEGLE lives in Philadelphia and draws things. He is responsible for the mini-comics Is It Bacon?, Ayaje's Wives, and Seven More Days of Not Getting Eaten, and is the 2010 recipient of the Ignatz Award for "Promising New Talent." He is cocreator of the webcomic Destructor with writer Sean T. Collins. When facing a deadline, he will draw during a hurricane. See more at destructorcomics.com, wiegle.com, and partykausa.com.

YIEN YIP is currently a freelance illustrator and screen-printing artist who was born and bred in Alberta, Canada. She has been drawing and painting ever since she was a kid; however, like every other member of her family, she decided to be "realistic" and took up accountancy for a bit. After five years in the field and one quarter-life crisis, she packed her bags and got her BAA in illustration at Sheridan College. With a deep love for drawing, screen-printing, some animation, and noodles, she is taking on the illustration world one step at a time.

YEJI YUN is an illustrator born and raised in Seoul, South Korea. She studied graphic design and illustration in Seoul, then Baltimore, and lastly in London, where she now lives and continues to work. She has produced illustrations for many different fields, including magazines, books, logos, posters, T-shirts, and advertising. She also makes her own zines and exhibits her personal projects. Yeji is influenced by poetic and nostalgic material and likes to draw inspiration from her own imagination and emotions. Her favorite color is turquoise. See more at seeouterspace.com.

CREDITS AND PERMISSIONS

"Advice to a Young Man on the Choice of a Mistress" by Benjamin Franklin was created especially for this volume. Copyright © 2012 by Cortney Skinner. Printed by permission of the artist.

Aeneid by Virgil was created especially for this volume. Copyright © 2012 by Michael Lagocki. Printed by permission of the artist.

The *Analects* and Other Writings by Confucius first appeared in the *Action Philosophers!* comics series by Fred Van Lente and Ryan Dunlavey. Copyright 2006 by Fred Van Lente and Ryan Dunlavey. Reprinted by permission of the artists.

Apu Ollantay (an Incan play) was created especially for this volume. Copyright © 2012 by Caroline Picard. Printed by permission of the artist.

Beowulf was originally self-published by Gareth Hinds, then all three volumes were collected by Candlewick Press. This condensation of Part One was created by Hinds especially for this volume. Copyright © 2007 by Gareth Hinds. Reproduced by permission of the publisher, Candlewick Press, Somerville, MA.

The Book of Daniel ("The Three Youths and the Fiery Furnace") from the Hebrew Bible was previously published only on the artist's website in 2009. Copyright © 2009 by Benjamin Frisch. Reprinted by permission of the artist

The Book of Esther from the Hebrew Bible was originally published in *Megillat Esther* by J. T. Waldman (Jewish Publication Society, 2005). Copyright © 2005 by J. T. Waldman. Reprinted by permission of the publisher.

The Book of Revelation from the New Testament was created especially for this volume. Copyright © 2012 by Rick Geary. Printed by permission of the artist.

Candide by Voltaire was created especially for this volume. Copyright © 2012 by Ian Ball. Printed by permission of the artist.

The Canterbury Tales by Geoffrey Chaucer was originally published as part of *The Canterbury Tales* by Seymour Chwast (Bloomsbury USA, 2011). Copyright © 2011 by Seymour Chwast. Reprinted by permission of the publisher.

"Coyote and the Pebbles" originally appeared in *Trickster: Native American Tales: A Graphic Collection*, edited by Michael Dembicki (Fulcrum Publishing, 2010). Copyright © 2010 by Dayton Edmonds and Micah Farritor. Reprinted by permission of the publisher and the artists.

Dangerous Liaisons by Choderlos de Laclos was created especially for this volume. Copyright © 2012 by Molly Crabapple. Printed by permission of the artist.

The Divine Comedy by Dante Alighieri was originally published as parts of *Dante's Divine Comedy* by Seymour Chwast (Bloomsbury USA, 2010). Copyright © 2010 by Seymour Chwast. Reprinted by permission of the publisher.

Don Quixote by Miguel Cervantes was originally published as part of *The Last Knight* by Will Eisner (NBM, 2003). Copyright © 2003 by Will Eisner. Reprinted by permission of the artist.

The Epic of Gilgamesh was originally published in October 2007 as issue #3 of the *Gilgamesh* comics series by Kevin and Kent Dixon. Copyright © 2007 by Kevin and Kent Dixon. Reprinted by permission of the artists.

The Faerie Queene by Edmund Spenser was created especially for this volume. It is the first stage of an ongoing project for web and print. Copyright © 2012 by Michael Stanyer and Eric Johnson. Printed by permission of the artists.

"Letter to the Royal Academy of Brussels" (a.k.a. "Fart Proudly") from a text by Benjamin Franklin was created especially for this volume. Copyright © 2012 by Stan Shaw. Printed by permission of the artist.

"The Fisherman and the Genie" from *The Arabian Nights* first appeared in *Scheherazade: Stories of Love, Treachery, Mothers, and Monsters*, edited by Megan Kelso (Soft Skull Press, 2004). Copyright © 2004 by Andrice Arp. Reprinted by permission of the artist.

"The Flea" by John Donne was created especially for this volume. Copyright © 2012 by Noah Patrick Pfarr. Printed by permission of the artist.

"Forgive Us Our Trespasses" by Aphra Behn was created especially for this volume. Copyright © 2012 by Alex Eckman-Lawn. Printed by permission of the artist.

Gulliver's Travels by Jonathan Swift first appeared in *SPX*, the Small Press Expo 2003 anthology. Copyright © 2003 by Gareth Hinds. Reprinted by permission of the artist.

Hagoromo (*Celestial Feather Robe*) was created especially for this volume. Copyright © 2012 by Isabel Greenberg. Printed by permission of the artist.

"Hot Sun, Cool Fire" by George Peele originally appeared in Dave Morice's *Poetry Comics* zine. Copyright © 1982 by Dave Morice. Reprinted by permission of the artist.

The Iliad by Homer was created especially for this volume. Copyright © 2012 by Alice Duke. Printed by permission of the artist.

The Inferno by Dante Alighieri is part of a work in progress, to eventually be published by Knockabout Comics (London). It appears here for the first time. Copyright © 2012 by Hunt Emerson. Printed by permission of the artist.

Journey to the West by Wu Cheng'en was created especially for this volume. Copyright © 2012 by Conor Hughes. Printed by permission of the artist.

King Lear by William Shakespeare was first published as part of *King Lear* by Ian Pollock (Can of Worms Enterprises Ltd., 1984). Copyright © 1984 by Ian Pollock. Reprinted by permission of Can of Worms Enterprises Ltd.

"The Last Ballad" by François Villon was first published in French on Julian Peters' website. The English version was created especially for this volume. English language copyright © 2012 by Julian Peters. Printed by permission of the artist.

"The letters of Héloïse and Abelard" was created especially for this volume. Copyright © 2012 by Ellen Lindner. Printed by permission of the artist.

London Journal by James Boswell first appeared in *Weirdo* #3. Copyright © 2011 by Robert Crumb. Used by permission of the Agence Littéraire Lora Fountain & Associates, Paris, France.

Lysistrata by Aristophanes was created especially for this volume. Copyright © 2012 by Valerie Schrag. Printed by permission of the artist.

Mahabharata by Vyasa was created especially for this volume. Copyright © 2012 by Matt Wiegle. Printed by permission of the artist.

Medea by Euripides appears for the first time in this volume. Copyright © 2012 by Tori McKenna. Printed by permission of the artist.

A Midsummer Night's Dream by William Shakespeare was created especially for this volume. Copyright © 2012 by Maxx Kelly. Printed by permission of the artist.

"A Modest Proposal" by Jonathan Swift first appeared in *World War 3 Illustrated*. Copyright © 1994 by Peter Kuper. Reprinted by permission of the artist.

Le Morte d'Arthur by Sir Thomas Malory was created especially for this volume. Copyright © 2012 by Omaha Perez. Printed by permission of the artist.

"O nobilissima viriditas" by Hildegard of Bingen was created especially for this volume. Copyright © 2012 by Molly Kiely. Printed by permission of the artist.

The Odyssey by Homer first appeared in *The Odyssey* by Gareth Hinds (Candlewick Press, 2009). Copyright © 2009 by Gareth Hinds. Reproduced by permission of the publisher, Candlewick Press, Somerville, MA.

On the Nature of Things by Lucretius was originally published as *The Ancient Ploughman* in a limited edition of 200 by Two Fine Chaps. Copyright © 2007 by Tom Biby and Jonathan Fetter-Vorm (a.k.a. Two Fine Chaps). Reprinted by permission of the artists.

Outlaws of the Water Margin by Shi Nai'an first appears in this volume. Copyright © 2012 by Shawn Cheng. Printed by permission of the artist.

Paradise Lost by John Milton was created especially for this volume. Copyright © 2012 by Rebecca Dart. Printed by permission of the artist.

Poem fragments (Sappho) was created especially for this volume. Copyright © 2012 by Alessandro Bonaccorsi. Printed by permission of the artist.

Poems (Rumi) is an excerpt from *One Song: A New Illuminated Rumi* by Rumi, Michael Green, and Coleman Barks (Running Press, 2005). Copyright © 2005 by Michael Green and Coleman Barks. Reprinted by permission of the publisher.

Popol Vuh was created especially for this volume. Copyright © 2012 by Roberta Gregory. Printed by permission of the artist.

Sonnet 18 by William Shakespeare was created especially for this volume. Copyright © 2012 by Robert Berry. Printed by permission of the artist.

Sonnet 20 by William Shakespeare was created especially for this volume. Copyright © 2012 by Aidan Koch. Printed by permission of the artist.

Symposium by Plato first appears in this volume. Copyright © 2012 by Yeji Yun. Printed by permission of the artist.

The Tale of Genji by Murasaki Shikibu was created especially for this volume. Copyright © 2012 by Molly Kiely. Printed by permission of the artist.

Three Tang poems by Wang Han, Cui Hu, and Li Bai was created especially for this volume. Copyright © 2012 by Sharon Rudahl. Printed by permission of the artist.

Tao Te Ching by Lao Tzu first appeared in the *Action Philosophers!* comics series by Fred Van Lente and Ryan Dunlavey. Copyright © 2006 by Fred Van Lente and Ryan Dunlavey. Reprinted by permission of the artists.

The Tibetan Book of the Dead (*Bardo Thodol*) by Padmasambhava and Karma Lingpa was created especially for this volume. Copyright © 2012 by Sanya Glisic. Printed by permission of the artist.

"To His Coy Mistress" by Andrew Marvell was created especially for this volume. Copyright © 2012 by Yien Yip. Printed by permission of the artist.

A Vindication of the Rights of Woman by Mary Wollstonecraft first appeared in the *Action Philosophers!* comics series by Fred Van Lente and Ryan Dunlavey. Copyright © 2007 by Fred Van Lente and Ryan Dunlavey. Reprinted by permission of the artists.

The visions of St. Teresa of Ávila from her autobiography was created especially for this volume. Copyright © 2012 by Edie Fake. Printed by permission of the artist.

"The Woman with Two Coyntes" from *The Arabian Nights* was created especially for this volume. Copyright © 2012 by Vicki Nerino. Printed by permission of the artist.

INDEX TO VOLUME 1

TITLE

AUTHOR/POET

ARTIST/ADAPTER

COUNTRY/AREA OF O.

Photo by Ross Smith

RUSS KICK is the author of the bestselling anthologies *You Are Being Lied To* and *Everything You Know is Wrong*, which have sold over half a million copies. *The New York Times* has dubbed Kick "an information archaeologist," *Details* magazine described Kick as "a Renaissance man," and *Utne Reader* named him one of its "50 Visionaries Who Are Changing Your World." Russ Kick lives in Nashville, Tennessee, and Tucson, Arizona.

SEVEN STORIES PRESS is an independent book publisher based in New York City. We publish works of the imagination by such writers as Nelson Algren, Russell Banks, Octavia E. Butler, Ani DiFranco, Assia Djebar, Ariel Dorfman, Coco Fusco, Barry Gifford, Hwang Sok-yong, Lee Stringer, and Kurt Vonnegut, to name a few, together with political titles by voices of conscience, including the Boston Women's Health Collective, Noam Chomsky, Angela Y. Davis, Human Rights Watch, Derrick Jensen, Ralph Nader, Loretta Napoleoni, Gary Null, Project Censored, Barbara Seaman, Alice Walker, Gary Webb, and Howard Zinn, among many others. Seven Stories Press believes publishers have a special responsibility to defend free speech and human rights, and to celebrate the gifts of the human imagination, wherever we can. For additional information, visit www.sevenstories.com.